THE CRIMSON CAMPAIGN

THE POWDER MAGE TRILOGY:
BOOK 2

BRIAN McCLELLAN

www.orbitbooks.net

ORBIT

First published in Great Britain in 2014 by Orbit
This paperback edition published in 2014 by Orbit

9 11 12 10 8

Copyright © 2014 by Brian McClellan

Maps by Isaac Stewart

Excerpt from *Blood Song* by Anthony Ryan
Copyright © 2011 by Anthony Ryan

The moral right of the author has been asserted.

A CIP catalogue record for this book
is available from the British Library.

ISBN 978-0-356-50204-5

Printed and bound in Italy by Elcograf S.p.A.

Papers used by Orbit are from well-managed forests
and other responsible sources.

For Michele,
My one and only
My friend, my collaborator, and my love

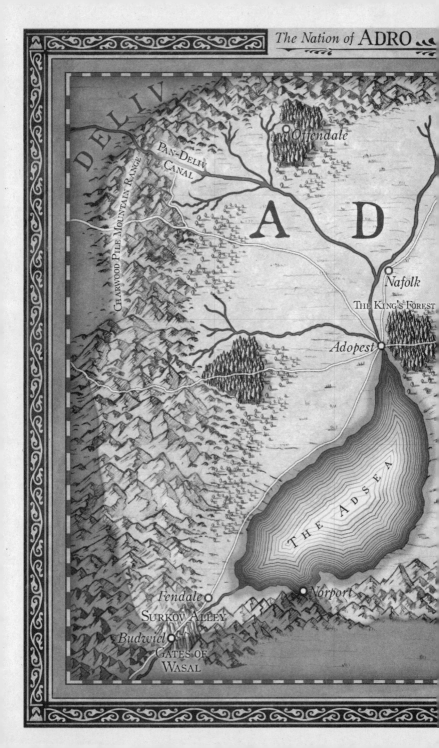

Tileman
University

R O

I

O

V

Kresim Kurga

N

South Pike
Mountain

Z

K E

Scale in Miles

0   50   100

2013

CITY OF
❧ ADOPEST ❧
AND SURROUNDINGS

1. Kirkamshire
   Adopest University
2. Adom's Wall
3. The Samalian Market
4. Samalian District
5. Lighthouse of Gostaun
6. Dwightwich Belltower
7. Kresim Cathedral

8. Baker's Town
9. The Routs
10. Elections Square
11. Public Archives
12. Centestershire
13. Black Street
14. Hrusch Ave.
15. Skyline Palace

16. Union Headquarters

HIGH
TALIEN

NEW
CITY

FACTORY
DISTRICT

WEST
LADEN

OLD CITY

Scale in Miles

0   1   2

THE ADSEA

CHAPTER
1

Adamat stood perfectly still in the middle of a deep hedgerow outside of his own summer house and stared through the windows at the men in the dining room. The house was a two-story, three-bedroom affair sitting by itself in the woods at the end of a dirt path. It was a twenty-minute walk into town from here. Unlikely anyone would hear gunshots.

Or screams.

Four of Lord Vetas's men milled about in the dining room, drinking and playing cards. Two of them were large and well-muscled as draft horses. A third was of middling height, with a heavy gut hanging out of his shirt and a thick black beard.

The final man was the only one Adamat recognized. He had a square face and a head that was almost comically small. His name was Roja the Fox, and he was the smallest boxer in the bareknuckle-boxing circuit run by the Proprietor back in Adopest. He could move faster than most boxers, by necessity, but he wasn't popular with the crowds and did not fight often. What he was doing here, Adamat had no idea.

What he did know was that he feared for the safety of his children—especially his daughters—with a group of malcontents like this.

"Sergeant," Adamat whispered.

The hedgerow rustled, and Adamat caught a glimpse of Sergeant Oldrich's face. He had a sharp jawline, and the dim moonlight betrayed the bulge of tobacco in one cheek. "My men are in place," Oldrich responded. "Are they all in the dining room?"

"Yes." Adamat had observed the house for three days now. All that time he'd stood by and watched these men yell at his children and smoke cigars in his house, dropping ash and spilling beer on Faye's good tablecloth. He knew their habits.

He knew that the fat, bearded one stayed upstairs, keeping an eye on the children all day. He knew the two big thugs escorted the children to the outhouse while Roja the Fox kept watch. He knew the four of them wouldn't leave the children by themselves until after dark, when they'd set up their nightly card game on the dining room table.

He also knew that in three days, he'd seen no sign of his wife or his oldest son.

Sergeant Oldrich pressed a loaded pistol into Adamat's hand. "Are you sure you want to lead on this? My men are good. They'll get the children out unharmed."

"I'm sure," Adamat said. "They're my family. My responsibility."

"Don't hesitate to pull the trigger if they head toward the stairs," Oldrich said. "We don't want them to take hostages."

The children were already hostages, Adamat wanted to say. He bit back his words and smoothed the front of his shirt with one hand. The sky was cloudy, and now that the sun had set there would be no light to betray his presence to those inside. He stepped out of the hedgerow and was suddenly reminded of the night he'd been summoned to Skyline Palace. That was the night all this had begun: the coup, then the traitor, then Lord Vetas. Silently, he cursed Field Marshal Tamas for drawing him and his family into this.

Sergeant Oldrich's soldiers crept out across the worn dirt path with Adamat, heading toward the front of the house. Adamat knew there were another eight behind the house. Sixteen men in total. They had the numbers. They had the element of surprise.

Lord Vetas's goons had Adamat's children.

Adamat paused at the front door. Adran soldiers, their dark-blue uniforms almost impossible to see in the darkness, took up spots beneath the dining room windows, their muskets at the ready. Adamat looked down at the door. Faye had chosen this house, instead of one closer to town, in part because of the door. It was a sturdy oak door with iron hinges. She felt that a strong door made her family safer.

He'd never had the heart to tell her the door frame was riddled with termites. In fact, Adamat had always meant to have it replaced.

Adamat stepped back and kicked right next to the doorknob.

The rotten wood exploded with the impact. Adamat ducked into the front hall and brought his pistol up as he rounded the corner.

All four of the goons burst into action. One of the big men leapt toward the back doorway leading to the staircase. Adamat held his pistol steady and fired and the man dropped.

"Don't move," Adamat said. "You're surrounded!"

The remaining three goons stared back at him, frozen in place. He saw their eyes go to his spent pistol, and then they all went for him at once.

The volley of musket balls from the soldiers outside burst the window and glass showered the room like frost. The remaining goons went down, except for Roja the Fox. He stumbled toward Adamat with a knife drawn, blood soaking the sleeve of one arm.

Adamat reversed the grip on his pistol and brought the butt down on Roja's head.

Just like that, it was over.

Soldiers spilled into the dining room. Adamat pushed past them and bolted up the stairs. He checked the children's rooms first: all empty. Finally, the master bedroom. He flung the door open with such force it nearly flew off the hinges.

The children were huddled together in the narrow space between the bed and the wall. The older siblings embraced the younger ones, shielding them in their arms as best they could. Seven frightened faces stared up at Adamat. One of the twins was crying, no doubt from the crack of the muskets. Silent tears streamed down his chubby cheeks. The other poked his head out timidly from his hiding place beneath the bed.

Adamat breathed a sigh of relief and fell to his knees. They were alive. His children. He felt the tears come unbidden as he was mobbed by small bodies. Tiny hands reached out and touched his face. He threw his arms wide, grabbing as many of them as possible and pulling them closer.

Adamat wiped the tears from his cheeks. It wasn't seemly to cry in front of the children. He took a great breath to compose himself and said, "I'm here. You're safe. I've come with Field Marshal Tamas's men."

Another round of happy sobs and hugs followed before Adamat was able to restore order.

"Where is your mother? Where's Josep?"

Fanish, his second oldest, helped to shush the other children. "They took Astrit a few weeks ago," she said, pulling at her long black braid with shaking fingers. "Just last week they came and took Mama and Josep."

"Astrit is safe," Adamat said. "Don't worry. Did they say where they were taking Mama and Josep?"

Fanish shook her head.

Adamat felt his heart fall, but he didn't let it show on his face. "Did they hurt you? Any of you?" He was most concerned for Fanish. She was fourteen, practically a woman. Her shoulders were bare beneath her thin nightgown. Adamat searched for bruises and breathed a word of thanks there were none.

"No, Papa," Fanish said. "I heard the men talking. They wanted to, but..."

"But what?"

"A man came when they took away Mama and Josep. I didn't hear his name, but he was dressed as a gentleman and he spoke very quietly. He told them that if they touched us before he gave them permission, he'd..." She trailed off and her face went pale.

Adamat patted her on the cheek. "You've been very brave," he reassured her gently. Inside, Adamat fumed. Once Adamat was no longer any use to him, Vetas no doubt would have turned those goons loose on the children without a second thought.

"I'm going to find them," he said. He patted Fanish on the cheek again and stood up. One of the twins grabbed his hand.

"Don't go," he begged.

Adamat wiped the little one's tears. "I'll be right back. Stay with Fanish." Adamat wrenched himself away. There was still one more child and his wife to save—more battles to win before they were all safely reunited.

He found Sergeant Oldrich just outside the upstairs bedroom, waiting respectfully with his hat in his hands.

"They took Faye and my oldest son," Adamat said. "The rest of the children are safe. Are any of those animals alive?"

Oldrich kept his voice low so the children wouldn't overhear. "One of them took a bullet to the eye. Another, the heart. It was a lucky volley." He scratched the back of his head. Oldrich wasn't old by any means, but his hair was already graying just above his ears. His cheeks were flushed from the storm of violence. His voice, though, was even.

"Too lucky," Adamat said. "I needed one of them alive."

"One's alive," Oldrich said.

When Adamat reached the kitchen, he found Roja sitting in one of the chairs, his hands tied behind his back, bleeding from bullet wounds to the shoulder and hip.

Adamat retrieved a cane from the umbrella stand beside the front door. Roja stared balefully at the floor. He was a boxer, a fighter. He wouldn't go down easy.

"You're lucky, Roja," Adamat said, pointing to the bullet wounds with the tip of his cane. "You might survive these. If you receive medical attention quickly enough."

"I know you?" Roja said, snorting. Blood speckled his dirty linen shirt.

"No, you don't. But I know you. I've watched you fight. Where's Vetas?"

Roja turned his neck to the side and popped it. His eyes held a challenge. "Vetas? Don't know him."

Beneath the feigned ignorance, Adamat thought he caught a note of recognition in the boxer's voice.

Adamat placed the tip of his cane against Roja's shoulder, right next to the bullet wound. "Your employer."

"Eat shit," Roja said.

Adamat pressed on his cane. He could feel the ball still in there, up against the bone. Roja squirmed. To his credit, he didn't make a sound. A bareknuckle boxer, if he was any good, learned to embrace pain.

"Where's Vetas?"

Roja didn't respond. Adamat stepped closer. "You want to live through the night, don't you?"

"He'll do worse to me than you ever could," Roja said. "Besides, I don't know nothin'."

Adamat stepped away from Roja, turning his back. He heard Oldrich step forward, followed by the heavy thump of a musket butt slamming into Roja's gut. He let the beating continue for a few moments before turning back and waving Oldrich away.

Roja's face looked like he'd been through a few rounds with Sou-Smith. He doubled over, spitting blood.

"Where did they take Faye?" *Tell me*, Adamat begged silently. *For your sake, hers, and mine. Tell me where she is.* "The boy, Josep? Where is he?"

Roja spit on the floor. "You're him, aren't you? The father of these stupid brats?" He didn't wait for Adamat to answer. "We were gonna bugger all those kids. Startin' with the small ones first. Vetas wouldn't let us. But your wife…" Roja ran his tongue along his broken lips. "She was willing. Thought we'd go easy on the babies if she took us all."

Oldrich stepped forward and slammed the butt of his musket across Roja's face. Roja jerked to one side and let out a choked groan.

Adamat felt his whole body shaking with rage. Not Faye. Not his beautiful wife, his friend and partner, his confidante and the mother of his children. He held up his hand when Oldrich wound up to hit Roja again.

"No," Adamat said. "That's just an average day for this one. Get me a lantern."

He grabbed Roja by the back of the neck and dragged him out of the chair, pushing him outside through the back door. Roja stumbled into an overgrown rosebush in the garden. Adamat lifted him to his feet, sure to use his wounded shoulder, and shoved him along. Toward the outhouse.

"Keep the children inside," Adamat said to Oldrich, "and bring a few men."

The outhouse was wide enough for two seats, a necessity for a household with nine children. Adamat opened the door while two of Oldrich's soldiers held Roja up between them. He took a lantern from Oldrich and let it illuminate the inside of the outhouse for Roja to see.

Adamat grabbed the board that covered the outhouse hole and tossed it on the ground. The smell was putrid. Even after sundown the walls crawled with flies.

"I dug this hole myself," Adamat said. "It's eight feet deep. I should have cut a new one years ago, and the family has been using it a lot lately. They were here all summer." He shined the lantern into the hole and gave an exaggerated sniff. "Almost full," he said. "Where is Vetas? Where did they take Faye?"

Roja sneered at Adamat. "Go to the pit."

"We're already there," Adamat said. He grabbed Roja by the back of the neck and forced him into the outhouse. It was barely big enough for the two of them. Roja struggled, but Adamat's strength was fueled by his rage. He kicked Roja's knees out from under him and shoved the boxer's head into the hole.

"Tell me where he is," Adamat hissed.

No answer.

"Tell me!"

"No!" Roja's voice echoed in the box that formed the outhouse seat.

Adamat pushed on the back of Roja's head. A few more inches and Roja would get a face full of human waste. Adamat choked back his own disgust. This was cruel. Inhuman. Then again, so was taking a man's wife and children hostage.

Roja's forehead touched the top of the shit and he let out a sob.

"Where is Vetas? I won't ask again!"

"I don't know! He didn't tell me anything. Just paid me to keep the kids here."

"How were you paid?" Adamat heard Roja retch. The boxer's body shuddered.

"Krana notes."

"You're one of the Proprietor's boxers," Adamat said. "Does he know about any of this?"

"Vetas said we were recommended. No one hires us for the job unless the Proprietor gives the go-ahead."

Adamat gritted his teeth. The Proprietor. The head of the Adran criminal world, and a member of Tamas's council. He was one of the most powerful men in Adro. If he knew about Lord Vetas, it could mean he'd been a traitor all along.

"What else do you know?"

"I barely spoke twenty words with the guy," Roja said. His words were coming out in broken gasps as he sputtered through his tears. "Don't know anything else!"

Adamat struck Roja on the back of the head. He sagged, but he was not unconscious. Adamat lifted him by his belt and shoved his face down into the muck. He lifted him again and pushed. Roja flailed, his legs kicking hard as he tried to breathe through the piss and shit. Adamat grabbed the boxer by the ankles and pushed down, jamming Roja in the hole.

Adamat turned and walked out of the outhouse. He couldn't think through his fury. He was going to destroy Vetas for putting his wife and children through this.

Oldrich and his men stood by, watching Roja drown in filth. One of them looked ill in the dim lantern light. Another was nodding in approval. The night was quiet now, and Adamat could hear the steady chirp of crickets in the forest.

"Aren't you going to ask him more questions?" Oldrich said.

"He said himself, he doesn't know anything else." Adamat felt his stomach turn and he looked back at Roja's kicking legs. The mental image of Roja forcing himself on Faye almost stopped Adamat, and then he said to Oldrich, "Pull him out before he dies. Then ship him to the deepest coal mine you can find on the Mountainwatch."

Adamat swore to do worse to Vetas when he caught him.

CHAPTER

2

Field Marshal Tamas stood above Budwiel's southern gate and surveyed the Kez army. This wall marked the southernmost point of Adro. If he tossed a stone in front of him, it would land on Kez soil, perhaps rolling down the slope of the Great Northern Road until it reached the Kez pickets on the edge of their army.

The Gates of Wasal, a pair of five-hundred-foot-tall cliffs, rose to either side of him, divided by thousands of years of flowing water coming out of the Adsea, cutting through Surkov's Alley, and feeding the grain fields of the Amber Expanse in northern Kez.

The Kez army had left the smoldering ruins of South Pike Mountain only three weeks ago. Official reports estimated the number of men in the army that had besieged Shouldercrown as two hundred thousand soldiers, accompanied by camp followers that swelled that number to almost three-quarters of a million.

His scouts told him that the total number was over a million now.

A small part of Tamas cowered at such a number. The world had not seen an army of that size since the wars of the Bleakening over fourteen hundred years ago. And here it was at his doorstep, trying to take his country from him.

Tamas could recognize a new soldier on the walls by how loud they gasped upon seeing the Kez army. He could smell the fear of his own men. The anticipation. The dread. This was not Shouldercrown, a fortress easily held by a few companies of soldiers. This was Budwiel, a trading city of some hundred thousand people. The walls were in disrepair, the gates too numerous and too wide.

Tamas did not let that fear show on his own face. He didn't dare. He buried his tactical concerns; the terror he felt that his only son lay in Adopest deep in a coma; the pain that still ached in his leg despite the healing powers of a god. Nothing showed on his countenance but contempt for the audacity of the Kez commanders.

Steady footfalls sounded on the stone stairs behind him, and Tamas was joined by General Hilanska, the commander of Budwiel's artillery and the Second Brigade.

Hilanska was an extremely portly man of about forty years old, a widower of ten years, and a veteran of the Gurlish Campaigns. He was missing his left arm at the shoulder, taken clean off by a cannonball thirty years ago when Hilanska was not yet a captain. He had never let his arm nor his weight affect his performance on a battlefield, and for that alone he had Tamas's respect. Never mind that his gun crews could knock the head off a charging cavalryman at eight hundred yards.

Among Tamas's General Staff, most of whom had been chosen for their skill and not their personalities, Hilanska was the closest thing Tamas had to a friend.

"Been watching them gather there for weeks and it still doesn't cease to impress me," Hilanska said.

"Their numbers?" Tamas asked.

Hilanska leaned over the edge of the wall and spit. "Their discipline." He removed his looking glass from his belt and slid it open with a well-practiced jerk of his one hand, then held it up to his eye. "All those damned paper-white tents lined up as far as the eye can see. Looks like a model."

"Lining up a half-million tents doesn't make an army disciplined," Tamas said. "I've worked with Kez commanders before. In Gurla. They keep their men in line with fear. It makes for a clean and pretty camp, but when armies clash, there's no steel in their spine. They break by the third volley." *Not like my men*, he thought. *Not like the Adran brigades.*

"Hope you're right," Hilanska said.

Tamas watched the Kez sentries make their rounds a half mile away, well in range of Hilanska's guns, but not worth the ammunition. The main army camped almost two whole miles back; their officers feared Tamas's powder mages more than they did Hilanska's guns.

Tamas gripped the lip of the stone wall and opened his third eye. A wave of dizziness passed over him before he could see clearly into the Else. The world took on a pastel glow. In the distance there were lights, glimmering like the fires of an enemy patrol at night— the glow of Kez Privileged and Wardens. He closed his third eye and rubbed at his temple.

"You're still thinking about it, aren't you?" Hilanska asked.

"What?"

"Invading."

"Invade?" Tamas scoffed. "I'd have to be mad to launch an attack against an army ten times our size."

"You've got that look to you, Tamas," Hilanska said. "Like a dog pulling at its chain. I've known you too long. You've made no secret that you intend to invade Kez given the opportunity."

Tamas eyed those pickets. The Kez army was set so far back it would be almost impossible to catch them unawares. The terrain gave no good cover for a night attack.

"If I could get the Seventh and Ninth in there with the element of surprise, I could carve through the heart of their army and be back in Budwiel before they knew what hit them," Tamas said quietly. His heart quickened at the thought. The Kez were not to be underestimated. They had the numbers. They still had a few Privileged, even after the Battle of Shouldercrown.

But Tamas knew what his best brigades were capable of. He knew Kez strategies, and he knew their weaknesses. Kez soldiers were levies from their immense peasant population. Their officers were nobles who'd bought their commissions. Not like his men: patriots, men of steel and iron.

"A few of my boys did some exploring," Hilanska said.

"They did?" Tamas quelled the annoyance of having his thoughts interrupted.

"You know about Budwiel's catacombs?"

Tamas grunted in acknowledgment. The catacombs stretched under the West Pillar, one of the two mountains that made up the Gates of Wasal. They were a mixture of natural and man-made caverns used to house Budwiel's dead.

"They're off limits to soldiers," Tamas said, unable to keep the reproach from his voice.

"I'll deal with my boys, but you might want to hear what they have to say before we have them flogged."

"Unless they discovered a Kez spy ring, I doubt it's relevant."

"Better," Hilanska said. "They found a way for you to get your men into Kez."

Tamas felt his heart jump at the possibility. "Take me to them."

CHAPTER
3

Taniel stared at the ceiling only a foot above him, counting each time he swung, side to side, in the hemp-rope hammock, listening to the Gurlish pipes that filled the room with a soft, whistling music.

He hated that music. It seemed to echo in his ears, all at once too soft to hear well but loud enough to make him grind his molars together. He lost count of the hammock swings somewhere around ten and exhaled. Warm smoke curled out from between his lips and against the crumbling mortar in the ceiling. He watched the smoke escape the roof of his niche and swirl into the middle of the mala den.

There were a dozen such niches in the room. Two were occupied. In the two weeks he'd been there, Taniel had yet to see the occupants get up to piss or eat or do anything other than suck on the long-stemmed mala pipes and flag the den's owner over for a refill.

He leaned over, his hand reaching for a refill for his own mala pipe. The table next to his hammock held a plate with a few scraps of dark mala, an empty purse, and a pistol. He couldn't remember where the pistol came from.

Taniel gathered the bits of mala together into one small, sticky ball and pushed it into the end of his pipe. It lit instantly, and he took a long pull into his lungs.

"Want more?"

The den's owner sidled up to Taniel's hammock. He was Gurlish, his skin brown but not as dark as a Deliv's, with a lighter tone under his eyes and on his palms. He was tall, like most Gurlish, and skinny, his back bent from years of leaning into the niches of his mala den to clean them out or light an addict's pipe. His name was Kin.

Taniel reached for his purse, wiggled his fingers around inside before remembering that it was empty. "No money," he said, his own voice ragged in his ears.

How long had he been here? Two weeks, Taniel decided after putting his mind to the question. More importantly, how did he get here?

Not *here*, the mala den, but here in Adopest. Taniel remembered the fight on top of Kresimir's palace as Ka-poel destroyed the Kez Cabal, and he remembered pulling the trigger of his rifle and watching a bullet take the god Kresimir in the eye.

It was all darkness after that until he woke up, covered in sweat, Ka-poel straddling him with fresh blood on her hands. He remembered bodies in the hallway of the hotel—his father's soldiers with an unfamiliar insignia on their jackets. He'd left the hotel and stumbled here, where he'd hoped to forget.

Of course, if he still remembered all that, then the mala wasn't doing its job.

"Army jacket," Kin said, fingering his lapel. "Your buttons."

Taniel looked down at the jacket he wore. It was Adran-army

dark blue, with silver trim and buttons. He'd taken it from the hotel. It wasn't his—too big. There was a powder mage pin—a silver powder keg—pinned to the lapel. Maybe it *was* his. Had he lost weight?

The jacket had been clean two days ago. He remembered that much. Now it was stained with drool, bits of food, and small burns from mala embers. When the pit had he eaten?

Taniel pulled his belt knife and took one of the buttons in his fingers. He paused. Kin's daughter walked through the room. She wore a faded white dress, clean despite the squalor of the den. She must have been a few years older than Taniel, but no children clung to her skirts.

"Do you like my daughter?" Kin asked. "She will dance for you. Two buttons!" He held up two fingers for emphasis. "Much prettier than the Fatrastan witch."

Kin's wife, sitting in the corner and playing the Gurlish pipes, stopped the music long enough to say something to Kin. They exchanged a few words in Gurlish, then Kin turned back to Taniel. "Two buttons!" he reiterated.

Taniel cut a button loose and put it in Kin's hand. Dance, eh? Taniel wondered if Kin had a strong enough grasp of Adran for euphemism, or if dance was indeed all she'd do.

"Maybe later," Taniel said, settling back in the hammock with a fresh ball of mala the size of a child's fist. "Ka-poel isn't a witch. She's…" He paused, trying to figure out a way to describe her to a Gurlish. His thoughts moved slowly, sluggish from the mala. "All right," he conceded. "She's a witch."

Taniel topped off his mala pipe. Kin's daughter was watching him. He returned her open stare with a half-lidded gaze. She was pretty, by some standards. Too tall by far for Taniel, and much too gaunt—most Gurlish were. She stayed there, laundry balanced on her hip, until her father shooed her out.

How long had it been since he'd had a woman?

A woman? He laughed, smoke curling out his nose. The laugh ended in a cough and received no more than a curious glance from Kin. No, not *a* woman. *The* woman. Vlora. How long had it been? Two and a half years now? Three?

He sat back up and fished around in his pocket for a powder charge, wondering where Vlora was now. Probably still with Tamas and the rest of the powder cabal.

Tamas would want Taniel back on the front line.

To the pit with that. Let Tamas come to Adopest looking for Taniel. The last place he'd look was a mala den.

There wasn't a powder charge in Taniel's pocket. Ka-poel had cleaned him out. He'd not had a smidgen of powder since she brought him out of that goddamned coma. Not even his pistol was loaded. He could go out and get some. Find a barracks, show them his powder-mage pin.

The very idea of getting out of the hammock made his head spin.

Ka-poel came down the steps into the mala den just as Taniel was beginning to drift off. He kept his eyes mostly closed, the smoke curling from his lips. She stopped and examined him.

She was short, her features petite. Her skin was white, with ashen freckles and her red hair was no more than an inch long. He didn't like it so short, it made her look boyish. *No mistaking her for a boy*, Taniel thought as she shrugged out of her long black duster. Underneath she wore a white sleeveless shirt, scrounged from who-knew-where, and close-fitting black pants.

Ka-poel touched Taniel's shoulder. He ignored her. Let her think him asleep, or too deep in a mala haze to notice her. All the better.

She reached out and squeezed his nose shut with one hand, pushing his mouth closed with the other.

He jerked up, taking a breath when she let go. "What the pit, Pole? Trying to kill me?"

She smiled, and it wasn't the first time under the mala haze that he'd stared into those glass-green eyes with less than proper thoughts. He shook them away. She was his ward. He was her protector. Or was it the other way around? She was the one who'd done the protecting up on South Pike.

Taniel settled back into the hammock. "What do you want?"

She held up a thick pad of paper, bound in leather. A sketchbook. To replace the one lost on South Pike Mountain. He felt a pang at that. Sketches from eight years of his life. People he'd known, many of them long dead. Some friends, some enemies. Losing that sketchbook hurt almost as much as losing his genuine Hrusch rifle.

Almost as much as . . .

He pushed the stem of his mala pipe between his teeth and sucked in hard. He shivered as the smoke burned his throat and lungs and seeped into his body, deadening the memories.

When he reached out for the sketchbook, he saw that his hand was shaking. He snatched it back quickly.

Ka-poel's eyes narrowed. She set the sketchbook on his stomach, followed by a pack of charcoal pencils. Finer sketching tools than he'd ever had in Fatrasta. She pointed at them, and mimed him sketching.

Taniel made his right hand into a fist. He didn't want her to see him shaking. "I . . . not now, Pole."

She pointed again, more insistently.

Taniel took another deep breath of mala and closed his eyes. He felt tears roll down his cheeks.

He felt her take the book and pencils off his chest. Heard the table move. He expected a reproach. A punch. Something. When he opened his eyes again, he saw her bare feet disappearing up the stairs of the mala den and she was gone. He took another deep breath of mala and wiped the tears off his face.

The room began to fade into the mala haze along with his memories; all the people he'd killed, all the friends he'd seen die. The god he'd seen with his own eyes, and then put down with an ensorcelled bullet. He didn't want to remember any of that.

Just another few days in the mala den, then he'd be fine. Back to his old self. He'd report to Tamas and get back to what he was good at: killing Kez.

Tamas found himself a quarter mile under a thousand tons of rock just a few hours after leaving Budwiel's walls. His torch flickered in the darkness, casting light and shadows across the row after row of recessed graves carved into the walls of the caverns. Skulls hung from the ceilings by the hundred in a grisly tribute to the dead, and he wondered if this was what the pathway to the afterlife looked like.

More fire, he imagined.

He fought off his initial claustrophobia by reminding himself that these catacombs had been used for a thousand years. They weren't likely to collapse anytime soon.

The size of the passageway surprised him. At times the rooms were wide enough to hold hundreds of men. At their narrowest, even a carriage could pass through them without scraping the sides.

The two artillery men Hilanska had spoken of walked on ahead. They carried their own torches and they talked excitedly, their voices echoing as they passed through the varied chambers. Beside Tamas, his bodyguard Olem kept pace with a hand on his pistol and a suspicious eye on the two soldiers ahead of him. Bringing up the rear were two of Tamas's best powder mages: Vlora and Andriya.

"These caverns," Olem said, running his fingers along the stone walls, "were widened with tools. But look at the ceiling." He pointed upward. "No tool marks."

"They were carved out by water," Tamas said. "Probably thousands of years ago." He let his eyes run over the ceiling and then down to the floor. Their path sloped gently downward, punctuated from time to time by steps cut into the floor and worn by the passing of thousands of pilgrims, families, and priests every year. Despite these signs of use, these catacombs were empty of anything living—the priests had suspended burials during the siege, worried that artillery fire might collapse some of the caves.

Tamas used to play in caverns like these when his father, an apothecary, searched the mountains every summer for rare flowers, mushrooms, and fungus. Some cave systems went incredibly deep into the heart of the mountain. Others ended abruptly, just when things seemed to be getting interesting.

The passageway opened up into a wide cavern. The torchlight no longer danced on the ceiling and far walls, but disappeared into the darkness above. They stood on the edge of a pool of still water blacker than a moonless night. Their voices echoed in the great hollow space.

Tamas came to a stop beside the waiting artillery men. He cracked a powder charge in between his fingers and sprinkled it on his tongue. The trance swept through him, bringing dizziness and clarity all at once. The ache of his leg disappeared and the tendrils of light caused by the torches were suddenly more than enough for him to examine the cavern in its entirety.

The walls were lined with stone sarcophagi, stacked almost haphazardly upon one another thirty, maybe forty feet into the air. A dripping sound echoed through the chamber: the source of the underground lake. Tamas could see no exit but the one through which they'd come.

"Sir?" one of the artillerymen said. His name was Ludik, and he held his torch over the pool, trying to gauge the depths.

"We're thousands of feet beneath the West Pillar," Tamas said. "And no closer to Kez. I don't like being led into strange places."

The cock of Olem's pistol stirred the silence of the cave. Behind Tamas, Vlora and Andriya stood with their rifles at the ready. Ludik exchanged a nervous glance with his comrade and swallowed hard.

"It looks like the cave system ends," Ludik said, pointing with his torch across the pond. "But it doesn't. It keeps going, and goes straight toward Kez."

"How do you know?" Tamas asked.

Ludik hesitated, expecting reproach. "Because, sir, we followed it through."

"Show me."

They passed behind a pair of sarcophagi on the other side of the pond and ducked beneath a ledge that proved deeper than it looked. A moment later, and Tamas was standing on the other side. The cavern opened up again and led down into the dark.

Tamas turned to the bodyguard at his shoulder. "Try not to shoot anyone unless I say so."

Olem stroked his neatly trimmed beard, eyeing the artillerymen. "Of course, sir." His hand didn't leave the butt of his pistol. Olem wasn't the trusting sort these days.

An hour later, Tamas left the cavern and climbed up through brush and scree into daylight. The sun had passed over the mountains to the east and the valley was in shadow.

"All clear, sir," Olem said, helping him up to steady footing.

Tamas checked his pistol, then absently thumbed the contents of another powder charge onto his tongue. They stood in a steep valley on the southern slope of the Adran Mountains. By his guess, they were less than two miles from Budwiel. If that was correct, they now flanked the Kez army perfectly.

"An old riverbed, sir," Vlora said, picking her way among the small boulders. "It points to the west, then cuts south. The base of the valley is obscured by a hillock. We're not more than a half mile from the Kez right now, but there's no sign they've even bothered scouting this valley."

"Sir!" a voice called from within the cave.

Tamas whirled. Vlora, Olem, and Andriya all raised their rifles, pointing into the darkness.

An Adran soldier emerged. His shoulder sported a chevron with a powder horn beneath it. The man was a lance corporal, one of Olem's new company of elite soldiers, the Riflejacks.

"Quiet, fool," Olem hissed. "You want all of Kez to hear?"

The messenger wiped the sweat from his brow, blinking up at the brightness of day. "Sorry, sir," he said to Tamas. "I got lost in the mountain. General Hilanska sent me after you not more than a moment after you left."

"What is it, man?" Tamas demanded. Gasping messengers were never a good sign. They never hurried unless it was of utmost importance.

"The Kez, sir," the messenger said. "Our spies report they will attack en masse the day after tomorrow. General Hilanska requests you back at the wall immediately."

Tamas ran his eyes across the steep valley in which they stood. "How many men do you think we could bring through here in two days?"

"Thousands," Vlora said.

"Ten thousand," Olem added.

"A hammer of two brigades," Tamas said. "And Budwiel will be the anvil."

Vlora seemed doubtful. "That's a small hammer, sir, compared with that monstrous force out there."

"Then we'll have to strike hard and fast." Tamas examined the valley one more time. "Let's head back. Have the engineers start widening the tunnel. Get some men up here to shore up this scree so our passage won't cause a ruckus. When the Kez attack, we'll smash them against the gates of Budwiel."

CHAPTER
4

There were few things in the world more tedious, Nila reflected as she sat on the kitchen floor and watched flames curl around the base of the immense iron pot hanging over the fire, than waiting for water to boil.

Most manor houses would be silent at this hour. She'd always relished the quiet—the still night air that insulated her from the chaos of a servant's life when the master and mistress were at home and the house bustled with movement. There was a night not more than a few months past, though it felt like years, that Nila had known no life but the one in which she boiled water and did the laundry every week for Duke Eldaminse's family and the serving staff.

Lord Eldaminse was dead now, his servants scattered and his home burned. Everything Nila had ever known was gone.

Here in Lord Vetas's city manor on a side street in the middle of Adopest, the household never slept.

Somewhere in the enormous house a man was shouting. Nila couldn't make out the words, but they were spoken in anger. Probably Dourford, the Privileged. He was one of Lord Vetas's lieutenants, and he had a temper like Nila had never seen. He had a habit of beating the cooks. Everyone in the house feared him, even the hulking bodyguards who accompanied Lord Vetas on his errands.

Everyone feared Dourford except, of course, for Vetas.

As far as Nila could tell, Lord Vetas feared nothing.

"Jakob," Nila said, speaking to the six-year-old boy sitting beside her on the kitchen floor, "hand me the lye."

Jakob got to his feet and paused, frowning at her. "Where?" he asked.

"Under the washbasin," Nila said. "The glass jar."

Jakob rummaged around beneath the washbasin before finding the jar. He grabbed it by the lid and pulled.

"Careful!" Nila said. She was on her feet and beside him in a moment, and caught him by the shoulders as the jar came loose and he stumbled backward. She put a hand beneath the jar. "Got you," she said, and took the jar. It wasn't very heavy, but Jakob had never been the strongest child.

She unscrewed the lid and doled out a measure for the laundry with a spoon.

"No," she said when Jakob reached for the open jar. "You don't want to touch that. It's very poisonous. It'll eat right through your pink fingers." She snatched him by the hand and playfully bit at his fingers. "Like an angry dog!"

Jakob giggled and retreated across the room. Nila put the lye away on a high shelf. They shouldn't keep materials like this within reach of children. Even if Jakob *was* the only child in the house.

Nila wondered what life would be like if she was still in the Eldaminse manor. There would have been a party for Jakob's sixth birthday two weeks ago. The house staff would have been given a stipend and an extra afternoon off. Duke Eldaminse would have likely made another pass at Nila—or two, or three—and Lady Eldaminse would have considered putting her out on the street.

Nila missed the quiet of the nights doing laundry for the Eldaminse house. She didn't miss backbiting and jealousy among the serving staff, or Lord Eldaminse's groping hands. But she'd exchanged it for something worse.

Lord Vetas's manor.

There was a scream from somewhere in the basement, where Lord Vetas kept his . . . room.

"Pit," Nila said softly to herself, eyes back on the flame of the kitchen fire.

"A lady doesn't curse."

Nila felt her spine stiffen. The voice was quiet, calm. Deceptively placid, like the surface of the ocean undisturbed by the sharks circling beneath.

"Lord Vetas." She turned and curtsied to the man standing in the kitchen door.

Vetas was a Rosvelean with dusty-yellow skin. His back was straight, one hand tucked into his vest pocket and the other holding his evening glass of red wine with casual familiarity. Seen on the street, he might be mistaken for a well-dressed clerk or merchant with his white shirt, dark-blue vest, and black pants that she'd neatly pressed herself.

Nila knew that to assume anything about Vetas was a deadly mistake. He was a killer. She'd felt his hands on her throat. She'd looked into his eyes—eyes that seemed to see everything at once— and seen the dispassion with which he regarded living things.

"I'm not a lady, my lord," Nila said.

Vetas's eyes examined her clinically. Nila felt stripped beneath that gaze. She felt like a piece of meat on the butcher's block. It frightened her.

And it made her angry. She wondered for a moment if Lord Vetas would look that calm and collected in his casket.

"Do you know why you're here?" Vetas said.

"To watch over Jakob." She cast a glance at the boy. Jakob watched Vetas curiously.

"That's right." A smile suddenly split Vetas's face, warmth flooding his expression without touching his eyes. "Come here, boy," Vetas said, kneeling. "It's all right, Jakob. Don't be afraid."

Jakob's training as a noble's son left him no choice but to obey. He started toward Vetas, looking back to Nila for direction.

Nila felt her chest go cold. She wanted to throw herself between them, to take a hot iron from the fire and beat Vetas back. The false smile on his face was far more frightening to her than his customary stoic gaze.

"Go ahead," she heard herself say in a small voice.

"I brought you a candy." Vetas handed Jakob a treat wrapped in colored paper.

"Jakob, don't . . ." Nila started.

Vetas fixed her with his eyes. There was no threat behind them, no emotion. Just a cold glance.

"You can have it," Nila said, "but you should save it for tomorrow, after breakfast."

Vetas gave Jakob the candy and tousled his hair.

Don't touch him, Nila screamed inside. She forced herself to smile at Vetas.

"Why is Jakob here, my lord?" Nila said, pushing the question through her fear.

Vetas got to his feet. "That's no concern of yours. Do you know how to behave like a lady, Nila?" he asked.

"I . . . I suppose. I'm just a laundress."

"I think you're more than that," Vetas said. "Everyone has the ability to rise above their station. You survived the royalist barricades, then infiltrated Field Marshal Tamas's headquarters with the aim of rescuing young Jakob here. And you're pretty. No one ever looks past beauty, if it's dressed right."

Nila wondered how Vetas could possibly have known about the royalist barricades. She'd told him about Tamas's headquarters, but . . . what exactly did he mean about beauty?

"I may have further use for you than just"—he made a gesture toward Jakob and the laundry—"this."

Jakob was too busy trying to nibble at his candy as discreetly as possible to notice the disdain in Vetas's voice. Nila wasn't. And she feared what he meant by "further use."

"My lord." She curtsied again, and tried not to let her hatred show on her face. She might be able to kill him in the bath. Like she'd read in those mystery novels she'd borrowed from the butler's son at the Eldaminse house.

"In the meantime," Vetas said. He stepped into the hall outside the kitchen, keeping the door open with one foot. "Bring her in here," he called.

Someone cursed. A woman screamed in anger—an angry-wildcat yell. There was a struggle in the hall and two of Vetas's bodyguards dragged a woman into the kitchen. She was in her forties perhaps, her body sagging in all the wrong places from having had too many children, her skin wrinkled from work but unweathered by the sun. Her curly black hair was tucked back behind her head in a bun and the bags beneath her eyes spoke of little sleep.

The woman stopped when she caught sight of Nila and Jakob.

"Where is my son?" she spat at Vetas.

"In the basement," Vetas said, "and he won't be harmed as long as you cooperate."

"Liar!"

A patronizing smile touched Vetas's lips. "Nila, Jakob. This is Faye. She is unwell and must be watched at all times, lest she hurt herself. She's going to share your room, Jakob. Can you help watch her, my boy?"

Jakob nodded solemnly.

"Good lad."

"I'll kill you," Faye said to Vetas.

Vetas stepped to Faye and whispered something in her ear. She stiffened, the color draining from her face.

"Now," Vetas said, "Faye is going to take over your responsibilities, Nila. She'll do the laundry, and help with Jakob."

Nila exchanged a glance with the woman. She felt the knot of fear in her belly reflected on Faye's face.

"And me?" Nila knew what Vetas would do with someone who didn't have a use. She still remembered Jakob's dead nurse—the one who'd refused to go along with Vetas's schemes.

Vetas suddenly crossed the room. He took Nila by the chin, turning her face one way and then another. He forced his thumb into her mouth and she had to keep herself from biting down as he examined her teeth. He stepped away suddenly, and wiped his hands on a kitchen towel as if he'd just handled an animal.

"Your hands show very little wear from the laundering. Remarkably little, to be honest. I'll give you some lotion in the morning and you'll apply it every hour. We'll have those hands looking soft, like a noblewoman's, in no time." He patted her on the cheek.

Nila resisted the urge to spit in his eye.

Vetas leaned forward and spoke quietly so that Jakob could not hear. "This woman," Vetas said, pointing to Faye, "is your responsibility, Nila. If she displeases me, you'll suffer for it. Jakob will suffer for it. And believe me, I know how to make people suffer."

Vetas stepped away, throwing a smile toward Jakob. More loudly he said, "I think you need some new clothes, Jakob. Would you like that?"

"Very much, sir," Jakob said.

"We'll do that tomorrow. Some toys, too."

Vetas glanced at Nila, his eyes holding a silent warning, and he left the room with his bodyguards.

Faye adjusted her dress and took a deep breath. Her eyes traveled around the room. A mix of emotions ranged across her face: anger, panic, and fear. For a moment Nila thought she might snatch up a frying pan and attack her.

Nila wondered who she was. Why was she here? Obviously another prisoner. Another player in Vetas's schemes. Could Nila trust her?

"I'm Nila," she said. "And this is Jakob."

Faye's eyes settled on Nila and she nodded with a frown. "I'm Faye. And I'm going to kill that bastard."

CHAPTER
5

Adamat slipped through the side door of one of the dilapidated buildings in Adopest's dock district. He moved down hallways, brushing past secretaries and bookkeepers, always looking straight ahead. In his experience, no one questioned a man who knew where he was going.

Adamat knew that Lord Vetas was looking for him.

It wasn't hard to surmise. Vetas still had Faye. He still had leverage, and no doubt he wanted Adamat dead or under his thumb.

So Adamat stayed low. Field Marshal Tamas's soldiers were protecting his family—part of the bargain Adamat had struck with the field marshal in order to keep his neck from the guillotine. Adamat had to work from the shadows now, finding Lord Vetas and discovering his plans, and freeing Faye before any more harm could come to her. If she was even still alive.

He couldn't do it alone.

The headquarters for the Noble Warriors of Labor was a squat, ugly brick building not far from the Adopest docks. It didn't look like much, but it housed the offices of the biggest union in all the Nine. Every subdivision of the Warriors moved through this hub: bankers, steelworkers, miners, bakers, millers, and more.

But Adamat only needed to speak with one man, and he didn't want to be noticed on his way in. He went down a low-ceilinged hallway on the third floor and paused outside an office door. He could hear voices inside.

"I don't care what you think of the idea," came the voice of Ricard Tumblar, head of the entire union. "I'm going to find him and persuade him. He's the best man for the job."

"Man?" a woman's voice returned. "You don't think a *woman* can do it?"

"Don't start with me, Cheris," Ricard said. "It was a turn of phrase. And don't make this about men or women. You don't like it because he's a soldier."

"And you bloody well know why."

Ricard's retort was lost as Adamat heard the creak of the floor-boards behind him. He turned to find a woman standing behind him.

She looked to be in her midthirties, with straight blond hair tied back in a ponytail behind her head. She wore a dress uniform with loose pants and a white frilled shirt of the type that might be worn by a footman. Her hands were clasped behind her back.

A secretary. The last thing Adamat needed.

"Can I help you, sir?" she said. Her tone was brusque, and her eyes never left Adamat's face.

"Oh, my," Adamat said. "This must look terrible. I didn't mean to eavesdrop, I just needed to speak with Ricard."

She didn't sound at all like she believed him. "The secretary should have kept you in the waiting room."

"I came in the side door," Adamat admitted. So she wasn't the secretary?

The woman said, "Come with me to the lobby and we'll make you an appointment. Mr. Tumblar is terribly busy."

Adamat gave a half bow at the waist. "I'd rather not make an appointment. I just need to speak with Ricard. It's a terribly urgent matter."

"Please, sir."

"I just need to speak with Ricard."

Her voice dropped slightly—instantly more threatening. "If you do not come with me, I will have you taken to the police for trespassing."

"Now look here!" Adamat raised his voice. The last thing he wanted to do was cause a commotion, but he desperately needed Ricard's attention.

"Fell!" Ricard's voice called from inside the office. "Fell! Damn it, Fell, what is that ruckus!"

Fell narrowed her eyes at Adamat. "What is your name?" she asked sternly.

"Inspector Adamat."

Fell's demeanor changed instantly. Gone was the severe gaze that brooked no argument. She let out a soft sigh. "Why didn't you say so to begin with? Ricard has us looking all over the city for you." She stepped past Adamat and opened the door. "It's Inspector Adamat here to see you, sir."

"Well, don't leave him in the hallway. Send him in!"

The room was cluttered but clean—for once. Bookshelves ran the length of each wall, and an ironwood desk framed the center of the room. Ricard was sitting behind his desk, facing a woman who looked to be about fifty. Adamat could immediately tell she was wealthy. Her rings were gold, set with precious gems, and her dress made from the finest cut of muslin. She fanned her face with a fine lace handkerchief and pointedly looked away from Adamat.

"You'll have to excuse me, Cheris," Ricard said. "This is very important."

The woman pushed past Adamat and left the room. Adamat

heard the door slam behind him and they were alone. Adamat thought briefly to ask what that had been about—then decided against it. Ricard was just as likely to spend an hour explaining as he was to tell Adamat it was private business. Adamat removed his hat and coat and returned Ricard's embrace.

Ricard sat back down behind his desk and gestured to the vacant chair. They spoke at the exact same moment:

"Adamat, I need your help."

"Ricard, I need your help."

They both fell silent, and then Ricard laughed and ran a hand across the bald spot on the front of his scalp. "You haven't needed my help for years," he said. He took a deep breath. "First, I want to tell you how sorry I am about the Barbers."

The Black Street Barbers. The street gang that supposedly reported to Ricard, but that had come after Adamat in his own home. Had that really been only a month ago? It seemed like years.

"Tamas wiped them out," Adamat said. "The survivors are rotting in Sablethorn."

"With my blessing."

Adamat nodded. He didn't trust himself to say more about the topic. He didn't precisely blame Ricard for the incident, but he now had far less faith in Ricard's people.

"Is Faye still out of the city?" Ricard said.

Something must have showed in Adamat's eyes. Ricard was a man who'd made his living reading facial tics and knowing what to say at the right moment. He stood up and opened the door a crack. "Fell," he said. "I don't want to be bothered. No people. No sound."

He closed the door and slid the latch, returning to his desk.

"Tell me everything," Ricard said.

Adamat paused. He'd fought with himself for days about whether to come to Ricard at all, and what exactly to say. It wasn't as if he didn't trust Ricard—it was that he didn't trust Ricard's people. Lord

Vetas had spies everywhere. But if he couldn't trust Ricard himself, then there was no one left in his life to turn to for help.

"Faye and the children were taken by a man named Lord Vetas," Adamat said. "They were held against their will to guarantee my cooperation. I gave Vetas information about my conversations with Tamas and my investigation."

Ricard tensed. Whatever he'd expected, this was not it. "You crossed Tamas?" *And you're still alive?* was the unspoken question.

"I've told Tamas all of it," Adamat said. "He has forgiven me—for now—and sent me on a hunt for Lord Vetas. I managed to rescue some of the children, but Vetas still has Faye and Josep."

"Can't you use Tamas's soldiers to go after Vetas?"

"I'd have to find him first. Once I do, I wish it were that simple. The moment Vetas finds out where I am, he will no doubt threaten me with Faye's life. I need to find him silently, track him, and get her out of his hands before I bring down Tamas's wrath upon him."

Ricard nodded slowly. "So you don't know where he is?"

"He's like a ghost. I looked into him when he first started blackmailing me. He doesn't even exist."

"If *you* can't find him, I doubt any of my people can."

"I don't need you to find him. I need information." Adamat reached into his pocket and removed the card Vetas had left him months ago. It had an address on it. "This is the only lead I have. It's an old warehouse not all that far from here. I need to know everything about it. Who owns it? Who owns the properties around it? When was it last sold? Everything. Your people have access to records I can't easily get my hands on."

Ricard nodded. "Of course. Anything." He reached to take the card.

Adamat stopped him, clutching Ricard's hand. "This is deadly serious. The lives of my wife and my son depend on it. If you don't think you can trust your people, just tell me now and I'll find him myself." *Remember what happened with the Barbers*, Adamat said silently.

Ricard seemed to get the message. "I have some people," Ricard said. "Don't worry. This will be safe."

"One more thing," Adamat said. "There are two people involved in this somehow that you might blanch at crossing."

Ricard smiled. "If it's not Tamas, I can't imagine who."

"Lord Claremonte and the Proprietor."

Ricard's smile disappeared. "Lord Claremonte doesn't surprise me," he said. "The Brudania-Gurla Trading Company has been trying to move in on the union since our inception. He's tricky, but he doesn't scare me."

"Don't be so quick to dismiss him. Lord Vetas works for him." And Vetas was holding Adamat's wife and son hostage. Clare-monte, as far as Adamat was concerned, might as well have been holding Faye and Josep personally.

Ricard made a dismissive gesture. "You say that the Proprietor might be involved? I don't trust him, of course, but I thought you cleared him of treachery yourself."

"I never cleared him," Adamat said. "I just found out that Char-lemund was the one trying to kill Tamas. One of the Proprietor's boxers was holding my family hostage. You know how he is about his boxers finding work elsewhere—no one works for someone else without the Proprietor's permission." Which meant that the Pro-prietor may be in league with Lord Claremonte.

"Tread carefully on this, my friend," Ricard warned. "Vetas may be trying to use you, but the Proprietor will cut and bury your entire family without so much as a thought." He glanced at the card Adamat had given him and put it in his vest pocket. "I'll look into this, don't worry. But I need a favor from you."

"Go on."

"Do you know Taniel Two-Shot?"

"I know *of* him," Adamat said. "Everyone in the Nine does. The newspapers were saying he was in a coma after a battle of sorcery on top of South Pike Mountain."

"He's not in a coma anymore," Ricard said. "He woke up a week ago, and he's disappeared."

Adamat's first thoughts went to Lord Vetas. The man was working actively against Tamas. He would leap at the chance to capture the field marshal's son. "Any sign of violence?"

Ricard shook his head. "Well, yes. But it's not like that. He left his guard duty of his own volition. Tamas had his own men guarding him, but my people were keeping an eye on him as well. That he slipped both our nets is rather embarrassing. I need him found quietly."

"Do you want him returned?" Adamat said. "I'm not about to make a powder mage do something he doesn't want to do."

"No, just find out where he is and let me know."

Adamat stood up. "I'll see what I can do."

"And I'll look into this Lord Vetas." Ricard held up a hand to forestall Adamat's protests. "Discreetly. I promise."

Tamas entered Budwiel's biggest mess hall and was nearly knocked over by the swirl of enticing smells wafting from inside.

He swept past the tables where hundreds of his men were having their evening repast and headed toward the kitchens, trying to ignore his hunger pangs.

The man he was looking for was hard to miss: big, fat, taller than most, with waist-length black hair tied behind his head and his olive skin showing just a touch of Rosvelean ancestry. He stood in one corner of the kitchens, on his toes to be able to see into the highest row of ovens.

Mihali was, officially, Tamas's chef. He and his cadre of assistants provided food of the highest caliber for Tamas's entire army, and even for the city of Budwiel. The people loved Mihali; the men worshipped him.

Well, perhaps they *should* worship him.

He was Adom reborn, patron saint of Adro, and brother to the god Kresimir. Which made him a god in his own right.

Mihali turned to Tamas and waved across the myriad of assistants, flour going up in a cloud around him.

"Field Marshal," the chef called. "Come over here."

Tamas stifled the annoyance at being summoned like a common soldier and made his way through the tables of bread.

"Mihali—"

The god-chef cut him off. "Field Marshal, I'm so glad you're here. I have a matter of great importance to discuss with you."

Great importance? Tamas had never seen Mihali so distressed. He leaned forward. What could possibly worry a god? "What is it?"

"I can't decide what to make for lunch tomorrow."

"You git!" Tamas exclaimed, taking a step back. His heart thundered in his ears, as if he'd expected Mihali to announce that the world would end on the morrow.

Mihali didn't seem to notice the insult. "I haven't not known what to cook for decades. I normally have it all planned out but... I'm sorry, are you mad about something?"

"I'm trying to fight a war here, Mihali! The Kez are knocking at Budwiel's front door."

"And hunger is knocking at mine!"

Mihali seemed so out of sorts that Tamas forced himself to calm down. He put a hand on Mihali's arm. "The men will love whatever you make."

"I'd planned poached eggs with asparagus tips, filet of salmon, lamb chops glazed with honey, and a selection of fruit."

"That's three meals you just named there," Tamas said.

"Three meals? *Three meals?* That's four courses, barely enough for a proper lunch, and I did the same thing five days ago. What kind of a chef serves the same meal more than once a week?" Mihali tapped flour-covered fingers against his chin. "How could I have messed up? Maybe it's a leap year."

Tamas counted to ten silently to keep his temper contained—something he'd not done since Taniel was a boy. "Mihali, we're going into battle the day after tomorrow. Will you help me?"

The god appeared nervous. "I'm not going to kill anyone, if that's what you're asking," Mihali said.

"Can you do anything for us? We're outnumbered ten to one out there."

"What is your plan?"

"I'm going to take the Seventh and the Ninth through the catacombs and flank the Kez position. When they try to attack Budwiel, we'll smash them against the gates and route them."

"That sounds very military."

"Mihali, please focus!"

Mihali finally stopped casting about the mess tent as if searching for tomorrow's menu and gave Tamas a level stare. "Kresimir was a commander. Brude was a commander. *I* am a chef. But since you ask: The strategy sounds very high-risk with an equally high payoff. It suits you perfectly."

"Can you do anything to help?" Tamas asked gently.

Mihali seemed to think on this. "I can make sure that your men remain unnoticed until the moment you charge."

Tamas felt a wave of relief. "That would be perfect." He waited for a few moments. "Mihali, you appear agitated."

Mihali took Tamas by the elbow and pulled him into one corner of the tent. In a low voice, he said, "Kresimir is gone."

"That's right," Tamas said. "Taniel killed him."

"No, no. Kresimir is *gone*, but I didn't feel him die."

"But the whole of the Nine felt it. Privileged Borbador told me that every Knacked and Privileged in the world felt it when he died."

"That wasn't him dying," Mihali said, waving the lump of bread dough still in one hand. "That was his counterstroke against Taniel for shooting him in the head."

Tamas's mouth was suddenly dry. "You mean Kresimir is still alive?" Privileged Borbador had warned Tamas that a god couldn't be killed. Tamas had hoped that Borbador was wrong.

"I don't know," Mihali said, "and that's what worries me. I've always been able to sense him, even when half the cosmos separated us."

"Is he with the Kez army?" Tamas would have to cancel all his plans. Rethink every strategy. If Kresimir was with the Kez army, they might all be swept away.

"No, he's not," Mihali said. "I would know."

"But you said that..."

"I assure you," Mihali said. "I would know if he was that close. Besides, he wouldn't risk an open confrontation between us."

Tamas balled his fists. The uncertainties were the worst part of planning for a battle. It always put him on edge, knowing he couldn't plan for everything, and this was a god-sized uncertainty. He'd have to go forward with his plans and hope that Mihali's help in concealing the troops would be enough.

"Now," Mihali said, "if we're quite through with that, I need help with tomorrow's menu."

Tamas poked the god in the chest. "*You* are the chef," he said. "*I* am the commander, and I have a battle to plan."

He left the mess hall and was halfway to his command tent when he cursed himself for not snagging a bowl of Mihali's squash soup.

Less than twenty-four hours after Ricard sent him looking for Taniel Two-Shot, Adamat found himself sitting back in Ricard's office near the docks.

Ricard chewed on the end of a rough-cut pencil and stared across at Adamat. What little hair he had left stuck up from the top of his head like a wind-blown haystack, and Adamat wondered if he'd slept at all in the time between their meetings. At least he was wearing a different shirt and jacket. The room smelled of incense, burned paper, and foul meat. Adamat wondered if there was an uneaten sandwich beneath one of the stacks of records.

"You didn't go home last night, did you?" Adamat asked.

"How could you tell?"

"Besides the fact that you look like the pit? You didn't change your boots. I haven't seen you wear the same pair of boots two days in a row since I met you."

Ricard looked down at his feet. "You would notice that, wouldn't you?" He wiped fatigue from his eyes. "Don't tell me you've already found Two-Shot?"

Adamat held up a piece of paper. On it, he'd written the address of the mala den where he'd found the hero of the Adran army wallowing in his own self-pity. He held the note out to Ricard. When Ricard reached for it, he pulled it back at the last second, as if suddenly changing his mind.

"I read something interesting in the newspaper this morning," Adamat said. When Ricard didn't respond, he took the newspaper in question from under his arm and threw it on the desk. " 'Ricard Tumblar to Run for First Minister of the Republic of Adro,' " he said, reading the headline out loud.

"Oh," Ricard said blandly. "That."

"Why didn't you tell me?"

"You seemed to have a lot on your plate."

"And you're vying to become leader of our new government. What the pit are you doing business down at the docks for?"

Ricard perked up. "I've built a new place. Moving into it tomorrow, actually. Still in the factory district, but it'll be fantastic for entertaining dignitaries. Would you like to see it?"

"I'm a little busy now," Adamat said. When Ricard's face fell, he added, "Some other time, I'm sure."

"You'll like it. Gaudy. Grand. But stylish."

Adamat snorted. Knowing Ricard, "gaudy" only began to describe it. He tossed the paper on Ricard's desk. "Either you had less people looking for him than you made me believe, or your people are idiots."

"I don't recognize the address," Ricard said, grinning so hard it made his cheeks red.

Adamat wasn't in the mood for the enthusiasm. "After a battle, soldiers go straight for one of two things: either home or vice. Taniel Two-Shot is a career soldier, so I guessed vice. The quickest place to find that near the People's Court is to head northwest into the Gurlish Quarter. He was in the sixth mala den I checked."

"You got lucky," Ricard said. "Admit it. He could have gone anywhere. You just looked in the Gurlish Quarter first."

Adamat shrugged. Investigative work depended more on luck than he cared to admit, but he'd never tell that to a client. "Any chance you found the record for the address I gave you yesterday?"

Ricard sifted through the papers on his desk. A moment later he handed Adamat back Vetas's card. It had a name and address written on it in pencil.

"Fell checked herself," Ricard said. "The warehouse was bought by a tailor—of all things—two years ago. There are no records to indicate it had been sold after the tailor bought it, which means it didn't fall into the hands of the union. Must have been purchased privately. I'm sorry I couldn't do more to help."

"This is a start," Adamat said. He stood up and retrieved his hat and cane.

"You'll be taking SouSmith with you, won't you?" Ricard asked. "I don't want you going after this Vetas alone."

"SouSmith is still laid up," Adamat said. "He took some bloody damage from the Barbers."

Ricard grimaced. "He could go see Lady Parkeur."

Lady Parkeur was an eccentric middle-aged woman who lived with thousands of birds in an old church in High Talien. She always had feathers in her hair and smelled like a henhouse, but she was also the only Knacked in the city with the ability to heal wounds. She could knit together broken tissue and bone with the force of her will, and she cost more money than a Privileged healer.

"I spent every penny I had left to get myself healed by her after the beating I took from Charlemund," Adamat said. "I had to so I could go after my family."

"Fell!" Ricard yelled, making Adamat jump.

The woman appeared a moment later. "Mr. Tumblar?"

"Send a message to Lady Parkeur. Tell her I'm calling in that favor she owes me. There's a boxer, name of SouSmith, who needs mending. Tell her she needs to make a house call today."

"She doesn't do house calls," Fell said.

"She bloody well better for me. If she gives you any lip, remind her about that incident with the goat."

"Right away," Fell said.

"Incident with a goat?" Adamat said.

Ricard looked around. "Don't ask. I need a bloody drink."

"Ricard, you don't have to call in favors for me," Adamat said. He knew by experience how much Lady Parkeur cost for healing. The wait to see her was usually weeks. Adamat had only gotten in through a personal request from Field Marshal Tamas.

"Think nothing of it," Ricard said. "You've saved my ass more times than I can count." He recovered a bottle from behind a stack of books and drained the last finger of cloudy liquid from the bottle, then made a face. It was another moment before he ceased his search for more alcohol and dropped into his seat. "But don't think I won't ask you for more favors. This 'First Minister' business is going to be a rough time."

"I'll do what I can."

"Good. Now go find out about Lord Whatshisname. I've been thinking of a really big gift for you and Faye for your anniversary next year. I'd prefer that you're both around to give it to."

CHAPTER

6

Taniel cut the last silver button off his jacket and handed it to Kin. The stooped Gurlish examined the button closely in the light of a candle before sliding it into his pocket, just like he had all the others, and set a ball of mala on the table next to Taniel's hammock.

Despite the greed apparent on Kin's face, he had a worried look in his eyes.

"Don't go through it so fast. Savor. Taste. *Enjoy*," Kin said.

Taniel pushed a large piece of mala into his pipe. It lit instantly off the embers of the old mala, and he breathed in deep.

"You smoke more in a day than any man does in twenty," Kin said. He settled back on his haunches, watching Taniel smoke.

Taniel lifted his silver powder-mage button and rolled it between his fingers. "Must be the sorcery," he said. "Ever had a powder mage in here before?"

Kin shook his head.

"Never known a powder mage who smoked mala myself," Taniel said. "We all take the powder. Never need more to feel alive."

"Why the mala?" Kin busied himself sweeping the center of the den.

Taniel took a deep breath. "Powder doesn't make you forget."

"Ah. Forget. Every man takes mala to forget." Kin nodded knowingly.

Taniel stared at the ceiling of his niche, counting the hammock swings.

"Going to bed," Kin said, setting his broom in one corner.

"Wait," Taniel reached out with one hand, only to draw it back when he realized how pathetic he must look. "Give me enough to get through the night."

"Night?" Kin shook his head. "It's morning now. I work through the night. Most smokers come then."

"Give me enough for that, then."

Kin seemed to consider this, looking at the ball he just gave Taniel. From what he said, a ball like that should have lasted four or five days.

"Give me the powder keg, and I'll give you as much you can smoke for three weeks."

Taniel clenched the powder-keg pin in his fist. "No. What else?"

"I'll give you my daughter for the whole three weeks, too."

Taniel's stomach turned at the thought of the Gurlish mala man pimping his daughter to his customers.

"No."

"You like art?" Kin picked up the sketchbook and pencil Ka-poel had brought for Taniel.

"Put those down."

Kin dropped the sketchbook with a sigh. "You no have value. No money."

Taniel checked the pockets of his coat. Nothing. He ran his fingers over the silver embroidery.

"How much for my coat?"

Kin sniffed and touched the fabric. "Tiny bit."

"Give me that." Taniel set his mala pipe on the table and wriggled out of the coat, handing it over to Kin.

"You'll die of cold, and I won't pay for funeral."

"It's the middle of summer. Give me the damned mala."

Kin handed him a disappointingly small ball of the sticky black mala before disappearing up the stairs with Taniel's coat. Taniel heard the creak of feet on the floorboards above him, and Kin's voice speaking in Gurlish.

He settled back into his hammock and took a long draw at his mala pipe.

It was said that mala would make a man forget for hours at a time. Taniel tried to think back on the hours he'd lost. How long had he been down here? Days? Weeks? It didn't seem like a long time.

He took the pipe out of his mouth and examined it in the dim light of the den's candles. "Damned stuff doesn't work," he said to himself. He could still see Kresimir stepping out of that cloud after descending from the sky. A god! A real, live god. Taniel wondered what his childhood priest would have done had he known Taniel would one day grow up to shoot the god of the Nine.

Time hadn't stopped when the ensorcelled bullet went through Kresimir's eye, so it seemed the world could live without its god. But how many people had died trying to keep Kresimir from returning to the world? Hundreds of Adran. Friends. Allies. Thousands of Kez—hundreds by Taniel's own hand.

Every time he closed his eyes, he saw a new face. Sometimes it was a man or a woman he'd killed. Sometimes it was Tamas, or Vlora. And sometimes it was Ka-poel. Maybe it was the mala, but, by the pit, it made his heart beat faster when he saw the savage girl's face.

The steps creaked. Taniel looked up. Through the haze he could see Ka-poel come down the stairs. She crossed the room to his side, frowned at him.

"What?" he said.

She tugged on his shirt, then pinched her own long duster. *Jacket.* Damn. First thing she noticed.

He wrapped his hand around his ball of mala protectively.

Quicker than he could see, her hand darted forward and snatched the mala pipe from between his teeth.

"You little bitch," he hissed. "Give it back."

She danced away from his grasping hands to stand in the middle of the room, grinning.

"Ka-poel, bring me that pipe."

She shook her head.

His breathing came harder. He blinked against a sudden cloud in his vision, unable to tell if it was the mala or his own fury. After a moment of struggle, he sat up in the hammock.

"Give it back to me *now*." He swung his legs over the edge of the hammock, but when he tried to stand up, a wave of nausea struck him harder than it ever had when he opened his third eye to see into the Else. He sank back into the hammock, his heart hammering in his ears.

"Pit," he whispered, clutching at his temples. "I'm all sorts of buggered."

Ka-poel set the mala pipe on a stool on the other side of the room.

"Don't put that there," Taniel said, his own voice now weak. "Bring it to me."

She just shook her head and shrugged out of her duster. Before he could protest, she crossed to him and swept it up over his hammock and up to his shoulders.

He pushed it away. "You'll get cold," he said.

She pointed at him.

"It's summer, damn it. I'm fine."

She drew the duster back up over his chest.

Again, he gave it back to her. "I'm not a child."

Something seemed to light in her eyes at that. She pulled the duster off him and threw it to the ground.

"Pole, what the..." His next words were lost in his own strangled cry as she lifted one leg over the hammock and straddled him, sitting directly on his lap. His heart beat a little faster as she wiggled her ass to get comfortable. In the closeness of the niche, their faces were almost touching. "Pole...," he said, suddenly breathless. The mala pipe, and even the little ball of mala in his hands, were suddenly forgotten.

Her tongue darted out and wet her lips. She seemed poised, watchful—like an animal.

Taniel almost didn't hear the sound of the door to the house upstairs being thrown open. Feet thumped on the floorboards. A woman began shouting in Gurlish.

Ka-poel lowered her head. Taniel's shoulders flexed, pushing him toward her.

"Captain Taniel Two-Shot!" The stairs rattled under a pair of determined boots. A woman in a dress suit, hat in hand, entered the room. "Captain!" she said. "Captain, I..."

She froze when she saw Taniel with Ka-poel in his lap. Taniel felt the color rise in his cheeks. A quick glance at Ka-poel. She gave him a small, knowing smile, but annoyance flashed in her eyes. She rolled off of him and swept her duster off the floor and over her shoulders in one quick movement.

The woman turned to one side, staring at the far wall. "Sir, I'm sorry, I didn't know you were indisposed."

"She's not undressed," Taniel retorted. His voice cracked and he cleared his throat. "Who the pit are you?"

The woman gave a slight bow. "I am Fell Baker, undersecretary for the Holy Warriors of Labor." Despite having found them in a compromising situation, she didn't seem the least bit embarrassed.

"The union? How the pit did you find me?" Taniel pulled himself to a sitting position in the hammock, though it made his stomach turn something fierce. He wondered how long it had been since he ate.

"I'm Ricard Tumblar's aide, sir. He sent me to find you. He would very much like to meet with you."

"Tumblar? Don't know the name." He settled back into the hammock and eyed Ka-poel. She'd sat on the stool on the far side of the mala den, tapping his pipe against her palm as she studied the undersecretary.

Fell raised an eyebrow. "He's the head of the union, sir."

"I don't care."

"He's asked me to extend to you an invitation to lunch."

"Go away."

"He says there's a great deal of money at stake."

"I don't care."

Fell examined him for a few moments before turning and heading up the creaking stairs just as abruptly as she'd arrived. The hushed sound of voices came down through the floor. They were speaking in Gurlish. Taniel glanced at Ka-poel. She returned his stare for a moment, then winked.

What the pit?

A few moments later the undersecretary came back downstairs.

"Sir, it appears you're out of money."

Taniel looked for his mala pipe. Oh. Ka-poel still had it. Right.

"Take that from her and give it to me, would you?" Taniel said to Fell.

Fell faced Ka-poel. The two women exchanged a glance that seemed full of meaning. Taniel didn't like that at all.

The undersecretary clasped her hands together. "I will not, sir." She crossed the room in two strides and grabbed Taniel by the chin, forcing his face toward her. Taniel grasped the woman's wrist, but Fell was stronger than she looked. She examined his eyes.

"Let go of me, or I will bloody well kill you," Taniel growled.

Fell took her hands away and stepped back. "How much have you smoked since you got here?"

"Don't know," Tamas grumbled. Ka-poel hadn't so much as moved when the undersecretary had rushed him. Some help she was.

"Eight pounds of the stuff in four days. That's what the owner told me."

Taniel shrugged.

"That's enough to kill a warhorse, sir."

Taniel sniffed. "Didn't seem to do much."

A perplexed look crossed Fell's face. She opened her mouth, shut it again, and then said, "Didn't do much? I . . ." She grasped her hat and went back upstairs, only to return again after a few minutes.

"The owner," Fell said, "insists he watched you smoke it himself. I examined your eyes. Not even a hint of mala poisoning. Pit, I've probably gotten mala poisoning just standing in the smoke and talking to you. You're god-touched."

Taniel surged to his feet. One moment he was in the hammock, and the next he had Fell by the lapels with both fists. His head spun, his vision warped, and his hands trembled with rage. "I am not god-touched," Taniel said. "I've not . . . I'm . . ."

"Kindly unhand me, sir," Fell said gently.

Taniel felt his hands drop to his sides. He took a step back and mumbled to himself.

"I'll give you a moment to clean up," Fell said. "We'll get you a new jacket on the way to see Ricard."

"I'm not going," Taniel said weakly. He stumbled to the corner, grateful for a wall to lean against. It might be that he *couldn't* go. He doubted he could walk more than twenty feet.

Fell sighed. "Mr. Tumblar offers the hospitality of his own mala den, sir. It is a much more comfortable location, and his denkeeper won't take your jacket. If you refuse that invitation, we are instructed to bring you there by force."

Taniel looked over to Ka-poel. She was cleaning her fingernails with what looked to be a sharpened knitting needle, almost as long as her forearm. She met his eyes briefly. Again that small, knowing smile. Again the annoyance in her eyes.

"Ricard's den has significantly more privacy than this, sir," Fell said, coughing once into her hand.

Taniel was not sure that whatever had just happened with Ka-poel was bound to repeat itself. "All right, Fell. But one thing."

"Sir?"

"I don't think I've eaten in two days. I could use some lunch."

Two hours later, Taniel was in the Adopest docks. The docks traditionally ran Adran commerce, governing the transport of cargo from the Ad River and its tributaries in the north all the way down through Surkov's Alley and across the Amber Expanse. With the war on, trade through Kez was at a standstill, and cargo that usually used the river was now sent over the mountains by mule and packhorse.

Despite the change in transportation, the docks were still the center of commerce in Adopest. Barges brought iron ore and raw lumber down the river to supply the Adran mills and gunsmiths, who turned out weapons and ammunition in the hundreds every day.

The docks stank of fish, sewage, and smoke, and Taniel was starting to miss the cool, sweet smell of mala in Kin's den. His escort consisted of Fell Baker the undersecretary and a pair of wide-shouldered steelworkers. Taniel wondered if the steelworkers were there to carry him to the meeting with Ricard if he decided not to go.

Ka-poel trailed along behind the group. The steelworkers ignored her; Fell kept a wary eye on her at all times. She seemed to suspect that Ka-poel was more than just a mute savage, while Taniel had a hunch that Fell might be more than an undersecretary.

Fell stopped in front of a dockside warehouse within spitting distance of the water. Taniel looked out from between the alleyways and across the Adsea. Even during the day he could see a glow on the horizon, and the conspicuous absence of South Pike Mountain. The view made him want to hide beneath a rock. The death throes of a god had leveled a mountain, and he'd gotten away with a month-long coma. He wasn't certain why he wasn't dead, but he suspected it had to do with Ka-poel.

He wondered if everyone else had been so lucky. Where was Bo? Where were the men and women of the Mountainwatch he'd befriended during the defense of Shouldercrown?

An image flashed through his mind of clutching Ka-poel to his chest as Kresimir's palace collapsed around him. Fire and stone, the burning heat of lava as the mountain collapsed.

"Hard to believe it's gone, isn't it," Fell said, nodding across the water as she opened the door to the warehouse and gestured for Taniel to go in.

Taniel gave one last glance to the east and jerked his head toward Fell. "You first."

"Fine," Fell said. She looked to the steelworkers, offering them cigars from a gunmetal case in her vest pocket. "Back to work for you, boys." The two men tipped their hats to Fell, took a light for their cigars and then headed back into the street. "Come on," Fell said. Once they were all in, she closed the door behind Ka-poel. "Welcome to Ricard's new offices."

Taniel had to keep himself from whistling. On the outside, the building looked like an old warehouse. The windows were shuttered, the brick long in need of refacing. The inside was another matter.

The floors were of black marble, and the walls were whitewashed behind crimson satin curtains. The building appeared to have but one main room, an echoing chamber two stories high and at least two hundred paces long, lit by a half-dozen crystal chandeliers. At the near end of the room there was a long bar, complete with uniformed barman and well-endowed woman in nothing more than a petticoat.

"Your coat, sir," the woman said.

Taniel handed her his new dark-blue uniform jacket. He felt his gaze rest on her a little longer than was proper. Without looking at Ka-poel, he turned to examine the room. Artwork adorned the walls, sculptures were set at even intervals inside shallow recesses. This was the kind of wealth displayed by the highest echelons of nobility, even that of the king. Taniel thought that Tamas had stamped out this kind of wealth when he slaughtered the nobility. A thought occurred that perhaps Tamas had just changed the very rich and powerful for a new set of the same.

A man crossed the marble floor toward them. He wore a white smoking jacket, a cigar clenched between his teeth. He looked to be about forty years old, with a hairline receding well past the middle of his head. He wore a long beard in the Fatrastan style, and the grin on his face reached his ears and even touched his eyes.

"Taniel Two-Shot," the man said, holding out his hand. "Ricard Tumblar. I'm a great admirer of yours."

Taniel took his hand with hesitation.

"Mr. Tumblar."

"Mister? Bah, call me Ricard. I'm at your service. And this must be your ever-present companion. The Dynize. My lady?" Ricard swept into a deep bow and took Ka-poel's hand in his, bending to kiss it gently. Despite his forward nature, he eyed her as one might something pretty but far from tame, something that might bite at any moment.

Ka-poel didn't seem to know how to react to this.

"I'd heard you were a handsome woman," Ricard said, "but the stories didn't do you justice." He broke away from them and crossed to the bar. "Drink?"

"What do you have?" Taniel felt his mood brighten a little.

"Anything," Ricard said.

Taniel doubted that. "Fatrastan ale, then."

Ricard nodded to the barman. "Two, please. For the lady?"

Ka-poel flashed three fingers.

"Make that three," Ricard said to the barman. A moment later, he handed Taniel a mug.

"Son of a bitch," Taniel said after a sip. "You really do have Fatrastan ale."

"I did say anything. Can we take a seat?"

He led them toward the far end of the room. Taniel blamed his mala-addled mind for not noticing earlier that they weren't alone. A dozen men and half again as many women lounged on divans, drinking and smoking, talking quietly among themselves.

Ricard spoke as they approached the group. "Oh, I had a question for you, Taniel. How much black powder does the army use?"

Taniel rubbed his eyes. His head hurt, and he didn't come here to meet Ricard's cronies. "Quite a lot, I'd imagine. I'm not a quartermaster. Why do you ask?"

"Been getting more and more powder orders from the General Staff," Ricard said, waving his hand like it was a trifle. "I just thought it strange. It almost seems as if their requisitions double every week. Nothing to worry about, I'm sure."

The talking died down when Taniel reached the group at the end of the room, and he felt suddenly uncomfortable.

"I thought this was going to be a private meeting," Taniel said quietly, stopping Ricard with a hand to his arm.

Ricard didn't even glance down at the hand Taniel laid on him. "Give me a moment to make introductions and we'll get down to business."

He went around the room, giving names that Taniel immediately forgot, and titles that Taniel took no great note of. These men and women were the heads of the various factions within the unions: bakers, steelworkers, millers, ironsmiths, blacksmiths, and goldsmiths.

True to his word, when the introductions were finished, Ricard led them toward a quiet corner of the vast room, where they were joined by just one other woman. She was one of the first Ricard had introduced, and Taniel couldn't remember her name.

"Cigarette?" Ricard offered as they took their seats. A man in a jacket matching the barman's brought them a silver tray lined with cigarettes, cigars, and pipes. Taniel noticed a mala pipe among the recreation. His fingers twitched to take it, but he fought down the urge and waved away the servant.

"Your secretary said you wanted to meet with me," Taniel said, realizing with a start that Fell had disappeared. "She didn't say why. I'd like to know."

"I have a proposition."

Taniel looked at the woman again. She was older, with an air of disdain particular to the very wealthy. What was her name? And who did she represent? The bakers? No. Goldsmiths?

"I'm not interested," Taniel said.

"I haven't even told you what it is," Ricard said.

"Look," Taniel said. "I came because your undersecretary made it clear that she'd make me come even if I didn't want to. I've been polite. I've come. Now I'd like to go." He stood.

"Is this what you brought me here for, Ricard?" the woman said, looking down her nose at Taniel. "To see a mala-drunk soldier piss on your hospitality? I fear for this country, Ricard. We've handed it over to the uneducated soldiers. They don't know anything but vice and killing."

Taniel clenched his fists and felt his lip curl. "You don't know me, madam. You don't know who the pit I am or what I've seen. Don't pretend to understand soldiers when you've never looked into another man's eyes and seen that one of you would die."

Ricard leaned back on his divan and relit his cigar with a matchstick. He had the air of a man at the boxing ring. Had he expected this?

The woman fairly bristled. "I know soldiers," she said. "Sick, stupid brutes. You rape and steal, and you kill when you can't do that. I've known many soldiers and I don't have to kill a man to know you're nothing more than a churlish brigand in a uniform."

Ricard sighed. "Please, Cheris, not now."

"Not now?" Cheris asked. "If not now, then when? I've had enough of Tamas's iron grip on the city. I didn't want you to bring this so-called war hero here."

Taniel turned to go.

"Taniel," Ricard said. "Give me just a few more moments."

"Not with her here," Taniel said. He headed toward the door, only to find his way blocked by Ka-poel. "I'm leaving, Pole."

She returned his grimace with a cool-eyed shake of the head.

"Look at that!" Cheris said behind him. "The coward flees back to his mala den. He can't face truth. And you want this man at your side, Ricard? He's led around by a savage girl."

Taniel whirled. He'd had enough. His rage piqued, he advanced toward Cheris, one hand held in the air.

"Strike me!" she said, leaning forward to offer a cheek. "It'll show how much of a man you are."

Taniel froze. Had he just been ready to hit her? "I killed a god," he fumed. "I put a bullet through his eye and watched him die to save this country!"

"Lies," Cheris said. "You lie to me to my face? You think I believe this tripe about Kresimir returning?"

Taniel would have let his hand fly right then if Ka-poel hadn't slipped around him. She faced Cheris, eyes narrowed. Taniel suddenly felt fear. As much as he wanted to hurt this woman, he knew what Ka-poel was capable of.

"Pole," he said.

"Out of my face, you savage whore," Cheris said, getting to her feet.

Ka-poel's fist connected with her nose hard enough to send

Cheris tumbling over the back of the divan. Cheris screamed. Ricard shot to his feet. The group of union bosses still speaking quietly on the other side of the room fell silent, and stared, shocked, toward them.

Cheris climbed to her feet, pushing away Ricard's attempt to help. Without a look back, she fled the room, blood streaming from her nose.

Ricard turned to Taniel, his expression caught somewhere between horror and amusement.

"I won't apologize," Taniel said. "Neither for me nor for Pole." Ka-poel took a place at his side, arms crossed.

"She was my guest," Ricard said. He paused, examined his cigar. "More ale," he called to the barkeep. "But you are my guests as well. She's going to make me pay for that later. I'd hoped she would be an ally in the coming months, but it appears that is not the case."

Taniel looked to Ricard, then to the main door, where Cheris was demanding her coachman.

"I should go," Taniel said.

"No, no. Ale!" Ricard shouted again, though Taniel could see the barkeep heading toward them. "You're more important than she is."

Taniel slowly lowered himself back into his seat. "I killed Kresimir," he said. Part of him wanted to be proud of it, but saying it aloud made him feel ill.

"That's what Tamas told me," Ricard said.

"You don't believe me."

The barkeep arrived and changed Taniel's mug for another one, though he'd only finished half. New mugs all around and the man disappeared. Ricard drank deeply of his before he began to speak.

"I'm a practical man," Ricard said. "I know that sorcery exists, though I am not a Privileged or a Knacked or a Marked. Two months ago, if you'd told me that Kresimir would return, I would have wondered what asylum you'd escaped from.

"But I was there when the Barbers tried to kill Mihali. I saw your father—a man twice as pragmatic as I—go ghost white. He felt something from the chef and—"

"I'm sorry," Taniel interrupted. "Mihali?"

Ricard tapped the ash from the end of his cigar. "Oh. You're very much out of the loop, aren't you? Mihali is Adom reborn. Kresimir's brother, here in the flesh."

Taniel felt the hair on the back of his neck stand on end. Another god? Kresimir's own brother?

"What I'm trying to get at," Ricard went on, "is that your father believes that Mihali is Adom reborn. And if Adom has returned, why not Kresimir? So, yes. I believe you shot Kresimir. Is it possible to kill a god? I don't know."

He scowled into his mug. "As for the newspapers and the people, they are skeptical. Rumors fly. People are taking sides. Right now it all comes down to a matter of faith, and we have only your word and the word of a few Mountainwatchers that Kresimir returned and took a bullet in the eye."

Taniel felt his strength leave him. To be thought a fraud after all he went through? It was the final blow. He pointed to the door. "How do they explain South Pike? The entire mountain collapsed." He heard his voice rise with anger.

"You won't change anyone's mind by shouting," Ricard said. "Believe me. I'm the head of the union. I've tried."

"Then what can I do?"

"Convince them. Show them what kind of a man you are and then, only when they trust you, tell them the truth."

"That seems...dishonest."

Ricard spread his hands. "That's up to your own moral judgment. But me, I think a man who sees it like that is a fool."

Taniel clenched his fists. How could they not believe him? How could they not know what happened up there? Hadn't Tamas told the newspapers? Did even Tamas not believe what had happened?

Taniel didn't know where Tamas was. Budwiel, according to the soldiers who had been watching him when he awoke. Was Tamas even still there?

"Do you know where Bo is?" Taniel asked.

"Bo?"

"Privileged Borbador. Is he still alive?"

Ricard spread his hands. "I can't help you."

"You're not much good, Tumblar, are you?" Taniel wanted to punch something. He leapt to his feet and stalked back and forth the length of the room. No friends. No family. What could he do now? "Who was that woman?" he asked.

"Cheris? The head of the bankers' union."

"I thought you were the head of the union."

"The Noble Warriors of Labor has many subdivisions. I speak for the group as a whole, but each trade has their own union boss."

"You said I was more important than her."

Ricard nodded. "I did."

"How so?"

"How much do you know about politics in Adro?" Ricard countered with his own question.

"The power used to be with the king. Now?" Taniel shrugged. "No idea."

"No one knows where the power is now," Ricard said. "The people assume it's with Tamas. Tamas thinks it's with his council when in fact the council is all but fractured. Lady Winceslav is in seclusion after her scandal with a traitorous brigadier, the Arch Diocel has been arrested, and Prime Lektor is in the east, studying the remains of South Pike for some sign of the god Kresimir."

"So who is running Adro?"

Ricard chuckled. "That leaves myself, the Proprietor, and Ondraus the Reeve. Not exactly a noble group. The truth is, Adro is doing fine for now. Tamas and his men keep the peace. But that will only last so long. We need to continue with our plans. Since the beginning of all this, the council decided that as soon as Manhouch was out of the way, we'd set up a democracy: a system of government that was voted upon by the people. The country would be divided into principalities, each with its own elected governor, and those men would meet in Adro and vote upon policy for the country."

"Much like a ministry without the king at the head."

"Indeed," Ricard said. "Of course there must be someone to stand as the king."

Taniel narrowed his eyes. "I can't imagine Tamas taking that well."

"We won't call him a king, of course. And he would have little real power. He would serve as a figurehead. A single man the country can look to for leadership and guidance, even if the policy is determined by the governors—we are going to call him the First Minister of the People."

"I remember Tamas striking down an idea just like this that the royalists presented him with."

"Tamas approved this," Ricard said. "Believe me. None of us on the council has any interest in crossing him, especially not in such a public way. The key is that, like the governors, this new First Minister of the People will be replaced every three years. We've set the mechanism in place. It just needs to be carried out."

Taniel could easily tell where this was going. "And you intend to put yourself forward as a candidate."

"Of course."

"Why?"

Ricard sucked hard on his cigar and let the smoke curl out through his nostrils. It reminded Taniel of the smoke of his mala pipe. He could feel the lure of that blissful smoke pulling at him.

"The First Minister of the People will have little power of his own, but he'll have the eyes of all the Nine directed at him. His name will go down in the history books forever." Ricard sighed. "I don't have any children. I've been left by"—he stopped to count—"six wives, and deserved it every time. All I have left is my name. And I want it taught to every Adran schoolchild for the rest of time."

Taniel drained the last of his ale. The dregs of the hops at the bottom of the glass were bitter. It reminded him of Fatrasta, of hunting down Kez Privileged in the wilds. "Where do I fit into all of this? I'm just a soldier who killed a god that no one believes even returned."

"You?" Ricard threw his head back and laughed. Taniel didn't see what was so funny.

"I'm sorry," Ricard said as he wiped his eyes. "You're Taniel Two-Shot! You're the hero of two continents. A soldier who's killed more Privileged than any man in the history of the Nine. The way the newspapers tell it, you held Shouldercrown Fortress against half a million Kez all by yourself."

"Wasn't just me," Taniel muttered, thinking of the men and women he'd watched die on that mountain.

"But the common people think so. They adore you. They love you more than they love Tamas, and he's been the darling of Adro since he single-handedly saved the Gurlish Campaign decades ago."

"So what do you want from me? A sponsorship?"

"Pit, no," Ricard said, passing his empty ale mug to the barkeep. "I want you to be my Second Minister. You'll be one of the most famous men in the world."

CHAPTER 7

In northeastern Adopest there was a small section of the Samalian District that hadn't been burned when Field Marshal Tamas allowed the pillage of the nobility's property after Manhouch's execution. It was a commercial area, filled with goods and service shops that catered to the nobility. Rumor had it that during the riots the owners of these shops set up their own barricades and held off the rioters themselves.

Now, five months after the riots, the former emporium of the rich had been transformed into a marketplace for the middle class. Prices had been lowered, but not quality, and people traveled halfway across the city to wait in line for cobblers, tailors, bakers, and jewelers.

Adamat came early in the morning, before the larger crowds arrived, and found the tailor who had purchased Vetas's warehouse. Adamat sat down in a small café across the street from the tailor's and ordered breakfast, keeping an eye out for expected company. It wasn't long until he spotted it.

Adamat rose from his seat and crossed the street. He discreetly sidled up beside SouSmith and said, "Were you followed?"

To his credit, SouSmith barely started. "Bloody pit," SouSmith said. "Didn't recognize ya."

"That's the idea." Adamat had dyed his hair gray. A dry dusting of powder on his face made his skin appear cracked, making him look twenty years older, and he affected a limp. He leaned heavily on a new, silver-headed cane. His jacket and pants were the finest money could by—he'd had to call in favors just to procure them. But he needed to look the part of a wealthy gentleman.

SouSmith shook his head. "Wasn't followed," he said. "Been staying low."

"Good," Adamat said. "How do you feel?"

"Like pit. Bloody healing Knacked."

Despite what he said, SouSmith looked better. Just five weeks ago he'd been shot twice and stabbed, and had barely made it through alive. It would have been a long recovery without Ricard's largesse.

"Go to that café over there," Adamat said, "and get breakfast. Take a seat facing that store there." He indicated the tailor's shop. "I'm going in to make some inquiries."

As much as he wanted SouSmith to come inside the tailor shop with him in case it was merely a front for Vetas and Vetas had men stationed inside, SouSmith was too memorable of a man, and there was no disguising a boxer of his size. No sense in bringing him in until needed.

Adamat crossed the street and entered the shop. A quick perusal told him that this tailor specialized in high-end jackets. Mannequins were placed around the edges of the room, wearing everything from smoking and evening jackets to the kind a duke might wear to a ball. The shop smelled strongly of peppermint oil that the owner used to mask the scent of stored cloth.

"May I help you?"

The tailor came in from the back room. He was a dark-skinned Deliv; a small man with long, steady fingers. He wore a pair of thin-rimmed spectacles and a vest with protruding lapels stuck through with a variety of needles and pins.

"Haime?" Adamat said, affecting an accent common in Adopest's southern suburbs.

"I am he," the tailor said with a short bow. "Jackets and suits. May I take your measurements for a new jacket today?"

"I haven't come in search of clothing," Adamat said. He looked down the end of his nose and made a show of perusing the mannequins. "At least, not today."

Haime clasped his hands behind his back. "Some other business?"

Adamat pulled a piece of paper from his breast pocket and unfolded it. "My employers are looking to purchase a piece of property," he said. "Records show that you are the owner."

Haime seemed genuinely puzzled. "I don't own any property."

"You did not buy a warehouse on Donavi Street in the factory district two years ago?"

"No, I..." Haime suddenly stopped and tapped his chin with one finger. "I did. That's right. One of my clients asked me to make a purchase and then transfer the title into his name. He wanted to keep the affair quiet. Something about not wanting the newspapers getting wind of his employer's purchases."

Adamat felt his heart jump. There were very few organizations that could make the news with a simple purchase of property. One of them was the Brudania-Gurla Trading Company. And their head was Lord Claremonte, Vetas's employer.

"Could I get his name, please?" Adamat said. He pulled a fountain pen from his pocket and poised it above his piece of paper.

Haime gave him an apologetic look. "I'm very sorry, but my client requested I keep that information in confidence."

"My employer would very much like to purchase that building," Adamat said. "I'm sure that something could be arranged..." He removed a checkbook from his pocket.

"No, no," Haime said. "I'm sorry, it's not a matter of money. I'm a man of my word."

Adamat gave a long-suffering sigh. "I'm sure." He put away the checkbook and pen and gathered his hat and cane. He paused, making a show of looking around the mannequins once more with an admiring eye. His gaze stopped on one and he almost choked.

It was the same jacket Lord Vetas had been wearing the last time they spoke.

"I see you've a fine eye," Haime said, slipping over toward the mannequin. "This jacket is discerning and subtle. It would look fantastic on you."

Adamat felt his heart begin to beat faster. Vetas must have been the same client to purchase that warehouse and the jacket. If Haime knew that he knew, the tailor might become suspicious.

"No, I don't think it's my style."

"Nonsense," Haime said. "The jacket has a slimming effect and draws the eyes up to your face. I could make an entire suit to match."

Adamat pretended to think on this for several moments. The jacket was obviously tailored. He could see a slight discoloration at the waist, where a rip had been patched, and he realized that this might be the actual jacket Lord Vetas had been wearing. "This looks like the right size. Can you tailor it for me now?"

"Unfortunately, no. This particular jacket belongs to someone. He's picking it up in a few days. I could have a new one made up for you in..." He paused to think. "A week. Just let me take your measurements."

Adamat patted his pockets. "I seem to have left my own checks at home. I only have my employers'. I will not be able to make a payment today."

"You're obviously a gentleman, sir," Haime said. "You may just give me your address."

Adamat didn't have an address to give to him. He didn't want to risk any word of this reaching Vetas. That risk was already high, as Haime might mention the attempted purchase to Vetas just as a matter of course. Adamat withdrew his pocket watch. "I have an appointment in less than an hour," he said. "I must make it. Let me come back early next week for measurements."

Haime's face fell. A good salesman never let a mark go out the door without a commitment to buy. "If that works best for you."

"It does," Adamat said. "I'll be back, don't worry."

Adamat hurried across the street and found SouSmith waiting at the café.

"Any sign of Vetas or any of his eyes?"

SouSmith shook his head.

"Let's go," Adamat said.

"Breakfast still coming."

Adamat checked to make sure the tailor wasn't watching him through the window of his shop before taking a seat next to Sou-Smith. "The tailor isn't involved directly," Adamat said. "He bought and sold the property for one of his clients: I think it's Vetas. I saw the same jacket Vetas was wearing the last time I saw him, all the way down to the tailoring."

"You sure?"

"I don't forget, remember?" Adamat tapped the side of his head. "I could tell that the lines of that jacket matched perfectly. Unfortunately, the tailor wouldn't give me Vetas's name or address."

"Dead end."

"No. Vetas—or, more likely, one of his men—is coming to pick up that jacket in the next few days. It was being mended. I'm going to stake out the tailor and watch for who picks up the jacket. I'll follow them and find out where Vetas lives."

"Where you want me?" SouSmith's breakfast arrived: four

poached eggs with Novi goat cheese. He grinned as it was set in front of him and set about eating quickly.

"Nowhere," Adamat said. "I can't risk you being recognized. I can wear a disguise. You, however, can't."

SouSmith sniffed. Through a mouthful of egg, he said, "Can't leave you to follow him alone."

Adamat knew the risks. If Vetas or his man was good enough to mark Adamat, he could very well be a dead man. But SouSmith was a liability in this kind of work. He was easily recognized, and even if he wasn't, his size made him less than ideal for following someone.

"I'll do it alone," Adamat said.

Tamas lay in the tall grass of a knoll beneath the Adran Mountains and watched through his looking glass as the Kez army prepared to assault Budwiel.

Morning dew soaked his combat uniform. The cloud cover was low on this day and a rolling fog clung to plains outside of Budwiel. The air was heavy with moisture. He knew it would foul guns on both sides, but when Tamas looked toward Budwiel, he noted a ray of sunshine peeking through the clouds to bathe the city and clear the air.

No doubt Mihali's indirect participation in the battle.

And they would need every bit of his help. Tamas swung his looking glass back toward the Kez. His breath caught in his throat at the sight of their army. Rank upon rank of tan uniforms with green trim stretched for what seemed like forever. Long experience let him count their ranks with only a cursory glance.

One hundred and twenty thousand at least. And that was just their infantry.

They would send their recruits first to act as so much cannon fodder in order to test Budwiel's defenses. Five, maybe ten thousand of them would pour out across the fields, tramping down the wet grass and receiving the full brunt of grapeshot. They'd be followed quickly by the more experienced men, who'd form a strong backbone to the main assault and push the recruits on hard in front of them, even at the tip of their bayonets. Sorcery-warped Wardens would accompany the front of the second wave.

It was a foolish method of attack, in Tamas's opinion, but the Kez commanders had always favored a massed rush—no matter the cost in lives—above guile.

And it just might work. The key to throwing back the Kez assault would be to break the resolve of their second wave. To kill the Wardens and send the veterans running for cover. It would be hard to break such a sizable force.

But not impossible.

Which is where the Seventh and the Ninth came in. Once the Kez committed the main body, Tamas would order his men over the knoll at a dead charge into the Kez flank.

No matter the size of a crowd, they'd run if panic seized them.

The Kez cannon had been moved forward before dawn. They pounded away at Budwiel's fortifications, answered in turn by Hilanska's heavy artillery.

Tamas watched as the Kez infantry fell into rank a few hundred yards behind their artillery. He felt his stomach lurch.

"That's a lot of men, sir," Olem said from beside him.

"A great many," Tamas agreed. Was that unease in Olem's voice? Tamas couldn't blame him if it was. That many soldiers would make anyone nervous.

"Think we can break them?"

"We'd better. The cavalry will help."

"We've only two hundred, though," Olem said.

"All we need is the illusion of a brigade of cavalry. We're here to cause panic, and then slaughter. Not the other way around."

During the night, they'd had enough time to bring two hundred cavalry through the caverns. It was a testament to Tamas's engineers that they'd managed to get the caverns wide enough to accommodate the passage of ten thousand men plus a platoon of horse in just one night.

The real victory of the night, however, had been six field guns. Small, firing six-pound balls, and with five-foot wheels that would allow them to be moved easily, they were just enough to give the impression of an entire army on the Kez flank.

Tamas let his mind wander to the aftermath of the battle. They could rout the Kez, but they wouldn't be able to pursue for long. Tens of thousands would be dead, but to the Kez that was just another number. They would still have hundreds of thousands left. This battle would be to break the morale of their army. The Kez couldn't afford another loss on the psychological level of the Battle of Shouldercrown.

Tamas's spies already reported that there were grumblings in Ipille's ministry. Given enough of a spark, the army might even turn on Ipille, though that seemed too much to even hope.

"Sir," Olem said. "The columns are advancing."

Tamas pulled himself back to the present. It was bad luck to think of victory as the battle started. He had plans in place. If triumph came, then it would be time to implement them. Not now.

"Signal the men to get ready."

Vlora crawled onto the knoll next to Tamas as Olem hurried away.

"Are your men in place?" Tamas asked.

"You mean Andriya's men, sir?"

Tamas could hear the bitterness in her voice. He'd given Andriya command of the powder cabal for this battle, and it irked her. Tamas fought down his own annoyance. When would she learn that, skilled though she was, she did not have the experience to be in command?

"My powder mages," Tamas said sternly. "Are they in place?"

"Yes, sir."

"And you've sighted the last of the Kez Privileged?"

"They're hanging back," Vlora said. "They think we're on Bud-wiel's walls, waiting for them, so they're well behind the columns. Quite within range of us here. You signal the attack, sir, and we'll drop the Privileged."

"Excellent. Get to your position."

Vlora crawled off the knoll without another word. Tamas looked over his shoulder to watch her go.

"All ready, sir." Olem came jogging up the hill and threw him-self to the ground beside Tamas. "Time to hurry up and wait." He caught the way Tamas was looking.

"Still thinking of punching her, sir?"

Tamas gave Olem a wry look. Since when had his men gotten away with speaking that way to him? "No."

"You seem angry, sir."

"She has a lot of growing up to do still. I'm mostly sad. Had things gone differently, she might be my daughter-in-law by now." He sighed and brought the looking glass back to his eye. "Tan-iel might not have been on that damned mountain and lying in a coma under the House of Nobles."

Olem's voice was quiet. "He might not have been there to put a bullet in Kresimir's eye and save us all, sir."

Tamas drummed his fingers against his looking glass. Olem was right, of course. Change one event in history, and you might as well change everything that followed. What concerned him now was trying to find a way to bring Taniel out of his coma, and to keep his body safe until he did.

As if he could read Tamas's thoughts, Olem said, "He'll be all right, sir. I've got some of my best Riflejacks keeping an eye on him."

Tamas wanted to turn to Olem, to thank him for the reassur-ance. But now was not the time for worry or sentiment. "The lines are beginning to advance," Tamas said. "Make sure the men hold. I don't want the Kez to know we're coming until the right moment."

"They'll hold," Olem said with confidence.

"Make certain. Personally."

Olem moved off to check on the brigades, leaving Tamas alone on the knoll for a few precious moments. Soon, an unending stream of messengers would be requesting further orders as the battle began and raged throughout the day.

Tamas closed his eyes and envisioned the battlefield as a crow might.

Kez infantry formed a half circle facing Budwiel's walls. Their ranks would tighten as they advanced to account for the terrain, and fill in the gaps from casualties caused by Adran cannon. A single line of Kez cavalry, perhaps one thousand strong, waited on the Great Northern Road for the infantry to take the walls and throw open the gates, at which time they would charge into the city. The rest of their cavalry camped over two miles behind the battlefield. Most of them weren't even on their horses. They didn't think they'd be needed today.

The Kez reserves waited behind the rest of the army. Their numbers were a terrible sight, but Tamas's looking glass and his spies told another story: They were there for show only. Only one out of five had a musket. Their uniforms were mismatched and off-color. Tamas shook his head. The Kez had more men than they had guns. The reserves would break and run at the first sign of his troops.

The *rat-tat-tat-tat* of Kez drummers reverberated against the mountains, and Tamas felt the ground tremble as the mass of Kez infantry began their advance. He directed his glass toward the walls of Budwiel.

The heavy artillery, already firing on the Kez field guns, redoubled their efforts as the wall of infantry crept closer. Tamas could see soldiers of the Second on the walls, their Adran blues looking sharp, their discipline steady.

As the lines of Kez infantry reached the killing field, artillery blasted holes in their ranks. Those holes were quickly closed, and the tan-and-green uniforms marched onward, leaving a hundred dead for every dozen paces they gained. The smell of gunpowder reached Tamas on the wind and he took a deep breath, savoring the bitter sulfur.

He climbed to his feet and motioned over his signal-flag man. On the field below their vantage point, he watched as the mass of Kez reserves shifted forward to take places behind the infantry. Tamas scowled. If they were to take the city, it would be with the mass of infantry. Why would they even move the reserves into position…?

He felt a cold tingle down his spine. The Kez thought they'd be able to sack Budwiel today. They would secure the walls with their infantry and then signal the reserves into the city to burn, rape, and plunder. Tamas had seen them do the same in Gurla. If they breached the walls, it would be a horror beyond imagining.

To think they'd do it in a single day was beyond optimistic on the part of the Kez commanders.

He couldn't let that happen.

"Signal at the ready," Tamas said. The flagger beside him waved out the order. Tamas could see the eagerness in the man's face. The Seventh and Ninth were ready. They'd tear into the Kez flank with gusto. Tamas felt his blood begin to rise. "Wait… wait…"

Tamas blinked. What was that?

He put his looking glass to his eye. When he focused on the fields directly before Budwiel, he saw dozens of twisted men running toward the walls. They wore black coats and bowler caps. Wardens.

But these Wardens… Tamas swallowed. He'd never seen anyone run this fast, not even one of those sorcery-spawned killers. They covered the last few hundred yards to the wall with the speed of a racing Thoroughbred.

In his glass, Tamas could see the wall commanders bellowing. Muskets opened fire. Not a single Warden went down. They reached the base of the wall and leapt, clinging to its vertical face like insects and scurrying to the top. In a flash, they were among the gun crews, brandishing swords and pistols.

Wait, pistols? Wardens didn't carry pistols. Privileged had an aversion to gunpowder, and they were the ones who created the sorcery-spawned monsters.

Small explosions rocked the top of the walls. Bodies fell from the fortifications, and one by one, the cannons ceased firing.

Tamas rocked back on his heels. What was happening? How could those Wardens have gained the wall so easily? He smacked his looking glass in his hand. Without the cannons to keep them at bay, the Kez infantry would take the walls easily. They wouldn't have the threat of artillery at their backs to keep them from turning to face Tamas's brigades head-on.

"Sir," the flagger said, "should I signal the attack?"

"No," Tamas said. The word came out a strangled cry.

He continued to watch as the infantry reached the base of the wall. Ladders went up, and by the time the tan-and-green uniforms reached the top of the wall, Tamas could not see a single Adran soldier left standing. The Wardens had cut them all down.

"Sir." Olem appeared at Tamas's side. He drew his own looking glass to his eye. "What...what happened?" Tamas could hear his own disbelief reflected in Olem's voice.

"Wardens," Tamas choked out. He wanted to spit, but his mouth was too dry. They were soon joined by officers of the Seventh and Ninth. They all looked out at the battle together.

Kez infantry flooded the walls. Minutes later the front gates were thrown open. The Kez cavalry charged up the road toward the gates.

"We must attack, sir," said a major whose name Tamas couldn't recall.

Tamas whirled to his officers when he heard mutters of agreement.

"It's suicide," he said. His voice cracked. "Budwiel is lost."

"We could salvage the day," another voice said.

Tamas ground his teeth. He agreed with them. By god, he agreed with them. "Perhaps," he said. "Maybe we would be able to rout the tail end of the Kez army. We could destroy the reserves and set fire to the Kez camp. But then we'd be caught out on the empty plain, easily surrounded, and cut off from reinforcement."

Silence. These officers were brave, but they weren't fools. They could see he was right.

"Then what do we do?"

Tamas heard a boom echo out from Budwiel. Smoke and dust erupted from the base of the West Pillar. He yelled for a scout to check the tunnels, but already knew what had happened. The catacombs. Someone had set off an explosion inside of them, cutting off Tamas's entry back into Budwiel.

"I've been betrayed again," he whispered. More loudly, "We keep our backs to the mountain." He tried to think of the closest Mountainwatch pass into Adro. It would be a nightmare to move ten thousand men over any of the passes. "We march toward the pass at Alvation. Tell your men."

General Cethal of the Ninth Brigade caught Tamas's arm.

"Alvation?" he asked. "That will take over a month of hard marching."

"Maybe two," Tamas said. "And we'll be pursued." He eyed Budwiel. Smoke rose from the city. "We have no choice."

His stomach turned. Many of his men had family in the city, camp followers of the army. The Kez would put the city to the torch. The same fear techniques they'd used in Gurla. His men would hate him for marching away while the city burned, but it was their only hope for survival. He swore to get them back to Adro—to deliver them their vengeance.

CHAPTER
8

Adamat waited just a few shops down from the tailor's. He sat on a stoop, a newspaper in his hands. His disguise today was younger, with black hair neatly greased to one side of his head in the latest style of coffee shop owners. He wore pressed brown trousers and a dress shirt with cuffs rolled up to his elbows. A matching brown jacket lay across his knee. Before he'd left that morning a quick application of Dortmoth whale ointment had given his skin a youthful glow. A false black mustache and tinted spectacles hid his face.

Adamat watched over the top of his newspaper as traffic moved through the street between shops and cafés. For two days he'd watched Haime's shop. It was nearly three o'clock on the third day and he had yet to lay eyes on Lord Vetas.

His position gave him the perfect view of Haime's shop. He could see not only the exit and approach clearly but through the front window and nearly everything that went on inside as well. Men came and went from the shop. There were very few women. At around two thirty a trio of big, hard-looking men entered the shop. Adamat was sure they were Vetas's goons, but when they exited just a few minutes later, he could still see Vetas's jacket still hanging on the mannequin.

Adamat half read the articles in the newspaper. The standoff in Budwiel continued, though since the news was three or four days old, anything could have happened.

The paper reported that a sudden loss of income had caused Lady Winceslav to disband two of the eight brigades of the Wings of Adom. That could only bode ill for the war effort. Four more brigades held position north of Budwiel, while the last two stood guard at the smoldering remains of South Pike, should the Kez army try a crossing of the volcanic wasteland.

As Adamat began to read through a story on the effect of the war on Adran economics, the movement of Haime's door across the street caught his eye. He looked up in time to see a dress disappear through the door. A moment later a woman appeared in the window and began to speak with Haime.

She was a young woman with auburn curls. She couldn't have been more than eighteen or nineteen and, though young, she wouldn't be mistaken for a mere girl. She had a confident bearing with a straight back and raised chin, and the red evening dress she wore looked tailored for her figure.

Haime turned to Vetas's jacket and gestured. He waved his hand up and down the jacket and then motioned to the bottom corner, where Adamat had noticed the repaired rip. The woman nodded and Haime took the jacket down and wrapped it carefully in tissue paper.

The woman emerged a moment later with a brown box under her arm. She looked both ways, and Adamat resisted the urge to duck behind his newspaper. *Look casual*, he reminded himself. He didn't know her face. She most certainly did not know his.

She headed west down the street. Adamat climbed to his feet, folding the newspaper and tucking it under his arm, and picking up his cane.

He followed her at a respectable distance. The key to trailing someone was to stay far enough back not to be noticed but close enough that he wouldn't lose her if she deviated from her course suddenly. It helped to know whether she suspected that she was being followed. Adamat thought not, but one could never be too careful.

Adamat expected her to take a carriage within a block or two. She was dressed like a lady in that evening dress, and her heeled boots were not meant for long walks. But she stayed in the street and veered northwest, picking her way along slowly. She stopped by a street vendor's stall once to purchase a fruit tart, then continued on her way.

She turned down a quiet street in the Routs. It was a wealthy part of town, predominantly known for the banking district at its center. The street itself had less foot traffic, which worried Adamat. At some point he would become noticeable, and that would be the last thing he wanted.

He fell back another forty feet before turning onto the same street. He was just in time to see the woman disappear into a large three-story townhouse.

The house had a broad front that came all the way up to the street. The walls were white brick, and the shutters blue. It was quite large, of the type built to house several families of the growing middle class. If it involved anyone else but Vetas, Adamat would have passed the house by as being too out in the open and ordinary.

As it was, he wondered if perhaps he'd made a mistake. Maybe the jacket did not belong to Vetas. Maybe he'd been watching the wrong jacket through the window of Haime's shop. Perhaps the woman had noticed him following her and had come here to give him the slip.

Adamat cursed under his breath. There were too many variables.

He walked down the street at a slow pace, taking long, casual steps as if admiring the houses. He drew close to the house and made a mental note as to the number and street name, and let his eyes wander past each of the windows. Surely, Vetas would have a man keeping watch if this was his headquarters.

Nothing. Adamat tried not to dwell on disappointment, but there was absolutely nothing to mark this house as belonging to Vetas. He would have to check the property records.

Just as Adamat was passing by the last window, he caught sight of a face. It was a boy of six, watching as the traffic passed his home. He waved to Adamat.

Adamat waved back.

No. This couldn't be Lord Vetas's house. What use could he possibly have for a small boy?

Unless Lord Vetas had a son. That seemed unlikely. The boy shared nothing of Vetas's facial structure. A ward? No. Vetas was a spy for Lord Claremonte. He wouldn't keep a ward. Perhaps another hostage? That did seem a possibility.

Adamat continued down the street. He'd take the next carriage and come back and stake out the house. It was his only lead at this point.

He climbed into a carriage and took his seat, only to find someone else climb in behind him. It was a street sweeper, his face and clothes grimy from a long day at work in the sun.

"Pardon me," Adamat started to say, when he saw the pistol in the street sweeper's hand.

He felt a cold bead of sweat trickle down the small of his back.

"What's this all about?" Adamat said.

"Your pocketbook," the man said, his voice a growl.

Relief swept over Adamat. A mugging. That's all this was. Not one of Vetas's men, having recognized him going past. Adamat slowly removed his pocketbook from his vest and handed it to the thief. It wouldn't do the man much good. Only fifty krana in banknotes inside. No checks or identification.

The man flipped through the pocketbook with one hand, sure to keep the pistol on Adamat. A few moments and the man would exit the carriage and disappear into the afternoon crowds.

But then, this was the Routs. Who had the stones to pull a mugging on a residential street in the Routs in the middle of the afternoon? Adamat opened his mouth.

That's when he recognized the child in the window.

That boy was the son of Duke Eldaminse. The royalists had fought a small war with Tamas in the city center with the goal of putting him on the throne after Manhouch's execution. Adamat remembered the boy from a job he did for the Eldaminse family almost a year ago.

The thief looked up at Adamat. "Not good enough," he said.

"What?"

The thief flipped the pistol around in his hand, and the last thing Adamat saw was the butt of the weapon coming at his face.

When Taniel awoke, Fell was sitting next to his hammock.

They were back in Kin's mala den. Smoke curled through the air, but it wasn't mala. Cherry tobacco, by the smell. He could see Fell out of the corner of his eye, a short-stemmed pipe hanging from the corner of her mouth.

A woman smoking a pipe. Not something Taniel had seen often. Most of the women he knew preferred Fatrastan cigarettes.

The union undersecretary was a handsome woman. Far too severe for Taniel. With her hair back and thin face she reminded him of a governess he'd once had. He watched her for several moments through half-closed eyes, wondering what she was thinking. She didn't seem to notice that Taniel was awake. She was staring across the room. Taniel shifted in his hammock to see what Fell was looking at.

Ka-poel. Of course. She sat next to the stairs, forming a wax figurine with her fingers. Her satchel sat on her lap. She glanced up at the undersecretary every so often. She was making a doll. Of Fell.

Taniel wondered if the undersecretary seemed enough of a threat to her to warrant a doll, or if she had just started making one for every person they met. She was going to run out of room in her satchel if the latter proved to be the case.

The last four days were a blur. Taniel reached into his memory, but the only thing he found was mala smoke and the ceiling of Kin's mala den. Before that . . .

Ricard Tumblar wanted Taniel to run for the First Ministry with him.

That meant politics.

Taniel hated politics. He had witnessed firsthand the power grabs of the mercantile elite in Fatrasta as their war for independence marched toward success; the backstabbing, the conniving. Ricard claimed that none of that was to happen. Ricard claimed that these would be elections, open and fair to the public; that the government would be chosen by the people.

Ricard, like most politicians, couldn't be trusted.

But that didn't seem enough for a four-day mala binge. Why would Taniel come back to this hole and—

Oh yes. Ricard had mentioned something about informing Field Marshal Tamas that Taniel was awake and doing well. Ricard, no matter what Taniel had said, did not seem to understand that Tamas would demand Taniel's immediate presence on the front lines.

That was a good thing, Taniel tried to tell himself. He was useful. He could get back there and help defend his country.

By killing. The one thing Taniel seemed to be any good at. Pit, he'd even killed a god. Not that anyone believed it.

He shifted in his hammock, reaching for his mala pipe and the enormous ball of the sticky substance Kin had left him.

The mala was gone.

"Awake?" Fell said, her attention leaving Ka-poel.

Taniel pushed himself up. He checked his coat pocket—he still had a coat, that was good—then his trousers and the lip of the hammock.

"What are you looking for?" Fell asked. By her expression, she knew exactly what Taniel was looking for.

"Where's my mala?"

"From what Kin said, you smoked it all. You ran out sometime last night." Fell tossed something into her mouth and crunched. "Cashews?" she asked, holding out a paper bag made from an old newspaper toward Taniel.

Taniel shook his head. He checked the mala pipe. Nothing left. Then the floor. "That thieving Gurlish must have taken the rest of the ball. I got enough to last me weeks."

"I know the rate you were smoking that stuff," Fell said. "I don't think Kin gypped you. He knows where the money came from."

Taniel frowned. Where had the money come from? He looked up at Fell. Ah, that's right. Ricard.

"You know," Fell said, "Ricard's mala den has much better quality mala. The mats are silk, and the entertainment is better than Kin's daughter."

Taniel felt his stomach lurch. He fell back into his hammock. Kin's daughter. Taniel didn't remember anything. "Did I...?"

Fell shrugged and looked to Ka-poel. Ka-poel gave a slight shake of her head.

Taniel let out a small sigh. The last thing he needed to do right now was bed a Gurlish mala-den owner's daughter.

"What do you want?" he asked Fell.

Fell tapped her pipe out on her shoe and put it in her pocket, then tossed more cashews into her mouth. "We got word from your father today."

Taniel sat up straight. "And?"

"A few things of note to report. The Kez were preparing to attack the next day. That would be three days ago. He was planning on leading a counteroffensive with his best men."

"How many Kez soldiers?"

"Rumors say a million. Tamas didn't say."

His best soldiers meant the Seventh and Ninth brigades. And rumors of a million? That was twice the size of the army at the Battle of Shouldercrown. Even if it were exaggerated ten times, Tamas was still leading ten thousand men against a hundred thousand. Bloody brash fool.

It somehow made it worse that Tamas would probably win.

"Oh," Fell added, as if as an afterthought. "He asked after you."

Taniel sniffed. "'Where's my damned useless son? I need him on the line.' Something like that?"

"He asked if you'd made any recovery and if the doctors thought his presence would help in any way."

"Now I know you're lying," Taniel said. "Tamas wouldn't leave a battlefield for anyone." *Not even me. Especially not me.*

"He's been very worried. We sent word that you seemed better, but who knows if it reached him before the battle." Fell reached into her paper bag for another cashew, a small smile on her lips.

"But you didn't tell him I'm awake?"

"No. Ricard thought that perhaps you'd like some time to recover."

So Taniel's entreaties to keep his father in the dark *had* done some good.

"More like he's worried that Tamas will send for me the minute he knows I'm not laid out."

"That too," Fell admitted.

"Of course." Taniel fell back into his hammock and sighed. He felt tired and used. What was he, other than a tool for others? "That old bastard Tamas—"

He was cut off by the sound of a door upstairs banging open.

The stairs into the den shook, and a young man burst into the room. Fell got to her feet.

"What is it?" she said.

The messenger looked around wildly at the den. His chest heaved from hard running. "Ricard wants you at the People's Court immediately."

Fell crumpled up the empty cashew bag and tossed it to the floor. "What has happened?"

The messenger looked at Taniel, then at Ka-poel, and back to Fell. He seemed on the verge of collapse.

"We've word from Budwiel. The city has fallen, put to the torch. Field Marshal Tamas is dead."

Nila sat beside the window, the curtains only slightly parted, and watched the world stroll by in top hats and coats, canes clicking on the cobbles, women tipping their bonnets back to enjoy the sun on their faces. The summer heat bore down on Adro, but no one seemed to notice. The weather was far too nice to care.

She wished she was out there enjoying it. Her room was too stuffy, and Vetas's men had nailed shut all the windows in the house. The air was thick and humid, stifling, and moment to moment she felt as if she was going to faint. Vetas had sent her on errands just yesterday, and the freedom of the sun on her face had felt so wonderful she'd almost left the city, forgetting Vetas and Jakob and all the terrible memories of the last few months.

Her heart leapt into her throat at the sound of the bedroom door opening, but she forced herself not to react outwardly. It wasn't Vetas. He came in from the hallway. Not from the door to the nursery, where Jakob played quietly with a small army of wooden horses and complained frequently about the warmth.

"Nila," a voice said. "You must get dressed."

Nila glanced at the dress laid out on her bed. One of Vetas's goons had brought it up for her an hour ago. It was a long chemise dress of white muslin with a high waistline. The trim was crimson, giving it a flair of color at the hem and the bust, and the ends of the short sleeves. It looked incredibly comfortable, and much cooler than the evening dress he'd told her to wear during her errands yesterday.

There was a silver chain on her bedside table with a single pearl the size of a musket ball, and in a box a pair of new black knee-high boots that she could tell with a glance would fit her perfectly. Three more outfits, each more expensive than the last, hung in the closet.

Presents from Lord Vetas. She'd never owned such fine clothing. The dress was plain enough, nothing gaudy, but the lines were absolutely perfect. A glance inside the hem had shown her the initials D.H.—Madame Dellehart, the finest seamstress in Adopest. The dress cost more than any regular laundress would earn in a year.

"Nila," the voice insisted. "Get dressed."

The expensive clothes and the jewelry made Nila sick to her stomach. She might as well accept presents from a demon as from Lord Vetas. She knew they came with a price.

"I'm not going to," Nila said.

Footsteps creaked across the floorboards. Faye knelt in front of Nila and took her hand.

They'd been cooped up in this manor together for six days and Nila still didn't know much about the woman. She knew that Faye's son was being held as a prisoner in the basement, and that she had other children elsewhere, also prisoners of Lord Vetas. She also knew that Faye would kill Vetas, given the opportunity.

At least, she'd try. Nila was beginning to wonder whether Vetas could be killed. He didn't seem human; he barely ate, he didn't sleep, and he didn't get drunk no matter how much wine he consumed.

Faye tugged at Nila's hand. "Up," she said. "Get dressed."

"You're not my mother," Nila said. The words came out as a snarl.

"She'd tell you the same thing if she were here."

Nila leaned forward. "She's dead. I never knew her, and neither did you. Maybe she'd tell me to break this window and cut my own wrists rather than give in to Vetas's demands."

Faye stood up. The kindly entreaty written across her face seemed to disappear and her expression hardened. "Maybe," she said. "If so, she was a fool." Faye began to pace the room.

Nila had guessed her to be a housewife of some middle-class merchant. She wondered what value Faye had to Lord Vetas. Faye hadn't spoken of it. And only a few words here and there about her children. In fact, the woman was far too calm. Ever since her initial outburst the night she'd been brought in, Faye had been meek as a dormouse. Nila imagined that if she had children, she'd not rest until they were out of danger. Faye was either very patient—and a stronger woman than Nila gave her credit for—or something else. Perhaps a ruse by Vetas? A spy?

That didn't make sense. Nila wasn't worth spying on. If Vetas wanted something from her, he was the type of man to torture it out.

Either way, Nila didn't trust Faye. She couldn't trust anyone here in the Vetas's lair.

"If you don't get dressed," Faye said, "Vetas will take out his anger on you or the boy. Maybe both."

"I'm not his whore," Nila said.

"He's not asked you to do anything degrading." The silent "yet" hung in the air for a moment. "Just to accompany him on his errands. It'll get you out of this damned house again. I'll keep an eye on Jakob while you're gone. Here," Faye said, "let me help you."

Nila let Faye pull her to her feet and strip off her old dress.

"There's new undergarments," Faye said, lifting a small box from the bed.

Nila snatched the box and threw it to the floor. "I've seen them, thank you," she snapped. "Only a whore wears a shift like that." She took a deep breath, realizing that her hands were shaking.

Faye let her arms drop to her side. She stepped to the nursery door, looking in on Jakob, and then closed it. She turned to Nila, hands on her hips.

"Have you seen the room in the basement?" Faye asked.

Nila stared back defiantly. Who was this old woman to demand things of her?

"Well?" Faye said.

Nila nodded sharply and tried not to think of the room with the long tables and blood stains and sharp knives on the bench.

"He showed them to me, too," Faye said. "When I first got here. I don't want to go to that room and I imagine you don't, either. So keep him happy."

"I'm…"

"I don't care who you are," Faye said, "or why you're here. But you seem to care for Jakob. Vetas is not the kind of man to hesitate in turning his insidious practices on children."

"He wouldn't."

Faye took a step closer to Nila. Nila made herself stand her ground, but a look in the woman's eye frightened her.

Faye said, "He cut off my boy's finger while I watched. While my children watched. We all screamed, and his goons held us back. Then he sent the finger to my husband, to ensure his cooperation in one of Vetas's plans." Faye spit on the floor.

"And what are you doing now?" Nila said.

"I'm waiting."

"For what?" Nila scoffed.

"My chance." The words were barely audible. Faye wiped a tear from the corner of her eye and took a deep breath. "There's time for fury. And there's time for patience. And Vetas's reckoning will come."

"What if I were to tell him what you said? How do you know you can trust me?"

Faye tilted her head to one side. "Go ahead and tell him if you want. You think he doesn't know that I'd pull his guts out through his ass if I got the chance?" Faye shook her head in disgust. "My husband is an inspector. He's a smart man, a principled man. He's always thought the nobility were a load of inbred fools. I once asked him how he could put up with a baron's mockery or the obtuse idiocy of a duchess long enough to finish a high-profile case."

Nila remained silent, watching the side of Faye's face while she talked.

"He said," Faye went on, "that swallowing his pride and being patient in the face of adversity had allowed him to feed and protect his family for years, whereas giving in to his instincts to fight back would only land him in prison, or worse. Waiting is all I can do right now. So I wait. And you should, too. Put on the damned dress."

Nila watched the woman for any sign of dishonesty. There was fire in her eyes. Fury. The kind only a mother is capable of.

"Give me some privacy," Nila said.

She was dressed by the time there was a knock on the door. Not from Jakob's nursery but from the hallway. Nila swallowed her fear as she heard the door open and was glad that she had put on the clothes.

"That's progress," Lord Vetas said. "Turn around."

She turned to face him, forcing herself to meet his eyes.

He looked her up and down and slowly swirled the wine in the glass in his right hand. "You'll do," he said.

"For what?" she asked.

If he heard the anger in her voice, he ignored it. "I've been trying to secure a luncheon with a woman named Lady Winceslav for some time. I have finally succeeded. You will accompany me to the luncheon as my niece. You are a shy girl, and will say nothing more than 'yes, ma'am' or 'no, ma'am.' I intend on courting her, and she'll be more amiable to the idea if I have a close female relative. I'll only need you for a few weeks, at most."

"Who is—"

"That is of no concern of yours. Play your part well and you'll find I allow you to keep the small measure of freedom I've permitted. Play it poorly and I will punish you. Understand?"

"Yes," Nila said.

"Good. Where's the boy?"

Nila wished there was some kind of lie she could tell him. But where else would Jakob be but in his nursery? "Jakob," she called, "come in here, please!"

The door to the nursery opened and Jakob skipped across the room. He looked up at Vetas with a smile on his face. "Hello!"

Vetas grinned at him. The expression reminded Nila of a polished skull she'd seen once in an apothecary's shop. "Hello, my boy," Vetas said. "How are you enjoying your new clothes?"

Jakob spun around, arms out, to show off a smart suit of a blue jacket, matching knee-length pants, and high socks. "They're very nice," Jakob said. "Thank you."

"My pleasure, child," Vetas said. "I brought you something." He stepped back into the hallway and came back with a box not much bigger than the one Nila's boots had arrived in. Setting the box on the floor, he flipped off the top to reveal a set of wooden soldiers and horses, twenty in all.

Jakob gasped with delight and set about pulling them from the box all at once, scattering them across the floor.

"Take them to your room," Nila said.

Jakob stopped unpacking and cast Nila a scowl. He put the toys back in and began to drag the box toward the nursery.

"Do you like them?" Vetas asked.

"Of course! Thank you, Uncle Vetas!"

"You're welcome, child."

Vetas's grin disappeared the moment Jakob was out of sight. He took a sip of his wine. "Be ready in half an hour," he said. He left the room, and Nila heard the door lock from the outside.

"*Uncle* Vetas," Jakob had said.

Nila wondered how Faye planned on killing Vetas, and if perhaps Nila would get her chance first.

CHAPTER
9

Taniel hurried through the streets of Adopest, blinded by disbelief. Tamas dead? It couldn't be. The old bastard was too stubborn to die. It was late morning and the traffic was thick, and he had to shoulder his way past pedestrians and dodge carriages and carts. He could hear Fell apologizing to the people Taniel bowled over.

Taniel paused momentarily to make sure Ka-poel was still with them. She was right beside him, faithful as his own shadow. Fell appeared out of the crowd. Of the messenger who'd found them in the mala den, there was no sign.

"Pole," he said. "Do you know if he's dead?"

Ka-poel seemed taken aback.

He took her by the shoulders and pulled her closer. "Did you ever make a doll of him? Do you have some kind of connection?"

Her frown cleared and she shook her head. Nothing.

"Pit." Taniel turned around.

"I'm sorry about your father," Fell said, coming up beside him.

"I'll believe the old bastard is dead when I see his body," Taniel said. He suddenly felt ill as a vision of Tamas lying cold and stiff in an open coffin filled his mind. He pushed the vision aside, but found himself leaning on Ka-poel for support.

She looked up at him with her glass-green eyes. They contained a mix of emotions: anger, confusion, sympathy, resolve. Her eyes hardened and he looked away.

"Where the pit are we, anyway?" he asked. "I don't recognize anything."

"Because you've been charging headlong through the crowds," Fell said. "This way to the People's Court." She pointed east. They'd been going north.

Taniel nodded. "Lead on," he said. He still had his hand on Ka-poel's shoulder. She hadn't moved it. "Pole," he said, "I . . ." He stopped. His mind was a haze, but the man coming toward him along the street looked familiar. Taniel could have sworn he'd seen him hanging around Kin's mala den. He was tall, with wide shoulders and a slight limp. Something was off about him.

The man looked up and into Taniel's eyes. It was all the warning Taniel got.

The man took two great strides toward Taniel. He shouldered Ka-poel out of the way and then Taniel felt the man's fist connect with his sternum. He was thrown up, above the heads of the crowd, and then tumbled to the ground, landing shoulder-first on the hard cobbles.

Taniel gasped in ragged breaths. Had his ribs been broken?

A small crowd gathered around Taniel. He heard voices asking if he was all right. A gentleman nudged Taniel's arm with his cane. A woman screamed.

Only one kind of creature could have hit Taniel that hard.

A Warden.

Taniel snatched the gentleman's cane, ignoring a shout of protest, and pushed himself to his feet in time to see a young woman thrown to the ground as the Warden pushed past her and grasped Taniel by the throat with both hands.

Steel jutted from the Warden's throat and stopped mere inches from Taniel's eyes. The Warden threw him to the ground and whirled, to reveal a stiletto jammed into the back of his neck right at the spine. The Warden gurgled, and attacked Fell, who danced out of the way quicker than Taniel would have given her credit for.

Taniel leapt to his feet and brought the cane down on the back of the Warden's head. The hardwood cane splintered from the force of the blow.

The Warden barely flinched. He turned toward Taniel, then back at Fell, as if trying to decide which threat to attack. While they watched, he pulled a handkerchief from his pocket and with the other hand reached back and slid the stiletto from his own spine. Vile, black blood spurted from the hole in his neck. Taniel heard someone be violently sick on the street.

The Warden pushed his handkerchief into his wound to stop the bleeding. The whole grisly procedure had taken less than five or six seconds. The Warden then turned on Fell, leaping quickly.

Taniel was ready. He jumped forward, holding the jagged end of the broken cane like a dagger in one hand. He drew back his arm to ram it into the Warden's back.

Something hit Taniel from the side. His teeth rattled. His vision went dark.

A second later and Taniel was staring up into the distorted face of another Warden. The Warden had his knee on Taniel's chest and his hands closed around Taniel's throat. Taniel squirmed, but he didn't have the strength to fight. He needed powder.

Taniel was able to bring his knee up between them, pushing the Warden's weight off his chest. He brought the broken cane around with his one free arm and stabbed it deep into the Warden's arm. The Warden laughed and put his knee back on Taniel's chest.

Taniel groaned as the knee was pushed into his sternum with additional weight. Ka-poel was on the Warden's back. She stabbed her long needle into the Warden's spine again and again. The Warden shook like a bull trying to throw off an unwanted rider. Taniel thought he felt something pop in his chest.

The Warden stood, unable to get Ka-poel off his back, and Taniel gasped, feeling the air rush back into his lungs with exhilaration. He needed to get out. To get away. He needed powder.

He rolled onto his belly and lurched up to his knees. The Warden lashed out with one boot, kicking Taniel back to the cobbles. Taniel struggled to his feet. Behind him, Ka-poel fought to stay on the Warden's back as he reached his over-long arms out behind him to try to peel her off.

People were calling for the city police now. The crowds had gathered, but kept their distance.

Ka-poel couldn't win this fight. But then, neither could Taniel. He reached out with his senses. There had to be powder around here somewhere. Someone had to have some.

He stumbled over to a young man in a bowler cap who was carrying a rifle over one shoulder. It was a Hrusch, and it looked freshly bought—it hadn't once been fired. Taniel grasped the young man by the front of his shirt. "Your powder horn! Give it to me!"

The young man tried to pull away. Taniel reached into his kit and felt his hand close around the smooth cylindrical shape of the powder horn. He wrenched it out of the bag triumphantly and spun back to see Ka-poel still on the Warden's back, if only barely.

"Pole, down!"

Ka-poel released her grip and was thrown to one side. Taniel held the powder horn like a grenade and threw it overhand. He reached out with his mind to ignite the powder and warp the blast to blow the creature to bits.

Nothing happened.

The Warden caught the powder horn in one hand. He stared

Taniel in the eye and flipped the horn around so the tapered end pointed toward himself, and *bit* through the horn. Powder spilled out from between his lips. His tongue lapped at the powder, grinding it between his teeth.

Taniel backed up until he thumped against the young man he'd stolen the powder horn from.

"Charges," he said. "I need powder charges!" A cold sweat broke out on Taniel's forehead. This Warden. This thing…

The young man turned and ran. Taniel heard screams and saw more people fleeing. He felt his boot hit something as he tried to step back again. The young man had dropped both his kit and his rifle.

Taniel rummaged inside the kit quickly, sure not to take his eyes off the Warden. There was a handful of powder charges. He crushed the end of one between his fingers and drew a line of the black powder on the back of his hand. The Warden was still eating the powder from the powder horn. *All of it.*

It didn't make sense, but somehow the Warden was a twisted reflection of Taniel himself. This Warden was a powder mage.

Taniel snorted the powder.

For a few moments, Taniel thought he might faint. At the edge of his vision the world went dark before suddenly becoming so stark it hurt his eyes. He flexed his hands, then felt his chest. No pain. He gritted his teeth and took the rifle in both hands.

The Warden charged him without warning. Taniel stepped to one side and gripped the barrel with both hands, bringing the stock back over his shoulder and whipping it out and around into the Warden's face.

The hickory stock shattered and the Warden went down with a satisfying thump. He flopped onto his stomach and pushed himself to his knees, then rammed himself into Taniel's chest.

Taniel backpedaled, trying to stay on his feet. He wouldn't be able to wrestle a Warden down on the ground—not if the Warden was in a powder trance. Taniel set one foot behind him to stop his backward movement and wrapped his arms around the Warden's middle. He jerked the Warden off balance and let go.

The Warden rolled away from Taniel and slowly got to his feet.

The creature's face was a mess of pulped flesh and slivers of wood. Blood streamed from his nose and mouth, and one of his eyes was swollen shut. He bared his teeth at Taniel. Half of them were missing.

"What the pit are you?" Taniel said.

The Warden cocked his head to one side. He lifted his brown hair, which was tied loosely over his right shoulder in a ponytail, to reveal the raised red welt of a brand. The image of a rifle about the length of a man's finger had been burned into his skin.

It was the brand that Kez Privileged gave to powder mages before their execution.

The Warden let his hair fall back into place. He watched Taniel for a moment, then looked to his side. Ka-poel was there, her long needle in hand, crouched low. She snarled at the Warden.

"Pole, get back..."

The Warden leapt toward Ka-poel. He moved with incredible speed, crossing the distance in the blink of an eye.

Taniel was faster now that he was in his powder trance. He shot toward the Warden, only to see the Warden twist at the last second. Taniel's fist soared past the Warden's face and he felt the Warden's fingers tighten around his neck once again.

The Warden wouldn't try to choke him this time. He'd wring Taniel's neck, snapping it like a child snaps a matchstick.

Taniel jabbed his hand at the Warden's chest. The Warden barely grunted. Taniel jabbed again and again, lightning fast. He felt the Warden's fingers lose their strength. Ka-poel threw herself at the Warden. He backhanded her, tossing her to the cobbles.

Taniel saw red in the corner of his vision. His mind's eye saw

Ka-poel's body in the street, her neck bent at the wrong angle, lifeless eyes staring into the sky.

The Warden suddenly sagged. Taniel made a fist with his hand, pulled it back...

And stopped in horror. His hand was covered in the Warden's black blood. Between his fingers, the flesh still clinging to it, he held one of the Warden's thick ribs. He looked down. The Warden, collapsed, stared back up at him. His coat was soaked through with blood.

Taniel saw the vision of Ka-poel's lifeless body again in his mind and rammed the Warden's own rib through its eye.

He stood for several moments, gasping in ragged breaths. Something touched him and he nearly screamed, his body was so tense. It was Ka-poel. She wasn't dead. She put one small hand on his, heedless of the Warden's blood.

"I've never seen a powder mage do that," Fell said, breathless, as she approached them through the empty street. The front of her secretary's smock was covered in black Warden's blood, as well as in some of her own. One cheek was red and swollen, but she didn't seem to notice.

"Where's the other Warden?" Taniel asked.

"He ran," Fell said.

"You're not just an undersecretary," Taniel said, remembering the long stiletto Fell had fearlessly jammed into a Warden's throat. "Wardens don't run."

"He did when he saw what you did to his friend," Fell said. "I kept him busy until then." She sniffed. "You're not an ordinary powder mage."

Taniel looked down at his hands. He'd punched through the Warden's skin and ripped out its rib. No one could do that. Not even he could, in the deepest powder trance. Then again, maybe a god killer could. Something had happened to him up on South Pike.

"I guess not." He looked around at the carnage. The closest people were over a hundred paces away, watching and pointing. He heard Adran police blowing their whistles as they grew close.

"This was a trap," Taniel said. "A Kez trap. How are they in the city? I thought Tamas rooted out the traitor Charlemund and his Kez accomplice."

"He did," Fell said. She seemed troubled.

Taniel fingered a powder charge and closed his eyes. Back in a powder trance. It felt incredible. His senses were alive. He could smell every scent on the air, hear every sound in the street.

His heart still thundered from the fight.

"I'm leaving," he said, taking Ka-poel by the hand.

"Ricard . . ." Fell began.

"Can go to the pit," Taniel said. "I'm going south. If Tamas is truly dead, and the Kez are making Wardens out of powder mages, then the army will need me."

Tamas rode beside Olem at the head of the Seventh Brigade. The column stretched out behind them, twisting along the Great Northern Highway as it rose and fell through the foothills of the Adran Mountains. His men were already dusty and tired, and the journey to get back into Adro had barely begun.

They marched northwest, unsheltered by Mihali's sorcerous fog that had allowed them to escape the Kez army four days before. To the east, the Adran Mountain Range cut into the sky with craggy, snow-topped peaks, while the sweltering summer heat beat down on Tamas's army. To the south and west, the Amber Expanse—the breadbasket of the Nine, and the source of the Kez's great wealth—spread out as far as the eye could see.

Tamas would have preferred to march on foot beside his men. But his leg still had a twinge to it, and he needed to be able to get up and down the column quickly. His orders had seen many officers' horses redistributed to the pickets, joining his two hundred cavalry in scouting.

"We're running out of food," Olem said from horseback beside Tamas.

It wasn't the first time Olem had mentioned rations, and it wouldn't be the last.

"I know," Tamas said. His men had their basic kit with a week's worth of road rations. No camp followers, no supply train. They'd marched double-time for four days now, and he had no doubt that some of his men had already finished their reserve against orders. "Give the order for half rations," Tamas said.

"We already did, sir." Olem chewed nervously on the butt of a cigarette.

"Halve it again."

Tamas looked west. It was infuriating. Millions of acres of farmland within sight, seemingly within a stone's throw. The reality was they couldn't be any farther away. The closest crops might be eight miles distant, without roads to reach them. No way to traverse the foothills and get down on the plain, forage with over ten thousand soldiers, and get back up to the road without losing a full two days' worth of marching.

It was their lead on the Kez armies that Tamas could not risk, even for food.

"Put together more foraging parties," Tamas said. "Twenty men each. Tell them not to range more than a single mile off the Northern Highway."

"We'll have to drop our pace," Olem said. He spit out his cigarette butt and reached in his pocket for another, only to examine it for a moment and slip it back in his jacket. He muttered something under his breath.

"What's that?" Tamas asked.

"I said I'm going to run out of cigarettes sooner or later."

Cigarettes were the least of Tamas's worries. "The men are exhausted." He turned in his saddle to look back along the column. "I can't push them double-time another day. The only way they've been able to go so fast for so long is thanks to the residuals of Mihali's food."

Olem saluted and headed down the column.

Tamas wished that the god had accompanied them on the ill-fated flanking maneuver. He ran his eyes over the faces of the men of the Seventh and Ninth. For the most part, his men met his gaze. These were hard men. His very best. They'd done twenty-five miles a day for four days. Kez infantry averaged twelve.

He caught sight of a rider coming up along the column. The figure looked huge, even on a cavalry charger.

Gavril.

Tamas tipped his hat to his brother-in-law as he came up alongside.

Gavril wiped the sweat from his face with one long sleeve and took a few gulps from his canteen. He'd discarded his grungy Mountainwatcher's furs on the heat of the high plains and wore only his faded Watchmaster's vest and a pair of dark-blue pants from an old cavalry uniform.

He grunted a hello. No salute from Gavril. Tamas would have been surprised to get one.

"What news?" Tamas asked.

"We've spotted the Kez," Gavril said. No "sir" either.

Tamas felt his heart leap into his throat. He knew the Kez were on his trail. It would be stupid not to realize that. But for four days they'd not seen any sign of the Kez armies.

"And?" Tamas lifted his own canteen to his lips.

"At least two brigades of Kez cavalry," Gavril said.

Tamas spit water all down the front of him. "Did you say *brigades*?"

"Brigades."

Tamas let out a shaky breath. "How far?"

"I'd guess fifty-five miles."

"Did you get close enough for an accurate count?"

"No."

"How hard are they pushing?"

"Can't be sure. Kez cavalry will make forty miles a day on the open plain if they push hard. An army of that size, and in the foothills—twenty-five, maybe thirty miles a day."

Which meant that if Tamas allowed his men rest and forage, the Kez would catch them in seven days. If Tamas was lucky.

"In six days," Gavril said, "you'll hit the edge of the Hune Dora Forest. The terrain will be too steep for cavalry to surround us. They'll be able to dog our heels, but nothing more. Not till we reach the Fingers of Kresimir."

Tamas closed his eyes, trying to remember the geography of northern Kez. This was Gavril's old haunt, back when he was Jakola of Pensbrook, the most famous womanizer in all of Kez.

"The Fingers of Kresimir," Tamas said. He knew the location, but it sounded familiar for more than just its mark on a map . . .

"Camenir," Gavril said quietly.

Tamas felt a sliver of ice creep down his spine despite the heat. A flash of memory, and once again he was standing beside a shallow grave, dug with bare hands in the cold of night beside the torrent of a raging river. The end of a daring—but ultimately failed—plan, and the most harrowing escape of Tamas's long career.

Gavril tugged at the front of his sweat-soaked vest. "We'll be going right by. I'm going to stop and pay my respects."

"I don't think I could find him," Tamas said, though he knew it was a lie. The location of the grave was burned into his memory.

"I can," Gavril said.

"It's quite a ways off the road. If I remember right."

"You'll stop too."

Tamas looked back at his column of soldiers again. They

marched on, the dust rising above them carried into the sky by a light breeze.

"I have men on the march, Jakola," he said. "I'm not stopping for anything."

Gavril sniffed. "It's 'Gavril' now, and yes, you will be stopping." He went on, not giving Tamas the chance to object. "You can lose the Kez entirely at the Fingers. We just have to reach the first bridge before them."

The Fingers of Kresimir were a series of deep, powerful snow-fed rivers off the Adran Mountains. They were impossible to ford, even on horseback. The Great Northern Road traversed them by a series of bridges built almost a hundred years ago.

"*If* we can reach the bridge before them," Tamas said, thankful to leave the topic of that lonely grave behind. "Even if we do, the cavalry can go west and around and be waiting for us when we come down onto the plains."

"You'll think of something."

Tamas ground his teeth together. He had eleven thousand infantry and two hundred cavalry, and just a four-day lead on a group of Kez cavalry that could very well equal his numbers. Dragoons and cuirassiers had more than just an edge on infantry in open battle.

"We need food," Tamas said.

Gavril looked toward the west and the tantalizing wheat fields of the Amber Expanse. "If we slow down too much to forage, the cavalry will reach us before Hune Dora Forest. Once we reach the forest, there are few farms. Foragers might bag deer and rabbits, but not enough to go around."

"And the city itself?"

Tamas remembered there was a settlement just south of Hune Dora Forest. Whether the forest took its name from the settlement, or the other way around, Tamas did not know.

"It's generous calling it a 'city.' It has walls, sure, but there can't be more than a few hundred people. We might be able to buy or steal enough food for a day or two." Gavril paused. "I hope you're not planning on stripping the countryside of everything. The people here have it hard enough. Ipille treats his serfs worse than Manhouch ever did."

"An army needs food, Jak…Gavril."

Tamas stared toward the mountains, barely noticing the white peaks. He had to balance this army perfectly. They needed food and safety. If they reached Hune Dora Forest without food, his men would begin to starve and desert. If they took too long to forage, the cavalry would reach them before the forest and have their way with the entire column.

Olem returned from his task, cantering up beside Tamas and Gavril.

"Olem," Tamas said. "Signal the column to stop." He paused to examine the countryside. To the left of the road an overgrown field sloped down toward a ravine a half mile off. "This here, it'll do."

"For what, sir?"

Tamas steeled himself. "It's time I talk to the men. Assemble them in ranks."

It took nearly an hour for the last of the columns to catch up. It was valuable time lost, but thus far Tamas had left the officers to tend to their men and keep them informed. If he was going to keep command of this lot—retain their discipline and loyalty over the next few weeks—he needed to speak to them himself.

He stood on the edge of the road and looked down the slope. The field had been trampled, the green replaced by Adran blue, standing at ease in ranks like so many blades of grass.

Tamas knew that many of these men would die without reaching their homes.

"'Tention!" Olem bellowed.

There was an audible shifting of legs and straightening of backs as eleven thousand soldiers snapped to attention.

The world was silent. A breeze picked up, blowing down from

the mountains and pushing gently on Tamas's back. To their credit, not a single soldier reached to steady his hat.

"Soldiers of the Seventh and Ninth," he began, shouting to be heard by all. "You know what's happened. You know that Budwiel has fallen and that the Kez push in to Adro, checked only by the Adran army.

"I grieve for Budwiel. I know that you grieve with me. Many of you question why we didn't stay and fight." Tamas paused. "We were outnumbered and outclassed. The fall of Budwiel's walls made our initial strategy obsolete and we could not have won that battle. As you all know, I do not fight battles that I will not win."

There was a murmur of agreement. The anger at abandoning Budwiel had dulled in the six days since. The men understood. There was no need to dwell on it further.

"Budwiel may have fallen, but Adro has not. I promise you—I *swear* to you—that Budwiel will be avenged. We will return to Adro and join our brothers and we will defend our country!"

A cheer went up among the men. To be honest, it was half-hearted, but at least it was something. He raised his arms for quiet.

"First," he said when the noise had died down, "we have a perilous journey ahead of us. I won't lie to you. We have little food, no baggage train or resupply. No reinforcements. Our ammunition will dwindle and our nights will be cold. We are utterly alone in a foreign land. Even now, the enemy has set their dogs on us.

"Kez cavalry are on our trail, my friends. Cuirassiers and dragoons, at least our number's worth and maybe more. I'd wager my hat that they are led by Beon je Ipille, the king's favorite son. Beon is a brave man and he will not be beaten easily."

Tamas could see the fear in his men's eyes. Tamas let it stew for a moment, watched the growing sense of panic. And then he reached out his hand and pointed to his men.

"You are the Seventh and the Ninth. You are Adro's finest, and that makes you the greatest infantry the world has ever seen. It is my pleasure, and my honor, to command you on the field of battle, and if it comes to it, to die with you. But I say we will not die here—on Kez soil.

"Let the Kez come," Tamas roared. "Let them send their greatest generals after us. Let them stack the odds against us. Let them come upon us with all their fury, because these hounds at our heels will soon know we are lions!"

Tamas finished, his throat raw from shouting, his fist held over his head.

His men stared back at him. No one made a sound. He could hear his heart beating in his ears, and then somewhere near the back of the assembled troops someone shouted, "Huzzah!"

Another voice joined it. Then another. It turned into a cheer, then a chant, and eleven thousand men raised their rifles over their heads and bellowed their defiance back at him, buckles and swords rattling in a sound that could have drowned out cannon fire.

These were his men. His soldiers. His sons and daughters. They would stare into the eyes of the pit itself for him. He stepped back away from the road so that they would not see his tears.

"Good speech, sir," Olem said, sheltering a match from the wind as he lit the cigarette pinched between his lips.

Tamas cleared his throat. "Wipe that grin off your face, soldier."

"Right away, sir."

"Once this quiets down, get the head of the column moving. We need to make more headway before night comes."

Olem went off about his duties, and Tamas took another few moments to gather himself. He stared to the southeast. Was that his imagination, or could he see movement in the distant foothills? No. The Kez weren't that close. Not yet.

CHAPTER

10

Adamat had spent the night in darkness, tied to a chair. At some point he hadn't been able to hold back any longer and had soiled himself. The air smelled of piss and mold and dirt. He was in a basement of a heavily trafficked building and could hear the creak and moan of floorboards as feet moved across them.

He'd yelled out loud when he first awoke in utter darkness. Someone had come to tell him to shut up. He had recognized the grizzled voice of the thief and called him a bloody dog.

The thief had left, laughing to himself.

Morning had come hours ago. Adamat could tell by the light coming in through the cracks of the floor above him. He could hear his own stomach grumbling for food. His throat was parched, his tongue swollen. His neck, legs, and back were all sore from sitting tied to the chair for fourteen hours or more.

The whale ointment he'd used to smooth his wrinkles and hide his age was beginning to burn. The stuff was supposed to be wiped off in less than twelve hours.

He felt himself begin to drift and shook his head to keep himself awake. Sleeping in this situation was deadly. He needed to be awake. To be alert. He had a head injury. It would take more light to tell if his eyes were focusing properly.

It was difficult to tell where he was. Voices above him were muffled, and no particular smells—aside from those of his own piss and the cold damp of a basement—stood out.

Adamat heard the creak of a door, then saw a light off in the corner of his vision. He turned his head—a painful movement—to watch as a lamp bobbed down a flight of stairs. He could hear two voices. The thief was not one of them.

"He hasn't said much except call Toak a bloody dog," a man said. The voice was nasal and high. "Didn't have anything in his pocketbook but a fifty-krana note and a false mustache. No checkbook. No identification. He could be a copper."

A voice answered him, too low for Adamat to hear.

"Well, yeah," the first voice said. "Most coppers carry a city mark on 'em, even if they're trying for a bust. Could be one of those undercover-spy types. The field marshal has been using them to root out Kez spies."

Another murmured answer.

The first voice had an edge of panic when he resumed speaking. "We didn't know," he said. "Toak said to grab 'im, so we did. He followed the lady back to the house."

The speaker arrived in front of Adamat with the lamp. He held it to Adamat's face. Adamat couldn't help but shy away from the flickering candlelight. He blinked against the brightness and tried to see the speaker's face and that of the murmuring man. It could be Vetas. Vetas would recognize Adamat in a second, and then he'd be a dead man, or worse.

"My name is Tinny," the first voice said. "Look up at the gov'na."

Tinny grabbed Adamat's chin and turned it toward the light. Adamat hawked the phlegm from his throat into Tinny's eye. He was rewarded with a sharp crack across the face that knocked his chair over.

Adamat lay on his back, his hands crushed underneath him, stars floating across his vision. He couldn't help the moan of pain that escaped his lips. He wondered if his wrists were broken.

"Pick him up," the murmuring voice said.

Tinny hung the lamp from the ceiling and righted Adamat's chair. Adamat considered head-butting the man, but thought his head had taken enough damage lately.

"What do you want from me?" Adamat tried to growl the words, but they came out as a rasp from his dry throat.

"That depends," the murmured voice continued. "Why were you following the woman in the red dress?"

Why . . . ? So it wasn't Vetas. Or Vetas hadn't recognized him yet.

"Wasn't following anyone," Adamat said. He tried to maintain a northwestern drawl. "Just shopping and going for a walk."

"Without any identification? And a false mustache? Put the light to his face."

Tinny grabbed Adamat's chin again and shoved the lantern up next to it.

The murmuring voice gave a soft chuckle. "Ah, you bloody fool."

"Fool for what? Going for a walk?" Adamat said.

"I wasn't talking to you."

The lantern pulled away from Adamat's face, and he could see Tinny clearly in the light. Tinny's eyes were wide, his complexion pale. "It was an honest mistake, gov'na. I swear."

"Leave," the voice murmured. "Wait. Tell the master we have Inspector Adamat."

Tinny hung the lamp back on the ceiling and left the room. Adamat couldn't help the cold fear that spidered up the back of his neck. He squinted in the poor light, trying to see the source of that murmured voice.

"Adamat," the murmuring voice said suddenly in his ear.

Adamat started. He hadn't heard the man move, and there wasn't another person in this dank basement. "Who, now?" Adamat said. Hold the pose. Play dumb. Don't let them break you.

A soft sigh in his ear. A sudden blade against his naked throat. He had the all-too-vivid recollection of a razor blade breezing past his throat not more than two months ago. He pulled back instinctively, a sharp breath escaping him. The knife did not follow. A sudden tug at his bound wrists and they were free.

He rubbed some feeling back into them and stared straight ahead. He didn't dare assume that he'd been released. He might take a knife in the ribs or across the throat at any time. No doubt the man behind him was ready for sudden moves, and even if Adamat overpowered him, Adamat was still in a basement beneath someone's headquarters.

Adamat still didn't know where he was. The murmuring voice belonged to someone who recognized him, even in such ill light. He cycled through the names of hundreds of men, trying to match a face to the voice, but to no avail.

He felt, more than heard, the presence move back in front of him. He could make out a heavyset shadow in a sleeveless shirt. A bald head shone in the candlelight. *Definitely* not Lord Vetas.

Adamat tried to blink the blurriness from his eyes and took in a deep breath. It caught in his throat at the slight scent of sweetbell and the recollection of a similar scent in his own home the same night that the Black Street Barbers had attacked him.

"Eunuch." The word came out of his throat with a strangled sigh of relief. He felt his body sag against the ropes still tying his ankles to the chair, only to stiffen again a moment later as the realization set in that the Proprietor's eunuch might very well be working with Lord Vetas.

The eunuch turned toward Adamat. "There," he said. "Pretense dropped. Now, what were you doing following the woman in the red dress?"

Adamat sniffed. The smell of his own piss was somehow less bearable now this his hands were untied.

"Working," he said.

"On?"

"I report to Field Marshal Tamas, and him only. You should know that."

The eunuch tapped the side of his jaw with one finger, considering Adamat through narrow, unfeeling eyes.

"We're on the same side, aren't we?" Adamat said. The question came out just a little too desperate for his liking.

"In a few minutes my master will have decided what to do with you. If he decides to let you live, I suggest that you keep this little run-in to yourself."

" 'If'?"

The eunuch shrugged. "I would like to know if we are working at cross-purposes. There are rumors about you, Adamat. Finding you where we did could mean one of two things."

Adamat waited for the eunuch to elaborate on what those two things were. He didn't. "That I'm with you, or against you?" Adamat hazarded a guess.

"These things are rarely so simple as 'with or against.' "

"I was following a hunch," Adamat said. "Trying to find someone."

"Lord Vetas?"

Adamat watched the eunuch for several long seconds. No tic. No hint. No giveaways. He was as unreadable as polished marble. Was the Proprietor working with Vetas, providing enforcement and tails, as Adamat feared?

"Yes."

"Why?"

Adamat looked at his hands. In the dim light he could see the dark welts where they'd been bound. His fingers all still worked. For that he should be grateful. He knew he wouldn't feel the real pain and ache until he tried to walk. He looked back up at the eunuch.

Still unreadable. The truth could get him killed in this situation. There were a hundred lies he could tell. Adamat considered himself a good liar. But he could get himself killed with the wrong lie, even one told well, or if the eunuch even suspected a lie.

The truth it was.

"He took my family," Adamat said. "Blackmailed me, and he still has my wife and oldest son. I want to get them back, and then kill him slowly."

"A lot of violence planned, for a family man," the eunuch said.

Adamat leaned forward. "'Family,'" he said. "Remember that word. There is nothing that will make a man more desperate and more capable of violence than endangering his family."

"Interesting." The eunuch seemed unmoved.

A door opened. Light poured into the opposite side of the cellar, and footfalls thumped down the steps.

"The master says bring him up, gov'na," Tinny said.

The eunuch scowled. "Now?"

"Yeah. Wants to see him."

Adamat smoothed the front of his soiled jacket. He didn't think he could be more nervous than he'd been when sitting in a basement, tied to a chair, at the mercy of who-knew-who, but he was.

"I'm to meet the Proprietor?"

"It appears so." The eunuch extended a hand and helped Adamat to his feet. "Don't worry," he said. "There are three men who know his face in all the Nine. You won't be one of them."

Adamat wasn't reassured. He looked down at his pants, at the cold, wet stain sticking his trousers to his legs. "How will..."

"Ah." The eunuch gestured Tinny over. "Adamat is now a guest. Have a couple of the girls clean him up, and take him to the master in twenty minutes."

Tinny shifted from one foot to the other. "He seemed awfully insistent."

"Have you seen the master's new rug?"

Tinny nodded uncertainly.

"Do you want it to smell like this cellar?"

"No, gov'na."

"Clean him up, and *then* take him to the master."

Adamat's first order of business was to get a feel for his new location. He studied the decoration and architecture, but both were utterly useless to him. Polished wood floors creaked beneath his feet. The walls were plaster over wood, the candelabras of brass. It was a spacious affair, but demurely utilitarian.

Adamat was led into a bathing room with hot running water. His clothes were stripped from him without ceremony by a pair of handmaids, so quickly he couldn't protest the impropriety of it all. When the eunuch had instructed he be bathed by a couple of girls, Adamat had expected whores. These were sturdy washing women.

His back and hair were scrubbed quickly, cold water splashed over him to rinse off the soap, and a fresh pair of trousers presented to him. When Adamat emerged from the bathing room, the same two women combed his hair and straightened his collar.

Tinny was waiting beside the door. In better light, Adamat could see he was a sickly man of medium height. He wore a cut-across, double-breasted coat with squared tails and a starched cravat. The coat, along with the cream pants and knee-high boots, were so incredibly ordinary that Adamat doubted he could pick Tinny out in a line of men on the street, despite Adamat's having memorized his face.

It was Adamat's Knack, after all. He never forgot a face, and he wouldn't forget the Proprietor's either. Just one glance was all he needed.

Tinny handed Adamat his pocketbook.

Adamat flipped it open. The fifty-krana note was still inside. Along with Adamat's false mustache.

Adamat took a proffered coat from one of the women and stuffed the pocketbook inside. He did it all without looking away from Tinny. The man returned his gaze with a slight sneer and looked Adamat up and down.

"It'll be good enough," Tinny said. "At least you don't smell of piss no more." He gave Adamat a mean grin. "You've got a mark there on your face."

From where Tinny had struck him. Charming.

"I see you cleaned the spit from yours."

Tinny's grin turned down at the corners, and he gripped Adamat's coat. In a low voice he said, "Master gives the word and I'll carve you up. It'll take me three days to kill you. I know who you are. Copper. Don't like your kind."

This close Adamat could smell the wine on Tinny's breath. That hadn't been there before. Was Tinny so terrified of the eunuch he'd gone to get a drink? Interesting. Of more interest was the way Tinny stood; a slight lean to his left, caused either by his left leg being shorter than the right or by favoring an injury to his right.

Adamat jerked his coat from Tinny's grip.

"After you," Tinny said.

"I insist." Adamat waved his hand forward.

Tinny gave him a mocking bow and stepped into the hallway. Adamat watched his legs. A definite limp, favoring his right.

Adamat lashed out without warning, his boot connecting solidly with the side of Tinny's right leg. Tinny folded sideways, his yell of surprise muffled by Adamat's hand over his mouth. Adamat took most of his weight and lowered him to the floor, putting one hand firmly against his throat.

"Don't threaten to kill a man unless you know without a doubt you'll have the opportunity," Adamat whispered. "Now, I've spent the entire summer with the most powerful people in all the Nine breathing down my neck. Do you think I care about one limping henchman? Do you think I have the time for you?

"I'm going to go talk to your master. If it goes badly, he'll kill me, I have no doubt. But I promise, if they put me alone in a room with you, that it doesn't matter how securely they bind me—I'll get loose and I'll kill you."

Adamat released Tinny's neck and mouth.

Different kinds of men responded differently to those with power over them. Some got angry. Some took it silently. Some were so terrified they'd believe anything you said, no matter how outlandish.

From the look in Tinny's eyes, Adamat believed him to be the last of these.

Adamat made his way into the grand hall. His whole body ached from the night spent tied to a chair, and he worked to suppress his own limp. He passed a dozen men and women. Dressed unremarkably, just like Tinny. Probably messengers and the like.

Adamat had been in the lairs of perhaps half a dozen crime bosses in his life. Every one had either been an opulent palace or a scum-ridden den of iniquity. The Proprietor's headquarters was so ordinary that it almost shocked him. It might have been the offices of some powerful but money-conscious nobleman, for all he could tell.

In the grand hall there were enforcers. Big men, scowling at everyone, pistols in their belts. They flanked the front windows and door. Adamat saw a woman he recognized, a whorehouse madame from the east side of Adopest who'd once told Adamat where to find a killer. She was dressed in her very best, and she sat on a bench beside the front door. She looked like a girl waiting to see the headmaster.

Someone gripped Adamat's arm. He surprised himself by not leaping out of his skin, and turned to look up into the face of one of the big enforcers.

Before the man could speak, Adamat said, "I'm looking for the eunuch. He just sent me for a bath and I seem to have lost my handler. I'm to see the Proprietor now."

The enforcer opened his mouth, then closed it. He scowled. Obviously not what he'd been expecting.

"Adamat," a voice came.

The eunuch drifted across the grand hall and nodded to the enforcer. In the light of the day, Adamat could see that he was wearing a tailored brown suit with long coattails and an emerald cravat. The big man stepped away, and Adamat let himself be led down a side corridor by the eunuch.

"Where is Tinny?" the eunuch asked.

"He tripped. Fell down some stairs. I told him I'd find you myself."

"Ah." The eunuch didn't seem like he would dispute Adamat's story. "Well, if you'd step inside, the master will see you now."

They'd stopped in front of a door at the side of the corridor. Nondescript. Unadorned. Adamat looked up and down the hall.

"Here?"

"Yes."

"I see."

"You were expecting something else?" the eunuch asked. "Something more grand, perhaps?"

Adamat examined the plain trappings of the hall, caught sight of a woman with a bundle of papers in her arms, wearing a long, plain dress and looking so ordinary it hurt his brain.

"No, I suppose not."

The eunuch rapped on the door.

"Come," came the brisk order.

Adamat stepped into the room and closed the door behind him.

The room was very well lit, much to Adamat's surprise. It was a significantly sized office with fine wood paneling, high-arched windows, and a fireplace framed by ornate brickwork. Two well-worn chairs sat next to the fireplace, not far from the door. At the opposite end of the room was a wide desk, partially blocked by a screen. Adamat took note that, aside from the fine rug on the floor, there were no decorations.

Beside the desk sat a severe-looking woman with a sharp jawline and pronounced crow's-feet in the corners of her eyes. Her posture was immaculate, her dress smoothed over her legs. A half-knitted scarf sat in her lap.

"Inspector Adamat?" the woman asked.

Adamat nodded, looking curiously at the screen. He could hear pen scratches from behind it.

"My name is Amber," the woman said. She pronounced the word like "amba." "You must first know that if you see the master's face, even by accident, you will die."

Adamat found himself suddenly less curious as to what was behind the screen.

"Sit," the woman said, gesturing to one of the chairs beside the fire. Adamat sat.

Amber went on. "I speak for the master. I am his mouthpiece, and you may address yourself to me as if I were he, and I will address myself to you also as if I were he. Now, I'd like to apologize for the evening you spent in our cellar. Most unfortunate."

The scratching of the pen had stopped. Adamat noticed that Amber was no longer looked at him, but behind the screen. Perhaps reading some kind of hand language from the master?

"It was wholly unpleasant, I assure you."

"To the matter at hand," the Proprietor said through Amber. "There is a man by the name of Lord Vetas that has been causing my organization no small amount of problems."

"I don't know the name," Adamat lied, wondering why he bothered. He'd already told the eunuch about Vetas and his family.

"Come now. He's kept it very quiet, but the name has been passed around the very top levels of Tamas's military cabinet. Along with yours. I'd find it a very large coincidence that my men stumbled across you following one of Lord Vetas's spies."

"Stranger things have happened," Adamat said.

"Such as Taniel Two-Shot," the Proprietor said, "a celebrated war hero, putting a bullet between the eyes of a god on top of South Pike Mountain? Or Field Marshal Tamas, one of the most reasonable men in Adro, declaring a chef the god of Adro?"

Adamat drummed his fingers on his pantleg and watched Amber as she watched behind the screen. It was disconcerting to carry on a conversation this way, but he seemed to have no alternative. "You don't believe that tripe, do you?"

"I didn't say I believed it," said the Proprietor through his interpreter. "I tend to only believe hard facts, but if I only *acted* on hard facts, I wouldn't be here. Half of my trade is whispers and rumors. Information."

"Information is power," Adamat agreed. "You've certainly made your living well enough."

"It's not just power, it's money. But I'll give you this for free: Field Marshal Tamas is dead."

Adamat clasped his hands together to hide the sudden shaking of his fingers. Was this true? Could the field marshal be dead? If that was the case, Adamat was suddenly without a sponsor. His campaign against Lord Vetas already had little enough backing for a man that dangerous, but sixteen soldiers and an open checkbook was nothing to scoff at. Adamat wasn't sure he was prepared to take on Vetas alone.

"How do you know?" Adamat said when he trusted himself to speak. His voice wavered.

"I received this missive from General Hilanska of the Second Brigade just this morning." A hand reached out from behind the screen and gave a note to Amber. She in turn gave it to Adamat. "I assume his other councillors—Lady Winceslav, Prime Lektor, Ondraus the Reeve, and Ricard Tumblar—all received the same note."

Adamat slipped the silk ribbon off the note and unrolled it. The letters were Adran, but the single paragraph gibberish.

"A cipher?" Adamat said.

"Indeed. It says—"

Adamat cut him off. "That Kresimir has returned and Field Marshal Tamas was cut off behind enemy lines with only two brigades. He's presumed dead."

Silence from the Proprietor. Amber stared behind the screen for several moments. Her eyes opened a little wider before she delivered the Proprietor's response. "That was...impressive."

Adamat gave the missive back to Amber. "A perfect memory makes ciphers very easy to decode. I spent two summers as a boy memorizing the keys to over four hundred different ciphers, both common and uncommon. That one is extremely rare, but I don't forget. Kresimir. I thought Taniel Two-Shot put a bullet through his eye?"

"Gods. Rumors. I've built this empire in Adro's underworld by making very good guesses, and my guess here is that General Hilanska wouldn't say such a thing unless he believes it fully."

Adamat leaned back. He stared at the screen, feeling less intimidated for some reason. What was behind that screen? What kind of a person? The hand Adamat had seen reach out was old, obviously male, with manicured nails. The Proprietor didn't spend his whole life behind a screen. Somewhere else he had an assumed identity. One that allowed him to move about in public.

"Only a handful of people in Adopest know this information," Adamat said. "Why tell me?"

The Proprietor seemed to hesitate. "Because it puts you to the wind. Tamas was your employer."

"And you want to employ me?" Adamat felt his hackles rise. In all his life he never thought he'd have a job offer from the Proprietor himself.

"Ricard Tumblar will ask you to help with his campaign for the new ministry. He'll offer to pay well. I can pay better. Other than that, what role could you possibly fill? A place back on the police force? I don't think you want to be walking the streets in uniform over the next few years."

"What would you hire me to do?"

"That brings me around to my first question. What interest do you have in Lord Vetas?"

Adamat tilted his head to the side. The Proprietor didn't know about Adamat's wife. Which meant the eunuch hadn't told him yet. It also meant either the Proprietor wasn't working for Lord Vetas or that he was not close enough that Vetas had told him about Adamat.

"He has my wife. I'm going to find him, rescue my wife, and kill Lord Vetas."

Adamat heard a low chuckle from behind the screen. He couldn't help but scowl.

"Perfect," the Proprietor said through Amber. "Just perfect."

"Why should you care about Lord Vetas?"

"As I said, he's been causing problems for my organization."

"What kind of problems?"

"Ones that I can't handle without things becoming very noisy. He has at least sixty enforcers, and one of them is a Privileged."

Adamat's heart jumped. A Privileged? Pit, how could he deal with something like that? "It might help if you were more specific about the problems."

"None that concern you."

Adamat smoothed the front of his shirt again. "A turf war, maybe? Vetas is moving in on your sources of revenue? Stirring up trouble in the underworld? Stealing your manpower, maybe?" That would explain why Roja the Fox was one of the guards holding Adamat's children hostage—but if Roja had gone over to Vetas *without* the Proprietor's blessing, it meant that Roja thought Vetas the stronger of the two.

A scary thought indeed.

"None," the Proprietor said, Amber's translation somewhat icy, "that concern you. This meeting is over. You may leave."

Adamat blinked at the abruptness of it. "You don't want to hire me?"

"Not anymore."

"And you're not going to kill me?"

"No. Out."

Adamat stood and examined the room once more, careful not to focus too much on the screen. Everything here was of a very fine quality, but not handcrafted. The paneling was milled, the candelabras secondhand. Even the desk looked like the kind that were made a dozen-a-day at a large carpenter's workshop. Nothing here that could be traced.

Except the rug. Gurlish, by the design, and even to an inexperienced eye the fibers were finely woven.

Adamat fished inside his jacket for a handkerchief. He blew his nose noisily and dropped it, then bent and snatched it from the floor, making sure to look away from the Proprietor's desk.

When he stood, Amber still had the expectant look on her face that told him he'd overstayed his welcome. She glanced toward the door and he nodded.

Outside, the eunuch stood by the door.

"Stay here," he said, going into the Proprietor's office.

Adamat took the moment alone to examine the fibers in between his fingers. There were only a few, all crinkled and dry. He couldn't tell them from the lint in his pocket. But he knew a woman who might be able to identify them.

The eunuch emerged from the office, pulling the door closed behind him with a click. He seemed troubled. "You're free to go," he said. "Of course, we can't just have you walk out the front door. Keep the clothes."

Adamat opened his mouth to respond, when someone grabbed him from behind. A rag was shoved over his mouth and nose, and the last thing he remembered was the overpowering smell of ether.

CHAPTER

11

Taniel was awakened from his half doze at the reins by the distant report of cannon fire.

Dark thoughts swirled in his mind, thick as the clouds of smoke in the mala den. He could still see the Warden eating black powder. He could still feel the powder-enhanced strength in the monster's twisted limbs. How could the Kez have made one of those creatures out of a powder mage? From what he knew of Wardens and Privileged, that seemed impossible.

Then again, so did stabbing a Warden with its own rib after ripping it from the creature's chest.

The sudden sensation of falling made him grip the saddle horn in a panic, startling the horse. The world seemed to spin around him. He took several deep, ragged breaths. Even once he knew that he wasn't actually falling, his heart still raced. Five days without mala. His hands shook, his mouth was dry, and his head pounded. The heat of the sun beating down didn't help any of it.

A cool hand suddenly touched his cheek. Ka-poel sat in the saddle behind him, arms wrapped around his waist for most of the journey, for she didn't know the first thing about riding a horse. It should have been terribly uncomfortable to have her clinging to him in this heat, but somehow it was the only thing that gave him relief.

Not that he'd admit it to her.

It was early afternoon and the mountains were closing in on either side as they traveled into Surkov's Alley. They'd spent the night in Fendale, a large city of some hundred thousand that was swelled to four times that number with army reserves and the refugees from Budwiel.

What little sleep Taniel had managed in Fendale was restless and plagued with nightmares. He'd read once that the only way to sleep well after forming a mala addiction was with more mala.

Ka-poel removed her hand from his cheek, to his decidedly uncomfortable regret. What would he do with this girl? She seemed to think he belonged to her in some way. He could sleep with her, he supposed, but the thought of it made him feel . . . conflicted. She was a savage, and his servant. A companion and nothing more. There wasn't a soul in polite Adran society who wouldn't think it most improper.

When had he ever cared about what society thought proper, he reminded himself. And a savage? Taniel had seen Ka-poel's sorcery. She'd saved his life on several occasions. She was anything but "just a savage girl."

Taniel tried to blink away the fog that permeated his mind, but with little success. Drifting off like that could be dangerous. They would reach the front by tomorrow evening, and from there he'd have to find out if there were any other powder mages left in the army, and news of his father. And of course, he'd have to report to . . . to who? Taniel had never reported to anyone but Field Marshal Tamas.

Could Tamas really be dead? Taniel was a little surprised to feel a lump in the back of his throat at the idea. He loved Tamas, admired him even, but he didn't like him, and they had never been especially close. After all, the old bastard had ordered him to kill his best friend. Taniel didn't even know where Bo was now. Maybe he'd died on the mountain, or been executed by Tamas weeks ago.

Taniel hoped they were both alive—Tamas and Bo. There were still things that needed to be said.

As for Ka-poel . . . Respect. That's all Taniel was feeling. And a feeling of hopelessness, for Tamas had been Adro's best chance at winning the war.

They stopped to rest in one of the many little towns in Surkov's Alley between Fendale and Budwiel. Normally a town like this would have a couple thousand residents. With the war on, it was overflowing. Supply trains flowed through the city, and infantry reserves walked the streets in their uniforms, enjoying a few days away from the front. Taniel watched as dozens of carts rolled by, carrying wounded and dead soldiers from the front. He'd seen hundreds of such carts since leaving Adopest. It didn't bode well for the war.

"Captain, if you ignore me for another moment, I'll have you flogged."

Ka-poel, seated next to him on a grassy bank while they ate their lunch, elbowed Taniel in the ribs. Taniel looked up, feeling genuine surprise that someone was talking to him.

A colonel sat on horseback, his narrow features twisted in a scowl. He pointed his riding crop at Taniel. "Captain, what brigade are you with?" He gave Taniel a moment to answer, and then, "Wipe that stupid look off your face. Is that such a hard question?"

"I don't have one," Taniel said.

"Don't have a . . . are you daft? Are you a captain in the Adran army or not? Be careful how you answer, son, or I'll have you brought up on charges of impersonating an officer!"

Taniel fingered the captain's stars on his lapel. They were gold, as he'd used his silver buttons to buy mala and these were the only replacements he could get on short notice. His powder-keg pin was in his pocket. Who the bloody pit was this man? Taniel had never answered to anyone other than the field marshal. He supposed that technically he was attached to a brigade. The Seventh, maybe?

Taniel shrugged.

The colonel's face turned red. "Major!"

A woman in her midthirties rode up beside the colonel. "Sir?" She had long brown hair tied back behind her head in a single braid, and a thin face with a beauty mark on her left cheek. She saluted the colonel and then looked down at Taniel.

"Have this man arrested," the colonel said.

"Charges, sir?"

"Disrespecting a superior officer. The man didn't salute me, or answer my questions, or stand in my presence."

The major climbed down from her horse and gestured to a pair of neatly dressed soldiers to join her.

Taniel watched the three of them approach. He took a bite of mutton and cheese, chewing slowly.

"Stand up, Captain," the major said. When Taniel didn't respond, she jerked her head to one of the soldiers. He bent to grab Taniel by the arm.

Taniel lifted the pistol from his lap and cocked back the hammer, pointing it at the soldier. "Bad idea, soldier." Taniel almost cracked a smile at the looks on the faces of the major and colonel, but he doubted that would help his position.

"Uh, sir," one of the soldiers said, "are you Taniel Two-Shot?"

"Yes," Taniel said, "I am."

"I used to be with the Seventh. It's a pleasure to meet you, sir, but it seems we're supposed to arrest you."

Taniel locked eyes with the major. "That's not going to happen today."

The major retreated for a moment and held a quiet conference with the colonel. A few moments later the colonel nodded and the major and the soldiers were dismissed.

Taniel returned to his lunch, only to find the colonel still sitting on his horse not ten feet away. The man rode a little closer. Taniel looked up. He wasn't in the mood for this.

The colonel's expression was still disapproving. "Captain, I'm sorry, I didn't recognize you. We've met before, but it was years ago. Your father was a great man."

Taniel swallowed a mouthful of food. How was he supposed to answer that? "Yes, he was."

"Captain, I should warn you. The field marshal was quite lenient with all his soldiers, especially his mages. With his death there's been a shift in policy in that regard. I doubt the General Staff will make an exception for you, even with your reputation. Point a pistol at a ranking officer again and you'll be—"

"Shot?" Taniel asked, not able to keep the smirk from his face.

The colonel scowled. "Hanged."

"Thank you for the warning. *Sir.*"

The colonel nodded. "I'm glad to hear you're on your feet again, Captain. We need you on the front." He paused for a moment, as if waiting for Taniel to stand and salute him. He could have waited all day for that, as far as Taniel was concerned. After nearly a minute he turned his horse and was off at a canter.

Taniel couldn't help but wonder why the colonel wasn't on the front with the rest of the army.

"Pole," he said. "I don't know if it's a good idea for you to come with me."

She rolled her eyes at him.

"I'm serious, Pole. It's a war zone. I know you've been in war before." Pit, she'd been with him facing down the same Kez Grand

Army just a couple months ago. He'd watched her butcher half the Kez royal cabal up on South Pike. "But I've felt...strange since you brought me back. I don't know what I'll do. I'd rather not get you killed."

Taniel again remembered the blood on her hands when he awoke from the coma. He had seen dead soldiers, and a man he felt he should recognize lying on the ground unconscious. Ka-poel had tried to explain it with hand gestures. Taniel had surmised that she'd traded a life for his. Whose, he didn't know, but the thought made him sick.

Ka-poel took the piece of cheese from his hand and tossed it in her mouth. That seemed like all the answer that Taniel was going to get.

"Oh well," he said. "I had to try. It'll be good to have you at my side."

Ka-poel pursed her lips in a sly smile.

"My *side*, Ka-poel. I don't—"

She put her finger to his lips, her smile widening.

"They won't like you being with me," Taniel said. "There are some women soldiers, and fraternization is strictly prohibited. It happens all the time, of course, but the officers like to keep up appearances. They might try to make you sleep in a different tent."

Ka-poel spread her hands, questioning.

"What? Fraternization? You know. Men and women being... together. Intimately."

She pointed between them, then made a flat, chopping motion with her hand. *But we aren't.* The grin on her face made the motion appear mocking, like a child denying that they'd done something wrong when they'd been caught doing it.

It made Taniel's heart beat faster, and he could feel his face go red. "All right, girl, we're going now. Just after I piss."

When he got back to the horse, he found her sitting in the saddle already, but toward the front, as if she expected him to sit behind her.

"Move back," he said.

She ignored him. He pulled himself up into the saddle behind her, and to take the reins, he had to wrap his arms around her waist. She snuggled up against his chest and he flicked the reins with a sigh.

The number of people along the road increased as they got closer and closer to the front. In the last ten miles there were so many tents that they filled the entire valley from one side to the other. It seemed like a sea of people—soldiers, smiths, whores, cooks, laundresses, and merchants. He saw soldiers with the stripes of just about every brigade in Adro, including all of the Wings of Adom, Lady Winceslav's mercenaries. By now she'd know that Tamas was dead. Taniel wondered if she'd pull her mercenaries out of the war.

The road seemed to disappear beneath the crowd, and Taniel knew they were just one good rainstorm away from it becoming a shit hole of mud. The Addown River cut through the whole thing, a dirty mess clogged with the waste of hundreds of thousands of people. There were barges moored here and there along the river—supply ships from Adopest, no doubt bringing food, weapons, and fresh recruits.

The tents gained some order as he finally reached the army proper. He didn't think he'd ever look forward to straight lines and discipline again, but after having to push his way through the final few miles he was glad to leave the reserves and hangers-on behind him.

For most of the trip down the Alley the cannon fire had rumbled together like thunder in the distance. Now he could pick out individual blasts. The artillery crew were working full-time, it seemed. That didn't surprise him; he'd seen the Kez Grand Army.

What did surprise him was the crack and spark of sorcery he noticed as he got closer. There were Privileged fighting on the front—on both sides. Most of the Kez Cabal had been wiped out at the Battle for South Pike or at Kresim Kurga by Ka-poel. And where had Adro gotten any Privileged?

It took some questioning, but Taniel was soon able to find the closest officers' mess. It was mostly full of officers from the Third Brigade. He tossed his powder-keg pin on the bar.

"I need a room," he said.

The barkeep eyed him suspiciously. "No rooms here, sir. All full up."

"Kick someone out," Taniel said. "I'm not sleeping in a tent in this mess." Pit. He'd skin a man who tried to do something like that to him. But Taniel wasn't about to leave Ka-poel anywhere in an army this size that didn't have a locking door.

"I'm sorry, sir. I can't do that."

Taniel looked down at his powder-keg pin. "You see that, right?"

The barkeep slid the powder-mage pin back across the bar toward Taniel. "Look, '*sir.*' There aren't any powder mages left in the army. They've all been wiped out. So don't try to pull one over on me."

Taniel rocked back on his barstool. All of them? Gone? "What do you mean 'wiped out'? How could they be wiped out?"

"They were with Field Marshal Tamas when he was lost behind the enemy lines."

"There's not a single Marked this side of Budwiel?"

"Not just this side of Budwiel. They're dead."

"Have you seen the bodies?" Taniel demanded. "Well, have you? Do you know anyone who has? Has there been recent news from Kez? I thought not. Now get me a drink, and have someone find out about getting me a room."

The barkeep folded his arms across his dirty apron and didn't move.

"Look," Taniel said, "if I'm the last living powder mage north of Budwiel, then I'm a damned celebrity. There are Privilegeds out there who need to be killed. I'll need a drink and eventually some sleep to be able to do that."

"Is this man bothering you, Frederik?"

A woman positioned herself at the bar and looked at Taniel, bemused. Taniel recognized her as the major with the beauty mark on her cheek. The one who'd tried to arrest him earlier that day. Had she followed him?

"Ma'am," Frederik said. "He claims he's a powder mage."

"He is. This is Taniel Two-Shot."

The barkeep ducked a quick bow. "Sorry, sir. What will you have?"

"Gin." Taniel cleared his throat. "No apology needed."

"And for the savage?"

Ka-poel was drumming her fingers on the bar, looking bored.

"Her name is Ka-poel, and she'll have water."

She smacked him in the shoulder.

"Wine," Taniel amended. "Something with a light taste."

The major regarded Taniel warily, sizing him up the way she might an enemy on the battlefield. "You let your servants treat you like that?" she asked.

"I'm sorry," Taniel said, trying not to let his irritation show. "I must have missed your name?"

"I'm Major Doravir, of the Third, adjutant to General Ket."

"My 'servant' is a Bone-eye, Major. A sorcerer more powerful than half the Kez Cabal put together."

Doravir seemed doubtful. "Is she your wife?"

"No."

"Your fiancée?"

Taniel glanced at Ka-poel. Had he given this major that impression? "No."

"Does she have a rank?"

"No."

"Then she doesn't belong in the officers' mess. She can wait for you outside."

"She's my guest, Major."

"With all the crowds, General Ket has declared that only spouses may stay with officers at the mess. Too many men bringing their whores back to sleep with them."

Taniel felt his fingers creeping toward the pistol at his belt, but remembered the advice the colonel had given him earlier in the day. No, he couldn't do that here. He turned to Ka-poel. "Pole, will you marry me?"

Ka-poel gave one serious nod.

Pit. Taniel hoped she saw what he was playing at. He turned back to Doravir. "She's my fiancée." He glanced at the barkeep. "Get me a room."

Doravir snorted out her nose. "You're funny, Two-Shot. You can stay with me in my room. Frederik, give him a key."

"And my fiancée here?"

"She can stay in the closet." Doravir gave Ka-poel a mocking smile. That did not bode well.

Taniel took the glass of gin from the bar and drained it in one swallow. It almost knocked him clean off his feet. How long had it been since he'd drunk hard liquor? He blinked a few times, hoping his eyes weren't visibly watering. "I'll stay somewhere else, thank you."

"Good luck." Doravir snorted. "There's not an empty room within five miles of the front, and with Tamas gone, no one will put up with a mere captain shoving them out. You'll have to push a private from his tent."

Taniel took some pleasure in the annoyance in Doravir's voice. "I think I'll do that, then. Come on, Ka-poel."

Adamat was slapped awake with rough hands. He jerked forward, reaching for a cane that wasn't there, and groggily took stock of his surroundings.

He was in the back of a carriage with one other man—the same pickpocket who'd pistol-whipped him before taking him to the

Proprietor's. The carriage wasn't moving. Outside, he could hear the general bustle of an evening crowd.

"Toak, was it?" Adamat asked.

The man nodded. He held a pistol in his right hand, hammer back, pointed at Adamat. "Get out."

"Where am I?"

"Quarter mile north of Elections Square," Toak said. "Get out."

Adamat climbed from the carriage and held his hand up to shade his eyes from the afternoon sun. As soon as he was off the running board, the carriage took off, disappearing down the street. Adamat rubbed his eyes and tried to get his mind working. He felt nauseous. What had they given him? Ah, yes. Ether. He'd be in a fog for hours yet.

He spent until just before dark at a nearby café, nursing a soda water to settle his stomach.

Why had the Proprietor offered him employment and then simply dumped him back on the street? A very strange way to act. The Proprietor was known for secrecy and efficiency. For keeping his promises and destroying his competition. He was not known for behaving strangely.

It had to be something Adamat had said.

Adamat blamed the ether when it took him well over an hour to realize the obvious.

The Proprietor had intended on paying him to go after Lord Vetas. But why pay a man to do something he already plans to do? Adamat shook his head. Stupid. On both his part and the Proprietor's. If Tamas was truly dead, Adamat would lose the few soldiers Tamas had granted him. Adamat couldn't take Lord Vetas alone.

Adamat knew where Lord Vetas was holing up. The house with the woman in the red dress. The house where he had seen the Eldaminse boy.

Now that he knew that, a frontal assault would be necessary. The same as they had done to rescue Adamat's family. Smash open the doors, take them by surprise. A man like Lord Vetas would have guards. What had the Proprietor said? At least sixty men and a Privileged.

Adamat needed manpower. He needed help. The Proprietor's help.

No doubt the Proprietor would have had him followed. The location of Adamat's safe house, and the errands he needed to run, were not things he wanted the Proprietor to know. Adamat climbed to his feet and called for a hackney cab.

He changed cabs three times and cut through half a dozen buildings before he felt confident no one was following him anymore.

It was well after dark when he arrived at the textile mill. The looms were still working despite the late hour. Adamat talked his way inside and climbed rickety wrought-iron stairs up to a room overlooking the mill's work floor. Inside he could see a woman leaning over a brass microscope. She was about forty, with hair dyed black to hide the gray roots. The walls of her office were lined with fabric samples of every kind—from cheap canvas to fine silks that cost a hundred krana for a yard.

He rapped on the door.

The woman waved him in without looking up from her microscope.

"Hello, Margy," Adamat said.

The woman finally looked up. "Adamat," she said in surprise. "What a pleasure."

"Good to see you." Adamat removed his hat.

"You as well."

Adamat took her hand a moment. Margy was one of Faye's oldest friends. Adamat considered telling her about the whole predicament before dismissing the thought. "I need some help," he said.

"Not a social visit, then?"

"Unfortunately."

Margy turned back to her microscope. "Don't you usually send Faye on these kinds of tasks? How is she, by the by? I haven't heard from her all summer."

Adamat cringed. "Not well. What with everything going on with the revolution and all that. It's played like the pit on her."

"Sorry to hear that." Margy suddenly spit on the floor, her face turning sour. "Damn that Tamas and his damned coup!"

"Margy?" Adamat couldn't keep the shock from his voice. Margy had always been outspoken, but he wouldn't have put her as a royalist by any means. She'd risen to be head foreman of the biggest textile mill in all of Adro by her own hand, not by any kind of appointment.

"He's gonna take us all to the pit," Margy said, wagging her finger at Adamat. "Just you wait. I hope you don't buy into all this nonsense about him trying to make a better world. It's just a power grab, that's all."

Adamat raised his hands. "I stay out of politics."

"We all have to choose sides one day, Adamat." She tucked a stray wisp of hair behind her ear and cleared her throat. Adamat could tell she was a little embarrassed by her outburst. "Now what did you need?"

Adamat removed the fibers from his pocket carefully, hoping he was giving her bits of the Proprietor's rug and not string from his borrowed jacket. "I need to find this rug," he said.

She took the fibers carefully. "This isn't pocket lint, is it? Faye brought me pocket lint more than once."

"I do hope not."

Margy put the fibers under her microscope and spent a moment adjusting knobs on the side. "Vanduvian wool," she said.

"High grade?"

"The finest. Whoever owns this rug is very, very rich."

"Any chance of tracing the rug?"

Margy stepped away from her microscope. "I'd say so. Only a few rug dealers sell Vanduvians. I'll ask around. Stop by in a couple weeks and maybe I'll have something for you."

"That long?" Adamat said.

"You need it sooner?"

"If at all possible. It's a rather urgent matter."

Margy sighed. "It'll cost you."

"I don't have much money on me."

"I don't want money," Margy said. "You tell Faye that she's taking me out for dinner at the Café Palms sometime before the leaves turn, and we'll call it square."

Adamat swallowed and forced a smile on his face. "I'll do that."

Margy turned back to her microscope. "Come by in a week and I'll know where the rug is from."

CHAPTER

12

As Taniel drew closer to the front, he realized that the Privileged sorcery he saw from afar was in fact coming from the Wings of Adom mercenaries.

The Wings of Adom held the western edge of the front, sandwiched between the rising mountains and the Adran army. They had four brigades on the front, their uniforms brilliant in red, gold, and white.

The Privileged sorcery from both sides was weak at best. Fire splashed against shields of hardened air, and lightning sprang from the sky to strike among the ranks, but the blasts of power seemed halfhearted. Even a mercenary army as prestigious as the Wings couldn't pay as well as a royal cabal, and it seemed the Kez were making use of the weakest and the youngest sorcerers. After the carnage at Kresim Kurga, who did they have left?

Taniel swung his kit over one shoulder and frowned at the west side of the Addown. The hillock on which he stood would make a good marksman's spot—high above and several hundred paces behind the fighting. But from what he could tell, the Kez had been pushing back the Adran army every day.

The front was about five miles north of Budwiel. The city smoked, flames visible over the poorest quarters of the city. Taniel wondered what the Kez had done with all those people. Many, certainly, had fled north when the city fell, but not all of them could have gotten out. Now they were slaves, or dead.

The Kez had a reputation for brutality toward the people they conquered.

Ka-poel sat down on the hillock and opened her satchel in her lap. She removed a stick of wax and began to shape it slowly with her fingers. Taniel wondered who she was making this time.

"Can you do sorcery without those?" Taniel lowered himself cross-legged beside her. "Without the dolls, I mean. And some bit of a person?"

She raised her chin and looked down her nose at him for a moment before returning to her work.

"And where the pit do you get the wax? I never see you buy anything. Do you even have any money?"

Ka-poel reached inside her shirt and withdrew a roll of banknotes. She shook it under Taniel's nose before putting it back.

"Where did you get that?"

She flicked him on the nose. Hard.

"Ow. Hey. Answer me, girl."

She raised her fingers, ready to flick again.

"OK, OK. Kresimir, I'm just asking a question." Taniel pulled his rifle into his lap and ran his fingers along the stock. No notches. A clean barrel. Brand-new, this was. Test-fired, according to the soldier who'd given it to him. *Never take a rifle you didn't fire yourself into battle.* It was Tamas who'd told him that. Tamas, who was most likely dead and buried in a mass grave along with the rest of the Seventh and Ninth.

Where did that leave the Adran army? Where did that leave Taniel? He wondered briefly if Tamas had left behind a will of some kind. Taniel had never thought about that before. Since he was a boy he'd always thought Tamas would live forever.

The fighting below consisted of nothing but an exchange of artillery. Some of the shells hit the soft ground, skipping through the Adran ranks, while others smacked into unseen sorcery and split apart, falling harmlessly to the ground.

The exchange seemed almost like a formality. Neither side was losing more than a few men, and none of the artillery pieces were being hit.

"Do you have any redstripes?" Taniel asked.

Ka-poel shook her head.

"Can you make me more?"

She scowled at him and pointed at the wax in her hand as if to say, *Can't you see I'm working on something?*

"I need my powder now," Taniel said.

Ka-poel stopped shaping the wax and looked at him for several moments, her green eyes unreadable. She nodded suddenly and pulled his powder horn from her pack.

Taniel's hands were shaking when he poured the first bit of powder into the paper to make a powder charge. The black grit between his fingers felt good. Almost too good. It felt like…power. He licked his lips and poured a line out on the back of his hand, lifting it to his face.

He stopped. Ka-poel was watching him.

One long snort, and it felt like his brain was on fire. Taniel rocked back, his body shuddering, shaking. He heard a whimper—pitiful and low. Did he make that noise? Taniel put his head in his hands and waited for what seemed like several minutes before the shaking finally stopped.

When he raised his head, the world glowed.

Taniel blinked. He hadn't opened his third eye. He wasn't looking into the Else. But everything seemed to glow regardless. No, he decided. Not glow. It was like the lines stood out sharper than they'd ever been. The world was clear in a way that a regular man could never understand. As if every moment out of a powder trance was spent under water and only now had he surfaced.

Was it like this when he took the powder to fight that Warden in Adopest? Had he just not noticed?

How had mala ever felt like a good alternative to this? How could any drug compare?

Taniel felt the grin on his face and didn't try to hide it. "Oh, pit. That's good." He finished loading a dozen powder charges before stowing them in his kit and hanging his powder horn from his shoulder. He got down on his chest and began to scan the enemy lines.

There were Privileged on the east side of the Addown. Most of them wore colorful uniforms and were surrounded by bannermen and bodyguards. A lot of Wardens, too. The Kez weren't scared of powder mages, not with Tamas gone. They'd relearn that fear in the coming days.

Primary targets.

There were officers. Practically anyone on a horse, it seemed. Where were all their cavalry? Strange that the Kez hadn't brought any of their cavalry north of Budwiel. Oh well. The officers would do.

Secondary targets.

There were artillerymen.

Tertiary targets.

Taniel felt the rumble in the ground before he heard the sound of hoofbeats. A few dozen yards to his left a group of some twenty Adran cavalry had gathered. Adran officers. A couple of generals. Taniel recognized a few of them.

General Ket was a handsome woman of about fifty—handsome, that is, if he didn't account for the ragged bit of skin where her right ear had been. Her broad face seemed somehow familiar, as if Taniel had seen her recently, when he knew for a fact it'd been years since their last meeting. She was the general of the Third Brigade.

Ket wasn't the only member of the group to have lost a bit of herself in battle. General Hilanska of the Second Brigade was morbidly obese and was missing his left arm at the shoulder.

None of them noticed Taniel.

They seemed agitated about something. Pointing and gesturing, all of them watching the battlefield through their looking glasses. Hilanska shouted for the artillery to be moved back.

Moved back? That was tantamount to conceding ground. Why would they...?

Taniel saw it now. Movement among the Kez lines. Whole companies coming up just behind their artillery. An assault. The Kez intended to push them back this day.

Taniel narrowed his eyes. There were huge men among those companies. Giant, twisted forms.

Taniel didn't know if these were regular Wardens, or the new kind made from powder mages, like the kind that had attacked him in Adopest.

Either way, this would go poorly for the Adran army.

Taniel noted that the Adran artillery was staggered every couple hundred feet. The artillery out front could be pulled back while those beside kept firing. This was planned. Perhaps this was what they'd been doing the last ten days. It made sense, if they knew they were going to lose the front line anyway.

Taniel didn't like it.

He left Ka-poel and headed down the hillock to join the officers, approaching General Hilanska.

"Sir, what's going on?"

The general gave Taniel a dismissive glance, then a second, longer stare. "We're pulling back, son."

"That's foolish, sir. We have the high ground. We can hold."

General Ket brought her horse around behind Taniel, looking

him up and down. He wondered if she remembered him. He must look different after four years.

"Are you questioning your betters, Captain?" General Ket asked.

"It's a stupid tactic, ma'am. It assumes loss."

"Captain, you'll earn yourself a demotion without an instant apology."

Another general, a blond man with a stiff bearing, added, "I'd imagine this is why he's still a captain."

General Hilanska held up his remaining arm. "Calm down, Ket. You don't recognize our boy here, do you? Taniel Two-Shot, hero of the Fatrastan War for Independence. I'm glad to see you among the living."

"General." Taniel dipped his head. Tamas had told him a tale or two when he was a boy about what kind of man Hilanska was—loyal, passionate. The best kind of companion to have with you on the line. He was fat and and old now, but Taniel imagined him to be the same kind of person.

"I don't care who he is," Ket said. "No one disregards rank in this army and gets away with it."

"Tamas—" Hilanska began.

"Tamas is dead," Ket said. "It's not his army anymore. If you'd—"

The argument was cut off by a messenger.

"Sirs, the enemy is advancing."

Ket spurred her mount down the embankment toward the front, shouting orders.

Hilanska's stallion pranced to one side as if in excitement. "Get my artillery out of there!" He looked down at Taniel. "I wouldn't go down there," he said. "They've got a new kind of Warden. Smaller. Smarter. Faster. Never seen anything like it. 'Black Wardens,' we've been calling them."

"They've been turning powder mages into Wardens," Taniel said. "They sent two to kill me in Adopest."

"Glad to see they failed. Powder-mage Wardens. How is that even possible?" Hilanska gave him a weighing gaze. "All right, Captain. Go down there and hold that line and I'll move my artillery back."

Taniel returned to Ka-poel at the top of the hillock. She was making progress on her doll.

"The Kez are attacking," Taniel said. "I'm going to fight." Why was he telling her? Was she going to stop him? Go with him?

She didn't answer him, so he grabbed his kit and headed down toward the front. Ka-poel would be safer back here out of the melee, he decided. But would he? Ever since Shouldercrown, he had wondered who was protecting who.

The Kez soldiers were already on their way, marching to the steady sound of the snare drums. Trumpets were sounding in the Adran camp, and more men rushed toward the front.

Taniel paused and scanned the approaching Kez. None of the Kez Privileged were advancing, but... there.

The Wardens in their black bowler caps and black jackets came through marching Kez infantry like dogs running out ahead of the pack. They practically flew across the empty field. Some carried small swords, others long pikes. They howled like animals, an eerie sound that lifted above the cannon fire and the snares and trumpets and made Taniel shudder.

Taniel dropped to one knee and sighted along his rifle. One breath. Two. Fire.

He willed the bullet on through the sky, burning the smallest bit of powder to keep it in the air. He focused on one of the Black Wardens. The bullet took only two or three seconds to bridge the space and...

He missed.

Taniel couldn't believe it. He was far behind the line, steady as a rock, with no distractions. How could he miss?

He reloaded his rifle. The Wardens were coming fast. Once they reached the Adran line they'd cause untold chaos. Taniel lined up another shot and squeezed the trigger.

The bullet tore through a Warden's eye, laying the creature out on the ground. None of the Warden's companions seemed to notice. One even snagged the small sword out of the still-twitching hand, barely slowing his charge.

There was no way Taniel was going to be able to stop any more. He had...what? Another two shots before the Wardens reached the earthworks that marked the Adran line?

Taniel drew the bayonet from his kit and unwrapped it, fitting the ring tightly around the end of his rifle. He stood, ready to charge, pausing only to scratch a mark in the butt of his rifle with an old nail he kept in his pocket. He thought suddenly of Ka-poel and wondered if he should have left her alone.

He joined the flood of Adran infantry heading to the front, elbowing and shoving his way through. They weren't moving fast enough.

A call went out to hold the line. Taniel wasn't going to be there in time for the initial shock. His legs pumped beneath him, covering ground three times faster than any of the others. He felt a snarl rise to his throat.

"Aim! Fire!" a nearby officer yelled.

A plume of smoke rose from the front of the Adran line. Many of the Wardens staggered. Some of them fell. Not nearly enough.

There was one section along the Adran earthworks that rose higher than the others. Taniel could see that several officers had taken the high ground. It was precisely where the Wardens would head. They'd leave the flat ground to the regular infantry and go straight for the strongest spots.

Even as the thought went through Taniel's head, he saw several of the Wardens change direction to run straight for the highest earthworks. One of the big brutes outstripped them all. He had several dark spots on his coat and his body twitched as more musket shots hit him, but nothing could take him down. He raised his sword and flew up the side of the earthworks, leaping over the top.

Taniel slammed into him in midair. The impact tore the air from his lungs, and they were both flung back over the earthworks, rolling down the side. He felt strong hands on his chest and was thrown off the Warden. He hit the ground and rolled to his feet to find the Warden already thrusting a small sword at his face.

Taniel parried with his bayonet and then thrust. The blade slid into the Warden almost up to the barrel, but seemed to have as much effect as the musket shots had.

The Warden threw itself backward, off of Taniel's bayonet and out of range of another stab.

Taniel whirled as another Warden came at him from the side. Taniel ducked and thrust, putting the tip of his bayonet into the tender spot below the creature's chin. He had to let go of his rifle and leap to one side to avoid the thrust of the first Warden's sword. Taniel drew his own short sword and waited for the attack.

The Warden paused to throw a whole powder charge into his mouth. He gnashed at the powder with blackened teeth and spit the paper on the ground.

Taniel had never been all that good with a short sword. He was fast and competent, but if this creature had any amount of training, he'd cut right through Taniel.

Taniel caught one thrust and pushed the Warden's sword to one side. The Warden bridged the gap with his other fist. Taniel was ready for it.

He caught the Warden's fist and slammed his forehead against the Warden's nose. He could feel the bone move back into the creature's brain. That alone should have killed it, but Taniel still felt struggle in the Warden's muscles. Taniel stepped back and slashed across the Warden's throat. It gurgled and collapsed, clinging to life, but it wouldn't be any more of a problem.

Taniel could feel the Warden's black, sticky blood all across his face.

"Oi!" Someone called from the earthworks above him. "They're coming!"

Taniel realized with a start that the rest of the Kez army was almost upon him. He snatched his rifle and scrambled up the earthworks, kicking dirt and swearing. The Warden had made it look easy. It most certainly wasn't.

Several hands helped pull Taniel to the relative safety of the earthworks, then thumped him on the back.

"Back to the line!" someone shouted.

Taniel shook his head, resting for a moment on the earthworks barricade. He clutched his rifle to his chest to keep his hands from shaking, and wondered if going over the earthworks like that had been a mistake.

Someone smacked him across the face. He half expected it to be Ka-poel, but when he lifted his eyes, he recognized Major Doravir. She looked furious.

"Do you have a death wish, Captain?" She grabbed him by the collar, shaking him like an errant schoolboy. "Well, do you? No one goes over that embankment without orders. No one!"

"Piss on your orders!"

Taniel shoved her away. He might have put his bayonet through her chest if he'd had any less control over himself.

She stared at him, a cold rage in her eyes. "I'll see you hanged, Captain."

"Try it."

"Load," came an officer's call. Taniel took a moment to orient himself. From the high earthworks he could see up and down the jagged line. Wardens were fighting behind the earthworks, clearing out whole groups of men, but the two he'd killed seemed to have tipped things in Adro's favor in the immediate vicinity. Soldiers bent to reload their rifles, readying for the Kez onslaught.

Taniel turned away from Doravir and stuffed a bullet down his rifle. Out of the corner of his eye he watched her storm away, yelling orders.

"Careful, Captain," a nearby soldier whispered. "If that one turns her eyes on you, she'll sleep with you or see you dead. Or both."

"She can go to the pit, for all I care."

"She's General Ket's sister," the soldier said. "She does what she wants. But she's a damned good officer. Don't let anyone tell you otherwise."

Ket's sister. That's why he thought he'd seen Ket more recently. The resemblance was strong, even if Doravir had a thinner build. "A damned good officer would let me do my job," Taniel said. He dropped a second bullet down his rifle and secured it with a scrap of cloth.

The soldier stared at him. "You feeling all right, Captain? You just loaded that twice, and without powder."

"Ask yourself," Taniel said with confidence he didn't feel, "what type of a man would leap the earthworks and go fight two Wardens by himself, then load his rifle without powder." He licked the powder off his fingers to keep the edge on his powder trance, and set the rifle against his shoulder. He sighted along the barrel. The Kez front line was still some two hundred yards distant. Well out of range of the muskets, while the Adran riflemen would open fire any moment.

Taniel found a pair of officers well back from the line and squeezed the trigger. He floated the two bullets simultaneously, pushing them toward their respective targets.

He caught one of the officers in the chest. The man clutched at the wound and slumped in his saddle, causing panic in his bodyguard. Taniel winced. The other bullet had missed the target. How could he be missing? Had the mala made him lose his edge?

"Kresimir be damned," the soldier beside him said. "You're

Taniel Two-Shot. Hey"—he tapped the man beside him on the shoulder—"This is Taniel Two-Shot."

"Yeah," the other soldier responded, "and I'm a general."

"He was just down in front of the barricade. Took on four Wardens all by himself."

"Nah."

"Saw it with my own eyes."

"Sure you did."

Taniel focused on the Kez lines. The *rat-tat-tatting* of their snares seemed to echo in his brain. He opened his third eye for a moment, watching as the earth was bathed in glowing pastels, splashes of sorcery covering every part of the battlefield.

"You ready to die with us, Two-Shot?" the second soldier asked, breaking Taniel's concentration. It wasn't phrased as a threat. Just a question.

"No, not particularly."

"We've been falling back every day. Sometimes twice. Every time the damned Kez advance like this. And each time, we lose three hundred men or more."

Taniel couldn't believe that. "Every time?"

The man nodded solemnly.

"Falling back..." Taniel craned his neck. The artillery had been wheeled away by now, back to the next row of trenches and earthen barricades. "Stupid bloody fools. We have to hold. We can't let them push us back like this. We're practically hemorrhaging troops."

"I don't know what an 'hemorg' is, but we're bleedin' men something fierce. We can't hold. We tried, but can't. Nothing stops those Black Wardens. No matter how many we kill, there seems to be more."

"You're awfully calm," Taniel said.

"Something peaceful about that, I think. Knowing you're going to die. That lad over on your other side—"

Taniel took a glance. The kid next to him didn't seem old

enough to shave. His hands shook so hard his musket was swaying from side to side.

"—that lad doesn't have the same opinion I do."

"It's just the jitters," Taniel said. "We all get them." Taniel glanced at the Kez. A hundred and fifty yards. He reloaded his rifle, lifted it to his shoulder, and fired.

"Not you," the first soldier said. "I heard you put a round in a Privileged's eye for your first kill."

"That I did. But I learned to shoot from Field Marshal Tamas himself." He paused. "They teach you to shoot at targets," he said to the young man beside him. "It's different when you realize there's a man on the other end, shooting back at you. I was sitting two miles away. I had surprise on my side. But, lad, you take a deep breath and pull that trigger. Fire straight and true, because you might not get another shot."

"Lad," Taniel had said. The boy was no more than five years his junior.

Taniel loaded his rifle while he spoke, set, and fired. Another officer dropped.

The boy looked at Taniel. His hands hadn't stopped shaking.

"I don't think your pep talk helped much," the first soldier said.

"Quiet down on the line!" That was Major Doravir. She had her sword raised above her head, a pistol in the other hand. "Aim!"

The Kez were almost in musket range. There were thousands of them. Rank upon rank upon rank. Taniel could see now why it was impossible to hold the line. He remembered the Battle of South Pike and how they'd almost lost the bastion a dozen times. They'd been guarding a pass from an enchanted bulwark only a hundred paces wide. Here, with nothing but earthworks between them and the Kez, it would be next to impossible to hold.

"Fire!"

The front line and much of the second of the Kez offensive fell beneath the volley. The Adran infantry began to reload.

Before a second volley could be fired, the Kez lines came to a stop. The new front line dropped to their knees and lined up their shots before firing.

Taniel threw himself behind the safety of the earthworks. He pulled the young soldier down with him and listened to the volley, and then the *thwap* of musket balls ricocheting off the dirt. The young soldier struggled to get back up. Taniel held him down.

"Line fire," Taniel said. "They'll fire that shot, then the next before they charge. You wait..."

The second volley sounded. Taniel counted to three before he let the boy back up and came up himself, ready to fire.

The Kez charged with a mighty roar, their bayonets leveled.

"Fire at will!" came the call.

Taniel took a deep breath of the smoke from the powder. It made his head buzz, his blood pump faster. His hands weren't shaking from mala withdrawal anymore. His body had found something so much better. He poured a bit of powder onto the back of his hand and snorted.

The Kez reached the bottom of the earthworks and began the steep climb. Taniel rose up high enough to fire down at them, when he spotted a Privileged about a hundred yards away with her hands twitching up sorcery. Taniel adjusted his aim and pulled the trigger.

The woman went down in a spray of blood, clutching at her throat.

Kez infantry poured over the earthworks like a flood breaching a levy. Taniel thrust his bayonet into a man's stomach, cracked another soldier across the face with the butt of his rifle. He leapt onto the rise to keep them from coming over, swinging and stabbing.

He barely heard the call for retreat.

"Hold!" he screamed, knocking a grenadier off the earthworks with his rifle stock. "We can hold!"

The young soldier who had been beside him went down with a bayonet through his chest. Taniel leapt off the bulwark to his aid, skewering the Kez infantryman like a side of beef.

The boy might die from a wound like that. It had gone straight between his ribs—likely through a lung. If so, he'd drown in his own blood.

But Taniel couldn't leave him there. The Adran soldiers were retreating.

"Hold! Hold, you bloody bastards!"

Taniel was almost alone on the earthworks. The boy lay at Taniel's feet. The first soldier he'd spoken to lay against the rear of the earthworks, dead eyes fixed blindly on the sky. Major Doravir was gone.

He reached out and felt the powder of the Kez infantry. A thought was all it took to light it. He used his mind to warp the blast away from him and away from the earthworks. The sound rang in his ears, sending him to his knees. Every ounce of powder within a dozen yards went up.

Powder smoke rose in the air, and charred corpses littered the earthworks. Groans and cries for mercy rose from the wounded. Men farther down the line had stopped their fighting to stare at Taniel. He took a step toward them, going to help hold the earthworks at the next spot, when he realized he couldn't see an infantryman in a blue jacket on his feet anywhere.

It was just a sea of sandy uniforms. The Kez had taken the earthworks.

The boy was still alive and coughing blood. Taniel slung his rifle over his shoulder and grasped the young soldier under the arms, pulling him backward toward the Adran camp.

It was a long haul, half carrying the boy over a hundred paces to the next set of earthworks. Most of the Kez ignored him. A few potshots skipped off the dirt nearby, but the Kez were too busy securing the new ground. They'd level the earthworks and move back to their own camp, where they'd push their artillery forward another hundred paces and prepare for tomorrow's charge.

Exhausted, his head still buzzing from the powder trance, Taniel reached the Adran army. "See to him," Taniel said when a surgeon came running. The surgeon balked and her eyes were wide.

"He's dead, sir."

"Just bloody see to him! Make him comfortable!"

"No, sir. He's not just dying. He's dead already."

Taniel dropped to his knee beside the young soldier and put his fingers on the lad's throat. No pulse. He used the same two fingers to close the young soldier's eyes.

"Damn it," he said.

The surgeon got on her knees next to him.

"I'm fine!" He pushed away her fingers.

"Your arm, sir."

Taniel looked down. His uniform had been torn through, leaving a bloody, jagged cut along his left arm. He'd not even felt it.

"Surgeon," a voice said, "tend to someone who's worth it." Major Doravir stalked toward them, her brown hair wild and her cheeks black with powder burns. Her jacket was gone, her white shirt stained with sweat and blood.

Taniel got to his feet. "Major Doravir," he said. "Didn't have the decency to die with your men, eh?"

Her backhand jerked his head to the side. He touched his cheek. That had been hard enough to rattle his teeth. "Do that again and I'll break your hand."

"I was the last one away from the front on the retreat," Major Doravir snarled.

"No," Taniel said. "I was. We could have held that bulwark. Instead we lost ground and who knows how many hundred men."

"I obey orders. You don't. No more warnings, Captain. I'll see you hanged." The major spun on her heel and marched off, shouting for the provosts.

Taniel rubbed at his chin and caught Ka-poel watching him from a distance. She headed toward the battlefield, where Kez soldiers were leveling the earthworks and civilians from both sides were already collecting the dead and wounded.

"Where the pit are you going?" Taniel shouted.

She pointed toward the battlefield and held up a doll. Damned girl. That wouldn't work like it did on Kresim Kurga. There were too many enemies here, and not enough dolls.

Taniel glanced toward Major Doravir. She was speaking to two soldiers with the insignia of Adran provosts on their shoulders. Military police. Doravir pointed to Taniel.

He decided it was a good time to make himself scarce.

CHAPTER

13

Tamas climbed out of his tent and finished buttoning up the front of his uniform. He adjusted the gold epaulets on his shoulders and he wondered if they'd have rain that day. The sky over the Adran Mountains to the east had just barely taken on a light halo, while the rest of the world slept on in darkness.

Tamas gazed at that slight brightening and wondered how things went on the other side of the mountains. Budwiel had fallen. The Kez were no doubt pushing their way up Surkov's Alley. Tamas hoped that his generals could handle the defense. He grimaced to himself. With Budwiel gone, the fight could only go in Kez's favor. His men needed him. His country needed him. His son needed him. He had to get across these damned mountains.

He could hear rustling in the camp, and the low whistles of sergeants as they kicked their men from their beds. The smell of smoke came from cookfires that no doubt had little over them.

Olem sat beside Tamas's tent. His forage cap was pulled over his eyes, his legs propped on a log in front of him, and his hands thrust deep in his pockets. The pose was an affected one. Olem's Knack eliminated the need for sleep.

"Quiet night?" Tamas asked, squatting beside the small, smoldering fire and rubbing his hands together. The heat of the summer didn't touch the early morning, not in foothills like this. He poked the coals with a twig, then tossed in the twig. No more than ash. There wasn't much to burn on the high steppe.

"Little bit of rustling, sir. Some grumbling, too." Olem sniffed as if the grumbling were no more than an annoyance.

His men were hungry. Tamas knew it, and it pained him.

"I put a stop to it, sir," Olem said.

"Good."

Tamas heard soft footfalls on the dirt. Olem shifted, and his hand emerged just a little from his coat. He had a pistol.

A carcass thumped to the ground beside Tamas. He started.

"Elk, sir," Vlora said as she squatted down next to him.

Tamas felt a little spell of relief. Meat.

"Any more?" he asked, his voice a little too hopeful.

"Andriya bagged one, too. He's portioning it out to the powder mages. This one's for the officers."

Tamas chewed on the inside of his lip. "Olem. Have it butchered and distributed to the men. A small, raw piece for each. Let them cook it themselves. We break camp in two hours."

Olem climbed to his feet and stretched. He returned his pistol to his belt and headed off, calling a few names.

"We'll reach Hune Dora tomorrow by midday, sir," Vlora said. Her shoulders were stained with blood from the elk. She had to have been burning a powder trance, otherwise there was no way a girl of her size could have carried an entire elk over her shoulders.

"How far?"

"About sixteen miles. Went up that way while hunting."

"And?"

"A small town, just like Gavril said."

"Walled?"

"The wall is an old ruin. Eight feet high, maybe. I wouldn't worry about it, though, sir. The city looks abandoned."

Abandoned? Tamas had hoped there would be some population, just so he could loot their stores of powder and food.

"Anything else up that direction?

"The terrain turns steep. The road seems to follow the contours of the mountain ridges. Lots of bridges, from what I could see. Once we're in the forest, the dragoons will have a hard time encircling us."

"As I'd hoped."

"The bad news is, the road narrows considerably. We'll be able to march maybe just three or four men abreast."

That would require Tamas's column to extend to almost four miles long. Not conducive to an army being dogged by dragoons. Tamas swore under his breath.

He watched the sky for a moment. There wouldn't be rain today, he decided.

"I lied, before," Tamas said.

Vlora frowned at the embers of the fire. "Sir?"

"Back in Budwiel you asked me if there was any news about Taniel. I lied."

Vlora opened her mouth, but Tamas went on before she could say anything.

"A few days before we went through the caves, I received a message from Adopest. Taniel's savage was awake."

"And Taniel?"

"Nothing. But if one of them can come out of it, presumably the other. And I wouldn't think that little savage girl is stronger than my boy. He'll..." He heard his voice crack. "He'll make it."

He examined Vlora out of the corner of his eye. He thought he saw a tear on her face.

"How is your leg, sir?" she asked.

Tamas looked down at his leg. Mihali had healed it. He could walk. He could ride. Pit, he could dance if he wanted to. But deep inside the calf, it still hurt. The pain throbbed, right where they'd taken that blasted star of gold out of his flesh. Despite the healing powers of a god, there was still something wrong with it.

"It's fine," he said. "Good as new."

"You still walk with a limp," Vlora said.

"Do I? Just habit."

Vlora leaned back on her haunches. "I've heard that healed tissue has a problem readjusting itself. It needs help. Plenty of exercise and massage. If you'd like..."

"I don't think I need the gossip that would come out of you rubbing my leg," Tamas said. He chuckled, and was relieved when Vlora laughed as well.

"I was going to say have Olem do it, sir."

"I'm sure I'll be fine." Tamas watched Vlora a little longer. She glanced up at him, then back at the fire. She still wouldn't meet his eyes.

He found he missed their old familiarity. If things had gone better, she might be his daughter-in-law by now. Back before she went off to the university, she'd been the one soldier with the gall to call him Tamas. She'd hung on his arm, even hugged him in public.

Before she slept with that fop in Jileman and Taniel broke off their engagement.

Tamas climbed to his feet. "I want you and Andriya to keep on hunting. We need as much meat as we can get."

"We're going to run out of powder eventually, sir," she said.

"Get some from the Seventh's quartermaster."

"I meant the whole army."

Tamas drummed his fingers on his belt. An army on the march, without resupply or even wagons and camp followers. They would run out of everything. Sooner, rather than later. Their only advantage was a swift march, and that was lost with having to forage and the exhaustion brought on by hunger.

"I'll be sure the mages get what they need." His powder mages were still each worth more than a dozen men.

Vlora nodded. "I'll check with the quartermaster." She stood and abruptly headed off into the camp.

Tamas watched her go, and felt himself an old man, burdened with regret.

The camp grew louder over the next few minutes as the last of the soldiers were roused from their beds. A few cheers went up, and Tamas guessed Olem must have distributed the elk meat. It wasn't much, not when spread so thinly, but it was a bite more than they'd had.

Tamas broke down and stowed his own tent. He'd just finished tying his bedroll when Olem returned with a bundle of bloody canvas.

"I would have done that, sir," Olem said.

Tamas eyed the bloody canvas and felt his mouth watering. "I have you doing more important things. I was a soldier once, Olem. I can break camp as well as any man."

"If you insist, sir." Olem knelt beside the coals and produced a skewer, then unwrapped the bloody canvas to reveal a hunk of elk meat.

Tamas stood and looked to the south. Somewhere out there, the Kez cavalry were breaking their camp, probably hoping to overtake the Adran brigades before they were able to reach the relative safety of the forest.

Tamas heard, more than saw, a horse galloping through the camp. A few moments later and Gavril emerged from the still-dark morning on a shuddering charger.

Tamas grabbed the horse by the bridle as his brother-in-law swung down. The horse's sides were lathered, its eyes wild. Gavril had been riding hard.

"Sixteen thousand," Gavril said. "Ten and a half thousand dragoons and another five and a half of cuirassiers. Three full brigades of cavalry."

Kresimir. How could they possibly fight that many cavalry? "How far?"

"We can beat them to the forest if we leave now. I've not spoken with my northern outriders."

"Vlora just came from the north. We're sixteen miles from Hune Dora."

Gavril accepted an offered canteen from Olem and took a swig, then poured the rest over his head. His body steamed. "We won't have time to sack the city."

"She says it's abandoned. I'll have some men take a look, but we'll probably head right past it."

"Abandoned, eh?" Gavril scratched his bearded chin. "We could make a stand there."

Tamas cast an anxious glance to the south. He couldn't see the Kez cavalry, but it seemed to him he could *sense* them. "Maybe."

Olem stood and held out a pewter plate. On it was a steaming cut of elk.

"Burned on the edges and raw in the middle, but it's delicious," Olem said with a grin.

Tamas heard his stomach growl. There must have been two pounds of meat on that plate.

"Share it with Gavril," Tamas said. "I'm not hungry."

Olem cocked an eyebrow. "I can hear your stomach making bear calls from here, sir. You have to keep up your strength."

"Really, I'm fine."

Gavril grabbed the meat with his bare hands. "Suit yourself." He tore it in half and plopped one half back on the plate. He began to cram the rest into his mouth. Around bites, he yelled out to another rider who'd just come into camp.

"Sir," Olem said as Gavril strode off, "you need to eat."

"Get the men on their feet," Tamas said. A sudden urgency rose within him as a gust of wind nearly tore off his hat. "Have the advance column marching out of the camp in twenty minutes." He stared south until Olem was gone.

Sixteen thousand Kez cavalry. His two brigades of infantry would be ridden down. They'd die hungry, exhausted, and in a foreign land while the Kez burned their homes.

He couldn't let that happen.

He *wouldn't* let that happen.

Tamas strode toward the nearest tents. "Companies," he shouted. "Prepare for march!"

Sergeant Oldrich and his squad of Riflejacks were staying at a retired barracks on the southeast side of the Ad River, not far from the Lighthouse of Gostaun. The barracks was a big building, abandoned and empty but for the odd feral dog. The front doors were barred and chained, but one of the many side entries had been left unlocked.

Adamat entered the barracks through that door and crossed two empty parade grounds before he found the small mess hall where the captain and his squad were watching Adamat's four youngest children put on a play in the center of the mess.

Adamat stood in the door quietly, unable to keep the smile from his face as Astrit absently played with her black curls while she tried to remember the lines of the princess trapped in a tall tower by the evil Privileged who, judging by the costumes composed of robes and bedsheets, was being played by one of the twins.

"Daddy!" Astrit cried, catching sight of him.

He was mobbed by all the children crowding around him with hugs and kisses. He made sure to give each one a kiss, saying each of their names—except for the twins. He could never tell them apart, and he wasn't about to admit it.

Adamat wrestled on the floor with his children for several minutes before he was able to extract himself. He bid them return to their play, and joined Sergeant Oldrich at the table in the corner of the room.

"Coffee?" the sergeant offered, chewing absently at the tobacco tucked in his cheek.

"Tea, if you have it."

Oldrich called over to one of his men. "Tea!" He fixed Adamat with a frown. "You look awful. You got rolled, didn't you?"

"Yeah." Adamat found himself watching his children. They were beautiful kids. They really were. The thought of anything happening to them made his blood begin to boil and he forced himself to look away. "Got out of it fine, and I've found Vetas's headquarters."

"I didn't think you could." Oldrich lifted his coffee cup in a salute. "I figured the bastard would be in the wind after what you did to his boys in Offendale."

Adamat sniffed. "He's not afraid of me," Adamat said. "I don't think he's afraid of anything. You ever seen a machine powered by steam? They've got looms, hammers, printing presses..." Adamat was briefly reminded of his own failed foray into publishing but managed to push the thought away.

"Yeah," Oldrich said. "They have them in ships now, too."

"Exactly. He's like a steam engine. Just keeps going. No feeling, no thought. Just a task to do and he's going to do it."

Oldrich sipped his coffee. "Damn. Almost makes you feel bad for him."

"No," Adamat said. "I'll still rip his heart out when I find him."

"And I hope you get your chance. Shall we go get him?"

"How many men do you have again?" Adamat asked, though he knew well enough.

"Fifteen," Oldrich said. "Two to guard the children..."

"Five."

"Five to guard the children, that leaves us with twelve, counting you and me."

"Not enough."

"He's got enough goons to take on a squad of the field marshal's best?"

"He's got at least sixty enforcers and a Privileged."

Oldrich whistled. "Ah. I don't think there's anything we can do about that."

"Pit. Thank you," Adamat said as a cup of tea was set in front of him. He added two lumps of sugar and stirred it to cool. "Have you seen the morning paper?"

"No. You want one? Oi! Someone get the investigator a paper!"

Adamat cringed inwardly. He was hoping to find out that Oldrich *hadn't* seen a paper today. Not draw attention to one. Oh well. "Do you remember a Privileged by the name of Borbador?" Adamat changed the subject.

"I do," Oldrich said. His normally pleasant face was suddenly guarded.

"I think he'd do it for us. Borbador was one of the cabal's best and brightest. He held Shouldercrown against the Kez Cabal virtually by himself. I know Tamas left him alive and has him stashed in the city. If we could—"

"No," Oldrich said.

"'No' what?"

"Privileged Borbador has a gaes to compel him to kill the field marshal."

"I know. I'm the one who told Tamas about the gaes."

"Then why would you ask me that? Releasing him would endanger Tamas and I won't do it."

Adamat held his head in his hands. He felt like he was doing that a lot lately. "It's our only chance against a Privileged under Lord Vetas."

"You could ask Taniel Two-Shot," Oldrich said. "He kills Privileges as a hobby, and rumor has it he's in the city."

"Newspaper said this morning he left for the front." Adamat realized his mistake as the words left his mouth.

"So you have seen a paper?" Oldrich nudged a spittoon from beneath the table with one toe, leaning over to spit into it. "Was there something in it you wanted me to see?"

"Sir," one of Oldrich's men called from the doorway. He was a young man, probably not much older than Adamat's son Josep. "Sir, you should see this." He rushed over to Oldrich and dropped a paper into his lap.

Oldrich lifted the paper. The headline read, "Budwiel Sacked, Field Marshal Tamas Dead." Oldrich was silent for several minutes as he read the article. The young soldier stayed by his side the whole time. When Oldrich finished, he handed the newspaper back to the soldier.

"You weren't going to tell me?"

Adamat felt like a child who'd been caught robbing the pantry. "I was," Adamat said. "After I figured out how to convince you to stay and help me." Adamat swallowed hard. He was about to lose the last bit of help he had to get Faye back. Once Oldrich was gone, it would be just Adamat with eight children to look after, and a wife and son still in his enemy's hands.

"There's no convincing," Oldrich said. "I was given an order. Tamas is my commanding officer and an old friend. He told me to see this thing through to the end regardless of whether he lived through the war."

"And you will?"

"Yes."

Adamat couldn't help but breathe a sigh of relief. He dabbed at his forehead with a handkerchief, realizing that he'd been sweating. "Thank you." He paused. "You seem to be taking this awfully well."

"The headline is sensational," Oldrich said, pointing to the paper. "It's actually 'presumed dead.' Tamas went behind enemy lines with the Seventh and Ninth and hasn't been seen since. Those are the two hard-as-nails brigades in the Adran army. Until I see a body, I'm going to believe that Tamas is in Kez, chewing up their army and spitting them out like toothpicks."

"So I won't be able to convince you to release Privileged Borbador with Tamas dead?"

"Sorry. You'll have to think of something else. And do it quick, because I can only help you take down Vetas until there's an army knocking on Adopest's front door."

Adamat stood. "I'll think of something."

"Also," Oldrich said, "with Tamas presumed dead, that means the clerks will tighten the noose on the checkbook he gave you. We'll need money for bribes or supplies sooner rather than later. If you've got some money stashed away..."

"I'll see what I can do," Adamat said. He reluctantly said goodbye to his children and headed for the door, only to have Oldrich join him in the hallway. "Sergeant?"

"I wanted to tell you something," Oldrich said in a hushed voice. He glanced into the mess. "If only to make you feel a little reassured. I don't want you to worry about your children. The boys have taken a real shine to them. Anyone finds us, comes in here looking for those kids, my boys'll scramble 'em good, and they won't be kind about it."

Adamat fought back the sudden tears in the corners of his eyes. "Thank you," he managed. "It does... it does mean a lot. Thank you."

Adamat got to his safe house by about one in the morning. He wearily climbed the stairs to the apartment above the landlady's, listening to the creak of his boots on the old wooden steps. Had it really been five days since he'd been here? He'd slept on a park bench, a hospice bunk, and a chair in a bar over the days since his meeting with the Proprietor as he planned his next move on Lord Vetas.

He needed a bath.

SouSmith sat next to a low-burning lamp on the sofa. The boxer looked up from a game of cards laid out in front of him, his brow furrowed.

"Bloody worried," SouSmith said.

Adamat closed the door with a sigh. He was hoping he'd have a good night's sleep before having to face SouSmith. He felt like the pit. His body hurt, he'd had little sleep in ten days, and he needed a good meal. He'd felt like this only once or twice before in his life, back when Manhouch succeeded his father and the commoners were restless and all police officers were working eighteen-hour days.

He never thought he'd feel like that again. He thought he'd left it all behind.

"Sorry," Adamat said.

SouSmith looked back at his game. He moved one card on top of another and pulled two off the table, setting them beside him on the sofa.

"Look like pit," SouSmith said.

"Feel like it, too."

"Where you been?" His beady eyes searched Adamat's face.

"The Proprietor reeled me in." Adamat limped over to a chair by the sofa and collapsed into it. "His boys worked me over all night before I got to see him. Turns out the whole thing was a big bloody mistake. Tossed me back out on the cobbles with 'sorry.'"

"You saw the Proprietor?"

Was that worry in SouSmith's voice?

"I came as close as one gets. Sat in the same room with him behind a black screen. Spoke to him through some knitting woman, like he's mute or something." Adamat frowned. Maybe the Proprietor *was* mute. Maybe the woman wasn't just a security measure but an interpreter. "Do we have any food?"

SouSmith jerked his thumb to a platter next to the sofa. Underneath the cover was a sandwich. The meat and cheese were warm, but it seemed like the best thing Adamat had ever tasted as he collected it and sank back into his chair.

Adamat felt a little strength return as he finished the meal. "He wants the same thing I want, it seems," Adamat said between the final few bites. "Lord Vetas has been causing him trouble. The Proprietor's boys only pulled me in because we were following the same woman." Adamat licked his fingers clean. "But now that the Proprietor knows we're after the same thing, it seems he's content to just step back and let me go at Vetas. Which is a bloody shame, because I need his help!" Adamat heard his own voice rise as he finished the sentence, and he grabbed the platter the sandwich was on and hurled it across the room. It clattered into one corner.

SouSmith leaned back on the sofa, his game forgotten, watching Adamat.

"I've never wanted to kill a man so badly as I do Lord Vetas," Adamat whispered. "I know where he is. I found his headquarters. I have a chance, and with the Proprietor's help I could do it, and he just pushed me back on the street." He took a shaky breath. "I'm going to do something very foolish, SouSmith, and I think you should walk away from me. Consider this the end of your employment."

SouSmith's eyebrows rose. "I'll decide that."

"I'm going to blackmail the Proprietor."

SouSmith began collecting his cards in one hand. A moment later he was done and he stood up. "For once," he said, "I agree with ya."

Adamat closed his eyes. He didn't blame SouSmith. Not one bit. But he'd been hoping against hope that SouSmith would once again refuse to leave. That he'd stay by Adamat's side and see this thing through.

SouSmith fetched his jacket from the rack by the door. "Sorry, friend," he said, "I'll die for ya, but the Proprietor won't stop with me."

Of course. SouSmith had his brother's family to worry about.

They shook hands, and Adamat heard SouSmith's heavy step down the stairs and out the front door.

Adamat fell back into his chair with his head in his hands.

SouSmith was big and powerful and he was worth five men in a fight, but he was also a friend. Adamat couldn't afford to have friends. Not with what he was about to do.

Adamat dragged himself to his feet just long enough to go find his bed. He didn't bother removing his clothes before he dropped into it.

CHAPTER
14

Taniel rubbed at his eyes and tried to remember what it felt like to sleep.

Five times in three days he'd fought in a bloody melee on the front lines. Five times he'd been the last one to leave the earthen defenses when the Kez proved too strong. Five times he'd been forced to make the long trek across the corpse-strewn fields dragging the wounded and dying, furious that they'd once again let the front fall beneath a Kez onslaught.

How many times could they retreat before the army was nothing but dead and wounded?

Taniel paused to look to the south. Budwiel was getting farther away every day. The front—or what had been the front until half an hour ago—was about a quarter mile away and obscured in powder smoke. The Kez soldiers were already leveling the earthworks and carting away their dead.

This last offensive had been a bad one. The infantry from the Seventeenth Brigade was mostly green and they'd broken and run before the retreat was even sounded. Taniel wondered if there was a single man unharmed after that mess. The groaning of the wounded in the surgeons' tents made his skin crawl.

He found Ka-poel sitting by the fire next to their tent. She stared at the coals, absently cleaning beneath her fingernails with the tip of one of her long needles. A pot of water boiled over the flames. She looked Taniel over once, then stared back at the fire.

Taniel dropped to the ground next to her. His whole body hurt. He was covered in countless cuts and bruises. A particularly nasty Warden had almost done him in, and he had a clean slice across the side of his stomach to show for it.

Ka-poel stood silently and moved around behind him, where she began to pull him out of the jacket. He didn't like when she undressed him—well, he *liked* it, but he'd heard officers muttering about the impropriety of their relationship already—but tonight he was far too tired to argue. She unbuttoned his shirt and cleaned his neck and torso with a hot, wet washcloth.

He lay on his side while she stitched the wound on his stomach, wincing every time the needle went in.

"Pole," he said while he lay there, "do you remember something being mentioned about Tamas putting together a school for powder mages in Adopest?"

She drummed two fingers on his arm. *Yes.*

"I think Sabon was in charge of it. I wonder if he's still up there. Pit, I could use his help." Taniel paused to think. Sabon's face floated in front of him, perfect teeth standing out against his black skin. Sabon was the only one Tamas ever listened to. He'd taught Taniel to shoot. A good soldier; a good man. "Damn it, I should have asked Ricard. Even if Sabon is with Tamas, there had to be a couple other powder mages left in Adopest. We need them on the front."

Ka-poel finished the stitching and Taniel climbed to his feet.

His shirt was nearly black, stiff with dried blood. He smelled like a slaughterhouse. He left it on the ground. Ka-poel would find some-one to wash it for him. He fetched his one spare shirt from the tent and buttoned it up.

His tent was on the side of one of the mountain ridges that frames Surkov's Alley. It meant he had to sleep at an incline, but he also had a vantage over most of the valley, and right now he watched the Wings of Adom camp. The Wings' camp sat closer to the front than the Adran, and they held the east side of the valley with their flank against the river.

Reports were that the Wings were holding their front every day, but were forced to withdraw when the Adrans retreated so that the Kez couldn't flank them.

Tamas would have been furious had he been here to see it, that the mercenaries were putting forth a better defensive than the Adran army.

A pair of Wings brigadiers were making their way from their own camp toward the big, white-and-blue command tent at the rear of the Adran army. A few other officers seemed to be heading in the same direction. A meeting, it seemed. If Tamas were here, Taniel would be at that meeting.

A great many things were different with Tamas gone.

Not far from the command tent was the mess tent. In most armies the cooking was done by soldiers for their company, or sometimes even their squad. Here at the front, all the cooking was being done by one chef, or so the rumor went.

Mihali.

It wasn't hard to pick out the tall, fat figure making his way between the cookfires, checking on his small regiment of female assistants. Taniel frowned. Who was this man who claimed he was a god? Taniel had seen a god's face—Kresimir's—and put a bullet through his eye. Kresimir had looked like a god. Mihali did not.

Taniel took his jacket and headed down the mountainside toward the command tent.

Soldiers seemed to watch him everywhere he went. Some tipped their hats. Some saluted. Some just stared as he walked by, but Taniel didn't welcome the attention. Was he some kind of curiosity for them to gawk at? For years he'd always felt at home in the army, but now, with Tamas and the powder mages gone, Taniel felt alone, a foreigner.

He wondered what he looked like to them. He smelled like the alley behind a butcher, and he probably looked like one too. His body was covered in nicks and cuts, his black hair singed from a powder blast yesterday, his face dirty and bruised.

And he wondered what he was. He'd managed to escape serious injury in five hard, bloody fights. He'd been grazed by bullets seven times in the last two days. He'd been inches from being run through on half a dozen occasions. Was he just that fast? Or something else?

That kind of luck didn't happen. It was uncanny. Had it been like this in Fatrasta? No, he'd never been in an ongoing fight this bloody. He remembered ripping a rib from the Warden in Adopest and wondered if this luck was somehow connected to his newfound strength.

He reached the command tent, ignoring the guard who asked him to stop.

The tent was filled. There were perhaps twenty officers inside—what seemed like all the Wings brigadiers and Adran generals and colonels. Voices were raised, fists being shaken. Taniel slipped along the edge of the tent, trying to make some kind of sense of the argument.

He caught sight of a familiar face and moved up through the crowd.

Colonel Etan was ten years older than Taniel. He was a tall man with wide shoulders and brown hair cut short over a flat, ugly face. Not that anyone would tell him that he was ugly. The grenadiers of the Twelfth Brigade were the biggest, strongest men in the Adran army and one word against their colonel would find you at odds with all two thousand of them.

"What's going on?" Taniel whispered.

Colonel Etan gave him a quick glance. "Something about..." He paused to look again. "Taniel? Pit, Taniel, I heard you'd joined us at the front, but I didn't believe it. Where have you been?"

"Later," Taniel said. "What's the argument about?"

Etan's welcoming grin faded. "A messenger from the Kez. Demands that we surrender."

"So?" Taniel snorted. "There's nothing to argue about. No surrender."

"I agree, but some of the higher-ups don't. Something has them scared."

"Of course they're scared. They've been retreating from every fight! If they'd hold the line just once, we could break these Kez bastards."

"It's not that," Etan said. "The Kez are claiming they have Kresimir on their side. Not just in spirit, either, but that he's there in their camp!"

Taniel felt his whole body go cold. "Oh, pit."

"Are you all right? You don't look well."

"Kresimir can't be there. I killed him myself."

Etan's attention was now fully on Taniel. "You... killed him? I heard some wild rumors of a fight on South Pike before it collapsed, but you..."

"Yes," Taniel said. "I put a bullet in his eye and his heart. Watched him go down in a spray of godly blood."

"General Ket!" Etan shouted. "General Ket!" He grabbed Taniel's arm and shoved his way through the assembled officers. They all scrambled to get clear of him—no one stood their ground before a grenadier of his size.

"No, Etan..."

Etan pulled him out into the opening in the middle of the room, where the unfriendly faces of two dozen officers waited in tense expectation. "Tell them what you told me," Etan said to Taniel.

Taniel was once again terribly conscious of his frayed, bloody clothes and dirty face. The room seemed to spin slightly, the air hot and close.

He cleared his throat. "Kresimir is dead," Taniel said. "I killed him myself."

The clamor of voices made his head hurt worse than the sound of a musket volley. He looked around, trying to find an ally. He saw General Ket in the group, but she was no friend of his. Where was General Hilanska?

"Let him speak!" a woman shouted. Brigadier Abrax, of the Wings mercenaries. She was ten years younger than Taniel's father with a face twice as severe and short hair cropped above her ears. Her uniform was white, with red-and-gold trim.

General Ket took the sudden silence to sneer at Taniel. "You can't kill a god."

"I did," Taniel said. "I watched him die. I fired two ensorcelled bullets. I saw them hit. Saw him crumple. I was on that mountain when it began to collapse."

"Oh?" Ket demanded. "Then how'd you get down?"

Taniel opened his mouth, only to shut it again. How did he get down? The last thing he remembered was cradling Ka-poel's unconscious body as the building they were in began to buckle and fall.

"That's what I thought," Ket said. "The powder has gone to your head."

"He's a hero, sir!" Colonel Etan said.

"Even heroes can go mad! Provosts! Get him out of here! This meeting is no place for a captain."

Taniel was shoved to the side by someone, and he heard another voice say, "Kresimir isn't here! What kind of poppycock is that?"

"I've seen him."

Everything went still. Taniel recognized that voice. General Hilanska.

Hilanska was still seated while everyone else stood. He wore his dress uniform, decked out in dozens of medals, the collar freshly starched, his empty left sleeve pinned to his chest. The general looked tired, his immense weight sagging over the edge of the chair, his face pulled down from weariness.

Hilanska went on, his voice deep and level. "You've all seen him! At the parley this morning. He was there, you bloody fools, and you ignored him. The man at the back, who didn't speak. He wore a gold mask with only one eyehole. If any of you had bothered to listen, the Wings Privileged said he reeked of sorcery, more powerful than any they'd ever witnessed."

"That was only a Privileged," Ket said. "Not a god."

Hilanska struggled to his feet. "Call me mad, Ket. I dare you. Tamas believed Kresimir had returned. He believed Two-Shot here had shot him. But the bullets weren't fatal. Kresimir is, after all, a god."

Ket regarded Hilanska warily. "And yet Tamas still led the Seventh and Ninth behind the Kez lines to their deaths."

"He's not dead," Taniel said, feeling his blood rise.

Ket turned on him. "Says our dead field marshal's whelp."

"Whelp?" Taniel's vision went blurry. "I've killed hundreds of men. I've nearly held that damned line out there by myself the last two days. I feel like I'm the only one who wants to win this war, and you call me a whelp?"

Ket spat at his feet. "You'll take all the credit yourself? What an ego! Just because you sprang from Tamas's loins doesn't mean you have his skill, boy."

Taniel could barely think. He'd been on the front line every day fighting for this? Rage took control of him. "I'll kill you, you stupid bitch!"

Taniel felt his muscles tense to leap at General Ket, when something struck him in the side of the head. He staggered and tried to run at Ket. Hands grabbed him, arms pulled him away. He was hit again in the head. Thrashing and yelling, he was forced out of the command tent.

"Taniel," he heard Colonel Etan say in his ear, "calm down, Taniel, please!"

It took the sight of a half-dozen sharpened pikes leveled at his face to bring Taniel back from the brink of rage. The provosts—Adran military police—behind those pikes wore expressions that said they'd poke him full of holes in an instant.

"That's enough of that," Etan said, pushing away a pike. He was able to get the provosts to back off a few steps.

Now that the rage had passed, Taniel felt cold, weak. His whole body began to shake. Had he really just called Ket a bitch in front of the entire General Staff? What had come over him?

"Are you trying to get yourself killed?" Etan demanded. "I've heard rumors that there was a powder mage out on the front each of the last few days, throwing himself into the teeth of the enemy like he wanted to die. I'd never imagined it was you. You'll be lucky to get off with a flogging for this. Attacking General Ket! I can't believe it."

Taniel pulled his knees to his chest and tried to get his body to stop shaking. "Are you done?" Why was he shaking so much? It scared him worse than looking down the wrong end of a Warden's sword. Was it the mala withdrawal? His powder?

"Taniel..." Etan stared at him, and Taniel could tell there was genuine concern in his eyes. "Taniel, you dragged me five feet before I managed to clock you in the side of the head. I've dropped men twice your size with that punch, and I had to do it three times to even faze you. Pit, *I'm* twice your size! I know that powder mages are strong, but..."

"I'll take full responsibility," Taniel said. "Hopefully you'll not be reprimanded."

"I'm not worried about me."

"Captain?"

They both looked up. General Hilanska stood over them. The provosts were gone.

"Colonel, I'd like a word with the captain in private, please."

Etan left them, and Taniel slowly climbed to his feet, unsure as to whether he'd be able to stand but certain that General Hilanska might be his only ally left in this camp. "Sir?" He swayed to the side and stumbled. Hilanska caught him with his one good arm.

"Ket wants your head," Hilanska said.

"I'd imagine."

"You know," the old general said, "with Tamas gone, powder mages don't have any pull anymore. Some of the ranking officers seem to want to pretend you never existed."

Taniel leaned his head back and looked up at the darkening sky. Some stars were beginning to show, and the moon glowed bright on the eastern horizon. "Do you believe he's dead?"

Hilanska began to walk, forcing Taniel to follow him on wobbly legs. Taniel's hands were shaking a little less, now.

"I don't want to believe it," Hilanska said. "None of us do, despite how the others are acting. We all loved your father. He was a brilliant strategist. But all contact was lost. We haven't heard from any of our spies in the Kez army for three weeks now. We have to face the facts. Tamas is likely dead."

If Tamas was dead, so were Vlora and Sabon and the rest of the powder cabal and the Seventh and Ninth. Taniel felt his chest tighten. No tears. There wouldn't be any of those. Not for Tamas. But for him to be gone forever... "And Kresimir?"

"Whatever you did to him, he survived it."

"What of this Mihali? This god-chef?"

Hilanska shrugged. "Your father seemed to think he was Adom reborn."

"And you?"

"I don't have any evidence either way. His cooking is amazing. Supposedly, he and Kresimir have some kind of a truce. Something about letting the mortals fight it out." Hilanska spit out of the corner of his mouth. "I don't like the idea that we're being used in some kind of cosmic battle."

"No," Taniel said. "Neither do I." His head was starting to clear. Things weren't spinning anymore. "What can Ket do to me?"

"She's a general. You're a captain. A roomful of people just watched you try to kill her."

"I wouldn't have killed her. And I'm not just a captain. I'm a powder mage."

Hilanska said, "I know. Tamas kept you outside the rank system. If he was still here, you would have gotten away with it. Ket is a good general, but she has a narrow vision of things. Tamas knew that. You're just a captain now, though."

"Who has been ordering the retreats along the front?"

Hilanska stopped and turned toward Taniel. "I have."

"You?" Taniel had to keep himself from stepping back.

Hilanska set his hand on Taniel's shoulder, as a father might to his son. "We can't hold them," Hilanska said. "Up until you arrived, we had no answer to those Black Wardens. They just cut right through the infantry like nothing I've ever seen. They're faster and stronger than regular Wardens, and powder won't ignite near them. Even with you here, we can't hold the line."

"What about sorcery? The Wings have Privileged."

"Sorcery doesn't do a thing to the new Wardens. It's baffling, really. I can't imagine that the Kez Cabal would create something they might not be able to control."

Taniel mulled over that for a moment. His brain was starting to work again. That seemed a good sign. The rage was becoming a distant memory. "Maybe they didn't create them."

"What do you mean?"

"Well, we've never seen a Warden created out of a powder mage before. Maybe Kresimir did that. Maybe the remnants of the Kez Cabal have no say."

"It makes sense." Hilanska watched him for a few moments. "Where are you sleeping?"

Taniel looked up to the side of the mountain. "Have a tent set up there."

"I'll get you a real room," Hilanska said. "You need some sleep. Come find me in an hour, and I'll have something arranged. Now, though, I need to try to convince Ket not to have you hanged."

Taniel's heart had finally stopped pounding. He felt deflated, ill. "Thank you. General?"

Hilanska paused and looked back.

"I've been turned down for more powder by a dozen different quartermasters. They claim we don't have enough black powder and the General Staff is rationing it. Is there really a shortage?" Taniel thought back to Ricard Tumblar. The union boss had mentioned something about the supply demands from the front being unusually high.

"It's not as bad as all that," Hilanska said quietly. "I'll make sure you get what you need. Anything else?"

"Yes." Taniel hesitated, not sure if he wanted to know the answer to his next question. "Are there any powder mages left in Adopest? I know Tamas was training some new ones."

"They all went with him. Even the trainees."

"Pit. I'd hoped that Sabon was still here somewhere."

Hilanska's face fell and he let out a soft sigh. "You haven't heard?"

"Heard what?"

"Sabon's dead, my boy. Took a bullet from an air rifle to the side of the head over a month ago."

Hilanska patted Taniel on the shoulder and headed off into the night.

It was several moments before Taniel could manage to take another deep, shaky breath. He looked at the sky again. The daylight was only a sliver on the western mountains now; the sky above, a blanket of brilliant stars on dark blue.

Sabon, dead. His mentor. His teacher.

That had to have shaken Tamas. Perhaps enough that Tamas had made mistakes.

If Sabon was dead, then maybe Tamas was as well.

Was Taniel the last powder mage left in Adro? It seemed that way. The army retreated more every day. Kresimir was alive, and demanding their surrender. What could he do?

Fight.

The only answer.

CHAPTER
15

Tamas stood in the stirrups, watching through a looking glass as Kez scouts crested the last hilltop between the Kez cavalry and Tamas's two ragged brigades of infantry.

After a few more moments of examining the enemy scouts he sat down and handed the looking glass to Olem.

"We'll have about two-thirds of our men inside the forest by the time they reach us."

Behind him, the Hune Dora Forest rose above the plains. The prairie up to the forest had been logged to the twig a century ago, but Hune Dora itself was a barricade of trees, protected by royal decree and declared a national property of Kez. The terrain changed drastically here, as the rolling foothills of the prairie gave way to sharp mountain ridges that crept like mighty old roots toward the Amber Expanse.

Tamas suspected the difficulty in logging Hune Dora had as

much to do with the forest being protected as the king's hunting practices.

He spurred his mount around and rode to catch up with the rear of the column. The men marched at half-time as the elements of the column ahead of them adjusted from six abreast to four abreast in order to smoothly transition to the forest roadway.

"Colonel Arbor," Tamas said as he joined the rear guard.

Colonel Arbor was ancient as army standards went. He was ten years older than Tamas, and had long since lost most of his hearing and all of his teeth. Despite his age he could march, fight, and drink like a man of thirty, a fact he attributed to a glass of wine and fine cigar before bed every night. The colonel walked beside the very last men of the rear guard, rifle slung over his shoulder like a common soldier, cavalry saber at his side. The First Battalion of the Seventh Brigade was Tamas's very best. It was no accident they carried the rear.

"Eh?" the colonel said.

"I wish you'd ride." Tamas nearly had to shout, just to be sure the colonel would hear him.

The colonel flexed his jaw and popped out his false teeth into one hand. "Won't do it," he said. "My old bollocks hurt like the pit in a saddle. Besides, sir, we need horses for scouting." He eyed Tamas and Olem's mounts as if he thought they'd find better use with the rangers.

"We're going to have company in about fifteen minutes," Tamas said. "You've the rear guard. I want a walking retreat. Steady and brave."

Arbor cleared his throat and spit out a wad of phlegm. "Battalion!" he screamed. Farther up the line, a captain jumped half a foot in surprise. "Fix sword bayonets! Interlocking windmill. Livers in ten!"

The orders were passed up the column by sergeants, though half the brigade had probably already heard them. Arbor brushed his false teeth off on his uniform jacket and then slipped them into his back pocket. "Wouldn't want them to get damaged in the coming melee." He winked at Tamas.

"Right." Tamas urged his mount forward to join his powder mages farther up the column. Behind him, Arbor's battalion fanned out across the prairie, forming a half-moon shield around the rear of the column.

"Sir!" Andriya turned to Tamas with a salute as Tamas rode up to the group. Five powder mages gathered around Andriya. They'd all spent the night hunting and scouting, and looked like the pit, with bags beneath their eyes. Tamas could smell the black powder hanging around them like a cloud.

Tamas reined in. "The Kez van is just over that hill. About twelve hundred dragoons coming on hard."

"We going to stay and fight?" Andriya asked. He had the same hungry look he always did when it came time to shed Kez blood.

"No," Tamas said. "The van will be here about an hour before the rest. I want us to be well into the forest by that time. Don't worry," he added upon seeing the disappointment on Andriya's face. "We'll have plenty to kill."

He looked over the field of battle—for it was that. No doubt now that blood would be shed within the hour. He examined the tree line and the contour of the land, then the old stone walls of the abandoned city of Hune Dora. With more time to plan—a day, or even a few hours—he'd have been able to set up a trap and exterminate the Kez vanguard. As it was, he needed his men off the plains.

He pointed to where the forest rose sharply from the prairie. "Andriya, I want your team a few hundred yards out from the tree line. Vlora, put yours on those rocks over there." He pointed to the north. "As soon as they're within range, take horses off the front. Try to stumble the whole column. When they spread for a charge, kill their officers. Dismissed."

The powder mages scattered at a run. They'd be in place and

begin firing within a few minutes. It might buy his brigades a little extra time to get into the forest.

He'd placed his powder mages at high points to be able to make long shots, but the road itself fell into a wide, flat gully before rising once more into the trees. The Kez vanguard would have an easy charge.

Just inside the forest, the Seventh's Fourth Battalion had taken up firing positions. They'd give the First Battalion some cover if it came to a sprint into the woods.

Tamas whirled his horse to face northwest, toward the forest, then dismounted. He cracked a powder charge between his fingers and sprinkled some on his tongue. He felt the powder trance take hold.

"Carbine," he ordered.

Olem, who had been shadowing him silently this whole time, handed him a loaded carbine. Tamas lowered himself to one knee. The carbine was a shortened rifle, able to be fired and be reloaded on horseback easier than a long rifle, but it was still best to fire dismounted. Instead of an elongated stock to hold it steady, it had a steel handle attached to the barrel.

Tamas gripped the carbine tightly and lined up his shot on the horizon. He watched as the dragoon scouts drew closer.

A Kez dragoon was typically armed with a carbine, one pistol, and a straight sword. The older Kez commanders treated them as mounted infantry—that is, they rode horses but fought on foot. Younger commanders utilized them as light cavalry.

The current scenario would see them firing carbine, then pistol, and then making an open charge with the hope of breaking Tamas's rear guard. Tamas was willing to bet his horse on the tactic.

It wasn't long until the main company of the Kez vanguard breached the far hill. Tamas breathed out gently, sighting down his carbine. The dragoons were a little over a mile away and still in formation at four abreast. The horsehair on their spiked cavalry helmets waved in the wind, jostling as they rode.

Tamas heard the crack of a rifle come from his left and knew Andriya had taken the first shot. Several long seconds passed, filled with the reports of rifle fire.

The first dragoon stumbled. The horse fell, twisting as it went down. Another, then another fell. They slammed into the road in a cloud of dust. The horses immediately behind the front line became entangled and many of them went down, tumbling and thrashing beneath the hooves of their own allies.

Tamas didn't have to hear the screams of the horses for them to echo in his head.

They had to have known Tamas had his powder mages, yet they'd kept close formation. Tamas wanted to shake his head at the mistake. The dragoons should have been ready for it.

But then again, who is ready for a bullet to take them when the enemy is only a dot on the horizon?

He pulled his trigger.

A few seconds later his bullet entered a horse's eye. The beast jerked and fell. The rider went up and over his horse, hitting the ground hard enough to break his neck.

Tamas handed Olem his carbine and took a loaded one in its place.

The Kez column spread out from the road, widening their formation. More came over the hilltop. Tamas's initial elation at seeing a dozen brought down so quickly disappeared. He had twelve hundred more to deal with. Tripping up a few at the head of the column was hardly a victory.

He searched the breadth of the dragoons for an officer's epaulets. He found them quickly and rested his carbine against his shoulder. A deep breath. Let it out. Squeeze the trigger.

The bullet caught the young officer in the throat. He was thrown from the saddle, and Tamas was instantly on to the next target.

For the next couple of minutes, his powder mages fired at will, each bullet finding a deadly mark with few exceptions. The Kez vanguard drew closer.

"Better mount up, sir," Olem said, not a hint of nervousness in his voice.

Tamas could read the dragoon formation. They spread on the eastern side of the road in columns six deep. They would hit the First Battalion's flank, driving them away from the possible protection of the city of Hune Dora's walls. The dragoons would strike hard and fast, avoiding entanglement, and be back out of range of conventional musket fire within a few moments. They would be able to pull back around behind Hune Dora's walls, shielding them from powder mages, and then sweep an attack against the column's flank.

Tamas saw carbines lifted to shoulders. He swung up into his saddle and cleared the barrel of his carbine.

"Watch the wall," he said to Olem. "Let's go."

Arbor's First Battalion slowed to a crawl. Every other man suddenly stopped, whirled, and lowered to one knee. Tamas could hear Arbor scream the order to fire, and a cloud of powder smoke rose in the air. Fifty or more dragoons fell. The soldiers leapt to their feet, reloading as they resumed their march.

Tamas galloped toward the rear guard and drew his curved cavalry saber.

The dragoons let loose with their carbines, leaving their own clouds of powder smoke like a memory behind them.

The line of soldiers staggered. Some fell, some limped along, crying for help. None of them broke to tend to the wounded.

They'd been trained well.

The dragoons holstered their carbines in the saddle. Pistols were drawn, aim taken.

The second line of Adran soldiers turned, knelt, and fired.

A cloud of smoke went up from the dragoons as they returned shots with their pistols. They were out of the cloud only a moment later, swords drawn, as they came in for the charge.

Arbor's First Battalion turned to meet the charge. Their sword bayonets were fixed on the ends of their muskets, making the weapons long enough to act as pikes. Tamas cursed. Their formation was too loose...

The dragoons' thunderous charge was upon Tamas's soldiers.

Horses screamed as they were impaled upon sword bayonets. Men fell from their mounts. Adran soldiers were cut about the neck and face by straight-edged cavalry swords. The lines of infantry and cavalry met, disappearing in a bloody tangle.

Tamas leaned forward, urging more speed out of his charger, Olem right beside him. Across the field of battle, opposite him where the old walls of Hune Dora turned around a hill, another cavalry charge appeared.

Gavril was at the head of these cavalry. Two hundred cuirassiers in the dark-blue pants and crimson coats of the Adran heavy cavalry raced across the prairie just as the tattered remains of the Kez dragoons extracted themselves from the First Battalion.

Though still outnumbered three to one, Gavril's cuirassiers hit the dragoons with the force of an artillery shell. The collision was audible, the yells of the dragoons turning desperate at the sudden appearance of an enemy at their flank. Somewhere in the midst of the tangle a Kez trumpet belted out a desperate retreat.

A moment later and Tamas hit the fray himself. He swung his cavalry sword out and across, neatly severing the carotid artery of a Kez dragoon. He whirled in the saddle, barely catching the sword strike of another dragoon. He reached out with his senses and detonated a powder charge in the dragoon's breast pocket and immediately urged his charger forward, looking for the next target.

The last of the dragoon vanguard extracted themselves and fled back toward their brigades.

A cheer went up among Tamas's men. It carried from the First Battalion down the column and on to the Ninth Brigade, which was already safe inside the forest.

Tamas caught his breath as his charger picked its way through the bodies of men and horses to join Gavril. "Rein in your cuirassiers," Tamas shouted to Gavril. Gavril nodded and gave the orders.

"The main body of cavalry will be here in an hour," Tamas said, gasping, his heart still pounding, the powder smoke stinging his eyes and reminding him that he was an old man.

Gavril brought his mount close to Tamas and lowered his voice. "What will we do with the dead and wounded?"

Tamas examined the field of battle. There were at least a thousand dead and wounded, counting the Kez and Adrans together. The Kez couldn't have retreated with more than three hundred of their men. There was no way Tamas could march with his wounded.

"Arbor!" Tamas said, searching. "Olem, find Arbor."

A few moments later, the old colonel joined him on the field. He had a new cut on his cheek and powder burns on his sleeves. He'd seen action himself, it seemed.

"Sir?"

"Status of the First Battalion?"

"Fine and kicking, sir. We gave 'em pit. No exact count yet, but I lost no more than two hundred men."

Two hundred men from Tamas's best battalion. Almost a fourth of them. It was a staggering victory against almost twelve hundred dragoons, but Tamas couldn't afford to lose a single man, let alone two hundred of his very best.

"Pack up your wounded. Send them up the column. Strip the battlefield of everything useful."

"Permission to slaughter the horses, sir?" Arbor said. "We need the meat."

"Granted. Give your men a battlefield burial. I wish we had more time, but I mean to be off this prairie when the rest of the Kez get here."

Arbor gave a brisk nod and headed off, giving orders.

"A battlefield burial, sir?" Olem asked.

"Something we did on the march in Gurla. When another army pressed on us after a fight, we'd wrap our dead in their canvas tents with their names marked on the canvas and hope the enemy had the decency to give them a proper burial." Tamas sighed. He didn't like battlefield burials. The dead deserved more respect than that.

"Did they?"

"What?"

"Did they give them a proper burial, sir?"

"Four times out of five...no. They'd leave them to rot in the Gurlish sun."

Tamas swung out of his saddle and knelt down beside a wounded Adran soldier. The man stared into the sky, teeth clenched, his knee a bloody mess. A single glance told Tamas that the leg would most likely have to be amputated. Until then, how to move the man at all? Tamas drew his knife and held the handle to the wounded man.

"Bite down on this," he said. "It'll ease the pain a bit. Olem, have a few boys check the city. Maybe there are some abandoned wagons. Gavril, have your men catch any of the unwounded Kez horses. We might need them."

He looked toward the southern horizon. Soon enough, fifteen thousand cavalry would breach that hill.

It took four whole days of searching and over a thousand krana in bribes before Adamat found where Field Marshal Tamas had stashed Borbador, the last living Privileged from Manhouch's royal cabal.

It was funny, Adamat decided, that he was using the field marshal's own money to try to undo his orders.

Colonel Verundish stood beside him. She was a smart-looking Deliv woman in her fifties, her ebony skin a complement to the dark blue of her Adran uniform, with straight black hair tied back.

"He's here?" Adamat asked.

"He is," she confirmed.

They stood on a bluff at the very northernmost district of Adopest, where the rows of houses abruptly gave way to farmland. Here, the streets didn't smell so much like shit and soot. Here, there were fewer factories and people.

Not a bad place to live. If Adamat survived long enough to retire, maybe he could move his family out here.

Verundish nodded down to the manor below them. The grounds were overgrown, most of the windows broken, the walls vandalized. Like so many other manors belonging to the nobility, it had been gutted by Tamas's troops of anything of value and then opened to the public after the execution of its former owner.

Adamat followed Verundish down from the bluff and entered the manor grounds by a back gate. The sorry state of the place made Adamat sad. He had no love of the nobility, not by any stretch, but many of these manors had been architectural works of art. Some had been burned to the ground, some crushed to rubble for their stone. This one had got off lightly with mere vandalism.

They entered through the servants' quarters and made their way to the second floor. Adamat counted two dozen men and women, all soldiers by their look. They wore greatcoats over their uniforms, despite the summer heat, and each one gave Adamat a cursory glance as he went by.

A glimpse of a chevron over a powder horn told Adamat that these were Riflejacks—more of Tamas's best soldiers.

Verundish stopped outside the last room toward the rear of the servants' quarters. "You've got five minutes," she said.

"What will you do with him?" Adamat asked. "Now that Tamas is dead?"

The colonel's lips curled into a scowl. "*If* Tamas is dead—we'll wait for his generals to return to Adopest and hand him over to them. They'll decide his fate."

"Tamas isn't in danger from him anymore."

"I don't care what you think you know, Inspector," Verundish said. "The field marshal slaughtered the cabal for a reason, and this man is its last living member. Now go on." Verundish lifted a pocket watch in one hand and looked down at it. "Your five minutes is ticking."

Adamat opened the door and slipped inside.

Privileged Borbador sat tied to a chair in the corner of the room. His feet were bound tight against the posts of the chair, his hands locked in stiff iron gloves that would prevent his fingers from moving. He looked comfortable, for all the tightness of the ropes. He was thinner than the last time Adamat had seen him, and his chin sported a full-grown beard. In front of him was a stand, like the kind that musicians used to hold their music. Bo looked up from it.

"Bo," Adamat said, taking his hat in his hands.

Bo cleared his throat. "Yes?"

"My name is Adamat. We met a few months ago at Shouldercrown."

"Inspector. Yes. I remember you. You're the one who brought my gaes to Tamas's attention."

Adamat grimaced. "I'm sorry. I was working for him."

"You're not anymore?"

"Well, the rumors are that he's dead."

Bo stretched his neck out and tilted his head from side to side. It was about the only part of him he could move. He didn't respond.

"Bo," Adamat said. "Has the necklace around your neck—the one supporting the gaes—loosened since his reported death?"

Bo's eyes narrowed. Not much, but just enough to give Adamat his answer. The gaes was still in place. Tamas was alive. And Bo hadn't told the soldiers guarding him.

"Interesting," Adamat said aloud.

"Think you could turn the page for me?" Bo nodded at the stand in front of him.

Adamat moved around to see a book propped on the stand. He

obliged by turning it to the next page and then smoothing the page out with one hand.

"Many thanks. I've been staring at that one page for about half an hour now."

Adamat asked, "How strong is the compulsion to kill Tamas?"

"Why do you ask?"

"Could you resist it? He's quite far from here. Could you resist the compulsion to go looking for him?"

"For a time," Bo said. "Yes. It's only six months since Manhouch's death. I think I have a year until the gaes kills me."

"Two minutes!" Verundish called from the hallway.

Adamat lowered his voice. "If I get you out, will you help me?"

"Help you do what?"

"I need to rescue my wife and kill a man who is a threat to this entire country." Adamat had no idea if Bo was a patriot of any kind, but the addendum sounded good.

"What is this, some kind of pulp novel?" Bo smirked at him.

"It's very serious, actually."

Bo's smirk dissolved. "Why do you need my help?"

"The man I need to kill has over sixty men guarding him—one of them is a Privileged."

"Really, now? You work for Field Marshal Tamas—who is reported as dead—and you're going after a man who's kidnapped your wife and has the kind of resources to have sixty enforcers and a Privileged at his disposal?" Adamat could practically sense Bo's desire to flex his fingers. "Have you ever thought of getting out of the investigating business?"

"You don't know the half of it," Adamat said.

"Get me out of here and I'll spend a week as a mime in the King's Garden," Bo said, "whatever you want."

Adamat regarded the Privileged for a moment. Was he in any shape to fight another sorcerer? Adamat knew a Privileged needed gloves to do his magic, to protect his hands from being burned by the Else, but there was no sign of Bo's. Could a Privileged even be trusted?

"All right," Adamat said. "I'll do what I can."

Verundish opened the door. "Time is up, Inspector."

Adamat followed Verundish back out of the servants' quarters. She stopped him once they'd reached the edge of the manor grounds. "You can find your own way back?" she asked.

"Yes." Adamat examined her for a long moment. She watched him, her brown eyes unreadable. He would have guessed her as the military type even without the uniform—her back was straight, her hands clasped behind her like a soldier at ease.

This was a great risk he was taking, but he had no other choice if he wanted to free Borbador—and then Faye.

"I need Privileged Borbador," Adamat said.

"Pardon?" Verundish was just turning to go. She stopped and looked back at him.

"I need you to free him."

Verundish cleared her throat. "That's not happening, Inspector."

"Name your price. Field Marshal Tamas is dead. Let Bo go and you and your men can join the defensive at Surkov's Alley. Or leave the country. That might be the best idea, with what I've heard from the front."

"That"—her words were angry, clipped—"is treason."

"Please," Adamat said. "Privileged Borbador is my only chance to save my wife—maybe even to save this country. Free, he's of value. Under guard, he just ties up you and your men."

"You should go now, Inspector," Verundish said.

Adamat let out a small sigh. He'd half expected her to arrest him right then and there. He should be glad she was letting him go.

"Inspector."

He paused. "Yes?"

"Seventy-five thousand krana. Banknotes. You have a week."

CHAPTER

16

Taniel walked among the corpses on the battlefield and wondered how many had died that day.

A few hundred? A few thousand?

Surgeons, thieves, the families of soldiers—they all picked their way among the bodies, finding the wounded first and getting them back to their respective armies before bothering to stack the dead into carts like so much firewood, then taking them to be buried in mass graves.

There were always far more wounded than dead. That's how it always was, even when sorcery was involved. At least, that's how it was immediately after a battle. Over the next week well over half of the wounded would die. Even more would end up crippled for life.

He'd picked a horrid profession, Taniel reflected.

Well. Not so much "picked." There's no picking your profession when Tamas is your father. Taniel couldn't think of a time when he didn't want to be a soldier. Vlora, the girl he'd thought was the love of his life, wanted to be a soldier, too. So Taniel had gone along with his father's wishes and trained to be a powder mage. It was the only life he'd ever known.

And now Tamas, Vlora, Sabon, and everyone else who'd ever influenced Taniel in his youth were all dead and gone.

Taniel tried to shake the weight of that thought from his shoulders and kept walking.

Soldiers weren't supposed to come onto the battlefield after a skirmish like this. The temporary truce after each battle that allowed either side to collect their own dead and wounded was tentative enough without armed, hot-tempered men taking to the field.

That didn't stop some of them from coming. Taniel watched a fistfight break out between a sobbing Kez soldier and a wounded Adran sergeant. It was put down quickly by both Kez and Adran provosts, and the offending parties hauled off.

"How long do you usually stay out here?" Taniel asked.

Ka-poel knelt beside the dead body of an Adran soldier. She looked up at him briefly before lifting the dead man's left hand and using her long needle to pick something out of the man's chewed fingernails. What was it? Hair from a Kez officer? Blood of someone still alive? Only she knew.

Taniel didn't really expect an answer. She'd been less than communicative lately, even for her.

She moved to the next body. Taniel followed, watching as she cut a bit of bloody shirt off a dead Kez officer.

Taniel had left his jacket and weapons back at camp. No need for anyone to know he was out here. Regardless, some of the Adran surgeons gave him respectful nods. Others a respectful distance.

He lifted his eyes to the Kez camp. Where was Kresimir? he wondered, a little thrill of fear working up his spine. The god was lying low. Unseen. Even when Taniel opened his third eye, there was no sign of the overwhelming glow of power that should surround a god.

At this point, Taniel worried more about being killed by the Kez than about falling into the god's hands.

The Kez marched forward every day. Sometimes only a few hundred feet. Other times as much as a quarter mile, but always a little closer to Adopest. Eventually the valley would open up into the Adran basin and the Kez would use their hugely superior numbers to surround the Adran army and strike at several cities at once. They'd ravage the countryside, and Adro would be forced to capitulate.

What would Tamas have done?

Bah. Tamas would have held the damned line. That's all the Adran army needed to do: keep from losing their front every damned day.

All Taniel could do was fight. He couldn't keep the generals from sounding a retreat, even when he felt the Kez about to break and run. He couldn't hold the whole thing by himself.

"That stuff you gather," Taniel asked as Ka-poel rose to her feet, "is it just from men who are alive?"

She nodded, depositing something into one of the tiny leather bags in her satchel.

Even the living left a bit of themselves behind on the battlefield. Blood, hair, nails. Sometimes a finger or bit of skin. Ka-poel gathered it all up and stored it for later.

Taniel jumped a little at the sudden crack of a musket, but it was just the sound of a provost shooting a looter. He licked his lips and looked at the Kez camp again. What if Kresimir was out here, walking among the dead? What if he saw Taniel? Knew who he was? What he'd done?

"I'm going back to camp," Taniel said. He looked over his shoulder several times on the long walk back, watching Ka-poel continue to pick her way among the bodies.

Dinner was being served as Taniel worked his way through the camp. Quartermasters were returning to their companies with rations of meat, kettles of soup, loaves of bread. Far better fare than soldiers usually saw on the battlefield. Taniel could smell the food, making his mouth water. This chef, Mihali, god or not, created incredible dishes. Taniel didn't know that bread could have the swirls of flavor and buttery softness that this stuff did.

Taniel stopped at his room. General Hilanska had found him a shed to bed down in. It wasn't much, but it was private. He snatched his jacket, slipping a few powder charges into his pocket, then hesitated at his belt. He should be able to wander his own camp without fear, but something told him to go armed. Perhaps just paranoia. Or maybe it was the idea that General Ket's provosts were still looking for him. Why they'd not found him yet was anyone's guess.

Taniel buckled the belt, with two pistols, around his waist.

He'd only taken a few steps from his tent when a soldier accosted him.

"Sir!"

Taniel paused. The soldier was a young man, maybe twenty-five. Still older than Taniel himself. A private in the Eleventh Brigade, by his insignia.

When Taniel didn't answer, the soldier went on hesitantly. "Sir, the fellows and I, we were wondering if you'd do us the honor of joining us for dinner. It's all the same food, sir, and the company is good." He held his flat-top forage cap in both hands, wringing it.

"Where?" Taniel asked.

"Just right over there, sir." The soldier perked up a little. "We've got a fifth of Doubin rum, and Finley plays the flute something fierce."

Taniel couldn't help but feel suspicious. He set a hand on one of his pistols. "Why are you so nervous, soldier?"

The soldier ducked his head. "Sorry, sir, I didn't mean to bother you." He turned to slink away, obviously distraught.

Taniel caught up to him in just a few quick steps. "Doubin rum, you say?"

"Aye, sir."

"Horrid shit. That's the stuff sailors drink."

The soldier's forehead wrinkled in a frown. "It's the best we can do, sir." There was a flash of anger in his eyes.

They both stopped in the middle of the path, the soldier still holding his hat. He glared at Taniel now. Taniel could imagine what was going through his head: *Damned officers. Think they're so high and mighty. Plenty of good stuff to drink at the officers' mess. Won't sit with a soldier, not for a moment.*

"What's your name, soldier?"

"Flint."

No "sir" on the end of that. Taniel nodded, as if he'd not noticed. "I got a taste for Doubin rum on the ship from Fatrasta. Haven't tasted it all summer. I'd be honored, if you'd have me."

"You mocking me?"

"No," Taniel said. "Not a bit. Lead on."

Flint's frown slowly began to slide. "This way, sir."

It wasn't more than twenty yards to Flint's fire. There were two men beside the fire, keeping Mihali's soup warm in an old iron pot. One had a large nose, crooked off to the side from not being set after breaking, while the other was a short, round man practically bursting from his uniform. The one with the nose froze at the sight of Taniel, a spoon lifted halfway to his mouth.

"Captain, sir," Flint said, gesturing to the two men by the fire. "The one with the nose there is Finley. Ugliest man in the Eleventh. And that round bit of meat there is Faint, on account that she fainted the first time she fired a musket. Finley, Flint, and Faint. We're the fellows of the Eleventh Brigade."

Taniel lifted his eyebrows. He'd not in a hundred years have guessed that Faint was a woman.

"Fellows, this is Captain Taniel Two-Shot, hero of the Fatrastan War and the Battle for South Pike."

Faint seemed skeptical. "You sure this is Taniel Two-Shot?"

"That's him, all right," Finley said. "I was with Captain Ajucare when we went after the Privileged at the university."

"I thought you looked familiar," Taniel said. "I never forget a nose."

Flint laughed and punched Finley in the arm. Finley fell off his chair, and Taniel heard himself chuckle. It was a raspy, nasty sound, like an instrument desperately in need of tuning. How long had it been since he'd laughed?

Flint fetched a folding cloth chair and brought it to Taniel. Finley poured them each a pewter tin of soup, and then bread and mutton was passed around.

They ate in quiet for several minutes. Taniel was the first one to break the silence. "I heard the Second took a beating a couple of weeks ago."

"Aye," Flint said. "That we did."

"We were on the wall," Faint said. "The wall in Budwiel when the Black Wardens came over."

Finley stared quietly into his soup.

"Faint here," Flint said. "She punched one of those Wardens in the nose with that ham fist of hers. Knocked him right off the bulwark."

"I'd imagine that gave him quite the shock. I heard it was bad," Taniel said. "I'm glad to see you got out."

"Most weren't so lucky," Finley said quietly. Flint and Faint's smiles disappeared.

Taniel cleared his throat, looking around. Usually a squad would eat together. "All that's left of your squad?" he asked as respectfully as he could.

Faint chuckled. Finley pushed her. "It's not funny," Finley said.

"It's a little funny," Faint said.

Taniel wondered whether to smile at the joke. "What?"

"Not our squad, sir," Flint spoke up. "This is all that's left of our company."

Taniel felt his mouth go dry. A company was usually about two hundred men. To lose all but three...

"No wounded?" he asked.

"Probably," Faint said. She ladled herself another tin of soup. "But not that we've seen. This deal with the Kez, where we clean up our own dead and wounded after each battle, only came about after Budwiel. We left Budwiel at a run. Left behind supplies, ammunition, weapons...loved ones. Everyone who couldn't run is now a slave, or worse."

"What's worse than being a slave?" Flint asked.

Finley looked up from rolling a cigarette. "Where do you think they keep getting those Wardens? Why torture and twist your own people if you've got prisoners?"

"It takes years to make and train a Warden," Taniel said.

"Does it?" Finley asked. He lit his cigarette with a burning stick from the fire. "Rumors are going around the men, rumors that they've got Kresimir himself in the camp."

Flint shook his head. "If they had Kresimir, we'd all be dead."

"We've got Adom reborn," Faint said. She held up her mutton and bread. "Mihali is keeping Kresimir from destroying us all."

Flint rolled his eyes. "Come on, now."

"There's another rumor," Finley said. He looked up, meeting Taniel's eyes across the fire. "There's a rumor Taniel Two-Shot put a bullet in Kresimir's eye, and now Kresimir wears a mask that covers half his face—and it don't have no eyehole in it." He leaned over, offering his smoking cigarette to Taniel.

Taniel took a long drag at the cigarette. Nasty things, he'd always thought, but he made exceptions for nights like this, when it was more about camaraderie than habit. "I heard a rumor," he said, coughing and turning his head toward Flint, "that there was Doubin rum at this fire."

"Now that"—Faint pointed at Taniel—"is fact." She retreated to her tent for a moment and came back with an earthen jug. "Get your flute, Finley," she said. "I've had enough of this dark talk."

Taniel was offered the jug first. He took a sip of the stuff and felt his whole body shudder. "Gah," he said, wiping his mouth on his sleeve.

"My da works for Doubin and Company," Faint said, taking the jug. "Tastes like a demon's own piss, don't it!" She threw back the jug, taking a long, hard drink.

Taniel leaned back, watching the fire, unable to keep from laughing when Flint spat a mouthful of the rum into the fire and the flames flared up momentarily.

"Don't waste it!" Faint shouted, nabbing the jug.

It didn't take more than a few more passes before Taniel could feel the stuff working through his system. His body loosened and his mind became bleary. He leaned back and watched the fire, and before long Finley began to play his flute.

It was a low, mournful sound. Not at all the kind of shrill dance Taniel had heard from that kind of instrument before. It didn't take long until Faint began to sing. Her voice, much to Taniel's surprise, was a clear tenor that cut through the night.

He found himself drifting in his own mind. The aches in his body dissolved and the front seemed a hundred miles away.

There was a rustle of sound, so very slight he could have imagined it, and then Ka-poel slid into his lap. Just like that. No asking or hesitation, but as quick as a long-familiar lover. Taniel would have been uncomfortable if he didn't already feel so warm. Content. Happy, even.

Taniel drifted for what seemed like hours, and woke with a shiver. He didn't know how long he'd been gone, but the sun had set and the starry sky spread out above them. Had he dreamed that moment of contentment?

No.

Flint stared into the red coals. Finley was putting away his flute, and Faint snored softly on the ground beside the fire. Ka-poel was nestled in the crook of Taniel's arm. Her eyes were closed, a small smile on her face.

Taniel lifted his free arm and brushed a bit of red hair from her forehead. It was growing back after the fight on the mountain, and it seemed a deeper, more vibrant red than before.

Taniel felt eyes upon him. Flint was watching.

"She's a pretty little thing," Flint said.

Taniel didn't answer. He didn't trust himself to. Words like *impropriety* and *savage* went through his head, but they didn't have the bite they usually did. What did those things matter? He might die tomorrow.

"Thank you," Taniel said to Flint, "for inviting me."

"It was our pleasure, sir. Not often soldiers get to dine with a hero like you."

"No hero. Not me. Just a man with nothing but rage in his heart."

"If you really had nothing but rage in your heart, that girl wouldn't be sleeping there sound as can be," Flint said. He winked at Taniel, and Taniel felt his cheeks grow warm.

"I should warn you, sir," Flint said.

"Yes?"

"The provosts are looking for you. Rumor is General Ket wants to hang you."

Taniel scoffed. "If they were looking for me, they could have found me. I'm on the front line every day."

"They don't want to arrest you in front of the men. You've saved a right large number of soldiers every day on the line. The men aren't sure whether you're a demon or an angel, but they think you're watching over them—fighting while the senior officers sit farther back and watch us die. There might be a riot if they arrest you on the line."

"It's not hard to find my room," Taniel said, glancing toward the little shed he and Ka-poel were staying in.

"The provosts are questioning around all quiet-like. They've asked us a couple times." Flint shook his head with a little smile. "Everyone tells them to look on the front."

Taniel picked at a bit of gristle stuck between his teeth. So, the infantry were watching his back. It made him feel sad, more than anything. He didn't deserve to be looked out for. He was only on the front because he knew nothing but killing. Not because he wanted to save the soldiers.

"Then I have something else to thank you for."

"Don't thank me, sir," Flint said. "Just keep looking out for us out there. No one else is."

"I'll try."

"Also, sir, avoid the Third. General Ket's brigade love her. Don't know why, but her men are loyal, and they might just turn you over to the provosts themselves."

Taniel shifted Ka-poel's weight on his shoulder and climbed to his feet, balancing her in his arms. She didn't respond to the jostling except to nuzzle her face closer to his neck. It was a feather's touch, soft and warm, and Taniel felt his body react to it.

"Good night, Flint," he said.

"Good night, sir."

Taniel carried Ka-poel back to their shed. He laid her down in his bed and covered her with a blanket before pulling a powder charge from his pocket.

He stared at the charge for several moments. A small hit of the powder and he'd see better in the dark. He wouldn't have to light a lamp. It wasn't like he was sleeping these days anyway. How long had it been? Two weeks since a proper night's sleep? Could humans exist like that? He felt wooden and sluggish, as if walking in a dream.

But when he had a bit of powder, he was as alive and awake as always.

Taniel took a pinch of the powder and raised it to his nose. He stopped. Lowered it and rewrapped the powder charge. He found a match and struck it, touching it to the lamp beside the bed. The shed was suddenly thrown into the light.

He got his rifle out from beneath the bed and began to clean it. The process calmed him, let him think. He pulled his mind away from Ka-poel, lying there in his bed, and away from the provosts and General Ket, and away from his father's death and the Kez army's inexorable push into Adro.

Taniel finished with the rifle and cleaned his pistols, then wrapped a few dozen powder charges. He looked at that powder. He needed it. Wanted it.

He didn't let himself take any.

His bayonet was last. He took it out of its leather wrappings and examined it in the light of the lamp. There was a bit of dried blood in one of the grooves. He picked it off, then polished the metal. He felt the bed move a little and looked up.

Ka-poel lay on her side, one hand resting on her hip, the other propped beneath her head. She watched him with those green eyes. Her shirt had ridden up a bit and he could see the ashen freckles at her waist and the sharp curve of her hips. He felt his heart beat faster.

"I have to kill Kresimir," Taniel said. "For good this time. But I don't know how to do it."

Ka-poel moved to the edge of the bed. She leaned over, reaching beneath the bed, and opened her satchel. She fished around a little bit before coming back up with a doll.

Taniel swallowed hard. The doll had been shaped from wax into the perfect resemblance of a person. Gold hair, a handsome face, stout shoulders, and almost feminine lips. Taniel knew that face. He'd seen it on the man who'd stepped out of a cloud after descending from the heavens.

Kresimir.

She'd never seen Kresimir. At least, so he thought. How could she know what he looks like?

"I don't think even *your* magic is strong enough to kill a god," Taniel said. "I shot him with two redstripes."

Ka-poel touched a finger to her chin thoughtfully. She slowly drew the finger down her throat and then over her shirt, between her breasts. It stopped, then back to her throat. She made a cutting motion, then spread her hand.

"Blood?" Taniel asked, his throat dry.

She nodded.

"Kresimir's blood?"

Another nod.

"I'll never get close enough."

She mouthed a word. *Try.*

"You want me to throw myself at a god, hoping I can draw his blood?"

Ka-poel swung her legs around to the edge of the bed. She took the bayonet out of his hands and set it on the bedside table. She lowered herself into his lap, legs straddling his own.

"Pole, I don't..."

She put a finger to his lips. He remembered the mala den back in Adopest. With her pressed firmly against him in the hammock, her face so close. He shuddered.

Ka-poel put two fingers to her lips, then pushed them against his forehead. She mouthed a word.

It wasn't spoken, but still seemed to echo in his mind.

Sleep.

Sleep.

He felt his back hit the bed and his eyelids shut, suddenly weighty as millstones.

Sleep.

"Why are you courting Lady Winceslav?" Nila asked.

The centerpiece of the dining room of Lord Vetas's city manor was a long ironwood table that could seat sixteen. Vetas sat at the head of the table, his plate empty, a glass of red wine in his right hand, his left lying flat on the table with fingers spread. Nila sat on his right. Jakob sat on his left, and Faye sat beside Nila.

When Nila was a girl, she used to dream of attending fine dinner parties, admiring her reflection in the polished silverware and drinking from a wineglass rimmed with gold. She never imagined that dream would turn into a nightmare.

For ten days now they'd been eating with Vetas every evening. Despite the normal bustle and the number of men around the house—upward of sixty some days—dinnertime was always quiet. He used the time to instruct Nila in proper dining etiquette, and to shower Jakob with compliments, praise, and gifts. Nila hated every minute of it. Vetas filled every moment with mundane chatter, going on with some instruction or asking them all questions about themselves.

Nila knew better than to take this as some kind of friendliness. Vetas was prying. Finding out new things about them and filing them away in that insidious mind of his.

He never let anything slip about himself, of course. He was a master at deflecting questions. Which was why Nila was surprised when he answered hers.

"Lady Winceslav," he said, "owns the Wings of Adom mercenary company. You've heard of them, I trust?"

"Everyone has," Nila said. She glanced at Faye. The housewife sat stiff in her chair, staring at the empty place setting beside Jakob. Each of the last ten nights, that place had been occupied by her son, Josep, a boy of fifteen or sixteen, who was missing the ring finger of his right hand. Tonight that chair was empty.

"Most everyone, yes," Vetas said. "Right now they are employed against the Kez army. I'd like to employ them elsewhere."

Nila moved the food around on her porcelain plate. She didn't want to be here. Didn't want to look at Vetas's soulless face anymore. "And that's it? They're mercenaries. Can't you just...hire them?"

"That's it," Vetas said. He gave her a tight smile.

That wasn't it, of course. There was some other reason why he was courting the Lady. Perhaps he wanted to hire the mercenaries as well, but his plans couldn't be that simple. Nila didn't care. She just wanted dinner to be over. It wouldn't be, though. Not until Vetas said it was.

"You want to use her," Nila said.

"Hmm?" Vetas lifted his wineglass to his lips.

"For whatever all this is about." Nila gestured down the table. Aside from the place settings here at one end, the table was covered with papers—correspondence, receipts, lists; everything involved with Lord Vetas's affairs. She'd read a few, when she'd gotten the chance. None of them seemed to mean anything.

Vetas smiled at Jakob. "The Lady Winceslav is an eligible widow and a very intelligent woman. She'd make a wonderful wife."

"A wife?" The word came out in a burst of laughter. Nila covered her mouth, petrified at the outburst.

"Yes," Vetas said, as if he'd not heard the disbelief in her voice. "A wife." He leaned toward Jakob. "You understand that every lord needs a good wife, and it's important to marry someone with connections."

"Yes, Uncle Vetas."

"Good child."

"Uncle Vetas, I thought that the nobility of Adro no longer existed."

Vetas gave the boy a nod. "The nobility of Adro is in hiding, my boy. Remember, you're heir to the crown. Someday the nobility will return, and when it does, you will be at their head."

Nila ceased moving the fork around her plate. This was the first she'd heard Vetas say anything about the nobility. She'd always assumed that Jakob, in his capacity as next in line for the crown, fit into Vetas's plans somehow, but he'd never spoken of it.

She waited for Vetas to go on. Instead, Vetas took a sip of his wine.

Faye was still staring at the empty place setting across from her. She'd begun to rock back and forth slightly, her mouth hanging open, her forehead wrinkled.

"You're just using everyone," Nila said. "Me. Jakob. Lady Winceslav." *What is your plan?* Nila wanted to shout. *Why are you in Adopest?*

Vetas looked slightly surprised. "Of course I am. That's what nobles do. But," he said, reaching over and patting Jakob affectionately on one hand, "it's all for your protection. The duty of the nobility is to protect the people, no matter what kind of distasteful things they have to do."

Nila slammed her hand down on the table, making Jakob jump. "Don't!" she said. She gripped the lip of the table to keep herself from shaking.

"Don't what?" Vetas asked innocently.

"Nila," Jakob said, "why are you shouting at Uncle Vetas?"

Vetas gave Nila that tight smile again.

She would have snatched up her knife and leapt at Vetas then and there if Faye hadn't spoken.

"Where is my son?"

Vetas's fingers drummed once on the table. His attention shifted from Nila to Faye. "Nila," he said without looking at her, "I think that you should take Jakob to his room, now."

"Isn't there dessert, Uncle Vetas?" Jakob asked.

"Of course, my child. I'll have some brought up to you. Run along."

Nila still wanted to grab that knife and leap at him. She waited, contemplating, wondering if she could move fast enough. "Jakob," she said, getting up from her chair and holding out her hand. "Come along."

She took Jakob upstairs and put him in his room, helping him get out a number of toys before going into her own room and rushing out into the hallway, stepping carefully to avoid the creakiest boards, until she reached the servants' stairs that descended into the kitchens. She descended halfway down the stairs and pressed her ear to the wall.

"...was burned down," Vetas was saying calmly, his voice muddled through the plaster. "There were eleven graves. Seems the fire took them all in their beds. The townspeople claimed there was nothing but bone and ash left."

A loud sob startled Nila. It was followed by the low sound of crying. Faye.

Vetas went on as if he hadn't noticed Faye's reaction. "I won't have time to go up and investigate it myself, but it seems as if your children are all dead."

"Where is my son?" Faye demanded. The crying dried up, followed by a few sniffs.

"I've also received reliable word that your husband has been imprisoned by Tamas. It seems that he confessed to being blackmailed, and the field marshal plans on having him executed for treason." Vetas's voice droned on, as if he were talking about the weather. "My contacts within Sablethorn are few enough, but I should have better information within a week or so."

"Where"—the table rattled as if someone had pounded it with a fist—"is my son?"

Vetas said, "With your husband arrested, you and your son are of no use to me anymore. I'll keep you around for another couple of weeks, but I've sold your son to the Kez. He'll be smuggled—"

There was a sudden scream and then a crash. The walls rattled once, and then there was silence. Nila held her breath. Had Faye attacked Vetas? Had she succeeded?

The silence dragged on. Nila thought she could hear the labored sound of heavy breathing coming from the dining room.

"That," Vetas said, "was not very smart." The dining room door opened, and Vetas spoke to one of his men. "Take her downstairs. I'll join you shortly."

Heavy footsteps entered the dining room. The sound of a struggle resumed.

"I'll kill you, bastard!" Faye said. "I'll take your eyes! I'll take your tongue! There won't be anything left when I'm done!" A slew of curses and screams followed Faye out of the dining room and soon became muffled as she was carried into the basement.

Nila listened for several minutes before hearing Vetas leave the dining room. His soft, measured footfalls traveled down the hall, and the basement door opened. Nila counted to one hundred before she descended the servants' stairs into the kitchen.

She looked around quickly. The kitchen had been rearranged since she was last here. She brought a stool over to the washbasin and got on it, rummaging around in the high cupboards. Nothing. She swore under her breath and got back down. There, under the sink. Back in reach of children.

She snatched the large jar of lye and set it on the kitchen table. It didn't take long to find an empty spice pot. She blew the leaves of spices out of the bottom and poured half a cup of lye into it.

"What are you doing?"

Nila nearly dropped the lye jar. She looked up.

Privileged Dourford stood in the doorway. His height and Privileged's gloves made him imposing, and all the house staff knew his temper.

"Just getting some lye, my lord," Nila said.

"For what?"

"Some of the sauce got on my sleeve from dinner." She pinched one sleeve of her dress, hoping he wouldn't actually look closely. "I want to wash it before it stains."

"I thought Lord Vetas made it clear you're not to be doing any of the laundry anymore."

"It's just a small stain, my lord." Nila smiled in a way she hoped would be shy and tucked her shoulders forward, squeezing her breasts together to accent her cleavage. "I didn't want to bother any of the house staff."

Dourford's eyes lingered on her bust. "All right. But make sure that boy is asleep. That damned harpy is going to get what's coming to her tonight, and it'll be hard to keep her quiet." Dourford rummaged in the cupboards until he found half a loaf of bread and left the room, chewing thoughtfully.

Nila put the large lye jar back and tucked the spice pot into her dress pocket. She returned to her room, wondering how hard it would be to poison both Vetas and Dourford at the same time.

CHAPTER
17

Adamat was wary as his hackney cab pulled onto the long suburban street that led to his house.

He hadn't been there for almost two months—not since the day he told Vetas that Field Marshal Tamas was on his way to arrest Arch-Diocel Charlemund. Adamat had been forced to trick Vetas and still almost gotten Tamas killed. Vetas would want Adamat back—either dead or alive.

Adamat was willing to bet that Vetas was having the house watched.

He kept an eye on the street on the approach to the house. No suspicious men, no figures lurking in windows with an undue interest in his home. Foot traffic was minimal in this part of town, just a family heading to the market and a single old man strolling briskly in the sun.

The carriage rolled to a stop three houses down from his own.

Adamat checked the snub-nosed pistol in his pocket. Loaded and primed.

He flipped the collar of his jacket up around his face, pulled his hat low, and stepped into the street. Handing a few krana to the driver, Adamat headed warily toward his house, his cane held firmly in one hand.

The shutters were closed, the blinds drawn as he'd left them. Adamat searched the front of the house for any sign that things had been touched or tampered with. Nothing.

Adamat opened the gate to the alleyway between houses and went back to his garden. Another short inspection showed him nothing out of order. He waited for several minutes, examining the house again and again. No new scratches on the lock, no footprints in the garden.

It slowly began to dawn on him that perhaps he wasn't as important to Vetas as he thought. Lord Vetas was playing some kind of larger game on behalf of his master, Lord Claremonte. Did Adamat matter anymore? After all, as far as Vetas knew, Tamas had had Adamat quietly executed for treason. What if Vetas had written Adamat off entirely? Maybe Faye and Josep were already dead, buried in a shallow grave somewhere.

Adamat clenched and unclenched his fists. No. He couldn't think like that. Faye was alive. Vetas still held her. And Adamat was going to get her back.

Adamat unlocked the back door and stepped into the house. He closed his eyes and took a deep breath. The rooms were warm and stuffy with the windows closed up, but it still smelled like old wood, books, dust, and a slight hint of lavender from the incense Faye used to burn. He drew his pistol and carefully searched each of the rooms.

Everything was just as it had been left: the bloodstains on the sofa and carpet from one of Lord Vetas's men, a bullet hole in the ceiling. Another in the hall and one in the floor, along with the rest of the unrepaired damage done in the fight with the Black Street Barbers.

Pistol in one hand, cane in the other, Adamat climbed the stairs to the second floor. Here was where the Barbers had attacked him. There was SouSmith's blood, almost black on the dark hickory stairs.

No one upstairs. No sign anyone had gone through his belongings or searched the house.

Adamat sighed and lowered the pistol. He was almost disappointed. It was as if Lord Vetas had forgotten him entirely.

He put his cane in the umbrella stand by the front door and headed to the kitchen. There might be some canned beans or something to eat in the pantry. Get some food, then find his shovel, and then...

Adamat was not nearly fast enough to react as something swung around the corner and took him full in the nose. Pain blossomed all over his face and he was suddenly blinking up at the ceiling through tears.

Someone towered over him. He was grasped by the lapels of his jacket and lifted off the ground and a moment later slammed into the wall. Adamat swallowed a mouthful of his own blood and tried to breathe through his nose, only to utter a whimper.

Adamat was held against the wall by two strong arms. He batted at them to no effect, then lifted his hand to wipe his eyes. He looked into the face of a man with coal stains on his cheeks and shirt. Adamat recognized this man—one of Lord Vetas's goons.

Adamat cleared his throat and tried to sound casual. "Kale, was it?"

"That's right." The coal shoveler's mouth twisted. "Been waiting for you for a long time."

Adamat's whole head hurt. His nose had to be broken. He probably looked an absolute mess. The second set of clothes ruined in a week.

"Lord Vetas wants a word with you," Kale said. "You come along quietly now, or I start breaking your teeth."

Where the pit had he come from? Adamat had checked the whole house. Man must have been hiding in the cellar. And what on earth had he hit Adamat with? A cudgel?

"Right," Adamat said.

Kale's grip loosened. Adamat felt himself slide down the wall until his feet were touching the ground. This man was fast. And strong. Pit, what Adamat would have given to have SouSmith here now.

"Clean yourself up," Kale said. He let go of Adamat's jacket.

Adamat felt his knees give out from beneath him and he collapsed to the floor. He'd landed on something. Just under his chest—his pistol. He wrapped his fingers around the butt blindly.

He felt a strong hand on his back. "I'm all right," Adamat said. "Just. Hurts. I'll get another shirt from my bedroom and then I'll come, no fight." His words were gurgled and nasal.

He pushed himself to his feet with some struggle. Pit, the pain in his face. It would take more than three fingers of whiskey to dull this. Adamat took three steps down the hall and turned, lifting the pistol, and pulled the trigger.

The sound of the gunshot made his head—somehow—hurt even more.

Kale regarded the pistol, then looked at Adamat.

Adamat looked at the pistol, then at Kale. Then at the floor.

The bullet was on the ground. It must have fallen out of the barrel when Adamat dropped the pistol.

Kale crossed the space between them in two long strides, knocking the pistol out of Adamat's hand and grabbing Adamat by the throat, lifting him into the air and slamming him against the front door. The walls rattled from the impact.

Adamat struggled to breathe. He kicked. He punched. Nothing he could do would loosen Kale's grip.

"That's going to cost you a thumb," Kale said.

Adamat flailed around with his right hand. He had to do something, he had to ... he felt his hand touch the head of his cane where it sat in the umbrella stand. He gripped the cane as far down as he could, lifted it, and slammed it into Kale's temple.

Kale staggered to one side, letting up on his grip. Adamat shoved him away with one arm and brought the cane down as hard as he could.

The coal shoveler caught the blow with one hand even as he stumbled away from Adamat. He grabbed the end of the cane and jerked.

Adamat found himself in a sudden tug-of-war. Kale jerked again, almost pulling Adamat over. Adamat could see the coal shoveler's eyes tighten at the corners and knew he'd not keep ahold of the cane the next time.

So Adamat twisted the head of the cane. There was a quiet *click*.

Kale yanked hard on the cane. He tumbled to the ground and looked with some surprise at the end of the cane in his hand.

Adamat threw himself forward, cane-sword-first, ramming the short blade into Kale's stomach. He pulled back and rammed again, then again. Adamat stumbled to one side after the final thrust, staring at Kale.

The coal shoveler stared back. He held both arms across his stomach, whimpering from the pain.

"He'll know," Kale said. "Lord Vetas will know you're back, and he'll kill your wife."

Adamat stood up straight and leveled his cane sword at Kale. "She's still alive?"

Kale didn't respond.

"And Josep? My boy?"

"Get me a doctor," Kale said. "Do it now and I'll tell you about your boy."

"My next-door neighbor is a doctor. Tell me and I'll fetch him."

Kale let out a long, anguished sigh. "Your boy...your boy is gone. They took...I don't know where, but he's gone. Your wife is there...she..."

"She what?"

"Get me a doctor."

"Tell me." The pain in Adamat's head seemed to climb to a crescendo. It was agonizing, and by the look of his soaked shirt and jacket he must have lost a great deal of blood from his nose.

"Vetas...he'll know. He thought maybe Tamas took you in...that you were arrested, or shot...but now he'll know you're alive."

Adamat gritted his teeth. "Not if they don't find the body." He barely trusted himself to thrust straight and true, but his cane sword went into Kale's eye and only stopped when it hit the back of his skull. He pulled it out and waited until the body stopped twitching before he cleaned the blade on Kale's coat.

Adamat stripped to the waist and and tossed his bloody clothes onto Kale's body. He hunted about the house for any other sign that the coal shoveler had ever been here, then went and found his shaving mirror.

His bleary eyes and bloody face stared back at him. He barely recognized himself.

Adamat's nose was bent nearly perpendicular to his head. Every gentle touch as he probed his face forced him to choke down a scream.

He put one hand on either side of his nose and stared at himself in the eyes. It was now or never.

He grasped his nose and straightened it.

Adamat woke up on the floor of his kitchen to the sound of someone pounding on his front door. He slowly got to his feet and glanced in the mirror. Through all the blood and grime he could tell his nose was straight again. He wondered if it was worth the excruciating pain that even now made him want to collapse.

It took him a full minute with shaking hands to reload his pistol.

When it was primed, he went to the front door and peeked out the window.

It was one of his neighbors. An older woman, stooped from age and wearing a day dress with a shawl hastily thrown over her head. He didn't think he'd ever learned her name.

Adamat cracked the door.

The woman nearly screamed at the sight of him.

"Yes?" he asked.

"Are you . . . are you all right?" she asked in a trembling voice. "I thought I heard a gunshot, and then not five minutes ago came the most terrible scream."

"Gunshot? No, no gunshot. I'm terribly sorry at my appearance. I fell and broke my nose. I was just setting it. Probably the scream you heard."

She stared at him like he was some kind of specter. "Are you sure you're fine?"

"Just a broken nose," Adamat said, gesturing at his face. "An accident, I assure you."

"I'll run and fetch the doctor."

"No, please," Adamat said. "I'll go myself soon. No need to do that."

"Now, now, I must insist."

"Madame!" Adamat made his voice as firm as he could. It made his nasal passage vibrate, and the pain nearly dropped him to the floor again. "If you mind, I will attend to myself. Do not, under any circumstance, summon a doctor."

"If you are certain . . . ?"

Damned busybodies. "Quite, thank you, madame." Adamat closed the door and surveyed the mess in his hallway. Blood everywhere. The rug, the floor, the walls. All over the door behind him.

It took Adamat several hours and quite a lot of Faye's spare linens to clean up all the blood. He worked urgently—no telling if another of Vetas's goons would arrive at any time. But he had to have the house cleaned out. There had to be no sign that he'd ever been here.

When it was done, Adamat finally cleaned himself. A full bottle of wine, and the pain in his head was a dull hum instead of a constant hammering. Night had fallen. He wrapped Kale's body in the soiled linens and dragged it out the back door, thinking how furious Faye would be once she found out what he'd used the linens for.

In the corner of Adamat's small garden was a toolshed, and under the toolshed an unused root cellar no larger than the inside of a small carriage. Adamat entered the root cellar and felt around in the dark for several minutes before he found what he was looking for: a rope on the cellar floor in a layer of loose dirt. He grabbed the rope and hauled, pulling free a stout wooden box.

He took the strongbox into the garden and returned to drop the body inside the root cellar. He rearranged the tools so it looked like no one had been in there for some time and closed the door behind him.

Inside the lockbox was every krana he'd saved since he first found out he owed Palagyi for the loan that had started Adamat and Friends Publishing. Adamat didn't trust bankers anymore. Not since his loan had been sold to Palagyi.

The sum came out to a little under twenty-five thousand. Not enough. Not nearly enough.

Adamat spent another several hours cleaning the house of all traces of blood and then gathered a travel case full of children's clothes, the strongbox, and his cane and pistol before he headed out into the street to look for a hackney cab.

Taniel lay against the earthen battlements and glanced up at the overcast sky.

Mountainous white clouds moved ponderously through the sky, rolling like foam on top of a wave as it crashed upon the beach. Bits of gray mixed into the clouds, here and there. Rain, maybe? He hoped not. The earthworks would turn to mud and the rain would foul powder on both sides.

Taniel could hear the distant drumming of the Kez. It seemed far away, from where he lay against the cool, hard earth. The shouts of the Adran commanders—those were closer. He wanted to tell them to stuff it. Every man on the line knew they'd likely die today. Every man on the line knew that the Kez would succeed in their attack, taking the earthworks again like they did yesterday, and the day before that.

Morale wasn't just dead; it had been hanged, shot, then drawn and quartered and buried in a rocky grave.

"Well?" Taniel said.

Colonel Etan stood a few feet back from the edge of the earthworks, waving his sword and lending his own reassurances to the meaningless chatter of the officers. He wore a bearskin hat with a purple plume, befitting an officer of the Twelfth Grenadiers. His eyes were fixed on the approaching Kez infantry, still well beyond the earthworks.

"Coming," Etan said.

Taniel scanned the clouds. "Wake me when they get here." He closed his eyes.

Some of Etan's grenadiers chuckled at that. Taniel opened his eyes to see who'd laughed, and flashed them a grin. He surprised himself at how easily he smiled. Just a few days ago the very act had seemed foreign. Now...

He caught sight of Ka-poel back behind Etan. She sat on the earthworks, her knee raised up, chin in her hand. She was watching the Kez advance. Even the grenadiers—the strongest, bravest men in the Adran army—had a wild, nervous look in their eyes. They knew what it meant to be on the front. But Ka-poel's eyes were thoughtful, piercing. Not a hint of fear. She looked as deadly as a Fatrastan wildcat.

Taniel wondered what she saw that the others didn't.

"Getting close," Etan said. His body was tense and he kept a white-knuckle grip on his sword.

Taniel wondered where Kresimir was. Why hadn't the god shown himself? Why hadn't he killed them all, scattering them with sorcery, instead of letting his army chip away slowly at the Adran defenses day after day?

"Here they come!"

Taniel gripped his rifle in both hands. The timing for this had to be perfect. No hesitation. He had to—

"Now!"

There was just a hint of a shadow in the corner of Taniel's eyes. Taniel thrust his rifle upward, ramming two and a half spans of steel straight up between the legs of a leaping Warden.

Taniel felt the rifle stock twist in his hands. He gave a shout and pushed up harder, lifting the Warden like some kind of macabre trophy and then slamming him onto the earthwork floor.

Even a Warden could be taken by surprise, it seemed. The creature lay still in utter shock for several moments, eyes wide, a look of panic on his face. Then it began to thrash, trying to pull off the bayonet that Taniel had rammed up its ass.

A dozen grenadiers fell on the Warden with bayonets and swords. It only took a few moments before all that remained of the Warden was a bloody mess of meat. Taniel pulled his bayonet out of the dead creature just as the Adran line opened fire.

"Get rid of it," Etan said. He and a pair of his men grabbed the dead Warden and hefted it over the earthworks, letting it roll down to the field below.

The advancing Kez wavered in the onslaught of musket fire. Hundreds dropped to the ground, but the Kez war machine marched right over them. They dropped their bayoneted muskets into a ready position and charged at a run.

Taniel got up on the earthworks and fired his rifle, dropping a Kez major from the back of his horse.

Etan stepped up beside Taniel. "It's been a pleasure knowing you, my friend," he said, eyes on the charging Kez.

"We're not losing today." Taniel rammed a cotton-wrapped bullet down his rifle, then cracked open a powder charge with his thumb. He snorted the charge in one long drag and rubbed his nose with the back of his hand. "Not today," he said. Then, louder, "We're not losing today."

Taniel felt a rising wave of anger. Why should they lose? Why should they turn and run? They were better than the Kez. The Adran army was feared all over the Nine.

He turned toward the grenadiers. "Are you Field Marshal Tamas's men? Are you?"

"The field marshal is dead," someone said.

Taniel felt the spittle fly out of his mouth. "Are you?"

"I'm the field marshal's man!" Etan lifted his sword. "Dead or alive, I'll always be!"

"Are you?" Taniel screamed at the grenadiers.

"Yes!" They answered with one voice, muskets raised.

"The Adran army—Tamas's army—doesn't lose. You can flee if you want"—Taniel pointed at the grenadiers—"when the trumpet sounds. Run back to those armchair generals, let the Kez shoot you in the back. But I'll be here until the Kez break."

"So will I," Etan said. He swung his saber.

"And I!" the grenadiers shouted in unison.

Taniel turned back to the Kez. "Send them to the pit!"

Taniel saw his father's face float before his vision like a tattered flag. He saw Vlora, and Sabon and Andriya, and all the rest of his fellow powder mages. He could see his friends in the Seventh and Ninth. Then they were gone, and the world was drenched in red as Taniel felt his legs carry him over the edge of the earthworks and straight into the teeth of the Kez infantry.

The crack of muskets and blasts of artillery were suddenly lost in the thunder of the charging infantry. Taniel gutted a Kez soldier with his bayonet, then locked the stock of his rifle with another. He shoved, sending the soldier reeling.

An officer's sword sliced neatly along his cheek, just beneath the eye. He felt the blade, but pain seemed a distant thing from within the powder trance, with so much adrenaline coursing through his body. He smacked the officer across the chin with his rifle then stabbed an infantryman.

The Kez were all around him and he felt a sudden panic. It didn't matter how quick or how powerful he was, he could be felled by sheer force of numbers, just like the Warden he and the grenadiers had hacked apart.

Taniel saw a bayonet aim at his heart. He dropped his shoulder and felt the point snag his jacket, ripping clean through, then slammed his fist into the soldier's face.

And suddenly Taniel was not alone. Adran grenadiers with their bearskin hats and crimson-cuffed jackets were beside him, muskets at the ready to push back the Kez assault.

"Shove!" Etan's voice rose above the din. "Step! Thrust! Shove! Step! Thrust!"

While the Kez infantry threw themselves forward with reckless abandon, the Twelfth Grenadiers moved in lockstep, every man chosen for his immense size and trained to meet the enemy unflinchingly. They'd come over the earthworks behind Taniel and now they pushed forward, bayonets working, chewing through the Kez infantry like so many farmers cutting hay.

Taniel forced himself into the line of grenadiers and joined their march. To his surprise, the Kez infantry seemed to melt before them. Taniel knew power. He knew speed. But the pure strength of these grenadiers working together shocked him. He felt the rhythm of their push deep down in his chest.

A Kez soldier threw himself over the line, crashing into Taniel and sending him back. The grenadiers closed up the empty spot, not missing a beat. Taniel wrestled with the soldier, throwing him to the ground and pressing his boot to the man's throat. A glance at the line, and then...

Out of the corner of his eye he saw a Warden tear through the grenadiers. The biggest and strongest that Adro had to offer were scattered like toys as the creature breached the line.

Another Warden crashed through. Colonel Etan staggered back, his brow bloodied. He recovered quickly, slashing with his heavy saber, taking the Warden's hand off at the wrist. The Warden threw himself forward and snatched Etan by the throat, picking up a man of fifteen stone and shaking him as a dog might a rat.

A trumpet sounded.

Retreat.

Fury tore through Taniel. No. He wouldn't fall back. He wasn't leaving this field without a victory.

Taniel snarled, the soldier beneath his boot forgotten. He could see Etan's eyes roll back as he went into shock. Taniel hefted his rifle, bayonet ready, and charged.

Something slammed into him from the side. He flew, a few moments of uncontrolled tumble sending his heart lurching before he hit the ground, bouncing off an infantryman's body. The jolt sent Taniel's rifle sliding from his hands, and when he came to his feet, he was unarmed.

There wasn't time to react. This new Warden was too fast. A heavy fist pummeled his face, sending him spinning.

Taniel righted himself, bracing for another blow. Mentally, he touched a bit of powder. There was no reaction. This was a Black Warden.

The next blow failed to land as the Warden thrashed about, Ka-poel on his back. She hung on by one of her long needles, which was buried deep into the meat of the creature's shoulder. She'd missed his spine by inches, and the needle could do nothing but infuriate him.

Taniel drew his boot knife. He squared his shoulders, ready to leap, when the Warden suddenly stiffened. He lurched forward, dropping to his knees. Ka-poel calmly withdrew her needle and stepped away from the Warden. She wore a vicious smile and in one hand held a half-formed wax doll. Her fingers worked furiously to finish the doll.

The Warden came to its feet, still wobbling, still lurching. It staggered to one side and then suddenly flew forward, charging the Kez.

Perhaps half the grenadiers still stood, their line ragged and broken, with more of them dropping beneath Kez infantry every second. The Warden cleared them with a single leap, landing among the Kez.

Most of the infantry ignored him. They were used to the Wardens, of course. It wasn't until this one took a discarded saber in his hand and began slicing up the Kez ranks that horror began to spread.

The panic was palpable. Taniel watched as the Kez began to scream and back away from the Warden. Some tried to stand and fight. Some even attacked him. A bayonet speared the Warden through the neck and the creature snapped the steel bayonet off the end of the musket and kept fighting. The Kez began to waver.

Taniel had killed Wardens in hand-to-hand combat, the same creatures that terrorized the Adran army, and now Ka-poel had turned one on the Kez. A thrill worked its way up from his toes until it reached his fingertips, and Taniel wondered just what he'd become that allowed him to fight a ferocious monster like that.

"To me!" He lifted his rifle over his head. "To me!" he shouted above the sound of the trumpets, blaring louder and louder for the grenadiers to retreat. "Bugger the trumpets, we fight!"

The Kez began to crumple. None of their snare drums were calling a retreat, but they fled all the same. The few Wardens left on the field were finally overpowered and mercilessly slaughtered. Some of the Kez threw down their weapons and fell to their knees in surrender.

The Warden that Ka-poel controlled chased the Kez almost the whole way back to their camp. A dozen other Wardens had congregated to try to put it down.

Ka-poel's eyes were alight with glee, and the wax figurine in her hands twitched and spun. Her lips opened in a silent laugh.

The Warden fought on. Stabbed, shot, sliced: it would not fall.

And then Ka-poel lifted the doll and pushed the head off with one thumb.

The Warden collapsed.

Taniel stared, openmouthed, at Ka-poel. How could this girl, the same woman who had pressed herself against him so intimately, fall asleep in his arms like a child one minute and then take to the battlefield with the power of a vengeful goddess the next?

She turned, as if feeling his gaze, and flashed him a shy smile. In an instant she was once again the girl he'd rescued from a dirty hut in the swamps of Fatrasta.

Taniel wanted to rush to her, to carry her away from this madness, to make sure that she was all right. But she wasn't his to protect, not anymore. Not since Kresim Kurga. He had a feeling that who—or what—Ka-poel really was had just begun to show itself.

Ignoring his own wounds, Taniel began to cast about for Colonel Etan. He found the grenadier beneath a dead Warden. Taniel rolled the corpse away. Etan was still breathing, much to Taniel's relief, but there was a profound look of panic in his eyes.

"I can't move my legs," Etan said.

Taniel dropped to his knees beside Etan and felt that same panic begin to rise within him. "It's all right," Taniel said. "We'll get you a surgeon."

"I can't feel my legs!" Etan gripped Taniel's arm. He gasped, and Taniel could see the strain on his face as he tried to move. "I can't feel them!"

Taniel felt his heart crack. Etan was one of the strongest men he knew. To die in battle was one thing, but to be broken...

"Get me a surgeon!" Taniel yelled. "And tell them to stop with the bloody trumpets. We won already, damn it!"

Etan seemed to sag. "We won?"

"We won." Taniel looked around the field. He could see soldiers running from the Adran side, coming to provide backup. If there wasn't a surgeon among them, he'd strangle someone.

"You held it," Etan said. "You held the line."

"No. You did. You and your grenadiers."

"Couldn't have done it without you." Etan was blinking rapidly now. Taniel searched him for a wound, trying to find something. Etan's fingers grasped the sleeve of Taniel's jacket, his knuckles bone white, his face drawn in pain. "I saw the way my boys looked at you. They would have followed you all the way to the pit just now. Just like Tamas. Just like your father."

"Don't say horrid shit like that," Taniel said. He felt hot tears on his cheeks. "I'm nothing like that old bastard."

"Taniel. Promise me you'll win this thing. Promise me you'll finish this. That this won't be the last victory Adro has."

"No need for promises," Taniel said. "You're not dying."

Etan pulled Taniel close. "I can't feel my bloody legs. I know what that means, you ass. I won't see a battlefield again. So you promise me now that you'll win this thing."

"I don't know if I can," Taniel said.

Etan slapped him. Taniel felt his cheek burn from the force of the blow. "Promise me." Another sharp blow nearly turned Taniel around. Even lying on the ground, unable to move his legs, Etan was strong. "Promise it!"

A woman, one of the surgeons, threw herself to the ground on Etan's opposite side. She looked him over, a frown on her face. "Where's the wound?"

"My back's broken," Etan said. His voice cracked. He looked Taniel in the eyes. "Promise me."

"No."

Etan's eyes were glassy with tears. "Coward. If I were dying, you'd promise me. Because you wouldn't have to answer to me then. But I'm not dying, and you won't promise it. Bloody coward."

Taniel turned his face away. He knew it was true.

They brought out a cart, one of the ambulances with a covered top and four cots to hold the wounded, to take Etan back to camp. Etan turned his head away from Taniel, and Taniel didn't walk beside him as they carted him away.

They had destroyed the Kez attack. Probably a thousand of the enemy soldiers dead. Twice that many wounded and another few hundred taken prisoner. It took Taniel a moment to realize he was surrounded by soldiers. The Twelfth Grenadiers. The smallest of them was a hand taller than Taniel. He wondered how many had died in the melee. Their losses had to be staggering.

One of them approached him. Taniel thought about turning away. He could push through them and head back to camp. Had they been listening? Did they hear their colonel tell Taniel he was a coward?

The stout man had his bearskin hat in one hand. His other hand was empty. Clenched in a fist. Taniel lifted his chin and waited to be punched.

"Sir," the grenadier said.

"Go ahead. I deserve it."

The grenadier seemed confused. He looked down at his fist, then flattened his hand. "Sir, you're not a coward. The colonel... no man wants to end up like that. The things he said... you're not a coward. We just watched you charge a brigade of Kez infantry *by yourself.* I want you to know: If you need something, anything, you just say so. I'll be there. I suspect most of these boys will say the same."

There was a round of nodding, and then the grenadiers began to trudge wearily back to camp.

Taniel stood alone in the field for several minutes, watching the surgeons cart off the dead and wounded. He felt someone behind him. He didn't have to turn around. Ka-poel.

He wiped the tears from his face with the sleeve of his jacket. "Don't you have bodies to examine, or some such thing?" he asked.

She took his hand. He wanted to pull away, but couldn't.

They stood together in silence as the blood of the living and the dead and the dying mingled together and made a red sea of Adran soil. Taniel lifted her hand in his. The movement was impulsive, sudden, and he wondered later what thought drove him, but he touched her hand to his lips firmly.

"I'm going to end this," he said. "I'm going to kill Kresimir. For good. You need his blood? I'll get it, even if I die doing it."

Out of the corner of his eye he saw her give a slight shake of her head.

Without warning she stepped in front of him and wrapped one hand around the back of his head and pulled him down to her, pressing her warm lips against his. It seemed as if fire raced through his veins at the touch, and when she finally stepped away, he was breathless. He fought the impulse to drop to his knees, telling himself it was just blood loss that left him so weak.

Then the moment was past, and silent as always, Ka-poel went about her business, leaning over the body of a dead Adran soldier.

Stunned, Taniel watched her for several minutes until something far behind the Kez line brought him out of his reverie. In an instant he was a soldier again: vigilant, watchful, ready to defend against new threats from the enemy.

The Kez soldiers were raising something into the sky above their camp, just north of Budwiel's city walls. It must have been eight stories high for him to be able to see it from this distance. He took a small hit of powder, sharpening his eyes.

It was an immense beam, hewn from what looked to be one giant tree. Soldiers and prisoners milled about the base and spread out in a fan behind it, pulling on long ropes tied to the top of the beam. It was lifted high and then suddenly it dropped ten or twenty feet—probably into a slot dug out of the ground—to stand straight in the air.

Taniel frowned. He could see something on the side of the beam. A person?

He focused his powder-heightened eyes. Yes. A woman, it seemed. Stripped naked, she was nailed to the beam by her wrists, and her hands were missing. A rope about her waist secured her to the beam.

Taniel was taken aback. Was she a traitor of some kind, put up there as a warning? The missing hands would indicate she'd been a Privileged. What could…

The body moved. Bloody pit, she was alive.

Her head lifted, and Taniel felt his blood go cold. He knew her. She'd fought him in Kresim Kurga, the holy city, when he tried to keep her from summoning Kresimir.

It was Julene.

CHAPTER
18

Tamas waited for the return of his night scouts and listened to the familiar sounds of his soldiers breaking camp.

There was a light chatter this morning—something missing over the last two weeks' worth of march since the fall of Budwiel. Someone laughed in the distance. Nothing like a full belly to bring a man's spirits up. Combine that with elation at the victory over the Kez vanguard, and Tamas could almost call his men happy.

Almost.

Tamas didn't like eating horse. It reminded him of hard times in Gurla, of starvation and disease and the desert heat, when they'd been forced to slaughter their own healthy horses to stay alive. The taste was slightly sweet, and gamier than beef. Meat that came from cavalry chargers tended to be tough.

Then again, at least his stomach didn't rumble.

"What is it, soldier?"

Vlora stood at attention on the other side of his cook fire. She snapped off a salute.

"Kez spotted, sir. Riding under a white flag."

Tamas flicked a bit of fat into the fire and watched it sizzle. He stood up, wiping his hands on an already soiled handkerchief. Another problem they faced—no camp followers meant no laundresses. Both his uniforms were dirty and stained, and he smelled like a cesspool.

Adom forbid you do your own laundry, a little voice in the back of his head said. Tamas chuckled.

"Sir?" Vlora asked.

"Nothing, soldier. I'll meet them on the edge of camp. Olem!"

"Coming, sir."

Tamas was joined by Olem and a small bodyguard of Olem's Riflejacks. Among the Ninth, stationed as the rear guard, the last tents were being rolled and stowed in packs and cook fires put out. They'd be on the march in twenty minutes. The advance elements of the Seventh were already half a mile down the road.

He passed a row of wagons. They'd been able to salvage them from the abandoned remains of Hune Dora. The bottoms were already stained from the blood of the wounded, and they smelled like death at ten paces. Today, they would carry the wounded that had survived the last two days.

"Have those washed out," Tamas said to Olem. "In fact, I want bathing mandatory. There's plenty of mountain streams in these woods. Organize it with the scouts. I want fifty men to stop and bathe in every mountain stream we pass. If we don't look to ourselves, we'll have disease rampant in the camp."

"Yes, sir." Olem rubbed at his dust-caked uniform. "I could use a little freshening up myself."

They left the edge of the Adran camp and passed the rear pickets. The forest beyond was still, the only sounds that of chattering squirrels and the call of birds. Tamas welcomed the birdsong.

It reminded him of peace, distracted him from the harsh call of the carrion crows and the memory of piled corpses that lingered behind his eyes.

Tamas saw the Kez riders before they saw him.

There were a dozen of them. They were still mounted upon their chargers in the middle of the road, watching the Adran pickets impassively. They wore the heavy breastplates of cuirassiers over tan uniforms with green trim. They dismounted as Tamas drew closer and one of them removed his helmet and approached.

"Field Marshal Tamas?"

"I am he," Tamas said.

"I am General Beon je Ipille," he said in Adran with a light accent. He extended his hand. "The pleasure is mine."

Tamas took the general's hand. Beon was a young man, perhaps in his late twenties. His face was boyish, touched by the same cabal sorceries that kept every king of the Nine looking young far beyond their years. That alone would have told Tamas that Beon was one of Ipille's sons, if not for the name and reputation.

"The king's favored son. Your reputation precedes you."

Beon tilted his head modestly. "And you, yours."

"To what do I owe the honor?" Tamas said. This was all a formality, of course. Tamas knew why Beon was here.

"I've come to inquire as to your intentions in my country."

"Only to return to my own, and defend it from the aggression of a tyrant."

Beon didn't even blink at the insult against his father. Tamas made a mental note of that. He was more levelheaded than his older brothers, it seemed. "I'm afraid I can't let you do that."

"So we are at an impasse."

"Not an impasse, I think," Beon said. "I've come to request your surrender."

"An impasse. I will not surrender," Tamas said flatly.

Beon nodded, as if to himself. "I was afraid you would say that."

"Afraid?" Tamas knew Beon's reputation. Fear didn't enter into it. Beon was almost recklessly brave. He seized opportunities a lesser commander might balk at. His courage had served him well.

"I do not relish chasing the great Field Marshal Tamas. You've already seen to my vanguard—how do you say, sending them back with their tails tucked between their legs?" He looked over his shoulder at one of the other riders. The rider was a dragoon, with a straight sword and lacking the breastplate of a cuirassier. "Their commanders barely escaped with their lives."

"You could just let me go on my way," Tamas said jovially. "I'll be out of your country in a few weeks."

Beon chuckled. "And my father would have my head. Your men are hungry, Tamas. You have no food, other than the horsemeat you salvaged from my vanguard. I'll be fair. I'll tell you what you face, and then you can decide whether to surrender. Yes?"

Tamas snorted. "That is more than fair."

"Good. I have ten thousand dragoons and fifty-five hundred cuirassiers under my command. My elder brother is about a week's march behind me with thirty thousand infantry. I know you have eleven thousand men. We outnumber you four to one. You have no hope of escaping this country. Surrender now, and your men will be treated with respect as prisoners of war." He paused and lifted his hand, as if swearing upon the Rope. "I've studied you, Tamas. You do not throw your men's lives away in needless causes."

"If you've studied me," Tamas said quietly, "you'll know that I do not lose."

Beon's expression was bemused. "You are a dead man, Tamas. Do you have any requests?"

"Yes. I have over a hundred wounded. If I hand them over to you, will they be treated with respect as prisoners of war?"

"So that you may travel faster? No. Any wounded that fall into our hands will be executed as criminals."

Beon was a gentleman through and through. It was entirely likely he was bluffing. Did Tamas dare risk it?

"Then, General, I have no more to say to you."

Beon gave a respectful nod. "I would wish you good luck, but . . ."

"I understand."

The Kez remounted and were off down the road within minutes. Tamas watched them go. That general would be trouble. Incompetence was practically bred into the Kez army, where nobles could purchase their commission or find themselves a general at the whim of the king.

Once in a while, though, talent rose above the chaff.

"Olem," Tamas said.

The bodyguard snapped to attention, but his eyes never left the direction the Kez had gone. Tamas knew he was itching for a fight.

"Sir?"

"Get me an ax and meet me at the head of the column."

The basic kits of all Adran infantry included a hand ax and a shovel. They were meant for cutting firewood and digging latrine pits.

A good commander utilized them for far more.

Tamas gathered his horse and rode to the front of the column. He found Colonel Arbor at the vanguard with his First Battalion. The colonel flexed his jaw, popping his false teeth out into one hand as Tamas fell in beside him.

"Nice day, sir. Trees keep the forest cool."

Tamas examined the road. It winded along a steep, heavily forested hillside. Enough light reached the ground for there to be a thick undergrowth; thorny and tangled. Without the road, the terrain would be nearly impossible to traverse.

"A word, Colonel," Tamas said. "Pick two platoons and bring them off to the side."

Arbor hollered for the Nineteenth and Thirty-Fourth Platoons. By the time they'd shuffled off the road and into the forest, Olem had joined them. He dismounted and handed Tamas an ax.

Tamas removed his jacket and his shirt and looked around at the men. "We have fifteen thousand cavalry dogging our tails," he said. "On horseback, they travel faster and easier than us. I mean to change that. Every time there's a narrowing in the terrain, like that one there"—he pointed to where the road cut into the hillside up ahead—"we're going to drop a few tons of rubble there. Gather rocks, fell trees. Any kind of debris. As soon as the column has passed, we're going to stop it up."

Tamas picked a nearby tree. It was wide enough that three men couldn't have reached around its base. It would do perfectly. He positioned himself on the side of the tree facing the road and began to chop.

The two platoons set about hacking at trees with axes and billhooks and gathering everything they could from the nearby forest. They stacked great piles beside the road. Tamas pulled two more platoons out of the column, and by the time the last of his men had passed, they had half a dozen immense trees ready to fall across the road.

Tamas turned his head at the sound of an approaching rider.

It was only Gavril. He reined in beside Tamas.

"You the last of our scouts back there?" Tamas asked.

"Aye," Gavril said. "The Kez are a mile behind me. They're not coming hard. I don't think they're in a hurry." He examined the work Tamas had been doing. "Cutting trees like a logger. I like this side of you. I hope all this work was worth it."

"It'll take them hours to clear this," Tamas said.

"Or they'll go around."

Tamas wiped the sweat from his brow. If they found a way through the forest, all of this was for naught. "Can they?"

"They'll have to scout it," Gavril said. "And they'll be cautious in case you've laid a trap. You might have bought us some time."

Tamas took his shirt from Olem, and a soldier brought him his charger. He climbed into the saddle. "Bring 'em down!" he shouted to the soldiers.

A few minutes later the trees crashed to the ground. They were felled so that they lay across each other, wedged to block the road. It wouldn't be as simple as throwing a rope around them and dragging them away with teams of horses.

The rest of the rubble was thrown to block the way, and Tamas ordered the platoons to march double-time to catch up with the rest of the column.

"Have your scouts find me good spots to block the road," Tamas said to Gavril.

"Consider it done."

"Olem, see that those two platoons are given a double ration of horsemeat tonight. They earned it."

"Yes, sir."

Tamas shrugged into his shirt. "Put your mind to anything else we can use to slow down the Kez. They might still dog us with a company or two, but I want to keep the bulk of their numbers as far behind us as possible."

"I heard you met with the Kez general," Gavril said.

"I did. It was Beon je Ipille. Ipille's youngest son."

Gavril grunted. "I've heard he's a decent sort—for Ipille's spawn, anyway."

"He is."

"How did it go?" Gavril asked.

"I have one regret and one hope."

Gavril seemed intrigued. "Your hope?"

"That I didn't make a grave mistake refusing to surrender."

"And your regret?"

"It's too bad Beon wasn't Ipille's first son. He'd have made a terrific king. I'm going to regret killing him."

"I came as quickly as I could," Adamat said.

"Have a seat."

Adamat took a chair opposite Ricard and leaned back. Ricard's face was grave. What hair remained on his balding head stuck out everywhere in unkempt wisps, and his eyes were tired, his beard uncombed, clothes rumpled. Very unlike Ricard.

Ricard stared at the floor. "You heard the news?" he asked, gesturing to the newspaper on his desk.

The paper proclaiming the death of Field Marshal Tamas was a week old now.

"All of Adro has heard it," Adamat said.

Ricard finally looked up. When he glimpsed Adamat's face, he nearly fell out of his chair. "What the pit happened to you?"

Adamat would have snorted if it didn't hurt so badly to do so. He imagined he looked far worse off than Ricard. Little sleep, his nose recently broken and reset, cuts and bruises all across his face. Adamat was a horror, and it was interfering with his work. No one liked being seen doing business with someone who'd had the piss beaten out of them.

"I've had a few run-ins lately," Adamat said.

Ricard waited for an explanation. Adamat wasn't about to give him one.

"Yes, well..." Ricard slowly tore his gaze from Adamat's face. "The country is in an uproar. The Kez are pushing the southern front, and with Tamas gone a few royalists have come out of the woodwork. He was the glue holding this whole nation together." Ricard ran his fingers through his hair. "Tamas's remaining councillors... we've already started bickering among ourselves. I don't know what we're going to do."

"Are you going ahead with the election?"

Ricard threw up his hands in exasperation. "We have no choice. We could declare martial law and delay the election, but the entire army is on the southern front trying to fight back the Kez." Ricard rubbed his eyes. "Which brings me to why I asked you to come in: Lord Claremonte is making his move."

Adamat sat up straighter. "And?"

Ricard spit on the floor, then seemed to immediately regret having done so. "He's declared his intention to run for prime minister of Adro."

"How could he?" Adamat breathed in disbelief. "He's not even Adran!"

"Ah, but he is. Or at least that's what the records he provided to the Ministerial Review Board says. Fell! Fell, get in here!"

The young woman Adamat had previously met slipped into the room. Her hair was done up in a braid that went over one shoulder, and she wore a frilled blouse loose about the neck. "Sir?"

"Fell, what have you got on Claremonte?"

"Nothing," Fell said. "If his birth records are forgeries, they're extremely good. We have people going over all the information we have on him. He's never actually claimed to be Brudanian, and the Brudania-Gurla Trading Company doesn't require Brudanian citizenship to become the head."

Adamat found himself watching Fell, suddenly suspicious, and he wasn't quite sure why. "Keep . . . keep talking," Adamat said.

"Sir?" Fell asked.

"Have you found a stronger connection to Lord Vetas?" Adamat's own knowledge about Vetas and Claremonte's relationship came through the Proprietor's eunuch, and through Vetas's own admission. If he'd been misled in some way, it could derail his entire line of inquiry.

"None that we can find."

"Why could he possibly want to be prime minister of Adro? Ricard, didn't you tell me yourself that the prime minister will be a figurehead?"

Ricard shifted uncomfortably in his chair. "That is *my* vision of the prime minster, yes."

"The truth is," Fell said, without waiting for Ricard's instruction, "the first prime minister will be the one to set the standard for every one to follow him. How much power the prime minister holds, and how he wields it, will depend entirely on how aggressive the first man to hold the office decides to be."

Adamat smoothed the front of his jacket. What was bothering him so much about this woman? There was something about her mannerisms that he'd not noticed before...something he couldn't quite put his finger on. "So if Claremonte is elected, there is the potential for him to wield as much power in Adro as a king?"

"Not as much as a king," Ricard said. "The design of the system has put parameters on that. However...quite a lot of power."

"Pit," Adamat said.

Fell crossed to Ricard's side. "Sir, if I may..."

"That's it!" Adamat stared at her.

"What?" Ricard asked.

Adamat reached in his pocket slowly, grasping the butt of his pistol. "You have the same way of speaking," he said to Fell. "Some of the same cadence as he does. It's not readily noticeable. Not like you're family or anything, but as if you've been trained at the same finishing school."

"As who?" Ricard asked.

"Lord Vetas."

Ricard and Fell exchanged a look.

"This is bad," Fell said.

Ricard agreed. "Very bad."

Adamat's gaze moved between the two. He found himself squeezing the butt of his pistol in one hand and the head of his cane with the other. He felt his jaw clench. What was going on here? What did they know that he didn't?

Ricard said to Fell, "I'm going to tell him."

"This isn't common knowledge," Fell said with a frown.

"What the pit are you two talking about?" Adamat asked.

Ricard leaned forward on his desk, leaning his chin on one hand. "Have you heard of the Fontain Academy in Starland?"

"No," Adamat said. Neither Ricard nor Fell seemed unduly ready to leap at him, so he loosened his grip on his pistol and cane. "A finishing school?" he guessed.

"Of a sort," Ricard said. "It's a very exclusive place. Of every thousand students they have, only one graduates."

"What makes it so difficult?" Adamat asked.

"The rigors," Fell spoke up. "Eighteen hours of work every day for twenty years. Training of every sort: martial, sexual, memory retention, etiquette, mathematics, science, politics, philosophy. Exposure to every school of thought in the known world. No contact with friends or family for the rest of your life. The willingness to become beholden to one man or organization against bribery or threat of pain or death."

"Sounds awful," Adamat said. "I would have heard of such a place."

"No," Ricard said. "You wouldn't have."

Fell was looking at her fingernails. "Only prospective clients know about the Fontain Academy. It costs as much as thirty million krana to purchase a graduate."

"Purchase? So it's slavery?" Adamat rocked back in his chair. Thirty million krana. That was a kingly sum. There were less than fifty people in all the Nine with access to that much money, and he didn't think Ricard was one of them.

Adamat wasn't sure if he believed this. How could an organization like that exist? Certainly slavery was still openly practiced in the world, but in the Nine? Not for hundreds of years. "Are you asking me to believe that you and Lord Vetas are graduates of the Fontain Academy?"

"It appears that way," Fell said. "I couldn't confirm it for certain, but for you to make the observation you did transcends coincidence."

"Then what can you tell me about him?"

"Every graduate has different specialties. But if he is a graduate, then he's dangerous. He'll be adept at blackmail and sabotage. He'll be smarter than most of the people in this city, including you. Proficient with all weapons, but likely favoring knives and pistols."

"What's your specialty?" Adamat asked.

Fell gave him a thin smile but didn't answer.

"Can we speak alone?" he asked Ricard.

Ricard nodded to Fell.

"Sir," Fell said. "The Fontain Academy is not a secret, strictly, but we do not advertise ourselves. This information is to be kept private."

"I'll respect that," Adamat said.

Fell left the room, leaving him alone with Ricard.

Adamat watched his friend for nearly a minute before he spoke. "You *purchased* a woman?"

"Adamat..."

"I didn't think even you would stoop to that."

"It's not like that, I—"

"It's not, is it?" Adamat raised his eyebrows.

"Well, maybe a little. But that's not why I did it."

"Then why?"

Ricard's face grew grim. "I love this country. I love my union. I will not see either torn apart by the machinations of a foreigner. I'll be the first prime minister if it kills me—or if I have to kill to do it."

"When?"

"When what?"

"When did you...purchase...her?"

"I finalized it over the summer. She arrived four weeks ago."

"And where the pit did you get thirty million krana?"

"She was ten million," Ricard said. "About half my fortune. She's only had ten years of schooling at the academy—it's normally twenty years."

Adamat shook his head. "Ten million for that girl. What were you thinking?"

"She runs my organization better than I can," Ricard said quietly. "In one month—just one—she's made me fifty thousand krana. She's straightened my ministerial campaign. Before her I had some good ideas, but now I have a serious chance at being the prime minister of Adro. She's worth every penny I spent on her."

"Can you trust her? What's to stop her from killing you and taking control of the union, if she's so smart."

Ricard said, "Loyalty. For the next thirty years of her life she belongs to me. It's the price of schooling at the Fontain Academy. And reputation. If she were to turn on me in some way, the academy would kill her themselves."

Adamat smoothed the front of his coat again. This was all too much. "That reminds me," Adamat said. "I need to borrow money."

"You still owe Palagyi money?" Ricard said, seemingly relieved to steer the conversation away from Fell. "I'm glad you finally got some sense into you. What the pit was that all about, refusing to let me pay him?"

"Palagyi is dead. And no, not that. I need fifty thousand krana. Now. In banknotes."

Ricard blinked at him. "Fifty? I can write a check for fifty. I'd do it in a heartbeat for you."

"It needs to be cash."

"Can't do it. No bank in Adro would let me take out fifty thousand all at once. I could have it for you in a couple of weeks."

"That's too long," Adamat said. He rubbed his eyes. Ricard was his only hope of getting the money to pay Colonel Verundish to release Bo. How could he himself possibly come up with that sum in a week?

Well, perhaps Ricard wasn't the only hope.

"You smell like the southbound end of a northbound ass," Gavril said.

Tamas sat and watched his charger nibble on a bit of dry grass beside the road. The column had stopped for a short rest, and he was up near the vanguard.

In the distance Tamas could hear the crack of rifles. Another Kez scouting party close enough to engage. The Kez had been dogging their heels ever since Tamas's meeting with General Beon. Their dragoons stayed close, traveling in groups of ten or twenty, flanking the rear guard and causing whatever mayhem they could.

Tamas was weary of it. He'd set a dozen traps, killed hundreds of Kez dragoons, but his men couldn't even stop to scavenge or they risked finding themselves flanked by more than just a few squads.

Gavril sniffed at the wind, as if to punctuate his previous statement.

Tamas looked down at his uniform. The dark blue didn't show stains badly, but the silver-and-gold trim had seen better days, and the linen shirt beneath the jacket was yellowed from sweat, the cuffs stained dark from powder burns and dirt. A thin crust of dirt covered his face and hands like a second skin, and he didn't dare imagine how his feet might smell once he peeled off his boots.

"I smell fine," he told his brother-in-law.

"First rule of bathing," Gavril said. "If you can't smell yourself anymore, it's time to wash. We're stopped for lunch. The last of the horsemeat is gone, so the least we can do is give the men an hour of rest. Follow that stream back there up a few hundred yards and there's a waterfall. Might give you some privacy."

"Are you going to give me your report?"

"After you bathe."

Tamas examined Gavril for a few moments. He was a different man from the one Tamas had met so many years ago. Jakola of Pensbrook had been a svelte, dashing character with a clean-shaven chin and broad shoulders. Gavril had gained a lot of weight during his time at the Mountainwatch. He carried it well, but Gavril would still be here long after the rest of them had starved to death.

The morbid thought gave Tamas a chuckle.

"I'm serious," Gavril said.

Tamas climbed to his feet. It couldn't be helped. A sudden boyish impulse struck him and he flipped Gavril a rude gesture before heading down the column. Men lay about the road, their uniforms soaked with sweat. No one saluted him. Tamas didn't make an issue of it. A ways down the resting column, two men broke out in a fistfight. Their sergeant broke it up quickly. People were growing hungry again, and tensions would only get higher.

He found the stream where a few dozen soldiers had stripped to nothing, washing themselves in the cold mountain water. Tamas passed them and headed upstream.

The stream cut through a gully, surrounded on either side by steep earthen walls. The trees rose even farther, towering hundreds of feet above him, giving Tamas the slight feeling of claustrophobia.

As the stream cut around a corner, Tamas could hear the rush of falling water. He stopped and examined the top of the gully. This was a horrible place to be. An army could come upon him, and he wouldn't hear it over the sound of the waterfall.

Every stop had pickets out a quarter of a mile. No one would come upon him without warning.

Tamas rounded the bend to find Olem was there already, stripped down to his trousers, standing with his face up against the shower of falling water.

Tamas stepped toward him, and a word of greeting died on his lips.

Vlora stood under the waterfall with Olem. She was completely nude, her uniform discarded with the rest of her gear on the bank of the stream. Olem had his hands in her dark hair, pulling them through the knots and tangles. She said something and Olem laughed, and then she turned toward him. She pushed her body up against Olem's. She opened her mouth, and Olem tilted his head down toward hers.

Her eyes flickered open. She stepped smoothly past Olem and turned her body away from Tamas. Olem said something, then stole a furtive glance at Tamas. He was suddenly washing his own hair vigorously.

"What's wrong?" A hand thumped Tamas's shoulder. "Haven't seen a naked woman before?" Gavril passed Tamas, heading toward the waterfall, already stripping off his shirt.

Tamas's heart leapt, and he said a silent prayer of thanks that he didn't jump two feet in the air. He quickly grew conscious of his voyeurism. He could feel his face growing red, so he strode to the waterfall, stripping off his uniform.

Vlora left the water and gathered her knapsack, dressing quickly. A minute later and Tamas was alone with Gavril and Olem.

"You know," Gavril said to Olem, tossing his uniform on the rocks beside the stream, "you're supposed to take your pants off when you shower."

Olem cleared his throat and gave an uncomfortable laugh. He glanced in the direction Vlora had gone.

Gavril gave a belly-shaking laugh. "That is a good-looking woman. I can see why you left 'em on." He elbowed Olem in the ribs, nearly knocking him over. Olem gave him a lopsided grin. A glance at Tamas and his grin disappeared.

"Vlora was engaged to Taniel," Tamas said. "Up until the beginning of this summer." He stared at Olem. What had he walked in upon? Had this been going on long, or was it a chance thing?

If Gavril noticed the tension, he ignored it. "Not engaged to him anymore, is she?" He shrugged his big shoulders. "Fine-looking woman is a fine-looking woman. Her being unpromised is only a bonus."

"I sometimes forget your . . . habits . . . with women."

Gavril squared his body to Tamas, unashamed of his nudity. "You also forgot about that string of seventeen-year-old noble daughters trying to bag the most eligible bachelor in the Nine the year after Erika died . . . before we went to Kez. How many of those did you bed?"

Tamas had forgotten all about bathing. He clutched his jacket in one hand, jaw clenched. "Watch your mouth, Jakola."

At some point Olem had left the waterfall and gathered his shirt, jacket, and pistol from the ground. He began to slink downstream.

"We're going to have a talk, Olem," Tamas said.

Olem froze. Drops of water hung in his sandy beard.

Gavril's thick finger prodded Tamas in the chest. "You've had your share of women, Tamas. Including my sister. That means I can say what I want."

Tamas looked down at Gavril's finger, seriously considering snapping it off. Who the pit did he think he was, speaking to Tamas like that? If they'd been in public, Tamas would have had no choice but to call him out. As it were, he wanted to punch him in the nose. In a fight, Gavril had the strength and weight. Tamas had the speed, and if he had powder, it was no contest. He could...

He stopped himself. Here he was, deep in Kez territory, pursued by an army four times the size of his, and all he wanted was to feel clean again before the next battle. What was he doing? Gavril wasn't his enemy.

A glance over his shoulder told him Olem had gone.

"You're too much of a hard-ass, Tamas," Gavril said.

Tamas hung his uniform on the protruding root of a tree and stepped under the waterfall. The initial shock struck him to the core. The water was cold as ice, runoff from the mountain peaks towering over them to the east.

"Sweet Kresimir!" He felt his leg stiffen with the cold.

"I've taken colder baths at the Mountainwatch," Gavril said.

Tamas looked downstream, the way Olem had gone. "Vlora was engaged to my Taniel. He could be dead now, for all I know. I'll not have—"

"The engagement was broken off," Gavril cut him off. "You told me so yourself. Let it go. How many times did you fool around behind Erika's back?"

"None," Tamas said. His voice came out colder than the stream.

Gavril made a face like he didn't believe a word of it. He opened his mouth, but Tamas spoke first.

"Question my honor," Tamas said. "Just try it."

"Won't say another word about it."

"Good. Now give me your damned report."

"The Kez have fallen back almost eight miles. Some of your road-blocks have worked, some haven't. The cavalry can't be more than two abreast on these roads, so their own column is miles long. They've got scouts ranging everywhere they can through the woods to try to find shortcuts. I have my rangers keeping an eye out for small companies that try to flank us, but so far our worst enemy is the lack of food."

"How long until we reach the Fingers of Kresimir?" Tamas scrubbed his fingers through his mustache. He needed a shave, badly.

"Six days."

"Good."

"About that, I have bad news."

Tamas sighed. "Just what I was hoping to hear."

"The Kez have sent their cuirassiers around to the west to cut across the plains. That's fifty-five hundred heavy cavalry. What they lose in going around Hune Dora they'll gain by having flat ground. If my guess is right, they'll reach the Fingers right about the time we do.

"Last time I went through the Fingers," Gavril continued, "the forest ended about a mile from the first river. Open, flat plain all the way to the water, then a narrow wooden bridge."

"A perfect place for the Kez to trap us."

"Exactly."

Tamas closed his eyes, trying to see the space in his mind. It had been thirteen years since he last passed through the area. "I need to break the Kez."

"What?"

"Break them. I can't have the cavalry dogging us all the way to Deliv. Even if we lose them for a time crossing the Fingers, they'll be there waiting for us in the Northern Expanse, and on the open plateau we won't stand a chance against three brigades of cavalry."

"How are you going to break that many cavalry? You've only got eleven thousand men, Tamas. I've seen you work miracles before, but this is out of your league."

Tamas stepped out from under the cold water and snatched his uniform from the roots. He pulled his pants on over his wet body.

"We're going to march double-time. We can make it in four days. That'll give us preparation time."

"You can't march double for four days on empty stomachs."

Tamas ignored him. "Take twenty of your fastest riders. Take extra horses—some of those we captured from the Kez. Go ahead to the Fingers."

"I thought we were going to slaughter the horses so the men could eat."

"Slaughter them when you get there. I want you to destroy the bridge."

Gavril stepped out of the water and shook his great head, spraying water everywhere. It reminded Tamas of watching a bear fishing in a river. "Are you mad?" Gavril asked.

"Do you trust me?"

Gavril hesitated a few seconds too long. "Yes?"

"Destroy the bridge, slaughter the horses, and start making rafts. Swear your men to silence about the bridge. Once we catch up to you, the story is that the bridge was washed out and you were sent on ahead to build rafts."

"You better have a damned good reason for destroying that bridge before we cross it," Gavril said. "Otherwise my men will string me up for trying to get our whole army killed."

Tamas pulled his jacket on. "Do it. Only take men you trust."

He began walking down the stream as Gavril began to dress. He paused when Gavril called out behind him.

"Tamas," his brother-in-law said. "Try not to get us all slaughtered."

CHAPTER

19

Have you wondered," Taniel said, "why they always sound the retreat?"

He sat at Colonel Etan's bedside in a small inn off the main road in the town of Rue, about two miles behind the front line. It was a quiet town, though the echo of distant artillery still reminded Taniel that there was a war carrying on without them.

Etan was propped up in his bed by a pile of feather pillows. A nurse was stationed just outside the door to see to his needs, while a steady stream of Etan's grenadiers had been coming and going all day, wishing him well and taking orders to the front.

Only a wounded colonel would get this kind of treatment, Taniel knew. He'd heard of a few infantrymen who'd broken their backs. Most died from neglect within a few months.

Taniel watched his friend out of the corner of his eye and made a few marks in his sketchbook, outlining Etan's strong jaw in charcoal.

Etan had refused the offer to step down from his post. Said he could—and would—still command the Twelfth Grenadiers, even if he had to do it from a chair. Rumors were that General Hilanska was going to force Etan's resignation.

Taniel hoped not. Retaining command of his grenadiers was the only thing keeping Etan from surrendering to despair.

"We retreat," Etan said, "because we're always overwhelmed." He dipped a feather pen in an inkwell and finished a sentence on the paper in his lap. He'd cursed and shouted when Taniel had first pulled out his sketchbook. Now he seemed to be doing his best to ignore the fact that Taniel was sketching him.

Taniel studied Etan's face, his mind elsewhere. Something seemed wrong about the trumpets. The retreats. Every damned time. "You know Tamas's campaign history as well as any historian. How many times has he sounded a retreat?"

"Seven, if memory serves."

"Out of how many battles?"

"Hundreds."

"And the last few weeks how many times have we fallen back before the Kez?"

Etan sighed, setting down his feather pen and rubbing his eyes. "Taniel, what does it matter? The generals don't have a choice. It's either fall back with heavy losses or suffer the deaths of every man on the front."

"What if one of the generals is in league with the Kez?" Taniel mused aloud. "Ordering the retreat early each time?"

"Those are dangerous accusations."

"Tamas believed there was a traitor—"

Etan cut him off. "And he was right. He caught the bastard. Charlemund won't see the light of day again, no matter what threats the Church makes."

"Tamas might not have caught all the traitors," Taniel said quietly.

"These generals were handpicked by Tamas. Every one of them has supported him for years, even through the coup—where the risks of failure were high, and they'd all be labeled traitors. They are capable and loyal."

Taniel took a small pinch of powder and snorted it off the back of his hand. He fought to clear his mind. There was a time when the tiniest bit of powder would allow him to focus and think, but it seemed harder and harder to do so.

Powder. That was the other thing bothering him.

"Do you have access to quartermaster reports?" Taniel asked.

Etan finished writing another missive and set it on the table beside his bed. "For my regiment, certainly."

"I don't need them for your regiment. I need them for the entire army. Can you get them?"

"I'd need to pull some strings..."

"Do it."

Etan's mouth hardened into a flat line. "Because I'm so disposed to doing you favors right now."

"Please?" Taniel said, sketching Etan's shoulders.

"Why?"

"Something that's been niggling in the back of my mind. I just want to see how much black powder the army has been using."

"All right," Etan agreed with a sigh. "I'll see what I can do." He fell silent and for several minutes there was nothing but the sound of Etan's feather pen scratching away at the paper. Etan seemed enthralled by his work. Since his paralysis, Etan had rushed head-long into the administrative duties of his rank. He'd spent the last three days checking on supply reports, reading recruitment numbers, and leafing through dossiers of men who might be considered for rank advancement.

Taniel was glad Etan had something to do to keep his mind off his injury.

The sound of Etan's pen suddenly stopped. "How do the Kez

have so many bloody Black Wardens?" he asked. "Didn't—doesn't—your father have a hard time finding them as it is?"

"Can't say for sure," Taniel said as he gave a little more shape to Etan's chin in his drawing. He'd wondered the same thing himself. "The Kez purge their countryside of powder mages every two years and make regular sweeps in the meantime. Tamas always assumed the mages they rounded up were executed. His spies never reported anything else."

Etan tapped the feather pen on the paper. "You think that maybe the Kez have been imprisoning them?"

"That's my thought," Taniel said. "Kez has a much greater population than Adro, which could partly account for their numbers. And I think Kresimir is the one turning them into Powder Wardens. It can't be coincidence that these new bastards appeared at the same time as Kresimir."

Etan began to write again, only to stop a moment later. "Oh," he said. "I got something for you."

"Eh?"

Etan produced a silver snuffbox and handed it to Taniel. "I heard you lost your old one on South Pike. Thought you'd like it."

Taniel flipped open the lid. Inside, it was engraved with the words "Taniel Two-Shot, the Unkillable."

"The Unkillable?" Taniel scoffed.

"That's what the boys have taken to calling you."

"That's absurd. Anyone can be killed." He held out the snuffbox. "I can't take this."

Etan began to cough. He fell back with a grimace, clutching his side. "Take it, you stubborn bastard, or I'll start screaming at you for being a coward again. You and that girl of yours saved our asses out there."

"She's not my girl."

Etan snorted. "Oh, really? Rumors are getting around, Taniel." Etan looked down at his hands. "I shouldn't tell you this, but the

General Staff wants you two separated. Says it's bad for morale, having a war hero gallivanting around with a savage."

"You believe all that? Agree with it?" Taniel stiffened. He didn't have to sit here and listen to this drivel.

Etan made a calming motion. "I see your face when you look at her. Same way you used to look at Vlora." Etan shrugged. "I won't judge. Just warning you about the rumors."

Taniel forced himself to relax. The way he used to look at Vlora? This was almost as preposterous as the grenadiers calling Taniel "unkillable." "What should I do? I'm not going to send her away."

"Marry her?"

Taniel laughed, shaking his head at the absurdity of the statement.

"I'm not joking," Etan said. "The General Staff can say anything they want about propriety, but if she's your wife, they have to stuff it." He began to cough again, harder this time.

"You need rest," Taniel said. Etan's face had turned as pale as Taniel's sketch paper. In the hours of the afternoon Taniel had almost forgotten the severity of Etan's injury. His sudden frailty brought it all back.

"I need to write out more orders."

"Rest." Taniel took the paper and quill from Etan and set them beside the bed. He put the snuffbox there with them and headed for the door.

"Taniel."

"Yes?"

Etan plucked the snuffbox off his bedside table and tossed it to Taniel, who caught it in one hand.

"Take it," Etan said. "Or I'll have you shot."

"All right, all right. I'll take it." He closed the door behind him.

Ka-poel was waiting in the hallway, sitting on the ground just outside the door with her legs crossed, one of her wax dolls in hand.

She stowed it and stood up. If she'd heard what Etan had to say about her, she gave no indication.

"Can you do anything for him?" Taniel asked.

A slight shake of her head.

"Damn it, Pole. You practically brought me back from the dead, and you can't…"

She held up a finger, her forehead wrinkling in a frown. Taniel thought she might go on, but instead she turned and walked away.

He followed her down and through the common room of the inn, where wounded soldiers talked and drank while they waited to be sent home or back to the front. There was a somber air to the room. A woman sat in one corner, alone, her leg amputated at the knee. She moaned to herself, a lonely keening sound that everyone tried to ignore.

The weather outside didn't improve Taniel's mood. The sky had threatened rain for a week now, every day a little cloudier. Yesterday there'd been a misting drizzle in the evening—just enough to make the grass slick and the fighting all the more treacherous.

Taniel stopped just outside the inn and wondered if he should have gotten a drink before heading back to the front.

A pair of provosts approached from the street. Both carried heavy steel pikes and wore Adran blues with green trim and the insignia of mountains crossed by cudgels.

Coincidence, Taniel wondered, or were they waiting for him?

"Captain Taniel Two-Shot?"

"What?"

"You're to come with us, sir."

Definitely waiting for him. "On whose authority?"

"General Ket's."

"I don't think I'll do that." Taniel touched the butt of his pistol.

"We're placing you under arrest, sir."

Arrest? This had gone too far. "On what charge?"

"That's for General Ket to say."

One stepped forward, taking Taniel by the arm.

Taniel jerked away. "Get your hands off me. I know my rights as a soldier of the Adran army. You'll tell me the charges or you'll go to the pit." Taniel's senses told him that they didn't have an ounce of powder. They'd come ready. For him.

Or had they? The provost jerked hard on Taniel's arm, like he was some kind of unruly child. "Come quiet-like now. We're to bring the girl as well. Where is she?"

Where had Ka-poel gone? Taniel looked around, pulling his arm away from the provost.

"Now, sir! Don't make us—"

Taniel's fist connected with the provost's chin, sending the man to the ground. The other provost lowered his pike and stepped forward threateningly. Taniel shifted to one side, grabbed the pike by the shaft, and jerked the man off balance. The provost stumbled forward, and Taniel planted a fist into the side of his head.

The first provost came to his feet, already swinging. His ears were red, his face twisted in an angry grimace at having been sucker punched to the ground. The provost was easily a head taller than Taniel and weighed four stone more.

Taniel caught the provost's fist and slammed his opposite hand into the man's elbow. He heard the snap, saw the blood and the white bone sticking out of the flesh.

The provost's scream drew more attention than Taniel wanted. He let the man fall to the ground and then started walking briskly toward the front.

Arrest him? General Ket had the gall to arrest him? It seemed like Taniel was the only thing left between the Kez and Adopest. He'd killed half of their remaining Privileged, giving the Wings a clear advantage on the field, and he'd run out of room for notches on his rifle, he'd killed so many infantry.

Ka-poel joined him a few moments later. One minute he was walking alone, trying to ignore the stares of anyone who'd seen him break a provost's arm, and the next she was beside him, strolling along as if nothing had happened.

"Where the pit were you?"

Ka-poel didn't respond.

"Well…" Taniel gritted his teeth. Pit. A general had an arrest warrant out for him. They'd come sooner or later, in force. What could he do? Break the arms of every provost in the army? "If they come again, disappear just like that. I don't want them getting their damned hands on you."

She nodded.

Taniel felt his steps grow in purpose as he headed back toward the front. He changed his course a little and went toward the cooking tents.

Taniel found his goal in the third mess tent he looked inside.

The master chef, Mihali, was alone inventorying barrels. He held a piece of charcoal in one hand and paper in the other. His long black hair was tied behind his head in a ponytail.

"Good afternoon, Taniel," Mihali said without turning around.

Taniel came up short as the tent flap fell closed behind him. "Have we met?"

"No. But I'm friends with your father. Please, come in."

Taniel stayed warily near the tent flap. Ka-poel had come inside behind him, and she seemed to have no reservations about plopping down on a barrel in one corner.

"Tamas is dead," Taniel said.

"Oh, don't be silly. You don't believe that."

"I've come to accept it."

Mihali still hadn't turned around. Even with his back toward Taniel, he had a kind of presence that made Taniel second-guess his decision to come there. There was something about him. A smell, maybe? No. Something more subtle. Just the slightest sense of familiarity.

"Tamas is very much alive," Mihali said. His lips moved silently, finger wagging as he counted barrels in one corner of the tent. "Along with most of the Seventh and the Ninth. They're being pursued heavily right now by three full brigades of cavalry and six brigades of infantry."

Taniel snorted. "How can you know all that?"

"I *am* Adom reborn."

"So. You *do* claim to be a god?"

Mihali finally turned around with a sigh, making marks on his paper. He had a pudgy, elongated face that spoke of a mix of Adran and Rosvelean ancestry. His white apron was stained with flour and blood, and there was a piece of potato peel stuck to the side of his clean-shaven chin. "Is it that hard to believe? You've attempted to kill one god."

"I saw Kresimir descend from the clouds. I saw his face. I looked upon Kresimir and I knew with every bit of me that he was a god. You…" Taniel trailed off, watching the master chef for the anger that was sure to come.

"Not so much?" Instead of taking offense, Mihali laughed. "Kresimir was always so much better at appearing effortlessly grand. Your father needed to come to believe on his own. You, I think, need a more direct approach." Mihali approached him and held a hand out toward his head. He stopped suddenly, recoiling. Taniel noticed that Mihali's hand was trembling.

"May I?" Mihali asked Ka-poel.

Ka-poel returned his stare, her eyes daring him to try.

Mihali extended his hand once more toward Taniel. As it drew closer, it trembled harder and harder, as if affected by some unseen force. Finally, the chef's fingers brushed Taniel's skin.

Taniel felt a spark.

Then it seemed as if the universe flashed before his eyes. Countless years zoomed by, filling Taniel's memories like they were his own. He saw Kresimir's original descent from the heavens, and then felt Kresimir call to his brothers and sisters to aid him in rebuilding the Nine. He witnessed the chaos of the Bleakening, and the relentless march of the centuries. Lifetimes rushed past in a blink of an eye.

And then it was all gone.

Taniel staggered backward, gasping.

Ka-poel had done something similar to him once, several months ago. It had left him breathless in its emotion and magnitude, though it had only been a few moments' worth of memories.

This was two thousand years' worth.

It took him some time to recover. When he did, he said, "You are a god." Not a question this time.

" 'God' is a funny word," Mihali said, turning back to his inventory. He made a mark on his paper and silently counted sacks of onions. "It implies omnipotence and omniscience. Let me assure you, I am neither."

"Then what are you?" Bo had once said that the gods were nothing more than powerful Privileged. With memories like that, how could Mihali be anything but a god?

"Semantics, semantics!" Mihali threw up his hands. "For the sake of argument, let's say yes, I am a god. I don't think either of us has the time for a theo-philosophical argument right now. Please, have a seat." Mihali picked up a wine barrel like it weighed no more than a couple pounds and set it beside Taniel, then went to get another.

Taniel tried to nudge the barrel over a few inches. He couldn't. He frowned, then looked at Mihali as the chef fetched a barrel for himself and one for Ka-poel.

Ka-poel's hand casually brushed Mihali's arm.

"Now, girl," Mihali said as a man might gently reprimand a daughter, "none of that." He gently touched her fingers.

There was a flare of fire, and Ka-poel danced away, blowing on her fingertips and scowling at Mihali. Had she been trying to collect a hair from the chef?

Mihali deposited himself on his wine barrel. "Unlike my brothers and sisters, I decided to stay on in this world after organizing the Nine. Hidden, of course. But learning." There was a far-off look in Mihali's eye as he stared at something Taniel could not see. "Distant stars are beautiful and curious, but I found the people here so varied and enchanting I couldn't leave."

Mihali glanced at Ka-poel. "I've studied the Bone-eyes. Not in depth. Being in Dynize and Fatrasta, so far away from Adro, taxes my strength. I never knew how Kresimir and the rest left the planet. They always called me a homebody for not wanting to explore the cosmos. Anyway, the Bone-eyes have incredible magic. So very different from anything Kresimir or the others could imagine. You, my dear, are truly terrifying. So much potential."

Mihali didn't look terrified. If anything, he seemed intrigued.

The chef turned to Taniel. "And powder mages! Kresimir wouldn't have expected that. After all, gunpowder wasn't invented until hundreds of years after he left." Mihali drummed a pudgy finger on his chin. "He's going mad, you know. That Bone-eye bullet you put in his eye was never removed. It's in his brain, causing him incredible pain every day."

Taniel tried to work moisture into his mouth. Kresimir, a god, was going mad. All because of him. "Does he know who shot him?"

"I believe he knows. What you did on South Pike is barely a rumor in the Adran army, and the only two to survive that battle on the Kez side were Julene and Kresimir." Mihali paused. "Of course, he has Julene. Then he must know."

"He nailed Julene to a beam. Cut off her hands. Why would he do that?"

Mihali frowned. "Julene. Misguided child. She may or may not have deserved that, but I don't think torture does anyone any good."

Taniel noticed that Mihali had sidestepped the question about Julene. He decided not to press it.

"How can I kill him?"

"Kresimir? Hmm. What makes you think I'd tell you?"

Taniel rocked back. "But...you're on our side. Aren't you?" He felt his muscles tense, a bit of fear touching his heart.

"I defend Adro. It's my country, after all. However, Kresimir is still my brother. I love him. I will not see him dead. I would, however, like to stop him. Help him. If I can get that bullet out of his brain, I might even be able to reason with him and end this whole thing."

Taniel's fingers curled into fists. "I'm going to kill him."

"That may be your path." Mihali examined his inventory paper. Once again, he seemed to be counting.

It was several moments before Taniel spoke again. "The generals. Do they know...?"

"Oh, Tamas told them. Most of them don't believe it."

"But they know you're a powerful Privileged?"

Mihali nodded. "An uncomfortable truth. They asked me to participate in the fighting and I refused. After all, the Privileged with the Wings of Adom are doing a fine job keeping the remainder of the Kez Cabal in check."

"Did you tell them that Tamas was alive?"

"Of course."

Taniel blinked at this. "Then why haven't they told me? Hilanska...surely he would have said something if there were hope."

"Not even a god sees everything," Mihali said. "I do not know. But I don't trust the generals. I'm sure that most of them have Adro's best interests at heart. But a few..."

"General Ket."

Mihali shrugged. "The provosts are here, by the way."

Taniel stepped to the tent flap and took a peek. Dozens of them had gathered outside.

"Pit. Can I get out the back way?"

"They've surrounded the tent. It's probably best that you go with them."

"I won't let them arrest me. The bastards. I—"

Mihali cleared his throat. "As I said. It's probably for the best. For now, anyway."

Taniel's mind raced. What to do? Run for it? Go out, dignified, and let them take him away? "Answer me this, first: What has happened to me? I'm stronger and faster than before. I've never felt this kind of power. It took enough mala to kill a horse just to get me buzzed. I know it's more than just being a powder mage. Is it because of her?" He flung his finger toward Ka-poel, who raised an eyebrow in response.

Mihali hesitated for several moments. "You've been tempered," he said. "This girl here has you wrapped in protective sorceries. Kresimir's returning strike after you shot him was enough to bring down South Pike Mountain. It should have shattered your mortal body. That blow he gave you could very well have killed me, for all my knowledge of sorcery. But you..." Mihali chuckled, as if something was funny. "You, it just made stronger."

"That doesn't make any sense, it—"

"It's time to go," Mihali said.

Taniel took a deep breath. "All right. Ka-poel, stay here. I don't want them touching you." Without waiting for an answer, he stepped out of the tent and into daylight.

The provosts surrounded him quickly, their pikes leveled.

"All right, you bastards. Take me to General Ket, I—"

Someone brought a truncheon down on his head, hard. Taniel staggered forward, spitting blood from the blow. Another hit his stomach, then his knee. He collapsed to the ground. He was cursed and kicked and beaten, and when he thought he could take no more, he was pulled to his feet and struck about the face and head until he lost consciousness.

CHAPTER

20

Tamas listened to his stomach growl as his charger trotted along the road at the rear of the column. Ahead of him, the men of the Ninth Brigade shuffled to the crack of a single drummer boy's snare. The air was hot and oppressive, even with the cover of tall pine trees. The summer humidity soaked through Tamas's soiled jacket and made every breath a labor.

He watched one of the infantry in the column ahead of him. The man was tall, with dirty-blond hair pulled back in a ponytail over one shoulder. About twenty minutes ago his shoulders had started to sway dangerously as he marched. He'd be the next to faint. Tamas would have put money on it.

Every so often the soldiers would glance back at Tamas's charger with hungry eyes. They watched with the same looks every scout and officer who was still riding. It was unsettling.

They'd slaughtered the last of the Kez horses two days ago and distributed the meat. Tamas heard rumor that some of the company quartermasters were holding back and selling the last precious pounds. He'd tried to get to the bottom of it, but no one would confess. Every stream they passed saw a dozen men leave the line, throwing themselves into the mud in search of tiny fish and crawdads. Their sergeants had to beat them back into the column.

"They think they're going to get a meal soon," Olem said.

Tamas shook himself from his reverie. He felt light-headed, weak. He'd not eaten in four days. The men on their feet needed it more than he did. At least there was some periodic grazing for the horses.

Olem pointed up to a pair of buzzards circling high above the treetops.

"Ah," Tamas said.

"They've been following us for fifty miles," Olem said.

"You can't be sure it's the same vultures."

"One of 'em has red on the tips of his feathers."

Tamas grunted. Words were coming slow out of his mouth. The heat didn't make him feel much like talking.

"That red-tipped buzzard kept on when most of the others stayed behind at the camp two mornings ago, when we slaughtered the horses." Olem pursed his lips. "I think he's hoping for the big payday."

Tamas looked up at the buzzards. He didn't want to talk about them. He'd seen far too many on far too many battlefields. "I haven't seen you smoke for a week," he said.

"Too bloody hot, pardon the language, sir." Olem patted his breast pocket. "Besides. I'm saving my last one."

"A special occasion of some kind?"

Olem continued to watch the buzzards. "Gavril told me we might be making a stand at the Fingers. I figure it'll be nice to die with a cigarette between my lips."

Tamas couldn't help but scowl. "Have you told anyone? About the stand, I mean."

"No, sir."

"Damned Gavril. Needs to keep his mouth shut."

"So it's true, then?"

"I don't intend to make a last stand, Olem. I intend to break the Kez. Last stands are for men who plan on losing."

"Quite right, sir."

Tamas sighed inwardly. Soldiers had a strange sense of fatalism. Most of them didn't realize that any odds could be beaten with the right maneuvering.

"Olem..." Tamas began.

"Sir?"

"About what I saw the other day..."

A muscle jumped in Olem's jaw. "What do you mean, sir?"

"I think you know what I mean. *Vlora*. If I'd come a few minutes later, I think I would have found the two of you in a much more compromising position."

"That was the hope, sir."

Tamas blinked. He'd not expected that kind of bluntness. "Can't hold your tongue to save face, can you?"

"Not to save my life, sir."

"I won't have that kind of fraternization, Olem."

"What kind, sir?" The corners of Olem's eyes tightened.

"You and Vlora. She is a captain, you are—"

"A captain," Olem said. "You made me one yourself." He touched the gold pins on his lapels helpfully.

Tamas cleared his throat and looked up. Those damned buzzards were still there. "I mean that she is a powder mage. You know my mages are a different contingent of the army. I won't have you crossing that line."

Olem looked like he wanted to say something. He worked his jaw around, chewing on a phantom cigarette. "Yes, sir. Whatever you say, sir."

The sarcasm in Olem's tone leaked through like water through paper. It nearly shocked Tamas. Olem was normally so loyal, so quick to obey. He opened his mouth, a rebuke on his tongue.

The soldier with a ponytail staggered and fell out of line, hitting the ground hard. Two of his companions stopped to help him.

"Head up the line," Tamas said. "Call for rest. The men need a sit-down."

Only too grateful to get away, Olem spurred his mount on, calling out, "Field Marshal orders the column to halt! Fall out!"

Tamas could hear the order repeated farther up the column. Slowly, the line of soldiers came to a stop. Some men went looking for the closest stream, some men relieved themselves in the woods, and others slumped to the ground where they were, too exhausted to move.

Tamas opened his canteen and drained the last few drops. The water was hot and tasted of the metal. "Soldier," Tamas said, pointing to a man who looked the least worse for the wear. "Find me some clean, cold water and fill this, then tell your sergeant you're off latrine duty tonight."

The soldier took the canteen. "Aye, sir."

Tamas climbed down from his charger and hung the reins from a tree limb. He paced the width of the road, trying to work some feeling back into his legs after riding half the day. He stopped once and looked south. No sign of the Kez. The woods were too thick. According to the latest reports, the head of the Kez column was ten miles back. They had dragoons ranging in the area in between, trying to catch Adran stragglers and harass the end of the Adran column, but what mattered to Tamas was where the bulk of the cavalry were.

He was going to need that heavy lead.

"Sir."

Tamas turned to find Vlora standing next to his charger. Her uniform was dirty, jacket loosened at the neck, her black hair tied back behind her head. He had the brief image of her naked beneath the waterfall, leaning in to kiss Olem. He willed the image away, trying not to let his embarrassment show on his face.

"Captain."

"How is the leg, sir?"

Tamas flexed the muscles in his leg, felt them twinge. Riding hadn't helped it loosen at all, but the pain wasn't too bad. "It's fine, thank you. Any luck hunting?"

"The deer are keeping well away from the column. If we range more than a mile or two from the road, we won't be able to carry our prey back. A few squirrels and rabbits. Enough to keep the powder mages fed."

At least his mages were keeping up their strength. He felt his stomach twist at the mention of rabbit.

"If we camped for more than one night, or even slowed down a bit, we might be able to bag some deer."

"Sorry, Captain. I can't allow that. We have to reach the Fingers well ahead of the Kez."

"The scouts say we'll be there in two days, sir."

"That's right," Tamas said. "Once we cross the first river, we'll burn the bridge and take it easy for a couple of days. Rest and restock."

"I certainly hope so, sir. The men are looking poor."

Tamas turned his attention to the soldier who had fainted. He was sitting up now, drinking out of a canteen, talking to one of his fellows. Tamas clasped his hands behind his back and faced Vlora.

"Captain, you and I both know that what happened the other day was completely out of order."

Vlora didn't even blink. "You mean, when you watched me bathe?"

Tamas could have slapped her for that. Damned girl. She knew what he wanted to say, and she wasn't going to make it easy.

"You and Olem..."

"Sir, I don't think that's any of your business. With all due respect."

"I am your commanding officer—"

"Yes, sir. And you've always made it very clear that what two soldiers want to do in their spare time is up to them, as long as it doesn't break convention between the ranks."

"This is different." This *was* different, Tamas told himself. "I won't have one of my Marked gallivanting around with my bodyguard, do you understand? I won't have my bodyguard going around with... with..."

"A whore?"

She had spoken quietly, but Tamas felt the breath taken from him.

"That's what you want to say, isn't it, sir? You want to call me a whore for what I did to Taniel? A slut? I can hear the words on the tip of your tongue, even if you don't speak them."

"Watch your tone, soldier," Tamas warned.

"Permission to speak freely, sir?"

"Permission denied."

Vlora ignored him. "You don't think I know what I did to Taniel? You don't think it kills me inside knowing that I threw away everything we had for a few months of passion with some idiot?"

"Permission denied, Captain."

"You don't hear the men talk." Vlora's voice rose. "You don't hear what everyone says about me behind my back—even to my face. You don't see the sneers. 'Vlora, she'll spread her legs for anyone now.' You don't hear them whisper that outside your tent at night, placing bets on who can be the first to get me on my back."

"Permission denied!" Tamas stepped forward. Any other soldier would have shrunk beneath the red fury in Tamas's eyes, but Vlora refused to back down.

"I spent eighteen months alone while Taniel was in Fatrasta because *you* sent him there. Taniel, the war hero. People talked about how every woman in Fatrasta was ready to throw themselves on him. And then to hear he had a little savage girl, following him everywhere. What was I supposed to think of that? No man would look twice at me at the university. They knew who I was. They were too afraid of Taniel to say any nice thing to me."

Vlora spat the words in Tamas's face, her voice dripping with bitterness, her whole body trembling with rage. "Then a man appears who doesn't care whose fiancée I am. He charms me, loves me, and assures me there's not another in the world that can make him so happy. I trusted him." Vlora's face twisted in disgust. "Then I find out he was bedding me just to *make you look bad*."

The pain in Vlora's eyes and the malice in her voice was more than Tamas could bear. Once, he had been her father, her friend, her mentor. But now he had become nothing more to her than an object of hatred, an enemy to despise.

"Get out of my sight, Captain. If we weren't at war, I'd have you court-martialed."

Vlora leaned forward, closer than anyone who didn't know Tamas as well as she did would have dared. Close enough to embrace him. Close enough to stick a knife in his ribs if she wanted. "Kill me yourself, if you want it done so badly," she said. "Don't hand the job over to lesser men."

She whirled on her heel and strode down the column. Soldiers stared openmouthed at her as she went past, then turned to look toward Tamas, waiting for his wrath to follow like thunder after lightning.

Tamas watched Vlora almost disappear around a bend in the road. She made an abrupt stop as Olem rode into view. The bodyguard leaned over his horse, said something to her. She put her hand on his thigh. He pushed it away gently and gave a meaningful glance at Tamas.

Vlora grabbed Olem by the belt and pulled him off his horse, pushing him into the woods off the trail. Tamas swore under his breath and took two steps down the column.

Someone cleared their throat. Tamas looked around.

It was the soldier he'd sent for water. "Your canteen, sir."

Tamas snatched the canteen. When he looked again, Olem and Vlora were gone.

He took several deep breaths and went back to his horse.

"Sir, you mind if I ask how long until we march again?" the soldier asked.

Tamas took a long draw of water. It was so frigid it seemed to burn his throat going down. It made his teeth hurt.

"Thirty minutes, damn it. Get some rest."

Adamat rapped on the door of the foreman's office in the textile mill. Below him, dozens of steam-powered looms thundered at full tilt throughout the day, creating a racket that drowned out all but the loudest shouts. Hundreds of workers tended the millworks, moving about the floor like so many insects.

Adamat let himself into the foreman's office. Inside, the sound was greatly reduced.

"Margy," he called.

The woman emerged from the back of the room and smiled when she saw Adamat. He leaned in and kissed her on the cheek.

She stepped back from him in shock. "What in all the Nine have you done to yourself?"

"Fell down the stairs," Adamat said. His voice whined nasally, and his face still hurt as if the broken nose had happened only an hour ago.

Margy harrumphed. "Looks more like you got it punched in," she said. "I alway told you putting your nose in other people's business was going to get it broken."

Adamat threw his hands up in mock surrender. "I've only got a moment, Margy. I just dropped by to see if you had a lead on that rug."

"Fine, fine." Margy moved over to the desk beside her microscope and began leafing through papers. "I sent Faye a letter last week," she said.

"I'll ask if she got it." Adamat leaned against the doorpost and closed his eyes. His face hurt. His back hurt. His hands and his head hurt. Everything hurt, and he wasn't getting enough sleep. He couldn't recall the last time he'd eaten more than toast and tea. He opened his eyes again when Margy pushed a piece of paper into his hand.

"That's the buyer," she said. "I couldn't get a name, just the address from a check receipt."

"Thanks, Margy."

"Tell Faye to come visit soon, will you?"

"Of course."

Adamat left the textile mill and didn't look at the paper until he was outside. With no name, it would be more work for him to find out the owner of the address, and knowing the Proprietor, Adamat would have to go through several layers of fake names *and* addresses before he found the Proprietor's identity.

He hailed a hackney cab and looked at the address.

He had to look again, blinking to be sure his eyes weren't playing tricks on him.

This was an address he knew.

The weather had grown overcast as the morning progressed, and Adamat stopped by his safe house in western Adopest to get an umbrella. He paused in the hallway. The door to the flat was open.

Part of him screamed to just turn and walk away. He might not survive the next run-in with Vetas's goons.

He drew his pistol and checked to see if it was loaded before pushing gently on the door.

SouSmith sat on the sofa. His arms were folded over his stomach, his chin resting on his chest as he dozed. His shirt was covered in blood.

"SouSmith?"

The big boxer jerked awake. "Ah."

"What happened?"

SouSmith cocked an eyebrow at him, as if it were strange of Adamat to ask after his bloody shirt. "What happened yourself? Someone break your nose?"

Adamat called for the landlady to put a kettle on, and closed the door behind him. "You're soaked with blood."

"None of it's mine," SouSmith said. "Least, not much. Nose?"

"One of Vetas's goons was waiting at my old house. Hit me in the face with a cudgel. Now what's this? You can't be sitting in a man's living room covered in someone else's blood without an explanation."

"Four o' Vetas's men came by my brother's place," SouSmith said. "Shot one of my nephews. Me and Daviel...we killed all four."

"Pit, SouSmith. I'm sorry. Is your nephew...?"

"Kid was twelve. Daviel had just got it together to send 'im to school." SouSmith stood up and stretched. The blood on his shirt was black and dry, probably hours old. His piggish eyes glinted with anger. "I'm in," he said. "Proprietor or no, I'm 'a see Vetas burn. Then I've got to see to my family."

Adamat was about to ask what they did with the bodies when he remembered SouSmith's brother was a butcher. He probably did not want to know. He gave a wary nod.

Could he trust SouSmith? What if Vetas's goons had turned him? What if, like Adamat, SouSmith's family was being held by Vetas?

Could he even afford to ask these questions? Adamat needed every man he could get on his side.

"Get cleaned up," Adamat said. "You left some clothes here."

"We going somewhere?"

"I have to see a man about fifty thousand krana."

Adamat stepped out of the carriage in the Routs—the very best part of town, filled with large brick bankers' houses. The streets were wide, paved with flat cobbles, and lined with towering elms. Adamat tilted his hat up and looked for the house he wanted.

There—in between two of the immense city townhouses owned by the wealthy bankers sat a small, austere house with a well-kept garden. Adamat headed up the walk to the house, followed closely by SouSmith.

"The Reeve, right?" SouSmith asked.

"Yes." Ondraus the Reeve. One of Tamas's councillors, and an architect of the coup that overthrew Manhouch. He was a sour, unfriendly old man. Adamat did not relish a second meeting. He pounded on the door.

He pounded for ten minutes before he finally heard the latch inside move, and the door opened a crack.

"For a wealthy man," Adamat said, "I'm surprised you answer the door yourself."

Ondraus the Reeve glared at Adamat through narrowed eyes. "Get off my front step, or I'll have you jailed for harassment." Ondraus was wearing a robe and slippers. His hair was unkempt.

"I need money," Adamat said. "Your accountants told me I've been cut off."

Ondraus sneered at him. "Tamas is dead. Whatever access to funds he promised you is gone. I'd suggest you find employment elsewhere."

"See, that's a problem. May I come in?"

"No."

Adamat leaned on the door. Ondraus started, reeling back into his tiny foyer.

"Wait out here, please," Adamat said to SouSmith. The boxer nodded.

Ondraus stormed toward his office. Adamat drew the pistol from his pocket and cleared his throat.

The Reeve froze when he saw the pistol. "What is the meaning of this?" he demanded.

Adamat drew his eyes across the room. It had changed little in the months since Adamat's last visit. The mantel had been dusted, the fireplace cleaned, but the carpet showed no more wear and the smells were exactly the same. The house seemed almost unused.

"I can see through the open door to your office there," Adamat said, "a bell cord. Hardly worth noticing on my last visit, but I find myself wondering, in a house with three rooms and no servants, why you have a bell cord." Adamat motioned toward the only chair beside the fireplace. Ondraus took a seat.

"Are you here to rob me?" Ondraus said. "All my money is in investments. As you can see, there's nothing of worth here. I don't even keep a checkbook in my home."

"See," Adamat continued without acknowledging the interruption, "my guess is that bell cord leads to a system of rooms beneath your house, and in one of those rooms you have a permanent staff of four large, dangerous men ready to come to your defense if you need it. And off of those rooms leads a tunnel, likely going to one of these nearby manors that you own under a false name. You don't live in it, of course. You just use it to conceal your comings and goings under your other name."

Ondraus watched Adamat from the chair, saying nothing. His glare was less angry now and more...calculating. For some reason the change made him far more frightening.

"You haven't yet told me that I'm a dead man," Adamat said. He considered Ondraus for a moment. "I suppose you're not the type."

"What is your insurance?" Ondraus asked.

"Letters. Sent to certain friends I have in the police force."

"Telling them that I am the Proprietor?"

It was a thrill to hear Ondraus say it out loud. No denial. No admission. A simple statement, and it made the hair on the back of Adamat's neck stand up. "No, of course not. Telling them that if I disappear, my body can be found beneath your house. No one wants to investigate the Proprietor. But my friends on the force will have no problem combing through the affairs of one accountant. You're known as a shut-in. Shut-ins are always interesting. My friends might even find it fun. And when they find out about the rooms beneath your house, and the bodyguards, and the manor and the huge amounts of money in your portfolio, they will become extremely interested indeed."

Ondraus scoffed. "You think that will save you?"

"Yes, I do." Adamat felt a crack in his confidence. What if Ondraus just didn't care? A man with his connections could just disappear if an investigation started on him. "I think that my life is a trivial thing to spare, if it will save you even a few months' worth of scrutiny and trouble.

"If that is not the case," Adamat added, "I have sent another letter to a friend in the publishing business, telling him I know who the Proprietor is. If I wind up dead, and he hears of an investigation of my death involving you, he'll draw conclusions and, let me say, he's not a very smart man. He values headlines far more than his own life."

Ondraus began to chuckle. It was a dry sound, and for a moment Adamat thought he was coughing. "Very clever," he said.

"If you'd given me help, instead of deciding to let me take Vetas on my own, I wouldn't have even wondered about your identity."

"You'd have still wondered," Ondraus said, waving one hand dismissively. "What do you want?"

"Fifty—no, seventy-five thousand krana in cash, and your help killing Lord Vetas and rescuing my wife."

Ondraus steepled his fingers and leaned back. "You need to learn to get more out of your blackmail. I'm one of the richest men in the Nine."

"I'm not interested in your money. I just want to get Faye back."

"Vetas still has a Privileged."

"That's what the money is for. If I have the money, I'll have my own Privileged."

Ondraus mulled this over. "Resourceful. And if I decide to let you live once Vetas is dead?"

"I'll forget you exist."

"You surprise me, Adamat," Ondraus said. His body was no longer tensed and angry. He lounged back in the chair, steepling his fingers. "The lengths you're going to. I was warned years ago that you were the most principled, tenacious man on the Adopest police force. I actually have gone to a few small lengths to avoid you."

"Believe me," Adamat said. "If this didn't involve my family, I wouldn't be here."

"Well, in that case, I have a stipulation. After this is over, you promise to work for me when I have need of you."

"No."

Ondraus held up his hand to forestall the protest. "I'll pay you, if it happens. The work will likely be dangerous. But agree to this, or I'll kill you and SouSmith, and see what happens."

Adamat searched Ondraus's eyes. There was an iron resolve there that told him Ondraus would do just that. And maybe...a hint of humor? A touch of a smile on his lips? Was Ondraus enjoying this?

"Agreed," Adamat said.

"Wonderful." Ondraus paused. "Does SouSmith know?"

"He thinks I'm here to ask for money," Adamat said. He left out that he'd told SouSmith he planned on blackmailing the Proprietor. SouSmith might make his own deductions, or he might not. If he did, he was smart enough to keep quiet. No need telling Ondraus any of that.

"You'll have it tomorrow," Ondraus said. "I'll have it delivered to...?"

"I'll meet your man in Elections Square. By the stains."

"You're not to come here ever again," Ondraus said. "Our contact will be through my eunuch. You may go now."

Adamat slid his pistol into his pocket with the sudden realization that he was no longer in control.

"And Adamat," Ondraus said, "if I ever have need to regret this, everyone you've ever loved will regret it too."

CHAPTER
21

At some point during the beating they'd put a black hood over Taniel's head and now he tripped and struggled as he was shoved through the camp by the provosts. He could hear their warning to those who passed to stay clear, and their quiet curses when he stumbled. Disoriented, he would have fallen but for the strong arms beneath his armpits. His head pounded, his body a knot of pain.

They forced him up a set of stairs and dragged him inside a building. An inn? Officers' mess? He didn't know. He was thrown into a chair, then tied down. He tried to struggle. The effort earned him a cuff on the back of the head.

Taniel slumped against his bonds and strained to hear some sound that would tell him his location. Nothing but the chatter of soldiers outside the building, too low to hear the voices. He might have been anywhere in the Adran camp.

How much time passed, he couldn't be sure. The air grew cooler, so it must have been night. His face was completely numb. They had to have beaten it into a mess. He felt along his teeth. All there. His shirt was soaked—probably his own blood, and as he sat there, it grew cold.

The numbness in his body began to fade, along with his last powder trance, leaving him to feel the full pain of the beating, when he finally heard the door open. Multiple sets of heavy footsteps. Then another set. Lighter, but no less military.

His hood was pulled off. A match was struck and the lanterns on the wall lit. The room was no bigger than three yards square and was bare but for two chairs and the lanterns on the wall.

General Ket stood above him, arms crossed, her face impassive. She was flanked by two of her provosts. The men glared at him, cudgels held in such a way as if they were daring him to move.

"You'll need more men," Taniel said.

She seemed taken off guard that he spoke first. "What?"

"If you're going to beat me into submission, or whatever it is you're here to do."

"Shut up, Two-Shot." Ket scratched at the stub of her missing ear and then began to pace. "I should have you shot."

"You'll have to hang me," Taniel said. He couldn't help but chuckle. Shot. These officers all acted like they knew everything, but you can't put a powder mage in front of a firing squad. Not one armed with conventional rifles, anyway.

One of the provosts put his full weight behind his fist and slammed it into Taniel's jaw. Taniel's head snapped to the side and his vision spun. The provost became a fuzzy blur. Taniel hawked a wad of bloody phlegm at the provost, and the man drew back for another punch.

Ket held up a hand. "That's not necessary, provost." She rounded on Taniel. "Is this a joke to you? You're looking at being executed!"

"For what?" Taniel scoffed. "Holding the line?"

"For what?" she echoed incredulously. Ket stopped her pacing to face him. "Insubordination, conduct unfitting an officer, disobeying direct orders. Physically assaulting an officer. The way you act verges on treason."

"Go to the pit," Taniel said. He was proud when he didn't flinch at the provost coming toward him.

Ket stopped the man again.

"Keep it up," Taniel said. "I can do this all night. Treason? Is it treason to be the only officer in this bloody army that seems to care about winning a battle? Is it treason to rally the men? Give them something to stand up for? You talk to me about treason, when the trumpets sound a retreat every time we're about to win a battle."

"That's a lie!" Ket stepped forward, and for a moment Taniel thought she'd hit him herself. "We sound the alarm when the battle goes against us. You're down on the lines. You don't see the desperation of the fight where you are."

Taniel leaned forward, straining at his bonds. "I don't see it because I'm winning." He leaned back. "You're scared of me. Have you gone over to the Kez? Is that why? You're scared I'll—"

Ket didn't stop the provost this time. Taniel's words were cut off by the blow, and he was genuinely surprised to find his teeth still there when his head stopped ringing.

Taniel tasted blood. He swallowed. "Is that why you arrested me in secret?" Taniel spoke around a swollen tongue. "Had me dragged through the camp in a hood? So no one could see me?" Taniel snorted and looked the provost in the eye, daring him to hit again.

General Ket scratched at her ear. "You are very popular," she admitted as she began to pace again. "But even the popular— someone like you, who the common soldiers call a hero—need to be disciplined. Otherwise the army falls apart. It's unfortunate, but that's the way it is. I'd make you a public display, but the other generals don't agree with me. They think if the men see you flogged, it'll hurt morale and, Kresimir knows, it's already low enough."

"So you're not going to kill me."

"No. At least, not yet. This is your one and only warning."

"And you expect an apology?"

"Indeed. Several, in fact. Starting with Major Doravir, and ending with me."

Taniel shrugged. "Not going to happen."

"Excuse me?" Ket's eyebrows rose in genuine surprise.

"I nearly killed a god. I've slaughtered dozens of Privileged. Maybe over a hundred. I've lost count. In the absence of Field Marshal Tamas—by the way, why was I told he was dead? I have it from the mouth of a god that he's not. Ah, yes. The god we have in our own camp. The god that the high command are pretending doesn't exist.

"Where was I? In the absence of Tamas, I'm your best tool against the Kez. I'm rallying the men and killing the remaining Kez Privileged and Wardens. So no. I won't bloody well apologize to anyone. My father didn't abide fools. I may not like my father much, but we share that in common."

General Ket remained silent through the whole speech. Taniel was surprised by that. He expected to be cut off by a provost's fist halfway in. He was ready to spit the words through his broken jaw if he had to.

"Tamas is lost to us," Ket said. "There's no way he'll survive in Kez. It's better to assume he's dead. And as for Mihali... if he wasn't so popular among the men, we'd have him removed. He's a very persuasive madman, nothing more."

"Then why are we fighting this war at all?" Taniel asked. "If Kresimir is on the Kez side, we can't win. Unless. Ah. Unless you don't think Kresimir is there at all. You don't think any of this supernatural stuff is real."

"I believe what I see with my own eyes," Ket said. "I see two opposing armies. If there was a god present, we'd all be dead. Now." She paused to drag a chair over in front of Taniel and sat down, crossing her legs. "The threat of physical pain obviously means nothing to you. Death?" She examined him for a moment. "No, not that either."

She continued. "This is what's going to happen: Your records will be transferred to the Third Brigade. You'll keep your rank—but commanding a company of picked riflemen who will take on the tasks I assign. No more of this mucking about on the front line. You're not an infantryman."

"You want your own pet powder mage, eh?"

Ket went on as if she hadn't noticed him speak. "You'll apologize to Major Doravir. In public. After which you will read a prepared note—again, in public—that apologizes for your misconduct and swear on your father's grave that you will keep the regulations of the Adran army."

"I'll do no such thing."

"The savage girl is no longer to share your room. I don't approve of such illicit relationships among my officers. Especially not with a savage."

Taniel sneered. "There's nothing illicit going on."

"I wasn't finished! The girl will be placed with the laundresses of the Third. You'll be allowed to speak with her ten minutes each day. No more."

"That's preposterous!" Taniel leaned forward. "She's not Adran army, she's—"

He was silenced by the provost's fist. The blow nearly knocked him over, but the other provost stepped up and held the chair steady.

"Do not interrupt me again," Ket said coldly. "I've put up with your insubordination long enough. Rumors are the girl is some kind of sorcerer. I'll have her watched. If she attempts to leave the camp, she'll be beaten. If she attempts to find you, she'll be beaten. Understand? Oh, and before you say anything—yes, I can keep her here. This is a time of war. Conscription is a reality."

Taniel waited for a few moments before speaking. "I'll kill any man who lays a hand on her."

"You make any threat you want, but you can't protect her all the time. You'll do all these things for me, or I'll hand your girl over to the Dredgers. You've heard of them, haven't you? The scum of the

Third. Men so low that the Mountainwatch wouldn't take them. I reform such men, and if I don't succeed, I execute them." General Ket stood up and walked over until she was right next to Taniel. She whispered, "I don't approve of rape, nor encourage it. But I understand it's a powerful psychological tool, and don't think I won't give your little savage girl to the Dredgers to do with what they will."

Taniel wondered if he could kill her right then. He'd have to use his teeth to do it. Tear out her throat. The provosts could be fast enough to stop him. But it might be worth a try.

"I'm not a monster, Captain. I'm not doing this on a whim. It is my duty to impose order upon this camp and I will do it even if it costs your little savage her innocence. Do you understand?"

Taniel felt the fury leave him. He wouldn't—he couldn't subject Ka-poel to that.

"Yes," he said.

General Ket headed toward the door. "Untie him. Clean him up. He's confined to quarters until he apologizes to Major Doravir."

Tamas watched the slow march of his column as they emerged from the trees of Hune Dora Forest and onto the floodplain of the river known locally as the Big Finger.

The plain was perhaps a half mile across, from the forest to the edge of the river. The ground was rocky, but not overly so, and filled with rich, sandy silt. During a wet summer it might have been impassable by large numbers of cavalry and so given them a greater advantage, but as it was, the plain was dry and hard.

The Big Finger was the first in a succession of mountain-fed rivers collectively known as the Fingers of Kresimir. It was deep and fast-flowing and impossible to cross without sturdy rafts that could be pushed across and land on the other side farther downstream. Or by way of the bridge.

The bridge was nowhere to be seen.

Tamas heard the cries of dismay as the news was passed on down the column. He felt a twinge of pain for his men. They were starving, tired, beaten by the heat, and they'd just arrived at their one hope of delivery and found it gone.

They didn't know that Tamas had ordered the bridge destroyed.

Across the floodplain, near the river, Tamas could see smoldering bonfires. Flanks of meat roasted above them, the last of the horses taken from the Kez a week ago. Enough for a meal for ten thousand men.

Gavril rode across the floodplain, and Tamas noted he'd kept his own horse alive. He gave Tamas a salute, then said loudly, "Damned bridge washed away."

"Bloody pit!" Tamas slapped a fist into the palm of one hand.

Gavril went on. "We slaughtered the rest of the horses and scouted for wood for rafts. I'll need men to build them."

"All right. We've got half a day until the Kez reach us. Olem!"

The bodyguard nearly jumped out of his saddle. He brought his horse up alongside Tamas. He'd been hanging back ever since the incident with Vlora.

"Sir?"

"Organize getting the men fed. Gather the officers so I can brief them."

"Yes, sir." Olem flicked his reins and headed down the column, slumped in his saddle like a boy whose dog had just died.

Gavril brought his horse up closer to Tamas. "What the pit did you say to that man? I've not seen someone look that guilty since the Lady Femore's face when her husband caught me in bed with her and his sister."

"I told him I didn't want him continuing relations with Vlora."

Tamas watched Olem as he shouted for men to help him distribute food. He'd have to keep it organized. Eleven thousand hungry men were liable to start a riot. "I ordered Vlora to stop as well. She...vehemently...disobeyed." Tamas couldn't tolerate that kind of insubordination, not in a time of war. He didn't know what he was going to do about that. He'd been avoiding it for two days.

Gavril let out a loud guffaw and slapped his knee. Tamas thought about reaching across and punching him off his horse, but decided against it. Wouldn't want to risk breaking his neck, even if it would have done him good.

"Did everything go smoothly?" Tamas asked in a low voice, jerking his head toward the river.

"It did," Gavril said. "Knocked out the bridge yesterday, though the boys weren't happy about it. I can't promise they won't say anything."

"Last thing I need is rumors going around that I gave the order."

"I'll do my best to keep them quiet," Gavril said, "but if this turns into a death trap, I'm going to curse your name with my dying breath." The expression he wore told Tamas he was only partially joking.

"That seems fair. How close are the cuirassiers?"

"My outriders say a day." Gavril scratched his beard. "I hope you're certain about this. We could have gotten the army across the river and been safe for another two weeks, foraging and resting, and then faced them on the north side of the Fingers in better shape."

"I am certain," Tamas said. He looked to the west. The Big Finger meandered out of sight behind Hune Dora Forest about a mile downriver. Tomorrow he'd have a whole brigade of heavy cavalry riding upstream on that floodplain. He'd be boxed in and outnumbered. "I won't face three brigades of cavalry under Beon je Ipille on the open plains of the Northern Expanse. It would be suicide, even for me. Are you coming to my meeting?"

Gavril looked toward the bonfires. "I'll give Olem a hand organizing lunch."

"Good. The men will need their strength. I'm putting them to work next. It's going to be a long night."

Tamas rode toward the gathering of his officers, only a stone's throw from the river. Some of them were still on horseback. The rest were on foot, having given their mounts over to Gavril's rangers two weeks ago.

He ran his eyes over the assembled men. Every one of his generals, colonels, and majors were present. He dismounted.

"Gentlemen," he said. "Gather round. Forgive me for not providing refreshment. I left my god-chef back in Budwiel."

The comment received a few forced chuckles. Tamas felt his heart fall a little and made himself reevaluate his officers. They were a sorry lot. They were gaunt and unshaven, their uniforms dirty. Several wore the fresh scars of their skirmishes with Kez dragoons. Those still in possession of their horses had followed his example and given the better portion of their rations to the marching soldiers. They were tired, hungry, and he could see the fear in their eyes. Fear that hadn't been so stark before finding out the bridge was gone.

"As you can see, the bridge we'd hoped to cross to escape our pursuers is washed away. This has forced me to make a change in our plans. The Kez dragoons will be here in full force by the end of the day. The cuirassiers will be here tomorrow."

"That's not enough time to get everyone across the river," someone said.

Tamas searched for the source of the voice. It was a major, commandant of the quartermasters of the Ninth Brigade. He was missing his epaulets, and he bore a two-day-old gash across the bridge of his nose, the congealed blood almost black.

"No, it's not," Tamas admitted.

A clamor of voices went up. Tamas sighed. On a normal day these were his best officers. Not one of them would have interrupted him. Today was not a normal day.

He raised his hand. A few moments passed, but the hubbub died down.

"A panicked crossing of the river on hastily made rafts will leave our army fractured and in disarray. Beon's dragoon commanders would not hesitate to attack en masse the moment they arrived. So we're going to wait, and make a panicked crossing of the river tomorrow afternoon."

His officers stared back at him, uncomprehending. No one said a word until Colonel Arbor flexed his jaw and popped his false teeth into one hand.

"You're setting a trap," Arbor said.

"Precisely."

"How can we set a trap for half again our number of cavalry?" protested General Cethal of the Ninth Brigade. He was a stout man of medium height. He had a particular wariness for cavalry, since a flanking maneuver by Gurlish cavalry had cost him two regiments and his left eye ten years ago.

"By making ourselves a ripe target." Tamas picked up a straight stick and cleared away some of the tall grass so he could draw in the sandy dirt of the floodplain.

"But we *are* a ripe target," General Cethal said.

Tamas ignored him. "Here is our position." He drew a line to represent the river, and then chevrons for the mountains. "The smaller division of heavy cavalry will come from the west. The larger number of dragoons, from the south. General Cethal, what is the first thing we teach prospective officers at the academy?"

"Terrain is key."

"Indeed."

"But sir," General Cethal insisted, "you've put us on a flat floodplain with almost seventeen thousand cavalry bearing down on us. I can't think of many worse situations."

"We have our backs to the river," Tamas said. "And we have significant manpower. The terrain will be very different tomorrow."

"You mean to shape the terrain to your needs?" General Cethal shook his head. "It can't be done. We'd need a week to prepare."

Tamas stared hard at General Cethal. "Expecting defeat will surely bring it," he said quietly.

"I'm sorry, sir," Cethal said.

Tamas took a moment to look each officer in the eye before going on. "The ancient Deliv, back before the Time of Kresimir, were foreigners to the Nine. Our own ancestors were just some of the barbarians the Deliv faced. The Deliv had barely a fraction of the fighting men, but they were better organized. A Deliv legion could march thirty miles and create an entire fortification to camp all in one day. They survived because they had the discipline and the will. We shall do the same."

As he spoke, Tamas had been drawing lines in the dirt with his stick. He pointed at one line. "The soil is somewhat rocky, but the dirt is loose and easy to dig." He pointed to a series of Xs. "Hune Dora Forest has an abundance of wood."

Colonel Arbor squatted beside the crude drawing and examined it for a moment. He suddenly laughed. "It might work. Should I get my boys digging?"

"Your battalion has the first rest. We'll be working all night, so it'll be done in shifts. Then you'll chop trees. General Cethal, your men will be digging."

"My men? The Ninth?"

"Yes. All of them."

"Do you intend to create a palisade?" General Cethal asked.

"Not quite," Tamas said. "Get digging. I'll come around in an hour and give each company specific instructions." He made a shooing gesture with his stick. "Get to work."

Tamas watched his officers head off toward their men. It was going to be a long night. He hoped that when morning came, and battle was joined, his efforts would be worth it. Otherwise he would have exhausted all of his men for nothing.

"Mihali," he whispered to himself, "if you're still with us . . . I need some help."

It was the closest thing to a prayer he'd ever spoken.

*   *   *

Adamat and SouSmith watched the abandoned manor where Privileged Borbador was being kept. The street was empty, the air silent. Dark clouds threatened on the southern horizon, and the wind was beginning to pick up. They were in for a stormy night.

There were no signs of Verundish's soldiers in the manor. Adamat wasn't sure whether that was a good thing or not. He'd left the money yesterday at an address the Deliv colonel had given him. He couldn't help but think of all the things that could go wrong, or wonder whether she had taken the money and simply changed where they were hiding Bo.

Adamat headed down the hill and navigated the ruin until he found the servants' quarters. Bedding was gone, debris picked up. The only sign soldiers had ever been there was warm ashes in one of the fireplaces. Adamat grew more nervous with each step. Was it all for naught, blackmailing the Proprietor and gathering the money?

The door to the room where they'd kept Bo was closed. He turned the knob and stepped inside.

Privileged Borbador was gone. The chair, the bed, even the stand and the book were still there, but Bo was gone.

"Bloody pit!" Adamat kicked over the book stand. "That bloody..." He dropped into the chair, head in his hands. She'd just taken the money and left, just like that. And with her, Privileged Borbador, and any hope Adamat had of getting his wife back.

SouSmith leaned in the doorway, watching Adamat with a frown. "What'll you do?" he asked.

Adamat wanted to gouge his own eyes out. What could he do? He thought he'd known despair, but this...

The hall floorboards creaked. SouSmith turned. Adamat pulled the pistol from his pocket. If that was Verundish, he'd shoot her without a second thought.

Bo stepped past SouSmith and into the room. His hair was brushed back, his lapels straightened, and his beard shaved and styled into thick muttonchops.

Adamat felt the strength go from his limbs. He slumped back in the chair and stared at the Privileged.

"I thought you looked beat up the last time we spoke," Bo said. "What happened to your nose?"

"I'm going to hit the next person who asks me that." As long as they weren't a Privileged, Adamat added silently.

Bo gave a thin smile. "Thank you," he said, "for getting me released. They treated me well enough, but no one likes being tied up like that, not even able to move my hands." He flexed his fingers. "So stiff."

"You're welcome," Adamat said. "Now you'll hold up your part of the bargain?"

"I have some things to do." Bo stepped to the window and looked out.

Adamat felt his chest tighten. Things to do? "I need you now."

"You'll have me tomorrow."

"You're not going anywhere without me," Adamat said. "I need to make sure I have your help."

"You don't trust me?"

"I can't afford to," Adamat said.

"If I decide to ignore our deal, you wouldn't be able to stop me." It wasn't a question, but a statement.

"Probably not," Adamat agreed.

They locked gaze for a few moments, and Adamat had to remind himself how young Bo really was. Twenty? Maybe twenty-two? His eyes were so much older, like a man who'd seen more than his share of suffering and lived to talk about it.

"Suit yourself," Bo said.

"You'll only need one night?"

"Yes."

"SouSmith," Adamat said, "go to Sergeant Oldrich, and then the eunuch. Tell them I plan on acting tomorrow, then meet me at the safe house."

The big boxer nodded and left.

Adamat followed Bo out into the street. The Privileged walked with a purpose, like he had things to do, his head held high and his eyes alert. They had to walk for half an hour before they found a carriage. Bo gave the driver directions and they got inside.

"The eunuch," Bo said, taking his hands out of his pockets. Adamat realized he wasn't wearing Privileged's gloves. "As in 'the Proprietor's eunuch'?"

Adamat smoothed the front of his coat. "Indeed."

"That's a dangerous friend you have. The cabal tried to kill him a couple times. Failed, obviously."

"The Proprietor or the eunuch?"

"The eunuch," Bo said. "The Proprietor had an uneasy truce with the cabal, but Zakary never liked the eunuch. Didn't try to kill him again after a Privileged he sent after the eunuch wound up dead."

"The eunuch killed a Privileged?"

"It's not common knowledge," Bo said, "but yes." The Privileged fell silent for the rest of their trip, looking out the window and fingering something beneath his jacket.

The demon's carbuncle, Adamat guessed. The jewel around his neck that would eventually kill him if he didn't avenge the death of Manhouch.

"We're here," Bo suddenly said.

They climbed out of the carriage in the middle of Bakerstown. The air smelled of hot bread and meat pies, making Adamat's mouth water. "I'm going to get something to eat," he said, stopping beside a pie vendor.

"Get me one too," Bo replied, "then come upstairs." He disappeared inside a squat brick building sandwiched between two bakeries.

Adamat paid for two meat pies and followed Bo inside. When he reached the top of the stairs, he found himself in a one-room flat. There was a table and a bed, with an old mattress stuffed with straw, and one window looking out into an alley behind the bakery.

Bo stood on a chair in the middle of the room, pressing his fingers gently against the ceiling.

"What are you doing?"

Bo didn't answer him, but hit the ceiling once, hard. The plaster gave way and a box suddenly dropped into the room, hitting the floor with a crash.

Adamat waved plaster dust away from his face as Bo opened the box. Inside was a pair of Privileged's gloves and what appeared to be thousands of crisp banknotes, bundled together by silk ribbon.

"I would have expected something a little more…magical," Adamat said.

Bo pulled on the Privileged's gloves and flexed his fingers, then began setting stacks of banknotes on the floor next to the box. "I wasn't raised as a Privileged," Bo said. "Not like most of the others. I came off the streets originally."

"So…a box in the ceiling?"

"I'm not stupid. The wards on this box will blow anyone that's not me halfway across the room if they touch it."

"Ah."

"How much did you pay Verundish to let me go?"

"Why?"

"How much?"

"Seventy-five thousand," Adamat said.

Bo handed him two stacks of banknotes. "Here's a hundred."

"I can't take these," Adamat said, trying to give them back. "I still need your help, I…"

Bo rolled his eyes. "Take them. I'll still help you. I don't care how you got the money, but it couldn't have been easy. I pay my debts back double, when I can."

Adamat only put the banknotes in his pockets when he realized Bo wasn't going to take no for an answer. At a quick guess, Bo had over a million krana in that box. It was a mind-boggling number for a man like Adamat. But to a man like Bo, who'd been a member of the royal cabal, it was probably a trifle.

The Privileged bundled it all up in brown paper and wrapped it with a bow like it was one big package he'd just acquired at the store, keeping back four stacks of krana and secreting them about his person. When he was finished, he stood and nodded to Adamat. "Let's go."

Bo wouldn't let Adamat come with him inside the next time they stopped, nor the time after that. It was the fourth stop, well after dark, when Adamat finally got curious enough to follow him.

They were in one of the more pleasant parts of town, where the growing middle class lived in smart, two-story houses and walked the line between the nobility and the poor. It was not unlike where Adamat himself lived, if a little more crowded.

Bo left the carriage and headed down a long alley between two tenement buildings of spacious flats. Adamat waited for a moment before slipping out after him.

He paused by the edge of the alley, watching around the corner, as Bo knocked on a door. A moment later he was admitted inside.

Adamat inched his way down the alley until he reached a window looking into the flat.

Inside, he could see a pair of children playing next to a large fireplace. A boy and a girl, maybe eight and ten years of age. The window was open to take advantage of the stiff evening winds. Adamat moved to the next window that looked into a kitchen.

A man with a long mustache and burly shoulders stood next to the kitchen table, frowning at Bo. The woman sat at the table, busy with her knitting.

"Just ten minutes of your time," Bo was saying. He drew a stack of banknotes from his pocket and tossed it on the table.

The woman dropped her knitting needles and held a hand to her mouth. The man sputtered over the amount. Bo drew another stack and added it to the first.

"Whatever you say," the man said. "Just let me get my coat."

The door opened, and Adamat was forced to press himself against the wall, hoping the darkness would conceal him from Bo's eyes.

Bo followed the man out into the alleyway and gestured for him to come down farther. They weren't ten feet from Adamat when they stopped.

"Now what's this all about?" the man asked.

Bo lifted his gloved fingers in the air and snapped them.

The man's head twisted around a hundred and eighty degrees. Bo deftly stepped out of the way as the body staggered and fell. He seemed to regard the dead man for a few moments before he turned and headed back toward the carriage.

Adamat couldn't help himself. He'd seen gruesome murders in his time, and bad men do terrible things, but the abruptness…He stepped from the darkness. "What the pit is the meaning of this?" he hissed.

"Keep walking." Bo grabbed him by the arm in a surprisingly firm grip and spun him about, pushing him toward the carriage.

Adamat had no choice but to allow himself to be dragged along. The carriage was soon heading down the street, and Adamat struggled to find a voice to express what he'd just seen. The murder had been quick and cold. A trained assassin couldn't have done it better.

"Here," Bo said. He grasped something beneath his shirt and yanked, then tossed it into Adamat's lap. "Take this. I don't want the bloody thing anymore."

Adamat stared down at the ruby-red jewel sitting in his lap. "Is that the demon's carbuncle?" He wasn't sure if he wanted to touch it.

"It is," Bo said.

"I thought you had to kill Tamas," Adamat said. "How did…?"

Bo looked rather pleased with himself. Not at all like someone who'd just snapped a man's neck not two dozen paces from his wife and children. "I had to avenge the king. That man there was the headsman who loaded Manhouch into the guillotine."

Adamat finally drew a handkerchief from his pocket and lifted the jewel to see it better by the light of the streetlamps outside the carriage. It was warm—no, hot—to the touch and seemed to throb with its own inner light. He wondered how much a jeweler would pay for a sorcerous piece of art like this.

"Gorgeous, isn't it?" Bo said.

"It can't have been that simple. A god made the precedence for the gaes. You can't just kill the executioner and have it be all. Can you?"

"Kresimir was just a man," Bo said. His eyes narrowed as if at something that made him angry. "Just a damned man with a bloody huge amount of power. He may be smarter than most, and have more time to think and plan, but even the so-called gods make mistakes."

"Is this thing...safe?" Adamat asked.

"Quite."

Adamat wrapped it in his handkerchief and put it in his pocket. "Why didn't you just tell Tamas?"

"I wasn't sure," Bo said. "I only had the thought recently, and I would have looked a damn fool if his soldiers had killed an innocent man only for the carbuncle not to come off."

"You weren't sure? What the bloody pit kind of man—?"

Bo held up his hand and gave Adamat a cold, long stare. "At what point have you ever gotten the impression that there are good people in the royal cabal?"

"You've given me that impression," Adamat said. He swallowed hard. "Yes. You have."

"Well, get past it." Bo turned toward the carriage window. "Because I'm not a good man. Not in the slightest. I just pay my debts."

Adamat watched the Privileged for several minutes. Was that regret in his voice? A frown at the edges of his mouth? It was impossible to tell. Members of the royal cabal were dangerous men, he reminded himself, and were not to be trusted.

He just hoped that Bo really was on his side.

CHAPTER

22

Tamas judged he had two hours before night fell and the Kez dragoons would be close enough to scout his position.

The sound of his soldiers chopping great trees on the edge of the Hune Dora Forest echoed across the floodplains, and teams of men dragged the trees by hand across the dusty grassland to where Tamas had decided to make his stand. Closer, the scrape of a thousand shovels on sandy dirt made Tamas's skin crawl. He hated that sound. It felt like someone scraping a nail across his molars.

He found Andriya cleaning his rifle down near the river. The Marked's belt had become decorated with squirrel tails over the last few days. He didn't have the same look as the rest of the soldiers. His cheeks were slightly rounded from eating well and his face lacked the lines of exhaustion.

His eyes, though, betrayed him. They were wide and bright, shifting constantly. Like the rest of Tamas's mages, Andriya had been floating in a powder trance for weeks running. It was a terribly dangerous thing to do. Going powder blind could see any of the mages dizzy, disoriented, unconscious, or even dead.

"I'd back off on the powder, soldier," Tamas said gently.

Andriya looked him up and down. His lips twisted, and for a moment Tamas thought Andriya would snap at him.

"Right, sir," Andriya said. "Probably should."

"Where is Vlora?"

Andriya shrugged. Tamas couldn't help but wonder where the discipline was going in his army.

"What was that?"

"Don't know, sir."

"Find her."

"She won't talk to you, sir."

"Come again, soldier?"

"She said—and of course, I'm only quoting—that you could go to the pit."

Tamas inhaled sharply. This wouldn't do. This wouldn't do at all. He quickly thought over his options. He could have her flogged. Had a regular soldier said something like that to him, he wouldn't have hesitated. Vlora was...was what? Another time, he might have thought she was kin. But she'd made it clear that was no longer the case.

Besides, a public flogging on the eve of a major battle? He rolled his eyes to himself. *That* would help morale.

He could give her a public reprimand. What if she defied him? He'd have no choice but to impose more severe punishment. With her temper, he might have to have her hanged.

"Get the powder cabal together," Tamas said. "I've got assignments for you. Tell Vlora to be there."

Andriya saluted and went about cleaning his rifle. Tamas headed toward the bonfires to find something to eat.

The soldiers had been organized into lines. Olem stood at the head of the lines along with the better part of his Riflejacks—all trusted men that could keep the infantry in line. The last of the horsemeat was distributed quickly as soldiers approached with their pewter dishes.

The camp was coming together even as work continued on Tamas's preparations. Tents were pitched, small fires made. Parties were sent out to forage the woods or fish the river. Fights broke out and were quickly put down, only to start up again somewhere else. Food seemed to be the main instigator as soldiers tried to get in line for seconds. The meat might keep them going through the night, but morale was low, and the food wouldn't last through tomorrow.

"Sir."

Andriya's voice broke through Tamas's thoughts. Nineteen men and women stood assembled before him: the entirety of his powder cabal, including the recruits Sabon had managed to gather before his death.

"We're running low on powder and bullets," Tamas said without preamble. He caught sight of Vlora at the back of the group, but did not wait to hold her eye. "Tomorrow we'll be fighting almost sixteen thousand cavalry. I'm setting a trap that should even the odds, but it's going to be a brutal battle."

Tamas looked around, suddenly feeling weary. His leg ached. He thought to take some powder, but stopped himself. Save it for the soldiers. He walked to a large rock and sat down, gesturing for the powder mages to be at ease. Most of them sat on the sandy ground. Vlora remained standing, her arms crossed. Tamas ignored her.

"I'm going to redistribute bullets and powder among the men so that you have enough for the next twenty-four hours. Your first job: Do not let Kez scouts get within a half mile of us. Do not let them take the high ground along the mountain." He pointed east to the slope of the Adran Mountains. "Do not let them see what we're up to. The life of every soldier depends on this.

"However," he went on, "I want them to see we're doing *some-*

thing. A little digging. Preparations and rafts. Perhaps trying to rebuild the bridge. Every so often, let one of their scouts get closer, and then let him get away with a bullet in the arm, or something equally convincing."

"Tomorrow should be much of the same. I expect Beon to attack as soon as his cuirassiers arrive. He knows an opportunity when he sees one, and he never hesitates to take it."

"And if he senses the trap?" Andriya asked.

"Then we cross the river tomorrow night, and deal with Beon on the other side of the Fingers." Tamas had a very good feeling that would not be the case. Beon needed to stop them now. The farther north they got, the better chance they had of finding succor in Deliv and crossing back into Adro. Tamas prayed that would spur on Beon. He dreaded the idea of facing the Kez on the open plains of the Northern Expanse.

"We'll have teams," Tamas said. "Nine and three. Nine on watch, killing Kez scouts, and three resting."

"We don't need rest," Andriya said. He grinned at Tamas. His crooked teeth were stained yellow. "We just need powder."

Tamas held his hand up toward Andriya. "You'll have your time to kill Kez," he said. "You all need some rest tonight."

It was perhaps six o'clock, and the hot sun burned red over the Amber Expanse to the west. Tamas wondered if the coming night would be his last in this world.

The Kez outnumbered him. He was growing old. Not as fast or as sharp as he'd once been. Beon might see through the trap and outmaneuver him, or circle at a distance, content to pick off Tamas's troops until Tamas made it across the river, then head west around the Fingers and wait for Tamas on the Northern Expanse.

Had it been a mistake to order Gavril to destroy the bridge?

"Sir?"

Tamas jolted out of his reverie. The powder mages were gone, all but Vlora. For a moment he imagined she was a little girl again—ten years old—seeking his approval. The sun had sunk in the western sky and the camp was completely pitched. The bonfires had burned low, all sign of the horse carcasses gone. Thousands of men worked on the floodplain while thousands more chopped trees on the edge of the Hune Dora Forest.

"Where are they?"

"Sir?"

"The powder mages."

Vlora had a hint of worry in her eyes. "You dismissed them over an hour ago. Told me to stay."

"And you've been waiting this whole time?"

"You seemed preoccupied."

Tamas took a shaky breath. He suddenly remembered dismissing Andriya and the rest of the mages, but it was like looking back in time through a thick fog.

Getting old indeed.

"Have you been eating, sir?"

Tamas's stomach growled. "I had some horsemeat earlier."

"I was watching you, sir. You didn't take anything when you went to check on the bonfires."

"I'm sure I did."

Vlora dug in her belt, then handed him a white tuber. "Found these truffles in the forest yesterday. You should eat. Take them, Tamas."

Tamas put out a hand reluctantly and she dropped them there.

He hesitated, staring at the truffles. Truffles grown in forests of the Adran Mountains were delicacies in most of the Nine. They were small and pale-cream colored. He'd never much liked truffles.

"Thank you," he said.

Vlora leaned on her rifle, staring over toward the forest. He gazed at the side of her face. He'd watched her grow from a fledgling powder mage into a capable soldier, one of his best. She was strong, with a beauty that the years would dim but never fully diminish. He felt a pang of loss, once again, that this girl would never bear him a grandson. He looked again at the truffles in his hand.

"What I said, Tamas—sir, I shouldn't have spoken to you that way. Not in front of the men."

"No, you shouldn't have."

Vlora stiffened. "I'll accept whatever reprimand you see fit."

Tamas didn't know his heart was capable of breaking. Not after all these years. He took a deep breath. "You're a grown woman. Olem is a good man. He'll make you happy."

She seemed surprised by this. But not in the way Tamas expected. "He's just another man," she said. "Someone to warm the nights." She closed her eyes. "We're soldiers. Tomorrow, one of us might be dead. Even if we both survive the battle, we'll move on and find others. It's the life we've chosen." Her eyes opened again and she looked across the camp. "All of us."

Ah. What every soldier knew so well. Lovers were brief, passion burning like a candle—hot at the center and easily doused. It was too hard to keep the flame kindled longer than a season or a campaign. "It can be a lonely life," Tamas agreed.

"You think we can win tomorrow?" Vlora asked.

Tamas looked toward the forest. At his soldiers going about their tasks. They were dragging trees across the floodplains now, toward the camp. The sound of billhooks hitting wood carried in the night. A rifle fired somewhere. Soldiers foraging, or powder mages scaring off Kez scouts?

"I think we can win every battle," Tamas said. "This . . . this will be difficult. The whole fulcrum of my plan could topple if the Kez catch too good a look at my preparations. We are low on powder and bullets, and the men are half-starved. We have to win tomorrow, or we'll die here."

He felt cold suddenly, despite the heat, and very old.

"I don't want to die here, sir," Vlora said. She hugged her rifle.

"Neither do I."

"Sir."

"Yes?"

"Gavril... he said you buried someone beside the Little Finger, long ago. Who was it?"

Tamas felt himself whisked away. Felt the spray of the raging river on his face, the mud and blood caked on his fingers from digging a grave by hand.

He forced himself to stand, trying not to favor his bad leg. It needed the exercise. "I've buried countless friends. More enemies. Kin, and those close enough they might as well be. I want to see Adro again. I want to know if my son survived his ordeals. But before then, there is a lot of work to do. That is all, Captain. Dismissed."

Taniel sat brooding in his quarters, watching out the window as a line of wagons carried wounded soldiers away from the front. He thought about opening the window and asking how the battle was going. But he already had a guess: badly. This lot had probably taken a mortar round—their wounds were bloody and varied, and by their uniforms they were all from the same company.

General Ket had sent him to an inn about five miles behind the line, under guard twenty-four hours a day. It seemed like weeks since Ket had given Taniel her ultimatum. He knew it had been a single night.

The provosts had demanded to know where Ka-poel was. Taniel had shrugged and told them to stuff it, but inside he'd worried about what they'd do when they caught her. Had they been given orders to give her a beating like the one they'd given Taniel? Or worse? Without dolls of them, would Ka-poel be able to fend off the provosts?

General Ket had come by his quarters early this morning to tell him that every day he refused to apologize to Major Doravir was another day that men died on the line.

Taniel would be up there now if it weren't for General Ket. He wouldn't let her convince him it was his fault that the line was being pushed back again.

Outside his window, Taniel caught sight of a young man. It was a boy, really. Couldn't have been more than fifteen. His leg had been taken off at the knee. Whether by a cannonball or a surgeon, Taniel didn't know, but he was struck by the calm on the boy's face. While men three times his age wailed over any number of flesh wounds, the boy sat stoically in the back of a wagon, his stump hanging off the edge, watching serenely while a fresh group of conscripts were sent to the front.

Taniel lifted his sketchbook and began to outline the boy's face.

A knock sounded at the door. Taniel ignored it, wanting to give the boy's portrait some shape so that he could finish it later.

He'd almost forgotten there even had been a knock, when it sounded again. The wagon outside was moving on, and the wounded boy with it. Taniel dropped his sketchbook on the table and went to the door.

He was surprised to find Mihali there. The big chef held a silver platter aloft in one hand, a towel over the opposite arm. His apron was dirty with flour and what looked like smudges of chocolate.

"Sorry to bother you," Mihali said, sweeping past Taniel. Two provosts followed the chef inside. One held a folding table, the other a bottle of wine. "Right there," Mihali told them. "Next to the window. Now some privacy, please."

The provosts grumbled, setting up the table and then retreating into the hallway.

"Sit," Mihali instructed, pointing at the only chair in the room. He deposited himself on the edge of the bed.

"What's this?" Taniel asked.

"Dinner." Mihali swept the lid off the silver tray. "Braised side of beef with quail's egg quiche and sweet goat cheese, and served with a red wine. Nothing fancy, I'm afraid, but the wine is a lovely 'forty-seven and has been chilled."

Nothing fancy? The smell rising from the platter made Taniel shudder with pleasure. His mouth watered immediately, and he found himself at the table unable to remember sitting down, with a piece of beef already on his fork. He paused. "May I?"

"Please, please," Mihali encouraged. He popped the wine cork and poured two glasses.

It was a little unnerving that Mihali watched him while he ate, but Taniel quickly learned to ignore the chef's presence and was soon reaching for seconds.

"What," Taniel asked, eyeing Mihali, who was on his third glass of wine, "is the occasion?"

Mihali poured Taniel another glass. "Occasion? Does there need to be an occasion to eat well?"

"I thought so."

Mihali shook his head. "I heard they'd relegated you to quarters and were feeding you soldier's rations. That qualifies as a war crime in my book."

"Ah." Taniel smiled, but couldn't be sure that Mihali was actually joking. He leaned forward, taking his wineglass, and noted that the wine bottle was still full after, what, five glasses between the two of them? Perhaps Mihali had a second bottle hidden somewhere.

"I have a letter for you," Mihali said, removing an envelope from his apron.

Taniel paused, a fork halfway to his mouth. "From?" he mumbled around a mouthful of quail's egg.

"Colonel Etan."

Taniel tossed his fork down and snatched the letter. He tore it open and ran his eyes over the contents. When he was finished, he pushed his chair back and took a deep breath. He wasn't hungry anymore, not even for Mihali's food.

"What is it?" Mihali asked.

"None of your..." Taniel swallowed his retort. Mihali had come all this way from the front with a full meal, and delivered a letter that would likely not have reached Taniel otherwise. The chef deserved his thanks, not his anger. "I asked Colonel Etan to pull the quartermaster records regarding black-powder use in the army."

"Oh?"

"He also pulled requisition orders. They don't match up. The army has requisitioned three times as much powder as they've used, and nearly twice what has actually reached the front line."

"It's getting lost somewhere?" Mihali asked.

"More likely stolen. Corruption's not unheard of in any army, even ours, but Tamas cracks down on it hard during wartime. These records"—he tossed the envelope on his bed—"mean that the quartermasters are in on it. And at least one member of the General Staff. Someone is making millions off this war."

"As you said," Mihali responded, "it's not unheard of."

"But powder...we'll run out quickly at this rate. The whole country, and then it doesn't matter how much better our troops are, we'll be ground beneath Kez's heel. Damn it!" Taniel drummed his fingers on the silver platter in front of him. He wanted to throw it across the room, but there was still a bit of beef left. "Can you get me out of here?"

"I'm sorry, but I don't think so," Mihali said with a sigh. "As I told you before, the General Staff doesn't listen to a word I say." Mihali patted his belly. "Tamas—now he has an ear for good sense, even if he is mistrustful of the person giving it. These generals can't see past the ends of their noses."

Taniel leaned back and sipped his wine. Something about Mihali's steady tone and unruffled attitude helped calm his nerves. "They're some of the best in the Nine, believe it or not." To his surprise, there was no grudge in his tone. "Though I can't say that speaks well for Adro, or against the rest of the Nine."

Mihali chuckled. "That certainly explains why we haven't lost yet. Despite being so heavily outnumbered."

"How is it going on the front?" Taniel asked. "I mean, I can see…" He gestured out the window, the memory of the wagons full of dead and wounded still fresh. "But I've had no real news for two days."

"Not well. We lost almost a mile yesterday." Mihali's face grew serious. "You were about to change things, you know. Stopping that advance last week gave the men their first victory in months. They had heart. I could sense it. They would have charged after you, right down Kresimir's throat."

"Pit. I have to get out of here. Back on the front. And I need to find out who's profiteering off our black powder."

"How?"

"I'll strangle every quartermaster in the army until one tells me. You're sure you can't get me released?"

"Most of the General Staff doesn't even believe I'm a god. To them, I'm a mad chef. The only way you'll get out of here, Taniel, is if you apologize to Major Doravir."

Taniel stood up and went to the window. "Absolutely not."

"Don't pit your pride against General Ket's," Mihali said. "That woman makes Brude look humble."

Brude. One of the saints—er, gods. Taniel watched Mihali down a fourth glass of wine out of the corner of his eye. It was easy to forget what Mihali was. After all, one would expect a god to look, and act, as grand as any king. Not dribble wine out of the corner of his mouth and then clean it up with a shirtsleeve.

"What can I do?" Taniel asked. He wondered if Mihali had given advice to his father. He couldn't imagine Tamas soliciting advice from a chef, even if he did believe that Mihali was a god.

"Apologize to Doravir."

Taniel blew air out through his nose.

"I can't see much," Mihali said quietly, looking into his wineglass. "The future is always moving, always blurry, even to those with the vision to see it. What I can see is that if you stay in this room, we'll continue to lose ground every day. The Kez will push us out of the valley and surround us, eventually forcing a surrender. Or we'll run out of powder, and the same will happen."

Taniel scoffed. "I'm just one man. I can't make that much of a difference."

"One man always makes a difference. Sometimes it's a small one. Other times, he tips a war. And you . . . you're not human. Not anymore."

"Oh? Then what am I?" Taniel asked. Mihali made less and less sense as he continued to speak.

"Hmm," Mihali said. "I don't think there's a word for it. After all, you're the first of your kind. You've become like Julene."

Taniel heard his own sharp intake of breath. "I'm not a Predeii."

"No. Not precisely. You're not immortal, after all. Then again, neither is Julene. She's just ageless. I don't think your sorcery would ever let you become ageless. Even with Ka-poel's help. But you're the powder-mage equivalent of a Predeii."

"This is ridiculous. Where *is* Ka-poel?"

"Hiding. I offered her my protection—with some reservations, of course. That girl makes my skin crawl. She didn't accept it. I might need her help at some point, though."

Taniel rubbed his temples.

"Another glass of wine?"

"I think I've had enough."

"Suit yourself." Mihali poured himself another one. His cheeks were flushed, but other than that there was no sign he'd drunk seven glasses. The wine bottle, Taniel noted, was still full.

"You said that you can see a little of the future," Taniel said. "If I apologize to Major Doravir, what then?"

Mihali stared into his wineglass. "Motion. That's what I see. It's a small event, but it stirs things up. It makes the certain uncertain. And right now, the certain does not bode well for us."

Taniel snatched a quill pen and took the back of Etan's letter. Quickly, ink smudging the page, he scrawled out a note. "Can you get this to Ricard Tumblar?" he asked. "I can't send it regular post. If someone on the General Staff is profiteering, they'll have eyes everywhere."

"I can send one of my girls," Mihali said, taking the letter.

"Thank you. Do you know where can I find Major Doravir?"

"As it happens . . . yes."

CHAPTER

23

Tamas watched the sunrise over the Adran Mountains to the east and wondered if it would be the last he would ever see.

The Kez dragoons had caught up with them late the day before. They made camp over a mile into Hune Dora Forest. He'd spent half the night watching their campfires flicker in the night and listening to them sing cavalry battle hymns. Every so often a gunshot would punctuate the distant sound as one of their scouts got too close and met a powder mage's bullet.

Now, the world was quiet but for the sound of the swift river on the rocks behind him. Tamas lay on the ground, leaning against his saddle about a hundred paces from the river. He held a powder charge in his hand, kneading the paper between his fingers.

In his mind he could see the dragoons climbing from their tents, stretching in the crisp morning air and preparing Fatrastan coffee over their cookfires. They'd be unhurried. Restful. They knew that their heavy cavalry wouldn't be here for some time yet, and that Beon wouldn't attack before he had his full force.

"Where are the cuirassiers?" Tamas asked. His breath fogged as he spoke. Despite the heat of the summer days, the mornings were still chill this close to the mountains.

Gavril stared sullenly toward the tree line as if he expected the dragoons to appear any moment. "Not more than a few hours away. I'd expect them here by noon."

"They'll be in formation by two o'clock. One, if Beon's generals are organized."

"Not long to get ready."

"Long enough. Olem."

The bodyguard stirred from his lookout position a few paces from Tamas's side. "Sir?"

"Pull our pickets back from the forest. Are the rafts done?"

"Aye, sir. Three big ones."

"Begin ferrying troops across the river. Start with the wounded, then the greenest troops. Take your time at it. I expect the Kez to attack between one and two o'clock. I want about a thousand of our men across the river by then. Enough to be convincing, but not enough to destroy our ability to fight."

"Very good, sir. Anything else?" Olem's tone was crisp. Ready for battle.

"Does everyone know where they are meant to be when the fighting starts?"

"Yes, sir. We drilled them half the night."

"Make things chaotic. I want lots of milling about. Fistfights. If you have to 'lose' one of the rafts in the river, so be it. This has to be convincing."

"I spoke to Colonel Arbor last night, sir. His men are going to hide their kits and rifles. Make like they've abandoned them."

"Good. Dismissed. Wait. Find me Andriya and Vlora."

Olem flinched at the mention of Vlora's name. He saluted and was off.

The wind was blowing westerly, and Tamas could see a low cloud cover inching its way off the Adran Mountains. If rain was coming, it would make this a miserable fight. Beon might even delay his attack, making all of Tamas's preparations be for nothing.

He wondered idly if Mihali had heard his prayer last night.

"What are you up to, Tamas?" Gavril asked.

"Kind of obvious from this end, isn't it?"

"I've been ranging since you arrived yesterday. To me, it looks like a half-finished defense."

"Perfect." Tamas climbed to his feet. The camp was shaped in a square. To the north, the Big Finger raged along its banks. To the east, a scree slope leading up to the mountain prevented a flanking maneuver by Kez cavalry. To the west and south, a mound of earth about three feet tall had been piled all around the camp. It was a standard short defense, from behind which infantry could take easy cover.

It would barely slow a cavalry charge.

To the west, the mound had been topped with tree trunks, propped together to form giant Xs. Between them, sharpened stakes had been driven into the ground. It was a thick, deadly defense against cavalry. A few hundred men worked hard at adding to those stakes as the mound of dirt swung around to defend the south. It wasn't nearly enough men. There would be a gap in their defenses about an eighth of a mile long. A gap through which ten thousand dragoons would charge.

"Sir."

Tamas broke away from his examination of the camp. Andriya and Vlora stood at attention. Neither looked like they'd slept all night. Damned fools.

"Gather the powder mages," Tamas said. "I'm sending you across the river."

They stared back at him blankly. "Sir?" Andriya said. His hands twitched on his rifle. "You promised we'd be killing Kez."

"You can do that from the other side of the river. I'm not risking any of my mages in the melee. I want you where you can shoot without being shot—or stabbed."

"You want us to cross in shifts to keep the Kez scouts at bay?" Vlora asked.

Tamas hesitated. A chill wind cut through the camp and he noticed a low fog creeping its way down from the mountains and across the floodplain.

"No. I want the Kez scouts getting a good look at the camp now. They're welcome to get as close as they dare."

"Sir, I'd rather be on this side of the river," Andriya said.

Tamas sighed. "Not today, Andriya."

Andriya gripped his rifle. "Please, sir." He bared his teeth. "You promised I would get to kill Kez."

"From a distance." Tamas clipped the words off firmly. "Besides, they'll be watching for the Marked. They'll feel more confident with you on the other side of the river."

"You're coming with us, then?" Vlora said.

Tamas frowned. "No. Why would I?"

"You're one of the powder mages, sir."

"No. I have to remain in close in order to command."

"That's not fair." Andriya was livid. He stared toward the forest, straining like a hound that could smell its quarry. "I've got every right to put my bayonet through a Kez noble's eye. I want blood on my hands."

"'Blood on my hands, *sir*,'" Tamas corrected. He didn't need this. He had fifteen thousand cavalry about to rain down on him, and just when he thought he might have sorted things out with Vlora, Andriya was becoming insubordinate. "Cross the river. That's an order, soldier."

He turned away from Andriya to make it clear that the conversation was over. The two powder mages left him alone with Gavril. Tamas and Gavril remained silent for a few minutes, watching the organized chaos evolve in the camp. Men shouted. Tamas thought he saw a punch thrown. A little while later, the first raft was launched. It got away from the handlers and was pulled downstream with no one on it. A cry of dismay went up from the brigades, and Tamas didn't think it was feigned.

"Where do you want me?" Gavril asked.

"On your horse," Tamas said. "You and your rangers should take the eastern flank, in case some of Beon's dragoons attempt the scree."

"All right," Gavril said.

"Here." Tamas unhooked the cavalry saber from his belt and handed it to Gavril. "Better to swing from horseback."

"You're not going to be mounted?"

Tamas smiled, though he didn't feel any mirth behind it. "I'm taking the center. If I'm not mounted, the men won't see when I fall."

Gavril seemed to think on the gravity behind those words before accepting the cavalry saber.

Tamas took the small sword from his saddle and hooked it to his belt.

"I'll see you after the battle," Gavril said.

Tamas clasped hands, then was surprised when Gavril pulled him into an embrace. Gavril held him for a moment, then headed off to join his rangers.

Olem returned an hour later.

"Any of the men eat this morning?" Tamas asked.

"Caught a lot of fish in the river, actually. Andriya bagged a pair of goats on the mountainside. There was a little leftover horse. Every man had a bite of something."

"Let's hope it's enough," Tamas said.

Olem looked up. "At least the buzzards will eat well."

Tamas watched as the fog he'd seen earlier moving in slowly enveloped the entire camp. It wasn't thick—barely two feet deep. Enough to obscure the ground but not the camp itself. The clouds had moved in from above. They threatened rain, but Tamas had seen this kind of weather before. There'd be nothing more than a light mist.

Strange weather for a summer day.

At eleven thirty, Tamas caught sight of a pair of horsemen to the west, nearly a mile away at the bend in the river. He sprinkled some black powder on his tongue, and the men came into sharp relief. Tan-and-green uniforms under shining breastplates, and wearing plumed helmets.

The cuirassiers had arrived.

Adamat stood on the sixth floor of the Dwightwich bell tower with a looking glass at his eye. He was examining a fellow with shifty eyes who was wearing a faded red waistcoat and knee-length trousers and sitting on the stoop about a hundred paces from Lord Vetas's headquarters.

"They have another lookout on the corner of Seventh and May-flew Avenue," Adamat said. He could hear the scratching of a pen behind him. He scanned the streets once more with the looking glass and then handed it to a young woman by the name of Riplas—the eunuch's second-in-command. She took his spot at the window while he turned to the assembled group in the cramped bell tower room.

"You're sure you have everyone?" the eunuch asked Adamat.

Adamat looked at the eunuch out of the corner of his eye. If he had any idea Adamat was blackmailing his master, he'd given no indication when he showed up the day before with forty of the meanest street scum Adamat had ever seen: boxers, gang members, dockworkers, pimps, and bodyguards.

"I've been watching them on and off for almost two weeks," Adamat said. "They change their posts, but between your reports and mine I think we have everyone."

He guessed that Vetas was employing over a hundred heads, based on the comings and goings from his headquarters. That was no small operation, and any thirty of them could be in the head-quarters at any given time. The Proprietor had said Vetas had sixty enforcers.

Adamat looked over at Bo. The Privileged was down on his haunches in one corner of the room, his eyes closed, hands folded inside the sleeves of his jacket. He opened his eyes, as if he'd felt Adamat's gaze upon him. Adamat shuddered. He was still unnerved by the casual murder of Manhouch's headsman the day before.

"Vetas's pet Privileged is there," Bo said. "Right now. She's not some hired fool, either. She's got cabal-level stuff at her beck and call."

A bird burst from the bells above their heads, causing Adamat to jump. He noticed that he was the only one to do so and smoothed the front of his coat. A powerful Privileged? That wasn't good. Not at all. He was depending on Bo to be able to neutralize Vetas's Privileged even as Adamat's men seized the place.

Bo must have sensed the unasked question. "I'll kill her. Don't worry about that."

"If it turns into any kind of a fight between you two, we're all dead men," the eunuch said.

"Well, you're not exactly a man," Bo said with a smirk. He nod-ded to Riplas. "And she's not." His smirk suddenly turned to a frown. "And she's *definitely* not."

Adamat turned to see Fell standing on the bell tower stairs. The Fontain Academy graduate wore a fitted waistcoat, sans tails, and a pair of tight men's pants tucked into her boots.

"Ricard can't spare any men right now," Fell said, "but he sent me."

The eunuch turned toward her with a look of disgust. "Does he know the resources the Proprietor is shifting for this operation?" he asked.

"As a matter of fact," Fell said, cocking her eyebrow, "he doesn't. I'm sure he'll be interested to know."

Adamat stepped between them. "It's more help than you realize," he said to the eunuch. For Ricard to send his ten-million-krana servant into harm's way meant a great deal.

"Bah," the eunuch sneered. His fingers tapped rapidly against the side of his leg. He seemed on edge—not the quiet, thoughtful killer Adamat had met months ago.

Adamat stepped back to the window and took the looking glass from Riplas. "Any more lookouts?" he asked.

"None."

"Then take the final assignments down."

Riplas left the room. She had the positions and descriptions of all of Lord Vetas's lookouts. She'd hand them over to the eunuch's goons, and they'd do the rest.

Everything was in place. Now Adamat just had to wait.

He lifted the looking glass to his eye and returned his gaze to Vetas's headquarters. Over an hour passed, and he watched from his vantage point as the eunuch's goons took care of Vetas's lookouts. He felt the sweat roll down the back of his neck as he waited. So much could go wrong. The slightest slip, and Faye was dead.

"What if he doesn't come outside today?" Bo asked.

The front door to Vetas's headquarters opened, and a familiar figure stepped outside. He wore his sharp black coat, top hat, and carried a cane in one hand. Adamat felt his heart jump at the sight.

"That's not going to be a problem," Adamat said. "He's leaving now."

Lord Vetas checked the street with the smallest twitches of his head. Probably receiving signals from his lookouts—the closest of whom Adamat had left undisturbed.

Vetas gave an almost imperceptible nod. A woman came through the door—the same one he'd seen in the red dress weeks ago, with the auburn curls—and together they headed south down the avenue. They were followed two steps back by a pair of well-dressed and well-muscled men. A few seconds later a third came out the door, waited for a moment, then followed.

"I'll keep on his trail," Fell said, disappearing down the stairs.

"Take his tail," Adamat said to the eunuch, "and then meet us at the house. Bo?"

Bo stood up, stretching his gloved fingers. "I'll get a little closer and unravel the Privileged's wards. It'll take me some time, but I'll be ready when you get back."

Sergeant Oldrich was waiting for Adamat in the chapel beneath the bell tower. He sat in a pew, legs up, a wad of tobacco in one cheek. He tipped his hat back, watching as Bo slid out one exit.

"So," Oldrich said, turning to Adamat, "you got yourself a Privileged."

Adamat steeled himself. He couldn't be sure how Oldrich would react after having specifically stated he wouldn't help Adamat rescue Bo. "I did."

"I heard Verundish dismissed her men and left town yesterday. I thought that might have been the cause."

"I did what I needed to. He's freed of his gaes, if that makes a difference."

"Oh?"

"He killed the guillotine operator who took off Manhouch's head."

"Huh," Oldrich said. "Well, I'm sure the field marshal will be delighted. You ready?"

"Let's go."

Oldrich's soldiers fell in with them as they left the chapel, and Adamat told them to stay back a hundred paces.

Adamat, in turn, trailed Fell. He saw her weaving in and out of foot traffic as they headed farther into the city. The streets were crowded just after lunch—that would make it harder for Vetas's men to spot Adamat, but just as hard for Adamat to keep track of them.

It was a little over thirty minutes before Fell stopped and waved Adamat forward. They stood at a busy intersection, just around the corner from a flower market. Fell had her back against the wall, her shoulders slumped as if she didn't have a care in the world. Adamat came up beside her and mimicked her body language.

"His tail is over there," she said, slowly tilting her chin upward in one direction.

Adamat saw the man right away. He was eating a meat pie and scanning the crowd with a mistrusting leer. Not subtle, but an effective lookout. Not far behind him, Adamat spotted the eunuch.

"Vetas is inside the flower stall around the corner," Fell said. "Leave him to me. Have your soldiers take his goons."

"I want him alive."

"So do I," Fell said.

Adamat needed him alive so Vetas could tell him where Josep was. He wondered why Fell would want him breathing.

"I'm going," Fell said. She disappeared around the corner, casual and graceful as a cat.

Adamat gave the signal to Oldrich, then tilted his hat forward to hide his face and followed Fell.

He made his way to the middle of the street and was soon joined by Oldrich and six of his men. They each examined bouquets or pretended to talk, but he couldn't help but think they looked far too obvious.

Vetas's two goons were standing outside of the Parkside Flower Boutique, watching the crowd, their arms crossed, not the least bit subtle. Adamat glanced toward the tail. The man was gone. Adamat hoped that meant the eunuch had taken care of him.

Adamat could feel every muscle tighten as he watched the flower shop entrance out of the corner of his eye. Maybe Vetas had already spotted them and disappeared out the side. What if his goons warned him, or Vetas was able to slip into the crowd?

His hands were beginning to shake from nervousness when Lord Vetas finally emerged from the flower shop with the woman in the red dress. She carried a bouquet of flowers. He handed a package to one of his goons and scanned the flower market.

His eyes locked onto Adamat's. Adamat felt a cold sweat break at the corner of his brow. He tensed, ready to chase Vetas through the streets.

Fell emerged from the flower shop, strolling out like a paying customer. A stiletto dropped from her sleeve and she gracefully swung it around over Vetas's shoulder and pressed it to his throat.

The two goons stepped back, shouting. Both drew pistols. The crowd split apart.

Adamat felt like he was in a dream. He watched himself draw his own pistol and fire it. One of the goons went down. The other took a cudgel to the back of the head from one of Oldrich's soldiers, and the rest of the soldiers quickly fell in around Vetas, obscuring him from the crowd.

Adamat shouldered his way through the soldiers until he reached Vetas.

Lord Vetas was on his knees in front of Fell, a stiletto still to his throat. She'd relieved him of two very similar-looking daggers and a small pistol, both of which were lying on the ground behind her.

Adamat took great pleasure in the mild look of surprise on Vetas's face. It died quickly when Vetas saw Adamat.

Vetas smiled. "Adamat! I suspected you might still be alive."

"Is she still alive?" Adamat pressed the hot barrel of his pistol against Vetas's face.

"Every pain you do to me," Vetas said, not flinching at the heat of the pistol barrel, "I will return to you and your wife tenfold. I want you to remember that, Adamat."

"So she is alive?"

"Quite," Vetas said. "Though she won't be in an hour and forty-two minutes if I haven't returned." He paused, looking around at the soldiers. "I suspect you know where my headquarters is. You've probably been watching me very closely. Bravo. But do you have enough men to get in there?"

"You mean past your Privileged?" Adamat asked. "Yes. Yes, I think I do. Where is my boy?"

Vetas gave a sickeningly self-satisfied smile. "An hour and forty-one minutes. Are you sure you have time for this?"

Adamat looked at the woman in the red dress. Oldrich held her tightly by the arm. She glared at him through narrowed eyes, but he could see that her hands trembled. "Who are you?" he demanded.

"Nila," she said.

"What do you do for him?" He pointed at Vetas.

"Nothing! I . . . nothing. I don't work for him. I'm just there to watch Jakob. He's only a boy!"

"What was Vetas buying in there?"

"Flowers!"

"For who?"

"Lady Windeldwas, or something like that." Nila brushed the hair out of her face.

"Lady Winceslav?"

"Yes, that was it."

"Why?"

"I don't know." For all her fright, she was remarkably calm beneath the torrent of questions.

Adamat turned back to Vetas. "Why?"

"An hour and forty minutes, Adamat," he said.

Adamat brought his pistol back and slammed the butt across Vetas's face. "Secure them," he said to Fell. To Oldrich, "Sergeant, give her four of your men. We need to get off the street before the police get here."

Fell dragged Vetas to his feet, still holding the stiletto to his throat. Oldrich sent four of the men with her, along with Nila and the two wounded goons, and the rest of the soldiers followed Adamat.

They met up with the eunuch three blocks down from Vetas's headquarters.

"My men are in position," the eunuch said.

"Where's Bo?" Adamat asked, wheezing from the effort of the run.

He found the Privileged around the corner, standing in the middle of the street. Bo wore black gloves over his Privileged gloves to conceal them. He was muttering to himself, his gloved fingers working silently in the air in front of him, as if he was playing an invisible piano with one hand and plucking a harp with the other. There were three or four people watching him as if he was some kind of madman. He certainly looked the part.

"We have to go in now," Adamat said. He hunched over his pistol, trying to conceal it from view while he reloaded it.

Bo's fingers continued to work the air. "I said I'd need time."

"We don't have much time," Adamat said. "His men have orders to kill Faye if he doesn't return at a prescribed time."

"Unfortunate," Bo said with a scowl. "Tell the eunuch to get his men in place."

The order was given, and five minutes later the eunuch joined Adamat and Bo.

"We're ready," the eunuch said.

Bo looked him up and down, eyes lingering on the tailored suit and the bald head. "You make my skin crawl."

"I'll take that as a compliment."

Adamat smoothed the front of his jacket. "Sergeant?"

Oldrich's remaining soldiers had fetched their rifles. They beginning to get looks from the passersby. "We're ready," Oldrich said.

"Let's make it a parade, then." Bo turned on his heel and marched down the middle of the street, heading toward Lord Vetas's headquarters. His fingers twitched, making music that only he could hear. Adamat exchanged a look with Captain Oldrich. This was not how they'd taken the house in Offendale.

Bo didn't slow as he rounded the corner and stepped his way toward Vetas's house. When he reached the middle of the street directly in front of the house, he turned and faced it. He raised his hands above his head. In one of the windows, a lookout shouted a warning.

Even though Adamat couldn't open his third eye, he could still feel it when a Privileged standing at his elbow reached into the Else. Sorcery flowed into the world, and Bo threw his arms wide, and the entire face of the building collapsed like a piece of cake sliced by a giant knife.

Adamat stared at the dust rising from the rubble. Men inside the house stared back, coughing and waving away plaster dust. The shock was plain on their faces.

Sergeant Oldrich drew his sword. "Charge!" he screamed.

All pit broke loose.

CHAPTER

24

A column of heavy cavalry appeared on the floodplain down-river, west of Tamas. The plumes on their helmets waved gently in the breeze, their mounts stepping with confidence despite the low cover of fog.

Tamas lifted his looking glass and examined the enemy.

The officers were out front with their red epaulets, shouting orders, sabers raised.

Fools.

A rifle cracked from somewhere across the river. A few moments later a Kez officer tumbled from his horse.

They advanced at a leisurely pace, as if it were nothing more than a parade drill. More rifle shots rang out from Tamas's powder mages, and cuirassiers began to fall. The column continued to advance.

Brian McClellan

"This weather might foul our powder, sir," Olem said, looking up at the clouds.

Tamas said, "It won't rain."

"It's awfully damp, sir. Strange, this fog. Never seen it sweep down off the mountains so quickly."

"That's because this is an answer to a prayer."

Tamas heard a trumpet echo through Hune Dora Forest and looked to the south. There was movement among the trees half a mile away across the floodplain where only hours ago Tamas's infantry had been cutting trees and dragging them to camp.

The dragoons emerged from the forest.

Tamas felt his breath catch in his throat. So many cavalry in one place.

He'd seen a force like this perhaps three times in his life. Each time, he'd been numbered among those cavalry, and the enemy had been swept before them. The horses stepped in line, well trained and fearless. Unlike the cuirassiers, someone among the dragoons had the foresight to remove the officer's epaulets, so they would be harder to pick out for Tamas's powder mages.

Behind him, the panic among the Seventh and Ninth Brigades seemed to rise in pitch, and Tamas worried that the act had outgrown itself. He'd witnessed hard infantry of the line break at the sight of a magnificent cavalry formation before.

And the Kez cavalry *were* magnificent. The armored breasts of the cuirassier warhorses seemed to form a wall of moving steel. Their plumes quivered with the movement, and the immaculate uniforms of their riders only added to their majesty.

Tamas searched the line of cuirassiers. In a powder trance, he could see the faces of each man, even at this distance. But picking out one face among so many was nearly impossible. "I wonder where Beon will position himself," Tamas said. He pointed with his small sword to the southwest. "There, likely, so that he can sweep with his cuirassiers around the barriers we've set up and join his dragoons in the slaughter." Tamas turned to his bodyguard. "Tell me we're going to win, Olem."

" 'We're going to win, Olem,' " Olem said, putting his last cigarette in his mouth.

Tamas stepped onto a rocky outcropping to give himself a better view of the battlefield.

"Men," he shouted, "take the line!"

Nila was pushed into a doorway by one of the soldiers.

She squeezed her eyes closed, fighting tears she knew so desperately wanted to come. To have escaped soldiers so many times and then fall into Lord Vetas's clutches, and now this? Who were these people? What did they want?

A man grabbed her by the arm and shoved her up a narrow flight of stairs. They went up two floors, shouting and cursing the whole way. Nila fought them out of instinct more than anything else. She clawed at a soldier's face, only for her arm to be bent around behind her and her face shoved up against the wall.

"Pit, this girl is a hellion," the man said. She tried to twist in his grip. He put pressure on her arm and she gasped from the sudden pain. It felt as if it would snap at any moment.

She was thrown into the corner of a small, windowless room. The plaster was yellow and bare, the only furniture a squat table with a stub of candle.

They hadn't gone far before finding this building, not more than a couple of blocks. Nila had no idea if this was planned, but there seemed some confusion among the soldiers.

Lord Vetas was pushed to the ground beside her. She stared at him—the only familiar face in this chaos. He was calm, collected. Completely unperturbed. Nila hated that she looked to him for some kind of reassurance. She knew none would come.

"Watch him," the woman said. She was young, and could not

have been more than ten years older than Nila, but her eyes were as cold as Vetas's. Nila had heard someone call her Fell. The soldiers seemed hesitant to follow her orders, but after Fell gave them a long stare, they turned to watch Vetas.

Fell had drawn a pair of wrist irons from beneath her coat. They weren't typical irons, even Nila could see that. Instead of a horseshoe-looking metal with a crosspiece, they were thick bands with only a single loop of chain between them. The two soldiers turned Vetas roughly onto his stomach, and the irons were snapped around his wrists. He rolled over, examining Fell.

"Drovian irons," he said. "Very professional."

"Turn around," Fell said to Nila.

"No," Nila said.

Fell grasped her by the arm and jerked her forward onto her knees. Fell stepped behind her, and Nila felt the cold metal of the wrist irons close on her skin.

There was a shout from downstairs. Fell turned to one of the soldiers. "Do not take your eyes off of him," she said, and disappeared down the stairs.

Despite Fell's instructions, the two soldiers retreated to the hallway, where they stood near the door, leaning on their rifles.

"What is happening?" Nila asked Vetas.

Vetas's face was impassive, unmoving as always. He didn't so much as glance at her.

He watched the two soldiers for a moment before rocking back on his hips and deftly sliding his shackled wrists beneath his legs and out in front of him, like a contortionist performing a trick. Nila felt her eyes widen a bit. The wrist irons hurt like all pit, and even if they hadn't been so tight, she couldn't have done that—and Vetas was a man well over forty.

Nila glanced nervously between Vetas and the soldiers. How could they not see him? Did they just not care?

Vetas pulled something off the bottom of his shoe: a wooden

knob. It looked like the handle of an ice pick Nila had seen men use to move blocks of ice in the winter, but it had no pick attached to it.

Another handle came off the bottom of his other shoe, and Vetas searched through his slicked hair with his fingers, drawing out a long wire after only a moment of searching. He wrapped the wire around one handle and then the other.

Nila had been with Lord Vetas long enough to know what it was: a garrote.

Vetas got to his feet in one smooth motion, like a snake rising from the grass. He crossed the room in a few silent steps.

One of the soldiers must have seen him coming out of the corner of his eye. The soldier whirled, raising his rifle. Vetas slammed an elbow into the soldier's throat. The soldier staggered to one side, gurgling painfully for air. The other soldier had his rifle up in time, but the long bayonet was impossible to use in such close quarters. Vetas grabbed the stock of the rifle and smacked the soldier in the nose with it. When the man reeled back, Vetas slid around him, dropping the garrote into place.

Nila's mind whirled. She eyed the soldier's fallen rifle—she could have used it on Vetas if not for the irons locking her hands behind her back. The two soldiers soon lay dead in the hall. Blood trickled across the floorboards, flowing to fill the grooves.

Vetas, his face still and unmoving as stone, searched the soldier for keys.

The creaking of the floorboards was the only warning. Vetas looked up and suddenly fell back into the hallway, out of Nila's line of sight. Fell soared past, knife at the ready.

Nila could hear the dull thumps of flesh on flesh. Grunts, a few quiet curses—those came from the woman.

The pair tumbled back into the room. Nila screamed as both of them tumbled over her outstretched feet.

They struggled on the floor, legs intertwined, the knife pressed flat between them. Nila kicked indiscriminately. She wanted them away from her. The knives, the anger—one slip, and Nila could be dead.

Fell rolled off of Vetas and sprang to her feet.

She struck at him, fast as a viper. Vetas, still on his knees, caught the knife on the metal of his wrist irons. She struck again, and again, and each time Vetas moved impossibly fast to block her. Between the strikes he managed to regain his footing.

They circled warily, and Nila pulled herself into the corner as much as possible.

She hoped they'd kill each other. But what then? She had no way of getting the irons off her hands.

Fell and Vetas seemed at an impasse. Their circling stopped. Fell changed hands with her dagger, then changed back.

Nila didn't hesitate. Months of anger and fear came to a head, and with a shriek of rage she kicked Vetas in the back of the leg.

Fell struck out at Lord Vetas at the same time. The blow to Vetas's leg sent him leaning backward. The knife slid past his eye, cutting one cheek badly. He caught Fell's hand, deftly sliding the garrote around her wrist, and swung about.

Fell had no choice but to follow his swing, or risk losing her hand. Vetas stepped close to her, and she tried to step away. It was like some kind of grisly dance.

Vetas slammed his head forward into Fell's cheek. The woman staggered backward, hitting the window.

Vetas had let go of his garrote. Dazed, Fell couldn't have seen the kick coming. She took a boot square to the chest, and tumbled out the window.

Vetas turned to Nila. There was a quiet click, and his wrist irons fell off. He held the key up in one hand.

Nila shrank away from the darkness in his eyes.

"You bet the wrong way, laundress," he said. He tossed the key on the floor. "You'll pay for that tonight. I promise. If not you, then the boy will."

He left the room, leaving Nila to let the sobs wrench themselves from her throat. Her whole body shook. She crawled over to the key. It took a few minutes with her trembling hands to get it into the lock and free herself.

She stared at the destruction. Two dead soldiers, a broken window, and Lord Vetas was gone. She took the time to collect herself. Deep breaths stopped the sobs, and she dried her tears. This wasn't the time to give in to emotion.

She could run. She knew that.

But if she ran, Vetas would do unspeakable things to Jakob. It was no empty threat. He wouldn't hesitate.

Nila crept down the stairs, only to find the other two soldiers dead in the hallway on the first floor. One's head was twisted at an impossible angle. The other had been bayoneted with his own rifle.

There was a crowd gathering in the street looking at the bodies through the open door. A woman was screaming for the police. Someone pointed at Nila.

It only took a moment to find a back door to the building. Nila took it, slipping down an alleyway and into the crowd.

She had to make her way back to Vetas's house and try to get Jakob away.

Adamat put his head down and charged into the gaping hole left in Vetas's headquarters by Bo's sorcery.

He shot the first man to raise a weapon, and then tossed aside his spent pistol and drew his cane sword.

Oldrich's soldiers were the first to follow Adamat into the fray, their bayonets making short work of Vetas's goons. The eunuch's men followed them in, and Adamat could hear pistol shots and the sounds of fighting from the other side of the buildings. They'd formed a cordon around Vetas's headquarters. Now they just had to tighten it.

A horizontal pillar of flame shot through the wall of one of the rooms inside, missing Adamat by not more than a few feet, the heat of it sending him reeling to one side.

The flame splashed over one of the eunuch's men, sending him screaming, running into the street. The pillar grew longer by the second, extending into the street and completely enveloping Privileged Borbador.

Adamat felt his heart leap into his throat. If Bo died, Vetas's Privileged would kill them all . . .

The flames abated, leaving Bo standing unhurt, like a rock that had been pounded by the surf. Bo advanced, his hands held out in front of him, fingers plucking at invisible strings.

Wind tore at Adamat's coat and buffeted through the innards of the building, knocking men from both sides off their feet before slamming through the wall and pushing back the pillar of flame. Bo raised his hands above his head and was suddenly running forward, his jaw locked and determined.

Lightning shot at Bo. He batted it aside with one hand as he scaled the rubble into the building, then leapt through the inner wall with a roar.

The house shuddered and shook as the two Privileged locked in battle. Adamat stopped in his tracks as he realized they could all be killed by the slightest mistake by either of the Privileged. One finger twitched the wrong way, one hand pushed aside accidentally, and every one of them would be dead.

The Privileged's flames had lit curtains on one side of the house. The fire spread to the table, quickly, and black smoke filled the ruined building.

He had to find Faye.

A man with a scar cutting across his lips stumbled toward Adamat, half blinded by the smoke. He swung a small sword wildly, crashing into a chair. Adamat leapt back, blocking a second swing with his cane sword, then a third. He felt the handle of his cane shift beneath his fingers—it was not meant to block the flailing sword of a man this big, and would splinter from the shock.

He leapt inside the scarred man's guard and drove the cane sword between his ribs. The man lurched back, bellowing in pain, and Adamat let him go.

"Faye!" he yelled. "Faye!"

The smoke was getting thicker. Where would Vetas have kept her? The basement? Did he have other prisoners here? The boy had been on the second floor when Adamat saw him in the window weeks ago, but the boy was not his concern.

Adamat heard a woman's scream. It was coming from upstairs.

The building was being quickly abandoned. Men ran past Adamat, some of them fighting the flames, some of them fighting each other. Adamat blinked through the tears brought on by the smoke. There, the staircase.

He made his way to the stairs. The house creaked. The flames were moving quickly now, spreading across the furniture at alarming speeds. There was paper everywhere, even in the foyer. Parchments and books, tables against all the walls. It looked more like a clerk's office than a place where Lord Vetas planned whatever campaign he was waging.

What if he wasn't keeping Faye here? What if she was somewhere else and the scream Adamat had heard was another?

Smoke filled the staircase as Adamat made his way up it. He pulled a handkerchief from his pocket, pressing it over his face. He stood dismayed at the top of the stairs, staring down a long hallway and a row of at least a dozen doors. The heat from downstairs was growing. It would spread up the stairs at any moment—if the smoke didn't kill him, the flames would. It would take too long to search the place. How could he find Faye in time?

"Faye! Faye!"

Adamat tried the first door. Locked. He kicked it open. A small room with two soiled beds and a nightstand. Empty.

He drew his foot back to kick open the next door when a scream came from farther down the hall. He rushed toward the source of the sound. One of the doors was open. He swung around the corner, cane sword raised.

Faye stood over the body of a man, a bloody candlestick in one hand. On her face she wore a look so vicious that Adamat scarcely recognized her. Adamat saw the face of a small boy peeking out from behind a curtain on the other side of the room.

"Faye!"

She looked up and nearly collapsed when she saw him. She dropped the candlestick and might have fallen had Adamat not caught her.

They stared at each other for one long moment, and Adamat wondered if it was perhaps she who was supporting him and not the other way around, as his knees felt like so much jelly.

"Where's Josep?" Adamat asked.

"Gone. They took him."

"I'll get him back," Adamat said. He looked at the boy. "That's the Eldaminse child, isn't it?"

"It is," Faye said. "Come on." She held out a hand to the boy. "Don't be afraid, this is my husband."

Adamat stared at his wife. "I . . ." he said.

"Shh." She pressed a finger to his lips. There were tears in her eyes. "We have to go."

Adamat nodded. "Quickly, let's—" He stopped in the hallway. The smoke was too thick, and there were flames leaping from the staircase. He tore off his jacket. "Press this to your face," he said to Faye, and gave his handkerchief to the boy. He led them away from the stairs, down the hallway and toward the front of the building. They might have to jump to the rubble below, but a broken leg was much preferable to being roasted alive.

Adamat froze as a great groaning noise rose above the sound of the flames. Was it the house creaking under the strain of the battle or some kind of sorcery?

"This way," Faye said, pulling him back into action. She led him around the corner, where another staircase went down to the first floor. There were no flames shooting up this one, but he took it cautiously.

Something slammed through the staircase wall and tumbled down the stairs into a pile of smoldering clothes. Adamat thrust Faye behind him, pointing at the pile with his sword.

Coughing, sputtering, it stood up.

It was Bo. Flames still licked at his clothes, and his muttonchops were singed. He beat at the flames for a moment, and then scowled through the smoking ruins of the stairwell wall.

Bo held a hand over his head. A *whump* split the air, making Adamat's ears pop. The flames died instantly. Bo's fingers jerked to one side, and wind whipped through the house, sucking smoke away like a giant bellows inhaling above a fire.

The staircase was suddenly full of cool, clean air. Adamat gasped in a great breath of it, holding Faye tightly. She clutched the Eldaminse boy to her skirts.

Fire whipped past Bo, over his shoulder. The Privileged turned his head, as if mildly perturbed. Slivers of ice the size of daggers shot from above his head and *thwapped* into something out of Adamat's sight. Bo nodded to himself.

"You can come down now," Bo said. "I think it's safe."

"You think?" Adamat crept slowly down the stairs until he reached the base.

They passed the kitchen and entered the sitting room at the back of the house. On the near wall, impaled to the masonry by icicles dripping blood, was the other Privileged. It was a woman, Deliv by her dark skin. Bo didn't spare her a second glance. Faye shielded the Eldaminse boy's eyes.

"Faye," Adamat said, "this is Privileged Borbador, the last remaining member of the Adran royal cabal."

"Forgive me if I don't shake your hand," Faye said. "I don't think I want to touch your hands."

Bo's black gloves had been burned off by the flames, but his rune-covered Privileged's gloves were white and pristine, as if brand-new. He clasped his hands and rocked back on his heels. "Understandable. Where's Vetas?" he asked.

"Fell has him," Adamat said.

"That woman, I'd very much like to meet her. Properly, that is."

Adamat couldn't help but wonder what that meant. "I don't think you do," he said.

"I think I'll be—"

A scream from outside cut off Bo's sentence. He cocked his head, like a dog listening for a whistle. "Oh, pit," he said. "You didn't tell me there were two."

"What, another Privileged?" Adamat began casting around for somewhere to hide. But what could protect them? There was no hiding from a Privileged.

Bo sneered, rolling up his sleeves. "Yes," he said. "Get down!"

The world exploded in a blast of plaster and wood. Adamat was thrown from his feet and knocked about, buffeted by forces beyond his control. He tried to grab for Faye—for anything, but found himself on the ground a moment later.

Everything was silent. Had the attack killed Faye? Or Bo, for that matter? Adamat moved cautiously, not sure whether all the parts of him were intact. A beam had fallen across his chest, the air swirling with smoke and dust. It felt like the whole house had landed on him.

He didn't feel anything broken, and he was able to move the beam just enough to wriggle out from beneath the rubble. He used his fingers to gingerly feel across the whole surface of his chest. Not much pain.

Adamat climbed to his feet. The Eldaminse boy was nearby, apparently unhurt. Adamat wasn't sure whether to be relieved or worried that through all the excitement the boy had hardly made a noise.

"Go on," Adamat said to him, "hide in the kitchen!" The Privileged might still be here. The boy rushed past, and Adamat shook his head to clear it. Where was Faye?

Panic rose inside of him. Faye. She was gone. Separated from him by the blast. The roof had caved in, and he'd avoided most of it . . . sweet Kresimir, was she beneath the rubble?

"Faye! Faye!"

"She's right here," a voice said.

Adamat turned to find the eunuch standing in the doorway. He was holding Faye up beneath one arm. It looked like she'd injured her ankle. They were both covered in plaster dust.

Adamat eyed the eunuch. They'd done it. Taken Vetas. Saved Faye. Would the eunuch turn on him now for blackmailing the Proprietor? Bo wasn't here. Adamat didn't even know if the Privileged was alive. Adamat didn't know where Sergeant Oldrich was. No one would ask questions if the eunuch quietly killed them both and disappeared.

"She's safe," the eunuch said.

"Thank you."

The eunuch was surprisingly gentle as he helped Faye into the room. Adamat stepped toward them, arms out.

The stiletto handle seemed to materialize in the side of the eunuch's neck. When he opened his mouth, blood poured out, and he dropped to his knees. Faye, suddenly unsupported, toppled to the side, only to be caught by Lord Vetas.

CHAPTER
25

No one moved at Tamas's shouted order. The thick chaos of soldiers milling against the edge of the river did not change.

Tamas felt his heart begin to beat faster.

"Men of the Seventh! Take the line!"

Nothing. His hands shook. He'd overplayed himself. This false panic he'd meant to create had become real. He'd defeated himself before the battle even began.

"First Battalion!" a voice cut through the crowd. Someone shoved their way out of the press. It was old Colonel Arbor. He held his rifle in one hand, his teeth in the other. "To the line, First Battalion!"

Tamas swung around. The Kez cavalry continued to advance slowly. They were a half a mile out on the western front. The dragoons to the south began to move forward. Vlora and the rest of the powder mages continued to fire from across the river, whittling away at their numbers.

Adran infantry began to peel away from the mob by the river and get to their positions. Too few of them. Too slowly.

Then more. And more. Soldiers left the riverside and raced across the camp to the mound of dirt separating them from the Kez cavalry. They threw themselves to the safe side of the mound and readied their rifles, loading bullets and fixing bayonets. Tamas took a deep breath. He felt his heart soar. If he could have kissed every one of his men then and there, he would have.

He turned back to the Kez advance and his heart stopped.

The advance had ceased less than a quarter of a mile from Tamas's position.

Fifteen thousand Kez cavalry wedged Tamas's army completely against the river and the mountains.

He saw a man ride to the front of the cuirassiers. Had Beon figured out Tamas's game? Did he sense a trap?

The man, Tamas recognized, was Beon je Ipille himself. Brave, to come out to the front of his heavy cavalry, when he knew a powder mage's bullet might end him any second.

Beon seemed to cock his head at Tamas's position. His lips moved briefly, then he kissed his sword and raised it.

A salute. Beon was saluting Tamas. The motion stunned him. *You stand and fight*, the salute seemed to say, *when you could have run*.

Beon's sword fell and the earth trembled as fifteen thousand sets of hooves thundered toward Tamas.

"Hold!" Tamas yelled, gripping his rifle. He turned away from the cuirassiers. Their charge would be stopped by the sharpened stakes and crosses. They'd pull up hard and exchange fire with the Ninth, or advance slowly to try to navigate the defenses.

Between Tamas and the dragoons, however, there were no such

apparent obstacles—only a thin layer of white fog over the ground and then the raised earthworks behind which his men crouched.

Three hundred yards. The dragoons leaned over their mounts, urging them faster. A bullet whistled over Tamas's head and took a dragoon between the eyes. Tamas raised his rifle, lined up a shot, and fired. He lowered, reloaded, and repeated.

Two hundred yards. Dragoons raised their carbines and twisted their faces in wordless cries.

One hundred yards. Tamas's lines opened fire. Hundreds of dragoons fell from the first volley alone. The rest charged on, heedless of their comrades' fall.

Seventy yards. The dragoons opened fire with their carbines. Tamas's soldiers crouched behind their earthen wall, reloading.

Fifty yards. Dragoons let their carbines drop and raised their pistols.

Thirty yards. The line of dragoons aimed pistols.

Twenty yards.

Ten yards.

The front line of dragoons disappeared.

Tamas closed his eyes for a brief moment as the screams reached him.

The momentum of the cavalry unit at full gallop had carried them headfirst into a concealed trench. Almost twenty feet wide and just as deep, it stretched the entire length of the "opening" Tamas had left in his defenses. The trench was topped with stakes covered in grass and other debris. A poor disguise in the light of the day, but the fog had covered them completely. They cracked under the weight of the warhorses.

Tamas had once seen a row of carriages go straight into the Adsea. The first carriage had plunged around a steep corner and off the end of a pier. The second had followed, the driver seeing the drop only at the last second, while the third driver's attempts to slow his horses had failed.

This was much like that, but instead of three carriages, it was thousands and thousands of dragoons heading straight into his trench.

By the time the dragoons had managed to arrest their charge, the trench was nearly filled with screaming, thrashing horses and writhing men trying to escape the press. The line of Kez dragoons stared in horror at their fallen comrades.

Tamas shuddered at the thought of being at the bottom of that trench.

"Fire!" Tamas yelled.

The Seventh Brigade opened fire at the Kez dragoons. Their horses milled in panic at the edge of the trench, officers shouting and waving their swords, trying to get the horses at the rear of the column to back up so they could organize a withdrawal.

Tamas reloaded and fired again. The dragoons began to organize. If they were given a chance to disengage, they still had thousands left. They could reorganize and hound Tamas's flank when he turned to deal with the cuirassiers.

"Bayonets!" Tamas ordered, lifting his rifle in the air.

Every forty paces of the trench, they'd left a ten-foot-wide path of solid ground. They were unmarked, and the way would be unsure in the fog, but Tamas had to counterattack.

Tamas headed across the closest of these paths, straight into the flank of the withdrawing Kez dragoons.

He reached out with his senses, taking in the closest powder charges and igniting them with his mind. The small explosions killed men and horse alike, rattling Tamas's teeth from their proximity. His soldiers flooded around him, howling as they set upon the dragoons with their long-sword bayonets.

The melee erupted along the whole line as the five thousand men of the Seventh Brigade slammed into the Kez dragoons. Without the impact of their charge, and against the long reach of sword bayonets, the dragoons lost their advantage.

Tamas ran toward the closest dragoon. He thrust his bayonet up and into the man's exposed side, then jerked his rifle savagely to tear open the wound. The man fell from his horse, and Tamas danced back out of the way as the animal panicked and bolted.

Something hit him hard from the side, knocking him off his feet. He landed on the ground, the breath knocked from him, and was immediately pushing himself back up.

"Sir!" Olem had lost his rifle and drawn his sword. He rammed it into the thigh of a dragoon and made a dash for Tamas.

Tamas got to his feet, only to have Olem hit him full on in the chest. They both went down as a straight cavalry sword whooshed through the air where Tamas's head had been.

Olem rolled off of Tamas and helped him to his feet.

Tamas's own rifle had disappeared in the melee. He drew his sword.

"Time to back off, sir," Olem shouted over the din of gunfire.

"We're not done here yet. Seventh!" Tamas slid his sword into its scabbard and pulled a rifle out of the mud. It still had its bayonet fixed. He pointed it at the closest dragoon and ran, hoping Olem was behind him.

He reached out, detonating more powder as he drew closer to the dragoons once more. On either side of him, his infantry pressed the attack.

Tamas felt a stinging breeze along the right side of his head, just above his ear. He felt suddenly dizzy, but charged on. Each step, however, the dragoons seemed to get farther away.

It took Olem yelling into his ear to bring him back to reality. "They've retreated, sir!"

Tamas stopped and looked about him, taking in the carnage. Thousands had died in that charge, and thousands more were stuck in that trench—broken men and horses dying a slow death. The screams rang in his ears. "Right. Back to the line." He grabbed Olem's arm to steady himself.

They took a safe path across the trench. The rest of the Seventh had turned away from the retreating dragoons and were making sure none of the rest would get out of the trench alive. Tamas saw one dragoon grab an Adran soldier's foot and beg for mercy. The soldier put his bayonet through the dragoon's eye.

Tamas felt Olem's hand on his shoulder.

"You've taken a bullet along the side of your head, sir," Olem said.

Tamas touched his head and his fingers came back crimson.

"A straight crease," Olem said. "Bloody, but doesn't look deep."

Olem's left arm hung at his side. His sleeve was in bloody tatters, nearly cut from him. He noted Tamas's questioning gaze. "Just a flesh wound, sir."

"Tamas, you bloody dog!" a voice bellowed. "The Ninth has crumbled! Our flank is lost!"

The words brought Tamas's head up and around. Gavril rode by at full tilt, followed by the rest of his rangers heading to the west.

"Colonel Arbor!" Tamas cast about for the colonel, finding him near the edge of the trench, taking a pair of wounded Kez officers prisoner.

"Sir!"

"Hold this position." Tamas waved his sword over his head. "Men of the Seventh, to me!"

Tamas began to sprint to the west, fueled by adrenaline and the powder of the battle. Already, he could see the damage. There were countless cuirassiers inside the line of defenses. Some of the Ninth had already begun to flee, running deeper into the camp or throwing themselves into the river.

The cuirassiers pressed hard on the southwestern corner. The defenses had all but collapsed, except for a small knot of men. Tamas recognized General Cethal on horseback. Even as he caught sight of the general, Cethal's horse was pulled down.

Tamas came up short. He stamped the butt of his rifle on the ground and shouted to be heard.

"Line, form!"

Olem fell in beside him. To his left and right, soldiers of the Seventh stood shoulder to shoulder.

"Load!"

Rifles and muskets were quickly loaded.

"Aim!"

His men brought their weapons to their shoulders.

"Fire!"

The Seventh fired above the heads of the milling members of the Ninth. A slew of cuirassiers fell from their horses.

"Bayonets, forward!"

The "aim and fire" had given the rest of the Seventh time to fall in behind him. Tamas now had an infantry wall six lines deep, bayonets bristling. They marched forward, lockstep. Soldiers of the Ninth fell in or were pushed aside. He aimed his line directly toward where he'd seen General Cethal fall.

They encountered the heavy cavalry thirty paces later.

Cuirassiers locked in combat had lost their greatest weapon—the charge—but they had some advantages over dragoons. They were armored, providing protection against bayonets, and their heavy sabers were more effective against armed infantry.

"Hold the line!" Tamas ordered as his men began to bring down cuirassiers. They stabbed and slashed, putting the men and horses down before stepping past them and continuing the push.

Tamas spotted General Cethal through a break in the fighting. Cethal was on the ground, twenty paces away. His face and hands were bloody, his saber raised above him. A dismounted cuirassier knocked Cethal's sword to one side and thrust with his own.

Tamas broke his formation, charging between two men on horseback. The cuirassier above Cethal drew his sword back and thrust again. Cethal's body twitched.

The cuirassier didn't even see Tamas.

Tamas's bayonet entered the spot beneath his arm where the

straps of his breastplate met. Tamas rammed the bayonet in deeper, pushing it until the barrel of his rifle was soaked in blood. He pushed a final time and let go of the rifle, throwing himself to his knees at Cethal's side.

Cethal stared back up at him in horror, his hands crimson with his own blood.

Tamas heard the clash of swords and Olem's challenging yell, but they all seemed distant to him.

Cethal had been stabbed at least four times through the chest and stomach. His hands were covered with countless cuts, and his face was a mess. He blinked at Tamas through the blood.

"My boys," he gasped, "they broke."

Tamas took Cethal's hand in his and squeezed.

The ultimate betrayal. Your men breaking and running, fleeing around you.

"You didn't," Tamas said. "You stood."

"I'm not a coward," Cethal said. "Bloody Beon. Never seen cuirassiers so nimble. They danced between the trench and our . . . our fortifications." Cethal rammed his empty hand into one of the wounds in a futile attempt to staunch the bleeding. "You stop the dragoons?"

"We did."

Cethal drew in a sharp breath. "Don't be hard on my boys. I wanted to . . . to run, myself. Damned cuirassiers." He blinked again. "You find Beon and . . ." He coughed, and cleared his throat. ". . . give him my regards. That was a bloody fine bit of horsemanship." He pulled his hand out of Tamas's and used it to try and staunch another wound. "Go on. Men need you. I'll be . . . fine."

Tamas stripped off his coat and put it beneath Cethal's head. He stood up. His line of infantry had passed him and pushed on. He wrenched his bayonet out of the cuirassier's body and ran to catch up.

The heavy cavalry had fallen back. All but a handful had been unhorsed, and those had turned tail to flee. One by one, pockets of Kez cuirassiers surrendered.

He caught sight of the last of the fighting. His soldiers pressed in, presenting a wall of bristling bayonets to the remaining Kez. Tamas shouldered his way into the melee, and was not the least bit surprised to find Beon at the center of it.

Beon's helmet was gone. His breastplate hung off him by one strap, and the side of his cheek had been laid open. He favored one arm. Beside him the last of his bodyguards was run through and thrown to the ground. Beon stepped back, hair soaked with blood and sweat, and threw down his sword.

"I surrender," he said loudly. "We surrender."

One of the Adran soldiers stepped forward. He cocked his rifle back and aimed his bayonet at Beon's neck.

Tamas could stand it no more. The blood. The neglect of mercy. He dashed forward and grabbed the soldier's rifle by the hot muzzle and thrust it aside.

"He said," Tamas proclaimed loudly, "that he surrenders."

Adamat lurched forward, a curse on his lips, only to stop when Vetas pressed the stiletto against Faye's neck.

"I promised you pain tenfold," Vetas said. "I want you to remember that." His forearm flexed, and Adamat closed his eyes, unwilling to watch Faye's life blood spill from her throat.

"Step away from him."

Adamat opened his eyes. Vetas looked slightly confused. His forearm strained, but the stiletto got no closer to Faye's throat.

"Please," Bo said, coming around the corner, "just step off to one side."

Adamat snatched Faye, pulling her away from Vetas. Lord Vetas's nostrils flared, eyes flashing anger, but it was clear he couldn't move.

Bo's fingers twitched. Invisible sorcery tossed Vetas across the room, slamming him into the wall beside the impaled Privileged. Bo walked up beside Vetas and took the man's chin in hand roughly, turning his head to see the dead Privileged.

"She was good," Bo said. "Real worthy of cabal membership. That's what I did to her. The other one—your backup—he wasn't that skilled. It only took a moment. And you." Bo tapped a gloved finger beneath Vetas's chin. "I don't like you. I saw that room you keep in the cellar. I've known men like that in the cabal. I was overjoyed to hear that Tamas had slaughtered them."

Bo stepped back and looked at Vetas thoughtfully. Vetas was still pinned to the wall by Bo's sorcery. Bo said, "I bet you were the type of child who tortured animals for fun. Tell me, did you ever pull the wings off of insects?"

Vetas didn't respond.

"Answer me!" Bo bellowed.

Vetas flinched. "Yes."

"That's what I thought. How does it feel?"

A single twitch of Bo's finger. That's all it took and Vetas's right arm was ripped off by invisible forces. Adamat didn't know who screamed louder: Vetas, from the pain, or Faye from the shock. Adamat clutched Faye to his chest, worried he'd fall at any moment, and his stomach felt like it might turn inside out.

Bo's finger twitched again. Vetas's other arm dropped to the ground beside him. There was a flare of fire at his shoulders.

"We'll cauterize those wounds," Bo said. "Wouldn't want you to die too quickly. That's the point among you types, isn't it? To keep them alive as long as possible?" Bo smacked Vetas once, then again. "Isn't it? Tell me! Isn't it?"

Adamat lurched forward and grabbed Bo's arm. Bo whirled on him, hands raised, fire in his eyes. Adamat did his best not to shy away. "That's enough, man! Enough!" He couldn't believe himself. Dashing forward to spare Vetas. An hour ago, Adamat was ready to do every pain in the world to Vetas. Now, he just felt ill.

Bo lowered his hands, nodding, muttering to himself. "Take them," he said, pointing to Faye and the boy. "Vetas isn't going anywhere. Get them out of here."

Adamat put an arm around Faye's waist, letting her take the weight off her ankle as he led her out of the smoldering ruin of a building.

The street was filled with people. Onlookers stood well back, a hundred paces at least, their curiosity warring with their fear of the sorcery. Immediately in front of the building, the eunuch's men had gathered with their wounded and prisoners, and some were heading inside now that the fire and smoke were gone. Adamat saw Sergeant Oldrich and Riplas, moving among them, giving orders.

Adamat gestured Riplas over. "The eunuch is dead," he said quietly.

The eunuch's second-in-command rocked back a step, eyes wide. "What? How?"

"It was Lord Vetas. He must have gotten away from Fell. Speaking of which…"

Fell emerged from the groups of onlookers. She held her arm carefully to one side, her body covered in cuts. She limped over to him.

"Vetas, he…"

"He's inside," Adamat said, choking back anger. Fell had told him she could hold Vetas. She had obviously been overpowered. Oldrich's soldiers had probably been killed as well. He didn't trust himself to say more.

When Fell returned, her cold demeanor was somewhat sobered.

"What are you going to do with him?"

"I want to know what he did with my boy…other than that, I don't care."

Fell and Riplas seemed to size each other up for a moment. "You're the eunuch's second in command?" Fell asked.

"Yes."

"Let's talk." Fell jerked her head, and the two women moved aside for a private conference.

Adamat squeezed Faye, as if to reassure himself that she was still there. She nestled against his chest, her eyes closed, her face wet with tears.

"The children?" she asked suddenly.

"Safe," Adamat said. "I'm sorry I couldn't come sooner."

"You came. That's all that matters."

Adamat fell to his knees beside her, pressing her hand to his lips. "I could die now. I have you back."

"Please," Faye said. "Not yet. My ankle hurts quite a lot."

CHAPTER

26

Taniel found Major Doravir in the Wine's End, an upper-class gentleman's club that had been appropriated for use by the army as an officers' mess hall. The room was lined with rich crimson damask and smelled heavily of cigar smoke. The armchairs scattered throughout the club had been upholstered with the furs of big cats from the Gurlish continent. In one corner, a sergeant was playing a grand piano. The conversation was somber and muted, though a few officers seemed to note Taniel's entrance.

Taniel paused in the doorway and adjusted the collar of his dress uniform—a gift from Mihali. Most of his possessions had been lost when South Pike collapsed, including his various uniforms. Somehow the fat chef had gotten Taniel's measurements and had had a new one made for him. It even had the proper silver buttons with powder kegs on them.

He examined the room slowly, hat tucked under his arm, and tried not to think about the provosts waiting outside for him. If he failed to apologize, he imagined they'd take him straight back to his quarters.

Taniel spotted Major Doravir near the bar, playing cards with an older officer of about fifty and two other majors. He took a deep breath and crossed the room, weaving his way through the chairs, giving a small nod to the few men who called out to him.

Major Doravir, her back to the wall, couldn't possibly have missed his presence, but she didn't bother to look up when Taniel stopped beside her table.

The older officer—a colonel by his uniform, though Taniel couldn't place the face—was speaking.

"And I said to them, it's the lack of noble blood. I understand Tamas's cull was a political thing, but there's no arguing that the lack of nobility among his officers has cheapened the whole army. By Kresimir, if he couldn't . . ." The old officer paused, frowning at Taniel. "Ah, Captain. Fetch me another beer. Now, where was I? If he couldn't . . . get to it, Captain, I'm thirsty."

Taniel ignored the colonel. "Major Doravir," Taniel said.

Doravir glanced up from her cards. "You're being rude to Colonel Bertthur."

Bertthur? Where did he know that name from? "My apologies, Colonel"—Taniel didn't look at the man—"but I must speak with Major Doravir."

"It's 'Colonel' now," Doravir said, touching the bars at her collar. "And whatever you have to say to me"—she set her cards facedown on the table and leaned back in her chair—"can be said in public."

Taniel swallowed a mouthful of bile. "Congratulations on your promotion, Colonel."

"I say," Bertthur stood up.

"Sit down, sir," Taniel snapped. "This has nothing to do with you. Colonel Doravir, I'd like to offer my deepest apologies for any"—Taniel rolled the sentence around in his head, trying not to spit it out—"insult I may have given you with my recent conduct."

Taniel couldn't help but notice that the murmur of conversation had completely disappeared. It felt as if a hundred sets of eyes were staring at him. They probably were.

"Colonel Bertthur is my husband," Doravir said. "Apologize to him."

Husband? The man must have been twenty years her senior.

"I did," Taniel said. "And I apologized to you. Now if you'll excuse me." Taniel turned on his heel.

He paused when Bertthur cleared his throat. "Was that Taniel? Tamas's brat?"

Keep walking, Taniel told himself.

"Two-Shot," Bertthur said. "Come back here this instant. Colonel Etan!"

Taniel froze. Etan was here?

"Colonel, isn't this the man who got you crippled?"

"He's the man who saved my life," Etan's voice returned.

"He saved my life, too!" someone shouted.

"And mine!"

"Bah. I remember you now, Two-Shot," Bertthur said. "It must have been five, six years ago. A whiny little bastard. A piss-poor soldier. You'd rather run off with that dark-haired whore of yours, neglecting your training. I never saw anything in you. Huh. Looks like she didn't either."

A whore? Vlora? He might have wanted to call her that and worse when he'd caught her with that fop at the university, but Taniel would be damned if he'd let some fool officer go on about his love life. He balled his hands into fists and slowly took a breath to calm himself. He didn't have to listen to this. He could just walk away.

"Bertthur, I think you've had enough," Etan's voice said. "Perhaps it's time to retire for the evening."

"Go to the pit, Etan," Bertthur went on. "Taniel, I can see that things haven't changed. No respect for authority. No military decorum. You've just traded one whore for another."

"Bertthur!" Etan's voice held some warning.

"But now it's a savage whore! What will he think of next? I bet your father is rolling over in his grave every time you bed that bitch."

Taniel's whole body shook. The fury threatened to overwhelm him. He forced himself to remain calm. Slowly, he turned around.

"Bertthur," Taniel said. "I don't remember a Colonel Bertthur. I remember a *Captain* Bertthur. An ass of a man who held his rank only because he was the bastard son of a duke. Field Marshal Tamas swore that man would never hold a higher rank as long as he was left alive."

Bertthur turned red. "That's a week in the stocks for you, Two-Shot."

"You're a braggart and a fool, Bertthur. You're a disgrace to the uniform."

"Two weeks!"

Taniel charged toward Bertthur and the officer shrank back, as if expecting to be punched. Taniel gripped the colonel's bars on his collar and ripped them off, tossing them to the side.

"A month!" Bertthur roared.

Something soared through the air and struck Bertthur in the side of the face. It looked like mashed potatoes.

"Who did that?" Doravir demanded.

A dinner roll hit Bertthur on the nose. He reeled back, suddenly under assault from every manner of dinner food. Someone flung a whole dish of sauce on him, staining his uniform.

"You're not a free man anymore, Two-Shot!" Bertthur fumed. "Your father is dead. You'll see two months in the stocks, and I'll hand your little savage whore over to my men!"

Taniel took a step forward and plowed his fist into Bertthur's chin, sending the older man to the ground. He could hear the crack of the bastard's jaw breaking.

"Provosts!" Doravir shouted.

Damn this. Damn them all. Taniel righted Berrthur's chair with his foot and leapt up on it.

"Friends," he shouted, raising his arms for quiet. The officers' mess suddenly calmed, and to Taniel's surprise, he had silence within moments. "The General Staff has deceived us all," Taniel said. "Field Marshal Tamas is not dead. He hasn't even been captured. He's leading the Seventh and Ninth through Kez as we speak."

"A lie!" Doravir shouted.

Tamas raised his voice to drown her out. "Haven't you wondered where the Kez cavalry are? They're chasing Tamas!"

Taniel was shoved off the chair by a provost. The man had no sooner laid his hands on Taniel than a major tackled him to the floor. Taniel got to his feet. "We only have to hold these Kez bastards for a few more months! Fall will be here soon and then winter, and Field Marshal Tamas with it!"

A musket butt slammed Taniel in the stomach. He doubled over in pain, but forced himself up. "No retreat! No surrender!"

The officers' mess erupted in a roar of cheering. Food was flying everywhere. Taniel was forced to the floor by the back of his neck, his face ground into the carpet.

"You're finished, Two-Shot," Doravir hissed. "You're a dead man!"

Taniel didn't care. The officers would all tell their men, and their men would hold the line. They'd do it for Taniel. They'd do it for Tamas.

Nila felt a sense of dread grow in the pit of her stomach as she neared Vetas's manor. Black smoke billowed above the street, and men's screams carried on the wind. The sound of fighting grew more distinct as she drew closer, and above it all a sound that she'd only heard once or twice in her life but was unmistakable—the thump of sorcery.

It had to be Privileged Dourford. She could see the tall Privileged in her mind's eye, laughing gleefully as he slung sorcery at unknown attackers, burning men to a crisp with the flick of his fingers.

The sorcery seemed to have an echo. There'd be a thump, and then another one just as loud if not louder almost immediately after. The combat was still going on as she rounded the corner of the next street over and approached the manor from the rear. Smoke poured from the windows on all three stories of the manor. Flames licked the smoke, curling like fingers around the window frames. A crash, and then another.

No, this wasn't any echo.

Sorcery fought sorcery inside the building.

Nila ran toward the manor, her dress gathered in both hands. She remembered hearing the kitchen staff say that Lord Vetas had called a second Privileged from somewhere down south. She was supposed to have arrived this morning. Was that woman fighting Dourford?

There was a great *whump* and Nila felt her ears pop. She staggered to one side of the street, trying to keep her feet. The flames had disappeared from the manor. Another *whump*, and the smoke burst from the windows as if propelled by a giant bellows, and no more followed it out.

Nila froze in her tracks, more frightened by the sudden silence than she had been by the sorcery. Who had won? Who had even been fighting? Was Vetas in there? Was he still alive? Could Jakob have survived all of that?

She didn't know if she could make herself go inside. She took several deep breaths, gathering her courage.

A crack split the air, throwing Nila off her feet. She landed on the street hard enough to scrape the skin off her palm.

One side of the house collapsed, crashing in on itself. She stared, openmouthed, as the walls crumpled and part of the roof slid off one side, clay shingles falling into the alley with a sound like a thousand wind chimes in a hurricane.

Nila climbed to her feet and was running toward the house before she could think. Her palm throbbed, her dress bloody, but she didn't care about that. Jakob was still inside, up on the second floor. His nursery faced the other street, and even at this angle she could tell that if he was inside, he'd been crushed. But maybe he was lucky. Maybe he'd been under the bed, or protected by the door frame, or…

The back wall of the manor suddenly blew outward, sending plaster, furniture, and bits of what looked to have once been a human out into the street.

A man stood in the wreckage. He was of medium height, with ruddy muttonchops on an otherwise clean-shaven face and loose pants and matching jacket that wouldn't have looked out of place on a street in the bankers' quarter. He wasn't particularly handsome, nor was he ugly, but Nila felt a jolt when she first saw him.

He held his hands high, fingers poised in white Privileged's gloves as he looked down on the mess he'd just made all over the thoroughfare. The gathering crowd pulled back in fear. A woman fainted when she realized what the juicy red meat scattered in the street was. A man vomited.

The Privileged surveyed the gathered crowd and lowered his hands. He turned and disappeared inside the wreckage of the house. Before he did, however, Nila caught sight of something on his gloves: the symbol of the Adran Mountains with the teardrop of the Adsea beneath them.

This wasn't just any Privileged. This was a member of the Adran royal cabal.

Something told Nila that Dourford hadn't stood a chance.

Nila picked her way through the wreckage and ducked beneath a beam, entering the house as close as she could get to the servants' stairs.

The sitting room was completely crushed. She could hear a man calling for help, and another moaning. A body lay in the mangled timber, covered in plaster dust, unmoving. She heard someone speaking from the other room. It sounded like Lord Vetas.

Nila moved slowly into the kitchen. It remained almost completely untouched by the collapse, but it seemed that the servants' stairs had taken the worst of it. She wouldn't be climbing up to the second floor that way.

She stepped over to the door to the dining room and listened. Silence, but she could hear someone moving. She looked through a crack in the door. She heard herself gasp at the sight of a woman, body hanging limply from dripping shards of ice, nailed to the back wall of the dining room. She wore Privileged's gloves. Vetas's other Privileged?

Someone spoke. A man's voice. He was saying…

Lord Vetas slammed into the back wall of the dining room hard enough to rattle the remains of the house. Something shifted in the wreckage, and Nila heard someone scream. Lord Vetas, though, didn't make a sound. The Adran Privileged stepped into view. He spoke quietly, his face angry. He grabbed Lord Vetas by the chin and forced him to look at the dead Privileged.

The Adran Privileged stepped back suddenly. His voice was suddenly calm and collected. Nila heard him say, "I bet you were the type of child who tortured animals for fun. Tell me, did you ever pull the wings off of insects? Answer me!"

Nila had some satisfaction in seeing Vetas pull back in fear. His mouth moved, the word too low to hear.

"That's what I thought. How does it feel?"

Nila pulled away from the door. Vetas's scream drowned out the calls of the wounded and dying in the rest of the house. She turned toward the kitchen, looking for another way to get through the wreckage. Panic set in. She had to find Jakob. She had to get away from the house. Even as she began to breathe harder, the adrenaline setting in, a wave of relief swept over her. Vetas was gone. If he wasn't dead yet, he would be. That bastard had finally found someone stronger and crueler.

She put him from her mind. He wasn't worth another thought. Jakob, though...

"Nila?"

Nila's gaze darted around the kitchen. A child's voice. Where had it come from?

"Nila, quick, hide in here."

She found Jakob in the bottom of the pantry, tucked behind a sack of flour. She glanced at the door to the dining room. "There's no room for me in there," she said, helping him out of the pantry.

"What about Faye?" Jakob asked. "And Uncle Vetas."

A moan emanated from the dining room. Nila took Jakob by the shoulder and pushed him out through the broken wall the same way she'd come in.

The crowd outside had retreated to what they deemed a safe distance from the house, seemingly content to wait for the police and fire brigades to arrive. Someone grabbed Nila by the arm as she pushed her way through the throng. She shoved them off without a comment, not bothering to look back, and kept her grip on Jakob's shoulder.

Her mind was already racing. She still had her buried silver outside the city. She had no money, no clothes but the ones on her back. They'd have to walk all the way to the city limits, find the silver, and then tomorrow they could come back into the city and find a place to sell it.

A night or two spent sleeping in the street wouldn't kill them.

They were four blocks away, when Nila noticed that everyone she passed was staring at her. It was another block before Jakob pointed at her dress and she realized that the blood from her palm was everywhere. It looked like she'd been rolling in it. Two more streets down and they reached a string of shops.

"Do you need help, ma'am?" a passing gentleman asked, pressing a handkerchief to his mouth. He looked queasy at the sight of her.

She showed him her palm. "Just skinned it, is all," she said, trying to keep her tone level. "Looks worse than it is."

The gentleman seemed relieved. "There's a doctor right over there," he said, pointing two shops down. "She accepts walk-ins."

"Thank you so much," Nila said.

She waited for a moment until the gentleman continued on his way. She had no way to pay for a doctor. She'd have to deal with the pain until . . .

Nila remembered the silver necklace with the large pearl hanging about her neck. A "gift" from Vetas.

The doctor was an older woman in a white dress and sharp eyeglasses perched on her nose. She was seeing a patient, but one look at Nila's bloody dress and she rushed to see what was the matter.

Nila did her best to make small talk as the doctor cleaned and then wrapped her wound. She had fallen, Nila told the doctor. A nasty fall, but nothing was sprained. Payment? "Oh, my. I seem to have left my pocketbook at home. Can you keep this necklace until I return to pay you?"

The arrangement was struck, and Nila even borrowed a fifty-krana note against the necklace. She pulled Jakob out the door, relieved that he'd stayed quiet through the entire exchange.

Nila had only gone another half a block before a thought struck her.

The Privileged. The one who'd come out victorious and then torn Vetas's arms off—he was a member of the Adran royal cabal.

"Jakob," Nila said, directing him over to a street side café, "can you wait here for a few minutes?"

Jakob's eyes grew wide. "Don't leave me alone."

"Just for a few minutes. Here, let me buy you glass of milk. Sit right here, inside, and wait for me to come back." She paused, thinking. "If I don't come back, I want you to ask directions to the nearest barracks. Tell the commanding officer that you're looking for Captain Olem. He'll be away, fighting on the front, but the officer will help you find someplace to stay."

"You're not coming back for me?"

"I am," Nila said, "but just in case I don't, that's what you're to do."

The boy seemed to take stock of her confidence and straightened his back. "Yes, Nila."

She bought him a glass of milk and put him on a chair just inside the café, asking the waiter to keep an eye on him for half an hour. Ten krana bought her an old apron from the café, and she wrapped it around her middle. It concealed the blood on her dress nicely.

Then Nila backtracked her way to Lord Vetas's manor.

The police had arrived, and the fire brigades were crawling all over the manor. A white sheet had been laid over the remains of Dourford, and the fire brigades pulled a twisted body from the wreckage. All of Lord Vetas's men had disappeared, along with whomever they were fighting. The number of police kept her from wanting to get any closer to the building.

She began to make a circuit of the area, checking each of the nearby streets. Surely there were lookouts, or . . . or . . . someone!

Nila found nothing. Lord Vetas's men, the Adran soldiers, the cabal Privileged; they'd scattered to the wind.

She widened her search.

It wasn't until five streets over that she caught sight of a man with ruddy muttonchops and a pressed suit of clothes walking along the thoroughfare with a wide rug, rolled thick enough that it might have a body inside, over his shoulder. He wasn't wearing any Privileged's gloves, but Nila knew it was the same man—the cabal Privileged.

She ran to catch up with him. He walked slowly under the weight of the rug and he was whistling loudly to himself. Surely this couldn't be the same man?

He turned a corner.

Slowly, Nila crept up to the edge of the building. Maybe it wasn't him. Privileged didn't carry things themselves. They had servants for that.

She rounded the corner and nearly screamed.

About ten feet down the alley, the man was sitting on his rolled rug. He had his feet up on an old wine barrel as if he'd been there all day.

"Can I help you?" he asked.

Nila glanced into the street. Surely he wouldn't harm her. Not on a busy street in broad daylight.

"Sir," she said. How to talk to a Privileged? She'd spent some time with Rozalia when she was with the royalists months ago, but that had made her just as uncomfortable. Privileged were not to be trusted. "My lord?"

His eyes narrowed, but he didn't correct her. This was the same man, all right. And he didn't like someone noticing that he was a Privileged. She braced herself, ready to run.

"Yes?" he asked, his voice amiable.

"You're a Privileged," she said. "From the Adran Cabal."

The man raised an eyebrow. "What makes you think that?"

"I saw you splatter Lord Dourford across the cobbles about an hour ago."

"That was his name?" the Privileged said. "I thought he looked familiar. That pompous prick was a member of the Kez Cabal. Bah, I'm surprised they let him in. Less talent than a Knacked." He looked her up and down. "Now what can I do for you? Make it good, because I'll have to kill you after."

Kill her? Nila had no doubt he would, given the need. Members of the royal cabals were notoriously cruel. She cleared her throat and straightened her back. "Due to your duty as a member of the royal cabal, I will give into your protection Jakob Eldaminse, next in line for the crown of Adro." She let out a sharp breath, only now realizing that she'd been holding it.

The Privileged's eyebrow remained cocked. Slowly, as if realizing that she was serious, the eyebrow lowered. He threw his head back and laughed.

Nila felt a nervous smile dance upon her lips. Had she said something funny? "You'll do it, then?"

"What? Oh, pit no. You think I want some noble brat hanging on my hip? That kid is, what, four?"

"Six."

"Six. Right." The Privileged stood up. "The Adran nobility is dead. They're not coming back." He paused and looked around. "Where is the boy, anyway?"

"Hiding."

"Smart."

"Sir," Nila said. "My lord, you have to. He has no one else to protect him."

"He seems to have you."

"I'm just a laundress."

"You dress like a waiter."

"The apron? No, I'm a laundress."

"I'm pretty sure that you're a waiter," the Privileged said.

It took her several moments to realize that she was being teased.

"My lord!" she said in a voice that she hoped was commanding, "you have to protect Jakob Eldaminse."

"No, I don't." The Privileged sighed as if suddenly tired, and though he'd looked to be in his midtwenties just a moment ago, he suddenly seemed elderly. "I'm done with the Adran nobility." He blinked and then seemed to look more closely at her. "Have we met before?"

She shook her head.

"Oh well. I should be off. This rug won't keep all day."

Nila felt a rising panic inside her. It hadn't worked. The Privileged wouldn't protect Jakob. It wasn't as if she were trying to hand the boy off, she told herself. It was that he needed better protectors than she. "You're not going to..."

"Kill you? No. You're trying to hide one of the last living members of Manhouch's extended family. You're not going to tell anyone about me anytime soon."

"I will," Nila said.

"Excuse me?"

"I will tell them. Unless you swear to protect Jakob."

"You're adorable."

"I'm serious."

"I'm sure you are." The Privileged bent and lifted one edge of the rug, tipping it upward against the wall and examining it for a moment as if figuring out the best way to get it back on his shoulders.

Nila felt numb. What would she do now? Sure, she could get ahold of some money, but what then? "Your rug is bleeding."

"So it is," the Privileged said, glancing at the dark stain soaking through the fabric. "I thought I cauterized those wounds."

A cold finger crept its way up Nila's spine. "Who is that?" she asked.

"Him? Some idiot named Vetal or something."

"Vetas?"

"Yeah. Him."

Nila stormed over to the rug and kicked it. Then again, then again.

The Privileged grabbed her by the arm, pulling her away. "He's unconscious," he said, "and I want him alive so that I can torture him some more. For information," he added.

Nila stumbled away from the rug and leaned up against the wall of the alley. She felt like she was going to be ill. Everything had been so clear in her mind as she'd escaped Vetas's grasp. Now it was full of questions. Part of her wanted to cry. She quelled the feeling and stared at the wall, trying to come up with some kind of plan.

She was surprised to find the Privileged still standing there a few moments later.

"Don't you have something to do with *that*?" she said, jerking her chin at the rug.

The Privileged stepped closer. Nila refused to step back.

"My name's Bo," he said.

Nila sniffed.

"Look, I won't keep the boy," Bo said. "I'm not in any position to protect him. I'm a hunted man myself. But I can give you two a few days of safety while you figure out what to do."

"Why?"

Bo chuckled. "Because you're brave enough to demand things of a Privileged on your own, and from what I gather, you know this fellow"—he tapped the rug with his toe—"and because you're rather attractive. A few days is all, though." He pulled a pencil and paper from his breast pocket and scribbled something on it. "I have to go put my rug into storage. Gather the boy and meet me at this address. For Kresimir's sake, make sure you're not followed."

CHAPTER
27

"You have to hold still, sir."

Tamas resisted the urge to twitch away from Olem's needle. Olem had shaved the side of Tamas's head and cleaned the bullet gash with frigid mountain water and now he made tight stitches with catgut. The wound ran almost the entire length of the side of Tamas's head. It was an eerie feeling, knowing that had the path of the bullet been an inch to one side, it would have turned Tamas's head into a canoe.

"Sorry," Tamas muttered.

The air reeked of death as the corpses of thousands of men and horses stank in the midmorning sun. His soldiers had labored the entire rest of the day after the battle and all this morning in an effort to dig all the bodies from the trench. The men had been laid out, their kits and supplies stripped from them, while the horses were prepared for eating.

War may need decorum, but his army needed food and supplies.

The moans and cries of the wounded reached him. Both Kez and Adran were being treated to field surgery in an impromptu hospital. Neither army had a proper team of doctors beyond the rudimentary skills of soldiers who'd seen countless wounds.

Tamas watched as Gavril picked his way through the camp toward him.

All signs of the chaos and disorganization they'd used to lure in the Kez cavalry were gone. A team of engineers was hard at work making a proper bridge over the Big Finger. Cook fires everywhere smoked with horsemeat. Quartermasters took stock of supplies they'd stripped from both Kez and Adran dead. There were piles of boots, kits, blankets, and tents, along with rifles, ammunition, even powder horns and charges.

Gavril reached Tamas and sat down on the ground beside him. "General Cethal is dead."

Tamas bowed his head for a moment of silence, further frustrating Olem's attempts at stitching.

"I'm surprised he lasted this long," Tamas said. "Tough old dog. What reports?"

"Based on the bodies so far, we're guessing about two thousand dead on our side. Another three thousand wounded. About a quarter of those will join the dead within a week. Half our wounded are incapacitated."

Thirty-five hundred casualties to this battle. Over a fourth of Tamas's fighting force. It was a heavy blow.

"And the Kez?"

"Based on bodies alone, we can guess that only twenty-five hundred of them got away. The rest are either dead or captured."

Tamas let out a long breath. A decisive victory in anyone's book. Most of the enemy, including all of their high officers, either killed or captured.

"Give our boys a rest," Tamas said. "Any Kez who can stand, put him to work burying the bodies."

"What are we going to do with all these captives?" Gavril asked. "We can't take them with us. Pit, we can't even carry our own wounded—don't forget that Beon's brother is still coming on hard with thirty thousand infantry."

"When will he reach us?"

"Our prisoners are being sketchy about time frames, but piecing things together, I'd guess they are about a week behind us."

Close enough that if Tamas allowed himself to be slowed by wounded and prisoners, the Kez infantry would catch him before he could get to Deliv.

"How is Beon?"

"Asked to see you," Gavril said.

"Right. Olem?"

Olem wiped the needle off on his jacket. "All done, sir. Doesn't look pretty, but the stitches are tight. Try not to do any strenuous thinking in the near future."

Tamas held up a field mirror. "I look like a bloody invalid. Bring me my hat."

"It'll rub against the stitches."

"Wrap it in a handkerchief. I'm not going to parley with the enemy looking like this."

Olem wrapped Tamas's head, and Tamas gingerly sat his bicorne hat on top of it.

"How does it feel, sir?"

"Hurts like the bloody pit. Let's go see Beon."

Tamas let Gavril and Olem walk out in front of him as they crossed the camp. Gavril had come through the battle with little more than a black eye, while Olem had a tendency to ignore his own wounds. His left hand was wrapped tightly, and fresh blood soaked through his white shirt at the shoulder. "Olem, see to yourself," Tamas said as they neared the prisoners.

"I'm all right, sir," Olem said.

"That's an order."

Olem relented and limped back to camp. Tamas was sorry to see him go, but Olem needed rest and medical attention.

The prisoners had been put in a makeshift stockade overnight. They were bound hand and foot and watched over by the Seventh Brigade. The Ninth couldn't be trusted with prisoners right now—they'd taken the worst of it in the cuirassier charge, and most of them still wanted blood.

"Field Marshal to see General Beon," Gavril said to one of the guards. The man headed into the stockade. He emerged a few minutes later with Beon in tow.

The Kez general didn't look so well. His left arm was in a sling. Stitches on his forehead and the back of his right hand looked crooked and painful. He walked with a pronounced limp.

"General," Tamas said.

Beon gave him a weary nod. "Field Marshal. I should thank you for saving my life from your men yesterday."

"You are most welcome."

"Ah," Beon said. "I *should* thank you. But I won't." He let his head sag. "I don't know if I can live with the shame of such a defeat."

Gavril leaned against one of the wooden stakes that made the stockade. "Don't be so hard on yourself," Gavril said. "It's Tamas, after all."

Tamas suppressed his annoyance to keep it from reaching his face. "Deceit may not be a gentleman's tool, but in the end, victory is all that matters on the field of battle."

"Too true," Beon said. "The trench. It was well done. Dug and concealed, all in one afternoon. My scouts kept at bay, and that bit of fog concealed it completely. You played me, Field Marshal. You knew I'd order the charge when I saw you trying to cross the river."

Tamas allowed himself a small nod.

"Bravo," Beon said with a sigh. "What now? As you can see,

you've taken thousands of us hostage. We're hundreds of miles from the nearest city that might afford ransom. Thousands of both sides will die of improper treatment and disease within the next couple of weeks."

"I've sent a man to your camp and called for a parley," Tamas said. "I intend to ransom all of your soldiers and and most of your officers in exchange for food, supplies, and a promise of parole."

"Parole?" Beon seemed surprised. "As a man of honor, I must tell you that a great number of my officers will not adhere to the conditions of parole. The moment your prisoners are free of your hands, they will be set back to fighting you."

"As a man of honor, I expect you to tell me which of your highest officers are, in fact, men of honor."

Beon chuckled. "Ah. And those are the ones you will ransom back to the remnants of my army? I see. You realize, of course, that the honor will only stand until my brother catches up with his infantry, and relieves me and my officers of our command?"

"I do. And I never said I would ransom *you*."

Beon tilted his head to one side. "I can't imagine any use you would have for me. My presence will not prevent my brother from launching an attack when he catches you."

"Still. I'd rather you not be on the other side for the time being."

"You don't trust me not to break my parole?"

"It's not that, either. By the way, General Cethal sends his regards."

"He mounted a valiant defense. I've broken greater numbers of infantry with fewer cuirassiers. Tell him it was a fine stand."

"He's dead," Tamas said.

Beon lowered his head.

Someone cleared his throat. Tamas turned to find a messenger at his shoulder.

"Sir, the Kez are here for the parley."

"Of course. General Beon, if you will?"

The Kez had sent what remained of their officer corps. A colonel, five majors, and six captains. Tamas ran his eyes over them. The Kez retreat had been last-minute. Only two of the majors had wounds on them. That meant the rest had fled before even entering the melee.

The parley proceeded much as he expected. The Kez rattled their sabers and made demands, but in the end, they knew they were beaten. They traded powder and ammunition in exchange for having their surviving officers returned to them—with a few notable exceptions. Food, and information regarding how things went back in Adro, were exchanged in return for their soldiers.

"You cannot possibly think we will allow you to keep Beon je Ipille," the Kez colonel said. "He is third in line for the crown!"

"'Allow' me?" Tamas said. "It is I who am allowing you to leave with your lives. Almost four thousand men in exchange for road rations, information, and a shaky promise of parole? I'm the one being robbed. I'll keep General Beon until his father offers to trade safe passage back to Adro for his son's life. We will make the exchange of prisoners at first light tomorrow."

They exchanged information about the landscape in northern Kez and the position of the infantry brigades under Beon's brother. The Kez returned to their camp, noses raised, proud even in defeat.

"My father hates you," Beon said as they walked back to the Adran camp. "There isn't a chance in the pit he'd trade my life for those of your army. Especially after my failure here."

"I know." Tamas stopped and turned to Beon. "You will be accorded every respect due to a prisoner of your status. I expect your word of honor that you will not attempt to escape my camp and that you will not attempt to transfer information about the disposition of my army to your own. In exchange, you will be given a tent, full freedom of the camp, and the choice of any two menservants from your own army."

"I give my word of honor," Beon said.

"Very good."

Beon was escorted to the stockade to select his menservants, leaving Tamas alone with Gavril.

"You really trust him?" Gavril asked.

"Yes."

"Then why are you keeping him here?"

Tamas removed his hat and gingerly touched at the fresh stitches on his scalp. It would be months before the hair grew back properly to conceal the wound. In the meantime, he would look like some half-mad fool.

"He's the only one of Ipille's sons worth anything as a human being. I intend to return to Adro and throw back Ipille's army. According to them"—he jerked his head in the direction of the retreating Kez officers—"Ipille is personally in Adro. If I can manage to kill him and his two oldest sons, Beon will be king of Kez and he might actually listen to reason and help me end this war."

"Ah." Gavril scratched at his beard. "What else did you find out about Adro?"

"Last the Kez cavalry heard, Ipille had burned Budwiel and was slowly but steadily advancing up Surkov's Alley. Hilanska and the rest of the generals are holding fast with the help of the Wings of Adom. Supposedly, Kresimir himself is there, but he's not using his powers to aid the Kez army."

"I thought Kresimir was dead."

"That's not what the Kez think. After South Pike collapsed, Privileged Borbador told me that you can't kill a god."

"If he's alive," Gavril reasoned, "he probably wants whoever shot him in the face."

"I know," Tamas said. "We march tomorrow afternoon. I need to get back to Adro and put myself between the Kez army and my son. If Kresimir is alive, I'll make him wish he had been destroyed at South Pike."

* * *

Adamat stopped with his hand on the door to a decommissioned grain mill in the factory district of Adopest. He looked over his shoulder and tried to tell himself he was no longer at risk of being followed. Lord Vetas was captured, his men taken or scattered, Adamat's family now safe. He was being paranoid, he reasoned, and pushed the door in.

Or was he? He made his way past a secretary's desk, long empty and half-rotted, and past the millworkers' bunk rooms, which smelled like an animal had made a nest in them and then died.

Adamat had successfully blackmailed the Proprietor. Lord Vetas's master, Lord Claremonte, might have other spies in the city. And there was still the Kez army pushing its way north through Surkov's Alley.

Would Adamat and his family ever really be safe again?

He went through another door that led to the mill's main workroom. The room was several hundred feet long with over a dozen millstones placed at intervals along one wall. Most of them were either broken or missing completely, the machinery left to rot when the mill was abandoned. The sound of the river, over which this portion of the mill was suspended, filled the room.

Bo sat with his chair tilted back on two legs, leaning against the wall next to the door. Beside him, Fell held a pipe between her lips and stared at something in the distance. Her shirtsleeves were rolled up, and there were flecks of blood on her arms.

"You missed the morning's festivities," Bo said to Adamat.

"You call torturing a man 'festivities'?" Adamat asked.

"I'm not a good person," Bo said.

Adamat cast a glance over Bo's clothes. "You've blood on your shoes."

Bo swore, then licked his thumb and ran it over the top of one of his shoes.

"How is your wife?" Fell asked, taking the pipe from her mouth.

Adamat hesitated. "She has . . . had a rough time of things." That was as much of an understatement as Adamat had ever made. Faye had been beaten and abused. She'd cried for two days straight and wouldn't allow any of the children out of her sight for more than a few minutes. She grew from melancholy to cheerful and back again in seconds, but Adamat wouldn't expect anything different from someone who'd been through what she had. "She's strong," Adamat said. "She'll be fine."

Bo let his chair thump down onto four legs and stood up, stretching. "I'm happy to hear that."

Strangely enough, Bo sounded sincere. Privilegeds weren't known for their empathy.

"Hit me," Bo said to Fell.

A smile flickered across Fell's face. She reached into her pocket and withdrew a cashew, then tossed it in the air. Bo caught it in his mouth.

"I need to get back to Ricard," Fell said, gathering her bag of cashews and a leather satchel at her feet.

"Go on," Bo said. "We'll take it from here. It was good working with you this morning."

Adamat held up a hand. "A question."

"Yes?" Fell asked.

"Did either of you see a young woman or a boy after we vacated Vetas's manor?"

"The girl in the red dress?" Fell asked.

The one she'd let escape, along with Vetas, very nearly getting Faye killed? "Yes. Her."

Fell shook her head.

Bo hesitated a moment. "Maybe . . . no. No, I don't think I saw them."

"Pity," Adamat said. "Faye asked me to look for her. She was another prisoner of Vetas, and the boy may be a royal heir."

"I'll put my ear to the ground," Fell said. She gave them each a nod, her glance lingering on Bo, and then made her exit.

"How was the 'work' this morning?" Adamat asked after Fell had left.

"She's very good at putting a man to the question," Bo said, either missing or ignoring the innuendo in Adamat's tone. He cracked his knuckles and headed down the long line of millstones. "Not as good as I am, but then, I am a cabal Privileged." Bo glanced over his shoulder as if to be sure Fell was gone, then said, "Don't trust that woman."

"I wasn't planning on it."

"Good. She's loyal to Ricard and to her precious Academy. Nothing else. And I'm not even sure if she's more loyal to Ricard than she is to the Academy."

"I imagine she'd say the same thing to me about you," Adamat said.

"Oh," Bo said, "I don't think you should trust me, either. But you only have to deal with me for another couple of days. As soon as this Vetas business is cleaned up and I think your family is safe, I'm in the wind."

Bo led Adamat down the stairs at the end of the room and into the wheel room beneath the mill. For each of the millstones above them, there was a wheel down here with one end dipped in the water. Or at least, there used to be. Most of them were missing, leaving an empty channel of water flowing through one side of the floor.

Lord Vetas was strapped to an upright gurney in one corner. His arms were missing—of course, Bo had taken those off two days ago. A bloody blanket covered his body; likely more for Adamat's sake than for Vetas's. His eyes were closed, his breathing shallow.

Bo kicked the gurney and Vetas's eyes shot open. He immediately tried to recoil from Bo, but his bonds kept that from happening.

"You remember our friend Adamat?" Bo asked.

"Yes," Vetas whispered, not taking his eyes from Bo.

"He has a few questions. Answer them."

Adamat centered himself before his former tormentor and tried to force himself to remember what Vetas had done to his family. This pitiful creature before him didn't deserve pity or compassion.

"Where is my son?" Adamat asked.

"I don't know."

"What happened to him?"

"Sold him."

Adamat rocked back on his heels. "Sold him? What do you mean?"

"Slavers."

"There are no slavers in Adopest!"

A hideous giggle wormed its way up through Vetas's throat, only for him to swallow it when Bo took a step forward. "Kez smugglers," Vetas said, his voice still quiet. "Used to take powder mages out from under Tamas's nose and send them in to Kez."

"My boy is not a powder mage," Adamat said.

Vetas blinked back at him. His eyes, once serpentine and unfeeling, were now just...dead, was the only way to describe them. They showed fear when they glanced toward Bo, but other than that, nothing.

"Why would you sell him to the Kez?"

"My Privileged said he was a powder mage."

Adamat began to pace. Josep, a Marked? That seemed impossible. "How long ago?"

"A week."

"Have they taken him from the country?" Adamat felt his chest tighten as he began to panic. Smugglers dealing in human beings—especially powder mages—wouldn't wait to get their cargo out of the country. In all likelihood, Josep was gone already, far beyond Adamat's reach.

"I'd imagine," Vetas said.

"What do they want them for?" Adamat said. "The Kez don't want powder mages alive. They've no need for smugglers. They use assassins."

"Experimentation," Vetas said.

"What do you mean?"

"I don't know. Just a guess."

"Where can I find them?"

Vetas looked away for a moment. Adamat stepped forward menacingly. There was no fear in Vetas's eyes. Not until Bo began to rub his thumb and forefinger together.

"A pub near the waterfront," Vetas said, his eyes twitching toward the water flowing through the mill trough.

A pub, eh? Probably not more than half a mile from this very place. "Tell me everything," Adamat said.

He questioned Vetas for half an hour, getting the names of contacts, locations, and passwords. He had to be thorough. Slavers in a place as civilized as Adopest tended to operate in utmost secrecy, and would have taken dozens of precautions.

Adamat finished his questions and headed immediately toward the door. He couldn't get away from Vetas fast enough. The man revolted him. He'd taken Adamat's wife and children and put them through unspeakable trials. He'd plotted against Adro, and he'd dealt with the lowliest of scum.

Bo jogged to catch up with Adamat as he climbed the stairs back to the mill's main floor.

"You didn't ask him anything else," Bo said.

"I don't need to know anything else."

"Claremonte's plans? His designs on Adro? You don't want to know all that?"

Adamat stopped and turned to the Privileged. "Later. I have to get my son back."

"It's too late. If slavers have him, he'll be out of the country by now."

"How would you know?" Adamat demanded.

"Common sense," Bo said. "And remember. The royal cabal was a dark place. Dealing with slaves was one of many things they did."

"Bah!" Adamat strode toward the front of the mill.

Bo kept up, much to his annoyance. "We've been questioning Vetas for two days. Claremonte is planning something big. Not even Vetas knows it all, but Claremonte might even have plans of invasion!"

"And I suppose you're going to help stop him?"

Bo's silence made Adamat sigh. The Privileged had no interest in helping. He'd probably leave the country now that his debt to Adamat was paid. It seemed that Bo had just enough civic sense of duty to try to convince Adamat to help stop Claremonte.

"Even Vetas said that your son would be gone by now," Bo said.

"And you trust him? That's awfully naïve for a cabal Privileged."

Bo leaned in toward Adamat. "I *broke* him," he said in words that were nearly a growl. "He wouldn't dare lie to me."

"It was too easy," Adamat said. "I know what type of man Vetas is. He's keeping something back."

Doubt flickered across Bo's face, then resolved itself in a scowl. "No. He won't. He can't. Like I said, I broke him."

"You should keep at it." Adamat's stomach twisted at the words. This kind of torture made him sick. Even when applied to Lord Vetas. "There's no telling what else he has in that head of his."

"He'll be dead within hours," Bo said.

"Ricard's orders?" Perhaps Ricard thought Vetas was too much of a liability to keep alive for long. If Claremonte managed to find and rescue him, the following wrath would be terrible indeed.

"I don't take orders from Ricard. No, nature will finish what I started. It's taken what little knowledge I have of healing to keep him alive. I tore his arms off, and then spent the last two days questioning him. You think he'll live long? No. By nightfall I'm throwing his corpse into the Adsea and getting the pit out of this country."

"Well, then." Adamat took a deep breath and smoothed the front of his coat. Here he was, back to square one. All his allies were gone. The Proprietor had cut off contact. Ricard was busy dealing with the fallout of Vetas's capture, and Bo was leaving the country. Adamat was alone again. "I guess this is good-bye."

Bo tugged at the fingers of his right glove and pulled it off. He extended his hand. "Thank you."

"No," Adamat said, clasping the hand. He felt his heart skip a beat. Privileged did not shake hands with anyone. Not ever. "Thank you."

Bo headed back toward the mill basement. Adamat watched him go, hoping that perhaps he'd change his mind and stay in the country. Maybe he'd even help Adamat rescue Josep. But after a moment Bo disappeared downstairs.

Adamat headed into the street. This would be difficult. Maybe, just maybe, he had one friend left in Adopest.

Adamat paused on his doorstep and looked through the front window.

The blinds were drawn, but through the cracks he could see the twins playing on the rug in the living room. One of them had a wooden boat. The other one wanted it, and pushed the first over, snatching for the toy.

Adamat felt a smile tug at the corner of his mouth. They'd been through so much, but they still played and argued like regular children. He'd expected them to be worse for the wear after their ordeals. Fanish, his oldest daughter, shouted from the back room, and a moment later she entered and separated the two, then berated them soundly.

He pushed the door open and stepped inside. It didn't take long for all the children to mob him as they all sought for a hug or a kiss. He knelt and let them fawn over him. Felt the relief to have them back home. He never would have thought he'd welcome the shouting and shoving after a long day of walking the street... but he finally had his family back.

The smile slid from his face. No sign of Faye.

"Where's your mother?" Adamat asked Fanish, gently prying Astrit off his leg.

"She's in bed, Papa."

"Has she been down today?" Fanish looked at the younger children and shook her head. She was old enough to know her mother had been through a lot, and to notice readily that she was acting strange. She was also smart enough to want to keep the other children from worrying.

Adamat took his daughter aside. "Has she eaten?"

"No."

"What did you have for dinner?"

"Soup. It's still over the fire."

"Where'd it come from?"

"Ricard's assistant brought it by. Enough for three days for the whole family."

"Fell?"

"Her. Yes."

Adamat's fists tightened. The woman who almost cost Adamat his wife by letting Vetas escape. He'd never forget that. He stopped himself from getting worked up. This was no time to hold a grudge. "Get me a bowl of soup."

He set his cane next to the front door and hung up his hat, then took the soup from his daughter and headed upstairs. In their bedroom, Faye was lying with her back to the door, blankets pulled up around her shoulders even though it was summer and the house was quite warm.

"Faye," he said gently.

No response.

He went around to her side of the bed and sat gently on the edge. He could see the rise and fall of her shoulders as she breathed softly. Her eyes were closed, but long intimacy told him she was still awake.

"Love," he said, "you need to eat something."

Again, no response.

"Sit up," he said. "You need to eat."

"You didn't take your boots off." Her voice was quiet and timid. Not at all the scolding brashness that he was used to, and that worried him.

"I'm sorry, I'll sweep up. You need to eat now."

"I'm not hungry."

"You haven't eaten all day."

"I did."

"I talked to Fanish."

She was lying to him, and now she knew that he knew. "Oh."

"You have to keep up your strength."

"Why?" She pulled the blanket tighter around her shoulders.

"For the children. For me. For yourself."

Faye didn't say anything. Adamat could see tears rolling down her cheeks, her eyes squeezed closed. He put a hand gently on her arm. Didn't she know she was safe now? Couldn't she tell that the children needed her more than ever? That *he* needed her?

"I'm going to find Josep," he said.

Her eyes opened. "You know where he is?"

"I have a lead."

"What is it?"

Adamat patted her arm and stood. "Nothing to worry about. I'll be back late tonight, though."

There was a knock on the door downstairs, and Faye shifted around in the bed, her movements jerking, her eyes wide and wild.

"It's just SouSmith," Adamat said, trying to calm her. "He's going with me."

"What is this lead? Where is my boy?" Faye demanded.

"It's nothing to—"

She grabbed him by the arm, her grip vice-like. "Tell me."

Adamat sank back onto the bed. He didn't want to worry her, but it seemed it couldn't be helped. "Vetas sold him to Kez slavers. Supposedly, Josep is a powder mage. I'm going to go meet with the slavers and try to get him back."

"No," Faye said, surprising Adamat with the force of the word. "You'll do no such thing. You've already scraped through so much danger. I'll not wait here for word of your death."

"I've dealt with worse than slavers," Adamat said.

"I know the type of men Vetas did... *business* with." Faye spat the word. There was panic in her eyes. Adamat could see that her desire to get her son back was warring with the need to protect her husband and her remaining children.

"I have to get Josep back. I won't leave him to the Kez."

Faye squeezed his arm tighter. "Be careful."

"I will." Adamat extricated himself from Faye's grip as gently as he could. Tears were streaming down her face as he left the room and headed down the stairs. SouSmith stood in the front hall, coat buttoned tight, smiling at the children playing in the living room.

The boxer nodded to Adamat. "Ready?"

"Yes." Adamat glanced up the stairs to his bedroom and took his cane from beside the door. "Fanish, check on your mother in a half hour or so."

"Yes, Papa."

"Good girl. SouSmith, let's go."

CHAPTER
28

Everything OK?" SouSmith asked as they took a hackney cab away from Adamat's home. The evening air was warm and windy. Adamat decided there would be a storm tomorrow.

"Fine," Adamat said.

SouSmith didn't seem to believe him, cocking an eyebrow.

"Fine!" Adamat said, louder.

SouSmith nodded to himself and settled against the side of the hackney cab.

Adamat looked out the window and watched the people going about their nightly errands. There was a small boy on the corner, trying to sell the last of his newspapers, and an older couple out for a stroll before it turned dark. Adamat wondered if they had any inkling of what was going on in their city. The chaos. The war.

He wondered if they cared.

Night was falling when the hackney cab dropped Adamat and

SouSmith off two blocks from the dockside pub called The Salty Maiden. Adamat could see the beaten sign, rocking in the wind from its post. What a stupid name. The Adsea wasn't salt water.

He checked the snub-nosed pistols in his pocket while SouSmith did the same. The boxer frowned during their preperations, not looking at Adamat.

"Sorry," Adamat said when he was ready to go.

"Eh?"

"I didn't mean to snap at you," Adamat said. "You're a good man. A good friend, for coming with me to do this. It could be very dangerous."

SouSmith grunted. "You still paying me, ain't you?"

"Yes."

The boxer nodded, as if it were a matter of course that he'd come with, but his frown dissolved.

They headed toward the pub, and Adamat listened to the click of his cane on the cobbles, then on the wood as they entered the boardwalk. This pub was out on the pier—a bad location. Only one exit, though no doubt smugglers had a boat hidden underneath for a quick getaway.

Not the ideal place to confront slavers.

Adamat pushed the door open and was met with silence.

A half-dozen sailors lounged around the dimly lit, one-room building. Not a mean-looking lot. Most of them were young men in their prime wearing white cotton shirts, open at the chest, and knee-length trousers. They all blinked at Adamat as if he were a three-eyed fish.

Acting inconspicuous was out of the question.

Adamat sidled up to the bar, while SouSmith leaned up against the door frame, taking in the sailors with his piggish eyes. Adamat slid a fifty-krana note across the bar. "I'm looking for Doles," he said.

The barkeep's expression didn't change. "I'm Doles. What'll you have?"

"Brudanian whiskey, if you have it," he said.

Doles, who was dressed like an ordinary sailor—and probably was—took the banknote and stuffed it in his pocket. He reached beneath the bar, not taking his eyes off Adamat, and brought up a decanter of dark liquid. He slammed it on the bar with enough force to make Adamat jump, then poured a shot into a small, dirty cup.

"Bad season for it," Doles said.

The script was just as Vetas had said. Adamat's mouth was dry, and he had to concentrate to keep his hand from shaking as he reached out and took the glass of whiskey in one hand. "Never a bad season for Brudanian whiskey," he replied.

Adamat had had a cudgel pulled on him enough times to know the signs. Dole's wrist twitched behind the bar. A moment later his hand came up, cocked back and swinging a piece of polished wood the length of a man's forearm.

Adamat drew his pistol with his left hand and raised his right to grab Doles's wrist, arresting the swing of the cudgel.

"I think we should settle down," Adamat said, his pistol aimed at the barkeep's nose.

Doles didn't even blink. "Yes. We should."

Adamat blanched. He felt the cold barrel of a pistol touch the back of his neck, and his hackles went up.

"Drop it," Doles said.

Adamat rolled his tongue around his parched gums. His heart hammered in his ears. "I die, you die," he said.

"I'll take the risk." Doles didn't seem concerned.

The pistol barrel pressed harder against the back of his neck. Adamat slowly lowered his own pistol and set it on the bar. Doles picked it up and unloaded it. "Kill them, dump the bodies out beyond the breakers."

Adamat felt rough hands grab him by the arms. He was pulled around to see SouSmith receiving similar treatment. Three of the sailors held him, knives drawn to his throat, while two others manhandled Adamat down to his knees.

"Don't do it here," Doles said with some annoyance, gesturing to the sailors. "I don't want blood on me floorboards. Do it downstairs."

"I'm here about a boy," Adamat said as he was shoved toward one corner of the room.

Doles didn't answer him.

"Someone you smuggled into Kez," Adamat said.

A rug was pulled back to reveal a trapdoor. SouSmith began to struggle violently, and one of the men holding Adamat joined the other three to wrestle SouSmith toward the corner.

"Vetas is dead!" Adamat said.

The sailor stopped pushing him toward the trapdoor. Adamat jerked away from his grip and faced Doles, who was holding up one hand.

"Dead? Really?"

"Yes," Adamat said. "We took him and his men, and Vetas is dead."

Doles sighed. "Damn it. We'll have to move again." He twitched his head, and Adamat was grabbed and pushed. Adamat tried to struggle, but the sailor was far stronger than he. His cane had been lost by the bar, and his hat knocked off. He snagged a handful of the sailor's hair and fought back.

Doles walked around the bar and watched the struggle impassively. "Either up here or down there," Doles said. "Don't make no difference to me. 'Cept I'll have to clean the blood up if you die here." He paused. "Well, we're moving anyway. Guess it doesn't matter."

"He's my son!" Adamat said. "Please, I just want him back. Don't you have children?"

"Nope," Doles said, leaning against the bar. He seemed amused by the struggle between SouSmith and his sailors.

"A father? You had a father! Please!"

"I did," Doles said. "Bastard and a drunk. Woulda killed him myself had he not fallen off a dock and drowned."

Adamat stepped back, and his foot touched air as he fell into the trapdoor. He snagged one arm on the ladder leading down beneath the pier, and the other on the floor. A sailor stomped on his hand, and Adamat let out a yell.

"I'll pay you!" Adamat said. "For my boy, I'll pay to get him back."

Doles chuckled. "You can't afford it."

"A hundred thousand krana. In cash!"

Doles's eyebrows climbed his forehead. "Well. Let up, boys." He stepped forward and kicked the sailor still grinding his heel into Adamat's fingers. "I said, let up!"

The sailor stepped away from Adamat, and the others ceased wrestling with SouSmith. The moment they'd loosened their hold, SouSmith grabbed one by the face and picked him off the floor, tossing him through the window. There was a strangled scream and a splash.

"Let up!" Doles bellowed.

SouSmith froze, a snarl on his face, the arm of a sailor grasped between two hands as if he was ready to snap a twig.

Doles glanced out the broken window, then frowned at Sou-Smith. "A strong bugger," he muttered. Louder, "Three hundred thousand," Doles said. "That's the price for your boy."

"Three hundred...?"

"Take it or leave it," Doles said. "And by 'leave it' I mean we'll kill you now."

Adamat felt his mouth work soundlessly. Even with the money Bo had given him, he didn't have three hundred thousand krana. He'd have to borrow from Ricard.

"I'll do it."

Doles seemed skeptical, but he spit in his hand and reached down. Adamat took the offered handshake and choked down a scream when Doles gripped his freshly crushed hand and squeezed. Doles lifted him out of the hole, stronger than Adamat would have expected.

"What's his name?" Doles asked.

"Josep."

"Ah, I remember him. Stubborn lad." Doles's face soured. "He's already in Norpoint."

Norpoint was the only Kez harbor on the Adsea, far to the south. Adamat felt his heart skip a beat. If Josep was already in Norpoint...

Doles said, "It'll take me about six days to go down and get him back. I'll have to grease some palms. The Kez never like losing a powder mage they thought they had under wraps," Doles mused out loud, speaking for all the world as if this was a business meeting, and he hadn't just been about to have Adamat killed.

"Fifty thousand tomorrow," Doles said. "Here, before sunup. Then two hundred and fifty when I get back from Norpoint."

"And then?"

"We'll meet at The Flaming Cuttlefish," Doles said. "It's a pub close by."

"I know it."

"Good."

Adamat nursed his crushed hand and hoped that none of the fingers were broken. It would certainly be stiff in the morning.

"How can I trust you?" he asked.

Doles made an openhanded gesture. "You can't. Want your boy back?"

"Yes."

"Then this is your only chance."

Adamat examined the man. A slaver. Nothing respectable or trustworthy about him. He had an honest face, though Adamat found that honest faces were almost always deceptive. "I'll be back here in a few hours with the money."

Brian McClellan

"I'll see you then," Doles said. He gestured to the door. They were dismissed.

The sailor SouSmith had thrown through the window suddenly stuck his head up through the trapdoor. His face was bloody from the glass, his clothes and hair soaked, silt on one shoulder. "I'll kill you!" he screamed at SouSmith, hefting himself up through the trapdoor.

Doles tripped the man on his mad dash toward SouSmith, then set a boot on the sailor's backside. He waved good-bye to Adamat, then said to his man, "Stay down, or I'll let the big one tear you apart."

Outside, SouSmith turned a sneer toward the pub.

"That could have gone better," Adamat said. "Then again... it could have gone worse."

SouSmith's sneer slowly left his face. "Yeah. You need me to come back with ya?"

"Yes. Yes, I think that would be a good idea."

"I'll be ready for 'em next time," SouSmith said, and for a moment he looked as if he considered going back in and killing the lot.

Adamat looked the big man over. He didn't seem worse for the wear. His shirt had ripped. Not many people get the drop on SouSmith.

"I'm sure," Adamat said. "Let's go get the money."

Taniel sat in a chair in the middle of the tent, his hands clasped in irons and his legs shackled. There wasn't an ounce of powder anywhere within fifty feet of the command tent, and above all the cautions that the General Staff had taken with his arrest, that concerned him the most. They were being careful with him. Too damned careful.

He was flanked by a pair of provosts. Two more stood behind

him, and another four were at the back of the command tent. Each man held a truncheon at the ready and was eyeing him like he was some kind of dangerous degenerate.

The tent was barren, austere. There were a dozen chairs in the back, most of them empty, and at the front a table with five places—one for each of the senior General Staff of the Adran army.

Taniel inspected the tent with a quick glance. Colonels Doravir and Bertthur were seated just behind him. Bertthur's broken jaw was held in place by a linen tied around his head. To Taniel's surprise, Brigadier Abrax, the senior commander of the Wings of Adom, sat near the tent flap. What interest could she have in these proceedings?

In the back corner, Colonel Etan sat in his wheeled chair, nodding encouragement. Taniel forced a confident smile he didn't feel. No one else had come to support him.

Then again, perhaps they wouldn't let anyone else in the tent.

This was, after all, a court-martial.

Cloth whispered as the front of the tent parted and the generals filed in. Everyone stood. The provosts grasped Taniel roughly beneath the arms and pulled him to his feet, the chains on his ankles nearly making him trip and fall.

Generals Ket and Hilanska were the only two Taniel recognized. He should know more of the senior staff than this, shouldn't he? Or had Ket stacked the cards against him by selecting new generals to serve on the jury? Taniel tried to meet Hilanska's eye, but the one-armed general kept his gaze on the floor, a scowl on his face. This didn't bode well.

The generals sat, and Taniel was allowed back in his chair. General Ket took the middle seat, scratching furiously at the stub of her missing ear. Her eyes traveled about the tent for a moment and then came to rest on Taniel. She gave a slight shake of her head, like a prison warden denying parole.

"This court-martial is in session," Ket said. "I will be presiding.

As you all know, this is a time of war. In such cases, Adran military law allows us to proceed with a drumhead court-martial. No prosecutor or defensive council was consulted. An investigation was carried out swiftly and privately over the course of the last seven days, and now, according to Adran military law, we will determine guilt and sentencing."

Taniel heard the tent flap at the back of the room part, and the sounds of the camp outside grew momentarily louder before the flap was closed again.

A frown passed over Ket's face at what she saw. Taniel thought about turning around, but Ket was still speaking.

"We've lost eight miles of ground and over three thousand men over the last seven days due directly to the chaos caused by Captain Taniel and his proclamation that Field Marshal Tamas is still alive, and that the General Staff is in league with the enemy. Captain Taniel is accused of fomenting rebellion among the ranks. The charge: treason. Does the accused enter a plea?"

"Not guilty," Taniel said. He knew the customs of the court. This was standard procedure—or at least, that's what Colonel Etan had told him, and Etan had studied military law at the university. Taniel couldn't help the feeling, however, that everything was going to go against him.

General Ket went on to read another dozen charges, including insubordination and assaulting a superior officer. Taniel responded with "not guilty" to every charge.

There was a clink of silverware behind him, and General Ket scowled. Taniel turned around to find Mihali passing out small plates to everyone sitting in the back—even to the provosts. Mihali came to the front with a stack of plates balanced on his arm and began to set them on the general's table.

"Provosts," Ket said, "remove this man."

"Oh, it's just refreshments," Mihali scolded, bringing a plate to Taniel. "Wine cake sprinkled with chocolate shavings and a touch of pepper powder. There will be hot coffee outside after the court-martial." His back to the generals, Mihali winked at Taniel.

None of the provosts had responded to Ket's command. They were too busy eating.

Taniel couldn't quite muster the strength to smile. He took a proffered slice of cake and tasted a bite, his chains clinking, and found it absolutely perfect. When everyone had finished, Mihali gathered the plates and retreated to the back of the tent.

Ket's cake remained untouched. "The investigation has concluded and the evidence has been presented to the judges, each of whom has made his or her own private determination. On the charge of treason, how do we find?"

"Guilty."

"Not guilty," General Hilanska said.

Ket stared into Taniel's eyes. "Guilty."

"Guilty."

"Guilty."

Taniel felt as if the bottom of his stomach had dropped out.

Ket went on. "By a majority, the defendant is found guilty of treason. The court-martial has reached its verdict. The penalty for treason is death by firing squad."

"That won't work on a powder mage," Mihali said helpfully from somewhere in the back.

"Silence in the court!" Ket pounded her gavel on the table.

"I'm not allowed to speak for myself?" Taniel demanded. "To address these idiotic charges?"

Ket sneered. "Were you or were you not given a full briefing by Colonel Etan on how a wartime court-martial is carried out?"

"I was."

"Then you'll know that you are not permitted to speak. Another outburst like that and I'll have you removed."

Taniel bit his tongue. Removed from his own trial? This was a load of buggery!

"In the case of a powder mage," Ket said, "the execution will be carried out by hanging."

General Hilanska leaned over to Ket and whispered something in her ear. She nodded slowly. Ket took a deep breath, as if collecting herself.

"I've been remiss by jumping to the inevitable conclusion of this court. The judges will now retire in order to discuss the sentencing of the guilty party. Court is in recess for one hour." The generals stood.

"May I speak to the court?"

General Ket paused, about to exit the back, and frowned past Taniel's shoulder. "This is a military court. I do not know who you are, ma'am, but civilians are not permitted."

"It will just take a moment. My name is Fell, undersecretary of the Noble Warriors of Labor and personal assistant to Ricard Tumblar. I am here to speak on behalf of Mr. Tumblar."

Taniel turned in his seat. Fell stood at the back of the room. She wore a tan suit jacket and sharply pressed shirt and trousers, her hands tucked casually into the pockets of her vest.

"Absolutely not," Ket said. "Provosts, remove this woman."

The gendarmes had no qualms about heading toward Fell.

"General Ket!" Fell said loudly. "This man who you seem so eager to sentence to death for the love of his country is in the running for second chair to the first prime minister of Adro!"

"Politics has no place in the Adran military," Ket said. The provosts paused, unsure as to whether to remove Fell now that Ket was facing her directly.

"Captain Taniel Two-Shot is a military hero on two continents," Fell said. "You might eschew politics, but you will destroy popular opinion of this war and of your command if the captain is executed."

"I don't care for public opinion. Leave this court."

"General Ket," Fell said emphatically, "if Taniel Two-Shot is executed, the factories will shut down in protest. Replacement boots, uniforms, buttons, musket kits, shirts, and hats will stop coming to the front. Hrusch Avenue will cease to produce rifles and muskets. The newspapers will make sure every single soul in Adopest knows that Taniel Two-Shot, hero of Adro, son of the supposedly late, and most definitely great Field Marshal Tamas, has been executed on trumped-up charges."

"Are you threatening me, Miss . . . ?"

"Fell."

"Fell." Ket rounded the table and crossed the room, gesturing to the provosts. "Are you threatening this war effort?"

Fell put a hand to her chest in shock. "Me? Threaten you? By Kresimir, General Ket, I would never think to threaten you. After all, I can see Taniel's face right there, tenderized like a side of beef by your provosts. I wouldn't want to end up like that. No, I am merely providing context for the consequences of the decision of this court."

"Your master controls the unions. Therefore, you're threatening me."

"No." Fell waggled her finger like a parent scolding a child. "My master heads the unions. The unions have the power to strike, and Mr. Tumblar cannot stop them if they so desire. Do you want that to happen?"

Ket leaned in toward Fell. To her credit, the undersecretary did not so much as flinch.

"This court is in recess for one hour!" Ket whirled and stormed out of the tent, followed by the other generals.

Fell dragged a chair up to the middle of the room. She waved her hand at the provosts flanking Taniel, and they hesitantly took a step back. Fell deposited the chair beside Taniel and sat down.

Taniel studied Fell for a moment. She was dressed sharply, looking far more a businesswoman than an undersecretary or personal assistant. Her eyes, though, were tired, and Taniel could see a recent scar on her cheek covered by a layer of face powder. She reached into her pocket and removed a brown bag. "Cashew?"

Taniel didn't know what to make of the woman. She, and her master, could have very well just saved Taniel's life...but a man like Ricard always had his price.

"You're going to owe Ricard a great deal if you live through this," Fell said in a low voice.

And there it was. "I didn't ask for his help."

"No, but he gave it. You're an honorable man, aren't you, Taniel?"

The idea of owing Ricard Tumblar anything made Taniel's stomach turn.

"What's Ricard's price?"

"Three years," Fell said. "As a politician. You'll be expected to attend galas and address the public. Everything will be scheduled for you. When you're not in the public eye, you can do anything you want—bed whomever, smoke all the mala in the world. Not a hard life at all." Fell shrugged. "But if Ricard happens to die or be killed, you'll have to step up as prime minister of Adro."

"I don't want that."

Fell gave him a tight smile. "Then you're more qualified for the job than Ricard is."

Taniel wondered if that was something that Ricard himself would have said, or if the undersecretary had just made a jab at her master.

"I thought that Hrusch Avenue hadn't unionized." Taniel glanced meaningfully toward the tent flap where the generals had exited.

"*They* don't know that."

"Is Ricard serious about those threats?"

"I'd rather not find out."

A bluff, then. Taniel had to give credit to Ricard. Bluffing the senior staff of the Adran army took courage. "Has Ricard ever tried blackmailing Tamas?"

"Oh, pit no. Tamas would have strung Ricard up like a marionette."

"I'm glad to hear he has limits."

The hour-long recess for the court stretched into two hours, and then into three. Mihali served coffee and another round of cake.

Taniel couldn't help wondering where the pit the generals had gotten to. What could be taking them so long?

"This is a good thing, you know," Fell said between bites of cake.

Colonel Etan, his chair wheeled up beside Taniel, agreed. "At this point, the sentencing requires a four-out-of-five vote. If they'd returned at the hour, or earlier, it would not have looked good for you. They've been arguing this whole time, which means that more generals than just General Hilanska are trying to save your skin."

The tent flap was swept aside, and the generals reentered the room. Fell and Etan both retreated to the back, and the generals took their chairs.

Ket examined Taniel for several moments before speaking. The anger had left her eyes. Steely determination replaced it. "This court," she said, "has found the defendant guilty of treason. We have decided to drop the remainder of the charges and commute upon the guilty one sentence, to be carried out immediately:

"Captain Taniel is hereby stripped of his rank in the Adran army and dishonorably discharged. As this is a closed court, the verdict is private—however much I'd like to announce to the world that Taniel is no longer one of us, he will be allowed twelve hours to gather his things and quietly leave the camp. Any failure to do so will be met with swift reprisal. Court is adjourned."

Taniel could hear Doravir protesting from the back that the sentence was too light. Etan loudly argued that the sentence was too harsh. The provosts released Taniel from the irons and stripped him out of his uniform jacket.

He didn't argue. He couldn't argue. He barely noticed when the generals had left.

How could they do this to him? After all he'd done? All he'd given?

"Taniel."

He looked up. Etan sat in front of him, an orderly waiting to wheel him off.

"Taniel, you know I don't believe any of this treason garbage. None of them do either. If they did, they'd have executed you, regardless of Tumblar's threats. They just wanted you out of the way. If there's anything you need, just let me know. I have a house in North Umpshire if you need someplace quiet to recover. Bring the girl if you'd like."

Ka-poel. Taniel let out a shaky sigh. What should he do with Ka-poel? Send her back to Fatrasta? Would she even go?

"Thanks," Taniel said.

It was some time before he realized that the tent was empty. Fell was gone. It occurred to him that he should have asked her if Ricard received his letter regarding the missing gunpowder.

Taniel managed to climb to his feet. His legs shook, and he wondered where he could get some mala. No. Not mala. He needed powder. That would be easier to find anyway. He had to gather his things. What did he even have? His sketchbook and charcoals. The rifle wasn't even his—army issued, though he might be able to slip off with it anyway. He could sell the buttons off his army jacket.

Taniel cursed. The provosts had taken his jacket.

He cursed again when he noticed the tent was not, in fact, empty.

Mihali sat at the back, sipping a cup of coffee. He met Taniel's glance with the slight rise of his eyebrows.

Taniel wondered what it would be like to punch a god. "Did you see that, you bastard?" Taniel said. "'Apologize to Doravir.' That's what you told me. 'Save the war.' How the pit does this save anything? Stripped of everything I know?"

"The future is always changing," Mihali said. "Coffee?"

"Go to the pit."

Taniel left the command tent and headed toward his quarters. He wasn't two dozen steps outside when he was joined by Brigadier Abrax. It only took him a few moments to realize why she was there.

"Do the Wings of Adom usually perch at a court-martial, waiting to recruit new mercenaries?"

Brigadier Abrax was a serious woman in her forties, with short blond hair and a sharp white-and-red uniform. "Awfully full of yourself, Two-Shot. I can see why Ket wanted to be rid of you. What makes you think I've come along recruiting?"

"Nothing. Sorry, ma'am." Taniel reminded himself that he was not in a position to insult the senior commander of the best mercenary army in the world.

"I have, of course," Abrax said. "Come recruiting, that is. I want to offer you a spot in the Wings of Adom."

Taniel had never thought highly of mercenaries. At best, they took your money and did everything they could to avoid actually fighting. However, he had to grudgingly admit that the Wings had a reputation for slogging into the melee along with the ordinary infantry. He'd seen them do it himself during this war.

Taniel stopped and turned to the brigadier. "The General Staff would be furious."

"What do I care?" Abrax said. "I don't report to anyone but Lady Winceslav and Tamas. Not to the General Staff. Besides, I just watched them court-martial their best soldier. I don't have a lot of faith in their ability to do anything right. Even if you are a pompous ass with no respect for authority, you're worth fifty men, and I mean to see you in my army."

"That was an incredibly backhanded compliment," Taniel said.

Abrax gave him a shallow smile. "I meant every word."

"Ricard Tumblar seems to think he's bought me."

"If you feel as if you must repay him," Abrax said with a shrug, "feel free to do so. But after this war is over. I have the feeling you would much rather be on the front than in Adopest trying to win over the snakes in politics. At least here you're allowed to shoot your enemies."

Taniel looked around the camp. It was muddy and chaotic, the moans of the wounded rising from the field hospitals and the crack of gunfire drifting back from the front. Still, he couldn't imagine leaving it for a desk or a podium in Adopest.

"What do you propose?" he asked.

"You'll be a major in the Wings of Adom with full pay and benefits. I'll place you outside the chain of command and you'll only report to me. Your sole mission will be to kill enemy Privileged and Wardens. I don't like to complicate things further than that."

"And the other brigadiers will agree to this?"

"They love the idea," Abrax said. She leaned toward him. "Tamas recently stole one of our very best. He did it fairly, I think, but it still stung. The brigadiers consider this revenge."

Taniel examined Abrax. She seemed sincere. Tamas had had nothing but good things to say about the Wings, and being in a mercenary company was certainly preferable to having to sit out the rest of the war.

"Who did Tamas steal?"

"A young brigadier by the name of Sabastenien," Abrax said.

The name rang a bell, but Taniel could not give it a face.

"How long do you want me in the Wings?"

"Until the end of the war. We disband between assignments. You'll be paid in full and disbanded, with the option to muster for our next assignment."

"Ka-poel?"

Abrax frowned. "Your savage?"

"Yes."

"Bring her with if you want. I don't care who you're bedding. I put on a good front, but I'm not a prude."

"I'm not sleeping with her. She accompanies me on the battle-field as my spotter."

Abrax seemed to mull this over for a few moments. "I can't promise any more than a private's wages for her."

"Oh, ah..." Taniel almost stepped back. No one had even con-sidered actually *paying* Ka-poel in the Adran army. "That sounds fair."

"We have a deal?"

"I think so."

"Report to our camp in two hours," she said. "We'll get you bed-ded down in temporary quarters and then outfit you in the morn-ing. I want you on the field killing Kez by noon tomorrow."

CHAPTER
29

Tamas climbed from his bedroll. He paused once, taking a deep breath.

"Getting old," he muttered.

Every morning his limbs ached a little more, especially his leg. Every day it took him just another couple of seconds to climb from the bed. Worse now, sleeping on the hard ground. Every night for the last five weeks.

Five weeks. Hard to believe it had only been that long since he'd faced the Kez Grand Army, planning how he'd take them from the side and smash them against the gates of Budwiel. Bloody stupid, now that he looked back on it, thinking he could take the entire Grand Army with two brigades.

His arrogance got him into this. Had he been there, manning the walls beside Hilanska and the rest, they would have fought off those Wardens and sent the Kez army to the pit.

Tamas got to his feet. He pulled on his shirt, long since yellowed and stained with blood—his own blood, and that of others—then on came his uniform pants and boots. Olem had polished the boots during the night, like he did every night. He understood that a field marshal needed to keep up appearances. Finally, Tamas put on his jacket, and he stepped out into the morning air with his bicorne tucked under one arm.

Gavril stared down at him from on horseback. Somehow, he kept that Watchmaster's vest of his immaculate. His pants were ripped and stained, his arms and shoulders covered with powder burns, nicks, and cuts, but the faded colors of the Watchmaster's vest showed no wear but that of time and washing.

Gavril had Tamas's charger saddled and ready, and held the reins out to Tamas.

"I'm not going on some bloody jaunt with you," Tamas said.

"Then why are you dressed?" Gavril looked around the camp. No one had stirred yet. Tamas let them off easy the last couple of days, sleeping until past eight in the morning. They'd earned their rest, and with the Kez cavalry broken, their remnants sworn to leave Tamas be, and the infantry still a week off, Tamas could afford to give his men some slack.

"The army is marching today," Tamas said.

"We'll catch up."

Stubborn bastard. Why did Gavril need this? Why did he need to drag Tamas along with him? The dead were best left buried, undisturbed. They cared not for the sentiments of the living.

Tamas would rather have tipped his hat to the west and bowed his head in respect for a few minutes. It would have been more practical.

"Get on your damn horse," Gavril said.

Tamas climbed onto his mount.

They rode west in silence along one of the many rivers that made up the Fingers of Kresimir. Tamas didn't know if this one had a name. The locals probably called it something—not that there were many locals in this part of Kez.

Northern Kez, with its countless farms and ranches, had once been filled with people. The alternating droughts and floods of the last ten years that had caused Adro so many problems had also affected Kez, and huge portions of the Kez population had gone to the eastern cities in search of work. He imagined those cities even more crowded and dirty than Adopest.

Tamas wondered how Adopest had fared in the war. The canal over the mountains should be finished by this time, alleviating some of the strain off the Mountainwatch for trade. With war with the Kez, food would have to come from Novi and Deliv.

Tamas and Gavril came down out of the highest foothills to where Kresimir's Fingers began to meet. The Fingers didn't all converge, not all at once. It was several days' ride to the place where they did, and their destination was not that far out onto the plains.

The ground turned rocky—great boulders and sudden ravines that made Tamas wonder if the mountains had once come out this far, and if so, what god or force of nature had knocked them down.

The terrain had provided a good place to hide from Ipille's Wardens, long ago.

They crossed a rocky bluff and then descended into a gully where two of Kresimir's Fingers met. Tamas rubbed at his shoulders, suddenly cold despite the summer sun beating down upon them.

He saw it then. A cairn, not more than fifty paces from where the two rivers met. It was about four feet high and six feet across, sandstone rocks gathered from the area and stacked.

It had changed little in the last thirteen years. The bloody fingerprints both Tamas and Gavril had left, their hands raw from digging the stony earth, had been washed away. A necklace—a treasured possession of the dead that Tamas had left on the highest stone—was gone, but the rest of the cairn remained undisturbed.

Tamas climbed down from his horse and tied the reins to a

stunted tree. He approached the cairn slowly. Thoughtfully. Now that he was here, the dread he'd felt in coming seemed silly.

He turned to Gavril.

The big man, with all his stubbornness in making Tamas accompany him on this pilgrimage, seemed reluctant to get any closer.

Tamas took a shaky breath. He reached out and touched the top stone of the cairn.

"Camenir," he said, and found it felt good to say it aloud.

A crunch of footsteps sounded on the rocky soil as Gavril finally joined him.

"I doubt anyone but you or me remember the name." In his head, it had been a musing thought. Aloud, it sounded callous, and Tamas instantly regretted saying it. Gavril was the last of Camenir's kin. His relatives on the Kez side, dead by Ipille's orders. The ones on the Adran side not numerous, and those alive having long disowned him.

Tamas tried to picture Camenir in his mind, and found he could not. He looked a lot like Gavril, he thought. Not as big. Quite a bit younger. A sloppy, casual manner and a genuine smile that most found endearing.

"How did you do it?" Gavril stood beside the cairn, head bowed.

"Do what?"

"How did you go on? After what happened?"

Tamas was surprised to hear accusation in Gavril's voice.

"What choice did I have?"

What did Gavril want him to say? Did Gavril want him to admit he'd slept his way through half the eligible ladies in Adopest, and quite a few ineligible ones? Did Gavril want him to point out that he'd killed more men in duels in the short time following Erika's death than he had in all his angry youth?

"I saw grief in you," Gavril said. "I saw it eating through you after Erika's murder. After Manhouch denied your demands that we go to war. When you came and said you wanted to kill Ipille, I knew it had to be done. But…but after we failed, after Camenir died, you changed. All those signs of grief I'd seen in you were gone. You went back to society. Smiled at all those fools who'd laughed behind their hands at the box containing Erika's head. You entertained guests and walked the streets laughing."

"What choice did I have?" Tamas repeated.

Gavril gripped his shoulder and turned him around to look him in the eye. "You never grieved for Camenir. You never cared that my little brother died." Tears sprang up in Gavril's eyes, his face red.

"What did you want?" Tamas was suddenly angry. Had Gavril held this against him all these years? Did Gavril think that Camenir meant nothing to him? "Did you want me to turn to the bottle, like you did?"

"I wanted you to show some decorum!" Gavril's voice rose sharply. "Show some regret. Any sign of emotion for my brother! A man who died for you!"

This close, Gavril towered over him, but Tamas felt no fear. Only rage and regret. "That's rich, coming from you," Tamas spat. "Do you think climbing into an ale cask showed decorum?"

Tamas barely saw the fist coming. One moment it loomed, big as a ham, and the next his ears rang as he stared at the ground from his knees. He blinked away a sudden haze. Blood leaked from his mouth and nose, spattering on the dusty ground. Not the first blood he'd left on this spot.

He climbed to his feet, wobbling on his knees. Gavril glared at him, daring him to hit back.

So he did.

The look of surprise on Gavril's face as Tamas's fist connected with his stomach gave Tamas a jolt of satisfaction. He followed it up with another punch, doubling Gavril over.

"I lost my wife, you bastard," he growled.

Gavril wrapped his arms around Tamas and lifted him with a

bellow. Tamas felt a thrill of fear as his feet left the ground. To a man with Gavril's strength, he might as well have been a child.

He brought his elbow down on Gavril's back, eliciting a yell from the big man.

Gavril lifted him high, then pounded him into the ground. Tamas felt the air leave his lungs, the feeling leave his legs, and his vision blurred. He hacked out a cough and dug one hand into the fat of Gavril's stomach.

They rolled in the dirt for what felt like hours. Swearing, kicking, punching. It didn't matter how hard Tamas hit Gavril, nothing seemed to stop him. Even without a powder trance, Tamas still considered himself a pit of a fighter. Gavril broke his holds. Absorbed his punches. And he gave as good—or better—than he got.

Tamas climbed to his feet and kicked Gavril. His brother-in-law shoved him backward, and Tamas felt his back hit the rocks of the cairn.

"Stop!" he said.

Gavril looked up, his face bruised, one eye blackened and his nose bloody. He saw the cairn behind Tamas and lowered his fist.

Tamas limped away from the cairn and lowered himself against an old fallen log.

He felt along his ribs. One of them might have gotten cracked. His face felt like a rug after the housekeeper had beat it for an hour. The back of his jacket had ripped—he could tell just by moving his shoulders. One of his boots was on the other side of the cairn, and Tamas didn't even remember it coming off.

"You want to know what happened to me?" Tamas said.

Gavril grunted. He lay on the ground across from Tamas, legs splayed.

"That night we buried Camenir is the night I decided to kill Manhouch." Tamas gathered up a wad of spit and hawked it into the dirt. It was red. "I decided to start a war. Not for the people's rights or because Manhouch was evil or any of the other drivel I tell my supporters. I started a war to avenge my wife and my brother."

Tamas took a deep breath and stared at his stockinged foot. His sock had ripped a week ago and his big toe stuck through it. "I couldn't do it in a world of grief. I had to feel out my friends. Charm my enemies. That was the first step: to convince them I was still Adro's favored son. Manhouch's protector. The next step was putting Manhouch's head in a basket.

"Then, of course, the war. Which"—Tamas held up one finger—"I almost didn't go through with. The earthquake and the royalists nearly knocked me off my course. My heart bled when I saw the shambles in which Adopest had been left. But Ipille sent Nikslaus and put me back on my path to vengeance."

Tamas let his finger drop. "The path will end when I cut out Ipille's heart for taking my family."

The air was still. The only sound that of the water where the two rivers met.

"That was a nice speech," Gavril said.

"I thought so."

"Had that memorized long?"

"Most of it for years," Tamas said. "Had to do a little improvising. Never thought I'd be giving it to you."

"Who, then?"

Tamas shrugged. "My grandchildren? My executioner? Taniel's the only one who knew the real reasons I planned the things I did."

The sound of a horse whinnying brought Tamas's head around. Up on the bluff, perhaps a hundred feet away, were two riders. He squinted into the afternoon sun as his fingers looked for his pistol. It had come out of his belt and lay a dozen paces to his left.

The riders began to head down the bluff toward him. The glare of the sun lessened, and he recognized two familiar faces: Olem and Beon je Ipille.

"Company," Tamas said.

Gavril craned his neck and looked toward the bluff. "Is that Beon and Olem?"

"Yes."

"I could break Beon's neck. Bury him next to Camenir. Would be poetic justice in that."

"My—our—quarrel isn't with Beon. It's with his father."

"I've heard Beon is Ipille's favorite."

"Ipille's 'favorite' son changes every six months or so. Beon just lost a major battle with me. I think if we killed him now, Ipille would say he deserved it."

"Not a loving father."

"No."

Olem and Beon came to a halt some dozen paces off. Olem looked down at Tamas's dislodged boot, then around the gully. "Seems there was a fight," he said.

"Ambushed. We dumped the bodies in the river," Tamas said.

"Of course," Olem said. He didn't sound convinced.

"I thought that you were given orders to stay in the camp?" Tamas said to Olem.

"Sorry, sir," Olem said. "The general here asked me to accompany him as his chaperone so that he did not break his word of honor in leaving the camp."

"And why did you feel the need to follow me?" Tamas turned to Beon.

Beon frowned toward the cairn. "I have heard a story," he said. "Regarding a powder mage, and two huge brothers with great strength." His eyes flicked to Gavril. "An old story, passed around in my father's court. One that my father has taken great pains to stamp out."

"So?" Gavril said, his tone petulant.

Beon seemed unperturbed. "The story caught my childhood imagination. It comes to an end when an entire company of my father's Elite disappeared in the Fingers of Kresimir. Some of their bodies were found. Some weren't. I always wondered if that was really the end of the story."

Tamas and Gavril looked at each other.

Tamas asked, "And you thought you might find the end of the story by following us out here?"

Beon was looking at the cairn again. "I thought, perhaps. I see a powder mage, a widower by my father's orders, and one very large man with great strength. I predict that the story I heard has a sadder ending than my childhood imagination would have hoped." He bowed his head toward them and turned his horse around. "I'm sorry to have disturbed you."

"It did," Gavril called out.

Beon stopped and looked back. "Did what?"

"The story. It had a sad ending."

"No," Beon said. "The story is not over yet. But the ending will be very sad regardless."

CHAPTER
30

The Flaming Cuttlefish was a fisherman's pub. Like The Salty Maiden, it was located out at the end of a pier, suspended about ten feet above the water. Unlike The Salty Maiden, it was packed with all kinds. There were factory workers, seamstresses, millers, and even a few gunsmiths. The pub was known throughout the city for cheap, delicious freshwater oysters. In one corner of the room a fiddler was sawing away a seaman's tune, and the whole pier swayed with the stamp of a hundred feet.

The barmaid had assured Adamat that that was normal.

Adamat nursed his beer and let his eyes wander around the room again. He sat with his back to the wall, watching the exits. No signs of the slaver, Doles, or any of his men. No sign of Adamat's son.

It was near midnight. Doles was supposed to meet him here yesterday, but had never come. Riding out his optimism, Adamat had come back and waited all day, a case filled with two hundred fifty thousand krana in cash sitting on his knee. He was tired and nervous, and every minute that passed he grew angrier.

SouSmith, sitting beside him, stifled a yawn. He was drumming his fingers to the tune of the fiddler, his eyes wandering. Adamat could tell he was losing focus.

"Pit!" Adamat swore, getting to his feet.

SouSmith started. "Huh?" He came alert, looking around for signs of danger.

"He's not coming," Adamat shouted above the music and stamping. "We're done here."

SouSmith followed him out into the night, and for the second time in a week Adamat found himself standing in the dark, on a pier, with nothing to show for himself. He kicked a pier piling and swore when it bruised his toe. He nearly threw his case into the water, but SouSmith grabbed his arm.

"You'll be sorry 'bout that."

Adamat looked down at the case. All of his money; his savings, the money Bo had given him, plus another fifty thousand from Ricard. Yes. He *would* have been sorry.

"I'll have to go to Norport now," Adamat said. He was already doing the math in his head. He'd have to charter a boat—and not just any boat, but a smuggler to get him into the Kez-held town—then he'd need to locate Josep and free him from the Kez. There might be Privileged involved, though rumor had it Taniel Two-Shot had killed most of the Kez Cabal on South Pike. Then he'd . . .

SouSmith shook him by the arm.

"What is it?" Adamat asked, annoyed that his thoughts had been interrupted.

"Norport? You mad?"

"No. I have to get my son back."

SouSmith sighed. He pulled a pipe from his pocket and set it between his teeth, then packed it with tobacco. "Have to let it go," he grunted.

"He's my boy," Adamat said. "How can I let him go?" He slumped against the same pier piling that he'd just kicked.

"He's outta reach," SouSmith said gently.

"No. He can't be." Adamat tried to resume his previous train of thought. So much he'd have to do. "Will you come with me?"

SouSmith puffed on his pipe for a moment. "Yeah."

"Thank you," Adamat said, relief washing over him. Norport would be dangerous, but going alone into Kez territory might be suicide.

"One condition."

"What's that?"

"Sleep on it."

Adamat hesitated for a moment. He should prepare tonight. Get his supplies together, find a smuggler...then again, finding a smuggler *would* be far easier in the morning. Most of Adamat's contacts were asleep by this hour. "Fine," he said. "I'll sleep on it."

SouSmith accompanied Adamat home before taking his own leave. Adamat watched SouSmith's hackney cab clatter down the street, then headed inside.

The house was quiet but for the soft sound of one of the children crying. Adamat removed his boots and hat, and hung his jacket by the door. He passed the children's rooms, pausing briefly beside Astrit's. She was the one crying. Fanish sung softly to her, holding her tight and rocking her back and forth. Neither of them saw Adamat.

He crept into his own room. The lamp was burning low, like it always was when Adamat was still out late.

Faye sat up in bed. Her eyes were red, her long, bedraggled curls framing her haggard face. The faint light of hope in her eyes died when she saw him, and Adamat felt his shoulders slump in defeat. He sat down on the bed beside her and buried his face in his hands.

"You tried," Faye said. She was better, he thought. Despite her appearance, she'd been growing stronger over the last week, spending time with the children. She still stayed away from the windows and avoided going outside, though Adamat couldn't determine the reason. Perhaps she feared being seen by one of her former captors?

"I'm going to Norport," Adamat said when he'd regained his composure.

Faye's hand, gently stroking his arm, froze. "Why?"

"To get Josep back. I can find him there, and if I can't find him, I can pick up his trail."

"No."

"What do you mean?"

"I mean no." Faye's tone was firm. "I'll not have you risking your life over this. Not anymore. I've lost Josep, but I have eight more children, and I can't provide for them and protect them without you."

"You won't—"

"I said no."

Adamat could tell by her tone there'd be no argument. No hope at all. She'd do everything in her power to keep him from going. "But—"

"No."

He tried to find the courage to tell her off. To tell her that he had a duty to his son, that he could still get his boy back.

The courage never came.

In the morning, Adamat went to return the money he'd borrowed from Ricard.

A secretary met him in the lobby of Ricard's new headquarters. She opened her mouth with a word of greeting, but something on his face must have stilled her tongue, and she led him back to the room off the side of the building that was Ricard's office.

The room was much larger than his old office, but no cleaner. The whole room reeked. There were oysters on one shelf, probably from the same pub that Adamat had been to last night, and from the smell of them they were three days old. The scent was made worse by some kind of incense burning on Ricard's desk.

He ignored Ricard's greeting and threw himself into the chair across from him.

Ricard frowned and leaned back in his seat, and the two of them regarded each other for a few moments. Ricard's eyes went to the case on Adamat's lap.

"They never showed," Adamat said, tossing the case on the ground. "They took my fifty-thousand-krana deposit and disappeared. Now my boy is gone forever, along with any hope I have of getting him back. I should never have trusted them." Adamat could hear the disgust in his own voice.

Ricard got that look on his face when he was about to say "I told you so," but instead quietly said, "We all make mistakes."

Adamat wanted to break things. He wanted to go on a violent rampage, destroying Ricard's expensive furniture and chandeliers and crystal decanters, then throw himself on the ground in the middle of the mess and sob.

"I don't know what to do now," he said.

Ricard said, "I have something I could have you look into."

Adamat fixed Ricard with a long look. How could Ricard think he'd want to take a case right now?

"It would keep your mind off things," Ricard went on. "There are accusations of profiteering within the ranks of the Adran army. I need to follow up on those accusations and find some evidence."

"That's a job for the provosts," Adamat said.

"Not when the corruption runs all the way up to the General Staff."

"No," Adamat said. "I'm done with military dealings. Find someone braver and stupider."

Ricard stifled a smile. "You're the bravest and stupidest man I know."

"I can attest to that," a voice said from the back of the room.

Privileged Borbador stood in the doorway. He wore a slimming day jacket, his face pink from a morning shave, a cane in one hand. His Privileged's gloves were nowhere to be seen.

"Who the pit are you?" Ricard asked.

"Privileged Borbador, at your service." Bo bowed his head slightly. "I understand you have a letter for me."

"Oh," Ricard said in surprise. A confused look crossed his face. "How could you possibly know that I have a letter for you?"

Bo smiled.

"Right. From Taniel Two-Shot," Ricard said. He searched through his papers until he discovered the letter, then brought it to Bo.

Bo leaned up against the doorway as he read the note. He turned it around, looking at some kind of report that had been written on the back. His eyes narrowed, and he glanced at Adamat. "Did you tell him that Tamas is still alive?"

"I did," Adamat said.

"We have no evidence of that." Ricard spread his hands.

"He is," Bo said. "And when he gets back, he's going to gut his General Staff."

"If the army runs out of powder, Adro will have been conquered long before Tamas returns."

Bo chewed on his lip. "Any word from Taniel Two-Shot? Other than this letter, I mean."

"He is being court-martialed as we speak. I sent my undersecretary down to intervene on my behalf, but I won't know the results for days."

"Court-martialed? For what?" Bo's tone was flat. Adamat thought it his imagination, but the temperature of the room seemed to have dropped.

"Mostly trumped-up charges," Ricard said. "Disobeying orders, attacking one of the General Staff. But Taniel suspects that some of the General Staff are war-profiteering, and may even be in league with the Kez, which would explain why they're court-martialing their only powder mage."

Bo waved the letter. "Yes, I read that. Pit. Pit, pit, pit. I suppose I could go kill them all, if they haven't hanged him by the time I get there."

"That wouldn't be very good for the war effort," Adamat pointed out. "And we don't know which of the generals are profiteering."

"You think I give a damn about who it is?" Bo snapped. Bo raised his hand, and even though he wasn't wearing his Privileged's gloves, Adamat felt himself shrink into his chair. Bo took a deep breath and closed his eyes for a few minutes before speaking again. "I'll take care of this," he said. To Ricard, "I may need your help."

"My organization is at your disposal."

"Good."

Bo left as quickly as he'd arrived, and Adamat found himself alone with Ricard once again.

"Well, that's interesting. You've made yourself some rather fascinating friends." Ricard plucked a half-smoked cigar from an ashtray and examined it, as if deciding whether to finish it off. He tossed it into the rubbish bin at his feet.

"I'd rather not have had to," Adamat murmured.

"You need a break. Not more work. I see that now. You should come on a trip with me," Ricard said.

"What? Where?"

"The grand opening of the Pan-Deliv Canal!" Ricard stood up and threw back the curtains on his window to reveal the ugliness of the factory dock-fronts with the backdrop of a rainstorm raging across the Adsea. He cocked an eyebrow at the weather and closed the curtains.

"I thought it was called the King Manhouch Canal?"

"No king, no King Manhouch Canal." Ricard opened his cigar box and offered one to Adamat, which he refused.

"I will not let you cheer me up," Adamat said.

Ricard waved his hand in front of him as if envisioning a sign hanging from the wall. "I wanted to call it the Tumblar Crossing, but my Ministerial Election Committee seems to think that humility looks better to the voting public, while the council wanted something to strengthen ties with Deliv." Ricard struck a match and lit his cigar. "I give up so much for the greater good."

"You poor man," Adamat said.

"You'll come to the grand opening?"

"No." What could possibly make Ricard think that Adamat would want to travel, after all his ordeals? He closed his eyes, trying to escape the stink of those oysters. "What about Privileged Borbador?"

"I'll leave word for my people to help him. Come with me. I insist," Ricard said.

"Absolutely not. My wife is in no shape to travel. My children—"

"Your children can come. I'll hire the nannies, and you and Faye can ride in my carriage. We leave this afternoon."

"Faye will not go!"

"She's already agreed."

Adamat narrowed his eyes. "Liar."

"Cross my heart," Ricard said. "I visited her yesterday."

"She would have said something."

"She didn't, apparently. Go home and ask her. My bet is that she's already packed. It'll do you both good to get out of the city."

"If you planned this all out, why that rubbish about the profiteering generals?"

"I wanted to get your thoughts on it. You weren't very helpful."

"I couldn't possibly—"

"All expenses are on me," Ricard said. He leaned over his desk, his nose wrinkling as incense wafted in his face. "Go home and get ready. My carriage will pick you up in three hours. No more arguments."

"I won't be bullied." Adamat tried to get angry. He wanted to lean across the desk and smack Ricard, but the fury just wasn't there. Ricard was right. He needed to get out of the city and have some fresh air. If the children could come, and Faye had already agreed, perhaps it would do them all some good.

"Three hours," Ricard said.

Adamat kicked the travel case, sending stacks of banknotes across the floor. "All right, damn it! Just throw out those damned oysters!"

Ricard stood up straight and nodded, pinching his nose at the pungent odor. "Agreed."

Taniel didn't know whether to curse his luck or to praise it.

General Ket could very well have sent him to the noose. She had the backing of the rest of the senior staff—all but General Hilanska, it seemed. Fell's arrival couldn't have been more timely, and Abrax's offer of employment with the Wings would let him stay on the front.

But to be thrown out of the Adran army? The thought still made him stumble. He'd been raised in the army. He'd marched and killed and bled for them for nearly half his life and now they tossed him aside like unwanted trash, all because he accused the General Staff of helping Kez.

And perhaps they were. Their retreat orders were suspiciously well timed, and their refusal to hold the line even when the Kez were beaten was baffling.

Nothing Taniel could do about it now except join the Wings of Adom. He'd have a chance to finally finish off the Kez Privileged, and maybe once all those damned sorcerers were dead, they'd stop making Wardens of any kind. Of course, Taniel also needed a way to get Kresimir's blood so that Ka-poel could kill him.

That seemed like the easy part.

An explosion sent Taniel reeling. He regained his feet a moment later. Where had it come from?

There was confusion in the Adran camp, but it seemed the explosion had come from the south. Taniel rushed to a hillock and looked south to the Kez camp.

In the far distance, miles away, beyond the Kez camp and the immense beam where Julene hung in the sun, he could see the city of Budwiel. The walls of the city smoldered. Low clouds hung above it—or was that smoke? A gunpowder explosion? Possible.

The Kez camp was a flurry of activity, all of it directed back toward Budwiel. Was that Tamas, finally returning? No, it couldn't be. Tamas wouldn't attack the Kez rear unless he was damned certain that the Adran brigades would attack from the front.

It *would* have been an opportune moment to strike. Taniel cocked his head, listening for the trumpets to call the men to arms.

His gaze drifted to the beam erected in the middle of the Kez camp and Julene's body hanging from it and he wondered again how she'd ended up there. She had been so willful, so powerful. Had Kresimir done it? Taniel couldn't imagine anyone else having the power to subdue her like that.

Taniel waited. Silence. There wasn't even an alarm in case the Kez attempted a surprise attack.

The sun was just setting when Taniel reached his quarters in a small shed. He had a couple hours to find Ka-poel and gather his things. Should he say good-bye to anyone? Etan would remain in contact. Was there anyone else?

Taniel leaned against the door to the shed he'd been using as quarters. No. There wasn't anyone else. For all his time in the Adran army, Taniel had few friends. That should have made it easier to leave.

It should have . . .

Taniel opened the door. The waning sunlight slashed across the inside of the room.

Ka-poel lay naked on the cot, her hands stretched above her head, her face hidden in the shadows. Taniel felt his face turn red. He averted his eyes.

"Pole, what are you doing?"

A fist connected with his stomach, doubling him over. A pair of hands shoved him inside. He fell to the floor, trying to gather his wits as the door closed behind him.

Taniel scrambled to get to his feet. Something hard slammed into his back and he felt a blade against his throat. His mouth went dry.

"Don't move, powder mage."

A match was struck and the lantern beside the bed lit. There were five men crowded into the small room. They leered down at Taniel. Each one carried a truncheon or a knife. The lot of them reeked of whiskey. They wore Adran military jackets with a patch on the shoulder that showed the emblem of a shovel.

Dredgers. Third Brigade. The lowest of the low in the entire Adran military.

General Ket's men.

One of the soldiers took a swig from a bottle in his hand and punched Taniel in the face. The blow was hard and well placed, forcing Taniel down farther. By the soldier's stripes on his shoulder, he was a captain.

Taniel stared at the floor, watching long tendrils of bloody saliva drop on the wood. "Who the pit are you?" he spat.

The captain sniffed. "General Ket told us we'd get this little piece here. We thought we'd start early." He set the bottle on the nightstand and began to loosen his trousers. "And you're going to watch."

Taniel looked at Ka-poel out of the corner of his eye, trying to ignore her nudity. Her face was bruised and black, her lip split and bloody. She'd been beaten badly.

He surged to his feet. Someone was quick enough with a truncheon to bash him across the shoulders. Taniel didn't even feel it. His right hand grasped the captain's chin, fingers in the man's mouth. His left hand grabbed the captain by the forehead.

Taniel felt the pop and tear of muscles, bone, and tendon as he tore the captain's jaw off. Deep inside, the sound frightened him, but all objections were silenced by his rage.

He took a truncheon blow across the side of the face and turned on the wielder. His fist hit the soldier's nose hard enough to kill him instantly. Red filled Taniel's vision like a thick fog, and his body moved as if on its own accord.

Taniel couldn't remember killing the last three, but he was soon surrounded by five corpses, their blood still warm on his hands and shirt. He dropped to his knees beside Ka-poel. She was breathing lightly. Her eyes fluttered open.

"Shh," Taniel said when her mouth opened. He covered her with a blanket and then snatched his only other jacket from the bedpost, throwing it on over his blood-soaked shirt. He grabbed his sketch-book and his kit and threw them in his bag, then lifted Ka-poel in his arms. There was nothing else in this room that mattered.

He spotted her satchel, discarded in the corner, and grabbed it as he left.

Taniel sprinted the entire way to the Wings camp. As soon as he reached the pickets, he began to call for a doctor. Confused infantrymen regarded him from their posts as he raced by.

The brigadiers' tents were not hard to find in the center of the camp.

"Is this Abrax's tent?" Taniel demanded.

The two sentries exchanged a glance.

"Brigadier Abrax! I must see her now!"

"Two-Shot?"

Taniel whirled to see Abrax approaching from the way he'd come. She was probably just returning from the Adran camp, and he realized they'd spoken less than twenty minutes ago.

"What the pit are you..." Her eyes took in his bloody shirt and Ka-poel's bruised body. "What happened?"

"I need a doctor for her. Now!"

"Get a doctor," Abrax barked at the sentries. "Bring her into my tent. There, set her on the cot. What happened to her? Holy saints, what happened to you? You're covered in blood. Did you do this to her?"

"No!" Taniel roared the word before he was able to control himself. "No. I didn't. She's all that matters. See to her, please."

"It'll be done," Abrax said.

"I've just killed five men," Taniel said. "Soldiers in the Third Brigade. It was in self-defense, but they'll be coming for me shortly."

Abrax blinked at the news. She opened her mouth, then shut it. "You were attacked?" she finally managed.

"Yes."

"Details, man. *Now!*"

"Five men jumped me in my quarters. They had Ka-poel like this...they were going to...while I watched." Taniel heard his words flow out in broken, rushed sentences.

"You were unarmed?"

Taniel nodded.

Abrax put her hand to her mouth and studied Taniel. "You're in shock. Sit down. Were you in a powder trance?"

"No."

"Five men," she breathed, almost too low for Taniel to hear. "With his bare hands." She glanced at Ka-poel. "The doctors will be here soon. Stay here."

Abrax crossed to the head of the tent. "Stewart!" she bellowed as she went. Abrax stepped outside, but she spoke loudly enough that Taniel could hear her clearly. "Ah, there you are. Get our best internal investigators. Send them to the Adran camp immediately. There has been a quintuple murder and I want to know the exact circumstances leading up to it."

"We going after someone? Or trying to determine how the victims arrived at their deaths?" a male voice asked. Stewart, Taniel assumed.

"We're not going after anything but the truth. And they're not victims, they're potential rapists. Dig up everything you can on them. I want to know exactly what type of people they were and what they were doing before their deaths."

"Yes, ma'am."

"And close the camp to the Adran provosts and stifle any rumors going around."

"Of course. Anything else?"

"Stay close. I'm sure I'll need something."

Abrax returned to the tent a moment later. Taniel thought to stand, and realized that he'd taken Ka-poel's hand at some point. He decided to stay by her side.

"Thank you," he said.

"Believe me this," Abrax said, her face flushed, her brow furrowed. "If you've lied to me, I'll put the noose around your neck myself. But I won't see a man lose his life because he defended himself and his loved one."

The doctor came moments later. Taniel refused to leave the tent, but did avert his eyes as the doctor examined Ka-poel. She struggled a little—he hoped that was a good sign.

"I've given her something to help her sleep," the doctor said after her examination. She glared at Taniel. "She's suffered a brutal assault."

"It wasn't him," Abrax snapped.

The doctor's glare lost its bite. "She wasn't raped, and she had blood beneath her nails, and her knuckles are bruised. She gave them a good fight. That might help you catch them."

"They're dead already," Taniel said flatly.

"Good. Her languid state is from exhaustion. She might have

fought them for hours. Her left arm is broken, and she might lose an ear. No concussion, though, and that's remarkable."

Taniel returned to Ka-poel's side, barely noticing that Abrax lowered herself into a chair nearby to watch them.

Taniel wasn't sure how late it was when he heard angry shouting outside the tent. Abrax lifted herself warily from her chair and went outside.

"What did I say about a closed camp?" Abrax demanded.

"Brigadier Abrax," a sharp voice said.

Taniel put his head in his hands. Doravir.

"You're harboring a man wanted for the murder of four infantrymen and a captain of the Third Brigade. Release him to our custody now."

CHAPTER
31

Nila felt her fingers shaking as she tried to position the needle beside her target.

"Don't be nervous," Bo said. His voice was soft and soothing. He sat cross-legged on a faded pillow in one corner of the room beside the only window, a musty old tome of a book cradled in his lap while he watched her. "If you mess up, it's all right. I'll only be burned from the inside out by otherworldly fire, consumed like a bale of hay soaked in lantern oil."

"You're not making this any easier," Nila said. She took a deep breath and stabbed the needle into one of his Privileged's gloves. The positioning looked right. It had to be perfect for the gloves to work properly.

"I know," Bo said. She could hear his grin in his tone.

"Why can't you do this yourself?"

"Because I hate sewing. And you're a laundress. You're probably far better at it than I am anyway."

And Nila owed him. Even if he didn't say it, Nila was certain it had crossed his mind.

She was painfully aware that Bo had offered to shelter her and Jakob for three days. That had been nine days ago, and she wasn't entirely certain why he hadn't forced them out into the street. A Privileged seemed the last type of person to whom she would want to owe a favor, so when he mentioned that he had several pairs of ripped gloves that needed mending, she volunteered.

That was before she knew that the stitching on Privileged's gloves had to be perfect. Absolutely perfect.

She wondered why else he'd let them stay. Perhaps he expected to bed her. Out of the corner of her eye, she could see that he was watching her. He seemed to do that a lot, but only when he thought she wouldn't notice. It made her nervous.

But he'd given her and Jakob food, shelter, and the first pleasant company she'd had in a long time. He was calm, quiet, and hadn't tried to force himself on her. Yet.

Every time she started to wonder what it would be like to let herself sleep with him, she had to remind herself of Dourford, splattered across the street. Bo wasn't just a man. He was a Privileged. Privileged were dangerous people.

"This requires a skilled seamstress," Nila said. "I can sew, but this is—"

"You're doing fine."

She returned to her task. She'd managed to finish three of the twelve gloves he'd stashed away for repair. Whether any of them could be used...

"Will you really burn from the inside out if I do these wrong?" Nila asked.

"No."

"You git!"

"They won't work, though. Which is just as likely to get me killed." Bo set his book to one side and climbed to his feet, joining her at the table. He put on one of the finished gloves and snapped his fingers. "Nothing. This one won't do." He tried on another glove. "Nor this." He tossed the two useless gloves in their own pile and put on the third. Again, he snapped his fingers.

A small flame appeared at the tips of his fingers. The flame went out and he removed the glove, putting it in his pocket. "This will. Excellent."

"Do you want me to..." Nila reached for the two useless gloves.

"Don't worry about it. I'll dispose of those ones."

For a moment she thought he was going to return to his pillow and his book. Instead, he pulled out a chair and sat down. He kicked out another chair with his feet and put them up, leaning back with his hands folded behind his head. "Where's the boy? I haven't heard a peep out of him all day."

"He's playing in his room. I told him to keep quiet so that you could read."

"Very considerate of you."

Nila made a mistake in her stitching. She cursed under her breath and pulled the needle back out to try again. Why was he watching her? What did he want?

"You're a very good-looking girl. Did you know that?"

Oh. That was why. Nila felt her heart skip a beat. She'd heard rumors that Privileges had a powerful sex drive. That cabal Privileged each had several concubines, and that few women could resist them.

"I've been told that before," Nila said.

"You should wear your hair back more often. It helps display those cheekbones."

Nila didn't trust herself to speak. Had he asked about Jakob because he was hoping to get her alone? Would he give her an ultimatum: Either get out or come to my bed? Nila resolved not to do it. She still had her silver hidden outside the city. She'd been thinking about this ever since Bo first took them in. She'd get the silver and take Jakob northeast into Novi. They would head to the capital and get a small house there, and she'd take up as a laundress.

Bo opened his mouth.

Here it comes, Nila thought.

"Do your parents live in the city?"

"I won't...! What?"

"Your parents," Bo said. "Do they live in the city?"

Nila was taken aback by the question. "My parents are dead," she answered curtly. This wasn't what she'd expected him to say. "I'm an orphan."

"Oh," Bo said. "Sorry to hear that."

"I never knew them."

Bo was staring at the ceiling. His tone was wistful. "I knew my father a little before he died. I spent some time in an orphanage, too. Then out on the streets for me."

Nila almost laughed. Was this how he'd try to get her to bed? Make them feel some kind of kinship? "And then the royal cabal?"

"No. First Taniel Two-Shot. And then his father, Tamas, took me in. That's where the dowsers found me. Did you ever get tested as a child?"

Bo knew Field Marshal Tamas? He'd been adopted by him? That seemed far-fetched. "Tested?"

"By the cabal dowsers. For ability."

Nila saw another mistake she'd made. She pulled out the needle and used the tip to pick out the thread. "Of course. They came to the orphanage every year."

"You should try again," Bo said. He removed a pair of gloves from his pockets and tossed them on the table. "Sometimes the dowsers miss someone."

Nila wanted to roll her eyes. He was still flirting with her. She could tell by the tiny smile at the corners of his mouth, and by the playful tone of his voice. "I don't think so."

"Suit yourself." Bo put the gloves back in his pocket.

There were several blissful minutes of silence while Nila sewed and Bo sat in his chair, rocking back on two legs and staring at the ceiling. Nila's mind began to wander. Maybe she shouldn't go to Novi. Perhaps she should head across the ocean to faraway Fatrasta. Less likely she or Jakob would ever be found or recognized.

"Jakob," Bo suddenly said. "His last name was Eldaminse, right?"

"Yes."

"And you worked for his family?"

Nila nodded. The Eldaminse house. That seemed like so long ago. Had it really only been four months? Memories of that place felt like visions of a world from a dream.

"Did you know anything about his father's business?"

"I was a laundress."

"Servants hear everything. That's why so many of them spy for the cabals."

Nila blinked. "They do?"

"Well. Indirectly. They don't know *who* they're spying for, they just know they're being paid for information."

"I never did. I was taught never to snoop."

"Pity." Bo rocked his chair down onto all four legs and stood up. "Jakob," he called, heading down a short hall toward the room Nila and Jakob were sharing.

Nila paused in her sewing and cocked her head to one side.

"Jakob," Bo said, his voice muffled, "do you remember if your father was ever visited by any military men?"

Nila couldn't hear Jakob's answer.

"Really? Interesting. How long ago was that?" There was a pause, and then, "Thank you, Jakob. You were very helpful."

Bo returned to the room. He grabbed his jacket off the hook.

"Where are you going?" Nila said.

"For someone taught never to snoop, you sure look like you were listening hard."

Nila felt her cheeks redden.

Bo smiled. "I'm heading to the Public Archives. I'll likely not be back until tomorrow. There's a small stack of banknotes hidden under the windowsill. Feel free to get you and the boy some food." He stopped in the door, his gloves in one hand. He seemed preoccupied. "Are you sure you don't want to try on my gloves?"

Nila pushed her chair back and stood up.

"I've had enough of this," she said.

Bo's eyebrows rose. He seemed genuinely surprised. "Of...?"

"Your flirting. I'll leave if you want us to, but I'm not going to bed with you."

Bo took several quick steps across the room, coming to a stop with less than a handbreadth between them. He leaned forward, and Nila could hear her heart thumping in her ears. She became acutely aware that if Bo did try to force himself on her, or to hurt her or Jakob, she couldn't do a thing about it.

"I flirt with everyone," Bo whispered in her ear. "And if you wanted to go to bed with me, I wouldn't say no. But I've never raped a woman and never will. So stop cringing every time you catch me looking at you. I like looking at people. I find them fascinating."

Nila's throat was dry. A glance down showed her that Bo still wasn't wearing his gloves. "If you don't expect me to go to bed with you, why haven't you made us leave?"

"Because I like you," Bo said. "And I like the kid. But I'm leaving the city soon and you should figure out your plans. I won't be here longer than a week." He stepped away. "See you tomorrow?"

Nila swallowed. "Yes."

"Glad to hear it."

Tamas's army crossed the last of Kresimir's Fingers and ascended the wide plateau of the Northern Expanse almost seven weeks after they'd left Budwiel.

The Northern Expanse, like the Amber Expanse to the south, was a breadbasket of the Nine. Unlike the Amber Expanse, it was not home to cattle farms or wheat fields but to immense bean fields, which could survive better with little water.

Tamas ordered forage teams to spread out across the plateau, under the command of the most levelheaded sergeants in the army. He needed to strip the land of its resources while making this as painless to the native population as possible.

He rode at the head of the column, eyes on the northern horizon. It would be several days before they crossed the Deliv border and could see the city of Alvation, but he couldn't help that his heart beat faster with every step. Soon, they'd find relief. Soon, they'd cross the Charwood Pile Mountains and descend into Adro, taking the fight back to the Kez.

Gavril rode up beside Tamas. He and his horse were coated in dust from coming up behind the column. Not far behind him, an old man rode a pack mule. He had a hard time keeping up with Gavril's charger. Tamas reined in his mount. Olem stopped too, his eyes vigilant despite the plateau being empty but for their army.

"Who is this?" Tamas said, nodding at the old man, who was still fifty paces off.

"A Kez bean farmer."

"Why is he here?"

"Wanted to talk to you."

Tamas cocked an eyebrow at Gavril. This was the last thing he needed. Why on earth would Gavril bring him here? "Does he know who I am?"

"Yes, and he has some interesting things to say."

What could an old bean farmer on the Northern Expanse have to say of interest?

The old man brought his burro up beside their horses.

"Are you the field marshal?" the old man said in Adran. The Kez accent was so thick that the words were barely distinguishable. His face was wrinkled, his skin brown from the hot sun of the plateau and perhaps a mix of Deliv blood. Labor and trade went on freely between the Deliv to the north and Kez farmers on the plateau.

The old bean farmer was emaciated. He might have been plump at one point, but the skin now sagged from his cheeks and sickly splotches on his face spoke to malnutrition.

The man's eyes held a smoldering anger that surprised Tamas.

"I speak Kez," Tamas said in Kez.

"Are you the field marshal?" the bean farmer said again in Kez.

"I am. Good afternoon."

The bean farmer spit at the feet of Tamas's charger. He bared his teeth and glared, as if daring Tamas to do anything about it.

Tamas looked at Gavril. His brother-in-law, still bruised from their fight last week, just shrugged his shoulders.

"Something wrong?" Tamas asked.

"You tell me."

Tamas shot another glance at Gavril. What was this all about?

"I can't imagine."

"You took my crop," the old man said. "It was a good one this year, considering the drought. You took my wife and daughters. Your blasted men broke my son's legs when he refused to serve them!"

Tamas scowled. Damned infantry. Even the best couldn't keep themselves under control. He'd ordered that women be left alone under penalty of death. The food, they needed, but Tamas didn't need his soldiers raping and killing their way across the Kez countryside.

"What company did this?" he asked Gavril.

"None of ours. The man and his son were alone in his hut when the forage teams found him. The place had been stripped bare, all the furniture broken. The boy's legs were broken, like he says. The lad will be a cripple for life. Looks like it happened weeks ago."

"I'm sorry about your wife and daughters," Tamas said, "but it wasn't my men."

"Are you calling me a liar?" The bean farmer edged his mule closer to Tamas.

Tamas took a deep breath and reminded himself that striking an old man wasn't the best way to end a conversation. "When did this happen?"

"Eighteen days ago," the bean farmer said.

"It couldn't have been us. We just arrived."

"Then who was it? I know Adran troops when I see them." The bean farmer leaned over to pluck at Tamas's jacket. "Adran blues, with silver trim. I'm not a fool!"

"How many men?"

"Thousands of ya!" The bean farmer spit again.

"Gavril, any sign an army came through here recently?"

Gavril rode off a few feet to confer with one of his scouts. He came back a moment later. "Foraging teams are all reporting the same thing—the land's been stripped clean. All the crops were harvested early, or burned, and the men have come across dozens of empty farmsteads."

Tamas drummed his fingers on his saddle horn. The forage he'd been expecting on the Northern Expanse—gone. All of it. Nothing for his men to eat on the way to Alvation.

"Well?" the bean farmer demanded. "What do you have to say for yourself?"

"Which way were they headed?" Tamas asked.

The bean farmer seemed taken aback. "North."

"Olem, give this man enough food for him and his son and send him back to his home. Let him keep the mule." Tamas flicked the reins. "Gavril."

Tamas left the cursing old bean farmer in Olem's hands and rode back to the head of the column. Gavril came up beside him, letting his charger keep pace with Tamas's.

"This doesn't make sense," Tamas said. "We don't have any troops in northern Kez."

"I'd say the old man isn't right in the head, but the place has been swept clean. It would have taken a great number of men to come through and strip the plateau like this."

Tamas gripped his saddle horn. How was he going to feed his men with no forage?

"How many?" Tamas asked.

Gavril scratched the stubble on his chin. "At least a brigade or two."

"Wearing Adran blue, but not Adran." Tamas mused it over in his head. "Shit! They're trying to slip into Adro."

"The Kez?"

"It must be. They come through here, acting like an invading army—bluff their way through Alvation and then take an unsuspecting Mountainwatch. They might be in Adro already."

"What should we do?" Gavril asked.

Tamas let his fingers play upon the butt of one of the saw-handled dueling pistols stuck in his belt. A gift from his son. "We keep going. We catch up to them and take them from behind."

CHAPTER
32

Ricard Tumblar's carriage jolted along the winding highway at the base of the Charwood Pile Mountain Range, headed north toward the Pan-Deliv Canal. Mountains rose above them immediately to the west, and there were more in the distance to the north, their white tops looking like frosting on peaked cakes. The carriage thumped, then clattered over a stone bridge crossing a tributary of the Ad River and then it was back to the pitted dirt road.

Adamat stared out the window and tried not to think of the jarring of the ground. The last thing he needed was to throw up all over the velvet interior.

Five days in a carriage was no pleasant prospect, even one as fancy as Ricard's. The undercarriage employed the very newest leaf-spring suspension and the thick, padded seats helped absorb some rocking of the road, but nothing prevented Adamat's head from hitting the roof when they hit a particularly deep hole in the road.

Damn these northern roads.

At least Faye seemed to be enjoying herself, as much as she could under the circumstance. She had become even more withdrawn after her decision not to go after Josep. Her weeping had stopped, though, and she seemed more resolved to put on a good face for the other children.

"We'll have these roads fixed up better once the canal comes into more use," Ricard was saying, his head craned out the window. "I'd like to see the whole thing cobbled, with a full-time union crew to tend to maintenance year-round."

Adamat longed to reach their destination. Just a couple hours away, or so Ricard had said. They'd be staying at the finest hotel in northern Adro. Room service, massages, hot running water. The hotel was brand-new, built to accommodate dignitaries and businessmen taking the canal over the Charwood Pile.

"Couldn't you just leave it to the Mountainwatch?" Adamat asked. "The maintenance, I mean. We're in the foothills. That counts as their territory."

Ricard wagged a finger under his nose. "No! No, no, no. I fought tooth and nail for the canal to be a union project. The Mountainwatch wanted in on it. Claimed it was their jurisdiction, or some such tripe, but this is a union job! The union employs good, hardworking Adrans. Not the convicts and malcontents of forced labor like the Mountainwatch."

"Surely they're guarding the pass," Adamat said.

"No," Ricard said proudly. "Purely union, even down to the lock guards."

That surprised Adamat. The Mountainwatch was more than just a forced-labor institution. It had a long tradition of guarding the high places—they were the gatekeepers of Adro, and they'd proved that again in the recent defense of Shouldercrown Fortress.

Adamat understood that Ricard was proud of his unions, but unionizing the defense of the country seemed strange.

They stopped for a midday meal several miles south of the canal. Adamat and Faye dined with their children and their hired nannies while Ricard met with Fell about plans for the mountain. When lunch was over, Adamat wandered outside to stretch his legs.

The inn sat next to a small stream—runoff from the mountains. Adamat listened to the bubbling sound it made as it meandered under the road and down toward the river, then looked north.

Adamat could see the locks of the canal from where he stood. They worked their way up the side of the mountain like steps, the road zigzagging its way up beside them. The whole setup looked like a model at this distance, and even seeing it with his own eyes, he scarcely believed it to be real. A canal going over an entire mountain range!

The locks themselves were a feat of engineering never before seen in this world. They were built purely by the labor of men, no sorcery at all, unless you count the few Knacked that the union no doubt employed for their various skills. Despite the rigors of the journey, Adamat knew that touring the locks prior to the grand opening was going to be worth the whole trip.

Josep would have loved to have seen the canal.

Ricard and Fell came outside, studying a map together and pointing at the road. He could hear them discussing the benefits of cobbles versus brick or poured concrete.

Something on the mountainside caught Adamat's eye. At this distance, he couldn't be sure, but . . .

"Ricard," he said, interrupting the two, "do you have a looking glass?"

Fell said, "I do." She went back to the carriage and returned a moment later, handing Adamat a looking glass.

"I thought you said that the grand opening wasn't until tomorrow," Adamat said to Ricard.

Ricard squinted toward the canal. "It's not."

"You're not supposed to have any traffic on the canal?"

"Not yet. I mean, they've been tested, but no commercial traffic until after the grand opening. Why, what do you see?"

Adamat put the looking glass to his eye and found the locks. They came into focus, and then he saw what had caught his eye.

Each of those locks held a ship—and not just any ships, but oceangoing merchantmen with rows of cannon and tall masts. There had to be dozens of them, and he could see the tiny figures of men working the locks as the entire row of ships slowly descended the side of the mountain.

The ships bore green-and-white-striped flags, marked in the center with a laurel wreath. Adamat felt his legs grow weak and a growing dread in the pit of his stomach.

He thrust the looking glass into Fell's hands. "Get the children back in the carriages. We're going back to Adopest. Now!"

"What?" Ricard demanded, snatching the looking glass. "What is wrong with you? The grand opening is tomorrow, we're..." He fell silent as he put the looking glass to his eye.

"It's a good thing you didn't let the Mountainwatch guard your canal," Adamat shouted over his shoulder as he ran toward the inn. "Otherwise it would have been harder for the Brudania-Gurla Trading Company to bring their whole damn fleet across it."

"They're going to send me to Adopest," Taniel said.

One of Ka-poel's eyes opened. The one that wasn't swollen shut.

Taniel went on. "General Ket says this is a civil matter because I'm no longer in the Adran army and I'm not officially in the Wings of Adom yet. I'm to be sent back to Adopest under house arrest to await trial." Taniel paced the short length of the tent. He held in his hand a note from Brigadier Abrax telling him the conditions of his house arrest. "That could take months. The war might be over by then, and we'll have lost."

Taniel stopped pacing and dropped onto his cot. What could

he do? He'd spent the last hour arguing with Abrax. The brigadier claimed her hands were tied, that she could do nothing but provide Taniel with a small house in Adopest. The Wings of Adom's charter did not allow them to admit anyone awaiting trial.

"I'm going to kill her," Taniel said.

Ka-poel struggled to sit up in her cot. They'd been given a tent in the corner of the Wings' camp at the farthest point from the Adran army. Her green eyes were wet. Taniel suspected she'd cried during the night.

He thought that perhaps his rage would fade as the days passed and Ka-poel was sitting up and able to move. If anything, seeing her wounds heal slowly made him even angrier. Her lips were swollen and cracked, her face still bruised.

She spread her hands, awkwardly because her arm was in a sling. *Who?*

"General Ket. She must have ordered what they...what they did to you. She must have known she wouldn't be able to send me to the noose so easily. Those men had you for hours."

Ka-poel shook her head.

"No? 'No' what? The doctor said you fought back. That you..."

Another emphatic shake of her head. She motioned with her thumb over her shoulder and then made a snatching motion. She pointed to herself.

"They caught you?"

She thought for a moment, and then made a walking motion with her fingers.

"Followed you?"

A nod.

She reached for her satchel and winced. Taniel lifted it for her. She took it from him and began to rummage around inside.

Ka-poel began to lay out dolls on the cot. They were instantly recognizable: General Hilanska, General Ket; the entire General Staff of the Adran army.

Taniel stared at the dolls. Each time he saw one, he was amazed by the detail she put into the wax, but here it was something more. He *knew* all of these people. Some of them, like Hilanska, he'd known since childhood. Bits of real hair protruded from the wax in places. A drop of blood was rubbed on one of them. It made his skin crawl.

"Why were you making dolls for them?" Taniel asked.

Ka-poel tilted her head to the side as if to tell him it was a stupid question.

"Just in case, right?"

A nod.

"And the Dredgers caught you while you were getting something of Ket's to use in her doll?"

Another nod.

If she wasn't already bruised, Taniel would have smacked her. What she'd done was incredibly dangerous. If people suspected the nature of her sorcery and saw her skulking about the general's quarters, she could have been beaten *and* locked up.

"Still," he went on, "they said that she'd told them they could have you." The anger ebbed. Only a little, but it was enough to make his muscles relax. He leaned back in his chair, putting his hands over his face. "I should still kill her."

Ka-poel thrust her thumb at herself. *I will.* A flat hand, as if to stop, and she mouthed the words "*If I need to.*"

"Pit, Pole, I—"

"Knock, knock!" The voice came from outside the front of the tent. "May I come in?"

Mihali. The damned chef. If it weren't for him, none of this would have ever happened. Taniel would still be in the Adran army and Ka-poel would never have been beaten by Ket's thugs.

"Go to—!" Taniel started, when Ka-poel lay a soft hand on his arm.

She nodded. Taniel took a deep, calming breath. It didn't help.

"Yes," he called.

The flap was swept back and Mihali ducked into the tent, carrying a wide platter. Steam rose from beneath the platter cover with the smell of warm bread and, what was that? Eggs.

Taniel looked away. He wouldn't give Mihali the satisfaction of eating his food.

Mihali set the platter on Taniel's cot and removed the lid. He leaned over it, wafting the smell of it toward him. "Warm cornmeal cake with a sweet crust drizzled in maple honey with poached eggs on the side."

Ka-poel's face lit up. Cornmeal cake was a Fatrastan staple, uncommon in the Nine. She snatched one up immediately, tossing it between her hands until it cooled enough to hold.

Taniel smiled, though he tried to cover it with a cough. He wasn't about to let Mihali see him pleased.

"What do you want, Adom?"

"Oh, please," Mihali said. "Call me Mihali. 'Adom' has such a high-and-mighty connotation."

"Well"—Taniel's mouth watered at the smell of the cornbread— "what do you want?"

"I've come to apologize," Mihali said.

Ka-poel patted the cot beside her.

"Thank you!" Mihali took a seat, and Taniel felt a stab of jealousy.

"Apologize? For telling me to make amends with Doravir and getting me kicked out of the Adran army?"

Mihali's eyebrows rose. "Heavens, no. That needed to happen."

"It *what*?" Taniel sputtered.

Mihali waved a hand as if it were of little consequence.

"I came to apologize because I told you that I would not help you kill Kresimir and that I did not think he needed to die."

Taniel couldn't help it any longer. His hand reached out, as if it had a mind of its own, and took a piece of cornbread. He bit in and was instantly glad. The cornbread was soft and moist, seemingly melting in his mouth, and the honey tasted as if it were straight from the comb.

"You changed your mind?" Taniel asked around bites.

"I wish," Mihali said, plucking a piece of cornbread from the platter and smearing it with fruit spread, "that this could be solved amicably. Or even at all. A couple of months ago I made a deal with Kresimir that neither of us would contribute to the war directly. Since then it's gone badly for the Adran side—as you can tell—but things are not well in the Kez camp either." Mihali paused to lick honey and crumbs off his fingertips. "Kresimir has taken to killing his own people at an alarming rate."

"Good," Taniel snorted.

"No," Mihali said. "Not good. I speak with Kresimir often. We can bridge space for that purpose, and when we do, I can see a bit into his mind. He's going mad." Mihali swallowed and looked down at his cornbread sadly. "Quite thoroughly mad."

"I don't care."

"Taniel, how long do you think a mad god would stick to killing his own people? He might very well try to destroy the Nine. Perhaps even the whole world. I don't think he could—not even Kresimir is that powerful—but if he tried, it would probably kill every living thing in this part of the world."

"I already stopped him once," Taniel said.

"Which makes you particularly suited to the task."

"Couldn't you stop him?"

"Sorcery is predictable in some ways," Mihali said. "There are patterns that all Privileged use, from the lowliest sorcerer all the way up to Kresimir. I can predict those patterns and counter them. However, if Kresimir lashes out in his madness, it will be completely random. I could protect myself, but no one else."

Taniel thought on this for a few moments. Could a god actually go mad?

"It's from the bullet, isn't it?"

Mihali seemed to think on this for a moment. "I have heard reports—when I lurk about the generals' staff meetings—from their spies. There is a rumor in the Kez camp that Kresimir coughs blood into his pillow. That he wanders the halls of his compound at night and accosts his own guards, demanding to know whether they are the eye behind the flintlock."

Taniel's mouth went dry. The eye behind the flintlock. Who else could it possibly be but him? Kresimir was looking for him in his madness. The words felt like bile coming out, but Taniel asked, "Can he be healed? At least enough to see reason?"

"I don't know," Mihali said. "I broached the subject with him last night. He was furious. The explosion over in Budwiel? You must have heard it. That was him. It killed thousands of Kez camp followers."

"No great loss."

Mihali scowled. Taniel felt a flicker at the edge of his senses, like sorcery was being used. He suddenly wondered whether he should be this close to Mihali.

"Those people," Mihali said, visibly restraining himself, "were not soldiers. They were laundresses and bakers and boot makers. Their lives were snuffed out in an instant because I asked Kresimir the wrong question and he grew angry." Mihali shook his head. "I understand that killing is your profession, but every loss of life is great. Especially so many, and all on the..."

Mihali fell silent. He helped himself to another piece of corn-bread and chewed thoughtfully. His eyes fell on the dolls laid out opposite him by Ka-poel, and his fingers twitched as if he were nervous.

"He's coherent enough to create these Powder Wardens," Taniel said.

Mihali said, "It's the only thing that gives me hope for his recovery. He's not all gone. I might be able to heal him. I would need to restrain Kresimir, though, and I can't do that on my own."

Mihali was looking at Ka-poel when he said that. Taniel didn't like it one bit.

"How?"

"She can do it," Mihali said, nodding at Ka-poel. "I think I mentioned that in my varied lives I have had some contact with Bone-eyes. Their magic is uniquely suited to fighting, harming, protecting, and even controlling individuals. I've never known one with even a fraction of Ka-poel's power. And to think, she taught herself to do all this..." Mihali trailed off. He was breathless, his face flushed.

Controlling individuals, Mihali had said. Did Ka-poel control Taniel? He knew that she had protected him before, and he'd seen what she could do with those dolls of hers.

"And if he's healed?" Taniel asked. "Will he end this war? Leave Adro alone?"

"I believe so. He's not been well."

"You *believe* so? Or you *know* so? He made a promise to destroy Adro."

"A promise that will not be kept. I'll see to it." Mihali spread his pudgy hands, looking from Ka-poel to Taniel. "Please. Help me. Help my brother."

Ka-poel pointed to her broken arm, and then to Mihali.

Mihali's eyebrows went up. "Of course. I've been remiss." He closed his eyes, and Ka-poel suddenly gasped.

Taniel lurched forward, putting his arm behind her back so that she wouldn't fall. "What did you do to her?"

Ka-poel shrugged Taniel away from her and undid the sling around her arm. She flexed and moved it, nodding to herself. He looked at her face. The bruises were gone.

"I can heal your wounds as well," Mihali said.

Taniel flinched away. "I'll keep them, thank you." Silently, Taniel called himself a fool. Why refuse the healing powers of a god? Was he afraid of Mihali's sorcery? Or perhaps afraid of owing someone else? Abrax and Ricard has already done Taniel favors that would require years to pay off.

Taniel touched his fingers to the tender swelling on his face from the beatings given to him by Ket's gendarmes. "I'll keep it as a reminder."

"I ask," Mihali said, standing up, "that you consider my request. In exchange, I have a gift—freely given."

Taniel was wary of any gift given by a god. After all, nothing was free. "What?"

Mihali removed a handkerchief and a knife from his pocket. He pressed one thumb against his knife, then into the handkerchief for a moment, and then handed it to Ka-poel.

His blood. The blood of a god. Taniel felt his heart beat a little faster. What could Ka-poel do with this? Could she control Mihali? Kill him?

Ka-poel tucked the handkerchief silently into her satchel, her face unreadable.

Mihali stepped away from them both and busied himself putting the remaining cornbread and eggs on a tin plate, which he handed to Ka-poel. He lifted his empty platter and gave a bow. "Please," he said, "consider my request—my plea—for help." He bowed low and then left.

Taniel took a shaky breath and looked down, only just realizing that he still held the letter regarding his house arrest. He was to be escorted to Adopest early in the morning. They'd assigned him eight provosts—four from the Wings of Adom, four from the Adran army.

There would be no fighting the Kez or killing their gods for Taniel.

Ka-poel reached out and touched Taniel's chest. She thumped him several times above the heart.

"What?"

She pointed to him and then spread her hands, questioning. Then back at him.

"I don't know what you're getting at, girl," he said, trying to quell his frustration.

She indicated his heart again and pointed emphatically.

"What do I want?"

A nod.

Taniel took a deep breath. "I want to kill something right now. I'm furious. I should be out there fighting. I was born to fight—born to protect Adro."

She pointed at him again, then at the floor. *What do you want now?*

"I want to protect you."

Ka-poel smiled then, and Taniel felt his heart jump. She leaned toward him and pressed her lips to his.

"I'm going after Kresimir's blood," Taniel said.

Mihali paused over an immense pot of soup, the ladle halfway to his lips.

"I see."

"Ka-poel has agreed to subdue him, but she needs his blood. I'll need help getting into the Kez camp."

Mihali considered this for a few moments before taking a sip of his soup. "Mmm. That's good. Needs a little more pepper, though." He brought a jar of whole peppercorns from his apron and poured a measure into the palm of his hand. He ground his hands together, watching the pepper fall into the pot. He stirred the soup, then took another sip. "Perfect."

"It can be hard to take you seriously sometimes," Taniel said. "No. I misspoke. All of the time."

Mihali chuckled, but Taniel hadn't been making a joke.

"The Kez camp," Taniel urged.

"I can conceal you so that you walk right through the Kez sentries,"

Mihali said, moving to a wide iron grill in the middle of the cooking yard. He began flipping turkey legs with practiced speed.

Taniel ducked as he heard the sound of a shout behind him. A glance over his shoulder told him it wasn't directed at him. Walking through the Adran camp was dangerous, even in civilian clothes with a tricorn hat pulled down to conceal his face. He was supposed to be under guard by the provosts right now.

"They won't notice you here, either. Have a turkey leg." Mihali picked up a leg with his tongs and handed it to Taniel.

"That looks hot."

"Nonsense. A chef would never give a guest something that would burn them."

Taniel took the turkey leg with some trepidation. The bone was only warm, despite having just come off the flames, and when he bit into it, juice ran down his unshaved chin. He didn't speak until he was done eating. "How can you make me unseen?" Taniel asked. "Before, you had to ask Ka-poel's permission to touch my mind."

"I just did," Mihali said.

Taniel froze in the midst of picking the last bits of flavor off the turkey leg. He looked around. "I don't feel unseen." He glanced down at the turkey bone. "Did you..."

"Yes," Mihali said. "Doing any kind of constructive sorcery directly to the human body is one of the most difficult things a Privileged can accomplish. That's why healers are so rare. I figured out about a thousand years ago that the easiest way to get a spell into a person was through their stomach." Mihali picked up a turkey leg and took a bite. A sudden look of worry crossed his face. "Let's have that be our secret, hmm?"

Taniel snorted. "I won't tell on you."

"Oh, thank you." Mihali finished his turkey leg noisily and then lifted another off the grill. "Care to take one to Ka-poel?"

"Will it make her unseen? And if I'm unseen now, how will she see me? Or how are you seeing me?"

"I can see you because I'm a god. Ka-poel will be able to sense where you are, and the spell doesn't muffle your voice."

"If I sneeze?"

"Uh"—Mihali tapped the tongs against his apron, leaving a greasy stain—"Don't. The spell does have its drawbacks. For instance, it is designed to drop as soon as you get close to Kresimir's sphere of influence. It would backfire to have Kresimir sense my intrusion."

Taniel looked at his hand. He certainly didn't feel unseen. "How long did it take you to come up with this?"

"A few moments."

"Really?"

Mihali raised an eyebrow. "We're not called gods necessarily because we're the most powerful Privileged—though that is an interpretation. We're called gods because the things that regular mortals struggle for days, weeks, or months to accomplish take us only the effort of a thought."

"Ah. Well, I'm going now."

"Wait." Mihali produced a deep pewter mug seemingly out of nowhere and crossed to his pot of soup. He ladled the mug full and set a lid on it. "Take this to Ka-poel. It'll help her sleep while you're gone."

Taniel turned to go, when he thought better of it. "Adom—Mihali?"

"Hmm?"

"Will you protect her?"

"I feel after giving her my blood, that it is I who need protection," Mihali said. He winked. "That girl is like a glass teapot filled with gunpowder. So fragile, but with such a power for destruction." He straightened up and swung the ladle into a salute. Soup spattered on his apron. "No harm will come to her."

"Thank you," Taniel said. "Now I'm going to get some of your brother's blood."

CHAPTER
33

Tamas watched Olem rub down his horse as the camp settled in for the night. A low fire of brush and prairie twigs crackled in a stone ring in front of him. The sun still shone in the western sky, lighting the plateau with a brilliant hue of reds, oranges, and pinks.

Their second day on the plateau, and their supplies were already running low. They'd slaughtered thousands of Kez horses after the battle fourteen days before, but only been able to carry a limited amount. What little food they had needed to be rationed. A pound of meat per man per day was not much.

Tamas lifted his head at a sound carried on the wind. He waited a few seconds, then returned to gazing at the flames. Beside him, Olem was snapping twigs and feeding them into the fire.

His rangers still hadn't found this mysterious Adran army, but there were plenty of signs of their passing. Stripped bean fields, burned farms. The dead and the dying, the old and the infirm of what was left of the farmers of the Northern Expanse. The plateau was already a dry, exhausted land. Whatever army had come through two weeks ago had killed everything living.

Per his orders, the army had dug a six-foot trench around the entire camp. It was backbreaking work, but he'd be damned if he'd be caught at night by an army he didn't see coming. Some of his soldiers were still digging. The sound of shovels scraping rocks and dirt, the curses of infantry working after a long day's march.

Tamas lifted his head again. That sound. What was it? He cocked his head to one side, trying to find a location.

Nothing.

Had the Deliv turned on him? The king of Deliv had been firm in his response earlier this summer when Tamas had asked for allies against the Kez. They'd promised to stay out of the war entirely.

"May I join you, Field Marshal?"

Tamas looked up. The lengthening shadows tricked his eyes for a moment before he made out Beon je Ipille. Tamas gestured to the bare ground on the other side of the fire. Beon lowered himself gingerly to the ground, crossing his legs beneath him. The Kez general's eyes were sunken, his face pale. He was one of the few Kez officers that Tamas had kept with him as prisoners—the rest were paroled to the Kez army.

"How is your arm?" Tamas asked.

Beon looked down at his left arm where it hung in a sling. "It is well, thank you. My physician says that the arm is not broken, but I lost quite a lot of blood in the melee. I should recover in time. Your injuries?"

"Fine." Tamas ran a couple of fingers over his ribs, wincing at the tenderness. He didn't think they'd cracked from his fight with Gavril, but his body felt like one big bruise. "I'm wishing I'd brought Dr. Petrik along when I left Budwiel. But then again, my plans at the time were greatly different from how things ended up."

Beon nodded, staring into the fire. He took a deep breath and opened his mouth, only to close it again. It was several minutes before he finally spoke.

"I remember riding through the Northern Expanse once," Beon said. "It must have been six or seven years ago. I went along with some of my father's Privileged on a delegation to Deliv. This land was greener, more full." Beon smiled sadly. "Towns threw festivals in our honor. There were thousands of people—proud, happy farmers.

"Now I can't help but wonder: what has happened to my country?" Beon looked around. "The last two days, I've seen countless abandoned farms. The bean fields are all gone. The land is brown and dry. I've heard reports of the droughts, both here and in the rest of the Nine, but I didn't imagine it to be so bad.

"What's more, where are all my people? We passed a farm this morning. The crop—and there had been a crop, I'm not so removed that I can't see that—was trampled, and the farm buildings burned remnants. I must ask you, Field Marshal. Have you sent men on ahead? Are you destroying these lands?"

"The desolation you see," Tamas said, his pride pricked at the accusation, "was not caused by my men. I swear it."

"It must have been bandits, then."

Tamas wondered how much he should tell Beon of his suspicions. "I don't think so."

Beon didn't seem to hear him. "Two days ago," Beon said, "I rode past an old man on a pack mule. He begged me to right the wrongs and expel the Adran foreigners that were ravishing our lands." Beon spoke carefully, as if testing the waters before a swim.

"My scouts tell me another army has come through this way," Tamas said. "And reports from what serfs remain in the area say that they wear Adran blues. This makes me wonder, as I know for a fact that I have no men in northern Kez."

Beon gazed at Tamas, brow furrowed, as if trying to decide whether Tamas was speaking the truth.

Tamas asked, "Do you know whether your father sent legions north, disguised as Adrans, in order to sneak through Deliv and over the mountains?"

"I don't. Besides, our soldiers wouldn't do this to their own land."

Tamas wondered where Beon got such a high regard for the morals of infantry.

Olem suddenly grabbed his rifle and surged to his feet. "Sir," he said, "did you hear that?"

Tamas paused and listened. Nothing.

Wait. There. It sounded like a shout. Very distant. He climbed to his feet. Nearby, a slight rise in the terrain gave him a better vantage point. He scanned the horizon, listening for the shout again.

"There," Olem said, pointing north.

Dust rose off the plateau, a billowing trail of the kind made when multiple riders were coming hard. "Saddle my mount," Tamas said to Olem. "Quickly!"

Tamas ran through the camp. A few hundred yards from his own tent, the powder mages were camped together. Most of them were there, their legs splayed, boots off, talking as they passed around a bottle they'd got from who knew where. Vlora stood when she saw Tamas.

"Andriya, Vlora," Tamas barked. "With me! The rest of you, raise the general alarm. Riders on the northern horizon."

"How many, sir?" Vlora asked as they headed back to the north end of the camp.

"That's what we're going to find out," Tamas said. "Do you know where Gavril is?"

"Ranging," Andriya answered.

"Where?"

"North, I think."

"Pit. You two, get horses."

Olem brought Tamas his horse and rifle. He threw himself into the saddle and headed north, not waiting for anyone else. Olem caught up to him quickly enough—he'd not yet unsaddled his own mount from the day.

"What's happening, sir?" Olem shouted over the sound of hooves thundering on the dusty soil.

"Riders," Tamas said. "A lot of them."

"Could it just be Gavril's rangers?"

Tamas wanted to say yes, but he fixed his eyes on the cloud of dust rising in the distance. It was getting larger. Too big to be less than twenty horses, and Gavril's rangers worked in pairs.

They left camp behind and headed north along the main road. A glance over his shoulder told Tamas that more riders were following him out of the camp, a few hundred yards behind him.

Tamas fumbled in his pocket for a powder charge as his body rocked up and down with the motion of the stallion beneath him. He put it straight in his mouth and bit down, tasting the bitter sulfur and the grit between his teeth. He spit the soggy charge paper out as the powder trance coursed through his veins.

The ground rushed by beneath his charger's hooves and the horizon came into stark relief. He found the cloud of dust and traced it to the source. There, miles away, a single horseman.

Tamas frowned. Just one? The horseman lay low on his mount, clinging to the horse's neck. Tamas thought he recognized him as one of Gavril's rangers.

A few moments later, breasting a rise in terrain behind the ranger, came more riders.

Their uniforms were blue with silver trim, and they wore the conical, horsehair helmets of Adran dragoons.

Tamas swore. Adran dragoons? It couldn't be. If they were, the ranger wouldn't be fleeing before them. Tamas looked over at Olem, but the bodyguard couldn't see that far.

"Dragoons," Tamas shouted at him. "Chasing one of our rangers! They're wearing Adran blues, but they're not friendly."

Olem responded by urging his mount harder.

Tamas put his head down and counted the beats of the hooves as they closed the distance between themselves and the ranger. As he drew closer, he was able to tell that the dragoons were perhaps a half mile behind the ranger. The ranger's horse frothed at the mouth, shaking its head hard. It wouldn't last much longer.

Tamas waved his pistol at the ranger, motioning for him to stop. The ranger's horse shuddered and swayed, eyes rolling as the ranger reined in beside Tamas. The ranger's face and front were covered in dust, smeared and muddy from his sweat.

"Where's Gavril?" Tamas demanded.

The ranger gasped for breath, trying to speak, before he threw his hand out behind him. "Far...back...fought so I could... escape."

"Who are they?"

"Kez! We thought they were friendlies, but they fell on us the moment Gavril spoke in Adran."

Tamas whirled toward the dragoons and quickly counted. Sixteen. They waved their carbines and hollered, showing no sign of slowing at the sight of Tamas and Olem. They'd be upon him in minutes. He raised his off hand to steady his pistol and closed one eye. He squeezed the trigger.

In his head, he counted seconds, concentrating on the powder, keeping the bullet flying far beyond when it should have fallen. At the same time, his hands worked to holster one pistol and draw the other.

One. Two. Thr...

A dragoon near the rear of the group fell, the bullet taking him neatly in the eye.

Tamas steadied his second pistol and fired. Another dragoon fell. Again, at the rear of the group. Tamas didn't want to scare off the dragoons, and it didn't seem like they noticed their comrades' fall.

"Olem! With me!"

Tamas dug his heels in and spurred his horse forward. He holstered his second pistol and drew his heavy cavalry saber. It felt good in his grip, the old leather handle worn and strong.

The dragoons aimed their carbines at seventy yards. They fired, and Tamas heard one bullet whistle past his ear.

Hitting a single riding target from horseback was difficult at best, if you weren't a powder mage.

He cocked his saber back and eyed the lead dragoon. The man was missing an ear. Earless stowed his carbine and drew his straight cavalry sword in one quick motion.

Hand still on the reins, Tamas dug into his front uniform pocket for a small handful of bullets.

Tamas studied the position of Earless's sword, then ran his eyes over the next few dragoons, all in a pair of seconds. Tamas leaned to his right, bringing his saber up high.

Then they were upon each other.

Tamas slid to his left in the saddle, narrowly avoiding the stroke of Earless's sword. His cavalry saber bit through soft flesh, the top three inches cleaving through Earless's neck. Tamas worked a bullet up to the top of his fist and flicked it in the air with his thumb, burning powder from a spare charge to send it into the heart of the next dragoon. He followed through with his saber cut, bringing it over his horse's head and deflecting the stab from a dragoon on his left.

He flicked another bullet into the air and burned powder, sending it backward and into Earless's spine.

Back over his mount's head with his saber, Tamas sawed on the reins. A dragoon at the rear of the group leaned toward him with a savage slice.

Parry. Parry again.

The dragoon was fast, and skilled. Tamas flicked a bullet into the air, sending it into the dragoon's shoulder. The dragoon dropped his sword, clutching at his arm, and Tamas rammed his saber into the man's chest.

Tamas spun around, looking for the next enemy, only to see two of the dragoons surrender to Olem. In the distance to the south, puffs of powder smoke rose from a pair of figures—Vlora and Andriya. Tamas rode to one of the surrendered dragoons.

"Where is Gavril?" he said in Kez.

The dragoon stared back at him.

"Where is Gavril? A big man! Where is he?"

The dragoon shook his head.

"Pit." Tamas cleaned and sheathed his sword. "Olem, with me!"

"Sir, my horse is lame." Olem was already dismounting. His horse was in a panic, blood streaming from a wound beneath its neck.

"Then take one of theirs!"

"The prisoners..."

"Leave them! I'll not lose another brother in this forsaken country!"

Tamas pushed on without waiting for an answer. A while later, he looked over his shoulder to see Olem and the powder mages struggling to keep up.

The sun set on the western horizon, bathing Tamas in twilight. He kept on, the hot night air whipping his hair and jacket, drying the blood on his cheeks. His charger began to struggle, breathing hard, slowing despite his continued urging.

Olem was lost to him as darkness spread on the plateau. The eerie sound of howling brush wolves reached his ears above the whistling of the wind. His powder trance wore off, and he chewed another powder charge to bring it back again. The road passed in a blur and the pounding of hooves.

He did not know how far or how long he'd ridden when his charger stumbled. He jolted from the saddle, thrown for several feet, and landed hard on his shoulder.

Tamas staggered to his feet. Silence. Nothing in the night. No sound of hooves from his soldiers following. No sign or sound of dragoons. Just the desperate gasping of his charger.

Where was Gavril? What had happened to him? Tamas ran a hand through his sweaty, dirty hair. His hat was gone, blown off he knew not when. He stumbled over to examine the horse, his legs wobbly from riding too long and too hard.

The charger lay on its side. It rolled its eyes at him, foam and blood at its nose and the corner of its mouth. Tamas blinked away tears and tried to calm the beast with a hand on its flank. It twitched and tried to stand up, only to let out a shuddering scream. The sound shook Tamas's soul.

The horse's leg had shattered, bone sticking out from the side. It must have stepped in a hole and stumbled from exhaustion.

Tamas drew his pistol. He loaded it slowly, carefully.

The shot rang out across the plateau.

Tamas gathered his saddlebags, ammunition, pistols, and rifle. He began to walk north.

He didn't know when he'd stopped. Only that he was suddenly on his knees, staring at his hands. They were raw from the reins. Where had his riding gloves gone? He shook his head and thought to stand and keep going.

Instead, he dropped his head into his hands. Another brother. All that remained of his family gone except, perhaps, his son. Tamas had failed again.

He should have stopped. Interrogated those Kez dragoons. Found out if Gavril was even alive, and where they'd taken him. How many dragoons in their company.

Tamas knew he'd been a fool, riding on like that. A desperate fool, trying to save his brother. Alone.

Tamas wept.

The tears were dry when Tamas heard hoofbeats on the road. They came on at a steady canter from the south. One set, from the sound of things.

"Tamas?" a female voice called.

Vlora.

She shouted his name again. The hoofbeats grew closer, then stopped. The crunch of gravel as she leapt from her horse. Then hands on his shoulders, shaking him.

"Sir, please. Answer me. Tamas!"

Tamas took a long breath, holding it for several beats before letting it out.

"I'm here." His voice surprised him, coming out a whispered croak.

He felt something forced into his hands. He looked down. A canteen. He took a sip.

"Your horse..."

"Broke its leg," Tamas said. "I had to put it down."

"I know. I saw it. Almost two miles back. You kept walking, all this way?"

"Poor creature. Died because I wouldn't stop."

Vlora put her cool hand on the back of his neck. "Drink more."

"Couldn't find Gavril," Tamas said. "Tried. Couldn't. Failed again. Another brother, gone. My last. I..." He felt the tears coming again and stopped to take several deep breaths. "Where's Olem?"

"His horse threw a shoe nearly fifteen miles ago."

"Fifteen miles..."

Vlora took his face in her hands, forcing him to look up at her. He wondered what she saw then, in his eyes. A broken old man, dirty from the road?

"Tamas," Vlora said, "you rode nearly forty miles. It will be dawn in an hour."

Tamas blinked the tears out of his eyes and looked up. It felt like he was looking at a different world. The moon was high overhead, the stars bright.

She examined him for several moments. He knew she could see that he was low on powder and ammunition. He'd dropped his rifle at some point. But not the pistols. Not the ones Taniel had given him. No, he wouldn't leave those behind for the world. Taniel—his boy—had given them to him.

Tamas struggled to his feet, letting Vlora take some of his weight. He looked north. Forty miles. He was in Deliv now. Closer to Alvation than he was to his own army.

Foolish. Bloody foolish of him.

Vlora went to her horse and began unloading her saddle.

"What are you doing?"

"We're camping here," Vlora said.

"I've got to return..."

"Don't be stupid, Tamas. The army will catch up in two days. If you keep going tonight, you'll be utterly useless when we reach Alvation."

She was right, of course. Not that he liked it.

He drew himself up. "I'm your—"

"My commanding officer. I know. Here's a bedroll. I'll take first watch."

Tamas looked down at the bedroll thrust into his hands, then up at the moon, and finally to the north, where Alvation sat somewhere in the darkness, just off the edge of the plateau.

"Another brother," he heard himself say again. "Another."

CHAPTER
34

Tamas didn't wake until the heat of the noonday sun finally drove him out of a restless sleep. He sat up suddenly, looking down stupidly at the hat in his lap. He lifted it, turned it around. It wasn't his. Far too small.

Vlora. She was gone, and Tamas wondered if her coming to find him the night before had been just a fevered dream.

"She went looking for water for the horses, sir."

Tamas looked behind him. Olem sat on a rock, carefully cleaning his carbine. He had saddlebags and canteens. Tamas rolled his tongue around inside his mouth. It felt dry and hot, his tongue two sizes too big.

"Canteen," Tamas said.

Olem tossed him a canteen and Tamas drank hungrily.

"When did you catch up?"

"Just after dawn," Olem said. He was looking at Tamas strangely. "You don't look so well, sir."

Tamas ran his hand through what was left of his hair and gingerly felt along the stitches in his scalp. "Lost my hat last night."

"Ah." Olem's gaze seemed to say, *What, we're not going to mention you rode off like a madman last night? What the pit is wrong with you?*

Tamas looked away. "There's not much water on this damned plateau."

"We passed an old river bed in the night," Olem said. "I couldn't tell if there was anything in the bottom. Vlora has gone to check."

Tamas got to his feet and walked a few circles around the camp. He felt awful. His legs were sore and cramped—especially his bad one—his crotch chafed, his face wind-burned and hands raw. He had a pounding headache, from too little water and too little rest. Every time he stopped his circuit, he couldn't help but look north, toward Alvation, then again to the south.

Vlora returned an hour later with the horses and full waterskins.

Late in the afternoon, they were joined by the rest of the powder mages and ten of Olem's Riflejacks. Not long after that, several of the rangers caught up with them. Tamas immediately sent them out scouting to the north.

Late in the day, Tamas saw riders on the northern horizon, miles off. They never came closer, but Tamas could see they were wearing blue uniforms with silver trim. Who were these impostors? Were they Kez, as he suspected?

The army reached Tamas by late the next day. They pitched camp there, and Tamas's first order of business was to find the Kez dragoons he'd fought two days earlier.

There were three of them. They were a ragged lot, their horses, weapons, supplies, and helmets confiscated. Their faces were burned from the sun. One of them walked with a heavy limp, and dried blood on his trousers said the wound was recent. Another was missing two front teeth.

The third was missing his boots. He'd wrapped the bloody remnants of his jacket around his feet.

One of their guards pointed at the man with his jacket wrapped around his feet. His white undershirt was stained brown and yellow from sweat and blood. He had short brown hair and large muttonchops. "That's their lieutenant," the guard said. "That's what his jacket said, before he tore it."

"Where are his boots?" Tamas asked.

"Took them away," the guard said. "To try to get him to talk."

Tamas sighed. "Go find them. No way to treat an officer, even a prisoner of war." He turned to the lieutenant and spoke to him in his own language: "What is your name?"

The man stared past Tamas.

"Tell me your name, and I'll give you your boots back."

"What?" the man said with a thick Adran accent. "I don't speak Kez."

Tamas rolled his eyes. "I know you're a Kez officer. Keep pretending to be Adran and I'll have you shot for desertion." He leaned forward. "I can do things to my own men that I can't do to a prisoner of war."

The man's eyes flicked to Tamas. He flinched. "Lieutenant Mernoble," he said. "The King's Thirty-Fourth Dragoons."

"What are you doing here, Mernoble?" Tamas asked. "We are in Deliv."

"Weren't in Deliv when you caught us," Mernoble said.

"You came from the north. The only thing north at the time was Deliv."

Mernoble returned his gaze to the spot over Tamas's shoulder and didn't speak. A few moments later, the guard returned with Mernoble's boots. Tamas took them and handed them over to Mernoble.

Mernoble took the boots. "With your leave?"

Tamas nodded.

Mernoble sat on the ground and gingerly unwrapped his feet. Tamas winced at the sight. The lieutenant's socks were torn and soaked with blood, his feet raw. It looked like he'd been walking without boots for miles. He slipped the boots on carefully, unable to suppress a groan when he returned to his feet.

"Have they been given water?" Tamas asked. When the guard didn't answer, Tamas turned to him. "Well? Water, or food?"

The guard shook his head.

"Damn it, man, go get them food. They're soldiers, just like you."

The guard scurried off.

"He's getting you some food," Tamas said in Kez.

Mernoble nodded gratefully.

"Why were you in Deliv?" Tamas asked again.

Mernoble took a deep breath and returned to staring past Tamas.

Tamas scowled. "Do you know who I am?"

The man shook his head.

"I am Field Marshal Tamas."

Mernoble swallowed. Hard.

"Come with me," Tamas said. To one of the other guards, "Where is General Beon's tent?"

"Are you sure that's wise, sir?" The guard seemed confused.

"What do you mean, man? Where is the general's tent?"

"Just over there."

Tamas walked through the camp until he found Beon sitting beside a low fire of twigs and old horse dung. The general struggled to stand when he saw Tamas. At the sight of the prisoner, his eyes narrowed.

"General Beon," Tamas said, "I have gathered by your demeanor that you would be greatly interested in knowing who has been burning, raping, and robbing their way through the bean farms on the plateau."

"I would," Beon said. His tone was icy. "I discovered it last night, in fact. These men are Kez officers, pretending to be Adran." He looked down at Mernoble's feet. "Who gave him back his boots?"

Tamas looked from Beon to Mernoble. The lieutenant's eyes were wide with fear, and suddenly Tamas understood. It had been Beon who ordered Mernoble's boots taken away. Likely, he'd ordered the lieutenant be left unfed as well. Tamas's own men would have been more than happy to go along with it. "I did."

"I demand that this man's boots be removed, and that you organize a firing squad. I want these men executed tomorrow morning for crimes against the people of Kez."

Tamas bit back a reply. He'd not be ordered around by a prisoner, even if he did respect Beon. Instead, he turned to Mernoble. "It seems time to explain yourself, Lieutenant."

Mernoble's hands were shaking. "What would you like to know?"

"Everything," Beon said. For his youth, his demeanor was commanding.

Tamas put a hand on Mernoble's shoulder. "First, tell me where Gavril is. He was a big man. Captured by your unit two days ago, before you chased my ranger back to my camp."

"They took him back to Alvation," Mernoble said.

"Alive?"

"Yes."

Tamas let out a small sigh. That was the first thing he needed to know. Now to find out the rest.

"Is that all, sir?"

"No. Start with your brigade," Tamas said.

"I am with the Thirty-Fourth Dragoons, attached to the Nineteenth Brigade of His Majesty's Grand Army," Mernoble said. "We were sent north..."

"Who?" Tamas asked. "How many?"

"Two brigades. The Nineteenth and the Twenty-Fourth. We

were sent north seven weeks ago with the aim of capturing the Deliv city of Alvation."

"For what purpose?" Tamas asked. Now was his chance to ask questions. This man might clam up once he realized how his answers benefited the enemy.

"So that we could besiege the Mountainwatch above Alvation. We were to take Alvation, then the Mountainwatch, then come over the Charwood Pile and down into Adro."

"And the uniforms?" Tamas asked.

"A ruse. To make the Deliv think that an Adran army had sacked Alvation."

Tamas's breath caught in his throat. If the Kez attacked Deliv while masquerading as Adran, it might force Deliv into the war on the Kez side.

"Have you succeeded?"

Mernoble looked at Beon, but only got an icy stare for the effort. "We took Alvation," he said. "About a week and a half ago. The Mountainwatch commander saw through our disguise, so we haven't entered Adro yet. The Mountainwatch is under siege."

"How do you explain this treatment of my people, Lieutenant?" Beon asked. "Of *our* people?"

"I'm not proud of it, sir," Mernoble said, casting his eyes downward. "When we left the Grand Army, we were ordered to travel lightly and quickly. Live off the land with a limited supply caravan. Conscript as needed. The order came from His Majesty himself. When we found the Adran rangers, we were on a scouting mission, looking for more food and conscripts."

"My father sanctioned this treatment?" Beon growled the question.

Mernoble nodded.

"Who is the general in charge of the Nineteenth?"

"It was Field Marshal—I mean, General Tine," Mernoble said. General, after being demoted because of his failure to take the

South Pike Mountainwatch. "Was?" Tamas asked. Tine was a capable commander, but pragmatic and often cavalier with his men's lives. Tamas would not have been surprised to see him act in this manner.

"He was hanged, sir. For treason."

"Hanged?" Beon said.

"That's what I heard, sir. And I saw the body. Last week."

"He was a general," Tamas said. "The orders would have had to come straight from Ipille." He stepped away, taking a deep breath of the evening air. This was strange. Very strange. Ipille was a tyrant, but he was no idiot. He wouldn't have wanted to provoke war with Deliv.

Tamas returned to the pair. "Who the pit would convince Ipille it's a good idea to attack Alvation?"

"I don't know sir, I . . ."

"Yes?"

"Well, I'm not privy to that information, but I had heard rumors."

"Go on."

"It was the Privileged."

"What Privileged?" Tamas felt his hackles rise. Most of the Kez Cabal had died on South Pike, or so he'd been told.

"Rumors were he came out of Adro. His Majesty's own envoy. Only took him two days to convince His Majesty to attack Deliv."

Tamas put his hands on Mernoble's shoulders, feeling suddenly desperate. "His name, damn it. What was it?"

"He's the same that hanged Field Marshal Tine. The same in Alvation right now."

"Tell me his bloody name."

"Duke Nikslaus, sir."

Adamat paced his living room and tried to decide what to do with his family.

It had taken them four days' hard travel to return to Adopest. He'd not seen Ricard since that afternoon when Adamat had spotted Brudania-Gurla Trading Company ships coming down the canal lock system. Ricard had insisted on going to find out what the devil was going on, while Adamat had taken his family back to Adopest right away.

He feared that Ricard had been captured.

Adamat tried to remind himself that he had far too little information with which to make informed decisions. Perhaps there was another explanation for the Trading Company ships. But his mind kept going back to one thing: Adro had been invaded by Brudania.

It was as if all of Adamat's nightmares were coming true. Claremonte was bringing the might of the Trading Company fleet down on Adopest. With the entire army tied up against the Kez in southern Adro, the capital city was completely defenseless. The Mountainwatch had been muscled out of defending the canal by Ricard himself. There was absolutely nothing to stop Claremonte from sailing down the Ad River and taking the city.

How long had Claremonte been planning this? He must have quietly captured the lock system weeks ago, and bribed the Deliv navy to let him sail his fleet up the canal from the ocean.

What did Claremonte want with Adro? To conquer it? Did he want their resources? Was the Brudania-Gurla Trading Company in the employ of the Kez? Or were they operating on their own? Adamat found the latter thought somehow more terrifying than the former. If both Brudania and Kez wanted Adro, Adopest would be torn apart between them.

He had to get his family out of the city. Who knew what an occupying army would do?

But where to go?

They were trapped. One army to the south, one to the north.

He could send them to Novi. Adamat didn't know anyone in Novi. Perhaps he could...

There was a knock on the door. Adamat snatched the pistol from his desk and took a sip of wine before heading to the front hallway.

"Stay upstairs," he said when he saw Astrit looking curiously down from the landing.

He opened the door to find a servant there. Adamat recognized him, though he'd never heard the man's name. One of Ricard's.

"Inspector Adamat?" the servant said.

"Yes?" Adamat said cautiously.

"Mr. Tumblar requests you at the Warriors' headquarters, sir. There's a carriage waiting."

"He's back?"

"Arrived less than an hour ago, sir," the servant said.

Could this be a trap? Were agents of Lord Claremonte there now, waiting to kill Adamat when he showed his face? Or was Adamat just being paranoid? "Did he say anything else?"

"No, sir. Just requested your presence."

"I'll be a moment."

Adamat went out to the garden behind the house where Faye was sitting alone with a book. The sun shone down between the rooftops, and Faye had her head tilted back, face to the light, her book sitting in her lap.

"Love," Adamat said gently.

Faye jumped. The book slid from her grasp, and she put a hand to her chest.

"Don't sneak up on me like that," she said. "Was someone at the door?"

Adamat fetched the book and gave it back to her. "Yes. A messenger from Ricard. He's asked to see me."

"Well?"

"I want you to go to Novi," he said.

"I will not."

"Please, no more arguing." They'd fought the entire trip back from the north over what she and the children should do. She wanted to stay in the city. He wanted her to get out. "You'll be safer in Novi."

"Just like I was safer in Nafolk?" she asked, bristling.

"Faye..."

"Don't 'Faye' me," she said. "We'll stay together. No more sending us off for our own good. Me. The children. We're not going anywhere."

Adamat opened his mouth to protest, but couldn't think of what to say. He wasn't going to win, he knew that, but he still wanted to fight. Couldn't she see it was better for her to be somewhere safe?

Adamat leaned forward to kiss the top of her head. "I'm going to see what Ricard has to say," he said.

CHAPTER
35

Taniel crossed the no-man's-land between the Adran and Kez armies under the cover of dark.

He supposed he could have done it during the day. He'd walked unseen through the Adran camp just to try out Mihali's spell. It worked. But some deep reservation kept him from trusting Mihali completely.

He arrived just after midnight. There were sentries stationed a half mile out from the Kez camp. If the Kez operated anything like the Adran army, many of the sentries would be Knacked—men who could see in the dark or hear quiet noises and had the third eye. Taniel had forgotten to ask if the spell worked against the third eye.

Or if he made sounds when he walked.

He stopped a few dozen yards from the closest sentry and poured a measure of black powder across the back of his hand. A single, long snort and the powder was gone.

Taniel dusted off his nose and crouched in a shallow streambed. There wasn't much cover to speak of in the valley. What little brush there was had been stripped by the Adran camp for burning or to make space for tents or just because soldiers got bored. Taniel could smell that a latrine had been dug nearby.

He measured the space between the two closest sentries. Fifty paces, give or take. He headed for the gap.

A twig snapped beneath his foot, and one of the sentries turned toward Taniel.

"Password!" the sentry demanded in Kez.

The sentry waited for a few moments. The barrel of his musket wavered, and he squinted into the dark.

"Powell?" the sentry called. "Powell!"

"Heh?"

The reply came from less than ten feet away. Taniel could feel his heart beating in his throat.

"You see anyone out there?"

"What kind of fool question is that? I'd a-raised the alarm if I did."

"I thought I heard something. Coulda been a spy."

"Idiot. If it was a spy, he knows I'm here now."

"Oh." The first sentry seemed pleased with himself. "Then we scared him off, did we?"

"By Kresimir, you're daft. Just watch the night."

Taniel skirted the spot he'd heard the voice come from. Even with his Marked eyesight he couldn't make out a figure in the darkness. The sentry must have been damned good at hiding.

Taniel passed a few dozen more sentries without incident and then he was in the heart of the Kez camp. He wasn't sure when Mihali's sorcerous invisibility would cease, so he did his best to keep low as he crept through the camp.

It was desolate. In the Adran camp there was always someone awake. Men telling stories or women doing laundry, no matter the hour. The fires were kept going most of the night, and there was always the hum of quiet voices. The Kez camp, however...

The tents were in perfectly straight lines, giving Taniel good vision down the aisles. He didn't spot a soul for five minutes, when he finally caught sight of a squad of Kez guards. They marched double-time through the center of the camp, eyes straight ahead, muskets held over their heads. It looked more like they were being punished than that they were on guard duty.

Taniel avoided the few patrols and made his way toward the rear of the camp. It wasn't hard to find his objective.

The command tent was as big as a city administration building and was made up of a dozen smaller tents. Guards were posted at even intervals around the entire tent complex. Light shone through the walls, and Taniel's Marked hearing could make out the sound—if not the words themselves—of heated argument.

Someone was still up. That suited Taniel fine.

He hunkered down behind a soldier's tent and watched the main entrance. He didn't need anything fancy. Just someone who'd know their way around the Kez camp. A high-ranking officer would be the best.

It didn't take long before whatever argument had been taking place died down. Five minutes later, officers began exiting the tent.

Taniel watched them go, noting what direction they went.

A major. Another major. A colonel—good. A general. Even better.

He shifted in his hiding spot, ready to follow the general at a distance, when someone else caught his eye.

Taniel recognized the man. Field Marshal Goutlit—Tine's replacement. Tamas had always referred to Goutlit as a competent bureaucrat, a man who thought of losses as nothing more than numbers on paper and had no qualms about sending ten thousand men to their deaths if it would win him even a trivial victory.

Goutlit immediately headed south, toward the rear of the Kez camp. One of the guards broke off from the command tent and followed.

So did Taniel.

Goutlit's sleeping quarters was a farmhouse only a few hundred yards from the command tent. The field marshal went inside while the guard took up a station beside the front door.

Taniel rounded the farmhouse once. Two windows, both with shutters fastened tight. No other door but the front.

He pressed himself up against the wall of the farmhouse and crept back around to the front. A hand over the guard's mouth and a knife between the ribs and into the man's left lung was enough to keep him from making noise. Taniel removed the knife and rammed it into the guard's heart, then slowly lowered the body to the ground.

"Pouli," Goutlit called from inside. "Get in here."

The door creaked when it opened. The farmhouse was dark but for a light coming from the only other room.

"Pouli," Goutlit said from the other room. "They didn't bring the girl I asked for. Damned quartermasters can't do a thing right. Go and fetch her this instant. It's late enough as it is, I want to be asleep in half an hour."

Taniel grabbed the dead guard by the belt and dragged him inside, then closed the door.

"I said this instant, man. If I have to—"

Goutlit came out of his room carrying a lantern. He was a balding man of medium height and square shoulders and a strong gaze. He'd removed his jacket and was shaking his head, obviously in a bout of anger. He froze when he saw the body of his guard.

Taniel was on him in a moment, bloody knife in one hand, the other pressing over Goutlit's mouth to cut off a strangled cry.

"Shh," Taniel said. "Quiet now, or I cut out your heart." He waved the knife in front of Goutlit's eyes. "This is how it works: If you call out, I kill you. If you try to run, I kill you. I'm faster and stronger than you and I won't hesitate. Do you understand?"

Behind Taniel's hand, Goutlit whispered, "I only speak Kez."

"Don't lie to me. I met you years ago at a ball thrown by Manhouch and you spoke Adran fine. Now tell me, do you understand?"

Goutlit inhaled sharply. "Yes."

Taniel stepped away from Goutlit, but watched him carefully out of the corner of his eye. He checked outside the door. No alarm. No one suspicious that the guard was not at his post.

"Can you see me?"

"What?" Goutlit said. "Of course."

So Mihali's invisibility was gone for certain.

Goutlit slowly sagged into a chair. "Who are you?" he asked in Adran. "Are you here to kill me? I have money. I can make you a rich man."

"I don't care about your money," Taniel said. "I won't kill you if you cooperate."

Goutlit, Taniel remembered his father saying, was not a brave man. His strength was arithmetic. He stayed as far from the fighting as possible and only engaged the enemy when he had overwhelming force.

"I will not betray my country," Goutlit said, chin up.

Taniel left the dead guard and pounced on Goutlit. The man let out a high whimper and tried to press himself into his chair. "If you don't help me, I won't think any more about snuffing out your life than you would of killing a mouse in your pantry."

Another whimper.

"No need to betray anything," Taniel said. "No one will ever question your loyalty. Though you may want to come up with some reason as to why Pouli here wound up dead." Taniel left

Goutlit, smelling mildly like piss, in his chair and finished getting Pouli's boots off and then took the man's pants and jacket. They'd be a bit too big, but they'd have to do.

"Tell me about Kresimir," Taniel said.

Goutlit remained silent.

"The god," Taniel said roughly, "living in your camp. Where is he?"

"He's living in the old keep. About a mile south of here. He was in Budwiel, living in the mayor's mansion, but two days ago it was destroyed by Adran sorcery."

Taniel chuckled. "Adran sorcery, huh? Does the General Staff believe that?"

Goutlit licked his lips. Enough of an answer.

"So he's in Midway Keep?"

Goutlit said, "That's it."

"Guards?"

"Prielights."

Elite guards of the Kresim Church. As far as Taniel knew, the Church had made no public proclamation about the war. It seemed like they were ready to defend their god, though. "How many?"

"I don't know."

"Inside or out?"

"Both."

"Does Kresimir ever come into the camp?"

Goutlit shook his head. "Never. We always go to him."

"Is it true he wears a mask with no right eyehole?"

"Yes."

Taniel tongued his teeth. Interesting.

"Who are you?" Goutlit asked as Taniel put on the dead guard's pants.

Taniel tightened his belt. "Change your pants. You smell like piss. And get your jacket."

Goutlit's hands shook as he changed his clothes. Taniel watched, just to be sure the man wouldn't try to slip out a window.

Taniel spotted the liquor cabinet in the corner. He crossed to it and found a bottle of Starlish whiskey, pouring out half a measure. He held the glass out to Goutlit.

The Kez field marshal drank it hungrily in two great gulps, then doubled over coughing. Taniel cringed and listened for any voices outside the farmhouse. Nothing.

"You're him, aren't you?" Goutlit asked.

"Who?"

"The eye behind the flintlock. Taniel Two-Shot."

Taniel felt his chest grow cold. So. The rumors Mihali had heard were true. Kresimir was looking for him. "Let's go," Taniel said, shouldering the guard's musket. "Remember—any false word or movement and you are a dead man."

Goutlet straightened his jacket. The whiskey seemed to have given him courage. "What do you want of me?"

Taniel opened the front door. The god was coughing blood at night, Mihali had said.

"You're going to help me steal Kresimir's bedsheets."

CHAPTER
36

"Are you sure this is wise, sir?" Olem asked. "We're awfully close to the city."

Tamas gazed through his looking glass at the city of Alvation. It was an unwalled city, spilling along the north side of a shallow river that flowed from the northeast and wound along the Northern Expanse. Most of the buildings were two or three stories, smoke rising from their chimneys, with stone-shingled roofs. It was a major intersection of the Great Northern Highway and the Charwood Pass—a Mountainwatch toll road that took trade up over the Charwood Pile and into Adro.

He guessed Alvation to number around a hundred thousand souls. Not as large a city as those in the south of Kez or on the coast of Deliv, but not a small one, by any means.

"No, not entirely," Tamas answered.

Olem lay at Tamas's side. Vlora on his left. Behind him, the rest of his powder mages made camp in an abandoned farmhouse while Tamas, Olem, and Vlora crouched in a dry irrigation ditch and observed the city from three miles out.

An abandoned farmhouse. This close to the city. Something was surely wrong here.

"I don't see any sign of the Kez army," Olem said.

"There." Vlora pointed. "Do you see where the Charwood Pass first enters the city from the west? A little way east of that. Blue-and-silver uniforms. The Kez impostors." Vlora was in a powder trance, like Tamas himself. They'd both be able to see farther and clearer than Olem.

Tamas searched until he found the spot she'd indicated. A group of some fifty soldiers moved through the stalls of an open market, pointing and shouting. They had several large carts and were filling them from the vendors' stalls.

"Nikslaus is bleeding the city for all they've got," Tamas said. "Sending his men out to collect a tax."

Tamas traced the outside of the city with his looking glass, then to where the city met the Charwood Pass. He squinted to see into the long shadows cast by the late-day sun. Figures milled about. More soldiers. Tamas spotted barrels, carts, horses.

"I sense a lot of powder in the city," Vlora said.

"There's an army camped there."

"More than usual."

Tamas didn't know what that could mean. Perhaps the Deliv had been stockpiling powder here in preparation for a war with Kez or Adro. "Interesting."

Vlora said, "At the base of the mountain. Looks like their head-quarters for besieging the Mountainwatch."

"I see it," Tamas said.

"Where the pit is the Deliv army?" Olem asked.

Tamas continued to examine the city. It was a question he'd asked himself a few times. "King Sulam might be gathering an army even now. Or Nikslaus took the city fast enough that word hasn't yet reached Sulam." It was a possibility he didn't want to consider. The Deliv had a proud history of having a swift, efficient army—even if their current one was rather outdated. "Likely, Nikslaus plans on being over the mountains before Sulam responds. Then he can pin it on the Adran army and bring Deliv into the war."

Olem said, "They're occupying the city, sir. The people *have* to know that it's Kez soldiers in disguise." He chewed on his fingernails— he'd been doing that ever since smoking his last cigarette.

"I don't know," Tamas said. "Nikslaus isn't an idiot. He'll think of something."

"Should we bring the army forward? Call for an attack?" Olem asked. "If we position at night, we may be able to blindside them."

"If they don't already know we're here." Tamas cursed quietly under his breath. "They've got Gavril, remember?" The city had no walls, which made it easier to take without artillery, but the Kez were entrenched. They had all the supplies, and knew the lay of the land. Urban warfare would be chaos.

"Sir," Vlora said. "Look at the church steeple near the center of the city."

Tamas scanned along until he found the church.

"Above the bell tower," Vlora said.

Tamas took a sharp breath. Above the bell tower of an old stone Kresim church hung dozens of bodies. Men, women, white Kez, and black Deliv. Children. He felt his stomach turn, and for a moment Sabon's dead face flashed before him.

"Bloody Nikslaus," Tamas said.

"Should we go back, sir?"

"Back?"

"To the army. We'll have to come up with something to take the Kez by surprise."

Tamas examined the bell tower again, then the city as a whole. He ran his gaze along the tops of the buildings, considering angles of attack. He would have to get his men close to the city under cover of night, then cross the shallow river and catch as many of the Kez out in the open as they could.

The best he could hope for in that situation, even if the Deliv rose up and sided with Tamas, would be a weeks-long urban melee with the Kez. And he couldn't afford that, not with thirty thousand Kez infantry still coming on from the south.

"Congratulations, Olem. You've just been promoted to colonel."

"Sir?" Olem's mouth hung open.

"I need someone to head back and give commands to the Seventh and Ninth, and they're not going to take it from a captain."

"But sir, the ranks?"

"I think we can skip 'major' and all that."

"Thank you, sir, but I think—"

Tamas held up a hand to forestall any protestations.

"I have things to do, Olem. First"—Tamas collapsed his looking glass—"I'm going in to find Gavril and get him out. I have an old friend in the city who might help me. Then I'll kill Nikslaus. Then, and only then, we'll go to battle."

Nila sat beside Jakob's bed and listened to the soft sound of his snores. The boy's chest rose and fell slowly, his face peaceful. It reminded her of the cherubs she'd once seen painted on the ceiling of a church. Outside the open window she could hear the sound of a carriage clattering by on the cobbles.

They'd moved from Bo's apartment in the factory district to a small house in one of the few fashionable areas of High Talien, in Adopest's northwest side. From what Bo had said, he had several such "safe houses" scattered around the city. She had wondered at one point where he had gotten the money for all this before remembering that he was a member of the Adran royal cabal.

It was easy to forget, sometimes. Cabal Privileged were known for their cruelty and power. Not for their quiet humor, flirting smiles, and silent generosity.

But he was leaving tomorrow. Heading south, he'd said, to rescue Taniel Two-Shot.

Nila would find herself alone once again, sole guardian to the little boy sleeping before her. What was she going to do with him? Go to Fatrasta? To Novi? Live out the quiet life of a single laundress and tell everyone that Jakob was her little brother?

Would Jakob be able to live with that as he grew older? After all, he'd been a duke's son. Not more than a couple of months ago there had been the very real possibility of him becoming king. She would have been his caretaker and surrogate mother, maybe even a noblewoman by decree of the new king. She would have had wealthy suitors and servants and actual power.

How life would have been different.

But it wasn't.

Now she had to figure out where they would go when Bo left the city. It occurred to her that the silver she'd buried in a graveyard outside the city might not even still be there. Someone might have found it and taken it, and then where would she be? She didn't want to think about it.

She heard the front door of the house open and shut, and her heart beat faster until she reminded herself that they were under Bo's protection—at least for another day—and that Lord Vetas could no longer harm them.

Bo stepped into the room, treading quietly. He knew that Jakob went to bed by eight in the evening. He gestured for her to join him in the kitchen.

"Can the boy watch himself for a few hours?" Bo asked after she'd closed the door to Jakob's room. The words were rushed, and his eyes were alight. He was excited about something.

He wanted to take her somewhere. Where could it be? She felt her cheeks grow a little warm. "Well, he's sleeping. He might get scared if he wakes up and no one's in the house with him."

"Can he read?"

"A little."

"Good. Write him a note. I need your help. We'll be back in just a few hours."

"I could wake him and take him with us."

"You won't want him with us," Bo said.

Nila felt her cheeks flush.

"Not for that," Bo said, giving her a lopsided smile.

Nila's cheeks felt on fire. Was that disappointment in the pit of her stomach?

She suddenly wondered how young Bo really was. He seemed so confident, and his status as an Adran Cabal member made her think of him as quite a bit older, but there were times he looked barely twenty.

"Come on," Bo said.

She wrote a note for Jakob and left it on the kitchen table beside a glass of water, then joined Bo in the carriage. He pounded on the roof, and they were off.

"Do you know what you're going to do when I leave?" Bo asked as the carriage jostled along through the streets.

Nila looked down. She had hoped that, perhaps, he would stay a little longer. "I haven't decided yet."

"I can't imagine you have much money," Bo said.

"A little. I have some silver buried outside of the city that I took the night Tamas's soldiers came to the Eldaminse house. I hope it's still there."

"And if it's not?"

Nila swallowed. "I don't know."

They rode along for several moments in silence, and then, "I'll leave a couple hundred for you when I go," Bo said.

A couple hundred could buy her and Jakob passage to Novi, or pay for a week in an inn.

"Thank you," Nila said, not sure what else to say. "That will go a long way toward helping us start a new life."

"A long way? It should go the whole way."

Nila frowned at Bo.

"A couple hundred thousand krana?"

"Hundred thousand..." Nila sputtered. She and Jakob could live the rest of their lives comfortably off a couple hundred thousand krana. "What, why would you...?"

Bo waved a hand as if it were nothing. Nila turned to stare out the window, partially so that Bo could not see the tears forming in her eyes.

"The house, too," Bo said. "The one we're in now. If you decide to stay in Adro, the house is yours. I've already put the title in your name."

She couldn't help but stare at Bo. Who was this man? Why was he doing this? He was a Privileged of a royal cabal—some of the most powerful men in all the Nine. People like that didn't take notice of orphan boys or lonely laundresses.

"Why?" she asked.

Bo shrugged. Several moments passed before Nila realized that she wasn't going to get a real answer. She dried the tears in the corners of her eyes and took a deep breath, letting it out slowly.

"Thank you," she said.

Bo was looking at his feet. He seemed uncomfortable with the thanks, as if he didn't feel he deserved it. Another shrug.

"Where are we going?" Nila asked.

"When I was a boy," Bo said, apparently happy to change the subject—he lifted his finger to the carriage curtain to look at the darkening sky outside—"Field Marshal Tamas took me in off the streets. He didn't want Taniel playing with an uneducated ruffian. He gave me a place to sleep and hired tutors for me and Taniel."

Nila remembered watching Field Marshal Tamas sleep, her knife ready to kill the man who'd brought so much suffering to Adro and killed the king, before she'd been distracted by Captain Olem. "That seems very kind of him," she said.

"I hated those damn tutors. I abhorred reading and writing, but Tamas told me I had to practice my letters. So I did. By copying all of his correspondence while he slept. His old ones, his new ones. Tamas kept all his letters in a strongbox, the lock of which I picked easily."

Nila couldn't help but give a shocked laugh at that.

Bo smiled too. "I kept all the copies I made. Just in case. I've always been good at planning ahead. Part of being a successful street rat, I suppose. Anyway, in one of those letters, from when he was a young man, Tamas talked about forcing the nobility out of the army in order to combat corruption. It seems that many of the nobles were purchasing supplies with government money and then selling them elsewhere in order to line their own pockets."

"And what does this have to do with me?" Nila asked. Bo had spoken at length over the last week about his quest to find evidence of profiteering among the General Staff in order to exonerate Taniel Two-Shot after his court-martial. Nila was willing to help if she could, but it worried her to leave Jakob by himself.

"Tamas's letter mentioned one name in particular. Duke Eldaminse."

Nila breathed in sharply.

"We're going to Duke Eldaminse's manor," Bo said. "Or what's left of it, anyway."

Nila hadn't been back to the Eldaminse manor since the night the soldiers had come and taken away Lord and Lady Eldaminse. Nila had barely escaped being raped before taking Jakob and fleeing into the darkness of the early morning. "I . . . don't know how I can help you."

"Well, I hope you can," Bo said. "I've not heard word from the south since finding out that Taniel was being court-martialed. At best he's in prison. At worst, he's already dead. I need evidence to condemn the General Staff that court-martialed him, or I'm going to have to go down there and kill a lot of soldiers to get him out." Bo scowled at his ungloved hands. "I'd rather not do that. So inconvenient."

They arrived at the manor an hour later. The sun had set and the streets were dark. Rows of city manor houses rose like ghosts of ages past out of the shadows. Less than six months ago this street had been well lit and home to dozens of noble families and hundreds of servants. Now the windows were dark, the yards silent. A chill went up Nila's spine at the sight of the Eldaminse manor. Even in the darkness she could tell that fire had destroyed part of the roof, and one of the chimneys had collapsed.

"Are you all right," Bo asked. She felt his hand touch her shoulder. He was wearing his Privileged's gloves.

Nila cleared her throat. "Yes."

He handed her a lantern and then lifted his own, lighting it with the snap of his fingers.

"Thank you," Nila said. The light illuminated the drive and threw the yard into deeper shadows. Somehow, it reassured her. "This way."

She led him up the front drive and in through the main door. The grand hall had been ransacked. The paintings and sculptures were gone or defaced, and the chandelier had been cut down and stripped of semiprecious stones. Someone had written illegible words on the wall with what might have been feces. The house smelled like a farmyard.

"What are we looking for?" she asked.

"A safe," Bo said. "Somewhere Eldaminse would have kept his correspondence and books."

Nila lifted her lantern high and headed toward the stairs. "It'll be gone already. Everything of value has been looted."

"I have to try."

The rest of the house looked much like the grand hall. The furniture was smashed or missing, everything of value removed, the walls covered in graffiti. Nila couldn't help but feel sorrow at that. The house had once been a happy place, full of life and riches. Jakob had once run down these halls, chasing the servants with a wooden musket. She was glad Bo had left the boy in his bed.

The duke's office was on the second floor in the southeastern corner of the house. The moment she entered the room, she knew they weren't going to find anything. The room was covered in scorch marks, and part of the floor and outer wall were missing. Someone had tried blowing open the safe with gunpowder. They'd used a lot, by the looks of it. The duke's desk had been reduced to splinters by the explosion.

She pointed to the mangled lump of metal over a dozen paces from where the safe had once sat.

"That's it," she said. "The duke's safe."

Bo stooped to examine the safe. Anything that had been inside it would have been destroyed by the explosion, or stolen after. He kicked the metal, then swore, hopping around the room on one foot while he held his toe. "Pit, pit, pit!" Bo stumbled toward the hole in the floor and Nila found herself grabbing him by the back of his jacket, pulling him back before he could fall.

He let out an exasperated sigh. "Ten days of work and this was my best lead." He dropped onto the floor, cross-legged. "Are you sure there's nothing else?"

"I was just a laundress," Nila said. "I've only been in this office a couple of times, and I was always trying to think of a way to keep Eldaminse from taking me to his bed."

Bo pounded a fist on the floor. "Damn!"

"Can't you just go down south and . . ." She made a gesture with her hands.

"And what? Magic Taniel out of whatever cell they've locked him in? It's a bit more involved than that."

Nila sat on the floor next to Bo.

"If I don't have the evidence to convict the General Staff, I'll have to use sorcery," Bo said. "Well, I'll start with bribes. Bribes might work, but they're notoriously unreliable. Someone is just as likely to take your money and then turn you in as they are to help you. If bribes don't work, I'll have to kill people. I don't *actually* enjoy killing people, despite what some might think of royal cabalists. And I certainly don't want to kill Adran soldiers. Taniel wouldn't ever forgive me."

Bo stared at the floor, looking angry and sad all at the same time.

"Wait!" Nila got to her feet.

"What...?"

"I came in here once and Lord Eldaminse was kneeling by the fire."

"Most people do," Bo said, his tone a little annoyed.

"No. Eldaminse always sat by the fire. He had this great big chair." Nila skirted the hole in the floor and approached the fireplace. "Right here. And he never put the wood in himself. Always summoned a servant to do it. So when I saw him kneeling there, I thought it was strange."

Bo was on his feet now, too. "A lockbox, you think? Hidden under the flagstones?"

"Maybe," Nila said. It had to be. It was all Bo had left, and Nila suddenly found herself wanting him to find the answers he needed. She dropped to her knees beside the fireplace and began trying to squeeze her fingers between the cracks. She searched for a hidden switch or a recess she could grab to move the stone. Nothing.

"Move," Bo said. He tugged on his Privileged's gloves and raised his hands. Nila scrambled out of the way. The flagstone suddenly cracked, and the pieces—each far bigger than Nila could have lifted herself—flew to the side. Bo grinned down at the floor. Beneath the flagstone, untouched by the explosion that had destroyed the safe, was a small lockbox. She grabbed it by the straps on the sides and lifted it out.

Bo destroyed the lock with a flick of his gloved fingers and the lid sprang open. Inside were several leather-bound books, each about the size of a pocket ledger, and Nila realized that could very well be what they were.

Bo opened one of the books and flipped through it. The grin on his face grew wider. "Yes," he said. "This is exactly what I needed." He dropped the book back into the lockbox. Then he closed his eyes, hands flat on the lid of the lockbox. He almost looked like he was praying.

A thought occurred to Nila. "Bo," she said.

"Yes?" He didn't open his eyes.

"Won't they arrest you when they find out who you are?"

"More than likely."

"And won't they kill you if you try to rescue Taniel with sorcery?"

Bo's eyes opened. "Almost certainly. I'll be right back." He left the room, hurrying like a man who had just realized he'd left the kettle on in the kitchen.

Nila listened to his footfalls down the hallway and then down the stairs. She could hear the sound of his boots crunching on the gravel drive outside.

She was alone now, in this great manor that had once been her home. She lifted her lantern and did a slow circuit of the duke's office. Several minutes passed, and Nila began to wonder where Bo had gone. Had he abandoned her?

No. She realized that the lockbox was still sitting on the floor, and beside it a pair of Bo's Privileged's gloves.

She sat down next to the lockbox and flipped open the lid. Taking a book in one hand, she began to leaf through it slowly. She recognized the duke's penmanship on each page. There were what appeared to be diary entries and then, later on, columns and figures.

Once in a while there would be a name, underlined. None of it made any sense to her.

She put the book back. The next one was much the same, and again with the third. Bo would have to sort these out and find what he was looking for, but he seemed happy to have these. She picked up his gloves. Strange that he would leave them here.

Nila listened for the sound of his footfalls in the house or on the drive. Nothing.

She stared at the gloves by the light of the candle. This was one of the pairs she'd mended. She could tell by the coffee stain next to one of the runes. On an impulse, she slid the glove over her hand.

She'd expected a shock. Perhaps something that would hurt her. There were stories about Privileges who warded everything they owned so that other people couldn't use them. But nothing happened when she put the glove on. She slid the other over her left hand.

They were too big for her by quite a bit. Why had Bo been so eager for her to put them on? She didn't remember ever having to put on gloves when the Privileged dowsers had visited her orphanage when she was young.

Nila held her hand away from her face and shied away, closing her eyes. She snapped her fingers.

Again, nothing.

"I really thought that would work."

Nila nearly leapt out of her skin. She tore the gloves off her hands and threw them on the floor.

Bo stood in the doorway, watching her.

"What?" Nila said, getting to her feet. "You thought what would work?"

Bo strolled into the room. How had he gotten back upstairs without making any sound? "You don't have the glow in the Else," Bo said, "but people who haven't before tapped their potential rarely do. I thought there was something about you. Perhaps a Knack, or maybe even sorcery. I've been waiting almost two weeks for you to finally try on a pair of Privileged's gloves."

Nila smoothed the front of her dress and turned up her nose. Trickery! "Well, I'm not a Privileged," she said. "Get that out of your head."

Bo crossed the room quickly. She took a half step back, and suddenly she felt the sting of his palm across her cheek.

Fury rose up inside her. He had slapped her! Unprovoked. She drew back her fist.

"Wait!" Bo said.

Nila wasn't sure why she'd stopped.

"Look."

Nila looked at her hand, the one cocked back in a fist, ready to beat Bo to a pulp. It was wreathed in blue flame. She could feel the heat of the flame on her face but not on her hand. She gave a shout and leapt back, shaking the hand until the flame went out. What had happened? How had she done that?

"Sorry about the slap," Bo said, his eyes both gleeful and wary at the same time. "I needed to elicit an emotional reaction from you."

"You could have just kissed me," Nila snapped.

"Oh? I'll keep that in mind next time." Bo rubbed his chin. "It appears, young lady, that you are a Privileged. You can tap into the Else. What's more—and this is really interesting—you weren't wearing gloves just then."

CHAPTER
37

Tamas and Vlora slipped into Alvation under the cover of night.

The river was easy enough to cross—slippery and treacherous, and cold as Novi's frosted toes, being runoff from the mountains—but no more than thigh-deep.

As they made their way past the mills and into the tenement district, Tamas realized he'd never heard streets so quiet in the middle of the night. If he closed his eyes, he might imagine himself out on the plateau but for the infrequent step of boots on cobbles from patrolling Kez and the occasional bark of a dog. There was no one about but the patrols. He didn't even hear the familiar slosh of chamber pots being emptied out of windows.

Nikslaus had the city under martial law, and from the look of the bodies hanging from the bell tower in the city center, he was serious about punishing infractions.

Tamas took note of the powder that Vlora had sensed. There

did seem to be quite a lot of it scattered throughout the city, and not just in munition caches. They had enough to supply twenty brigades—which seemed strange, because there weren't any Deliv soldiers around and it was far more than the Kez could carry.

As they passed through the market district, there was a sudden shout nearby. Tamas stopped to listen, and a moment later the crack of muskets filled the air.

Tamas motioned for Vlora to follow and sprinted toward the sound. It couldn't have been more than two or three streets over. He climbed a nearby market building and headed quietly toward the edge.

The street below was a war zone.

Bodies littered the cobbles, no more than lumps in the darkness, lying in pools of their own blood.

An experienced eye told Tamas that the Deliv had sprung a trap on a Kez patrol. The initial volley had done its work, cutting down half the patrol, but the rest had taken the fight to the Deliv partisans and were making short work with their bayoneted muskets.

Tamas drew his pistols.

"Not our fight," Vlora whispered urgently in his ear.

He hesitated a few moments, and that was long enough for the Kez patrol to finish cleaning up the partisans. What remained of the Deliv fled into the night. The patrol regrouped to tend to their dead and make prisoners of the wounded partisans.

Tamas descended from the rooftop and headed back down the street. When they'd gone far enough, he said, "An organized resistance. They're trying to take back the city."

Vlora had her nose to the wind, her ear cocked. She nodded slowly as her eyes searched the night. Like him, she was in a powder trance, listening, smelling—trying to get a bearing on the state of the city.

"But how organized?" she asked. "We're trying to liberate the city in one day. Not help a small group of partisans."

Of course she was right. Tamas needed to keep perspective. He had a goal for the night, and needed to reach it.

They passed out of the market district, then a small suburb of close-packed houses, before they reached a wealthier part of town. Along the way they passed two more fights between Deliv and false Adran soldiers. The houses became farther apart, most of them surrounded by gardens with high walls, and the street was wide enough for six carriages. Tamas felt like he finally knew where he was.

Hailona's home was one of these manors.

Tamas heard the sudden sound of a man shouting. Another voice joined the first and then a musket blast. The racket grew louder—it was coming up the street behind them. Tamas cast about for someplace to hide but saw only the empty, wide street and walled yards.

"Quick," Tamas said. He dropped to one knee, making a hammock of his fingers, and jerked his head at the wall beside them. Vlora put her foot in his hands, and he pushed her up and over the brick wall. She put her hand back down, but even when he jumped, it was well out of reach. Tamas looked back down the street.

A small group of Deliv appeared around the bend. There were eight—no, nine—of them. Most limped desperately as they fled from an unseen foe. They wore greatcoats and wide-brimmed hats, concealing their features. One stopped and fired a pistol around the corner of the walled yard they'd just rounded. He leapt back from returning fire.

Tamas dropped to the ground, pulling his legs up and covering his face with his coat and hat. The only place to hide was in plain sight. At best, they'd think him a drunk or vagrant.

He watched beneath the brim of his hat as the Deliv worked their way along the other side of the street, looking over their shoulders continuously.

The source of their fear revealed itself a few moments later. A man ducked around the corner behind them, aimed his musket, and fired. He wore the Adran blues—but he was no Adran. He was followed by more of the same. They ran across the street, taking cover behind the thick-grown trees beside the street, firing haphazardly at the Deliv as they retreated.

One Deliv staggered and fell. He waved on the rest of them, cursing loudly when others stopped to help.

Tamas felt his fingers close around the hilt of his small sword. His heart began to beat harder. Could he just watch this slaughter and stand idly by?

The Deliv were outnumbered two to one, and most of them were wounded. Wherever they were retreating to, they wouldn't make it.

A Kez soldier dashed behind one of the decorative oaks that lined the street. He was less than a dozen feet away and hadn't seemed to notice Tamas's huddled form. He stopped to reload his musket, clearing his barrel and priming the powder. Tamas felt his knuckles so tight on his sword they chafed. His trance-attuned hearing picked up Vlora's whisper from on top of the wall: "Not our fight."

Tamas's sword entered the Kez soldier's throat from the side, right between his esophagus and his spine. The man dropped without even a gurgling protest. Tamas felt his legs pump hard, the pain to his right barely registering as he crossed the street in a dozen long strides.

One of the soldiers turned toward him. Tamas slashed his sword upward, cutting through the front of the man's face, then followed through by plunging his sword into the ribs of the next soldier.

They all knew he was here now. Panicked shouting rose in the street.

The world seemed to move at a snail's pace. Tamas sensed a spark hit the powder pan of a pistol, traveling toward the barrel. In the instant before the weapon fired, Tamas reached out and absorbed the energy of the blast, throwing it behind the swipe of his sword as it took a man's head clear off.

A soldier—a woman—drew her sword, only to fall from a bullet in the eye. Tamas's mind barely registered Vlora's help as he switched to the next target. A man with a captain's silver collar dashed up the street toward Tamas, his small sword at the ready.

Tamas threw himself forward, breaking inside the man's guard in two quick strokes and disemboweling him. Tamas spun for the next Kez soldier and...

None were left. The street was clear. The only sounds were the moaning of the wounded and dying, and Tamas's own panting. He felt his heart hammer at the inside of his chest. He cracked a powder charge and sprinkled it on his tongue. The hammering began to subside.

The Deliv were still retreating up the street. One even turned toward Tamas, pistol raised, and fired. Tamas felt his heart skip a beat as the bullet ricocheted off the street not far from his feet. The Deliv swore loudly enough to be heard across fifty paces and dropped his pistol. He grabbed one of the other Deliv by the shoulder and pointed toward Tamas.

The small group came to a stop. They all stared toward Tamas as he stood among the Kez bodies.

Tamas looked over the group. How well could they see him in the dark?

Regardless, he didn't have time for this. He had a mission to finish. Halley's manor was just down the street. Unfortunately, the Deliv group was in between him and Hailona's manor.

He looked across the street. The shadow of Vlora's head was just visible at the top of the wall. He reassessed the height.

Tamas broke out in a run across the street. One of the Deliv shouted for him to stop.

His foot hit the wall about two feet up. His boot caught just enough friction to send him up, and he pushed off with all his strength. He grabbed the top of the wall, felt Vlora's hand grasp his arm, and then he pulled himself up and rolled over, falling with a thump to the garden below.

Tamas rolled over onto his back, hoping he hadn't just cracked a rib in his fall. He took a deep breath. He felt some pain, but not too much.

"You all right?" Vlora asked, crouching beside him.

"Getting too damn old for fights like that." He climbed to his feet and ran his fingers along the hilt of his small sword. "But that felt good. Very good. I needed a fight like that." He paused, saw that Vlora was looking at him strangely. "What?"

"Now I know where Taniel gets it," she said. After a few seconds, she added, "You're the only other one I've seen move as fast as him. None of the other powder mages can do it. We're all stronger and faster than regular men, but you and Taniel...damn."

Tamas's heart hammered in his chest, too hard. He wasn't just *getting* old. He *was* old.

They headed across the garden and crossed the wall again a hundred yards later. The group of Deliv was still in the street, now behind Tamas, and were checking the dead and finishing off the wounded Kez soldiers. Tamas and Vlora crossed the street farther down, unnoticed.

They kept on down the same street and turned two corners before they reached Hailona's city manor.

It was a grand affair with a short gravel drive, manicured lawn, and a brick façade with evenly spaced windows. The roof was tall and steeply slanted and must have had over a dozen chimneys.

The windows of the manor were dark, the driveway lanterns unlit. Tamas ran across the lawn and around the back of the house. He passed by the servants' quarters, where there would likely be someone still up, and found the observatory porch.

The observatory had belonged to Hailona's husband before he died twenty years ago. The last time Tamas had been here it was

Hailona's study. He paused at the glass door to the observatory as a thought occurred to him.

He didn't even know if she still lived here.

Tamas sought to recall if Sabon had ever mentioned Hailona selling her city manor. Not likely. He was usually taciturn when it came to the subject of his sister.

It was better that way.

Tamas forced the door with his shoulder, wincing when it made a loud noise. He paused, listening for the sound of footsteps or of a servant sounding the alarm.

Nothing.

He stepped inside. Vlora followed after him a moment later.

The study was different from the last time he'd been here. No telescope. A different desk. Where it had been, a large globe of the world rested on a stand in the corner.

Tamas felt the creeping fingers of panic in his bowels. What if she wasn't here? She was his only link in this city. How would he find Gavril?

"This," Tamas whispered, "might not be her home."

Vlora touched his arm. "Is that her?"

There was a portrait above the mantel. It was a Deliv man that Tamas didn't recognize. He wore a military uniform, and his head was shaved bald. Behind him stood Hailona.

Tamas let out a soft sigh of relief. This was the right place after all.

"I'll have to go wake her up," Tamas said. He wasn't looking forward to this part. A gross invasion, entering her bedchamber at this time of night was not the best way to reignite a long-forgotten acquaintance.

Especially if she'd remarried.

Vlora hissed at him. She stood beside the window, her fingers on the curtain.

He went to her side. There were people outside, coming straight for the observatory portico. Tamas blinked. It was the same group he'd saved from the Kez soldiers. Was her husband among them?

"Hide!"

Tamas made for the closest door, sliding inside and closing it all the way but for the slightest crack. He checked his surroundings. A closet, albeit a big one. Vlora barely moved, electing to slide behind a thick curtain. Tamas swore quietly. Neither of them could extricate themselves without alerting the occupants of the room.

Tamas watched the room through a crack in the door. He could hear hushed voices outside, but not make out what they were saying. The glass door opened and the group filed in.

Most seemed wounded in some way. Two of them had to be carried. Tamas could smell the gunpowder and blood—but then again, that may have just been him.

"Get us some lights," a woman's voice said. "Ruper, take them to the sitting room. Fetch towels. Get a fire going. We need hot water."

Tamas recognized that voice. Even after fifteen years he recognized the voice, and it surprised him.

Hailona.

Doors opened and shut, feet pounded frantically into the rest of the manor house. There was grunting and cursing as the wounded were carried to another room.

A male voice spoke up as someone fumbled around in the dark. "They'll come for us."

"I know," Hailona said. She sounded miserable.

A lantern was lit, casting the room into light and shadow. Tamas blinked his eyes to let them adjust. Through the crack in the door he could see a Deliv with a black braided ponytail over one shoulder. The man suddenly swept his arm across a desk, throwing parchments, weights, and a small stack of coins to the floor.

"Someone must have sold us out!" he said. "I'll find them, I'll kill them with my bare hands."

"Calm down, Demasolin," Hailona said.

"I will not! All is lost. They were ready for us. You saw it as well as I. The bloody Adrans! Indier took a bullet through the eye the moment she stepped into that room! A dozen musket men, all concealed in the shadows. Someone had betrayed us."

"They're not bloody Adrans," Hailona said. She sounded uncertain. "You heard them speak in Kez."

"A ruse! Two brigades in Adran blues! You think we wouldn't have heard about two brigades of the Grand Army splitting off from Budwiel to come up here? Our spies are better than that."

"And our spies in Adro?"

"We have few spies in Adro! They're supposed to be allies."

"Tamas would never—"

Demasolin whirled on Hailona. "Don't you defend him! That damned butcher would do anything, and you know it."

"And Sabon?" There was steel in Hailona's voice. "You think Sabon would let him attack Deliv?"

Tamas felt his breath seize in his chest. Oh, pit. She didn't know Sabon was dead. He'd sent her a message, but it must not have reached her. He squeezed his eyes closed, trying to control his breathing.

"There's a reason your parents disowned him," Demasolin said.

Tamas heard a loud crack. Demasolin reeled back into view, clutching his cheek. Hailona stormed after him. It was the first time Tamas had gotten a good look at her.

She had not aged well. Her features were wrinkled, her hair gone gray. There were well-defined crow's-feet in the corners of eyes red from unshed tears. Her jaw was set, her hand raised to strike again.

"Speak ill of my brother again," she said quietly, her voice a challenge.

Demasolin squared his shoulders. "You dare strike a duke of the king?"

A duke. No wonder he thought Tamas a butcher. The nobility of all the Nine feared and hated Tamas, even his supposed allies. Just what Tamas needed.

Hailona was about to speak when Demasolin held up one hand. He sniffed the air. His eyes suddenly darted around the room.

"There's someone here," he whispered.

Tamas could see Vlora's hiding spot from his own. The curtains shifted slightly. Tamas laid his hand on the hilt of his sword and took a long, quiet breath. He put his other hand on the closet door, ready to push it open at any moment.

Demasolin drew his sword and began to make a long circuit of the room, sniffing and casting about. Tamas let himself relax and opened his third eye. Demasolin glowed faintly in the Else.

He had a Knack.

Demasolin had just passed Vlora's hiding spot when he suddenly whirled and thrust his sword into the curtains with a shout.

Tamas choked down a startled cry.

Nothing had happened. Demasolin pulled back the curtains.

"An open window," Hailona said. "Really?"

"There!" Demasolin said, gazing out into the night. "Someone flees!" He dashed out the door, sword at the ready, and into the night.

The room was empty but for Hailona. He could see her rush to the door, watching Demasolin disappear. A moment later she came back into the room, her shoulders slumped, and dropped into a divan.

Tamas felt a great dread in the pit of his stomach. His heart thundered in his ears, and he paused for a moment to gather his nerve. Charging into a brigade of Kez was easier than this.

He took his hand off his sword and pushed the closet door open.

"Hello, Halley," he said.

When Adamat arrived at the headquarters of the Noble Warriors of Labor, Ricard wasn't there. In fact, no one was there but the porter and the bartender, and the latter poured Adamat a glass of Gurlish beer from a chilled cask and directed him to wait in the foyer.

Adamat elected to let himself into Ricard's study.

He waited for almost three hours, growing more and more nervous as he watched the light begin to wane and darkness fall over the Adsea, before the sound of the doors in the foyer bursting open brought him to his feet.

Adamat went to the door of Ricard's office and nudged it open with his toe. Through the crack, he could see Ricard striding through the foyer, tossing his coat angrily on the floor. The union boss's thinning hair was standing straight off his head, and his white shirt was wet with sweat. "Get me a drink!" he yelled. Fell trailed behind him, along with a half-dozen other assistants.

No sign of Lord Claremonte's men. Adamat stepped out of Ricard's office, feeling a little sheepish about his suspicions.

Ricard strode past him into the office and threw himself into his desk chair.

"We're buggered, Adamat," he said.

Instead of asking why he'd been left waiting for three hours, Adamat said, "Why?"

"The Brudania-Gurla Trading Company has invaded our country."

"What did you find out?" Adamat asked.

The porter brought Ricard a bottle of dark whiskey and a glass. Ricard threw the glass in the fireplace, where it exploded in a tinkle of shiny shards, then grabbed the bottle and pulled out the stopper, downing a quarter of the bottle in several long swallows.

Adamat yanked it from his fingers. "You getting shit-faced isn't going to help anyone."

"You don't understand," Ricard said. "Claremonte's coming, and he's bringing everything he has with him." Adamat could see in Ricard's eyes that he wasn't just angry or flustered; he was scared. Adamat had never seen his old friend like this. There was real fear in his eyes.

"Has Brudania invaded?" Adamat asked.

"Pit if I know. Not a damn shot was fired. No one even tried to stop me when I went up to the locks to ask questions. Claremonte just bribed every union member on the canal and brought his fleet over. Simple as that. They'll be here tomorrow."

"Tomorrow?" Adamat blanched. "How could they possibly be here that quickly?"

Ricard pointed out the window, though it didn't even face the direction of the canal. "We built the canal to bring goods over the mountains quickly. It can support the draft of Claremonte's merchantmen, and the Ad River has been deepened the entire way down. The union has spent the last five years replacing every bridge on the Ad just so that we can do exactly what Claremonte is doing now. Nothing can stop him."

"Surely there's something."

"I've spent every minute since I returned trying to come up with an option. I wasted an hour talking to blacksmiths to see if we could build an immense chain fast enough to stop him, but it can't be done."

Ricard looked like a drowning man who couldn't quite reach the rope being lowered to him. His face was flushed, and Adamat now noticed that his pants were torn up one leg at the calf.

"You're bleeding," Adamat said.

Ricard looked at his leg and gave a sigh. He made no motion to staunch the wound.

Fell came into the room. Her hair was back, her uniform tidy. Not an eyelash out of place.

"He's bleeding," Adamat told her.

She knelt by Ricard's side and exposed the wound, tying it up.

"Anything?" Ricard asked her.

"We're still working on it."

"We have to organize a defense," Adamat said.

Ricard hiccuped. He reached toward the whiskey bottle. "There's no time."

"There's police," Adamat said, pulling the bottle out of Ricard's reach. "Some soldiers. Call on the people. You have the newspapers. Use them."

"A militia," Ricard said, sitting up, his ears perking like a dog's.

"Yes." Adamat felt his heart begin to race. "This city is not indefensible. There's a million people here. Use the newspapers. You remember the crowd at Elections Square when Tamas put Manhouch's head in a basket. There's the will. The manpower. People will rise up to defend their homes."

Ricard leapt to his feet, knocking Fell back on her ass. "Fell," he said, helping her up. "Draft a letter. Inform the newspapers. I want the front page first thing in the morning. Tell them every home in Adopest is to have a newspaper by sunup. I want the presses working all night! Get me the union bosses. I want everyone involved. We'll do it. We'll defend this city!"

Adamat felt a smile spread over his face. This was the Ricard he knew.

Ricard snatched him by the hand. "Adamat, thank you. I knew you had it in you. Whatever I'm paying you, double it."

"You aren't..." Adamat said, but Ricard was already racing out of his office. Adamat stood there for a moment, dumbfounded. Ricard shouted to his footmen and assistants, giving orders like a line commander. He was in full swing now, and he wouldn't stop until he'd organized a defense of the city.

The office was suddenly quiet and cold, and Adamat looked around for a glass to pour himself some whiskey. Finding none, he took a sip from the bottle.

"Sir," Fell said, breaking the silence.

"Hmm?"

She stood with her hands behind her back, chin up. "I never apologized, sir. I want to do that now."

"For what?" Adamat felt his anger stir. He knew for what: for almost getting his wife killed. For not containing Lord Vetas like she said she would.

"Lord Vetas," she said. "He got the best of me. I should have taken more men."

Adamat fought down his anger, forced himself to remain calm. Another swig of whiskey helped. "He was good at what he did. He got the best of me far too many times." As he said the words, he felt something shift in the back of his mind. He frowned.

"Sir?" Fell asked when he'd been silent for several moments.

He held up a hand for quiet. He needed to think. Vetas had gotten the better of him on many occasions. All evidence said that he was a genius planner with no heart for remorse and no hesitation considering lives lost.

"Is he dead?" Adamat asked.

"Vetas? Yes. He died two weeks ago. Bo got rid of the body."

"And where is Bo?"

"He's disappeared," Fell said. "Ricard even offered him a job, but he wouldn't take it."

Adamat smoothed the front of his jacket. He'd told Bo about his reservations over Vetas. That perhaps Vetas hadn't told them the entire truth, or even led them astray. He even . . .

"Damn!" Adamat said. "Vetas. He knew everything. He got the better of us one last time. Not even Bo could get it out of him."

"How do you know?" Fell asked.

"The pier." Adamat shook his head. She wouldn't know what he was talking about. "I asked Vetas for a way to track down my boy, and he sent me to the slavers that Josep was sold to. He told me who to ask for, and the passwords to use. But he gave me the wrong password! The slavers attacked me. I barely got out with my life, and I was so intent on getting Josep back that it didn't occur to me until now."

Adamat slumped against the wall. There was nothing he could

do about it now. Vetas was dead. There'd be no reckoning, no confrontation. What little advantage Adamat thought they may have gained over Claremonte was gone—if that wasn't made apparent enough by Claremonte's sailing his fleet over the Charwood Pile Mountains.

"What information did you get from Vetas?" Adamat asked.

Fell frowned. "Reports. His master's plans."

"What plans?"

"Campaign plans for the ministerial election. His platform for reformation within the city."

"They're all trash," Adamat said.

"But there was good information there. We found other hideouts. More of his men in the city."

"He wants us to think we have some kind of advantage. We don't. Everything we learned from Vetas is suspect."

Adamat took his hat from the peg beside the door and gathered his cane. He felt so very tired.

"What are you doing?" Fell asked.

Their only hope was Ricard's ability to rouse the city. Otherwise it would be in Claremonte's hands by tomorrow night.

"Going home. I'm going home to my wife. I'll see you at the north gate of the city tomorrow morning."

CHAPTER

38

Midway Keep was a historical monument, a castle of vanity built not for comfort or even defense but to look imposing. Its walls were tall but easily scaled, the indefensible number of entrances brimming with fortifications. The keep towered over the Addown River and menaced the main highway. To the peasants it may have been breathtaking.

To anyone skilled in warfare it was a joke.

It had been built some three hundred years ago by a juvenile king who considered himself an architect. To Taniel, it seemed the perfect place to house a mad god.

Taniel watched the keep from the shadow of a sprawling oak standing solitary in the middle of the Kez army. He could hear the soft sounds of a snoring infantryman nearby. Otherwise, the night was still.

He checked that last thought when he realized he could also

hear Field Marshal Goutlit's unsteady, terrified breaths. The Kez officer crouched beside him, still smelling faintly of piss, and fidgeted with the collar of his jacket. Taniel watched him out of the corner of his eye. A wrong move here, a suspicious noise, and Taniel was a dead man.

Of course, he'd be sure to take Goutlit with him.

"Where's the servants' entrance?" Taniel whispered.

"I don't know."

Taniel drew his belt knife.

"I, uh, think it's over there. To the right."

Taniel pushed the knife back in its sheath. "Is it guarded?"

Goutlit swallowed hard and eyed Taniel, as if afraid to say he didn't know.

A light caught Taniel's eye, just in the corner of his vision. He crouched a little farther down and watched the keep for several moments. There. He saw a light moving in a high-arched window.

Goutlit saw it too. He scooted back, pressing himself up against the big oak behind him. Taniel grabbed a handful of Goutlit's jacket to keep him from moving farther.

"Where's Kresimir's room?" Taniel asked.

"There," Goutlit's voice came out dry and raspy. He lifted a finger. "That tower there, just above the light."

A sudden whine cut through the night. It was a low keening that rose sharply into a wail. A low thump accompanied it, and then a human scream that grew louder and louder until Taniel was sure that a banshee was going to come out of the tree above them.

Just as quickly as it began, the sound was over. Distantly, from the keep, he heard a sound like crashing furniture.

"What the pit?"

"Kresimir," Goutlit said, his voice barely a whisper. "Every night." Goutlit turned to stare at Taniel. "Every night he's looking for the eye behind the flintlock."

Taniel shivered involuntarily.

"Every morning they find bodies," Goutlit said. "Usually just a few, but sometimes as many as a dozen. Prielight Guards, servants. Kresimir's concubines. Some of them are strangled while others have been burned through by sorcery."

"Shut up," Taniel said. His skin was beginning to crawl. He set his musket against the tree and watched while the light in the keep moved farther and farther away from Kresimir's tower.

"You can't kill him," Goutlit said.

"What?" Taniel snapped.

"That stuff about Kresimir's bedsheets. Do you think I'm a fool? You're going to try to finish the job you started on South Pike, aren't you?"

Taniel remained silent. There was fear in Goutlit's voice.

Goutlit went on, "He can't be killed. About twenty have tried so far. Assassins from your own army. From the Church, and even one of Ipille's—though Kresimir doesn't know that."

The Church had tried to have Kresimir killed? Even while their Prielights guarded him? Now, that was interesting. There must be a division within the Kresim Church.

"No one's gotten close enough, I'd imagine," Taniel said.

"Oh, they have." Goutlit swallowed hard. "I saw one assassin with my own eyes. A woman. She tried to open his throat. Her knife bent on his skin."

Taniel remembered shooting at Julene once, in her cave-lion form. The bullet had simply skimmed off her skin like a smooth stone off of water. And now Taniel was trying to steal from the god who'd managed to nail her to a beam.

"Not enough force."

"He was hit by a cannonball, walking the front. It shattered on him! Killed half a nearby gun crew and a colonel!"

Goutlit had begun to talk louder. His voice was high-pitched, and he breathed heavily. His whole body began to tremble. Taniel shook him by the front of his jacket. It didn't seem to help.

Taniel realized he had a problem. He would need to scale the walls of the keep. Easy enough by himself, but impossible for Goutlit.

The simplest thing would be to just kill the man. He was an enemy, after all. A Kez. Their field marshal.

Taniel lay a hand on his knife. Goutlit didn't seem to notice. A quick stroke, silent as can be. It wouldn't be the first man Taniel had killed, nor the last.

Then again, this was butchery. Goutlit was his prisoner.

"Take off your clothes," Taniel said.

Goutlit seemed to snap out of whatever fear had been racing through his mind. "I beg your pardon?"

"Clothes. Off."

"I refuse."

"This is me saving your life," Taniel said. "I can either tie you up, to be found in the morning, or I can kill you. Tell me now, but decide quickly."

Taniel thought for a moment that Goutlit would cry out. Was this the indignity to break him? Goutlit watched Taniel in silence and then removed his jacket.

"You can keep your underclothes on," Taniel said, "but make it quick." When the field marshal had stripped to his underwear, Taniel motioned with his knife at the tree. "Climb."

Goutlit's eyes widened. "I can't possibly . . ."

Taniel grabbed Goutlit by the back of his neck and shoved him at the trunk of the giant oak. Goutlit scrambled up to the lowest branch awkwardly. Taniel gathered Goutlit's clothes and followed him up.

"Keep going."

Goutlit was about thirty feet in the air before he clutched a thick branch and absolutely refused to climb farther. His eyes rolled wildly, and Taniel could hear his teeth chatter.

"I won't go higher. Kill me now."

"This will do." Taniel fastened Goutlit to the tree branch tightly, using Goutlit's own belt and pants as restraints. "It's not comfortable, but you'll live."

Taniel stuffed one of Goutlit's socks into the field marshal's mouth.

He ignored Goutlit's squeals of protest and began to descend. By the time he reached the ground, he couldn't even hear the man, and once he'd taken a few dozen steps, Goutlit was all but forgotten.

Taniel timed the Prielight patrols around the base of the keep and slipped up to the wall after the last patrol had passed. The keep had once had a moat, but that had long ago filled in, leaving only a swampy lowland and a few ponds behind.

The walls of the keep were easily sixty feet high, and the one leading up to the tower that was Taniel's target couldn't have been less than a hundred. No small climb.

He left the musket in some weeds and secured his pistols and dagger before beginning the climb. Immense blocks of granite, half Taniel's height, were stacked at a slight incline, each one with a lip that gave his fingers a couple inches of room to hold on to. Taniel tested his grip with both hands, then hauled himself up.

He was halfway up the wall when a Prielight patrol passed under where he'd been. He hung off the wall, breathing quietly and praying they'd not stumble across his musket. A raised voice, even a suspicious glance upward, and he'd be finished. He silently cursed himself for taking the dead guard's uniform. The Kez military tan stood out against the dark granite of the keep like a beacon.

The patrol kept moving, and Taniel resumed his climb.

He reached the top of the wall, just under the parapets. He could hear the steady tread of a patrolling guard just above him, and then another sound. It seemed quiet and distant at first, and then grew louder.

Taniel pressed himself against the stone, his fingers and arms aching from the climb. What was that sound? He looked down.

502   *Brian McClellan*

Far below, another Prielight patrol. Was someone sounding an alarm?

He let go of the wall with one hand and carefully dipped into his pocket, taking a powder charge between his fingers. He'd make noise if he snorted it, so he crushed the end of the charge and sprinkled it in his mouth.

That infernal sound would not go away.

His powder trance intensified and he clung to the wall for a moment of dizziness.

Taniel almost began to laugh.

The guard above him was whistling.

A scream shattered the quiet of the night, nearly making Taniel lose his grip in surprise. It came from one of the windows below him.

His heart hammering in his ears, Taniel heard the guard on the parapet curse softly to himself, and then the sound of running footsteps as the man went to see what was wrong.

There was no time to waste. Taniel couldn't be sure if the scream had been Kresimir, or one of the god's victims, or even someone raising the alarm on Taniel. He pulled himself up to the parapet and peeked over. No one.

On the parapet, Taniel padded quietly toward Kresimir's tower. He could make out other guards on the opposite walls of the keep, all of them looking down toward the source of the scream. None of them seemed to have noticed him.

He reached the tower and swore. No door on this level. He looked up. Another fifty feet of climbing, in full view of the guards on the parapet. Wait. A window, not fifteen feet above him.

Taniel threw himself up the stone wall, climbing as quickly as he dared, and in only a few moments he was through the window.

He found himself in the spiral staircase of the tower. He glanced back the way he'd come and had to stop to blink away a dizzy spell.

It was a long way to fall.

Taniel climbed the tower stairs until the stairs ended in a thick iron-bound door. He paused there and wondered what kind of a ward a god would put on his bedroom. He looked down and was grateful that his hands were not shaking. No sound of footsteps below him. No breathing from inside the room. Kresimir must be out.

Taniel pressed gently on the door. It opened with a single long creak that made him cringe.

He paused at the sight of the room.

Taniel had expected something like he'd seen in Kresimir's palace on South Pike: a fine bed with expensive silk and lush carpeting and wall hangings, preserved against nature and time. But this... this was not the opulent quarters of a god.

The rug was nothing more than a soiled sheet. The curtains— perhaps once fine—were now torn and bedraggled. There was a full body mirror, shattered. A four-poster bed lay slanted against one wall, two of the posts destroyed.

Was this really Kresimir's room? It showed signs of habitation. There was a table by one window, set with a meal. Taniel crossed to that and glanced out. He was just above the Addown. On the table was a tankard, half full of beer. A mouse, unafraid of Taniel, nibbled on the bread.

This had to be a mistake. Taniel had seen Kresimir's palace. He'd seen Kresimir's city. The god who created those things would not live in a tower like this.

What could he do? Goutlit must have lied to him. Taniel gritted his teeth. He'd climb back down and go skin that worm. Half the night, wasted, just because...

His eyes fell on the bed. The sheets were covered in blood; spattered rust-colored stains.

Taniel opened his third eye.

He dropped to his knees, staggered by the kaleidoscope of colors within the Else. Thousands of pastels swirled and moved, as if sorcery itself was born in this room. Taniel had to breathe deeply, suppressing the urge to vomit. The whole mountainside of South Pike hadn't looked like this after months of Kez Privileged slinging their strongest sorcery at Shouldercrown Fortress.

Taniel forced his third eye to close and slowly got back to his feet. He drew his dagger and staggered to the bed.

He grabbed the sheet and tore it off the bed. One or two long strips would do it. He could wrap them around his waist, beneath his jacket, and be out the window in less than a minute.

Taniel stopped. He'd heard something. Just the wind, or...

Footsteps on the stairs.

He finished his cuts and grabbed a handful of bloody linens. He made a dash for the window.

The door opened.

A Prielight Guard stood in the door, a platter with fresh bread and cheese and a bottle of wine. He stopped, mouth open in surprise, at the sight of Taniel.

The silence was broken as the guard threw the platter to the floor and drew his sword, running forward with a shout.

CHAPTER

39

Tamas wasn't sure which bothered him more: the look of sudden fear in Hailona's eyes, or what she said immediately afterward.

"It's true. Adro has invaded Deliv!" The words came out as a gasp. Hailona put one hand to her mouth. "You're here, so it must be true." She rocked back in her seat, and for a moment Tamas thought she might fall.

He rushed to her side and tried to take her hand, but she pulled back as if it were a serpent.

"Get back," she said breathlessly.

"It's not true," he said. "None of that."

"How can I be sure? Where is Sabon?"

The question Tamas dreaded the most. He evaded it. "Look at me. Am I in uniform? Have you seen me in public since this army took Alvation? They're not my men!"

Hailona stared at him as if in shock.

Tamas went on. "Do you think I'd be stupid enough to attack Deliv? To risk them joining the war when Kez has sacked Budwiel and threatens the very heart of Adro? No, Hailona, this is a plot by the Kez to turn our nations against each other."

Hailona visibly steeled herself. She stood, taking a deep breath and squaring her shoulders. Some of her old regality returned then and she seemed younger.

"Explain yourself," she said. Her gaze was hard, accusing.

Tamas felt himself flinch. Fifteen years since they'd last spoken. How could he convince her?

"I have two brigades of men camped a day outside the city. We were trapped in Kez after the battle of Budwiel. My men are bloodied, tired, and starving. We came north for succor in Alvation. Imagine my surprise to see soldiers in Adran blue holding the city."

"Can you prove it?"

"Prove it? Those soldiers out there—I'd bet half of them only speak Kez. The ones who speak Adran do it with an accent thicker than my Deliv. I don't know what's happening here any more than you do, but I have my suspicions."

"You'll have to do better than 'suspicions,'" Hailona said. "Demasolin will be back any moment. He won't believe you." She said the words as if she didn't believe him either.

"Who is he?" Tamas glanced toward the door Demasolin had taken to chase Vlora.

"My brother-in-law. The duke of Vindren."

"You remarried? I didn't know."

"Ten years ago. I asked Sabon not to tell you. Where is he? Demasolin will not trust him either, but a countryman is more believable than an Adran."

Tamas pulled back. He felt like he'd been slapped in the face. She'd asked Sabon not to tell him that she'd gotten remarried? Sabon was like a brother to Tamas. At one point, he'd been close to marrying Hailona and now she glossed past it like it wasn't any kind of issue.

He mentally checked himself. He had more important things to worry about.

He heard steps coming down the hallway. The door opened, and an older Deliv gentleman in a servant's evening jacket stood in the doorway. He seemed startled to find Tamas there and glanced between Hailona and Tamas quickly. He tensed, as if ready to spring between them.

"It's all right, Ruper," Hailona said. "How is everyone?"

"Ferhulia will die before the night is over," Ruper said. His voice had the educated politeness of a butler. "Inel might make it, but we have to move him. We can't stay here. They'll come for us."

"Who?" Tamas demanded. "Who is coming for you?"

"The general in command of the . . ." She hesitated just a moment before saying, "Adran army. His name is Saulkin. We tried to kill him tonight but it was a trap. He saw me clearly when we retreated and he knows who I am."

"We could have barely minutes, ma'am," Ruper said.

The glass door to the observatory portico opened. Demasolin strode through the door. He removed black gloves and threw them to the table, only to freeze in place when he saw Tamas.

"Who is this?" His gaze cut through Tamas, his eyes narrowed. Tamas was able to see him better now. Demasolin was in his thirties, perhaps, with a clean-shaven face and strong jawline. He had the bearing of a duke, Tamas decided.

"An old . . . friend," Hailona said. "Did you catch the intruder?"

Demasolin continued to stare at Tamas. "Apparently not." His nose twitched as he sniffed. "She got away," he said. "Leapt the garden wall like it was nothing. A powder mage. I'd bet my life on it." Another sniff. "As is this one."

In one quick motion Demasolin discarded his pistol and a belt of powder charges, throwing them away from Tamas. He drew his sword. "Powder mage or not, I will gut you. Remove your weapons."

"You think you can?" Tamas asked quietly.

Tamas was tired. He'd made this entire trek north just to reach Alvation, where he thought he'd find succor, only to find the city held by the enemy and the very people that he'd looked to for help now suspicious of him.

He knew he should disarm. Let them see he wasn't a threat. Take the time to explain himself.

But if what Ruper said was true, more soldiers would arrive any minute. Tamas would not disarm for one man with a sword.

Tamas laid a hand gently on the hilt of his sword.

Demasolin darted forward.

Tamas drew his sword and set his back foot in less time than it took to blink. Demasolin came on quickly.

"Stop! He'll kill you!"

Demasolin slowed. Tamas relaxed, suddenly wary. Was Hailona talking to him? She knew who he was. What he was capable of.

"Demasolin," Hailona said. "Please, wait. He'll kill you."

"I've killed powder mages before," Demasolin said between gritted teeth. "I've killed a Privileged. I am the duke of Vindren!" He said it like the name would mean something to Tamas.

It did, finally. A tickle in the back of his memory. Vindren. A man with a Knack for smells. Nose like a bloodhound. Quick as a powder mage in full trance.

Tamas lowered his sword.

"You surrender?" Demasolin said.

"No."

Demasolin took another step forward.

"I feel like this is a waste of our time," Tamas said.

"It was you, wasn't it?" Hailona suddenly said. "Outside in the street. Who killed all of those soldiers. I told you it was a powder mage," she said to her brother-in-law.

"I only saw a shadow," Demasolin said. The tip of his sword wavered.

"It was I," Tamas said. "Do you want a demonstration?"

"I don't take well to threats, old man."

Tamas examined Demasolin. Muscles taut, ready to lunge. His bearing, confidence, and stance all said that he was a gifted swordsman.

A young woman suddenly burst through the door. She wore her hair up, a greatcoat over her shoulders, and Tamas could sense two pistols under the coat. "Ma'am," she said, with only one quick glance at the two men pointing their swords at each other, "there are soldiers in the street."

"Put your swords up!" Hailona hissed at Tamas and Demasolin. To the young woman, she said, "How many?"

"Eight, ma'am, but…"

"What is it?"

"They're all dead, ma'am. Freshly dead."

Hailona looked at Tamas.

Tamas shrugged. "I only killed the ones chasing you."

There was a low knock on the glass door to the portico. Everyone looked that way. From Tamas's position he could see Vlora. She was carrying something large. He gestured her in.

She kicked the door open and swung through, tossing a body to the observatory floor with a thump. "This might answer your questions," she said.

"One of my captains," Tamas said by way of introduction. "Vlora, meet Lady Hailona, former governor of Alvation."

Vlora spared Hailona a look. "Taniel told me about her. One of your past lovers. She was pretty back then, wasn't she?"

Hailona gasped. Tamas groaned. Demasolin spun toward Tamas.

"Field Marshal Tamas," Demasolin roared. "On guard, you dog!"

He leapt at Tamas with startling speed. Tamas was barely able to bring the point of his sword up in time. Immediately on the retreat, he parried twice and danced backward. He could feel his leg protest in sudden agony when he twisted away from a particularly savage thrust.

Tamas was suddenly falling. He landed on his ass, crashing into a potted plant and knocking it over. He kept his sword up in a defensive position as Demasolin pressed forward.

A pistol fired, bringing Demasolin up short. Tamas stared at the tip of Demasolin's sword, barely able to register how fast the man moved. It was like fighting a Warden, with all their speed and none of their clumsiness.

Vlora held a smoking pistol pointed at the ceiling in one hand. In the other, a loaded pistol aimed at Demasolin. Plaster drifted down from the ceiling. "Stop," she said. "Drop the sword. I won't miss."

Demasolin looked once at Vlora, then once at Tamas, lying as he was at a disadvantage on the ground. Tamas tried not to let his pain reach his eyes.

Show no weakness.

Demasolin threw his sword to the floor with a snort of disgust.

Tamas heard several sets of footsteps in the hallway outside. Faces appeared at the door. Swords and pistols were drawn. Vlora kept her pistol trained on Demasolin.

Hailona made a calming gesture with both hands. To the people at the door, she said, "Everything is fine here. Prepare to leave. We have to get out of the manor."

Vlora nudged the body at her feet with one toe. It was a man in an Adran coat, with brown hair and a mustache. He was alive, his eyes wide, looking at Vlora in fear. "This one can answer some questions," Vlora said.

Demasolin crossed the room and grabbed the front of the man's coat with both hands, pulling him into a sitting position on the floor. The soldier's hands had been tied with his own belt.

"Why are his boots missing?" Demasolin said.

Vlora lowered her pistol. "Less willing to run if he doesn't have boots."

Tamas slowly climbed to his feet while the attention was away from him. He couldn't tell which hurt more—his leg or his pride. *Too old for this.* He tested the leg gently. It seemed to take weight. A momentary bout of weakness? He better not risk it.

He sheathed his sword and limped to the large desk in the middle of the room so he'd have something to lean on. Hailona watching him. Her eyes held something between suspicion and fear.

"Who," Demasolin demanded of the prisoner, "are you?"

The man's eyes remained wide as they flitted between the unfriendly faces in the room. He remained silent.

Demasolin shook him by the front of his coat and switched from Deliv to Adran. "Who are you? Speak, now!"

Nothing.

Demasolin slapped the soldier, openhanded. The soldier suddenly struggled, grappling with Demasolin, trying to throw him off, only to stop immediately when Vlora set the barrel of her pistol against his neck.

Vlora leaned over the soldier. In Kez, she said, "Do you understand me?" It was a soft tone, almost seductive, and Tamas wouldn't have heard it if he wasn't in a powder trance still.

The soldier nodded.

"Do you value your life?"

He nodded emphatically.

"Darling, if you want to live through the night, you'll answer the good man's questions. If not..." She gently rubbed the end of the pistol barrel against the soldier's neck.

Again with the tone, almost seductive. It was a side of Vlora Tamas had not seen before.

"I...I am Galhof of Adopest. Adran soldier," the man said in Adran. His accent was thick, the words broken.

"Try again," Vlora said in Kez. She hadn't stopped caressing the soldier's neck with her pistol. "You'll either have to get a better Adran accent or develop a sudden immunity to bullets."

The soldier's eyes almost seemed to bulge out of his head as he tried to look at the pistol touching his neck without turning his head. He cleared his throat. "My name *is* Galhof," he said in Kez, "but...I am a Kez soldier."

"What are you doing in Alvation?" Demasolin asked. "What are your orders?"

"We're to take the Mountainwatch above the city."

"Why the ruse, then? Why the Adran coats?"

"Don't know, sir," Galhof said. "I'm just a soldier."

Tamas didn't have time for this. "Guess," he growled.

"So that Deliv blames Adro for the attack."

"But," Hailona spoke up suddenly, "how did they expect the ruse to hold? There are already suspicions." She shot a glance at Demasolin. "I've been saying for a week I thought you were Kez."

The soldier looked around the room again as if seeking allies. He said nothing.

Tamas felt a sudden dread in the pit of his stomach. It grew heavier as certainty within him grew. When he spoke, it came out a croak. "They plan on putting Alvation to the torch. Oh, pit. All of it. They're going to burn it all, kill every man, woman, and child. They'll leave behind just enough evidence to condemn Adro. By the time anyone has stopped to think about it, Deliv will already be at war with Adro."

"Not even the Kez would stoop to that," Demasolin said.

Tamas was certain now. "The man in command of this army is a monster."

"Who?"

"Duke Nikslaus. The king's favorite Privileged. He'll stop at nothing to win this war."

"I know that name," Hailona said softly.

Tamas shot her a warning glance. Now was not the time to bring up his history with Nikslaus.

Ruper suddenly appeared in the doorway again. "Ma'am," he said, "we have to go. The lookout has spotted soldiers coming down the main street. Over a hundred of them. We have to go now."

"The wounded?" Hailona asked.

"We'll have to carry them, or leave them for the Adrans."

"They're not Adrans," Hailona said. "They are Kez. Quickly now. Get everyone to the cellar. We'll take the old passage across the street to Wyn Manor and go to Millertown."

The butler didn't even blink at the correction. "Very good, ma'am." Ruper disappeared again.

Demasolin retrieved his sword from the floor and stopped beside Tamas. "We're not done, old man," he said, sliding it into its sheath with a click. "They call you a savior in the Adran papers. I name you a butcher and a traitor to your own crown."

"I'm all of them," Tamas said with a shrug.

Demasolin seemed taken aback by that. He strode from the room.

Tamas looked over at the Kez soldier. "He knows where we're going," he said.

"Right," Vlora said. She grabbed the soldier by the back of the neck and forced him outside.

Hailona put a hand to her mouth. "That man..."

A shot rang out on the porch.

"A soldier's lot in life is to die for his country," Tamas said.

"He was our prisoner."

"He's spent the last couple of weeks terrorizing your city, along with his countrymen. Justice must fall swiftly, or it might not fall at all."

"Is that what you said about the Adran nobility when you sent them to the guillotine?"

"Yes."

"You always said you were a soldier," Hailona said. Her voice was accusing. "Do you accept your own death as inevitable?"

Tamas leaned over to rub his leg. "Death is always inevitable. I gave up on the idea I'd die surrounded by my grandchildren earlier this year." He couldn't help but look toward the door Vlora had just left by. His thoughts leapt to Taniel. Was he alive? Had he come out of the coma? So far away. Nothing Tamas could do. "One day," he said, "I'll die for my country. I'd rather it be on the battlefield than at the hands of a Kez headsman."

"You really believe it, don't you?"

"What?" Tamas asked.

"That you are in the right."

"Of course."

"Could there have been a better way than killing all those people?"

"Likely," Tamas said. "But I didn't take it."

Tell her, something said inside of him. *Tell her about Sabon's death. It has to happen sooner or later.* Better she find out from him than from someone else.

"I need your help," Hailona said.

"I was about to say the same thing."

Hailona frowned. "My husband—Demasolin's brother—was taken by the Ad...the Kez. He's being held in the city's main prison. Tonight we tried to rescue him and free all the prisoners there. It was one of over twenty attacks all across the city we've been planning for over a week. We failed, and if our failure was any indication, so did the other attacks."

"The prison—are they holding all of their prisoners there?" Tamas asked. "They captured one of my outriders on the edge of the plateau a few days ago. That's why I came here with just Vlora. To try to rescue him."

"I don't know. Demasolin has eyes all around the city. You may ask him."

But whether he'd answer a question from Tamas was another thing.

Tamas found Demasolin watching out the front door for any

sign of the Kez. Tamas could hear the sound of soldiers in the street, beyond the manor walls. They were moving quietly, probably too low for Demasolin to hear.

The Deliv gave Tamas a glance filled with disdain.

Tamas ignored it.

"Four days ago," Tamas said, "the Kez took one of my outriders as we crossed the plateau coming north. I came to the city to get him back. I understand your brother is a prisoner as well. I think we could help each other."

Demasolin didn't so much as look toward him. "I don't think I want your help," he said coldly.

Tamas bit back a retort, gritting his teeth. Shortsighted bastard. Typical nobleman.

"My son," Tamas said quietly, "lies half-dead because he chose to save Adro instead of himself. He is in Adopest, and I don't know whether he still lives. The man the Kez hold prisoner is my late wife's brother. He may be the last kin I have left alive."

Tamas went on. "You think me a beast. You might be right. But the Kez hold your brother, and they hold mine. I think if we work together we can get them both back."

Demasolin didn't reply. Tamas waited for a few heartbeats before turning away.

Nothing else he could say would sway the man.

"Wait," Demasolin said suddenly. "Three days ago they brought in a prisoner by the south gate. A giant of a man, wearing a Mountainwatch Watchmaster's vest."

"That was him."

"My contacts say he's in the same prison. I'll help you."

"Thank you," Tamas said.

"I'll help you, but I will not hesitate to kill you if I need to."

CHAPTER
40

Taniel drew his knife and threw himself forward.

He grasped the Prielight Guard by the chest and pushed both himself and the guard backward through the door. They tumbled down the stairs, a jumble of limbs and grunts and curses. Taniel was able to arrest his own fall by grabbing onto the walls of the spiral staircase.

The Prielight went down a few more steps and landed with his back against the wall, dagger drawn. He wiped blood from the corner of his mouth.

"Guards!" the Prielight yelled.

The Prielight sprang upward, swinging his knife. Taniel dodged one blow and then another. Despite being at a disadvantage in the tower stairs, the Prielight was incredibly fast, forcing Taniel to dance away from quick jabs at his feet.

Taniel swung down for the Prielight's head, only to have the guard move out of the way. The counterstrike sparked against the stone steps beside Taniel's foot.

Taniel stomped on the Prielight's wrist to trap his hand, and leaned over, stabbing quickly at the neck.

He felt the Prielight's fist slam into his groin. Nausea swept through him as he fell with his back to the stairs. His stomach felt like it had flipped. The Prielight Guard scrambled up the stairs and raised his knife.

Taniel planted both feet on the Prielight's chest and shoved.

The guard cried out in dismay as he tumbled back down the stairs.

Taniel turned to run back up to the tower when something caught his eye. There was a figure on the stairs, just down from where he and the Prielight were fighting. In the darkness it seemed no more than a shadow, and Taniel felt cold fingers creep up his spine.

The specter wore a mask with a single eyehole, and long white robes.

Kresimir.

Taniel flew up the stairs, propelled by fear. He slammed the tower door behind him and checked the far window. A straight drop into the Addown. No telling how deep the river was there. The fall could still kill him, and even if he survived it, he'd be swept down the river into Budwiel.

But better to take his chances than face certain death at Kresimir's sorcery.

Taniel felt his pockets. The bloody sheet was gone. If he left without it, all this was for nothing.

There, in the middle of the floor. He must have dropped it when he attacked the Prielight. Taniel snatched up the strip of linen and stuffed it into his belt.

The tower door opened.

The Prielight charged him without hesitation. Taniel grappled with the guard, shoving them both toward the far window.

Over the Prielight's shoulder he caught a glimpse of Kresimir.

"Stop," the god said.

The voice was like the toll of a bell echoing in Taniel's head.

The Prielight staggered away from Taniel, clutching at his ears. Taniel grabbed the Prielight by the shoulders and shoved him toward Kresimir, then sprinted for the window.

Just a few steps and he lunged, throwing himself as far from the keep walls as possible. The wind whistled by his ears as he fell, his heart in his throat, the dark water of the Addown rushing up to meet him.

Taniel plunged into the inky depths, the force of the impact pushing the breath from his body. His feet sank into the silt at the bottom of the river and he could feel himself torn by the current as his fingers desperately groped for the surface. His lungs burned. His jaw ached from trying to force himself to keep it closed.

A moment later and he breached the surface, gasping for air.

The keep was already behind him and pulling away quickly as he was swept along by the river. It didn't take long to realize that he was being dragged toward the banks. He felt his leg slam into a rock and then he was again plunged beneath the water for a moment. He sputtered back to the surface.

People in the keep were shouting and pointing after him. He'd have to strike for the opposite bank of the river and float it all the way down to Budwiel. The current was fast enough to keep him ahead of any pursuing Prielight Guards, and he might be able to disappear in the ruins of the city until the next night. He set his eye on the other bank.

Taniel blinked. Something was wrong.

The river bank no longer slid by. The water was moving—Taniel could feel the current pull at him—but he wasn't.

Taniel's stomach lurched as he was suddenly viewing the bank from above it. How could that be? He was still in the water.

Confusion, then realization set in.

He—and a whole lake's worth of water—had been scooped out of the river by sorcery. It was as if a giant had fetched a drink with a cupped hand and Taniel was in that hand. His stomach lurched as he was lifted higher and then began moving back toward the keep.

Taniel swam to the edge. There was nothing there but a long drop to the hard ground. He reached out probing fingers. They bumped against a wall of hardened air.

A few moments later and Taniel—along with thousands of gallons of water—was dropped unceremoniously in the courtyard of the keep.

Muddy water from the Addown cascaded across the limestone cobbles. Taniel got to his feet, ankle-deep in water, and looked around wildly.

"On your knees!"

Prielight Guards poured into the courtyard, shouting in Kez. There were dozens, and when Taniel reached out with his senses, he was dismayed to find they were carrying air rifles—no powder on any of them.

He reached for his knife, only to find it gone, lost in the river. One of his pistols was missing as well, and the other one soaked through. The powder would be useless. He drew it from his belt anyhow and flipped it over. On the walls above, Prielight Guards aimed their air rifles.

"Down!" The first guard to reach Taniel menaced him with a long pike. "On your knees, swine."

He seemed surprised when Taniel darted forward, past the head of the pike, and cracked his pistol butt across the man's face. Taniel discarded the pistol and plucked the pike from the Prielight's fingers. He braced himself. This, he realized, was a fight he could not win.

An air rifle popped, and then another. Bullets ricocheted off the courtyard cobbles. Taniel sprinted toward the closest Prielight. *Keep moving*, he told himself. *Make a harder target. And get among the guards so that, at the very least, some might get hit by friendly fire in the confusion.*

"Stop."

Taniel staggered, almost dropping the pike. He suddenly felt woozy and out of breath. Again, the word tolled like a giant bell.

Prielight Guards threw down their weapons and shrank to their knees, clutching at their ears.

Taniel forced himself to keep going. Every step was like slogging through a bog.

"I said stop." Kresimir appeared at one of the courtyard doors. The water of the Addown he'd dumped in the courtyard seemed to shrink beneath his feet and dry up, so that when he stepped it was on parched cobbles.

Taniel kept moving. His body wanted to stop, but he knew he couldn't. He had to press on. To get away from the god.

"Why do you not obey my orders?" Kresimir's voice was the deepest bass Taniel had ever heard. It rang within his ears. The god tilted his head to one side, as if curious. He pointed at the cobbles. "Kneel."

"Go to the pit," Taniel spat. His whole body shook from the effort of moving.

"Kneel!"

The keep quaked. One of the Prielight Guards screamed. Taniel could feel Kresimir's confusion behind the mask.

"Take him," Kresimir whispered.

Prielight Guards surged to their feet. It was a struggle for Taniel just to move as he tried to react to their advance.

Fighting was out of the question.

Taniel's pike was taken from him. Someone slammed the butt of an air rifle into his back, dropping him to his knees.

"A spy, my lord," the guard captain said. "Another assassin."

"From who?"

Fingers curled into Taniel's hair and his head was wrenched back so that he looked up at Kresimir. "Answer your god, cur," the guard captain said.

Taniel cleared his throat and spit the contents at Kresimir's feet.

The butt of a rifle smacked across his face.

"Amateurs," Taniel said. General Ket's provosts had hit him harder than that.

"Adran, my lord," the guard captain said.

Kresimir took a small step back. "Who ordered you here?" He paused a moment, and then, "Why does he not answer? His god *compels* him."

The next blow was a pike handle to Taniel's chin that he feared had dislocated his jaw. Something hit him in the stomach. He was dragged up by the hair and hit again, then again. Amateurs these were not. Compared with these, the first blow had been gentle.

"Answer your god," the guard captain said.

Taniel remained silent.

"Break his arm."

One Prielight took ahold of Taniel's wrist, bending it painfully back, and then brought a knee up against his elbow as one might break a branch for the fire. Taniel gritted his teeth, trying not to scream. Once. Twice. Three times.

"Break it," the guard captain said again.

"I can't. It's like trying to break a cannon barrel." The Prielight rubbed at his knee.

"Get a hammer."

"Fools." Kresimir's voice made the Prielights cower. He stepped up and looked down on Taniel.

Taniel felt the warmth of sorcery like the slow approach of a flame.

"Beg," Kresimir said.

Taniel shook his head.

"Beg!" Kresimir's jaw twisted with sudden strain, and Taniel felt the heat come on quickly. He drew back involuntarily, ready for the worst kind of pain.

Kresimir suddenly threw himself backward, a wail escaping his lips. It grew louder and louder, and might have shattered the stones of the keep had it been longer. As it was, Taniel thought that for a moment it would drive him mad. The god fell to the ground, swatting at invisible flames, whimpering.

Taniel felt the chuckle rise within him. It burst forth from his mouth like a funny thought at an inopportune moment.

Ka-poel's wards. It had to be.

Kresimir couldn't break them.

Kresimir cowered on the cobbles. His mask had fallen off. He stared at Taniel through one eye of fear. The other eye was pus-filled, oozing black liquid over a swollen, purple cheek. "What did you do to me?" Kresimir asked.

Taniel couldn't stop laughing. "Oh," he said. "That wasn't me. You met Pole."

Taniel tried to move. He still couldn't.

Kresimir groped blindly for his mask. He returned it to his face and climbed to his feet, but did not approach Taniel again.

"Fetch the Adran traitor," Kresimir said. There was fear in his voice. "Have him identify this spy."

Taniel waited on his hands and knees, head sagged from exhaustion. Kresimir had sent his men out just thirty minutes ago.

"A traitor," Kresimir had said. Who was it? Taniel had suspected all along that it might be Ket. She'd been too enthusiastic about ordering the retreats. Maybe Doravir.

Of course, it might be someone lower. A general's aid, or even courier. Plenty of people had access to the kind of sensitive information that would give the Kez the edge.

Taniel had a feeling it wasn't a lower-ranking officer, though. He suspected a colonel, or maybe even a general.

Kresimir paced slowly in one corner of the keep courtyard. Every few minutes he'd turn his one good eye toward Taniel.

Taniel stared back in defiance. He'd brought down this god. He'd put a bullet in Kresimir's eye. He'd proved a god could feel pain.

He wouldn't give Kresimir the satisfaction of watching him grovel.

Of course, Taniel knew he might think otherwise after a few days of torture. He had to be realistic. Ka-poel's wards seemed to protect him from sorcery. Perhaps even from permanent physical damage. But he knew from experience that he could still feel pain.

Funny, that. Her protection might just be his undoing. The Kez could torture him indefinitely.

Footsteps approached from a hallway adjoining the courtyard. Taniel rocked back on his knees. He'd see this traitor and spit in his eye before he died.

"My lord, you summoned me?"

Taniel's head jerked around.

The traitor was an older, heavyset man. He wore the epaulets of a general, and the left sleeve of his blue Adran uniform was pinned across the shoulder to make up for the missing arm.

General Hilanska.

"Who is this assassin?" Kresimir gestured toward Taniel.

"My lord?" Hilanska turned. His eyes grew wide at the sight of Taniel, and his mouth worked silently for a moment.

"You know him?"

"I do indeed, my lord. He is the very man you seek: the eye behind the flintlock. Taniel Two-Shot."

"I feared..." The words came from Kresimir's mouth as a whisper.

Taniel got to his feet. It was like trying to stand beneath the weight of the entire keep, his knees buckling beneath him, legs shaking from the effort.

"I'll kill you," he said to Hilanska.

"Was he sent here?" Kresimir asked.

The general seemed troubled. "No, my lord. He should be under arrest in the Wings of Adom camp right now."

"Why?" Taniel demanded. "My father trusted you!" Everything that had happened: the arrest, the court-martial, the attack on Ka-poel. Had that all been Hilanska?

"He mentioned someone named Pole," Kresimir said.

Hilanska frowned. "I don't know anyone...ah. There is a girl named Ka-poel."

"Is she a great sorcerer? Why did I not know of her?"

Taniel surged forward. The guards clustered around, menacing him with pikes and air rifles. "Not another word, Hilanska!"

"She's just a child, practically. Two-Shot's companion. A savage."

"And a sorcerer?"

"A Bone-eye. A savage magician of some kind. Negligible powers."

"Kill her."

Taniel snarled wordlessly. He felt a pike blade catch his shoulder, tearing through his skin and flesh as he forced his way through the circle of Prielight Guards. One of the guards threw himself in front of Taniel. Barely even slowing down, Taniel snatched the guard by the throat and crushed his windpipe.

Hilanska turned to run, but he was too slow. Taniel leapt after him, fingers grasping, ready to crush the traitor's skull between his palms.

And he would have, had Kresimir not stepped between them.

The god raised a hand, and Taniel felt that same sluggish weight fall upon him.

He tore through it, batting away Kresimir's hand. His body didn't feel like it was his own, and he gave in to the rage flowing through him.

Taniel expected his fists to strike steel when he touched the flesh of the god. Instead, Kresimir crumpled before him, crying out. Taniel's knuckles cracked hard against Kresimir's jaw, then his face. Kresimir's mask clattered to the ground, and Taniel found himself straddling the god, pounding away.

Kresimir's nose was a fountain of blood, and his teeth gave way to the beating.

Taniel's fingers curled around the god's throat when the Prielights pulled him away. He flailed about with his fists, sending several of the Prielights to the floor before he himself was beaten down.

"Don't kill him!" Kresimir shrieked, scrambling to get to his feet. His face was crimson, his white robes soaked with blood. "Don't kill him," he said again. Kresimir returned the mask to his face and backed slowly away from Taniel. "Hang him high. I want the world to see what becomes of a man who thought he could kill God."

The Prielights dragged Taniel across the hall. He kicked and screamed, throwing what punches he could. As he was pulled out of the hall, he could hear Kresimir speaking once again to Hilanska:

"Tomorrow I burn the Adran army."

"Are you sure, my lord? What about Adom?"

"He will burn with the rest."

Adamat spent the night in the arms of his wife and rose early to make his way to the riverfront.

It was only about seven o'clock, but a thin crowd had already turned out. By the blaze of the sun rising in the east over the abandoned Skyline Palace, Adamat could tell it would be a beautiful day. Few clouds hung above him. The sky was blue and gold.

He found a spot where the crumbling wall of the old city overlooked the Ad River as it came into Adopest but before it hooked around the bend and met up with the Adsea. Adamat sat on the wall and dangled his feet over the edge, eating a meat pie he'd bought from a vendor in the street. He still felt burdened by the loss of Josep. Perhaps Faye was right—the other children needed him now. He had to somehow protect them from this new threat.

He hoped that Josep would forgive him.

No sign of ships on the river to the north. Perhaps Ricard had oversold it. Surely the Trading Company merchantmen couldn't sail all the way down the Ad River so quickly?

Yet still he waited. Ricard had not given an estimate of when Lord Claremonte's ships would arrive, and Adamat did not want to miss it. He had no plans, no grand schemes to throw Lord Claremonte from his goals. Adamat could only watch. Something told him that this day would be one to live in his mind forever.

By eleven o'clock, the crowd had thickened to the point that carriages could no longer navigate the streets. Noise filled the air as people shouted among themselves. No one really seemed to know what was going on. Their only information came from the newspaper article that Ricard had run the night before.

There was certainly excitement in the streets, and the police were out in full force. More than one old veteran wore faded Adran blues and sported a fifty-year-old musket on his shoulder. Other men had brought their whole families out and were picnicking on the old city wall. Pastry bakers and meat pie vendors were hawking their snacks to the crowd.

Adamat bought a newspaper from a newsie lad and perused Ricard's front-page article. It was a rousing speech that called the people out to defend their city against the oppressions of foreign invasion and tyranny. Adamat lowered the newspaper to watch a pair of children splashing in the muddy water of the Ad like it was a carnival day.

He flipped through the newspaper while he waited for Claremonte's ships. Unsubstantiated rumors out of Kez that Field Marshal Tamas was still alive. Fresh news from Deliv that an Adran army was besieging one of their cities—preposterous.

The slow rise of shouts throughout the throng brought Adamat's nose out of his newspaper.

Ships on the horizon.

They began as white dots slowly creeping down the river and steadily drew closer as the afternoon went on. They were moving at an almost reckless pace, especially for merchantmen navigating a freshwater river. They came on at full sail with the current, the wind at their backs.

It was two o'clock before the ships finally reached Adopest. Adamat had never sailed on an oceangoing vessel and had only been to ocean port cities a handful of times in his life. Most of his knowledge of them came from books, but he could tell the lead vessel was a fourth-rate ship of the line, and he counted twenty-three gun ports on just one side. It seemed to be the biggest of the ships, and it waved the green-and-white-striped flag, in the center of which was a laurel wreath, that was the emblem of the Brudania-Gurla Trading Company.

The ships furled their sails and drifted downriver. Adamat could see sailors rushing about the deck, and Brudanian infantry staring passively back at the crowd awaiting them in Adopest. The gun ports were open.

If Claremonte was invading, his ships could destroy most of the city without even disembarking crews and soldiers.

There was no motion among the longboats. The infantry seemed content to stand on the ships and do nothing, and the sailors were…

Adamat watched them carefully. What was going on? He cursed his limited knowledge of seafaring. Crossbeams were lowered, sails unhooked and stowed, and very soon it dawned on Adamat that they were taking down the mast.

He didn't even know that ships could *do* that. It made sense, though. While the bridges along the northern Ad had been replaced for the passage of masted ships, the ones in downtown Adopest had not. If Claremonte wanted to get his fleet onto the Adsea, where it would be most effective, he'd have to drop the masts completely, float down the river, and reinstall them on the open water.

Adamat desperately wanted to do something. This immense crowd of people seemed to have no direction. Like him, they simply watched while the masts were lowered. What more could they do? The ships sat at anchor out in the river, and they were heavily armed. It would have taken the Adran army to stop them.

He was surprised at how quickly the masts were removed, and Adamat gave up his seat on the edge of the wall to walk with the ships as the anchors were raised and they headed downriver.

He was even more surprised when the ships weighed anchor once more between the bridges, coming to stop just a half mile from the outlet to the Adsea.

They'd stopped, he noted, next to the towering Kresim Cathedral in the new city.

Adamat descended the old city wall and fought his way through the throng to cross the bridge and head toward the Kresim Cathedral. He cast his gaze toward the ships every so often, but nothing had changed. Still a flurry of activity on board. Still no sign of lowering the longboats or firing the cannons.

Between the Kresim Cathedral and the Ad River was an amphitheater where the Diocels of the Church could address significant crowds. By the time Adamat reached it, the amphitheater was overflowing with people trying to get a better look at the tall ships.

It was a death trap. Adamat cursed everyone inside that amphitheater for their stupidity. Hundreds would die if Claremonte opened up with a single salvo.

Adamat thought he spied a familiar face nearby, and muscled his way toward the river. There was Ricard, surrounded by his assistants and the other union bosses, Fell at his side.

"Ricard, what the pit is going on?" Adamat demanded.

"No idea," Ricard said. He seemed just as confused as the rest of the crowd, and regarded the ship with caution. "I've got my boys out in force, armed to the teeth with whatever they could find, but if Claremonte opens fire, there's not a damn thing we can do about it. We can only stop him if he tries to come ashore."

"And who would be stupid enough to do that?" Adamat asked.

"Look," one of the union bosses said, "they're lowering a longboat."

Adamat peered toward the ship. Sailors scurried about the deck, and suddenly a longboat swung out and was lowered into the river. A rope ladder was dropped, and men began to descend onto it.

"Give me a looking glass," Adamat said. Fell handed him hers.

He found the longboat and examined it for a few moments. There were a half-dozen Brudanian soldiers. Some rowers. A few men in top hats.

Adamat stopped and focused on one face in particular.

"He's here," Adamat said. "In the longboat."

"Who?"

"Claremonte."

"How the pit would you know?"

"I saw his likeness once. A small portrait at a Trading Company stock house, back before he rose to be head of the company."

"Let him come, the bastard," Ricard said. "We'll be ready for him."

Claremonte looked anything but worried. He laughed at something one of the rowers said, then clapped a soldier on the back. He was a striking man, with high cheekbones that contrasted with a body grown soft with age and wealth. His eyes were alive and happy, nothing like his late lackey, Lord Vetas.

The longboat rowed away from the ship, Lord Claremonte standing in the bow like a commander leading the invasion of a foreign land.

Which, unless Adamat was completely wrong, was what he was.

But where were his men? Why would he come to land practically alone, into the teeth of a waiting mob who'd been told he was coming to take their homes from them?

The longboat stopped about some distance from the shore and threw down an anchor. Lord Claremonte stood up straight, facing the amphitheater, and spread his hands.

"Citizens of Adopest," he began, a smile on his face, the words booming inhumanly across the river.

CHAPTER
41

Tamas watched from the vantage of an old church tower as rain fell in thick sheets across Alvation.

The early morning was dim and cloudy, and Tamas didn't think that it would get much lighter outside as the day went on. Tamas couldn't even see the Charwood Mountains, though they rose less than a mile from his current position.

An excellent day for his army to sneak up on the city.

A terrible day for a battle.

Powder would be wet, the ground muddy, and with the Kez wearing Adran uniforms, neither side would be able to tell friend from foe.

The street below was full of Kez soldiers moving supplies.

He watched them work with no small amount of trepidation. If he was right, and he feared he was, Nikslaus's last act when he pulled out of the city would be to put it to the torch, slaughtering civilians and leaving enough chaos behind that no one would bother to question who was behind the attack.

The Mountainwatch above Alvation was about twenty-five miles away. Early this morning, Tamas had heard the faint report of cannon fire from that direction. Nikslaus had the Mountainwatch under siege.

It wasn't a strong Mountainwatch. Not a bastion like South Pike; more of a fortified toll road. It wouldn't hold long against two brigades of Kez soldiers.

Tamas had sent Vlora back to the Seventh and Ninth hours ago.

He missed her now. No one to watch his back. The Deliv partisans didn't trust him, so he spent most of his time watching the Kez soldiers—watching for patterns, waiting for Nikslaus to make his move. One eye always on the road, on the chance Tamas would see Gavril among the prisoners being forced to do hard labor for the Kez.

Tamas heard a noise in the chapel beneath the tower. The large main door opened and closed again. A moment later, a set of footsteps rang on the stone stairs. Tamas brushed his fingers along the grip of one pistol and then took a powder charge between his fingers. He opened it carefully, only taking the tiniest pinch, and sprinkled the black powder on his tongue.

Just enough to keep him going. To fend off exhaustion and sharpen his eyes. Not enough for him to risk going powder blind.

He hoped.

Hailona ascended the belfry steps and joined Tamas at the top, where he stood beside the enormous bronze bell. He tipped his hat to her.

"Halley," he said.

"Tamas."

They stood in silence for several minutes.

Tamas stole a glance at her once or twice. He'd been unfair in his first assessment last night. She was still a regal woman. Stately, her back straight, arms held just so in a way that said she was equally comfortable in a silk gown worth more than a soldier makes in a year and in the plain brown wool that she wore now.

It wasn't that she had aged *poorly*. She had just aged.

They all had, he reflected. He himself, Hailona, Gavril. She'd been the governor of Alvation for almost three decades. She'd ruled beside her first husband for twenty years, then alone at the king's bequest for another ten. That was more than enough to age a woman beyond her years.

"You never came back," she said suddenly.

"Halley…"

She spoke over him. "I never really expected you to. I don't blame you. Not terribly, anyway. I see now what your goals were, what has driven you the last fifteen years. I can't say I agree with them, but I understand, at least."

Tamas had had dozens of lovers over the few years immediately after Erika died.

He only regretted one of them.

"You caused me a lot of pain after you left," Hailona went on, "when I still thought you might come back for me. You came and stayed for a few months, and then disappeared. But…I want you to know something. I want you to know that you made me feel amazing in those few weeks. Like a woman who could stand up against the world. That in my long life, only two men made me feel that way: you and my first husband."

"Your second husband…"

Hailona gave a choked laugh. Tamas glanced out of the corner of his eye to find that her face was red and she held a handkerchief to her mouth. "My husband is a coward. Pit, I can't even say his name." She sighed, leaning against a column beside the bell. "I respect him. He's one of the finest merchants in southern Deliv, but he's also one of the biggest cowards in southern Deliv. I do not love him."

Tamas stared out into the pouring rain and pondered the unsaid words. She didn't love her husband—but she loved Tamas. He swallowed a lump in his throat.

He cleared his throat. "I'm sorry, Halley. For what it's worth. I'm sorry."

"You're sorry..." She laughed again. It came out a half sob.

Tamas felt his heart being torn in two. This woman beside him was a powerful creature. She could stand up beside Lady Winceslav among the best women to seek his hand in marriage, before the world found out just how bitter of an old widower he really was.

Hailona smoothed the front of her dress and visibly calmed herself. "I met the general of the Kez army when they first arrived," she said, her tone suddenly businesslike.

"They took us by surprise. Marched in, pretending to be Adrans. He gathered all the nobility together at the governor's mansion that first night. Told us we were prisoners in the city. He had an impeccable Adran accent. Spoke Deliv equally well. Not a trace of Kez. I was convinced, at first.

"Then I started thinking. I knew you. From Sabon's letters I guessed he had great influence in your decision making. Neither of you would ever attack Deliv. Then I thought maybe one of your generals had gone mad. Gone rogue. This general—he seems a madman. Dangerous and deadly."

"Did you see his hands?" Tamas interrupted softly.

Hailona frowned. "No. He kept them tucked away beneath his coat. I thought it strange, now that you mention it, but didn't give it a second glance."

"He doesn't have any," Tamas said.

"No hands?" Hailona seemed taken aback. "I feel like I would have heard of a Kez general with no hands."

"It was a...recent development," Tamas said. "And he's not a general. He's a Privileged."

"How could a Privileged have no...oh." She stared at him in

silence for several moments. "You took them, didn't you?" Another long pause. "You hate Privileged so much?"

"I hate *him* so much." Tamas tried to keep the emotion out of his voice. He wasn't successful. "Duke Nikslaus was the one who arrested and beheaded Erika, and then brought me her...her..."

He felt her hand touch his shoulder gently. He squeezed his eyes shut. Felt the tears swelling within them. He would never forgive himself for failing Erika.

"Tamas," Hailona said.

He cleared his throat. "Was Sabon really disowned?"

She removed her hand from his shoulder and returned to lean against the column. "Being a powder mage was never illegal here in Deliv. Nor was it ever state-sponsored, like in Adro. Our parents thought he should have joined the Deliv army. But if he had, they would ignore his gifts. As if he wasn't a powder mage at all. When you came along and asked him to join you and be in the first powder cabal in the world, he was ecstatic. I've never seen him so happy. My parents didn't understand."

"He never told me," Tamas said.

"He wouldn't," Hailona said. She smiled at Tamas, and he remembered how beautiful she had been all those years ago. "You're his best friend."

"And he was mine."

The smile disappeared. "Was?"

"He's dead, Halley."

She took a quick step back, then another. "What? No. Not Sabon."

"Shot. By a Kez Warden. One of Duke Nikslaus's men."

"You...you let him die?"

"I didn't. It was an ambush, I..."

The softness in her eyes a moment ago was gone. Any love, any feeling, also gone. She breathed heavily, clutching at her dress, her eyes filled with horror. She turned and fled down the belfry stairs.

"Halley!"

Tamas heard the door to the chapel slam below. He fell back against the bell, felt it rock slightly from his weight without making a sound. He shook his head and stared out into the rain sightlessly.

Was all he left behind misery and death? Sorrow, widows, and grieving families? He made his hands into fists. How dare she blame him? Sabon was his best friend. His closest confidant for the last fifteen years.

No, she was right to blame him. He was a harbinger of death, it seemed. Not to be trusted with the lives of anyone dear.

It was perhaps an hour before Tamas heard the chapel door open below. A slow, measured step lit upon the stairs. Tamas frowned, wondering who it was for only a moment before the mint-tinged smell of cigarette smoke wafted up the stairwell.

"Sir," Olem said as he joined Tamas. He wore a greatcoat and forage cap pulled down over his eyes, soaked from the rain. Beneath the coat, his Adran blues. He wore the colonel's pins Tamas had given him last night. That seemed like an eternity ago.

"I thought you ran out of those." Tamas looked at the cigarette between Olem's lips.

Olem drew it from his mouth, turned it sideways as if it were a peculiar thing, and blew smoke out his nose slowly before returning the cigarette to its place. "Stopped at a tobacconist on the way through town."

"I see you have your priorities straight."

"Of course. You don't look so well, sir."

Tamas looked back out across the city. "Sometimes I feel like a pestilence."

"That argument," Olem said after a moment's consideration, "could be made."

"You make me feel so much better."

"I try, sir."

"What are you doing here? I told Vlora to give the signal, not order you here. And how the bloody pit did you get past the river in broad daylight?"

"I pretended I was a Kez colonel pretending to be an Adran colonel," Olem said. "It was disturbingly easy."

"They didn't ask for papers or proof?"

"In this rain?" Olem gestured at the downpour. "You don't understand an enlisted man, sir. Nobody asks for bloody papers in this kind of weather."

"Sloppy."

"I call it lucky. I also have news."

Tamas straightened up. "What kind of news?"

"A Deliv army is about a day and a half outside the city. Coming from the west. Our outriders spotted them just a few hours ago."

"How big?"

"Several brigades, at least."

"Pit."

"That's not a good thing, sir?"

"Maybe. We need to launch an attack soon."

"We won't be ready, sir."

"We have to. Something to tell the Deliv that there is more going on here than meets the eye. Otherwise their brigades will fall on us, thinking we are the ones holding the city.

"Come with me," he said, heading for the belfry stairs. "And keep a hand on your pistol. I might be starting a fight I can't win."

Vlora was waiting at the bottom of the stairs.

"My powder mages?" he asked.

"Waiting in an abandoned factory a quarter mile from here."

Tamas gestured for her to join him. He checked the street outside the chapel before crossing over to Millertown. The ground was muddy from the rain, a frothy slurry of refuse and garbage. They cut through several alleyways to avoid Kez patrols and then entered one of the larger mills.

A pair of Deliv partisans guarded the door. They let Tamas pass through, eyeing Vlora and Olem suspiciously. Tamas climbed the stairs to the second floor.

Demasolin was examining a report while a few of his captains and spies looked on. He glanced up when Tamas entered, but did not greet him.

Tamas counted the men in the room. Six of them, if it came to a fight.

Tamas removed his gloves and threw them on the table for emphasis. "Why didn't you tell me about the army?" he demanded.

Demasolin glanced up again. "What army?"

"Don't be bloody coy with me. You've got the entire city running with your spies. I know you can get people in and out. There's a Deliv army just over a day's march from here."

"You didn't need to know." Demasolin returned to reading his report.

Tamas planted both hands on the table in front of Demasolin and leaned over it until his face was only a few inches from Demasolin's. "You want to go another round? You willing to bet my leg will go again? Because you're putting my whole army in danger."

He heard the creak of movement behind him as Demasolin's underlings shifted uncomfortably. Tamas would leave them to Olem and Vlora if it came to blows.

Demasolin set the report facedown on the table. He leaned back in his chair, and his fingers crept slowly toward the sword at his hip.

"If the Kez know," Tamas said, "which they undoubtedly do, they'll torch the city tonight and be gone by morning."

"They won't torch anything in this weather."

"Nikslaus will find a way. That leaves you all dead, and my army sitting there looking guilty while whoever survives the Kez slaughter will say Adro did it. No one wins if your king attacks my army. Would you risk the lives of everyone in this city, and the lives of Deliv soldiers, because you think I'm a butcher?"

Demasolin's fingers stopped their movement toward his sword. "We'll have to act tonight. Just after dark."

"Have you found where they moved the prisoners?"

"We have."

Tamas bit his tongue. How long had Demasolin been sitting on that information, too?

"Can you provide a distraction?" Tamas asked.

"No," Demasolin said. "You have one man in there," he said. "I have dozens. Including my brother. I'll be going after them, and it'll be you who provides a distraction."

"Where are they being held?"

"I don't think you need to know that."

Tamas wanted to reach across the table and strangle Demasolin. Even so, he wasn't sure if that was a fight he wanted to start, and he wasn't keen on risking his leg going out again. He had better people to strangle.

Demasolin produced a map of the city and spread it out across the table. "The main city barracks is here. There are about two hundred men stationed there. Get close enough to detonate their powder reserves and it'll bring every soldier within a half mile running."

Tamas spun the map around so the south end was facing him. He ran his eyes around the marks, then spaced his fingers and did some math.

"No," Tamas said. "You've tried this already. Your failed attack last night. Someone is feeding the Kez information. They'll be ready for your attack on the prison and for mine on the barracks."

"What else can we do?" Demasolin said. "I don't know who the damned traitor is."

"You want a distraction? I'll give you a distraction. This General Saulkin. He's staying at the governor's manor, correct?"

Demasolin answered hesitantly. "Yes."

"Is he still there?"

"As of an hour ago, yes."

"Tell your spies that Field Marshal Tamas is going to kill Saulkin."

"And how will that help?"

"Because Saulkin is Duke Nikslaus, and I cut his bloody hands off. If he knows I'm in the city, he'll forget about everything else."

"Then you'll walk into a trap." Demasolin held up one hand. "Don't get me wrong. The world will be a better place if you die today. But if he kills you right away, this city may die with you."

Tamas ran his fingers along the map, memorizing the streets of the city. "I walked into one of his traps twice now. I don't intend to do it again. Do me a favor, though . . . don't give this information to your men until about six o'clock."

"Are you going to tell me how you plan on avoiding a trap?" Demasolin asked.

Tamas tapped the map absently. "I don't think you need to know that. Remember. Six o'clock. I'm going to kill this bastard once and for all."

CHAPTER

42

The beatings lasted through the night.

They pummeled Taniel with cudgels and fists. He faded in and out of consciousness but was, mercifully, out for most of it. He could feel the cold air on his skin when they finally took him outside. Through bloody eyes he could tell that the sun barely touched the tips of the eastern mountains.

Dawn was here.

Ka-poel might already be dead.

Taniel's feet dragged behind him as the Prielight Guards carried him through the Kez camp. A thousand voices reached his ears along with the sounds of an army preparing breakfast. Taniel wondered if any of them knew—or cared—who he was.

He was dropped unceremoniously on the ground. Taniel lay facedown, groaning into the dirt. His whole body felt numb and destroyed, smashed to a pulp by Prielight Guards. His body would be one giant bruise in a day or two. If he lived that long.

He felt along the inside of his mouth and wondered at the resiliency of his teeth. Was that Ka-poel's sorcery at work? Keeping him from breaking bones? His ribs *felt* broken, though Taniel didn't think he had the strength in him to check.

Did he?

Taniel opened his eyes. Men moved and worked all around him. A sea of legs and feet.

"One, two, pull! One, two, pull!"

The mantra was repeated again and again. What could they be doing?

He dragged his hand along through the dirt until he could see it. Moved a finger, then another. They were all still working. That was something, wasn't it? Those cuts on his knuckles. Where had they come from?

Oh. Right.

Those were from Kresimir's teeth.

Strong hands lifted Taniel to his feet. He swayed back, nearly falling. His arms were lifted, wrists bound together by strong cord.

"Make it tight," someone said. "He'll be up there a while."

Up where?

Taniel's arms were lifted above his head. He felt the rope between his wrists snag on something and the guards stepped away. Taniel's legs gave out beneath him, but he didn't fall.

"One, two, pull!"

Taniel's whole body jerked as he was lifted from the ground by his wrists.

"One, two, pull!"

Panic caused Taniel to flail about with his legs, but there was nothing beneath him but air. He looked up.

He hung from a hook fastened to an immense beam being lifted perpendicular to the ground. Teams of men pulled on ropes to raise the beam until it pointed at the sky.

The vision of Julene, nailed to a beam in the middle of the Kez camp, her hands gone at the wrists, haunted his memory.

He vomited down the front of himself.

"One, two, pull!"

It took the workers some time to get the beam in place. Taniel's back finally hit the wood and his feet scrambled for purchase on the beam. There was none to be had.

He was facing the Adran camp. In the early dawn light he could see soldiers gathering on the front lines, pointing and talking. A few officers were examining him through looking glasses. He closed his eyes, unable to bear looking back. Those men he'd thought to lead to victory would see him here now.

He had to warn them. What had Kresimir said last night? He planned to burn the army, and Mihali with it.

A rasping noise reached him. It was guttural and base, but it had a pattern to it. Slowly, Taniel realized someone was laughing.

"Two-Shot," the voice said.

Taniel craned his neck.

There, not much farther than spitting distance to his left, was another immense beam. They must have moved it up closer to the lines during the night. And still hanging there, the seared stumps of her wrists crossed in some kind of sick entreaty, was Julene.

"Didn't think I'd see you here, Two-Shot," she said.

Taniel looked away from the Predeii.

"Sorry, is it my voice? They haven't given me water in two months." She stopped and cleared her throat. Another long, raspy laugh. "The problem with not being able to die is just that." A cough, and then another laugh.

Taniel closed his eyes, hoping she would stop talking.

"You look good, Two-Shot," Julene said. "I mean it. Look at me.

Kresimir tortured me for weeks before he hung me up here. I'm curious why he didn't do the same to you. Don't worry. A couple of weeks and you'll be good as new. Me, though. I'll never heal. Kresimir made sure of that. I haven't seen a mirror lately, but tell me, can you still see that charming scar on my face?"

Had she gone mad from hanging from the beam for so long, unable to die? Taniel's arms were beginning to ache from the strain of holding his weight. They could only get worse as long as he was up here. He finally turned to look at Julene.

She was hideous. Most of her hair was gone. Her skin, which once looked young and supple, was now cracked like old leather. Her face had been particularly savaged—the tip of her nose cut off, most of her teeth gone. She grinned at Taniel, as if she knew what must be going through his mind.

There was madness in her eyes.

"Charming as always," he said. He looked up at his hands, tied about the wrist. They were starting to hurt more now. He tried lifting his legs but gave up after several moments with a groan—half pain, half anger.

"The pain doesn't go away," Julene said. "Even after months. Even after your arms are numb it will still throb deep down in your shoulders. I find"—she moved her head slowly to one side, a look of agony moving across her face—"that switching the arm that holds all the weight gives you some relief."

Taniel closed his eyes. Would he last that long? Would he still be alive in months, watching his country burn, unable to do a thing?

From the Adran army he saw a rider heading toward the Kez lines with a white flag billowing above him.

A call for truce? Or had that traitor Hilanska finally convinced the General Staff to surrender?

Taniel began to struggle harder. He had to get off this rope.

*   *   *

Tamas found Hailona in the mill's basement, an old granary. It was the only private room in the place. It smelled of dry old wheat, the scent dusty in Tamas's nostrils.

Hailona looked up when he knocked on the door frame of the open door. Ruper, the butler, was just inside. He stood when he saw Tamas.

"You killed my little brother," Hailona said.

Tamas knew that wasn't fair. Knew he wasn't in the wrong. Sabon had known the risks of being one of Tamas's soldiers. But Tamas also knew that convincing Hailona of that would be next to impossible.

"I need your help."

"Go to the pit. Get out of my sight."

"Hailona..." Tamas took a step forward.

Ruper got between them, blocking the path to his mistress with his body.

Tamas narrowed his eyes at the butler. "Hailona, I need a way into the governor's mansion. I'm going to kill the man who killed my wife *and* your brother."

Ruper moved forward until his chest touched Tamas's. "My lady has said for you to leave, sir."

Hailona held up a hand. "Ruper, it's all right." She dried her eyes with a handkerchief. Her hand remained up, as if asking for time to think. After a few moments, she let it drop. "Ruper, I want you to show Tamas the secret passage into the mansion."

"Are you sure, ma'am?"

"Yes."

Tamas stepped back from the butler. "Thank you, Halley."

"Kill the bastard, Tamas," Hailona said. "Make him suffer." She took a shaky breath. "Then I don't ever want to see you again."

"I understand."

Tamas left the mill. Vlora was waiting for him out in the rain. She wore a tricorn hat and a greatcoat. She tipped the hat toward Tamas, water pouring off the front. She leaned against a rifle, and he could see her blue uniform beneath the greatcoat and a pistol at her hip.

"Did Olem head back to the army?"

She nodded.

"Where are the others?"

"Waiting."

Tamas nodded. A few minutes later Ruper joined them in the street and they made their way out of Millertown. At the edge of the mill district, lounging around the outdoor seating of an otherwise abandoned streetside café, was Tamas's powder cabal.

He'd only brought the best. The ones that Sabon had been training during the summer in Adopest were still in the city. They didn't have the experience or training for a mission like this.

His powder cabal was outfitted much the same as Vlora, in greatcoats and tricorn hats. Every one of them had as much weaponry and powder at they could carry, from pistols to swords and daggers. Tamas felt a smile touch his lips. Eight men and women, every one of them a talented powder mage. As good as an army, as far as he was concerned. Tamas checked the streets quickly for any sign of Kez patrols, then turned to his mages.

"We're going to provide a distraction so that the Deliv can rescue the political prisoners being held by the Kez," Tamas said. "Gavril is among those prisoners. I'd like to be there to get our man out, but we have a more important task.

"Ours is to cut the head off this Kez abomination of an occupying army. We're going straight for the throat. You all know my history with Duke Nikslaus, so you all know that I choose to do this with some...relish."

There was a low chuckle among the powder mages.

"But as I said, we're to provide a distraction. I intend on luring in as many soldiers as possible. There will be Wardens, no doubt. Perhaps several dozen. The odds, despite our skills and talents, will be very heavily against us. This mission smacks of revenge for me. I won't ask you to throw your lives away for my vengeance."

One of his mages, a girl not much older than Vlora by the name of Leone, spoke up. "You expect to die here, sir?"

"I never expect to die in battle. An expectation like that has a habit of coming true. However...there are times, more than others, when the chances I'll lose are much greater."

"That's a fancy way of saying he expects to die," Vlora said.

Tamas shot her a look.

"Sir." Andriya raised his hand.

"Yes?"

"I signed on to kill Kez. I've got fifty-seven notches on my rifle from the last two months. I wanted a hundred by the end of the campaign. Will there be forty-seven Kez there?"

"I'd expect."

"Very good, sir. I'm coming."

"The rest of us are, too," Vlora said quietly.

"Thank you."

"Not doing it for you, sir," Andriya said. "Doing it to kill Kez."

"I appreciate it all the same. Ruper. If you please?"

They followed the butler through the streets, dodging Kez patrols as they went. Tamas watched the patrols from the shadows. There was an urgency in their step, and an extra vigilance. Tamas recognized the look. He'd seen it before in the eyes of comrades in Gurla, patrolling an unfriendly city on the last day before a withdrawal with the expectation—and fear—that anything could happen.

The governor's mansion was back in the same wealthy part of town as Hailona's manor. Their small group dashed from walled garden to walled garden until they reached a small wooded park well off the main street. Ruper led them into the woods to a groundskeeper's shack.

It was a small building, barely large enough for all of them standing. Ruper moved a table, then pulled up an old rug and tossed it aside to reveal a trapdoor. He lit a lantern, and they descended into a cellar.

The cellar was rough-cut, descending past topsoil and into the clay earth. From a quick glance, it could have been any root cellar, about four feet wide and a dozen long, with a small room at the far end. When they reached the room and turned the corner, a sharply angled tunnel led off into the darkness.

Tamas counted nearly four hundred paces, sloshing through mud, trying to keep his greatcoat from scraping the damp sides of the tunnel, before they ascended a set of stone steps and came out in a somewhat more spacious basement. It was a stone room, with a dust-covered wardrobe in one corner, a double bed, and an empty musket rack. At the opposite side of the room a spiral staircase led upward.

"This room and passage," Ruper said, his first words since joining them, "were made as an escape route long ago, when unrest was common in this part of Deliv." Ruper gestured toward the staircase. "That will take you up to the second floor. It comes out from behind a false bookshelf into the main office of the governor. I'll return to my mistress now."

Tamas caught Ruper by the shoulder before he could go back down into the passage. "Tell Halley that... tell her I'm truly sorry I never came back."

Ruper pulled himself from Tamas's grip and headed down into the passage with the only lantern, leaving Tamas and his mages in darkness.

Tamas took a small touch of powder to his tongue, letting him see ever so slightly in the utter blackness. He headed up the staircase slowly, as quietly as he could. It creaked beneath him as the wrought iron ground together beneath his weight.

At the top of the staircase there was light. It came in through a pair of holes just a couple inches too short for Tamas to look through comfortably. He set his face against the wall, gazing through the looking-holes.

He could see very little. A double door on the opposite side of the room. A candelabra. The top of a sofa. He opened his third eye.

There were blots of color in the Else. Just bright enough to be Wardens, but too far away from him to be inside the governor's office. No sign of a Privileged.

Tamas pushed gently on the door.

It rolled forward silently, then slid to the side with nothing more than a touch of a finger. Tamas stepped out into the governor's office. It was a large room, with dozens of gilded candelabras, shelves full of books, two magnificent fireplaces, and a grand window that looked out over the courtyard in front of the manor.

The room was empty.

Tamas let out a sigh of relief and called softly for his Marked to come up. They filed into the room, tracking mud on the pristine red carpets. He directed them with hand signals to cover the doors and windows.

They checked the adjoining rooms and the hallway immediately outside.

Vlora joined him by the bay window a few minutes later. "No one in these office suites, sir," she said. "A couple of Wardens downstairs by the front door. Andriya says he can hear soldiers talking in the servants' quarters on the first floor."

"Good work."

"What now?"

"We wait."

"Are you sure Nikslaus will come back here, sir?"

"I have a good guess."

Andriya returned to the room at that moment. "Sir, luggage in the master bedroom."

Tamas checked his pocket watch. It was just after six o'clock. "Timing will be everything."

Tamas watched out the bay window. There were a dozen or so soldiers in the yard. They stood at attention, facing the gate, muskets on their shoulders. Tamas spotted a Warden in one corner of the yard, barely visible from his vantage point.

He checked his watch every few minutes. Would Nikslaus come back here? Had the news already reached him that Tamas was coming for him? Maybe he'd read Nikslaus wrong. Maybe Nikslaus would rather flee than attempt to catch Tamas.

Tamas brought his attention back to the courtyard outside as several horsemen came through the front gate. They were followed closely by a carriage decked out with lace curtains and fine gilding. It pulled around the turnabout and came to a stop. Tamas was so close he could have tossed a rock through the window and hit the top of the carriage.

The door opened and a Deliv woman stepped out. She looked about sixteen. She wore a fine gown that displayed her ample bosom. Tamas felt a wave of disappointment as she got her feet on the gravel drive and looked around regally.

Not Nikslaus.

Tamas stepped away from the window.

"Sir!" Vlora motioned him back over. Someone else was getting out of the carriage. It seemed a struggle for him, leaning his forearms against the door frame. It was a man. He wore white Privileged's gloves. A Warden appeared from the mansion, grasping one of the arms and helping the man down. His face was partially concealed by a tricorne hat.

Tamas prayed the Privileged would turn his head just a little bit so Tamas could get a look at his identity.

The Privileged stopped to talk to one of the soldiers. The voices were too low for Tamas to make out. The soldier gave the Privileged a brisk nod, then turned to the others. "We leave in two hours!" he said loudly. "Anyone who's not ready to move out by dark will be shot."

Tamas's gaze was still locked on the Privileged in the tricorne. It had to be Nikslaus! But Tamas still couldn't see his face. Whoever he was, he chatted amiably with the young lady beside him.

They had just mounted the steps to the mansion when a messenger came galloping hard into the courtyard and came to a stop in a spray of gravel. The messenger leapt from his horse and ran to the Privileged.

Tamas felt his heart begin to beat faster.

The messenger saluted and breathlessly gave his report. The Privileged pushed him away with an elbow and spun toward the mansion.

Tamas heard the doors below burst open. The Privileged's voice echoed through the building.

"Get everyone!" he screamed. "All my Wardens, to me! I want five hundred soldiers here in twenty minutes. Give the order! We leave within the hour!"

"But, sir," Tamas heard someone say, "the city!"

"I don't give a pit about the city. Deliv can enter the war with Adro for all I care. He's here, you fool! He's here!"

"Nikslaus," Tamas whispered.

Tamas watched as messengers scrambled out the front mansion drive, going out to give Nikslaus's orders.

"Well, Demasolin," Tamas muttered, "you have your distraction."

Urgent steps sounded on the staircase in the foyer accompanied by Nikslaus's frantic orders.

Tamas looked down to find one hand already on the grip of a pistol, the other on the hilt of his sword. His fingers itched.

"He's coming," Andriya hissed from his station by the door.

"Do we wait for him here?" Vlora said.

Tamas blinked and saw the bodies of Deliv politicians hanging from the steeple of the Alvation cathedral. He saw Sabon's dead eyes gazing up at him from Charlemund's gravel drive, and the countless soldiers Tamas had lost trying to catch Nikslaus.

He saw Erika's head floating before him. Her face, frozen in horror, blond hair caked with blood, skin severed neatly at the neck. He saw Nikslaus's grin as he presented Tamas with the head of his dead wife.

Tamas poured an entire powder charge into his mouth. His body felt like it was on fire as energy coursed through him. Vlora must have seen something on his face.

"Pit," Vlora swore. "Andriya, get out of the way."

Tamas burst through the double doors of the office, drawing his pistol in one hand.

"Nikslaus!" he bellowed.

CHAPTER

43

"Citizens of Adopest," Lord Claremonte's voice boomed.

The shock of the amplified sound made Adamat's knees grow weak. "Pit," he hissed, "he has Privileged with him!" It was the only way he could be heard above the roar of the crowd like this.

"My friends," Lord Claremonte continued, "my brothers and sisters. My countrymen! I bring you greetings from the farthest corners of the world. I have come today to meet you, my fellow Adrans, and to lower myself humbly before you on gracious knee to offer myself as candidate for the post of First Minister of our fair country." At this, Claremonte lowered himself down on one knee and bowed his head. A moment passed and he rose back up, spreading his arms as if to embrace every man, woman, and child on the riverbank.

"This is a great nation! We have so much. We have the unions, the army, the Wings of Adom, the banks, and the Mountainwatch.

We have industry unparalleled in the modern world. We have the mightiest heroes that any country could hope for in the likes of Taniel Two-Shot and the late Field Marshal Tamas."

Lord Claremonte sighed and bowed his head, as if overcome with emotion. "Field Marshal Tamas died for you, my friends. He died for me. For all of us to be free of the Kez tyranny. He had such incredible vision and stride, and I will not let it die with him!"

The crowd was utterly silent now. Adamat heard someone drop a coin, and he cursed himself for waiting with bated breath for Claremonte's next words.

"For what this country needs now is hope. And for that, I have brought with me nine thousand of Brudania's finest soldiers to throw in with the Adran army and push back the Kez aggressors." He threw his hand back toward the line of Trading Company ships waiting in the river. "I have brought cannon, and rifles, and supplies. I have brought food, and money. I bring treasures from the four corners of the world, all of which will be put toward the war effort against the Kez."

"I do this freely. I ask no thanks, nor hold back any of my wealth on reservation. I only ask that you consider me a worthy candidate for the coming election."

Adamat noticed that other longboats were being lowered now. These ones were filled with Brudanian soldiers, and they were free once they hit the water and began rowing toward the riverbank. Claremonte's own longboat had drawn anchor and was slowly drifting closer to the amphitheater.

"My countrymen," Claremonte continued in the silence that followed, "this country needs change. This is a forward-thinking nation! A place of intellectual and industrial prowess. In my ministerial duties, I will continue to support that change and push us forward into the coming century. We will forget the old ways. The superstitions. The foolishness.

"Gods—what have they done for you?" He shook his head.

"Nothing. These rumors you've heard about Kresimir and Adom returning? They are true! But know this; we will not tolerate them. They have no place in this world of ours, and I mean to show them that.

"We may be mortal, but we are fierce and we are proud, and even the gods will tremble at this mighty nation of Adro.

"It starts today, my friends. Our new world."

The final word seemed barely a whisper, but Adamat felt his heart hammering in his chest. Something was happening. What was Claremonte about to do? What could he possibly be...? Adamat brought the looking glass in his hands, hitherto forgotten, back to his eye and focused on Claremonte.

Claremonte turned to a woman at his shoulder. The woman raised her hands to reveal white gloves covered in crimson runes—a Privileged.

Adamat read the inaudible words on Claremonte's lips: "Bring it down."

Sorcery cut through the clear sky, eliciting a gasp of terror from the assembled crowds. White lightning, like knives flashing, cut through the air above the amphitheater and smashed into the Kresim Cathedral. Dust billowed in great clouds above the immense building as invisible blades sliced clean through the stone façade.

An invisible fist smashed into the dome of the cathedral, and all at once the building collapsed in on itself. People ran from the falling stonework, screaming in terror, but the destruction was contained by sorcery, and to Adamat's eyes it looked as if no one was harmed.

When the dust had settled, Adamat turned his eyes back on Claremonte. Once again the man stepped to the prow of the boat to address the crowd. He raised his arms.

"This is only the beginning, my brothers and sisters. This world. We will take it back!"

*   *   *

Tamas's first bullet would have taken Nikslaus through the eye if a Warden hadn't flung the Privileged aside. The bullet slammed into the Warden's shoulder, making him jerk. The twisted creature drew his sword and bounded up the stairs toward Tamas.

Tamas drew his sword and charged the Warden. The creature bellowed a challenge, and Tamas answered with a silent snarl. Their swords clashed loudly once, twice, and then Tamas was inside the Warden's guard. He grabbed the Warden by the neck, feeling the strength of the powder coursing through him, and tossed it off the hallway balcony to the foyer below.

Nikslaus had rolled down the stairs and picked himself off the marble floors. One of his gloves had come off—Tamas paused at that. No, the whole hand had come off.

He had been wearing false hands. A ruse to fool his own soldiers into thinking he could still do sorcery? Perhaps. Tamas didn't care as he flew down the stairs three at a time.

Nikslaus fled toward the front door, gesturing wildly at Tamas and screaming at his men, "Kill him!"

The air was already bitter with the scent of black powder. Tamas felt a surge of energy, and an explosion tore through the Kez soldiers as Vlora ignited their powder.

Soldiers came at him with swords drawn. Nikslaus was smart enough to keep some of his soldiers without powder, it seemed. Tamas caught a thrust with the tip of his sword, flipping it to the side and ramming his own sword into the soldier's chest. He kept moving forward. Nikslaus backed away from him, face painted with terror.

A knife spun past Tamas's face and clattered against the marble banister behind him. He spun toward its owner, a Warden, and grunted as the creature hit him with the force of a charging bull.

Tamas felt himself lifted into the air and then slammed into the banister. It cracked from the force of the blow, sending him and the Warden tumbling over the edge of the stairs and a short drop to the floor.

He felt the creature's fingers close on his throat. Tamas grasped it by the wrist and slammed his other palm into the Warden's elbow. The creature's arm snapped, bending ninety degrees the wrong way. Tamas grabbed the Warden by the lapels and kicked, flipping it off of him.

By the time Tamas had gotten back to his feet, the room was filled with soldiers. Most of them were dead or dying, shot by a mage or blown to bits by their own powder horns, but there were still enough of the Kez to get in the way.

Tamas spotted Nikslaus as he fled down a side hallway.

"Pit!" Tamas swore. He lurched to his feet only to fall again. The Warden with the broken arm had grabbed Tamas's leg. It swung a knife at Tamas.

Tamas jerked his leg out of the Warden's grip, and its knife slammed into the marble floor. The beast surged forward, and Tamas deflected the knife with the guard of his sword. He pummeled the Warden's face with his hilt, then danced back out of range of another knife thrust.

The creature got to its feet.

And came crashing down again as Andriya leapt from the upstairs hallway and landed behind it, bayonet ramming through its skull and brain.

"Well," Andriya said, running toward the Kez infantry, "go kill the duke!"

Tamas dashed toward the hallway where Nikslaus had disappeared. It was a long hall, perhaps a hundred yards into another wing of the manor. Tamas opened his third eye, fighting off the dizziness, and searched for signs of Wardens or the Privileged.

A soldier leapt out of a side room with a shout. Tamas closed his third eye, reeling back as he felt a sword slice cleanly along the side of his stomach. He fended off another thrust and drew his second pistol, firing from the hip. The shot took the Kez soldier in the chest. The man lurched forward, then tried to step back. A look of surprise crossed his face as he fell to the ground.

Tamas left him where he was and sprinted along the hallway. The pain of his bad leg throbbed like the beat of a drum and the cut along his side stung in the open air. He slowed as he rounded the corner at the end of the hallway, only to find another hall leading off a hundred paces long.

No sign of Nikslaus.

"Sir!" Vlora came up beside him, breathing hard.

"He came this way," he said.

She nodded and trotted out ahead of him.

Vlora was about fifteen paces ahead of him when a Warden burst out of the cover of a doorway and slammed into her. His momentum took them both across the hallway and out of sight, into another room.

"Vlora!" Tamas ran forward, only to stop when a voice called out.

"No closer." Nikslaus. The voice came from just inside the doorway where Vlora and the Warden had disappeared.

"I'm coming to kill you," Tamas said.

"Not if you want this one alive."

Tamas looked down. Both pistols were spent. He might be able to angle a bullet around the corner. No. He *knew* he could.

"Vlora?" Tamas called out.

No answer.

"If she's dead," Tamas said, "I've no reason to stop myself from coming around this corner."

Tamas heard a deep, angry grunt, and then Vlora's voice. "I'm all right, sir."

"For now," Nikslaus said, "but if she bites my Warden again, I'll let him snap her neck. I'm using her as a shield, Tamas. If you angle a bullet around that wall, it'll hit her."

Tamas sheathed his sword and drew a pistol. He reloaded quickly, steadily, and then shoved it in his belt so he could reload the other.

"How is your leg?" Nikslaus called. "I'm surprised you can put that much weight on it."

"It was healed by a god. It feels fantastic. How are your hands? Did Kresimir grow them back for you?"

Tamas was satisfied to hear a low curse.

"Surrender, Tamas, or I kill the girl."

"Kill her," Tamas said. "I don't care."

"I think you do. I recognize this one. Vlora. I never told you that was one of my little schemes, did I? Having her seduced." Tamas heard another low grunt—the Warden—and then Nikslaus's laugh. "You probably thought it was the nobility. Well, that's what the fop thought, too."

"She betrayed Taniel," Tamas said. "Like I said: kill her."

Nikslaus clicked his tongue disapprovingly. "Oh, Tamas. I know everything about you. I know your hopes and your fears. I know your favorites. She's always been one of your favorites. Did you think about bedding her after Taniel canceled the wedding? I know you did. So suddenly available. How that must have tempted you."

Tamas opened his third eye and stepped away from the wall. He could see Nikslaus's bright glow in the Else through the wall. It was several dozen paces back from the corner. Closer, he could see the dull glow of the Warden and the barely perceptible glow that Vlora gave off in the Else. The Warden was using Vlora as a shield. Tamas would likely hit Vlora if he tried to angle a bullet around the corner.

"Throw your pistol down, Tamas, and I'll let her live," Nikslaus said.

"Why should I trust you?"

"You've no choice. The courtyard is filling up with soldiers. I don't care how many mages you brought, you're outnumbered and outmatched. You throw down your weapons and come out, and I give my word that this girl lives."

"Why so magnanimous?" Tamas said. He drew his second pistol. He aimed one at the glow of the Privileged and one at that of the Warden.

"Not sure what's come over me," Nikslaus said. "Maybe it's the prospect of your head on a pike!" His voice rose to a shout. "Think of it, Tamas. Only a couple months ago, it was me trapped inside a manor, while your soldiers filed into the courtyard. What a reversal of fortunes! Maybe I'll cut off your hands before I kill you."

Tamas examined the walls. Marble over limestone, most likely. To pierce it, he'd have to put half a horn's worth of powder behind a bullet, and concentrate energy around the bullet to keep it from fragmenting. One, he could do. Not two.

"I wouldn't take the time," Tamas said. He lowered the pistol aimed at Nikslaus and uncocked the hammer. He set it on the floor and slid it out into the middle of the hall where the Warden could see it.

"I'm unarmed. Now let her go," Tamas said.

"When I see you on your knees!" Nikslaus screamed.

Tamas focused on the smudge of color in the Else that was the Warden. He concentrated on his bullet, and set the barrel of his other pistol against the wall and pulled the trigger.

He dropped the pistol as soon as he'd pulled the trigger and leapt and rolled into the hallway, snatching up the other pistol and coming up into a crouch. The pistol kicked back in his hand as he touched the powder with his mind.

Both shots had hit the Warden. The first, through the wall, had gone low, cutting through the creature's neck. The second took it between the eyes, just over Vlora's shoulder. The Warden collapsed backward, Vlora still in its grip.

Tamas caught sight of Nikslaus running across the room behind the Warden.

Tamas gently wrested Vlora from the dead Warden's grip. The

creature had been holding a knife to her throat. She had a cut there, leaking crimson, but Tamas could not tell how deep.

"Vlora. Vlora!"

Her eyes were slightly glazed, her face panicked. There was a shard of marble embedded in her cheek. Tamas pulled it out, brushing her hair out of the way with one hand.

She shook her head suddenly, as if coming out of a dream. "I'm alive," she said. "I'm alive. I'm fine." She seemed to be speaking more to herself than him.

Tamas removed a handkerchief from his pocket and pressed it to her throat. She could still speak, so the cut wasn't too deep. "Keep pressure on it."

"Go," Vlora said. "Go after him."

Tamas took off his greatcoat and wadded it into a ball. He lifted Vlora's head and put it underneath. "Andriya! Pit, where is he? Andriya!"

Leone appeared suddenly, her bayoneted rifle held at the ready. She set her rifle on the ground and squatted beside Vlora.

"Stay with her," Tamas said. "Vidalslav makes the cleanest stitches. When the fighting dies down, make sure she sees Vlora first."

Tamas retrieved his other pistol and checked the room. Nikslaus had fled through a side door. He caught sight of the Privileged running across the lawn, heading for the front gate.

"Sir," Leone said, "we've taken the house, but the courtyard is filled with soldiers."

Tamas dropped a bullet down the barrel of one of his pistols and rammed cotton batting down to keep it stable. "I don't care," he said. "I have a man to kill."

Taniel sagged against the rough-hewn wood of the beam from which he hung, what little strength he had sapped from his struggles.

He'd tried to loosen his bonds. No amount of wiggling would get him out of them. What else could he do? He looked down. No use anyway, he supposed. Kez guards stood at the foot of the beam at the bottom of a fifty-foot drop. Could he survive that far of a fall? Would he land, only to have the Kez finish off his broken body?

How would Tamas have gotten out of this? The old bastard may have been mean, but he was clever, too.

Julene had watched him struggle for all of an hour. She seemed amused by it, if anything, and the madness in her eyes seemed to come and go.

"Why did he do this to you?" Taniel asked.

Julene gave that choking laugh again. "I ask myself that every day."

There'd be no help from her, Taniel decided. She was clearly as mad as the god who put her there. He looked up at the hook from which he hung, and then toward the Adran camp. Even at this distance, without a powder trance, he could tell that the General Staff was gathering. Equal commotion was going through the Kez camp. Both sides were preparing for a parlay.

Was that when Kresimir planned to kill them all?

"Kresimir didn't want to come back," Julene said.

Taniel turned his head sharply toward her. The madness was gone from her, and her eyes were suddenly lucid.

"He wouldn't have, if I hadn't summoned him like I did," she went on. "He doesn't care that Tamas killed Manhouch. The fate of the mortals of this world don't concern him. I was so wrong." Julene coughed, then swallowed hard, her broken face somehow twisting to look more bitter. "If I live another twenty thousand years, I could not possibly make a mistake again like I did by summoning Kresimir." Her whole body shuddered, and she threw back her head, moaning in agony.

Taniel turned away. He couldn't look at that. Cruelty for the sake of cruelty. Gods, it seemed, were capable of pettiness just as much as the next man.

Taniel scanned the Adran camp, looking for familiar faces. It was too far to make out individuals.

By now Ka-poel would know what had happened to him.

If she was still alive.

Taniel flexed his arms and pulled against his rope. He lifted a few inches, and then fell back. His struggling all morning had exhausted him.

"What are you doing, powder mage?" Julene said.

"Trying to get away." He pulled himself up again. He gained an inch. Maybe two.

"You can't. You fall from here and you'll break your legs."

"Maybe I can shimmy down."

Julene rasped out a laugh. "They'll just put you back up."

Taniel spotted a movement in the Kez camp. It wasn't significant, and he knew not what drew his eye in that direction. He willed himself to see farther.

A small figure was winding its way through the soldiers. A hooded shape—it could have been a child. But Taniel knew that build. He knew how to read the sway of the walk, from long familiarity.

Ka-poel. What was she doing here? She had to get out, to leave the camp before she was caught!

No one paid her any mind. The soldiers were preparing for something big. She was a few hundred yards away, just working her way through the camp in no particular hurry.

Taniel flexed again. He lifted himself up until his face nearly touched the hook. Every fiber of his body trembled from the effort, his bruised flesh crying out in pain.

"What do you plan to do, powder mage?" Julene's voice was steady. The rasp was gone. A glance in her direction showed her staring intently at him.

Taniel let himself drop, gasping at the effort. "I'm going to kill Kresimir."

Ka-poel was getting closer. What did she plan on doing when she got to him? Her sorcery couldn't get him off this beam.

In the distance, in the no-man's-land between the armies, Taniel saw a lone figure head out from the Adran camp. Tall and fat, wearing a white apron. Mihali.

It only took a moment of searching before Taniel found Kresimir standing at the head of the Kez lines. The god had changed his bloody clothes for clean ones and still wore his mask. He, too, began heading toward the middle of the field.

Taniel lifted himself up until he reached the hook. Inch by inch, he felt with his fingers. His struggles *had* loosened his bonds. Perhaps not enough to slip out of them, but...

Taniel grasped the hook with both hands and placed his feet flat against the beam. He pressed with his legs, working his toes against the wood like the feet of a clamp. Firmly braced on the beam, he pushed up, willing even more strength from his already burning thighs. Just a couple inches was all he needed...

And he was there! He worked his bonds along the curve of the hook until suddenly the rope was free. A wave of giddiness swept over him, nearly making him fall. He was free of the hook! He could drop from this height anytime he wanted.

He looked down and his stomach lurched. That didn't seem like such a good idea.

Grasping the hook, he turned himself around so that he was facing the beam.

"You're a stubborn bastard," Julene said.

Taniel didn't answer her. Slowly, he began working his way down the rough-hewn beam. He dug his fingernails and the toes of his boots into the wood as if he were scaling a cliff face. Every muscle protested in agony. There was no way he could scrape his fingernails the entire way down.

He worked down the first few feet and stopped, gasping for breath.

"Can you really do it?" Julene asked. "Kill Kresimir?"

Taniel worked his way down another foot.

"It's the savage, isn't it? By pit, her sorcery is potent. She might be able to kill him."

Taniel remained silent. Another foot. He could do it.

He looked down. There were four guards stationed around the base of the beam. None of them noticed his descent. He'd have to get near enough to the ground to drop on one of them, and then fight the other three—his hands still bound. Ka-poel would be there by now. She could . . .

She entered his line of vision suddenly, approaching one of the guards at a quick pace. The guard straightened and said something, holding out a hand. Her small fist darted out, slamming into his throat. The guard fell to his knees, gurgling blood.

Another foot. Taniel's heart thundered in his ears. He had to keep moving.

"Make me a promise," Julene said.

"Faster, faster, I have to go faster," Taniel whispered to himself.

"Promise you'll kill me. Shoot me in the head with one of those bullets you used to blind Kresimir. I won't survive that. Not in my weakened state. Consider it an act of vengeance, if you like."

Taniel looked down. Ka-poel was grappling with another guard. A third grabbed her by the shoulders.

"Promise me, Taniel."

Taniel was struck by the pleading in her voice. He stopped just long enough to look at her. "I promise," he said.

Julene gave a shrill laugh.

Below, the three guards had forced Ka-poel to the ground. Taniel took a deep breath and closed his eyes.

Then he let himself fall.

CHAPTER
44

Tamas followed Nikslaus through a side door of the mansion and out onto the lawn. The ground was soaked, rain coming down in thick sheets. Even though it was only half past six in the afternoon, the sky was darkening. A grandfather of a storm was blowing in.

The Privileged was just rounding the corner to the front of the mansion as Tamas came out the door. He set off in pursuit.

He reached the corner of the building and stopped. A quick glance showed fifty, maybe sixty soldiers in the courtyard. They hid behind carriages and sculptures, exchanging fire with the powder mages inside.

Nikslaus leapt onto the running board of a carriage, hooking one arm through a handstrap. Tamas could hear him yelling between the volleys of musket fire:

"Go!" Nikslaus pounded on the roof of the carriage with one

stub and ducked inside. The carriage took off down the short drive and turned into the street.

A bullet took a chip out of the masonry just above Tamas's head. He flinched away. They'd spotted him.

Tamas examined the soldiers. Too many. Even at his best. Most of his powder was gone, used in that shot through the limestone. He checked the garden wall about fifty paces away. Too tall.

Tamas heard a commotion around the corner and risked a glance.

The powder horn of a Kez soldier suddenly exploded, ripping the man in half. Another followed, and then another. Men began to throw their muskets, horns, and charges away to avoid being killed. It had to be Vlora. Only she had the range igniting powder to kill men all the way by the gates. She must have gotten to a window, or had someone directing her. It was dangerously stupid to ignite powder blind, both for yourself and for your allies.

The front doors of the manor suddenly burst open. Andriya flew through them. He held a bayoneted rifle in both hands and was screaming at the top of his lungs. His eyes were wild, his hat gone, his greatcoat billowing around him. He leapt on the closest Kez soldier, skewering the man mercilessly.

It was the best Tamas was going to get for cover.

He set off at a sprint across the lawn, cutting behind the Kez soldiers. Most ignored him, their eyes all on Andriya.

Tamas neared the gate. A soldier turned toward Tamas, desperately trying to fix the bayonet to the end of his musket. Tamas sprinted toward the soldier, put his foot on a rock near the driveway, and launched himself in the air. He cracked the man in the chin with one boot and was past him and through the gate.

There were more soldiers in the street. Tamas realized he was alone in the midst of twenty or more Kez infantry.

He ignited all the powder nearby. He used his mind to warp the blast away from him, but he'd never been as good at that as some, and the shock wave knocked him off his feet.

Tamas crawled to his knees, then to his feet. He tried to shake the dizziness. The ache of his leg suddenly pushed through his powder trance, making him stumble as he searched for Nikslaus's carriage.

The ground was littered with bodies. Nearly every one of the soldiers had been killed outright. Only a few moaned in agony, clutching at missing limbs. Gore and blood filled the street. The sight of it—the smell of powder and blood—made him retch.

There, at the end of the street. Nikslaus's carriage was heading down the main thoroughfare of the city toward the mountains, disappearing into the deluge. Tamas could see the driver frantically whipping his horses. Civilians leapt out of the way as the carriage surged forward.

Tamas tried to run. He lurched sideways, catching himself with one hand on the lip of an overflowing rain barrel. He pushed back to standing and kept on, moving slower, trying to get his head to stop pounding. He felt something dribble down his cheek and touched his face. There was blood there. It felt like it was coming from his ears.

He couldn't stop now. The carriage was getting farther and farther away. Before too long it would break out of the city and head up into the mountains. Nikslaus would get away again.

Tamas crunched one of his few remaining powder charges between his teeth and forced himself to run.

The street cobbles pounded away beneath his feet. He let the powder trance take him over completely, feeling the burn of powder through his veins. Shops and houses flew by him. Tears formed in the corners of his eyes as he ran faster than a horse, his heart thumping in his ears. His hat came off, whipped away by the wind, and rain pelted his face.

The carriage reached the eastern edge of the city well ahead of him. Tamas could see the land in his mind's eye. A few hundred yards of sloped parade grounds, filled with Nikslaus's soldiers and their ill-gotten gains from looting the city, before the mountains rose steeply and the road entered a valley, where it crept gradually higher into the Charwood Pile.

There'd be thousands of Kez soldiers in that parade ground. Tamas had to kill Nikslaus before he reached the mountain. He stopped to catch his breath, and leveled his pistol at the back of the carriage. No. Not now. Too many Deliv in the streets. He needed a clean shot.

Tamas neared the edge of the city. The downpour had become a deluge. The carriage was lost to him, but he had no doubt of Nikslaus's destination. No doubt, also, that the powder in his pistol pan was wet.

A crowd began to emerge out of the rain, and the sound of shouting suddenly rose above the thrum of rain against the ground. There were men everywhere, choking the street.

It took Tamas a few moments to realize they were fighting. A brawl? No. A battle, a bloody melee. Every one of them wore the dark-blue coats of Adran infantry, but he was able to make out two sides. It appeared that every man on one side had torn off their white shirtsleeves and wrapped them around their right arms.

Tamas grabbed a man without a white band on his arm. "Kez?" he asked in Kez.

The man seemed taken off guard. "Yes," he answered in Kez.

Tamas ran the man through and shoved him off the end of his sword with one boot. He turned just in time to parry the thrust of a bayonet. It came from a soldier with a white band. The soldier was about to lunge again when he came up short. "Field Marshal!"

"Where's Colonel Olem?" Tamas asked, saying a silent prayer of thanks that his men recognized him.

"No idea, sir. He led the charge."

"The bands?" Tamas gestured to the shirtsleeve tied around the soldier's arm.

"Colonel Olem's idea, sir. Keep us all straight."

"Good."

The soldier suddenly stripped off his jacket and tore the other arm off his undershirt. "Here, sir."

Tamas let him wrap his arm. "Thank you. What are your orders?"

"Slaughter the Kez," the soldier said. He lifted his rifle and charged off with a yell.

Tamas stood, still in a little bit of shock at the melee. He'd not heard horns or drums or seen any kind of panic in the Kez soldiers that said that the Seventh and Ninth had arrived. Didn't Nikslaus have scouts? Then again, who could see anything in this rain?

Despite the ferocity of the battle, not a shot was being fired. It was too wet for that. Olem must have convinced the other generals and colonels of the need to charge straight in.

It was a commander's nightmare. Already the parade grounds had been turned into a muddy quagmire. The downpour was so thick Tamas could barely see twenty feet in front of him.

Nikslaus's carriage must have been slowed by the rain. It had to have followed the road, otherwise it would get bogged down in the mud.

Tamas set off at a trot along the cobbles.

The fighting raged all around him. The sound of screams and yells, the ring of sword on sword, rose intermittently above the pounding rain. The cobbles were slick with rain and blood.

He fought his way through, sword out in front of him, right arm raised so that his soldiers could see the dirty white band tied just below his shoulder. He shoved and stabbed, paused for only a moment to urge on infantry from the Seventh, and then moved on down the road, searching for Nikslaus.

How had the duke's carriage gotten through this melee? Had his driver shoved forward, trampling soldiers on both sides, desperate to escape Tamas's wrath? Or had the duke given him the slip, and somehow concealed the carriage from Tamas in order to escape back into the city?

Tamas caught sight of Colonel Arbor, his uniform soaked through, holding his false teeth in one hand while he used his cavalry saber to give a pit of a fight to a Kez captain. A particularly thick sheet of rain came down, concealing the colonel. Both men were gone the next time Tamas looked.

Tamas fended off a bayonet thrust and opened his third eye, fighting the dizziness that came with it. Specks of color rose out of the storm, dancing like candles in a drafty room—Knacked soldiers on both sides of the fighting.

He swept his gaze back toward the city. Nothing that way but Knacked. No Privileged. A few Wardens.

The rain fell harder. Lightning lit the darkening sky, giving Tamas a brief glimpse through the deluge and across the entire battlefield.

Men struggled in the mire of the parade field, boots sliding and squelching. They were a sea of blue uniforms, drenched and muddy. Tamas wondered if the strips of white were even helping them tell friend from foe. He guessed that thousands would die this night to the swords of their own comrades.

Lightning flashed again, and Tamas saw something forty or fifty paces ahead, just off the road. A crash of thunder followed immediately. He felt his whole chest shake from the sound. His third eye had shown him a fire among the wreckage—not of flame but of light in the Else that betrayed the presence of a Privileged.

What he'd seen a moment before resolved itself into the wreckage of a carriage as Tamas drew closer.

It looked like the driver had swerved, one wheel going off the cobbles and into the soft, wet mud. The carriage had tipped over and slid down an embankment, ending top-down in two feet of water at the bottom of a ditch, wheels still spinning.

Infantry fought around the carriage as if they didn't notice it was there, despite the fresh skid marks in the mud and the driver frantically trying to cut loose six crazed horses.

Tamas slid down the embankment some fifteen paces away,

watching the carriage warily. No sign of Nikslaus. Tamas's third eye told him the Privileged was still within. No Wardens, either. Was this an accident? Or a trap?

Tamas approached, one hand on the muddy bank to keep his balance, the other holding one of his pistols. The powder in the pan might be wet, but the residue in the muzzle would still be dry and he could light it with a thought. One shot. That's all he had.

That's all he needed.

Tamas wrenched the door off the carriage and stooped to look inside. Nikslaus lay in the rising water of the ditch, his back against one side of the carriage. Tamas snagged the Privileged's coat with one hand and pulled him through the door, out of the water, and up onto the bank.

"I'm going to watch you die," Tamas shouted above the rain. He rammed his pistol into his belt and grasped Nikslaus's coat by the collar. He'd do it with his own hands. For Erika. For Sabon. For all the powder mages who'd died in the duke's grasp.

Tamas blinked the rain out of his eyes as he lifted Nikslaus up in front of him. Once more, to look his enemy in the eye.

Something was wrong.

Nikslaus's head lolled at an impossible angle, eyes staring blankly toward the sky. Muddy water poured from his mouth.

The man who'd haunted Tamas's dreams for well over a decade—who'd killed his wife and his best friend and caused a war that threatened to destroy his country—had broken his neck and drowned in a ditch.

Tamas dropped the body. He opened his third eye, just to be sure. The light of the Else was gone from Nikslaus.

He took a few steps back, stumbling in the water, and fell against the opposite bank. Nikslaus had died, from an accident no less, just moments before Tamas reached him.

Tamas hammered his fists into the mud. He kicked a carriage wheel hard enough to break several spokes and bend the iron strake that held the wheel together. He slipped in the mud, falling to his knees.

He slumped forward in the same water that had just drowned Nikslaus, rain falling in his eyes. He still had his shot—for a moment, he considered putting it in his own brain. He'd lost Erika, he'd lost Sabon, he'd lost Gavril. And now he would never avenge them. He gripped his pistol, Taniel's gift. No. Not everything. He still had his son.

"Please! Please, help me!"

The call brought Tamas back. He looked down to see that Nikslaus's body was being carried away down the ditch with the force of the storm waters. A fitting end, even if Tamas hadn't brought it about himself.

He climbed the embankment in time to hear the voice again.

"Please! I've lost my knife!"

The carriage driver was struggling in the mud, kicked and shoved by frightened horses as he tried to cut them loose. It looked like he'd managed to free all but two of the panicked beasts.

The fighting continued around them. Tamas knew he needed to get back to level ground and find his officers, to bring some kind of cohesion into the melee. With Nikslaus gone, the Kez might very well break and run.

A horse screamed, and Tamas again heard the sound of the pleading driver.

Tamas climbed the wreckage of the carriage and lowered himself down just behind the driver. The man was on his knees, trying to dodge thrashing hooves as he cast about in the water for his knife.

"Here," Tamas said. He pushed the man aside and drew his sword, and with two quick strokes, the horses were free. They rolled to their feet and were off, splashing upstream through the ditch, away from the carriage. They would be impossible to catch until they calmed down, and one of them might very well break a leg in these conditions, but at least they were free.

Tamas turned to the driver. The man cowered before him, blinking in fear at the epaulets on Tamas's uniform.

"Thank you, sir," the driver said.

"Find the closest Adran officer," Tamas plucked at the white sleeve tied around his arm, "and surrender yourself. That's the only way you'll survive the night."

The driver ducked his head, the water dripping off the brim of his forage cap. "Sir, thank you, sir. The duke, is he ...?"

"He's dead."

It may have been the darkness and the rain, but it seemed that relief washed across the driver's face. "What about the powder, sir?"

"Powder?" Tamas asked. "What powder?"

The color drained from the driver's face. "The whole city. It's filled with it. The duke was going to kill all those people!"

Tamas turned toward Alvation. Black powder! That's why he sensed so much. Nikslaus must have strung it through every building, ready to be touched off at his command. That's the only way he could have leveled the city in one night.

Tamas struggled up the embankment and began to run back the way he'd come. The Wardens would probably set it off, even if it meant dying themselves. No hope that a conscientious officer would countermand Nikslaus's orders.

There'd have to be tens of thousands of pounds of powder throughout Alvation to destroy the whole city. They could have set it off and then swept through the wreckage, slaughtering the survivors. What better way to frame Adro for the attack? No one would suspect a Privileged like Nikslaus of using black powder.

Tamas would never make it in time.

The first blast was so large it shook the ground. A cloud of fire rose up over the market district as high as a four-story building and the shock wave knocked hundreds of fighting soldiers off their feet.

Tamas tripped and fell, bashing one knee on the cobbles. He was back running with a limp a moment later, eyes on the city, waiting for the next blast. The fire was gone almost as quickly as it had risen, but Tamas could see the outline of a plume of smoke and steam rising into the evening sky.

That wouldn't be all of it. He had to get back into the city and...

And what? Stop the Wardens from lighting the powder? He didn't know where they were, and the city was quite large. He could try to find the powder caches, but no doubt the Wardens would have blown them up already.

Another blast rocked the city, this time on its far side. Tamas was ready for it, and managed to keep his footing despite the rumbling of the ground.

Each one of the blasts was no doubt killing hundreds. He could suppress the blasts, or redirect the energy, but trying to contain that much powder would be like boiling water in a sealed teakettle—it would rip him apart.

Tamas entered the city, shoving his way through the melee, and spread his senses outward. There was a munitions dump on the next street, he could feel it. Enough powder to level ten city blocks.

Tamas sensed the match being touched to powder somewhere inside the munitions dump, and already it was too late to suppress the explosion. The pressure built in Tamas's mind, the explosion rocketing outward from the gunpowder.

Tamas grasped the energy, ready to redirect it. His mind reached out for the rest of the powder to see how much he'd have to stop.

A scattering of powder charges was easy. A powder horn was no problem. Even a barrel of powder, Tamas could redirect.

Fifty barrels of powder went at once.

Tamas grasped the energy and pushed it straight down beneath him. It felt like he'd attached a hundred cannons to his boots and fired them all at once. The energy coursed out, throwing up dirt, rock, and cobbles, and Tamas could see the shocked faces of the soldiers closest to him just before they were vaporized in an instant.

It was too much. He couldn't contain so much powder. His body groaned and twisted, and his skin felt ready to split.

All of this took less than a heartbeat. Tamas could feel consciousness slipping, and with it the will to control the force of the explosion.

He'd failed his wife. He'd failed his soldiers, his son, the people of Alvation and Adro.

He'd failed them all.

The world went black.

Taniel landed square on the shoulders of one of his guards. The man crumpled beneath him, absorbing some of the impact, but Taniel's legs still buckled beneath him and he rolled, howling in pain, up against the base of the beam.

The two remaining guards froze, their eyes wide, in the midst of trying to bring Ka-poel under control.

Taniel forced himself to his feet and caught the swing of a musket butt on the rope binding his hands. He lashed out with one boot, kicking in the side of a guard's knee, and then slammed his tied hands across the face of the other.

Ka-poel's hood had fallen back in the struggle. Her eyes were wide, her short red hair wild. She lifted her chin under Taniel's brief scrutiny. The moment was over, and she wicked a drop of blood off the end of her long needle and darted forward, drawing her belt knife to saw through Taniel's bonds.

"You shouldn't have come," Taniel said.

She finished cutting his bonds and thrust a powder horn into his hands. He tore the plug out with his teeth. The powder poured into his mouth, tasting sulfuric on his tongue, crunching between his teeth. He sputtered and choked, but forced himself to swallow a mouthful of black powder.

The powder trance raced through him, warming his body,

tightening his muscles. The pain of his wounds and bruises faded to the back of his mind.

Ka-poel finished dispatching the four guards with her belt knife. She stood up and sniffed, wiping the blood off.

Taniel looked around. Despite the activity in the camp, plenty of soldiers had begun to notice their fight. An officer was running toward them at the head of a squad, pointing and shouting for others.

Taniel rubbed at his wrists. He and Ka-poel were in the center of the Kez army, completely cut off and with no hope of rescue. He'd have to kill a hundred thousand men to escape this.

"Pole." He bent at the knee, fetching one of the guard's muskets, and winced. Not enough powder in the world to completely drown out the pain. "I don't think we're going to get through this."

Ka-poel surveyed the Kez army, like a general surveying her troops.

Taniel hefted the musket. It was a cheap make, nothing like the Hrusch rifle he was used to. He retrieved the bayonet from the guard's kit and fitted it into place. It would have to do. The Kez were coming—fifty, maybe more now. And any fighting would bring the notice of the rest of the army.

"Pole," he said, "I love you."

Ka-poel touched one finger to her heart, then pointed at him. She tossed her satchel on the ground in front of her. It landed with the top open, and she lifted her hand.

Her dolls began to rise out of the satchel. Taniel remembered the fight at Kresim Kurga and the power she had shown.

"It won't be enough this time, Pole."

The dolls kept coming. Ten. Fifty. A hundred. A thousand.

An impossible number rose out of the satchel and spread out evenly in the air surrounding them.

The Kez soldiers had come to a stop twenty paces away and were watching her sorcery, perplexed. A Kez captain lifted his hand. "Load!"

Taniel ignited their powder with a thought. Muskets ripped apart and powder horns exploded and the air filled with the scent of spent powder and the sound of screams.

"A powder mage!" someone yelled. The call went on through the camp as soldiers discarded their muskets and scrambled for swords and knives. More men came running—first a trickle, then in force. Taniel gripped the barrel of his musket and prepared for the fight.

It started as a small, out-of-place movement in the corner of his eye. A Kez soldier stopped in the middle of the camp and rammed his bayonet into the neck of the man beside him. The soldier seemed perplexed at what he'd just done before he suddenly turned and cracked his musket butt across the teeth of another Kez infantryman.

Another soldier suddenly held his powder horn up to his flint-lock and pulled the trigger, blowing himself and three of his companions to the pit.

Fistfights broke out, and the tide of Kez soldiers heading toward Taniel and Ka-poel began to ebb as they turned on one another.

Ka-poel stood, legs braced, eyes on her dolls as if she were examining a chessboard. Around her, the dolls were moving of their own accord. Some of them fought each other, while others tumbled and stabbed at shadows. Taniel felt a terrible fear grip him. She was controlling an entire army, thousands all at once!

An unoccupied infantryman charged Taniel.

Taniel slapped aside the thrust of a bayonet and rammed his own through the infantryman's eye.

"We should go," he said to Pole. "You can't keep them forever."

Ka-poel caught his sleeve and made the shape of a gun with one hand, pointing at her dolls.

"You want me to shoot them?"

A nod.

Taniel dropped the butt of the musket to the ground and quickly loaded it. Lifting it to his shoulder, he looked to Ka-poel for confirmation.

She made a hurrying motion with one hand.

Taniel aimed at her field of dolls and pulled the trigger.

A sound like thunder cracked out of the late-morning air, sending Kez soldiers diving for cover. A nearby soldier suddenly splattered across a tent like he'd been hit by a cannonball. Taniel could hear the cries of dismay, and someone shouted, "Artillery fire!"

Ka-poel threw her head back in a silent laugh.

"That's sadistic," Taniel said. He grabbed her by the hand. "Let's go."

They raced through the Kez camp, heading toward the eastern mountains that lined Surkov's Alley. Ka-poel's dolls kept pace with them, floating, fighting shadows. By the time they reached the edge of the Kez camp and began to climb the nearest hill, the number of dolls had diminished.

Ka-poel panted heavily as they climbed. Taniel looked behind them. No one was following, but it wouldn't be long until they did. He pulled on her arm and felt her sag to the ground, her eyes suddenly cloudy from exhaustion. Taniel swung his musket onto his shoulder and then lifted Ka-poel in his arms, continuing to run.

The hill grew steeper, and Taniel soon found himself climbing more than running. He was forced to set Ka-poel on a large rock in the scree and pause to rest, turning to look at the valley.

They weren't being chased.

The entire Kez camp was in an uproar. Brother fought brother. A weak Privileged was slinging sorcery in a panic. Wardens were trying to restore order by killing "ringleaders" in a perceived uprising among the troops—it only added to the chaos.

All because of Ka-poel's dolls.

Taniel uncorked his powder horn and poured a measure onto the back of his hand. He snorted it. The immediate danger may have passed, but the Kez could still send infantry or even riders after them. There'd be no getting away if they did. He could feel fatigue circling him, like a pack of wolves around a wounded deer.

The burning flame of his powder trance would go out soon. No amount of fuel would keep it going, and then he would be useless.

He and Ka-poel would need to walk the steepest part of the scree north for over three miles to get even with the Adran camp.

Then there was the matter of the traitor Hilanska.

Near the front line, the chaos seemed the least pronounced, and plenty of the Kez soldiers were still watching as Kresimir and Mihali spoke alone between the camps. The two gods faced each other, no more than a few feet apart. Taniel would have given a fair amount to read their lips. Neither seemed to notice or care about the confusion in the Kez camp.

Mihali reached out, resting a hand on Kresimir's shoulder.

Kresimir shrugged it off.

Mihali spread his hands in a calming gesture. Kresimir raised one hand in the air, pointing at the sky, shouting something.

Mihali kept speaking. His lips barely moved and his face was serene.

It was several minutes that Mihali spoke. Much to Taniel's surprise, Kresimir seemed to listen. The god's hand fell to his side.

Back at the camp, chaos continued. Ka-poel's floating dolls had dwindled to no more than a few dozen. She sat up, looking haggard and bruised, but a victorious smile played on her lips. Her attention seemed to be focused on the last dolls, and they were not disappearing as quickly as the earlier ones. She was fighting hard to keep those last few puppets alive.

Taniel watched the two gods. Kresimir and Mihali had edged closer to each other. Mihali was pointing to his opposite hand as if explaining something. Kresimir listened, brow furrowed.

Mihali appeared to finish his explanation.

Kresimir shook his head adamantly.

Mihali frowned. A sad smile crept onto his face and he opened his arms.

Taniel suddenly felt his heart beating faster. He lifted his musket to his shoulder and sighted down the barrel at Kresimir. Two miles. Not a hard shot for him, but the bullet was a regular ball and it would take far too long to reach Kresimir. Taniel could only provide a distraction.

Kresimir suddenly threw his arms wide. For a brief moment, he looked as if he was ready to embrace his brother.

Taniel clutched his hands to his face and stumbled back, falling to the ground as a light brighter than a thousand suns erupted from Kresimir. Taniel braced himself, waiting for a shock wave and the deafening boom of an explosion.

Neither came. The light blazed on so brightly that though Taniel covered his face, he still felt as if he was staring into the heart of the sun.

A hand touched him. He reached out, grabbing Ka-poel. What did she see? Was there anything *to* see? She had to be as blind as he was. He pulled her to him and clutched her to his chest, trying to protect her eyes from the blaze. Sweet gods, what was this sorcery?

Taniel felt the brightness begin to fade after what seemed an eternity. Fear crept through him when he opened his eyes and saw nothing. Had he been blinded?

It must have been twenty minutes before shapes began to manifest themselves in his vision. He blinked rapidly, trying to dispel pools of color, trying to grasp what he'd just seen. That blaze—so bright and intense, but without heat or sound. Not an explosion.

Taniel tried to recall his knowledge of Privileged sorcery. What had Kresimir done?

Slowly, it dawned on him.

Kresimir had opened the Else itself to the world.

Taniel's returning sight began to show him that both the Kez and Adran camps were in chaos now. It seemed that no one could see. Hundreds of thousands of men crept on their hands and knees, wailing and crying out.

In the center of the field, positioned between the two camps, Kresimir stood alone. Mihali was completely gone, not even ash where he'd once stood. Kresimir's mouth was open, his face frozen in a silent scream.

Taniel watched as Kresimir's shoulders slumped. Kresimir stared blindly for a moment at the spot where Mihali had been. Then the god dropped to his knees and wept.

Taniel sagged against the mountainside, overcome with exaustion, his body racked with the pain of his wounds. A few minutes passed in silence before he looked down at his bloody, vomit-stained shirt. There was a rushing sound in his ears, and his hands shook with sudden excitement.

"Pole," he said. "My shirt is soaked with Kresimir's blood."

Adamat couldn't take his eyes off Lord Claremonte as he finished his speech. He'd worked the crowd perfectly. There weren't cheers or shouts—no, not even Claremonte would have expected that.

There were grumbles. Murmurs of discontent. Someone near Adamat told the woman next to him that Claremonte had a point. A rising sense of indignation washed through the assembled masses, and Adamat knew that Claremonte had convinced them. Maybe not all of them. Maybe not now. But the few screams of protest when Claremonte's Privileged destroyed the Kresim Cathedral had been stifled quickly.

All up and down the Ad, Brudanian soldiers pushed their longboats up onto the riverbank and disembarked. At quick glance they seemed to be working in teams of about fifteen, each one accompanied by a Privileged. They carried bayoneted muskets and barrels of black powder, and Adamat saw the first team reach a church on the other side of the Ad and begin pushing people away.

They were preparing it for demolition.

If Adamat wasn't so horrified he'd be impressed. Claremonte

had arrived with reinforcements and supplies, given a brilliant speech for his ministerial candidacy, and now he was setting about destroying the religious buildings of Adro. He'd taken the horror of the people—the fear of the Brudanians invading the capital—and turned it on its head. Everyone would be so relieved that Claremonte was not pillaging the city that he could do just about anything he wanted.

Adamat wasn't a religious man by any stretch, but he wanted to rush to the nearest church and stop the soldiers from destroying it. These were historical icons, some of them close to a thousand years old! He had the feeling that any move to stop the soldiers would see him killed.

Less than forty paces away, Claremonte's longboat was pushed onto the bank. Ricard was already hurrying toward it, his assistants and bodyguards following cautiously. Adamat shouted at him to stop.

A sailor helped Claremonte onto the muddy ground and then up the shore and onto the street.

Adamat knew from the set of Ricard's shoulders that he was about to do something stupid.

"Fell! Grab him!"

It was too late. Ricard cocked his fist back and punched Claremonte in the nose, dropping him like a sack of potatoes.

Brudanian soldiers surged forward, and Claremonte's Privileged raised a gloved hand, fingers held together as if about to snap them. Adamat's heart leapt into his throat.

"Stop!" Claremonte climbed to his feet. He laid a calming hand on the Privileged's arm. "No need for violence," he said, holding his nose with two fingers.

"What the pit do you think you're doing?" Ricard demanded, cocking his arm back as if about to swing again.

"Doing?" Claremonte said as he tilted his head back to keep his nose from bleeding. "I'm running for First Minister of Adro. You are Ricard Tumblar, I presume?"

"Yes," Ricard said icily.

Claremonte stuck his hand out. "Lord Claremonte. It's a delight to meet you."

"That delight," Ricard said, "is not shared."

"Well, that is too bad." Claremonte let his hand drop. "I assumed we were friends!"

"Why would you assume that?"

"Because," Claremonte said, "you brought out half the city to greet me and hear my speech. That's the kind of thing friends do." Claremonte's smile had dropped on one side—only slightly, but it now came across as a leer. His eyes swept past Ricard and Fell and over the other union bosses and came to rest on Adamat. The corner of his mouth lifted back into a full smile. "Really," he said, still speaking to Ricard, "I must thank you for that. Now if you'll excuse me, I have an election to win."

Tamas felt the familiar jolt and rocking of a carriage as he fought his way back to consciousness.

It brought a panic in him. Where was he being taken? Who was driving the carriage? Where were his men?

Memory of the battle outside of Alvation, of finding Nikslaus's body, and of trying to stop the explosion of thousands of pounds of gunpowder all came back to Tamas at once.

He was on his back, and when he opened his eyes, he stared up at the roof of a stagecoach. It was light outside, so he must have been out for some time. The air was cool and thin, and that brought another wave of worry to Tamas's muddled mind. Was it winter? Had he been out for months?

His arms wouldn't move on his command. After fighting down yet more panic, he decided that yes, his arms could move but they were restrained, and it was a struggle just to shift. Had he been taken captive by the Kez?

The first face that Tamas saw was not one he expected.

It belonged to an ebony-skinned Deliv man with gray hair curled tight against his scalp. He wore a kelly-green Deliv uniform without epaulets or insignia. The man leaned over Tamas, regarding him contemplatively.

"Good. You're awake. The doctors were beginning to think you might be out indefinitely. We're almost to the summit."

Tamas closed his eyes again. Perhaps his mind was too foggy to hear correctly. Had the Deliv said "summit"?

"Who the bloody pit are you?" Tamas asked. The face seemed familiar in a long-absent way, like a painting seen above a mantelpiece or a figure from his childhood. One of Sabon's relatives? No, he didn't look a thing like Sabon.

The Deliv bowed his head. "I am Deliv."

"I said who are you, not where are you from. Bloody fool." Tamas's brain pounded inside his skull like a military parade. He flexed his fingers and tested his bonds. Wait. He didn't have any bonds. Then why couldn't he move? He lifted his head and looked down at the tight-fitting blanket wrapped around his chest.

A little wiggling and Tamas was able to pull his arms free. He pushed the blanket aside and sat up.

He was wearing his spare uniform—at least, he thought it was his spare. This one wasn't soiled from the battle outside Alvation.

The carriage came to a stop suddenly, pitching Tamas to one side. The Deliv reached out a hand to steady him. Tamas waved him off.

"What do you mean, 'summit'?" he asked.

The door to the carriage opened to reveal Olem standing outside. He snapped to attention and his face split into a grin at the sight of Tamas.

"Sir! Glad to see you awake. How is your head?"

Tamas felt a wave of relief. He was still in the hands of his own men, it seemed, and Olem was still armed. He cast a glance toward the Deliv and stepped out of the carriage.

"Feels like I was thrown off the top of Sablethorn and landed on my face," Tamas said.

He looked to either side and noted they were in the mountains. Well, that explained "the summit."

"Are we past the Alvation Mountainwatch?"

"We've passed the first Mountainwatch post, sir." Olem pointed up the path. "The main Alvation Mountainwatch fortress is up ahead. We'll spend the night there before resuming the march."

Tamas felt emotions flow over him like the surf on a windy day. His legs were already weak, and news that he was already on Adran soil nearly made him fall. He pushed away Olem's offered hand and began to walk up the path. He thought through the calculations in his head. This time of year the pass would be quite clear and likely dry. They could descend back onto the Adran plains and head toward Surkov's Alley. They'd be back defending the country in a week and a half of hard march.

"Sir, you should continue to rest."

"I can walk fine," Tamas said, though his legs had more than a little wobble to them and his head was dizzy. Up ahead, the Alvation Mountainwatch fortress looked tall and imposing. The doors had been thrown open, and Mountainwatchers were cheering at the soldiers marching up the pass. "The fresh air will do me good. Now report. How long have I been out?"

"Two days, sir."

"The battle?"

"It went..."—Olem hesitated—"well enough."

"Our losses?"

Olem plucked a cigarette from his the curl of his jacket cuff and stuck it in his mouth without lighting it. "We have less than two thousand men in fighting condition left between the Seventh and the Ninth."

"That's it?" Tamas came to a stop and turned to Olem. He looked back down the path and noted that their baggage train led far beyond his sight. Where had that come from? They'd not had a baggage train in their march north.

"Gavril?"

"Recovered by Demasolin."

Tamas felt relief wash over him. "My powder mages?"

"Vidaslav took a bayonet to the stomach. We don't know if he'll survive. Leone was killed defending Vlora from a Warden."

"And Vlora?" Tamas felt his heart stop.

"She's wounded, but alive."

Tamas sagged against Olem. It was several moments before he regained his composure and stepped away.

He noticed that the old man from the carriage was following them up the path.

"How are we going to make a dent in the Kez army in Adro with just two thousand men?" Tamas asked. He couldn't help the annoyance in his voice when he jerked his head at the old Deliv and said, "And who the pit is this?"

Olem took his cigarette out of his mouth and twirled it between his fingers. "Please excuse the field marshal," he said to the old Deliv. "He's not in his right mind."

The Deliv seemed amused by this. "I hope he gets into his right mind before we go up against the Kez." He bowed his head. "I am Deliv," he said, "but you may call me Sulem the Ninth."

Sulem the... "Oh. My lord." Tamas inclined his head, shaking off the urge to drop to one knee. His mouth had gone dry. Sulem IX, king of Deliv, and Tamas had sworn at him for being a bloody fool in the carriage. "I meant no offense. I didn't realize..."

"None taken, Field Marshal." The king raised an eyebrow and glanced toward the ground as if expecting Tamas to kneel, but did not pursue the idea further.

Tamas didn't know what to say. How much did the king know? Why was he here, marching along with Tamas and a brand-new baggage train?

"I'm sorry, my lord," Tamas said, "but I am very much out of touch. I'm not sure what has gone on in the days while I was out."

The king clasped his hands behind his back. "Colonel," he said to Olem, "do you mind if I give your report?"

"Not at all, Your Eminence."

"Shall we?" the king asked, extending his arm toward the fortress rising above them.

"Yes," Tamas said.

They continued walking up the mountain road, past the remnants of Tamas's cavalry, with Olem trailing a few feet behind.

The Deliv king said, "Let me tell you how things have come from my side, and then later you can finish your conversation with Colonel Olem. I came to Alvation expecting an Adran army, but instead found two. The day after your battle with Duke Nikslaus's troops was a little confusing, but between my generals and your Colonel Olem and Colonel Arbor, everything got sorted out." Sulem paused for a moment.

"I'm sorry for Alvation, my lord," Tamas said.

"Sorry? What for? You saved a Deliv city, Tamas. I am greatly in your debt."

"The gunpowder?"

"You and your powder mages stopped it before too much damage could be dealt. There were casualties, of course, but the city remains and with it a debt of gratitude."

"I see"—Tamas glanced over his shoulder at the baggage train—"that you've supplied us for our journey. For that, *I* am grateful."

There was a twinkle in Sulem's eye, and for the first time since the carriage, a smile crept onto the old king's face. "Supplies and more," he said.

"More?"

"Field Marshal," Sulem said, "this is the vanguard. We're coming over the mountains with fifty thousand men. There would be more if I hadn't sent the better part of my army down the Great Northern Road into Kez. You have my soldiers at your service, and I intend to see you through this war. The kind of treachery plotted by Nikslaus and Ipille does not befit a brother king." Sulem's smile disappeared, his voice gaining a dangerous edge. "You may have sent Manhouch to the guillotine, and I do not approve, but Ipille made an attack upon my people."

Fifty thousand Deliv troops! *That*, Tamas knew, could send the Kez reeling. Tamas felt his heart soar. This would turn the tide of the war. Adro had more than just a chance now, they had an ally.

For the first time in weeks his step was light. He neared the Alvation Mountainwatch feeling as if a great weight had been lifted off his shoulders.

There was a clamor on the walls of the Mountainwatch fortress, and a horseman suddenly burst through the gate at a reckless speed. The messenger saw Tamas and sawed at the reins, bringing his mount to a stop in a spray of gravel. The man leapt from horseback.

"Sir," he said. His cheeks were red, frost-burned from navigating the cold heights at great speeds, and his hand trembled as he saluted.

"Breathe, soldier," Tamas said.

"Sir," the messenger gasped, "we have word from one of our posts on the eastern side of the mountains. Adopest, sir. It's burning."

EPILOGUE

Privileged Borbador stood on the front step of a medium-sized house in the Adran suburbs and wondered when the last time was that he'd asked someone for help. It wasn't something most Privileged were accustomed to doing. They either did everything themselves or they gave orders.

An explosion rocked the evening air, causing Bo to flinch. Another church. Those Brudanian bastards had been demolishing religious buildings all over the city. They'd dragged priests out into the street and beat them to death in public, and the Adran people had just stood by and watched it all happen. They were too shell-shocked by the war, too relieved that the Brudanians hadn't sacked the city, to do anything to stop it.

Some had even joined in.

Bo didn't like the Kresim Church very much, but he hated the idea of standing by and watching while a foreign army destroyed the cultural icons of the city. He'd been in the crowd, watching while they tore down the Kresim Cathedral. He'd listened to Claremonte's speech and seen the Trading Company army come onshore, unopposed by people who should have been defending their city.

It made Bo nervous for the Trading Company Privileged to be in the city. He'd spent every day since their arrival going to great lengths to avoid them. At best, they'd try to press him into service, thinking he had no allegiances left to Adro. At worse, they'd see him as a loose end and do their best to kill him.

Bo might have thrown his all at them the day they arrived, sinking several of the ships—maybe even killing Claremonte—before being put down by the Brudanian Privileged. But he was finished with other people's crusades. He had his own problems to worry about now.

A friend and brother to save.

The sound of children's laughter reached him from inside the house. It almost made him pause. Almost.

Bo rapped on the door. The laughter stopped.

"Stay here, children," a nervous voice commanded. Floorboards creaked as someone came down the front hall of the house. Bo's third eye told him it was the very Knacked he was coming to see. He could sense someone peering through the eyehole at him, and then a deadbolt was turned. The door opened a crack.

"Privileged Borbador," Adamat said.

Bo bowed his head. "Inspector Adamat."

Adamat's eyes searched the street, slightly wild, as if looking for a trap. "To what do I owe the pleasure? I didn't think I'd ever see you again."

"I brought gifts," Bo said, indicating the paper-wrapped packages beneath his arms. "May I come in?"

Adamat scanned the street once more. Conflict raged across his face. He was a nervous man these days, it seemed. Bo could relate.

And nobody wanted to invite a Privileged into their home.

"Love," a woman's voice came, "who is it?"

"Privileged Borbador."

The door opened the rest of the way and Bo saw Faye standing in the hallway. She looked somewhat better than that day in Vetas's manor. She'd gotten some sleep, and though Bo guessed from the red in the corner of her eyes that she'd been crying recently, she hid it well.

"Privileged," Faye said, "please come in."

Bo brought his bundle of packages inside with him and deposited them in the living room. "Call me Bo," he said. "I brought gifts for your family."

"You shouldn't have," Faye said, giving him a gracious smile.

Adamat looked less pleased with the idea. There was a wariness in his eyes. He didn't trust Bo.

Bo couldn't exactly blame him for that.

"Did you feel it?" Bo asked.

Adamat seemed taken aback. "Feel what?"

"It would have been an unexplained shock," Bo said. "Like being alone in a room and a cold glass of water thrown in your face."

Adamat slowly shook his head. "I don't know what you mean."

Strange, Bo thought, that Knacked couldn't sense it when a god died. Mihali—Adom reborn—had been murdered six days ago. It wasn't the same as when Taniel had shot Kresimir in the eye, though. This had felt more...permanent.

"Nothing," Bo said. "No need to worry yourselves over it."

"We were just having dinner," Faye said, giving her husband a warning look. "Would you join us?"

"Thank you, but no. I was hoping to talk to your husband alone."

Adamat cleared his throat. "Faye can hear anything I would," he said.

Bo could tell at a glance that Faye wasn't going to leave the room. So much for divide and conquer. He wondered if he should have brought Nila and Jakob inside with him. Bo had asked them to wait in the carriage, but now he thought their presence might have helped put Adamat at ease.

He still wasn't sure what he was going to do with that girl. She was a Privileged, it seemed. A Privileged who didn't need gloves. Bo didn't think that she understood the gravity of what she really was. No Privileged in all the Nine could touch the Else without gloves. Not even the Predeii.

Only the so-called gods could do that.

"I need your help," Bo said.

"I'm not for hire," Adamat said, glancing at his wife. "My family has gone through greater trials the last few months than any family ought. I will not leave them for anything."

Faye narrowed her eyes at Bo, her gracious welcome suddenly gone. To Bo it felt as if the warmth had been sucked out of the room.

"Two things," Bo said, holding up his hands. He'd left his gloves off for this. The last thing he needed was for Adamat to think he was trying to threaten him. "First, I need you, Faye, to watch over Jakob Eldaminse for a time."

"The boy's alive?" Faye asked.

"Second," Bo added, "I need Adamat to help me rescue my best friend—my only friend. I have evidence that condemns General Ket and her sister of selling army property for their own profit. I need you, Sergeant Oldrich, and Oldrich's men to come with me to arrest General Ket and get Taniel Two-Shot released."

This whole thing made Bo nervous. He'd not heard a word from the front since finding out that Taniel was being court-martialed. Taniel could be in prison, he could have been hanged. Bo cursed himself for not acting fast enough on this, but he'd had to find evidence before he could do anything about it. He should have left for the front as soon as he'd found evidence of Ket's involvement a week ago, but he'd had to gather more evidence than just one dead noble's records.

"Arresting a member of the General Staff during wartime?" Adamat scoffed. "That's suicide. No. I won't do it. As I said, I have a family to care for and protect. I am not for hire."

"Please," Faye said, her jaw stiff, "we'd like to get back to dinner with our children now."

Bo ignored them. He hated himself, sometimes, for the things he had to do. For the killing, the lying and stealing. For having to manipulate people. "In exchange for your help, Adamat, I will give you one favor from myself."

"What could I possibly..."

"One favor!" Bo said, holding up a finger. "Anything you want from the last living member of the Adran royal cabal."

Faye frowned. Bo could see her mind working behind her eyes.

"No," Adamat said. "I don't think—"

"Love," Faye said, tugging on Adamat's arm.

Bo took a deep breath. "One favor," he said again. "Anything you want. Even if it means I have to slaughter my way through Kez to find your missing son."

There would be protestations. Arguments. They would try several more excuses, but Bo could see in their eyes that he had them.

ACKNOWLEDGMENTS

Thanks to my fantastic agent, Caitlin Blasdell, for her editorial advice and her willingness to talk it out when I was having problems with the book—and of course for selling the book in the first place. To my editor, Devi Pillai, who had the patience and faith to let me work through the book at my own pace and kept pushing out the deadline so I could be truly happy with the final product.

My wife, Michele, was great during the whole process. She is always my first brainstormer and editor, and nothing gets to either Caitlin or Devi without Michele's grudging approval.

Thanks to my parents, who have always been incredibly supportive of my writing and were no exception during the writing of this book. My dad was the first "fan" to give his stamp of approval on this book, reading most of the final draft in a single afternoon.

Thanks to Isaac Stewart, who did the maps and interior art for *Promise of Blood*. He not only did a fantastic job on yet another map for *The Crimson Campaign* but updated the old ones to better fit the narrative.

Thanks to all the awesome folks at Orbit for their support with Book One and Book Two: Susan Barnes, Lauren Panepinto, Alex Lencicki, Laura Fitzgerald, Ellen Wright, and everyone else. These books wouldn't be the success they are without all their editing, artistic, and marketing wizardry.

Thanks to Ethan Kinney, who forced me to think about things from a different perspective due to all his damn questions about the powder mage universe.

Of course, thanks to all of my friends and family who supported me along the way, especially Sunny Morton for listening to me chatter about the process and gave great advice to a newly published author.

extras

about the author

Brian McClellan is an avid reader of fantasy and graduate of Orson Scott Card's Literary Bookcamp. When he is not writing, he loves baking, making jam from fruit grown in northeast Ohio, and playing video games. He currently lives in Cleveland, Ohio with his wife. Find out more about Brian McClellan at www.brianmcclellan.com.

Find out more about Brian McClellan and other Orbit authors by registering for the free monthly newsletter at www.orbitbooks.net.

if you enjoyed
THE CRIMSON CAMPAIGN

look out for

BLOOD SONG

book one of Raven's Shadow

by

Anthony Ryan

VERNIERS' ACCOUNT

He had many names. Although yet to reach his thirtieth year, history had seen fit to bestow upon him titles aplenty: Sword of the Realm to the mad king who sent him to plague us, the Young Hawk to the men who followed him through the trials of war, Darkblade to his Cumbraelin enemies and, as I was to learn much later, Beral Shak Ur to the enigmatic tribes of the Great Northern Forest – the Shadow of the Raven.

But my people knew him by only one name and it was this that sang in my head continually the morning they brought him to the docks: *Hope Killer*. Soon you will die and I will see it. *Hope Killer*.

Although he was certainly taller than most men, I was surprised to find that, contrary to the tales I had heard, he was no giant, and whilst his features were strong they could hardly be called handsome. His frame was muscular but not possessed of the massive thews described so vividly by the storytellers. The only aspect of his appearance to match his legend was his eyes: black as jet and piercing as a hawk's. They said his eyes could strip a man's soul bare, that no secret could be hidden if he met your gaze. I had never believed it but seeing him now, I could see why others would.

The prisoner was accompanied by a full company of the Imperial Guard, riding in close escort, lances ready, hard eyes scanning the watching crowd for trouble. The crowd, however, were silent. They stopped to stare at him as he rode through, but there were no shouts, no insults or missiles hurled. I recalled that they knew this man, for a brief time he had ruled their city and commanded a foreign army within its walls, yet I saw no hate in their faces, no desire for vengeance. Mostly they seemed curious. Why was he here? Why was he alive at all?

The company reined in on the wharf, the prisoner dismounting to be led to the waiting vessel. I put my notes away and rose from my resting place atop a spice barrel, nodding at the captain. 'Honour to you, sir.'

The captain, a veteran Guards officer with a pale scar running along his jawline and the ebony skin of the southern Empire, returned the nod with practised formality. 'Lord Verniers.'

'I trust you had an untroubled journey?'

The captain shrugged. 'A few threats here and there. Had to crack a few heads in Jesseria, the locals wanted to hang the Hope Killer's carcass from their temple spire.'

I bridled at the disloyalty. The Emperor's Edict had been read in all towns through which the prisoner would travel, its meaning plain: no harm will come to the Hope Killer. 'The Emperor will hear of it,' I said.

'As you wish, but it was a small matter.' He turned to the prisoner. 'Lord Verniers, I present the Imperial prisoner Vaelin Al Sorna.'

I nodded formally to the tall man, the name a steady refrain in my head. Hope Killer, Hope Killer . . . 'Honour to you, sir,' I forced the greeting out.

His black eyes met mine for a second, piercing, enquiring. For a moment I wondered if the more outlandish stories were true, if there was magic in the gaze of this savage. Could he truly strip the truth from a man's soul? Since the war, stories had abounded of the Hope Killer's mysterious powers. He could talk to animals, command the Nameless and shape the weather to his will. His steel was tempered with the blood of fallen enemies and would never break in battle. And worst of all, he and his people worshipped the dead, communing with the shades of their forebears to conjure forth all manner of foulness. I gave little credence to such folly, reasoning that if the Northmen's magics were so powerful, how had they contrived to suffer such a crushing defeat at our hands?

'My lord.' Vaelin Al Sorna's voice was harsh and thickly accented, his Alpiran had been learned in a dungeon and his tones were no doubt coarsened by years of shouting above the clash of weapons and screams of the fallen to win victory in a hundred battles, one of which had cost me my closest friend and the future of this Empire.

I turned to the captain. 'Why is he shackled? The Emperor ordered he be treated with respect.'

'The people didn't like seeing him riding unfettered,' the captain explained. 'The prisoner suggested we shackle him to avoid trouble.' He moved to Al Sorna and unlocked the restraints. The big man massaged his wrists with scarred hands.

'My lord!' A shout from the crowd. I turned to see a portly man in a

*white robe hurrying towards us, face wet with unaccustomed exertion.
'A moment, please!'*

The captain's hand inched closer to his sabre but Al Sorna was unconcerned, smiling as the portly man approached. 'Governor Aruan.'

*The portly man halted, wiping sweat from his face with a lace scarf.
In his left hand he carried a long bundle wrapped in cloth. He nodded
at the captain and myself but addressed himself to the prisoner. 'My lord.
I never thought to see you again. Are you well?'*

'I am, Governor. And you?'

*The portly man spread his right hand, lace scarf dangling from his
thumb, jewelled rings on every finger. 'Governor no longer. Merely a
poor merchant these days. Trade is not what it was, but we make our
way.'*

*'Lord Verniers.' Vaelin Al Sorna gestured at me. 'This is Holus Nester
Aruan, former Governor of the City of Linesh.'*

'Honoured Sir.' Aruan greeted me with a short bow.

*'Honoured Sir,' I replied formally. So this was the man from whom
the Hope Killer had seized the city. Aruan's failure to take his own life
in dishonour had been widely remarked upon in the aftermath of the
war but the Emperor (Gods preserve him in his wisdom and mercy) had
granted clemency in light of the extraordinary circumstances of the Hope
Killer's occupation. Clemency, however, had not extended to a continuance of his Governorship.*

*Aruan turned back to Al Sorna. 'It pleases me to find you well. I
wrote to the Emperor begging mercy.'*

'I know, your letter was read at my trial.'

*I knew from the trial records that Aruan's letter, written at no small
risk to his life, had formed part of the evidence describing curiously
uncharacteristic acts of generosity and mercy by the Hope Killer during
the war. The Emperor had listened patiently to it all before ruling that
the prisoner was on trial for his crimes, not his virtues.*

'Your daughter is well?' the prisoner asked Aruan.

'Very, she weds this summer. A feckless son of a shipbuilder, but what can a poor father do? Thanks to you, at least she is alive to break my heart.'

'I am glad. About the wedding, not your broken heart. I can offer no gift except my best wishes.'

'Actually, my lord, I come with a gift of my own.'

Aruan lifted the long, cloth-covered bundle in both hands, presenting it to the Hope Killer with a strangely grave expression. 'I hear you will have need of this again soon.'

There was a definite hesitation in the Northman's demeanour before he reached out to take the bundle, undoing the ties with his scarred hands. The cloth came away to reveal a sword of unfamiliar design, the scabbard-clad blade was a yard or so in the length and straight, unlike the curved sabres favoured by Alpiran soldiery. A single tine arched around the hilt to form a guard and the only ornamentation to the weapon was a plain steel pommel. The hilt and the scabbard bore many small nicks and scratches that spoke of years of hard use. This was no ceremonial weapon and I realised with a sickening rush that it was his sword. The sword he had carried to our shores. The sword that made him the Hope Killer.

'You kept that?' I sputtered at Aruan, appalled.

The portly man's expression grew cold as he turned to me. 'My honour demanded no less, my lord.'

'My thanks,' Al Sorna said, before any further outrage could spill from my lips. He hefted the sword and I saw the Guard Captain stiffen as Al Sorna drew the blade an inch or so from the scabbard, testing the edge with his thumb. 'Still sharp.'

'It's been well cared for. Oiled and sharpened regularly. I also have another small token.' Aruan extended his hand. In his palm sat a single ruby, a well-cut stone of medium weight, no doubt one of the more valued gems in the family collection. I knew the story behind Aruan's gratitude, but his evident regard for this savage and the sickening presence of the sword still irked me greatly.

Al Sorna seemed at a loss, shaking his head. 'Governor, I cannot . . .'

I moved closer, speaking softly. 'He does you a greater honour than you deserve, Northman. Refusing will insult him and dishonour you.'

He flicked his black eyes over me briefly before smiling at Aruan, 'I cannot refuse such generosity.' He took the gem. 'I'll keep it always.'

'I hope not,' Aruan responded with a laugh. 'A man only keeps a jewel when he has no need to sell it.'

'You there!' A voice came from the vessel moored a short distance along the quay, a sizeable Meldenean galley, the number of oars and the width of the hull showing it to be a freighter rather than one of their fabled warships. A stocky man with an extensive black beard, marked as the captain by the red scarf on his head, was waving from the bow. 'Bring the Hope Killer aboard, you Alpiran dogs!' he shouted with customary Meldenean civility. 'Any more dithering and we'll miss the tide.'

'Our passage to the Islands awaits,' I told the prisoner, gathering my possessions. 'We'd best avoid the ire of our captain.'

'So it's true then,' Aruan said. 'You go to the Islands to fight for the lady?' I found myself disliking the tone in his voice, it sounded uncomfortably like awe.

'It's true.' He clasped hands briefly with Aruan and nodded at the captain of his guard before turning to me. 'My lord. Shall we?'

'You may be one of the first in line to lick your Emperor's feet, scribbler' – the ship's captain stabbed a finger into my chest – 'but this ship is my kingdom. You berth here or you can spend the voyage roped to the mainmast.'

He had shown us to our quarters, a curtained-off section of the hold near the prow of the ship. The hold stank of brine, bilge water and the intermingled odour of the cargo, a sickly, cloying mélange of fruit, dried fish and the myriad spices for which the Empire was famous. It was all I could do to keep from gagging.

'I am Lord Verniers Alishe Someren, Imperial Chronicler, First of the Learned and honoured servant of the Emperor,' I responded, the handkerchief over my mouth muffling my words somewhat. 'I am emissary to the Ship Lords and official escort to the Imperial prisoner. You will treat me with respect, pirate, or I'll have twenty guardsmen aboard in a trice to flog you in front of your crew.'

The captain leaned closer; incredibly his breath smelt worse than the hold. 'Then I'll have twenty-one bodies to feed to the orcas when we leave the harbour, scribbler.'

Al Sorna prodded one of the bedrolls on the deck with his foot and glanced around briefly. 'This'll do. We'll need food and water.'

I bristled. 'You seriously suggest we sleep in this rat-hole? It's disgusting.'

'You should try a dungeon. Plenty of rats there too.' He turned to the captain. 'The water barrel is on the foredeck?'

The captain ran a stubby finger through the mass of his beard, contemplating the tall man, no doubt wondering if he was being mocked and calculating if he could kill him if he had to. They have a saying on the northern Alpiran coast: turn your back on a cobra but never a Meldenean. 'So you're the one who's going to cross swords with the Shield? They're offering twenty to one against you in Ildera. Think I should risk a copper on you? The Shield is the keenest blade in the Islands, can slice a fly in half with a sabre.'

'Such renown does him credit.' Vaelin Al Sorna smiled. 'The water barrel?'

'It's there. You can have one gourd a day each, no more. My crew won't go short for the likes of you two. You can get food from the galley, if you don't mind eating with scum like us.'

'No doubt I've eaten with worse. If you need an extra man at the oars, I am at your disposal.'

'Rowed before have you?'

'Once.'

The captain grunted, 'We'll manage.' He turned to go, muttering over his shoulder, 'We sail within the hour, stay out of the way until we clear the harbour.'

'Island savage!' I fumed, unpacking my belongings, laying out my quills and ink. I checked there were no rats lurking under my bedroll before sitting down to compose a letter to the Emperor. I intended to let him know the full extent of this insult. 'He'll find no berth in an Alpiran harbour again, mark you.'

Vaelin Al Sorna sat down, resting his back against the hull. 'You speak my language?' he asked, slipping into the Northern tongue.

'I study languages,' I replied in kind. 'I can speak the seven major tongues of the Empire fluently and communicate in five more.'

'Impressive. Do you know the Seordah language?'

I looked up from my parchment. 'Seordah?'

'The Seordah Sil of the Great Northern Forest. You've heard of them?'

'My knowledge of northern savages is far from comprehensive. As yet I see little reason to complete it.'

'For a learned man you seem happy with your ignorance.'

'I feel I speak for my entire nation when I say I wish we had all remained in ignorance of you.'

He tilted his head, studying me. 'That's hate in your voice.'

I ignored him, my quill moving rapidly over the parchment, setting out the formal opening for Imperial correspondence.

'You knew him, didn't you?' Vaelin Al Sorna went on.

My quill stopped. I refused to meet his eye.

'You knew the Hope.'

I put my quill aside and rose. Suddenly the stench of the hold and the proximity of this savage were unbearable. 'Yes, I knew him,' I grated. 'I knew him to be the best of us. I knew he would be the greatest Emperor this land has ever seen. But that's not the reason for my hate, Northman. I hate you because I knew the Hope as my friend, and you killed him.'

I stalked away, climbing the steps to the main deck, wishing for the first time in my life that I could be a warrior, that my arms were thick with muscle and my heart hard as stone, that I could wield a sword and take bloody vengeance. But such things were beyond me. My body was trim but not strong, my wits quick but not ruthless. I was no warrior. So there would be no vengeance for me. All I could do for my friend was witness the death of his killer and write the formal end to his story for the pleasure of my Emperor and the eternal truth of our archive.

I stayed on the deck for hours, leaning on the rail, watching the green-tinged waters of the north Alpiran coast deepen into the blue of the inner Erinean Sea as the ship's bosun beat the drum for the oarsmen and our journey began. Once clear of the coast the captain ordered the mainsail unfurled and our speed increased, the sharp prow of the vessel cutting through the gentle swell, the figurehead, a traditional Meldenean carving of the winged serpent, one of their innumerable sea gods, dipping its many-toothed head amidst a haze of spume. The oarsmen rowed for two hours before the bosun called a rest and they shipped oars, trooping off to their meal. The day watch stayed on deck, running the rigging and undertaking the never-ending chores of ship life. A few favoured me with a customary glare or two, but none attempted to converse, a mercy for which I was grateful.

We were several leagues from the harbour when they came into view, black fins knifing through the swell, heralded by a cheerful shout from the crow's nest. 'Orcas!'

I couldn't tell how many there were, they moved too fast and too fluidly through the sea, occasionally breaking the surface to spout a cloud of steam before diving below. It was only when they came closer that I fully realised their size, over twenty feet from nose to tail. I had seen dolphins before in the southern seas, silvery, playful creatures that could be taught simple tricks. These were different, their size and the dark, flickering shadows they traced through the water seemed ominous to me, threatening shades of nature's indifferent cruelty. My shipmates clearly felt differently, yelling greetings from the rigging as if hailing old friends. Even the captain's habitual scowl seemed to have softened somewhat.

One of the orcas broke the surface in a spectacular display of foam, twisting in midair before crashing into the sea with a boom that shook the ship. The Meldeneans roared their appreciation. Oh Seliesen, I thought. The poem you would have written to honour such a sight.

'They think of them as sacred.' I turned to find that the Hope Killer had joined me at the rail. 'They say when a Meldenean dies at sea the orcas will carry his spirit to the endless ocean beyond the edge of the world.'

'Superstition,' I sniffed.

'Your people have their gods, do they not?'

'My people do, I do not. Gods are a myth, a comforting story for children.'

'Such words would make you welcome in my homeland.'

'We are not in your homeland, Northman. Nor would I ever wish to be.'

Another orca rose from the sea, rising fully ten feet into the air before plunging back down. 'It's strange,' Al Sorna mused. 'When our ships came across this sea the orcas ignored them and made only for the Meldeneans. Perhaps they share the same belief.'

'Perhaps,' I said. 'Or perhaps they appreciate a free meal.' I nodded at the prow, where the captain was throwing salmon into the sea, the orcas swooping on them faster than I could follow.

'Why are you here, Lord Verniers?' Al Sorna asked. 'Why did the Emperor send you? You're no gaoler.'

'The Emperor graciously consented to my request to witness your upcoming duel. And to accompany the Lady Emeren home of course.'

'You came to see me die.'

'I came to write an account of this event for the Imperial Archive. I am the Imperial Chronicler after all.'

'So they told me. Gerish, my gaoler, was a great admirer of your history of the war with my people, considered it the finest work in Alpiran literature. He knew a lot for a man who spends his life in a dungeon. He would sit outside my cell for hours reading out page after page, especially the battles, he liked those.'

'Accurate research is the key to the historian's art.'

'Then it's a pity you got it so wrong.'

Once again I found myself wishing for a warrior's strength. 'Wrong?'

'Very.'

'I see. Perhaps if you work your savage's brain, you could tell me which sections were so very wrong.'

'Oh, you got the small things right, mostly. Except you said my command was the Legion of the Wolf. In fact it was the Thirty-fifth Regiment of Foot, known amongst the Realm Guard as the Wolfrunners.'

'I'll be sure to rush out a revised edition on my return to the capital,' I said dryly.

He closed his eyes, remembering. '"King Janus's invasion of the northern coast was but the first step in pursuit of his greater ambition, the annexation of the entire Empire."'

It was a verbatim recitation. I was impressed by his memory, but was damned if I'd say so. 'A simple statement of fact. You came here to steal the Empire. Janus was a madman to think such a scheme could succeed.'

Al Sorna shook his head. 'We came for the northern coastal ports. Janus wanted the trade routes through the Erinean. And he was no madman. He was old and desperate, but not mad.'

I was surprised at the sympathy evident in his voice; Janus was the great betrayer after all, it was part of the Hope Killer's legend. 'And how do you know the man's mind so well?'

'He told me.'

'Told you?' I laughed. 'I wrote a thousand letters of enquiry to every ambassador and Realm official I could think of. The few who bothered to reply all agreed on one thing: Janus never confided his plans to anyone, not even his family.'

'And yet you claim he wanted to conquer your whole Empire.'

'A reasonable deduction based on the available evidence.'

'Reasonable, maybe, but wrong. Janus had a king's heart, hard and cold when he needed it to be. But he wasn't greedy and he was no dreamer. He knew the Realm could never muster the men and treasure needed to conquer your Empire. We came for the ports. He said it was the only way we could secure our future.'

'Why would he confide such intelligence to you?'

'We had . . . an arrangement. He told me many things he would tell no other. Some of his commands required an explanation before I would obey them. But sometimes I think he just needed to talk to someone. Even kings get lonely.'

I felt a curious sense of seduction; the Northman knew I hungered for the information he could give me. My respect for him grew, as did my dislike. He was using me, he wanted me to write the story he had to tell. Quite why I had no idea. I knew it was something to do with Janus and the duel he would fight in the Islands. Perhaps he needed to unburden himself before his end, leave a legacy of truth so he would be known to history as more than just the Hope Killer. A final attempt to redeem both his spirit and that of his dead king.

I let the silence string out, watching the orcas until they had eaten their fill of free fish and departed to the east. Finally, as the sun began to dip towards the horizon and the shadows grew long, I said, 'So tell me.'

Enter the monthly
Orbit sweepstakes at
www.orbitloot.com

With a different prize every month,
from advance copies of books by
your favourite authors to exclusive
merchandise packs,
**we think you'll find something
you love.**

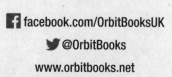

LETHAL WHITE

ROBERT
GALBRAITH

sphere

SPHERE

First published in Great Britain in 2018 by Sphere

1 3 5 7 9 10 8 6 4 2

A CIP catalogue record for this book
is available from the British Library.

Hardback ISBN 978-0-7515-7285-8
Trade paperback ISBN 978-0-7515-7286-5

Typeset in Bembo by M Rules
Printed and bound in Great Britain by
Clays Ltd, Elcograf S.p.A.

Papers used by Sphere are from well-managed forests
and other responsible sources.

MIX
Paper from
responsible sources
FSC® C104740

Sphere
An imprint of
Little, Brown Book Group
Carmelite House
50 Victoria Embankment
London EC4Y 0DZ

An Hachette UK Company
www.hachette.co.uk

www.littlebrown.co.uk

To Di and Roger,

and in memory

of the lovely white Spike

PROLOGUE

Happiness, dear Rebecca, means first and foremost the calm, joyous sense of innocence.

Henrik Ibsen, *Rosmersholm*

If only the swans would swim side by side on the dark green lake, this picture might turn out to be the crowning achievement of the wedding photographer's career.

He was loath to change the couple's position, because the soft light beneath the canopy of trees was turning the bride, with her loose red-gold curls, into a pre-Raphaelite angel and emphasising the chiselled cheekbones of her husband. He couldn't remember when he had last been commissioned to photograph so handsome a couple. There was no need for tactful tricks with the new Mr and Mrs Matthew Cunliffe, no need to angle the lady so that rolls of back fat were hidden (she was, if anything, fractionally too slender, but that would photograph well), no need to suggest the groom 'try one with your mouth closed', because Mr Cunliffe's teeth were straight and white. The only thing that needed concealing, and it could be retouched out of the final pictures, was the ugly scar running down the bride's forearm: purple and livid, with the puncture marks of stitches still visible.

She had been wearing a rubber and stockinette brace when the photographer arrived at her parents' house that morning. It had given him quite a start when she had removed it for the photographs. He had even wondered whether she had made a botched attempt to kill herself before the wedding, because he had seen it all. You did, after twenty years in the game.

1

'I was assaulted,' Mrs Cunliffe – or Robin Ellacott, as she had been two hours ago – had said. The photographer was a squeamish man. He had fought off the mental image of steel slicing into that soft, pale flesh. Thankfully, the ugly mark was now hidden in the shadow cast by Mrs Cunliffe's bouquet of creamy roses.

The swans, the damned swans. If both would clear out of the background it wouldn't matter, but one of them was repeatedly diving, its fluffy pyramid of a backside jutting out of the middle of the lake like a feathered iceberg, its contortions ruffling the surface of the water so that its digital removal would be far more complicated than young Mr Cunliffe, who had already suggested this remedy, realised. The swan's mate, meanwhile, continued to lurk over by the bank: graceful, serene and determinedly out of shot.

'Have you got it?' asked the bride, her impatience palpable.

'You look gorgeous, flower,' said the groom's father, Geoffrey, from behind the photographer. He sounded tipsy already. The couple's parents, best man and bridesmaids were all watching from the shade of nearby trees. The smallest bridesmaid, a toddler, had had to be restrained from throwing pebbles into the lake, and was now whining to her mother, who talked to her in a constant, irritating whisper.

'Have you got it?' Robin asked again, ignoring her father-in-law.

'Almost,' lied the photographer. 'Turn in to him a little bit more, please, Robin. That's it. Nice big smiles. Big smiles, now!'

There was a tension about the couple that could not be wholly attributed to the difficulty of getting the shot. The photographer didn't care. He wasn't a marriage counsellor. He had known couples to start screaming at each other while he read his light meter. One bride had stormed out of her own reception. He still kept, for the amusement of friends, the blurred shot from 1998 that showed a groom head-butting his best man.

Good-looking as they were, he didn't fancy the Cunliffes' chances. That long scar down the bride's arm had put him off her from the start. He found the whole thing ominous and distasteful.

'Let's leave it,' said the groom suddenly, releasing Robin. 'We've got enough, haven't we?'

'Wait, wait, the other one's coming now!' said the photographer crossly.

The moment Matthew had released Robin, the swan by the far shore had begun to paddle its way across the dark green water towards its mate.

'You'd think the buggers were doing it on purpose, eh, Linda?' said Geoffrey with a fat chuckle to the bride's mother. 'Bloody things.'

'It doesn't matter,' said Robin, pulling her long skirt up clear of her shoes, the heels of which were a little too low. 'I'm sure we've got something.'

She strode out of the copse of trees into the blazing sunlight and off across the lawn towards the seventeenth-century castle, where most of the wedding guests were already milling, drinking champagne as they admired the view of the hotel grounds.

'I think her arm's hurting her,' the bride's mother told the groom's father.

Bollocks it is, thought the photographer with a certain cold pleasure. *They rowed in the car.*

The couple had looked happy enough beneath the shower of confetti in which they had departed the church, but on arrival at the country house hotel they had worn the rigid expressions of those barely repressing their rage.

'She'll be all right. Just needs a drink,' said Geoffrey comfortably. 'Go keep her company, Matt.'

Matthew had already set off after his bride, gaining on her easily as she navigated the lawn in her stilettos. The rest of the party followed, the bridesmaids' mint-green chiffon dresses rippling in the hot breeze.

'Robin, we need to talk.'

'Go on, then.'

'Wait a minute, can't you?'

'If I wait, we'll have the family on us.'

Matthew glanced behind him. She was right.

'Robin—'

'Don't touch my arm!'

3

Her wound was throbbing in the heat. Robin wanted to find the holdall containing the sturdy rubber protective brace, but it would be somewhere out of reach in the bridal suite, wherever that was.

The crowd of guests standing in the shadow of the hotel was coming into clearer view. The women were easy to tell apart, because of their hats. Matthew's Aunt Sue wore an electric blue wagon wheel, Robin's sister-in-law, Jenny, a startling confection of yellow feathers. The male guests blurred into conformity in their dark suits. It was impossible to see from this distance whether Cormoran Strike was among them.

'Just stop, will you?' said Matthew, because they had fast outstripped the family, who were matching their pace to his toddler niece.

Robin paused.

'I was shocked to see him, that's all,' said Matthew carefully.

'I suppose you think I was expecting him to burst in halfway through the service and knock over the flowers?' asked Robin.

Matthew could have borne this response if not for the smile she was trying to suppress. He had not forgotten the joy in her face when her ex-boss had crashed into their wedding ceremony. He wondered whether he would ever be able to forgive the fact that she had said 'I do' with her eyes fastened upon the big, ugly, shambolic figure of Cormoran Strike, rather than her new husband. The entire congregation must have seen how she had beamed at him.

Their families were gaining on them again. Matthew took Robin's upper arm gently, his fingers inches above the knife wound, and walked her on. She came willingly, but he suspected that this was because she hoped she was moving closer to Strike.

'I said in the car, if you want to go back to work for him—'

'—I'm an "effing idiot",' said Robin.

The men grouped on the terrace were becoming distinguishable now, but Robin could not see Strike anywhere. He was a big man. She ought to have been able to make him out even among her brothers and uncles, who were all over six foot. Her spirits, which had soared when Strike had appeared, tumbled earthwards like rain-soaked fledglings. He must have left after the service rather than boarding a minibus to the hotel. His brief appearance had signified a gesture of goodwill, but nothing more. He had not come to rehire her, merely to congratulate her on a new life.

'Look,' said Matthew, more warmly. She knew that he, too, had scanned the crowd, found it Strike-less and drawn the same conclusion. 'All I was trying to say in the car was: it's up to you what you do, Robin. If he wanted – if he wants you back – I was just worried, for Christ's sake. Working for him wasn't exactly safe, was it?'

'No,' said Robin, with her knife wound throbbing. 'It wasn't safe.'

She turned back towards her parents and the rest of the family group, waiting for them to catch up. The sweet, ticklish smell of hot grass filled her nostrils as the sun beat down on her uncovered shoulders.

'Do you want to go to Auntie Robin?' said Matthew's sister.

Toddler Grace obligingly seized Robin's injured arm and swung on it, eliciting a yelp of pain.

'Oh, I'm so sorry, Robin – Gracie, let go—'

'Champagne!' shouted Geoffrey. He put his arm around Robin's shoulders and steered her on towards the expectant crowd.

The gents' bathroom was, as Strike would have expected of this upmarket country hotel, odour-free and spotless. He wished he could have brought a pint into the cool, quiet toilet cubicle, but that might have reinforced the impression that he was some disreputable alcoholic who had been bailed from jail to attend the wedding. Reception staff had met his assurances that he was part of the Cunliffe-Ellacott wedding party with barely veiled scepticism as it was.

Even in an uninjured state Strike tended to intimidate, given that he was large, dark, naturally surly-looking and sported a boxer's profile. Today he might have just climbed out of the ring. His nose was broken, purple and swollen to twice its usual size, both eyes were bruised and puffy, and one ear was inflamed and sticky with fresh black stitches. At least the knife wound across the palm of his hand was concealed by bandages, although his best suit was crumpled and stained from a wine spill on the last occasion he had worn it. The best you could say for his appearance was that he had managed to grab matching shoes before heading for Yorkshire.

He yawned, closed his aching eyes and rested his head momentarily against the cold partition wall. He was so tired he might easily fall asleep here, sitting on the toilet. He needed to find Robin, though, and ask her – beg her, if necessary – to forgive him for sacking her and come back to work. He had thought he read delight in her face when their eyes met in church. She had certainly beamed at him as she walked past on Matthew's arm on the way out, so he had hurried back through the graveyard to ask his friend Shanker, who was now asleep in the car park in the Mercedes he had borrowed for the journey, to follow the minibuses to the reception.

Strike had no desire to stay for a meal and speeches: he had not RSVPed the invitation he had received before sacking Robin. All he wanted was a few minutes to talk to her, but so far this had proved impossible. He had forgotten what weddings were like. As he sought Robin on the crowded terrace he had found himself the uncomfortable focus of a hundred pairs of curious eyes. Turning down champagne, which he disliked, he had retreated into the bar in search of a pint. A dark-haired young man who had a look of Robin about the mouth and forehead had followed, a gaggle of other young people trailing in his wake, all of them wearing similar expressions of barely suppressed excitement.

'You're Strike, aye?' said the young man.

The detective agreed to it.

'Martin Ellacott,' said the other. 'Robin's brother.'

'How d'you do?' said Strike, raising his bandaged hand to show that he could not shake without pain. 'Where is she, d'you know?'

'Having photos done,' said Martin. He pointed at the iPhone clutched in his other hand. 'You're on the news. You caught the Shacklewell Ripper.'

'Oh,' said Strike. 'Yeah.'

In spite of the fresh knife wounds on his palm and ear, he felt as though the violent events of twelve hours previously had happened long ago. The contrast between the sordid hideout where he had cornered the killer and this four-star hotel was so jarring that they seemed separate realities.

A woman whose turquoise fascinator was trembling in her

white-blonde hair now arrived in the bar. She, too, was holding a phone, her eyes moving rapidly upwards and downwards, checking the living Strike against what he was sure was a picture of him on her screen.

'Sorry, need a pee,' Strike had told Martin, edging away before anybody else could approach him. After talking his way past the suspicious reception staff, he had taken refuge in the bathroom.

Yawning again, he checked his watch. Robin must, surely, have finished having pictures taken by now. With a grimace of pain, because the painkillers they had given him at the hospital had long since worn off, Strike got up, unbolted the door and headed back out among the gawping strangers.

A string quartet had been set up at the end of the empty dining room. They started to play while the wedding group organised themselves into a receiving line that Robin assumed she must have agreed to at some point during the wedding preparations. She had abnegated so much responsibility for the day's arrangements that she kept receiving little surprises like this. She had forgotten, for instance, that they had agreed to have photographs taken at the hotel rather than the church. If only they had not sped away in the Daimler immediately after the service, she might have had a chance to speak to Strike and to ask him – beg him, if necessary – to take her back. But he had left without talking to her, leaving her wondering whether she had the courage, or the humility, to call him after this and plead for her job.

The room seemed dark after the brilliance of the sunlit gardens. It was wood-panelled, with brocade curtains and gilt-framed oil paintings. Scent from the flower arrangements lay heavy in the air, and glass and silverware gleamed on snow-white tablecloths. The string quartet, which had sounded loud in the echoing wooden box of a room, was soon drowned out by the sound of guests clambering up the stairs outside, crowding onto the landing, talking and laughing, already full of champagne and beer.

'Here we go, then!' roared Geoffrey, who seemed to be enjoying the day more than anybody else. 'Bring 'em on!'

If Matthew's mother had been alive, Robin doubted that Geoffrey would have felt able to give his ebullience full expression. The late Mrs Cunliffe had been full of cool side-stares and nudges, constantly checking any signs of unbridled emotion. Mrs Cunliffe's sister, Sue, was one of the first down the receiving line, bringing a fine frost with her, for she had wanted to sit at the top table and been denied that privilege.

'How are you, Robin?' she asked, pecking the air near Robin's ear. Miserable, disappointed and guilty that she was not feeling happy, Robin suddenly sensed how much this woman, her new aunt-in-law, disliked her. 'Lovely dress,' said Aunt Sue, but her eyes were already on handsome Matthew.

'I wish your mother—' she began, then, with a gasp, she buried her face in the handkerchief that she held ready in her hand.

More friends and relatives shuffled inside, beaming, kissing, shaking hands. Geoffrey kept holding up the line, bestowing bear hugs on everybody who did not actively resist.

'He came, then,' said Robin's favourite cousin, Katie. She would have been a bridesmaid had she not been hugely pregnant. Today was her due date. Robin marvelled that she could still walk. Her belly was watermelon-hard as she leaned in for a kiss.

'Who came?' asked Robin, as Katie sidestepped to hug Matthew.

'Your boss. Strike. Martin was just haranguing him down in the—'

'You're over there, I think, Katie,' said Matthew, pointing her towards a table in the middle of the room. 'You'll want to get off your feet, must be difficult in the heat, I guess?'

Robin barely registered the passage of several more guests down the line. She responded to their good wishes at random, her eyes constantly drawn to the doorway through which they were all filing. Had Katie meant that Strike was here at the hotel, after all? Had he followed her from the church? Was he about to appear? Where had he been hiding? She had searched everywhere – on the terrace, in the hallway, in the bar. Hope surged only to fail again. Perhaps Martin, famous for his lack of tact, had driven him away? Then she reminded herself that Strike was not such a feeble creature as that and hope bubbled up once more, and while her inner self performed these peregrinations of expectation and dread, it was impossible to simulate the more conventional wedding day emotions whose absence, she knew, Matthew felt and resented.

'Martin!' Robin said joyfully, as her younger brother appeared, already three pints to the bad, accompanied by his mates.

'S'pose you already knew?' said Martin, taking it for granted that she must. He was holding his mobile in his hand. He had slept at a friend's house the previous evening, so that his bedroom could be given to relatives from Down South.

'Knew what?'

'That he caught the Ripper last night.'

Martin held up the screen to show her the news story. She gasped at the sight of the Ripper's identity. The knife wound that man had inflicted was throbbing on her forearm.

'Is he still here?' asked Robin, throwing pretence to the wind. 'Strike? Did he say he was staying, Mart?'

'For Christ's sake,' muttered Matthew.

'Sorry,' said Martin, registering Matthew's irritation. 'Holding up the queue.'

He slouched off. Robin turned to look at Matthew and saw, as though in thermal image, the guilt glowing through him.

'You knew,' she said, shaking hands absently with a great aunt who had leaned in, expecting to be kissed.

'Knew what?' he snapped.

'That Strike had caught—'

But her attention was now demanded by Matthew's old university friend and workmate, Tom, and his fiancée, Sarah. She barely heard a word that Tom said, because she was constantly watching the door, where she hoped to see Strike.

'You knew,' Robin repeated, once Tom and Sarah had walked away. There was another hiatus. Geoffrey had met a cousin from Canada. 'Didn't you?'

'I heard the tail end of it on the news this morning,' muttered Matthew. His expression hardened as he looked over Robin's head towards the doorway. 'Well, here he is. You've got your wish.'

Robin turned. Strike had just ducked into the room, one eye grey and purple above his heavy stubble, one ear swollen and stitched. He raised a bandaged hand when their eyes met and attempted a rueful smile, which ended in a wince.

'Robin,' said Matthew. 'Listen, I need—'

'In a minute,' she said, with a joyfulness that had been conspicuously absent all day.

'Before you talk to him, I need to tell—'

'Matt, please, can't it wait?'

Nobody in the family wanted to detain Strike, whose injury meant that he could not shake hands. He held the bandaged one in front of him and shuffled sideways down the line. Geoffrey glared at him and even Robin's mother, who had liked him on their only previous encounter, was unable to muster a smile as he greeted her by name. Every guest in the dining room seemed to be watching.

'You didn't have to be so dramatic,' Robin said, smiling up into his swollen face when at last he was standing in front of her. He grinned back, painful though it was: the two-hundred-mile journey he had undertaken so recklessly had been worth it, after all, to see her smile at him like that. 'Bursting into church. You could have just called.'

'Yeah, sorry about knocking over the flowers,' said Strike, including the sullen Matthew in his apology. 'I did call, but—'

'I haven't had my phone on this morning,' said Robin, aware that she was holding up the queue, but past caring. 'Go round us,' she said gaily to Matthew's boss, a tall redheaded woman.

'No, I called – two days ago, was it?' said Strike.

'What?' said Robin, while Matthew had a stilted conversation with Jemima.

'A couple of times,' said Strike. 'I left a message.'

'I didn't get any calls,' said Robin, 'or a message.'

The chattering, chinking, tinkling sounds of a hundred guests and the gentle melody of the string quartet seemed suddenly muffled, as though a thick bubble of shock had pressed in upon her.

'When did – what did you – two days ago?'

Since arriving at her parents' house she had been occupied non-stop with tedious wedding chores, yet she had still managed to check her phone frequently and surreptitiously, hoping that Strike had called or texted. Alone in bed at one that morning she had

10

checked her entire call history in the vain hope that she would find a missed communication, but had found the history deleted. Having barely slept in the last couple of weeks, she had concluded that she had made an exhausted blunder, pressed the wrong button, erased it accidentally . . .

'I don't want to stay,' Strike mumbled. 'I just wanted to say I'm sorry, and ask you to come—'

'You've got to stay,' she said, reaching out and seizing his arm as though he might escape.

Her heart was thudding so fast that she felt breathless. She knew that she had lost colour as the buzzing room seemed to wobble around her.

'Please stay,' she said, still holding tight to his arm, ignoring Matthew as he bristled beside her. 'I need – I want to talk to you. Mum?' she called.

Linda stepped out of the receiving line. She seemed to have been waiting for the summons, and she didn't look happy.

'Please could you add Cormoran to a table?' said Robin. 'Maybe put him with Stephen and Jenny?'

Unsmiling, Linda led Strike away. There were a few last guests waiting to offer their congratulations. Robin could no longer muster smiles and small talk.

'Why didn't I get Cormoran's calls?' she asked Matthew, as an elderly man shuffled away towards the tables, neither welcomed nor greeted.

'I've been trying to tell you—'

'Why didn't I get the calls, Matthew?'

'Robin, can we talk about this later?'

The truth burst upon her so suddenly that she gasped.

'*You* deleted my call history,' she said, her mind leaping rapidly from deduction to deduction. 'You asked for my passcode number when I came back from the bathroom at the service station.' The last two guests took one look at the bride and groom's expressions and hurried past without demanding their greeting. 'You took my phone away. You said it was about the honeymoon. Did you listen to his message?'

'Yes,' said Matthew. 'I deleted it.'

The silence that seemed to have pressed in on her had become a high-pitched whine. She felt light-headed. Here she stood in the big white lace dress she didn't like, the dress she had had altered because the wedding had been delayed once, pinned to the spot by ceremonial obligations. On the periphery of her vision, a hundred blurred faces swayed. The guests were hungry and expectant.

Her eyes found Strike, who was standing with his back to her, waiting beside Linda while an extra place was laid at her elder brother Stephen's table. Robin imagined striding over to him and saying: 'Let's get out of here.' What would he say if she did?

Her parents had spent thousands on the day. The packed room was waiting for the bride and groom to take their seats at the top table. Paler than her wedding dress, Robin followed her new husband to their seats as the room burst into applause.

The finicky waiter seemed determined to prolong Strike's discomfort. He had no choice but to stand in full view of every table while he waited for his extra place to be laid. Linda, who was almost a foot shorter than the detective, remained at Strike's elbow while the youth made imperceptible adjustments to the dessert fork and turned the plate so that the design aligned with its neighbours'. The little Strike could see of Linda's face below the silvery hat looked angry.

'Thanks very much,' he said at long last, as the waiter stepped out of the way, but as he took hold of the back of his chair, Linda laid a light hand on his sleeve. Her gentle touch might as well have been a shackle, accompanied as it was by an aura of outraged motherhood and offended hospitality. She greatly resembled her daughter. Linda's fading hair was red-gold, too, the clear grey-blue of her eyes enhanced by her silvery hat.

'Why are you here?' she asked through clenched teeth, while waiters bustled around them, delivering starters. At least the arrival of food had distracted the other guests. Conversation broke out as people's attention turned to their long-awaited meal.

'To ask Robin to come back to work with me.'

'You sacked her. It broke her heart.'

There was much he could have said to that, but he chose not to say it out of respect for what Linda must have suffered when she had seen that eight-inch knife wound.

'Three times she's been attacked, working for you,' said Linda, her colour rising. 'Three times.'

Strike could, with truth, have told Linda that he accepted liability only for the first of those attacks. The second had happened after Robin disregarded his explicit instructions and the third as a consequence of her not only disobeying him, but endangering a murder investigation and his entire business.

'She hasn't been sleeping. I've heard her at night . . .'

Linda's eyes were over-bright. She let go of him, but whispered, 'You haven't got a daughter. You can't understand what we've been through.'

Before Strike could muster his exhausted faculties, she had marched away to the top table. He caught Robin's eye over her untouched starter. She pulled an anguished expression, as though afraid that he might walk out. He raised his eyebrows slightly and dropped, at last, into his seat.

A large shape to his left shifted ominously. Strike turned to see more eyes like Robin's, set over a pugnacious jaw and surmounted by bristling brows.

'You must be Stephen,' said Strike.

Robin's elder brother grunted, still glaring. They were both large men; packed together, Stephen's elbow grazed Strike's as he reached for his pint. The rest of the table was staring at Strike. He raised his right hand in a kind of half-hearted salute, remembered that it was bandaged only when he saw it, and felt that he was drawing even more attention to himself.

'Hi, I'm Jenny, Stephen's wife,' said the broad-shouldered brunette on Stephen's other side. 'You look as though you could use this.'

She passed an untouched pint across Stephen's plate. Strike was so grateful he could have kissed her. In deference to Stephen's scowl, he confined himself to a heartfelt 'thanks' and downed half of it in one go. Out of the corner of his eye he saw Jenny mutter something in Stephen's ear. The latter watched Strike set the pint glass down again, cleared his throat and said gruffly:

'Congratulations in order, I s'pose.'

'Why?' said Strike blankly.

Stephen's expression became a degree less fierce.

'You caught that killer.'

'Oh yeah,' said Strike, picking up his fork in his left hand and stabbing the salmon starter. Only after he had swallowed it in its entirety and noticed Jenny laughing did he realise he ought to have treated it with more respect. 'Sorry,' he muttered. 'Very hungry.'

Stephen was now contemplating him with a glimmer of approval.

'No point in it, is there?' he said, looking down at his own mousse. 'Mostly air.'

'Cormoran,' said Jenny, 'would you mind just waving at Jonathan? Robin's other brother – over there.'

Strike looked in the direction indicated. A slender youth with the same colouring as Robin waved enthusiastically from the next table. Strike gave a brief, sheepish salute.

'Want her back, then, do you?' Stephen fired at him.

'Yeah,' said Strike. 'I do.'

He half-expected an angry response, but instead Stephen heaved a long sigh.

'S'pose I've got to be glad. Never seen her happier than when she was working for you. I took the piss out of her when we were kids for saying she wanted to be a policewoman,' he added. 'Wish I hadn't,' he said, accepting a fresh pint from the waiter and managing to down an impressive amount before continuing. 'We were dicks to her, looking back, and then she ... well, she stands up for herself a bit better these days.'

Stephen's gaze wandered to the top table and Strike, who had his back to it, felt justified in stealing a look at Robin, too. She was silent, neither eating nor looking at Matthew.

'Not now, mate,' he heard Stephen say and turned to see his neighbour holding out a long thick arm to form a barrier between Strike and one of Martin's friends, who was on his feet and already bending low to ask Strike a question. The friend retreated, abashed.

'Cheers,' said Strike, finishing Jenny's pint.

'Get used to it,' said Stephen, demolishing his own mousse in a mouthful. 'You caught the Shacklewell Ripper. You're going to be famous, mate.'

People talked of things passing in a blur after a shock, but it was not like that for Robin. The room around her remained only too visible, every detail distinct: the brilliant squares of light that fell through the curtained windows, the enamel brightness of the azure sky beyond the glass, the damask tablecloths obscured by elbows and disarranged glasses, the gradually flushing cheeks of the scoffing and quaffing guests, Aunt Sue's patrician profile unsoftened by her neighbours' chat, Jenny's silly yellow hat quivering as she joked with Strike. She saw Strike. Her eyes returned so often to his back that she could have sketched with perfect accuracy the creases in his suit jacket, the dense dark curls of the back of his head, the difference in the thickness of his ears due to the knife injury to the left.

No, the shock of what she had discovered in the receiving line had not rendered her surroundings blurred. It had instead affected her perception of both sound and time. At one point, she knew that Matthew had urged her to eat, but it did not register with her until after her full plate had been removed by a solicitous waiter, because everything said to her had to permeate the thick walls that had closed in on her in the aftermath of Matthew's admission of perfidy. Within the invisible cell that separated her entirely from everyone else in the room, adrenaline thundered through her, urging her again and again to stand up and walk out.

If Strike had not arrived today, she might never have known that he wanted her back, and that she might be spared the shame, the anger, the humiliation, the hurt with which she had been racked since that awful night when he had sacked her. Matthew had sought to deny her the thing that might save her, the thing for which she had cried in the small hours of the night when everybody else was asleep: the restoration of her self-respect, of the job that had meant everything to her, of the friendship she had not known was one of the prizes of her life until it was torn away from her. Matthew had lied and kept lying. He had smiled and laughed as she dragged herself through the days before the wedding trying to pretend that she was happy that she had lost a life she had loved. Had she fooled him? Did he believe that she was truly glad her life with Strike was over? If he did, she had married a man who did not know her at all, and if he didn't . . .

The puddings were cleared away and Robin had to fake a smile for the concerned waiter who this time asked whether he could bring her something else, as this was the third course that she had left uneaten.

'I don't suppose you've got a loaded gun?' Robin asked him.

Fooled by her serious manner, he smiled, then looked confused.

'It doesn't matter,' she said. 'Never mind.'

'For Christ's sake, Robin,' Matthew said, and she knew, with a throb of fury and pleasure, that he was panicking, scared of what she would do, scared of what was going to happen next.

Coffee was arriving in sleek silver pots. Robin watched the waiters pouring, saw the little trays of petits fours placed upon the tables. She saw Sarah Shadlock in a tight turquoise sleeveless dress, hurrying across the room to the bathroom ahead of the speeches, watched heavily pregnant Katie following her in her flat shoes, swollen and tired, her enormous belly to the fore, and, again, Robin's eyes returned to Strike's back. He was scoffing petits fours and talking to Stephen. She was glad she had put him beside Stephen. She had always thought they would get on.

Then came the call for quiet, followed by rustling, fidgeting and a mass scraping of chairs as all those who had their backs to the top table dragged themselves around to watch the speakers. Robin's eyes met Strike's. She could not read his expression. He didn't look away from her until her father stood up, straightened his glasses and began to speak.

Strike was longing to lie down or, failing that, to get back into the car with Shanker, where he could at least recline the seat. He had had barely two hours' slumber in the past forty-eight, and a mixture of heavy-duty painkillers and what was now four pints was rendering him so sleepy that he kept dozing off against the hand supporting his head, jerking back awake as his temple slid off his knuckles.

He had never asked Robin what either of her parents did for a living. If Michael Ellacott alluded to his profession at any point during his speech, Strike missed it. He was a mild-looking man, almost professorial, with his horn-rimmed glasses. The children had all got his height, but only Martin had inherited his dark hair and hazel eyes.

The speech had been written, or perhaps rewritten, when Robin was jobless. Michael dwelled with patent love and appreciation on Robin's personal qualities, on her intelligence, her resilience, her generosity and her kindness. He had to stop and clear his throat when he started to speak of his pride in his only daughter, but there was a blank where her achievements ought to have been, an empty space for what she had actually done, or lived through. Of course, some of the things that Robin had survived were unfit to be spoken in this giant humidor of a room, or heard by these feathered and buttonholed guests, but the fact of her survival was, for Strike, the highest proof of those qualities and to him it seemed, sleep-befuddled though he was, that an acknowledgement ought to have been made.

Nobody else seemed to think so. He even detected a faint relief in the crowd as Michael drew to a conclusion without alluding to knives or scars, gorilla masks or balaclavas.

The time had come for the bridegroom to speak. Matthew got to his feet amid enthusiastic applause, but Robin's hands remained in her lap as she stared at the window opposite, where the sun now hung low in the cloudless sky, casting long dark shadows over the lawn.

Somewhere in the room, a bee was buzzing. Far less concerned about offending Matthew than he had been about Michael, Strike adjusted his position in his chair, folding his arms and closing his eyes. For a minute or so, he listened as Matthew told how he and Robin had known each other since childhood, but only in their sixth form had he noticed how very good-looking the little girl who had once beaten him in the egg-and-spoon race had become . . .

'Cormoran!'

He jerked awake suddenly and, judging by the wet patch on his chest, knew that he had been drooling. Blearily he looked around at Stephen, who had elbowed him.

'You were snoring,' Stephen muttered.

Before he could reply the room broke into applause again. Matthew was sitting down, unsmiling.

Surely it had to be nearly over . . . but no, Matthew's best man was getting to his feet. Now that he was awake again, Strike had become aware just how full his bladder was. He hoped to Christ this bloke would speak fast.

'Matt and I first met on the rugby pitch,' he said and a table towards the rear of the room broke into drunken cheers.

'Upstairs,' said Robin. 'Now.'

They were the first words she had spoken to her husband since they had sat down at the top table. The applause for the best man's speech had barely died away. Strike was standing, but she could tell that he was only heading for the bathroom because she saw him stop a waiter and ask directions. In any case, she knew, now, that he wanted her back, and was convinced that he would stay long enough to hear her agreement. The look they had exchanged during the starters had told her as much.

'They'll be bringing in the band in half an hour,' said Matthew. 'We're s'posed to—'

But Robin walked off towards the door, taking with her the invisible isolation cell that had kept her cold and tearless through her father's speech, through Matthew's nervous utterings, through the tedium of the familiar old anecdotes from the rugby club regurgitated by the best man. She had the vague impression that her mother tried to waylay her as she ploughed through the guests, but paid no attention. She had sat obediently through the meal and the speeches. The universe owed her an interlude of privacy and freedom.

Up the staircase she marched, her skirt held out of the way of her cheap shoes, and off along a plush carpeted corridor, unsure where she was going, with Matthew's footsteps hurrying behind her.

'Excuse me,' she said to a waistcoated teenager who was wheeling a linen basket out of a cupboard, 'where's the bridal suite?'

He looked from her to Matthew and smirked, actually smirked.

'Don't be a jerk,' said Robin coldly.

'Robin!' said Matthew, as the teenager blushed.

'That way,' said the youth hoarsely, pointing.

Robin marched on. Matthew, she knew, had the key. He had stayed at the hotel with his best man the previous evening, though not in the bridal suite.

When Matthew opened the door, she strode inside, registering the rose petals on the bed, the champagne standing in its cooler, the large envelope inscribed to Mr and Mrs Cunliffe. With relief, she saw the holdall that she had intended to take as hand luggage to their mystery honeymoon. Unzipping it, she thrust her uninjured arm inside and found the brace that she had removed for the photographs. When she had pulled it back over her aching forearm, with its barely healed wound, she wrenched the new wedding ring off her finger and slammed it down on the bedside table beside the champagne bucket.

'What are you doing?' said Matthew, sounding both scared and aggressive. 'What – you want to call it off? You don't want to be married?'

Robin stared at him. She had expected to feel release once they were alone and she could speak freely, but the enormity of what he had done mocked her attempts to express it. She read his fear of her silence in his darting eyes, his squared shoulders. Whether he was aware of it or not, he had placed himself precisely between her and the door.

'All right,' he said loudly, 'I know I should've—'

'You knew what that job meant to me. You knew.'

'I didn't want you to go back, all right?' Matthew shouted. 'You got attacked and stabbed, Robin!'

'That was my own fault!'

'He fucking sacked you!'

'Because I did something he'd told me not to do—'

'*I knew you'd fucking defend him!*' Matthew bellowed, all control gone. 'I knew if you spoke to him you'd go scurrying back like some fucking lapdog!'

'You don't get to make those decisions for me!' she yelled. 'Nobody's got the right to intercept my fucking calls and delete my messages, Matthew!'

Restraint and pretence were gone. They heard each other only

19

by accident, in brief pauses for breath, each of them howling their resentment and pain across the room like flaming spears that burned into dust before touching their target. Robin gesticulated wildly, then screeched with pain as her arm protested sharply, and Matthew pointed with self-righteous rage at the scar she would carry for ever because of her reckless stupidity in working with Strike. Nothing was achieved, nothing was excused, nothing was apologised for: the arguments that had defaced their last twelve months had all led to this conflagration, the border skirmishes that presage war. Beyond the window, afternoon dissolved rapidly into evening. Robin's head throbbed, her stomach churned, her sense of being stifled threatened to overcome her.

'You hated me working those hours – you didn't give a damn that I was happy in my job for the first time in my life, so you *lied*! You knew what it meant to me, and you *lied*! How could you delete my call history, how could you delete my voicemail—?'

She sat down suddenly in a deep, fringed chair, her head in her hands, dizzy with the force of her anger and shock on an empty stomach.

Somewhere, distantly in the carpeted hush of the hotel corridors, a door closed, a woman giggled.

'Robin,' said Matthew hoarsely.

She heard him approaching her, but she put out a hand, holding him away.

'Don't touch me.'

'Robin, I shouldn't have done it, I know that. I didn't want you hurt again.'

She barely heard him. Her anger was not only for Matthew, but also for Strike. He should have called back. He should have tried and kept trying. *If he had, I might not be here now.*

The thought scared her.

If I'd known Strike wanted me back, would I have married Matthew?

She heard the rustle of Matthew's jacket and guessed that he was checking his watch. Perhaps the guests waiting downstairs would think that they had disappeared to consummate the marriage. She could imagine Geoffrey making ribald jokes in their absence. The band must have been in place for an hour. Again she remembered how much this was all costing her parents. Again, she remembered that they had lost deposits on the wedding that had been postponed.

'All right,' she said, in a colourless voice. 'Let's go back down and dance.'

She stood up, automatically smoothing her skirt. Matthew looked suspicious.

'You're sure?'

'We've got to get through today,' she said. 'People have come a long way. Mum and Dad have paid a lot of money.'

Hoisting her skirt up again, she set off for the suite door.

'Robin!'

She turned back, expecting him to say 'I love you', expecting him to smile, to beg, to urge a truer reconciliation.

'You'd better wear this,' he said, holding out the wedding ring she had removed, his expression as cold as hers.

Strike had not been able to think of a better course of action, given that he intended to stay until he had spoken to Robin again, than continuing to drink. He had removed himself from Stephen and Jenny's willing protection, feeling that they ought to be free to enjoy the company of friends and family, and fallen back on the methods by which he usually repelled strangers' curiosity: his own intimidating size and habitually surly expression. For a while he lurked at the end of the bar, nursing a pint on his own, and then repaired to the terrace, where he had stood apart from the other smokers and contemplated the dappled evening, breathing in the sweet meadow smell beneath a coral sky. Even Martin and his friends, now full of drink themselves and smoking in a circle like teenagers, failed to muster sufficient nerve to badger him.

After a while, the guests were skilfully rounded up and ushered *en masse* back into the wood-panelled room, which had been transformed in their absence into a dance floor. Half the tables had been removed, the others shifted to the sides. A band stood ready behind amplifiers, but the bride and groom remained absent. A man whom Strike understood to be Matthew's father, sweaty, rotund and red-faced, had already made several jokes about what they might be getting up to when Strike found himself addressed by a woman in a tight turquoise dress whose feathery hair adornment tickled his nose as she closed in for a handshake.

'It's Cormoran Strike, isn't it?' she said. 'What an honour! Sarah Shadlock.'

Strike knew all about Sarah Shadlock. She had slept with Matthew at university, while he was in a long-distance relationship with Robin. Once again, Strike indicated his bandage to show why he could not shake her hand.

'Oh, you poor thing!'

A drunk, balding man who was probably younger than he looked loomed up behind Sarah.

'Tom Turvey,' he said, fixing Strike with unfocused eyes. 'Bloody good job. Well done, mate. *Bloody good job.*'

'We've wanted to meet you for ages,' said Sarah. 'We're old friends of Matt and Robin's.'

'Shacklewell Rip – Ripper,' said Tom, on a slight hiccough. 'Bloody good job.'

'*Look* at you, you poor thing,' said Sarah again, touching Strike on the bicep as she smiled up into his bruised face. '*He* didn't do that to you, did he?'

'Ev'ryone wants to know,' said Tom, grinning blearily. 'Can hardly contain their bloody selves. You should've made a speech instead of Henry.'

'Ha ha,' said Sarah. 'Last thing you'd want to do, I expect. You must have come here straight from catching – well, I don't know – *did* you?'

'Sorry,' said Strike, unsmiling, 'police have asked me not to talk about it.'

'Ladies and gentlemen,' said the harried MC, who had been caught unawares by Matthew and Robin's unobtrusive entrance into the room, 'please welcome Mr and Mrs Cunliffe!'

As the newlyweds moved unsmilingly into the middle of the dance floor, everybody but Strike began to applaud. The lead singer of the band took the microphone from the MC.

'This is a song from their past that means a lot to Matthew and Robin,' the singer announced, as Matthew slid his hand around Robin's waist and grasped her other hand.

The wedding photographer moved out of the shadows and began clicking away again, frowning a little at the reappearance of the ugly rubber brace on the bride's arm.

The first acoustic bars of 'Wherever You Will Go' by The Calling struck up. Robin and Matthew began to revolve on the spot, their faces averted from each other.

So lately, been wondering,
Who will be there to take my place
When I'm gone, you'll need love
To light the shadows on your face . . .

Strange choice for an 'our song', Strike thought . . . but as he watched he saw Matthew move closer to Robin, saw his hand tighten on her narrow waist as he bent his handsome face to whisper something in her ear.

A jolt somewhere around the solar plexus pierced the fug of exhaustion, relief and alcohol that had cushioned Strike all day long from the reality of what this wedding meant. Now, as Strike watched the newlyweds turn on the dance floor, Robin in her long white dress, with a circlet of roses in her hair, Matthew in his dark suit, his face close to his bride's cheek, Strike was forced to recognise how long, and how deeply, he had hoped that Robin would not marry. He had wanted her free, free to be what they had been together. Free, so that if circumstances changed . . . so the possibility was there . . . free, so that one day, they might find out what else they could be to each other.

Fuck this.

If she wanted to talk, she would have to call him. Setting down his empty glass on a windowsill, he turned and made his way through the other guests, who shuffled aside to let him pass, so dark was his expression.

*

23

As she turned, staring into space, Robin saw Strike leaving. The door opened. He was gone.

'Let go of me.'

'What?'

She pulled free, hoisted up her dress once more for freedom of movement, then half-walked, half-ran off the dance floor, almost careering into her father and Aunt Sue, who were waltzing sedately nearby. Matthew was left standing alone in the middle of the room as Robin fought her way through the startled onlookers towards the door that had just swung shut.

'Cormoran!'

He was already halfway down the stairs, but on hearing his name he turned back. He liked her hair in its long loose waves beneath the crown of Yorkshire roses.

'Congratulations.'

She walked down another couple of steps, fighting the lump in her throat.

'You really want me back?'

He forced a smile.

'I've just driven for bloody hours with Shanker in what I strongly suspect is a stolen car. Of course I want you back.'

She laughed, though tears sprang to her eyes.

'Shanker's here? You should have brought him in!'

'Shanker? In here? He'd have been through everyone's pockets then nicked the reception till.'

She laughed some more, but tears spilled out of her brimming eyes and bounced down her cheek.

'Where are you going to sleep?'

'In the car, while Shanker drives me home. He's going to charge me a fortune for this. Doesn't matter,' he added gruffly, as she opened her mouth. 'Worth it if you're coming back. More than worth it.'

'I want a contract this time,' said Robin, the severity of her tone belied by the expression of her eyes. 'A proper one.'

'You've got it.'

'OK, then. Well, I'll see you . . .'

When would she see him? She was supposed to be on honeymoon for two weeks.

'Let me know,' said Strike.

He turned and began to descend the stairs again.

'Cormoran!'

'What?'

She walked towards him until she stood on the step above. Their eyes were on a level now.

'I want to hear all about how you caught him and everything.'

He smiled.

'It'll keep. Couldn't have done it without you, though.'

Neither of them could tell who had made the first move, or whether they acted in unison. They were holding each other tightly before they knew what had happened, Robin's chin on Strike's shoulder, his face in her hair. He smelled of sweat, beer and surgical spirits, she, of roses and the faint perfume that he had missed when she was no longer in the office. The feel of her was both new and familiar, as though he had held her a long time ago, as though he had missed it without knowing it for years. Through the closed door upstairs the band played on:

I'll go wherever you will go
If I could make you mine . . .

As suddenly as they had reached for each other, they broke apart. Tears were rolling down Robin's face. For one moment of madness, Strike yearned to say, 'Come with me', but there are words that can never be unsaid or forgotten, and those, he knew, were some of them.

'Let me know,' he repeated. He tried to smile, but it hurt his face. With a wave of his bandaged hand, he continued down the stairs without looking back.

She watched him go, wiping the hot tears frantically from her face. If he had said 'come with me', she knew she would have gone: but then what? Gulping, wiping her nose on the back of her hand, Robin turned, hoisted up her skirts again, and climbed slowly back towards her husband.

ONE YEAR LATER

1

*I hear that he means to enlarge . . . that he is looking for a
competent assistant.*

Henrik Ibsen, *Rosmersholm*

Such is the universal desire for fame that those who achieve it accidentally or unwillingly will wait in vain for pity.

For many weeks after the capture of the Shacklewell Ripper,
Strike had feared that his greatest detective triumph might have
dealt his career a fatal blow. The smatterings of publicity his agency
had hitherto attracted seemed now like the two submersions of the
drowning man before his final descent to the depths. The business
for which he had sacrificed so much, and worked so hard, relied
largely on his ability to pass unrecognised in the streets of London,
but with the capture of a serial killer he had become lodged in the
public imagination, a sensational oddity, a jokey aside on quiz shows,
an object of curiosity all the more fascinating because he refused to
satisfy it.

Having wrung every last drop of interest out of Strike's ingenuity in catching the Ripper, the papers had exhumed Strike's family
history. They called it 'colourful', though to him it was a lumpen
internal mass that he had carried with him all his life and preferred
not to probe: the rock star father, the dead groupie mother, the
army career that ended with the loss of half his right leg. Grinning
journalists bearing chequebooks had descended on the only sibling
with whom he had shared a childhood, his half-sister, Lucy. Army
acquaintances had given off-the-cuff remarks that, shorn of what

Strike knew was rough humour, assumed the appearance of envy and disparagement. The father whom Strike had only met twice, and whose surname he did not use, released a statement through a publicist, implying a non-existent, amicable relationship that was proceeding far from prying eyes. The aftershocks of the Ripper's capture had reverberated through Strike's life for a year, and he was not sure they were spent yet.

Of course, there was an upside to becoming the best-known private detective in London. New clients had swarmed to Strike in the aftermath of the trial, so that it had become physically impossible for him and Robin to cover all the jobs themselves. Given that it was advisable for Strike to keep a low profile for a while, he had remained largely office-bound for several months while sub-contracted employees – mostly ex-police and military, many from the world of private security – took on the bulk of the work, Strike covering nights and paperwork. After a year of working on as many jobs as the enlarged agency could handle, Strike had managed to give Robin an overdue pay rise, settle the last of his outstanding debts and buy a thirteen-year-old BMW 3 series.

Lucy and his friends assumed that the presence of the car and additional employees meant that Strike had at last achieved a state of prosperous security. In fact, once he had paid the exorbitant costs of garaging the car in central London and met payroll, Strike was left with almost nothing to spend on himself and continued to live in two rooms over the office, cooking on a single-ringed hob.

The administrative demands freelance contractors made and the patchy quality of the men and women available to the agency were a constant headache. Strike had found only one man whom he had kept on semi-permanently: Andy Hutchins, a thin, saturnine ex-policeman ten years older than his new boss, who had come highly recommended by Strike's friend in the Met, Detective Inspector Eric Wardle. Hutchins had taken early retirement when he had been struck by a sudden bout of near-paralysis of his left leg, followed by a diagnosis of multiple sclerosis. When he had applied for contract work, Hutchins had warned Strike that he might not always be fit; it was, he explained, an unpredictable disease, but he had not relapsed in three years. He followed a special low-fat diet that to Strike sounded positively punitive: no red meat, no cheese, no chocolate, nothing deep-fried. Methodical and patient, Andy could be trusted to get the job done without constant supervision, which was more than could be said for any of Strike's other hires apart from Robin. It seemed incredible to him, still, that she had walked into his life as a temporary secretary to become his partner and outstanding colleague.

Whether they were still friends, though, was another question.

Two days after Robin and Matthew's wedding, when the press had driven him out of his flat, while it was still impossible to turn on the TV without hearing his own name, Strike had sought refuge, in spite of invitations from friends and his sister, in a Travelodge near Monument station. There he had attained the solitude and privacy he craved; there he had been free to sleep for hours undisturbed; and there he had downed nine cans of lager and become increasingly desirous of speaking to Robin with each empty can that he threw, with diminishing accuracy, across the room into the bin.

They had had no contact since their hug on the stairs, to which Strike's thoughts had turned repeatedly in the ensuing days. He was sure that Robin would be going through a hellish time, holed up in Masham while deciding whether to pursue a divorce or an annulment, arranging the sale of their flat while dealing with both press and family fallout. What exactly he was going to say when he reached her, Strike did not know. He only knew that he wanted to hear her voice. It was at this point, drunkenly searching his kit bag, that he discovered that in his sleep-deprived haste to leave his flat, he had not packed a recharging lead for his mobile, which was out of battery. Undeterred, he had dialled directory enquiries and succeeded, after many requests to repeat himself more clearly, in getting connected to Robin's parents' house.

Her father had answered.

'Hi, c'n'I speak t'Robinplease?'

'To Robin? I'm afraid she's on her honeymoon.'

For a muzzy moment or two, Strike had not quite comprehended what he had been told.

31

'Hello?' Michael Ellacott had said, and then, angrily, 'I suppose this is another journalist. My daughter's abroad and I would like you to stop calling my house.'

Strike had hung up, then continued to drink until he passed out.

His anger and disappointment had lingered for days and were in no way abated by his awareness that many would say that he had no claims upon his employee's private life. Robin wasn't the woman he had thought her if she could have got meekly on a plane with the man he mentally referred to as 'that twat'. Nevertheless, something close to depression weighed upon him while he sat in his Travelodge with his brand-new recharging lead and more lager, waiting for his name to disappear from the news.

Consciously seeking to distract himself from thoughts of Robin, he had ended his self-imposed isolation by accepting an invitation that he would usually have avoided: dinner with Detective Inspector Eric Wardle, Wardle's wife April and their friend Coco. Strike knew perfectly well that he was being set up. Coco had previously tried to find out through Wardle whether Strike was single.

She was a small, lithe, very pretty girl with tomato-red hair, a tattoo artist by trade and a part-time burlesque dancer. He ought to have read the danger signs. She was giggly and slightly hysterical even before they started drinking. Strike had taken her to bed in the Travelodge in the same way he had drunk nine cans of Tennent's.

Coco had taken some shaking loose in the weeks that followed. Strike did not feel good about it, but one advantage of being on the run from the press was that one-night stands found it far harder to track you down.

One year on, Strike had no idea why Robin had chosen to remain with Matthew. He supposed her feelings for her husband ran so deep that she was blind to what he really was. He was in a new relationship himself, now. It had lasted ten months, the longest since he had split up with Charlotte, who had been the only woman whom he had ever contemplated marrying.

The emotional distance between the detective partners had become a simple fact of daily existence. Strike could not fault Robin's work. She did everything she was told promptly, meticulously and with initiative and ingenuity. Nevertheless, he had noticed a pinched look that had never been there before. He thought her slightly jumpier than usual and, once or twice while parcelling out work between his partner and subcontractors, he had caught an uncharacteristic blank, unfocused expression that troubled him. He knew some of the signs of post-traumatic stress disorder and she had now survived two near-fatal attacks. In the immediate aftermath of losing half his leg in Afghanistan, he, too, had experienced dissociation, finding himself suddenly and abruptly removed from his present surroundings to those few seconds of acute foreboding and terror that had preceded the disintegration of the Viking in which he had been sitting, and of his body and military career. He had been left with a deep dislike of being driven by anybody else and, to this day, with dreams of blood and agony that sometimes woke him, bathed in sweat.

However, when he had attempted to discuss Robin's mental health in the calm, responsible tones of her employer, she had cut him off with a finality and a resentment that he suspected could be traced to the sacking. Thereafter, he had noticed her volunteering for trickier, after-dark assignments and it had been something of a headache to arrange work so that he did not appear to be trying, as in fact he was, to keep her on the safest, most mundane jobs.

They were polite, pleasant and formal with each other, talking about their private lives in the broadest brushstrokes, and then only when necessary. Robin and Matthew had just moved house and Strike had insisted that she take a full week off to do it. Robin had been resistant, but Strike had overruled her. She had taken very little leave all year, he reminded her, in a tone that brooked no argument.

On Monday, the latest of Strike's unsatisfactory subcontractors, a cocky ex-Red Cap Strike had not known while in the service, had driven his moped into the rear of a taxi he was supposed to be tailing. Strike had enjoyed sacking him. It had given him somebody on whom to vent his anger, because his landlord had also chosen this week to inform Strike that, along with nearly every other owner of office space in Denmark Street, he had sold out to a developer.

The threat of losing both office and home now loomed over the detective.

To set the seal on a particularly shitty few days, the temp he had hired to cover basic paperwork and answer the phone in Robin's absence was as irritating a woman as Strike had ever met. Denise talked nonstop in a whiny, nasal voice that carried even through the closed door of his inner office. Strike had latterly resorted to listening to music on headphones, with the result that she had had to bang on the door repeatedly and shout before he heard her.

'What?'

'I've just found this,' said Denise, brandishing a scribbled note in front of him. 'It says "clinic" ... there's a word beginning with "V" in front ... the appointment's for half an hour's time – should I have reminded you?'

Strike saw Robin's handwriting. The first word was indeed illegible.

'No,' he said. 'Just throw it away.'

Mildly hopeful that Robin was quietly seeking professional help for any mental problems she might be suffering, Strike replaced his earphones and returned to the report he was reading, but found it hard to concentrate. He therefore decided to leave early for the interview he had scheduled with a possible new subcontractor. Mainly to get away from Denise, he was meeting the man in his favourite pub.

Strike had had to avoid the Tottenham for months in the aftermath of his capture of the Shacklewell Ripper, because journalists had lain in wait for him here, word having got out that he was a regular. Even today, he glanced around suspiciously before deciding that it was safe to advance on the bar, order his usual pint of Doom Bar and retire to a corner table.

Partly because he had made an effort to give up the chips that were a staple of his diet, partly because of his workload, Strike was thinner now than he had been a year ago. The weight loss had relieved pressure on his amputated leg, so that both the effort and the relief of sitting were less noticeable. Strike took a swig of his pint, stretching his knee from force of habit and enjoying the relative ease of movement, then opened the cardboard file he had brought with him.

The notes within had been made by the idiot who had crashed his moped into the back of the taxi, and they were barely adequate. Strike couldn't afford to lose this client, but he and Hutchins were struggling to cover workload as it was. He urgently needed a new hire, and yet he wasn't entirely sure that the interview he was about to conduct was wise. He had not consulted Robin before making the bold decision to hunt down a man he had not seen for five years, and even as the door of the Tottenham opened to admit Sam Barclay, who was punctual to the minute, Strike was wondering whether he was about to make an almighty mistake.

He would have known the Glaswegian almost anywhere as an ex-squaddie, with his T-shirt under his thin V-neck jumper, his close-cropped hair, his tight jeans and over-white trainers. As Strike stood up and held out his hand, Barclay, who appeared to have rec-ognised him with similar ease, grinned and said:

'Already drinking, aye?'

'Want one?' asked Strike.

While waiting for Barclay's pint, he watched the ex-Rifleman in the mirror behind the bar. Barclay was only a little over thirty, but his hair was prematurely greying. He was otherwise exactly as Strike remembered. Heavy browed, with large round blue eyes and a strong jaw, he had the slightly beaky appearance of an affable owl. Strike had liked Barclay even while working to court-martial him.

'Still smoking?' Strike asked, once he'd handed over the beer and sat down.

'Vapin' now,' said Barclay. 'We've had a baby.'

'Congratulations,' said Strike. 'On a health kick, then?'

'Aye, somethin' like that.'

'Dealing?'

'I wasnae dealin',' said Barclay hotly, 'as you fuckin' well know. Recreational use only, pal.'

'Where are you buying it now, then?'

'Online,' said Barclay, sipping his pint. 'Easy. First time I did it, I thought, this cannae fuckin' work, can it? But then I thought, "Och, well, it's an adventure." They send it to you disguised in fag packets and that. Choose off a whole menu. Internet's a great thing.'

He laughed and said, 'So whut's this all about? Wasnae expectin' to hear from *you* any time soon.'

Strike hesitated.

'I was thinking of offering you a job.'

There was a beat as Barclay stared at him, then he threw back his head and roared with laughter.

'Fuck,' he said. 'Why didn't ye say that straight off, like?'

'Why d'you think?'

'I'm no vapin' every night,' said Barclay earnestly. 'I'm no, seriously. The wife doesnae like it.'

Strike kept his hand closed on the file, thinking.

He had been working a drugs case in Germany when he had run across Barclay. Drugs were bought and sold within the British army as in every other part of society, but the Special Investigation Branch had been called in to investigate what appeared to be a rather more professional operation than most. Barclay had been fingered as a key player and the discovery of a kilo brick of prime Moroccan hash among his effects had certainly justified an interview.

Barclay insisted that he had been stitched up and Strike, who was sitting in on his interrogation, was inclined to agree, not least because the Rifleman seemed far too intelligent not to have found a better hiding place for his hashish than the bottom of an army kit bag. On the other hand, there was ample evidence that Barclay had been using regularly, and there was more than one witness to the fact that his behaviour was becoming erratic. Strike felt that Barclay had been lined up as a convenient scapegoat, and decided to undertake a little side excavation on his own.

This threw up interesting information relating to building materials and engineering supplies that were being reordered at a thoroughly implausible rate. While it was not the first time that Strike had uncovered this kind of corruption, it so happened that the two officers in charge of these mysteriously vanishing and highly resaleable commodities were the very men so keen to secure Barclay's court martial.

Barclay was startled, during a one-to-one interview with Strike, to find the SIB sergeant suddenly interested, not in hashish, but in anomalies relating to building contracts. At first wary, and sure he would not be believed given the situation in which he found himself, Barclay finally admitted to Strike that he had not only noticed what others had failed to see, or chosen not to enquire into, but begun to tabulate and document exactly how much these officers were stealing. Unfortunately for Barclay, the officers in question had got wind of the fact that he was a little too interested in their activities, and it was shortly after this that a kilo of hashish had turned up in Barclay's effects.

When Barclay showed Strike the record he had been keeping (the notebook had been hidden a good deal more skilfully than the hashish), Strike had been impressed by the method and initiative it displayed, given that Barclay had never been trained in investigative technique. Asked why he had undertaken the investigation for which nobody was paying, and which had landed him in so much trouble, Barclay had shrugged his broad shoulders and said 'no right, is it? That's the army they're robbin'. Taxpayers' money they're fuckin' pocketin'.'

Strike had put in many more hours on the case than his colleagues felt was merited, but finally, with Strike's additional investigations into the matter to add weight, the dossier on his superiors' activities that Barclay had compiled led to their conviction. The SIB took credit for it, of course, but Strike had made sure that accusations against Barclay were quietly laid to rest.

'When ye say "work",' Barclay wondered aloud now, as the pub hummed and tinkled around them, 'ye mean detective stuff?'

Strike could see that the idea appealed.

'Yeah,' said Strike. 'What have you been doing since I last saw you?'

The answer was depressing, though not unexpected. Barclay had found it hard to get or keep a regular job in the first couple of years out of the army and had been doing a bit of painting and decorating for his brother-in-law's company.

'The wife's bringin' in most o' the money,' he said. 'She's got a good job.'

'OK,' said Strike, 'I reckon I can give you a couple of days a week for starters. You'll bill me as a freelancer. If it doesn't work out, either of us can walk away at any time. Sound fair?'

'Aye,' said Barclay, 'aye, fair enough. What are you paying, like?'

They discussed money for five minutes. Strike explained how his other employees set themselves up as private contractors and how receipts and other professional expenses should be brought into the office for reimbursement. Finally he opened the file and slid it around to show Barclay the contents.

'I need this guy followed,' he said, pointing out a photograph of a chubby youth with thick curly hair. 'Pictures of whoever he's with and what he's up to.'

'Aye, all right,' said Barclay, getting out his mobile and taking pictures of the target's photograph and address.

'He's being watched today by my other guy,' said Strike, 'but I need you outside his flat from six o'clock tomorrow morning.'

He was pleased to note that Barclay did not query the early start.

'Whut happened to that lassie, though?' Barclay enquired as he put his phone back into his pocket. 'The one who was in the papers with ye?'

'Robin?' said Strike. 'She's on holiday. Back next week.'

They parted with a handshake, Strike enjoying a moment's fleeting optimism before remembering that he would now have to return to the office, which meant proximity to Denise, with her parrot-like chatter, her habit of talking with her mouth full and her inability to remember that he detested pale, milky tea.

He had to pick his way through the ever-present roadworks at the top of Tottenham Court Road to get back to his office. Waiting until he was past the noisiest stretch, he called Robin to tell her that he had hired Barclay, but his call went straight to voicemail. Remembering that she was supposed to be at the mysterious clinic right now, he cut the call without leaving a message.

Walking on, a sudden thought occurred to him. He had assumed that the clinic related to Robin's mental health, but what if—?

The phone in his hand rang: the office number.

'Hello?'

'Mr Strike?' said Denise's terrified squawk in his ear. 'Mr Strike, could you come back quickly, please? Please – there's a gentleman – he wants to see you very urgently—'

Behind her, Strike heard a loud bang and a man shouting.

'Please come back as soon as you can!' screamed Denise.

'On my way!' Strike shouted and he broke into an ungainly run.

2

… he doesn't look the sort of man one ought to allow in here.
                                      Henrik Ibsen, *Rosmersholm*

Panting, his right knee aching, Strike used the handrail to pull himself up the last few steps of the metal staircase leading to his office. Two raised voices were reverberating through the glass door, one male, the other shrill, frightened and female. When Strike burst into the room, Denise, who was backed against the wall, gasped, 'Oh, thank God!'

Strike judged the man in the middle of the room to be in his mid-twenties. Dark hair fell in straggly wisps around a thin and dirty face that was dominated by burning, sunken eyes. His T-shirt, jeans and hoodie were all torn and filthy, the sole of one of his trainers peeling away from the leather. An unwashed animal stench hit the detective's nostrils.

That the stranger was mentally ill could be in no doubt. Every ten seconds or so, in what seemed to be an uncontrollable tic, he touched first the end of his nose, which had grown red with repeated tapping, then, with a faint hollow thud, the middle of his thin sternum, then let his hand drop to his side. Almost immediately, his hand would fly to the tip of his nose again. It was as though he had forgotten how to cross himself, or had simplified the action for speed's sake. Nose, chest, hand at his side; nose, chest, hand at his side; the mechanical movement was distressing to watch, and the more so as he seemed barely conscious that he was doing it. He was one of those ill and

40

desperate people you saw in the capital who were always some-body else's problem, like the traveller on the Tube everybody tried to avoid making eye contact with and the ranting woman on the street corner whom people crossed the street to avoid, fragments of shattered humanity who were too common to trouble the imagin-ation for long.

'You him?' said the burning-eyed man, as his hand touched nose and chest again. 'You Strike? You the detective?'

With the hand that was not constantly flying from nose to chest, he suddenly tugged at his flies. Denise whimpered, as if scared he might suddenly expose himself, and, indeed, it seemed entirely possible.

'I'm Strike, yeah,' said the detective, moving around to place him-self between the stranger and the temp. 'You OK, Denise?'

'Yes,' she whispered, still backed against the wall.

'I seen a kid killed,' said the stranger. 'Strangled.'

'OK,' said Strike, matter-of-factly. 'Why don't we go in here?'

He gestured to him that he should proceed into the inner office.

'I need a piss!' said the man, tugging at his zip.

'This way, then.'

Strike showed him the door to the toilet just outside the office. When the door had banged shut behind him, Strike returned quietly to Denise.

'What happened?'

'He wanted to see you, I said you weren't here and he got angry and started punching things!'

'Call the police,' said Strike quietly. 'Tell them we've got a very ill man here. Possibly psychotic. Wait until I've got him into my office, though.'

The bathroom door banged open. The stranger's flies were gaping. He did not seem to be wearing underpants. Denise whimpered again as he frantically touched nose and chest, nose and chest, unaware of the large patch of dark pubic hair he was exposing.

'This way,' said Strike pleasantly. The man shuffled through the inner door, the stench of him doubly potent after a brief respite.

On being invited to sit down, the stranger perched himself on the edge of the client's chair.

'What's your name?' Strike asked, sitting down on the other side of the desk.

'Billy,' said the man, his hand flying from nose to chest three times in quick succession. The third time his hand fell, he grabbed it with his other hand and held it tightly.

'And you saw a child strangled, Billy?' said Strike, as in the next room Denise gabbled:

'Police, quickly!'

'What did she say?' asked Billy, his sunken eyes huge in his face as he glanced nervously towards the outer office, one hand clasping the other in his effort to suppress his tic.

'That's nothing,' said Strike easily. 'I've got a few different cases on. Tell me about this child.'

Strike reached for a pad and paper, all his movements slow and cautious, as though Billy were a wild bird that might take fright.

'He strangled it, up by the horse.'

Denise was now gabbling loudly into the phone beyond the flimsy partition wall.

'When was this?' asked Strike, still writing.

'Ages ... I was a kid. Little girl it was, but after they said it was a little boy. Jimmy was there, he says I never saw it, but I did. I saw him do it. Strangled. I saw it.'

'And this was up by the horse, was it?'

'Right up by the horse. That's not where they buried her, though. Him. That was down in the dell, by our dad's. I seen them doing it, I can show you the place. She wouldn't let me dig, but she'd let you.'

'And Jimmy did it, did he?'

'Jimmy never strangled nobody!' said Billy angrily. 'He saw it with me. He says it didn't happen but he's lying, he was there. He's frightened, see.'

'I see,' lied Strike, continuing to take notes. 'Well, I'll need your address if I'm going to investigate.'

He half-expected resistance, but Billy reached eagerly for the proffered pad and pen. A further gust of body odour reached Strike. Billy began to write, but suddenly seemed to think better of it.

'You won't come to Jimmy's place, though? He'll fucking tan me. You can't come to Jimmy's.'

'No, no,' said Strike soothingly. 'I just need your address for my records.'

Through the door came Denise's grating voice.

'I need someone here quicker than that, he's very disturbed!'

'What's she saying?' asked Billy.

To Strike's chagrin, Billy suddenly ripped the top sheet from the pad, crumpled it, then began to touch nose and chest again with his fist enclosing the paper.

'Don't worry about Denise,' said Strike, 'she's dealing with another client. Can I get you a drink, Billy?'

'Drink of what?'

'Tea? Or coffee?'

'Why?' asked Billy. The offer seemed to have made him even more suspicious. 'Why do you want me to drink something?'

'Only if you fancy it. Doesn't matter if you don't.'

'I don't need medicine!'

'I haven't got any medicine to give you,' said Strike.

'I'm not mental! He strangled the kid and they buried it, down in the dell by our dad's house. Wrapped in a blanket it was. Pink blanket. It wasn't my fault. I was only a kid. I didn't want to be there. I was just a little kid.'

'How many years ago, do you know?'

'Ages ... years ... can't get it out of my head,' said Billy, his eyes burning in his thin face as the fist enclosing the piece of paper fluttered up and down, touching nose, touching chest. 'They buried her in a pink blanket, down in the dell by my dad's house. But afterwards they said it was a boy.'

'Where's your dad's house, Billy?'

'She won't let me back now. *You* could dig, though. *You* could go. Strangled her, they did,' said Billy, fixing Strike with his haunted eyes. 'But Jimmy said it was a boy. Strangled, up by the—'

There was a knock on the door. Before Strike could tell her not to enter, Denise had poked her head inside, much braver now that Strike was here, full of her own importance.

'They're coming,' she said, with a look of exaggerated meaning that would have spooked a man far less jumpy than Billy. 'On
their way now.'

'Who's coming?' demanded Billy, jumping up. 'Who's on
their way?'

Denise whipped her head out of the room and closed the door.
There was a soft thud against the wood, and Strike knew that she
was leaning against it, trying to hold Billy in.

'She's just talking about a delivery I'm expecting,' Strike said
soothingly, getting to his feet. 'Go on about the—'

'What have you done?' yelped Billy, backing away towards the
door while he repeatedly touched nose and chest. 'Who's coming?'

'Nobody's coming,' said Strike, but Billy was already trying to
push the door open. Meeting resistance, he flung himself hard against
it. There was a shriek from outside as Denise was thrown aside.
Before Strike could get out from around the desk, Billy had sprinted
through the outer door. They heard him jumping down the metal
stairs three at a time and Strike, infuriated, knowing that he had no
hope of catching a younger and, on the evidence, fitter man, turned
and ran back into his office. Throwing up the sash window, he leaned
outside just in time to see Billy whipping around the corner of the
street out of sight.

'*Bollocks!*'

A man heading inside the guitar shop opposite stared around in
some perplexity for the source of the noise.

Strike withdrew his head and turned to glare at Denise, who was
dusting herself down in the doorway to his office. Incredibly, she
looked pleased with herself.

'I tried to hold him in,' she said proudly.

'Yeah,' said Strike, exercising considerable self-restraint. 'I saw.'

'The police are on their way.'

'Fantastic.'

'Would you like a cup of tea?'

'No,' he said through gritted teeth.

'Then I think I'll go and freshen up the bathroom,' she said, adding
in a whisper, 'I don't think he used the flush.'

3

I fought out that fight alone and in the completest secrecy.

Henrik Ibsen, *Rosmersholm*

As she walked along the unfamiliar Deptford street, Robin was raised to temporary light-heartedness, then wondered when she had last felt this way and knew that it had been over a year. Energised and uplifted by the afternoon sunshine, the colourful shopfronts and general bustle and noise, she was currently celebrating the fact that she never need see the inside of the Villiers Trust Clinic again.

Her therapist had been unhappy that she was terminating treatment.

'We recommend a full course,' she had said.

'I know,' Robin replied, 'but, well, I'm sorry, I think this has done me as much good as it's going to.'

The therapist's smile had been chilly.

'The CBT's been great,' Robin had said. 'It's really helped with the anxiety, I'm going to keep that up . . . '

She had taken a deep breath, eyes fixed on the woman's low-heeled Mary Janes, then forced herself to look her in the eye.

' . . . but I'm not finding this part helpful.'

Another silence had ensued. After five sessions, Robin was used to them. In normal conversation, it would be considered rude or passive aggressive to leave these long pauses and simply watch the other person, waiting for them to speak, but in psychodynamic therapy, she had learned, it was standard.

45

Robin's doctor had given her a referral for free treatment on the NHS, but the waiting list had been so long that she had decided, with Matthew's tight-lipped support, to pay for treatment. Matthew, she knew, was barely refraining from saying that the ideal solution would be to give up the job that had landed her with PTSD and which in his view paid far too poorly considering the dangers to which she had been exposed.

'You see,' Robin had continued with the speech she had prepared, 'my life is pretty much wall to wall with people who think they know what's best for me.'

'Well, yes,' said the therapist, in a manner that Robin felt would have been considered condescending beyond the clinic walls, 'we've discussed—'

'—and . . .'

Robin was by nature conciliatory and polite. On the other hand, she had been urged repeatedly by the therapist to speak the unvarnished truth in this dingy little room with the spider plant in its dull green pot and the man-sized tissues on the low pine table.

'. . . and to be honest,' she said, 'you feel like just another one of them.'

Another pause.

'Well,' said the therapist, with a little laugh, 'I'm here to help you reach your own conclusions about—'

'Yes, but you do it by – by *pushing* me all the time,' said Robin. 'It's combative. You challenge everything I say.'

Robin closed her eyes, as a great wave of weariness swept her. Her muscles ached. She had spent all week putting together flat-pack furniture, heaving around boxes of books and hanging pictures.

'I come out of here,' said Robin, opening her eyes again, 'feeling wrung out. I go home to my husband, and he does it, too. He leaves big sulky silences and challenges me on the smallest things. Then I phone my mother, and it's more of the same. The only person who isn't *at me* all the time to sort myself out is—'

She pulled up short, then said:

'—is my work partner.'

'Mr Strike,' said the therapist sweetly.

It had been a matter of contention between Robin and the therapist that she had refused to discuss her relationship with Strike, other than to confirm that he was unaware of how much the Shacklewell Ripper case had affected her. Their personal relationship, she had stated firmly, was irrelevant to her present issues. The therapist had raised him in every session since, but Robin had consistently refused to engage on the subject.

'Yes,' said Robin. 'Him.'

'By your own admission you haven't told him the full extent of your anxiety.'

'So,' said Robin, ignoring the last comment, 'I really only came today to tell you I'm leaving. As I say, I've found the CBT really useful and I'm going to keep using the exercises.'

The therapist had seemed outraged that Robin wasn't even prepared to stay for the full hour, but Robin had paid for the entire session and therefore felt free to walk out, giving her what felt like a bonus hour in the day. She felt justified in not hurrying home to do more unpacking, but to buy herself a Cornetto and enjoy it as she wandered through the sun-drenched streets of her new area.

Chasing her own cheerfulness like a butterfly, because she was afraid it might escape, she turned up a quieter street, forcing herself to concentrate, to take in the unfamiliar scene. She was, after all, delighted to have left behind the old flat in West Ealing, with its many bad memories. It had become clear during his trial that the Shacklewell Ripper had been tailing and watching Robin for far longer than she had ever suspected. The police had even told her that they thought he had hung around Hastings Road, lurking behind parked cars, yards from her front door.

Desperate though she had been to move, it had taken her and Matthew eleven months to find a new place. The main problem was that Matthew had been determined to 'take a step up the property ladder', now that he had a better-paid new job and a legacy from his late mother. Robin's parents, too, had expressed a willingness to help them, given the awful associations of the old flat, but London was excruciatingly expensive. Three times had Matthew set his heart on flats that were, realistically, well out of their price range. Three times had they failed to buy what Robin could have told him would sell for thousands more than they could offer.

'It's ridiculous!' he kept saying, 'it isn't worth that!'

'It's worth whatever people are prepared to pay,' Robin had said, frustrated that an accountant didn't understand the operation of market forces. She had been ready to move anywhere, even a single room, to escape the shadow of the killer who continued to haunt her dreams.

On the point of doubling back towards the main road, her eye was caught by the opening in a brick wall, which was flanked by gateposts topped with the strangest finials she had ever seen.

A pair of gigantic, crumbling stone skulls sat on top of carved bones on gateposts, beyond which a tall square tower rose. The finials would have looked at home, Robin thought, moving closer to examine the empty black eye sockets, garnishing the front of a pirate's mansion in some fantasy film. Peering through the opening, Robin saw a church and mossy tombs lying amid an empty rose garden in full bloom.

She finished her ice cream while wandering around St Nicholas's, a strange amalgam of an old red-brick school grafted onto the rough stone tower. Finally she sat down on a wooden bench that had grown almost uncomfortably hot in the sun, stretched her aching back, drank in the delicious scent of warm roses and was suddenly transported, entirely against her will, back to the hotel suite in Yorkshire, almost a year ago, where a blood-red bouquet of roses had witnessed the aftermath of her abandonment of Matthew on the dance floor at her wedding reception.

Matthew, his father, his Aunt Sue, Robin's parents and brother Stephen had all converged on the bridal suite where Robin had retreated to escape Matthew's fury. She had been changing out of her wedding dress when they had burst in, one after another, all demanding to know what was going on.

A cacophony had ensued. Stephen, first to grasp what Matthew had done in deleting Strike's calls, started to shout at him. Geoffrey was drunkenly demanding to know why Strike had been allowed to stay for dinner given he hadn't RSVPed. Matthew was bellowing at all of them to butt out, that this was between him and Robin, while Aunt Sue said over and over, 'I've never seen a bride walk out of her first dance. *Never!* I've *never* seen a bride walk out of her first dance.'

Then Linda had finally grasped what Matthew had done, and began telling him off, too. Geoffrey had leapt to his son's defence, demanding to know why Linda wanted her daughter to go back to a man who allowed her to get stabbed. Martin had arrived, extremely drunk, and had taken a swing at Matthew for reasons that nobody had ever explained satisfactorily, and Robin had retreated to the bathroom where, incredibly, given that she had barely eaten all day, she had thrown up.

Five minutes later, she had been forced to let Matthew in because his nose was bleeding and there, with their families still shouting at each other in the next door bedroom, Matthew had asked her, a wodge of toilet roll pressed to his nostrils, to come with him to the Maldives, not as a honeymoon, not any more, but to sort things out in private, 'away,' as he put it thickly, gesturing towards the source of the yelling, 'from *this*. And there'll be press,' he added, accusingly. 'They'll be after you, for the Ripper business.'

He was cold-eyed over the bloody toilet paper, furious with her for humiliating him on the dance floor, livid with Martin for hitting him. There was nothing romantic in his invitation to board the plane. He was proposing a summit, a chance for calm discussion. If, after serious consideration, they came to the conclusion that the marriage was a mistake, they would come home at the end of the fortnight, make a joint announcement, and go their separate ways.

And at that moment, the wretched Robin, arm throbbing, shaken to the core by the feelings that had risen inside when she had felt Strike's arms around her, knowing that the press might even now be trying to track her down, had seen Matthew, if not as an ally, at least as an escape. The idea of getting on a plane, of flying out of reach of the tsunami of curiosity, gossip, anger, solicitude and unsought advice that she knew would engulf her as long as she remained in Yorkshire, was deeply appealing.

So they had left, barely speaking during the flight. What Matthew had been thinking through those long hours, she had never enquired.

She knew only that she had thought about Strike. Over and again, she had returned to the memory of their embrace as she watched the clouds slide past the window.

Am I in love with him? she had asked herself repeatedly, but without reaching any firm conclusion.

Her deliberations on the subject had lasted days, an inner torment she could not reveal to Matthew as they walked on white beaches, discussing the tensions and resentments that lay between the two of them. Matthew slept on the living-room sofa at night, Robin in the net-draped double bed upstairs. Sometimes they argued, at other times they retreated into hurt and furious silences. Matthew was keeping tabs on Robin's phone, wanting to know where it was, constantly picking it up and checking it, and she knew that he was looking for messages or calls from her boss.

What made things worse was that there were none. Apparently Strike wasn't interested in talking to her. The hug on the stairs, to which her thoughts kept scampering back like a dog to a blissfully pungent lamppost, seemed to have meant far less to him than it had to her.

Night after night, Robin walked by herself on the beach, listening to the sea's deep breathing, her injured arm sweating beneath its rubber protective brace, her phone left at the villa so that Matthew had no excuse to tail her and find out whether she was talking secretly to Strike.

But on the seventh night, with Matthew back at the villa, she had decided to call Strike. Almost without acknowledging it to herself, she had formulated a plan. There was a landline at the bar and she knew the office number off by heart. It would be diverted to Strike's mobile automatically. What she was going to say when she reached him, she didn't know, but she was sure that if she heard him speak, the truth about her feelings would be revealed to her. As the phone rang in distant London, Robin's mouth had become dry.

The phone was answered, but nobody spoke for a few seconds. Robin listened to the sounds of movement, then heard a giggle, and then at last somebody spoke.

'Hello? This is Cormy-Warmy—'

As the woman broke into loud, raucous laughter, Robin heard Strike somewhere in the background, half-amused, half-annoyed and certainly drunk:

'Gimme that! Seriously, give it—'

Robin had slammed the receiver back onto its rest. Sweat had broken out on her face and chest: she felt ashamed, foolish, humiliated. He was with another woman. The laughter had been unmistakably intimate. The unknown girl had been teasing him, answering his mobile, calling him (how revolting) 'Cormy'.

She would deny phoning him, she resolved, if ever Strike asked her about the dropped call. She would lie through her teeth, pretend not to know what he was talking about . . .

The sound of the woman on the phone had affected her like a hard slap. If Strike could have taken somebody to bed so soon after their hug – and she would have staked her life on the fact that the girl, whoever she was, had either just slept with Strike, or was about to – then he wasn't sitting in London torturing himself about his true feelings for Robin Ellacott.

The salt on her lips made her thirsty as she trudged through the night, wearing a deep groove in the soft white sand as the waves broke endlessly beside her. Wasn't it possible, she asked herself, when she was cried out at last, that she was confusing gratitude and friendship with something deeper? That she had mistaken her love of detection for love of the man who had given her the job? She admired Strike, of course, and was immensely fond of him. They had passed through many intense experiences together, so that it was natural to feel close to him, but was that love?

Alone in the balmy, mosquito-buzzing night, while the waves sighed on the shore and she cradled her aching arm, Robin reminded herself bleakly that she had had very little experience with men for a woman approaching her twenty-eighth birthday. Matthew was all she had ever known, her only sexual partner, a place of safety to her for ten long years now. If she *had* developed a crush on Strike – she employed the old-fashioned word her mother might have used – mightn't it also be the natural side effect of the lack of variety and experimentation most women of her age had enjoyed? For so long faithful to Matthew, hadn't she been bound to look up one day and remember that there were other lives, other choices? Hadn't she been long overdue to notice that Matthew was not the only man in the world? Strike, she told herself, was simply the one with whom she had been spending the most time, so naturally it had been he onto whom she projected her wondering, her curiosity, her dissatisfaction with Matthew.

Having, as she told herself, talked sense into that part of her that kept yearning for Strike, she reached a hard decision on the eighth evening of her honeymoon. She wanted to go home early and announce their separation to their families. She must tell Matthew that it had nothing to do with anybody else, but after agonising and serious reflection, she did not believe they were well suited enough to continue in the marriage.

She could still remember her feeling of mingled panic and dread as she had pushed open the cabin door, braced for a fight that had never materialised. Matthew had been sitting slumped on the sofa and when he saw her, he mumbled, 'Mum?'

His face, arms and legs had been shining with sweat. As she moved towards him, she saw an ugly black tracing of veins up the inside of his left arm, as though somebody had filled them with ink.

'Matt?'

Hearing her, he had realised that she was not his dead mother.

'Don't ... feel well, Rob ... '

She had dashed for the phone, called the hotel, asked for a doctor. By the time he arrived, Matthew was drifting in and out of delirium. They had found the scratch on the back of his hand and, worried, concluded that he might have cellulitis, which Robin could tell, from the faces of the worried doctor and nurse, was serious. Matthew kept seeing figures moving in the shadowy corners of the cabin, people who weren't there.

'Who's that?' he kept asking Robin. 'Who's that over there?'

'There's nobody else here, Matt.'

Now she was holding his hand while the nurse and doctor discussed hospitalisation.

'Don't leave me, Rob.'

'I'm not going to leave you.'

She had meant that she was going nowhere just now, not that she would stay for ever, but Matthew had begun to cry.

'Oh, thank God. I thought you were going to walk . . . I love you, Rob. I know I fucked up, but I love you . . .'

The doctor gave Matthew oral antibiotics and went to make telephone calls. Delirious, Matthew clung to his wife, thanking her. Sometimes he drifted into a state where, again, he thought he saw shadows moving in the empty corners of the room, and twice more he muttered about his dead mother. Alone in the velvety blackness of the tropical night, Robin listened to winged insects colliding with the screens at the windows, alternately comforting and watching over the man she had loved since she was seventeen.

It hadn't been cellulitis. The infection had responded, over the next twenty-four hours, to antibiotics. As he recovered from the sudden, violent illness, Matthew watched her constantly, weak and vulnerable as she had never seen him, afraid, she knew, that her promise to stay had been temporary.

'We can't throw it all away, can we?' he had asked her hoarsely from the bed where the doctor had insisted he stay. 'All these years?'

She had let him talk about the good times, the shared times, and she had reminded herself about the giggling girl who had called Strike 'Cormy'. She envisioned going home and asking for an annulment, because the marriage had still not been consummated. She remembered the money her parents had spent on the wedding day she had hated.

Bees buzzed in the churchyard roses around her as Robin wondered, for the thousandth time, where she would be right now if Matthew hadn't scratched himself on coral. Most of her now-terminated therapy sessions had been full of her need to talk about the doubts that had plagued her ever since she had agreed to remain married.

In the months that had followed, and especially when she and Matthew were getting on reasonably well, it seemed to her that it had been right to give the marriage a fair trial, but she never forgot to think of it in terms of a trial, and this in itself sometimes led her, sleepless at night, to castigate herself for the pusillanimous failure to pull herself free once Matthew had recovered.

She had never explained to Strike what had happened, why she had agreed to try and keep the marriage afloat. Perhaps that was why their friendship had grown so cold and distant. When she had returned from her honeymoon, it was to find Strike changed towards her – and perhaps, she acknowledged, she had changed towards him, too, because of what she had heard on the line when she had called, in desperation, from the Maldives bar.

'Sticking with it, then, are you?' he had said roughly, after a glance at her ring finger.

His tone had nettled her, as had the fact that he had never asked why she was trying, never asked about her home life from that point onwards, never so much as hinted that he remembered the hug on the stairs.

Whether because Strike had arranged matters that way or not, they had not worked a case together since that of the Shacklewell Ripper. Imitating her senior partner, Robin had retreated into a cool professionalism.

But sometimes she was afraid that he no longer valued her as he once had, now that she had proven herself so conventional and cowardly. There had been an awkward conversation a few months ago in which he had suggested that she take time off, asked whether she felt she was fully recovered after the knife attack. Taking this as a slight upon her bravery, afraid that she would again find herself sidelined, losing the only part of her life that she currently found fulfilling, she had insisted that she was perfectly well and redoubled her professional efforts.

The muted mobile in her bag vibrated. Robin slipped her hand inside and looked to see who was calling. Strike. She also noticed that he had called earlier, while she was saying a joyful goodbye to the Villiers Trust Clinic.

'Hi,' she said. 'I missed you earlier, sorry.'

'Not a problem. Move gone all right?'

'Fine,' she said.

'Just wanted to let you know, I've hired us a new subcontractor. Name of Sam Barclay.'

'Great,' said Robin, watching a fly shimmering on a fat, blush-pink rose. 'What's his background?'

'Army,' said Strike.

'Military police?'

'Er – not exactly.'

As he told her the story of Sam Barclay, Robin found herself grinning.

'So you've hired a dope-smoking painter and decorator?'

'Vaping, dope *vaping*,' Strike corrected her, and Robin could tell that he was grinning, too. 'He's on a health kick. New baby.'

'Well, he sounds ... interesting.'

She waited, but Strike did not speak.

'I'll see you Saturday night, then,' she said.

Robin had felt obliged to invite Strike to her and Matthew's house-warming party, because she had given their most regular and reliable subcontractor, Andy Hutchins, an invitation, and felt it would be odd to leave out Strike. She had been surprised when he had accepted.

'Yeah, see you then.'

'Is Lorelei coming?' Robin asked, striving for casualness, but not sure she had succeeded.

Back in central London, Strike thought he detected a sardonic note in the question, as though challenging him to admit that his girl-friend had a ludicrous moniker. He would once have pulled her up on it, asked what her problem was with the name 'Lorelei', enjoyed sparring with her, but this was dangerous territory.

'Yeah, she's coming. The invitation was to both—'

'Yes, of course it was,' said Robin hastily. 'All right, I'll see you—'

'Hang on,' said Strike.

He was alone in the office, because he had sent Denise home early. The temp had not wanted to leave: she was paid by the hour, after all, and only after Strike had assured her that he would pay for a full day had she gathered up all her possessions, talking nonstop all the while.

'Funny thing happened this afternoon,' said Strike.

Robin listened intently, without interrupting, to Strike's vivid account of the brief visit of Billy. By the end of it, she had forgotten to worry about Strike's coolness. Indeed, he now sounded like the Strike of a year ago.

'He was definitely mentally ill,' said Strike, his eyes on the clear sky beyond the window. 'Possibly psychotic.'

'Yeah, but—'

'I know,' said Strike. He picked up the pad from which Billy had ripped his half-written address and turned it absently in his free hand. 'Is he mentally ill, *so* he thinks he saw a kid strangled? Or is he mentally ill *and* he saw a kid strangled?'

Neither spoke for a while, during which time both turned over Billy's story in their minds, knowing that the other was doing the same. This brief, companionable spell of reflection ended abruptly when a cocker spaniel, which Robin had not noticed as it came snuffling through the roses, laid its cold nose without warning on her bare knee and she shrieked.

'What the fuck?'

'Nothing – a dog—'

'Where are you?'

'In a graveyard.'

'What? Why?'

'Just exploring the area. I'd better go,' she said, getting to her feet. 'There's another flat-pack waiting for me at home.'

'Right you are,' said Strike, with a return to his usual briskness. 'See you Saturday.'

'I'm so sorry,' said the cocker spaniel's elderly owner, as Robin slid her mobile back into her bag. 'Are you frightened of dogs?'

'Not at all,' said Robin, smiling and patting the dog's soft golden head. 'He surprised me, that's all.'

As she headed back past the giant skulls towards her new home, Robin thought about Billy, whom Strike had described with such vividness that Robin felt as though she had met him, too.

So deeply absorbed in her thoughts was she, that for the first time all week, Robin forgot to glance up at the White Swan pub as she passed it. High above the street, on the corner of the building, was a single carved swan, which reminded Robin, every time she passed it, of her calamitous wedding day.

4

But what do you propose to do in the town, then?

Henrik Ibsen, *Rosmersholm*

Six and a half miles away, Strike set his mobile down on his desk and lit a cigarette. Robin's interest in his story had been soothing after the interview he had endured half an hour after Billy had fled. The two policemen who had answered Denise's call had seemed to relish their opportunity to make the famous Cormoran Strike admit his fallibility, taking their time as they ascertained that he had succeeded in finding out neither full name nor address of the probably psychotic Billy.

The late afternoon sun hit the notebook on his desk at an angle, revealing faint indentations. Strike dropped his cigarette into an ashtray he had stolen long ago from a German bar, picked up the notepad and tilted it this way and that, trying to make out the letters formed by the impressions, then reached for a pencil and lightly shaded over them. Untidy capital letters were soon revealed, clearly spelling the words 'Charlemont Road'. Billy had pressed less hard on the house or flat number than the street name. One of the faint indents looked like either a 5 or an incomplete 8, but the spacing suggested more than one figure, or possibly a letter.

Strike's incurable predilection for getting to the root of puzzling incidents tended to inconvenience him quite as much as other people. Hungry and tired though he was, and despite the fact that he had sent his temp away so he could shut up the office, he tore the paper carrying the revealed street name off the pad and headed into the outer room, where he switched the computer back on.

There were several Charlemont Roads in the UK, but on the assumption that Billy was unlikely to have the means to travel very far, he suspected that the one in East Ham had to be the right one. Online records showed two Williams living there, but both were over sixty. Remembering that Billy had been scared that Strike might turn up at 'Jimmy's place', he had searched for Jimmy and then James, which turned up the details of James Farraday, 49.

Strike made a note of Farraday's address beneath Billy's indented scribbles, though not at all confident that Farraday was the man he sought. For one thing, his house number contained no fives or eights and, for another, Billy's extreme unkemptness suggested that whomever he lived with must take a fairly relaxed attitude to his personal hygiene. Farraday lived with a wife and what appeared to be two daughters.

Strike turned off the computer, but continued to stare abstractedly at the dark screen, thinking about Billy's story. It was the detail of the pink blanket that kept nagging at him. It seemed such a specific, unglamorous detail for a psychotic delusion.

Remembering that he needed to be up early in the morning for a paying job, he pulled himself to his feet. Before leaving the office, he inserted the piece of paper bearing both the impressions of Billy's handwriting and Farraday's address into his wallet.

London, which had recently been at the epicentre of the Queen's Diamond Jubilee celebrations, was preparing to host the Olympics. Union Jacks and the London 2012 logo were everywhere – on signs, banners, bunting, keyrings, mugs and umbrellas – while jumbles of Olympic merchandise cluttered virtually every shop window. In Strike's opinion, the logo resembled shards of fluorescent glass randomly thrown together and he was equally unenamoured of the official mascots, which looked to him like a pair of cycloptic molars.

There was a tinge of excitement and nervousness about the capital, born, no doubt, of the perennially British dread that the nation might make a fool of itself. Complaints about non-availability of Olympics tickets were a dominant theme in conversation, unsuccessful applicants decrying the lottery that was supposed to have given everybody a fair and equal chance of watching events live. Strike, who had hoped to see some boxing, had not managed to get tickets, but laughed out loud at his old school friend Nick's offer to take his place at the dressage, which Nick's wife Ilsa was overjoyed to have bagged.

Harley Street, where Strike was due to spend Friday running surveillance on a cosmetic surgeon, remained untouched by Olympic fever. The grand Victorian façades presented their usual implacable faces to the world, unsullied by garish logos or flags.

Strike, who was wearing his best Italian suit for the job, took up a position near the doorway of a building opposite and pretended to be talking on his mobile, actually keeping watch over the entrance of the expensive consulting rooms of two partners, one of whom was Strike's client.

'Dodgy Doc', as Strike had nicknamed his quarry, was taking his time living up to his name. Possibly he had been scared out of his unethical behaviour by his partner, who had confronted him after realising that Dodgy had recently performed two breast augmentations that had not been run through the business's books. Suspecting the worst, the senior partner had come to Strike for help.

'His justification was feeble, full of holes. He is,' said the white-haired surgeon, stiff-lipped but full of foreboding, 'and always has been a ... ah ... womaniser. I checked his internet history before confronting him and found a website where young women solicit cash contributions for their cosmetic enhancements, in return for explicit pictures. I fear ... I hardly know what ... but it might be that he has made an arrangement with these women that is not ... monetary. Two of the younger women had been asked to call a number I did not recognise, but which suggested surgery might be arranged free in return for an "exclusive arrangement".'

Strike had not so far witnessed Dodgy meeting any women outside his regular hours. He spent Mondays and Fridays in his Harley Street consulting rooms and the mid-week at the private hospital where he operated. Whenever Strike had tailed him outside his places of work, he had merely taken short walks to purchase chocolate, to which he seemed addicted. Every night, he drove his Bentley home to his wife and children in Gerrards Cross, tailed by Strike in his old blue BMW.

Tonight, both surgeons would be attending a Royal College of Surgeons dinner with their wives, so Strike had left his BMW in its expensive garage. The hours rolled by in tedium, Strike mostly concerned with shifting the weight off his prosthesis at regular intervals as he leaned up against railings, parking meters and doorways. A steady trickle of clients pressed the bell at Dodgy's door and were admitted, one by one. All were female and most were sleek and well-groomed. At five o'clock, Strike's mobile vibrated in his breast pocket and he saw a text from his client.

Safe to clock off, about to leave with him for the Dorchester.

Perversely, Strike hung around, watching as the partners left the building some fifteen minutes later. His client was tall and white-haired; Dodgy, a sleek, dapper olive-skinned man with shiny black hair, who wore three-piece suits. Strike watched them get into a taxi and leave, then yawned, stretched and contemplated heading home, possibly with a takeaway.

Almost against his will, he pulled out his wallet and extracted the piece of crumpled paper on which he had managed to reveal Billy's street name.

All day, at the back of his mind, he had thought he might go and seek out Billy in Charlemont Road if Dodgy Doc left work early, but he was tired and his leg sore. If Lorelei knew that he had the evening off, she would expect Strike to call. On the other hand, they were going to Robin's house-warming together tomorrow night and if he spent tonight at Lorelei's, it would be hard to extricate himself tomorrow, after the party. He never spent two nights in a row at Lorelei's flat, even when the opportunity had occurred. He liked to set limits on her rights to his time.

As though hoping to be dissuaded by the weather, he glanced up at the clear June sky and sighed. The evening was clear and perfect, the agency so busy that he did not know when he would next have a few hours to spare. If he wanted to visit Charlemont Road, it would have to be tonight.

5

*I can quite understand your having a horror of public meetings
and . . . of the rabble that frequents them.*

Henrik Ibsen, *Rosmersholm*

His journey coinciding with rush hour, it took Strike over an hour
to travel from Harley Street to East Ham. By the time he had located
Charlemont Road his stump was aching and the sight of the long
residential street made him regret that he was not the kind of man
who could simply write off Billy as a mental case.

The terraced houses had a motley appearance: some were bare
brick, others painted or pebble-dashed. Union Jacks hung at windows:
further evidence of Olympic fever or relics of the Royal Jubilee. The
small plots in front of the houses had been made into pocket gardens
or dumps for debris, according to preference. Halfway along the road
lay a dirty old mattress, abandoned to whoever wanted to deal with it.

His first glimpse of James Farraday's residence did not encourage
Strike to hope that he had reached journey's end, because it was
one of the best-maintained houses in the street. A tiny porch with
coloured glass had been added around the front door, ruched net
curtains hung at each window and the brass letterbox gleamed in the
sunshine. Strike pressed the plastic doorbell and waited.

After a short wait, a harried woman opened the door, releasing a
silver tabby, which appeared to have been waiting, coiled behind the
door, for the first chance to escape. The woman's cross expression sat
awkwardly above an apron printed with a 'Love Is . . . ' cartoon. A
strong odour of cooking meat wafted out of the house.

'Hi,' said Strike, salivating at the smell. 'Don't know whether you can help me. I'm trying to find Billy.'

'You've got the wrong address. There's no Billy here.'

She made to close the door.

'He said he was staying with Jimmy,' said Strike, as the gap narrowed.

'There's no Jimmy here, either.'

'Sorry, I thought somebody called James—'

'Nobody calls him Jimmy. You've got the wrong house.'

She closed the door.

Strike and the silver tabby eyed each other; in the cat's case, superciliously, before it sat down on the mat and began to groom itself with an air of dismissing Strike from its thoughts.

Strike returned to the pavement, where he lit a cigarette and looked up and down the street. By his estimate there were two hundred houses on Charlemont Road. How long would it take to knock on every household's door? More time than he had this evening, was the unfortunate answer, and more time than he was likely to have any time soon. He walked on, frustrated and increasingly sore, glancing in through windows and scrutinising passers-by for a resemblance to the man he had met the previous day. Twice, he asked people entering or leaving their houses whether they knew 'Jimmy and Billy', whose address he claimed to have lost. Both said no.

Strike trudged on, trying not to limp.

At last he reached a section of houses that had been bought up and converted into flats. Pairs of front doors stood crammed side by side and the front plots had been concreted over.

Strike slowed down. A torn sheet of A4 had been pinned to one of the shabbiest doors, from which the white paint was peeling. A faint but familiar prickle of interest that he would never have dignified with the name 'hunch' led Strike to the door.

The scribbled message read:

7.30 Meeting moved from pub to Well Community Centre in Vicarage Lane – end of street turn left
Jimmy Knight

Strike lifted the sheet of paper with a finger, saw a house number ending in 5, let the note fall again and moved to peer through the dusty downstairs window.

An old bed sheet had been pinned up to block out sunlight, but a corner had fallen down. Tall enough to squint through the uncovered portion of glass, Strike saw a slice of empty room containing an open sofa bed with a stained duvet on it, a pile of clothes in the corner and a portable TV standing on a cardboard box. The carpet was obscured by a multitude of empty beer cans and overflowing ashtrays. This seemed promising. He returned to the peeling front door, raised a large fist and knocked.

Nobody answered, nor did he hear any sign of movement within.

Strike checked the note on the door again, then set off. Turning left into Vicarage Lane, he saw the community centre right in front of him, 'The Well' spelled out boldly in shining Perspex letters.

An elderly man wearing a Mau cap and a wispy, greying beard was standing just outside the glass doors with a pile of leaflets in his hand. As Strike approached, the man, whose T-shirt bore the washed-out face of Che Guevara, eyed him askance. Though tieless, Strike's Italian suit struck an inappropriately formal note. When it became clear that the community centre was Strike's destination, the leaflet-holder shuffled sideways to bar the entrance.

'I know I'm late,' said Strike, with well-feigned annoyance, 'but I've only just found out the bloody venue's been changed.'

His assurance and his size both seemed to disconcert the man in the Mau cap, who nevertheless appeared to feel that instant capitulation to a man in a suit would be unworthy of him.

'Who are you representing?'

Strike had already taken a swift inventory of the capitalised words visible on the leaflets clutched against the other man's chest: DISSENT – DISOBEDIENCE – DISRUPTION and, rather incongruously, ALLOTMENTS. There was also a crude cartoon of five obese businessmen blowing cigar smoke to form the Olympic rings.

'My dad,' Strike said. 'He's worried they're going to concrete over his allotment.'

'Ah,' said the bearded man. He moved aside. Strike tugged a leaflet out of his hand and entered the community centre.

There was nobody in sight except for a grey-haired woman of West Indian origin, who was peering through an inner door that she had opened an inch. Strike could just hear a female voice in the room beyond. Her words were hard to distinguish, but her cadences suggested a tirade. Becoming aware that somebody was standing immediately behind her, the woman turned. The sight of Strike's suit seemed to affect her in opposite fashion to the bearded man at the door.

'Are you from the Olympics?' she whispered.

'No,' said Strike. 'Just interested.'

She eased the door open to admit him.

Around forty people were sitting on plastic chairs. Strike took the nearest vacant seat and scanned the backs of the heads in front of him for the matted, shoulder-length hair of Billy.

A table for speakers had been set up at the front. A young woman was currently pacing up and down in front of it as she addressed the audience. Her hair was dyed the same bright red shade as Coco's, Strike's hard-to-shake one-night stand, and she was speaking in a series of unfinished sentences, occasionally losing herself in secondary clauses and forgetting to drop her 'h's. Strike had the impression that she had been talking for a long time.

'. . . think of the squatters and artists who're all being – 'cause this is a proper community, right, and then in they come wiv like clipboards and it's, like, get out if you know what's good for you, thin end of the, innit, oppressive laws, it's the Trojan 'orse – it's a coordinated campaign of, like . . . '

Half the audience looked like students. Among the older members, Strike saw men and women who he marked down as committed protestors, some wearing T-shirts with leftist slogans like his friend on the door. Here and there he saw unlikely figures who he guessed were ordinary members of the community who had not taken kindly to the Olympics' arrival in East London: arty types who had perhaps been squatting, and an elderly couple, who were currently whispering to each other and who Strike thought might be gen-uinely worried about their allotment. Watching them resume the attitudes of meek endurance appropriate to those sitting in church, Strike guessed that they had agreed that they could not easily leave without drawing too much attention to themselves. A much-pierced boy covered in anarchist tattoos audibly picked his teeth.

Behind the girl who was speaking sat three others: an older woman and two men, who were talking quietly to each other. One of them was at least sixty, barrel-chested and lantern-jawed, with the pugnacious air of a man who had served his time on picket lines and in successful showdowns with recalcitrant management. Something about the dark, deep-set eyes of the other made Strike scan the leaflet in his hand, seeking confirmation of an immediate suspicion.

COMMUNITY OLYMPIC RESISTANCE (CORE)

15 June 2012

7.30pm White Horse Pub East Ham E6 6EJ

Speakers:

Lilian Sweeting	Wilderness Preservation, E. London
Walter Frett	Workers' Alliance/CORE activist
Flick Purdue	Anti-poverty campaigner/CORE activist
Jimmy Knight	Real Socialist Party/CORE organizer

Heavy stubble and a general air of scruffiness notwithstanding, the man with the sunken eyes was nowhere near as filthy as Billy and his hair had certainly been cut within the last couple of months. He appeared to be in his mid-thirties, and while squarer of face and more muscular, he had the same dark hair and pale skin as Strike's visitor. On the available evidence, Strike would have put a sizeable bet on Jimmy Knight being Billy's older brother.

Jimmy finished his muttered conversation with his Workers' Alliance colleague, then leaned back in his seat, thick arms folded, wearing an expression of abstraction that showed he was not listening to the young woman any more than her increasingly fidgety audience.

Strike now became aware that he was under observation from a nondescript man sitting in the row in front of him. When Strike met the man's pale blue gaze, he redirected his attention hastily towards Flick, who was still talking. Taking note of the blue-eyed man's clean jeans, plain T-shirt and the short, neat hair, Strike thought that he would have done better to have forgone the morning's close shave, but perhaps, for a ramshackle operation like CORE, the Met had not considered it worthwhile to send their best. The presence of a plain-clothes officer was to be expected, of course. Any group currently planning to disrupt or resist the arrangements for the Olympics was likely to be under surveillance.

A short distance from the plainclothes policeman sat a professional-looking young Asian man in shirtsleeves. Tall and thin, he was watching the speaker fixedly, chewing the fingernails of his left hand. As Strike watched, the man gave a little start and took his finger away from his mouth. He had made it bleed.

'All right,' said a man loudly. The audience, recognising a voice of authority, sat a little straighter. 'Thanks very much, Flick.'

Jimmy Knight got to his feet, leading the unenthusiastic applause for Flick, who walked back around the table and sat down in the empty chair between the two men.

In his well-worn jeans and unironed T-shirt, Jimmy Knight reminded Strike of the men his dead mother had taken as lovers. He might have been the bass player in a grime band or a good-looking roadie, with his muscled arms and tattoos. Strike noticed that the back of the nondescript blue-eyed man had tensed. He had been waiting for Jimmy.

'Evening, everyone, and thanks very much for coming.'

His personality filled the room like the first bar of a hit song. Strike knew him from those few words as the kind of man who, in the army, was either outstandingly useful or an insubordinate bastard. Jimmy's accent, like Flick's, revealed an uncertain provenance. Strike thought that Cockney might have been grafted, in his case more successfully, onto a faint, rural burr.

'So, the Olympic threshing machine's moved into East London!'

His burning eyes swept the newly attentive crowd.

'Flattening houses, knocking cyclists to their deaths, churning up land that belongs to all of us. Or it did.

'You've heard from Lilian what they're doing to animal and insect habitats. I'm here to talk about the encroachment on human communities. They're concreting over our common land, and for what? Are they putting up the social housing or the hospitals we need? Of course not! No, we're getting stadiums costing billions, showcases for the capitalist system, ladies and gentlemen. We're being asked to celebrate elitism while, beyond the barriers, ordinary people's freedoms are encroached, eroded, removed.

'They tell us we should be celebrating the Olympics, all the glossy press releases the right-wing media gobbles up and regurgitates. Fetishise the flag, whip up the middle classes into a frenzy of jingoism! Come worship our glorious medallists – a shiny gold for everyone who passes over a big enough bribe with a pot of someone else's piss!'

There was a murmur of agreement. A few people clapped.

'We're supposed to get excited about the public schoolboys and girls who got to practise sports while the rest of us were having our playing fields sold off for cash! Sycophancy should be our national Olympic sport! We deify people who've had millions invested in them because they can ride a bike, when they've sold themselves as fig leaves for all the planet-raping, tax-dodging bastards who are queuing up to get their names on the barriers – barriers shutting working people off their own land!'

The applause, in which Strike, the old couple beside him and the Asian man did not join, was as much for the performance as the words. Jimmy's slightly thuggish but handsome face was alive with righteous anger.

'See this?' he said, sweeping from the table behind him a piece of paper with the jagged '2012' that Strike disliked so much. 'Welcome to the Olympics, my friends, a fascist's wet dream. See the logo? D'you see it? It's a broken swastika!'

The crowd laughed and applauded some more, masking the loud rumble of Strike's stomach. He wondered whether there might be a takeaway nearby. He had even started to calculate whether he might have time to leave, buy food and return, when the grey-haired West Indian woman whom he had seen earlier opened the door to the hall and propped it open. Her expression clearly indicated that CORE had now outstayed its welcome.

Jimmy, however, was still in full flow.

'This so-called celebration of the Olympic spirit, of fair play and amateurism is normalising repression and authoritarianism! Wake up: London's being militarised! The British state, which has honed the tactics of colonisation and invasion for centuries, has seized on the Olympics as the perfect excuse to deploy police, army, helicopters and guns against ordinary citizens! One thousand extra CCTV cameras – extra laws hurried through – and you think they'll be repealed when this carnival of capitalism moves on?

'Join us!' shouted Jimmy, as the community centre worker edged along the wall towards the front of the hall, nervous but determined. 'CORE is part of a broader global justice movement that meets repression with resistance! We're making common cause with all left-ist, anti-oppressive movements across the capital! We're going to be staging lawful demonstrations and using every tool of peaceful protest still permitted to us in what is rapidly becoming an occupied city!'

More applause followed, though the elderly couple beside Strike seemed thoroughly miserable.

'All right, all right, I know,' added Jimmy to the community centre worker, who had now reached the front of the audience and was ges-turing timidly. 'They want us out,' Jimmy told the crowd, smirking and shaking his head. 'Of course they do. Of course.'

A few people hissed at the community centre worker.

'Anyone who wants to hear more,' said Jimmy, 'we'll be in the pub down the road. Address on your leaflets!'

Most of the crowd applauded. The plainclothes policeman got to his feet. The elderly couple was already scuttling towards the door.

6

I . . . have the reputation of being a wicked fanatic, I am told.
Henrik Ibsen, *Rosmersholm*

Chairs clattered, bags were hoisted onto shoulders. The bulk of the audience began to head for the doors at the back, but some appeared reluctant to leave. Strike took a few steps towards Jimmy, hoping to talk to him, but was outpaced by the young Asian man, who was striding jerkily towards the activist with an air of nervous determination. Jimmy exchanged a few more words with the man from the Workers' Alliance, then noticed the newcomer, bade Walter goodbye and moved forward with every appearance of goodwill to speak to what he clearly assumed was a convert.

As soon as the Asian man began to speak, however, Jimmy's expression clouded. As they talked in low voices in the middle of the rapidly emptying room, Flick and a cluster of young people loitered nearby, waiting for Jimmy. They seemed to consider themselves above manual labour. The community centre worker cleared away chairs alone.

'Let me do that,' Strike offered, taking three from her and ignoring the sharp twinge in his knee as he hoisted them onto a tall stack.

'Thanks very much,' she panted. 'I don't think we'll be letting this lot—'

She allowed Walter and a few others to pass before continuing. None of them thanked her.

'—use the centre again,' she finished resentfully. 'I didn't realise

69

what they were all about. Their leaflet's on about civil disobedience and I don't know what else.'

'Pro-Olympics, are you?' Strike asked, placing a chair onto a pile.

'My granddaughter's in a running club,' she said. 'We got tickets. She can't wait.'

Jimmy was still locked in conversation with the young Asian man. A minor argument seemed to have developed. Jimmy seemed tense, his eyes shifting constantly around the room, either seeking an escape or checking that nobody else was within earshot. The hall was emptying. The two men began to move towards the exit. Strike strained his ears to hear what they were saying to each other, but the clumping footsteps of Jimmy's acolytes on the wooden floor obliterated all but a few words.

'... for years, mate, all right?' Jimmy was saying angrily. 'So do whatever the fuck you want, you're the one who volunteered yourself...'

They passed out of earshot. Strike helped the community centre volunteer stack the last of the chairs and, as she turned off the light, asked for directions to the White Horse.

Five minutes later, and in spite of his recent resolution to eat more healthily, Strike bought a bag of chips at a takeaway and proceeded along White Horse Road, at the end of which he had been told he would find the eponymous pub.

As he ate, Strike pondered the best way to open conversation with Jimmy Knight. As the reaction of the elderly Che Guevara fan on the door had shown, Strike's current attire did not tend to foster trust with anti-capitalist protestors. Jimmy had the air of an experienced hard-left activist and was probably anticipating official interest in his activities in the highly charged atmosphere preceding the opening of the Games. Indeed, Strike could see the nondescript, blue-eyed man walking behind Jimmy, hands in his jean pockets. Strike's first job would be to reassure Jimmy that he was not there to investigate CORE.

The White Horse turned out to be an ugly prefabricated building, which stood on a busy junction facing a large park. A white war memorial with neatly ranged poppy wreaths at its base rose like an eternal reproach to the outside drinking area opposite, where old cigarette butts lay thickly on cracked concrete riven with weeds. Drinkers were milling around the front of the pub, all smoking. Strike spotted Jimmy, Flick and several others standing in a group in front of a window that was decorated with an enormous West Ham banner. The tall young Asian man was nowhere to be seen, but the plainclothes policeman loitered alone on the periphery of their group.

Strike went inside to fetch a pint. The décor inside the pub consisted mostly of Cross of St George flags and more West Ham paraphernalia. Having bought a pint of John Smith's, Strike returned to the forecourt, lit a fresh cigarette and advanced on the group around Jimmy. He was at Flick's shoulder before they realised that the large stranger in a suit wanted something from them. All talk ceased as suspicion flared on every face.

'Hi,' said Strike, 'my name's Cormoran Strike. Any chance of a quick word, Jimmy? It's about Billy.'

'Billy?' repeated Jimmy sharply. 'Why?'

'I met him yesterday. I'm a private detect—'

'Chizzle's sent him!' gasped Flick, turning, frightened, to Jimmy. ''K'up!' he growled.

While the rest of the group surveyed Strike with a mixture of curiosity and hostility, Jimmy beckoned to Strike to follow him to the edge of the crowd. To Strike's surprise, Flick tagged along. Men with buzz cuts and West Ham tops nodded at the activist as he passed. Jimmy came to a halt beside two old white bollards topped by horse heads, checked that nobody else was within earshot, then addressed Strike.

'What did you say your name was again?'

'Cormoran, Cormoran Strike. Is Billy your brother?'

'Younger brother, yeah,' said Jimmy. 'Did you say he came to see you?'

'Yep. Yesterday afternoon.'

'You're a private—?'

'Detective. Yes.'

Strike saw dawning recognition in Flick's eyes. She had a plump, pale face that would have been innocent without the savage eye-liner and the uncombed tomato-red hair. She turned quickly to Jimmy again.

'Jimmy, he's—'

'Shacklewell Ripper?' asked Jimmy, eyeing Strike over his lighter as he lit another cigarette. 'Lula Landry?'

'That's me,' said Strike.

Out of the corner of Strike's eye, he noticed Flick's eyes travelling down his body to his lower legs. Her mouth twisted in seeming contempt.

'Billy came to see you?' repeated Jimmy. 'Why?'

'He told me he'd witnessed a kid being strangled,' said Strike.

Jimmy blew out smoke in angry gusts.

'Yeah. He's fucked in the head. Schizoid affective disorder.'

'He seemed ill,' agreed Strike.

'Is that all he told you? That he saw a kid being strangled?'

'Seemed enough to be getting on with,' said Strike.

Jimmy's lips curved in a humourless smile.

'You didn't believe him, did you?'

'No,' said Strike truthfully, 'but I don't think he should be roaming the streets in that condition. He needs help.'

'I don't think he's any worse than usual, do you?' Jimmy asked Flick, with a somewhat artificial air of dispassionate enquiry.

'No,' she said, turning to address Strike with barely concealed animosity. 'He has ups and downs. He's all right if he takes his meds.'

Her accent had become markedly more middle-class away from the rest of their friends. Strike noticed that she had painted eyeliner over a clump of sleep in the corner of one eye. Strike, who had spent large portions of his childhood living in squalor, found a disregard for hygiene hard to like, except in those people so unhappy or ill that cleanliness became an irrelevance.

'Ex-army, aren't you?' she asked, but Jimmy spoke over her.

'How did Billy know how to find you?'

'Directory enquiries?' suggested Strike. 'I don't live in a bat cave.'

'Billy doesn't know how to use directory enquiries.'

'He managed to find my office OK.'

'There's no dead kid,' Jimmy said abruptly. 'It's all in his head. He goes on about it when he's having an episode. Didn't you see his tic?'

Jimmy imitated, with brutal accuracy, the compulsive nose to chest movement of a twitching hand. Flick laughed.

'Yeah, I saw that,' said Strike, unsmiling. 'You don't know where he is, then?'

'Haven't seen him since yesterday morning. What do you want him for?'

'Like I say, he didn't seem in any fit state to be wandering around on his own.'

'Very public spirited of you,' said Jimmy. 'Rich and famous detective worrying about our Bill.'

Strike said nothing.

'Army,' Flick repeated, 'weren't you?'

'I was,' said Strike, looking down at her. 'How's that relevant?'

'Just saying.' She had flushed a little in her righteous anger. 'Haven't always been this worried about people getting hurt, have you?'

Strike, who was familiar with people who shared Flick's views, said nothing. She would probably believe him if he told her he had joined the forces in the hope of bayoneting children.

Jimmy, who also seemed disinclined to hear more of Flick's opinions on the military, said:

'Billy'll be fine. He crashes at ours sometimes, then goes off. Does it all the time.'

'Where does he stay when he's not with you?'

'Friends,' said Jimmy, shrugging. 'I don't know all their names.' Then, contradicting himself, 'I'll ring around tonight, make sure he's OK.'

'Right you are,' said Strike, downing his pint and handing the empty to a tattooed bar worker, who was marching through the forecourt, grabbing glasses from all who had finished with them. Strike took a last drag on his cigarette, dropped it to join the thousands of its brethren on the cracked forecourt, ground it out beneath his prosthetic foot, then pulled out his wallet.

'Do me a favour,' he said to Jimmy, taking out a card and handing it over, 'and contact me when Billy turns up, will you? I'd like to know he's safe.'

Flick gave a derisive snort, but Jimmy seemed caught off guard.

'Yeah, all right. Yeah, I will.'

'D'you know which bus would get me back to Denmark Street quickest?' Strike asked them. He could not face another long walk to the Tube. Buses were rolling past the pub with inviting frequency. Jimmy, who seemed to know the area well, directed Strike to the appropriate stop.

'Thanks very much.' As he put his wallet back inside his jacket, Strike said casually, 'Billy told me you were there when the child was strangled, Jimmy.'

Flick's rapid turn of the head towards Jimmy was the giveaway. The latter was better prepared. His nostrils flared, but otherwise he did a creditable job of pretending not to be alarmed.

'Yeah, he's got the whole sick scene worked out in his poor fucked head,' he said. 'Some days he thinks our dead mum might've been there, too. Pope next, I expect.'

'Sad,' said Strike. 'Hope you manage to track him down.'

He raised a hand in farewell and left them standing on the forecourt. Hungry in spite of the chips, his stump now throbbing, he was limping by the time he reached the bus stop.

After a fifteen-minute wait, the bus arrived. Two drunk youths a few seats in front of Strike got into a long, repetitive argument about the merits of West Ham's new signing, Jussi Jääskeläinen, whose name neither of them could pronounce. Strike stared unseeingly out of the grimy window, leg sore, desperate for his bed, but unable to relax.

Irksome though it was to admit it, the trip to Charlemont Road had not rid him of the tiny niggling doubt about Billy's story. The memory of Flick's sudden, frightened peek at Jimmy, and above all her blurted exclamation 'Chizzle's sent him!' had turned that niggling doubt into a significant and possibly permanent impediment to the detective's peace of mind.

7

Do you think you will remain here? Permanently, I mean?
Henrik Ibsen, Rosmersholm

Robin would have been happy to spend the weekend relaxing after her long week unpacking and putting together furniture, but Matthew was looking forward to the house-warming party, to which he had invited a large number of colleagues. His pride was piqued by the interesting, romantic history of the street, which had been built for shipwrights and sea captains back when Deptford had been a shipbuilding centre. Matthew might not yet have arrived in the postcode of his dreams, but a short cobbled street full of pretty old houses was, as he had wanted, a 'step up', even if he and Robin were only renting the neat brick box with its sash windows and the mouldings of cherubs over the front door.

Matthew had objected when Robin first suggested renting again, but she had overridden him, saying that she could not stand another year in Hastings Road while further purchases of overpriced houses fell through. Between the legacy and Matthew's new job, they were just able to make rent on the smart little three-bedroomed house, leaving the money they had received from the sale of their Hastings Road flat untouched in the bank.

Their landlord, a publisher who was off to New York to work at head office, had been delighted with his new tenants. A gay man in his forties, he admired Matthew's clean-cut looks and made a point of handing over the keys personally on their moving day.

'I agree with Jane Austen on the ideal tenant,' he told Matthew, standing in the cobbled street. '"A married man, and without children; the very state to be wished for." A house is never well cared for without a lady! Or do you two share the hoovering?'

'Of course,' Matthew had said, smiling. Robin, who was carrying a box of plants over the threshold behind the two men, had bitten back a caustic retort.

She had a suspicion that Matthew was not disclosing to friends and workmates that they were tenants rather than owners. She deplored her own increasing tendency to watch Matthew for shabby or duplicitous behaviour, even in small matters, and imposed private penances on herself for thinking the worst of him all the time. It was in this spirit of self-castigation that she had agreed to the party, bought alcohol and plastic tumblers, made food and set everything up in the kitchen. Matthew had rearranged the furniture and, over several evenings, organised a playlist now blaring out of his iPod in its dock. The first few bars of 'Cutt Off' by Kasabian started as Robin hurried upstairs to change.

Robin's hair was in foam rollers, because she had decided to wear it as she had on their wedding day. Running out of time before guests were due, she pulled out the rollers one-handed as she yanked open the wardrobe door. She had a new dress, a form-fitting pale grey affair, but she was afraid that it drained her of colour. She hesitated, then took out the emerald-green Roberto Cavalli that she had never worn in public. It was the most expensive item of clothing she owned, and the most beautiful: the 'leaving' present that Strike had bought her after she had gone to him as a temp and helped him catch their first killer. The expression on Matthew's face when she had excitedly shown him the gift had prevented her ever wearing it.

For some reason her mind drifted to Strike's girlfriend, Lorelei, as she held the dress up against herself. Lorelei, who always wore jewel-bright colours, affected the style of a 1940s pin-up. As tall as Robin, she had glossy brunette hair that she wore over one eye like Veronica Lake. Robin knew that Lorelei was thirty-three, and that she co-owned and ran a vintage and theatrical clothing store on Chalk Farm Road. Strike had let slip this information one day and Robin, making a mental note of the name, had gone home and looked it up online. The shop appeared to be glamorous and successful.

'It's a quarter to,' said Matthew, hurrying into the bedroom, stripping off his T-shirt as he came. 'I might shower quickly.'

He caught sight of her, holding the green dress against herself.

'I thought you were wearing the grey one?'

Their eyes met in the mirror. Bare-chested, tanned and handsome, Matthew's features were so symmetrical that his reflection was almost identical to his real appearance.

'I think it makes me look pale,' said Robin.

'I prefer the grey one,' he said. 'I like you pale.'

She forced a smile.

'All right,' she said. 'I'll wear the grey.'

Once changed, she ran fingers through her curls to loosen them, pulled on a pair of strappy silver sandals and hurried back downstairs. She had barely reached the hall when the doorbell rang.

If she had been asked to guess who would arrive first, she would have said Sarah Shadlock and Tom Turvey, who had recently got engaged. It would be like Sarah to try and catch Robin on the hop, to make sure she had an opportunity to nose around the house before anybody else, and to stake out a spot where she could look over all the arrivals. Sure enough, when Robin opened up, there stood Sarah in shocking pink, a big bunch of flowers in her arms, Tom carrying beer and wine.

'Oh, it's *gorgeous*, Robin,' crooned Sarah, the moment she got over the doorstep, staring around the hall. She hugged Robin absent-mindedly, her eyes on the stairs as Matthew descended, doing up his shirt. '*Lovely*. These are for you.'

Robin found herself encumbered by an armful of stargazer lilies.

'Thanks,' she said. 'I'll just go and put them in water.'

They didn't have a vase big enough for the flowers, but Robin could hardly leave them in the sink. She could hear Sarah's laugh from the kitchen, even over Coldplay and Rihanna, who were now belting out 'Princess of China' from Matthew's iPod. Robin dragged a bucket out of the cupboard and began to fill it, splattering herself with water in the process.

The idea had once been mooted, she remembered, that Matthew would refrain from taking Sarah out for lunches during their office lunch hours. There had even been talk of stopping socialising with her, after Robin had found out that Matthew had been cheating with Sarah in their early twenties. However, Tom had helped Matthew get the higher-paid position he now enjoyed at Tom's firm, and now that Sarah was the proud owner of a large solitaire diamond, Matthew did not seem to think that there should be the slightest awkwardness attached to social events including the future Mr and Mrs Turvey.

Robin could hear the three of them moving around upstairs. Matthew was giving a tour of the bedrooms. She heaved the lily-filled bucket out of the sink and shoved it into a corner beside the kettle, wondering whether it was mean-spirited to suspect that Sarah had brought flowers just to get Robin out of the way for a bit. Sarah had never lost the flirtatious manner towards Matthew she had had since their shared years at university.

Robin poured herself a glass of wine and emerged from the kitchen as Matthew led Tom and Sarah into the sitting room.

'... and Lord Nelson and Lady Hamilton are supposed to have stayed in number 19, but it was called Union Street then,' he said. 'Right, who wants a drink? It's all set up in the kitchen.'

'Gorgeous place, Robin,' said Sarah. 'Houses like this don't come up that often. You must've got really lucky.'

'We're only renting,' said Robin.

'Really?' said Sarah beadily, and Robin knew that Sarah was drawing her own conclusions, not about the housing market, but about Robin and Matthew's marriage.

'Nice earrings,' said Robin, keen to change the subject.

'Aren't they?' said Sarah, pulling back her hair to give Robin a better view. 'Tom's birthday present.'

The doorbell rang again. Robin went to answer it, hoping that it would be one of the few people she had invited. She had no hope of Strike, of course. He was bound to be late, as he had been to every other personal event to which she had invited him.

'Oh, thank God,' said Robin, surprised at her own relief when she saw Vanessa Ekwensi.

Vanessa was a police officer: tall, black, with almond-shaped eyes, a model's figure and a self-possession Robin envied. She had come to the party alone. Her boyfriend, who worked in Forensic Services at the Met, had a prior commitment. Robin was disappointed: she had looked forward to meeting him.

'You all right?' Vanessa asked as she entered. She was carrying a bottle of red wine and wearing a deep purple slip dress. Robin thought again of the emerald-green Cavalli upstairs and wished she had worn it.

'I'm fine,' she said. 'Come through to the back, you can smoke there.'

She led Vanessa through the sitting room, past Sarah and Matthew, who were now mocking Tom's baldness to his face.

The rear wall of the small courtyard garden was covered in ivy. Well-maintained shrubs stood in terracotta tubs. Robin, who did not smoke, had put ashtrays and a few fold-up chairs out there, and dotted tea candles around. Matthew had asked her with an edge in his voice why she was taking so much trouble over the smokers. She had known perfectly well why he was saying it and pretended not to.

'I thought Jemima smoked?' she asked, with a feigned air of confusion. Jemima was Matthew's boss.

'Oh,' he said, caught off balance. 'Yeah – yeah, but only socially.'

'Well, I'm pretty sure this is a social occasion, Matt,' said Robin sweetly.

She fetched Vanessa a drink and came back to find her lighting up, her lovely eyes fixed on Sarah Shadlock, who was still mocking Tom's hairline, with Matthew her hearty accomplice.

'That's her, is it?' Vanessa asked.

'That's her,' said Robin.

She appreciated the small show of moral support. Robin and Vanessa had been friends for months before Robin had confided the history of her relationship with Matthew. Before that they had talked police work, politics and clothes on evenings that took them to the cinema, or to cheap restaurants. Robin found Vanessa better company than any other woman she knew. Matthew, who had met her twice, told Robin he found her 'cold', but said he could not explain why.

Vanessa had had a succession of partners; she had been engaged once, but broken it off when he had cheated. Robin sometimes wondered whether Vanessa found her laughably inexperienced: the woman who'd married her boyfriend from school.

A few moments later, a dozen people, colleagues of Matthew's with their partners, who had obviously been to the pub first, streamed into the sitting room. Robin watched Matthew greeting them and showing them where the drinks were. He had adopted the loud, bantering tone that she had heard him using on work nights out. It irritated her.

The party quickly became crowded. Robin effected introductions, showed people where to find drink, set out more plastic cups and handed a couple of plates of food around because the kitchen was becoming packed. Only when Andy Hutchins and his wife arrived did she feel she could relax for a moment and spend some more time with her own guests.

'I made you some special food,' Robin told Andy, after she had shown him and Louise out into the courtyard. 'This is Vanessa. She's Met. Vanessa, Andy and Louise – stay there, Andy, I'll get it, it's dairy-free.'

Tom was standing against the fridge when she got to the kitchen.

'Sorry, Tom, need to get in—'

He blinked at her, then moved aside. He was already drunk, she thought, and it was barely nine o'clock. Robin could hear Sarah's braying laugh from the middle of the crowd outside.

'Lemmelp,' said Tom, holding the fridge door that threatened to close on Robin as she bent down to the lower shelf to get the tray of dairy-free, non-fried food she had saved for Andy. 'God, you've got a nice arse, Robin.'

She straightened up without comment. In spite of the drunken grin, she could feel the unhappiness flowing from behind it, like a cool draught. Matthew had told her how self-conscious Tom was about his hairline, that he was even considering a transplant.

'That's a nice shirt,' said Robin.

'Wha' this? You like it? She bought it for me. Matt's got one like it, hasn't he?'

'Er – I'm not sure,' said Robin.

'You're not sure,' repeated Tom, with a short, nasty laugh. 'So much f' surveillance training. You wanna pay more attention at home, Rob.'

Robin contemplated him for a moment in equal amounts of pity and anger, then, deciding that he was too drunk to argue with, she left, carrying Andy's food.

The first thing she saw as people cleared out of the way to let her back into the courtyard was that Strike had arrived. He had his back to her and was talking to Andy. Lorelei was beside him, wearing a scarlet silk dress, the gleaming fall of dark hair down her back like an advertisement for expensive shampoo. Somehow, Sarah had inveigled her way into the group in Robin's brief absence. When Vanessa caught Robin's eye, the corner of her mouth twitched.

'Hi,' said Robin, setting the platter of food down on the wrought iron table beside Andy.

'Robin, hi!' said Lorelei. 'It's such a pretty street!'

'Yes, isn't it?' said Robin, as Lorelei kissed the air behind Robin's ear.

Strike bent down, too. His stubble grazed Robin's face, but his lips did not touch skin. He was already opening one of the six-pack of Doom Bar he had brought with him.

Robin had mentally rehearsed things to say to Strike once he was in her new house: calm, casual things that made it sound as though she had no regrets, as though there were some wonderful counter-weight that he couldn't appreciate that tipped the scales in Matthew's favour. She also wanted to question him about the strange matter of Billy and the strangled child. However, Sarah was currently holding forth on the subject of the auction house, Christie's, where she worked, and the whole group was listening to her.

'Yeah, we've got "The Lock" coming up at auction on the third,' she said. 'Constable,' she added kindly, for the benefit of anyone who did not know art as well as she did. 'We're expecting it to make over twenty.'

'Thousand?' asked Andy.

'Million,' said Sarah, with a patronising little snort of laughter.

Matthew laughed behind Robin and she moved automatically to let him join the circle. His expression was rapt, Robin noticed, as so often when large sums of money were under discussion. Perhaps, she thought, this is what he and Sarah talk about when they have lunch: money.

'"Gimcrack" went for over twenty-two last year. Stubbs. Third most valuable Old Master ever sold.'

Out of the corner of her eye, Robin saw Lorelei's scarlet-tipped hand slide into Strike's, which had been marked across the palm with the very same knife that had forever scarred Robin's arm.

'Anyway, boring, boring, boring!' said Sarah insincerely. 'Enough work chat! Anyone got Olympics tickets? Tom – my fiancé – he's furious. We got *ping pong*.' She pulled a droll face. 'How have you lot got on?'

Robin saw Strike and Lorelei exchange a fleeting look, and knew that they were mutually consoling each other for having to endure the tedium of the Olympics ticket conversation. Suddenly wishing that they hadn't come, Robin backed out of the group.

An hour later, Strike was in the sitting room, discussing the England football team's chances in the European Championships with one of Matthew's friends from work while Lorelei danced. Robin, with whom he had not exchanged a word since they had met outside, crossed the room with a plate of food, paused to talk to a redheaded woman, then continued to offer the plate around. The way she had done her hair reminded Strike of her wedding day.

The suspicions provoked by her visit to that unknown clinic uppermost in his mind, he appraised her figure in the clinging grey dress. She certainly didn't appear to be pregnant, and the fact that she was drinking wine seemed a further counter-indication, but they might only just have begun the process of IVF.

Directly opposite Strike, visible through the dancing bodies, stood DI Vanessa Ekwensi, whom Strike had been surprised to find at the party. She was leaning up against the wall, talking to a tall blond man who seemed, by his over-attentive attitude, to have temporarily forgotten that he was wearing a wedding ring. Vanessa glanced across the room at Strike and by a wry look signalled that she would not mind him breaking up the tête-à-tête. The football conversation was not so fascinating that he would be disappointed to leave it, and at the next convenient pause he circumnavigated the dancers to talk to Vanessa.

'Evening.'

'Hi,' she said, accepting his peck on the cheek with the elegance that characterised all her gestures. 'Cormoran, this is Owen – sorry, I didn't catch your surname?'

It didn't take long for Owen to lose hope of whatever he had wanted from Vanessa, whether the mere pleasure of flirting with a good-looking woman, or her phone number.

'Didn't realise you and Robin were this friendly,' said Strike, as Owen walked away.

'Yeah, we've been hanging out,' said Vanessa. 'I wrote her a note after I heard you sacked her.'

'Oh,' said Strike, swigging Doom Bar. 'Right.'

'She rang to thank me and we ended up going for a drink.'

Robin had never mentioned this to Strike, but then, as Strike knew perfectly well, he had been at pains to discourage anything but work talk since she had come back from her honeymoon.

'Nice house,' he commented, trying not to compare the tastefully decorated room with his combined kitchen and sitting room in the attic over the office. Matthew must be earning very good money to have afforded this, he thought. Robin's pay rise certainly couldn't have done it.

'Yeah, it is,' said Vanessa. 'They're renting.'

Strike watched Lorelei dance for a few moments while he pondered this interesting piece of information. An arch something in Vanessa's tone told him that she, too, read this as a choice not entirely related to the housing market.

'Blame sea-borne bacteria,' said Vanessa.

'Sorry?' said Strike, thoroughly confused.

She threw him a sharp look, then shook her head, laughing.

'Nothing. Forget it.'

'Yeah, we didn't do too badly,' Strike heard Matthew telling the redheaded woman in a lull in the music. 'Got tickets for the boxing.'

Of course you fucking did, thought Strike irritably, feeling in his pocket for more cigarettes.

'Enjoy yourself?' asked Lorelei in the taxi, at one in the morning.

'Not particularly,' said Strike, who was watching the headlights of oncoming cars.

He had had the impression that Robin had been avoiding him. After the relative warmth of their conversation on Thursday, he had expected – what? A conversation, a laugh? He had been curious to know how the marriage was progressing, but was not much the wiser. She and Matthew seemed amicable enough together, but the fact that they were renting was intriguing. Did it suggest, even subconsciously, a lack of investment in a joint future? An easier arrangement to untangle? And then there was Robin's friendship with Vanessa Ekwensi, which Strike saw as another stake in the life she led independently of Matthew.

Blame sea-borne bacteria.

What the hell did that mean? Was it connected to the mysterious clinic? Was Robin ill?

After a few minutes' silence it suddenly occurred to Strike that he ought to ask Lorelei how her evening had been.

'I've had better,' sighed Lorelei. 'I'm afraid your Robin's got a lot of boring friends.'

'Yeah,' said Strike. 'I think that's mainly her husband. He's an accountant. And a bit of a tit,' he added, enjoying saying it.

The taxi bowled on through the night, Strike remembering how Robin's figure had looked in the grey dress.

'Sorry?' he said suddenly, because he had the impression that Lorelei had spoken to him.

'I said, "What are you thinking about?"'

'Nothing,' lied Strike, and because it was preferable to talking, he slid an arm around her, pulled her close and kissed her.

8

... my word! Mortensgaard has risen in the world. There are lots of people who run after him now.

Henrik Ibsen, *Rosmersholm*

Robin texted Strike on Sunday evening to ask what he wanted her to do on Monday, because she had handed over all her jobs before taking a week's leave. His terse response had been 'come to office', which she duly entered at a quarter to nine the following day, glad, no matter how matters stood between her and her partner, to be back in the shabby old rooms.

The door to Strike's inner office was standing open when she arrived. He was sitting behind his desk, listening to someone on his mobile. Sunlight fell in treacle-gold pools across the worn carpet. The soft mumble of traffic was soon obliterated by the rattle of the old kettle and, five minutes after her arrival, Robin set a mug of steaming dark brown Typhoo in front of Strike, who gave her a thumbs up and a silent 'thanks'. She returned to her desk, where a light was flashing on the phone to indicate a recorded message. She dialled their answering service and listened while a cool female voice informed her that the call had been made ten minutes before Robin had arrived and, presumably, while Strike was either upstairs, or busy with the other call.

A cracked whisper hissed in Robin's ear.

'I'm sorry I ran out on you, Mr Strike, I'm sorry. I can't come back, though. He's keeping me here, I can't get out, he's wired the doors ...'

85

The end of the sentence was lost in sobs. Worried, Robin tried to attract Strike's attention, but he had turned in his swivel chair to look out of the window, still listening to his mobile. Random words reached Robin through the pitiable sounds of distress on the phone.

'. . . can't get out . . . I'm all alone . . .'

'Yeah, OK,' Strike was saying in his office. 'Wednesday, then, OK? Great. Have a good one.'

'. . . *please help me, Mr Strike!*' wailed the voice in Robin's ear.

She smacked the button to switch to speakerphone and at once the tortured voice filled the office.

'The doors will explode if I try and escape Mr Strike, please help me, please come and get me, I shouldn't have come, I told him I know about the little kid and it's bigger, much bigger, I thought I could trust him—'

Strike spun in his desk chair, got up and came striding through to the outer office. There was a clunk as though the receiver had been dropped. The sobbing continued at a distance, as though the distraught speaker was stumbling away from the phone.

'That's him again,' said Strike. 'Billy, Billy Knight.'

The sobbing and gasping grew louder again and Billy said in a frantic whisper, his lips evidently pressed against the mouthpiece.

'There's someone at the door. Help me. Help me, Mr Strike.'

The call was cut.

'Get the number,' said Strike. Robin reached for the receiver to dial 1471, but before she could do so, the phone rang again. She snatched it up, her eyes on Strike's.

'Cormoran Strike's office.'

'Ah . . . yes, good morning,' said a deep, patrician voice.

Robin grimaced at Strike and shook her head.

'Shit,' he muttered, and moved back into his office to get his tea.

'I'd like to speak to Mr Strike, please.'

'I'm afraid he's on another call right now,' lied Robin.

Their standard practice for a year had been to phone the client back. It weeded out journalists and cranks.

'I'll hold,' said the caller, who sounded captious, unused to not getting his way.

'He'll be a while, I'm afraid. Could I take a number and get him to call you back?'

'Well, it needs to be within the next ten minutes, because I'm about to go into a meeting. Tell him I want to discuss a job I'd like him to do for me.'

'I'm afraid I can't guarantee that Mr Strike will be able to undertake the job in person,' said Robin, which was also the standard response to deflect press. 'Our agency's quite booked up at the moment.'

She pulled pen and paper towards her.

'What kind of job are you—?'

'It has to be Mr Strike,' said the voice firmly. 'Make that clear to him. It has to be Mr Strike himself. My name's Chizzle.'

'How are you spelling that?' asked Robin, wondering whether she had heard correctly.

'C – H – I – S – W – E – L – L. Jasper Chiswell. Ask him to call me on the following number.'

Robin copied down the digits Chiswell gave her and bade him good morning. As she set down the receiver, Strike sat down on the fake leather sofa they kept in the outer room for clients. It had a disobliging habit of making unexpected farting noises when you shifted position.

'A man called Jasper Chizzle, spelled "Chiswell" wants you to take on a job for him. He says it's got to be you, nobody else.' Robin screwed up her forehead in perplexity. 'I know the name, don't I?'

'Yeah,' said Strike. 'He's Minister for Culture.'

'Oh my God,' said Robin, realisation dawning. '*Of course!* The big man with the weird hair!'

'That's him.'

A clutch of vague memories and associations assailed Robin. She seemed to remember an old affair, resignation in disgrace, rehabilitation and, somewhat more recently, a fresh scandal, another nasty news story . . .

'Didn't his son get sent to jail for manslaughter not that long ago?' she said. 'That was Chiswell, wasn't it? His son was stoned and driving and he killed a young mother?'

Strike recalled his attention, it seemed, from a distance. He was wearing a peculiar expression.

'Yeah, that rings a bell,' said Strike.

'What's the matter?'

'A few things, actually,' said Strike, running a hand over his stubbly chin. 'For starters: I tracked down Billy's brother on Friday.'

'How?'

'Long story,' said Strike, 'but turns out Jimmy's part of a group that's protesting against the Olympics. "CORE", they call themselves. Anyway, he was with a girl, and the first thing she said when I told them I was a private detective was: "Chiswell's sent him."'

Strike pondered this point while drinking his perfectly brewed tea.

'But Chiswell wouldn't need me to keep an eye on CORE,' he went on, thinking aloud. 'There was already a plainclothes guy there.'

Though keen to hear what other things troubled Strike about Chiswell's call, Robin did not prompt him, but sat in silence, allowing him to mull the new development. It was precisely this kind of tact that Strike had missed when she was out of the office.

'And get this,' he went on at last, as though there had been no interruption. 'The son who went to jail for manslaughter isn't – or wasn't – Chiswell's only boy. His eldest was called Freddie and he died in Afghanistan. Yeah. Major Freddie Chiswell, Queen's Royal Hussars. Killed in an attack on a convoy in Basra. I investigated his death in action while I was still SIB.'

'So you *know* Chiswell?'

'No, never met him. You don't meet families, usually ... I knew Chiswell's daughter years ago, as well. Only slightly, but I met her a few times. She was an old school friend of Charlotte's.'

Robin experienced a tiny frisson at the mention of Charlotte. She had a great curiosity, which she successfully concealed, about Charlotte, the woman Strike had been involved with on and off for sixteen years, whom he had been supposed to marry before the relationship ended messily and, apparently, permanently.

'Pity we couldn't get Billy's number,' said Strike, running a large, hairy-backed hand over his jaw again.

'I'll make sure I get it if he calls again,' Robin assured him. 'Are you going to ring Chiswell back? He said he was about to go into a meeting.'

'I'm keen to find out what he wants, but the question is whether we've got room for another client,' said Strike. 'Let's think . . . '

He put his hands behind his head, frowning up at the ceiling, on which many fine cracks were exposed by the sunlight. *Screw that now* . . . the office would soon be a developer's problem, after all . . .

'I've got Andy and Barclay watching the Webster kid. Barclay's doing well, by the way. I've had three solid days' surveillance out of him, pictures, the lot.

'Then there's old Dodgy Doc. He still hasn't done anything newsworthy.'

'Shame,' said Robin, then she caught herself. 'No, I don't mean that, I mean good.' She rubbed her eyes. 'This job,' she sighed. 'It messes with your ethics. Who's watching Dodgy today?'

'I was going to ask you to do it,' said Strike, 'but the client called yesterday afternoon. He'd forgotten to tell me Dodgy's at a symposium in Paris.'

Eyes still on the ceiling, brow furrowed in thought, Strike said:

'We've got two days at that tech conference starting tomorrow. Which do you want to do, Harley Street or a conference centre out in Epping Forest? We can swap over if you want. D'you want to spend tomorrow watching Dodgy, or with hundreds of stinking geeks in superhero T-shirts?'

'Not all tech people smell,' Robin reprimanded him. 'Your mate Spanner doesn't.'

'You don't want to judge Spanner by the amount of deodorant he puts on to come here,' said Strike.

Spanner, who had overhauled their computer and telephone system when the business had received its dramatic boost in business, was the younger brother of Strike's old friend Nick. He fancied Robin, as she and Strike were equally aware.

Strike mulled over options, rubbing his chin again.

'I'll call Chiswell back and find out what he's after,' he said at last. 'You never know, it might be a bigger job than that lawyer whose wife's sleeping around. He's next on the waiting list, right?'

'Him, or that American woman who's married to the Ferrari dealer. They're both waiting.'

Strike sighed. Infidelity formed the bulk of their workload.

'I hope Chiswell's wife isn't cheating. I fancy a change.'

The sofa made its usual flatulent noises as Strike quit it. As he strode back to the inner office, Robin called after him:

'Are you happy for me to finish up this paperwork, then?'

'If you don't mind,' said Strike, closing the door behind him.

Robin turned back to her computer feeling quite cheerful. A busker had just started singing 'No Woman, No Cry' in Denmark Street and for a while there, while they talked about Billy Knight and the Chiswells, she had felt as though they were the Strike and Robin of a year ago, before he had sacked her, before she had married Matthew.

Meanwhile, in the inner office, Strike's call to Jasper Chiswell had been answered almost instantly.

'Chiswell,' he barked.

'Cormoran Strike here,' said the detective. 'You spoke to my partner a short while ago.'

'Ah, yes,' said the Minister for Culture, who sounded as though he were in the back of a car. 'I've got a job for you. Nothing I want to discuss over the phone. I'm busy today and this evening, unfortunately, but tomorrow would suit.'

'*Ob-observing the hypocrites . . .*' sang the busker down in the street.

'Sorry, no chance tomorrow,' said Strike, watching motes of dust fall through the bright sunlight. 'No chance until Friday, actually. Can you give me an idea what kind of job we're talking about, Minister?'

Chiswell's response was both tense and angry.

'I can't discuss it over the phone. I'll make it worth your while to meet me, if that's what you want.'

'It isn't a question of money, it's time. I'm solidly booked until Friday.'

'Oh, for Christ's sake—'

Chiswell suddenly removed his phone from his mouth and Strike heard him talking furiously to somebody else.

'—*left* here, you moron! *Lef* – for fuck's sake! No, I'll walk. I'll bloody walk, open the door!'

In the background, Strike heard a nervous man say:

'I'm sorry, Minister, it was No Entry—'

'Never mind that! Open this – *open this bloody door!*'

Strike waited, eyebrows raised. He heard a car door slam, rapid footsteps and then Jasper Chiswell spoke again, his mouth close to the receiver.

'The job's urgent!' he hissed.

'If it can't wait until Friday, you'll have to find someone else, I'm afraid.'

'*My feet is my only carriage,*' sang the busker.

Chiswell said nothing for a few seconds; then, finally:

'It's got to be you. I'll explain when we meet, but – all right, if it *has* to be Friday, meet me at Pratt's Club. Park Place. Come at twelve, I'll give you lunch.'

'All right,' Strike agreed, now thoroughly intrigued. 'See you at Pratt's.'

He hung up and returned to the office where Robin was opening and sorting mail. When he told her the upshot of the conversation, she Googled Pratt's for him.

'I didn't think places like this still existed,' she said in disbelief, after a minute's reading off the monitor.

'Places like what?'

'It's a gentleman's club . . . very Tory . . . no women allowed, except as guests of club members at lunchtime . . . and "to avoid confusion",' Robin read from the Wikipedia page, '"all male staff members are called George".'

'What if they hire a woman?'

'Apparently they did in the eighties,' said Robin, her expression midway between amusement and disapproval. 'They called her Georgina.'

9

It is best for you not to know. Best for us both.

Henrik Ibsen, *Rosmersholm*

At half past eleven the following Friday, a suited and freshly shaven Strike emerged from Green Park Tube station and proceeded along Piccadilly. Double-deckers rolled past the windows of luxury shops, which were capitalising on Olympics fever to push an eclectic mix of goods: gold-wrapped chocolate medals, Union Jack brogues, antique sporting posters and, over and again, the jagged logo that Jimmy Knight had compared to a broken swastika.

Strike had allowed a generous margin of time to reach Pratt's, because his leg was again aching after two days in which he had rarely been able to take the weight off his prosthesis. He had hoped that the tech conference in Epping Forest, where he had spent the previous day, might have offered intervals of rest, but he had been disappointed. His target, the recently fired partner of a start-up, was suspected of trying to sell key features of their new app to competitors. For hours, Strike had tailed the young man from booth to booth, documenting all his movements and his interactions, hoping at some point that he would tire and sit. However, between the coffee bar where customers stood at high tables, to the sandwich bar where everyone stood and ate sushi with their fingers out of plastic boxes, the target had spent eight hours walking or standing. Coming after long hours of lurking in Harley Street the day before, it was hardly surprising that the removal of his prosthesis the previous evening had been an uncomfortable affair, the gel pad that separated stump from artificial shin difficult to prise off. As Strike passed the cool off-white arches of the Ritz, Strike hoped Pratt's contained at least one comfortable chair of generous proportions.

He turned right into St James's Street, which led him in a gentle slope straight down to the sixteenth-century St James's Palace. This was not an area of London that Strike usually visited on his own account, given that he had neither the means nor the inclination to buy from gentlemen's outfitters, long-established gun shops or centuries' old wine dealers. As he drew nearer to Park Place, though, he was visited by a personal memory. He had walked this street more than ten years previously, with Charlotte.

They had walked up the slope, not down it, heading for a lunch date with her father, who was now dead. Strike had been on leave from the army and they had recently resumed what was, to everyone who knew them, an incomprehensible and obviously doomed affair. On neither side of their relationship had there ever been a single supporter. His friends and family had viewed Charlotte with everything from mistrust to loathing, while hers had always considered Strike, the illegitimate son of an infamous rockstar, as one more manifestation of Charlotte's need to shock and rebel. Strike's military career had been nothing to her family, or rather, it had been just another sign of his plebeian unfitness to aspire to the well-bred beauty's hand, because gentlemen of Charlotte's class did not enter the Military Police, but Cavalry or Guards regiments.

She had clutched his hand very tightly as they entered an Italian restaurant somewhere nearby. Its precise location escaped Strike now. All he remembered was the expression of rage and disapproval on Sir Anthony Campbell's face as they had approached the table. Strike had known before a word was spoken that Charlotte had not told her father that she and Strike had resumed their affair, or that she would be bringing him with her. It had been a thoroughly Charlottian omission, prompting the usual Charlottian scene. Strike had long since come to believe that she engineered situations out of an apparently insatiable need for conflict. Prone to outbursts of lacerating honesty amid her general mythomania, she had told Strike towards the end of their relationship, that at least, while fighting, she knew she was alive.

As Strike drew level with Park Place, a line of cream-painted townhouses leading off St James's Street, he noted that the sudden memory of Charlotte clinging to his hand no longer hurt, and felt like an alcoholic who, for the first time, catches a whiff of beer without breaking into a sweat or having to grapple with his desperate craving. *Perhaps this is it*, he thought, as he approached the black door of Pratt's, with its wrought iron balustrade above. Perhaps, two years after she had told him the unforgivable lie and he had left for good, he was healed, clear of what he sometimes, even though not superstitious, saw as a kind of Bermuda triangle, a danger zone in which he feared being pulled back under, dragged to the depths of anguish and pain by the mysterious allure Charlotte had held for him.

With a faint sense of celebration, Strike knocked on the door of Pratt's.

A petite, motherly woman opened up. Her prominent bust and alert, bright-eyed mien put him in mind of a robin or a wren. When she spoke, he caught a trace of the West Country.

'You'll be Mr Strike. The minister's not here yet. Come along in.'

He followed her across the threshold into a hall through which could be glimpsed an enormous billiard table. Rich crimsons, greens and dark wood predominated. The stewardess, who he assumed was Georgina, led him down a set of steep stairs, which Strike took carefully, maintaining a firm grip on the banister.

The stairs led to a cosy basement. The ceiling had sunk so low that it appeared partially supported by a large dresser on which sundry porcelain platters were displayed, the topmost ones half embedded into the plaster.

'We aren't very big,' she said, stating the obvious. 'Six hundred members, but we can only serve fourteen a meal at a time. Would you like a drink, Mr Strike?'

He declined, but accepted an invitation to sit down in one of the leather chairs grouped around an aged cribbage board.

The small space was divided by an archway into sitting and dining areas. Two places had been set at the long table in the other half of the room, beneath small, shuttered windows. The only other person in the basement apart from himself and Georgina was a white-coated chef working in a minuscule kitchen a mere yard from where Strike sat. The chef bade Strike welcome in a French accent, then continued carving cold roast beef.

Here was the very antithesis of the smart restaurants where Strike tailed errant husbands and wives, where the lighting was chosen to complement glass and granite, and sharp-tongued restaurant critics sat like stylish vultures on uncomfortable modern chairs. Pratt's was dimly lit. Brass picture lights dotted walls papered in dark red, which was largely obscured by stuffed fish in glass cases, hunting prints and political cartoons. In a blue and white tiled niche along one side of the room sat an ancient iron stove. The china plates, the threadbare carpet, the table bearing its homely load of ketchup and mustard all contributed to an ambience of cosy informality, as though a bunch of aristocratic boys had dragged all the things they liked about the grown-up world – its games, its drink and its trophies – down into the basement where Nanny would dole out smiles, comfort and praise.

Twelve o'clock arrived, but Chiswell did not. 'Georgina', however, was friendly and informative about the club. She and her husband, the chef, lived on the premises. Strike could not help but reflect that this must be some of the most expensive real estate in London. To maintain the little club, which, Georgina told him, had been established in 1857, was costing somebody a lot of money.

'The Duke of Devonshire owns it, yes,' said Georgina brightly. 'Have you seen our betting book?'

Strike turned the pages of the heavy, leather-bound tome, where long ago wagers had been recorded. In a gigantic scrawl dating back to the seventies, he read: 'Mrs Thatcher to form the next government. Bet: one lobster dinner, the lobster to be larger than a man's erect cock.'

He was grinning over this when a bell rang overhead.

'That'll be the minister,' said Georgina, bustling away upstairs.

Strike replaced the betting book on its shelf and returned to his seat. From overhead came heavy footsteps and then, descending the stairs, the same irascible, impatient voice he had heard on Monday.

'—no, Kinvara, I can't. I've just told you why, I've got a lunch meeting ... no, you can't ... Five o'clock, then, yes ... yes ... *yes!* ... Goodbye!'

A pair of large, black-shod feet descended the stairs until Jasper Chiswell emerged into the basement, peering around with a truculent air. Strike rose from his armchair.

'Ah,' said Chiswell, scrutinising Strike from beneath his heavy eyebrows. 'You're here.'

Jasper Chiswell wore his sixty-eight years reasonably well. A big, broad man, though round-shouldered, he still had a full head of grey hair which, implausible though it seemed, was his own. This hair made Chiswell an easy target for cartoonists, because it was coarse, straight and rather long, standing out from his head in a manner that suggested a wig or, so the unkind suggested, a chimney brush. To the hair was added a large red face, small eyes and a protuberant lower lip, which gave him the air of an overgrown baby perpetually on the verge of a tantrum.

'M'wife,' he told Strike, brandishing the mobile still in his hand. 'Come up to town without warning. Sulking. Thinks I can drop everything.'

Chiswell stretched out a large, sweaty hand, which Strike shook, then eased off the heavy overcoat he was wearing despite the heat of the day. As he did so, Strike noticed the pin on his frayed regimental tie. The uninitiated might think it a rocking horse, but Strike recognised it at once as the White Horse of Hanover.

'Queen's Own Hussars,' said Strike, nodding at it as both men sat down.

'Yerse,' said Chiswell. 'Georgina, I'll have some of that sherry you gave me when I was in with Alastair. You?' he barked at Strike.

'No thanks.'

Though nowhere near as dirty as Billy Knight, Chiswell did not smell very fresh.

'Yerse, Queen's Own Hussars. Aden and Singapore. Happy days.'

He didn't seem happy at the moment. His ruddy skin had an odd, plaque-like appearance close up. Dandruff lay thick in the roots of his coarse hair and large patches of sweat spread around the underarms of his blue shirt. The minister bore the unmistakable appearance, not unusual in Strike's clients, of a man under intense strain, and when his sherry arrived, he swallowed most of it in a single gulp.

'Shall we move through?' he suggested, and without waiting for an answer he barked, 'We'll eat straight away, Georgina.'

Once they were seated at the table, which had a stiff, snowy-white tablecloth like those at Robin's wedding, Georgina brought them thick slices of cold roast beef and boiled potatoes. It was English nursery food, plain and unfussy, and none the worse for it. Only when the stewardess had left them in peace, in the dim dining room full of oil paintings and more dead fish, did Chiswell speak again.

'You were at Jimmy Knight's meeting,' he said, without preamble. 'A plainclothes officer there recognised you.'

Strike nodded. Chiswell shoved a boiled potato in his mouth, masticated angrily, and swallowed before saying:

'I don't know who's paying you to get dirt on Jimmy Knight, or what you may already have on him, but whoever it is and whatever you've got, I'm prepared to pay double for the information.'

'I haven't got anything on Jimmy Knight, I'm afraid,' said Strike. 'Nobody was paying me to be at the meeting.'

Chiswell looked stunned.

'But then, why were you there?' he demanded. 'You're not telling me *you* intend to protest against the Olympics?'

So plosive was the 'p' of 'protest' that a small piece of potato flew out of his mouth across the table.

'No,' said Strike. 'I was trying to find somebody I thought might be at the meeting. They weren't.'

Chiswell attacked his beef again as though it had personally wronged him. For a while, the only sounds were those of their knives and forks scraping the china. Chiswell speared the last of his boiled potatoes, put it whole into his mouth, let his knife and fork fall with a clatter onto his plate and said:

'I'd been thinking of hiring a detective before I heard you were watching Knight.'

Strike said nothing. Chiswell eyed him suspiciously.

'You have the reputation of being very good.'

'Kind of you to say so,' said Strike.

Chiswell continued to glare at Strike with a kind of furious desperation, as though wondering whether he dared hope that the detective would not prove yet another disappointment in a life beset with them.

'I'm being blackmailed, Mr Strike,' he said abruptly. 'Blackmailed by a pair of men who have come together in a temporary, though probably unstable, alliance. One of them is Jimmy Knight.'

'I see,' said Strike.

He, too, put his knife and fork together. Georgina appeared to know by some psychic process that Strike and Chiswell had eaten their fill of the main course. She arrived to clear away, reappearing with a treacle tart. Only once she had retired to the kitchen, and both men had helped themselves to large slices of pudding, did Chiswell resume his story.

'There's no need for sordid details,' he said, with an air of finality. 'All you need to know is that Jimmy Knight is aware that I did something that I would not wish to see shared with the gentlemen of the fourth estate.'

Strike said nothing, but Chiswell seemed to think his silence had an accusatory flavour, because he added sharply:

'No crime was committed. Some might not like it, but it wasn't illegal at the – but that's by the by,' said Chiswell, and took a large gulp of water. 'Knight came to me a couple of months ago and asked for forty thousand pounds in hush money. I refused to pay. He threatened me with exposure, but as he didn't appear to have any proof of his claim, I dared hope he would be unable to follow through on the threat.

'No press story resulted, so I concluded that I was right in thinking he had no proof. He returned a few weeks later and asked for half the former sum. Again, I refused.

'It was then, thinking to increase the pressure on me, I assume, that he approached Geraint Winn.'

'I'm sorry, I don't know who—?'

'Della Winn's husband.'

'Della Winn, the Minister for Sport?' said Strike, startled.

'Yes, of course Della-Winn-the-Minister-for-Sport,' snapped Chiswell.

The Right Honourable Della Winn, as Strike knew well, was a Welshwoman in her early sixties who had been blind since birth. No matter their party affiliation, people tended to admire the Liberal Democrat, who had been a human rights lawyer before standing for Parliament. Usually photographed with her guide dog, a pale yellow Labrador, she had been much in evidence in the press of late, her current bailiwick being the Paralympics. She had visited Selly Oak while Strike had been in the hospital, readjusting to the loss of his leg in Afghanistan. He had been left with a favourable impression of her intelligence and her empathy. Of her husband, Strike knew nothing.

'I don't know whether Della knows what Geraint's up to,' said Chiswell, spearing a piece of treacle tart and continuing to speak while he chewed it. 'Probably, but keeping her nose clean. Plausible deniability. Can't have the sainted Della involved in black-mail, can we?'

'Her husband's asked you for money?' asked Strike, incredulous.

'Oh no, no. Geraint wants to force me from office.'

'Any particular reason why?' said Strike.

'There's an enmity between us dating back many years, rooted in a wholly baseless – but that's irrelevant,' said Chiswell, with an angry shake of the head. 'Geraint approached me, "hoping it isn't true", and "offering me a chance to explain". He's a nasty, twisted little man who's spent his life holding his wife's handbag and answering her telephone calls. Naturally he's relishing the idea of wielding some actual power.'

Chiswell took a swig of sherry.

'So, as you can see, I'm in something of a cleft stick, Mr Strike. Even if I were minded to pay off Jimmy Knight, I still have to con-tend with a man who wants my disgrace, and who may well be able to lay hands on proof.'

'How could Winn get proof?'

Chiswell took another large mouthful of treacle tart and glanced over his shoulder to check that Georgina remained safely in the kitchen.

'I've heard,' he muttered, and a fine mist of pastry flew from the slack lips, 'that there may be photographs.'

'Photographs?' repeated Strike.

'Winn can't *have* them, of course. If he had, it would all be over. But he might be able to find a way of getting hold of them. Yerse.'

He shoved the last piece of tart into his mouth, then said:

'Of course, there's a chance the photographs don't incriminate me. There are no distinguishing marks, so far as I'm aware.'

Strike's imagination frankly boggled. He yearned to ask, 'Distinguishing marks on what, Minister?' but refrained.

'It all happened six years ago,' continued Chiswell. 'I've been over and over the damn thing in my head. There were others involved who might have talked, but I doubt it, I doubt it very much. Too much to lose. No, it's all going to come down to what Knight and Winn can dig up. I strongly suspect that if he gets hold of the photographs, Winn will go straight to the press. I don't think that would be Knight's first choice. He simply wants money.

'So here I am, Mr Strike, *a fronte praecipitium, a tergo lupi.* I've lived with this hanging over me for weeks now. It hasn't been enjoyable.'

He peered at Strike through his tiny eyes, and the detective was irresistibly put in mind of a mole, blinking up at a hovering spade that waited to crush it.

'When I heard you were at that meeting I assumed you were investigating Knight and had some dirt on him. I've come to the conclusion that the only way out of this diabolical situation is to find something that I can use against each of them, before they get their hands on those photographs. Fight fire with fire.'

'Blackmail with blackmail?' said Strike.

'I don't want anything from them except to leave me the hell alone,' snapped Chiswell. 'Bargaining chips, that's all I want. I acted within the law,' he said firmly, 'and in accordance with my conscience.'

Chiswell was not a particularly likeable man, but Strike could well imagine that the ongoing suspense of waiting for public exposure would be torture, especially to a man who had already endured his fair share of scandals. Strike's scant research on his prospective client the previous evening had unearthed gleeful accounts of the affair that had ended his first marriage, of the fact that his second wife had spent a week in a clinic for 'nervous exhaustion' and of the grisly drug-induced car crash in which his younger son had killed a young mother.

'This is a very big job, Mr Chiswell,' said Strike. 'It'll take two or three people to thoroughly investigate Knight and Winn, especially if there's time pressure.'

'I don't care what it costs,' said Chiswell. 'I don't care if you have to put your whole agency on it.

'I refuse to believe there isn't anything dodgy about Winn, sneaking little toad that he is. There's something funny about them as a couple. She, the blind angel of light,' Chiswell's lip curled, 'and he, her potbellied henchman, always scheming and backstabbing and grubbing up every freebie he can get. There must be something there. Must be.

'As for Knight, Commie rabble rouser, there's bound to be something the police haven't yet caught up with. He was always a tearaway, a thoroughly nasty piece of work.'

'You knew Jimmy Knight before he started trying to blackmail you?' asked Strike.

'Oh, yes,' said Chiswell. 'The Knights are from my constituency. The father was an odd-job man who did a certain amount of work for our family. I never knew the mother. I believe she died before the three of them moved into Steda Cottage.'

'I see,' said Strike.

He was recalling Billy's anguished words, '*I seen a child strangled and nobody believes me*', the nervous movement from nose to chest as he made his slipshod half-cross, and the prosaic, precise detail of the pink blanket in which the dead child had been buried.

'There's something I think I should tell you before we discuss terms, Mr Chiswell,' said Strike. 'I was at the CORE meeting because I was trying to find Knight's younger brother. His name's Billy.'

The crease between Chiswell's myopic eyes deepened a fraction.

'Yerse, I remember that there were two of them, but Jimmy was the elder by a considerable amount – a decade or more, I would guess. I haven't seen – Billy, is it? – in many years.'

'Well, he's seriously mentally ill,' said Strike. 'He came to me last Monday with a peculiar story, then bolted.'

Chiswell waited, and Strike was sure he detected tension.

'Billy claims,' said Strike, 'that he witnessed the strangling of a small child when he was very young.'

Chiswell did not recoil, horrified; he did not bluster or storm. He did not demand whether he was being accused, or ask what on earth that had to do with him. He responded with none of the flamboyant defences of the guilty man, and yet Strike could have sworn that to Chiswell, this was not a new story.

'And who does he claim strangled the child?' he asked, fingering the stem of his wine glass.

'He didn't tell me – or wouldn't.'

'You think this is what Knight is blackmailing me over? Infanticide?' asked Chiswell roughly.

'I thought you ought to know why I went looking for Jimmy,' said Strike.

'I have no deaths on my conscience,' said Jasper Chiswell forcefully. He swallowed the last of his water. 'One cannot,' he added, replacing the empty glass on the table, 'be held accountable for unintended consequences.'

10

I have believed that we two together would be equal to it.
Henrik Ibsen, *Rosmersholm*

The detective and the minister emerged from 14 Park Place an hour later and walked the few yards that took them back to St James's Street. Chiswell had become less curmudgeonly and gnomic over coffee, relieved, Strike suspected, to have put in train some action that might lift from him what had clearly become an almost intolerable burden of dread and suspense. They had agreed terms and Strike was pleased with the deal, because this promised to be a better-paid and more challenging job than the agency had been given in a while.

'Well, thank you, Mr Strike,' said Chiswell, staring off down St James's as they both paused on the corner. 'I must leave you here. I have an appointment with my son.'

Yet he did not move.

'You investigated Freddie's death,' he said abruptly, glancing at Strike out of the corner of his eyes.

Strike had not expected Chiswell to raise the subject, and especially not here, as an afterthought, after the intensity of their basement discussion.

'Yes,' he replied. 'I'm sorry.'

Chiswell's eyes remained fixed on a distant art gallery.

'I remembered your name on the report,' said Chiswell. 'It's an unusual one.'

He swallowed, still squinting at the gallery. He seemed strangely unwilling to depart for his appointment.

'Wonderful boy, Freddie,' he said. 'Wonderful. Went into my old regiment – well, as good as. Queen's Own Hussars amalgamated with the Queen's Royal Irish back in ninety-three, as you'll know. So it was the Queen's Royal Hussars he joined.

'Full of promise. Full of life. But of course, you never knew him.'

'No,' said Strike.

Some polite comment seemed necessary.

'He was your eldest, wasn't he?'

'Of four,' said Chiswell, nodding. 'Two girls,' and by his inflection he waved them away, mere females, chaff to wheat, 'and this other boy,' he added darkly. 'He went to jail. Perhaps you saw the newspapers?'

'No,' lied Strike, because he knew what it felt like to have your personal details strewn across the newspapers. It was kindest, if at all credible, to pretend you hadn't read it all, politest to let people tell their own story.

'Been trouble all his life, Raff,' said Chiswell. 'I got him a job in there.'

He pointed a thick finger at the distant gallery window.

'Dropped out of his History of Art degree,' said Chiswell. 'Friend of mine owns the place, agreed to take him on. M'wife thinks he's a lost cause. He killed a young mother in a car. He was high.'

Strike said nothing.

'Well, goodbye,' said Chiswell, appearing to come out of a melancholy trance. He offered his sweaty hand once more, which Strike shook, then strode away, bundled up in the thick coat that was so inappropriate on this fine June day.

Strike proceeded up St James's Street in the opposite direction, pulling out his mobile as he went. Robin picked up on the third ring.

'Need to meet you,' said Strike without preamble. 'We've got a new job, a big one.'

'Damn!' she said. 'I'm in Harley Street. I didn't want to bother you, knowing you were with Chiswell, but Andy's wife broke her wrist

104

falling off a stepladder. I said I'd cover Dodgy while Andy takes her to hospital.'

'Shit. Where's Barclay?'

'Still on Webster.'

'Is Dodgy in his consulting room?'

'Yes.'

'We'll risk it,' said Strike. 'He usually goes straight home on Fridays. This is urgent. I need to tell you about it face to face. Can you meet me in the Red Lion in Duke of York Street?'

Having refused all alcohol during his meal with Chiswell, Strike fancied a pint rather than returning to the office. If he had stuck out in his suit at the White Horse in East Ham, he was perfectly dressed for Mayfair, and two minutes later he entered the Red Lion in Duke of York Street, a snug Victorian pub whose brass fittings and etched glass reminded him of the Tottenham. Taking a pint of London Pride off to a corner table, he looked up Della Winn and her husband on his phone and began reading an article about the forthcoming Paralympics, in which Della was extensively quoted.

'Hi,' said Robin, twenty-five minutes later, dropping her bag onto the seat opposite him.

'Want a drink?' he asked.

'I'll get it,' said Robin. 'Well?' she said, rejoining him a couple of minutes later, holding an orange juice. Strike smiled at her barely contained impatience. 'What was it all about? What did Chiswell want?'

The pub, which comprised only a horseshoe space around a single bar, was already tightly packed with smartly dressed men and women, who had started their weekend early or, like Strike and Robin, were finishing work over a drink. Lowering his voice, Strike told her what had passed between him and Chiswell.

'Oh,' said Robin blankly, when at last Strike had finished filling her in. 'So we're ... we're going to try and get dirt on Della Winn?'

'On her husband,' Strike corrected her, 'and Chiswell prefers the phrase "bargaining chips".'

Robin said nothing, but sipped her orange juice.

'Blackmail's illegal, Robin,' said Strike, correctly reading her uneasy expression. 'Knight's trying to screw forty grand out of Chiswell and Winn wants to force him out of his job.'

'So he's going to blackmail them back and we're going to help him do it?'

'We get dirt on people every day,' said Strike roughly. 'It's a bit late to start getting a conscience about it.'

He took a long pull on his pint, annoyed not only by her attitude, but by the fact that he had let his resentment show. She lived with her husband in a desirable sash-windowed house in Albury Street, while he remained in two draughty rooms, from which he might soon be ejected by the redevelopment of the street. The agency had never before been offered a job that gave three people full employment, possibly for months. Strike was not about to apologise for being keen to take it. He was tired, after years of graft, of being plunged back into the red whenever the agency hit a lean patch. He had ambitions for his business that couldn't be achieved without building up a far healthier bank balance. Nevertheless, he felt compelled to defend his position.

'We're like lawyers, Robin. We're on the client's side.'

'You turned down that investment banker the other day, who wanted to find out where his wife—'

'—because it was bloody obvious he'd do her harm if he found her.'

'Well,' said Robin, a challenging look in her eye, 'what if the thing they've found out about Chiswell—'

But before she could finish her sentence, a tall man in deep conversation with a colleague walked straight into Robin's chair, flinging her forward into the table and knocking over her orange juice.

'Oi!' barked Strike, as Robin tried to wipe the juice off her sopping dress. 'Fancy apologising?'

'Oh dear,' said the man in a drawl, eyeing the juice-soaked Robin as several people turned to stare. 'Did I do that?'

'Yes, you bloody did,' said Strike, heaving himself up and moving around the table. 'And that's not an apology!'

'Cormoran!' said Robin warningly.

'Well, I'm sorry,' said the man, as though making an enormous concession, but taking in Strike's size, his regret seemed to become more sincere. 'Seriously, I do apol—'

106

'Bugger off,' snarled Strike. 'Swap seats,' he said to Robin. 'Then if some other clumsy tosser walks by they'll get me, not you.'

Half-embarrassed, half-touched, she picked up her hand-bag, which was also soaked, and did as he had requested. Strike returned to the table clutching a fistful of paper napkins, which he handed to her.

'Thanks.'

It was difficult to maintain a combative stance given that he was voluntarily sitting in a chair covered in orange juice to spare her. Still dabbing off the juice, Robin leaned in and said quietly:

'You know what I'm worried about. The thing Billy said.'

The thin cotton dress was sticking to her everywhere: Strike kept his gaze resolutely on her eyes.

'I asked Chiswell about that.'

'Did you?'

'Of course I did. What else was I going to think, when he said he was being blackmailed by Billy's brother?'

'And what did he say?'

'He said he had no deaths on his hands, but "one cannot be held accountable for unintended consequences".'

'What on earth does *that* mean?'

'I asked. He gave me the hypothetical example of a man dropping a mint, on which a small child later choked to death.'

'*What?*'

'Your guess is as good as mine. Billy hasn't called back, I suppose?'

Robin shook her head.

'Look, the overwhelming probability is Billy's delusional,' said Strike. 'When I told Chiswell what Billy had said, I didn't get any sense of guilt or fear . . .'

As he said it, he remembered the shadow that had passed over Chiswell's face, and the impression he had received that the story was not, to Chiswell, entirely new.

'So what are they blackmailing Chiswell about?' asked Robin.

'Search me,' said Strike. 'He said it happened six years ago, which doesn't fit with Billy's story, because he wouldn't have been a little kid six years ago. Chiswell said some people would think what he did was immoral, but it wasn't illegal. He seemed to be suggesting that it wasn't against the law when he did it, but is now.'

Strike suppressed a yawn. Beer and the heat of the afternoon were making him drowsy. He was due at Lorelei's later.

'So you trust him?' Robin asked.

'Do I trust Chiswell?' Strike wondered aloud, his eyes on the extravagantly engraved mirror behind Robin. 'If I had to bet on it, I'd say he was being truthful with me today because he's desperate. Do I think he's generally trustworthy? Probably no more than anyone else.'

'You didn't *like* him, did you?' asked Robin, incredulously. 'I've been reading about him.'

'And?'

'Pro-hanging, anti-immigration, voted against increasing maternity leave—'

She didn't notice Strike's involuntary glance down her figure as she continued:

'—banged on about family values, then left his wife for a journalist—'

'All right, I wouldn't choose him for a drinking buddy, but there's something slightly pitiable about him. He's lost one son, the other one's just killed a woman—'

'Well, yes, there you are,' said Robin. 'He advocates locking up petty criminals and throwing away the key, then his son runs over someone's mother and he pulls out all the stops to get him a short sen—'

She broke off suddenly as a loud female voice said: 'Robin! How lovely!'

Sarah Shadlock had entered the pub with two men.

'Oh God,' muttered Robin, before she could help herself, then, more loudly, 'Sarah, hi!'

She would have given much to avoid this encounter. Sarah would be delighted to tell Matthew that she had found Robin and Strike having a tête-à-tête in a Mayfair pub, when she herself had told Matthew by phone only an hour ago that she was alone in Harley Street.

Sarah insisted on wiggling around the table to embrace Robin, something the latter was sure she would not have done had she not been with men.

'Darling, what's happened to you? You're all sticky!'

She was just a little posher here, in Mayfair, than anywhere else Robin had met her, and several degrees warmer to Robin.

'Nothing,' muttered Robin. 'Spilled orange juice, that's all.'

'Cormoran!' said Sarah blithely, swooping in for a kiss on his cheek. Strike, Robin was pleased to note, sat impassive and did not respond. 'Bit of R and R?' said Sarah, embracing them both in her knowing smile.

'Work,' said Strike bluntly.

Receiving no encouragement to stay, Sarah moved along the bar, taking her colleagues with her.

'I forgot Christie's is round the corner,' muttered Robin.

Strike checked his watch. He didn't want to have to wear his suit to Lorelei's, and indeed, it was now stained with orange juice from having taken Robin's seat.

'We need to talk about how we're going to do this job, because it starts tomorrow.'

'OK,' said Robin with some trepidation, because it had been a long time since she had worked a weekend. Matthew had got used to her coming home.

'It's all right,' said Strike, apparently reading her mind, 'I won't need you till Monday.

'The job's going to take three people at a minimum. I reckon we've already got enough on Webster to keep the client happy, so we'll put Andy full time on Dodgy Doc, let the two waiting-list clients know we're not going to be able to do them this month and Barclay can come in with us on the Chiswell case.

'On Monday, you're going into the House of Commons.'

'I'm what?' said Robin, startled.

'You're going to go in as Chiswell's goddaughter, who's interested in a career in Parliament, and get started on Geraint, who runs Della's constituency office at the other end of the corridor to Chiswell's. Chat him up . . .'

He took a swig of beer, frowning at her over the top of the glass.

'What?' said Robin, unsure what was coming.

'How d'you feel,' said Strike, so quietly that she had to lean in to hear him, 'about breaking the law?'

'Well, I tend to be opposed to it,' said Robin, unsure whether to be amused or worried. 'That's sort of why I wanted to do investigative work.'

'And if the law's a bit of a grey area, and we can't get the information any other way? Bearing in mind that Winn's definitely breaking the law, trying to blackmail a Minister of the Crown out of his job?'

'Are you talking about bugging Winn's office?'

'Right in one,' said Strike. Correctly reading her dubious expression, he went on. 'Listen, by Chiswell's account, Winn's a slapdash loudmouth, which is why he's stuck in the constituency office and kept well away from his wife's work at the Department for Sport. Apparently he leaves his office door open most of the time, shouts about constituents' confidential affairs and leaves private papers lying around in the communal kitchen. There's a good chance you'll be able to inveigle indiscretions out of him without needing the bug, but I don't think we can count on it.'

Robin swilled the last of her orange juice in her glass, deliberating, then said:

'All right, I'll do it.'

'Sure?' said Strike. 'OK, well you won't be able to take devices in, because you'll have to go through a metal detector. I've said I'm going to get a handful to Chiswell tomorrow. He'll pass them to you once you're inside.

'You'll need a cover name. Text it to me when you've thought of one so I can let Chiswell know. You could use "Venetia Hall" again, actually. Chiswell's the kind of bloke who'd have a goddaughter called Venetia.'

'Venetia' was Robin's middle name, but Robin was too full of apprehension and excitement to care that Strike, from his smirk, continued to find it amusing.

'You're going to have to work a disguise as well,' said Strike. 'Nothing major, but Chiswell remembered what you look like from the Ripper coverage, so we've got to assume Winn might, too.'

'It'll be too hot for a wig,' she said. 'I might try coloured contact lenses. I could go and buy some now. Maybe some plain-lensed glasses on top.' A smile she could not suppress surfaced again. 'The House of Commons!' she repeated excitedly.

Robin's excited grin faded as Sarah Shadlock's white-blonde head intruded on the periphery of her vision, on the other side of the bar. Sarah had just repositioned herself to keep Robin and Strike in her sights.

'Let's go,' Robin said to Strike.

As they walked back towards the Tube, Strike explained that Barclay would be tailing Jimmy Knight.

'I can't do it,' said Strike regretfully. 'I've blown my cover with him and his CORE mates.'

'So what will you be up to?'

'Plug gaps, follow up leads, cover nights if we need them,' said Strike.

'Poor Lorelei,' said Robin.

It had slipped out before she could stop herself. Increasingly heavy traffic was rolling past, and when Strike did not answer, Robin hoped that he hadn't heard her.

'Did Chiswell mention his son who died in Iraq?' she asked, rather like a person hastily coughing to hide a laugh that has already escaped them.

'Yeah,' said Strike. 'Freddie was clearly his favourite child, which doesn't say much for his judgement.'

'What d'you mean?'

'Freddie Chiswell was a prize shit. I investigated a lot of Killed in Actions, and I never had so many people ask me whether the dead officer had been shot in the back by his own men.'

Robin looked shocked.

'*De mortuis nil nisi bonum?*' asked Strike.

Robin had learned quite a lot of Latin, working with Strike.

'Well,' she said quietly, for the first time finding some pity in her heart for Jasper Chiswell, 'you can't expect his father to speak ill of him.'

They parted at the top of the street, Robin to shop for coloured contact lenses, Strike heading for the Tube.

He felt unusually cheerful after the conversation with Robin: as they contemplated this challenging job, the familiar contours of their friendship had suddenly resurfaced. He had liked her excitement at the prospect of entering the House of Commons; liked being the one who had offered the chance. He had even enjoyed the way she stress-tested his assumptions about Chiswell's story.

On the point of entering the station, Strike turned suddenly aside, infuriating the irate businessman who had been walking six inches in his wake. Tutting furiously, the man barely avoided a collision and strode off huffily into the Underground while the indifferent Strike leaned up against the sun-soaked wall, enjoying the sensation of heat permeating his suit jacket as he phoned Detective Inspector Eric Wardle.

Strike had told Robin the truth. He didn't believe that Chiswell had ever strangled a child, yet there had been something undeniably odd about his reaction to Billy's story. Thanks to the minister's revelation that the Knight family had lived in proximity to his family home, Strike now knew that Billy had been a 'little kid' in Oxfordshire. The first logical step in assuaging his continued unease about that pink blanket was to find out whether any children in the area had disappeared a couple of decades ago, and never been found.

11

Lorelei Bevan lived in an eclectically furnished flat over her thriving vintage clothes store in Camden. Strike arrived that night at half past seven, a bottle of Pinot Noir in one hand and his mobile clamped to his ear with the other. Lorelei opened the door, smiled good-naturedly at the familiar sight of him on the phone, kissed him on the mouth, relieved him of his wine and returned to the kitchen, from which a welcome smell of Pad Thai was issuing.

'... or try and get into CORE itself,' Strike told Barclay, closing the door behind him and proceeding to Lorelei's sitting room, which was dominated by a large print of Warhol's Elizabeth Taylors. 'I'll send you everything I've got on Jimmy. He's involved with a couple of different groups. No idea whether he's working. His local's the White Horse in East Ham. Think he's a Hammers fan.'

'Could be worse,' said Barclay, who was speaking quietly, as he had just got the teething baby to sleep. 'Could be Chelsea.'

'You'll have to admit to being ex-army,' said Strike, sinking into an armchair and hoisting his leg up onto a conveniently positioned square pouffe. 'You look like a squaddie.'

'Nae problem,' said Barclay. 'I'll be the poor wee laddie who didnae know whut he was gettin' himself intae. Hard lefties love that shit. Let 'em patronise me.'

Grinning, Strike took out his cigarettes. For all his initial doubts, he was starting to think that Barclay might have been a good hire.

'All right, hang fire till you hear from me again. Should be some-time Sunday.'

As Strike rang off, Lorelei appeared with a glass of red for him.

'Want some help in the kitchen?' Strike asked, though with-out moving.

'No, stay there. I won't be long,' she replied, smiling. He liked her fifties-style apron.

As she returned to the kitchen, he lit up. Although Lorelei did not smoke, she had no objection to Strike's Benson & Hedges as long as he used the kitsch ashtray, decorated with cavorting poodles, that she had provided for the purpose.

Smoking, he admitted to himself that he envied Barclay infiltrat-ing Knight and his band of hard-left colleagues. It was the kind of job Strike had relished in the Military Police. He remembered the four soldiers in Germany who had become enamoured of a local far-right group. Strike had managed to persuade them that he shared their belief in a white ethno-nationalist super-state, infiltrated a meeting and secured four arrests and prosecutions that had given him par-ticular satisfaction.

Turning on the TV, he watched Channel 4 News for a while, drinking his wine, smoking in pleasurable anticipation of Pad Thai and other sensual delights, and for once enjoying what so many of his fellow workers took for granted, but which he had rarely experi-enced: the relief and release of a Friday night.

Strike and Lorelei had met at Eric Wardle's birthday party. It had been an awkward evening in some ways, because Strike had seen Coco there for the first time since telling her by phone that he had no interest in another date. Coco had got very drunk; at one in the morning, while he was sitting on a sofa deep in conversation with Lorelei, she had marched across the room, thrown a glass of wine over both of them and stormed off into the night. Strike had not been aware that Coco and Lorelei were old friends until the morning after he woke up in Lorelei's bed. He considered that this was really more Lorelei's problem than his. She seemed to think the exchange, for Coco wanted nothing more to do with her, more than fair.

'How d'you do it?' Wardle had asked, the next time they met, genuinely puzzled. 'Blimey, I'd like to know your—'

Strike raised his heavy eyebrows and Wardle appeared to gag on what had come perilously close to a compliment.

'There's no secret,' said Strike. 'Some women just like fat one-legged pube-headed men with broken noses.'

'Well, it's a sad indictment of our mental health services that they're loose on the streets,' Wardle had said, and Strike had laughed.

Lorelei was her real name, taken not from the mythical siren of the Rhine, but from Marilyn Monroe's character in *Gentlemen Prefer Blondes*, her mother's favourite film. Men's eyes swivelled when she passed them in the street, but she evoked neither the profound longing nor the searing pain that Charlotte had caused Strike. Whether this was because Charlotte had stunted his capacity to feel so intensely, or because Lorelei lacked some essential magic, he did not know. Neither Strike nor Lorelei had said 'I love you'. In Strike's case this was because, desirable and amusing though he found her, he could not have said it honestly. It was convenient to him to assume that Lorelei felt the same way.

She had recently ended a five-year-long live-in relationship when, after several lingering looks across Wardle's dark sitting room, he had strolled across to talk to her. He had wanted to believe her when she had told him how glorious it was to have her flat to herself and her freedom restored, yet lately he had felt tiny spots of displeasure when he had told her he had to work weekends, like the first heavy drops of rain that presage a storm. She denied it when challenged: *no, no, of course not, if you've got to work . . .*

But Strike had set out his uncompromising terms at the outset of the relationship: his work was unpredictable and his finances poor. Hers was the only bed he intended to visit, but if she sought predictability or permanence, he was not the man for her. She had appeared content with the deal, and if, over the course of ten months, she had grown less so, Strike was ready to call things off with no hard feelings. Perhaps she sensed this, because she had forced no argument. This pleased him, and not merely because he could do without the aggravation. He liked Lorelei, enjoyed sleeping with her and found it desirable – for a reason he did not bother to dwell on, being perfectly aware what it was – to be in a relationship just now.

The Pad Thai was excellent, their conversation light and amusing. Strike told Lorelei nothing about his new case, except that he hoped it would be both lucrative and interesting. After doing the dishes together, they repaired to the bedroom, with its candy-pink walls and its curtains printed with cartoonish cowgirls and ponies.

Lorelei liked to dress up. To bed that night, she wore stockings and a black corset. She had the talent, by no means usual, of staging an erotic scene without tipping into parody. Perhaps, with his one leg and his broken nose, Strike ought to have felt ludicrous in this boudoir, which was all frivolity and prettiness, but she played Aphrodite to his Hephaestus so adeptly that thoughts of Robin and Matthew were sometimes driven entirely from his mind.

There was, after all, little pleasure to compare with that given by a woman who really wanted you, he thought next day at lunchtime, as they sat side by side at a pavement café, reading separate papers, Strike smoking, Lorelei's perfectly painted nails trailing absently along the back of his hand. So why had he already told her that he needed to work this afternoon? It was true that he needed to drop off the listening devices at Chiswell's Belgravia flat, but he could easily have spent another night with her, returned to the bedroom, the stockings and the basque. The prospect was certainly tempting.

Yet something implacable inside him refused to give in. Two nights in a row would break the pattern; from there, it would be a short slide into true intimacy. In the depths of himself Strike could not imagine a future in which he lived with a woman, married or fathered children. He had planned some of those things with Charlotte, in the days when he had been readjusting to life minus half his leg. An IED on a dusty road in Afghanistan had blasted Strike out of his chosen life into an entirely new body and a new reality. Sometimes he saw his proposal to Charlotte as the most extreme manifestation of his temporary disorientation in the aftermath of his amputation. He had needed to relearn how to walk, and, almost as hard, to live a life outside the military. From a distance of two years, he saw himself trying to hold tight to some part of his past as everything else slipped away. The allegiance he had given the army, he had transferred to a future with Charlotte.

'Good move,' his old friend Dave Polworth had said without missing a beat, when Strike told him of the engagement. 'Shame to waste all that combat training. Slightly increased risk of getting killed, though, mate.'

Had he ever really thought the wedding would happen? Had he truly imagined Charlotte settling for the life he could give her? After everything they had been through, had he believed that they could achieve redemption together, each of them damaged in their own untidy, personal and peculiar ways? It seemed to the Strike sitting in the sunshine with Lorelei that for a few months he had both believed it wholeheartedly and known that it was impossible, never planning more than a few weeks ahead, holding Charlotte at night as though she were the last human on earth, as though only Armageddon could separate them.

'Want another coffee?' murmured Lorelei.

'I'd better make a move,' said Strike.

'When will I see you?' she asked, as Strike paid the waiter.

'Told you, I've got this big new job on,' he said. 'Timings are going to be a bit unpredictable for a while. I'll call you tomorrow. We'll go out as soon as I can get a clear evening.'

'All right,' she said, smiling, and added softly, 'Kiss me.'

He did so. She pressed her full lips against his, irresistibly recalling certain highlights of the early morning. They broke apart. Strike grinned, bade her goodbye and left her sitting in the sun with her newspaper.

The Minister for Culture did not invite Strike inside when he opened the door of his house in Ebury Street. Chiswell seemed keen, in fact, for the detective to leave as quickly as possible. After taking the box of listening devices, he muttered, 'Good, right, I'll make sure she gets them,' and was on the point of closing the door when he suddenly called after Strike, 'what's her name?'

'Venetia Hall,' said Strike.

Chiswell shut the door, and Strike turned his tired footsteps back along the street of quiet golden townhouses, towards the Tube and Denmark Street.

His office seemed stark and gloomy after Lorelei's flat. Strike threw open the windows to let in the noise of Denmark Street down below, where music lovers continued to visit the instrument stores and old record shops that Strike feared were doomed by the forthcoming redevelopment. The sound of engines and horns, of conversation and footsteps, of guitar riffs played by would-be purchasers and the distant bongos of another busker were pleasant to Strike as he settled to work, knowing that he had hours ahead in the computer chair if he were to wrest the bare bones of his targets' lives from the internet.

If you knew where to search and had time and expertise, the out-line of many existences could be unearthed in cyberspace: ghostly exoskeletons, sometimes partial, sometimes unnervingly complete, of the lives led by their flesh and blood counterparts. Strike had learned many tricks and secrets, become adept ferreting in even the darkest corners of the internet, but often the most innocent social media sites held untold wealth, a minor amount of cross-referencing all that was necessary to compile detailed private histories that their careless owners had never meant to share with the world.

Strike first consulted Google Maps to examine the place where Jimmy and Billy had grown up. Steda Cottage was evidently too small and insignificant to be named, but Chiswell House was clearly marked, a short way outside the village of Woolstone. Strike spent five minutes fruitlessly scanning the patches of woodland around Chiswell House, noticing a couple of tiny squares that might be estate cottages – *they buried it down in the dell by my dad's house* – before resuming his investigation of the older, saner brother.

CORE had a website where Strike found, sandwiched between lengthy polemics about celebration capitalism and neo-liberalism, a useful schedule of protests at which Jimmy was planning to demon-strate or speak, which the detective printed out and added to his file. He then followed a link to the Real Socialist Party website, which was an even busier and more cluttered affair than that of CORE. Here he found another lengthy article by Jimmy, arguing for the dissolution of the 'apartheid state' of Israel and the defeat of the 'Zionist lobby' which had a stranglehold on the Western capitalist establishment. Strike noted that Jasper Chiswell was among the 'Western Political Elite' listed at the bottom of this article as a 'publicly declared Zionist'.

Jimmy's girlfriend, Flick, appeared in a couple of photographs on the Real Socialist website, sporting black hair as she marched against Trident and blonde shaded to pink as she cheered Jimmy, who was speaking on an open-air stage at a Real Socialist Party rally. Following a link to Flick's Twitter handle, he perused her timeline, which was a strange mixture of the cloying and the vituperative. 'I hope you get fucking arse cancer, you Tory cunt' sat directly above a video clip of a kitten sneezing so hard that it fell out of its basket.

As far as Strike could tell, neither Jimmy nor Flick owned or ever had owned property, something that he had in common with both of them. He could find no indication online of how they were supporting themselves, unless writing for far-left websites paid better than he had imagined. Jimmy was renting the miserable flat in Charlemont Road from a man called Kasturi Kumar, and while Flick made casual mention on social media of living in Hackney, he could not find an address for her anywhere online.

Digging deeper into online records, Strike discovered a James Knight of the correct age who seemed to have cohabited for five years with a woman called Dawn Clancy, and upon delving into Dawn's highly informative, emoji-strewn Facebook page, Strike discovered that they had been married. Dawn was a hairdresser who had run a successful business in London before returning to her native Manchester. Thirteen years older than Jimmy, she seemed to have neither children nor any present-day contact with her ex-husband. However, a comment she had made to a jilted girlfriend's 'all men are trash' post, caught Strike's eye: 'Yeah, he's a shit, but at least he hasn't sued you! I win (again)!'

Intrigued, Strike turned his attention to court records and, after a little digging, found several useful nuggets of information. Jimmy had been charged with affray twice, once on an anti-capitalism march, once at an anti-Trident protest, but this, Strike had expected. What was far more interesting was to find Jimmy on a list of vexatious litigants on the website of HM Courts and Tribunals Service. Due to a longstanding habit of beginning frivolous legal actions, Knight was now 'forbidden from starting civil cases in courts without permission'.

Jimmy had certainly had a good run for his, or the state's, money. Over the past decade he had brought civil actions against sundry individuals and organisations. The law had taken his side only once, when, in 2007, he had won compensation from Zanet Industries, who were found not to have followed due process when dismissing him.

Jimmy had represented himself in court against Zanet and, presumably elated by his win, had gone on to represent himself in suing several others, among them a garage owner, two neighbours, a journalist he alleged had defamed him, two officers in the Metropolitan Police he claimed had assaulted him, two more employers and, finally, his ex-wife, who he said had harassed him and caused him loss of earnings.

In Strike's experience, those who disdained the use of representation in court were either unbalanced or so arrogant that it came to the same thing. Jimmy's litigious history suggested that he was greedy and unprincipled, sharp without being wise. It was always useful to have a handle on a man's vulnerabilities when trying to ferret out his secrets. Strike added the names of all the people Jimmy had tried to sue, plus the current address of his ex-wife, to the file beside him.

At close to midnight Strike retired to his flat for some much-needed sleep, rose early on Sunday, and transferred his attention to Geraint Winn, remaining hunched at the computer until the light began to fade again, by which time a new cardboard file labelled CHISWELL sat beside him, fat with miscellaneous but crosschecked information on Chiswell's two blackmailers.

Stretching and yawning, he became suddenly aware of the noises reaching him through the open windows. The music shops had closed at last, the bongos had ceased, but traffic continued to swish and rumble along Charing Cross Road. Strike heaved himself up, supporting himself on the desk because his remaining ankle was numb after hours in the computer chair, and stooped to look through the inner office window at a tangerine sky spread beyond the rooftops.

It was Sunday evening and in less than two hours England would be playing Italy at the quarter-finals of the European Football Championships in Kiev. One of the few personal indulgences Strike had allowed himself was a subscription to Sky so that he could watch football. The small portable TV that was all his flat upstairs could comfortably accommodate might not be the ideal medium on which to watch such an important game, but he could not justify a night in a pub given that he had an early start on Monday, covering Dodgy Doc again, a prospect that gave him little pleasure.

He checked his watch. He had time to get a Chinese takeaway before the match, but he still needed to call both Barclay and Robin with instructions for the next few days. As he was on the point of picking up the phone, a musical alert told him that he had received an email.

The subject line read: 'Missing Kids in Oxfordshire'. Strike laid his mobile and keys back on the desk and clicked it open.

Strike –
This is best I can do on a quick search. Obviously without exact time frame it's difficult. 2 missing child cases in Oxfordshire/ Wiltshire from the early/mid 90s unresolved as far as I can tell. Suki Lewis, 12, went missing from care October 1992.
Also Immamu Ibrahim, 5-year-old, disappeared 1996. Father disappeared at the same time, is believed to be in Algeria.
Without further information, not much to be done.
Best, E

12

The atmosphere we breathe is heavy with storms.

Henrik Ibsen, *Rosmersholm*

The sunset cast a ruddy glow across the duvet behind Robin as she sat at the dressing table in her and Matthew's spacious new bedroom. Next-door's barbecue was now smoking the air that had earlier been fragrant with honeysuckle. She had just left Matthew downstairs, lying on the sofa watching the warm-up to the England–Italy game, a cold bottle of Peroni in his hand.

Opening the dressing table drawer, she took out a pair of coloured contact lenses she had concealed there. After trial and error the previous day, she had decided the hazel ones appeared most natural with her strawberry-blonde hair. Gingerly, she extracted first one, then the other, placing them over her watering blue-grey irises. It was essential that she get used to wearing them. Ideally she would have had them in all weekend, but Matthew's reaction when he had seen her in them had dissuaded her.

'Your eyes!' he had said, after staring at her, perplexed, for a few seconds. 'Bloody hell, that looks horrible, take them out!'

As Saturday had already been ruined by one of their tense disagreements about her job, she had chosen not to wear the lenses all weekend, because they would serve as a constant reminder to Matthew about what she was up to the following week. He seemed to think that working undercover in the House of Commons was tantamount to treason, and her refusal to tell him who either her client or her targets were had further aggravated him.

Robin kept telling herself that Matthew was worried about her safety and that he could hardly be blamed for it. It had become a mental exercise she performed like a penance: *you can't blame him for being concerned, you nearly got killed last year, he wants you to be safe.* However, the fact that she had gone for a drink with Strike on Friday seemed to be worrying Matthew far more than any potential killer.

'Don't you think you're being bloody hypocritical?' he said.

Whenever he was angry, the skin around his nose and upper lip became taut. Robin had noticed it years ago, but lately it gave her a sensation close to revulsion. She had never mentioned this to her therapist. It had felt too nasty, too visceral.

'How am I hypocritical?'

'Going for cosy little drinks with him—'

'Matt, I work with—'

'—then complaining when I have lunch with Sarah.'

'Have lunch with her!' said Robin, her pulse quickening in anger. 'Do it! As a matter of fact, I met her in the Red Lion, out with some men from work. Do you want to call Tom and tell him his fiancée's drinking with colleagues? Or am I the only one who's not allowed to do it?'

The skin around his nose and mouth looked like a muzzle as it tightened, Robin thought: a pale muzzle on a snarling dog.

'Would you have told me you'd gone for a drink with him if Sarah hadn't seen you?'

'Yes,' said Robin, her temper snapping, 'and I'd've known you'd be a dick about it, too.'

The tense aftermath of this argument, by no means their most serious of the last month, had lingered all through Sunday. Only in the last couple of hours, with the prospect of the England game to cheer him, had Matthew become amiable again. Robin had even volunteered to fetch him a Peroni from the kitchen and kissed him on the forehead before leaving him, with a sense of liberation, for her coloured contact lenses and her preparations for the following day.

Her eyes felt gradually less uncomfortable with repeated blinking. Robin moved across to the bed, where her laptop lay. Pulling it towards her, she saw that an email from Strike had just arrived.

Robin,
Bit of research on the Winns attached. I'll call you shortly for
quick brief before tomorrow.
CS

Robin was annoyed. Strike was supposed to be 'plugging gaps' and working nights. Did he think she had done no research of her own over the weekend? Nevertheless, she clicked on the first of several attachments, a document summarising the fruits of Strike's online labour.

Geraint Winn

Geraint Ifon Winn, d.o.b. 15th July 1950. Born Cardiff. Father a miner. Grammar school educated, met Della at University of Cardiff. Was 'property consultant' prior to acting as her election agent and running her Parliamentary office post-election. No details of former career available online. No company ever registered in his name. Lives with Della, Southwark Park Road, Bermondsey.

Strike had managed to dig up a couple of poor-quality pictures of Geraint with his well-known wife, both of which Robin had already found and saved to her laptop. She knew how hard Strike had had to work to find an image of Geraint, because it had taken her a long time the previous night, while Matthew slept, to find them. Press photographers did not seem to feel he added much to pictures. A thin, balding man who wore heavy-framed glasses, he had a lipless mouth, a weak chin and a pronounced overbite, which taken together put Robin in mind of an overweight gecko.

Strike had also attached information on the Minister for Sport.

Della Winn

D.o.b. 8th August 1947. Née Jones. Born and raised Vale of Glamorgan, Wales. Both parents teachers. Blind from birth due to bilateral microphthalmia. Attended St Enodoch Royal School for the Blind from age 5 – 18. Won multiple swimming awards as teenager. (See attached articles for further details, also of The Playing Field charity).

Even though Robin had read as much as she could about Della over the weekend, she ploughed diligently through both articles. They told her little that she did not already know. Della had worked for a prominent human rights charity before successfully standing for election in the Welsh constituency in which she had been born. She was a long-time advocate for the benefit of sports in deprived areas, a champion of disabled athletes and a supporter for projects that used sport to rehabilitate injured veterans. The founding of her charity, the Level Playing Field, to support young athletes and sportspeople facing challenges, whether of poverty or physical impairment, had received a fair amount of press coverage. Many high-profile sportspeople had given their time to fundraisers.

The articles that Strike had attached both mentioned something that Robin already knew from her own research: the Winns, like the Chiswells, had lost a child. Della and Geraint's daughter and only offspring had killed herself at the age of sixteen, a year before Della had stood for Parliament. The tragedy was mentioned in every profile Robin had read on Della Winn, even those lauding her substantial achievements. Her maiden speech in Parliament had supported a proposed bullying hotline, but she had never otherwise discussed her child's suicide.

Robin's mobile rang. After checking that the bedroom door was closed, Robin answered.

'That was quick,' said Strike thickly, through a mouthful of Singapore noodles. 'Sorry – took me by surprise – just got a takeaway.'

'I've read your email,' said Robin. She heard a metallic snap and was sure he was opening a can of beer. 'Very useful, thanks.'

'Got your disguise sorted?' Strike asked.

'Yes,' said Robin, turning to examine herself at the mirror. It was strange how much a change of eye colour transformed your face. She was planning to wear a pair of clear-lensed glasses over her hazel eyes.

'And you know enough about Chiswell to pretend to be his goddaughter?'

'Of course,' said Robin.

'Go on then,' said Strike, 'impress me.'

'Born 1944,' Robin said at once, without reading her notes. 'Studied Classics at Merton College, Oxford, then joined Queen's Own Hussars, saw active service in Aden and Singapore.

'First wife, Lady Patricia Fleetwood, three children: Sophia, Isabella and Freddie. Sophia's married and lives in Northumberland, Isabella runs Chiswell's Parliamentary office—'

'Does she?' said Strike, sounding vaguely surprised, and Robin was pleased to know that she had discovered something he did not.

'Is she the daughter you knew?' she asked, remembering what Strike had said in the office.

'Wouldn't go as far as "knew". I met her a couple of times with Charlotte. Everyone called her "Izzy Chizzy". One of those upper-class nicknames.'

'Lady Patricia divorced Chiswell after he got a political journalist pregnant—'

'—which resulted in the disappointing son at the art gallery.'

'Exactly—'

Robin moved the mouse around to bring up a saved picture, this time of a dark and rather beautiful young man in a charcoal suit, heading up courtroom steps accompanied by a stylish, black-haired woman in sunglasses whom he closely resembled, though she looked hardly old enough to be his mother.

'—but Chiswell and the journalist split up not long after Raphael was born,' said Robin.

'The family calls him "Raff",' said Strike, 'and the second wife doesn't like him, thinks Chiswell should have disowned him after the car crash.'

126

Robin made a further note.

'Great, thanks. Chiswell's current wife, Kinvara, was unwell last year,' Robin continued, bringing up a picture of Kinvara, a curvaceous redhead in a slinky black dress and heavy diamond necklace. She was some thirty years younger than Chiswell and pouting at the camera. Had she not known, Robin would have guessed them father and daughter rather than a married couple.

'With nervous exhaustion,' said Strike, beating her to it. 'Yeah. Drink or drugs, d'you reckon?'

Robin heard a clang and surmised that Strike had just dropped an empty Tennent's can in the office bin. He was alone, then. Lorelei never stayed in the tiny flat upstairs.

'Who knows?' said Robin, her eyes still on Kinvara Chiswell.

'One last thing,' said Strike. 'Just in. A couple of kids went missing in Oxfordshire around the right time to tally with Billy's story.'

There was a brief pause.

'You still there?' asked Strike.

'Yes . . . I thought you don't believe Chiswell strangled a child?'

'I don't,' said Strike. 'The timescale doesn't fit, and if Jimmy knew a Tory minister had strangled a kid, he wouldn't have waited twenty years to try and monetise it. But I'd still like to know whether Billy's imagining that he saw someone throttled. I'm going to do a bit of digging on the names Wardle's given me and if either seem credible I might ask you to sound Izzy out. She might remember something about a kid disappearing in the vicinity of Chiswell House.'

Robin said nothing.

'Like I said in the pub, Billy's very ill. It's probably nothing,' said Strike, with a trace of defensiveness. As he and Robin were both well aware, he had previously jettisoned paid cases and rich clients to pursue mysteries that others might have let lie. 'I just—'

'—can't rest easy until you've looked into it,' said Robin. 'All right. I understand.'

Unseen by her, Strike grinned and rubbed his tired eyes.

'Well, best of luck tomorrow,' he said. 'I'll be on my mobile if you need me.'

'What are you going to be up to?'

'Paperwork. Jimmy Knight's ex doesn't work Mondays. I'm off to Manchester to find her on Tuesday.'

Robin experienced a sudden wave of nostalgia for the previous year, when she and Strike had undertaken a road trip together to interrogate women left behind in the wake of dangerous men. She wondered whether he had thought about it while he planned this journey.

'Watching England–Italy?' she asked.

'Yeah,' said Strike. 'There's nothing else, is there?'

'No,' said Robin hurriedly. She had not meant to sound as though she wanted to detain him. 'Speak soon, then.'

She cut the call on his farewell and tossed the mobile aside onto the bed.

13

I am not going to let myself be beaten to the ground by the dread of what may happen.

Henrik Ibsen, *Rosmersholm*

The following morning, Robin woke, gasping, her fingers at her own throat, trying to loosen a non-existent hold. She was already at the bedroom door when Matthew woke, confused.

'It's nothing, I'm fine,' she muttered, before he could articulate a question, groping to find the handle that would let her out of the bedroom.

The surprise was that it hadn't happened more often since she had heard the story of the strangled child. Robin knew exactly how it felt to have fingers close tightly around your neck, to feel your brain flood with darkness, to know that you were seconds from being blotted out of existence. She had been driven into therapy by sharp-edged fragments of recollection that were unlike normal memories and which had the power to drag her suddenly out of her body and plunge her back into a past where she could smell the strangler's nicotine-stained fingers, and feel the stabber's soft, sweatshirted belly against her back.

She locked the bathroom door and sat down on the floor in the loose T-shirt she had worn to bed, focusing on her breathing, on the feel of the cool tiles beneath her bare legs, observing, as she had been taught, the rapid beating of her heart, the adrenaline jolting through her veins, not fighting her panic, but watching it. After a while, she consciously noticed the faint smell of the lavender body wash she had used last night, and heard the distant passing of an aeroplane.

You're safe. Just a dream. Just a dream.

Through two closed doors, she heard Matthew's alarm go off. A few minutes later, he knocked on the door.

'You all right?'

'Fine,' Robin called back, over the running tap.

She opened the door.

'Everything OK?' he asked, watching her closely.

'Just needed a pee,' said Robin brightly, heading back to the bedroom for her coloured contact lenses.

Before starting work with Strike, Robin had signed on with an agency called Temporary Solutions. The offices to which they had sent her were jumbled in her memory now, so that only anomalies, eccentrics and oddities remained. She remembered the alcoholic boss whose dictated letters she had reworded out of kindness, the desk drawer she had opened to find a complete set of dentures and a pair of stained underpants, the hopeful young man who had nicknamed her 'Bobbie' and tried, ineptly, to flirt over their back-to-back monitors, the woman who had plastered the interior of her cubicle workspace with pictures of the actor Ian McShane and the girl who had broken up with her boyfriend on the telephone in the middle of the open-plan office, indifferent to the prurient hush falling over the rest of the room. Robin doubted whether any of the people with whom she had come into glancing contact remembered her any better than she remembered them, even the timid romancer who had called her 'Bobbie'.

However, from the moment that she arrived at the Palace of Westminster, she knew that what happened here would live in her memory for ever. She felt a ripple of pleasure simply to leave the tourists behind and pass through the gate where the policeman stood guard. As she approached the palace, with its intricate gold mouldings starkly shadowed in the early morning sun, the famous clock tower silhouetted against the sky, her nerves and her excitement mounted.

Strike had told her which side door to use. It led into a long, dimly lit stone hall, but first she must pass through a metal detector and X-ray machine of the kind used at airports. As she took off her shoulder bag to be scanned, Robin noticed a tall, slightly dishevelled natural blonde in her thirties waiting a short distance away, holding a small package wrapped in brown paper. The woman watched as Robin stood for an automated picture that would appear on a paper day pass, to be worn on a lanyard around her neck, and when the security man waved Robin on, stepped forwards.

'Venetia?'

'Yes,' said Robin.

'Izzy,' said the other, smiling and holding out a hand. She was wearing a loose blouse with a splashy pattern of oversize flowers on it, and wide-legged trousers. 'This is from Papa.' She pressed the package she was holding into Robin's hands. 'I'm *rilly* sorry, we've got to dash – so glad you got here on time—'

She set off at a brisk walk, and Robin hastened to follow.

'—I'm in the middle of printing off a bunch of papers to take over to Papa at DCMS – I'm *snowed under* just now. Papa being Minister for Culture, with the Olympics coming, it's just crazy—'

She led Robin at a near jog through the hall, which had stained-glass windows at the far end, and off along labyrinthine corridors, talking all the while in a confident, upper-class accent, leaving Robin impressed by her lungpower.

'Yah, I'm leaving at the summer recess – setting up a decorating company with my friend Jacks – I've been here for five years – Papa's not happy – he needs somebody *rilly* good and the only applicant he liked turned us down.'

She talked over her shoulder at Robin, who was hurrying to keep up.

'I don't s'pose you know any *fabulous* PAs?'

'I'm afraid not,' said Robin, who had retained no friends from her temping career.

'Nearly there,' said Izzy, who had led Robin through a bewildering number of narrow corridors, all carpeted in the same forest green as the leather seats Robin had seen in the Commons on TV. At last they reached a side-passage off which led several heavy wooden doors, arched in the gothic style.

'That,' said Izzy in a stage whisper, pointing as they passed the first door on the right, 'is Winn's. This,' she said, marching to the last door on the left, 'is ours.'

She stood aside to let Robin pass into the room first.

The office was cramped and cluttered. The arched stone windows were hung with net curtains, beyond which lay the terrace bar, where shadowy figures moved against the dazzling brightness of the Thames. There were two desks, a multitude of bookshelves and a sagging green armchair. Green drapes hung at the overflowing book-shelves that covered one wall, only partially concealing the untidy stacks of files stacked there. On top of a filing cabinet stood a TV monitor, showing the currently empty interior of the Commons, its green benches deserted. A kettle sat beside mismatched mugs on a low shelf and had stained the wallpaper above it. The desktop printer whirred wheezily in a corner. Some of the papers it was disgorging had slid onto the threadbare carpet.

'Oh, shit,' said Izzy, dashing over and scooping them up, while Robin closed the door behind her. As she tapped the fallen papers back into a neat stack on her desk, Izzy said:

'I'm *thrilled* Papa's brought you in. He's been under *so much* strain, which he really doesn't need with everything we've got on now, but you and Strike will sort it out, won't you? Winn's a horrible little man,' said Izzy, reaching for a leather folder. '*Inadequate*, you know. How long have you worked with Strike?'

'A couple of years,' said Robin, as she undid the package Izzy had given her.

'I've met him, did he tell you? Yah – I was at school with his ex, Charlie Campbell. Gorgeous but trouble, Charlie. D'you know her?'

'No,' said Robin. A long-ago near-collision outside Strike's office had been her only contact with Charlotte.

'I always quite fancied Strike,' said Izzy.

Robin glanced around, surprised, but Izzy was matter-of-factly inserting papers into the folder.

'Yah, people couldn't see it, but *I* could. He was so butch and so . . . well . . . unapologetic.'

'Unapologetic?' Robin repeated.

'Yah. He never took any crap from anyone. Didn't give a toss that people thought he wasn't, you know—'

'Good enough for her?'

As soon as the words escaped her, Robin felt embarrassed. She had felt suddenly strangely protective of Strike. It was absurd, of course: if anybody could look after themselves, it was he.

'S'pose so,' said Izzy, still waiting for her papers to print. 'It's been ghastly for Papa, these past couple of months. And it isn't as though what he did was wrong!' she said fiercely. 'One minute it's legal, the next it isn't. That's not Papa's fault.'

'What wasn't legal?' asked Robin innocently.

'Sorry,' Izzy replied, pleasantly but firmly. 'Papa says, the fewer people know, the better.'

She peeked through the net curtains at the sky. 'I won't need a jacket, will I? No . . . sorry to dash, but Papa needs these and he's off to meet Olympic sponsors at ten. Good luck.'

And in a rush of flowered fabric and tousled hair, she was gone, leaving Robin curious but strangely reassured. If Izzy could take this robust view of her father's misdemeanour, it surely could not be anything dreadful – always assuming, of course, that Chiswell had told his daughter the truth.

Robin ripped the last piece of wrapping from the small parcel Izzy had given her. It contained, as she had known it would, the half-dozen listening devices that Strike had given to Jasper Chiswell over the weekend. As a Minister of the Crown, Chiswell was not required to pass through the security scanner every morning, as Robin was. She examined the bugs carefully. They had the appearance of normal plastic power points, and were designed to be fitted over genuine plug sockets, allowing the latter to function as normal. They would begin to record only when somebody spoke in their vicinity. She could hear her own heartbeat in the silence left by Izzy's departure. The difficulty of her task was only just beginning to sink in.

She took off her coat, hung it up, then removed from her shoulder bag a large box of Tampax, which she had brought for the purpose of concealing the listening devices she wasn't using. After hiding all but one of the bugs inside it, she placed the box in the bottom drawer of her desk. Next, she searched the cluttered shelves until she found an empty box file, in which she hid the remaining device beneath a handful of letters with typos that she took out of a pile labelled 'for shredding'. Thus armed, Robin took a deep breath and left the room.

Winn's door had opened since she had arrived. As Robin walked past, she saw a tall young Asian man wearing thick-lensed glasses and carrying a kettle.

'Hi!' said Robin at once, imitating Izzy's bold, cheery approach. 'I'm Venetia Hall, we're neighbours! Who are you?'

'Aamir,' muttered the other, in a working-class London accent. 'Mallik.'

'Do you work for Della Winn?' asked Robin.

'Yeah.'

'Oh, she's *so* inspirational,' gushed Robin. 'One of my heroines, actually.'

Aamir did not reply, but radiated a desire to be left alone. Robin felt like a terrier trying to harass a racehorse.

'Have you worked here long?'

'Six months.'

'Are you going to the café?'

'No,' said Aamir, as though she had propositioned him, and he turned sharply away towards the bathroom.

Robin walked on, holding her box file, wondering whether she had imagined animosity rather than shyness in the young man's demeanour. It would have been helpful to make a friend in Winn's office. Having to pretend to be an Izzy-esque goddaughter of Jasper Chiswell was hampering her. She couldn't help but feel that Robin Ellacott from Yorkshire might have befriended Aamir more easily.

Having set off with fake purpose, she decided to explore for a while before returning to Izzy's office.

Chiswell's and Winn's offices were in the Palace of Westminster itself, which, with its vaulted ceilings, libraries, tearooms and air of comfortable grandeur, might have been an old university college.

A half-covered passageway, watched over by large stone statues of a unicorn and lion, led to an escalator to Portcullis House. This was a modern crystal palace, with a folded glass roof, triangular panes held in place by thick black struts. Beneath was a wide, open-plan area including a café, where MPs and civil servants mingled. Flanked by full-grown trees, large water features consisting of long blocks of covered-in shallow pools became dazzling strips of quicksilver in the June sunshine.

There was a shiver of ambition in the thrumming air, and the sense of being part of a vital world. Beneath the ceiling of artfully fragmented glass, Robin passed political journalists perched on leather benches, all of whom were checking or talking on their mobiles, typing onto laptops or intercepting politicians for comment. Robin wondered whether she might have enjoyed working here if she had never been sent to Strike.

Her explorations ended in the third, dingiest and least interesting of the buildings that housed MPs' offices, which resembled nothing so much as a three-star hotel, with worn carpets and cream walls and row upon row of identical doors. Robin doubled back, still clutching her file, and passed Winn's door again fifty minutes after she had last seen it. Quickly checking that the corridor was deserted, she pressed her ear against the thick oak and thought she heard movement within.

'How's it going?' asked Izzy, when Robin re-entered her office a couple of minutes later.

'I haven't seen Winn yet.'

'He might be over at DCMS. He goes to see Della on any excuse,' said Izzy. 'Fancy a coffee?'

But before she could leave her desk, her telephone rang.

While Izzy fielded a call from an irate constituent who had been unable to secure tickets for the Olympic diving – 'yes, I like Tom Daley, too,' she said, rolling her eyes at Robin, 'but it's a *lottery*, madam' – Robin spooned out instant coffee and poured UHT milk, wondering how many times she had done this in offices she hated, and feeling suddenly extraordinarily grateful that she had escaped that life for ever.

'Hung up,' said Izzy indifferently, setting down the receiver. 'What were we talking about? Oh, Geraint, yah. He's furious Della didn't make him a SPAD.'

'What's a SPAD?' Robin asked, setting Izzy's coffee down and taking a seat at the other desk.

'Special Advisor. They're like temporary civil servants. Lots more prestige, but you don't hand the posts out to family, it's not done. Anyway, Geraint's hopeless, she wouldn't want him even if it were possible.'

'I just met the man who works with Winn,' said Robin. 'Aamir. He wasn't too friendly.'

'Oh, he's odd,' said Izzy, dismissively. 'Barely civil to me. It's probably because Geraint and Della hate Papa. I've never really got to the bottom of why, but they seem to hate all of us – oh, that reminds me: Papa texted a minute ago. My brother Raff's going to be coming in later this week, to help out in here. Maybe,' Izzy added, though she did not sound particularly hopeful, 'if Raff's any good, he might be able to take over from me. But Raff doesn't know anything about the blackmail or who you really are, so don't say anything, will you? Papa's got about fourteen godchildren. Raff'll never know the difference.'

Izzy sipped her coffee again, then, suddenly subdued, she said:

'I suppose you know about Raff. It was all over the papers. That poor woman ... it was awful. She had a four-year-old daughter ... '

'I did see something,' said Robin, noncommittally.

'I was the only one in the family who visited him in jail,' said Izzy. 'Everyone was so disgusted by what he'd done. Kinvara – Papa's wife – said he should have got life, but she's got no idea,' she continued, 'how *ghastly* it was in there ... people don't realise what prison's like ... I mean, I *know* he did a terrible thing, but ... '

Her words trailed away. Robin wondered, perhaps ungenerously, whether Izzy was suggesting that jail was no place for a young man as refined as her half-brother. Doubtless it *had* been a horrible experience, Robin thought, but after all, he had taken drugs, climbed into a car and mown down a young mother.

'I thought he was working in an art gallery?' Robin asked.

'He's gone and messed up at Drummond's,' sighed Izzy. 'Papa's really taking him in to keep an eye on him.'

Public money paid for these salaries, Robin thought, remembering again the unusually short prison sentence the son of the minister had served for that drug-induced fatal accident.

'How did he mess up at the gallery?'

To her great surprise, Izzy's doleful expression vanished in a sudden spurt of laughter.

'Oh, God, I'm sorry, I shouldn't laugh. He shagged the other sales assistant in the loo,' she said, quaking with giggles. 'I know it isn't funny really – but he'd just got out of jail, and Raff's lovely looking and he's always pulled anyone he wants. They shoved him into a suit and put him in close proximity with some pretty little blonde art graduate, what did they think was going to happen? But as you can imagine, the gallery owner wasn't too chuffed. He heard them going at it and put Raff on a final warning. Then Raff and the girl went and did it again, so Papa had a total fit and says he's coming here instead.'

Robin didn't feel particularly amused, but Izzy appeared not to notice, lost in her own thoughts.

'You never know, it could be the making of them, Papa and Raff,' she said hopefully, then checked her watch.

'Better return some calls,' she sighed, setting down her coffee mug, but as she reached for her phone she froze, fingers on the receiver as a sing-song male voice rang out in the corridor beyond the closed door.

'That's him! Winn!'

'Well, here I go,' said Robin, snatching up her box file again.

'Good luck!' whispered Izzy.

Emerging into the corridor, Robin saw Winn standing in the doorway of his office, apparently talking to Aamir, who was inside. Winn was holding a folder with orange lettering on it saying 'The Level Playing Field'. At the sound of Robin's footsteps, he turned to face her.

'Well, hello there,' he said with a Cardiff lilt, stepping back into the corridor.

His gaze dribbled down Robin's neck, fell onto her breasts, then up again to her mouth and her eyes. Robin knew him from that single look. She had met plenty of them in offices, the type who watched you in a way that made you feel clumsy and self-conscious, who would place a hand in the small of the back as they sidled behind you or ushered you through doors, who peered over your shoulder on the excuse of reading your monitor and made chancy little comments on your clothes that progressed to comments on your figure during after-work drinks. They cried 'joke!' if you got angry, and became aggressive in the face of complaints.

'Where d'you fit in, then?' asked Geraint, making the question sound salacious.

'I'm interning for Uncle Jasper,' said Robin, smiling brightly.

'*Uncle* Jasper?'

'Jasper Chiswell, yes,' said Robin, pronouncing the name, as the Chiswells did themselves, 'Chizzle'. 'He's my godfather. Venetia Hall,' said Robin, holding out her hand.

Everything about Winn seemed faintly amphibian, down to his damp palm. He was less like a gecko in the flesh, she thought, and more like a frog, with a pronounced potbelly and spindly arms and legs, his thinning hair rather greasy.

'And how did it come about that you're Jasper's goddaughter?'

'Oh, Uncle Jasper and Daddy are old friends,' said Robin, who had a full backstory prepared.

'Army?'

'Land management,' said Robin, sticking to her prearranged story.

'Ah,' said Geraint; then, 'Lovely hair. Is it natural?'

'Yes,' said Robin.

His eyes slid down her body again. It cost Robin an effort to keep smiling at him. At last, gushing and giggling until her check muscles ached, agreeing that she would indeed give him a shout should she need any assistance, Robin walked on down the corridor. She could feel him watching her until she turned out of sight.

Just as Strike had felt after discovering Jimmy Knight's litigious habits, Robin was sure that she had just gained a valuable insight into Winn's weakness. In her experience, men like Geraint were astoundingly prone to believe that their scattergun sexual advances were appreciated and even reciprocated. She had spent no inconsiderable part of her temping career trying to rebuff and avoid such men, all of whom saw lubricious invitations in the merest pleasantry, and for whom youth and inexperience were an irresistible temptation.

How far, she asked herself, was she prepared to go in her quest to find out things to Winn's discredit? Walking with sham purpose through endless corridors to support her pretence of having papers to deliver, Robin pictured herself leaning over his desk while the inconvenient Aamir was elsewhere, breasts at eye-level, asking for help and advice, giggling at smutty jokes.

Then, with a sudden, dreadful lurch of imagination she saw, clearly, Winn's lunge, saw the sweaty face swooping for her, its lip-less mouth agape, felt hands gripping her arms, pinning them to her sides, felt the pot-belly press itself into her, squashing her backwards into a filing cabinet . . .

The endless green of carpet and chairs, the dark wood arches and the square panels seemed to blur and contract as Winn's imagined pass became an attack. She pushed through the door ahead as though she could physically force herself past her panic . . .

Breathe. Breathe. Breathe.

'Bit overwhelming the first time you see it, eh?'

The man sounded kindly and not very young.

'Yes,' said Robin, barely knowing what she said. *Breathe.*

'Temporary, eh?' And then, 'You all right, dear?'

'Asthma,' said Robin.

She had used the excuse before. It gave her an excuse to stop, to breathe deeply, to re-anchor herself to reality.

'Got an inhaler?' asked the elderly steward in concern.

He wore a frock coat, white tie and tails and an ornate badge of office. In his unexpected grandeur, Robin thought wildly of the white rabbit, popping up in the middle of madness.

'I left it in my office. I'll be fine. Just need a second . . .'

She had blundered into a blaze of gold and colour that was increasing her feeling of oppression. The Members' Lobby, that familiar, ornate, Victorian-gothic chamber she had seen on television, stood right outside the Commons, and on the periphery of her vision loomed four gigantic bronze statues of previous prime ministers – Thatcher, Atlee, Lloyd George and Churchill – while busts of all the others lined the walls. They appeared to Robin like severed heads and the gilding, with its intricate tracery and richly coloured embellishments, danced around her, jeering at her inability to cope with its ornate beauty.

She heard the scraping of a chair's legs. The steward had brought her a seat and was asking a colleague to fetch a glass of water.

'Thank you . . . thank you . . . ' said Robin numbly, feeling inadequate, ashamed and embarrassed. Strike must never know about this. He would send her home, tell her she wasn't fit to do the job. Nor must she tell Matthew, who treated these episodes as shameful, inevitable consequences of her stupidity in continuing surveillance work.

The steward talked to her kindly while she recovered and within a few minutes she was able to respond appropriately to his well-intentioned patter. While her breathing returned to normal, he told her the tale of how Edward Heath's bust had begun to turn green on the arrival of the full-sized Thatcher statue beside him, and how it had had to be treated to turn it back to its dark brown bronze.

Robin laughed politely, got to her feet and handed him the empty glass with renewed thanks.

What treatment would it take, she wondered as she set off again, to return her to what she had once been?

14

*... how happy I should feel if I could succeed in bringing a little
light into all this murky ugliness.*

Henrik Ibsen, *Rosmersholm*

Strike rose early on Tuesday morning. After showering, putting on
his prosthesis and dressing, he filled a thermos with dark brown tea,
took the sandwiches he had made the previous evening out of the
fridge, stowed them in a carrier bag along with two packets of Club
biscuits, chewing gum and a few bags of salt and vinegar crisps, then
headed out into the sunrise and off to the garage where he kept his
BMW. He had an appointment for a haircut at half past twelve, with
Jimmy Knight's ex-wife, in Manchester.

Once settled in the car, his bag of provisions within easy reach,
Strike pulled on the trainers he kept in the car, which gave his fake
foot better purchase on the brake. He then took out his mobile and
began to compose a text to Robin.

Starting with the names that Wardle had given him, Strike had
spent much of Monday researching, as best as he could, the two children the policemen had told him had vanished from the Oxfordshire
area twenty years previously. Wardle had misspelled the boy's first
name, which had cost Strike time, but Strike had finally dug out
archived press reports about Imamu Ibrahim, in which Imamu's
mother had asserted that her estranged husband had kidnapped the
boy and taken him to Algeria. Strike had finally dredged up two
lines about Imamu and his mother on the website of an organisation that worked to resolve international custody issues. From this,

Strike had to conclude that Imamu had been found alive and well with his father.

The fate of Suki Lewis, the twelve-year-old runaway from a care home, was more mysterious. Strike had finally discovered an image of her, buried in an old news story. Suki had vanished from her residential care home in Swindon in 1992 and Strike could find no other mention of her since. Her blurry picture showed a rather toothy, undersized child, fine-featured, with short dark hair.

Little girl it was, but after they said it was a little boy.

So a vulnerable, androgynous child might have disappeared off the face of the earth around the same time, and in the approximate area, that Billy Knight claimed to have witnessed the strangling of a boy-girl.

In the car, he composed a text to Robin.

If you can make it sound natural, ask Izzy if she remembers anything about a 12-year-old called Suki Lewis. She ran away 20 years ago from a care home near their family house.

The dirt on his windscreen shimmered and blurred in the rising sun as he left London. Driving was no longer the pleasure it had once been. Strike could not afford a specially adapted vehicle, and even though it was an automatic, the operation of the BMW's pedals remained challenging with his prosthesis. In challenging conditions, he sometimes reverted to operating brake and accelerator with his left foot.

When he finally joined the M6, Strike hoped to settle in at sixty miles an hour, but some arsehole in a Vauxhall Corsa decided to tailgate him.

'Fucking overtake,' growled Strike. He was not minded to alter his own speed, having settled in comfortably without needing to use his false foot more than was necessary, and for a while he glowered into his rear view mirror until the Vauxhall driver got the hint and took himself off.

Relaxing to the degree that was ever possible behind the wheel these days, Strike wound down the window to admit the fine, fresh summer's day and allowed his thoughts to return to Billy and the missing Suki Lewis.

She wouldn't let me dig, he had said in the office, compulsively tapping his nose and his chest, *but she'd let you.*

Who, Strike wondered, was 'she'? Perhaps the new owner of Steda Cottage? They might well object to Billy asking to dig up flowerbeds in search of bodies.

After feeling around with his left hand inside his provisions bag, extracting and ripping open a bag of crisps with his teeth, Strike reminded himself for the umpteenth time that Billy's whole story might be a chimera. Suki Lewis could be anywhere. Not every lost child was dead. Perhaps Suki, too, had been stolen away by an errant parent. Twenty years previously, in the infancy of the internet, imperfect communication between regional police forces could be exploited by those wishing to reinvent themselves or others. And even if Suki was no longer alive, there was nothing to suggest that she had been strangled, let alone that Billy Knight had witnessed it. Most people would surely conclude that this was a case of much smoke, but no fire.

Chewing crisps by the handful, Strike reflected that whenever it came to a question of what 'most people' would think, he usually envisaged his half-sister Lucy, the only one of his seven half-siblings with whom he had shared his chaotic and peripatetic childhood. To him, Lucy represented the acme of all that was conventional and unimaginative, even though they had both grown up on intimate terms with the macabre, the dangerous and the frightening.

Before Lucy had gone to live permanently with their aunt and uncle in Cornwall, at the age of fourteen, their mother had hauled her and Strike from squat to commune to rented flat to friend's floor, rarely remaining in the same place more than six months, exposing her children to a parade of eccentric, damaged and addicted human beings along the way. Right hand on the wheel, left hand now groping around for biscuits, Strike recalled some of the nightmarish spectacles that he and Lucy had witnessed as children: the psychotic youth fighting an invisible devil in a basement flat in Shoreditch, the teenager literally being whipped at a quasi-mystical commune in Norfolk (still, for Strike's money, the worst place that Leda had ever taken them) and Shayla, one of the most fragile of Leda's friends and a part-time prostitute, sobbing about the brain damage inflicted on her toddler son by a violent boyfriend.

That unpredictable and sometimes terrifying childhood had left Lucy with a craving for stability and conformity. Married to a quantity surveyor whom Strike disliked, with three sons he barely knew, she would probably dismiss Billy's story of the strangled boy-girl as the product of a broken mind, sweeping it swiftly away into the corner with all the other things she could not bear to think about. Lucy needed to pretend that violence and strangeness had vanished into a past as dead as their mother; that with Leda gone, life was unshakeably secure.

Strike understood. Profoundly different though they were, often though she exasperated him, he loved Lucy. Nevertheless, he could not help comparing her with Robin as he bowled towards Manchester. Robin had grown up in what seemed to Strike the very epitome of middle-class stability, but she was courageous in a way that Lucy was not. Both women had been touched by violence and sadism. Lucy had reacted by burying herself where she hoped it would never reach her again; Robin, by facing it almost daily, investigating and resolving other crimes and traumas, driven to do so by the same impulse to actively disentangle complications and disinter truths that Strike recognised in himself.

As the sun climbed higher, still dappling the grubby windscreen, he experienced a powerful regret that she wasn't here with him now. She was the best person he had ever met to run a theory past. She'd unscrew the thermos for him and pour him tea. *We'd have a laugh.*

They had slipped back into their old bantering ways a couple of times lately, since Billy had entered the office with a story troubling enough to break down the reserve that had, over a year, hardened into a permanent impediment to their friendship . . . *or whatever it was,* thought Strike, and for a moment or two he felt her again in his arms on the stairs, breathed in the scent of white roses and of the perfume that hung around the office when Robin was at her desk . . .

With a kind of mental grimace, he reached for another cigarette, lit up and forced his mind towards Manchester, and the line of questioning he intended to take with Dawn Clancy, who, for five years, had been Mrs Jimmy Knight.

15

Yes, she is a queer one, she is. She has always been very much on the high horse . . .

Henrik Ibsen, *Rosmersholm*

While Strike was speeding northwards, Robin was summoned without explanation to a personal meeting with the Minister for Culture himself.

Walking in the sunshine towards the Department for Culture, Media and Sport, which stood in a large white Edwardian building a few minutes away from the Palace of Westminster, Robin found herself almost wishing that she were one of the tourists cluttering the pavement, because Chiswell had sounded bad tempered on the phone.

Robin would have given a great deal to have something useful to tell the minister about his blackmailer, but as she had only been on the job a day and a half, all she could say with any certainty was that her first impressions of Geraint Winn had now been confirmed: he was lazy, lecherous, self-important and indiscreet. The door of his office stood open more often than not, and his sing-song voice rang down the corridor as he talked with injudicious levity about his constituents' petty concerns, name-dropped celebrities and senior politicians and generally sought to give the impression of a man for whom running a mere constituency office was an unimportant sideshow.

He hailed Robin jovially from his desk whenever she passed his open door, showing a pronounced eagerness for further contact.

146

However, whether by chance or design, Aamir Mallik kept thwarting Robin's attempts to turn these greetings into conversations, either interrupting with questions for Winn or, as he had done just an hour previously, simply closing the door in Robin's face.

The exterior of the great block that housed the DCMS, with its stone swags, its columns and its neoclassical façade, was not reassuring. The interior had been modernised and hung with contemporary art, including an abstract glass sculpture that hung from the cupola over the central staircase, up which Robin was led by an efficient-seeming young woman. Believing her to be the minister's goddaughter, her companion was at pains to show her points of interest.

'The Churchill Room,' she said, pointing left as they turned right. 'That's the balcony he gave his speech from, on VE Day. The minister's just along here ...'

She led Robin down a wide, curving corridor that doubled as an open-plan workspace. Smart young people sat at an array of desks in front of lengthy windows to the right, which looked out onto a quadrangle, which, in size and scale, bore the appearance of a colosseum, with its high white windowed walls. It was all very different from the cramped office where Izzy made their instant coffee from a kettle. Indeed, a large, expensive machine complete with pods sat on one desk for that purpose.

The offices to the left were separated from this curving space by glass walls and doors. Robin spotted the Minister for Culture from a distance, sitting at his desk beneath a contemporary painting of the Queen, talking on the telephone. He indicated by a brusque gesture that her escort should show Robin inside the office and continued talking on the telephone as Robin waited, somewhat awkwardly, for him to finish his call. A woman's voice was issuing from the earpiece, high-pitched and to Robin, even eight feet away, hysterical.

'I've got to go, Kinvara!' barked Chiswell into the mouthpiece. 'Yes ... we'll talk about this later. *I've got to go.*'

Setting down the receiver harder than was necessary, he pointed Robin to a chair opposite him. His coarse, straight grey hair stood out around his head in a wiry halo, his fat lower lip giving him an air of angry petulance.

'The newspapers are sniffing around,' he growled. 'That was m'wife. The *Sun* rang her this morning, asking whether the rumours are true. She said "what rumours?" but the fella didn't specify. Fishing, obviously. Trying to surprise something out of her.'

He frowned at Robin, whose appearance he seemed to find wanting.

'How old are you?'

'Twenty-seven,' she said.

'You look younger.'

It didn't sound like a compliment.

'Managed to plant the surveillance device yet?'

'I'm afraid not,' said Robin.

'Where's Strike?'

'In Manchester, interviewing Jimmy Knight's ex-wife,' said Robin.

Chiswell made the angry, subterranean noise usually rendered as 'harrumph', then got to his feet. Robin jumped up, too.

'Well, you'd better get back and get on with it,' said Chiswell. 'The National Health Service,' he added, with no change of tone, as he headed towards the door. 'People are going to think we're bloody mad.'

'Sorry?' said Robin, entirely thrown.

Chiswell pulled open the glass door and indicated that Robin should pass through it ahead of him, out into the open-plan area where all the smart young people sat working beside their sleek coffee machine.

'Olympics opening ceremony,' he explained, following her. 'Lefty bloody crap. We won two bloody world wars, but we're not supposed to celebrate that.'

'Nonsense, Jasper,' said a deep, melodious Welsh voice close at hand. 'We celebrate military victories all the time. This is a different kind of celebration.'

Della Winn, the Minister for Sport, was standing just outside Chiswell's door, holding the leash of her near-white Labrador. A woman of stately appearance, with grey hair swept back off a broad forehead, she wore sunglasses so dark that Robin could make out nothing behind them. Her blindness, Robin knew from her research, had been due to a rare condition in which neither eyeball had grown *in utero*. She sometimes wore prosthetic eyes, especially when she was to be photographed. Della was sporting a quantity of heavy, tactile jewellery in gold, with a large necklace of intaglios, and dressed from head to foot in sky blue. Robin had read in one of Strike's printed profiles of the politician that Geraint laid out Della's clothes for her every morning and that it was simplest for him, not having a great feel for fashion, to select things in the same colour. Robin had found this rather touching when she read it.

Chiswell did not appear to relish the sudden appearance of his colleague and indeed, given that her husband was blackmailing him, Robin supposed that this was hardly surprising. Della, on the other hand, gave no sign of embarrassment.

'I thought we might share the car over to Greenwich,' she said to Chiswell, while the pale Labrador snuffled gently at the hem of Robin's skirt. 'Give us a chance to go over the plans for the twelfth. What are you doing, Gwynn?' she added, feeling the Labrador's head tugging.

'She's sniffing me,' said Robin nervously, patting the Labrador.

'This is my goddaughter, ah ... '

'Venetia,' said Robin, as Chiswell was evidently struggling to remember her name.

'How do you do?' said Della, holding out her hand. 'Visiting Jasper?'

'No, I'm interning in the constituency office,' said Robin, shaking the warm, be-ringed hand, as Chiswell walked away to examine the document held by a hovering young man in a suit.

'Venetia,' repeated Della, her face still turned towards Robin. A faint frown appeared on the handsome face, half-masked behind the impenetrable black glasses. 'What's your surname?'

'Hall,' said Robin.

She felt a ridiculous flutter of panic, as though Della were about to unmask her. Still poring over the document he had been shown, Chiswell moved away, leaving Robin, or so it felt, entirely at Della's mercy.

'You're the fencer,' said Della.

'Sorry?' said Robin, totally confused again, her mind on posts and rails. Some of the young people around the space-age coffee machine had turned around to listen, expressions of polite interest on their faces.

'Yes,' said Della. 'Yes, I remember you. You were on the English team with Freddie.'

Her friendly expression had hardened. Chiswell was now leaning over a desk while he struck through phrases on the document.

'No, I never fenced,' said Robin, thoroughly out of her depth. She had realised at the mention of the word 'team' that swords were under discussion, rather than fields and livestock.

'You certainly did,' said Della flatly. 'I remember you. Jasper's goddaughter, on the team with Freddie.'

It was a slightly unnerving display of arrogance, of complete self-belief. Robin felt inadequate to the job of continuing to protest, because there were now several listeners. Instead, she merely said, 'Well, nice to have met you,' and walked away.

'*Again*, you mean,' said Della sharply, but Robin made no reply.

16

... a man with as dirty a record as his! ... This is the sort of
man that poses as a leader of the people! And successfully, too!
Henrik Ibsen, *Rosmersholm*

After four and a half hours in the driving seat, Strike's exit from the
BMW in Manchester was far from graceful. He stood for a while
in Burton Road, a broad, pleasant street with its mixture of shops
and houses, leaning on the car, stretching his back and leg, grateful
that he had managed to find a parking space only a short way from
'Stylz'. The bright pink shopfront stood out between a café and a
Tesco Express, pictures of moody models with unnaturally tinted
hair in the window.

With its black and white tiled floor and pink walls that reminded
Strike of Lorelei's bedroom, the interior of the small shop was
determinedly trendy, but it did not appear to cater to a particularly
youthful or adventurous clientele. There were currently only two
clients, one of whom was a large woman of at least sixty, who was
reading *Good Housekeeping* in front of a mirror, her hair a mass of
foil. Strike made a bet with himself as he entered that Dawn would
prove to be the slim peroxide blonde with her back to him, chatting
animatedly to an elderly lady whose blue hair she was perming.

'I've got an appointment with Dawn,' Strike told the young receptionist, who looked slightly startled to see anything so large and male
in this fug of perfumed ammonia. The peroxided blonde turned at
the sound of her name. She had the leathery, age-spotted skin of a
committed sunbed user.

'With you in a moment, cock,' she said, smiling. He settled to wait on a bench in the window.

Five minutes later, she was leading him to an upholstered pink chair at the back of the shop.

'What are you after, then?' she asked him, inviting him with a gesture to sit down.

'I'm not here for a haircut,' said Strike, still standing. 'I'll happily pay for one, I don't want to waste your time, but,' he pulled a card and his driver's licence from his pocket, 'my name's Cormoran Strike. I'm a private detective and I was hoping to talk to you about your ex-husband, Jimmy Knight.'

She looked stunned, as well she might, but then fascinated.

'Strike?' she repeated, gaping. 'You aren't him that caught that Ripper guy?'

'That's me.'

'Jesus, what's Jimmy done?'

'Nothing much,' said Strike easily. 'I'm just after background.'

She didn't believe him, of course. Her face, he suspected, was full of filler, her forehead suspiciously smooth and shiny above the carefully pencilled eyebrows. Only her stringy neck betrayed her age.

'That's over. It was over ages ago. I never talk about Jimmy. Least said, soonest mended, don't they say?'

But he could feel the curiosity and excitement radiating from her like heat. Radio 2 jangled in the background. She glanced towards the two women sitting at the mirrors.

'Sian!' she said loudly, and the receptionist jumped and turned. 'Take out her foils and keep an eye on the perm for me, love.' She hesitated, still holding Strike's card. 'I'm not sure I should,' she said, wanting to be talked into it.

'It's only background,' he said. 'No strings.'

Five minutes later she was handing him a milky coffee in a tiny staffroom at the rear of the shop, talking merrily, a little haggard in the fluorescent overhead light, but still good-looking enough to explain why Jimmy had first shown interest in a woman thirteen years his senior.

'... yeah, a demonstration against nuclear weapons. I went with this friend of mine, Wendy, she was big into all that. Vegetarian,' she added, nudging the door into the shop closed with her foot and taking out a pack of Silk Cut. 'You know the type.'

'Got my own,' said Strike, when she offered the pack. He lit her cigarette for her, then one of his Benson & Hedges. They blew out simultaneous streams of smoke. She crossed her legs towards him and rattled on.

'... yeah, so Jimmy gave a speech. Weapons and how much we could save, give to the NHS and everything, what was the point ... he talks well, you know,' said Dawn.

'He does,' agreed Strike, 'I've heard him.'

'Yeah, and I fell for it, hook, line and sinker. Thought he was some kind of Robin Hood.'

Strike heard the joke coming before she made it. He knew it was not the first time.

'*Robbing* Hood, more like,' she said.

She was already divorced when she had met Jimmy. Her first husband had left her for another girl at the London salon they had owned together. Dawn had done well out of the divorce, managing to retain the business. Jimmy had seemed a romantic figure after her wide-boy first husband and, on the rebound, she had fallen for him hard.

'But there were always girls,' she said. 'Lefties, you know. Some of them were really young. He was like a pop star to them or something. I only found out how many of them there were later, after he'd set up cards on all my accounts.'

Dawn told Strike at length how Jimmy had persuaded her to bankroll a lawsuit against his ex-employer, Zanet Industries, who had failed to follow due process in firing him.

'Very keen on his rights, Jimmy. He's not stupid, though, you know. Ten grand payout he got from Zanet. I never saw a penny of it. He pissed it all away, trying to sue other people. He tried to take me to court, after we split up. Loss of earnings, don't make me laugh. I'd kept him for five years and he claimed he'd been working with me, building up the business for no pay and left with occupational asthma from the chemicals – so much shit, he talked – they chucked it out of court, thank God. And then he tried to get me on a harassment charge. Said I'd keyed his car.'

She ground out her cigarette and reached for another one.

'I had, too,' she said, with a sudden, wicked smile. 'You know he's been put on a list, now? Can't sue anyone without permission.'

'I did know, yeah,' said Strike. 'Was he ever involved in any criminal activity while you were together, Dawn?'

She lit up again, watching Strike over her fingers, still hoping to hear what Jimmy was supposed to have done to have Strike after him. Finally she said:

'I'm not sure he was too careful about checking all the girls he was playing around with were sixteen. I heard, after, one of them . . . but we'd split up by then. It wasn't my problem any more,' said Dawn, as Strike made a note.

'And I wouldn't trust him if it was anything to do with Jews. He doesn't like them. Israel's the root of all evil, according to Jimmy. Zionism: I got sick of the bloody sound of the word. You'd think they'd suffered enough,' said Dawn vaguely. 'Yeah, his manager at Zanet was Jewish and they hated each other.'

'What was his name?'

'What was it?' Dawn drew heavily on her cigarette, frowning. 'Paul something . . . Lobstein, that's it. Paul Lobstein. He's probably still at Zanet.'

'D'you still have any contact with Jimmy, or any of his family?'

'Christ, no. Good riddance. The only one of his family I ever met was little Billy, his brother.'

She softened a little as she said the name.

'He wasn't right. He stayed with us for a bit at one point. He was a sweetheart, really, but not right. Jimmy said it was their father. Violent alkie. Raised them on his own and knocked the shit out of them, from what the boys said, used the belt and everything. Jimmy got away to London, and poor little Billy was left alone with him. No surprise he was how he was.'

'What d'you mean?'

'He 'ad a – a tic, do they call it?'

She mimicked with perfect accuracy the nose to chest tapping Strike had witnessed in his office.

'He was put on drugs, I know that. Then he left us, went to share a flat with some other lads for a bit. I never saw him again after Jimmy and I split. He was a sweet boy, yeah, but he annoyed Jimmy.'

'In what way?' Strike asked.

'Jimmy didn't like him talking about their childhood. I dunno, I think Jimmy felt guilty he'd left Billy in the house alone. There was something funny about that whole business . . . '

Strike could tell she hadn't thought about these things for a while.

'Funny?' he prompted.

'A couple of times, when he'd had a few, Jimmy went on about how his dad would burn for how he made his living.'

'I thought he was an odd-job man?'

'Was he? They told me he was a joiner. He worked for that politician's family, what's his name? The one with the hair.'

She mimed stiff bristles coming out of her head.

'Jasper Chiswell?' Strike suggested, pronouncing the name the way it was spelled.

'Him, yeah. Old Mr Knight had a rent-free cottage in the family grounds. The boys grew up there.'

'And he said his father would go to hell for what he did for a living?' repeated Strike.

'Yeah. It's probably just because he was working for Tories. It was all about politics with Jimmy. I don't get it,' said Dawn restlessly. 'You've got to live. Imagine me asking my clients how they vote before I'll—

'Bloody hell,' she gasped suddenly, grinding out her cigarette and jumping to her feet, 'Sian had better've taken out Mrs Horridge's rollers or she'll be bald.'

17

I see he is altogether incorrigible.

Henrik Ibsen, *Rosmersholm*

Watching for an opportunity to plant the bug in Winn's office, Robin spent most of the afternoon hanging around the quiet corridor on which both his and Izzy's offices lay, but her efforts were fruitless. Even though Winn had left for a lunchtime meeting, Aamir remained inside. Robin paced up and down, box file in her arms, waiting for the moment when Aamir might go to the bathroom and returning to Izzy's office whenever any passer-by tried to engage her in conversation.

Finally, at ten past four, her luck changed. Geraint Winn swaggered around the corner, rather tipsy after what seemed to have been a prolonged lunch, and in sharp contrast to his wife, he seemed delighted to meet her as she set off towards him.

'There she is!' he said, over-loudly. 'I wanted a word with you! Come in here, come in!'

He pushed open the door of his office. Puzzled, but only too eager to see the interior of the room she was hoping to bug, Robin followed him.

Aamir was working in shirtsleeves at his desk, which formed a tiny oasis of order in the general clutter. Stacks of folders lay around Winn's desk. Robin noticed the orange logo of the Level Playing Field on a pile of letters in front of him. There was a power point

156

directly under Geraint's desk that would be an ideal position for the listening device.

'Have you two met?' Geraint asked jovially. 'Venetia, Aamir.'

He sat down and invited Robin to take the armchair on which a sliding pile of card folders lay.

'Did Redgrave call back?' Winn asked Aamir, struggling out of his suit jacket.

'Who?' said the latter.

'Sir Steve Redgrave!' said Winn, with the suspicion of an eye roll in Robin's direction. She felt embarrassed for him, especially as Aamir's muttered 'no' was cold.

'Level Playing Field,' Winn told Robin.

He had managed to get his jacket off. With an attempted flourish, he threw it onto the back of his chair. It slid limply onto the floor, but Geraint appeared not to notice, and instead tapped the orange logo on the topmost letter in front of him. 'Our cha—' he belched. 'Pardon me – our charity. Disadvantaged and disabled athletes, you know. Lots of high profile supporters. Sir Steve keen to—' he belched again, '—pardon – help. Well, now. I wanted to apologise. For my poor wife.'

He seemed to be enjoying himself hugely. Out of the corner of her eye, Robin saw Aamir fling Geraint a sharp look, like the flash of a claw, swiftly retracted.

'I don't understand,' said Robin.

'Gets names wrong. Does it all the time. If I didn't keep an eye on her, we'd have all sorts going on, wrong letters going out to the wrong people ... she thought you were someone else. I had her on the phone over lunch, insisting you were somebody our daughter ran across years ago. Verity Pulham. 'Nother of your godfather's godchildren. Told her straight away it wasn't you, said I'd pass on her apologies. Silly girl, she is. Very stubborn when she thinks she's right, but,' he rolled his eyes again and tapped his forehead, the long-suffering husband of an infuriating wife, 'I managed to penetrate in the end.'

'Well,' said Robin carefully, 'I'm glad she knows she was mistaken, because she didn't seem to like Verity very much.'

'Truth to tell, Verity *was* a little bitch,' said Winn, still beaming. Robin could tell he enjoyed using the word. 'Nasty to our daughter, you see.'

'Oh dear,' said Robin, with a thud of dread beneath her ribs as she remembered that Rhiannon Winn had killed herself. 'I'm sorry. How awful.'

'You know,' said Winn, sitting down and tipping back his chair against the wall, hands behind his head, 'you seem far too sweet a girl to be associated with the Chiswell family.' He was definitely a little drunk. Robin could smell faint wine dregs on his breath and Aamir threw him another of those sharp, scathing looks. 'What were you doing before this, Venetia?'

'PR,' said Robin, 'but I'd like to do something more worthwhile. Politics, or maybe a charity. I was reading about the Level Playing Field,' she said truthfully. 'It seems wonderful. You do a lot with veterans, too, don't you? I saw an interview with Terry Byrne yesterday. The Paralympian cyclist?'

Her attention had been caught by the fact that Byrne had the same below the knee amputation as Strike.

'You'll have a personal interest in veterans, of course,' said Winn.

Robin's stomach swooped and fell again.

'Sorry?'

'Freddie Chiswell?' Winn prompted.

'Oh, yes, of course,' said Robin. 'Although I didn't know Freddie very well. He was a bit older than me. Obviously, it was dreadful when he – when he was killed.'

'Oh, yes, awful,' said Winn, though he sounded indifferent. 'Della was very much against the Iraq war. Very much against it. Your Uncle Jasper was all for it, mind you.'

For a moment, the air seemed to thrum with Winn's unexpressed implication that Chiswell had been well served for his enthusiasm.

'Well, I don't know about that,' said Robin carefully. 'Uncle Jasper thought military action justified on the evidence we had at the time. Anyway,' she said bravely, 'nobody can accuse him of acting out of self-interest, can they, when his son had to go and fight?'

'Ah, if you're going to take that line, who can argue?' said Winn.

He raised his hands in mock surrender, his chair slipped a little on the wall and for a few seconds he struggled to maintain balance, seizing the desk and pulling himself and the chair upright again. With a substantial effort, Robin managed not to laugh.

'Geraint,' said Aamir, 'we need those letters signed if we're going to get them off by five.'

''S'only half four,' said Winn, checking his watch. 'Yes, Rhiannon was on the British junior fencing team.'

'How marvellous,' said Robin.

'Sporty, like her mother. Fencing for the Welsh juniors at fourteen. I used to drive her all over the place for tournaments. Hours on the road together! She made the British juniors at sixteen.

'But the English lot were very stand-offish to her,' said Winn, with a glimmer of Celtic resentment. 'She wasn't at one of your big public schools, you see. It was all about connections with them. Verity Pulham, she didn't have the ability, not really. As a matter of fact, it was only when Verity broke her ankle that Rhiannon, who was a far better fencer, got on the British team at all.'

'I see,' said Robin, trying to balance sympathy with a feigned allegiance to the Chiswells. Surely this could not be the grievance that Winn had against the family? Yet Geraint's fanatic tone spoke of longstanding resentment. 'Well, these things should come down to ability, of course.'

'That's right,' said Winn. 'They should. Look at this, now ...'

He fumbled for his wallet and pulled from it an old photograph. Robin held out her hand, but Geraint, keeping a firm hold on the picture, got up clumsily, stumbled over a stack of books lying beside his chair, walked around the desk, came so close that Robin could feel his breath on her neck, and showed her the image of his daughter.

Dressed in fencing garb, Rhiannon Winn stood beaming and holding up the gold medal around her neck. She was pale and small-featured, and Robin could see very little of either parent in her face, although perhaps there was a hint of Della in the broad, intelligent brow. But with Geraint's loud breathing in her ear, trying to stop herself leaning away from him, Robin had a sudden vision of Geraint Winn striding, with his wide, lipless grin, through a large hall of sweaty teenage girls. Was it shameful to wonder whether it had been parental devotion that had spurred him to chauffeur his daughter all over the country?

'What have you done to yourself, eh?' Geraint asked, his hot breath in her ear. Leaning in, he touched the purple knife scar on her bare forearm.

Unable to prevent herself, Robin snatched her arm away. The nerves around the scar had not yet fully healed: she hated anyone touching it.

'I fell through a glass door when I was nine,' she said, but the confidential, confiding atmosphere had been dispersed like cigarette smoke.

Aamir hovered on the edge of her vision, rigid and silent at his desk. Geraint's smile had become forced. She had worked too long in offices not to know that a subtle transfer of power had just taken place within the room. Now she stood armed with his little drunken inappropriateness and Geraint was resentful and a little worried. She wished that she had not pulled away from him.

'I wonder, Mr Winn,' she said breathily, 'whether you'd mind giving me some advice about the charitable world? I just can't make up my mind, politics – charity – and I don't know anyone else who's done both.'

'Oh,' said Geraint, blinking behind his thick glasses. 'Oh, well . . . yes, I daresay I could . . . '

'Geraint,' said Aamir again, 'we really do need to get those letters—'

'Yes, all right, all right,' said Geraint loudly. 'We'll talk later,' he said to Robin, with a wink.

'Wonderful,' she said, with a smile.

As Robin walked out she threw Aamir a small smile, which he didn't return.

18

So matters have got as far as that already, have they!

Henrik Ibsen, *Rosmersholm*

After nearly nine hours at the wheel, Strike's neck, back and legs were stiff and sore and his bag of provisions long since empty. The first star was glimmering out of the pale, inky wash above when his mobile rang. It was the usual time for his sister, Lucy, to call 'for a chat'; he ignored three out of four of her calls, because, much as he loved her, he could muster no interest in her sons' schooling, the PTA's squabbles or the intricacies of her husband's career as a quantity surveyor. Seeing that it was Barclay on the line, however, he turned into a rough and ready lay-by, really the turnoff to a field, cut the engine and answered.

''M in,' said Barclay laconically. 'Wi' Jimmy.'

'Already?' said Strike, seriously impressed. 'How?'

'Pub,' said Barclay. 'Interrupted him. He was talkin' a load o' pish about Scottish independence. The grea' thing about English lefties,' he continued, 'is they love hearin' how shit England is. Havenae hadtae buy a pint all afternoon.'

'Bloody hell, Barclay,' said Strike, lighting himself another cigarette on top of the twenty he had already had that day, 'that was good work.'

'That was just fer starters,' said Barclay. 'You shoulda heard them when I told them how I've seen the error of the army's imperialist ways. Fuck me, they're gullible. I'm off tae a CORE meetin' the morrow.'

'How's Knight supporting himself? Any idea?'

'He told me he's a journalist on a couple o' lefty websites and he sells CORE T-shirts and a bit o' dope. Mind, his shit's worthless. We went back tae his place, after the pub. Ye'd be better off smokin' fuckin' Oxo cubes. I've said I'll get him better. We can run that through office expenses, aye?'

'I'll put it under "sundries",' said Strike. 'All right, keep me posted.'

Barclay rang off. Deciding to take the opportunity to stretch his legs, Strike got out of the car, still smoking, leaned on the five-bar gate facing a wide, dark field, and rang Robin.

'It's Vanessa,' Robin lied, when she saw Strike's number come up on her phone.

She and Matthew had just eaten a takeaway curry off their knees while watching the news. He had arrived home late and tired; she didn't need another argument.

Picking up the mobile, she headed out through the French doors onto the patio that had served as the smoking area for the party. After making sure that the doors were completely closed, she answered.

'Hi. Everything OK?'

'Fine. All right to talk for a moment?'

'Yes,' said Robin, leaning against the garden wall, and watching a moth banging fruitlessly against the bright glass, trying to enter the house. 'How did it go with Dawn Clancy?'

'Nothing useable,' said Strike. 'I thought I might have a lead, some Jewish ex-boss Jimmy had a vendetta against, but I rang the company and the poor bloke died of a stroke last September. Then I got a call from Chiswell just after I left her. He says the *Sun*'s sniffing around.'

'Yes,' said Robin. 'They called his wife.'

'We could've done without that,' said Strike, with what Robin felt was considerable understatement. 'I wonder who's tipped off the papers?'

'I'd bet on Winn,' said Robin, remembering the way that Geraint had talked that afternoon, the name-dropping, the self-importance. 'He's just the type to hint to a journalist that there's a story on Chiswell, even if he hasn't got proof of it yet. Seriously,' she said again, with no real hope of an answer, 'what d'you think Chiswell did?'

'Be nice to know, but it doesn't really matter,' said Strike, who sounded tired. 'We aren't being paid to get the goods on *him*. Speaking of which—'

'I haven't been able to plant the bug yet,' said Robin, anticipating the question. 'I hung around as late as possible, but Aamir locked the door after they both left.'

Strike sighed.

'Well, don't get overeager and balls it up,' he said, 'but we're up against it if the *Sun*'s involved. Anything you can do. Get in early or something.'

'I will, I'll try,' said Robin. 'I did get something odd about the Winns today, though,' and she told him about the confusion Della had made between herself and one of Chiswell's real goddaughters, and the story of Rhiannon on the fencing team. Strike seemed only distantly interested.

'Doubt that explains the Winns wanting Chiswell out of office. Anyway—'

'—means before motive,' she said, quoting Strike's own, oft-repeated words.

'Exactly. Listen, can you meet me after work tomorrow, and we'll have a proper debrief?'

'All right,' said Robin.

'Barclay's doing good work, though,' said Strike, as though the thought of it cheered him up. 'He's already well in with Jimmy.'

'Oh,' said Robin. 'Good.'

After telling her that he would text the name of a convenient pub, Strike rang off, leaving Robin alone and pensive in the quiet dark of the yard, while stars grew pin-bright overhead.

Barclay's doing good work, though.

As opposed to Robin, who had found out nothing but an irrelevancy about Rhiannon Winn.

The moth was still fluttering desperately against the sliding doors, frantic to get at the light.

Idiot, Robin thought. *It's better out here.*

The ease with which the lie about Vanessa being on the phone had slid out of her mouth ought, she reflected, to have made her feel guilty, but she was merely glad that she had got away with it. As she watched the moth continuing to bang its wings hopelessly against the brilliant glass, Robin remembered what her therapist had said to her during one of the sessions when Robin had dwelled at length on her need to discern where the real Matthew ended and her illusions about him began.

'People change in ten years,' the therapist had responded. 'Why does it have to be a question of you being mistaken in Matthew? Perhaps it's simply that you've both changed?'

The following Monday would mark their first wedding anniversary. At Matthew's suggestion, they were going to spend next weekend at a fancy hotel near Oxford. In a funny kind of way, Robin was looking forward to it, because she and Matthew seemed to get along better these days with a change of scene. Being surrounded by strangers nudged them out of their tendency to bicker. She had told him the story of Ted Heath's bust turning green, along with several other (to her) interesting facts about the House of Commons. He had maintained a bored expression through all of them, determined to signal his disapproval of the whole venture.

Reaching a decision, she opened the French window and the moth fluttered merrily inside.

'What did Vanessa want?' asked Matthew, his eyes on the news as Robin sat down again. Sarah Shadlock's stargazer lilies were sitting on a table beside her, still in bloom ten days after they had arrived in the house, and Robin could smell their heady scent even over the curry.

'I picked up her sunglasses by mistake last time we went out,' said Robin, feigning exasperation. 'She wants them back, they're Chanel. I said I'll meet her before work.'

'Chanel, eh?' said Matthew, with a smile that Robin found patronising. She knew that he thought he had discovered a weakness in Vanessa, but perhaps he liked her better to think that she valued designer labels and wanted to make sure she got them back.

'I'll have to leave at six,' said Robin.

'Six?' he said, annoyed. 'Christ, I'm knackered, I don't want to wake up at—'

'I was going to suggest I sleep in the spare room,' Robin said.

'Oh,' said Matthew, mollified. 'Yeah, OK. Thanks.'

19

I do not do it willingly – but, enfin – when needs must –
                                    Henrik Ibsen, *Rosmersholm*

Robin left the house at a quarter to six the next morning. The sky was a faint blush pink and the morning already warm, justifying her lack of jacket. Her eyes flickered towards the single carved swan as she passed their local pub, but she forced her thoughts back onto the day ahead and not the man she had left behind.

On arrival in Izzy's corridor an hour later, Robin saw that Geraint's office door was already open. A swift peek inside showed her an empty room, but Aamir's jacket hanging on the back of his chair.

Running to Izzy's office, Robin unlocked it, dashed to her desk, pulled one of the listening devices from the box of Tampax, scooped up a pile of out-of-date agendas as an alibi, then ran back out into the corridor.

As she approached Geraint's office, she slid off the gold bangle that she had worn for this purpose, and threw it lightly so that it rolled into Geraint's office.

'Oh damn,' she said out loud.

Nobody responded from inside the office. Robin knocked on the open door, said 'hello?' and put her head inside. The room was still empty.

Robin dashed across the room to the double power point just above the skirting board beside Geraint's desk. Kneeling, she took the listening device out of her bag, unplugged the fan on his desk, pressed the device into place over the dual socket, reinserted the fan's plug, checked that it worked, then, panting as though she had just sprinted a hundred yards, looked around for her bangle.

'What are you doing?'

Aamir was standing in the doorway in his shirtsleeves, a fresh tea in his hand.

'I did knock,' Robin said, sure that she was bright pink. 'I dropped my bangle and it rolled – oh, there it is.'

It was lying just beneath Aamir's computer chair. Robin scrambled to pick it up.

'It's my mother's,' she lied. 'I wouldn't be popular if that went missing.'

She slid the bangle back over her wrist, picked up the papers she had left on Geraint's desk, smiled as casually as she could manage, then walked out of the office past Aamir, whose eyes, she saw out of the corner of her own, were narrowed in suspicion.

Jubilant, Robin re-entered Izzy's office. At least she would have some good news for Strike when they met in the pub that evening. Barclay was no longer the only one doing good work. So absorbed was she in her thoughts that Robin didn't realise that there was somebody else in the room until a man said, right behind her: 'Who are you?'

The present dissolved. Both of her attackers had lunged at her from behind. With a scream, Robin spun around, ready to fight for her life: the papers flew into the air and her handbag slipped off her shoulder, fell to the floor and burst open, scattering its contents everywhere.

'Sorry!' said the man. 'Christ, I'm sorry!'

But Robin was finding it hard to draw breath. There was a thundering in her ears and sweat had broken out all over her body. She bent down to scoop everything back up, trembling so much that she kept dropping things.

Not now. Not now.

He was talking to her, but she couldn't understand a word. The world was fragmenting again, full of terror and danger, and he was a blur as he handed her eyeliner and a bottle of drops to moisten her contact lenses.

'Oh,' Robin gasped at random. 'Great. Excuse me. Bathroom.'

She stumbled to the door. Two people were coming towards her down the corridor, their voices fuzzy and indistinct as they greeted her. Hardly knowing what she responded, she half-ran past them towards the Ladies.

A woman from the Secretary for Health's office greeted her from the sink where she was applying lipstick. Robin blundered blindly past, locking the cubicle door with fumbling fingers.

It was no use trying to suppress the panic: that only made it fight back, trying to bend her to its will. She must ride it out, as though the fear was a bolting horse, easing it onto a more manageable course. So she stood motionless, palms pressed against the partition walls, speaking to herself inside her head as though she were an animal handler, and her body, in its irrational terror, a frantic prey creature.

You're safe, you're safe, you're safe . . .

Slowly, the panic began to ebb, though her heart was still leaping erratically. At last, Robin removed her numb hands from the walls of the cubicle and opened her eyes, blinking in the harsh lights. The bathroom was quiet.

Robin peered out of the cubicle. The woman had left. There was nobody there except her own pale reflection in the mirror. After splashing cold water on her face and patting it dry with paper towels, she readjusted her clear-lensed glasses and left the bathroom.

An argument seemed to be in progress in the office she had just left. Taking a deep breath, she re-entered the room.

Jasper Chiswell turned to glare at her, his wiry mass of grey hair sticking out around his pink face. Izzy was standing behind her desk. The stranger was still there. In her shaken state, Robin would have preferred not to be the focus of three pairs of curious eyes.

'What just happened?' Chiswell demanded of Robin.

'Nothing,' said Robin, feeling cold sweat erupting again under her dress.

'You ran out of the room. Did he—' Chiswell pointed at the dark man, '—do something to you? Make a pass?'

'Wha—? No! I didn't realise he was in here, that's all – he spoke and I jumped. And,' she could feel herself blushing harder than ever, 'then I needed the loo.'

Chiswell rounded on the dark man.

'So why are you here so early, eh?'

Now, at last, Robin realised that this was Raphael. She had known from the pictures she had found online that this half-Italian was an exotic in a family that was otherwise uniformly blond and very English in appearance, but had been wholly unprepared for how handsome he was in the flesh. His charcoal-grey suit, white shirt and a conventional dark blue spotted tie were worn with an air that none of the other men along the corridor could muster. So dark-skinned as to appear swarthy, he had high cheekbones, almost black eyes, dark hair worn long and floppy, and a wide mouth that, unlike his father's, had a full upper lip that added vulnerability to his face.

'I thought you liked punctuality, Dad,' he said, raising his arms and letting them fall in a slightly hopeless gesture.

His father turned to Izzy. 'Give him something to do.'

Chiswell marched out. Mortified, Robin headed for her desk. Nobody spoke until Chiswell's footsteps had died away, then Izzy spoke.

'He's under all kinds of stress just now, Raff, babes. It isn't you. He's honestly going berserk about the smallest things.'

'I'm so sorry,' Robin forced herself to say to Raphael. 'I completely overreacted.'

'No problem,' he replied, in the kind of accent that is routinely described as 'public school'. 'For the record, I'm not, in fact, a sex offender.'

Robin laughed nervously.

'You're the goddaughter I didn't know about? Nobody tells me anything. Venetia, yeah? I'm Raff.'

'Um – yes – hi.'

They shook hands and Robin retook her seat, busying herself with some pointless paper shuffling. She could feel her colour fluctuating.

'It's just crazy at the moment,' Izzy said, and Robin knew that she was trying, for not entirely unselfish reasons, to persuade Raphael that their father wasn't as bad to work with as he might appear. 'We're understaffed, we've got the Olympics coming up, TTS is constantly going off on Papa—'

'*What's* going off on him?' asked Raphael, dropping down into the sagging armchair, loosening his tie and crossing his long legs.

'TTS,' Izzy repeated. 'Lean over and put on the kettle while you're there, Raff, I'm dying for a coffee. TTS. It stands for Tinky the Second. It's what Fizz and I call Kinvara.'

The many nicknames of the Chiswell family had been explained to Robin during her office interludes with Izzy. Izzy's older sister Sophia was 'Fizzy', while Sophia's three children rejoiced in the pet names of 'Pringle', 'Flopsy' and 'Pong'.

'Why "Tinky the Second"?' asked Raff, unscrewing a jar of instant coffee with long fingers. Robin was still very aware of all his movements, though keeping her eyes on her supposed work. 'What was Tinky the First?'

'Oh, come on, Raff, you must have heard about Tinky,' said Izzy. 'That ghastly Australian nurse Grampy married last time round, when he was getting senile. He blew most of the money on her. He was the second silly old codger she'd married. Grampy bought her a dud racehorse and loads of horrible jewellery. Papa nearly had to go to court to get her out of the house when Grampy died. She dropped dead of breast cancer before it got really expensive, thank God.'

Startled by this sudden callousness, Robin looked up.

'How d'you take it, Venetia?' Raphael asked as he spooned coffee into mugs.

'White, no sugar, please,' said Robin. She thought it best if she maintained a low profile for a while, after her recent incursion into Winn's office.

'TTS married Papa for his dosh,' Izzy ploughed on, '*and* she's horse-mad like Tinky. You know she's got nine now? Nine!'

'Nine what?' said Raphael.

'Horses, Raff!' said Izzy impatiently. 'Bloody uncontrollable, bad-mannered, hot-blooded horses that she mollycoddles and keeps as child substitutes and spends all the money on! *God*, I wish Papa would leave her,' said Izzy. 'Pass the biscuit tin, babes.'

He did so. Robin, who could feel him looking at her, maintained the pretence of absorption in her work.

The telephone rang.

'Jasper Chiswell's office,' said Izzy, trying to prise off the lid of the biscuit tin one-handed, the receiver under her chin. 'Oh,' she said, suddenly cool. 'Hello, Kinvara. You've just missed Papa . . .'

Grinning at his half-sister's expression, Raphael took the biscuits from her, opened them and offered the tin to Robin, who shook her head. A torrent of indistinguishable words was pouring from Izzy's earpiece.

'No . . . no, he's gone . . . he only came over to say hello to Raff . . .'

The voice at the end of the phone seemed to become more strident.

'Back at DCMS, he's got a meeting at ten,' said Izzy. 'I can't – well, because he's very busy, you know, the Olymp – yes . . . goodbye.'

Izzy slammed the receiver down and struggled out of her jacket.

'She should take another *rest cure*. The last one doesn't seem to have done her much good.'

'Izzy doesn't believe in mental illness,' Raphael told Robin.

He was contemplating her, still slightly curious and, she guessed, trying to draw her out.

'Of course I believe in mental illness, Raff!' said Izzy, apparently stung. 'Of course I do! I was sorry for her when it happened – I *was*, Raff – Kinvara had a stillbirth two years ago,' Izzy explained, 'and *of course* that's sad, *of course* it is, and it was quite understandable that she was a bit, you know, afterwards, but – no, I'm sorry,' she said crossly, addressing Raphael, 'but she uses it. She *does*, Raff. She thinks it entitles her to everything she wants and – well, she'd have been a dreadful mother, anyway,' said Izzy defiantly. 'She can't stand not being the centre of attention. When she's not getting enough she starts her little girl act – *don't leave me alone, Jasper, I get scared when you're not here at night*. Telling stupid lies . . . funny phone calls to the house, men hiding in the flowerbeds, fiddling with the horses.'

'*What?*' said Raphael, half-laughing, but Izzy cut him short.

'Oh, Christ, look, Papa's left his briefing papers.'

She hurried out from behind her desk, snatched a leather folder off the top of the radiator and called over her shoulder, 'Raff, you can listen to the phone messages and transcribe them for me while I'm gone, OK?'

The heavy wooden door thudded shut behind her, leaving Robin and Raphael alone. If she had been hyperaware of Raphael before Izzy had gone, now he seemed to Robin to fill the entire room, his olive dark eyes on her.

He took Ecstasy and ran his car into a mother of a four-year-old. He barely served a third of his sentence and now his father's put him on the taxpayer's payroll.

'How do I do this, then?' asked Raphael, moving behind Izzy's desk.

'Just press play, I expect,' Robin muttered, sipping her coffee and pretending to make notes on a pad.

Canned messages began to issue from the answering machine, drowning out the faint hum of conversation from the terrace beyond the net-curtained window.

A man named Rupert asked Izzy to call him back about 'the AGM'.

A constituent called Mrs Ricketts spoke for two solid minutes about traffic along the Banbury road.

An irate woman said crossly that she ought to have expected an answering machine and that MPs ought to be answering to the public personally, then spoke until cut off by the machine about her neighbours' failure to lop overhanging branches from a tree, in spite of repeated requests from the council.

Then a man's growl, almost theatrically menacing, filled the quiet office:

'They say they piss themselves as they die, Chiswell, is that true? Forty grand, or I'll find out how much the papers will pay.'

20

*We two have worked our way forward in complete
companionship.*

Henrik Ibsen, *Rosmersholm*

Strike had selected the Two Chairmen for his Wednesday evening
catch-up with Robin because of its proximity to the Palace of
Westminster. The pub was tucked away on a junction of centuries-
old back streets – Old Queen Street, Cockpit Steps – amid a motley
collection of quaint, sedate buildings that stood at oblique angles to
each other. Only as he limped across the road and saw the hanging
metal sign over the front door did Strike realise that the 'two chairmen' for whom the pub was named were not, as he had assumed,
joint managers of a board, but lowly servants carrying the heavy
load of a sedan chair. Tired and sore as Strike was, the image seemed
appropriate, although the occupant of the sedan chair in the pub sign
was a refined lady in white, not a large, curmudgeonly minister with
wiry hair and a short temper.

The bar was crowded with after-work drinkers and Strike had a
sudden apprehension that he might not get a seat inside, an unwelcome prospect, because leg, back and neck were tight and sore after
yesterday's long drive and the hours he had spent in Harley Street
today, watching Dodgy Doc.

Strike had just bought a pint of London Pride when the table by
the window became free. With a turn of speed born of necessity, he
nabbed the high bench with its back to the street before the nearest
group of suited men and women could annexe it. There was no

question of anybody challenging his right to sole occupancy of a table made for four. Strike was large enough, and surly enough in appearance to make even this group of civil servants doubt their ability to negotiate a compromise.

The wooden-floored bar was what Strike mentally categorised as 'upmarket utilitarian'. A faded mural on the back wall depicted bewigged eighteenth-century men gossiping together, but otherwise all was pared-back wood and monochrome prints. He peered out of the window to see whether Robin was within sight, but as there was no sign of her he drank his beer, read the day's news on his phone and tried to ignore the menu lying on the table in front of him, which was taunting him with a picture of battered fish.

Robin, who had been due to arrive at six, was still absent at half past. Unable to resist the picture on the menu any longer, Strike ordered himself cod and chips and a second pint, and read a long article in *The Times* about the upcoming Olympics opening ceremony, which was really a long list of the ways in which the journalist feared it might misrepresent and humiliate the nation.

By a quarter to seven, Strike was starting to worry about Robin. He had just decided to call her when she came hurrying in through the door, flushed, wearing glasses that Strike knew she did not need and with an expression that he recognised as the barely contained excitement of one who has something worthwhile to impart.

'Hazel eyes,' he noted, as she sat down opposite him. 'Good one. Changes your whole look. What've you got?'

'How do you know I've—? Well, loads, actually,' she said, deciding it was not worthwhile toying with him. 'I nearly called you earlier but there have been people around all day, and I had a close shave this morning placing the listening device.'

'You did it? Bloody well done!'

'Thanks. I really want a drink, hang on.'

She came back with a glass of red wine and launched immediately into an account of the message that Raphael had found on the answering machine that morning.

'I had no chance of getting the caller's number, because there were four messages after it. The phone system's antiquated.'

Frowning, Strike asked: 'How did the caller pronounce "Chiswell", can you remember?'

'They said it right. *Chizzle.*'

'Fits with Jimmy,' said Strike. 'What happened after the call?'

'Raff told Izzy about it when she got back to the office,' said Robin, and Strike thought he detected a touch of self-consciousness as she said the name 'Raff'. 'He didn't understand what he was passing on, obviously. Izzy called her dad straight away and he went berserk. We could hear him shouting on the end of the line, though not much of what he was actually saying.'

Strike stroked his chin, thinking.

'What did the anonymous caller sound like?'

'London accent,' Robin said. 'Threatening.'

'"They piss themselves as they die",' repeated Strike in an undertone.

There was something that Robin wanted to say, but a brutal personal memory made it hard for her to articulate.

'Strangling victims—'

'Yeah,' said Strike, cutting her off. 'I know.'

Both of them drank.

'Well, assuming the call was Jimmy,' Robin went on, 'he's phoned the department twice today.'

She opened her handbag and showed Strike the listening device hidden inside it.

'You retrieved it?' he asked, staggered.

'And replaced it with another one,' said Robin, unable to suppress a triumphant smile. 'That's why I'm late. I took a chance. Aamir, who works with Winn, left and Geraint came into our office while I was packing up, to chat me up.'

'He did, did he?' asked Strike, amused.

'I'm glad you find it funny,' said Robin coolly. 'He isn't a nice man.'

'Sorry,' said Strike. 'In what way is he not a nice man?'

'Just take it from me,' said Robin. 'I've met plenty of them in offices. He's a pervert, but with creepy add-ons. He was just telling me,' she said, and her indignation showed in the rising tide of pink in her face, 'that I remind him of his dead daughter. Then he touched my hair.'

'Touched your hair?' repeated Strike, unamused.

'Picked a bit of it off my shoulder and ran it through his fingers,' said Robin. 'Then I think he saw what I thought of him and tried to pass it off as fatherly. Anyway, I said I needed the loo but asked him to stay put so we could keep chatting about charities. I nipped down the corridor and swapped the devices.'

'That was bloody good going, Robin.'

'I listened to it on the way here,' said Robin, pulling headphones out of her pocket, 'and—'

Robin handed Strike the headphones.

'—I've cued up the interesting bit.'

Strike obediently inserted the earbuds and Robin switched on the tape in her handbag.

'... at three thirty, Aamir.'

The Welsh male voice was interrupted by the sound of a mobile phone ringing. Feet scuffled near the power point, the ring ceased and Geraint said:

'Oh, hello Jimmy ... half a mo' – Aamir, close that door.'

More scuffling, footsteps.

'Jimmy, yes ... ?'

There followed a long stretch in which Geraint seemed to be attempting to stem the flow of a mounting tirade.

'Whoa – now, wai ... Jimmy, lis ... Jimmy, listen – *listen!* I know you've lost out, Jimmy, I understand how bitter you – *Jimmy, please!* We understand your feelings – that's unfair, Jimmy, neither Della nor I grew up wealth – my father was a coalminer, Jimmy! Now listen, please! *We're close to getting the pictures!*'

There followed a spell in which Strike thought he heard, very faintly, the rise and fall of Jimmy Knight's fluent speech at the end of the telephone.

'I take your point,' said Geraint finally, 'but I urge you to do nothing rash, Jimmy. He isn't going to give you – Jimmy, listen! He isn't going to give you your money, he's made that perfectly clear. It's the newspapers now or nothing, so ... proof, Jimmy! Proof!'

Another, shorter period of unintelligible gabbling followed.

'I've just told you, haven't I? Yes . . . no, but the Foreign Office . . . well, hardly . . . no, Aamir has a contact . . . yes . . . yes . . . all right then . . . I will, Jimmy. Good – yes, all right. Yes. Goodbye.'

The clunk of a mobile being set down was followed by Geraint's voice.

'Stupid prick,' he said.

There were more footsteps. Strike glanced at Robin, who by a rolling gesture of the hand indicated that he should keep listening. After perhaps thirty seconds, Aamir spoke, diffident and strained.

'Geraint, Christopher didn't promise anything about the pictures.'

Even on the tinny little tape, with the nearby shufflings of paper at Geraint's desk, the silence sounded charged.

'Geraint, did you h—?'

'Yes, I heard!' snapped Winn. 'Good God, boy, a first from the LSE and you can't think of a way to persuade that bastard to give you pictures? I'm not asking you to take them out of the department, just to get copies. That shouldn't be beyond the wit of man.'

'I don't want more trouble,' muttered Aamir.

'Well, I should have thought,' said Geraint, 'after everything Della in particular has done for you . . .'

'And I'm grateful,' said Aamir swiftly. 'You know I am . . . all right, I'll – I'll try.'

For the next minute there were no sounds but scuffing footsteps and papers, followed by a mechanical click. The device automatically switched off after a minute of no talking, activated again when somebody spoke. The next voice was that of a different man asking whether Della would be attending 'the sub-committee' this afternoon.

Strike removed the earbuds.

'Did you catch it all?' Robin asked.

'I think so,' said Strike.

She leaned back, watching Strike expectantly.

'The Foreign Office?' he repeated quietly. 'What the hell can he have done that means the *Foreign Office* has got pictures?'

'I thought we weren't supposed to be interested in what he did?' said Robin, eyebrows raised.

'I never said I wasn't interested. Just that I'm not being paid to find out.'

Strike's fish and chips arrived. He thanked the barmaid and proceeded to add a generous amount of ketchup to his plate.

'Izzy was completely matter of fact about whatever it is,' said Robin, thinking back. 'She couldn't possibly have spoken about it the way she did if he'd – you know – murdered anybody.'

She deliberately avoided the word 'strangled'. Three panic attacks in three days were quite sufficient.

'Got to say,' said Strike, now chewing chips, 'that anonymous call makes you – unless,' he said, struck by a thought, 'Jimmy's had the bright idea of trying to drag Chiswell into the Billy business on top of whatever else he's genuinely done. A child-killing doesn't have to be true to make trouble for a government minister who's already got the press on his tail. You know the internet. Plenty of people out there think being a Tory as tantamount to being a child killer. This might be Jimmy's idea of adding pressure.'

Strike stabbed a few chips moodily with his fork.

'I'd be glad to know where Billy is, if we had somebody free to look for him. Barclay hasn't seen any sign of him and says Jimmy hasn't mentioned having a brother.'

'Billy said he was being held captive,' Robin said tentatively.

'Don't think we can set much store on anything Billy's saying right now, to be honest. I knew a guy in the Shiners who had a psychotic episode on exercises. Thought he had cockroaches living under his skin.'

'In the—?'

'Shiners. Fusiliers. Want a chip?'

'I'd better not,' sighed Robin, though she was hungry. Matthew, whom she had warned by text that she would be late, had told her he would wait for her to get home, so they could eat dinner together. 'Listen, I haven't told you everything.'

'Suki Lewis?' asked Strike, hopefully.

'I haven't been able to work her into the conversation yet. No, it's that Chiswell's wife claims men have been lurking in the flowerbeds and fiddling with her horses.'

'Men?' Strike repeated. 'In the plural?'

'That's what Izzy said – but she also says Kinvara's hysterical and attention-seeking.'

'Getting to be a bit of a theme, that, isn't it? People who're supposed to be too crazy to know what they've seen.'

'D'you think that could have been Jimmy, as well? In the garden?'

Strike thought it over as he chewed.

'I can't see what he's got to gain from lurking in the garden or fiddling with horses, unless he's at the point where he just wants to frighten Chiswell. I'll check with Barclay and see whether Jimmy's got a car or mentioned going to Oxfordshire. Did Kinvara call the police?'

'Raff asked that, when Izzy got back,' said Robin, and once again, Strike thought he detected a trace of self-consciousness as she spoke the man's name. 'Kinvara claims the dogs barked, she saw the shadow of a man in the garden, but he ran away. She says there were footprints in the horses' field next morning and that one of them had been cut with a knife.'

'Did she call a vet?'

'I don't know. It's harder to ask questions with Raff in the office. I don't want to look too nosy, because he doesn't know who I am.'

Strike pushed his plate away from him and felt for his cigarettes.

'Photos,' he mused, returning to the central point. 'Photos at the Foreign Office. What the hell can they show that would incriminate Chiswell? He's never worked at the Foreign Office, has he?'

'No,' said Robin. 'The highest post he's ever held is Minister for Trade. He had to resign from there because of the affair with Raff's mother.'

The wooden clock over the fireplace was telling her it was time to leave. She didn't move.

'You're liking Raff, then?' Strike said suddenly, catching her off guard.

'What?'

Robin was scared that she had blushed.

'What do you mean, I'm "liking" him?'

179

'Just an impression I got,' said Strike. 'You disapproved of him before you met him.'

'D'you want me to be antagonistic towards him, when I'm supposed to be his father's goddaughter?' demanded Robin.

'No, of course not,' said Strike, though Robin had the sense that he was laughing at her, and resented it.

'I'd better get going,' she said, sweeping the headphones off the table and back into her bag. 'I told Matt I'd be home for dinner.'

She got up, bade Strike goodbye and left the pub.

Strike watched her go, dimly sorry that he had commented on her manner when mentioning Raphael Chiswell. After a few minutes' solitary beer consumption, he paid for his food and ambled out onto the pavement, where he lit a cigarette and called the Minister for Culture, who answered on the second ring.

'Wait there,' said Chiswell. Strike could hear a murmuring crowd behind him. 'Crowded room.'

The clunk of a door closing and the noise of the crowd was muted.

''M at a dinner,' said Chiswell. 'Anything for me?'

'It isn't good news, I'm afraid,' said Strike, walking away from the pub, up Queen Anne Street, between white painted buildings that gleamed in the dusk. 'My partner succeeded in planting the listening device in Mr Winn's office this morning. We've got a recording of him talking to Jimmy Knight. Winn's assistant – Aamir, is it? – is trying to get copies of those photographs you told me about. At the Foreign Office.'

The ensuring silence lasted so long that Strike wondered whether they had been cut off.

'Minist—?'

'I'm here!' snarled Chiswell. 'That boy Mallik, is it? Dirty little bastard. *Dirty little bastard.* He's already lost one job – let him try, that's all. Let him try! Does he think I won't – I know things about Aamir Mallik,' he said. 'Oh yes.'

Strike waited, in some surprise, for elucidation of these remarks, but none were forthcoming. Chiswell merely breathed heavily into the telephone. Soft, muffled thuds told Strike that Chiswell was pacing up and down on carpet.

'Is that all you had to say to me?' demanded the MP at last.

'There was one other thing,' said Strike. 'My partner says your wife's seen a man or men trespassing on your property at night.'

'Oh,' said Chiswell, 'yerse.' He did not sound particularly concerned. 'My wife keeps horses and she takes their security very seriously.'

'You don't think this has any connection with—?'

'Not in the slightest, not in the slightest. Kinvara's sometimes – well, to be candid,' said Chiswell, 'she can be bloody hysterical. Keeps a bunch of horses, always fretting they're going to be stolen. I don't want you wasting time chasing shadows through the undergrowth in Oxfordshire. My problems are in London. Is that everything?'

Strike said that it was and, after a curt farewell, Chiswell hung up, leaving Strike to limp towards St James's Park station.

Settled in a corner seat of the Tube ten minutes later, Strike folded his arms, stretched out his legs and stared unseeingly at the window opposite.

The nature of this investigation was highly unusual. He had never before had a blackmail case where the client was so unforthcoming about his offence – but then, Strike reasoned with himself, he had never had a government minister as a client before. Equally, it was not every day that a possibly psychotic young man burst into Strike's office and insisted that he had witnessed a child murder, though Strike had certainly received his fair share of unusual and unbalanced communications since hitting the newspapers: what he had once called, over Robin's occasional protests, 'the nutter drawer', now filled half a filing cabinet.

It was the precise relationship between the strangled child and Chiswell's case of blackmail that was preoccupying Strike, even though, on the face of it, the connection was obvious: it lay in the fact of Jimmy and Billy's brotherhood. Now somebody (and Strike thought it overwhelmingly likely to be Jimmy, judging from Robin's account of the call) seemed to have decided to tie Billy's story to Chiswell, even though the blackmailable offence that had brought Chiswell to Strike could not possibly have been infanticide, or Geraint Winn would have gone to the police. Like a tongue probing a pair of ulcers, Strike's thoughts kept returning fruitlessly to the Knight brothers: Jimmy, charismatic, articulate, thuggishly good-looking, a chancer and a hothead, and Billy, haunted, filthy, unquestionably ill, bedevilled by a memory no less dreadful for the fact that it might be false.

They piss themselves as they die.

Who did? Again, Strike seemed to hear Billy Knight.

They buried her in a pink blanket, down in the dell by my dad's house. But afterwards they said it was a boy . . .

He had just been specifically instructed by his client to restrict his investigations to London, not Oxfordshire.

As he checked the name of the station at which they had just arrived, Strike remembered Robin's self-consciousness when talking about Raphael Chiswell. Yawning, he took out his mobile again and succeeded in Googling the youngest of his client's offspring, of whom there were many pictures going up the courtroom steps to his trial for manslaughter.

As he scrolled through multiple pictures of Raphael, Strike felt a rising antipathy towards the handsome young man in his dark suit. Setting aside the fact that Chiswell's son resembled an Italian model more than anything British, the images caused a latent resentment, rooted in class and personal injuries, to glow a little redder inside Strike's chest. Raphael was of the same type as Jago Ross, the man whom Charlotte had married after splitting with Strike: upper class, expensively clothed and educated, their peccadillos treated more leniently for being able to afford the best lawyers, for resembling the sons of the judges deciding their fates.

The train set off again and Strike, losing his connection, stuffed his phone back into his pocket, folded his arms and resumed his blank stare at the dark window, trying to deny an uncomfortable idea headspace, but it nosed up against him like a dog demanding food, impossible to ignore.

He now realised that he had never imagined Robin being interested in any man other than Matthew, except, of course, for that moment when he himself had held her on the stairs at her wedding, when, briefly . . .

Angry with himself, he kicked the unhelpful thought aside, and forced his wandering mind back onto the curious case of a government minister, slashed horses and a body buried in a pink blanket, down in a dell.

21

... certain games are going on behind your back in this house.
Henrik Ibsen, *Rosmersholm*

'Why are you so busy and I've got bugger all to do?' Raphael asked
Robin, late on Friday morning.

She had just returned from tailing Geraint to Portcullis House.
Observing him from a distance, she had seen how the polite smiles of
the many young women he greeted turned to expressions of dislike as
he passed. Geraint had disappeared into a meeting room on the first
floor, so Robin had returned to Izzy's office. Approaching Geraint's
room she had hoped she might be able to slip inside and retrieve the
second listening device, but through the open door she saw Aamir
working at his computer.

'Raff, I'll give you something to do in a moment, babes,' muttered a fraught Izzy, who was hammering at her keyboard. 'I've got
to finish this, it's for the local party chairwoman. Papa's coming to
sign it in five minutes.'

She threw a harried glance at her brother, who was sprawled in
the armchair, his long legs spread out in front of him, shirtsleeves
rolled up, tie loosened, playing with the paper visitor's pass that hung
around his neck.

'Why don't you go and get yourself a coffee on the terrace?' Izzy
suggested. Robin knew she wanted him out the way when Chiswell
turned up.

'Want to come for a coffee, Venetia?' asked Raphael.

'Can't,' said Robin. 'Busy.'

The fan on Izzy's desk swept Robin's way and she enjoyed a few seconds of cool breeze. The net-curtained window gave but a misty impression of the glorious June day. Truncated parliamentarians appeared as glowing wraiths on the terrace beyond the glass. It was stuffy inside the cluttered office. Robin was wearing a cotton dress, her hair in a ponytail, but still she occasionally blotted her upper lip with the back of her hand as she pretended to be working.

Having Raphael in the office was, as she had told Strike, a disadvantage. There had been no need to come up with excuses for lurking in the corridor when she had been alone with Izzy. What was more, Raphael watched her a lot, in an entirely different way to Geraint's lewd up-and-down looks. She didn't approve of Raphael, but every now and then she found herself coming perilously close to feeling sorry for him. He seemed nervy around his father, and then – well, *anybody* would think him handsome. That was the main reason she avoided looking at him: it was best not to, if you wanted to preserve any objectivity.

He kept trying to foster a closer relationship with her, which she was attempting to discourage. Only the previous day he had interrupted her as she hovered outside Geraint and Aamir's door, listening with all her might to a conversation that Aamir was having on the phone about an 'inquiry'. From the scant details that Robin had so far heard, she was convinced that the Level Playing Field was under discussion.

'But this isn't a *statutory* inquiry?' Aamir was asking, sounding worried. 'It isn't official? I thought this was just a routine ... but Mr Winn understood that his letter to the fundraising regulator had answered all their concerns.'

Robin could not pass up the opportunity to listen, but knew her situation to be perilous. What she had not expected was to be surprised by Raphael rather than Winn.

'What are you doing, skulking there?' he had asked, laughing.

Robin walked hastily away, but she heard Aamir's door slam behind her and suspected that he, at least, would make sure that it was closed in future.

'Are you always this jumpy, or is it just me?' Raphael had asked, hurrying after her. 'Come for a coffee, come on, I'm so bloody bored.'

Robin had declined brusquely, but even as she pretended to be busy again, she had to admit that part of her – a tiny part – was flattered by his attentions.

There was a knock on the door and, to Robin's surprise, Aamir Mallik entered the room, holding a list of names. Nervous but determined, he addressed Izzy.

'Yeah, uh, hi. Geraint would like to add the Level Playing Field trustees to the Paralympian reception on the twelfth of July,' he said.

'I've got nothing to do with that reception,' snapped Izzy. 'DCMS are organising it, not me. *Why*,' she erupted, wiping her sweaty fringe off her forehead, 'does everyone come to *me*?'

'Geraint needs them to come,' said Aamir. The list of names quivered in his hand.

Robin wondered whether she dared creep into Aamir's empty office right now and swap the listening devices. She got to her feet quietly, trying not to draw attention to herself.

'Why doesn't he ask Della?' asked Izzy.

'Della's busy. It's only eight people,' said Aamir. 'He really needs—'

'"*Hear the word of Lachesis, the daughter of Necessity!*"'

The Minister for Culture's booming tones preceded him into the room. Chiswell stood in the doorway, wearing a crumpled suit and blocking Robin's exit. She sat down quietly again. Aamir, or so it seemed to Robin, braced himself.

'Know who Lachesis was, Mr Mallik?' asked Chiswell.

'Can't say I do,' said Aamir.

'No? Didn't study the Greeks in your Harringay Comprehensive? You seem to have time on your hands, Raff. Teach Mr Mallik about Lachesis.'

'I don't know, either,' said Raphael, peering up at his father through his thick, dark lashes.

'Playing stupid, eh? Lachesis,' said Chiswell, 'was one of the Fates. She measured out each man's allotted lifespan. Knew when everyone's number would be up. Not a fan of Plato, Mr Mallik? Catullus more up your street, I expect. He produced some fine poetry about men of your habits. *Pedicabo ego vos et irrumabo, Aurelia pathice et cinaede Furi*, eh? Poem 16, look it up, you'll enjoy it.'

Raphael and Izzy were both staring at their father. Aamir stood for a few seconds as though he had forgotten what he had come for, then stalked out of the room.

'A little Classics education for everyone,' said Chiswell, turning to watch him go with what appeared to be malicious satisfaction. 'We are never too old to learn, eh, Raff?'

Robin's mobile vibrated on her desk. Strike had texted. They had agreed not to contact each other during working hours unless it was urgent. She slid the phone into her bag.

'Where's my signing pile?' Chiswell asked Izzy. 'Have you finished that letter for Brenda Bloody Bailey?'

'Printing it now,' said Izzy.

While Chiswell scribbled his signature on a stack of letters, breathing like a bulldog in the otherwise quiet room, Robin muttered something about needing to get going, and hurried out into the corridor.

Wanting to read Strike's text without fear of interruption, she followed a wooden sign to the crypt, hastened down the narrow stone staircase indicated and found, at the bottom, a deserted chapel.

The crypt was decorated like a medieval jewel casket, every inch of gold wall embellished with motifs and symbols, heraldic and religious. There were jewel-bright saints' pictures above the altar and the sky-blue organ pipes were wrapped in gold ribbon and scarlet *fleurs-de-lys*. Robin hurried into a red velvet pew and opened Strike's text.

Need a favour. Barclay's done a 10-day stretch on Jimmy Knight, but he's just found out his wife's got to work over the weekend & he can't get anyone else to look after the baby. Andy leaves for a week in Alicante with the family tonight. I can't tail Jimmy, he knows me. CORE are joining an anti-missile march tomorrow. Starts at 2, in Bow. Can you do it?

Robin contemplated the message for several seconds, then let out a groan that echoed around the crypt.

It was the first time in over a year that Strike had asked her to work extra hours at such short notice, but this was her anniversary weekend. The pricey hotel was booked, the bags packed and ready in the car. She was supposed to be meeting Matthew after work in a couple of hours. They were to drive straight to Le Manoir aux Quat'Saisons. Matthew would be furious if she said she couldn't go.

In the gilded hush of the crypt, the words Strike had said to her when he had agreed to give her detective training came back to her.

I need someone who can work long hours, weekends ... you've got a lot of aptitude for the job, but you're getting married to someone who hates you doing it ...

And she had told him that it didn't matter what Matthew thought, that it was up to her what she did.

Where did her allegiance lie now? She had said that she would stay in the marriage, promised to give it a chance. Strike had had many hours of unpaid overtime out of her. He could not claim that she was workshy.

Slowly, deleting words, replacing them, overthinking every syllable, she typed out a response.

I'm really sorry, but it's my anniversary weekend. We've got a hotel booked, leaving this evening.

She wanted to write more, but what was there to say? 'My marriage isn't going well, so it's important I celebrate it'? 'I'd much rather disguise myself as a protestor and stalk Jimmy Knight'? She pressed 'send'.

Sitting waiting for his response, feeling as though she were about to get the results of medical tests, Robin's eyes followed the course of twisting vines that covered the ceiling. Strange faces peered down at her out of the moulding, like the wild Green Man of myth. Heraldic and pagan imagery mingled with angels and crosses. It was more than a place of God, this chapel. It harked back to an age of superstition, magic and feudal power.

The minutes slid by and still Strike hadn't answered. Robin got up and walked around the chapel. At the very back she found a cupboard. Opening it, she saw a plaque to suffragette Emily Davison. Apparently, she had slept there overnight so that she could give her place of residence as the House of Commons on the census of 1911, seven years before women were given the vote. Emily Davison, she could not help but feel, would not have approved of Robin's choice to place a failing marriage above freedom to work.

Robin's mobile buzzed again. She looked down, afraid of what she was going to read. Strike had answered with two letters:

OK

A lead weight seemed to slide from her chest to her stomach. Strike, as she was well aware, was still living in the glorified bedsit over the office and working through weekends. The only unmarried person at the agency, the boundary between his professional and private lives was, if not precisely non-existent, then flexible and porous, whereas hers, Barclay's and Hutchins' were not. And the worst of it was that Robin could think of no way of telling Strike that she was sorry, that she understood, that she wished things were different, without reminding both of them of that hug on the stairs at her wedding, now so long unmentioned that she wondered whether he even remembered it.

Feeling utterly miserable, she retraced her steps out of the crypt, still holding the papers she had been pretending to deliver.

Raphael was alone in the office when she returned, sitting at Izzy's PC and typing at a third of her speed.

'Izzy's gone with Dad to do something so tedious it just bounced off my brain,' he said. 'They'll be back in a bit.'

Robin forced a smile, returned to her desk, her mind on Strike.

'Bit weird, that poem, wasn't it?' Raphael asked.

'What? Oh – oh, that Latin thing? Yes,' said Robin. 'It was, a bit.'

'It was like he'd memorised it to use on Mallik. Nobody's got that at their fingertips.'

Reflecting that Strike seemed to know strange bits of Latin off by heart, too, Robin said, 'No, you wouldn't think so.'

'Has he got it in for that Mallik, or something?'

'I really don't know,' lied Robin.

Running out of ways to occupy her time at the desk, she shuffled papers again.

'How long are you staying, Venetia?'

'I'm not sure. Until Parliament goes into recess, probably.'

'You seriously want to work here? Permanently?'

'Yes,' she said. 'I think it's interesting.'

'What were you doing before this?'

'PR,' said Robin. 'It was quite fun, but I fancied a change.'

'Hoping to bag an MP?' he said, with a faint smile.

'I can't say I've seen anyone round here I'd like to marry,' said Robin.

'Hurtful,' said Raphael, with a mock sigh.

Afraid that she had blushed, Robin tried to cover up by bending down to open a drawer and taking a few objects out at random.

'So, is Venetia Hall seeing anyone?' he persisted, as she straightened up.

'Yes,' she said. 'His name's Tim. We've been together a year now.'

'Yeah? What does Tim do?'

'He works at Christie's,' said Robin.

She had got the idea from the men she had seen with Sarah Shadlock in the Red Lion: immaculate, suited public-school types of the kind she imagined Chiswell's goddaughter would know.

'What about you?' she asked. 'Izzy said something—'

'At the gallery?' said Raphael, cutting her off. 'That was nothing. She was too young for me. Her parents have sent her to Florence now, anyway.'

He had swung his chair around to face her, his expression grave and searching, contemplating her as though he wanted to know something that common conversation would not yield. Robin broke their mutual gaze. Holding a look that intense was not compatible with being the contented girlfriend of the imaginary Tim.

'D'you believe in redemption?'

The question caught Robin totally by surprise. It had a kind of gravity and beauty, like the gleaming jewel of the chapel at the foot of a winding stair.

'I . . . yes, I do,' she said.

He had picked up a pencil from Izzy's desk. His long fingers turned it over and over as he watched her intently. He seemed to be sizing her up.

'You know what I did? In the car?'

'Yes,' she answered.

The silence that unspooled between them seemed to Robin to be peopled with flashing lights and shadowy figures. She could imagine Raphael bloody at the steering wheel, and the broken figure of the young mother on the road, and the police cars and the incident tape and the gawpers in passing cars. He was watching her intently, hoping, she thought, for some kind of benison, as though her forgiveness mattered. And sometimes, she knew, the kindness of a stranger, or even a casual acquaintance, could be transformative, something to cling to while those closest to you dragged you under in their efforts to help. She thought of the elderly steward in the Members' Lobby, uncomprehending but immensely consoling, his hoarse, kindly words a thread to hold on to, which would lead her back to sanity.

The door opened again. Both Robin and Raphael jumped as a curvy redhead entered the room, a visitor's pass hanging around her neck on a lanyard. Robin recognised her at once from online photographs as Jasper Chiswell's wife, Kinvara.

'Hello,' said Robin, because Kinvara was merely staring blankly at Raphael, who had swung hastily back to his computer and began typing again.

'You must be Venetia,' said Kinvara, switching her clear golden gaze onto Robin. She had a high-pitched, girlish voice. Her eyes were catlike in a slightly puffy face. 'Aren't you pretty? Nobody told me you were so pretty.'

Robin had no idea how to respond to this. Kinvara dropped down into the sagging chair where Raff usually sat, took off the designer sunglasses holding her long red hair off her face and shook it loose. Her bare arms and legs were heavily freckled. The top buttons of her sleeveless green shirt-dress were straining across her heavy bust.

'*Whose* daughter are you?' asked Kinvara with a trace of petulance. 'Jasper didn't tell me. He doesn't tell me anything he doesn't *have* to tell me, actually. I'm used to it. He just said you're a goddaughter.'

Nobody had warned Robin that Kinvara did not know who she really was. Perhaps Izzy and Chiswell had not expected them to come face to face.

'I'm Jonathan Hall's daughter,' said Robin nervously. She had come up with a rudimentary background for Venetia-the-goddaughter, but had never expected to have to elaborate for the benefit of Chiswell's own wife, who presumably knew all Chiswell's friends and acquaintances.

'Who's he?' asked Kinvara. 'I should probably know, Jasper'll be cross I haven't paid attention—'

'He's in land management up in—'

'Oh, was it the Northumberland property?' interrupted Kinvara, whose interest had not seemed particularly profound. 'That was before my time.'

Thank God, thought Robin.

Kinvara crossed her legs and folded her arms across her large chest. Her foot bounced up and down. She shot Raphael a hard, almost spiteful look.

'Aren't you going to say hello, Raphael?'

'Hello,' he said.

'Jasper told me to meet him here, but if you'd rather I waited in the corridor I can,' Kinvara said in her high, tight voice.

'Of course not,' muttered Raphael, frowning determinedly at his monitor.

'Well, I wouldn't want to interrupt anything,' said Kinvara, turning from Raphael to Robin. The story of the blonde in the art gallery bathroom swam back into Robin's mind. For a second time she pretended to be searching for something in a drawer and it was with relief that she heard the sounds of Chiswell and Izzy coming along the corridor.

' . . . and by ten o'clock, no later, or I won't have time to read the whole bloody thing. And tell Haines *he'll* have to talk to the BBC, I haven't got time for a bunch of idiots talking about inclu – Kinvara.'

Chiswell stopped dead in the office door and said, without any trace of affection, 'I told you to meet me at DCMS, not here.'

'And it's lovely to see you, too, Jasper, after three days apart,' said Kinvara, getting to her feet and smoothing her crumpled dress.

'Hi, Kinvara,' said Izzy.

'I forgot you said DCMS,' Kinvara told Chiswell, ignoring her stepdaughter. 'I've been trying to call you all morning—'

'I told you,' growled Chiswell, 'I'd be in meetings till one, and if it's about those bloody stud fees again—'

'No, it isn't about the stud fees, Jasper, *actually*, and I'd have preferred to tell you in private, but if you want me to say it in front of your children, I will!'

'Oh, for heaven's sake,' Chiswell blustered. 'Come away, then, come on, we'll find a private room—'

'There was a man last night,' said Kinvara, 'who – *don't look at me like that, Isabella!*'

Izzy's expression was indeed conveying naked scepticism. She raised her eyebrows and walked into the room, acting as though Kinvara had become invisible to her.

'I said you can tell me in a private room!' snarled Chiswell, but Kinvara refused to be deflected.

'I saw a man in the woods by the house last night, Jasper!' she said, in a loud, high-pitched voice that Robin knew would be echoing all the way along the narrow corridor. 'I'm *not* imagining things – there was a man with a spade in the woods, I saw him, and he ran when the dogs chased him! You keep telling me not to make a fuss, but I'm alone in that house at night and if *you're* not going to do anything about this, Jasper, *I'm* going to call the police!'

22

*... don't you feel called upon to undertake it, for the sake of the
good cause?*

Henrik Ibsen, *Rosmersholm*

Strike was in a thoroughly bad temper.

Why the fuck, he asked himself, as he limped towards Mile End
Park the following morning, was *he*, the senior partner and founder
of the firm, having to stake out a protest march on a hot Saturday
morning, when he had three employees and a knackered leg?
Because, he answered himself, *he* didn't have a baby who needed
watching, or a wife who'd booked plane tickets or broken her wrist,
or a fucking anniversary weekend planned. *He* wasn't married, so it
was his downtime that had to be sacrificed, *his* weekend that became
just two more working days.

Everything that Robin feared Strike to be thinking about her, he
was, in fact, thinking: of her house on cobbled Albury Street versus
his draughty two rooms in a converted attic, of the rights and status
conferred by the little gold ring on her finger, set against Lorelei's disappointment when he had explained that lunch and possibly dinner
would now be impossible, of Robin's promises of equal responsibility
when he had taken her on as a partner, contrasted with the reality of
her rushing home to her husband.

Yes, Robin had worked many hours of unpaid overtime in her two
years at the agency. Yes, he knew that she had gone way beyond the
call of duty for him. Yes, he was, in theory, fucking grateful to her.
The fact remained that today, while he was limping along the street

towards hours of probably fruitless surveillance, she and her arsehole of a husband were speeding off to a country hotel weekend, a thought that made his sore leg and back no easier to bear.

Unshaven, clad in an old pair of jeans, a frayed, washed-out hoodie and ancient trainers, with a carrier bag swinging from his hand, Strike entered the park. He could see the massing protestors in the distance. The risk of Jimmy recognising him had almost decided Strike to let the march go unwatched, but the most recent text from Robin (which he had, out of sheer bad temper, left unanswered) had changed his mind.

> Kinvara Chiswell came into the office. She claims she saw a man with a spade in the woods near their house last night. From what she said, Chiswell's been telling her not to call the police about these intruders, but she says she's going to do it unless he does something about them. Kinvara didn't know Chiswell's called us in, btw, she thought I really was Venetia Hall. Also, there's a chance the charity commission's investigating the Level Playing Field. I'm trying to get more details.

This communication had served only to aggravate Strike. Nothing short of a concrete piece of evidence against Geraint Winn would have satisfied him right now, with the *Sun* on Chiswell's case and their client so tetchy and stressed.

According to Barclay, Jimmy Knight owned a ten-year-old Suzuki Alto, but it had failed its MOT and was currently off the road. Barclay could not absolutely guarantee that Jimmy wasn't sneaking out under cover of darkness to trespass in Chiswell's gardens and woods seventy miles away, but Strike thought it unlikely.

On the other hand, he thought it just possible that Jimmy might have sent a proxy to intimidate Chiswell's wife. He probably still had friends or acquaintances in the area where he grew up. An even more disturbing idea was that Billy had escaped from the prison, real or imaginary, in which he had told Strike he was being held, and decided to dig for proof that the child lay in a pink blanket by his father's old cottage or, gripped by who knew what paranoid fantasy, to slash one of Kinvara's horses.

Worried by these inexplicable features of the case, by the interest the *Sun* was taking in the minister, and aware that the agency was no closer to securing a 'bargaining chip' against either of Chiswell's blackmailers than on the day that Strike had accepted the minister as a client, he felt he had little choice but to leave no stone unturned. In spite of his tiredness, his aching muscles and his strong suspicion that the protest march would yield nothing useful, he had dragged himself out of bed on Saturday morning, strapped his prosthesis back onto a stump that was already slightly puffy and, unable to think of much he'd like to do less than walk for two hours, set off for Mile End Park.

Once close enough to the crowd of protestors to make out individuals, Strike pulled from the carrier bag swinging from his hand a plastic Guy Fawkes mask, white with curling eyebrows and moustache and now mainly associated with the hacking organisation Anonymous, and put it on. Balling up the carrier bag, he shoved it into a handy bin, then hobbled on towards the cluster of placards and banners: 'No missiles on homes!' 'No snipers on streets!' 'Don't play games with our lives!' and several 'He's got to go!' posters featuring the prime minister's face. Strike's fake foot always found grass one of the most difficult surfaces to navigate. He was sweating by the time he finally spotted the orange CORE banners, with their logo of broken Olympic rings.

There were about a dozen of them. Lurking behind a group of chattering youths, Strike readjusted the slipping plastic mask, which had not been constructed for a man whose nose had been broken, and spotted Jimmy Knight, who was talking to two young women, both of whom had just thrown back their heads, laughing delightedly at something Knight had just said. Clamping the mask to his face to make sure the slits aligned with his eyes, Strike scanned the rest of the CORE members and concluded that the absence of tomato-red hair was not because Flick had dyed it another colour, but because she wasn't there.

Stewards now started herding the crowd into something resembling a line. Strike moved into the mass of protestors, a silent, lumbering figure, acting a little obtusely so that the youthful organisers, intimidated by his size, treated him like a rock around which the current must be channelled as he took up a position right behind CORE. A skinny boy who was also wearing an Anonymous mask gave Strike a double thumbs up as he was shunted towards the rear of the line. Strike returned it.

Now smoking a roll-up, Jimmy continued to joke with the two young girls beside him, who were vying for his attention. The darker of the two, who was particularly attractive, was holding a double-sided banner carrying a highly detailed painting of David Cameron as Hitler overlooking the 1936 Olympic Stadium. It was quite an impressive piece of art, and Strike had time to admire it as the procession finally set off at a steady pace, flanked by police and stewards in high visibility jackets, moving gradually out of the park and onto the long, straight Roman Road.

The smooth tarmac was slightly easier on Strike's prosthesis, but his stump was still throbbing. After a few minutes a chant was got up: 'Missiles OUT! Missiles OUT!'

A couple of press photographers were walking backwards in the road ahead, taking pictures of the front of the march.

'Hey, Libby,' said Jimmy, to the girl with the hand-painted Hitler banner. 'Wanna get on my shoulders?'

Strike noted her friend's poorly concealed envy as Jimmy crouched down so that Libby could straddle his neck and be lifted up above the crowd, her banner raised high enough for the photographers in front to see.

'Show 'em your tits, we'll be front page!' Jimmy called up to her.

'*Jimmy!*' she squealed, in mock outrage. Her friend's smile was forced. The cameras clicked, and Strike, grimacing with pain behind the plastic mask, tried not to limp too obviously.

'Guy with the biggest camera was focused on you the whole time,' said Jimmy, when he finally lowered the girl back to the ground.

'Fuck, if I'm in the papers my mum'll go apeshit,' said the girl excitedly, and she fell into step on Jimmy's other side, taking any opportunity to nudge or slap him as he teased her about being scared of what her parents would say. She was, Strike judged, at least fifteen years younger than he was.

'Enjoying yourself, Jimmy?'

The mask restricted Strike's peripheral vision, so that it was only when the uncombed, tomato-red hair appeared immediately in front of him that Strike realised Flick had joined the march. Her sudden appearance had taken Jimmy by surprise, too.

'There you are!' he said, with a feeble show of pleasure.

Flick glared at the girl called Libby, who sped up, intimidated. Jimmy tried to put his arm around Flick, but she shrugged it off.

'Oi,' he said, feigning innocent indignation. 'What's up?'

'Three fucking guesses,' snarled Flick.

Strike could tell that Jimmy was debating which tack to take with her. His thuggishly handsome face showed irritation but also, Strike thought, a certain wariness. For a second time, he tried to put his arm around her. This time, she slapped it away.

'Oi,' he said again, this time aggressively. 'The fuck was that for?'

'I'm off doing your dirty work and you're fucking around with *her*? What kind of fucking idiot do you think I am, Jimmy?'

'Missiles OUT!' bellowed a steward with a megaphone, and the crowd took up the chant once more. The cries made by the Mohican-ed woman beside Strike were as shrill and raucous as a peacock's. The one bonus of the renewed shouting was that it left Strike at liberty to grunt with pain every time he set his prosthetic foot on the road, which was a kind of release and made the plastic mask reverberate in a ticklish fashion against his sweating face. Squinting through the eyeholes he watched Jimmy and Flick argue, but he couldn't hear a word over the din of the crowd. Only when the chant subsided at last could he make out a little of what they were saying to each other.

'I'm fucking sick of this,' Jimmy was saying. '*I'm* not the one who picks up students in bars when—'

'You'd ditched me!' said Flick, in a kind of whispered scream. 'You'd fucking ditched me! You told me you didn't want anything exclusive—'

'Heat of the moment, wasn't it?' said Jimmy roughly. 'I was stressed. Billy was doing my fucking head in. I didn't expect you to go straight to a bar and pick up some fucking—'

'You told me you were sick of—'

'Fuck's sake, I lost my temper and said a bunch of shit I didn't mean. If I went and shagged another woman every time you give me grief—'

'Yeah, well I sometimes think the only reason you even keep me around is Chis—'

'*Keep your fucking voice down!*'

'—and today, you think it was fun at that creep's house—'

'I said I was grateful, fuck's sake, we discussed this, didn't we? I had to get those leaflets printed or I'd've come with you—'

'*And* I do that cleaning,' she said, with a sudden sob, 'and it's disgusting and then today you send me – it was horrible, Jimmy, he should be in hospital, he's in a right state—'

Jimmy glanced around. Coming briefly within Jimmy's eye-line, Strike attempted to walk naturally, though every time he asked his stump to bear his full weight, he felt as though he was pressing it down on a thousand fire ants.

'We'll get him to hospital after,' said Jimmy. 'We will, but he'll screw it all up if we let him loose now, you know what he's like ... once Winn's got those photos ... hey,' said Jimmy gently, putting his arm around her for a third time. 'Listen. I'm so fucking grateful to you.'

'Yeah,' choked Flick, wiping her nose on the back of her hand, 'because of the money. Because you wouldn't even know what Chiswell had done if—'

Jimmy pulled her roughly towards him and kissed her. For a second she resisted, then opened her mouth. The kiss went on and on as they walked. Strike could see their tongues working in each other's mouths. They staggered slightly as they walked, locked together, while other CORE members grinned, and the girl whom Jimmy had lifted into the air looked crestfallen.

'Jimmy,' murmured Flick at last, when the kiss had ended, but his arm was still around her. She was doe-eyed with lust now, and soft-spoken. 'I think you should come and talk to him, seriously. He keeps talking about that bloody detective.'

'What?' said Jimmy, though Strike could tell he'd heard.

'Strike. That bastard soldier with the one leg. Billy's fixated on him. Thinks he's going to rescue him.'

The end point of the march came into sight at last: Bow Quarter in Fairfield Road, where the square brick tower of an old match factory, proposed site of some of the planned missiles, punctured the skyline.

'"Rescue him"?' repeated Jimmy scornfully. 'Fuck's sake. It's not like he's being fucking tortured.'

The marchers were breaking ranks now, dissolving back into a formless crowd that milled around a dark green pond in front of the proposed missile site. Strike would have given much to sit down on a bench or lean up against a tree, as many of the protestors were doing, so as to take the weight off his stump. Both the end, where skin that was never meant to bear his weight was irritated and inflamed, and the tendons in his knee were begging for ice and rest. Instead, he limped on after Jimmy and Flick as they walked around the edge of the crowd, away from their CORE colleagues.

'He wanted to see you and I told him you were busy,' he heard Flick say, 'and he cried. It was horrible, Jimmy.'

Pretending to be watching the young black man with a microphone, who was ascending a stage at the front of the crowd, Strike edged closer to Jimmy and Flick.

'I'll look after Billy when I get the money,' Jimmy was telling Flick. He seemed guilty and conflicted now. 'Obviously I'll look after him . . . and you. I won't forget what you've done.'

She liked hearing that. Out of the corner of his eye, Strike saw her grubby face flush with excitement. Jimmy took a pack of tobacco and some Rizlas from his jeans pocket and began to roll himself another cigarette.

'Still talking about that fucking detective, is he?'

'Yeah.'

Jimmy lit up and smoked in silence for a while, his eyes roving abstractedly over the crowd.

'Tell you what,' he said suddenly, 'I'll go see him now. Calm him down a bit. We just need him to stay put a bit longer. Coming?'

He held out his hand and Flick took it, smiling. They walked away.

Strike let them get a short head start, then stripped off the mask and the old grey hoodie, replaced the former with the sunglasses he had pocketed for this eventuality and set off after them, dumping the mask and hoodie on top of their banners.

The pace Jimmy now set was completely different to the leisurely march. Every few strides, Flick had to jog to keep up, and Strike was soon gritting his teeth as the nerve endings at the inflamed skin at the end of his stump rubbed against the prosthesis, his overworked thigh muscles groaning in protest.

He was perspiring hard, his gait becoming more and more unnatural. Passers-by were starting to stare. He could feel their curiosity and pity as he dragged his prosthetic leg along. He knew he should have been doing his bloody physio exercises, that he ought to have kept to the no chips rule, that in an ideal world he'd have taken the day off today, and rested up, the prosthesis off, an ice pack on his stump. On he limped, refusing to listen to the body pleading with him to stop, the distance between himself, Jimmy and Flick growing ever wider, the compensating movement of his upper body and arms becoming grotesque. He could only pray that neither Jimmy nor Flick would turn and look behind them, because there was no way Strike could remain incognito if they saw him hobbling along like this. They were already disappearing into the neat little brick box that was Bow station, while Strike was panting and swearing on the opposite side of the road.

As he stepped off the kerb, an excruciating pain shot through the back of his right thigh, as though a knife had sliced through the muscle. The leg buckled and he fell, his outstretched hand skidding along asphalt, hitting hip, shoulder and head on the open road. Somewhere in the vicinity a woman yelped in shock. Onlookers would think he was drunk. It had happened before when he had fallen. Humiliated, furious, groaning in agony, Strike crawled back onto the pavement, dragging his right leg out of the way of oncoming traffic. A young woman approached nervously to see whether he needed help, he barked at her, then felt guilty.

'Sorry,' he croaked, but she was gone, hurrying away with two friends.

He dragged himself to the railings bordering the pavement and sat there, back against metal, sweating and bleeding. He doubted whether he would be able to stand again without assistance. Running his hands over the back of his stump, he felt an egg-shaped swelling and, with a groan, guessed that he had torn a hamstring. The pain was so sharp that it was making him feel sick.

He tugged his mobile out of his pocket. The screen was cracked where he had fallen on it.

'Fuck. It. All,' he muttered, closing his eyes and leaning his head back against the cold metal.

He sat motionless for several minutes, dismissed as a tramp or a drunk by the people navigating around him, while he silently assessed his limited options. At last, with a sense of being utterly cornered, he opened his eyes, wiped his face with his forearm, and punched in Lorelei's number.

23

. . . ailing and languishing in the gloom of such a marriage . . .
                    Henrik Ibsen, *Rosmersholm*

In retrospect, Robin knew that her anniversary weekend had been doomed before it had even begun, down in the House of Commons crypt where she had turned down Strike's request to tail Jimmy.

Trying to throw off her sense of guilt, she had confided Strike's request to Matthew when he picked her up after work. Already tense due to the demands of navigating the Friday night traffic in the Land Rover, which he disliked, Matthew went on the offensive, demanding to know why she felt bad after all the slave labour Strike had had out of her over the past two years and proceeding to badmouth Strike so viciously that Robin had felt compelled to defend him. They were still arguing about her job an hour later, when Matthew suddenly noticed that there was neither wedding nor engagement ring on Robin's gesticulating left hand. She never wore these when playing the unmarried Venetia Hall, and had entirely forgotten that she would not be able to retrieve them from Albury Street before leaving for the hotel.

'It's our bloody anniversary and you can't even remember to put your rings back on?' Matthew had shouted.

They drew up outside the soft golden brick hotel an hour and a half later. A beaming man in uniform opened the door for Robin. Her 'thank you' was almost inaudible due to the hard, angry lump in her throat.

They barely spoke over their Michelin-starred dinner. Robin, who might as well have been eating polystyrene and dust, looked around at the surrounding tables. She and Matthew were by far the youngest couple there, and she wondered whether any of these husbands and wives had been through this kind of trough in their marriages, and survived it.

They slept back to back that night.

Robin woke on Saturday in the awareness that every moment in the hotel, every step through the beautifully cultivated grounds, with the lavender walk, the Japanese garden, the orchard and organic vegetable beds, was costing them a small fortune. Perhaps Matthew was thinking the same, because he became conciliatory over break-fast. Nevertheless, their conversation felt perilous, straying regularly into dangerous territory from which they retreated precipitately. A tension headache began pounding behind Robin's temple, but she did not want to ask hotel staff for painkillers, because any sign of dissatisfaction might lead to another argument. Robin wondered what it would be like to have a wedding day and honeymoon about which it was safe to reminisce. They eventually settled on talking about Matthew's job as they strolled the grounds.

There was to be a charity cricket match between his firm and another the following Saturday. Matthew, who was as good at cricket as he had been at rugby, was greatly looking forward to the game. Robin listened to his boasts about his own prowess and jokes about Tom's inadequate bowling, laughed at the appropriate moments and made sounds of agreement, and all the time a chilled and miserable part of her was wondering what was happening right now in Bow, whether Strike had gone on the march, whether he was getting any-thing useful on Jimmy and wondering how she, Robin, had ended up with the pompous, self-involved man beside her, who reminded her of a handsome boy she had once loved.

For the first time ever, Robin had sex with Matthew that night purely because she could not face the row that would ensue if she refused. It was their anniversary, so they had to have sex, like a nota-ry's stamp on the weekend, and about as pleasurable. Tears stung her eyes as Matthew climaxed, and that cold, unhappy self buried deep in her compliant body wondered why he could not feel her unhappiness even though she was trying so hard to dissemble, and how he could possibly imagine that the marriage was a success.

She put her arm over her wet eyes in the darkness after he had rolled off her and said all the things you were supposed to say. For the first time, when she said 'I love you, too', she knew, beyond doubt, that she was lying.

Very carefully, once Matthew was asleep, Robin reached out in the darkness for the phone that lay on her bedside table, and checked her texts. There was nothing from Strike. She Googled pictures of the march in Bow and thought she recognised, in the middle of the crowd, a tall man with familiar curly hair, who was wearing a Guy Fawkes mask. Robin turned her mobile face down on the bedside table to shut out its light, and closed her eyes.

24

*... her ungovernable, wild fits of passion – which she expected
me to reciprocate ...*

Henrik Ibsen, *Rosmersholm*

Strike returned to his two attic rooms in Denmark Street six days
later, early on Friday morning. Leaning on crutches, his prosthesis
in a holdall over his shoulder and his right trouser leg pinned up,
his expression tended to repel the sidelong glances of sympathy that
passers-by gave him as he swung along the short street to number
twenty-four.

He hadn't seen a doctor. Lorelei had called her local practice once
she and the lavishly tipped cabbie had succeeded in supporting Strike
upstairs to her flat, but the GP had asked Strike to come into his
surgery for an examination.

'What d'you want me to do, hop there? It's my hamstring, I can
feel it,' he had snapped down the phone. 'I know the drill: rest, ice,
all that bollocks. I've done it before.'

He had been forced to break his no-consecutive-overnights-at-a-
woman's rule, spending four full days and five nights at Lorelei's. He
now regretted it, but what choice had he had? He had been caught,
as Chiswell would have put it, *a fronte praecipitium, a tergo lupi*. He
and Lorelei had been supposed to have dinner on Saturday night.
Having chosen to tell her the truth rather than make an excuse not
to meet, he had been forced to let her help. Now he wished that he
had phoned his old friends Nick and Ilsa, or even Shanker, but it was
too late. The damage was done.

The knowledge that he was being unfair and ungrateful was hardly calculated to improve Strike's mood as he dragged himself and his holdall up the stairs. In spite of the fact that parts of the sojourn at Lorelei's flat had been thoroughly enjoyable, all had been ruined by what had happened the previous evening, and it was entirely his own fault. He had let it happen, the thing that he had tried to guard against ever since leaving Charlotte, let it happen because he'd dropped his guard, and accepted mugs of tea, home-cooked meals and gentle affection, until finally, last night in the darkness, she had whispered onto his bare chest, 'I love you'.

Grimacing again with the effort of balancing on his crutches as he unlocked his front door, Strike almost fell into his flat. Slamming the door behind him, he dropped the holdall, crossed to the small chair at the Formica table in his kitchen-cum-living room, fell into it and cast his crutches aside. It was a relief to be home and alone, however difficult it was to manage with his leg in this state. He ought to have returned sooner, of course, but being in no condition to tail anyone and in considerable discomfort, it had been easier to remain in a comfortable armchair, his stump resting on a large square pouffe, texting Robin and Barclay instructions while Lorelei fetched him food and drink.

Strike lit a cigarette and thought back over all the women there had been since he'd left Charlotte. First, Ciara Parker, a gorgeous one-night stand, with no regrets on either side. A few weeks after he had hit the press for solving the Landry case, Ciara had called him. He had become elevated in the model's mind from casual shag to possible boyfriend material by his newsworthiness, but he had turned down further meetings with her. Girlfriends who wanted to be photographed with him were no good to him in his line of work.

Next had come Nina, who had worked for a publisher, and whom he had used to get information on a case. He had liked her, but insufficiently, as he looked back on it, to treat her with common consideration. He had hurt Nina's feelings. He wasn't proud of it, but it hardly kept him up at nights.

Elin had been different, beautiful and, best of all, convenient, which was why he'd hung around. She had been in the process of divorcing a wealthy man and her need for discretion and compartmentalisation had been at least as great as his own. They had managed a few months together before he'd spilled wine all over her, and walked out of the restaurant where they were having dinner. He had called her afterwards to apologise and she had dumped him before he finished the sentence. Given that he had left her humiliated in Le Gavroche with a hefty dry-cleaning bill, he felt that it would have been in poor taste to respond with 'that's what I was going to say next'.

After Elin there had been Coco, on whom he preferred not to dwell, and now there was Lorelei. He liked her better than any of the others, which was why he was sorry that it had been she who said 'I love you'.

Strike had made a vow to himself two years previously, and he made very few vows, because he trusted himself to keep them. Having never said 'I love you' to any woman but Charlotte, he would not say it to another unless he knew, beyond reasonable doubt, that he wanted to stay with that woman and make a life with her. It would make a mockery of what he'd been through with Charlotte if he said it under circumstances any less serious. Only love could have justified the havoc they had lived together, or the many times he had resumed the relationship, even while he knew in his soul that it couldn't work. Love, to Strike, was pain and grief sought, accepted, endured. It was not in Lorelei's bedroom, with the cowgirls on the curtains.

And so he had said nothing after her whispered declaration, and then, when she'd asked whether he'd heard her, he'd said, 'Yeah, I did.'

Strike reached for his cigarettes. *Yeah, I did.* Well, that had been honest, as far as it went. There was nothing wrong with his hearing. After that, there'd been a fairly lengthy silence, then Lorelei had got out of bed and gone to the bathroom and stayed there for thirty minutes. Strike assumed that she'd gone there to cry, though she'd been kind enough to do it quietly, so that he couldn't hear her. He had lain in bed, wondering what he could say to her that was both kind and truthful, but he knew that nothing short of 'I love you, too' would be acceptable, and the fact was that he didn't love her, and he wasn't going to lie.

When she came back to bed, he had reached out for her in the bed. She'd let him stroke her shoulder for a while, then told him she was tired and needed some sleep.

What was I supposed to fucking do? he demanded of an imaginary female inquisitor who strongly resembled his sister, Lucy.

You could try not accepting tea and blow jobs, came the snide response, to which Strike, with his stump throbbing, answered, *fuck you.*

His mobile rang. He had sellotaped up the shattered screen, and through this distorted carapace he saw an unknown number.

'Strike.'

'Hi, Strike, Culpepper here.'

Dominic Culpepper, who had worked for the *News of the World* until its closure, had previously put work Strike's way. Relations between them, never personally warm, had become slightly antagonistic when Strike had refused Culpepper the inside story on his two most recent murder cases. Now working for the *Sun*, Culpepper had been one of those journalists who had most enthusiastically raked over Strike's personal life in the aftermath of the Shacklewell Ripper arrest.

'Wondered if you were free to do a job for us,' said Culpepper.

You've got a fucking nerve.

'What kind of thing're you after?'

'Digging up dirt on a government minister.'

'Which one?'

'You'll know if you take the job.'

'I'm pretty stretched just now. What kind of dirt are we talking?'

'That's what we need you to find out.'

'How do you know there's dirt there?'

'A well-placed source,' said Culpepper.

'Why do you need me if there's a well-placed source?'

'He's not ready to talk. He just hinted that there are beans to be spilled. Lots of them.'

'Sorry, can't do it, Culpepper,' said Strike. 'I'm booked solid.'

'Sure? We're paying good money, Strike.'

'I'm not doing too badly these days,' said the detective, lighting a second cigarette from the tip of his first.

'No, I'll bet you aren't, you jammy bastard,' said Culpepper. 'All right, it'll have to be Patterson. D'you know him?'

'The ex-Met guy? Run across him a couple of times,' said Strike.

The call finished with mutually insincere good wishes, leaving Strike with an increased feeling of foreboding. He Googled Culpepper's name and found his byline on a story about the Level Playing Field from two weeks previously.

Of course, it was possible that more than one government minister was currently in danger of being exposed by the *Sun* for an offence against public taste or morals, but the fact that Culpepper had recently been in close proximity with the Winns strongly suggested Robin had been right in suspecting Geraint of tipping off the *Sun*, and that it was Chiswell whom Patterson would shortly be investigating.

Strike wondered whether Culpepper knew that he, Strike, was already working for Chiswell, whether his call had been designed to startle information out of the detective, but it seemed unlikely. The newspaperman would have been very stupid to tell Strike whom he was about to hire, if he was aware that Strike was already in the minister's pay.

Strike knew of Mitch Patterson by reputation: they had twice been hired by different halves of divorcing couples in the last year. Previously a senior officer in the Metropolitan Police who had 'taken early retirement', Patterson was prematurely silver-haired and had the face of an angry pug. Though personally unpleasant, or so Eric Wardle had told Strike, Patterson was a man who 'got results'.

'Course, he won't be able to kick the shit out of people in his new career,' Wardle had commented, 'so that's one useful tool in his arsenal gone.'

Strike didn't much relish the thought that Patterson would shortly be on the case. Picking up his mobile again, he noted that neither Robin nor Barclay had called in an update within the last twelve hours. Only the previous day, he had had to reassure Chiswell, who had called to express his doubts about Robin, given her lack of results thus far.

Frustrated by his employees and his own incapacity, Strike texted Robin and Barclay the same message:

Sun just tried to hire me to investigate Chiswell. Call with update asap. Need useable info NOW.

Pulling his crutches back towards him, he got up to examine the contents of his fridge and kitchen cupboards, discovering that he would be eating nothing but tinned soup for the next four meals unless he made a trip to the supermarket. After pouring spoiled milk down the sink, he made himself a mug of black tea and returned to the Formica table, where he lit a third cigarette and contemplated, without pleasure, the prospect of doing his hamstring stretches.

His phone rang again. Seeing that it was Lucy, he let it go to voicemail. The last thing he needed right now was updates on the school board's last meeting.

A few minutes after that, when Strike was in the bathroom, she called back. He had hopped back into the kitchen with his trousers at half-mast, in the hope that it was either Robin or Barclay. When he saw his sister's number for a second time, he merely swore loudly and returned to the bathroom.

The third call told him that she was not about to give up. Slamming down the can of soup he had been opening, Strike swept up the mobile.

'Lucy, I'm busy, what is it?' he said testily.

'It's Barclay.'

'Ah, about time. Any news?'

'A bit on Jimmy's bird, if that helps. Flick.'

'It all helps,' said Strike. 'Why didn't you let me know earlier?'

'Only found out ten minutes ago,' said Barclay, unfazed. 'I've just heard her tellin' Jimmy in the kitchen. She's been bumpin' money from her work.'

'What work?'

'Didnae tell me. Trouble is, Jimmy's no that keen on her, from whut I've seen. I'm no sure he'd care if she got nicked.'

A distracting beeping sounded in Strike's ear. Another caller was trying to get him. Glancing at the phone, he saw that it was Lucy again.

'Tell ye somethin' else I got out o' him, though,' said Barclay. 'Last night, when he was stoned. He said he knew a government minister who had blood on his hands.'

Beep. Beep. Beep.

'Strike? Ye there?'

'Yeah, I'm here.'

Strike had never told Barclay about Billy's story.

'What exactly did he say, Barclay?'

'He was ramblin' on about the government, the Tories, whut a bunch o' bastards they are. Then, out o' nowhere, he says "and fuckin' killers". I says, what d'ye mean? An' he says, "I know one who's got blood on his fuckin' hands. Kids."'

Beep. Beep. Beep.

'Mind you, they're a bunch o' bampots, CORE. He might be talkin' about benefit cuts. That's as good as murder to this lot. Not that I think too much of Chiswell's politics meself, Strike.'

'Seen any sign of Billy? Jimmy's brother?'

'Nothin'. Naebody's mentioned him, neither.'

Beep. Beep. Beep.

'And no sign of Jimmy nipping off to Oxfordshire?'

'Not on my watch.'

Beep. Beep. Beep.

'All right,' said Strike. 'Keep digging. Let me know if you get anything.'

He rang off, jabbed at his phone's screen and brought up Lucy's call, instead.

'Lucy, hi,' he said impatiently. 'Bit busy now, can I—?'

But as she began to talk, his expression became blank. Before she had finished gasping out the reason for her call, he had grabbed his door keys and was scrabbling for his crutches.

25

We shall try if we cannot make you powerless to do any harm.

Henrik Ibsen, *Rosmersholm*

Strike's text requesting an update reached Robin at ten to nine, as she arrived in the corridor where Izzy and Winn's offices lay. So keen was she to see what he had to say that she stopped dead in the middle of the deserted passage to read it.

'Oh shit,' she murmured, reading that the *Sun* was becoming ever more interested in Chiswell. Leaning up against the wall of the corridor with its curved stone jambs, every oak door shut, she braced herself to call Strike back.

They had not spoken since she had refused to tail Jimmy. When she had phoned him on Monday to apologise directly, Lorelei had answered.

'Oh, hi, Robin, it's me!'

One of the awful things about Lorelei was that she was likeable. For reasons Robin preferred not to explore, she would have much preferred Lorelei to be unpleasant.

'He's in the shower, sorry! He's been here all weekend, he did his knee in following somebody. He won't tell me the details, but I suppose you know! He had to call me from the street, it was dreadful, he couldn't stand up. I got a cabbie to take me there and paid him to help me get Corm upstairs. He can't wear the prosthesis, he's on crutches ...'

'Just tell him I was checking in,' said Robin, her stomach like ice. 'Nothing important.'

Robin had replayed the conversation several times in her head since. There had been an unmistakably proprietorial note in Lorelei's voice as she talked about Strike. It had been Lorelei whom he had called when he was in trouble (*well, of course it was. What was he going to do, call you in Oxfordshire?*), Lorelei in whose flat he had spent the rest of the weekend (*they're dating, where else was he going to go?*), Lorelei who was looking after him, consoling him and, perhaps, uniting with him in abuse of Robin, without whom this injury might not have happened.

And now she had to call Strike and tell him that, five days on, she had no useful information. Winn's office, which had been so conveniently accessible when she had started work two weeks ago, was now carefully locked up whenever Geraint and Aamir had to leave it. Robin was sure that this was Aamir's doing, that he had become suspicious of her after the incidents of the dropped bangle, and of Raphael calling loud attention to her eavesdropping on Aamir's phone call.

'Post.'

Robin whirled around to see the cart trundling towards her, pushed by a genial grey-haired man.

'I'll take anything for Chiswell and Winn. We're having a meeting,' Robin heard herself say. The postman handed over a stack of letters, along with a box with a clear cellophane window, through which Robin saw a life-size and very realistic plastic foetus. The legend across the top read: *It Is Legal To Murder Me.*

'Oh God, that's horrible,' said Robin.

The postman chortled.

'That's nothing compared to some of what they get,' he said comfortably. 'Remember the white powder that was on the news? Anthrax, they claimed. Proper hoo-hah, that was. Oh, and I delivered a turd in a box once. Couldn't smell it through all the wrapping. The baby's for Winn, not Chiswell. She's the pro-choice one. Enjoying it here, are you?' he said, showing a disposition for chat.

'Loving it,' Robin said, whose attention had been caught by one of the envelopes she had so rashly taken. 'Excuse me.'

Turning her back on Izzy's office, she hurried past the postman, and five minutes later emerged onto the Terrace Café, which sat on the bank of the Thames. It was separated from the river by a low stone wall, which was punctuated with black iron lamps. To the left and right stood Westminster and Lambeth bridges respectively, the former painted the green of the seats in the House of Commons, the latter, scarlet like those in the House of Lords. On the opposite bank rose the white façade of County Hall, while between palace and hall rolled the broad Thames, its oily surface lucent grey over muddy depths.

Sitting down out of earshot of the few early morning coffee drinkers, Robin turned her attention to one of the letters addressed to Geraint Winn that she had so recklessly taken from the postman. The sender's name and address had been carefully inscribed on the reverse of the envelope in a shaky cursive: Sir Kevin Rodgers, 16 The Elms, Fleetwood, Kent and she happened to know, due to her extensive background reading on the Winns' charity, that the elderly Sir Kevin, who had won a silver at the hurdles in the 1956 Olympics, was one of the Level Playing Field's trustees.

What things, Robin asked herself, did people feel the need to put in writing these days, when phone calls and emails were so much easier and faster?

Using her mobile, she found a number for Sir Kevin and Lady Rodgers at the correct address. They were old enough, she thought, to still use a landline. Taking a fortifying gulp of coffee, she texted Strike back:

Following a lead, will call asap.

She then turned off caller ID on her mobile, took out a pen and the notebook in which she had written Sir Kevin's number and punched in the digits.

An elderly woman answered within three rings. Robin affected what she was afraid was a poor Welsh accent.

'Could I speak to Sir Kevin, please?'

'Is that Della?'

'Is Sir Kevin there?' asked Robin again, a little louder. She had been hoping to avoid actually claiming to be a government minister.

'Kevin!' called the woman. 'Kevin! It's Della!'

There was a noise of shuffling that made Robin think of tartan bedroom slippers.

'Hello?'

'Kevin, Geraint's just got your letter,' said Robin, wincing as her accent wobbled somewhere between Cardiff and Lahore.

'Sorry, Della, what?' said the man feebly.

He seemed to be deaf, which was both help and hindrance. Robin spoke more loudly, enunciating as clearly as she could. Sir Kevin grasped what she was saying on her third attempt.

'I told Geraint I'd have to resign unless he took urgent steps,' he said miserably. 'You're an old friend, Della, and it was – it is – a worthy cause, but I have to think of my own position. I did warn him.'

'But why, Kevin?' said Robin, picking up her pen.

'Hasn't he shown you my letter?'

'No,' said Robin truthfully, pen poised.

'Oh dear,' said Sir Kevin weakly. 'Well, for one thing . . . twenty-five thousand pounds unaccounted for is a serious matter.'

'What else?' asked Robin, making rapid notes.

'What's that?'

'You said "for one thing". What else are you worried about?'

Robin could hear the woman who'd answered the phone talking in the background. Her voice sounded irate.

'Della, I'd rather not go into it all on the phone,' said Sir Kevin, sounding embarrassed.

'Well, this is disappointing,' said Robin, with what she hoped was a touch of Della's mellifluous grandeur. 'I hoped you'd at least tell me why, Kevin.'

'Well, there's the Mo Farah business—'

'Mo Farah?' repeated Robin, in unaffected surprise.

'What was that?'

'*Mo – Farah?*'

'You didn't know?' said Sir Kevin. 'Oh dear. Oh dear . . .'

Robin heard footsteps and then the woman came back on the line, first muffled, then clear.

'Let me speak to her – Kevin, let go – look, Della, Kevin's very upset about all this. He suspected you didn't know what's been going on and, well, here we are, he was right. Nobody ever wants to worry you, Della,' she said, sounding as though she thought this a mistaken protectiveness, 'but the fact of the matter is – no, she's got to know, Kevin – Geraint's been promising people things he can't deliver. Disabled children and their families have been told they're getting visits from David Beckham and Mo Farah and I don't know who else. It's all going to come out, Della, now the Charity Commission's involved, and I'm not having Kevin's name dragged through the mud. He's a conscientious man and he's done his best. He's been urging Geraint to sort out the accounts for months now, and then there's what Elspeth ... no, Kevin, I'm *not*, I'm just telling her ... well, it could get very nasty, Della. It might yet come to the police as well as the press, and I'm sorry, but I'm thinking of Kevin's health.'

'What's Elspeth's story?' said Robin, still writing fast.

Sir Kevin said something plaintive in the background.

'I'm not going into that on the phone,' said Lady Rodgers repressively. 'You'll have to ask Elspeth.'

There was more shuffling and Sir Kevin took the receiver again. He sounded almost tearful.

'Della, you know how much I admire you. I wish it could have been otherwise.'

'Yes,' said Robin, 'well, I'll have to call Elspeth, then.'

'What was that?'

'I'll – call – Elspeth.'

'Oh dear,' said Sir Kevin. 'But you know, there might be nothing in it.'

Robin wondered whether she dared ask for Elspeth's number, but decided not. Della would surely have it.

'I wish you'd tell me what Elspeth's story is,' she said, her pen poised over her notebook.

'I don't like to,' said Sir Kevin wheezily. 'The damage these kinds of rumours do to a man's reputation—'

Lady Rodgers came back on the line.

'That's all we've got to say. This whole business has been very hard on Kevin, very stressful. I'm sorry, but that's our final word on the matter, Della. Goodbye.'

Robin set her mobile down on the table beside her and checked that nobody was looking her way. She picked up her mobile again and scrolled down the list of The Level Playing Field's trustees. One of them was called Dr Elspeth Curtis-Lacey, but her personal number was not listed on the charity's website and appeared, from a search of directory enquiries, to be unlisted.

Robin phoned Strike. The call went straight to voicemail. She waited a couple of minutes and tried again, with the same result. After her third failed attempt to reach him, she texted:

Got some stuff on GW. Call me.

The dank shadow that had lain on the terrace when she had first arrived was moving incrementally backwards. The warm sun slid over Robin's table as she eked out her coffee, waiting for Strike to call back. At last her phone vibrated to show that she had a text: heart leaping, she picked it up, but it was only Matthew.

Fancy a drink with Tom and Sarah tonight after work?

Robin contemplated the message with a mixture of lassitude and dread. Tomorrow was the charity cricket match about which Matthew was so excited. After-work drinks with Tom and Sarah would doubt-less mean plenty of banter on the subject. She could already picture the four of them at the bar: Sarah, with her perennially flirtatious attitude towards Matthew, Tom fending off Matthew's jokes about his lousy bowling with increasingly clumsy, angry ripostes, and Robin, as was increasingly the case these days, pretending to be amused and inter-ested, because that was the cost of not being harangued by Matthew for seeming bored, or feeling superior to her company or (as happened during their worst rows) wishing that she were drinking with Strike instead. At least, she consoled herself, it couldn't be a late or drunken night, because Matthew, who took all sporting fixtures seriously, would want a decent sleep before the match. So she texted back:

218

OK, where?

and continued to wait for Strike to ring her.

After forty minutes, Robin began to wonder whether Strike was somewhere he couldn't call, which left open the question of whether she ought to inform Chiswell of what she had just found out. Would Strike consider that a liberty, or would he be more annoyed if she failed to give Chiswell his bargaining chip, given the time pressure?

After debating the matter inwardly for a while longer, she called Izzy, the upper half of whose office window she could see from where she sat.

'Izzy, it's me. Venetia. I'm calling because I can't say this in front of Raphael. I think I've got some information on Winn for your father—'

'Oh, fabulous!' said Izzy loudly, and Robin heard Raphael in the background saying, 'Is that Venetia? Where is she?' and the clicking of computer keys.

'Checking the diary, Venetia ... He'll be at DCMS until eleven, but then he's in meetings all afternoon. Do you want me to call him? He could probably see you straight away if you hurry.'

So Robin replaced her mobile, notebook and pen in her bag, gulped down the last of her coffee and hurried off to the Department for Culture, Media and Sport.

Chiswell was pacing up and down his office, speaking on the phone, when Robin arrived outside the glass partition. He beckoned her inside, pointed to a low leather sofa at a short distance from his desk, and continued to talk to somebody who appeared to have displeased him.

'It was a gift,' he was saying distinctly into the receiver, 'from my eldest son. Twenty-four-carat gold, inscribed *Nec Aspera Terrent.* Bloody hell's bells!' he roared suddenly, and Robin saw the heads of the bright young people just outside the office turning towards Chiswell. 'It's Latin! Pass me to somebody who can speak *English*! *Jasper Chiswell*. I'm the *Minister for Culture*. I've given you the date ... no, you can't ... I haven't got all bloody day—'

Robin gathered, from the side of the conversation that she could hear, that Chiswell had lost a money clip of sentimental value, which he thought he might have left at a hotel where he and Kinvara had spent the night of her birthday. As far as she could hear, the hotel staff had not only failed to find the clip, they were showing insufficient deference to Chiswell for having deigned to stay at one of their hotels.

'I want somebody to call me back. Bloody useless,' muttered Chiswell, hanging up and peering at Robin as though he had forgotten who she was. Still breathing heavily, he dropped down on the sofa opposite her. 'I've got ten minutes, so this had better be worthwhile.'

'I've got some information on Mr Winn,' said Robin, taking out her notebook. Without waiting for his response, she gave him a succinct summary of the information she had gleaned from Sir Kevin.

'... and,' she concluded, barely a minute and a half later, 'there may be further impropriety on Mr Winn's part, but that information is allegedly held by Dr Elspeth Curtis-Lacey, whose number is unlisted. It shouldn't take us long to find a way of contacting her, but I thought,' Robin said apprehensively, because Chiswell's tiny eyes were screwed up in what might have been displeasure, 'I should bring you this immediately.'

For a few seconds he simply stared at her, his expression petulant as ever, but then he slapped his thigh in what was clearly pleasure.

'Well, well, well,' he said. 'He told me you were his best. Yerse. Said so.'

Pulling a crumpled handkerchief out of his pocket he wiped his face, which had become sweaty during his phone call with the unfortunate hotel.

'Well, well, well,' he said again, 'this is turning out to be a rather good day. One by one, they trip themselves up ... so Winn's a thief and a liar and maybe more?'

'Well,' said Robin cautiously, 'he can't account for the twenty-five thousand pounds, and he's certainly promised things he can't deliver ...'

'Dr Elspeth Curtis-Lacey,' said Chiswell, following his own train of thought. 'Name's familiar ...'

'She used to be a Liberal Democrat councillor from Northumberland,' said Robin, who had just read this on the Level Playing Field's website.

'Child abuse,' said Chiswell suddenly. 'That's how I know her. Child abuse. She was on some committee. She's a bloody crank about it, sees it everywhere. Course, it's full of cranks, the Lib Dems. It's where they congregate. Stuffed to the gunnels with oddballs.'

He stood up, leaving a smattering of dandruff behind him on the black leather, and paced up and down, frowning.

'All this charity stuff's bound to come out sooner or later,' he said, echoing Sir Kevin's wife. 'But, my Christ, they wouldn't want it to break right now, not with Della up to her neck in the Paralympics. Winn's going to panic when he finds out I know. Yerse. I think this might well neutralise him ... in the short term, anyway. If he's been fiddling with children, though—'

'There's no proof of that,' said Robin.

'—that would stymie him for good,' said Chiswell, pacing again. 'Well, well, well. This explains why Winn wanted to bring his trustees to our Paralympian reception next Thursday, doesn't it? He's clearly trying to keep them sweet, stop anyone else deserting the sinking ship. Prince Harry's going to be there. These charity people love a royal. Only reason half of them are in it.'

He scratched his thick mop of grey hair, revealing large patches of underarm sweat.

'Here's what we'll do,' he said. 'We'll add his trustees to the guest list and you can come too. Then you can corner this Curtis-Lacey, find out what she's got. All right? Night of the twelfth?'

'Yes,' said Robin, making a note, 'Fine.'

'In the meantime, I'll let Winn know I know he's had his fingers in the till.'

Robin was almost at the door when Chiswell said abruptly:

'You don't want a PA's job, I suppose?'

'Sorry?'

'Take over from Izzy? What does that detective pay you? I could probably match it. I need somebody with brains and a bit of backbone.'

'I'm ... happy where I am,' said Robin.

Chiswell grunted.

'Hmm. Well, perhaps it's better this way. I might well have a bit more work for you, once we've got rid of Winn and Knight. Off you go, then.'

He turned his back to her, his hand already on the phone.

Out in the sunshine, Robin took out her mobile again. Strike still hadn't called, but Matthew had texted the name of a pub in Mayfair, conveniently close to Sarah's work. Nevertheless, Robin was now able to contemplate the evening with slightly more cheerfulness than she had felt prior to her meeting with Chiswell. She even started humming Bob Marley as she walked back towards the Houses of Parliament.

He told me you were his best. Yerse. Said so.

26

I am not so entirely alone, even now. There are two of us to bear the solitude together here.

Henrik Ibsen, *Rosmersholm*

It was four in the morning, the hopeless hour when shivering insomniacs inhabit a world of hollow shadow, and existence seems frail and strange. Strike, who had fallen into a doze, woke abruptly in the hospital chair. For a second, all he felt was his aching body and the hunger that tore at his stomach. Then he saw his nine-year-old nephew, Jack, who lay motionless in the bed beside him, jelly pads over his eyes, a tube running down his throat, lines coming out of neck and wrist. A bag of urine hung from the side of the bed, while three separate drips fed their contents into a body that appeared tiny and vulnerable amid the softly humming machines, in the hushed, cavernous space of the intensive care ward.

He could hear the padding of a nurse's soft shoes somewhere beyond the curtain surrounding Jack's bed. They hadn't wanted Strike to spend the night in the chair, but he had dug in and his celebrity, minor though it was, combined with his disability, had worked in his favour. His crutches stood propped against the bedside cabinet. The ward was overwarm, as hospitals always were. Strike had spent many weeks in a series of iron beds after his leg had been blown off. The smell transported him back to a time of pain and brutal readjustment, when he had been forced to recalibrate his life against a backdrop of endless obstacles, indignities and privations.

The curtain rustled and a nurse entered the cubicle, stolid and practical in her overalls. Seeing that he was awake, she gave Strike a brief, professional smile, then took the clipboard off the end of Jack's bed and went to take readings from the screens monitoring his blood pressure and oxygen levels. When she had finished, she whispered, 'Fancy a cup of tea?'

'Is he doing all right?' Strike asked, not bothering to disguise the plea in his voice. 'How's everything looking?'

'He's stable. No need to worry. This is what we expect at this stage. Tea?'

'Yeah, that'd be great. Thanks very much.'

He realised that his bladder was full once the curtain had closed behind the nurse. Wishing he'd thought to ask her to pass his crutches, Strike hoisted himself up, holding the arm of the chair to steady himself, hopped to the wall and grabbed them, then swung out from behind the curtain and off towards the brightly lit rectangle at the far end of the dark ward.

Having relieved himself at a urinal beneath a blue light that was supposed to thwart junkies' ability to locate veins, he headed into the waiting room close to the ward where, late yesterday afternoon, he had sat waiting for Jack to come out of emergency surgery. The father of one of Jack's school friends, with whom Jack was meant to be staying the night when his appendix burst, had kept him company. The man had been determined not to leave Strike alone until they had 'seen the little chap out of the woods', and had talked nervously all the time Jack had been in surgery, saying things like 'they bounce at that age', 'he's a tough little bugger', 'lucky we only live five minutes from school' and, over and over again, 'Greg and Lucy'll be going frantic'. Strike had said nothing, barely listening, holding himself ready for the worst news, texting Lucy every thirty minutes with an update.

Not yet out of surgery.

No news yet.

At last the surgeon had come to tell them that Jack, who had had to be resuscitated on arrival at hospital, had made it through surgery, that he had had 'a nasty case of sepsis' and that he would shortly be arriving in intensive care.

'I'll bring his mates in to see him,' said Lucy and Greg's pal excitedly. 'Cheer him up – Pokémon cards—'

'He won't be ready for that,' said the surgeon repressively. 'He'll be under heavy sedation and on a ventilator for at least the next twenty-four hours. Are you the next of kin?'

'No, that's me,' croaked Strike, speaking at last, his mouth dry. 'I'm his uncle. His parents are in Rome for their wedding anniversary. They're trying to get a flight back right now.'

'Ah, I see. Well, he's not quite out of the woods yet, but the surgery was successful. We've cleaned out his abdomen and put a drain in. They'll be bringing him down shortly.'

'Told you,' said Lucy and Greg's friend, beaming at Strike with tears in his eyes, 'told you they bounce!'

'Yeah,' said Strike, 'I'd better let Lucy know.'

But in a calamity of errors, Jack's panic-stricken parents had arrived at the airport, only to realise that Lucy had somehow lost her passport between hotel room and departure gate. In fruitless desperation they retraced their steps, trying to explain their dilemma to everyone from hotel staff, police and the British embassy, with the upshot that they had missed the last flight of the night.

At ten past four in the morning, the waiting room was mercifully deserted. Strike turned on the mobile he had kept switched off while on the ward and saw a dozen missed calls from Robin and one from Lorelei. Ignoring them, he texted Lucy who, he knew, would be awake in the Rome hotel to which, shortly past midnight, her passport had been delivered by the taxi driver who had found it. Lucy had implored Strike to send a picture of Jack when he got out of surgery. Strike had pretended that the picture wouldn't load. After the stress of the day, Lucy didn't need to see her son ventilated, his eyes covered in pads, his body swamped by the baggy hospital gown.

All looking good, he typed. **Still sedated but nurse confident.**

He pressed send and waited. As he had expected, she responded within two minutes.

You must be exhausted. Have they given you a bed at the hospital?

No, I'm sitting next to him, Strike responded. **I'll stay here until you get back. Try and get some sleep and don't worry x.**

Strike switched off his mobile, dragged himself back onto his one foot, reorganised his crutches and returned to the ward.

The tea was waiting for him, as pale and milky as anything Denise had made, but after emptying two sachets of sugar into it, he drank it in a couple of gulps, eyes moving between Jack and the machines both supporting and monitoring him. He had never before examined the boy so closely. Indeed, he had never had much to do with him, in spite of the pictures he drew for Strike, which Lucy passed on.

'He hero-worships you,' Lucy had told Strike several times. 'He wants to be a soldier.'

But Strike avoided family get-togethers, partly because he disliked Jack's father, Greg, and partly because Lucy's desire to cajole her brother into some more conventional mode of existence was enervating even without the presence of her sons, the eldest of whom Strike found especially like his father. Strike had no desire to have children and while he was prepared to concede that some of them were likeable – was prepared to admit, in fact, that he had conceived a certain detached fondness for Jack, on the back of Lucy's tales of his ambition to join the Red Caps – he had steadfastly resisted birthday parties and Christmas get-togethers at which he might have forged a closer connection.

But now, as dawn crept through the thin curtains blocking Jack's bed from the rest of the ward, Strike saw for the first time the boy's resemblance to his grandmother, Strike's own mother, Leda. He had the same very dark hair, pale skin and finely drawn mouth. He would, in fact, have made a beautiful girl, but Leda's son knew what puberty was about to do to the boy's jaw and neck . . . if he lived.

Course he's going to bloody live. The nurse said—

He's in intensive fucking care. They don't put you in here for hiccoughs.

He's tough. Wants to join the military. He'll be OK.

He'd fucking better be. I never even sent him a text to say thank you for his pictures.

It took Strike a while to drop back into an uneasy doze.

He was woken by early morning sunshine penetrating his eyelids. Squinting against the light, he heard footsteps squeaking on the floor. Next came a loud rattle as the curtain was pulled back, opening Jack's bed to the ward again and revealing more motionless figures, lying in beds all around them. A new nurse stood beaming at him, younger, with a long dark ponytail.

'Hi!' she said brightly, taking Jack's clipboard. 'It's not often we get anyone famous in here! I know all about you, I read everything about how you caught that serial—'

'This is my nephew, Jack,' he said coldly. The idea of discussing the Shacklewell Ripper now was repugnant to him. The nurse's smile faltered.

'Would you mind waiting outside the curtain? We need to take bloods, change his drips and his catheter.'

Strike dragged himself back onto his crutches and made his way laboriously out of the ward again, trying not to focus on any of the other inert figures wired to their own buzzing machines.

The canteen was already half-full when he got there. Unshaven and heavy-eyed, he had slid his tray all the way to the till and paid before he realised he could not carry it and manage his crutches. A young girl clearing tables spotted his predicament and came to help.

'Cheers,' said Strike gruffly, when she had placed the tray on a table beside a window.

'No probs,' said the girl. 'Leave it there after, I'll get it.'

The small kindness made Strike feel disproportionately emotional. Ignoring the fry-up he had just bought, he took out his phone and texted Lucy again.

All fine, nurse changing his drip, will be back with him shortly. X

As he had half-expected, his phone rang as soon as he had cut into his fried egg.

'We've got a flight,' Lucy told him without preamble, 'but it's not until eleven.'

'No problem,' he told her. 'I'm not going anywhere.'

'Is he awake yet?'

'No, still sedated.'

'He'll be so chuffed to see you, if he wakes up before – before—'

She burst into tears. Strike could hear her still trying to talk through her sobs.

'. . . just want to get home . . . want to see him . . .'

For the first time in Strike's life, he was glad to hear Greg, who now took the phone from his wife.

'We're bloody grateful, Corm. This is our first weekend away together in five years, can you believe it?'

'Sod's law.'

'Yeah. He said his belly was sore, but I thought he was at it. Thought he didn't want us to go away. I feel a right bastard now, I can tell you.'

'Don't worry,' said Strike, and again, 'I'm going nowhere.'

After a few more exchanges and a tearful farewell from Lucy, Strike was left to his full English. He ate methodically and without pleasure amid the clatter and jangle of the canteen, surrounded by other miserable and anxious people tucking into fatty, sugar-laden food.

As he was finishing the last of his bacon, a text from Robin arrived.

I've been trying to call with an update on Winn. Let me know when it's convenient to talk.

The Chiswell case seemed a remote thing to Strike just now, but as he read her text he suddenly had a simultaneous craving for nicotine and to hear Robin's voice. Abandoning his tray with thanks to the kind girl who had helped him to his table, he set off again on his crutches.

A cluster of smokers stood around the entrance to the hospital, hunch-shouldered like hyenas in the clean morning air. Strike lit up, inhaled deeply, and called Robin back.

'Hi,' he said, when she answered. 'Sorry I haven't been in touch, I've been at a hospital—'

'What's happened? Are you OK?'

'Yeah, I'm fine. It's my nephew, Jack. His appendix burst yesterday and he – he's got—'

To Strike's mortification, his voice cracked. As he fought to conquer himself, he wondered how long it had been since he had cried. Perhaps not since the tears of pain and rage he had shed in the hospital in Germany to which he had been airlifted away from the patch of bloody ground where the IED had ripped off his leg.

'Fuck,' he muttered at last, the only syllable he seemed able to manage.

'Cormoran, what's happened?'

'He's – they've got him in intensive care,' said Strike, his face crumpled up in the effort to hold himself together, to speak normally. 'His mum – Lucy and Greg are stuck in Rome, so they asked me—'

'Who's with you? Is Lorelei there?'

'Christ, no.'

Lorelei saying 'I love you' seemed weeks in the past, though it was only two nights ago.

'What are the doctors saying?'

'They think he'll be OK, but, you know, he's – he's in intensive care. Shit,' croaked Strike, wiping his eyes, 'sorry. It's been a rough night.'

'Which hospital is it?'

He told her. Rather abruptly, she said goodbye and rang off. Strike was left to finish his cigarette, intermittently wiping his face and nose on the sleeve of his shirt.

The quiet ward was bright with sun when he returned. He propped his crutches against the wall, sat down again at Jack's bedside with the day-old newspaper he had just pilfered from the waiting room and read an article about how Arsenal might soon be losing Robin van Persie to Manchester United.

An hour later, the surgeon and the anaesthetist in charge of the ward arrived at the foot of Jack's bed to inspect him, while Strike listened uneasily to their muttered conversation.

'. . . haven't managed to get his oxygen levels below fifty per cent . . . persistent pyrexia . . . urine outputs have tailed off in the last four hours . . . '

'. . . another chest X-ray, check there's nothing going on in the lungs . . . '

Frustrated, Strike waited for somebody to throw him digestible information. At last the surgeon turned to speak to him.

'We'll be keeping him sedated just now. He's not ready to come off the oxygen and we need to get his fluid balance right.'

'What does that mean? Is he worse?'

'No, it often goes like this. He had a very nasty infection. We had to wash out the peritoneum pretty thoroughly. I'd just like to X-ray the chest as a precaution, make sure we haven't punctured anything resuscitating him. I'll pop in to see him again later.'

They walked away to a heavily bandaged teenager covered in even more tubes and lines than Jack, leaving Strike anxious and destabilised in their wake. Through the hours of the night Strike had come to see the machines as essentially friendly, assisting his nephew to recovery. Now they seemed implacable judges holding up numbers indicating that Jack was failing.

'Fuck,' Strike muttered again, shifting the chair nearer to the bed. 'Jack . . . your mum and dad . . . ' He could feel a traitorous prickle behind the eyelids. Two nurses were walking past. '. . . shit . . . '

With an almighty effort he controlled himself and cleared his throat.

'. . . sorry, Jack, your mum wouldn't like me swearing in your ear . . . it's Uncle Cormoran here, by the way, if you didn't . . . anyway, Mum and Dad are on their way back, OK? And I'll be with you until they—'

He stopped mid-sentence. Robin was framed in the distant doorway of the ward. He watched her asking directions from a ward sister, and then she came walking towards him, wearing jeans and a T-shirt, her eyes their usual blue-grey and her hair loose, and holding two polystyrene cups.

Seeing Strike's unguarded expression of happiness and gratitude, Robin felt amply repaid for the bruising argument with Matthew, the two changes of bus and the taxi it had taken to get here. Then the slight prone figure beside Strike came into view.

'Oh no,' she said softly, coming to a halt at the foot of the bed.

'Robin, you didn't have to—'

'I know I didn't,' said Robin. She pulled a chair up beside Strike's. 'But I wouldn't want to have to deal with this alone. Be careful, it's hot,' she added, passing him a tea.

He took the cup from her, set it down on the bedside cabinet, then reached out and gripped her hand painfully tightly. He had released her before she could squeeze back. Then both sat staring at Jack for a few seconds, until Robin, her fingers throbbing, asked:

'What's the latest?'

'He still needs the oxygen and he's not peeing enough,' said Strike. 'I don't know what that means. I'd rather have a score out of ten or – I don't fucking know. Oh, and they want to X-ray his chest in case they punctured his lungs putting that tube in.'

'When was the operation?'

'Yesterday afternoon. He collapsed doing cross-country at school. Some friend of Greg and Lucy's who lives right by the school came with him in the ambulance and I met them here.'

Neither spoke for a while, their eyes on Jack.

Then Strike said, 'I've been a bloody terrible uncle. I don't know any of their birthdays. I couldn't have told you how old he was. The dad of his mate's who brought him in knew more than me. Jack wants to be a soldier, Luce says he talks about me and he draws me pictures and I never even bloody thank him.'

'Well,' said Robin, pretending not to see that Strike was dabbing roughly at his eyes with his sleeve, 'you're here for him right now when he needs you and you've got plenty of time to make it up to him.'

'Yeah,' said Strike, blinking rapidly. 'You know what I'll do if he—? I'll take him to the Imperial War Museum. Day trip.'

'Good idea,' said Robin kindly.

'Have you ever been?'

'No,' said Robin.

'Good museum.'

Two nurses, one male, one the woman whom Strike had earlier snubbed, now approached.

'We need to X-ray him,' said the girl, addressing Robin rather than Strike. 'Would you mind waiting outside the ward?'

'How long will you be?' asked Strike.

'Half an hour. Forty minutes-ish.'

So Robin fetched Strike's crutches and they went to the canteen.

'This is really good of you, Robin,' Strike said over two more pallid teas and some ginger biscuits, 'but if you've got things to do—'

'I'll stay until Greg and Lucy come,' said Robin. 'It'll be awful for them, being so far away. Matt's twenty-seven and his dad was still worried sick when Matt was so ill in the Maldives.'

'Was he?'

'Yeah, you know, when he – oh, of course. I never told you, did I?'

'Told me what?'

'He got a nasty infection on our honeymoon. Scratched himself on some coral. They were talking about airlifting him off to hospital at one point, but it was OK. Wasn't as bad as they first thought.'

As she said it, she remembered pushing open the wooden door still hot from the daylong sun, her throat constricted with fear as she prepared to tell Matthew she wanted an annulment, little knowing what she was about to face.

'You know, Matt's mum died not that long ago, so Geoffrey was really scared about Matt ... but it was all OK,' Robin repeated, taking a sip of her tepid tea, her eyes on the woman behind the counter, who was ladling baked beans onto a skinny teenager's plate.

Strike watched her. He had sensed omissions in her story. *Blame sea-borne bacteria.*

'Must've been scary,' he said.

'Well, it wasn't fun,' said Robin, examining her short, clean fingernails, then checking her watch. 'If you want a cigarette we should go now, he'll be back soon.'

One of the smokers they joined outside was wearing pyjamas. He had brought his drip with him, and held it tightly like a shepherd's crook to keep himself steady. Strike lit up and exhaled towards a clear blue sky.

'I haven't asked about your anniversary weekend.'

'I'm sorry I couldn't work,' said Robin quickly. 'It had been booked and—'

'That's not why I was asking.'

She hesitated.

'It wasn't great, to be honest.'

'Ah, well. Sometimes when there's pressure to have a good time—'

'Yes, exactly,' said Robin.

After another short pause she asked:

'Lorelei's working today, I suppose?'

'Probably,' said Strike. 'What is this, Saturday? Yeah, I suppose so.'

They stood in silence while Strike's cigarette shrank, millimetre by millimetre, watching visitors and arriving ambulances. There was no awkwardness between them, but the air seemed charged, somehow, with things wondered and unspoken. Finally Strike pressed out the stub of his cigarette in a large open ashtray that most smokers had ignored and checked his phone.

'They boarded twenty minutes ago,' he said, reading Lucy's last text. 'They should be here by three.'

'What happened to your mobile?' asked Robin, looking at the heavily sellotaped screen.

'Fell on it,' said Strike. 'I'll get a new one when Chiswell pays us.'

They passed the X-ray machine being rolled out of the ward as they walked back inside.

'Chest looks fine!' said the radiographer pushing it.

They sat by Jack's side talking quietly for another hour, until Robin went to buy more tea and chocolate bars from nearby vending machines, which they consumed in the waiting room while Robin filled Strike in about everything she had discovered about Winn's charity.

'You've outdone yourself,' said Strike, halfway down his second Mars bar. 'That was excellent work, Robin.'

'You don't mind that I told Chiswell?'

'No, you had to. We're up against it time-wise with Mitch Patterson sniffing round. Has this Curtis-Lacey woman accepted the invitation to the reception?'

'I'll find out on Monday. What about Barclay? How's he getting on with Jimmy Knight?'

'Still nothing we can use,' Strike sighed, running a hand over the stubble that was rapidly becoming a beard, 'but I'm hopeful. He's good, Barclay. He's like you. Got an instinct for this stuff.'

A family shuffled into the waiting room, the father sniffing and the mother sobbing. The son, who looked barely older than six, stared at Strike's missing leg as though it was merely one more horrible detail in the nightmarish world he had suddenly entered. Strike and Robin glanced at each other and left, Robin carrying Strike's tea as he swung along on his crutches.

Once settled beside Jack again, Strike asked, 'How did Chiswell react when you told him everything you'd got on Winn?'

'He was delighted. As a matter of fact, he offered me a job.'

'I'm always surprised that doesn't happen more often,' said Strike, unperturbed.

Just then, the anaesthetist and surgeon converged at the foot of Jack's bed again.

'Well, things are looking up,' said the anaesthetist. 'His X-ray's clear and his temperature's coming down. That's the thing with children,' he said, smiling at Robin. 'They travel fast in both directions. We're going to see how he manages with a little less oxygen, but I think we're getting on top of things.'

'Oh, thank God,' said Robin.

'He's going to live?' said Strike.

'Oh yes, I think so,' said the surgeon, with a touch of patronage. 'We know what we're doing in here, you know.'

'Gotta let Lucy know,' muttered Strike, trying and failing to get up, feeling weaker at good news than he'd felt at bad. Robin fetched his crutches and helped him into a standing position. As she watched him swinging towards the waiting room, she sat back down, exhaled loudly and put her face briefly into her hands.

'Always worst for the mothers,' said the anaesthetist kindly.

She didn't bother to correct him.

Strike was away for twenty minutes. When he returned, he said:

'They've just landed. I've warned her how he looks, so they're prepared. They should be here in about an hour.'

'Great,' said Robin.

'You can head off, Robin. I didn't mean to balls up your Saturday.'

'Oh,' said Robin, feeling oddly deflated. 'OK.'

She stood up, took her jacket off the back of the chair and collected her bag.

'If you're sure?'

'Yeah, yeah, I'll probably try and get a kip in now we know he's going to be all right. I'll walk you out.'

'There's no need—'

'I want to. I can have another smoke.'

But when they reached the exit, Strike walked on with her, away from the huddled smokers, past the ambulances and the car park that seemed to stretch for miles, roofs glimmering like the backs of marine creatures, surfacing through a dusty haze.

'How did you get here?' he asked, once they were away from the crowds, beside a patch of lawn surrounded by stocks whose scent mingled with the smell of hot tarmac.

'Bus, then cab.'

'Let me give you the cab fare—'

'Don't be ridiculous. Seriously, no.'

'Well . . . thanks, Robin. It made all the difference.'

She smiled up at him.

''S'what friends are for.'

Awkwardly, leaning on his crutches, he bent towards her. The hug was brief and she broke away first, afraid that he was going to overbalance. The kiss that he had meant to plant on her cheek landed on her mouth as she turned her face towards him.

'Sorry,' he muttered.

'Don't be silly,' she said again, blushing.

'Well, I'd better get back.'

'Yes, of course.'

He turned away.

'Let me know how he is,' she called after him, and he raised one hand in acknowledgement.

Robin walked away without looking back. She could still feel the shape of his mouth on hers, her skin tingling where his stubble had scratched her, but she did not rub the sensation away.

Strike had forgotten that he had meant to have another cigarette. Whether because he was now confident that he would be able to take his nephew to the Imperial War Museum, or for some other reason, his exhaustion was now stippled with a crazy light-heartedness, as though he had just taken a shot of spirits. The dirt and heat of a London afternoon, with the smell of stocks in the air, seemed suddenly full of beauty.

It was a glorious thing, to be given hope, when all had seemed lost.

27

They cling to their dead a long time at Rosmersholm.

Henrik Ibsen, *Rosmersholm*

By the time Robin found her way back across London to the unfamiliar cricket ground, it was five in the afternoon and Matthew's charity match was over. She found him back in his street clothes in the bar, fuming and barely speaking to her. Matthew's side had lost. The other team was crowing.

Facing an evening of being ignored by her husband, and having no friends among his colleagues, Robin decided against going on to the restaurant with the two teams and their partners, and made her way home alone.

The following morning, she found Matthew fully dressed on the sofa, snoring drunkenly. They argued when he woke up, a row that lasted hours and resolved nothing. Matthew wanted to know why it was Robin's job to hurry off and hold Strike's hand, given that he had a girlfriend. Robin maintained that you were a lousy person if you left a friend alone to cope with a possibly dying child.

The row escalated, attaining levels of spite that had never yet been reached in a year of marital bickering. Robin lost her temper, and asked whether she was not owed time off for good behaviour, after a decade spent watching Matthew strut around various sports fields. He was genuinely stung.

'Well, if you don't enjoy it, you should have said!'

'Never occurred to you I might not, did it? Because I'm

supposed to see all your victories as mine, aren't I, Matt? Whereas *my* achievements—'

'Sorry, remind me what they are again?' Matthew said, a low blow he had never thrown at her before. 'Or are we counting *his* achievements as yours?'

Three days passed, and they had not forgiven each other. Robin had slept in the spare room every night since their row, rising early each morning so she could leave the house before Matthew was out of the shower. She felt a constant ache behind the eyes, an unhappiness which was easier to ignore while at work, but which settled back over her like a patch of low pressure once she turned her footsteps homewards each night. Matthew's silent anger pressed against the walls of their house, which, while twice the size of any space they had shared before, seemed darker and more cramped.

He was her husband. She had promised to try. Tired, angry, guilty and miserable, Robin felt as though she were waiting for something definitive to happen, something that would release them both with honour, without more filthy rows, with reasonableness. Over and again, her thoughts returned to the wedding day, when she had discovered that Matthew had deleted Strike's messages. With her whole heart, she regretted not leaving then, before he could scratch himself on coral, before she could be trapped, as she now saw it, by cowardice disguised as compassion.

As Robin approached the House of Commons on Wednesday morning, not yet focused on the day ahead, but pondering her marital problems, a large man in an overcoat peeled away from the railings where he had been mingling with the first tourists of the day and walked towards her. He was tall and broad-shouldered, with thick silver hair and a squashed, deeply pitted and lined face. Robin did not realise that she was his object until he halted right in front of her, large feet placed firmly at right angles, blocking her onward progress.

'Venetia? Can I have a quick word, love?'

She took a panicked half-step backwards, looking up into the hard, flat face, peppered with wide pores. He had to be press. Did he recognise her? The hazel contact lenses were a little more discernible at close quarters, even through her plain-lensed glasses.

'Just started working for Jasper Chiswell, haven't you, love? I was wondering how that came about. How much is he paying you? Known him long?'

'No comment,' said Robin, trying to sidestep him. He moved with her. Fighting the rising feeling of panic, Robin said firmly, 'Get out of my way. I need to get to work.'

A couple of tall Scandinavian youths with rucksacks were watching the encounter with clear concern.

'I'm only giving you a chance to tell your side of the story, darling,' said her accoster, quietly. 'Think about it. Might be your only chance.'

He moved aside. Robin knocked into her would-be rescuers as she pushed past them. *Shit, shit, shit . . .* who was he?

Once safely past the security scanner, she moved aside in the echoing stone hall where workers were striding past her and called Strike. He didn't pick up.

'Call me, please, urgently,' she muttered to his voicemail.

Rather than heading for Izzy's office, or the wide echoing space of Portcullis House, she took refuge in one of the smaller tearooms, which without its counter and till would have resembled a dons' common room, panelled in dark wood and carpeted in the ubiquitous forest green. A heavy oak screen divided the room, MPs sitting at the far end, away from the lesser employees. She bought a cup of coffee, took a table beside the window, hung her coat on the back of her chair and waited for Strike to call her. The quiet, sedate space did little to calm Robin's nerves.

It was nearly three-quarters of an hour before Strike phoned.

'Sorry, missed you, I was on the Tube,' he said, panting. 'Then Chiswell called. He's only just rung off. We've got trouble.'

'Oh God, what now?' said Robin, setting her coffee down as her stomach contracted in panic.

'The *Sun* think you're the story.'

And at once, Robin knew whom she had just met outside the Houses of Parliament: Mitch Patterson, the private detective the newspaper had hired.

'They've been digging for anything new in Chiswell's life, and there you are, good-looking new woman in his office, of course they're going to check you out. Chiswell's first marriage split up because he had an affair at work. Thing is, it isn't going to take them long to find out you aren't really his goddaughter. *Ouch – fuck—*'

'What's the matter?'

'First day back on two legs and Dodgy Doc's finally decided to go and meet a girl on the sly. Chelsea Physic Garden, Tube to Sloane Square and a bugger of a walk. Anyway,' he panted, 'what's *your* bad news?'

'It's more of the same,' said Robin. 'Mitch Patterson just accosted me outside Parliament.'

'Shit. D'you think he recognised you?'

'He didn't seem to, but I don't know. I should clear out, shouldn't I?' said Robin, contemplating the cream ceiling, which was stuccoed in a pattern of overlapping circles. 'We could put someone else in here. Andy, or Barclay?'

'Not yet,' said Strike. 'If you walk out the moment you meet Mitch Patterson, it'll look like you're the story for sure. Anyway, Chiswell wants you to go to this reception tomorrow night, to try and get the rest of the dirt on Winn from that other trustee – what was her name, Elspeth? *Bollocks* – sorry – having trouble here, it's a bloody woodchip path. Dodgy's taking the girl for a walk into the undergrowth. She looks about seventeen.'

'Don't you need your phone, to take photographs?'

'I'm wearing those glasses with the inbuilt camera ... oh, here we go,' he added quietly. 'Dodgy's copping a feel in some bushes.'

Robin waited. She could hear a very faint clicking.

'And here come some genuine horticulturalists,' Strike muttered. 'That's driven them back out into the open ...

'Listen,' he continued, 'meet me at the office tomorrow after work, before you go to that reception. We'll take stock of everything we've got so far and make a decision on what to do next. Try your best to get the second listening device back, but don't replace it, just in case we need to take you out of there.'

'All right,' said Robin, full of foreboding, 'but it's going to

240

be difficult. I'm sure Aamir is suspic— Cormoran, I'm going to have to go.'

Izzy and Raphael had just walked into the tearoom. Raphael had his arm around his half-sister, who, Robin saw at once, was distressed to the point of tears. He saw Robin, who hastily hung up on Strike, made a grimace indicating that Izzy was in a bad way, then muttered something to his sister, who nodded and headed towards Robin's table, leaving Raphael to buy drinks.

'Izzy!' said Robin, pulling out a chair for her. 'Are you all right?'

As Izzy sat down, tears leaked out of her eyes. Robin passed her a paper napkin.

'Thanks, Venetia,' she said huskily. 'I'm so sorry. Making a fuss. Silly.'

She took a deep shuddering breath and sat upright, with the posture of a girl who had been told for years to sit up straight and pull herself together.

'Just silly,' she repeated, tears welling again.

'Dad's just been a total bastard to her,' said Raphael, arriving with a tray.

'Don't say that, Raff,' hiccoughed Izzy, another tear trickling down her nose. 'I know he didn't mean it. He was upset when I arrived and then I made it worse. Did you know he's lost Freddie's gold money clip?'

'No,' said Raphael, without much interest.

'He thinks he left it at some hotel on Kinvara's birthday. They'd just called him back when I arrived. They haven't got it. You know what Papa's like about Freddie, even now.'

An odd look passed over Raphael's face, as though he had been struck by an unpleasant thought.

'And then,' said Izzy, shakily, 'I'd misdated a letter and he flew off the handle . . .'

Izzy twisted the damp napkin between her hands.

'Five years,' she burst out. 'Five years I've worked for him, and I can count on one hand how many times he's thanked me for anything. When I told him I was thinking of leaving he said "not till after the Olympics"',' her voice quavered, '"because I don't want to have to break in someone new before then".'

Raphael swore under his breath.

'Oh, but he's not that bad, really,' said Izzy quickly, in an almost comical *volte-face*. Robin knew that she had just remembered her hope that Raphael would take over her job. 'I'm just upset, making it sound worse than it—'

Her mobile rang. She read the caller's name and let out a moan.

'Not TTS, not now, I can't. Raff, you speak to her.'

She held out the mobile to him, but Raphael recoiled as though asked to hold a tarantula.

'Please, Raff – *please* . . .'

With extreme reluctance, Raphael took the phone.

'Hi, Kinvara. Raff here, Izzy's out of the office. No . . . Venetia's not here . . . no . . . I'm at the office, obviously, I just picked up Izzy's phone . . . He's just gone to the Olympic Park. No . . . no, I'm not . . . I don't know where Venetia is, all I know is, she's not here . . . yes . . . yes . . . OK . . . bye, then—' He raised his eyebrows. 'Hung up.'

He pushed the phone back across the table to Izzy, who asked:

'Why's she so interested in where Venetia is?'

'Three guesses,' said Raphael, amused. Catching his drift, Robin looked out of the window, feeling the colour rising in her face. She wondered whether Mitch Patterson had called Kinvara, and planted this idea in her head.

'Oh, come orf it,' said Izzy. 'She thinks Papa's . . . ? Venetia's young enough to be his daughter!'

'In case you haven't noticed, so's his wife,' said Raphael, 'and you know what she's like. The further down the tubes their marriage goes, the more jealous she gets. Dad's not picking up his phone to her, so she's drawing paranoid conclusions.'

'Papa doesn't pick up because she drives him crazy,' said Izzy, her resentment towards her father suddenly submerged by dislike for her stepmother. 'For the last two years she's refused to budge from home or leave her bloody horses. Suddenly the Olympics are nearly here and London's full of celebrities and all she wants to do is come up to town, dressed up to the nines and play the minister's wife.'

She took another deep breath, blotted her face again, then stood up.

'I'd better get back, we're so busy. Thanks, Raff,' she said, cuffing him lightly on the shoulder.

She walked away. Raphael watched her go, then turned back to Robin.

'Izzy was the only one who bothered to visit me when I was inside, you know.'

'Yes,' said Robin. 'She said.'

'And when I used to have to go to bloody Chiswell House as a kid, she was the only one who'd talk to me. I was the little bastard who'd broken up their family, so they all hated my guts, but Izzy used to let me help her groom her pony.'

He swilled the coffee in his cup, looking sullen.

'I suppose you were in love with swashbuckling Freddie, were you, like all the other girls? He hated me. Used to call me "Raphaela" and pretend Dad had told the family I was another girl.'

'How horrible,' said Robin and Raphael's scowl turned into a reluctant smile.

'You're so sweet.'

He seemed to be debating with himself whether or not to say something. Suddenly he asked:

'Ever meet Jack o'Kent when you were visiting?'

'Who?'

'Old boy who used to work for Dad. Lived in the grounds of Chiswell House. Scared the hell out of me when I was a kid. He had a kind of sunken face and mad eyes and he used to loom out of nowhere when I was in the gardens. He never said a word except to swear at me if I got in his way.'

'I . . . vaguely remember someone like that,' lied Robin.

'Jack o' Kent was Dad's nickname for him. Who *was* Jack o'Kent? Didn't he have something to do with the devil? Anyway, I used to have literal nightmares about the old boy. One time he caught me trying to get into a barn and gave me hell. He put his face up close to mine and said words to the effect of, I wouldn't like what I saw in there, or it was dangerous for little boys, or . . . I can't remember exactly. I was only a kid.'

'That sounds scary,' Robin agreed, her interest awakened now. 'What was he doing in there, did you ever find out?'

'Probably just storing farm machinery,' said Raphael, 'but he made it sound like he was conducting Satanic rituals.

'He was a good carpenter, mind you. He made Freddie's coffin. An English oak had come down ... Dad wanted Freddie buried in wood from the estate ...'

Again, he seemed to be wondering whether he ought to say what was on his mind. He scrutinised at her through his dark lashes and finally said:

'Does Dad seem ... well, normal to you at the moment?'

'What d'you mean?'

'You don't think he's acting a bit strangely? Why's he bawling Izzy out for nothing?'

'Pressure of work?' suggested Robin.

'Yeah ... maybe,' said Raphael. Then, frowning, he said, 'He phoned me the other night, which is strange in itself, because he can't normally stand the sight of me. Just to talk, he said, and that's never happened before. Mind you, he'd had a few too many, I could tell as soon as he spoke.

'Anyway, he started rambling on about Jack o'Kent. I couldn't make out what he was going on about. He mentioned Freddie dying, and Kinvara's baby dying and then,' Raphael leaned in closer. Robin felt his knees touch hers under the table, 'remember that phone call we got, my first day here? That bloody creepy message about people pissing themselves as they die?'

'Yes,' said Robin.

'He said, "It's all punishment. That was Jack o'Kent calling. He's coming for me."'

Robin stared at him.

'But whoever it was on the phone,' said Raphael, 'it can't have been Jack o' Kent. He died years ago.'

Robin said nothing. She had suddenly remembered Matthew's delirium, the depth of that subtropical night, when he had thought she was his dead mother. Raphael's knees seemed to press harder into hers. She moved her chair back slightly.

'I was awake half the night wondering whether he's cracking up. We can't afford to have Dad go bonkers as well, can we? We've already got Kinvara hallucinating horse slashers and gravediggers—'

'Gravediggers?' repeated Robin sharply.

'Did I say gravediggers?' said Raphael restlessly. 'Well, you know what I mean. Men with spades in the woods.'

'You think she's imagining them?' asked Robin.

'No idea. Izzy and the rest of them think she is, but then they've treated her like a hysteric ever since she lost that kid. She had to go through labour even though they knew it had died, did you know that? She wasn't right afterwards, but when you're a Chiswell you're supposed to suck that sort of thing up. Put on a hat and go open a fête or something.'

He seemed to read Robin's thoughts in her face, because he said:

'Did you expect me to hate her, just because the others do? She's a pain in the arse, and she thinks I'm a total waste of space, but I don't spend my life mentally subtracting everything she spends on her horses from my niece and nephews' inheritance. She's not a gold-digger, whatever Izzy and *Fizzy* think,' he said, laying arch emphasis on his other sister's nickname. 'They thought my mother was a gold-digger, too. It's the only motivation they understand. I'm not supposed to know they've got cosy Chiswell family nicknames for me and my mother, as well . . . ' His dark skin flushed. 'Unlikely as it might seem, Kinvara genuinely fell for Dad, I could tell. She could have done a damn sight better if it was money she was after. He's skint.'

Robin, whose definition of 'skint' did not comprise owning a large house in Oxfordshire, nine horses, a mews flat in London or the heavy diamond necklace she had seen around Kinvara's neck in photographs, maintained an impassive expression.

'Have you been to Chiswell House lately?'

'Not lately,' said Robin.

'It's falling apart. Everything's moth-eaten and miserable.'

'The one time I really remember being at Chiswell House, the grown-ups were talking about a little girl who'd disappeared.'

'Really?' said Raphael, surprised.

245

'Yes, I can't remember her name. I was young myself. Susan? Suki? Something like that.'

'Doesn't ring any bells,' said Raphael. His knees brushed hers again. 'Tell me, does everyone confide their dark family secrets to you after five minutes of knowing you, or is it just me?'

'Tim always says I look sympathetic,' said Robin. 'Perhaps I should forget politics and go into counselling.'

'Yeah, maybe you should,' he said, looking into her eyes. 'That isn't a very strong prescription. Why bother with glasses? Why not just wear contacts?'

'Oh, I . . . find these more comfortable,' said Robin, pushing the glasses back up her nose and gathering her things. 'You know, I really ought to get going.'

Raphael leaned back in his chair with a rueful smile.

'Message received . . . he's a lucky man, your Tim. Tell him so, from me.'

Robin gave a half-laugh and stood up, catching herself on the corner of the table as she did so. Self-conscious and slightly flustered, she walked out of the tearoom.

Making her way back to Izzy's office, she mulled over the Minister for Culture's behaviour. Explosions of bad temper and paranoid ram-blings were not, she thought, surprising in a man currently at the mercy of two blackmailers, but Chiswell's suggestion that a dead man had telephoned him was undeniably odd. He had not struck her on either of their two encounters as the kind of man who would believe in either ghosts or divine retribution, but then, Robin reflected, drink brought out strange things in people . . . and suddenly, she remembered Matthew's snarling face as he had shouted across the sitting room on Sunday.

She was almost level with Winn's office door when she regis-tered the fact that it was standing ajar again. Robin peered into the room beyond. It seemed to be empty. She knocked twice. Nobody answered.

It took her less than five seconds to reach the power socket beneath Geraint's desk. Unplugging the fan, she prised the recording device loose and had just opened her handbag when Aamir's voice said:

'What the hell do you think you're doing?'

Robin gasped, attempted to stand up, hit her head hard on the desk and yelped in pain. Aamir had just unfolded himself from an armchair angled away from the door, was taking headphones from his ears. He seemed to have been taking a few minutes for himself, while listening to an iPod.

'I knocked!' Robin said, her eyes watering as she rubbed the top of her head. The recording device was still in her hand and she hid it behind her back. 'I didn't think anyone was in here!'

'What,' he repeated, advancing on her, 'are you *doing?*'

Before she could answer, the door was pushed fully open. Geraint walked in.

There was no lipless grin this morning, no air of bustling self-importance, no ribald comment at finding Robin on the floor of his office. Winn seemed somehow smaller than usual, with purplish shadows beneath the lens-shrunken eyes. In perplexity he turned from Robin to Aamir, and as Aamir began to tell him that Robin had just walked in uninvited, the latter managed to stuff the recording device into her handbag.

'I'm so sorry,' she said, getting to her feet, sweating profusely. Panic lapped at the edges of her thought, but then an idea bobbed up like a life raft. 'I really am. I was going to leave a note. I was only going to borrow it.'

As the two men frowned at her, she gestured to the unplugged fan.

'Ours is broken. Our room's like an oven. I didn't think you'd mind,' she said, appealing to Geraint. 'I was just going to borrow it for thirty minutes.' She smiled piteously. 'Honestly, I felt faint earlier.'

She plucked the front of her shirt away from her skin, which was indeed clammy. His gaze fell to her chest and the usual lecherous grin resurfaced.

'Though I shouldn't say so, overheating rather suits you,' said Winn, with the ghost of a smirk, and Robin forced a giggle.

'Well, well, we can spare it for thirty minutes, can't we?' he said, turning to Aamir. The latter said nothing, but stood ramrod straight, staring at Robin with undisguised suspicion. Geraint lifted the fan carefully off the desk and passed it to Robin. As she turned to go, he patted her lightly on the lower back.

'Enjoy.'

'Oh, I will,' she said, her flesh crawling. 'Thank you so much, Mr Winn.'

28

Do I take it to heart, to find myself so hampered and thwarted in my life's work?

Henrik Ibsen, *Rosmersholm*

The long hike to and around Chelsea Physic Garden the previous day had not benefited Strike's hamstring injury. As his stomach was playing up from a constant diet of Ibuprofen, he had eschewed pain-killers for the past twenty-four hours, with the result that he was in what his doctors liked to describe as 'some discomfort' as he sat with his one and a half legs up on the office sofa on Thursday afternoon, his prosthesis leaning against the wall nearby while he reviewed the Chiswell file.

Silhouetted like a headless watchman against the window of his inner office was Strike's best suit, plus a shirt and tie, which hung from the curtain rail, shoes and clean socks sitting below the limp trouser legs. He was going out to dinner with Lorelei tonight and had organised himself so that he need not climb the stairs to his attic flat again before bed.

Lorelei had been typically understanding about his lack of communication during Jack's hospitalisation, saying with only the slightest edge to her voice that it must have been a horrible thing to go through on his own. Strike had too much sense to tell her that Robin had been there, too. Lorelei had then requested, sweetly and without rancour, dinner, 'to talk a few things through'.

They had been dating for just over ten months and she had just nursed him through five days of incapacity. Strike felt that it was neither fair, nor decent, to ask her to say what she had to say over the phone. Like the hanging suit, the prospect of having to find an answer to the inevitable question 'where do you see this relationship going?' loomed ominously on the periphery of Strike's consciousness.

Dominating his thoughts, however, was what he saw as the perilous state of the Chiswell case, for which he had so far seen not a penny in payment, but which was costing him a significant outlay in salaries and expenses. Robin might have succeeded in neutralising the immediate threat of Geraint Winn, but after a promising start Barclay had nothing whatsoever to use against Chiswell's first blackmailer, and Strike foresaw disastrous consequences should the *Sun* newspaper find its way to Jimmy Knight. Balked of the mysterious photographs at the Foreign Office that Winn had promised him, and notwithstanding Chiswell's assertion that Jimmy would not want the story in the press, Strike thought an angry and frustrated Jimmy was overwhelmingly likely to try and profit from a chance that seemed to be slipping through his fingers. His history of litigation told its own story: Jimmy was a man prone to cutting off his own nose to spite his face.

To compound Strike's bad mood, after several straight days and nights hanging out with Jimmy and his mates, Barclay had told Strike that unless he went home soon, his wife would be initiating divorce proceedings. Strike, who owed Barclay expenses, had told him to come into the office for a cheque, after which he could take a couple of days off. To his extreme annoyance, the normally reliable Hutchins had then cavilled at having to take over the tailing of Jimmy Knight at short notice, rather than hanging around Harley Street, where Dodgy Doc was once again consulting patients.

'What's the problem?' Strike had asked roughly, his stump throbbing. Much as he liked Hutchins, he had not forgotten that the ex-policeman had recently taken time off for a family holiday and to drive his wife to hospital when she broke her wrist. 'I'm asking you to switch targets, that's all. I can't follow Knight, he knows me.'

'Yeah, all right, I'll do it.'

'Decent of you,' Strike had said, angrily. 'Thanks.'

The sound of Robin and Barclay climbing the metal stairs to

the office at half past five made a welcome distraction from Strike's increasingly dark mood.

'Hi,' said Robin, walking into the office with a holdall over her shoulder. Answering Strike's questioning look, she explained, 'Outfit for the Paralympic reception. I'll change in the loo, I won't have time to go home.'

Barclay followed Robin into the room and closed the door.

'We met downstairs,' he told Strike cheerfully. 'Firs' time.'

'Sam was just telling me how much dope he's had to smoke to keep in with Jimmy,' said Robin, laughing.

'I've no been inhalin',' said Barclay, deadpan. 'That'd be remiss, on a job.'

The fact that the pair of them seemed to have hit it off was perversely annoying to Strike, who was now making heavy weather of hoisting himself off the fake leather cushions, which made their usual farting noises.

'It's the sofa,' he snapped at Barclay, who had looked around, grinning. 'I'll get your money.'

'Stay there, I'll do it,' Robin said, setting down her holdall and reaching for the chequebook in the lower drawer of the desk, which she handed to Strike, with a pen. 'Want some tea, Cormoran? Sam?'

'Aye, go on, then,' said Barclay.

'You're both bloody cheerful,' said Strike sourly, writing Barclay his cheque, 'considering we're about to lose the job that's keeping us all in employment. Unless either of you have got information I don't know about, of course.'

'Only excitin' thing tae happen in Knightville this week was Flick havin' a big bust up wi' one o' her flatmates,' said Barclay. 'Lassie called Laura. She reckoned Jimmy had stolen a credit card out o' her handbag.'

'Had he?' asked Strike sharply.

'I'd say it was more likely to be Flick herself. Told ye she was boastin' about helpin' herself to cash from her work, didn't I?'

'Yeah, you did.'

'It all kicked off in the pub. The girl, Laura, was scunnered. She and Flick got intae a row about who was more middle class.'

In spite of the pain he was in, and his grumpy mood, Strike grinned.

'Aye, it got nasty. Ponies and foreign holidays dragged in. Then this Laura said she reckoned Jimmy nicked her new credit card off her, months back. Jimmy got aggressive, said that was slander—'

'Shame he's banned, or he could've sued her,' said Strike, ripping out the cheque.

'—and Laura ran off intae the night, bawlin'. She's left the flat.'

'Got a surname for her?'

'I'll try and find out.'

'What's Flick's background, Barclay?' asked Strike as Barclay put his cheque into his wallet.

'Well, she told me she dropped out o' uni,' said Barclay. 'Failed her first-year exams and gave up.'

'Some of the best people drop out,' said Robin, carrying two mugs of tea over. She and Strike had both left their degree courses without a qualification.

'Cheers,' said Barclay, accepting a mug from Robin. 'Her parents are divorced,' he went on, 'and she's no speaking tae either of them. They don't like Jimmy. Cannae blame them. If my daughter ever hooks up wi' a bawbag like Knight, I'll know what tae do about it. When she's not around, he tells the lads what he gets up to wi' young girls. They all think they're shaggin' a great revolutionary, doin' it for the cause. Flick doesnae know the half o' what he's up tae.'

'Any of them underage? His wife suggested he's got form there. That'd be a bargaining chip.'

'All over sixteen so far's I know.'

'Pity,' said Strike. He caught Robin's eye, as she returned to them holding her own tea. 'You know what I mean.' He turned to Barclay again. 'From what I heard on that march, she's not so monogamous herself.'

'Aye, one o' her pals made a gag about an Indian waiter.'

'A waiter? I heard a student.'

'No reason it couldn'ta been both,' said Barclay. 'I'd say she's a—'

But catching Robin's eye, Barclay decided against saying the word, and instead drank his tea.

'Anything new your end?' Strike asked Robin.

'Yes. I got the second listening device back.'

'You're kidding,' said Strike, sitting up straighter.

'I've only just finished transcribing it all, there was hours of stuff on there. Most of it's useless, but ...'

She set down her tea, unzipped the holdall and took out the recording device.

'... there's one strange bit. Listen to this.'

Barclay sat down on the arm of the sofa. Robin straightened up in her desk chair and flicked the switch on the device.

Geraint's lilting accent filled the office.

'... keep them sweet, make sure I introduce Elspeth to Prince Harry,' said Geraint. 'Right, that's me off, I'll see you tomorrow.'

'G'night,' said Aamir.

Robin shook her head at Strike and Barclay and mouthed, 'Wait.'

They heard the door close. After the usual thirty-second silence, there was a click, where the tape had stopped then restarted. A deep, Welsh female voice spoke.

'Are you there, sweetheart?'

Strike raised his eyebrows. Barclay stopped chewing.

'Yes,' said Aamir, in his flat London accent.

'Come and give me a kiss,' said Della.

Barclay made a small choking noise into his tea. The sound of lips smacking emanated from the bug. Feet shuffled. A chair was moved. There was a faint, rhythmic thudding.

'What's that?' muttered Strike.

'The guide dog's tail wagging,' said Robin.

'Let me hold your hand,' said Della. 'Geraint won't be back, don't worry, I've sent him out to Chiswick. There. Thank you. Now, I needed a little private word with you. The thing is, darling, your neighbours have complained. They say they've been hearing funny noises through the walls.'

'Like what?' He sounded apprehensive.

'Well, they thought they *might* be animal,' said Della. 'A dog whining or whimpering. You haven't—?'

'Of course I haven't,' said Aamir. 'It must've been the telly. Why would I get a dog? I'm at work all day.'

'I thought it would be like you to bring home some poor little stray,' she said. 'Your soft heart . . . '

'Well, I haven't,' said Aamir. He sounded tense. 'You don't have to take my word for it. You can go and check if you want, you've got a key.'

'Darling, don't be like that,' said Della. 'I wouldn't dream of letting myself in without your permission. I don't snoop.'

'You're within your rights,' he said, and Strike thought he sounded bitter. 'It's your house.'

'You're upset. I knew you would be. I had to mention it, because if Geraint picks up the phone to them next time – it was the purest good luck the neighbour caught me—'

'I'll make sure and keep the volume down from now on,' said Aamir. 'OK? I'll be careful.'

'You understand, my love, that as far as I'm concerned, you're free to do whatever—'

'Look, I've been thinking,' Aamir interrupted. 'I really think I should be paying you some rent. What if—'

'We've been over this. Don't be silly, I don't want your money.'

'But—'

'Apart from everything else,' she said, 'you couldn't afford it. A three-bedroomed house, on your own?'

'But—'

'We've been through this. You seemed happy when you first moved in . . . I thought you liked it—'

'Obviously, I like it. It was very generous of you,' he said stiffly.

'Generous . . . it's not a question of generosity, for heaven's sake . . . Now, listen: how would you like to come and have a curry? I've got a late vote and I was going to nip over to the Kennington Tandoori. My treat.'

'Sorry, I can't,' said Aamir. He sounded stressed. 'I've got to get home.'

'Oh,' said Della, with a great deal less warmth. 'Oh . . . that's disappointing. What a pity.'

'I'm sorry,' he said again. 'I said I'd meet a friend. University friend.'

'Ah. I see. Well, next time, I'll make sure to call ahead. Find a slot in your diary.'

'Della, I—'

'Don't be silly, I'm only teasing. You can walk out with me, at least?'

'Yes. Yes, of course.'

There was more scuffling, then the sound of the door opening. Robin turned off the tape.

'They're *shaggin'*?' said Barclay loudly.

'Not necessarily,' said Robin. 'The kiss might've been on the cheek.'

'"Let me hold your hand"?' repeated Barclay. 'Since when's that normal office procedure?'

'How old's this Aamir bloke?' asked Strike.

'I'd guess mid-twenties,' said Robin.

'And she's, what . . . ?'

'Mid-sixties,' said Robin.

'And she's provided him with a house. He's not related to her, is he?'

'There's no family connection as far as I'm aware,' said Robin. 'But Jasper Chiswell knows something personal about him. He quoted a Latin poem at Aamir when they met in our office.'

'You didn't tell me that.'

'Sorry,' said Robin, remembering that this had happened shortly before she had refused to tail Jimmy on the march. 'I forgot. Yes, Chiswell quoted something Latin, then mentioned "a man of your habits".'

'What was the poem?'

'I don't know, I never did Latin.'

She checked her watch.

'I'd better get changed, I'm supposed to be at DCMS in forty minutes.'

'Aye, that's me off as well, Strike,' said Barclay.

'Two days, Barclay,' Strike said, as the other headed to the door, 'then you're back on Knight.'

'Nae bother,' said Barclay, 'I'll be wantin' a break from the wean by then.'

'I like him,' said Robin, as Barclay's footsteps died away down the metal stairs.

'Yeah,' grunted Strike, as he reached for his prosthesis. 'He's all right.'

He and Lorelei were meeting early, at his request. It was time to begin the onerous process of making himself presentable. Robin retired to the cramped toilet on the landing to change, and Strike, having put his prosthesis back on, withdrew to the inner office.

He had got as far as pulling on his suit trousers when his mobile rang. Half-hoping that it was Lorelei to say that she could not make dinner, he picked up the cracked phone and saw, with an inexplicable sense of foreboding, that it was Hutchins.

'Strike?'

'What's wrong?'

'Strike ... I've fucked up.'

Hutchins sounded weak.

'What's happened?'

'Knight's with some mates. I followed them into a pub. They're planning something. He's got a placard with Chiswell's face on it—'

'And?' said Strike loudly.

'Strike, I'm sorry ... my balance has gone ... I've lost them.'

'You stupid fucker!' roared Strike, losing his temper completely. 'Why didn't you tell me you were ill?'

'I've had a lot of time off lately ... knew you were stretched ...'

Strike switched Hutchins to speakerphone, laid his mobile onto his desk, took his shirt off the hanger and began to dress as fast as possible.

'Mate, I'm so sorry ... I'm having trouble walking ...'

'I know the fucking feeling!'

Fuming, Strike stabbed off the call.

'Cormoran?' Robin called through the door. 'Everything OK?'

'No, it's fucking not!'

He opened the office door.

In one part of his brain, he registered that Robin was wearing the green dress he had bought her two years ago, as a thank you for helping him catch their first killer. She looked stunning.

'Knight's got a placard with Chiswell's face on it. He's planning something with a bunch of mates. I *knew* it, I fucking *knew* this would happen now Winn's bailed on him ... I'll bet you anything he's heading for your reception. Shit,' said Strike, realising he didn't have shoes on and doubling back. 'And Hutchins has lost them,' he shouted over his shoulder. 'The stupid tit didn't tell me he's ill.'

'Maybe you can get Barclay back?' suggested Robin.

'He'll be on the Tube by now. I'm going to have to fucking do it, aren't I?' said Strike. He dropped back into the sofa and slid his feet into his shoes. 'There are going to be press all round that place tonight if Harry's going to be there. All it needs is for a journo to twig what Jimmy's stupid fucking sign means, and Chiswell's out of a job and so're we.' He heaved himself back to his feet. 'Where is this thing, tonight?'

'Lancaster House,' said Robin. 'Stable Yard.'

'Right,' said Strike, heading for the door. 'Stand by. You might have to bail me out. There's a good chance I'm going to have to punch him.'

29

*It became impossible for me to remain an idle spectator any
longer.*

Henrik Ibsen, *Rosmersholm*

The taxi that Strike had picked up in Charing Cross Road turned
into St James's Street twenty minutes later, while he was still talking
to the Minister for Culture on his mobile.

'A placard? What's on it?'

'Your face,' said Strike. 'That's all I know.'

'And he's heading for the reception? Well, this is bloody it, isn't
it?' shouted Chiswell, so loudly that Strike winced and removed the
phone from his ear. 'If the press see this, it's all over! You were supposed to stop something like this bloody happening!'

'And I'm going to try,' said Strike, 'but in your shoes I'd want to
be forewarned. I'd advise—'

'I don't pay you for advice!'

'I'll do whatever I can,' promised Strike, but Chiswell had
already hung up.

'I'm not going to be able to go any further, mate,' said the taxi-
driver, addressing Strike in the rear-view mirror from which dangled
a swinging mobile, outlined in tufts of multi-coloured cotton and
embossed with a golden Ganesh. The end of St James's Street had
been blocked off. A swelling crowd of royal watchers and Olympics
fans, many clutching small Union Jacks, was congregating behind
portable barriers, waiting for the arrival of Paralympians and
Prince Harry.

'OK, I'll get out here,' said Strike, fumbling for his wallet.

He was once again facing the crenellated frontage of St James's Palace, its gilded, diamond-shaped clock gleaming in the early evening sun. Strike limped down the slope again towards the crowd, passing the side street where Pratt's stood, while smartly dressed passers-by, workers and customers of galleries and wine merchants moved aside courteously as his uneven gait became progressively more pronounced.

'*Fuck, fuck, fuck*,' he muttered, pain shooting up into his groin every time he put his weight onto the prosthesis as he drew closer to the assembled sports fans and royal watchers. He could see no placards or banners of a political nature, but as he joined the back of the crowd and looked down Cleveland Row, he spotted a press pen and ranks of photographers, which stood waiting for the prince and famous athletes. It was only when a car slid past, containing a glossy-haired brunette Strike vaguely recognised from the television, that he remembered he had not called Lorelei to tell her he would be late to dinner. He hastily dialled her number.

'Hi, Corm.'

She sounded apprehensive. He guessed that she thought he was going to cancel.

'Hi,' he said, his eyes still darting around for some sign of Jimmy. 'I'm really sorry, but something's come up. I might be late.'

'Oh, that's fine,' she said, and he could tell that she was relieved that he was still intending to come. 'Shall I try and change the booking?'

'Yeah – maybe make it eight instead of seven?'

Turning for the third time to scan Pall Mall behind him, Strike spotted Flick's tomato-red hair. Eight CORE members were heading for the crowd, including a stringy, blond-dreadlocked youth and a short, thickset man who resembled a bouncer. Flick was the only woman. All bar Jimmy were holding placards with the broken Olympic rings on them, and slogans such as 'Fair Play Is Fair Pay' and 'Homes Not Bombs'. Jimmy was holding his own placard upside down, the picture on it turned inwards, parallel with his leg.

'Lorelei, I've got to go. Speak later.'

Uniformed police were walking around the perimeter fencing

keeping the crowds back, walkie-talkies in hand, eyes roving constantly over the cheerful spectators. They, too, had spotted CORE, who were trying to reach a spot opposite the press pen.

Gritting his teeth, Strike began to forge a path through the pressing crowd, eyes on Jimmy.

30

There is no denying it would have been more fortunate if we had succeeded in checking the stream at an earlier point.

Henrik Ibsen, *Rosmersholm*

Slightly self-conscious in her clinging green dress and heels, Robin attracted a considerable number of appreciative glances from male passers-by as she climbed out of her taxi at the entrance to the Department for Culture, Media and Sport. As she reached the doorway, she saw approaching from fifty yards away Izzy, who was wearing bright orange, and Kinvara, in what appeared to be the slinky black dress and heavy diamond necklace that she had worn in the photograph that Robin had seen of her online.

Acutely anxious about what was happening with Jimmy and Strike, Robin nevertheless registered that Kinvara appeared to be upset. Izzy rolled her eyes at Robin as they approached. Kinvara gave Robin a pointed up-and-down look that suggested she found the green dress inappropriate, if not indecent.

'We were supposed,' said a booming male voice in Robin's near vicinity, 'to be meeting *here.*'

Jasper Chiswell had just emerged from the building, carrying three engraved invitations, one of which he held out to Robin.

'Yes, I know that now, Jasper, thank you,' said Kinvara, puffing slightly as she approached. 'Very sorry for getting it wrong again. Nobody bothered to check I knew what the arrangements were.'

Passers-by stared at Chiswell, finding him vaguely familiar with his chimney-brush hair. Robin saw a suited man nudge his companion and point. A sleek black Mercedes drew up at the kerb. The chauffeur got out; Kinvara walked around the back of the car to sit behind him. Izzy wriggled over into the middle of the back seat, leaving Robin to take the back seat directly behind Chiswell.

The car pulled away from the kerb, the atmosphere inside unpleasant. Robin turned her head to watch the after-work drinkers and evening shoppers, wondering whether Strike had found Knight yet, scared of what might happen when he did, and wishing she could spirit the car directly to Lancaster House.

'You haven't invited Raphael, then?' Kinvara shot at the back of her husband's head.

'No,' said Chiswell. 'He angled for an invitation, but that will be because he's smitten with Venetia.'

Robin felt her face flood with colour.

'Venetia seems to have quite the fan base,' said Kinvara tersely.

'Going to have a little chat with Raphael tomorrow,' said Chiswell. 'I'm seeing him rather differently these days, I don't mind telling you.'

Out of the corner of her eye, Robin saw Kinvara's hands twist around the chain on her ugly evening bag, which sported a horse's head picked out in crystals. A tense silence settled over the car's interior as it purred on through the warm city.

31

... the result was, that he got a thrashing ...

Henrik Ibsen, *Rosmersholm*

Adrenaline made it easier for Strike to block out the mounting pain in his leg. He was closing on Jimmy and his companions, who were being thwarted in their desire to show themselves clearly to the press, because the excitable crowd had pressed forwards as the first official cars began to glide past, hoping to spot some celebrities. Late to the party, CORE now found themselves faced by an impenetrable mass.

Mercedes and Bentleys swished past, affording the crowd glimpses of the famous and the not-so-famous. A comedian got a loud cheer as he waved. A few flashes went off.

Clearly deciding that he could not hope for a more prominent spot, Jimmy began to drag his homemade banner out of the tangle of legs around him, preparatory to hoisting it aloft.

A woman ahead of Strike gave a shriek of indignation as he pushed her out of the way. In three strides, Strike had closed his large left hand around Jimmy's right wrist, preventing him from raising the placard above waist height, forcing it back towards the ground. Strike had time to see the recognition in his eyes before Jimmy's fist came hurtling at his throat. A second woman saw the punch coming and screamed.

Strike dodged it and brought his left foot down hard on the placard, splintering the pole, but his amputated leg was not equal to bearing all his weight, especially as Jimmy's second punch connected.

As Strike crumpled, he hit Jimmy in the balls. Knight gave a soft scream of pain, doubled up, hit the falling Strike and both of them toppled over, knocking bystanders sideways, all of whom shouted their indignation. As Strike hit the pavement, one of Jimmy's companions aimed a kick at his head. Strike caught his foot and twisted it. Through the mounting furore, he heard a third woman shriek:

'They're attacking that man!'

Strike was too intent on seizing hold of Jimmy's mangled cardboard banner to care whether he was being cast as victim or aggressor. Tugging on the banner, which like himself was being trampled underfoot, he succeeded in ripping it. One of the pieces attached to the spike heel of a panicking woman trying to get out of the way of the fight, and was carried away.

Fingers closed around his neck from behind. He aimed an elbow at Jimmy's face and his hold loosened, but then somebody kicked Strike in the stomach and another blow hit him on the back of the head. Red spots popped in front of his eyes.

More shouting, a whistle, and the crowd was suddenly thinning around them. Strike could taste blood, but, from what he could see, the splintered and torn remnants of Jimmy's placard had been scattered by the mêlée. Jimmy's hands were again scrabbling at Strike's neck, but then Jimmy was pulled away, swearing fluently at the top of his voice. The winded Strike was seized and dragged to his feet as well. He put up no resistance. He doubted he could have stood of his own accord.

32

… and now we can go in to supper. Will you come in, Mr. Kroll?

Henrik Ibsen, *Rosmersholm*

Chiswell's Mercedes turned the corner of St James's Street onto Pall Mall and set off along Cleveland Row.

'What's going on?' growled Chiswell, as the car slowed, then stopped.

The shouting ahead was not of the excited, enthusiastic kind that royalty or celebrities might expect. Several uniformed officers were converging on the crowd on the left-hand side of the street which was jostling and pushing as it tried to move away from what appeared to be a confrontation between police and protestors. Two dishevelled men in jeans and T-shirts emerged from the fray, both held in arm-locks by uniformed officers: Jimmy Knight, and a youth with limp blond dreadlocks.

Then Robin bit back a cry of dismay as a hobbling, bloody Strike appeared, also being led along by police. Behind them, an altercation in the crowd had not subsided, but was growing. A barrier swayed.

'Pull up, PULL UP!' bellowed Chiswell at the driver, who had just begun to accelerate again. Chiswell wound down his window. 'Door open – Venetia, open your door! – that man!' Chiswell roared at a nearby policeman, who turned, startled, to see the Minister for Culture shouting at him and pointing at Strike. 'He's my guest – that man – bloody well let him go!'

Confronted by an official car, a government minister, the steely, patrician voice, the brandishing of a thick embossed invitation, the policeman did as he was told. Most people's attention was focused on the increasingly violent brawl between police and CORE, and the consequent trampling and pushing of the crowd trying to get away from it. A couple of cameramen had broken away from the press pen up ahead, and were running towards the fracas.

'Izzy, move up – get in, GET IN!' Chiswell snarled at Strike through the window.

Robin squeezed backwards, half-sitting in Izzy's lap to accommodate Strike as he clambered into the back seat. The door slammed. The car rolled on.

'Who are you?' squealed the frightened Kinvara, who was now pinned against the opposite door by Izzy. 'What's going on?'

'He's a private detective,' growled Chiswell. His decision to bring Strike into the car seemed born of panic. Twisting around in his seat to glare at Strike, he said, 'How does it help me if you get bloody arrested?'

'They weren't arresting me,' said Strike, dabbing his nose with the back of his hand. 'They wanted to take a statement. Knight attacked me when I went for his placard. Cheers,' he added, as, with difficulty given how tightly compressed they all were, Robin passed him a box of tissues that had been lying on the ledge behind the rear seat. He pressed one to his nose. 'I got rid of the placard,' Strike added, through the blood-stained tissue, but nobody congratulated him.

'Jasper,' said Kinvara, 'what's going—?'

'Shut up,' snapped Chiswell, without looking at her. 'I can't let you out in front of all these people,' he told Strike angrily, as though the latter had suggested it. 'There are more photographers . . . You'll have to come in with us. I'll fix it.'

The car was now proceeding towards a barrier where police and security were checking ID and investigations.

'Nobody say anything,' Chiswell instructed. '*Shut up*,' he added pre-emptively to Kinvara, who had opened her mouth.

A Bentley up ahead was admitted and the Mercedes rolled forwards.

In pain, because she was bearing a good proportion of Strike's weight across her left hip and leg, Robin heard screeching from behind the car. Turning, she saw a young woman running after the car, a female police officer chasing her. The girl had wild tomato-red hair, a T-shirt with a logo of broken Olympic rings on it, and she screamed after Chiswell's car:

'He put the fucking horse on them, Chiswell! He put the horse on them, you cheating, thieving bastard, you *murderer*—'

'I have a guest here who didn't get his invitation,' Chiswell was shouting through his wound-down window to the armed policeman at the barrier. 'Cormoran Strike, the amputee. He's been in the papers. There was a balls-up at my department, his invitation didn't go. The prince,' he said, with breathtaking chutzpah, 'asked to meet him specifically!'

Strike and Robin were watching what was happening behind the car. Two policemen had seized the struggling Flick and were escorting her away. A few more cameras flashed. Caving under the weight of ministerial pressure, the armed policeman requested ID of Strike. Strike, who always carried a couple of forms of identification, though not necessarily in his own name, passed over his genuine driving licence. A queue of stationary cars grew longer behind them. The prince was due in fifteen minutes' time. Finally, the policeman waved them through.

'Shouldn't have done that,' said Strike in an undertone to Robin. 'Shouldn't have let me in. Bloody lax.'

The Mercedes swung around the inner courtyard and arrived, finally, at the foot of a shallow flight of red-carpeted steps, in front of an enormous, honey-coloured building that resembled a stately home. Wheelchair ramps had been set either side of the carpet, and a celebrated wheelchair basketball player was already manoeuvring his way up one.

Strike pushed open the door, clambered out of the car, then turned and reached back inside to assist Robin. She accepted the offer of help. Her left leg was almost completely numb from where he'd sat on her.

'Nice to see you again, Corm,' said Izzy, beaming, as she got out behind Robin.

'Hi, Izzy,' said Strike.

Now burdened with Strike whether he wanted him or not,

Chiswell hurried up the steps to explain to one of the liveried men standing outside the front door that Strike must be admitted without his invitation. They heard a recurrence of the word 'amputee'. All around them, more cars were releasing their smartly dressed passengers.

'What's all this about?' Kinvara said, who had marched around the rear of the Mercedes to address Strike. 'What's going on? What does my husband need a private detective for?'

'*Will you be quiet, you stupid, stupid bitch?*'

Stressed and disturbed though Chiswell undoubtedly was, his naked hostility shocked Robin. *He hates her*, she thought. *He genuinely hates her.*

'You two,' said the minister, pointing at his wife and daughter, 'get inside.'

'Give me one good reason I should keep paying you,' he added, turning on Strike as still more people spilled past them. 'You realise,' said Chiswell, and in his necessarily quiet fury, spit flew from his mouth onto Strike's tie, 'I've just been called a bloody murderer in front of twenty people, including press?'

'They'll think she's a crank,' said Strike.

If the suggestion brought Chiswell any comfort, it didn't show.

'I want to see you tomorrow morning at ten o'clock,' he told Strike. 'Not at my office. Come to the flat in Ebury Street.' He turned away, then, as an afterthought, turned back. 'You too,' he barked at Robin.

Side by side, they watched him lumbering up the steps.

'We're about to get sacked, aren't we?' whispered Robin.

'I'd say it's odds on,' said Strike, who, now that he was on his feet, was in considerable pain.

'Cormoran, what was on the placard?' said Robin.

Strike allowed a woman in peach chiffon to pass, then said quietly:

'Picture of Chiswell hanging from a gallows and, beneath him, a bunch of dead children. One odd thing, though.'

'What?'

'All the kids were black.'

Still dabbing at his nose, Strike reached inside his pocket for a cigarette, then remembered where he was and let his hand fall back to his side.

'Listen, if that Elspeth woman's in here, you might as well try and find out what else she knows about Winn. It'll help justify our final invoice.'

'OK,' said Robin. 'The back of your head's bleeding, by the way.'

Strike dabbed at it ineffectually with the tissues he had pocketed and began to limp up the steps beside Robin.

'We shouldn't be seen together any more tonight,' he told her, as they passed over the threshold into a blaze of ochre, scarlet and gold. 'There was a café in Ebury Street, not far from Chiswell's house. I'll meet you there at nine o'clock tomorrow, and we can face the firing squad together. Go on, you go ahead.'

But as she moved away from him, towards the grand staircase, he called after her:

'Nice dress, by the way.'

33

I believe you could bewitch any one – if you set yourself to do it.
                    Henrik Ibsen, *Rosmersholm*

The grand hallway of the mansion constituted a vast empty block of space. A red-and-gold-carpeted central staircase led to an upper balcony that split left and right. The walls, which appeared to be of marble, were ochre, dull green and rose. Sundry Paralympians were being shown to a lift on the left of the entrance, but the limping Strike made his way laboriously to the stairs and heaved himself upwards by liberal use of the banister. The sky visible through a huge and ornate skylight, supported by columns, was fading through technicolour variations that intensified the colours of the massive Venetian paintings of classical subjects hanging on every wall.

Doing his best to walk naturally, because he was afraid he might be mistaken for some veteran Paralympian and perhaps asked to expound on past triumphs, Strike followed the crowd up the right staircase, around the balcony and into a small anteroom overlooking the courtyard where the official cars were parked. From here, the guests were ushered left into a long and spacious picture gallery, where the carpet was apple green and decorated with a rosette pattern. Tall windows stood at either end of the room and almost every inch of white wall was covered in paintings.

'Drink, sir?' said a waiter just inside the doorway.

'Is it champagne?' asked Strike.

'English sparkling wine, sir,' said the waiter.

Strike helped himself, though without enthusiasm, and continued through the crowd, passing Chiswell and Kinvara, who were listening (or, Strike thought, pretending to listen) to a wheelchair-bound athlete. Kinvara shot Strike a swift, suspicious side glance as he passed, aiming for the far wall where he hoped to find either a chair, or something on which he could conveniently lean. Unfortunately, the gallery walls were so densely packed with pictures that leaning was impossible, nor were there any seats, so Strike came to rest beside an enormous painting by Count d'Orsay of Queen Victoria riding a dapple-grey horse. While he sipped his sparkling wine, he tried discreetly to staunch the blood still leaking from his nose, and wipe the worst of the dirt off his suit trousers.

Waiters were circulating, carrying trays of canapés. Strike managed to grab a couple of miniature crab cakes as they passed, then fell to examining his surroundings, noting another spectacular skylight, this one supported by a number of gilded palm trees.

The room had a peculiar energy. The prince's arrival was imminent and the guests' gaiety came and went in nervous spurts, with increasingly frequent glances at the doors. From his vantage point beside Queen Victoria, Strike spotted a stately figure in a primrose-yellow dress standing almost directly opposite him, close beside an ornate black and gold fireplace. One hand was keeping a gentle hold on the harness of a pale yellow Labrador, who sat panting gently at her feet in the overcrowded room. Strike had not immediately recognised Della, because she was not wearing sunglasses, but prosthetic eyes. Her slightly sunken, opaque, china-blue gaze gave her an odd innocence. Geraint stood a short distance from his wife, gabbling at a thin, mousy woman whose eyes darted around, searching for a rescuer.

A sudden hush fell near the doors through which Strike had entered. Strike saw the top of a ginger head and a flurry of suits. Self-consciousness spread through the packed room like a petrifying breeze. Strike watched the top of the ginger head move away, towards the far right side of the room. Still sipping his English wine and wondering which of the women in the room was the trustee with dirt on Geraint Winn, his attention was suddenly caught by a tall woman nearby with her back to him.

Her long dark hair was twisted up into a messy bun and, unlike every other woman present, her outfit gave no suggestion of party best. The straight black knee-length dress was plain to the point of severity, and though barelegged she wore a pair of spike-heeled, open-toed ankle boots. For a sliver of a second Strike thought he must be mistaken, but then she moved and he knew for sure that it was her. Before he could move away from her vicinity, she turned around and looked straight into his eyes.

Colour flooded her face, which as he knew was normally cameo pale. She was heavily pregnant. Her condition had not touched her anywhere but the swollen belly. She was as fine-boned as ever in face and limbs. Less adorned than any other woman in the room, she was easily the most beautiful. For a few seconds they contemplated each other, then she took a few tentative steps forwards, the colour ebbing from her cheeks as fast as it had come.

'Corm?'

'Hello, Charlotte.'

If she thought of kissing him, his stony face deterred her.

'What on earth are you doing here?'

'Invited,' lied Strike. 'Celebrity amputee. You?'

She seemed dazed.

'Jago's niece is a Paralympian. She's . . .'

Charlotte looked around, apparently trying to spot the niece, and took a sip of water. Her hand was shaking. A few drops spilled from the glass. He saw them break like glass beads on her swollen belly.

'. . . well, she's here somewhere,' she said, with a nervous laugh. 'She's got cerebral palsy and she's remarkable, actually, an incredible rider. Her father's in Hong Kong, so her mum invited me, instead.'

His silence was unnerving her. She rattled on:

'Jago's family like to make me go out and do things, only my sister-in-law's cross because I got the dates mixed up. I thought tonight was dinner at the Shard and this thing was Friday, tomorrow, I mean, so I'm not dressed properly for royalty, but I was late and I didn't have time to change.'

She gestured hopelessly at her plain black dress and her spike-heeled boots.

'Jago not here?'

Her gold-flecked green eyes flickered slightly.

'No, he's in the States.'

Her focus moved to his upper lip.

'Have you been in a fight?'

'No,' he said, dabbing at his nose with the back of his hand again. He straightened up, lowering his weight carefully back onto his prosthesis, ready to walk away. 'Well, nice to—'

'Corm, don't go,' she said, reaching out. Her fingers did not quite make contact with his sleeve; she let her hand fall back by her side. 'Don't, not yet, I – you've done such incredible things. I read about them all in the papers.'

The last time they had seen each other he had been bleeding, too, because of the flying ashtray that had caught him in the face as he left her. He remembered the text, 'It was yours', sent on the eve of her wedding to Ross, referring to another baby she had claimed to be bearing, which had vanished before he ever saw proof of its existence. He remembered, too, the picture she had sent to his office of herself, minutes after saying 'I do' to Jago Ross, beautiful and stricken, like a sacrificial victim.

'Congratulations,' he said, keeping his eyes on her face.

'I'm huge because it's twins.'

She did not, as he had seen other pregnant women do, touch her belly as she talked about the babies, but looked down as though slightly surprised to see her changed shape. She had never wanted children when they had been together. It was one of the things they had had in common. The baby that she had claimed was his had been an unwelcome surprise to both of them.

In Strike's imagination, Jago Ross's progeny were curled under the black dress like a pair of white whelps, not entirely human, emissaries of their father, who resembled a dissolute arctic fox. He was glad they were there, if such a joyless emotion could be called gladness. All impediments, all deterrents, were welcome, because it now became apparent to him that the gravitational pull Charlotte had so long exerted over him, even after hundreds of fights and scenes and a thousand lies, was not yet spent. As ever, he had the sense that behind the green and gold-flecked eyes, she knew exactly what he was thinking.

'They aren't due for ages. I had a scan, it's a boy and a girl. Jago's pleased about the boy. Are you here with anyone?'

'No.'

As he said it, he caught a flash of green over Charlotte's shoulder. Robin, who was now talking brightly to the mousy woman in purple brocade who had finally escaped Geraint.

'Pretty,' said Charlotte, who had looked to see what had caught his attention. She had always had a preternatural ability to detect the slightest flicker of interest towards other women. 'No, wait,' she said slowly, 'isn't that the girl who works with you? She was in all the papers – what's her name, Rob—?'

'No,' said Strike, 'that's not her.'

He wasn't remotely surprised that Charlotte knew Robin's name, or that she had recognised her, even with the hazel contact lenses. He had known Charlotte would keep tabs on him.

'You've always liked girls with that colouring, haven't you?' said Charlotte with a kind of synthetic gaiety. 'That little American you started dating after you pretended we'd broken up in Germany had the same kind of—'

There was a kind of hushed scream in their vicinity.

'Ohmigod, *Charlie!*'

Izzy Chiswell was bearing down upon them, beaming, her pink face clashing with her orange dress. She was, Strike suspected, not on her first glass of wine.

'Hello, Izz,' said Charlotte, forcing a smile. Strike could almost feel the effort it cost her to tug herself free of that tangle of ancient grudges and wounds in which their relationship had gradually strangled to death.

Again, he prepared to walk away, but the crowd parted and Prince Harry was suddenly revealed in all his hyper-real familiarity, some ten feet away from where Strike and the two women stood, so that moving away from the area would be done under the scrutiny of half the room. Trapped, Strike startled a passing waiter by reaching out a long arm and snatching another glass of wine from his tray. For a few seconds, both Charlotte and Izzy watched the prince. Then, when it became apparent that he was not about to approach them any time soon, they turned back to each other.

'Showing already!' Izzy said, admiring Charlotte's belly. 'Have you had a scan? D'you know what it is?'

'Twins,' said Charlotte, without enthusiasm. She indicated Strike, 'You remember—?'

'Corm, yah, of course, we brought him here!' said Izzy, beaming and clearly unconscious of any indiscretion.

Charlotte turned from her old schoolfriend to her ex, and Strike could feel her sniffing the air for the reason that Strike and Izzy would have travelled together. She shifted very slightly, apparently allowing Izzy into the conversation, but boxing Strike in so that he couldn't walk away without asking one of them to get out of his way. 'Oh, wait, of course. You investigated Freddie's death in action, didn't you?' she said. 'I remember you telling me about it. Poor Freddie.'

Izzy acknowledged this tribute to her brother with a slight tip of her glass, then peeked back over her shoulder at Prince Harry.

'He gets sexier every passing day, doesn't he?' she whispered.

'Ginger pubes, though, darling,' said Charlotte, deadpan.

Against his will, Strike grinned. Izzy snorted with laughter.

'Speaking of which,' said Charlotte (she never acknowledged that she had been funny), 'isn't that Kinvara Hanratty over there?'

'My ghastly stepmother? Yes,' said Izzy. 'D'you know her?'

'My sister sold her a horse.'

During the sixteen years of Strike's on-off relationship with Charlotte, he had been privy to countless conversations like this. People of Charlotte's class all seemed to know each other. Even if they had never met, they knew siblings or cousins or friends or classmates, or else their parents knew somebody else's parents: all were connected, forming a kind of web that constituted a hostile habitat for outsiders. Rarely did these web-dwellers leave to seek companionship or love among the rest of society. Charlotte had been unique in her circle in choosing somebody as unclassifiable as Strike, whose invisible appeal and low status had, he knew, been subjects of perennial, horrified debate among most of her friends and family.

'Well, I hope it wasn't a horse Amelia liked,' Izzy said, 'because Kinvara will ruin it. Awful hands and a horrible seat, but she thinks she's Charlotte Dujardin. D'you ride, Cormoran?' Izzy asked.

'No,' said Strike.

'He doesn't trust horses,' said Charlotte, smiling at him.

But he did not respond. He had no desire to touch upon old jokes or shared memories.

'Kinvara's livid, look at her,' said Izzy, with some satisfaction. 'Papa's just dropped a heavy hint he's going to try and talk my brother Raff into taking over from me, which is *fabulous*, and what I hoped would happen. Papa used to let Kinvara boss him around about Raff, but he's putting his foot down these days.'

'I think I've met Raphael,' said Charlotte. 'Wasn't he working at Henry Drummond's art gallery a couple of months ago?'

Strike checked at his watch and then back around the room. The prince was moving away from their part of the room and Robin was nowhere to be seen. With any luck, she had followed the trustee who had dirt on Winn into the bathroom and was eliciting confidences over the sink.

'Oh Lord,' said Izzy. 'Look out. Geraint Bloody – hello, Geraint!'

Geraint's object, it soon became clear, was Charlotte.

'Hello, hello,' he said, peering at her through heavily smudged glasses, his lipless smile a leer. 'You've just been pointed out to me by your niece. What an extraordinary young woman she is, quite extraordinary. Our charity's involved in supporting the equestrian team. Geraint Winn,' he said, holding out a hand, 'The Level Playing Field.'

'Oh,' said Charlotte. 'Hello.'

Strike had watched her repel lecherous men for years. Having acknowledged his presence, she stared coldly at Geraint, as though quite puzzled to know why he was still in her vicinity.

Strike's mobile vibrated in his pocket. Reaching for it, he saw an unknown number. This was his excuse to leave.

'Need to get going, sorry. 'Scuse me, Izzy.'

'Oh, that's a shame,' Izzy said, pouting. 'I wanted to ask you all about the Shacklewell Ripper!'

Strike saw Geraint's eyes widen. Inwardly cursing her, he said, 'Night. Bye,' he added to Charlotte.

Limping away as fast as he could manage, he accepted the call, but by the time he had raised it to his ear, the caller had gone.

'Corm.'

Somebody lightly touched his arm. He turned. Charlotte had followed him.

'I'm leaving, too.'

'What about your niece?'

'She's met Harry, she'll be thrilled. She doesn't actually like me that much. None of them do. What happened to your mobile?'

'I fell on it.'

He walked on, but, long-legged as she was, she caught up with him.

'I don't think I'm going your way, Charlotte.'

'Well, unless you're tunnelling out, we have to walk two hundred yards together.'

He limped on without answering. To his left, he caught another flash of green. As they reached the grand staircase in the hall, Charlotte reached out and lightly grasped his arm, wobbly in the heels that were so unsuitable for a pregnant woman. He resisted the urge to shake her loose.

His mobile rang again. The same unknown number had appeared on the screen. Charlotte drew up beside him, watching his face as he answered it.

The moment the mobile touched his ear he heard a desperate, haunting scream.

'They're going to kill me, Mr Strike, help me, help me, please help me . . .'

34

But who could really foresee what was coming? I am sure I could not.

Henrik Ibsen, *Rosmersholm*

The hazy, clear-skied promise of another summer's day hadn't yet translated itself into actual warmth when Robin arrived next morning at the café closest to Chiswell's house. She could have chosen one of the circular tables outside on the pavement, but instead she huddled down in a corner of the café where she was to meet Strike, hands clasped around her latte for comfort, her reflection in the espresso machine pale and heavy-eyed.

Somehow, she had known that Strike would not be here when she arrived. Her mood was simultaneously depressed and nervy. She would rather not have been alone with her thoughts, but here she was, with only the hiss of the coffeemaker for company, chilly in spite of the jacket she had grabbed on the way out of the house and full of anxiety about the imminent confrontation with Chiswell, who might quibble his bill, after the catastrophe of Strike's fight with Jimmy Knight.

But that wasn't all that was worrying Robin. She had woken that morning from a confused dream in which the dark, spike-booted figure of Charlotte Ross figured. Robin had recognised Charlotte immediately when she spotted her at the reception. She had tried not to watch the once-engaged couple as they'd talked, angry with herself for being so sharply interested in what was passing between them, yet, even as she had moved from group to group, shamelessly insinuating

278

herself into conversations in the hope of finding the elusive Elspeth Curtis-Lacey, her eyes had sought out Strike and Charlotte, and when they left the reception together she had experienced a nasty sensation in her stomach, akin to the drop of an elevator.

She had arrived home unable to think of anything else, which had made her feel guilty when Matthew emerged from the kitchen, eating a sandwich. She had the impression that he had not been home long. He subjected the green dress to an up-and-down look very like the one Kinvara had given her. She made to walk past him upstairs, but he had moved to block her.

'Robin, come on. Please. Let's talk.'

So they had gone into the sitting room and talked. Tired of conflict, she had apologised for hurting Matthew's feelings by missing the cricket match, and for forgetting her wedding ring on their anniversary weekend. Matthew in turn had expressed regret for the things he had said during Sunday's row, and especially for the remark about her lack of achievements.

Robin felt as though they were moving chess pieces on a board that was vibrating in the preliminary tremors of an earthquake. *It's too late. You know, surely, that none of this matters any more?*

But when the talk was finished, Matthew said, 'So we're OK?'

'Yes,' she replied. 'We're fine.'

He had stood up, held out a hand and helped her up from her chair. She had forced a smile and then he had kissed her, hard, on the mouth, and begun to tug at the green dress. She heard the fabric around the zip tear and when she began to protest, he clamped his mouth on hers again.

She knew that she could stop him, she knew that he was waiting for her to stop him, that she was being tested in an ugly, underhand way, that he would deny what he was really doing, that he would claim to be the victim. She hated him for doing it this way, and part of her wanted to be the kind of woman who could have disengaged from her own revulsion and from her own reluctant flesh, but she had fought too long and too hard to regain possession of her own body to barter it in this way.

'No,' she said, pushing him away. 'I don't want to.'

He released her at once, as she had known he would, with an expression compounded of anger and triumph. Suddenly, she knew that she had not fooled him when they had had sex on their anniversary weekend, and paradoxically that made her feel tender towards him.

'I'm sorry,' she said. 'I'm tired.'

'Yeah,' said Matthew. 'So am I.'

And he had walked out of the room, leaving Robin with a chill down her back where the green dress had torn.

Where the hell was Strike? It was five past nine and she wanted company. She also wanted to know what had happened after he left the reception with Charlotte. Anything would be preferable to sitting here, thinking about Matthew.

As though the thought had summoned him, her phone rang.

'Sorry,' he said, before she could speak. 'Suspicious package at bloody Green Park. I've been stuck on the Tube for twenty minutes and I've only just got reception. I'll be there as quick as I can, but you might have to start without me.'

'Oh, God,' said Robin, closing her tired eyes.

'Sorry,' Strike repeated, 'I'm on my way. Got something to tell you, actually. Funny thing happened last night – oh, hang on, we're moving. See you shortly.'

He hung up, leaving Robin with the prospect of having to deal alone with the first effusions of Jasper Chiswell's anger, and still grappling formless feelings of dread and misery that swirled around a dark, graceful woman who was sixteen years' worth of knowledge and memories ahead of her when it came to Cormoran Strike, which, Robin told herself, *shouldn't matter, for God's sake, haven't you got enough problems without worrying about Strike's love life, it's nothing whatsoever to do with you . . .*

She felt a sudden guilty prickle around her lips, where Strike's missed kiss had landed outside the hospital. As though she could wash it away, she downed the dregs of her coffee, got up and left the café for the broad, straight street, which comprised two symmetrical lines of identical nineteenth-century houses.

She walked briskly, not because she was in any hurry to bear the brunt of Chiswell's anger and disappointment, but because activity helped dispel her uncomfortable thoughts.

Arriving outside Chiswell's house precisely on time, she lingered for a few hopeful seconds beside the glossy black front door, just in case Strike were to appear at the last moment. He didn't. Robin therefore steadied herself, walked up the three clean white steps from the pavement and knocked on the front door, which was on the latch and opened a few inches. A man's muffled voice shouted something that might have been 'come in'.

Robin passed into a small, dingy hall dominated by vertiginous stairs. The olive-green wallpaper was drab and peeling in places. Leaving the front door as she had found it, she called out:

'Minister?'

He didn't answer. Robin knocked gently on the door to the right, and opened it.

Time froze. The scene seemed to fold in upon her, crashing through her retinas into a mind unprepared for it, and shock kept her standing in the doorway, her hand still on the handle and her mouth slightly open, trying to comprehend what she was seeing.

A man was sitting in a Queen Anne chair, his legs splayed, his arms dangling, and he seemed to have a shiny grey turnip for a head, in which a carved mouth gaped, but no eyes.

Then Robin's struggling comprehension grasped the fact that it was not a turnip, but a human head shrink-wrapped in a clear plastic bag, into which a tube ran from a large canister. The man looked as though he had suffocated. His left foot lay sideways on the rug, revealing a small hole in the sole, his thick fingers dangled, almost touching the carpet, and there was a stain at his groin where his bladder had emptied.

And next she understood that it was Chiswell himself who sat in the chair, and that his thick mass of grey hair was pressed flat against his face in the vacuum created by the bag, and that the gaping mouth had sucked the plastic into itself, which was why it gaped so darkly.

35

... the White Horse! In broad daylight!

Henrik Ibsen, Rosmersholm

Somewhere in the distance, outside the house, a man shouted. He sounded like a workman, and in some part of her brain Robin knew that that was who she had heard when she was expecting to hear 'come in'. Nobody had invited her into the house. The door had simply been left ajar.

Now, when it might have been expected, she didn't panic. There was no threat here, however horrifying the sight of that awful dummy, with the turnip head and the tube, this poor lifeless figure could not hurt her. Knowing that she must check that life was extinct, Robin approached Chiswell and gently touched his shoulder. It was easier, not being able to see his eyes, because of the coarse hair that obscured them like a horse's forelock. The flesh felt hard beneath his striped shirt and cooler than she had expected.

But then she imagined the gaping mouth speaking, and took several quick steps backwards, until her foot landed with a crunch on something hard on the carpet and she slipped. She had cracked a pale blue plastic tube of pills lying on the carpet. She recognised them as the sort of homeopathic tablets sold in her local chemist.

Taking out her mobile, she called 999 and asked for the police. After explaining that she had found a body and giving the address, she was told that someone would be with her shortly.

Trying not to focus on Chiswell, she took in the frayed curtains, which were of an indeterminate dun colour, trimmed with sad little bobbles, the antiquated TV in its faux wood cladding, the patch of darker wallpaper over the mantelpiece where a painting had once hung, and the silver-framed photographs. But the shrink-wrapped head, the rubber piping and the cold glint of the canister seemed to turn all of this everyday normality into pasteboard. The nightmare alone was real.

So Robin turned her mobile onto its camera function and began to take photographs. Putting a lens between herself and the scene mitigated the horror. Slowly and methodically, she documented the scene.

A glass sat on the coffee table in front of the body, with a few millimetres of what looked like orange juice in it. Scattered books and papers lay beside it. There was a piece of thick cream writing paper headed with a red Tudor rose, like a drop of blood, and the printed address of the house in which Robin stood. Somebody had written in a rounded, girlish hand.

> *Tonight was the final straw. How stupid do you think I am, putting that girl in your office right under my nose? I hope you realise how ridiculous you look, how much people are laughing at you, chasing a girl who's younger than your daughters.*
>
> *I've had enough. Make a fool of yourself, I don't care any more, it's over.*
>
> *I've gone back to Woolstone. Once I've made arrangements for the horses, I'll clear out for good. Your bloody horrible children will be happy, but will you, Jasper? I doubt it, but it's too late.*
>
> *K*

As Robin bent to take a picture of the note, she heard the front door snap shut, and with a gasp, she spun around. Strike was standing on the threshold, large, unshaven, still in the suit he had worn to the reception. He was staring at the figure in the chair.

'The police are on their way,' said Robin. 'I just called them.'

Strike moved carefully into the room.

'Holy shit.'

He spotted the cracked tube of pills on the floor, stepped over them, and scrutinised of the tubing and the plastic-covered face.

'Raff said he was behaving strangely,' said Robin, 'but I don't think he ever dreamed . . .'

Strike said nothing. He was still examining the body.

'Was that there yesterday evening?'

'What?'

'That,' said Strike, pointing.

There was a semi-circular mark on the back of Chiswell's hand, dark red against the coarse, pallid skin.

'I can't remember,' said Robin.

The full shock of what had happened was starting to hit her and she was finding it hard to arrange her thoughts, which floated, unmoored and disconnected, through her head: Chiswell barking through the car window to persuade the police to let Strike into last night's reception, Chiswell calling Kinvara a stupid bitch, Chiswell demanding that they meet him here this morning. It was unreasonable to expect her to remember the backs of his hands.

'Hmm,' said Strike. He noticed at the mobile in Robin's hand. 'Have you taken pictures of everything?'

She nodded.

'All of this?' he asked, waving a hand over the table. 'That?' he added, pointing at the cracked pills on the carpet.

'Yes. That was my fault. I trod on them.'

'How did you get in?'

'The door was open. I thought he'd left it on the latch for us,' said Robin. 'A workman shouted in the street and I thought it was Chiswell saying "come in". I was expecting—'

'Stay here,' said Strike.

He left the room. She heard him climbing the stairs and then his heavy footsteps on the ceiling above, but she knew that there was nobody there. She could feel the house's essential lifelessness, its flimsy cardboard unreality, and, sure enough, Strike returned less than five minutes later, shaking his head.

'Nobody.'

He walked past her through a door that led off the sitting room and, hearing his footsteps hit tile, Robin knew that it was the kitchen.

'Completely empty,' Strike said, re-emerging.

'What happened last night?' Robin asked. 'You said something funny happened.'

She wanted to discuss a subject other than the awful form that dominated the room in its grotesque lifelessness.

'Billy called me. He said people were trying to kill him – chasing him. He claimed to be in a phone box in Trafalgar Square. I went to try and find him, but he wasn't there.'

'Oh,' said Robin.

So he hadn't been with Charlotte. Even in this extremity, Robin registered the fact, and was glad.

'The hell?' said Strike quietly, looking past her into a corner of the room.

A buckled sword was leaning against the wall in a dark corner. It looked as though it had been forced or stood on and deliberately bent. Strike walked carefully around the body to examine it, but then they heard the police car pulling up outside the house and he straightened up.

'We'll tell them everything, obviously,' said Strike.

'Yes,' said Robin.

'Except the surveillance devices. Shit – they'll find them in your office—'

'They won't,' said Robin. 'I took them home yesterday, in case we decided I needed to clear out because of the *Sun*.'

Before Strike could express admiration for this clear-eyed fore-sight, somebody rapped hard on the front door.

'Well, it's been nice while it's lasted, hasn't it?' Strike said, with a grim smile, as he moved towards the hall. 'Being out of the papers?'

PART TWO

36

What has happened can be hushed up – or at any rate can be explained away . . .

Henrik Ibsen, *Rosmersholm*

The Chiswell case maintained its singular character even when their client was no more.

As the usual cumbersome procedures and formalities enveloped the corpse, Strike and Robin were escorted from Ebury Street to Scotland Yard, where they were separately interviewed. Strike knew that a tornado of speculation must be whirling through the newsrooms of London at the death of a government minister, and sure enough, by the time they emerged from Scotland Yard six hours later, the colourful details of Chiswell's private life were being broadcast across TV and radio, while opening the internet browsers on their phones revealed brief news items from news sites, as a tangle of baroque theories spread across blogs and social media, in which a multitude of cartoonish Chiswells died at the hand of myriad nebulous foes. As he rode in a taxi back to Denmark Street, Strike read how Chiswell the corrupt capitalist had been murdered by the Russian mafia after failing to pay back interest on some seedy, illegal transaction, while Chiswell the defender of solid English values had surely been dispatched by vengeful Islamists after his attempts to resist the rise of sharia law.

Strike returned to his attic flat only to collect his belongings, and decamped to the house of his old friends Nick and Ilsa, respectively a gastroenterologist and a lawyer. Robin, who at Strike's insistence had taken a taxi directly home to Albury Street, was given a peremptory hug by Matthew, whose tissue-thin pretence of sympathy was worse, Robin felt, than outright fury.

When he heard that Robin had been summoned back to Scotland Yard for further interrogation the next day, Matthew's self-control crumbled.

'Anyone could have seen this coming!'

'Funny, it seemed to take most people by surprise,' Robin said. She had just ignored her mother's fourth call of the morning.

'I don't mean Chiswell killing himself—'

'—it's pronounced "Chizzle"—'

'—I mean you getting yourself into trouble for sneaking around the Houses of Parliament!'

'Don't worry, Matt. I'll make sure the police know you were against it. Wouldn't want your promotion prospects compromised.'

But she wasn't sure that her second interviewer was a policeman. The softly spoken man in a dark grey suit didn't reveal whom he worked for. Robin found this gentleman far more intimidating than yesterday's police, even though they had, at times, been forceful to the point of aggression. Robin told her new interviewer everything she had seen and heard in the Commons, omitting only the strange conversation between Della Winn and Aamir Mallik, which had been captured on the second listening device. As the interaction had taken place behind a closed door after normal working hours, she could only have heard it by using surveillance equipment. Robin assuaged her conscience by telling herself that this conversation could not possibly have anything to do with Chiswell's death, but squirming feelings of guilt and terror pursued her as she left the building for the second time. So consumed was she by what she hoped was paranoia by this brush with the security services, that she called Strike from a payphone near the Tube, instead of using her mobile.

'I've just had another interview. I'm pretty sure it was MI5.'

'Bound to happen,' said Strike, and she took solace from his matter-of-fact tone. 'They've got to check you out, make sure you are who you claim to be. Isn't there anywhere you can go, other than home? I can't believe the press aren't onto us yet, but it must be imminent.'

'I could go back to Masham, I suppose,' Robin said, 'but they're bound to try there if they want to find me. That's where they came after the Ripper stuff.'

Unlike Strike, she had no friends of her own into whose anonymous homes she felt she could vanish. All her friends were Matthew's, too, and she had no doubt that, like her husband, they would be scared of harbouring anybody who was of interest to the security services. At a loss as to what to do, she went back to Albury Street.

Yet the press didn't come for her, even though the newspapers were hardly holding back on the subject of Chiswell. The *Mail* had already run a double-page spread on the various tribulations and scandals that had plagued Jasper Chiswell's life. '*Once mentioned as a possible prime minister*', '*sexy Italian Ornella Serafin, with whom he had the affair that broke up his first marriage*', '*voluptuous Kinvara Hanratty, who was thirty years his junior*', '*Lieutenant Freddie Chiswell, eldest son, died in the Iraq war his father had staunchly supported*', '*youngest child Raphael, whose drug-filled joy ride ended in the death of a young mother*'.

Broadsheets contained tributes from friends and colleagues: '*a fine mind, a supremely able minister, one of Thatcher's bright young men*', '*but for a somewhat tumultuous private life, there were no heights he might not have reached*', '*the public persona was irascible, even abrasive, but the Jasper Chiswell I knew at Harrow was a witty and intelligent boy*'.

Five days of lurid press coverage passed, yet still, the press's mysterious restraint on the subject of Strike and Robin's involvement held, and still, nobody had printed a word about blackmail.

On the Friday morning following the discovery of Chiswell's body, Strike was sitting quietly at Nick and Ilsa's kitchen table, sunlight pouring through the window behind him.

His host and hostess were at work. Nick and Ilsa, who had been trying for some years to have a baby, had recently adopted a pair of kittens whom Nick had insisted on calling Ossie and Ricky, after the two Spurs players he had revered in his teens. The cats, who had only recently consented to sit on the knees of their adoptive parents, had not appreciated the arrival of the large and unfamiliar Strike. Finding themselves alone with him, they had sought refuge on top of a kitchen wall cabinet. He was currently conscious of the scrutiny of four pale green eyes, which followed his every movement from on high.

Not that he was currently moving a great deal. Indeed, for much of the past half an hour he had been almost motionless, as he pored over the photographs that Robin had taken in Ebury Street, which he had printed out in Nick's study for convenience. Finally, causing Ricky to jump up in a flurry of upended fur, Strike isolated nine of the photographs and put the rest in a pile. While Strike scrutinised his selected images, Ricky settled back down, the tip of a black tail swaying as he awaited the detective's next move.

The first photograph that Strike had selected showed a close-up of the small, semi-circular puncture mark on Chiswell's left hand.

The second and third pictures showed different angles of the glass that had sat on the coffee table in front of Chiswell. A powdery residue was visible on the sides, above an inch of orange juice.

The fourth, fifth and sixth photographs Strike laid together side by side. Each showed a slightly different angle of the body, with slices of the surrounding room caught within its frame. Once again, Strike studied the ghostly outline of the buckled sword in the corner, the dark patch over the mantelpiece where a picture had previously hung and, beneath this, barely noticeable against the dark wallpaper, a pair of brass hooks spaced nearly a yard apart.

The seventh and eighth photographs, when placed side by side, showed the entirety of the coffee table. Kinvara's farewell letter sat on top of a number of papers and books, of which only a sliver of one letter was visible, signed by 'Brenda Bailey'. Of the books, Strike could see nothing but a partial title on an old cloth edition – 'CATUL' – and the lower part of a Penguin paperback. Also in shot was the upturned corner of the threadbare rug beneath the table.

The ninth and final picture, which Strike had enlarged from yet another shot of the body, showed Chiswell's gaping trouser pocket, in which something shiny and golden had been caught in the flash of Robin's camera. While he was still contemplating this gleaming object, Strike's mobile rang. It was his hostess, Ilsa.

'Hi,' he said, standing up and grabbing the packet of Benson &

Hedges and lighter that lay on the side behind him. With an eruption of claws on wood, Ossie and Ricky streaked along the top of the kitchen cabinets, in case Strike was about to start throwing things at them. Checking to see that they were too far away to make a break for the garden, Strike let himself outside and swiftly closed the back door. 'Any news?'

'Yes. Looks like you were right.'

Strike sat down on a wrought iron garden chair and lit up.

'Go on.'

'I've just had coffee with my contact. He can't speak freely, given the nature of what we're talking about, but I put your theory to him and he said "That sounds *very* plausible." Then I said, "Fellow politician?" and he said that sounded very likely, too, and I said I supposed that in that situation, the press would appeal, and he said, yes, he thought so, too.'

Strike exhaled.

'I owe you, Ilsa, thanks. The good news is, I'll be able to get out of your hair.'

'Corm, we don't mind you staying, you know that.'

'The cats don't like me.'

'Nick says they can tell you're a Gooner.'

'The comedy circuit lost a shining light when your husband decided on Medicine. Dinner's on me tonight and I'll clear out afterwards.'

Strike then rang Robin. She picked up on the second ring.

'Everything OK?'

'I've found out why the press aren't all over us. Della's taken out a super-injunction. The papers aren't allowed to report that Chiswell hired us, in case it breaks the blackmail story. Ilsa's just met her High Court contact and he confirmed it.'

There was a pause, while Robin digested this information.

'So Della convinced a judge that Chiswell made up the blackmail?'

'Exactly, that he was using us to dig dirt on enemies. I'm not surprised the judge swallowed it. The whole world thinks Della's whiter than white.'

'But Izzy knew why I was there,' protested Robin. 'The family will have confirmed that he was being blackmailed.'

Strike tapped ash absent-mindedly into Ilsa's pot of rosemary.

'Will they? Or will they want it all hushed up, now he's dead?'

He took her silence as reluctant agreement.

'The press will appeal the injunction, won't they?'

'They're already trying, according to Ilsa. If I were a tabloid editor, I'd be having us watched, so I think we'd better be careful. I'm going back to the office tonight, but I think you should stay home.'

'For how long?' said Robin.

He heard the strain in her voice and wondered whether it was entirely due to the stress of the case.

'We'll play it by ear. Robin, they know you were the one inside the Houses of Parliament. You became the story while he was alive and you're sure as hell the story now they know who you really are, and he's dead.'

She said nothing.

'How're you getting on with the accounts?' he asked.

She had insisted on being given this job, little though either of them enjoyed it.

'They'd look a lot healthier if Chiswell had paid his bill.'

'I'll try and tap the family,' said Strike, rubbing his eyes, 'but it feels tasteless asking for money before the funeral.'

'I've been looking through the photos again,' said Robin. In daily contact since finding the body, every one of their conversations wound its way back to the pictures of Chiswell's corpse and the room in which they had found him.

'Me too. Notice anything new?'

'Yes, two little brass hooks on the wall. I think the sword was usually—'

'—displayed beneath the missing painting?'

'Exactly. D'you think it was Chiswell's, from the army?'

'Very possibly. Or some ancestor's.'

'I wonder why it was taken down? And how it got bent?'

'You think Chiswell grabbed it off the wall to try and defend himself against his murderer?'

'That's the first time,' said Robin quietly, 'you've said it. "Murderer".'

A wasp swooped low over Strike but, repelled by his cigarette smoke, buzzed away again.

'I was joking.'

'Were you?'

Strike stretched out his legs in front of him, contemplating his feet. Stuck in the house, which was warm, he had not bothered with shoes and socks. His bare foot, which rarely saw sunlight, was pale and hairy. The prosthetic foot, a single piece of carbon fibre with no individual toes, had a dull gleam in the sunshine.

'There are odd features,' Strike said, as he waggled his remaining toes, 'but it's been a week and no arrest. The police will have noticed everything we did.'

'Hasn't Wardle heard anything? Vanessa's dad's ill. She's on compassionate leave, or I'd've asked her.'

'Wardle's deep in anti-terrorist stuff for the Olympics. Considerately spared the time to call my voicemail and piss himself laughing at my client dying on me, though.'

'Cormoran, did you notice the name on those homeopathic pills I trod on?'

'No,' said Strike. This wasn't one of the photographs he had isolated. 'What was it?'

'Lachesis. I saw it when I enlarged the picture.'

'Why's that significant?'

'When Chiswell came into our office and quoted that Latin poem at Aamir, and said something about a man of your habits, he mentioned Lachesis. He said she was—'

'One of the Fates.'

'—exactly. The one who "knew when everyone's number was up".'

Strike smoked in silence for a few seconds.

'Sounds like a threat.'

'I know.'

'You definitely can't remember which poem it was? Author, perhaps?'

'I've been trying, but no – wait—' said Robin suddenly. 'He gave it a number.'

'Catullus,' said Strike, sitting up straighter on the iron garden chair.

'How d'you know?'

'Because Catullus's poems are numbered, not titled, there was an old copy on Chiswell's coffee table. Catullus described plenty of interesting habits: incest, sodomy, child rape ... he might've missed out bestiality. There's a famous one about a sparrow, but nobody buggers it.'

'Funny coincidence, isn't it?' said Robin, ignoring the witticism.

'Maybe Chiswell was prescribed the pills and that put him in mind of the Fate?'

'Did he seem to you like the kind of man who'd trust homeopathy?'

'No,' admitted Strike, 'but if you're suggesting the killer dropped a tube of lachesis as an artistic flourish—'

He heard a distant trill of bells.

'There's someone at the door,' said Robin, 'I'd better—'

'Check who it is, before you answer,' said Strike. He had had a sudden presentiment.

Her footsteps were muffled by what he knew was carpet.

'Oh, God.'

'Who is it?'

'Mitch Patterson.'

'Has he seen you?'

'No, I'm upstairs.'

'Then don't answer.'

'I won't.'

But her breathing had become noisy and ragged.

'You all right?'

'Fine,' she said, her voice constricted.

'What's he—?'

'I'm going to go. I'll call you later.'

The line went dead.

Strike lowered the mobile. Feeling a sudden heat in the fingers of the hand not holding his phone, he realised his cigarette had burned to the filter. Stubbing it out on the hot paving stone, he flicked it over the wall into the garden of a neighbour whom Nick and Ilsa disliked, and immediately lit another, thinking about Robin.

He was concerned about her. It was to be expected, of course, that she was experiencing anxiety and stress after finding a body and being interviewed by the security services, but he had noticed lapses in concentration over the phone, where she asked him the same thing two or three times. There was also what he considered her unhealthy eagerness to get back to the office, or out on the street.

Convinced that she ought to be taking some time out, Strike hadn't told Robin about a line of investigation he was currently pursuing, because he was sure she would insist on being allowed to help.

The fact was that, for Strike, the Chiswell case had begun, not with the dead man's story of blackmail, but with Billy Knight's tale of a strangled child wrapped in a pink blanket in the ground. Ever since Billy's last plea for help, Strike had been phoning the telephone number from which it had been made. Finally, on the previous morning, he had got an answer from a curious passer-by, who had confirmed the phone box's position on the edge of Trafalgar Square.

Strike. That bastard soldier with the one leg. Billy's fixated on him. Thinks he's going to rescue him.

Surely there was a chance, however tiny, that Billy might gravitate back to the place where he had last sought help? Strike had spent a few hours wandering Trafalgar Square on the previous afternoon, knowing how remote was the possibility that Billy would show up, yet feeling compelled to do something, however pointless.

Strike's other decision, which was even harder to justify, because it cost money the agency could currently ill afford, was to keep Barclay embedded with Jimmy and Flick.

'It's your money,' the Glaswegian said, when the detective gave him this instruction, 'but what'm I looking for?'

'Billy,' said Strike, 'and in the absence of Billy, anything strange.'

Of course, the next lot of accounts would show Robin exactly what Barclay was up to.

Strike had a sudden feeling that he was being watched. Ossie, the bolder of Nick and Ilsa's kittens, was sitting at the kitchen window, beside the kitchen taps, staring through the window with eyes of pale jade. His gaze felt judgmental.

37

*I shall never conquer this completely. There will always be a
doubt confronting me – a question.*

Henrik Ibsen, *Rosmersholm*

Wary of breaching the conditions of the super-injunction, photographers stayed away from Chiswell's funeral in Woolstone. News
organisations restricted themselves to brief, factual announcements
that the service had taken place. Strike, who had considered sending
flowers, had decided against it on the basis that the gesture might be
taken as a tasteless reminder that his bill remained unpaid. Meanwhile
the inquest into Chiswell's death was opened and adjourned, pending
further investigations.

And then, quite suddenly, nobody was very interested in Jasper
Chiswell. It was as though the corpse that had been borne aloft for
a week upon a swell of newsprint, gossip and rumour, now sank
beneath stories of sportsmen and women, of Olympic preparations
and predictions, the country in the grip of an almost universal pre-
occupation, for whether they approved or disapproved of the event,
it was impossible to ignore or avoid.

Robin was still phoning Strike daily, pressuring him to let her
come back to work, but Strike continued to refuse. Not only had
Mitch Patterson twice more appeared in her street, but an unfamiliar
young busker had spent the whole week playing on the pavement
opposite Strike's office, missing chord changes every time he saw the
detective and regularly breaking off halfway through songs to answer
his mobile. The press, it seemed, had not forgotten that the Olympics

would eventually end, and that there was still a juicy story to be run on the reason Jasper Chiswell had hired private detectives.

None of Strike's police contacts knew anything about the progress of their colleagues' investigation into the case. Usually able to fall asleep under even the most unpropitious conditions, Strike found himself unusually restless and wakeful by night, listening to the increased noise from the London now heaving with Olympics visitors. The last time he had endured such a long stretch of sleeplessness had been his first week of consciousness after his leg had been borne off by the IED in Afghanistan. Then he had been kept awake by a tormenting itch impossible to scratch, because he felt it on his missing foot.

Strike hadn't seen Lorelei since the night of the Paralympic reception. After leaving Charlotte in the street, he had set off for Trafalgar Square to try and locate Billy, with the result that he had been even later to dinner with Lorelei than he had expected. Tired, sore, frustrated at his failure to find Billy and jarred by the unexpected meeting with his ex, he had arrived at the curry house in the expectation, and perhaps the hope, that Lorelei would have already left.

However, she had not only been waiting patiently at the table, she had immediately wrong-footed him with what he mentally characterised as a strategic retreat. Far from forcing a discussion about the future of their relationship, she had apologised for what she claimed to have been a foolish and precipitate declaration of love in bed, which she knew had embarrassed him and which she sincerely regretted.

Strike, who had drunk most of a pint on sitting down, bolstering himself, as he had imagined, for the unpleasant task of explaining that he did not want their relationship to become either more serious or permanent, was stymied. Her claim that she had said 'I love you' as a kind of *cri de joie* rendered his prepared speech useless, and given that she had looked very lovely in the lamp-lit restaurant, it had been easier and pleasanter to accept her explanation at face value rather than force a rupture that, clearly, neither of them wanted. They had texted and spoken a few times during the subsequent week apart, though nowhere near as often as he had talked to Robin. Lorelei had been perfectly understanding about his need to keep a low profile for a while once he explained that his late client had been the government minister who had suffocated in a plastic bag.

Lorelei had even been unfazed when he refused her invitation to watch the opening ceremony of the Olympics with her, because he'd already agreed to spend the evening at Lucy and Greg's. Strike's sister was as yet unwilling to let Jack out of her sight, and had therefore declined Strike's offer to take him to the Imperial War Museum over the weekend, offering dinner instead. When he explained to Lorelei how matters stood, Strike could tell that she was hoping that he would ask her to come with him to meet some of his family for the first time. He said, truthfully, that his motive for going alone was to spend time with the nephew whom he felt he had neglected, and Lorelei accepted this explanation good-naturedly, merely asking whether he was free the following night.

As the taxi bore him from Bromley South station towards Lucy and Greg's, Strike found himself mulling the situation with Lorelei, because Lucy usually demanded a bulletin on his love life. This was one of the reasons he avoided these kinds of get-togethers. It troubled Lucy that her brother was still, at the age of nearly thirty-eight, unmarried. She had gone so far, on one embarrassing occasion, as to invite to dinner a woman whom she imagined he might fancy, which had taught him only that his sister grossly misjudged his taste and needs.

As the taxi bore him deeper and deeper into middle-class suburbia, Strike found himself face to face with the uncomfortable truth, which was that Lorelei's willingness to accept the casualness of their current arrangement did not stem from a shared sense of disengagement, but from a desperation to keep him on almost any terms.

Staring out of the window at the roomy houses with double garages and neat lawns, his thoughts drifted to Robin, who called him daily when her husband was out, and then to Charlotte, holding lightly to his arm as she walked down the Lancaster House staircase in her spike-heeled boots. It had been convenient and pleasurable to have Lorelei in his life these past ten and a half months, affectionately undemanding, erotically gifted and pretending not to be in love with him. He could let the relationship continue, tell himself that he was, in that meaningless phrase, 'seeing how things went', or he could face the fact that he had merely postponed what must be done, and the longer he let things drift, the more mess and pain would result.

These reflections were hardly calculated to cheer him up, and as the taxi drew up outside his sister's house, with the magnolia tree in the front garden, and the net curtain twitching excitedly, he felt an irrational resentment towards his sister, as though all of it was her fault.

Jack opened the front door before Strike could even knock. Given his state the last time Strike had seen him, Jack looked remarkably well, and the detective was torn between pleasure at his recovery, and annoyance that he hadn't been allowed to take his nephew out, rather than making the long and inconvenient journey to Bromley.

However, Jack's delight in Strike's arrival, his eager questions about everything Strike remembered about their time together in hospital, because he himself had been glamorously unconscious, were touching, as was the fact that Jack insisted upon sitting next to his uncle at dinner, and monopolised his attention throughout. It was clear that Jack felt that they had become more closely bonded for each having passed through the tribulation of emergency surgery. He demanded so many details of Strike's amputation that Greg put down his knife and fork and pushed away his plate with a nauseated expression. Strike had previously formed the impression that Jack, the middle son, was Greg's least favourite. He took a slightly malicious pleasure in satisfying Jack's curiosity, especially as he knew that Greg, who would usually have shut the conversation down, was exercising unusual restraint given Jack's convalescent state. Unconscious of all undercurrents, Lucy beamed throughout, her eyes barely leaving Strike and Jack. She asked Strike nothing about his private life. All she seemed to ask was that he would be kind and patient with her son.

Uncle and nephew left the dinner table on excellent terms, Jack choosing a seat next to Strike on the sofa to watch the Olympics opening ceremony and chattering nonstop while they waited for the live broadcast to start, expressing the hope, among other things, that there would be guns, cannons and soldiers.

This innocent remark reminded Strike of Jasper Chiswell and his annoyance, reported by Robin, that Britain's military prowess was not to be celebrated on this largest of national stages. This made Strike wonder whether Jimmy Knight was sitting in front of a TV somewhere, readying himself to sneer at what he had castigated as a carnival of capitalism.

Greg handed Strike a bottle of Heineken.

'Here we go!' said Lucy excitedly.

The live broadcast began with a countdown. A few seconds in, a numbered balloon failed to burst. *Let it not be shit*, thought Strike, suddenly forgetting everything else in an upsurge of patriotic paranoia.

But the opening ceremony had been so very much the reverse of shit that Strike stayed to watch the whole thing, voluntarily missing his last train, accepting the offer of the sofa bed and breakfasting on Saturday morning with the family.

'Agency doing well, is it?' Greg asked him over the fry-up Lucy had cooked.

'Not bad,' said Strike.

He generally avoided discussing his business with Greg, who seemed to have been wrong-footed by Strike's success. His brother-in-law had always given the impression of being irritated by Strike's distinguished military career. As he fielded Greg's questions about the structure of the business, the rights and responsibilities of his free-lance hires, Robin's special status as salaried partner and the potential for expansion, Strike detected, not for the first time, Greg's barely disguised hope that there might be something Strike had forgotten or overlooked, too much the soldier to easily navigate the civilian business world.

'What's the ultimate aim, though?' he asked, while Jack sat patiently at Strike's side, clearly hoping to talk more about the military. 'I suppose you'll be looking to build up the business so that you don't need to be out on the street? Direct them all from the office?'

'No,' said Strike. 'If I'd wanted a desk job I'd've stayed in the army. The aim is to build up enough reliable employees that we can sustain a steady workload, and make some decent money. Short term, I want to build up enough money in the bank to see us through the lean times.'

'Seems under-ambitious,' said Greg. 'With the free advertising you got after the Ripper case—'

'We're not talking about that case now,' said Lucy sharply, from beside the frying pan, and with a glance at his son Greg fell silent, permitting Jack to re-enter the conversation with a question about assault courses.

Lucy, who had loved every moment of her brother's visit, glowed with pleasure as she hugged him goodbye after breakfast.

'Let me know when I can take Jack out,' said Strike, while his nephew beamed up at him.

'I will, and thanks so much, Stick. I'll never forget what you—'

'I didn't do anything,' Strike said, thumping her gently on the back. 'He did it himself. He's tough, aren't you, Jack? Thanks for a nice evening, Luce.'

Strike considered that he had got out just in time. Finishing his cigarette outside the station, with ten minutes to kill before the next train to central London, he reflected that Greg had reverted over breakfast to that combination of chirpiness and heartiness with which he usually treated his brother-in-law, while Lucy's enquiries after Robin as he put on his coat had shown signs of becoming a wide-ranging enquiry into his relationships with women in general. His thoughts had just returned dispiritedly towards Lorelei when his mobile rang.

'Hello?'

'Is this Cormoran?' said an upper-class female voice he did not immediately recognise.

'Yes. Who's this?'

'Izzy Chiswell,' she said, sounding as though she had a head cold.

'Izzy!' repeated Strike, surprised. 'Er . . . how are you?'

'Oh, bearing up. We, ah, got your invoice.'

'Right,' said Strike, wondering whether she was about to dispute the total, which was large.

'I'd be very happy to give you payment immediately, if you could ... I wonder whether you could possibly come and see me? Today, if that's convenient? How are you fixed?'

Strike checked his watch. For the first time in weeks he had nothing to do except make his way to Lorelei's later for dinner, and the prospect of collecting a large cheque was certainly welcome.

'Yeah, that should be fine,' he said. 'Where are you, Izzy?'

She gave him her address in Chelsea.

'I'll be about an hour.'

'Perfect,' she said, sounding relieved. 'I'll see you then.'

38

Oh, this killing doubt!

Henrik Ibsen, *Rosmersholm*

It was almost midday when Strike arrived at Izzy's mews house in Upper Cheyne Row in Chelsea, a quietly expensive stretch of houses which, unlike those of Ebury Street, were tastefully mismatched. Izzy's was small and painted white, with a carriage lamp beside the front door, and when Strike rang the doorbell she answered within a few seconds.

In her loose black trousers and a black sweater too warm for such a sunny day, Izzy reminded Strike of the first time he had met her father, who had been sporting an overcoat in June. A sapphire cross hung around her neck. Strike thought that she had gone as far into official mourning as modern-day dress and sensibilities would permit.

'Come in, come in,' she said nervously, not making eye contact, and standing back, waved him into an airy open-plan sitting and kitchen area, with white walls, brightly patterned sofas and an Art Nouveau fireplace with sinuous, moulded female figures supporting the mantelpiece. The long rear windows looked out onto a small, private courtyard, where expensive wrought iron furniture sat among carefully tended topiary.

'Sit down,' said Izzy, waving him towards one of the colourful sofas. 'Tea? Coffee?'

'Tea would be great, thanks.'

Strike sat down, unobtrusively extracted a number of uncomfortable, beaded cushions from beneath him, and took stock of the room. In spite of the cheery modern fabrics, a more traditional English taste predominated. Two hunting prints stood over a table laden with silver-framed photographs, including a large black and white study of Izzy's parents on their wedding day, Jasper Chiswell dressed in the uniform of the Queen's Own Hussars, Lady Patricia toothy and blonde in a cloud of tulle. Over the mantelpiece hung a large watercolour of three blond toddlers, which Strike assumed represented Izzy and her two older siblings, dead Freddie and the unknown Fizzy.

Izzy clattered around, dropping teaspoons and opening and closing cupboards without finding what she was looking for. At last, turning down Strike's offer of help, she carried a tray bearing a teapot, bone china mugs and biscuits the short distance between kitchenette and coffee table, and set it down.

'Did you watch the opening ceremony?' she asked politely, busy with teapot and strainer.

'I did, yeah,' said Strike. 'Great, wasn't it?'

'Well, I liked the first part,' said Izzy, 'all the industrial revolution bit, but I thought it went, well, a bit PC after that. I'm not sure foreigners will really get why we were talking about the National Health Service, and I must say, I could have done without all the rap music. Help yourself to milk and sugar.'

'Thanks.'

There was a brief silence, broken only by the tinkling of silver and china; that plush kind of silence achievable in London only by people with plenty of money. Even in winter, Strike's attic flat was never completely quiet: music, footsteps and voices filled the Soho street below, and when pedestrians forsook the area, traffic rumbled through the night, while the slightest breath of wind rattled his insecure windows.

'Oh, your cheque,' gasped Izzy, jumping up again to fetch an envelope on the kitchen side. 'Here.'

'Thanks very much,' said Strike, taking it from her.

Izzy sat down again, took a biscuit, changed her mind about eating it and put it on her plate instead. Strike sipped tea that he suspected was of the finest quality, but which, to him, tasted unpleasantly of dried flowers.

'Um,' said Izzy at last, 'it's quite hard to know where to begin.'

She examined her fingers, which were unmanicured.

'I'm scared you'll think I'm bonkers,' she muttered, glancing up at him through her fair lashes.

'I doubt that,' said Strike, putting down his tea and adopting what he hoped was an encouraging expression.

'Have you heard what they found in Papa's orange juice?'

'No,' said Strike.

'Amitriptyline tablets, ground up into powder. I don't know whether you – they're anti-depressants. The police say it's quite an efficient, painless suicide method. Sort of belt and – belt and braces, the pills and the – the bag.'

She took a sloppy gulp of tea.

'They were quite kind, really, the police. Well, they have training, don't they? They told us, if the helium's concentrated enough, one breath and you're . . . you're asleep.'

She pursed her lips together.

'The thing is,' she said loudly, in a sudden rush of words, 'I absolutely *know* that Papa would never have killed himself, because it was something he detested, he always said it was the coward's way out, awful for the family and everybody left behind.

'And it was strange: there was no packaging for the amitriptyline anywhere in the house. No empty boxes, no blister packs, nothing. Of course, a box would have Kinvara's name on it. Kinvara's the one who's prescribed amitriptyline. She's been taking them for over a year.'

Izzy glanced at Strike to see what effect her words had had. When he said nothing, she plunged on.

'Papa and Kinvara rowed the night before, at the reception, right before I came over to talk to you and Charlie. Papa had just told us he'd asked Raff to come over to the Ebury Street house next morning. Kinvara was furious. She asked why and Papa wouldn't tell her, he just smiled, and that infuriated her.'

'Why would—?'

307

'Because she hates all of us,' said Izzy, correctly anticipating Strike's question. Her hands were clutched together, the knuckles white. 'She's always hated anything and anyone that competed with her for Papa's attention or his affection, and she *particularly* hates Raff, because he looks just like his mother, and Kinvara's always been insecure about Ornella, because she's still very glamorous, but Kinvara doesn't like that Raff's a boy, either. She's always been frightened he'd replace Freddie, and maybe get put back in the will. Kinvara married Papa for his money. She never loved him.'

'When you say "put back"—'

'Papa wrote Raff out of his will when Raff ran – when he did the thing – in the car. Kinvara was behind that, of course, she was egging Papa on to have nothing more to do with Raff at all – anyway, Papa told us at Lancaster House he'd invited Raff around next day and Kinvara went quiet, and a couple of minutes later she suddenly announced that she was leaving and walked out. She claims she went back to Ebury Street, wrote Papa a farewell note – but you were there. Maybe you saw it?'

'Yes,' said Strike. 'I did.'

'Yes, so, she claims she wrote that note, packed her bag, then caught the train back to Woolstone.

'The way the police were questioning us, they seemed to think Kinvara leaving him would have made Papa kill himself, but that's just too ridiculous for words! Their marriage has been in trouble for ages. I think he'd been able to see through her for months and months before then. She's been telling crazy fibs and doing all kinds of melodramatic things to try and keep Papa's interest. I promise you, if Papa had believed she was about to leave him, he'd have been relieved, not suicidal, but of course, he wouldn't have taken that note seriously, he'd have known perfectly well it was more play-acting. Kinvara's got nine horses and no income. She'll have to be dragged out of Chiswell House, just like Tinky the First – my Grandpa's third wife,' Izzy explained. 'The Chiswell men seem to have a thing for women with big boobs and horses.'

Flushed beneath her freckles, Izzy drew breath, and said:

'I think Kinvara killed Papa. I can't get it out of my head, can't focus, can't think about anything else. She was convinced there was something going on between Papa and Venetia – she was suspicious from the first moment she saw Venetia, and then the *Sun* snooping around convinced her she was right to be worried – and she probably thought Papa reinstating Raff proved that he was getting ready for a new era, and I think she ground up her anti-depressants and put them in his orange juice when he wasn't looking – he always had a glass of juice first thing, that was his routine – then, when he became sleepy and couldn't fight her off, she put the bag over his head and *then*, after she'd killed him, she wrote that note to try and make it look as though she was the one who was going to divorce *him* and I think she sneaked out of the house after she'd done it, went home to Woolstone and pretended she'd been there when Papa died.'

Running out of breath, Izzy felt for the cross around her neck and played with it nervously, watching for Strike's reaction, her expression both nervous and defiant.

Strike, who had dealt with several military suicides, knew that survivors were nearly always left with a particularly noxious form of grief, a poisoned wound that festered even beyond that of those whose relatives had been dispatched by enemy bullets. He might have his own doubts about the way in which Chiswell had met his end, but he was not about to share them with the disorientated, grief-stricken woman beside him. What struck him chiefly about Izzy's diatribe was the hatred she appeared to feel for her stepmother. It was no trivial charge that she laid against Kinvara, and Strike wondered what it was that convinced Izzy that the rather childish, sulky woman with whom he had shared five minutes in a car could be capable of planning what amounted to a methodical execution.

'The police,' he said at last, 'will have looked into Kinvara's movements, Izzy. In a case like this, the spouse is usually the first one to be investigated.'

'But they're accepting her story,' said Izzy feverishly. 'I can tell they are.'

Then it's true, thought Strike. He had too high an opinion of the Met to imagine that they would be slapdash in confirming the movements of the wife who had had easy access to the murder scene, and who had been prescribed the drugs that had been found in the body.

'Who else knew Papa always drank orange juice in the mornings? Who else had access to amitriptyline and the helium—?'

'Does she admit to buying the helium?' Strike asked.

'No,' said Izzy, 'but she wouldn't, would she? She just sits there doing her hysterical little girl act.' Izzy affected a higher-pitched voice. '"I don't know how it got into the house! Why are you all pestering me, leave me alone, I've been widowed!"'

'I told the police, she attacked Papa with a hammer, over a year ago.'

Strike froze in the act of raising his unappetising tea to his lips.

'What?'

'She attacked Papa with a hammer,' said Izzy, her pale blue eyes boring into Strike, willing him to understand. 'They had a massive row, because – well, it doesn't matter why, but they were out in the stables – this was at home, at Chiswell House, obviously – and Kinvara grabbed the hammer off the top of a toolbox and smashed Papa over the head with it. She was bloody lucky she didn't kill him *then*. It left him with olfactory dysfunction. He couldn't smell and taste as well afterwards, and he got cross at the smallest things, but he insisted on hushing it all up. He bundled her off into some residential centre and told everyone she was ill, "nervous exhaustion".

'But the stable girl witnessed the whole thing and told us what had really happened. She had to call the local GP because Papa was bleeding so badly. It would have been all over the papers if Papa hadn't got Kinvara admitted to a psychiatric ward and warned the papers off.'

Izzy picked up her tea, but her hand was now shaking so badly that she was forced to put it back down again.

'She isn't what men think she is,' said Izzy vehemently. 'They all buy the little girl nonsense, even Raff. "She *did* lose a baby, Izzy ... " But if he heard a *quarter* of what Kinvara says about him behind his back, he'd soon change his tune.

'And what about the open front door?' Izzy said, jumping subject. 'You know all about that, it's how you and Venetia got in, isn't it? That door's never closed properly unless you slam it. Papa knew that. He'd have made sure he closed it properly if he'd been in the house alone, wouldn't he? But if Kinvara was sneaking out early in the morning without wanting to be heard, she'd have had to pull it to and leave it, wouldn't she?

'She isn't very bright, you know. She'd have tidied away all the amitriptyline packaging, thinking it would incriminate her if she left it. I know the police think the absence of packaging is odd, but I can tell they're all leaning towards suicide and that's why I wanted to speak to you, Cormoran,' Izzy finished, edging a little forward in her armchair. 'I want to hire you. I want you to investigate Papa's death.'

Strike had known the request was coming almost from the moment the tea had arrived. The prospect of being paid to investigate what was, in any case, preoccupying Strike to the point of obsession, was naturally inviting. However, clients who sought nothing but confirmation of their own theories were always troublesome. He could not accept the case on Izzy's terms, but compassion for her grief led him to seek a gentler mode of refusal.

'The police won't want me under their feet, Izzy.'

'They don't have to know it's Papa's death you're investigating,' said Izzy eagerly. 'We could pretend we want you to investigate all those stupid trespasses into the garden that Kinvara claims have been going on. It would serve her bloody well right if we took her seriously now.'

'Do the rest of the family know you're meeting me?'

'Oh, yes,' said Izzy eagerly. 'Fizzy's all for it.'

'Is she? Does she suspect Kinvara, too?'

'Well, no,' said Izzy, sounding faintly frustrated, 'but she agrees a hundred per cent that Papa couldn't have killed himself.'

'Who does she think did it, if not Kinvara?'

'Well,' said Izzy, who seemed uneasy at this line of questioning, 'actually, Fizz has got this crazy idea that Jimmy Knight was involved somehow, but obviously, that's ridiculous. Jimmy was in custody when Papa died, wasn't he? You and I saw him being led away by the police the evening before, but Fizz doesn't want to hear that, she's *fixated* on Jimmy! I've said to her, "how did Jimmy Knight know where the amitriptyline and the helium were?" but she won't listen, she keeps going on about how Knight was after revenge—'

311

'Revenge for what?'

'What?' said Izzy restlessly, though Strike knew she had heard him. 'Oh – that doesn't matter now. That's all over.'

Snatching up the teapot, Izzy marched away into the kitchen area, where she added more hot water from the kettle.

'Fizz is irrational about Jimmy,' she said, returning with her teapot refilled and setting it down with a bang on the table. 'She's never been able to stand him since we were teenagers.'

She poured herself a second cup of tea, her colour heightened. When Strike said nothing, she repeated nervously:

'The blackmail business can't have anything to do with Papa dying. That's all over.'

'You didn't tell the police about it, did you?' asked Strike quietly.

There was a pause. Izzy turned steadily pinker. She sipped her tea, then said:

'No.'

Then she said, in a rush, 'I'm sorry, I can imagine how you and Venetia feel about that, but we're more concerned about Papa's legacy now. We can't face it all getting into the press, Cormoran. The only way the blackmail can have any bearing on his death is if it drove him to suicide, and I just don't believe he'd have killed himself over that, or anything else.'

'Della must have found it easy to get her super-injunction,' said Strike, 'if Chiswell's own family were backing her up, saying nobody was blackmailing him.'

'We care more about how Papa's remembered. The blackmail . . . that's all over and done with.'

'But Fizzy still thinks Jimmy might've had something to do with your father's death.'

'That's not – that would be a separate matter, from what he was blackmailing about,' said Izzy incoherently. 'Jimmy had a grudge . . . it's hard to explain . . . Fizz is just silly about Jimmy.'

'How does the rest of the family feel about bringing me in again?'

'Well . . . Raff isn't awfully keen, but it's nothing to do with him. I'd be paying you.'

'Why isn't he keen?'

'Because,' said Izzy, 'well, because the police questioned Raff more than any of the rest of us, because – look, Raff doesn't matter,' she repeated. 'I'll be the client, I'm the one who wants you. Just break Kinvara's alibis, I know you can do it.'

'I'm afraid,' said Strike, 'I can't take the job on those terms, Izzy.'

'Why not?'

'The client doesn't get to tell me what I can and can't investigate. Unless you want the whole truth, I'm not your man.'

'You *are*, I know you're the best, that's why Papa hired you, and that's why I want you.'

'Then you'll need to answer questions when I ask them, instead of telling me what does and doesn't matter.'

She glared at him over the rim of her teacup, then, to his surprise, gave a brittle laugh.

'I don't know why I'm surprised. I knew you were like this. Remember when you argued with Jamie Maugham in Nam Long Le Shaker? Oh, you must remember. You wouldn't back down – the whole table was at you at one point – what was the argument about, d'you—?'

'The death penalty,' said Strike, caught off guard. 'Yeah. I remember.'

For the space of a blink, he seemed to see, not Izzy's clean, bright sitting room, with its relics of a wealthy English past, but the louche, dimly lit interior of a Vietnamese restaurant in Chelsea where, twelve years previously, he and one of Charlotte's friends had got into an argument over dinner. Jamie Maugham's face was smoothly porcine in his memory. He had wanted to show up the oik whom Charlotte had insisted on bringing to dinner instead of Jamie's old friend, Jago Ross.

'. . . and Jamie got rilly, rilly angry with you,' Izzy said. 'He's quite a successful QC now, you know.'

'Must've learned to keep his temper in an argument, then,' said Strike, and Izzy gave another little giggle. 'Izzy,' he said, returning to the main issue, 'if you mean what you say—'

'—I do—'

'—then you'll answer my questions,' said Strike, drawing a notebook out of his pocket.

Irresolute, she watched him take out a pen.

'I'm discreet,' said Strike. 'In the past couple of years, I've been told the secrets of a hundred families and not shared one of them. Nothing irrelevant to your father's death will ever be mentioned again outside my agency. But if you don't trust me—'

'I do,' said Izzy desperately, and to his slight surprise, she leaned forward and touched him on the knee. 'I do, Cormoran, honestly, but it's ... it's hard ... talking about Papa ... '

'I understand that,' he said, readying his pen. 'So let's start with why the police questioned Raphael so much more than the rest of you.'

He could tell that she didn't want to answer, but after a moment's hesitation she said:

'Well, I think it was partly because Papa phoned Raff early on the morning he died. It was the last call he made.'

'What did he say?'

'Nothing that mattered. It can't have had anything to do with Papa dying. But,' she rushed on, as though wanting to extinguish any impression her last words might have made, 'I think the *main* reason Raff isn't keen on me hiring you is that he rather fell for your Venetia while she was in the office and now, well, obviously, he feels a bit of an idiot that he poured his heart out to her.'

'Fell for her, did he?' said Strike.

'Yes, so it's hardly surprising he feels everyone's made a fool of him.'

'The fact remains—'

'I know what you're going to say, but—'

'—if you want me to investigate, it'll be me who decides what matters, Izzy. Not you. So I want to know,' he ticked off all the times she had said that information 'didn't matter' on his fingers as he named them, 'what your father called Raphael about the morning he died, what your father and Kinvara were rowing about when she hit him around the head with a hammer – and what your father was being blackmailed about.'

The sapphire cross winked darkly as Izzy's chest rose and fell. When at last she spoke, it was jerkily.

'It's not up to me to tell you about what Papa and Raff said to each other, the last t-time they spoke. That's for Raff to say.'

'Because it's private?'

'Yes,' she said, very pink in the face. He wondered whether she was telling the truth.

'You said your father had asked Raphael over to the house in Ebury Street the day he died. Was he rearranging the time? Cancelling?'

'Cancelling. Look, you'll have to ask Raff,' she reiterated.

'All right,' said Strike, making a note. 'What caused your stepmother to hit your father around the head with a hammer?'

Izzy's eyes filled with tears. Then, with a sob, she pulled a handkerchief out of her sleeve and pressed it to her face:

'I d–didn't want to tell you that b–because I d–didn't want you to think badly of Papa now he's ... now he's ... you see, he d–did something that ... '

Her broad shoulders shook as she emitted unromantic snorts. Strike, who found this frank and noisy anguish more touching than he would have found delicate eye dabbing, sat in impotent sympathy while she tried to gasp out her apologies.

'I'm – I'm s—'

'Don't be silly,' he said gruffly. 'Of course you're upset.'

But she seemed deeply ashamed of this loss of control, and her hiccoughing return to calm was punctuated with further flustered 'sorrys'. At last, she wiped her face dry as roughly as though cleaning a window, said one final 'I'm so sorry', she straightened her spine and said with a forcefulness Strike rather admired, given the circumstances:

'If you take the case ... once we've signed on the dotted line ... I'll tell you what Papa did that made Kinvara hit him.'

'I assume,' said Strike, 'the same goes for the reason that Winn and Knight were blackmailing your father?'

'Look,' she said, tears welling again, 'don't you see, it's Papa's memory, his legacy, now. I don't want those things to be the thing people remember about him – please help us, Corm. *Please*. I know it wasn't suicide, I *know* it wasn't ... '

He let his silence do the work for him. At last, her expression piteous, she said with a catch in her voice:

'All right. I'll tell you all about the blackmail, but only if Fizz and Torks agree.'

'Who's Torks?' enquired Strike.

'Torquil. Fizzy's husband. We swore we wouldn't ever tell anyone, but I'll t-talk to them and if they agree, I'll t-tell you everything.'

'Doesn't Raphael get consulted?'

'He never knew anything about the blackmail business. He was in jail when Jimmy first came to see Papa and anyway, he didn't grow up with us, so he couldn't – Raff never knew.'

'And what about Kinvara?' asked Strike. 'Did she know?'

'Oh, yes,' said Izzy, and a look of malice hardened her usually friendly features, 'but she *definitely* won't want us to tell you. Oh, not to protect Papa,' she said, correctly reading Strike's expression, 'to protect herself. Kinvara benefited, you see. She didn't mind what Papa was up to, so long as she reaped the rewards.'

39

*... naturally I talk as little about it as possible; it is better to be
silent about such things.*

Henrik Ibsen, *Rosmersholm*

Robin was having a bad Saturday, following an even worse night.

She had woken with a yelp at 4 a.m., with the sensation of being
still tangled in the nightmare in which she had been carrying a whole
bag full of listening devices through darkened streets, knowing that
men in masks were following her. The old knife wound on her arm
had been gaping open and it was the trail of her spurting blood that
her pursuers were following, and she knew she would never make it
to the place where Strike was waiting for the bag of bugs ...

'What?' Matthew had said groggily, half asleep.

'Nothing,' Robin had replied, before lying sleepless until seven,
when she felt entitled to get up.

A scruffy young blond man had been lurking in Albury Street
for the past two days. He barely bothered to conceal the fact that
he was keeping their house under observation. Robin had discussed
him with Strike, who was sure that he was a journalist rather than a
private detective, probably a junior one, dispatched to keep tabs on
her because Mitch Patterson's hourly rate had become an unjustifi-
able expense.

She and Matthew had moved to Albury Street to escape the place
where the Shacklewell Ripper had lurked. It was supposed to be
a place of safety, yet it, too, had become contaminated by contact
with unnatural death. Mid-morning, Robin had taken refuge in the

bathroom before Matthew could realise she was hyperventilating again. Sitting on the bathroom floor, she had recourse to the technique she had learned in therapy, cognitive restructuring, which sought to identify the automatic thoughts of pursuit, pain and danger that sprang into her mind given certain triggers. *He's just some idiot who works for the Sun. He wants a story, that's all. You're safe. He can't get at you. You're completely safe.*

When Robin emerged from the bathroom and went downstairs, she found her husband slamming kitchen doors and drawers as he threw together a sandwich. He did not offer to make one for her.

'What are we supposed to tell Tom and Sarah, with that bastard staring through the windows?'

'Why would we tell Tom and Sarah anything?' asked Robin blankly.

'We're going to theirs for dinner tonight!'

'Oh, no,' groaned Robin. 'I mean, yes. Sorry. I forgot.'

'Well, what if the bloody journalist follows us?'

'We ignore him,' said Robin. 'What else can we do?'

She heard her mobile ringing upstairs and, glad of the excuse to get out of Matthew's vicinity, went to answer it.

'Hi,' said Strike. 'Good news. Izzy's hired us to look into Chiswell's death. Well,' he corrected himself, 'what she actually wants is for us to prove Kinvara did it, but I managed to broaden the remit.'

'That's fantastic!' whispered Robin, carefully closing the bedroom door and sitting down on the bed.

'I thought you'd be pleased,' said Strike. 'Now, what we need for starters is a line on the police investigation, especially forensics. I've just tried Wardle, but he's been warned not to talk to us. They seem to have guessed I'd still be sniffing around. Then I tried Anstis, but nothing doing, he's full time on the Olympics and doesn't know anyone on the case. So I was going to ask, is Vanessa back off compassionate leave?'

'Yes!' said Robin, suddenly excited. It was the first time she had had the useful contact, rather than Strike. 'But even better than Vanessa – she's dating a guy in forensics, Oliver, I've never met him, but—'

'If Oliver would agree to talk to us,' said Strike, 'that would be fantastic. Tell you what, I'll call Shanker, see whether he'll sell me something we can offer in exchange. Call you back.'

He hung up. Though hungry, Robin did not go back downstairs, but stretched out on the smart mahogany bed, which had been a wedding gift from Matthew's father. It was so cumbersome and heavy that it had taken the full complement of removal men, sweating and swearing under their breath, to haul it up the stairs in pieces and reassemble it in the bedroom. Robin's dressing table, on the other hand, was old and cheap. Light as an orange crate without its drawers in, it had required only one man to pick it up and place it between the bedroom windows.

Ten minutes later, her mobile rang again.

'That was quick.'

'Yeah, we're in luck. Shanker's having a rest day. Our interests happen to coincide. There's somebody he wouldn't mind the police picking off. Tell Vanessa we're offering information on Ian Nash.'

'Ian Nash?' repeated Robin, sitting up to grab pen and paper and make a note of the name. 'Who exactly—?'

'Gangster. Vanessa will know who he is,' said Strike.

'How much did it cost?' asked Robin. The personal bond between Strike and Shanker, profound in its way, never interfered with Shanker's rules of business.

'Half the first week's fee,' said Strike, 'but it'll be money well spent if Oliver comes across with the goods. How're you?'

'What?' said Robin, disconcerted. 'I'm fine. Why d'you ask?'

'Don't suppose it's ever occurred to you that I've got a duty of care, as your employer?'

'We're partners.'

'You're a salaried partner. You could sue for poor working conditions.'

'Don't you think,' said Robin, examining the forearm where the eight-inch purple scar still stood out, livid, against her pale skin, 'I'd've already done that, if I was going to? But if you're offering to sort out the loo on the landing—'

'I'm just saying,' persisted Strike, 'it'd be natural if you'd had a bit of reaction. Finding a body isn't many people's idea of fun.'

'I'm absolutely fine,' lied Robin.

I have to be fine, she thought, after they had bidden each other goodbye. *I'm not losing everything, all over again.*

40

At six o'clock on Wednesday morning, Robin, who had again slept in the spare room, got up and dressed herself in jeans, T-shirt, sweatshirt and trainers. Her backpack contained a dark wig that she had bought online and which had been delivered the previous morning, under the very nose of the skulking journalist. She crept quietly downstairs, so as not to wake Matthew, with whom she had not discussed her plan. She knew perfectly well that he would disapprove.

There was a precarious peace between them, even though dinner on Saturday night with Tom and Sarah had been an awful affair: in fact, precisely because dinner had been so dreadful. It had started inauspiciously because the journalist had indeed followed them up the street. They had succeeded in shaking him off, largely due to Robin's counter-surveillance training, which had led them to dodge unseen out of a crowded Tube compartment just before the doors closed, leaving Matthew aggravated by what he considered undignified, childish tricks. But even Matthew could not lay the blame for the rest of the evening at Robin's door.

What had begun as light-hearted analysis over dinner of their failure to win the charity cricket match had turned suddenly nasty and aggressive. Tom had suddenly lashed out drunkenly at Matthew, telling him he was not half as good as he thought he was, that his arrogance had grated on the rest of the team, that, indeed, he was not popular in the office, that he put people's backs up, rubbed them the wrong way. Rocked by the sudden attack, Matthew had tried to ask what he had done wrong at work, but Tom, so drunk that Robin thought he must have started on the wine long before their arrival, had taken Matthew's hurt incredulity as provocation.

'Don't play the fucking innocent with me!' he had shouted. 'I'm not going to stand for it any more! Belittling me and fucking needling me—'

'Was I?' Matthew asked Robin, shaken, as they walked back towards the Tube in the darkness.

'No,' said Robin, honestly. 'You didn't say anything nasty to him at all.'

She added 'tonight' only in her head. It was a relief to be taking a hurt and bewildered Matthew home, rather than the man she usually lived with, and her sympathy and support had won her a couple of days' ceasefire at home. Robin was not about to jeopardise their truce by telling Matthew what she was planning this morning to throw the still-lurking journalist off her trail. She couldn't afford to be followed to a meeting with a forensic pathologist, especially as Oliver, according to Vanessa, had needed a great deal of persuasion to meet Strike and Robin in the first place.

Letting herself out quietly of the French windows into the courtyard behind the house, Robin used one of the garden chairs to clamber onto the top of the wall that divided their garden from that of the house directly behind them, of which the curtains were, mercifully, closed. With a muffled, earthy thud, she slid off the wall onto the neighbours' lawn.

The next part of her escape was a little trickier. She had first to drag a heavy ornamental bench in their neighbour's garden several feet, until it stood plumb with the fence, then, balancing on the back of it, she climbed over the top of the creosoted panel, which swayed precariously as she dropped down into a flowerbed on the other side, where she staggered and fell. Scrambling up again, she hurried across the new lawn to the opposite fence, in which there was a door to the car park on the other side.

To Robin's relief, the bolt opened easily. As she pulled the garden gate closed behind her, she thought ruefully of the footprints she had just left across the dewy lawns. If the neighbours woke early, it would be only too easy to discover whence had come the intruder who had invaded their gardens, shifted their garden furniture and squashed their begonias. Chiswell's killer, if killer there was, had been far more adept at covering their tracks.

Crouching down behind a parked Skoda in the deserted car park that served the garage-less street, Robin used the wing mirror to adjust the dark wig she had taken out of her backpack, then walked off briskly along the street that ran parallel with Albury Street, until she turned right into Deptford High Street.

Other than a couple of vans making early morning deliveries and the proprietor of a newsagent raising the metal security roller door from his shop front, there was hardly anybody around. Glancing over her shoulder, Robin felt a sudden rush, not of panic, but of elation: nobody was following her. Even so, she didn't remove her wig until she was safely on the Tube, giving the young man who had been eyeing her covertly over his Kindle something of a surprise.

Strike had chosen the Corner Café on Lambeth Road for its proximity to the forensics laboratory where Oliver Bargate worked. When Robin arrived, she found Strike standing outside, smoking. His gaze fell to the muddy knees of her jeans.

'Rough landing in a flowerbed,' she explained, as she came within earshot. 'That journalist is still hanging around.'

'Matthew give you a leg up?'

'No, I used garden furniture.'

Strike ground out his cigarette on the wall beside him and followed her into the café, which smelled pleasantly of frying food. In Strike's opinion, Robin looked paler and thinner than usual, but her manner was cheerful as she ordered coffee and two bacon rolls.

'One,' Strike corrected her. 'One,' he repeated regretfully to the man behind the counter. 'Trying to lose weight,' he told Robin, as they took a recently vacated table. 'Better for my leg.'

'Ah,' said Robin. 'Right.'

As he took a seat at a recently vacated table and swept crumbs from it with his sleeve, Strike reflected, not for the first time, that Robin was the only woman he had ever met who had shown no interest in improving him. He knew that he could have changed his mind now and ordered five bacon rolls, and she would simply have grinned and handed them over. This thought made him feel particularly affectionate towards her as she joined him at the table in her muddy jeans.

'Everything OK?' he asked, salivating as he watched her put ketchup on her roll.

'Yes,' lied Robin, 'all good. How *is* your leg?'

'Better than it was. What does this bloke we're meeting look like?'

'Tall, black, glasses,' said Robin thickly, through a mouthful of bread and bacon. Her early morning activity had made her hungrier than she had been in days.

'Vanessa back on Olympics duty?'

'Yeah,' said Robin. 'She's badgered Oliver into meeting us. I don't think he was that keen, but she's after promotion.'

'Dirt on Ian Nash will definitely help,' said Strike. 'From what Shanker told me, the Met's been trying—'

'I think this is him,' whispered Robin.

Strike turned to see a lanky, worried-looking black man in rimless glasses standing in the doorway. He was holding a briefcase. Strike raised a hand in greeting and Robin slid her sandwich and coffee over to the next seat, to allow Oliver to sit opposite Strike.

Robin was not sure what she had expected: he was handsome, with his high-rise hairstyle and pristine white shirt, but seemed suspicious and disapproving, neither of which trait she associated with Vanessa. Nevertheless, he shook the hand Strike proffered and, turning to Robin, said:

'You're Robin? We've always missed each other.'

'Yes,' said Robin, shaking hands, too. Oliver's spotless appearance was making her feel self-conscious about her dishevelled hair and muddy jeans. 'Nice to meet you, at last. It's counter service, shall I get you a tea or coffee?'

'Er – coffee, yeah, that'd be good,' said Oliver. 'Thanks.'

As Robin went to the counter, Oliver turned back to Strike.

'Vanessa says you've got some information for her.'

'Might have,' said Strike. 'It all depends on what you've got for us, Oliver.'

'I'd like to know exactly what you're offering before we take this any further.'

Strike drew an envelope out of his jacket pocket and held it up.

'A car registration number and a hand-drawn map.'

Apparently this meant something to Oliver.

'Can I ask where you got this?'

'You can ask,' said Strike cheerfully, 'but that information's not included in the deal. Eric Wardle will tell you my contact's got a record of hundred per cent reliability, though.'

A group of workmen entered the café, talking loudly.

'This'll all be off the record,' said Strike quietly. 'No one'll ever know you talked to us.'

Oliver sighed, then bent down, opened his briefcase and extracted a large notebook. As Robin returned with a mug of coffee for Oliver and sat back down at the table, Strike readied himself to make notes.

'I've spoken to one of the guys on the team who did forensics,' Oliver said, glancing at the workmen who were now bantering loudly at the next table, 'and Vanessa's had a word with someone who knows where the wider investigation's going.' He addressed Robin. 'They don't know Vanessa is friendly with you. If it gets out that we helped—'

'They won't hear it from us,' Robin assured him.

Frowning slightly, Oliver opened his notebook and consulted the details he had jotted there in a small but legible hand.

'Well, forensics are fairly clear-cut. I don't know how much technical detail you want—'

'Minimal,' said Strike. 'Give us the highlights.'

'Chiswell had ingested around 500mg of amitriptyline, dissolved in orange juice, on an empty stomach.'

'That's a sizeable dose, isn't it?' asked Strike.

'It could have been fatal on its own, even without the helium, but it wouldn't have been as quick. On the other hand, he had heart disease, which would have made him more susceptible. Amitriptyline causes dysrhythmia and cardiac arrest in overdose.'

'Popular suicide method?'

'Yeah,' said Oliver, 'but it's not always as painless as people hope. Most of it was still in his stomach. Very small traces in the duodenum. Suffocation is what actually killed him, on analysis of the lung and brain tissue. Presumably the amitriptyline was a back-up.'

'Prints on the glass and the orange juice carton?'

Oliver turned a page in his notebook.

'The glass only had Chiswell's prints on it. They found the carton in the bin, empty, also with Chiswell's prints on, and others. Nothing suspicious. Just as you'd expect if it had been handled during purchase. Juice inside tested negative for drugs. The drugs went directly into the glass.'

'The helium canister?'

'That had Chiswell's prints on it, and some others. Nothing suspicious. Same as the juice carton, like it had been handled during purchase.'

'Does amitriptyline have a taste?' asked Robin.

'Yeah, it's bitter,' said Oliver.

'Olfactory dysfunction,' Strike reminded Robin. 'After the head injury. He might not have tasted it.'

'Would it have made him groggy?' Robin asked Oliver.

'Probably, especially if he wasn't used to taking it, but people can have unexpected reactions. He might've become agitated.'

'Any sign of how or where the pills were crushed up?' asked Strike.

'In the kitchen. There were traces of powder found on the pestle and mortar there.'

'Prints?'

'His.'

'D'you know whether they tested the homeopathic pills?' asked Robin.

'The what?' said Oliver.

'There was a tube of homeopathic pills on the floor. I trod on them,' Robin explained. 'Lachesis.'

'I don't know anything about them,' said Oliver, and Robin felt a little foolish for mentioning them.

'There was a mark on the back of his left hand.'

'Yes,' said Oliver, turning back to his notes. 'Abrasions to face and a small mark on the hand.'

'On the face, too?' said Robin, freezing with her sandwich in her hand.

'Yes,' said Oliver.

'Any explanation?' asked Strike.

'You're wondering whether the bag was forced over his head,' said Oliver; it was a statement, not a question. 'So did MI5. They know he didn't make the marks himself. Nothing under his own nails. On the other hand, there was no bruising to the body to show force, nothing disarranged in the room, no signs of a struggle—'

'Other than the bent sword,' said Strike.

'I keep forgetting you were there,' said Oliver. 'You know all this.'

'Marks on the sword?'

'It had been cleaned recently, but Chiswell's prints were on the handle.'

'What time of death are we looking at?'

'Between 6 and 7 a.m.,' said Oliver.

'But he was fully dressed,' mused Robin.

'From what I've heard about him, he was quite literally the kind of bloke who wouldn't have been caught dead in pyjamas,' said Oliver drily.

'Met's inclining to suicide, then?' asked Strike.

'Off the record, I think an open verdict is quite likely. There are a few discrepancies that need explaining. You know about the open front door, of course. It's warped. It won't close unless you shut it with force, but it sometimes jumps back open again if you slam it too hard. So it could have been accidental, the fact that it was open. Chiswell might not have realised he'd left it ajar, but equally, a killer might not have known the trick to closing it.'

'You don't happen to know how many keys to the door there were?' asked Strike.

'No,' said Oliver. 'As I'm sure you'll appreciate, Van and I had to sound only casually interested, asking all these questions.'

'He's a dead government minister,' said Strike. 'Surely you didn't have to sound too casual?'

'I know one thing,' said Oliver. 'He had plenty of reasons to kill himself.'

'Such as?' enquired Strike, pen poised over his notebook.

'His wife was leaving him—'

'Allegedly,' said Strike, writing.

'—they'd lost a baby, his eldest son died in Iraq, the family say he was acting strangely, drinking heavily and so on, and he had serious money problems.'

'Yeah?' said Strike. 'Like what?'

'He was almost wiped out in the 2008 crash,' said Oliver. 'And then there was . . . well, that business you two were investigating.'

'D'you know where the blackmailers were, at the time of—?'

Oliver made a swift, convulsive movement that nearly knocked over his coffee. Leaned towards Strike he hissed:

'There's a super-injunction out, in case you haven't—'

'Yeah, we've heard,' said Strike.

'Well, I happen to like my job.'

'OK,' said Strike, unperturbed, but lowering his voice. 'I'll rephrase my question. Have they looked into the movements of Geraint Winn and Jimmy—?'

'Yes,' said Oliver curtly, 'and both have alibis.'

'What are they?'

'The former was in Bermondsey with—'

'Not Della?' blurted Robin, before she could stop herself. The idea of his blind wife being Geraint's alibi had struck her, somehow, as indecent. She had formed the impression, whether naively or not, that Della stood apart from Geraint's criminal activity.

'No,' said Oliver tersely, 'and do we have to use names?'

'Who, then?' asked Strike.

'Some employee. He claims he was with the employee and the bloke confirmed it.'

'Were there other witnesses?'

'I don't know,' said Oliver, with a trace of frustration. 'I assume so. They're happy with the alibi.'

'What about Ji – the other man?'

'He was in East Ham with his girlfriend.'

'Was he?' said Strike, making a note of it. 'I saw him being marched off to a police van, the night before Chiswell died.'

'He was let off with a caution. But,' Oliver said quietly, 'black-mailers don't generally kill their victims, do they?'

'Not if they're getting money out of them,' said Strike, still writing. 'But Knight wasn't.'

Oliver looked at his watch.

'Couple more things,' said Strike equably, his elbow still planted on the envelope containing Ian Nash's details. 'Does Vanessa know anything about a phone call to his son that Chiswell made on the morning of his death?'

'Yeah, she said something about that,' said Oliver, flicking backwards and forwards through his notebook to find the information. 'Yeah, he made two calls just after 6 a.m. First to his wife, then to his son.'

Strike and Robin looked at each other again.

'We knew about the call to Raphael. He called his wife as well?'

'Yeah, he called her first.'

Oliver seemed to read their reaction correctly, because he said:

'The wife's totally in the clear. She was the first person they investigated, once they were satisfied it wasn't politically motivated, obviously.

'A neighbour saw her go into the house on Ebury Street the evening before and come out shortly afterwards with a bag, two hours before her husband came back. A taxi driver picked her up half-way down the street and took her to Paddington. She was caught on camera on the train back to wherever she lives – is it Oxfordshire? – and apparently there was someone at the house when she got home, who can vouch for the fact that she arrived there before midnight and never left again until the police came round to tell her Chiswell was dead. Multiple witnesses to her whole journey.'

'Who was at the house with her?'

'That, I don't know.' Oliver's eyes moved to the envelope still lying beneath Strike's elbow. 'And that really is everything I've got.'

Strike had asked everything he had wanted to know, and had gained a couple of bits of information he had not expected, including the abrasions to Chiswell's face, his poor finances and the phone call to Kinvara in the early morning.

'You've been a big help,' he told Oliver, sliding the envelope across the table. 'Much appreciated.'

Oliver appeared relieved that the encounter was over. He stood up and, with one more hasty handshake and a nod to Robin, departed the café. Once Oliver had stridden out of sight, Robin sat back in her chair and sighed.

'What's that glum expression for?' asked Strike, draining his mug of tea.

'This is going to be the shortest job on record. Izzy wants us to prove it was Kinvara.'

'She wants the truth about her father's death,' said Strike, but he grinned at Robin's sceptical expression, 'and, yeah, she's hoping it was Kinvara. Well, we'll have to see whether we can break all those alibis, won't we? I'm going to Woolstone on Saturday. Izzy's invited me over to Chiswell House, so I can meet her sister. Are you in? I'd rather not drive, the state my leg's in at the moment.'

'Yes, of course,' said Robin immediately.

The idea of getting out of London with Strike, even for a day, was so appealing that she did not bother to consider whether she and Matthew had plans, but surely, in the glow of their unexpected rapprochement, he would raise no difficulties. After all, she had not worked for a week and a half. 'We can take the Land Rover. It'll be better on country roads than your BMW.'

'You might need diversionary tactics if that hack's still watching you,' said Strike.

'I think I could probably throw them off more easily in a car than on foot.'

'Yeah, you probably could,' said Strike.

Robin was in possession of an advanced driving qualification. Though he had never told her so, Robin was the only person by whom he would willingly be driven.

'What time are we supposed to be at Chiswell House?'

'Eleven,' said Strike, 'but plan to be away for the whole day. I fancy taking a look at the Knights' old place while we're there.' He hesitated. 'I can't remember whether I told you ... I kept Barclay undercover with Jimmy and Flick.'

He was braced for annoyance that he had not discussed it with her, resentment that Barclay had been working when she wasn't, or, perhaps most justifiably, a demand to know what he was playing at, given the state of the agency's finances, but she simply said, with more amusement than rancour:

'You know you didn't tell me. Why did you keep him there?'

'Because I've got a gut feeling there's a lot more to the Knight brothers than meets the eye.'

'You always tell me to mistrust gut feelings.'

'Never claimed not to be a hypocrite, though. And brace yourself,' Strike added, as they got up from the table, 'Raphael's not happy with you.'

'Why not?'

'Izzy says he fell for you. Quite upset you turned out to be an undercover detective.'

'Oh,' said Robin. A faint pink blush spread over her face. 'Well, I'm sure he'll bounce back fast enough. He's that type.'

41

I was thinking of what brought us together from the first, what
links us so closely to one another . . .

Henrik Ibsen, *Rosmersholm*

Strike had spent many hours of his life trying to guess what he had
done to cause the sullen silence of a woman in his vicinity. The best
that could be said for the prolonged sulk in which Lorelei spent most
of Friday evening was that he knew exactly how he had offended
her, and was even prepared to concede that her displeasure was, to
some extent, justified.

Within five minutes of his arrival at her flat in Camden, Izzy
had called his mobile, partly to tell him about a letter that she had
received from Geraint Winn, but mainly, he knew, to talk. She was
not the first of his clients to assume that they had purchased, along
with detective services, a mixture of father-confessor and therapist.
Izzy gave every sign that she was settling in to spend her entire
Friday evening talking to Strike, and the flirtatiousness that had been
apparent in the knee touching of their last encounter was even more
pronounced by phone.

A tendency to size Strike up as a potential lover was not uncommon in the sometimes fragile and lonely women he dealt with in his
professional life. He had never slept with a client, in spite of occasional temptation. The agency meant too much to him, but even had
Izzy held attraction for him, he would have been careful to keep his
manner on the antiseptic side of professional, because she would be
forever tainted in his mind by association with Charlotte.

332

In spite of his genuine desire to cut the call short – Lorelei had cooked, and was looking particularly lovely in a silky sapphire blue dress that resembled nightwear – Izzy had displayed the persistent adhesiveness of a teasel. It took Strike nearly three-quarters of an hour to disentangle himself from his client, who laughed long and loudly at even his mildest jokes, so that Lorelei could hardly fail to know that it was a woman who was at the end of the line. Hardly had he got rid of Izzy and begun to explain to Lorelei that she was a grief-stricken client, than Barclay had called with an update on Jimmy Knight. The mere fact that he had taken the second call, considerably briefer though it was, had, in Lorelei's eyes, compounded his original offence.

This was the first time he and Lorelei had met since she had retracted her declaration of love. Her wounded and affronted demeanour over dinner confirmed him in the unwilling belief that, far from wanting their no-strings arrangement to continue, she had clung to the hope that if she stopped pressuring him, he would be free to reach the realisation that he was, in fact, deeply in love with her. Talking on the phone for the best part of an hour, while dinner slowly shrivelled in the oven, had dashed her hopes of a perfect evening, and the reset of their relationship.

Had Lorelei only accepted his sincere apology, he might have felt like sex. However, by half-past two in the morning, at which time she finally burst into tears of mingled self-recrimination and self-justification, he was too tired and bad-tempered to accept physical overtures which would, he feared, assume an importance in her mind that he did not want to give them.

This has to end, he thought, as he rose, hollow-eyed and dark-jawed, at six o'clock, moving as quietly as possible in the hope that she would not wake before he made his way out of her flat. Forgoing breakfast, because Lorelei had replaced the kitchen door with an amusingly retro bead curtain that rattled loudly, Strike made it all the way to the top of the stairs to the street before Lorelei emerged from the dark bedroom, sleep tousled, sad and desirable in a short kimono.

'Weren't you even going to say goodbye?'

Don't cry. Please don't fucking cry.

'You looked very peaceful. I've got to go, Robin's picking me up at—'

'Ah,' said Lorelei. 'No, you wouldn't want to keep Robin hanging around.'

'I'll call you,' said Strike.

He thought he caught a sob as he reached the front door, but by making a noisy business of opening it, he could credibly claim not to have heard.

Having left in plenty of time, Strike made a detour to a handy McDonald's for an Egg McMuffin and a large coffee, which he consumed at an unwiped table, surrounded by other early Saturday risers. A young man with a boil on the back of his neck was reading the *Independent* right ahead of Strike, who read the words '*Sports Minister in Marriage Split*' over the youth's shoulder before he turned a page.

Drawing out his phone, Strike Googled 'Winn marriage'. The news stories popped up immediately: '*Minister for Sport Splits from Husband: Separation "Amicable"*', '*Della Winn Calls Time on Marriage*', '*Blind Paralympics Minister to Divorce*'.

The stories from major newspapers were all factual and on the short side, a few padded out with details of Della's impressive career within politics and outside. The press's lawyers would, of course, be particularly careful around the Winns just now, with their super-injunction still in place. Strike finished his McMuffin in two bites, jammed an unlit cigarette in his mouth and limped out of the restaurant. Out on the pavement he lit up, then brought up the website of a well-known and scurrilous political blogger on his phone.

The brief paragraph had been written only a few hours previously.

Which creepy Westminster couple known to share a predilection for youthful employees are rumoured to be splitting at last? He is about to lose access to the nubile political wannabes on whom he has preyed so long, but she has already found a handsome young 'helper' to ease the pain of separation.

Less than forty minutes later, Strike emerged from Barons Court Tube station to lean up against the pillar-box in front of the entrance. Cutting a solitary figure beneath the Art Nouveau lettering and open segmented pediment of the grand station behind him, he took out his phone again and continued to read about the Winns' separation. They had been married over thirty years. The only couple he knew who had been together that long were the aunt and uncle back in Cornwall, who had served as surrogate parents to Strike and his sister during those regular intervals when his mother had been unwilling or unable to care for them.

A familiar roar and rattle made Strike look up. The ancient Land Rover that Robin had taken off her parents' hands was trundling towards him. The sight of Robin's bright gold head behind the wheel caught the tired and faintly depressed Strike off-guard. He experienced a wave of unexpected happiness.

'Morning,' said Robin, thinking that Strike looked terrible as he opened the door and shoved in a holdall. 'Oh, sod off,' she added, as a driver behind her slammed on his horn, aggravated by the time Strike was taking to get inside.

'Sorry . . . leg's giving me trouble. Dressed in a hurry.'

'No problem – *and you!*' Robin shouted at the driver now overtaking them, who was gesticulating and mouthing obscenities at her.

Finally dropping down into the passenger seat, Strike slammed the door and Robin pulled away from the kerb.

'Any trouble getting away?' he asked.

'What d'you—?'

'The journalist.'

'Oh,' she said. 'No – he's gone. Given up.'

Strike wondered just how difficult Matthew had been about Robin giving up a Saturday for work.

'Heard about the Winns?' he asked her.

'No, what's happened?'

'They've split up.'

'*No!*'

'Yep. In all the papers. Listen to this . . .'

He read aloud the blind item on the political website.

'God,' said Robin quietly.

'I had a couple of interesting calls last night,' Strike said, as they sped towards the M4.

'Who from?'

'One from Izzy, the other from Barclay. Izzy got a letter from Geraint yesterday,' said Strike.

'Really?' said Robin.

'Yeah. It was sent to Chiswell House a few days back, not her London flat, so she only opened it when she went back to Woolstone. I got her to scan and email it to me. Want to hear?'

'Go on,' said Robin.

'"My very dear Isabella—"'

'Ugh,' said Robin, with a small shudder.

'"As I hope you will understand",' read Strike, '"Della and I did not feel it appropriate to contact you in the immediate, shocking aftermath of your father's death. We do so now in a spirit of friendliness and compassion".'

'If you need to point that out . . .'

'"Della and I may have had political and personal differences with Jasper, but I hope we never forgot that he was a family man, and we are aware that your personal loss will be severe. You ran his office with courtesy and efficiency and our little corridor will be the poorer for your absence".'

'He always cut Izzy dead!' said Robin.

'Exactly what Izzy said on the phone last night,' replied Strike. 'Stand by, you're about to get a mention.

'"I cannot believe that you had anything to do with the almost certainly illegal activities of the young woman calling herself 'Venetia'. We feel it only fair to inform you that we are currently investigating the possibility that she may have accessed confidential data on the multiple occasions she entered this office without consent."'

'I never looked at anything except the plug socket,' said Robin, 'and I didn't access the office on "multiple occasions". Three. That's "a few", at most.'

'"As you know, the tragedy of suicide has touched our own family. We know that this will be an extremely difficult and painful time for you. Our families certainly seem fated to bump into each other in their darkest hours.

'"Sending our very best wishes, our thoughts are with all of you, etc, etc".'

Strike closed the letter on his phone.

'That's not a letter of condolence,' said Robin.

'Nope, it's a threat. If the Chiswells blab about anything you found out about Geraint or the charity, he'll go after them, hard, using you.'

She turned onto the motorway.

'When did you say that letter was sent?'

'Five, six days ago,' said Strike, checking.

'It doesn't sound as though he knew his marriage was over then, does it? All that "our corridor will be poorer for your absence" guff. He's lost his job if he's split with Della, surely?'

'You'd think so,' agreed Strike. 'How handsome would you say Aamir Mallik is?'

'What?' said Robin, startled. 'Oh ... the "young helper"? Well, he's OK looking, but not model material.'

'It must be him. How many other young men's hands is she holding and calling darling?'

'I can't imagine him as her lover,' said Robin.

'"A man of your habits",' quoted Strike. 'Pity you can't remember what number that poem was.'

'Is there one about sleeping with an older woman?'

'The best-known ones are on that very subject,' said Strike. 'Catullus was in love with an older woman.'

'Aamir isn't in love,' said Robin. 'You heard the tape.'

'He didn't sound smitten, I grant you. I wouldn't mind knowing what causes the animal noises he makes at night, though. The ones the neighbours complain about.'

His leg was throbbing. Reaching down to feel the join between prosthesis and stump, he knew that part of the problem was having put on the former hurriedly, in the dark.

'D'you mind if I readjust—?'

'Carry on,' said Robin.

Strike rolled up his trouser leg and proceeded to remove the prosthesis. Ever since he had been forced to take two weeks off wearing it, the skin at the end of his stump had shown a tendency to object to renewed friction. Retrieving E45 cream from his holdall, he applied it liberally to the reddened skin.

'Should've done this earlier,' he said apologetically.

Deducing from the presence of Strike's holdall that he had come from Lorelei's, Robin found herself wondering whether he had been too pleasurably occupied to worry about his leg. She and Matthew had not had sex since their anniversary weekend.

'I'll leave it off for a bit,' said Strike, heaving both prosthesis and holdall into the back of the Land Rover, which he now saw was empty but for a tartan flask and two plastic cups. This was a disappointment. There had always been a carrier bag full of food on the previous occasions they had ventured out of London by car.

'No biscuits?'

'I thought you were trying to lose weight?'

'Nothing eaten on a car journey counts, any competent dietician will tell you that.'

Robin grinned.

'"Calories Are Bollocks: the Cormoran Strike Diet".'

'"Hunger Strike: Car Journeys I Have Starved On".'

'Well, you should've had breakfast,' said Robin, and to her own annoyance, she wondered for the second time whether he had been otherwise engaged.

'I did have breakfast. Now I want a biscuit.'

'We can stop somewhere if you're hungry,' said Robin. 'We should have plenty of time.'

As Robin accelerated smoothly to overtake a couple of dawdling cars, Strike was aware of an ease and restfulness that could not be entirely ascribed to the relief of removing his prosthesis, nor even of having escaped Lorelei's flat, with its kitschy décor and its heartsore occupant. The very fact that he had removed his leg while Robin drove, and was not sitting with all muscles clenched, was highly unusual. Not only had he had to work hard to overcome anxiety at being driven by other people in the aftermath of the explosion that had blown off his leg, he had a secret but deep-rooted aversion to women drivers, a prejudice he ascribed largely to early, nerve-wracking experiences with all his female relatives. Yet it was not merely a prosaic appreciation of her competence that had caused that sudden lifting of the heart when he had seen her driving towards him this morning. Now, watching the road, he experienced a spasm of memory, sharp with both pleasure and pain; his nostrils seemed to be full again with the smell of white roses, as he held her on the stairs at her wedding and he felt her mouth beneath his in the hot fug of a hospital car park.

'Could you pass me my sunglasses?' asked Robin. 'In my bag there.'

He handed them over.

'Want a tea?'

'I'll wait,' said Robin, 'you carry on.'

He reached into the back for the thermos and poured himself a plastic cup full. The tea was exactly as he liked it.

'I asked Izzy about Chiswell's will last night,' Strike told Robin.

'Did he leave a lot?' asked Robin, remembering the shabby interior of the house in Ebury Street.

'Much less than you might've thought,' said Strike, taking out the notebook in which he had jotted everything Izzy had told him. 'Oliver was right. The Chiswells are on their uppers – in a relative sense, obviously,' he added.

'Apparently Chiswell's father spent most of the capital on women and horses. Chiswell had a very messy divorce from Lady Patricia. Her family was wealthy and could afford better lawyers. Izzy and her sister are all right for cash through their mother's family. There's a trust fund, which explains Izzy's smart flat in Chelsea.

'Raphael's mother walked away with hefty child support, which seems to have nearly cleaned Chiswell out. After that, he plunged the little he had left into some risky equities advised by his stockbroker son-in-law. "Torks" feels pretty bad about that, apparently. Izzy would rather we didn't mention it today. The 2008 crash virtually wiped Chiswell out.

'He tried to do some planning against death duties. Shortly after he lost most of his cash, some valuable family heirlooms and Chiswell House itself were made over to the eldest grandson—'

'Pringle,' said Robin.

'What?'

'Pringle. That's what they call the eldest grandson. Fizzy's got three children,' Robin explained, 'Izzy was always banging on about them: Pringle, Flopsy and Pong.'

'Jesus Christ,' muttered Strike. 'It's like interviewing the Teletubbies.'

Robin laughed.

'—and otherwise, Chiswell seems to have been hoping he could put himself right by selling off land around Chiswell House and objects of less sentimental value. The house in Ebury Street's been remortgaged.'

'So Kinvara and all her horses are living in her step-grandson's house?' said Robin, changing up a gear to overtake a lorry.

'Yeah, Chiswell left a letter of wishes with his will, asking that Kinvara has the right to remain in the house lifelong, or until she remarries. How old's this Pringle?'

'About ten, I think.'

'Well, it'll be interesting to see whether the family honour Chiswell's request given that one of them thinks Kinvara killed him. Mind you, it's a moot point whether she'll have enough money to keep the place running, from what Izzy told me last night. Izzy and her sister were each left fifty grand, and the grandchildren get ten grand apiece, and there's hardly enough cash to honour those bequests. That leaves Kinvara with what's left from the house in Ebury Street once it's sold off and all other personal effects, minus the valuable stuff that was already put into the grandson's name. Basically, he's leaving her with the junk that wasn't worth selling and any personal gifts he gave her during the marriage.'

'And Raphael gets nothing?'

'I wouldn't feel too sorry for him. According to Izzy, his glamorous mother's made a career out of asset-stripping wealthy men. He's in line to inherit a flat in Chelsea from her.

'So all in all, it's hard to make a case for Chiswell being killed for his money,' said Strike. 'What *is* the other sister's bloody name? I'm not calling her Fizzy.'

'Sophia,' said Robin, amused.

'Right, well, we can rule her out. I've checked, she was taking a

Riding for the Disabled lesson in Northumberland on the morning
he died. Raphael had nothing to gain from his father's death, and Izzy
thinks he knew it, although we'll need to check that. Izzy herself got
what she called "a bit squiffy" at Lancaster House and felt a bit fragile
the following day. Her neighbour can vouch for the fact that she was
having tea in the shared courtyard behind their flats at the time of
death. She told me that quite naturally last night.'

'Which leaves Kinvara,' said Robin.

'Right. Now, if Chiswell didn't trust her with the information
that he'd called in a private detective, he might not have been honest
about the state of the family finances, either. It's possible she thought
she was going to get a lot more than she has, but—'

'—she's got the best alibi in the family,' said Robin.

'Exactly,' said Strike.

They had now left behind the clearly man-made border shrubs
and bushes that had lined the motorway as it passed Windsor and
Maidenhead. There were real old trees left and right now, trees that
had predated the road, and which would have seen their fellows felled
to make way for it.

'Barclay's call was interesting,' Strike went on, turning a couple
of pages in his notebook. 'Knight's been in a nasty mood ever since
Chiswell died, though he hasn't told Barclay why. On Wednesday
night he was goading Flick, apparently, said he agreed with her ex-
flatmate that Flick had bourgeois instincts – d'you mind if I smoke?
I'll wind down the window.'

The breeze was bracing, though it made his tired eyes water.
Holding his burning cigarette out of the car between drags,
he went on:

'So Flick got really angry, said she'd been doing "that shitty job
for you" and then said it wasn't her fault they hadn't got forty grand,
at which Jimmy went, to quote Barclay, "apeshit". Flick stormed out
and on Thursday morning, Jimmy texted Barclay and told him he was
going back to where he grew up, to visit his brother.'

'Billy's in Woolstone?' said Robin, startled. She realised that she
had come to think of the younger Knight brother as an almost mythical person.

341

'Jimmy might've been using him as a cover story. Who knows where he's really got to ... Anyway, Jimmy and Flick reappeared last night in the pub, all smiles. Barclay says they'd obviously made up over the phone and in the two days he was away, she's managed to find herself a nice non-bourgeois job.'

'That was good going,' said Robin.

'How d'you feel about shop work?'

'I did a bit in my teens,' said Robin. 'Why?'

'Flick's got herself a few hours part time in a jewellery shop in Camden. She told Barclay it's run by some mad Wiccan woman. It's minimum wage and the boss sounds barking mad, so they're having trouble finding anyone else.'

'Don't you think they might recognise me?'

'The Knight lot have never seen you in person,' said Strike. 'If you did something drastic with your hair, broke out the coloured contact lenses again ... I've got a feeling,' he said, drawing deeply on his cigarette, 'that Flick's hiding a lot. How did she know what Chiswell's blackmailable offence was? She was the one who told Jimmy, don't forget, which is strange.'

'Wait,' said Robin. 'What?'

'Yeah, she said, when I was following them on the march,' said Strike. 'Didn't I tell you?'

'No,' said Robin.

As she said it, Strike remembered that he had spent the week after the march at Lorelei's with his leg up, when he had still been so angry at Robin for refusing to work that he had barely spoken to her. Then they had met at the hospital, and he had been far too distracted and worried to pass on information in his usual methodical fashion.

'Sorry,' he said. 'It was that week after ...'

'Yes,' she said, cutting him off. She, too, preferred not to think about the weekend of the march. 'So what exactly did she say?'

'That he wouldn't know what Chiswell had done, but for her.'

'That's weird,' said Robin, 'seeing as he's the one who grew up right beside them.'

'But the thing they were blackmailing him about only happened six years ago, after Jimmy had left home,' Strike reminded her. 'If you ask me, Jimmy's been keeping Flick around because she knows too much. He might be scared of ending it, in case she starts talking.

'If you can't get anything useful out of her, you can pretend selling earrings isn't for you and leave, but the state their relationship's in, I think Flick might be in the mood to confide in a friendly stranger. Don't forget,' he said, throwing the end of his cigarette out of the window and winding it back up, 'she's also Jimmy's alibi for the time of death.'

Excited about the prospect of going back undercover, Robin said: 'I hadn't forgotten.'

She wondered how Matthew would react if she shaved the sides of her head, or dyed her hair blue. He had not put up much of a show of resentment at her spending Saturday with Strike. Her long days of effective house arrest, and her sympathy about the argument with Tom, seemed to have bought her credit.

Shortly after half past ten, they turned off the motorway onto a country road that wound down into the valley where the tiny village of Woolstone lay nestled. Robin parked beside a hedgerow full of Traveller's Joy, so that Strike could reattach his prosthesis. Replacing her sunglasses in her handbag, Robin noticed two texts from Matthew. They had arrived two hours earlier, but the alert of her mobile must have been drowned out by the racket of the Land Rover.

The first read:

All day. What about Tom?

The second, which had been sent ten minutes later, said:

Ignore last, was meant for work.

Robin was rereading these when Strike said:
'Shit.'
He had already reattached his prosthesis, and was staring through his window at something she could not see.
'What?'
'Look at that.'

343

Strike pointed back up the hill down which they had just driven. Robin ducked her head so that she could see what had caught his attention.

A gigantic prehistoric white chalk figure had been cut into the hillside. To Robin, it resembled a stylised leopard, but the realisation of what it was supposed to be had already hit her when Strike said:

"'Up by the horse. He strangled the kid, up by the horse.'"

42

In a family there is always something or other going awry . . .
Henrik Ibsen, *Rosmersholm*

A flaking wooden sign marked the turning to Chiswell House. The drive, which was overgrown and full of potholes, was bordered on the left by a dense patch of woodland and on the right, by a long field that had been separated into paddocks by electric fences, and contained a number of horses. As the Land Rover lurched and rumbled towards the out-of-sight house, two of the largest horses, spooked by the noisy and unfamiliar car, took off. A chain reaction then occurred, as most of their companions began to canter around, too, the original pair kicking out at each other as they went.

'Wow,' said Robin, watching the horses as the Land Rover swayed over the uneven ground. 'She's got stallions in together.'

'That's bad, is it?' asked Strike, as a hairy creature the colour of jet lashed out with teeth and back legs at an equally large animal he would have categorised as brown, though doubtless the coat colour had some rarefied equine name.

'It's not usually done,' said Robin, wincing as the black stallion's rear legs made contact with its companion's flank.

They turned a corner and saw a plain-faced neo–classical house of dirty yellow stone. The gravelled forecourt, like the drive, had several potholes and was strewn with weeds, the windows were grubby and a large tub of horse feed sat incongruously beside the front door. Three cars were already sitting there: a red Audi Q3, a racing green

345

Range Rover and an old and muddy Grand Vitara. To the right of the house lay a stable block and to the left, a wide croquet lawn that had long since been given over to the daisies. More dense woodland lay beyond.

As Robin braked, an overweight black Labrador and a rough-coated terrier came shooting out of the front door, both barking. The Labrador seemed keen to make friends but the Norfolk terrier, which had a face like a malevolent monkey, barked and growled until a fair-haired man, dressed in stripy shirt and mustard-coloured corduroy trousers, appeared at the doorway and bellowed:

'SHUT UP, RATTENBURY!'

Cowed, the dog subsided into low growls, all directed at Strike.

'Torquil D'Amery,' drawled the fair-haired man, approaching Strike with his hand outstretched. There were deep pockets beneath his pale blue eyes and his shiny pink face looked as though it never needed a razor. 'Ignore the dog, he's a bloody menace.'

'Cormoran Strike. This is—'

Robin had just held out her hand when Kinvara erupted out of the house, wearing old jodhpurs and a washed-out T-shirt, her loose red hair falling everywhere.

'For God's *sake* . . . don't you know *anything* about horses?' she shrieked at Strike and Robin. 'Why did you come up the drive so fast?'

'You should wear a hard hat if you're going in there, Kinvara!' Torquil called at her retreating figure, but she stormed away giving no sign that she had heard him. 'Not your fault,' he assured Strike and Robin, rolling his eyes. 'Got to take the drive at speed or you'll get stuck in one of the bloody holes, ha ha. Come on in – ah, here's Izzy.'

Izzy emerged from the house, wearing a navy shirtdress, the sapphire cross still around her neck. To Robin's slight surprise, she embraced Strike as though he was an old friend come to offer condolences.

'Hi, Izzy,' he said, taking half a step backwards to extricate himself from the embrace. 'You know Robin, obviously.'

'Oh, yah, got to get used to calling you "Robin" now,' said Izzy, smiling and kissing Robin on both cheeks. 'Sorry if I slip up and call you Venetia – I'm bound to, that's how I still think of you.

'Did you hear about the Winns?' she asked, in almost the same breath.

They nodded.

'Horrible, *horrible* little man,' said Izzy. 'I'm delighted Della's given him the push.

'Anyway, come along in ... where's Kinvara?' she asked her brother-in-law as she led them into the house, which seemed gloomy after the brightness outside.

'Bloody horses are upset again,' said Torquil, over the renewed barking of the Norfolk terrier. 'No, fuck off, Rattenbury, you're staying outside.'

He banged the front door closed on the terrier, which began to whine and scratch at it instead. The Labrador padded quietly in Izzy's wake as she led them through a dingy hallway with wide stone stairs, into a drawing room on the right.

Long windows faced out over the croquet lawn and the woods. As they entered, three white-blond children raced through the overgrown grass outside with raucous cries, then passed out of sight. There was nothing of modernity about them. In their dress and their hairstyles they might have walked straight out of the 1940s.

'They're Torquil and Fizzy's,' said Izzy fondly.

'Guilty as charged,' said Torquil, proudly. 'M'wife's upstairs, I'll go and get her.'

As Robin turned away from the window she caught a whiff of a strong, heady scent that gave her an unaccountable feeling of tension until she spotted the vase of stargazer lilies standing on a table behind a sofa. They matched the faded curtains, once scarlet and now a washed-out pale rose, and the frayed fabric on the walls, where two patches of darker crimson showed that pictures had been removed. Everything was threadbare and worn. Over the mantelpiece hung one of the few remaining paintings, which showed a stabled horse with a splashy brown and white coat, its nose touching a starkly white foal curled in the straw.

Beneath this painting, and standing so quietly that they had not immediately noticed him, was Raphael. With his back to the empty grate, hands in the pockets of his jeans, he appeared more Italian

347

than ever in this very English room, with its faded tapestry cushions, its gardening books piled in a heap on a small table and its chipped Chinoiserie lamps.

'Hi, Raff,' said Robin.

'Hello, Robin,' he said, unsmiling.

'This is Cormoran Strike, Raff,' said Izzy. Raphael didn't move, so Strike walked over to him to shake hands, which Raphael did reluctantly, returning his hand to his jeans immediately afterwards.

'Yah, so, Fizz and I were just talking about Winn,' said Izzy, who seemed greatly preoccupied with the news of the Winns' split. 'We just hope to God he's going to keep his mouth shut, because now Papa's gorn, he can say whatever he likes about him and get away with it, can't he?'

'You've got the goods on Winn, if he tries,' Strike reminded her.

She cast him a look of glowing gratitude.

'You're right, of course, and we wouldn't have that if it weren't for you . . . and Venetia – Robin, I mean,' she added, as an afterthought.

'Torks, I'm downstairs!' bellowed a woman from just outside the room, and a woman who was unmistakably Izzy's sister backed into the room carrying a laden tray. She was older, heavily freckled and weather-beaten, her blonde hair streaked with silver, and she wore a striped shirt very like her husband's, though she had twinned hers with pearls. 'TORKS!' she bellowed at the ceiling, making Robin jump. 'I'M DOWN HERE!'

She set the tray with a clatter on the needlepoint ottoman that stood in front of Raff and the fireplace.

'Hi, I'm Fizzy. Where's Kinvara gorn?'

'Faffing around with the horses,' said Izzy, edging around the sofa and sitting down. 'Excuse not to be here, I expect. Grab a pew, you two.'

Strike and Robin took two sagging armchairs that stood side by side, at right angles to the sofa. The springs beneath them seemed to have worn out decades ago. Robin felt Raphael's eyes on her.

'Izz tells me you know Charlie Campbell,' Fizzy said to Strike, pouring everybody tea.

'That's right,' said Strike.

'Lucky man,' said Torquil, who had just re-entered the room.

Strike gave no sign he had heard this.

'Did you ever meet Jonty Peters?' Fizzy continued. 'Friend of the Campbells? He had something to do with the police . . . no, Badger, these aren't for you . . . Torks, what did Jonty Peters do?'

'Magistrate,' said Torquil promptly.

'Yah, of course,' said Fizzy, 'magistrate. Did you ever meet Jonty, Cormoran?'

'No,' said Strike, 'afraid not.'

'He was married to what's-her-name, lovely gel, Annabel. Did masses for Save the Children, got her CBE last year, so well-deserved. Oh, but if you knew the Campbells, you must have met Rory Moncrieff?'

'Don't think so,' said Strike patiently, wondering what Fizzy would have said if he'd told her that the Campbells had kept him as far from their friends and family as was possible. Perhaps she was equal even to that: *oh, but then, you must have run across Basil Plumley? They loathed him, yah, violent alcoholic, but his wife did climb Kilimanjaro for Dogs Trust . . .*

Torquil pushed the fat Labrador away from the biscuits and it ambled away into a corner, where it flopped down for a doze. Fizzy sat down between her husband and Izzy on the sofa.

'I don't know whether Kinvara's intending to come back,' said Izzy. 'We might as well get started.'

Strike asked whether the family had heard any more about the progress of the police investigation. There was a tiny pause, during which the distant shrieks of children echoed across the overgrown lawn.

'We don't know much more than I've already told you,' said Izzy, 'though I think we all get the sense – don't we?' she appealed to the other family members, 'that the police think it's suicide. On the other hand, they clearly feel they have to investigate thoroughly—'

'That's because of who he was, Izz,' Torquil interrupted. 'Minister of the Crown, obviously they're going to look into it more deeply than they would for the bloke in the street. You should know, Cormoran,' he said portentously, adjusting his substantial weight on the sofa, 'sorry, gels, but I'm going to say it – personally, I think it *was* suicide.

'I understand, of course I do, that that's a hard thought to bear, and don't think I'm not happy you've been brought in!' he assured Strike. 'If it puts the gels' minds at rest, that's all to the good. But the, ah, male contingent of the family – eh, Raff? – think there's nothing more to it than, well, m'father-in-law felt he couldn't go on. Happens. Not in his right mind, clearly. Eh, Raff?' repeated Torquil.

Raphael did not seem to relish the implicit order. Ignoring his brother-in-law, he addressed Strike directly.

'My father was acting strangely in the last couple of weeks. I didn't understand why, at the time. Nobody had told me he was being blackm—'

'We're not going into that,' said Torquil quickly. 'We agreed. Family decision.'

Izzy said anxiously:

'Cormoran, I know you wanted to know what Papa was being blackmailed about—'

'Jasper broke no law,' said Torquil firmly, 'and that's the end of it. I'm sure you're discreet,' he said to Strike, 'but these things get out, they always do. We don't want the papers crawling all over us again. We're agreed, aren't we?' he demanded of his wife.

'I suppose so,' said Fizzy, who seemed conflicted. 'No, of course we don't want it all over the papers, but Jimmy Knight had good reason to wish Papa harm, Torks, and I think it's important Cormoran knows that, at least. You know he was *here*, in Woolstone, this week?'

'No,' said Torquil, 'I didn't.'

'Yah, Mrs Ankill saw him,' said Fizzy. 'He asked her whether she'd seen his brother.'

'Poor little Billy,' said Izzy vaguely. 'He wasn't right. Well, you wouldn't be, would you, if you were brought up by Jack o'Kent? Papa was out with the dogs one night years ago,' she told Strike and Robin, 'and he saw Jack *kicking* Billy, literally *kicking* him, all around their garden. The boy was naked. When he saw Papa, Jack o'Kent stopped, of course.'

The idea that this incident should have been reported to either police or social work seemed not to have occurred to Izzy, or indeed her father. It was as though Jack o'Kent and his son were wild creatures in the wood, behaving, regrettably, as such animals naturally behaved.

'I think the less said about Jack o'Kent,' said Torquil, 'the better. And you say Jimmy had reason to wish your father harm, Fizz, but what he really wanted was money, and killing your father certainly wasn't going—'

'He was angry with Papa, though,' said Fizzy determinedly. 'Maybe, when he realised Papa wasn't going to pay up, he saw red. He was a holy terror when he was a teenager,' she told Strike. 'Got into far-left politics early. He used to be down in the local pub with the Butcher brothers, telling everybody that Tories should be hung, drawn and quartered, trying to sell people the *Socialist Worker* . . .'

Fizzy glanced sideways at her younger sister, who rather determinedly, Strike thought, ignored her.

'He was trouble, always trouble,' Fizzy said. 'The girls liked him, but—'

The drawing room door opened and, to the rest of the family's evident surprise, Kinvara strode in, flushed and agitated. After a little difficulty extricating himself from his sagging armchair, Strike succeeded in standing up and held out a hand.

'Cormoran Strike. How do you do?'

Kinvara looked as though she would have liked to ignore his friendly overture, but shook the offered hand with bad grace. Torquil pulled up another chair beside the ottoman, and Fizzy poured an extra cup of tea.

'Horses all right, Kinvara?' Torquil asked heartily.

'Well, Mystic's taken another chunk out of Romano,' she said with a nasty glance at Robin, 'so I've had to call the vet again. He gets upset every time somebody comes up the drive too fast, otherwise he's absolutely fine.'

'I don't know why you've put the stallions in together, Kinvara,' said Fizzy.

'It's a myth that they don't get along,' Kinvara snapped back. 'Bachelor herds are perfectly common in the wild. There was a study in Switzerland that proved they can coexist peacefully once they've established the hierarchy among themselves.'

She spoke in dogmatic, almost fanatic, tones.

'We were just telling Cormoran about Jimmy Knight,' Fizzy told Kinvara.

'I thought you didn't want to go into—?'

'Not the blackmail,' said Torquil hastily, 'but what a horror he was when he was younger.'

'Oh,' said Kinvara, 'I see.'

'Your stepdaughter's worried that he may have had something to do with your husband's death,' said Strike, watching her for a reaction.

'I know,' said Kinvara, with apparent indifference, her eyes following Raphael, who had just walked away from the grate to fetch a pack of Marlboro Lights that lay beside a table lamp. 'I never knew Jimmy Knight. The first time I ever laid eyes on him was when he turned up at the house a year ago to speak to Jasper. There's an ashtray beneath that magazine, Raphael.'

Her stepson lit his cigarette and returned, carrying the ashtray, which he placed on a table beside Robin, before resuming his position in front of the empty fireplace.

'That was the start of it,' Kinvara continued. 'The blackmail. Jasper wasn't actually there that night, so Jimmy talked to me. Jasper was furious when he came home and I told him.'

Strike waited. He suspected that he wasn't the only one in the room who thought Kinvara might break the family vow of *omerta* and blurt out what Jimmy had come to say. She refrained, however, so Strike drew out his notebook.

'Would you mind if I run through a few routine questions? I doubt there'll be anything you haven't already been asked by the police. Just a couple of points I'd like clarified, if you don't mind.

'How many keys are there, to the house in Ebury Street?'

'Three, as far as *I'm* aware,' said Kinvara. The emphasis suggested that the rest of the family might have been hiding keys from her.

'And who had them?' asked Strike.

'Well, Jasper had his own,' she said, 'and I had one and there was a spare that Jasper had given to the cleaning woman.'

'What's her name?'

'I've no idea. Jasper let her go a couple of weeks before he – he died.'

'Why did he sack her?' asked Strike.

'Well, if you must know, we got rid of her because we were tightening our belts.'

'Had she come from an agency?'

'Oh no. Jasper was old-fashioned. He put up a card up in a local shop and she applied. I think she was Romanian or Polish or something.'

'Have you got her details?'

'No. Jasper hired and fired her. I never even met her.'

'What happened to her key?'

'It *was* in the kitchen drawer at Ebury Street, but after he died we found out that Jasper had removed it and locked it up in his desk at work,' said Kinvara. 'It was handed back by the ministry, with all his other personal effects.'

'That seems odd,' Strike said. 'Anyone know why he'd have done that?'

The rest of the family looked blank, but Kinvara said:

'He was always security conscious and he'd been paranoid lately – except when it came to the horses, of course. All the keys to Ebury Street are a special kind. Restricted. Impossible to copy.'

'Tricky to copy,' said Strike, making a note, 'but not impossible, if you know the right people. Where were the other two keys at the time of death?'

'Jasper's was in his jacket pocket and mine was here, in my handbag,' said Kinvara.

'The canister of helium,' said Strike, moving on. 'Does anybody know when it was purchased?'

Total silence greeted these words.

'Was there ever a party,' Strike asked, 'perhaps for one of the children—?'

'Never,' said Fizzy. 'Ebury Street was the place Papa used for work. He never hosted a party there that I can remember.'

'You, Mrs Chiswell,' Strike asked Kinvara. 'Can you remember any occasion—?'

'No,' she said, cutting across him. 'I've already told the police this. Jasper must have bought it himself, there's no other explanation.'

'Has a receipt been found? A credit card bill?'

'He probably paid cash,' said Torquil helpfully.

'Another thing I'd like to clear up,' Strike said, working down the list he had made himself, 'is this business of the phone calls the minister made on the morning of his death. Apparently he called you, Mrs Chiswell, and then you, Raphael.'

Raphael nodded. Kinvara said:

'He wanted to know whether I meant it when I said I was leaving and I said yes, I did. It wasn't a long conversation. I didn't know – I didn't know who your assistant really was. She appeared out of nowhere and Jasper was odd in his manner when I asked about her and I – I was very upset. I thought there was something going on.'

'Were you surprised that your husband waited until the morning to call you about the note you'd left?' asked Strike.

'He told me he hadn't spotted it when he came in.'

'Where had you left it?'

'On his bedside table. He was probably drunk when he got back. He's been – he *was* – drinking heavily. Ever since the blackmail business started.'

The Norfolk terrier that had been shut out of the house suddenly popped up at one of the long windows and began barking at them again.

'Bloody dog,' said Torquil.

'He misses Jasper,' said Kinvara. 'He was Jasper's d-dog—'

She stood up abruptly and walked away to snatch some tissues from a box sitting on top of the gardening books. Everybody looked uncomfortable. The terrier barked on and on. The sleeping Labrador woke and let out a single deep bark in return, before one of the tow-headed children reappeared on the lawn, shouting for the Norfolk terrier to come and play ball. It bounded off again.

'Good boy, Pringle!' shouted Torquil.

In the absence of barking, Kinvara's small gulps and the sounds of the Labrador flopping down to sleep again filled the room. Izzy, Fizzy and Torquil exchanged awkward glances, while Raphael stared rather stonily ahead. Little though she liked Kinvara, Robin found the family's inaction unfeeling.

'Where did that picture come from?' asked Torquil, with an artificial air of interest, squinting at the equine painting over Raphael's head. 'New, isn't it?'

'That was one of Tinky's,' said Fizzy, squinting up at it. 'She brought a bunch of horsey junk over from Ireland with her.'

'See that foal?' said Torquil, staring critically at the picture. 'You know what it looks like? Lethal white syndrome. Heard of it?' he asked his wife and sister-in-law. '*You'll* know all about that, Kinvara,' he said, clearly under the impression that he was graciously offering a way back into polite conversation. 'Pure white foal, seems healthy when it's born, but defective bowel. Can't pass faeces. M'father bred horses,' he explained to Strike. 'They can't survive, lethal whites. The tragedy is that they're born alive, so the mare feeds them, gets attached and then—'

'Torks,' said Fizzy tensely, but it was too late. Kinvara blundered out of the room. The door slammed.

'What?' said Torquil, surprised. 'What have I—?'

'*Baby*,' whispered Fizzy.

'Oh, Lord,' he said, 'I clean forgot.'

He got to his feet, hitched up his mustard corduroys, embarrassed and defensive.

'Oh, come on,' he said, to the room at large. 'I couldn't expect her to take it that way. Horses in a bloody painting!'

'You know what she's like,' said Fizzy, 'about *anything* connected with birth. Sorry,' she said to Strike and Robin. 'She had a baby that didn't survive, you see. Very sensitive on the subject.'

Torquil approached the painting and squinted over Raphael's head at words etched on a small plaque set into the frame.

'"Mare Mourning",' he read. 'There you are, you see,' he said, with an air of triumph. 'Foal *is* dead.'

'Kinvara likes it,' said Raphael unexpectedly, 'because the mare reminds her of Lady.'

'Who?' said Torquil.

'The mare that got laminitis.'

'What's laminitis?' asked Strike.

'A disease of the hoof,' Robin told him.

'Oh, do you ride?' asked Fizzy keenly.

'I used to.'

'Laminitis is serious,' Fizzy told Strike. 'It can cripple them. They need a lot of care, and sometimes nothing can be done, so it's kindest—'

'My stepmother had been nursing this mare for weeks,' Raphael told Strike, 'getting up in the middle of the night and so on. My father waited—'

'Raff, this really hasn't got anything to do with anything,' said Izzy.

'—waited,' continued Raphael doggedly, 'until Kinvara went out one day, called in the vet without telling her and had the horse put down.'

'Lady was suffering,' said Izzy. 'Papa told me what a state she was in. It was pure selfishness, keeping her alive.'

'Yeah, well,' said Raphael, his eyes on the lawn beyond the windows, 'if I'd gone out and come back to the corpse of an animal I loved, I might've reached for the nearest blunt instrument as well.'

'Raff,' said Izzy, 'please!'

'You're the one who wanted this, Izzy,' he said, with grim satisfaction. 'D'you really think Mr Strike and his glamorous assistant aren't going to find Tegan and talk to her? They'll soon know what a shit Dad could—'

'Raff!' said Fizzy sharply.

'Steady on, old chap,' said Torquil, something that Robin had never thought to hear outside a book. 'This whole thing's been bloody upsetting, but there's no need for that.'

Ignoring all of them, Raphael turned back to Strike.

'I suppose your next question was going to be, what did my father say to *me*, when he called me that morning?'

'That's right,' said Strike.

'He ordered me down here,' said Raphael.

'Here?' repeated Strike. 'Woolstone?'

'*Here*,' said Raphael. 'This house. He told me he thought Kinvara was going to do something stupid. He sounded woolly. A bit odd. Like he had a heavy hangover.'

'What did you understand by "something stupid"?' asked Strike, his pen poised over his pad.

'Well, she's got form at threatening to top herself,' said Raff, 'so that, I suppose. Or he might've been afraid she was going to torch what little he had left.' He gestured around the shabby room. 'As you can see, that wasn't much.'

'Did he tell you she was leaving him?'

'I got the impression that things were bad between them, but I can't remember his exact words. He wasn't very coherent.'

'Did you do as he asked?' asked Strike.

'Yep,' said Raphael. 'Got in my car like an obedient son, drove all the way here and found Kinvara alive and well in the kitchen, raging about Venetia – Robin, I mean,' he corrected himself. 'As you may have gathered, Kinvara thought Dad was fucking her.'

'Raff!' said Fizzy, sounding outraged.

'There's no need,' said Torquil, 'for that kind of language.'

Everybody was carefully avoiding catching Robin's eye. She knew she had turned red.

'Seems odd, doesn't it?' Strike asked. 'Your father asking you to come all the way down to Oxfordshire, when there were people far closer he could have asked to keep an eye on his wife? Didn't I hear that there was someone here overnight?'

Izzy piped up before Raphael could answer.

'Tegan *was* here that night – the stable girl – because Kinvara won't leave the horses without a sitter,' she said, and then, correctly anticipating Strike's next question, 'I'm afraid nobody's got any contact details for her, because Kinvara had a row with her right after Papa died, and Tegan walked out. I don't actually know where she's working now. Don't forget, though,' said Izzy, leaning forwards and addressing Strike earnestly, 'Tegan was probably fast asleep when Kinvara claims she came back here. This is a big house. Kinvara could have claimed to have come back any time and Tegan might not have known.'

'If Kinvara was there with him in Ebury Street, why would he tell me to come and find her here?' Raphael asked, exasperated. 'And how do you explain how she got here ahead of me?'

Izzy looked as though she would like to make a good retort to this, but appeared unable to think of one. Strike knew now why Izzy had said that the content of Chiswell's phone call to his son 'didn't matter': it further undermined the case for Kinvara as murderer.

'What's Tegan's surname?' he asked.

'Butcher,' said Izzy.

'Any relation to the Butcher brothers Jimmy Knight used to hang around with?' Strike asked.

Robin thought the three on the sofa seemed to be avoiding each other's eyes. Fizzy then answered.

'Yes, as a matter of fact, but—'

'I suppose I could try and contact the family, see whether they'll give me Tegan's number,' said Izzy. 'Yes, I'll do that, Cormoran, and let you know how I get on.'

Strike turned back to Raphael.

'So, did you set off immediately after your father asked you to go to Kinvara?'

'No, I ate something, first, and showered,' said Raphael. 'I wasn't exactly looking forward to dealing with her. She and I aren't each other's favourite people. I got here around nine.'

'How long did you stay?'

'Well, in the end, I was here for hours,' said Raphael quietly. 'A couple of police arrived to break the news that Dad was dead. I could hardly walk out after that, could I? Kinvara nearly coll—'

The door reopened and Kinvara walked back in, returned to her hard-backed chair, her face set, tissues clutched in her hand.

'I've only got five minutes,' she said. 'The vet's just called, he's in the area, so he'll pop in to see Romano. I can't stay.'

'Could I ask something?' Robin asked Strike. 'I know it might be nothing at all,' she said, to the room at large, 'but there was a small blue tube of homeopathic pills on the floor beside the minister when I found him. Homeopathy didn't seem to be the kind of thing he'd—'

'What kind of pills?' asked Kinvara sharply, to Robin's surprise.

'Lachesis,' said Robin.

'In a small blue tube?'

'Yes. Were they yours?'

'Yes, they were!'

'You left them in Ebury Street?' asked Strike.

'No, I lost them weeks ago . . . but I never had them *there*,' she said, frowning, more to herself than to the room. 'I bought them in London, because the pharmacy in Woolstone didn't have any.'

She frowned, clearly reconstructing events in her mind.

'I remember, I tasted a couple outside the chemists, because I wanted to know whether he'd notice them in his feed—'

'Sorry, what?' asked Robin, unsure she had heard correctly.

'Mystic's feed,' said Kinvara. 'I was going to give them to Mystic.'

'You were going to give homeopathic tablets to a *horse*?' said Torquil, inviting everyone else to agree that this was funny.

'Jasper thought it was a ludicrous idea, too,' said Kinvara vaguely, still lost in recollection. 'Yes, I opened them up right after I'd paid for them, took a couple, and,' she mimed the action, 'put the tube in my jacket pocket, but when I got home, they weren't there any more. I thought I must have dropped them somehow . . .'

Then she gave a little gasp and turned red. She seemed to be boggling at some inner, private realisation. Then, realising that everybody was still watching her, she said:

'I travelled home from London with Jasper that day. We met at the station, got the train together . . . he took them out of my pocket! He stole them, so I couldn't give them to Mystic!'

'Kinvara, don't be so utterly ridiculous!' said Fizzy, with a short laugh.

Raphael suddenly ground out his cigarette in the china ashtray at Robin's elbow. He seemed to be refraining from comment with difficulty.

'Did you buy more?' Robin asked Kinvara.

'Yes,' said Kinvara, who seemed almost disorientated with shock, though Robin thought her conclusion as to what had happened to her pills very strange. 'They were in a different bottle, though. That blue tube, that's the one I bought first.'

'Isn't homeopathy just placebo effect?' Torquil enquired of the room at large. 'How could a *horse*—?'

'Torks,' muttered Fizzy, through gritted teeth. 'Shut up.'

'Why would your husband have stolen a tube of homeopathic pills from you?' asked Strike curiously. 'It seems—'

'Pointlessly spiteful?' asked Raphael, arms folded beneath the picture of the dead foal. 'Because you're so convinced you're right, and the other person's wrong, that it's OK to stop them doing something harmless?'

'Raff,' said Izzy at once, 'I know you're upset—'

'I'm not upset, Izz,' said Raphael. 'Very liberating, really, going back through all the shitty things Dad did while he was alive—'

'That's enough, boy!' said Torquil.

'Don't call me "boy",' said Raphael, shaking another cigarette out of his packet. 'All right? Don't fucking call me "boy".'

'You'll have to excuse Raff,' Torquil told Strike loudly, 'he's upset with m'late father-in-law because of the will.'

'I already knew I'd been written out of the will!' snapped Raphael, pointing at Kinvara. '*She* saw to that!'

'Your father didn't need any persuasion from me, I promise you!' said Kinvara, scarlet in the face now. 'Anyway, you've got plenty of money, your mother spoils you rotten.' She turned to Robin. 'His mother left Jasper for a diamond merchant, after taking Jasper for everything she could lay her hands on—'

'Could I ask another couple of questions?' said Strike loudly, before a plainly fuming Raphael could speak.

'The vet will be here for Romano in a minute,' said Kinvara. 'I need to get back to the stable.'

'Just a couple, and I'm done,' Strike assured her. 'Did you ever miss any amitriptyline pills? I think you were prescribed them, weren't you?'

'The police asked me this. I might have lost some,' said Kinvara, with irritating vagueness, 'but I can't be sure. There was a box I thought I'd lost and then I found it again and it didn't have as many pills in as I remembered, and I know I meant to leave a pack at Ebury Street in case I ever forgot when I was coming up from London, but when the police asked me I couldn't remember whether I'd actually done it or not.'

'So you couldn't swear to it that you had pills missing?'

'No,' said Kinvara. 'Jasper might have stolen some, but I can't swear to it.'

'Have you had any more intruders in your garden since your husband died?' asked Strike.

'No,' said Kinvara. 'Nothing.'

'I heard that a friend of your husband's tried to call him early the morning that he died, but couldn't get through. D'you happen to know who the friend was?'

'Oh . . . yes. It was Henry Drummond,' said Kinvara.

'And who's—?'

'He's an art dealer, very old friend of Papa's,' interrupted Izzy. 'Raphael worked for him for a little while – didn't you, Raff? – until he came to help Papa at the House of Commons.'

'I can't see what Henry's got to do with anything,' said Torquil, with an angry little laugh.

'Well, I think that's everything,' said Strike, ignoring this comment as he closed his notebook, 'except that I'd be glad to know whether you think your husband's death was suicide, Mrs Chiswell.'

The hand grasping the tissue contracted tightly.

'Nobody's interested in what I think,' she said.

'I assure you, I am,' said Strike.

Kinvara's eyes flickered from Raphael, who was scowling at the lawn outside, to Torquil.

'Well, if you want my opinion, Jasper did a very stupid thing, right before he—'

'Kinvara,' said Torquil sharply, 'you'd be best advised—'

'I'm not interested in your advice!' said Kinvara, turning on him suddenly, eyes narrowed. 'After all, it's your advice that brought this family to financial ruin!'

Fizzy shot her husband a look across Izzy, warning him against retorting. Kinvara turned back to Strike.

'My husband provoked somebody, somebody I warned him he shouldn't upset, shortly before he died—'

'You mean Geraint Winn?' asked Strike.

'No,' said Kinvara, 'but you're close. Torquil doesn't want me to say anything about it, because it involves his good friend Christopher—'

'Bloody hell!' exploded Torquil. He got to his feet, again hitching up his mustard corduroys, and looking incensed. 'My God, are we dragging total outsiders into this fantasy, now? What the bloody hell has Christopher got to do with anything? M'father-in-law killed himself!' he told Strike loudly, before rounding on his wife and sister-in-law. 'I've tolerated this nonsense because you gels want peace of mind, but frankly, if this is where it's going to lead—'

Izzy and Fizzy set up an outcry, both trying to placate him and justify themselves, and in the midst of this mêlée, Kinvara got to her feet, tossed back her long red hair and walked towards the door, leaving Robin with the strong impression that she had lobbed this grenade into the conversation deliberately. At the door she paused, and the others' heads turned, as though she had called to them. In her high, clear, childish voice, Kinvara said:

'You all come back here and treat this house as though you're the real owners and I'm a guest, but Jasper said I could live here as long as I'm alive. Now I need to see the vet and when I get back, I'd like you all to have gone home. You aren't welcome here any more.'

43

*... I am afraid it will not be long before we hear something of
the family ghost.*

Henrik Ibsen, *Rosmersholm*

Robin asked whether she might use the bathroom before they
departed from Chiswell House and was shown across the hall by
Fizzy, who was still fuming at Kinvara.

'How dare she,' said Fizzy, as they crossed the hall. '*How dare she?*
This is Pringle's house, not hers.' And, in the next breath, '*Please* don't
pay any attention to what she said about Christopher, she's simply
trying to get a rise out of Torks, it was a disgusting thing to do, he's
simply *livid.*'

'Who *is* Christopher?' Robin asked.

'Well – I don't know whether I should say,' replied Fizzy. 'But
I suppose, if you – of course, he can't have anything to do with
it. It's just Kinvara's spite. She's talking about Sir Christopher
Barrowclough–Burns. Old friend of Torks' family. Christopher's
a senior civil servant and he was that boy Mallik's mentor at the
Foreign Office.'

The lavatory was chilly and antiquated. As she bolted the door,
Robin heard Fizzy striding back to the drawing room, doubtless
to placate the angry Torquil. She looked around: the chipped,
painted stone walls were bare except for many small dark holes in
which the occasional nail still stuck out. Robin presumed Kinvara
was responsible for the removal of a large number of Perspex
frames from the wall, which now stood stacked on the floor facing

the toilet. They contained a jumble of family photographs in messy collages.

After drying her hands on a damp towel that smelled of dog, Robin crouched down to flick through these frames. Izzy and Fizzy had been almost indistinguishable as children, making it impossible to tell which of them was cartwheeling on the croquet lawn, or jumping a pony at a local gymkhana, dancing in front of a Christmas tree in the hall or embracing the young Jasper Chiswell at a shooting picnic, the men all in tweeds and Barbours.

Freddie, however, was immediately recognisable, because unlike his sisters he had inherited his father's protuberant lower lip. As white-blond in youth as his niece and nephews, he featured frequently, beaming for the camera as a toddler, stony-faced as a child in a new prep school uniform, muddy and triumphant in rugby kit.

Robin paused to examine a group shot of teenagers, all dressed head to toe in white fencing jackets, Union Jacks ran down the sides of everyone's breeches. She recognised Freddie, who was standing in the middle of the group, holding a large silver cup. At the far end of the group was a miserable-looking girl whom Robin recognised immediately as Rhiannon Winn, older and thinner than she had been in the photograph her father had shown Robin, her slightly cringing air at odds with the proud smiles on every other face.

Continuing to search the boards, Robin stopped at the last one to examine the faded photograph of a large party.

It had been taken in a marquee, from what seemed to be a stage. Many bright blue helium balloons in the shape of the number eighteen danced over the crowd's heads. A hundred or so teenagers had clearly been bidden to face the camera. Robin scanned the scene carefully and found Freddie easily enough, surrounded by a large group of both boys and girls whose arms were slung around each other's shoulders, beaming and, in some cases, braying with laughter. After nearly a minute, Robin spotted the face she had instinctively sought: Rhiannon Winn, thin, pale and unsmiling beside the drinks table. Close behind her, half-hidden in shadow, were a couple of boys who were not in black tie, but jean and T-shirts. One in particular was darkly handsome and long-haired, his T-shirt bearing a picture of The Clash.

Robin got out her mobile and took a picture of both the fencing team and the eighteenth birthday party photographs, then carefully replaced the stack of Perspex boards as she had found them, and left the bathroom.

She thought for a second that the silent hall was deserted. Then she saw that Raphael was leaning up against a hall table, his arms folded.

'Well, goodbye,' said Robin, starting to walk towards the front door.

'Hang on a minute.'

As she paused, he pushed himself off the table and approached her.

'I've been quite angry with you, you know.'

'I can understand why,' said Robin quietly, 'but I was doing what your father hired me to do.'

He moved closer, coming to a halt beneath an old glass lantern hanging from the ceiling. Half the light bulbs were missing.

'I'd say you're bloody good at it, are you? Getting people to trust you?'

'That's the job,' said Robin.

'You're married,' he said, eyes on her left hand.

'Yes,' she said.

'To Tim?'

'No . . . there isn't any Tim.'

'You're not married to *him*?' said Raphael quickly, pointing outside.

'No. We just work together.'

'And that's your real accent,' said Raphael. 'Yorkshire.'

'Yes,' she said. 'This is it.'

She thought he was going to say something insulting. The olive dark eyes moved over her face, then he shook his head slightly.

'I quite like the voice, but I preferred "Venetia". Made me think of masked orgies.'

He turned and walked away, leaving Robin to hurry back out into the sunshine to rejoin Strike, who she presumed would be waiting impatiently in the Land Rover.

She was wrong. He was still standing beside the car's bonnet, while Izzy, who was standing very close to him, talked rapidly in an undertone. When she heard Robin's feet on the gravel behind her,

Izzy took a step backwards with what, to Robin, seemed a slightly guilty, embarrassed air.

'Lovely to see you again,' Izzy said, kissing Robin on both cheeks, as though this had been a simple social call. 'And you'll ring me, won't you?' she said to Strike.

'Yep, I'll keep you updated,' he said, moving around to the passenger seat.

Neither Strike nor Robin spoke as she turned the car around. Izzy waved them off, a slightly pathetic figure in her loose shirt dress. Strike raised a hand to her as they took the bend in the drive that hid her from their sight.

Trying not to upset the skittish stallions, Robin drove at a snail's pace. Glancing left, Strike saw that the injured horse had been removed from the field, but in spite of Robin's best intentions, as the noisy old car lurched past its field, the black stallion took off again.

'Who d'you reckon,' said Strike, watching the horse plunge and buck, 'first took a look at something like that and thought, "I should get on its back"?'

'There's an old saying,' said Robin, trying to steer around the worst of the potholes, '"the horse is your mirror". People say dogs resemble their owners, but I think it's truer of horses.'

'Making Kinvara highly strung and prone to lash out on slight provocation? Sounds about right. Turn right here. I want to get a look at Steda Cottage.'

A bare two minutes later, he said:

'Here. Go up here.'

The track to Steda Cottage was so overgrown that Robin had missed it entirely the first time they had passed it. It led deep into the woodland that lay hard up against the gardens of Chiswell House, but unfortunately, the Land Rover was only able to proceed for ten yards before the track became impassable by car. Robin cut the engine, privately worried about how Strike was going to manage a barely discernible path of earth and fallen leaves, overgrown with brambles and nettles, but as he was already getting out, she followed suit, slamming the driver's door behind her.

The ground was slippery, the tree canopy so dense that the track was in deep shade, dank and moist. A pungent, green, bitter smell filled their nostrils, and the air was alive with the rustle of birds and small creatures whose habitat was being rudely invaded.

'So,' said Strike, as they struggled through the bushes and weeds. 'Christopher Barrowclough-Burns. That's a new name.'

'No, it isn't,' said Robin.

Strike looked sideways at her, grinning, and immediately tripped on a root, remaining upright at some cost to his sore knee.

'*Shit* . . . I wondered whether you remembered.'

'"Christopher didn't promise anything about the pictures",' quoted Robin promptly. 'He's a civil servant who mentored Aamir Mallik at the Foreign Office. Fizzy just told me.'

'We're back to "a man of your habits", aren't we?'

Neither spoke for a short spell as they concentrated on a particularly treacherous stretch of path where whip-like branches clung willingly to fabric and skin. Robin's skin was a pale, dappled green in the sun filtered by the ceiling of leaves above them.

'See any more of Raphael, after I went outside?'

'Er – yes, actually,' said Robin, feeling slightly self-conscious. 'He came out of the sitting room as I was coming out of the loo.'

'Didn't think he'd pass up another chance of talking to you,' said Strike.

'It wasn't like that,' Robin said untruthfully, remembering the remark about masked orgies. 'Izzy whispering anything interesting, back there?' she asked.

Amused by the reciprocal jab, Strike took his eyes off the path, thereby failing to spot a muddy stump. He tripped for a second time, this time saving himself from a painful fall by grabbing a tree covered in a prickly climbing plant.

'*Fuck*—'

'Are you—?'

'I'm fine,' he said, angry with himself, examining the palm that was now full of thorns and starting to pull them out with his teeth. He heard a loud snap of wood behind him and turned to see Robin holding out a fallen branch, which she had broken to make a rough walking stick.

'Use this.'

'I don't—' he began, but catching sight of her stern expression, he gave in. 'Thanks.'

They set off again, Strike finding the stick more useful than he wanted to admit.

'Izzy was just trying to convince me that Kinvara could have sneaked back to Oxfordshire, after bumping off Chiswell between six and seven in the morning. I don't know whether she realises there are multiple witnesses to every stage of Kinvara's journey from Ebury Street. The police probably haven't gone into detail with the family yet, but I think, once the penny drops that Kinvara can't have done it in person, Izzy'll start suggesting she hired a hitman. What did you make of Raphael's various outbursts?'

'Well,' said Robin, navigating around a patch of nettles, 'I can't blame him, getting annoyed with Torquil.'

'No,' agreed Strike, 'I think old Torks would grate on me, too.'

'Raphael seems really angry with his father, doesn't he? He didn't *have* to tell us about Chiswell putting that mare down. I thought he was almost going out of his way to paint his father as ... well ... '

'A bit of a shit,' agreed Strike. 'He thought Chiswell had stolen those pills of Kinvara's out of malice, too. That whole episode was bloody strange, actually. What made you so interested in those pills?'

'They seemed so out of place for Chiswell.'

'Well, it was a good call. Nobody else seems to have asked questions about them. So what does the psychologist make of Raphael denigrating his dead father?'

Robin shook her head, smiling, as she usually did when Strike referred to her in this way. She had dropped out of her psychology course at university, as he well knew.

'I'm serious,' said Strike, grimacing as his false foot skidded on fallen leaves and he saved himself, this time with the aid of Robin's stick. '*Bollocks* ... go on. What d'you make of him putting the boot into Chiswell?'

'Well, I think he's hurt and furious,' said Robin, weighing her words. 'He and his father were getting on better than they ever had, from what he told me when I was at the House of Commons, but now Chiswell's dead, Raphael's never going to be able to get properly back on good terms with him, is he? He's left with the fact he was written out of the will and no idea of how Chiswell really felt about him. Chiswell was quite inconsistent with Raphael. When he was drunk and depressed, he seemed to lean on him, but otherwise he was pretty rude to him. Although I can't honestly say I saw Chiswell ever being nice to anybody, except maybe—'

She stopped short.

'Go on,' said Strike.

'Well, actually,' said Robin, 'I was going to say he was quite nice to me, the day I found out all about the Level Playing Field.'

'This was when he offered you a job?'

'Yes, and he said he might have a bit more work for me, once I'd got rid of Winn and Knight.'

'Did he?' said Strike, curiously. 'You never told me that.'

'Didn't I? No, I don't suppose I did.'

And like Strike, she remembered the week that he had been laid up at Lorelei's, followed by the hours at the hospital with Jack.

'I went over to his office, as I told you, and he was on the phone to some hotel about a money clip he'd lost. It was Freddie's. After Chiswell got off the phone, I told him about the Level Playing Field and he was happier than I ever saw him. "One by one, they trip themselves up",' he said.

'Interesting,' panted Strike, whose leg was now killing him. 'So you think Raphael's smarting about the will, do you?'

Robin, who thought she caught a sardonic note in Strike's voice, said:

'It isn't just money—'

'People always say that,' he grunted. 'It *is* the money, and it isn't. Because what *is* money? Freedom, security, pleasure, a fresh chance . . . I think there's more to be got out of Raphael,' said Strike, 'and I think you're going to have to be the one to do it.'

'What else can he tell us?'

'I'd like a bit more clarity on that phone call Chiswell made to him, right before that bag went over his head,' panted Strike, who was now in considerable pain. 'It doesn't make much sense to me, because even if Chiswell knew he was about to kill himself, there were people far better placed to keep Kinvara company than a stepson she didn't like who was miles away in London.

'Trouble is, the call makes even less sense if it was murder. There's something,' said Strike, 'we aren't being t – ah. Thank Christ.'

Steda Cottage had just come into view in a clearing ahead of them. The garden, which was surrounded by a broken-down fence, was now almost as overgrown as its surroundings. The building was squat, made of dark stone and clearly derelict, with a yawning hole in the roof and cracks in most of the windows.

'Sit down,' Robin advised Strike, pointing him towards a large tree stump just outside the cottage fence. In too much pain to argue, he did as she instructed, while Robin picked her way towards the front door and gave it a little push, but found it locked. Wading through knee-length grass, she peered one by one through the grimy windows. The rooms were thick with dust and empty. The only sign of any previous occupant was in the kitchen, where a filthy mug bearing a picture of Johnny Cash sat alone on a stained surface.

'Doesn't look as though anyone's lived here for years, and no sign of anyone sleeping rough,' she informed Strike, emerging from the other side of the cottage.

Strike, who had just lit a cigarette, made no answer. He was staring down into a large hollow in the woodland floor, around twenty feet square, bordered with trees and full of nettles, tangled thorn and towering weeds.

'Would you call that a dell?' he asked her.

Robin peered down into the basin-like indentation.

'I'd say it's more like a dell than anything else we've passed,' she said.

'"He strangled the kid and they buried it, down in the dell by our dad's house",' quoted Strike.

'I'll have a look,' said Robin. 'You stay here.'

'No,' said Strike, raising a hand to stop her, 'you're not going to find anything—'

But Robin was already sliding her way down the steep edges of the 'dell', the thorns snagging at her jeans as she descended.

It was extremely difficult to move around once she reached the bottom. Nettles came up almost to her waist and she held up her hands to avoid scratches and stings. Milk parsley and wood avens speckled the dark green with white and yellow. The long thorny branches of wild roses curled like barbed wire everywhere she trod.

'Watch yourself,' said Strike, feeling impotent as he watched her struggle along, scratching or stinging herself at every other step.

'I'm fine,' said Robin, peering at the ground beneath the wild vegetation. If anything had been buried here, it had long since been covered by plants, and digging would be a very difficult business. She said as much to Strike, as she bent low to see what lay underneath a dense patch of bramble.

'Doubt Kinvara would be happy with us digging, anyway,' said Strike, and as he said it, he remembered Billy's words: *She wouldn't let me dig, but she'd let you.*

'Wait,' said Robin, sounding tense.

In spite of the fact that he knew perfectly well she could not have found anything, Strike tensed.

'What?'

'There's something in there,' said Robin, moving her head from side to side, the better to see into a thick patch of nettles, right in the centre of the dell.

'Oh God.'

'What?' Strike repeated. Although far higher up than her, he could make out nothing whatsoever in the nettle patch. 'What can you see?'

'I don't know ... I might be imagining it.' She hesitated. 'You haven't got gloves, I suppose?'

'No. Robin, don't—'

But she had already walked into the patch of nettles, her hands raised, stamping them down at the base wherever she could, flattening them as much as possible. Strike saw her bend over and pull something out of the ground. Straightening up, she stood quite still, her red–gold head bowed over whatever she had found, until Strike said impatiently:

'What is it?'

Her hair fell away from a face that looked pale against the morass of dark green in which she stood, as she held up a small, wooden cross.

371

'No, stay there,' she ordered him, as he moved automatically towards the edge of the dell to help her climb out. 'I'm fine.'

She was, in fact, covered in scratches and nettle stings, but deciding that a few more would hardly count, Robin pushed her way more forcefully out of the dell, using her hands to pull herself up the steep sides until she came close enough for Strike to reach out a hand and help her the last few feet.

'Thanks,' she said breathlessly.

'Looks like it's been there years,' she said, rubbing earth from the bottom, which was pointed, the better to stick into the ground. The wood was damp and stained.

'Something was written on it,' said Strike, taking it from her and squinting at the slimy surface.

'Where?' said Robin. Her hair grazed his cheek as they stood close beside each other, staring at the very faint residue of what looked like felt tip, long since washed away by rain and dew.

'That looks like a kid's writing,' said Robin quietly.

'That's an "S",' said Strike, 'and at the end . . . is that a "g" or a "y"?'

'I don't know,' whispered Robin.

They stood in silence, contemplating the cross, until the faint, echoing barks of Rattenbury the Norfolk terrier pierced their reverie.

'We're still on Kinvara's property,' said Robin nervously.

'Yeah,' said Strike, keeping hold of the cross as he began to lumber back the way they had come, teeth gritted against the pain in his leg. 'Let's find a pub. I'm starving.'

44

But there are so many sorts of white horses in this world, Mrs.
Helseth . . .

Henrik Ibsen, *Rosmersholm*

'Of course,' said Robin, as they drove towards the village, 'a cross sticking out of the ground doesn't mean there's anything buried beneath it.'

'True,' said Strike, who had needed most of his breath on the return walk for the frequent obscenities he uttered as he stumbled and skidded on the forest floor, 'but it makes you think, doesn't it?'

Robin said nothing. Her hands on the steering wheel were covered in nettle stings that prickled and burned.

The country inn they reached five minutes later was the very image of picture-postcard England, a white, timbered building with leaded bay windows, moss-covered slates on the roof and climbing red roses around the door. A beer garden with parasols completed the picture. Robin turned the Land Rover into the small car park opposite.

'This is getting stupid,' muttered Strike, who had left the cross on the dashboard and was now climbing out of the car, staring at the pub.

'What is?' asked Robin, coming around the back of the car to join him.

'It's called the White Horse.'

'After the one up the hill,' said Robin, as they set off across the road together. 'Look at the sign.'

Painted on the board atop a wooden pole was the strange chalk figure they had seen earlier.

'The pub where I met Jimmy Knight the first time was called the White Horse, too,' said Strike.

'The White Horse,' said Robin, as they walked up the steps into the beer garden, Strike's limp now more pronounced than ever, 'is one of the ten most popular pub names in Britain. I read it in some article. Quick, those people are leaving – grab their table, I'll get the drinks.'

The low-ceilinged pub was busy inside. Robin headed first for the Ladies where she stripped off her jacket, tied it around her waist and washed her smarting hands. She wished that she had managed to find dock leaves on the journey back from Steda Cottage, but most of her attention on the return walk had been given to Strike who had nearly fallen twice more and hobbled on looking furious with himself, repelling offers of assistance with bad grace and leaning heavily on the walking stick she had fashioned from a branch.

The mirror showed Robin that she was dishevelled and grubby compared to the prosperous middle-aged people she had just seen in the bar, but being in a hurry to return to Strike and review the morning's activities, she merely dragged a brush through her hair, wiped a green stain off her neck and returned to queue for drinks.

'Cheers, Robin,' said Strike gratefully, when she returned to him with a pint of Arkell's Wiltshire Gold, shoving the menu across the table to her. 'Ah, that's good,' he sighed, taking a swig. 'So what's the most popular one?'

'Sorry?'

'The most popular pub name. You said the White Horse is in the top ten.'

'Oh, right ... it's either the Red Lion or the Crown, I can't remember which.'

'The Victory's my real local,' said Strike reminiscently.

He had not been back to Cornwall in two years. He saw the pub now in his mind's eye, a squat building of whitewashed Cornish stone, the steps beside it winding down to the bay. It was the pub in which he had first managed to get served without ID, sixteen years old and dumped back at his uncle and aunt's for a few weeks, while his mother's life went through one of its regular bouts of upheaval.

'Ours is the Bay Horse,' said Robin, and she, too, had a sudden vision of a pub from what she would always think of as home, also white, standing on a street that led off the market square in Masham. It was there that she had celebrated her A-level results with her friends, the same night that Matthew and she had got into a stupid row, and he had left, and she had refused to follow, but remained with her friends.

'Why "bay"?' asked Strike, now halfway down his pint and luxuriating in the sunshine, his sore leg stretched out in front of him. 'Why not just "brown"?'

'Well, there *are* brown horses,' said Robin, 'but bay means something different. Black points: legs, mane and tail.'

'What colour was your pony – Angus, wasn't it?'

'How did you remember that?' asked Robin, surprised.

'Dunno,' said Strike. 'Same as you remembering pub names. Some things stick, don't they?'

'He was grey.'

'Meaning white. It's all just jargon to confuse non-riding plebs, isn't it?'

'No,' said Robin, laughing. 'Grey horses have black skin under the white hair. True whites—'

'—die young,' said Strike, as a barmaid arrived to take their order. Having ordered a burger, Strike lit another cigarette and as the nicotine hit his brain, felt a wave of something close to euphoria. A pint, a hot day in August, a well-paid job, food on the way and Robin, sitting across from him, their friendship restored, if not entirely to what it had been before her honeymoon, then perhaps as close as was possible, now that she was married. Right now, in this sunny beer garden, and in spite of the pain in his leg, his tiredness and the unresolved mess that was his relationship with Lorelei, life felt simple and hopeful.

'Group interviews are never a good idea,' he said, exhaling away from Robin's face, 'but there were some interesting crosscurrents among the Chiswells, weren't there? I'm going to keep working on Izzy. I think she might be a bit more forthcoming without the family around.'

Izzy will like being worked on, Robin thought, as she took out her mobile.

'I've got something to show you. Look.'

She brought up her photograph of Freddie Chiswell's birthday party.

'That,' she said, pointing at the girl's pale, unhappy face, 'is Rhiannon Winn. She was at Freddie Chiswell's eighteenth birthday party. Turns out—' she scrolled back a picture, to show the group in white tunics, 'they were on the British fencing team together.'

'Christ, of course,' said Strike, taking the phone from Robin. 'The sword – the sword in Ebury Street. I bet it was Freddie's!'

'Of course!' echoed Robin, wondering why she hadn't realised that before.

'That can't be long before she killed herself,' said Strike, scrutinising more closely the miserable figure of Rhiannon Winn at the birthday party. 'And – bloody hell, that's Jimmy Knight behind her. What's he doing at a public schoolboy's eighteenth?'

'Free drink?' suggested Robin.

Strike gave a small snort of amusement as he handed back Robin's phone.

'Sometimes the obvious answer is the right one. Was I imagining Izzy looking self-conscious when the story of Jimmy's teenage sex appeal came up?'

'No,' said Robin, 'I noticed that, too.'

'Nobody wants us to talk to Jimmy's old mates the Butcher brothers, either.'

'Because they know more than where their sister works?'

Strike sipped his beer, thinking back to what Chiswell had told him the first time they'd met.

'Chiswell said other people were involved in whatever he did to get blackmailed, but they had a lot to lose if it got out.'

He took out his notebook and contemplated his own spiky, hard-to-read handwriting, while Robin sat peacefully enjoying the quiet chatter of the beer garden. A lazy bee buzzed nearby, reminding her of the lavender walk at Le Manoir aux Quat'Saisons, where she and Matthew had spent their anniversary. It was best not to compare how she felt now to the way she had felt then.

'Maybe,' said Strike, tapping the open notebook with his pen, 'the Butcher brothers agreed to take on horse-slashing duties for Jimmy while he was in London? I always thought he might have mates back down here who could've taken care of that side of things. But we'll let Izzy get Tegan's whereabouts out of them before we approach them. Don't want to upset the client unless it's absolutely necessary.'

'No,' agreed Robin. 'I wonder ... d'you think Jimmy met them when he came down here looking for Billy?'

'Could well have done,' said Strike, nodding over his notes. 'Very interesting, that. From what they said to each other on that march, Jimmy and Flick knew where Billy was at the time. They were off to see him when my hamstring went. Now they've lost him again ... you know, I'd give a hell of a lot to find Billy. That's where all of this started and we're still—'

He broke off as their food arrived: a burger with blue cheese on it for Strike, and a bowl of chilli for Robin.

'We're still?' prompted Robin, as the barmaid moved away.

' ... none the wiser,' said Strike, 'about the kid he claims he saw die. I didn't want to ask the Chiswells about Suki Lewis, or not yet. Best not to suggest I'm interested in anyone but Chiswell's death right now.'

He picked up his burger and took an enormous bite, his eyes unfocused, staring out over the road. After demolishing half of his burger, Strike turned back to his notes.

'Things to be done,' he announced, picking up his pen again. 'I want to find this cleaning woman Jasper Chiswell laid off. She had a key for a bit and she might be able to tell us how and when the helium got into the house.

'Hopefully Izzy will trace Tegan Butcher for us, and Tegan'll be able to shed some light on Raphael's trip down there on the morning his father died, because I'm still not buying that story.

'We'll leave Tegan's brothers for now, because the Chiswells clearly don't want us talking to them, but I might try and have a word with Henry Drummond, the art dealer.'

'Why?' asked Robin.

'He was an old friend, did Chiswell a favour hiring Raphael. They must've been reasonably close. You never know, Chiswell might've told him what the blackmail was about. And he tried to reach Chiswell early on the morning Chiswell died. I'd like to know why.

'So, going forwards: you're going to have a bash at Flick at her jewellery shop, Barclay can stay on Jimmy and Flick, and I'll tackle Geraint Winn and Aamir Mallik.'

'They'll never talk to you,' said Robin at once. 'Never.'

'Want to bet?'

'Tenner says they won't.'

'I don't pay you enough for you to throw tenners around,' said Strike. 'You can buy me a pint.'

Strike took care of the bill and they headed back across the road to the car, Robin secretly wishing that there was somewhere else they needed to go, because the prospect of returning to Albury Street was depressing.

'We might be better off going back on the M40,' said Strike, reading a map on his phone. 'There's been an accident on the M4.'

'OK,' said Robin.

This would take them past Le Manoir aux Quat'Saisons. As she reversed out of the car park, Robin suddenly remembered Matthew's texts from earlier. He had claimed to have been messaging work, but she couldn't remember him ever contacting his office at a weekend before. One of his regular complaints about her job was that its hours and responsibilities bled into Saturday and Sunday, unlike his.

'What?' she said, becoming aware that Strike had just spoken to her.

'I said, they're supposed to be bad luck, aren't they?' repeated Strike, as they drove away from the pub.

'What are?'

'White horses,' he said. 'Isn't there a play where white horses appear as a death omen?'

'I don't know,' said Robin, changing gear. 'Death rides a white horse in Revelations, though.'

'A pale horse,' Strike corrected her, winding down the window so that he could smoke again.

'Pedant.'

'Says the woman who won't call a brown horse "brown",' said Strike.

He reached for the grubby wooden cross, which was sliding about on the dashboard. Robin kept her eyes on the road ahead, determinedly focused on anything but the vivid image that had occurred to her when she had first spotted it, almost hidden in the thick, whiskered stems of the nettles: that of a child, rotting in the earth at the bottom of that dark basin in the woods, dead and forgotten by everyone except a man they said was mad.

45

It is a necessity for me to abandon a false and equivocal position.

Henrik Ibsen, *Rosmersholm*

Strike paid in pain for the walk through the woods at Chiswell House the next morning. So little did he fancy getting up out of bed and heading downstairs to work on a Sunday that he was forced to remind himself that, like the character of Hyman Roth in one of his favourite films, he had chosen this business freely. If, like the Mafia, private detection made demands beyond the ordinary, certain concomitants had to be accepted along with the rewards.

He had had a choice, after all. The army had been keen to keep him, even with half his leg missing. Friends of friends had offered everything from management roles in the close protection industry to business partnerships, but the itch to detect, solve and reimpose order upon the moral universe could not be extinguished in him, and he doubted it ever would be. The paperwork, the frequently obstreperous clients, the hiring and firing of subordinates gave him no intrinsic satisfaction – but the long hours, the physical priva-tions and the occasional risks of his job were accepted stoically and with occasional relish. And so he showered, put on his prosthesis and, yawning, made his painful way downstairs, remembering his brother-in-law's suggestion that his ultimate goal ought to be sitting in an office while others literally did the legwork.

Strike's thoughts drifted to Robin as he sat down at her computer. He had never asked her what her ultimate ambition for the agency was, assuming, perhaps arrogantly, that it was the same as his: build up a sufficient bank balance to ensure them both a decent income while they took the work that was most interesting, without fear of losing everything the moment they lost a client. But perhaps Robin was waiting for him to initiate a talk along the lines that Greg had suggested? He tried to imagine her reaction, if he invited her to sit down on the farting sofa while he subjected her to a PowerPoint display setting out long-term objectives and suggestions for branding.

As he set to work, thoughts of Robin metamorphosed into memories of Charlotte. He remembered how it had been on days like this while they had been together, when he had required uninterrupted hours alone at a computer. Sometimes Charlotte had taken herself out, often making an unnecessary mystery about where she was going, or invented reasons to interrupt him, or pick a fight that kept him pinned down while the precious hours trickled away. And he knew that he was reminding himself how difficult and exhausting that behaviour had been, because ever since he had seen her at Lancaster House, Charlotte had slid in and out of his disengaged mind like a stray cat.

A little under eight hours, seven cups of tea, three bathroom breaks, four cheese sandwiches, three bags of crisps, an apple and twenty-two cigarettes later, Strike had repaid all his subcontractors' expenses, ensured that the accountant had the firm's latest receipts, read Hutchins' updated report on Dodgy Doc and tracked several Aamir Malliks across cyberspace in search of the one he wanted to interview. By five o'clock he thought he had him, but the photograph was so far from 'handsome', which was how Mallik had been described in the blind item online, that he thought it best to email Robin a copy of the pictures he had found on Google Images, to confirm that this was the Mallik he sought.

Strike stretched, yawning, listening to a drum solo that a prospective purchaser was banging out in a shop below in Denmark Street. Looking forward to getting back upstairs and watching the day's Olympic highlights, which would include Usain Bolt running the hundred metres, he was on the point of shutting off his computer when a small 'ping' alerted him to the arrival of an email from Lorelei@VintageVamps.com, the subject line reading simply: 'You and me'.

Strike rubbed his eyes with the heels of his palms, as though the sight of the new email had been some temporary aberration of sight. However, there it sat at the top of his inbox when he raised his head and opened his eyes again.

'Oh, shit,' he muttered. Deciding that he might as well know the worst, he clicked on it.

The email ran to nearly a thousand words and gave the impression of having been carefully crafted. It was a methodical dissection of Strike's character, which read like the case notes for a psychiatric case that, while not hopeless, required urgent intervention. By Lorelei's analysis, Cormoran Strike was a fundamentally damaged and dysfunctional creature standing in the way of his own happiness. He caused pain to others due to the essential dishonesty of his emotional dealings. Never having experienced a healthy relationship, he ran from it when it was given to him. He took those who cared about him for granted and would probably only realise this when he hit rock bottom, alone, unloved and tortured by regrets.

This prediction was followed by a description of the soul-searching and doubts that had preceded Lorelei's decision to send the email, rather than simply tell Strike that their no-strings arrangement was at an end. She concluded that she thought it fairest to him to explain in writing why she, and by implication every other woman in the world, would find him unacceptable unless he changed his behaviour. She asked him to read and think about what she had said 'understanding that this doesn't come from a place of anger, but of sadness', and requested a further meeting so that they could 'decide whether you want this relationship enough to try a different way'.

After reaching the bottom of the email, Strike remained where he was, staring at the screen, not because he was contemplating a response, but because he was gathering himself for the physical pain he was anticipating upon standing up. At last he pushed himself up into a vertical position, flinching as he lowered his weight onto the prosthesis, then closed down his computer and locked up the office.

Why can't we can't end it by phone? he thought, heaving himself up the stairs by using the handrail. *It's obvious it's fucking dead, isn't it? Why do we have to have a post-mortem?*

Back in the flat, he lit another cigarette, dropped down onto a kitchen chair and called Robin, who answered almost immediately.

'Hi,' she said quietly. 'Just a moment.'

He heard a door close, footsteps, and another door closing.

'Did you get my email? Just sent you a couple of pictures.'

'No,' said Robin, keeping her voice low. 'Pictures of what?'

'I think I've found Mallik living in Battersea. Pudgy bloke with a monobrow.'

'That's not him. He's tall and thin with glasses.'

'So I've just wasted an hour,' said Strike, frustrated. 'Didn't he ever let slip where he was living? What he liked to do at the weekends? National Insurance number?'

'No,' said Robin, 'we barely spoke. I've already told you this.'

'How's the disguise coming along?'

Robin had already told Strike by text that she had an interview on Thursday with the 'mad Wiccan' who ran the jewellery shop in Camden.

'Not bad,' said Robin. 'I've been experimenting with—'

There was a muffled shout in the background.

'Sorry, I'm going to have to go,' Robin said hastily.

'Everything OK?'

'It's fine, speak tomorrow.'

She hung up. Strike remained with the mobile at his ear. He deduced that he had called during a difficult moment for Robin, possibly even a row, and lowered the mobile with faint disappointment at not having had a longer chat. For a moment or two, he contemplated the mobile in his hand. Lorelei would be expecting him to call as soon as he had read her email. Deciding that he could credibly claim not to have seen it yet, Strike put down his phone and reached instead for the TV remote control.

46

... I should have handled the affair more judiciously.

Henrik Ibsen, *Rosmersholm*

Four days later, at lunchtime, Strike was to be found leaning up against a counter in a tiny takeaway pizza restaurant, which was most conveniently situated for watching a house directly across the street. One of a pair of brown brick semi-detached houses, the name 'Ivy Cottages' was engraved in stone over the twin doors, which seemed to Strike more fitting for humbler dwellings than these houses, which had graceful arched windows and corniced keystones.

Chewing on a slice of pizza, Strike felt his phone vibrate in his pocket. He checked to see who was calling before answering, because he had already had one fraught conversation with Lorelei today. Seeing that it was Robin, he answered.

'I'm in,' said Robin. She sounded excited. 'Just had my interview. The owner's dreadful, I'm not surprised nobody wants to work for her. It's a zero-hours contract. Basically, she wants a couple of people to fill in whenever she fancies not working.'

'Flick still there?'

'Yes, she was manning the counter while I was talking to the shop owner. The woman wants to give me a trial tomorrow.'

'You weren't followed?'

'No, I think that journalist has given up. He wasn't here yesterday either. Mind you, he probably wouldn't have recognised me even if he'd seen me. You should see my hair.'

'Why, what have you done with it?'

'Chalk.'

'What?'

'Hair chalk,' said Robin. 'Temporary colour. It's black and blue. And I'm wearing a lot of eye make-up and some temporary tattoos.'

'Send us a selfie, I could do with some light relief.'

'Make your own. What's going on your end?'

'Bugger all. Mallik came out of Della's house with her this morning—'

'God, are they *living* together?'

'No idea. They went out somewhere in a taxi with the guide dog. They came back an hour ago and I'm waiting to see what happens next. One interesting thing, though: I've seen Mallik before. Recognised him the moment I saw him this morning.'

'Really?'

'Yeah, he was at Jimmy's CORE meeting. The one I went to, to try and find Billy.'

'How weird ... D'you think he was acting as a go-between for Geraint?'

'Maybe,' said Strike, 'but I can't see why the phone wouldn't have done if they wanted to keep in touch. You know, there's something funny about Mallik generally.'

'He's all right,' said Robin quickly. 'He didn't like me, but that was because he was suspicious. That just means he's sharper than most of the rest of them.'

'You don't fancy him as a killer?'

'Is this because of what Kinvara said?'

'"My husband provoked somebody, somebody I warned him he shouldn't upset",' Strike quoted.

'And why should anyone be particularly worried about upsetting Aamir? Because he's brown? I felt sorry for him, actually, having to work with—'

'Hang on,' said Strike, letting his last piece of pizza fall back onto the plate.

The front door of Della's house had opened again.

'We're off,' said Strike, as Mallik came out of the house alone, closed the door behind him, walked briskly down the garden path, and set off down the road. Strike headed out of the pizzeria in pursuit.

'Got a spring in his step now. He looks happy to be away from her ...'

'How's your leg?'

'It's been worse. Hang on, he's turning left ... Robin, I'm going to go, need to speed up a bit.'

'Good luck.'

'Cheers.'

Strike crossed Southwark Park Road as quickly as his leg permitted, then turned into Alma Grove, a long residential street with plane trees planted at regular intervals, and Victorian terraced houses on both sides. To Strike's surprise, Mallik stopped at a house on the right, with a turquoise door, and let himself inside. The distance between his place of residence and that of the Winns' was five minutes' walk at most.

The houses in Alma Grove were narrow and Strike could well imagine loud noises travelling easily through the walls. Giving Mallik what he judged to be sufficient time to remove his jacket and shoes, Strike approached the turquoise door and knocked.

After a few seconds' wait, Aamir opened up. His expression changed from pleasant enquiry to shock. Aamir evidently knew exactly who Strike was.

'Aamir Mallik?'

The younger man did not speak at first, but stood frozen with one hand on the door, the other on the hall wall, looking at Strike with dark eyes shrunken by the thickness of the lenses in his glasses.

'What do you want?'

'A chat,' said Strike.

'Why? What for?'

'Jasper Chiswell's family have hired me. They aren't sure he committed suicide.'

Appearing temporarily paralysed, Aamir neither moved nor spoke. Finally, he stood back from the door.

'All right, come in.'

In Aamir's position, Strike too would have wanted to know what the detective knew or suspected, rather than wondering through fretful nights why he had called. Strike entered and wiped his feet on the doormat.

The house was larger inside than it had appeared outside. Aamir led Strike through a door on the left into a sitting room. The décor was, very obviously, the taste of a person far older than Aamir. A thick, patterned carpet of swirling pinks and greens, a number of chintz-covered chairs, a wooden coffee table with a lace cloth laid over it and an ornamental edged mirror over the mantelpiece all spoke of geriatric occupants, while an ugly electric heater had been installed in the wrought iron fireplace. Shelves were bare, surfaces denuded of ornaments or other objects. A Stieg Larsson paperback lay on the arm of a chair.

Aamir turned to face Strike, hands in the pockets of his jeans.

'You're Cormoran Strike,' he said.

'That's right.'

'It was your partner who was pretending to be Venetia, at the Commons.'

'Right again.'

'What d'you want?' Aamir asked, for the second time.

'To ask you a few questions.'

'About what?'

'OK if I sit down?' asked Strike, doing so without waiting for permission. He noticed Aamir's eyes drop to his leg, and stretched out the prosthesis ostentatiously, so that a glint of the metal ankle could be seen above his sock. To a man so considerate of Della's disability, this might be sufficient reason not to ask Strike to get up again. 'As I said, the family doesn't think Jasper Chiswell killed himself.'

'You think I had something to do with his death?' asked Aamir, trying for incredulity and succeeding only in sounding scared.

'No,' said Strike, 'but if you want to blurt out a confession, feel free. It'll save me a lot of work.'

Aamir didn't smile.

'The only thing I know about you, Aamir,' said Strike, 'is that you were helping Geraint Winn blackmail Chiswell.'

'I wasn't,' said Aamir at once.

It was the automatic, ill-considered denial of a panicked man.

'You weren't trying to get hold of incriminating photographs to use against him?'

'I don't know what you're talking about.'

'The press are trying to break your bosses' super-injunction. Once the blackmail's out in the public domain, your part in it won't remain hidden for long. You and your friend Christopher—'

'*He's not my friend!*'

Aamir's vehemence interested Strike.

'D'you own this house, Aamir?'

'What?'

'Just seems a big place for a twenty-four-year-old on what can't be a big salary—'

'It's none of your business who owns this—'

'I don't care, personally,' said Strike, leaning forwards, 'but the papers will. You'll look beholden to the owners if you aren't paying a fair rent. It could seem like you owed them something, like you're in their pocket. The tax office will also consider it a benefit in kind if it's owned by your employers, which could cause problems for both—'

'How did you know where to find me?' Aamir demanded.

'Well, it wasn't easy,' Strike admitted. 'You don't have much of an online life, do you? But in the end,' he said, reaching for a sheaf of folded paper in the inside pocket of his jacket, and unfolding them, 'I found your sister's Facebook page. That *is* your sister, right?'

He laid the piece of paper, on which he had printed the Facebook post, on the coffee table. A plumply pretty woman in a hijab beamed up out of the poor reproduction of her photograph, surrounded by four young children. Taking Aamir's silence for assent, Strike said:

'I went back through a few years' worth of posts. That's you,' he said, laying a second printed page on top of the first. A younger Aamir stood smiling in academic robes, flanked by his parents. 'You took a first in politics and economics at LSE. Very impressive . . .

'And you got onto a graduate training programme at the Foreign Office,' Strike continued, placing a third sheet down on top of the first two. This showed an official, posed photograph of a small group of smartly dressed young men and women, all black or from other ethnic minorities, standing around a balding, florid-faced man. 'There you are,' said Strike, 'with senior civil servant Sir Christopher Barrowclough-Burns, who at that time was running a diversity recruitment drive.'

Aamir's eye twitched.

'And here you are again,' said Strike, laying down the last of his four printed Facebook pages, 'just a month ago, with your sister in that pizza place right opposite Della's house. Once I identified where it was and realised how close it was to the Winns' place, I thought it might be worth coming to Bermondsey to see whether I could spot you in the vicinity.'

Aamir stared down at the picture of himself and his sister. She had taken the selfie. Southwark Park Road was clearly visible behind them, through the window.

'Where were you at 6 a.m. on the thirteenth of July?' Strike asked Aamir.

'Here.'

'Could anyone corroborate that?'

'Yes. Geraint Winn.'

'Had he stayed the night?'

Aamir advanced a few steps, fists raised. It could not have been plainer that he had never boxed, but nevertheless, Strike tensed. Aamir looked close to breaking point.

'All I'm saying,' said Strike, holding up his hands pacifically, 'is that 6 a.m. is an odd time for Geraint Winn to be at your house.'

Aamir slowly lowered his fists, then, as though he did not know what else to do with himself, he backed away to sit down on the edge of the seat of the nearest armchair.

'Geraint came round to tell me Della had had a fall.'

'Couldn't he have phoned?'

'I suppose so, but he didn't,' said Aamir. 'He wanted me to help him persuade Della to go to casualty. She'd slipped down the last few stairs and her wrist was swelling up. I went round there – they only live round the corner – but I couldn't persuade her. She's stubborn. Anyway, it turned out to be only a sprain, not a break. She was fine.'

'So you're Geraint's alibi for the time Jasper Chiswell died?'

'I suppose so.'

'And he's yours.'

'Why would I want Jasper Chiswell dead?' asked Aamir.

'That's a good question,' said Strike.

'I barely knew the man,' said Aamir.

'Really?'

'Yes, really.'

'So what made him quote Catullus at you, and mention Fate, and intimate in front of a room full of people that he knew things about your private life?'

There was a long pause. Again, Aamir's eye twitched.

'That didn't happen,' he said.

'Really? My partner—'

'She's lying. Chiswell didn't know anything about my private life. Nothing.'

Strike heard the numb drone of a hoover next door. He had been right. The walls were not thick.

'I've seen you once before,' Strike told Mallik, who looked more frightened than ever. 'Jimmy Knight's meeting in East Ham, couple of months ago.'

'I don't know what you're talking about,' said Mallik. 'You've mistaken me for someone else.' Then, unconvincingly, 'Who's Jimmy Knight?'

'OK, Aamir,' said Strike, 'if that's how you want to play it, there's no point going on. Could I use your bathroom?'

'What?'

'Need a pee. Then I'll clear out, leave you in peace.'

Mallik clearly wanted to refuse, but seemed unable to find a reason to do so.

'All right,' said Aamir. 'But—'

A thought seemed to have occurred to him.

'—wait. I need to move – I was soaking some socks in the sink. Stay here.'

'Right you are,' said Strike.

Aamir left the room. Strike wanted an excuse to poke around upstairs for clues to the entity or activity that might have caused animal noises loud enough to disturb the neighbours, but the sound of Aamir's footsteps told him that the bathroom lay beyond the kitchen on the ground floor.

A couple of minutes later, Aamir returned.

'It's through here.'

He led Strike down the hall, through a nondescript, bare kitchen, and pointed him into the bathroom.

Strike entered, closed and locked the door, then placed his hand at the bottom of the sink. It was dry. The walls of the bathroom were pink and matched the pink bathroom suite. Grab rails beside the toilet and a floor-to-ceiling rail at the end of the bath suggested that this had been, some time in the recent past, the home of a frail or disabled person.

What was it that Aamir had wanted to remove or conceal before the detective entered? Strike opened the bathroom cabinet. It contained very little other than a young man's basic necessities: shaving kit, deodorant and aftershave.

Closing the cabinet, Strike saw his own reflection swing into view and, over his shoulder, the back of the door, where a thick navy towelling robe had been hung up carelessly, suspended from the arm hole rather than the loop designed for that purpose.

Flushing the toilet to maintain the fiction that he was too busy to nose around, Strike approached the dressing gown and felt the empty pockets. As he did so, the precariously placed robe slid off the hook.

Strike took a step backwards, the better to appreciate what had just been revealed. Somebody had gouged a crude, four-legged figure into the bathroom door, splintering the wood and paint. Strike turned on the cold tap, in case Aamir was listening, took a picture of the carving with his mobile, turned off the tap and replaced the towelling robe as he had found it.

Aamir was waiting at the end of the kitchen.

'All right if I take those papers with me?' Strike asked, and without waiting for an answer he returned to the sitting room and picked up the Facebook pages.

'What made you leave the Foreign Office, anyway?' he asked casually.

'I . . . didn't enjoy it.'

'How did it come about, you working for the Winns?'

'We'd met,' said Aamir. 'Della offered me a job. I took it.'

It happened, very occasionally, that Strike felt scruples about what he was driven to ask during an interview.

'I couldn't help noticing,' he said, holding up the wad of printed material, 'that you seemed to drop out of sight of your family for quite a long time after you left the Foreign Office. No more appearances in group shots, not even on your mother's seventieth birthday. Your sister stopped mentioning you, for a long time.'

Aamir said nothing.

'It was as if you'd been disowned,' said Strike.

'You can get out, now,' said Aamir, but Strike didn't move.

'When your sister posted this picture of the pair of you in the pizza place,' Strike continued, unfolding the last sheet again, 'the responses were—'

'I want you to leave,' repeated Aamir, more loudly.

'"What you doing with that scumbag?" "Your dad know you still seeing him?"' Strike read aloud from the messages beneath the picture of Aamir and his sister. '"If my brother permitted *liwat*—"'

Aamir charged at him, sending a wild right-handed punch to the side of Strike's head that the detective parried. But the studious-looking Aamir was full of the kind of blind rage that could make a dangerous opponent of almost any man. Tearing a nearby lamp from its socket he swung it so violently that had Strike not ducked in time, the lamp base could have shattered, not on the wall that half-divided the sitting room, but on his face.

'Enough!' bellowed Strike, as Aamir dropped the remnants of the lamp and came at him again. Strike fended off the windmilling fists, hooked his prosthetic leg around the back of Aamir's leg, and threw him to the floor. Swearing under his breath, because this action had done his aching stump no good at all, Strike straightened up, panting, and said:

'Any more and I'll fucking deck you.'

Aamir rolled out of Strike's reach and got to his feet. His glasses were hanging from one ear. Hands shaking, he took them off and examined the broken hinge. His eyes were suddenly huge.

'Aamir, I'm not interested in your private life,' panted Strike, 'I'm interested in who you're covering up for—'

'Get out,' whispered Aamir.

'—because if the police decide it's murder, everything you're trying to hide will come out. Murder inquiries respect no one's privacy.'

'*Get out!*'

'All right. Don't say I didn't warn you.'

At the front door, Strike turned one last time to face Aamir, who had followed him into the hall, and braced himself as Strike came to a halt.

'Who carved that mark on the inside of your bathroom door, Aamir?'

'*Out!*'

Strike knew there was no point persisting. As soon as he had crossed the threshold, the front door slammed behind him.

Several houses away, the wincing Strike leaned up against a tree to take the weight off his prosthesis, and texted Robin the picture he had just taken, along with the message:

Remind you of anything?

He lit a cigarette and waited for Robin's response, glad of an excuse to remain stationary, because quite apart from the pain in his stump, the side of his head was throbbing. In dodging the lamp he had hit it against the wall, and his back was aching because of the effort it had taken to throw the younger man to the floor.

Strike glanced back at the turquoise door. If he was honest, something else was hurting: his conscience. He had entered Mallik's house with the intention of shocking or intimidating him into the truth about his relationship with Chiswell and the Winns. While a private detective could not afford the doctor's dictum 'first, do no harm', Strike generally attempted to extract truth without causing unnecessary damage to the host. Reading out the comments at the bottom of that Facebook post had been a low blow. Brilliant, unhappy, undoubtedly tied to the Winns by something other than choice, Aamir Mallik's eruption into violence had been the reaction of a desperate man. Strike didn't need to consult the papers in his pocket to recall the picture of Mallik standing proudly in the Foreign Office, about to embark on a stellar career with his first-class degree with his mentor, Sir Christopher Barrowclough-Burns, by his side.

His mobile rang.

'Where on earth did you find that carving?' said Robin.

'The back of Aamir's bathroom door, hidden under a dressing gown.'

'You're joking.'

'No. What does it look like to you?'

'The white horse on the hill over Woolstone,' said Robin.

'Well, that's a relief,' said Strike, elbowing himself off the supporting tree and limping off along the street again. 'I was worried I'd started hallucinating the bloody things.'

47

... I want to try and play my humble part in the struggles of life.

Henrik Ibsen, *Rosmersholm*

Robin emerged from Camden Town station at half past eight on Friday morning and set off for the jewellery shop where she was to have her day's trial, furtively checking her appearance in every window that she passed.

In the months following the trial of the Shacklewell Ripper, she had become adept at make-up techniques such as altering the shape of her eyebrows or over-painting her lips in vermillion, which made a significant difference to her appearance when coupled with wigs and coloured contact lenses, but she had never before worn as much make-up as today. Her eyes, in which she was wearing dark brown contact lenses, were heavily rimmed with black kohl, her lips painted pale pink, her nails a metallic grey. Having only one conventional hole in each earlobe, she had bought a couple of cheap ear cuffs to simulate a more adventurous approach to piercing. The short black second-hand dress she had bought at the local Oxfam shop in Deptford still smelled slightly fusty, even though she had run it through the washing machine the previous day, and she wore it with thick black tights and a pair of flat black lace-up boots in spite of the warmth of the morning. Thus attired, she hoped that she resembled the other goth and emo girls who frequented Camden, an area of London that Robin had rarely visited and which she associated mainly with Lorelei and her vintage clothes store.

She had named her new alter ego Bobbi Cunliffe. When under-cover, it was best to assume names with a personal association, to which you responded instinctively. Bobbi sounded like Robin, and indeed people had sometimes tried to abbreviate her name that way, most notably her long-ago flirt in a temporary office, and her brother, Martin, when he wished to annoy her. Cunliffe was Matthew's surname.

To her relief, he had left for work early that day, because he was auditing an office out in Barnet, leaving Robin free to complete her physical transformation without undermining remarks and displeas-ure that she was, again, going undercover. Indeed, she thought she might derive a certain pleasure from using her married name – the first time she had ever offered it as her own – while embodying a girl whom Matthew would instinctively dislike. The older he got, the more Matthew was aggravated by and contemptuous of people who did not dress, think or live as he did.

The Wiccan's jewellery shop, Triquetra, was tucked away in Camden Market. Arriving outside at a quarter to nine, Robin found the stallholders of Camden Lock Place already busy, but the store locked up and empty. After a five-minute wait, her employer arrived, puffing slightly. A large woman whom Robin guessed to be in her late fifties, she had straggly dyed black hair that showed half an inch of silver root, had the same savage approach to eyeliner as Bobbi Cunliffe and wore a long green velvet dress.

During the cursory interview that had led to today's trial, the shop owner had asked very few questions, instead speaking at length about the husband of thirty years who had just left her to live in Thailand, the neighbour who was suing her over a boundary dispute and the stream of unsatisfactory and ungrateful employees who had walked out on Triquetra to take other jobs. Her undisguised desire to extract the maximum amount of work for the minimum amount of pay, coupled with her outpourings of self-pity, made Robin wonder why anybody had ever wanted to work for her in the first place.

'You're punctual,' she observed, when within earshot. 'Good. Where's the other one?'

'I don't know,' said Robin.

'I *don't need this*,' said the owner, with a slight note of hysteria. 'Not on the day I've got to meet Brian's lawyer!'

She unlocked the door and showed Robin into the shop, which was the size of a large kiosk, and as she raised her arms to start pulling up blinds, the smell of body odour and patchouli mingled with the dusty, incense-scented air. Daylight fell into the shop like a solid thing, rendering everything there more insubstantial and shabby by comparison. Dull silver necklaces and earrings hung in racks on the dark purple walls, many of them featuring pentagrams, peace symbols and marijuana leaves, while glass hookahs mingled with tarot cards, black candles, essential oils and ceremonial daggers on black shelves behind the counter.

'We've got *millions* of extra tourists coming through Camden right now,' said the owner, bustling around the back of the counter, 'and if she doesn't turn – *there you are*,' she said, as Flick, who looked sulky, sloped inside. Flick was wearing a yellow and green Hezbollah T-shirt and ripped jeans, and carrying a large leather messenger bag.

'Tube was late,' she said.

'Well, *I* managed to get here all right, and so did Bibi!'

'Bobbi,' Robin corrected her, deliberately broadening her Yorkshire accent.

She didn't want to pretend to be a Londoner this time. It was best not to have to talk about schools and locales that Flick might know.

'—well, I need you two to be on top of things *all – the – time*,' said the owner, beating out the last three words with one hand against the other. 'All right, Bibi—'

'—Bobbi—'

'—yes, come here and see how the till works.'

Robin had no difficulty grasping how the till worked, because she had had a Saturday job in her teens at a clothes shop in Harrogate. It was just as well that she did not need longer instruction, because a steady stream of shoppers began to arrive about ten minutes after they opened. To Robin's slight surprise, because there was nothing in the shop that she would have cared to buy, many visitors to Camden seemed to feel that their trip would be incomplete without a pair of pewter earrings, or a pentagram-embossed candle, or one of the small hessian bags that lay in a basket beside the till, each of which purported to contain a magic charm.

'All right, I need to be off,' the owner announced at eleven, while Flick was serving a tall German woman who was dithering between two packs of tarot cards. 'Don't forget: one of you needs to be focused on stock all the time, in case of pilfering. My friend Eddie will be keeping an eye out,' she said, pointing at the stall selling old LPs just outside. 'Twenty minutes each for lunch, taken separately. Don't forget,' she repeated ominously, 'Eddie's watching.'

She left in a whirl of velvet and body odour. The German customer departed with her tarot cards and Flick slammed the till drawer shut, the noise echoing in the temporarily empty shop.

'Old Steady Eddie,' she said venomously. 'He doesn't give a shit. He could rob her blind and he wouldn't care. Cow,' added Flick for good measure.

Robin laughed and Flick seemed gratified.

'What's tha name?' asked Robin, in broad Yorkshire. 'She never said.'

'Flick,' said Flick. 'You're Bobbi, yeah?'

'Yeah,' said Robin.

Flick took out her mobile from her messenger bag, which she had stowed beneath the counter, checked it, appeared not to see what she had hoped to see, then stuffed it out of sight again.

'You must've been hard up for work, were you?' she asked Robin.

'Had to take what I could,' Robin said. 'I were sacked.'

'Yeah?'

'Fookin' Amazon,' said Robin.

'Those tax-dodging bastards,' said Flick, slightly more interested. 'What happened?'

'Didn't make my daily rate.'

Robin had lifted her story directly from a recent news report about working conditions in one of the retail company's warehouses: the relentless pressure to make targets, packing and scanning thousands of products a day under unforgiving pressure from supervisors. Flick's expression wavered between sympathy and anger as Robin talked.

'That's outrageous!' she said, when Robin had finished.

'Yeah,' said Robin, 'and no union or nothing, obviously. Me dad were a big trade union man back in Yorkshire.'

'Bet he was furious.'

'He's dead,' said Robin, unblushingly. 'Lungs. Ex-miner.'

'Oh, shit,' said Flick. 'Sorry.'

She was looking upon Robin with respect and interest now.

'See, you'll have been a worker, not an employee. That's how the bastards get away with it.'

'What's the difference?'

'Fewer statutory rights,' said Flick. 'You might have a case against them if they deducted from your wages, though.'

'Dunno if I could prove that,' said Robin. 'How come you know all this?'

'I'm pretty active in the labour movement,' said Flick, with a shrug. She hesitated, 'And my mother's an employment lawyer.'

'Yeah?' said Robin, allowing herself to sound politely surprised.

'Yeah,' said Flick, picking her nails, 'but we don't get on. I don't see any of my family, actually. They don't like my partner. Or my politics.'

She smoothed out the Hezbollah T-shirt and showed Robin.

'What, are they Tories?' asked Robin.

'Might as well be,' said Flick. 'They loved bloody Blair.'

Robin felt her phone vibrate in the pocket of her second-hand dress.

'Is there a bog anywhere here?'

'Through here,' said Flick, pointing to a well-hidden purple painted door with more racks of jewellery nailed to it.

Beyond the purple door Robin found a small cubbyhole with a cracked, dirty window. A safe sat beside a dilapidated kitchen unit with a kettle, a couple of cleaning products and a stiff J-cloth on top. There was no room to sit down and barely room to stand, because a grubby toilet had been plumbed into the corner.

Robin shut herself inside the chipboard cubicle, put down the toilet lid and sat down to read the lengthy text that Barclay had just sent to both her and Strike.

Billy's been found. He was picked up off street 2 weeks ago. Psychotic episode, sectioned, hospital in north London, don't know which yet. Wouldn't tell docs his next of kin till yesterday. Social worker contacted Jimmy this morning. Jimmy wants me to go with him to persuade Billy to discharge himself. Scared what Billy's going to tell the doctors, says he talks too much. Also, Jimmy's lost bit of paper with Billy's name on & he's shitting himself about it. Asked me if I'd seen it. He says it's handwritten, no other details, I don't know why so important. Jimmy thinks Flick's nicked it. Things bad between them again.

As Robin was reading this for a second time, a response came in from Strike.

Barclay: find out visiting arrangements at the hospital, I want to see Billy. Robin: try and search Flick's bag.

Thanks, Robin texted back, exasperated. I'd never have thought of that on my own.

She got up, flushed the toilet and returned to the shop, where a gang of black-clad goths were picking over the stock like drooping crows. As she sidled past Flick, Robin saw that her messenger bag was sitting on a shelf beneath the counter. When the group had finally left in possession of essential oils and black candles, Flick took out her phone to check it again, before sinking once more into a morose silence.

Robin's experience in many temporary offices had taught her that little bonded women more than discovering that they were not alone in their particular man-related miseries. Taking out her own phone, she saw a further text from Strike:

That's why I get paid the big money. Brains.

Amused against her will, Robin suppressed a grin and said:
'He must think I'm fooking stupid.'
'Wassup?'

'Boyfriend. So-called,' said Robin, ramming her phone back into her pocket. 'S'posed to be separated from his wife. Guess where he was last night? Mate of mine saw him leaving hers this morning.' She exhaled loudly and slumped down on the counter.

'Yeah, my boyfriend likes old women and all,' said Flick, picking at her nails. Robin, who had not forgotten that Jimmy had been married to a woman thirteen years his senior, hoped for more confidences, but before she could ask more, another group of young women entered, chattering in a language that Robin did not recognise, though she thought it sounded Eastern European. They clustered around the basket of supposed charms.

'*Dziękuję ci*,' Flick said, as one of them handed over her money, and the girls laughed and complimented her on her accent.

'What did you just say?' asked Robin, as the party left. 'Was that Russian?'

'Polish. Learned a bit from my parents' cleaner.' Flick hurried on, as though she had given something away, 'Yeah, I always got on better with the cleaners than I did with my parents, actually, you can't call yourself a socialist and have a cleaner, can you? Nobody should be allowed to live in a house too big for them, we should have forcible repossessions, redistribution of land and housing to the people who need it.'

'Too right,' said Robin enthusiastically, and Flick seemed reassured to be forgiven her professional parents by Bobbi Cunliffe, daughter of a dead ex-miner and Yorkshire trade unionist.

'Want a tea?' she offered.

'Aye, that'd be great,' said Robin.

'Have you heard of the Real Socialist Party?' asked Flick, once she had come back into the shop with two mugs.

'No,' said Robin.

'It's not your normal political party,' Flick assured her. 'We're more like a proper community-based campaign, like, back to the Jarrow marchers, that kind of thing, the real spirit of Labour movement, not an imperialist Tory-lite shower of shite like fucking "New Labour". We don't want to play the same old politics game, we want to change the rules of the game in favour of ordinary working—'

401

Billy Bragg's version of the 'Internationale' rang out. As Flick reached into her bag, Robin realised that this was Flick's ringtone. Reading the caller's name, Flick became tense.

'You be all right on your own for a bit?'

'Course,' said Robin.

Flick slid into the back room. As the door swung shut Robin heard her say:

'What's going on? Have you seen him?'

As soon as the door was securely shut, Robin hurried to where Flick had been standing, crouched down and slid her hand under the leather flap of the messenger bag. The interior resembled the depths of a bin. Her fingers groped through sundry bits of crumpled paper, sweet wrappers, a sticky lump of something Robin thought might be chewed gum, various lid-less pens and tubes of make-up, a tin with a picture of Che Guevara on it, a pack of rolling tobacco that had leaked over the rest of the contents, some Rizlas, some spare tampons and a small, twisted ball of fabric that Robin was afraid might be a pair of worn pants. Trying to flatten out, read and then re-crumple each piece of paper was time-consuming. Most seemed to be abandoned drafts of articles. Then, through the door behind her, she heard Flick say loudly:

'*Strike?* What the hell . . . '

Robin froze, listening.

' . . . paranoid . . . it alone now . . . tell them he's . . . '

'Excuse me,' said a woman peering over the counter. Robin jumped up. The portly, grey-haired customer in a tie-dyed T-shirt pointed up at the shelf on the wall, 'could I see that rather special *athame*?'

'Which?' asked Robin, confused.

'The *athame*. The ceremonial dagger,' said the elderly woman, pointing.

Flick's voice rose and fell in the room behind Robin.

' . . . it, didn't you? . . . member you . . . pay me back . . . Chiswell's money . . . '

'Mmm,' said the customer, weighing the knife carefully in her hand, 'have you anything larger?'

'*You had it, not me!*' said Flick loudly, from behind the door.

'Um,' said Robin, squinting up at the shelf, 'I think this is all we've got. That one might be a bit bigger . . .'

She stood on tiptoe to reach the longer knife, as Flick said:

'*Fuck off, Jimmy!*'

'There you are,' said Robin, handing over the seven-inch-dagger.

With a clatter of falling necklaces, the door behind Robin flew open, hitting her in the back.

'Sorry,' said Flick, seizing her bag and shoving the phone back inside it, breathing hard, her eyes bright.

'Yes, you see, I like the triple moon marking on the smaller one,' said the elderly witch, pointing at the decoration on the hilt of the first dagger, unfazed by Flick's dramatic reappearance, 'but I prefer the longer blade.'

Flick was in that febrile state between fury and tears that Robin knew was one of the most amenable to indiscretion and confession. Desperate to get rid of her tiresome customer, she said bluntly in Bobbi's thick Yorkshire:

'Well, that's all we've got.'

The customer chuntered a little more, weighing the two knives in her hands, and at last took herself off without buying either.

'Y'all right?' Robin asked Flick at once.

'No,' said Flick. 'I need a smoke.'

She checked her watch.

'Tell her I'm taking lunch if she comes back, all right?'

Damn, thought Robin, as Flick disappeared, taking her bag and her promising mood with her.

For over an hour, Robin minded the shop alone, becoming increasingly hungry. Once or twice, Eddie at the record stall peered vaguely into the shop at Robin, but showed no other interest in her activities. In a brief lull between more customers, Robin nipped into the back room to make sure that there wasn't any food there that she had overlooked. There wasn't.

At ten to one, Flick strolled back into the shop with a dark, thuggishly handsome man in a tight blue T-shirt. He subjected Robin to the hard, arrogant stare of a certain brand of womaniser, melding appreciation and disdain to signal that she might be good-looking, but she would have to try a little harder than that to arouse his interest. It was a strategy that Robin had seen work on other young women in offices. It had never worked on her.

'Sorry I was so long,' Flick told Robin. Her bad mood did not seem entirely dissipated. 'Ran into Jimmy. Jimmy, this is Bobbi.'

'All right?' said Jimmy, holding out a hand.

Robin shook it.

'You go,' said Flick to Robin. 'Go and get something to eat.'

'Oh, right,' said Robin. 'Thanks.'

Jimmy and Flick waited while, under cover of checking her bag for money, Robin crouched down and, hidden by the counter, set her mobile to record before placing it carefully at the back of the dark shelf.

'See tha in a bit, then,' she said brightly, and strolled away into the market.

48

But what do you say to it all, Rebecca?

Henrik Ibsen, *Rosmersholm*

A whining wasp zigzagged from inner to outer rooms of Strike's office, passing between the two windows that were flung open to admit the fume-laden evening air. Barclay waved the insect away with the takeaway menu that had just arrived with a large delivery of Chinese food. Robin peeled lids off the cartons and laid them out on her desk. Over by the kettle, Strike was trying to find a third fork.

Matthew had been surprisingly accommodating when Robin had called him from Charing Cross Road three-quarters of an hour previously, to say that she needed to meet Strike and Barclay, and was likely to be back late.

'Fine,' he had said, 'Tom wants to go for a curry, anyway. I'll see you at home.'

'How was today?' Robin asked, before he could hang up. 'The office out in . . .'

Her mind went blank.

'Barnet,' he said. 'Games developer. Yeah, it was all right. How was yours?'

'Not bad,' said Robin.

Matthew was so determinedly uninterested in the details of the Chiswell job after their many arguments about it that there seemed no point in telling him where she had been, who she was impersonating, or what had happened that day. After they had said goodbye,

405

Robin walked on through meandering tourists and Friday night drinkers, knowing that a casual listener would have taken the conversation to be that of two people connected merely by proximity or circumstance, with no particular liking for each other.

'Want a beer?' Strike asked her, holding up a four pack of Tennent's.

'Yes, please,' said Robin.

She was still wearing her short black dress and lace-up boots, but had tied back her chalked hair, cleaned her face of its thick make-up and removed her dark lenses. Seeing Strike's face in a patch of evening sunlight, she thought he looked unwell. There were deeper lines than usual around his mouth and across his forehead, lines etched there, she suspected, by grinding, daily pain. He was also moving awkwardly, using his upper body to turn and trying to disguise his limp as he returned to her desk with the beer.

'What've you been up to today?' she asked Strike, as Barclay heaped his plate with food.

'Following Geraint Winn. He's holed up in a miserable B&B five minutes away from the marital home. He led me all the way into central London and back to Bermondsey again.'

'Risky, following him,' commented Robin. 'He knows what you look like.'

'All three of us could've been behind him and he wouldn't have noticed. He's lost about a stone since I last saw him.'

'What did he do?'

'Went to eat in a place right by the Commons, called the Cellarium. No windows, like a crypt.'

'Sounds cheerful,' said Barclay, settling down on the fake leather sofa and starting on his sweet and sour pork balls.

'He's like a sad homing pigeon,' said Strike, tipping the whole tub of Singapore noodles onto his own plate, 'returning to the place of his former glories with the tourists. Then we went to King's Cross.'

Robin paused in the act of helping herself to beansprouts.

'Blow job in a dark stairwell,' said Strike matter-of-factly.

'Eurgh,' muttered Robin, continuing to help herself to food.

'Did ye see it, aye?' asked Barclay with interest.

'Back view. Elbowed my way through the front door, then

backed out with apologies. He was in no state to recognise me. After that, he bought himself some new socks from Asda and went back to his B&B.'

'There are worse days out,' said Barclay, who had already eaten half the food on his plate. Catching Robin's eye, he said through a mouthful, 'Wife wants me home by half eight.'

'All right, Robin,' said Strike, lowering himself gingerly onto his own desk chair, which he had brought through to the outer office, 'let's hear what Jimmy and Flick had to say to each other when they thought no one was listening.'

He opened a notebook and took a pen from the pot on her desk, leaving his left hand free to fork Singapore noodles into his mouth. Still chewing vigorously, Barclay leaned forwards on the sofa, interested. Robin placed her mobile face up on the desk and pressed 'play'.

For a moment there was no sound except faint footsteps, which were Robin's, leaving the Wiccan's shop earlier in search of lunch.

'I thought you were here on your own?' said Jimmy's voice, faint but clear.

'She's having a day's trial,' said Flick. 'Where's Sam?'

'I told him I'll meet him at yours later. Right, where's your bag?'

'Jimmy, I haven't—'

'Maybe you picked it up by mistake.'

More footsteps, a scraping of wood and leather, clattering, thunks and furtive rustlings.

'This is a fucking tip.'

'I haven't got it, how many more times? And you've got no right to search that without my—'

'This is serious. I had it in my wallet. Where's it gone?'

'You've dropped it somewhere, haven't you?'

'Or someone's taken it.'

'Why would *I* take it?'

'Insurance policy.'

'That's a hell of an—'

'But if that's what you're thinking, you wanna remember, you fucking nicked it, so it incriminates you as much as me. More.'

'I was only there in the first place because of you, Jimmy!'

'Oh, *that's* going to be the story, is it? Nobody bloody made you. You're the one who started all this, remember.'

'Yeah and I wish I hadn't, now!'

'Too late for that. I want that paper back and so should you. It proves we had access to his place.'

'You mean it proves a connection between him and Bill – ouch!'

'Oh, fuck off, that didn't hurt! You demean women who really are knocked around, playing the victim. I'm not kidding, now. If you've taken it—'

'Don't threaten me—'

'What're you going to do, run off to Mummy and Daddy? How're they going to feel when they find out what their little girl's been up to?'

Flick's rapid breathing now became sobs.

'You nicked money from him, and all,' said Jimmy.

'You thought it was a laugh at the time, you said he deserved it—'

'Try that defence in court, see how far it gets you. If you try and save yourself by throwing me under the bus, I won't have any fucking problem telling the pigs you were in this thing *all the way*. So if that bit of paper turns up somewhere I don't want it to go—'

'I haven't got it, I don't know where it is!'

'—you've been fucking warned. Give me your front door key.'

'What? Why?'

'Because I'm going over to that shithole you call a flat right now and I'm searching it with Sam.'

'You're not going over there without me—'

'Why not? Got another Indian waiter sleeping off his hangover there, have you?'

'I never—'

'I don't give a shit,' said Jimmy. 'Screw whoever you like. Give me your key. *Give it me.*'

More footsteps; a tinkling of keys. The sound of Jimmy walking away and then a cascade of sobs that continued until Robin pressed pause.

'She cried until the shop owner came back,' said Robin, 'which was just before I did, and she hardly spoke this afternoon. I tried to walk back to the Tube with her, but she shook me off. Hopefully she'll be in a more talkative mood tomorrow.'

'So, did you and Jimmy search her flat?' Strike asked Barclay.

'Aye. Books, drawers, under her mattress. Nothing.'

'What exactly did he say you were looking for?'

'"Bit o' paper wi' handwriting an' Billy's name on", he says. "I had it in me wallet and it's gone". Claims it's somethin' tae do with a drugs deal. He thinks I'm some ned who'll believe anythin'.'

Strike put down his pen, swallowed a large mouthful of noodles and said:

'Well, I don't know about you two, but what jumps out at me is "it proves we had access".'

'I think I might know a bit more about that,' said Robin, who had so far successfully concealed her excitement about what she was about to reveal. 'I found out today that Flick can speak a bit of Polish, and we know she stole cash from her previous place of work. What if—?'

'"I do that cleaning",' said Strike, suddenly. 'That's what she said to Jimmy, on the march, when I was following them! "I do that cleaning, and it's disgusting" . . . Bloody hell – you think she was—?'

'Chiswell's Polish cleaner,' said Robin, determined not to be robbed of her moment of triumph. 'Yes. I do.'

Barclay was continuing to shovel pork balls into his mouth, though his eyes were suitably surprised.

'If that's true, it changes bloody everything,' said Strike. 'She'd have had access, been able to snoop around, take stuff into the house—'

'How'd she find out he wanted a cleaner?' asked Barclay.

'Must've seen the card he put in a newsagent's window.'

'They live miles apart. She's in Hackney.'

'Maybe Jimmy spotted it, snooping around Ebury Street, trying to collect his blackmail money,' suggested Robin, but Strike was now frowning.

'But that's back to front. If she found out about the blackmailable offence when she was a cleaner, her employment must've pre-dated Jimmy trying to collect money.'

'All right, maybe Jimmy didn't tip her off. Maybe they found out he wanted a cleaner while they were trying to dig dirt on him in general.'

'So they could run an exposé on the Real Socialist Party website?' suggested Barclay. 'That'd reach a good four or five people.'

Strike snorted in amusement.

'Main point is,' he said, 'this piece of paper's got Jimmy very worried.'

Barclay speared his last pork ball and stuck it in his mouth. 'Flick's taken it,' he said thickly. 'I guarantee it.'

'Why are you so sure?' asked Robin.

'She wants somethin' over him,' said Barclay, getting up to take his empty plate over to the sink. 'Only reason he's keepin' her around is because she knows too much. He told me the other day he'd be happy tae get shot of her if he could. I asked why he couldnae just dump her. He didnae answer.'

'Maybe she's destroyed it, if it's so incriminating?' suggested Robin.

'I don't think so,' said Strike. 'She's a lawyer's daughter, she's not going to destroy evidence. Something like that paper could be valuable, if the shit hits the fan and she decides she's going to cooperate with the police.'

Barclay returned to the sofa and picked up his beer.

'How's Billy?' Robin asked him, getting started at last on her own cooling meal.

'Poor wee bastard,' said Barclay. 'Skin and bone. The traffic cops caught him when he jumped a Tube barrier. He tried tae batter them, ended up bein' sectioned. The doctors say he's got delusions o' persecution. At first he thought he was bein' chased by the government and the medical staff were all part o' some giant conspiracy, but now he's back on his medication he's a wee bit more rational.

'Jimmy wanted tae take him home there and then, but the docs werenae gonna let that happen. What's really pissin' Jimmy off,' said Barclay, pausing to finish his can of Tennent's, 'is Billy's still obsessed wi' Strike. Keeps askin' for him. The doctors think it's part o' his delusion, that he's latched ontae the famous detective as part of his fantasy, like: the only person he can really trust. Couldnae tell them he and Strike have met. Not wi' Jimmy standin' there telling them it's all a load o' pish.

'The medics don't want anyone near him except family, and they're no keen on Jimmy any more, neither, not after he tried tae persuade Billy he's well enough to go home.'

Barclay crushed his beer can in his hand and checked his watch.

'Gotta go, Strike.'

'Yeah, all right,' said Strike. 'Thanks for staying. Thought it would be good to have a joint debrief.'

'Nae bother.'

With a wave to Robin, Barclay departed. Strike bent to pick up his own beer off the floor and winced.

'You all right?' asked Robin, who was helping herself to more prawn crackers.

'Fine,' he said, straightening up again. 'I did a lot of walking again today, and I could have done without the fight yesterday.'

'Fight? What fight?' asked Robin.

'Aamir Mallik.'

'What!'

'Don't worry. I didn't hurt him. Much.'

'You didn't tell me the argument got physical!'

'I wanted to do it in person, so I could enjoy you looking at me like I'm a complete bastard,' said Strike. 'How about a bit of sympathy for your one-legged partner?'

'You're an ex-boxer!' said Robin. 'And he probably weighs about nine stone soaking wet!'

'He came at me with a lamp.'

'*Aamir* did?'

She couldn't imagine the reserved, meticulous man she had known in the House of Commons using physical violence against anyone.

'Yeah. I was pushing him about Chiswell's "man of your habits" comment and he snapped. If it makes you feel any better, I don't feel good about it,' said Strike. 'Hang on a minute. Need a pee.'

He pulled himself awkwardly out of the chair and departed for the bathroom on the landing. As she heard the door close, Strike's mobile, which was charging on top of the filing cabinet beside Robin's desk, rang. She got up to check it and saw, through the cracked and sell-otaped screen, the name 'Lorelei'. Wondering whether to answer it, Robin hesitated too long and the call went to voicemail. Just as she was about to sit down again, a small *ping* declared that a text arrived.

If you want a hot meal and a shag with no human emotions involved, there are restaurants and brothels.

Robin heard the bang of the bathroom door outside and stumbled hastily back to her chair. Strike limped back inside the room, lowered himself into his chair and picked up his noodles.

'Your phone just rang,' said Robin. 'I didn't pick up—'

'Chuck it over,' said Strike.

She did so. He read the text with no change of expression, muted the phone and put it in his pocket.

'What were we saying?'

'That you didn't feel good about the fight—'

'I feel fine about the fight,' Strike corrected her. 'If I hadn't defended myself I'd have a face full of stitches.'

He pronged a forkful of noodles.

'The bit I don't feel great about is when I told him I know he's been ostracised by his family, barring one sister who's still talking to him. It's all on Facebook. It was when I mentioned his family dropping him that I nearly got my head taken off with a table lamp.'

'Maybe they're upset because they think he's with Della?' suggested Robin as Strike chewed his noodles.

He shrugged and made an expression indicative of 'maybe', swallowed, and said, 'Has it occurred to you that Aamir is literally the only person connected with this case who's got a motive? Chiswell threatened him, presumably with exposure. "A man of your habits." "Lachesis knew when everyone's time was up".'

'What happened to "forget about motive, concentrate on means"?'

'Yeah, yeah,' said Strike wearily. He set aside his plate, from which he had eaten nearly all the noodles, took out his cigarettes and lighter, and sat up a little straighter. 'OK, let's focus on means.

'Who had access to the house, to anti-depressants and helium? Who knew Jasper Chiswell's habits well enough to be sure he'd drink his orange juice that morning? Who had a key, or, who would he have trusted enough to let in in the early hours of the morning?'

'Members of his family.'

'Right,' said Strike, as his lighter flared, 'but we know Kinvara, Fizzy, Izzy and Torquil can't have done it, which leaves us with Raphael and his story of being ordered down to Woolstone that morning.'

'You really think he could have killed his father then driven coolly down to Woolstone to wait with Kinvara until the police arrived?'

'Forget psychology or probability: we're considering opportunity,' said Strike, blowing out a long jet of smoke. 'Nothing I've heard so far precludes Raphael being at Ebury Street at six in the morning. I know what you're going to say,' he forestalled her, 'but it wouldn't be the first time a phone call had been faked by a killer. He could have called his own mobile with Chiswell's to make it seem as though his father had ordered him down to Woolstone.'

'Which means that either Chiswell didn't have a passcode on his mobile, or that Raphael knew it.'

'Good point. That needs checking.'

Clicking out the nib of his pen, Strike made a note on his pad. As he did it, he wondered whether Robin's husband, who had previously deleted her call history without her knowledge, knew her current passcode. These small matters of trust were often powerful indicators of the strength of a relationship.

'There's another logistical problem if Raphael was the killer,' Robin said. 'He didn't have a key, and if his father let him in, it would mean Chiswell was awake and conscious while Raphael pounded up anti-depressants in the kitchen.'

'Another good point,' said Strike, 'but the pounding up of the pills has to be explained away with all of our suspects.

'Take Flick. If she was posing as the cleaner, she probably knew the house in Ebury Street better than most of the family. Loads of opportunities to poke around, and she had a restricted key for a while. They're hard to get copied, but let's say she managed it, so she could still let herself in and out of the house whenever she fancied.

'She creeps in in the early hours to doctor the orange juice, but crushing pills in a pestle and mortar is a noisy job—'

'—unless,' said Robin, 'she brought the pills already crushed up, in a bag or something, and dusted them around the pestle and mortar to make it look as though Chiswell had done it.'

'OK, but we still need to explain why there were no traces of amitriptyline in the empty orange juice carton in the bin. Raphael could plausibly have handed his father a glass of juice—'

'—except that Chiswell's prints were the only ones on there—'

'—but would Chiswell not find it odd to come downstairs in the morning to a pre-poured glass of juice? Would *you* drink a glass of something you hadn't poured, and which appeared mysteriously in what you thought was an empty house?'

Down in Denmark Street, a group of young women's voices rose over the constant swish and rumble of traffic, singing Rihanna's 'Where Have You Been?'

'*Where have you been? All my life, all my life . . .*'

'Maybe it *was* suicide,' said Robin.

'That attitude won't get the bills paid,' said Strike, tapping his cigarette ash onto his plate. 'Come on, people who had the means to get into Ebury Street that day: Raphael, Flick—'

'—and Jimmy,' said Robin. 'Everything that applies to Flick applies to him, because she would've been able to give him all the information she had about Chiswell's habits and his house, and given him her copied key.'

'Correct. So those are three people we know could have got in that morning,' said Strike, 'but this took much more than simply being able to get in through the door. The killer also had to know which anti-depressants Kinvara was taking, and arrange for the helium canister and rubber tubing to be there, which suggests close contact with the Chiswells, access to the house to get the stuff inside, or insider knowledge of the fact that the helium and tubing were already in there.'

'As far as we know, Raphael hadn't been in Ebury Street lately and wasn't on terms with Kinvara to know what pills she was taking, though I suppose his father might have mentioned it to him,' said

Robin. 'Judged on opportunity alone, the Winns and Aamir seem to be ruled out . . . so, assuming she *was* the cleaner, Jimmy and Flick go to the top of our suspect list.'

Strike heaved a sigh and closed his eyes.

'Bollocks to it,' he muttered, as he passed a hand across his face, 'I keep circling back to motive.'

Opening his eyes again, he stubbed out his cigarette on his dinner plate and immediately lit another one.

'I'm not surprised MI5 are interested, because there's no obvious gain here. Oliver was right – blackmailers don't generally kill their victims, it's the other way around. Hatred's a picturesque idea, but a hot-blooded hate killing is a hammer or a lamp to the head, not a meticulously planned fake suicide. If it was murder, it was more like a clinical execution, planned in every detail. Why? What did the killer get out of it? Which also makes me wonder, why *then?* Why did Chiswell die *then?*

'It was surely in Jimmy and Flick's best interests for Chiswell to stay alive until they could produce evidence that forced him to come across with the money they wanted. Same with Raphael: he'd been written out of the will, but his relationship with his father was showing some signs of improvement. It was in his interest for his father to stay alive.

'But Chiswell had covertly threatened Aamir with exposure of something unspecified, but probably sexual, given the Catullus quotation, and he'd recently come into possession of information about the Winns' dodgy charity. We shouldn't forget that Geraint Winn wasn't really a blackmailer: he didn't want money, he wanted Chiswell's resignation and disgrace. Is it beyond the realms of possibility that Winn or Mallik took a different kind of revenge when they realised the first plan had failed?'

Strike dragged heavily on his cigarette and said:

'We're missing something, Robin. The thing that ties all this together.'

'Maybe it doesn't tie together,' said Robin. 'That's life, isn't it? We've got a group of people who all had their own personal tribulations and secrets. Some of them had reason not to like Chiswell, to resent him, but that doesn't mean it all joins up neatly. Some of it must be irrelevant.'

'There's still something we don't know.'

'There's a lot we don't—'

'No, something big, something . . . fundamental. I can smell it. It keeps almost showing itself. Why did Chiswell say he might have more work for us after he'd scuppered Winn and Knight?'

'I don't know,' said Robin.

'"One by one, they trip themselves up",' Strike quoted. 'Who'd tripped themselves up?'

'Geraint Winn. I'd just told him about the missing money from the charity.'

'Chiswell had been on the phone, trying to find a money clip, you said. A money clip that belonged to Freddie.'

'That's right,' said Robin.

'Freddie,' repeated Strike, scratching his chin.

And for a moment he was back in the communal TV room of a German military hospital, with the television muted in the corner and copies of the *Army Times* lying on a low table. The young lieutenant who had witnessed Freddie Chiswell's death had been sitting there alone when Strike found him, wheelchair-bound, a Taliban bullet still lodged in his spine.

'. . . the convoy stopped, Major Chiswell told me to get out, see what was going on. I told him I could see movement up on the ridge. He told me to fucking well do as I was told.

'I hadn't gone more than a couple of feet when I got the bullet in the back. The last thing I remember was him yelling out of the lorry at me. Then the sniper took the top of his head off.'

The lieutenant had asked Strike for a cigarette. He wasn't supposed to be smoking, but Strike had given him the half pack he had on him.

'Chiswell was a cunt,' said the young man in the wheelchair.

In Strike's imagination he saw tall, blond Freddie swaggering up a country lane, slumming it with Jimmy Knight and his mates. He saw Freddie in fencing garb, out on the piste, watched by the indistinct figure of Rhiannon Winn, who was perhaps already entertaining suicidal thoughts.

Disliked by his soldiers, revered by his father: could Freddie be the thing that Strike sought, the element that tied everything together, that connected two blackmailers and the story of a strangled child? But the notion seemed to dissolve as he examined it, and the diverse strands of the investigation fell apart once more, stubbornly unconnected.

'I want to know what the photographs from the Foreign Office show,' said Strike aloud, his eyes on the purpling sky beyond the office window. 'I want to know who hacked the Uffington white horse onto the back of Aamir Mallik's bathroom door, and I want to know why there was a cross in the ground on the exact spot Billy said a kid was buried.'

'Well,' said Robin, standing up and beginning to clear away the debris of their Chinese takeaway, 'nobody ever said you weren't ambitious.'

'Leave that. I'll do it. You need to get home.'

I don't want to go home.

'It won't take long. What are you up to tomorrow?'

'Got an afternoon appointment with Chiswell's art dealer friend, Drummond.'

Having rinsed off the plates and cutlery, Robin took her handbag down from the peg where she'd hung it, then turned back. Strike tended to rebuff expressions of concern, but she had to say it.

'No offence, but you look terrible. Maybe rest your leg before you have to go out again? See you soon.'

She left before Strike could answer. He sat lost in thought until, finally, he knew he must begin the painful journey back upstairs to his attic flat. Having heaved himself upright again, he closed the windows, turned off the lights and locked up the office.

As he placed his false foot on the bottom stair to the floor above, his phone rang again. He knew, without checking, that it was Lorelei. She wasn't about to let him go without at least attempting to hurt him as badly as he had hurt her. Slowly, carefully, keeping his weight off his prosthesis as much as was practical, Strike climbed the stairs to bed.

49

*Rosmers of Rosmersholm – clergymen, soldiers, men who have
filled high places in the state – men of scrupulous honour, every
one of them . . .*

Henrik Ibsen, *Rosmersholm*

Lorelei didn't give up. She wanted to see Strike face to face, wanted
to know why she had given nearly a year of her life, as she saw it, to
an emotional vampire.

'You owe me a meeting,' she said, when he finally picked up the
phone at lunchtime next day. 'I want to see you. You owe me that.'

'And what will that achieve?' he asked her. 'I read your email,
you've made your feelings clear. I told you from the start what I
wanted and what I didn't want—'

'Don't give me that "I never pretended I wanted anything serious"
line. Who did you call when you couldn't walk? You were happy
enough for me to act like your wife when you were—'

'So let's both agree I'm a bastard,' he said, sitting in his combined
kitchen-sitting room with his amputated leg stretched out on a chair
in front of him. He was wearing only boxer shorts, but would soon
need to get his prosthesis on and dress smartly enough to blend in at
Henry Drummond's art gallery. 'Let's wish each other well and—'

'No,' she said, 'you don't get out of it that easily. I was happy, I
was doing fine—'

'I never wanted to make you miserable. I like you—'

'You *like* me,' she repeated shrilly. 'A year together and you
like me—'

418

'What do you want?' he said, losing his temper at last. 'Me to limp up the fucking aisle, not feeling what I should feel, not wanting it, wishing I was out of it? You're making me say what I don't want to say. I didn't want to hurt anyone—'

'But you did! You *did* hurt me! And now you want to walk away as though nothing happened!'

'Whereas you want a public scene in a restaurant?'

'I want,' she said, crying now, 'not to feel as though I could have been anyone. I want a memory of the end that doesn't make me feel disposable and cheap—'

'I never saw you that way. I don't see you like that now,' he said, eyes closed, wishing he had never crossed the room at Wardle's party. 'Truth is, you're too—'

'Don't tell me I'm too good for you,' she said. 'Leave us both with some dignity.'

She hung up. Strike's dominant emotion was relief.

No investigation had ever brought Strike so reliably back to the same small patch of London. The taxi disgorged him onto the gently sloping pavement of St James's Street a few hours later, with the red brick St James's Palace ahead and Pratt's on Park Place to his right. After paying off the driver, he headed for Drummond's Gallery, which lay between a wine dealer's and a hat shop on the left-hand side of the street. Although he had managed to put his prosthesis on, Strike was walking with the aid of a collapsible walking stick that Robin had bought him during another period when his leg had become almost too painful to bear his weight.

Even if it had marked the end of a relationship he wanted to escape, the call with Lorelei had left its mark. He knew in his heart that he was, in the spirit if not in the letter, guilty of some of the charges she had laid against him. While he had told Lorelei at the outset that he sought neither commitment nor permanence, he had known perfectly well that she had understood him to mean 'right now' rather than 'never' and he had not corrected that impression, because he wanted a distraction and a defence against the feelings that had dogged him after Robin's wedding.

However, the ability to section off his emotions, of which Charlotte had always complained, and to which Lorelei had dedicated a lengthy paragraph of the email dissecting his personality, had never failed him yet. Arriving two minutes early for his appointment with Henry Drummond, he transferred his attention with ease to the questions he intended to put to the late Jasper Chiswell's old friend.

Pausing beside the black marble exterior of the gallery, he saw himself reflected in the window and straightened his tie. He was wearing his best Italian suit. Behind his reflection, tastefully illuminated, a single painting in an ornate golden frame stood on an easel behind the spotless glass. It featured a pair of what, to Strike, looked like unrealistic horses with giraffe-like necks and staring eyes, ridden by eighteenth-century jockeys.

The gallery beyond the heavy door was cool and silent, with a floor of highly polished white marble. Strike walked carefully with his stick among the sporting and wildlife paintings, which were illuminated discreetly around the white walls, all of them in heavy gilded frames, until a well-groomed young blonde in a tight black dress emerged from a side door.

'Oh, good afternoon,' she said, without asking his name, and walked away towards the back of the gallery, her stilettos making a metallic click on the tiles. 'Henry! Mr Strike's here!'

A concealed door opened, and Drummond emerged: a curious-looking man, whose ascetic features of pinched nose and black brows were enclosed by rolls of fat around chin and neck, as though a puritan had been engulfed by the body of a jolly squire. With his mutton-chop whiskers and dark grey suit and waistcoat he had a timeless, irrefutably upper-class, appearance.

'How do you do?' he said, offering a warm, dry hand. 'Come into the office.'

'Henry, Mrs Ross just called,' said the blonde, as Strike walked into the small room beyond the discreet door, which was book-lined, mahogany-shelved and very tidy. 'She'd like to see the Munnings before we close. I've told her it's reserved, but she'd still like—'

'Let me know when she arrives,' said Drummond. 'And could we have some tea, Lucinda? Or coffee?' he enquired of Strike.

'Tea would be great, thank you.'

'Do sit down,' said Drummond, and Strike did so, grateful for a large and sturdy leather chair. The antique desk between them was bare but for a tray of engraved writing paper, a fountain pen and an ivory and silver letter opener. 'So,' said Henry Drummond heavily, 'you're looking into this appalling business for the family?'

'That's right. D'you mind if I take notes?'

'Carry on.'

Strike took out his notebook and pen. Drummond swivelled gently from side to side in his rotating chair.

'Terrible shock,' he said softly. 'Of course, one thought immediately of foreign interference. Government minister, eyes of the world on London with the Olympics and so forth ...'

'You didn't think he could have committed suicide?' asked Strike.

Drummond sighed heavily.

'I knew him for forty-five years. His life had not been devoid of vicissitudes. To have come through everything – the divorce from Patricia, Freddie's death, resignation from the government, Raphael's ghastly car accident – to end it *now*, when he was Minister for Culture, when everything seemed back on track ...

'Because the Conservative Party was his life's blood, you know,' said Drummond. 'Oh, yes. He'd bleed blue. Hated being out, delighted to get back in again, rise to minister ... we joked of him becoming PM in our younger days, of course, but that dream was gone. Jasper always said, "Tory faithful likes bastards or buffoons", and that he was neither one nor the other.'

'So you'd say he was in generally good spirits around the time he died?'

'Ah ... well, no, I couldn't say that. There were stresses, worries – but suicidal? Definitely not.'

'When was the last time you saw him?'

'The last time we met face to face was here, at the gallery,' said Drummond. 'I can tell you exactly what date it was: Friday the twenty-second of June.'

This, Strike knew, was the day that he had met Chiswell for the first time. He remembered the minister walking away towards Drummond's gallery after their lunch at Pratt's.

'And how did he seem to you that day?'

'Extremely angry,' said Drummond, 'but that was inevitable, given what he walked in on, here.'

Drummond picked up the letter opener and turned it delicately in his thick fingers.

'His son – Raphael – had just been caught, for the second time – ah—'

Drummond balked for a second.

'—*in flagrante*,' he said, 'with the other young person I employed at that time, in the bathroom behind me.'

He indicated a discreet black door.

'I had already caught them in there, a month prior to that. I hadn't told Jasper the first time, because I felt he had quite enough on his plate.'

'In what way?'

Drummond fingered the ornate ivory, cleared his throat and said:

'Jasper's marriage isn't – wasn't ... I mean to say, Kinvara is a handful. Difficult woman. She was badgering Jasper to put one of her mares in foal to Totilas at the time.'

When Strike looked blank, Drummond elucidated:

'Top dressage stallion. Nigh on ten thousand for semen.'

'Christ,' said Strike.

'Well, quite,' said Drummond. 'And when Kinvara doesn't get what she wants ... one doesn't know whether it's temperament or something deeper – actual mental instability – anyway, Jasper had a very difficult time with her.

'Then he'd been through the ghastly business of Raphael's, ah, accident – that poor young mother killed – the press, and so on and so forth, his son in jail ... as a friend, I didn't want to add to his troubles.

'I'd told Raphael the first time it happened that I wouldn't inform Jasper, but I also said he was on a final warning and if he stepped out of line again, he would be out on his ear, old friend of his father's or not. I had Francesca to consider, too. She's my goddaughter, eighteen years old and completely smitten with him. I didn't want to have to tell her parents.

'So when I walked in and heard them, I really had no choice. I'd thought I was safe to leave Raphael in charge for an hour because Francesca wasn't at work that day, but of course, she'd sneaked in specially to see him, on her day off.

'Jasper arrived to find me pounding on the door. There was no way to hide what was going on. Raphael was trying to block my entrance to the bathroom here while Francesca climbed out of the window. She couldn't face me. I rang her parents, told them everything. She never came back.

'Raphael Chiswell,' said Drummond heavily, 'is a Bad Lot. Freddie, the son who died – my godchild too, incidentally – was worth a million of . . . well, well,' he said, turning the penknife over and over in his fingers, 'one shouldn't say it, I know.'

The office door opened and the young blonde in the black dress entered with a tea tray. Strike compared it mentally to the tea he had in the office as she set down two silver pots, one containing hot water, bone china cups and saucers and a sugar bowl complete with tongs.

'Mrs Ross has just arrived, Henry.'

'Tell her I'm tied up for the next twenty minutes or so. Ask her to wait, if she's got time.'

'So I take it,' said Strike, when Lucinda had left, 'that there wasn't much time for conversation that day?'

'Well, no,' said Drummond, unhappily. 'Jasper had come to see Raphael at work, believing that all was going splendidly, and to arrive in the middle of that scene . . . Totally on my side, obviously, once he grasped what was going on. He was the one who actually shoved the boy out of the way to get the bathroom door open. Then he turned a nasty colour. He had a heart problem, you know, it had been grumbling on for years. Sat down on the toilet rather suddenly. I was very worried, but he wouldn't let me call Kinvara . . .

'Raphael had the decency to be ashamed of himself, then. Tried to help his father. Jasper told him to get out of it, made me close the door, leave him in there . . . '

Now sounding gruff, Drummond broke off and poured himself

and Strike tea. He was evidently in some distress. As he added three lumps to his own cup, the teaspoon rattled against the cup.

''Pologise. Last time I ever saw Jasper, you see. He came out of the bathroom, ghastly colour, still, shook my hand, apologised, said he'd let his oldest friend . . . let me down.'

Drummond coughed again, swallowed and continued with what seemed an effort:

'None of it was Jasper's fault. Raphael learned such morals as he's got from the mother, and she's best described as a high-class . . . well, well. Meeting Ornella was really the start of all Jasper's problems. If he'd only stayed with Patricia . . .

'Anyway, I never saw Jasper again. I had some difficulty bringing myself to shake Raphael's hand at the funeral, if you want the truth.'

Drummond took a sip of tea and Strike tried his own. It was far too weak.

'All sounds very unpleasant,' the detective said.

'You may well say so,' sighed Drummond.

'You'll appreciate that I have to ask about some sensitive matters.'

'Of course,' said Drummond.

'You've spoken to Izzy. Did she tell you that Jasper Chiswell was being blackmailed?'

'She mentioned it,' said Drummond, with a glance to check that the door was shut. 'He hadn't breathed a word to me. Izzy said it was one of the Knights . . . one remembers a family in the grounds. The father was an odd-job man, yes? As for the Winns, well, no, I don't think there was much liking between them and Jasper. Strange couple.'

'The Winns' daughter Rhiannon was a fencer,' said Strike. 'She was on the junior British fencing team with Freddie Chiswell—'

'Oh yes, Freddie was awfully good,' said Drummond.

'Rhiannon was a guest at Freddie's eighteenth birthday party, but she was a couple of years younger. She was only sixteen when she killed herself.'

'How ghastly,' said Drummond.

'You don't know anything about that?'

'How should I?' said Drummond, a fine crease between his dark eyes.

'You weren't at the eighteenth?'

'I was, as a matter of fact. Godfather, you know.'

'You can't remember Rhiannon?'

'Goodness, you can't expect me to remember all the names! There were upwards of a hundred young people there. Jasper had a marquee in the garden and Patricia ran a treasure hunt.'

'Really?' said Strike.

His own eighteenth birthday party, in a rundown pub in Shoreditch, had not included a treasure hunt.

'Just in the grounds, you know. Freddie always liked a competition. A glass of champagne at every clue, it was rather jolly, got things off with a swing. I was manning clue three, down by what the children always used to call the dell.'

'The hollow in the ground by the Knights' cottage?' asked Strike casually. 'It was full of nettles when I saw it.'

'We didn't put the clue *in* the dell, we put it under Jack o'Kent's doormat. He couldn't be trusted to take care of the champagne, because he had a drink problem. I sat on the edge of the dell in a deck chair and watched them hunt and everyone who found the clue got a glass of champagne and off they went.'

'Soft drinks for the under-eighteens?' asked Strike.

Faintly exasperated by this killjoy attitude, Drummond said:

'Nobody *had* to drink champagne. It was an eighteenth, a celebration.'

'So Jasper Chiswell never mentioned anything to you that he wouldn't want to get into the press?' asked Strike, returning to the main point.

'Nothing whatsoever.'

'When he asked me to find a way of countering his blackmailers, he told me that whatever he'd done happened six years ago. He implied to me that it wasn't illegal when he did it, but is now.'

'I've no idea what that could have been. Jasper was a very law-abiding type, you know. Whole family, pillars of the community, churchgoers, they've done masses for the local area ...'

A litany of Chiswellian beneficence followed, which rolled on for a couple of minutes and did not fool Strike in the slightest. Drummond was obfuscating, he was sure, because Drummond knew exactly what Chiswell had done. He became almost lyrical as he extolled the innate goodness of Jasper, and of the entire family, excepting, always, the scapegrace Raphael.

'. . . and hand always in his pocket,' Drummond concluded, 'mini-bus for the local Brownies, repairs to the church roof, even after the family finances . . . well, well,' he said again, in a little embarrassment.

'The blackmailable offence,' Strike began again, but Drummond interrupted.

'There was no offence.' He caught himself. 'You just said it your-self. Jasper told you he had done nothing illegal. No law was broken.'

Deciding that it would do no good to push Drummond harder about the blackmail, Strike turned a page in his notebook, and thought he saw the other relax.

'You called Chiswell on the morning he died,' said Strike.

'I did.'

'Would that have been the first time you'd spoken since sack-ing Raphael?'

'Actually, no. There had been a conversation a couple of weeks prior to that. M'wife wanted to invite Jasper and Kinvara over for dinner. I called him at DCMS, breaking the ice, you know, after the Raphael business. It wasn't a long conversation, but amicable enough. He said they couldn't make the night suggested. He also told me . . . well, to be frank, he told me he wasn't sure how much longer he and Kinvara would be together, that the marriage was in trouble. He sounded tired, exhausted . . . unhappy.'

'You had no more contact until the thirteenth?'

'We had no contact even then,' Drummond reminded him. 'I phoned Jasper, yes, but there was no answer. Izzy tells me—' He faltered. 'She tells me that he was probably already dead.'

'It was early for a call,' said Strike.

'I . . . had information I thought he should have.'

'Of what kind?'

'It was personal.'

Strike waited. Drummond sipped his tea.

'It related to the family finances, which as I imagine you know, were very poor at the time Jasper died.'

'Yes.'

'He'd sold off land and remortgaged the London property, offloaded all the good paintings through me. He was right down to the dregs, at the end, trying to sell me some of old Tinky's leavings. It was . . . a little embarrassing, actually.'

'How so?'

'I deal in Old Masters,' said Drummond. 'I do not buy paintings of spotted horses by unknown Australian folk artists. As a courtesy to Jasper, being an old friend, I had some of it valued with my usual man at Christie's. The only thing that had any monetary worth at all was a painting of a piebald mare and foal—'

'I think I've seen that,' said Strike.

'—but it was worth peanuts,' said Drummond. 'Peanuts.'

'How much, at a guess?'

'Five to eight thousand at a push,' said Drummond dismissively.

'Quite a lot of peanuts to some people,' said Strike.

'My dear fellow,' said Henry Drummond, 'that wouldn't have repaired a tenth of the roof at Chiswell House.'

'But he was considering selling it?' asked Strike.

'Along with half a dozen others,' said Drummond.

'I had the impression that Mrs Chiswell was particularly attached to that painting.'

'I don't think his wife's wishes were of much importance to him by the end . . . Oh dear,' sighed Drummond, 'this is all very difficult. I really don't wish to be responsible for telling the family something that I know will only cause hurt and anger. They're already suffering.'

He tapped his teeth with a nail.

'I assure you,' he said, 'that the reason for my call cannot have any bearing on Jasper's death.'

Yet he seemed in two minds.

'You must speak to Raphael,' he said, clearly choosing his words with care, 'because I think . . . possibly . . . I don't like Raphael,' he said, as though he had not already made that perfectly clear, 'but I

427

think, actually, he did an honourable thing on the morning his father died. At least, I can't see what he personally had to gain by it, and I think he's keeping silent about it for the same reason as myself. Being in the family, he is better placed to decide what to do than I can be. Speak to Raphael.'

Strike had the impression that Henry Drummond would rather Raphael made himself unpopular with the family.

There was a knock on the office door. Blonde Lucinda put her head inside.

'Mrs Ross isn't feeling terribly well, Henry; she's going to go, but she'd like to say goodbye.'

'Yes, all right,' said Drummond, getting to his feet. 'I don't think I can be of more use, I'm afraid, Mr Strike.'

'I'm very grateful for you seeing me,' said Strike, also rising, though with difficulty, and picking up his walking stick again. 'Could I ask one last thing?'

'Certainly,' said Drummond, pausing.

'Do you understand anything by the phrase "he put the horse on them"?'

Drummond appeared genuinely puzzled.

'Who put *what* horse ... where?'

'You don't know what that might mean?'

'I've really no idea. Terribly sorry, but as you've heard, I've got a client waiting.'

Strike had no alternative but to follow Drummond back into the gallery.

In the middle of the otherwise deserted gallery stood Lucinda, who was fussing over a dark, heavily pregnant woman sitting on a high chair, sipping water.

As he recognised Charlotte, Strike knew that this second encounter could not be a coincidence.

50

... you have branded me, once for all – branded me for life.

Henrik Ibsen, *Rosmersholm*

'Corm,' she said weakly, gaping at him over the rim of her glass. She was pale, but Strike, who would have put nothing past her to stage a situation that she could use to her advantage, including skipping food or applying white foundation, merely nodded.

'Oh, you know each other?' said Drummond, surprised.

'I must go,' mumbled Charlotte, getting to her feet while the concerned Lucinda hovered. 'I'm late, I'm meeting my sister.'

'Are you sure you're well enough?' said Lucinda.

Charlotte gave Strike a tremulous smile.

'Would you mind walking me up the road? It's only a block.'

Drummond and Lucinda turned to Strike, clearly delighted to offload responsibility for this wealthy, well-connected woman onto his shoulders.

'Not sure I'm the best person for the job,' said Strike, indicating his stick.

He felt Drummond and Lucinda's surprise.

'I'll give you plenty of warning if I think I'm actually going into labour,' said Charlotte. 'Please?'

He could have said 'No'. He might have said, 'Why don't you get your sister to meet you here?' A refusal, as she knew well, would make him appear churlish in front of people he might need to talk to again.

'Fine,' he said, keeping his voice just the right side of brusque.

'Thanks so much, Lucinda,' said Charlotte, sliding down from the chair.

She was wearing a beige silk trench coat over a black T-shirt, maternity jeans and sneakers. Everything she wore, even these casual things, was of fine quality. She had always favoured monochrome colours, stark or classic designs, against which her remarkable beauty was thrown into relief.

Strike held open the door for her, reminded by her pallor of the occasion when Robin had turned white and clammy at journey's end, after deftly steering a hire car out of what could have been a disastrous crash on black ice.

'Thank you,' he said to Henry Drummond.

'My pleasure,' said the art dealer formally.

'The restaurant's not far,' Charlotte said, pointing up the slope as the gallery door swung shut.

They walked side by side, passers-by perhaps assuming that he was responsible for her bulging stomach. He could smell what he knew was Shalimar on her skin. She had worn it ever since she was nineteen and he had sometimes bought it for her. Once again, he remembered walking this way towards the argument with her father in an Italian restaurant so many years ago.

'You think I arranged this.'

Strike said nothing. He had no desire to become enmeshed in disagreement or reminiscence. They had walked for two blocks before he spoke.

'Where is this place?'

'Jermyn Street. Franco's.'

The moment she said the name, he recognised it as the very same one in which they had met Charlotte's father all those years previously. The ensuing row had been short but exceedingly vicious, for a vein of incontinent spite ran right through every member of Charlotte's aristocratic family, but then she and Strike had gone back to her flat and made love with an intensity and urgency that he now wished he could expunge from his brain, the memory of her crying even as she climaxed, hot tears falling onto his face as she shouted with pleasure.

430

'Ouch. Stop,' she said sharply.

He turned. Cradling her belly with both hands, she backed into a doorway, frowning.

'Sit down,' he said, resenting even having to make suggestions to help her. 'On the step there.'

'No,' she said, taking deep breaths. 'Just get me to Franco's and you can go.'

They walked on.

The maître d'hôtel was all concern: it was clear that Charlotte was not well.

'Is my sister here?' Charlotte asked.

'Not yet,' said the maître d' anxiously, and like Henry Drummond and Lucinda, he looked to Strike to share responsibility for this alarming and unsought problem.

Barely a minute later, Strike was sitting in Amelia's seat at the table for two beside the window, and the waiter was bringing a bottle of water, and Charlotte was still taking deep breaths, and the maître d' was putting bread down between them, saying uncertainly that Charlotte might feel better if she ate something, but also suggesting quietly to Strike that he could call an ambulance at any moment, if that seemed desirable.

At last they were left alone. Still, Strike did not speak. He intended to leave the moment her colour improved, or her sister arrived. All around them sat well-heeled diners, enjoying wine and pasta amid tasteful wood, leather and glass, with black and white prints on the geometric white and red wallpaper.

'You think I arranged this,' mumbled Charlotte again.

Strike said nothing. He was keeping lookout for Charlotte's sister, whom he had not seen for years and who doubtless would be appalled to find them sitting together. Perhaps there would be another tight-lipped row, hidden from their fellow diners, in which fresh aspersions would be cast upon his personality, his background and his motives in escorting his wealthy, pregnant, married ex-girlfriend to her dinner date.

Charlotte took a breadstick and began to eat it, watching him.

'I really didn't know you were going to be there today, Corm.'

431

He didn't believe it for a second. The meeting at Lancaster House had been chance: he had seen her shock when their eyes met, but this was far too much of a coincidence. If he hadn't known it to be impossible, he would even have supposed that she knew he had split up with his girlfriend that morning.

'You don't believe me.'

'It doesn't matter,' he said, still scanning the street for Amelia.

'I got a real shock when Lucinda said you were there.'

Bollocks. She wouldn't have told you who was in the office. You already knew.

'This happens a lot lately,' she persisted. 'They call them Braxton Hicks contractions. I hate being pregnant.'

He knew he had not disguised his immediate thought when she leaned towards him and said quietly:

'I know what you're thinking. I didn't get rid of ours. I didn't.'

'Don't start, Charlotte,' he said, with the sensation that the firm ground beneath his feet was starting to crack and shift.

'I lost—'

'I'm not doing this again,' he said, a warning note in his voice. 'We're not going back over dates from two years ago. I don't care.'

'I took a test at my mother's—'

'*I said I don't care.*'

He wanted to leave, but she was if anything paler now, her lips trembling as she gazed at him with those horribly familiar, russet-flecked green eyes, now brimming with tears. The swollen belly still didn't seem part of her. He would not have been entirely surprised had she lifted her T-shirt to show a cushion.

'I wish they were yours.'

'Fuck's sake, Charlotte—'

'If they were yours, I'd be happy about it.'

'Don't give me that. You didn't want kids any more than I did.'

Tears now tipped over onto her cheeks. She wiped them away, her fingers shaking more violently than ever. A man at the next table was trying to pretend that he wasn't watching. Always hyperaware of the effect that she was having on those around her, Charlotte threw the eavesdropper a look that made him return hurriedly to his tortellini, then tore off a piece of bread and put it in her mouth, chewing while crying. Finally she gulped water to help her swallow, then pointed at her belly and whispered:

'I feel sorry for them. That's all I've got: pity. I feel sorry for them, because I'm their mother and Jago's their father. What a start in life. In the beginning I tried to think up ways of dying without killing them.'

'Don't be so fucking self-indulgent,' Strike said roughly. 'They're going to need you, aren't they?'

'I don't want to be needed, I never did. I want to be free.'

'To kill yourself?'

'Yes. Or to try and make you love me again.'

He leaned in towards her.

'You're married. You're having his children. We're finished, it's over.'

She leaned in, too, her tear-stained face the most beautiful he had ever seen. He could smell Shalimar on her skin.

'I'll always love you better than anyone in this world,' she said, stark white and stunning. 'You know that's the truth. I loved you better than anyone in my family, I'll love you better than my children, I'll love you on my deathbed. I think about you when Jago and I—'

'Keep this up and I'm leaving.'

She leaned back in her seat again and stared at him as though he were an approaching train and she was tied to the tracks.

'You know it's true,' she said hoarsely. 'You know it is.'

'Charlotte—'

'I know what you're going to say,' she said, 'that I'm a liar. I *am*. I *am* a liar, but not on the big things, never on the big ones, Bluey.'

'Don't call me that.'

'You didn't love me enough—'

'Don't you dare fucking blame me,' he said, in spite of himself. Nobody else did this to him: nobody even came close. 'The end – that was all you.'

'You wouldn't compromise—'

'Oh, I compromised. I came to live with you, like you wanted—'

'You wouldn't take the job Daddy—'

'I had a job. I had the agency.'

'I was wrong about the agency, I know that now. You've done such incredible things . . . I read everything about you, all the time. Jago found it all on my search history—'

'Should have covered your tracks, shouldn't you? You were a damn sight more careful with me, when you were screwing him on the side.'

'I wasn't sleeping with Jago while I was with you—'

'You got engaged to him two weeks after we finished.'

'It happened fast because I made it happen fast,' she said fiercely. 'You said I was lying about the baby and I was hurt, furious – you and I would be married now if you hadn't—'

'Menus,' said a waiter suddenly materialising beside their table, handing one to each of them. Strike waved his away.

'I'm not staying.'

'Take it for Amelia,' Charlotte instructed him, and he pulled the menu out of the waiter's hand and slapped it down on the table in front of him.

'We have a couple of specials today,' said the waiter.

'Do we look like we want to hear specials?' Strike growled. The waiter stood for a second, frozen in astonishment, then wound his way back through the crowded tables, his back view affronted.

'All this romantic bullshit,' Strike said, leaning in to Charlotte. 'You wanted things I couldn't give you. Every single fucking time, you hated the poverty.'

'I acted like a spoiled bitch,' she said, 'I know I did, then I married Jago and I got all those things I thought I deserved and I want to fucking die.'

'It goes beyond holidays and jewellery, Charlotte. You wanted to break me.'

Her expression became rigid, as it so often had before the worst outbursts, the truly horrifying scenes.

'You wanted to stop me wanting anything that wasn't you. That'd be the proof I loved you, if I gave up the army, the agency, Dave Polworth, every-bloody-thing that made me who I am.'

'I never, ever wanted to break you, that's a terrible thing to—'

'You wanted to smash me up because that's what you do. You have to break it, because if you don't, it might fade away. You've got to be in control. If you kill it, you don't have to watch it die.'

'Look me in the eye and tell me you've loved anyone, since, like you loved me.'

'No, I haven't,' he said, 'and thank fuck for that.'

'We had incredible times together—'

'You'll have to remind me what they were.'

'That night on Benjy's boat in Little France—'

'—your thirtieth? Christmas in Cornwall? They were a whole lot of fucking fun.'

Her hand fell to her belly. Strike thought he saw movement through the thin black T-shirt, and it seemed to him again that there was something alien and inhuman beneath her skin.

'Sixteen years, on and off, I gave you the best I had to give, and it was never enough,' he said. 'There comes a point where you stop trying to save the person who's determined to drag you down with them.'

'Oh, *please*,' she said, and suddenly, the vulnerable and desperate Charlotte vanished, to be replaced by somebody altogether tougher, cool-eyed and clever. 'You didn't want to save me, Bluey. You wanted to *solve* me. Big difference.'

He welcomed the reappearance of this second Charlotte, who was in every way as familiar as the fragile version, but whom he had far less compunction about hurting.

'I'm looking good to you now because I got famous and you married an arsehole.'

She absorbed the hit without blinking, though her face became a little pinker. Charlotte had always enjoyed a fight.

'You're so predictable. I knew you'd say I came back because you're famous.'

'Well, you do tend to resurface whenever there's drama, Charlotte,' Strike said. 'I seem to remember that the last time, I'd just got my leg blown off.'

'You bastard,' she said, with a cool smile. 'That's how you explain me taking care of you, all those months afterwards?'

His mobile rang: Robin.

'Hi,' he said, turning away from Charlotte to look out of the window. 'How's it going?'

'Hi, just telling tha I can't meet tha tonight,' said Robin, in a much thicker Yorkshire accent than usual. 'I'm going out with a friend. Party.'

'I take it Flick's listening?' said Strike.

'Yeah, well, why don't you try calling your wife if you're lonely?' said Robin.

'I'll do that,' said Strike, amused in spite of Charlotte's cool stare from across the table. 'D'you want me to yell at you? Give this some credibility?'

'No, *you* fook off,' said Robin loudly, and she hung up.

'Who was that?' asked Charlotte, eyes narrowed.

'I've got to go,' said Strike, pocketing the mobile and reaching for his walking stick, which had slipped and fallen under the table while he and Charlotte argued. Realising what he was after, she leaned sideways and succeeded in picking it up before he could reach it.

'Where's the cane I gave you?' she said. 'The Malacca one?'

'You kept it,' he reminded her.

'Who bought you this one? Robin?'

Amidst all of Charlotte's paranoid and frequently wild accusations, she had occasionally made uncannily accurate guesses.

'She did, as a matter of fact,' said Strike, but instantly regretted saying it. He was playing Charlotte's game and at once, she turned into a third and rare Charlotte, neither cold nor fragile, but honest to the point of recklessness.

'All that's kept me going through this pregnancy is the thought that once I've had them, I can leave.'

'You're going to walk out on your kids, the moment they exit the womb?'

'For another three months, I'm trapped. They all want the boy so much, they hardly let me out of their sight. Once I've given birth, it'll be different. I can go. We both know I'll be a lousy mother. They're better off with the Rosses. Jago's mother's already lining herself up as a surrogate.'

Strike held out his hand for the walking stick. She hesitated, then passed it over. He got up.

'Give my regards to Amelia.'

'She's not coming. I lied. I knew you'd be at Henry's. I was at a private viewing with him yesterday. He told me you were going to interview him.'

'Goodbye, Charlotte.'

'Wouldn't you rather have had advance warning that I want you back?'

'But I don't want you,' he said, looking down at her.

'Don't kid a kidder, Bluey.'

Strike limped out of the restaurant past the staring waiters, all of whom seemed to know how rude he had been to one of their colleagues. As he slammed his way out into the street, he felt as though he was pursued, as though Charlotte had projected after him a succubus that would tail him until they met again.

51

Can you spare me an ideal or two?

Henrik Ibsen, *Rosmersholm*

'You've been brainwashed to think it's got to be this way,' said the anarchist. 'See, you need to get your head around a world without leaders. No individual invested with more power than any other individual.'

'Right,' said Robin. 'So tha've *never* voted?'

The Duke of Wellington in Hackney was overflowing this Saturday evening, but the deepening darkness was still warm and a dozen or so of Flick's friends and comrades in CORE were happy to mill around on the pavement on Balls Pond Road, drinking before heading back to Flick's for a party. Many of the group were holding carrier bags containing cheap wine and beer.

The anarchist laughed and shook his head. He was stringy, blond and dreadlocked, with many piercings, and Robin thought she recognised him from the mêlée in the crowd on the night of the Paralympic reception. He had already shown her the squidgy lump of cannabis he had brought to contribute to the general amusement of the party. Robin, whose experience of drugs was restricted to a couple of long-ago tokes on a bong back in her interrupted university career, had feigned an intelligent interest.

'You're so naive!' he told her now. 'Voting's part of the great democratic con! Pointless ritual designed to make the masses think

438

they've got a say and influence! It's a power-sharing deal between the Red and Blue Tories!'

'What's th'answer, then, if it's not voting?' asked Robin, cradling her barely touched half of lager.

'Community organisation, resistance and mass protest,' said the anarchist.

''Oo organises it?'

'The communities themselves. You've been bloody brainwashed,' repeated the anarchist, mitigating the harshness of the statement with a small grin, because he liked Yorkshire socialist Bobbi Cunliffe's plain-spokenness, 'to think you need leaders, but people can do it for themselves once they've woken up.'

'An' who's gonna wake 'em up?'

'Activists,' he said, slapping his own thin chest, 'who aren't in it for money or power, who want *empowerment* of the people, not *control*. See, even unions – no offence,' he said, because he knew that Bobbi Cunliffe's father had been a trade union man, 'same power structures, the leaders start aping management—'

'Y'all right, Bobbi?' asked Flick, pushing to her side through the crowd. 'We'll head off in a minute, that was last orders. What're you telling her, Alf?' she added, with a trace of anxiety.

After a long Saturday in the jewellery shop, and the exchange of many (in Robin's case, wholly imaginary) confidences about their love lives, Flick had become enamoured of Bobbi Cunliffe to the point that her own speech had become slightly tinged with a Yorkshire accent. Towards the end of the afternoon she had extended a two-fold invitation, firstly to that night's party, and secondly, pending her friend Hayley's approval, a rented half-share in the bedroom recently vacated by their ex-flatmate, Laura. Robin had accepted both offers, placed her phone call to Strike, and agreed to Flick's suggestion that, in the absence of the Wiccan, they lock up the shop early.

''E's just telling me 'ow me dad was no better'n a capitalist,' said Robin.

'Fuck's sake, Alf,' said Flick, as the anarchist laughingly protested.

Their group straggled out along the pavement as they headed off through the night towards Flick's flat. In spite of his obvious desire to continue instructing Robin in the rudiments of a leaderless world, the anarchist was ousted from Robin's side by Flick herself, who wanted to talk about Jimmy. Ten yards ahead of them, a plump, bearded and pigeon-toed Marxist, who had been introduced to Robin as Digby, walked alone, leading the way to the party.

'Doubt Jimmy'll come,' she told Robin, and the latter thought she was arming herself against disappointment. 'He's in a bad mood. Worried about his brother.'

'What's wrong wi' him?'

'It's schizophrenic affection something,' said Flick. Robin was sure that Flick knew the correct term, but that she thought it appropriate, faced with a genuine member of the working classes, to feign a lack of education. She had let slip the fact that she had started a university course during the afternoon, seemed to regret it, and ever since had dropped her 'h's a little more consistently. 'I dunno. 'E 'as delusions.'

'Like what?'

'Thinks there's government conspiracies against him and that,' said Flick, with a little laugh.

'Bloody 'ell,' said Bobbi.

'Yeah, he's in 'ospital. He's caused Jimmy a lot of trouble,' said Flick. She stuck a thin roll-up in her mouth and lit it. 'You ever heard of Cormoran Strike?'

She said the name as though it were another medical condition.

'Who?'

'Private detective,' said Flick. 'He's been in the papers a lot. Remember that model who fell out of a window, Lula Landry?'

'Vaguely,' said Robin.

Flick glanced over her shoulder to check that Alf the anarchist was out of earshot.

'Well, Billy went to see 'im.'

'The fook for?'

'Because Billy's mental, keep up,' said Flick, with another little laugh. 'He thinks he saw something years ago—'

'What?' said Robin, quicker than she meant to.

'A murder,' said Flick.

'Christ.'

'He didn't, obviously,' said Flick. 'It's all bollocks. I mean, he *saw* something, but nobody bloody died. Jimmy was there, he knows. Anyway, Billy goes to this detective prick and now we can't get rid of him.'

'What d'you mean?'

''E beat Jimmy up.'

'The detective did?'

'Yeah. Followed Jimmy on a protest we were doing, beat him up, got Jimmy fooking arrested.'

'Bloody 'ell,' said Bobbi Cunliffe again.

'Deep state, innit?' said Flick. 'Ex-army. Queen and the flag and all that fucking shit. See, Jimmy and me had something on a Conservative minister—'

'Did you?'

'Yeah,' said Flick. 'I can't tell you what, but it was big, and then Billy fucked everything up. Sent Strike sniffing around, and we reckon he got in touch with the gov—'

She broke off suddenly, her eyes following a small car that had just passed them.

'Thought that was Jimmy's for a moment. It isn't. I forgot, it's off the road.'

Her mood sagged again. During the slack periods in the shop that day, Flick had told Robin the history of her and Jimmy's relationship, which in its endless fights and truces and renegotiations might have been the story of some disputed territory. They seemed never to have reached an agreement on the relationship's status and every treaty had fallen apart in rows and betrayals.

'You're well shot of him, if you ask me,' said Robin, who all day had pursued a cautious policy of trying to prise Flick free of the loyalty she clearly felt she owed the faithless Jimmy, in the hope of extracting confidences.

'Wish it were that easy,' said Flick, lapsing into the cod-Yorkshire she had adopted towards the end of the day. 'It's not like I wanna be *married* or anything—' she laughed at the very idea, '—he can sleep with who he likes and so can I. That's the deal and I'm fine with it.'

She had already explained to Robin at the shop that she identified as both genderqueer and pansexual, while monogamy, properly looked at, was a tool of patriarchal oppression, a line that Robin suspected had been originally Jimmy's. They walked in silence for a while. In the denser darkness they entered an underpass, when Flick said with a flicker of spirit:

'I mean, I've had my own fun.'

'Glad to hear it,' said Robin.

'Jimmy wouldn't like it if he knew all of them, either.'

The pigeon-toed Marxist walking ahead of them turned his head at that and Robin saw, by the light of a streetlamp, his little smirk as he glanced back at Flick, whose words he had clearly caught. The latter, being engaged in trying to dig her door keys out of the bottom of her cluttered messenger bag, seemed not to notice.

'We're up there,' Flick said, pointing at three lit windows above a small sports shop. 'Hayley's back already. Shit, I hope she remembered to hide my laptop.'

The flat was reached from a back entrance, up a cold, narrow stairwell. Even from the bottom of the stairs, they could hear the persistent bass of 'Niggas in Paris', and on reaching the landing, they found the flimsy door standing open and a number of people leaning up against the walls outside, sharing an enormous joint.

'*What's fifty grand to a muh-fucka like me*,' rapped Kanye West, from the dimly lit interior.

The dozen or so newcomers met a substantial number of people already inside. It was astonishing how many people could fit into such a small flat, which evidently comprised only two bedrooms, a minuscule shower room and a cupboard-sized kitchenette.

'We're using Hayley's room to dance in, it's the biggest, the one you'll share,' Flick shouted in Robin's ear as they forced their way towards the dark room.

Lit only by two strings of fairy lights, and the small rectangles of lights emanating from the phones of those checking their texts and social media, the room was already thick with the smell of cannabis and lined with people. Four young women and a man were managing to dance in the middle of the floor. Her eyes growing gradually accustomed to the darkness, Robin saw the skeletal frame of a bunk bed, already supporting a few people sharing a joint on the top mattress. She could just make out an LGBT rainbow flag and a poster of *True Blood*'s Tara Thornton on the wall behind them.

Jimmy and Barclay had already combed this flat for the piece of paper Flick had stolen from Chiswell and not found it, Robin reminded herself, peering through the darkness for likely hiding places. Robin wondered whether Flick kept it permanently on her person, but Jimmy would surely have thought of that, and in spite of Flick's avowed pansexuality, Robin thought Jimmy better placed than herself to persuade Flick to strip. Meanwhile, the darkness might be Robin's friend as she slid her hand beneath mattresses and rugs, but the party was so densely packed that she doubted it would be possible to do without alerting somebody to her odd behaviour.

'. . . find Hayley,' Flick bellowed in Robin's ear, pressing a can of lager into her hand, and they edged out of the room again into Flick's own bedroom, which seemed even smaller than it really was because every inch of the walls and ceiling had been covered in political flyers and posters, the orange of CORE and the black and red of the Real Socialist Party predominating. A gigantic Palestinian flag was pinned over the mattress on the floor.

Five people were already inside this room, which was lit by a solitary lamp. A pair of young women, one black, one white, lay entwined on the mattress on the floor, while podgy, bearded Digby had taken up a position on the floor, talking to them. Two teenage boys stood awkwardly against the wall, furtively watching the girls on the bed, their heads close together as they rolled a joint.

'Hayley, this is Bobbi,' said Flick. 'She's interested in Laura's half of the room.'

Both girls on the bed looked around: the tall, shaven-headed, sleepy-eyed peroxide blonde answered.

'I've already said Shanice can move in,' said the blonde, sounding stoned, and the petite black girl in her arms kissed her on the neck.

'Oh,' said Flick, turning in consternation to Robin. 'Shit. Sorry.'

'You're all right,' said Robin, feigning bravery in the face of disappointment.

'Flick,' someone called from the hall, 'it's Jimmy downstairs.'

'Oh, fuck,' said Flick, flustered, but Robin saw the pleasure flare in her face. 'Wait there,' she said to Robin, and left for the press of bodies in the hall.

'*Bougie girl, grab her hand,*' rapped Jay-Z from the other room.

Pretending to be interested in the conversation between the girls on the bed and Digby, Robin slid down the wall to sit on the laminate floor, sipping her lager while she covertly surveyed Flick's bedroom. It had evidently been tidied for the party. There was no wardrobe, but a clothes rail holding coats and the occasional dress, while T-shirts and sweaters were half-heartedly folded in a dark corner. A small number of Beanie Babies sat on top of the chest of drawers, along with a clutter of make-up, while various placards stood jumbled in a corner. Jimmy and Barclay must surely have been thoroughly through this room. Robin wondered whether they had thought of searching behind all these flyers. Unfortunately, even if they hadn't, she could hardly start unpinning them now.

'Look, this is basic stuff,' said Digby, addressing the girls on the bed. 'You'll agree that capitalism depends in part on the poorly paid labour of women, right? So feminism, if it's to be effective, *must* also be Marxist, the one implies the other.'

'Patriarchy is about more than capitalism,' said Shanice.

Out of the corner of her eye, Robin saw Jimmy fighting his way through the narrow hall, his arm around Flick's neck. The latter appeared happier than she had all evening.

'Women's oppression is inextricably linked to their inability to enter the labour force,' announced Digby.

The drowsy-eyed Hayley disentangled herself from Shanice to extend her hand towards the black-clad teenagers in a silent request. Their joint passed over Robin's head.

'Sorry 'bout the room,' Hayley said vaguely to Robin, after taking a long toke. 'Bastard getting a place in London, innit?'

'Total bastard,' said Robin.

'—because you want to subsume feminism within the larger ideology of Marxism.'

'There's no *subsuming*, the aims are identical!' said Digby, with an incredulous little laugh.

Hayley tried to give Shanice the joint, but the impassioned Shanice waved it away.

'Where are you Marxists when we're challenging the ideal of the heteronormative family?' she demanded of Digby.

'Hear, hear,' said Hayley vaguely, snuggling closer to Shanice and shoving the teenagers' joint at Robin, who passed it straight back to the boys. Interested though they had been in the lesbians, they promptly left the bedroom before anybody else could offer their meagre supply of drugs around.

'I used to have some of them,' Robin said aloud, getting to her feet, but nobody was listening. Digby took the opportunity to peek up Robin's short black skirt as she passed close to him on her way to the chest of drawers. Under cover of the increasingly heated conversation about feminism and Marxism, and with the appearance of vaguely nostalgic interest, Robin picked up and put down each of Flick's Beanie Babies in turn, feeling through the thin plush to the plastic beads and stuffing within. None of them felt as though they had been opened up and re-sewn to conceal a piece of paper.

With a sense of slight hopelessness, she returned to the dark hall, where people stood pressed together, spilling out onto the landing.

A girl was hammering on the door of the bathroom.

'Stop shagging in there, I need a piss!' she said, to amusement of various people standing around.

This is hopeless.

Robin slid into the kitchenette, which was hardly larger than two telephone boxes, where a couple was sitting on the side, the girl with her legs over the man's, who had his hand up her skirt, while the teenagers in black were now foraging with difficulty for something to eat. Under pretence of finding another drink, Robin sifted through empty cans and bottles, watching the progress of the teenagers through the cupboards and reflecting how insecure a hiding place a cereal box would make.

Alf the anarchist appeared in the kitchen doorway as Robin made to leave the room, now far more stoned than he had been in the pub.

'There she is,' he said loudly, trying to focus on Robin. 'Th' union leader's daughter.'

'That's me,' said Robin, as D'banj sang '*Oliver, Oliver, Oliver Twist*' from the second bedroom. She tried to duck under Alf's arm, but he lowered it, blocking her exit from the kitchen. The cheap laminate floor was vibrating with the stamping of the determined dancers in Hayley's room.

'You're hot,' said Alf. ''M'I allowed to say that? I mean it in a fucking feminist way.'

He laughed.

'Thanks,' said Robin, succeeding on her second pass in dodging around him and getting back into the tiny hall, where the desperate girl was still pounding on the bathroom door. Alf caught Robin's arm, bent down and said something incomprehensible in her ear. When he straightened up again, some of her hair chalk had left a black stain on the end of his sweaty nose.

'What?' said Robin.

'I said,' he shouted, '"wanna find somewhere quieter so we can talk more?"'

But then Alf noticed somebody standing behind her.

'All right, Jimmy?'

Knight had arrived in the hall. He smiled at Robin, then leaned up against the wall, smoking and holding a can of lager. He was ten years older than most of the people there, and some of the girls cast him sideways looks, in his tight black T-shirt and jeans.

'Waiting for the bog as well?' he asked Robin.

'Yeah,' said Robin, because that seemed the simplest way to extricate herself from both Jimmy and Alf the anarchist, should she need to. Through the open door of Hayley's room, she saw Flick dancing, now clearly delighted with life, laughing at whatever was said to her.

'Flick says your dad was a trade union man,' Jimmy said to Robin. 'Miner, yeah?'

'Yeah,' said Robin.

'Fuck's SAKE,' said the girl who had been hammering on the

bathroom door. She danced on the spot in desperation for a few more seconds, then pushed her way out of the flat.

'There are bins to the left!' called one of the other girls after her.

Jimmy leaned closer to Robin, so that she could hear him over the thumping bass. His expression was, as far as she could see, sympathetic, even gentle.

'Died, though, didn't he?' he asked Robin. 'Your dad. Lungs, Flick said?'

'Yeah,' said Robin.

'I'm sorry,' said Jimmy, quietly. 'Been through something similar myself.'

'Really?' said Robin.

'Yeah, my mum. Lungs, as well.'

'Workplace related?'

'Asbestos,' said Jimmy, nodding as he dragged on his cigarette. 'Wouldn't happen now, they've brought in legislation. I was twelve. My brother was two, he can't even remember her. My old man drank himself to death without her.'

'That's really rough,' said Robin sincerely. 'I'm sorry.'

Jimmy blew smoke away from her face and pulled a grimace.

'Two of a kind,' said Jimmy, clinking his can of lager against Robin's. 'Class war veterans.'

Alf the anarchist lurched away, swaying slightly, and disappeared into the dark room pierced with fairy lights.

'Family ever get compensation?' asked Jimmy.

'Tried,' said Robin. 'Mum's still pursuing it.'

'Good luck to her,' said Jimmy, raising his can and drinking. 'Good bloody luck to her.'

He banged on the bathroom door.

'Fucking hurry up, people are waiting,' he shouted.

'Maybe someone's ill?' Robin suggested.

'Nah, it'll be someone having a quickie,' said Jimmy.

Digby emerged from Flick's bedroom, looking disgruntled.

'I'm a tool of patriarchal oppression, apparently,' he announced loudly.

Nobody laughed. Digby scratched his belly under his T-shirt, which Robin now saw featured a picture of Groucho Marx, and ambled into the room where Flick was dancing.

'He's a tool, all right,' Jimmy muttered to Robin. 'Rudolf Steiner kid. Can't get over the fact that nobody gives him stars for effort any more.'

Robin laughed, but Jimmy didn't. His eyes held hers just a fraction too long, until the bathroom door opened a crack and a plump, red-faced young girl peeked out. Behind her, Robin saw a man with a wispy grey beard replacing his Mao cap.

'Larry, you filthy old bastard,' said Jimmy, grinning as the red-faced girl scuttled past Robin and disappeared into the dark room after Digby.

'Evening, Jimmy,' said the elderly Trotskyist, with a prim smile, and he, too, left the bathroom to a couple of cheers from the young men outside.

'Go on,' Jimmy told Robin, holding open the door and blocking anyone else's attempts to push past her.

'Thanks,' she said, as she slid into the bathroom.

The glare of the strip light was dazzling after the dinginess of the rest of the flat. The bathroom barely had standing room between the smallest shower Robin had ever seen, with a grimy transparent curtain hanging off half its hooks, a small toilet in which a large amount of sodden tissue and a cigarette end was floating. A used condom glistened in the wicker bin.

Above the sink were three rickety shelves crammed with half-used toiletries and general clutter, crammed together so that one touch seemed likely to dislodge everything.

Struck by a sudden idea, Robin moved closer to these shelves. She was remembering how she had relied on the squeamish ignorance and avoidance of most men towards matters pertaining to menstruation when she had hidden the listening devices in a box of Tampax. Her eyes ran swiftly over half-used bottles of supermarket-brand shampoo, an old tub of Vim, a dirty sponge, a pair of cheap deodorants and a few well-used toothbrushes in a chipped mug. Very carefully, because everything was so tightly packed together, Robin eased out a small box of Lil-Lets that proved to have only one sealed tampon inside it. As she reached up to replace the box, she spotted the corner of a small, squashy bundle, encased in a plastic wrapper and hidden behind the Vim and a bottle of fruity shower gel.

With a sudden stab of excitement, she reached up and wriggled the white polythene parcel carefully out of the place it had been wedged, trying not to knock everything over.

Somebody hammered on the door.

'I'm fucking bursting!' shouted a new girl.

'Won't be long!' Robin shouted back.

Two bulky sanitary towels had been rolled up in their own unromantic wrapping ('for Very Heavy Flow'): the sort of thing a young woman was unlikely to steal, especially if wearing skimpy clothing. Robin extracted them. There was nothing odd about the first. The second, however, emitted a small, crisp cracking noise as Robin bent it. Her excitement mounting, Robin turned it sideways and saw that it had been slit with what had probably been a razor blade. Wriggling her fingers into the tissue-like foam within, she felt a thick, folded piece of paper, which she eased out and unfolded.

The writing paper was exactly the same as that on which Kinvara had written her farewell note, with the name 'Chiswell' embossed across the top and a Tudor rose, like a drop of blood, beneath it. A few disjointed words and phrases were scrawled in the distinctive, cramped handwriting Robin had seen so often in Chiswell's office, and in the middle of the page one word had been circled many times.

251 Ebury Street
London
SW1W

Blanc de blanc

Suzuki ✔

~~*Mother?*~~

Bill

Odi et amo, quare id faciam, fortasse requiris? Nescio, sed fieri sentio et excrucior.

451

Hardly breathing in her excitement, Robin took out her mobile, took several pictures of the note, then refolded it, replaced it in the sanitary towel and returned the package to the place it had been on the shelf. She attempted to flush the toilet, but it was clogged and all she achieved was that the water rose ominously in the bowl, refusing to subside, the cigarette butt bobbing there in swirling tissue.

'Sorry,' Robin said, opening the door. 'Loo's blocked.'

'Whatever,' said the impatient, drunk girl outside, 'I'll do it in the sink.'

She pushed past Robin and slammed the door.

Jimmy was still standing outside.

'Think I'm going to take off,' Robin told him. 'I only really came t'see if that room was vacant, but soombody's got in ahead of me.'

'Shame,' said Jimmy lightly. 'Come to a meeting some time. We could use a bit of Northern soul.'

'Yeah, I might,' said Robin.

'Might what?'

Flick had arrived, holding a bottle of Budweiser.

'Come to a meeting,' said Jimmy, taking a fresh cigarette out of his pack. 'You were right, Flick, she's the real deal.'

Jimmy reached out and pulled Flick to him, pressing her to his side, and kissed her on the top of the head.

'Yeah, sh'iz,' said Flick, smiling with real warmth as she wound her arm around Jimmy's waist. 'Come to the next one, Bobbi.'

'Yeah, I might,' said Bobbi Cunliffe, the trade unionist's daughter, and she bade them goodbye, pushed her way out of the hall and out into the cold stairwell.

Not even the sight and smell of one of the black-clad teenagers vomiting copiously on the pavement just outside the main door could dampen Robin's jubilation. Unable to wait, she texted Strike the picture of Jasper Chiswell's note while hurrying towards the bus stop.

52

I can assure you, you have been on the wrong scent entirely,
Miss West.

Henrik Ibsen, *Rosmersholm*

Strike had fallen asleep, fully clothed, his prosthesis still attached, on top of the bedcovers in his attic bedroom. The cardboard folder containing everything pertaining to the Chiswell file was lying on his chest, vibrating gently as he snored, and he dreamed that he was walking hand in hand with Charlotte through an otherwise deserted Chiswell House, which they had bought together. Tall, slim and beautiful, she was no longer pregnant. She trailed Shalimar and black chiffon behind her, but their mutual happiness was evaporating in the damp chill of the shabby rooms through which they were wandering. What could have prompted the reckless, quixotic decision to purchase this draughty house, with the peeling walls and the wires dangling from the ceiling?

The loud buzz of a text arriving jerked Strike from sleep. For a fraction of a second he registered the fact that he was back in his attic room, alone, neither the owner of Chiswell House nor the lover of Charlotte Ross, before groping for the phone on which he was half lying in the full expectation that he was about to see a message from Charlotte.

He was wrong: it was Robin's name he saw when he peered groggily at the screen, and it was, moreover, one in the morning. Momentarily forgetting that she had been out at a party with Flick, Strike sat up hurriedly and the cardboard file that had been lying on his chest slid smoothly off him, scattering its various pages across the floorboards, while Strike squinted, blurry-eyed, at the photograph Robin had just sent him.

'Fuck me backwards.'

Ignoring the mess of notes at his feet, he called her back.

'Hi,' said Robin jubilantly, over the unmistakable sounds of a London night bus: the clatter and roar of the engine, the grinding of brakes, the tinny ding of the bell and the obligatory drunken laughter of what sounded like a gaggle of young women.

'How the *fuck* did you manage that?'

'I'm a woman,' said Robin. He could hear her smile. 'I know where we hide things when we really don't want them found. I thought you'd be asleep.'

'Where are you – a bus? Get off and grab a cab. We can charge it to the Chiswell account if you get a receipt.'

'There's no need—'

'Do as you're bloody told!' Strike repeated, a little more aggressively than he had intended, because while she had just pulled off quite a coup, she had also been knifed, out alone on the street after dark, a year previously.

'All right, all right, I'll get a cab,' said Robin. 'Have you read Chiswell's note?'

'Looking at it now,' said Strike, switching to speakerphone so that he could read Chiswell's note while talking to her. 'I hope you left it where you found it?'

'Yeah. I thought that was best?'

'Definitely. Where exactly—?'

'Inside a sanitary towel.'

'Christ,' said Strike, taken aback. 'I'd never've thought to—'

'No, nor did Jimmy and Barclay,' said Robin smugly. 'Can you read what it says at the bottom? The Latin?'

Squinting at the screen, Strike translated:

'"*I hate and I love. Why do I do it, you might ask? I don't know. I just feel it, and it crucifies me . . .*" that's Catullus again. A famous one.'

'Did you do Latin at university?'

'No.'

'Then how—?'

'Long story,' said Strike.

In fact, the story of his ability to read Latin wasn't long, merely (to most people) inexplicable. He didn't feel like telling it in the middle of the night, nor did he want to explain that Charlotte had studied Catullus at Oxford.

'"I hate and I love",' Robin repeated. 'Why would Chiswell have written that down?'

'Because he was feeling it?' Strike suggested.

His mouth was dry: he had smoked too much before falling asleep. He got up, feeling achy and stiff, and picked his way carefully around the fallen notes, heading for the sink in the other room, phone in hand.

'Feeling it for Kinvara?' asked Robin dubiously.

'Ever see another woman around while you were in close contact with him?'

'No. Of course, he might not have been talking about a woman.'

'True,' admitted Strike. 'Plenty of man love in Catullus. Maybe that's why Chiswell liked him so much.'

He filled a mug with cold tap water, drank it down in one, then threw in a tea bag and switched on the kettle, all the while peering down at the lit screen of his phone in the darkness.

'"Mother", crossed out,' he muttered.

'Chiswell's mother died twenty-two years ago,' said Robin. 'I've just looked her up.'

'Hmm,' said Strike. '"Bill", circled.'

'Not Billy,' Robin pointed out, 'but if Jimmy and Flick thought it meant his brother, people must sometimes call Billy "Bill".'

'Unless it's the thing you pay,' said Strike. 'Or a duck's beak, come to that . . . "Suzuki" . . . "Blanc de" . . . Hang on. Jimmy Knight's got an old Suzuki Alto.'

'It's off the road, according to Flick.'

'Yeah. Barclay says it failed its MOT.'

'There was a Grand Vitara parked outside Chiswell House when we visited, too. One of the Chiswells must own it.'

'Good spot,' said Strike.

He switched on the overhead light and crossed to the table by the window, where he had left his pen and notebook.

'You know,' said Robin thoughtfully, 'I think I've seen "Blanc de blanc" somewhere recently.'

'Yeah? Been drinking champagne?' asked Strike, who had sat down to make more notes.

'No, but . . . yeah, I suppose I must've seen it on a wine label, mustn't I? Blanc de blancs . . . what does it mean? "White from whites?"'

'Yeah,' said Strike.

For nearly a minute, neither of them spoke, both examining the note. 'You know, I hate to say this, Robin,' said Strike at last, 'but I think the most interesting thing about this is that Flick had it. Looks like a to-do list. Can't see anything here that proves wrongdoing or suggests grounds for blackmail or murder.'

'Mother, crossed out,' Robin repeated, as though determined to wring meaning out of the cryptic phrases. 'Jimmy Knight's mother died of asbestosis. He just told me so, at Flick's party.'

Strike tapped his notepad lightly with the end of his pen, thinking, until Robin voiced the question that he was grappling with.

'We're going to have to tell the police about this, aren't we?'

'Yeah, we are,' sighed Strike, rubbing his eyes. 'This proves she had access to Ebury Street. Unfortunately, that means we're going to have to pull you out of the jewellery shop. Once the police search her bathroom, it won't take her long to work out who must've tipped them off.'

'Bugger,' said Robin. 'I really felt like I was getting somewhere with her.'

'Yeah,' Strike agreed. 'This is the problem with having no official standing in an inquiry. I'd give a lot to have Flick in an interrogation room . . . This bloody case,' he said, yawning. 'I've been going through the file all evening. This note's like everything else: it raises more questions than it answers.'

'Hang on,' said Robin, and he heard sounds of movement, 'sorry – Cormoran, I'm going to get off here, I can see a taxi rank—'

'OK. Great work tonight. I'll call you tomorrow – later today, I mean.'

When she had hung up, Strike set his cigarette down in the ashtray, returned to his bedroom to pick up the scattered case notes off the floor, and took them back to the kitchen. Ignoring the freshly boiled kettle, he took a beer from the fridge, sat back down at the table with the file and, as an afterthought, opened the sash window beside him a few inches, to let some clean air into the room while he kept smoking.

The Military Police had trained him to organise interrogations and findings into three broad categories: people, places and things, and Strike had been applying this sound old principle to the Chiswell file before falling asleep on the bed. Now he spread the contents of the file out over the kitchen table and set to work again, while a cold night breeze laden with petrol fumes blew across the photographs and papers, so that their corners trembled.

'People,' Strike muttered.

He had written a list before he slept of the people who most interested him in connection with Chiswell's death. Now he saw that he had unconsciously ranked the names according to their degree of involvement in the dead man's blackmail. Jimmy Knight's name topped the list, followed by Geraint Winn's, and then by what Strike thought of as each man's respective deputy, Flick Purdue and Aamir Mallik. Next came Kinvara, who knew that Chiswell was being blackmailed, and why; Della Winn, whose super-injunction had kept the blackmail out of the press, but whose precise degree of involvement in the affair was otherwise unknown to Strike, and then Raphael, who had by all accounts been ignorant both of what his father had done, and of the blackmail itself. At the bottom of the list was Billy Knight, whose only known connection with the blackmail was the bond of blood between himself and the primary blackmailer.

Why, Strike asked himself, had he ranked the names in this particular order? There was no proven link between Chiswell's death and the blackmail, unless, of course, the threat of exposure of his unknown crime had indeed pushed Chiswell into killing himself.

It then occurred to Strike that a different hierarchy was revealed if he turned the list on its head. In this case Billy sat on top, a disinterested seeker, not of money or another man's disgrace, but of truth and justice. In the reversed order, Raphael came in second, with his strange and, to Strike, implausible story of being sent to his stepmother on the morning of his father's death, which Henry Drummond claimed grudgingly to have hidden some honourable motive as yet unknown. Della rose to third place, a widely admired woman of impeccable morality, whose true thoughts and feelings towards her blackmailing husband and to his victim remained inscrutable.

Read backwards, it seemed to Strike that each suspect's relation to the dead man became cruder, more transactional, until the list terminated with Jimmy Knight and his angry demand for forty thousand pounds.

Strike continued to pore over the list of names as though he might suddenly see something emerging out of his dense, spiky handwriting, the way unfocused eyes may spot the 3D image hidden in a series of brightly coloured dots. All that occurred to him, however, was the fact that there was an unusual number of pairs connected to Chiswell's death: couples – Geraint and Della, Jimmy and Flick; pairs of full siblings – Izzy and Fizzy, Jimmy and Billy; the duo of blackmailing collaborators – Jimmy and Geraint; and the subsets of each blackmailer and his deputy – Flick and Aamir. There was even the quasi-parental pairing of Della and Aamir. This left two people who formed a pair in being isolated within the otherwise close-knit family: the widowed Kinvara and Raphael, the unsatisfactory, outsider son.

Strike tapped his pen unconsciously against the notebook, thinking. *Pairs*. The whole business had begun with a pair of crimes: Chiswell's blackmail and Billy's allegation of infanticide. He had been trying to find the connection between them from the start, unable to believe that they could be entirely separate cases, even if on the face of it their only link was in the blood tie between the Knight brothers.

Turning the page, he examined the notes he had headed 'Places'. After a few minutes spent examining his own jottings concerning access to the house in Ebury Street, and the locations, in several cases unknown, of the suspects at the time of Chiswell's death, he made a note to remind himself that he still hadn't received from Izzy contact details for Tegan Butcher, the stable girl who could confirm that Kinvara had been at home in Woolstone while Chiswell was suffocating in a plastic bag in London.

He turned to the next page, headed 'Things', and now he set down his pen and spread Robin's photographs out so that they formed a collage of the death scene. He scrutinised the flash of gold in the pocket of the dead man, and then the bent sword, half hidden in shadow in the corner of the room.

It seemed to Strike that the case he was investigating was littered with objects that had been found in surprising places: the sword in the corner, the lachesis pills on the floor, the wooden cross found in a tangle of nettles at the bottom of the dell, the canister of helium and the rubber tubing in a house where no child's party had ever been held, but his tired mind could find neither answers nor patterns here.

Finally, Strike downed the rest of his beer, lobbed the empty can across the room into the kitchen bin, turned to a blank page in his notebook and began to write a to-do list for the Sunday of which two hours had already elapsed.

1. <u>Call Wardle</u>
Text note found in Flick's flat,
Update on police case if possible.
2. <u>Call Izzy</u>
Show her stolen note.
Ask: was Freddie's money clip ever found?
Tegan's details?
Need phone number for Raphael.
Also phone number, if poss, for Della Winn
3. <u>Call Barclay</u>
Give update.
Cover Jimmy & Flick again
When does Jimmy visit Billy?
4. <u>Call hospital</u>
Try and arrange interview with Billy when Jimmy not there.
5. <u>Call Robin</u>
Arrange interview with Raphael

6. _Call Della_
Try and arrange interview

After a little further thought, he finished the list with

7. Buy teabags/beer/bread

After tidying up the Chiswell file, tipping the overflowing ashtray into the bin, opening the window wider to admit more cold, fresh air, Strike went for a last pee, cleaned his teeth, switched off the lights and returned to his bedroom, where a single reading lamp still burned.

Now, with his defences weakened by beer and tiredness, the memories he had sought to bury in work forced their way to the forefront of his mind. As he undressed and removed his prosthetic leg, he found himself going back over every word Charlotte had said to him across the table for two in Franco's, remembering the expression of her green eyes, the scent of Shalimar reaching him through the garlic fumes of the restaurant, her thin white fingers playing with the bread.

He got into bed between the chilly sheets and lay, hands behind his head, staring up into the darkness. He wished he could feel indifferent, but in fact his ego had stretched luxuriously at the idea that she had read all about the cases that had made his name and that she thought about him while in bed with her husband. Now, though, reason and experience rolled up their sleeves, ready to conduct a professional post-mortem on the remembered conversation, methodically disinterring the unmistakable signs of Charlotte's perennial will to shock and her apparently insatiable need for conflict.

The abandonment of her titled husband and newborn children for a famous, one-legged detective would certainly constitute the crowning achievement of a career of disruption. Having an almost pathological hatred of routine, responsibility or obligation, she had sabotaged every possibility of permanence before she had to deal with the threats of boredom or compromise. Strike knew all this, because he knew her better than any other human being, and he knew that their final parting had happened at the exact moment where real sacrifice and hard choices had to be made.

But he also knew – and the knowledge was like ineradicable bacteria in a wound that stopped it ever healing – that she loved him as she had never loved anyone else. Of course, the sceptical girlfriends and wives of his friends, none of whom had liked Charlotte, had told him over and over again, 'That's not love, what she does to you', or, 'Not being funny, Corm, but how do you know she hasn't said exactly the same to all the others she's had?' Such women saw his confidence that Charlotte loved him as delusion or egotism. They had not been present for those times of total bliss and mutual understanding that remained some of the best of Strike's life. They had not shared jokes inexplicable to any other human being but himself and Charlotte, or felt the mutual need that had drawn them back together for sixteen years.

She had walked from him straight into the arms of the man she thought would hurt Strike worst, and indeed, it *had* hurt, because Ross was the absolute antithesis of him and had dated Charlotte before Strike had even met him. Yet Strike remained certain her flight to Ross had been self-immolation, done purely for spectacular effect, a Charlottian form of *sati*.

Difficile est longum subito deponere amorem,
Difficile est, verum hoc qua lubet efficias.

It is hard to abruptly shrug off a long-established love
Hard, but this, somehow, you must do.

Strike turned off the light, closed his eyes and sank, once more, into uneasy dreams of the empty house where squares of unfaded wallpaper bore witness to the removal of everything of value, but this time he walked alone, with the strange sensation that hidden eyes were watching.

53

And then, in the end, the poignant misery of her victory . . .
Henrik Ibsen, *Rosmersholm*

Robin arrived home just before 2 a.m. As she crept around the kitchen, making herself a sandwich, she noticed on the kitchen calendar that Matthew was planning to play five-a-side football later that morning. Accordingly, when she slipped into bed with him twenty minutes later, she set the alarm on her phone for eight o'clock before plugging it in to charge. As part of her effort to try and keep the atmosphere amicable, she wanted to get up to see him before he left.

He seemed happy that she'd made the effort to join him for breakfast, but when she asked whether he wanted her to come and cheer from the sidelines, or meet him for lunch afterwards, he declined both offers.

'I've got paperwork to do this afternoon. I don't want to drink at lunchtime. I'll come straight back,' he said, so Robin, secretly delighted, because she was so tired, told him to have a good time and kissed him goodbye.

Trying not to focus on how much lighter of heart she felt once Matthew had left the house, Robin occupied herself with laundry and other essentials until, shortly after midday, while she was changing the sheets on their bed, Strike called.

'Hi,' said Robin, gladly abandoning her task, 'any news?'

'Plenty. Ready to write some stuff down?'

'Yes,' said Robin, hurriedly grabbing notebook and pen off the

460

top of her dressing table and sitting down on the stripped mattress.

'I've been making some calls. First off, Wardle. Very impressed with your work in getting hold of that note—'

Robin smiled at her reflection in the mirror.

'—though he's warned me the police won't take kindly to us, as he put it, "clodhopping all over an open case". I've asked him not to say where he got the tip-off about the note, but I expect they'll put two and two together, given that Wardle and I are mates. Still, that's unavoidable. The interesting bit is that the police are still worried about the same features of the death scene as we are and they've been going deeper into Chiswell's finances.'

'Looking for evidence of blackmail?'

'Yeah, but they haven't got anything, because Chiswell never paid out. Here's the interesting bit. Chiswell got an unexplained payment in cash of forty thousand pounds last year. He opened a separate bank account for it, then seems to have spent it all on house repairs and other sundries.'

'He *received* forty thousand pounds?'

'Yep. And Kinvara and the rest of the family are claiming total ignorance. They say they don't know where the money came from or why Chiswell would've opened a separate account to take receipt of it.'

'The same amount Jimmy asked for before he scaled down his request,' said Robin. 'That's odd.'

'Certainly is. So then I called Izzy.'

'You've been busy,' said Robin.

'You haven't heard the half of it. Izzy denies knowledge of where the forty grand came from, but I'm not sure I believe her. Then I asked her about the note Flick stole. She's appalled that Flick might've been posing as her father's cleaner. Very shaken up. I think for the first time she's considering the possibility that Kinvara isn't guilty.'

'I take it she never met this so-called Polish woman?'

'Correct.'

'What did she make of the note?'

'She thinks it looks like a to-do list, as well. She assumes "Suzuki" meant the Grand Vitara, which was Chiswell's. No thoughts on "mother". The one thing of interest I got from her was in relation to "blanc de blanc". Chiswell was allergic to champagne. Apparently it made him go bright red and hyperventilate. What's odd about that is, there was a big empty box labelled Moët & Chandon in the kitchen when I checked it, the morning Chiswell died.'

'You never told me that.'

'We'd just found the body of a government minister. An empty box seemed relatively uninteresting at the time, and it never occurred to me it might be relevant to anything until I spoke to Izzy today.'

'Were there bottles inside?'

'Nothing, so far as I could see, and according to the family, Chiswell never entertained there. If he wasn't drinking champagne himself, why was the box there?'

'You don't think—'

'That's exactly what I think,' said Strike. 'I reckon that box was how the helium and the rubber tubing got into the house, disguised.'

'Wow,' said Robin, lying back on the unmade bed and looking up at the ceiling.

'Quite clever. The killer could've sent it to him as a gift, couldn't they, knowing he was highly unlikely to open and drink it?'

'Bit slapdash,' said Robin. 'What was to stop him opening it up anyway? Or re-gifting it?'

'We need to find out when it was sent,' Strike was saying. 'Meanwhile, one minor mystery's been cleared up. Freddie's money clip was found.'

'Where?'

'Chiswell's pocket. That was the flash of gold in the photograph you took.'

'Oh,' said Robin, blankly. 'So he must have found it, before he died?'

'Well, it'd be hard for him to find it *after* he died.'

'Ha ha,' said Robin sarcastically. 'There *is* another possibility.'

'That the killer planted it on the corpse? Funny you should say that. Izzy says she was very surprised when it turned up on the body, because if he'd found it, she would have assumed he'd have told her. He made a massive fuss about losing it, apparently.'

'He did,' Robin agreed. 'I heard him on the phone, ranting on about it. They fingerprinted it, presumably?'

'Yeah. Nothing suspicious. Only his – but at this point, that means nothing. If there was a killer, it's clear they wore gloves. I also asked Izzy about the bent sword, and we were right. It was Freddie's old sabre. Nobody knows how it got bent, but Chiswell's fingerprints were the only ones on there. I suppose it's possible Chiswell got it off the wall while drunk and sentimental and accidentally trod on it, but again, there's nothing to say a gloved killer couldn't have handled it as well.'

Robin sighed. Her elation at finding the note appeared to have been premature.

'So, still no real leads?'

'Hold your horses,' said Strike bracingly, 'I'm leading up to the good stuff.

'Izzy managed to get a new phone number for that stable girl who can confirm Kinvara's alibi, Tegan Butcher. I want you to give her a ring. I think you'll seem less intimidating to her than I will.'

Robin jotted down the digits Strike read out.

'And after you've called Tegan, I want you to phone Raphael,' said Strike, giving her the second number he had got from Izzy. 'I'd like to clear up once and for all what he was really up to, the morning his father died.'

'Will do,' said Robin, glad of something concrete to do.

'Barclay's going to go back onto Jimmy and Flick,' said Strike, 'and I . . .'

He left a small pause, deliberately dramatic, and Robin laughed.

'And you're . . .'

'. . . am going to interview Billy Knight and Della Winn.'

'What?' said Robin, amazed. 'How're you going to get into the hosp – and *she'll* never agree—'

'Well, that's where you're wrong,' said Strike. 'Izzy dug Della's number out of Chiswell's records for me. I just rang her. I admit, I was expecting her to tell me to piss off—'

'—in slightly more elevated language, if I know Della,' Robin suggested.

'—and she sounded initially as though she wanted to,' admitted Strike, 'but Aamir's disappeared.'

'What?' said Robin, sharply.

'Calm down. "Disappeared" is Della's word. In reality, he resigned the day before yesterday and vacated his house, which hardly makes him a missing person. He's not picking up the phone to her. She's blaming me, because – her words again – I did "a fine job" on him when I went round to question him. She says he's very fragile and it'll be my fault if he ends up doing himself a mischief. So—'

'You've offered to find him in exchange for her answering questions?'

'Right in one,' said Strike. 'She jumped at the offer. Says I'll be able to reassure him that he's not in trouble and that nothing unsavoury I might have heard about him will go any further.'

'I hope he's all right,' said Robin, concerned. 'He *really* didn't like me, but that just proves he's smarter than any of the rest of them. When are you meeting Della?'

'Seven o'clock this evening, at her house in Bermondsey. And tomorrow afternoon, if all goes to plan, I'm going to be talking to Billy. I checked with Barclay, and Jimmy's got no plans to visit then, so I called the hospital. I'm waiting for Billy's psychiatrist to call me back now and confirm.'

'You think they'll let you question him?'

'Supervised, yeah, I think they will. They're interested in seeing how lucid he is if he gets to talk to me. He's back on his meds and greatly improved, but he's still telling the story of the strangled kid. If the psychiatric team's in agreement, I'm going to be visiting the locked ward tomorrow.'

'Well, great. It's good to have things to be getting on with. God knows, we could use a breakthrough – even if it is about the death we're not being paid to investigate,' she sighed.

'There might not be a death at the bottom of Billy's story at all,' said Strike, 'but it's going to bug me for ever unless we find out. I'll let you know how I get on with Della.'

Robin wished him luck, bade him goodbye and ended the call, though she remained lying on her half-made bed. After a few seconds, she said aloud:

'Blanc de blancs.'

Once again, she had the sense of a buried memory shifting, issuing a gust of low mood. Where on earth had she seen that phrase, while feeling miserable?

'Blanc de blancs,' she repeated, getting off the bed. 'Blanc d – *ow!*'

She had put her bare foot down on something small and very sharp. Bending down, she picked up a backless diamond stud earring.

At first, she merely stared at it, her pulse unaltered. The earring wasn't hers. She owned no diamond studs. She wondered why she hadn't trodden on it when she climbed into bed with a sleeping Matthew in the early hours of the morning. Perhaps her bare foot had missed it, or, more probably, the earring had been in the bed and displaced only when Robin pulled off the undersheet.

Of course, there were many diamond stud earrings in the world. The fact remained that the pair to which Robin's attention had most recently been drawn had been Sarah Shadlock's. Sarah had been wearing them the last time Robin and Matthew had gone to dinner, the night that Tom had attacked Matthew with sudden and apparently unwarranted ferocity.

For what felt like a very long time, but was in reality little over a minute, Robin sat contemplating the diamond in her hand. Then she laid the earring carefully on her bedside cabinet, picked up her mobile, entered 'Settings', removed her caller ID, then phoned Tom's mobile.

He answered within a couple of rings, sounding grumpy. In the background, a presenter was wondering aloud what the forthcoming Olympic closing ceremony would be like.

'Yah, hello?'

Robin hung up. Tom wasn't playing five-a-side football. She continued to sit, motionless, her phone in her hand, on the heavy matrimonial bed that had been so difficult to move up the narrow stairs of this lovely rented house, while her mind moved back over the clear signs that she, the detective, had wilfully ignored.

'I'm so stupid,' Robin said quietly to the empty, sunlit room. '*So* bloody stupid.'

54

Your gentle and upright disposition, your polished mind, your
unimpeachable honour, are known to and appreciated by
everyone . . .

Henrik Ibsen, *Rosmersholm*

Though the early evening was still bright, Della's front garden lay in shadow, which gave it a placid, melancholy air in contrast to the busy, dusty road that ran beyond the gates. As Strike rang the doorbell, he noted two large dog turds on the otherwise immaculate front lawn and he wondered who was helping Della with such mundane tasks now that her marriage was over.

The door opened, revealing the Minister for Sport in her impenetrable black glasses. She was wearing what Strike's elderly aunt back in Cornwall would have called a housecoat, a knee-length purple fleece robe that buttoned to the high neck, giving her a vaguely ecclesiastic air. The guide dog stood behind her, looking up at Strike with dark, mournful eyes.

'Hi, it's Cormoran Strike,' said the detective, without moving. Given that she could neither recognise him by sight nor examine any of the identification he carried, the only way she could know whom she was admitting to her house was by the sound of his voice. 'We spoke on the phone earlier and you asked me to come and see you.'

'Yes,' she said, unsmiling. 'Come in, then.'

She stepped back to let him pass, one hand on the Labrador's collar. Strike entered, wiping his feet on the doormat. A swell of music, loud strings and woodwind instruments, cut through by the pounding of a kettle drum, issued from what Strike assumed was the sitting room. Strike, who had been raised by a mother who listened mainly to metal bands, knew very little about classical music, but there was a looming, ominous quality about this music that he didn't particularly care for. The hall was dark, because the lights hadn't been turned on, and otherwise nondescript, with a dark brown patterned carpet that, while practical, was rather ugly.

'I've made coffee,' said Della. 'I'll need you to carry the tray into the sitting room for me, if you wouldn't mind.'

'No problem,' said Strike.

He followed the Labrador, which padded along at Della's heels, its tail wagging vaguely. The symphony grew louder as they passed the sitting room, the doorframe of which Della touched lightly as she passed, feeling for familiar markers to orientate herself.

'Is that Beethoven?' asked Strike, for something to say.

'Brahms. Symphony Number One, C Minor.'

The edges of every surface in the kitchen were rounded. The knobs on the oven, Strike noticed, had raised numbers stuck to them. On a cork noticeboard was a list of phone numbers headed IN CASE OF EMERGENCY, that he imagined were for the use of a cleaner or home help. While Della crossed to the worktop opposite, Strike extracted his mobile from his coat pocket and took a picture of Geraint Winn's number. Della's outstretched hand reached the rim of the deep ceramic sink, and she moved sideways, where a tray sat already laden with a mug and a cafetière of freshly brewed coffee. Two bottles of wine stood beside it. Della felt for both of these, turned and held them out to Strike, still unsmiling.

'Which is which?' she asked.

'Châteauneuf-du-Pape, 2010, in your left hand,' said Strike, 'and Château Musar, 2006, in your right.'

'I'll have a glass of the Châteauneuf-du-Pape if you wouldn't mind opening the bottle and pouring it for me. I assumed that you wouldn't want a drink, but if you do, help yourself.'

'Thanks,' said Strike, picking up the corkscrew she had laid beside the tray, 'coffee will be fine.'

She set off silently for the sitting room, leaving him to follow with the tray. As he entered the room he caught the heavy scent of roses and was fleetingly reminded of Robin. While Della grazed furniture with her fingertips, feeling her way towards an armchair with wide wooden arms, Strike saw four large bunches of flowers positioned in vases around the room and punctuating the overall drabness with their vivid colours, red, yellow and pink.

Aligning herself by pressing the backs of her legs against the chair, Della sat down neatly, then turned her face towards Strike as he set the tray on the table.

'Would you put my glass here, on my right chair arm?' she said, patting it, and he did so, while the pale Labrador, which had flopped down beside Della's chair, watched him out of kind, sleepy eyes.

The strings of the violins in the symphony swooped and fell as Strike sat down. From the fawn carpet to the furniture, all of which might have been designed in the seventies, everything seemed to be in different shades of brown. Half of one wall was covered in built-in shelves holding what he thought must be at least a thousand CDs. On a table to the rear of the room was a stack of Braille manuscripts. A large, framed photograph of a teenage girl sat on the mantelpiece. It occurred to Strike that her mother could not even enjoy the bitter-sweet solace of looking at Rhiannon Winn every day, and he found himself filled with inconvenient compassion.

'Nice flowers,' he commented.

'Yes. It was my birthday a few days ago,' said Della.

'Ah. Many happy returns.'

'Are you from the West Country?'

'Partly. Cornwall.'

'I can hear it in your vowels,' said Della.

She waited while he dealt with the cafetière and poured himself coffee. When the sounds of clinking and pouring had ceased, she said:

'As I said on the phone, I'm very worried about Aamir. He'll still be in London, I'm sure, because it's all he's ever known. Not with his family,' she added, and Strike thought he heard a trace of contempt. 'I'm extremely concerned about him.'

She felt carefully for the wine glass next to her and took a sip.

'When you've reassured him that he isn't in any kind of trouble, and that anything Chiswell told you about him will go no further, you must tell him to contact me – urgently.'

The violins continued to screech and whine in what, to the untutored Strike, was a dissonant expression of foreboding. The guide dog scratched herself, her paw thudding off the carpet. Strike took out his notebook.

'Have you got the names or contact details of any friends Mallik might have gone to?'

'No,' said Della. 'I don't think he has many friends. Latterly he mentioned someone from university but I don't remember a name. I doubt it was anyone particularly close.'

The thought of this distant friend seemed to make her uneasy.

'He studied at the LSE, so that's an area of London he knows well.'

'He's on good terms with one of his sisters, isn't he?'

'Oh, no,' said Della, at once. 'No, no, they all disowned him. No, he's got nobody, really, other than me, which is what makes this situation so dangerous.'

'The sister posted a picture on Facebook of the two of them fairly recently. It was in that pizza joint opposite your house.'

Della's expression betrayed not merely surprise, but displeasure.

'Aamir told me you'd been snooping online. Which sister was it?'

'I'd have to ch—'

'But I doubt he'd be staying with her,' said Della, talking over him. 'Not with the way the family as a whole has treated him. He *might* have contacted her, I suppose. You might see what she knows.'

'I will,' said Strike. 'Any other ideas about where he might go?'

'He really doesn't have anyone else,' she said. 'That's what worries me. He's vulnerable. It's essential I find him.'

'Well, I'll certainly do my best,' Strike promised her. 'Now, you said on the phone that you'd answer a few questions.'

Her expression became slightly more forbidding.

'I doubt I can tell you anything of interest, but go on.'

'Can we start with Jasper Chiswell, and your and your husband's relationship with him?'

By her expression, she managed to convey that she found the question both impertinent and slightly ludicrous. With a cold smile and raised eyebrows, she responded:

'Well, Jasper and I had a professional relationship, obviously.'

'And how was that?' asked Strike, adding sugar to his coffee, stirring it and taking a sip.

'Given,' said Della, 'that Jasper hired you to try and discover disreputable information about us, I think you already know the answer to that question.'

'You maintain that your husband wasn't blackmailing Chiswell, then, do you?'

'Of course I do.'

Strike knew that pushing on this particular point, when Della's super-injunction had already shown what lengths she would go to in her own defence, would only alienate her. A temporary retreat seemed indicated.

'What about the rest of the Chiswells? Did you ever run across any of them?'

'Some,' she said, a little warily.

'And how did you find them?'

'I barely know them. Geraint says Izzy was hardworking.'

'Chiswell's late son was on the junior British fencing team with your daughter, I think?'

The muscles of her face seemed to contract. He was reminded of an anemone shutting in on itself when it senses a predator.

'Yes,' she said.

'Did you like Freddie?'

'I don't think I ever spoke to him. Geraint was the one who ferried Rhiannon around to her tournaments. He knew the team.'

The shadow stems of the roses closest to the window stretched like bars across the carpet. The Brahms symphony crashed stormily on in the background. Della's opaque lenses contributed to a feeling of inscrutable menace and Strike, though wholly unintimidated, was put in mind of the blind oracles and seers that peopled ancient myths, and the particular supernatural aura attributed by the able-bodied to this one particular disability.

'What was it that made Jasper Chiswell so eager to find out things to your disadvantage, would you say?'

'He didn't like me,' said Della simply. 'We disagreed frequently. He came from a background that finds anything that deviates from its own conventions and norms to be suspect, unnatural, even dangerous. He was a rich white Conservative male, Mr Strike, and he felt the corridors of power were best populated exclusively by rich white Conservative males. He sought, in everything, to restore a status quo he remembered in his youth. In pursuit of that objective, he was frequently unprincipled and certainly hypocritical.'

'In what way?'

'Ask his wife.'

'You know Kinvara, do you?'

'I wouldn't say I "know" her. I had an encounter with her a while ago that was certainly interesting in the light of Chiswell's public proclamations about the sanctity of marriage.'

Strike had the impression that beneath the lofty language, and in spite of her genuine anxiety about Aamir, Della was deriving pleasure from saying these things.

'What happened?' Strike asked.

'Kinvara turned up unexpectedly late one afternoon at the ministry, but Jasper had already left for Oxfordshire. I think it was her aim to surprise him.'

'When was this?'

'I should say ... a year ago, at least. Shortly before Parliament went into recess, I think. She was in a state of great distress. I heard a commotion outside and went to find out what was going on. I could tell by the silence of the outer office that they were all agog. She was very emotional, demanding to see her husband. Initially I thought she must have had dreadful news and perhaps needed Jasper as a source of comfort and support. I took her into my office.

'Once it was just the two of us, she broke down completely. She was barely coherent, but from the little I could understand,' said Della, 'she'd just found out there was another woman.'

'Did she say who?'

'I don't think so. She may have done, but she was – well, it was quite disturbing,' said Della austerely. 'More as though she had suffered a bereavement than the end of a marriage. "I was just part of his game", "He never loved me" and so forth.'

'What game did you take her to mean?' asked Strike.

'The political game, I suppose. She spoke of being humiliated, of being told, in so many words, that she had served her purpose . . .

'Jasper Chiswell was a very ambitious man, you know. He'd lost his career once over infidelity. I imagine he cast around quite clinically for the kind of new wife who'd burnish his image. No more Italian fly-by-nights now he was trying to get back into the cabinet. He probably thought Kinvara would go down very well with the county Conservatives. Well-bred. Horsey.

'I heard, later, that Jasper had bundled her off into some kind of psychiatric clinic not long afterwards. That's how families like the Chiswells deal with excessive emotion, I suppose,' said Della, taking another sip of wine. 'Yet she stayed with him. Of course, people do stay, even when they're treated abominably. He talked about her within my hearing as though she was a deficient, needy child. I remember him saying Kinvara's mother would be "babysitting" her for her birthday, because he had to be in Parliament for a vote. He could have paired his vote, of course – found a Labour MP and struck a deal. Simply couldn't be bothered.

'Women like Kinvara Chiswell, whose entire self-worth is predicated on the status and success of marriage, are naturally shattered when everything goes wrong. I think all those horses of hers were an outlet, a substitute and – oh yes,' said Della, 'I've just remembered – the *very* last thing she said to me that day was that in addition to everything else, she now had to go home to put down a beloved mare.'

Della felt for the broad, soft head of Gwynn, who was lying beside her chair.

'I felt very sorry for her, there. Animals have been an enormous consolation to me in my life. One can hardly overstate the comfort they give, sometimes.'

The hand that caressed the dog still sported a wedding ring, Strike noticed, along with a heavy amethyst ring that matched her housecoat. Somebody, he supposed Geraint, must have told her that it was the same colour and again, he felt an unwelcome pang of pity.

'Did Kinvara tell you how or when she'd found out that her husband had been unfaithful?'

'No, no, she simply gave way to an almost incoherent outpouring of rage and grief, like a small child. Kept saying, "I loved him and he never loved me, it was all a lie". I've never heard such a raw explosion of grief, even at a funeral or a deathbed. I never spoke to her again except for hello. She acted as though she had no memory of what had passed between us.'

Della took another sip of wine.

'Can we return to Mallik?' Strike asked.

'Yes, of course,' she said at once.

'The morning that Jasper Chiswell died – the thirteenth – you were here, at home?'

There was a lengthy silence.

'Why are you asking me that?' Della said, in a changed tone.

'Because I'd like to corroborate a story I've heard,' said Strike.

'You're mean, that Aamir was here with me, that morning?'

'Exactly.'

'Well, that's quite true. I'd slipped downstairs and sprained my wrist. I called Aamir and he came over. He wanted me to go to casualty, but there was no need. I could still move all my fingers. I simply needed some help managing breakfast and so on.'

'*You* called Mallik?'

'What?' she said.

It was the age-old, transparent 'what?' of the person who is afraid they've made a mistake. Strike guessed that some very rapid thinking was going on behind the dark glasses.

'*You* called Aamir?'

'Why? What does he say happened?'

'He says your husband went in person to fetch him from his house.'

'Oh,' said Della and then, 'of course, yes, I forgot.'

'Did you?' asked Strike gently. 'Or are you backing up their story?'

'I forgot,' Della repeated firmly. 'When I said I "called" him I wasn't talking about the telephone. I meant that I called "on" him. Via Geraint.'

'But if Geraint was here when you slipped, couldn't he have helped you with your breakfast?'

'I think Geraint wanted Aamir to help persuade me to go to casualty.'

'Right. So it was Geraint's idea to go to Aamir, rather than yours?'

'I can't remember now,' she said, but then, contradicting herself, 'I'd fallen rather heavily. Geraint has a bad back, naturally he wanted help and I thought of Aamir, and then the pair of them nagged me to go to A&E, but there was no need. It was a simple sprain.'

The light was now fading beyond the net curtains. Della's black lenses reflected the neon red of the dying sun above the rooftops.

'I'm extremely worried about Aamir,' she said again, in a strained voice.

'A couple more questions and I'm done,' Strike replied. 'Jasper Chiswell hinted in front of a roomful of people that he knew something disreputable about Mallik. What can you tell me anything about that?'

'Yes, well, it was that conversation,' said Della quietly, 'that first made Aamir think about resigning. I could feel him pulling away from me after it happened. And then *you* finished the job, didn't you? You went to his house, to taunt him further.'

'There was no taunting, Mrs Winn—'

'*Liwat*, Mr Strike, did you never learn what that meant all the time you were in the Middle East?'

'Yeah, I know what it means,' said Strike matter-of-factly. 'Sodomy. Chiswell seemed to be threatening Aamir with exposure—'

'Aamir wouldn't suffer from exposure of the truth, I assure you!' said Della fiercely. 'Not that it matters a jot, but he doesn't happen to be gay!'

The Brahms symphony continued on what, to Strike, was its gloomy and intermittently sinister course, horns and violins competing to jar the nerves.

'You want the truth?' said Della loudly. 'Aamir objected to being groped and harassed, *felt up* by a senior civil servant, whose inappropriate touching of young men passing through his office is an open secret, even a joke! And when a comprehensive-educated Muslim boy loses his cool and smacks a senior civil servant, which of the two do you imagine finds themselves smeared and stigmatised? Which of them, do you think, becomes the subject of derogatory rumours, and is forced out of a job?'

'I'm guessing,' said Strike, '*not* Sir Christopher Barrowclough-Burns.'

'How did you know whom I was talking about?' said Della sharply.

'Still in the post, is he?' asked Strike, ignoring the question.

'Of course he is! Everybody knows about his *harmless* little ways, but nobody wants to go on the record. I've been trying to get something done about Barrowclough-Burns for years. When I heard Aamir had left the diversity programme in murky circumstances, I made it my business to find him. He was in a pitiable state when I first made contact with him, absolutely pitiable. Quite apart from the derailing of what should have been a stellar career, there was a malicious cousin who'd heard some gossip and spread the rumour that Aamir had been fired for homosexual activity at work.

'Well, Aamir's father isn't the sort of man to look kindly on a gay son. Aamir had been resisting his parents' pressure to marry a girl they thought suitable. There was a terrible row and a complete breach. This brilliant young man lost everything, family, home and job, in the space of a couple of weeks.'

'So you stepped in?'

'Geraint and I had an empty property around the corner. Both our mothers used to live there. Neither Geraint nor I have siblings. It had become too difficult to manage our mothers' care from London, so we brought them up from Wales and housed them together, around the corner. Geraint's mother died two years ago, mine this, so the house was empty. We didn't need the rent. It seemed only sensible to let Aamir stay there.'

'And this was nothing but disinterested kindness?' Strike said. 'You weren't thinking of how useful he might be to you, when you gave him a job and a house?'

'What d'you mean, "useful"? He's a very intelligent young man, any office would be—'

'Your husband was pressuring Aamir to get incriminating information on Jasper Chiswell from the Foreign Office, Mrs Winn.

475

Photographs. He was pressuring Aamir to go to Sir Christopher for pictures.'

Della reached out for her glass of wine, missed the stem by inches and hit the glass with her knuckles. Strike lunged forwards to try and catch it, but too late: a whip-like trail of red wine described a parabola in the air and spattered the beige carpet, the glass falling with a thud beside it. Gwynn got up and approached the spill with mild interest, sniffing the spreading stain.

'How bad is it?' asked Della urgently, her fingers grasping the arms of her chair, her face inclined to the floor.

'Not good,' said Strike.

'Salt, please ... put salt on it. In the cupboard to the right of the cooker!'

Turning on the light as he entered the kitchen, Strike's attention was caught for the first time by an odd something he had failed to spot on his previous entry into the room: an envelope stuck high up on a wall-mounted cabinet to the right, too high for Della to reach. Having grabbed the salt out of the cupboard he made a detour to read the single word written on it: *Geraint.*

'To the right of the cooker!' Della called a little desperately from the sitting room.

'Ah, the right!' Strike shouted back, as he tugged down the envelope and slit it open.

Inside was a receipt from 'Kennedy Bros. Joiners', for the replacement of a bathroom door. Strike licked his finger, dampened down the envelope flap, resealed it as best he could and stuck it back where he had found it.

'Sorry,' he told Della, re-entering the room. 'It was right in front of me and I didn't notice.'

He twisted the top of the cardboard tub and poured salt liberally over the purple stain. The Brahms symphony came to an end as he straightened up, dubious as to the likely success of the home remedy.

'Have you done it?' Della whispered into the silence.

'Yeah,' said Strike, watching the wine rising into the white and turning it a dirty grey. 'I think you're still going to need a carpet cleaner, though.'

'Oh dear . . . the carpet was new this year.'

She seemed deeply shaken, though whether this was entirely due to the spilled wine was, Strike thought, debatable. As he returned to the sofa and set down the salt beside the coffee, music started up again, this time a Hungarian air that was no more restful than the symphony, but weirdly manic.

'Would you like more wine?' he asked her.

'I – yes, I think I would,' she said.

He poured her another and passed it directly into her hand. She drank a little, then said shakily:

'How could you know what you just told me, Mr Strike?'

'I'd rather not answer that, but I assure you it's true.'

Clutching her wine in both hands Della said:

'You *have* to find Aamir for me. If he thought *I* sanctioned Geraint telling him to go to Barrowclough-Burns for favours, it's no wonder he—'

Her self-control was visibly disintegrating. She tried to set the wine down on the arm of her chair and had to feel for it with the other hand before doing so successfully, all the while shaking her head in little jerks of disbelief.

'No wonder he what?' asked Strike quietly.

'Accused me of . . . of smothering . . . controlling . . . well, of course, this explains everything . . . we were so close – you wouldn't under-stand – it's hard to explain – but it was remarkable, how soon we became – well, like family. Sometimes, you know, there's an instant affinity – a connection that years couldn't forge, with other people—'

'But these past few weeks, it all changed – I could feel it – starting when Chiswell made that jibe in front of everyone – Aamir became distant. It was as though he no longer trusted me . . . I should have known . . . oh Lord, I should have known . . . you have to find him, you have to . . . '

Perhaps, Strike thought, the depth of her burning sense of need was sexual in origin, and perhaps on some subconscious level it had indeed been tinged with appreciation of Aamir's youthful mascu-linity. However, as Rhiannon Winn watched over them from her cheap gilt frame, wearing a smile that didn't reach her wide, anxious eyes, her teeth glinting with heavy braces, Strike thought it far more likely that Della was a woman possessed of that which Charlotte so conspicuously lacked: a burning, frustrated maternal drive tinged, in Della's case, with unassuageable regret.

'This as well,' she whispered. '*This as well*. What hasn't he ruined?'

'You're talking about—'

'My husband!' said Della numbly. 'Who else? My charity – our charity – but you know that, of course? It was you who told Chiswell about the missing twenty-five thousand, wasn't it? And the lies, the stupid lies, Geraint's been telling people? David Beckham, Mo Farah – all those impossible promises?'

'My partner found out.'

'Nobody will believe me,' said Della distractedly, 'but I didn't know, I had no idea. I've missed the last four board meetings – preparations for the Paralympics. Geraint only told me the truth after Chiswell threatened him with the press. Even then he claimed it was the accountant's fault, but he swore to me the other things weren't true. Swore it, on his mother's grave.'

She twisted the wedding ring on her finger, apparently distracted.

'I suppose your wretched partner tracked down Elspeth Lacey-Curtis, as well?'

'Afraid so,' lied Strike, judging that a gamble was indicated. 'Did Geraint deny that, too?'

'If he'd said anything to make the girls uncomfortable he felt awful, but he swore there was nothing else to it, no touching, just a couple of risqué jokes. But in this climate,' said Della furiously, 'a man ought to damned well think about what jokes he makes to a bunch of fifteen-year-old girls!'

Strike leaned forwards and grabbed Della's wine, which was in danger of being upended again.

'What are you doing?'

'Moving your glass onto the table,' said Strike.

'Oh,' said Della, 'thank you.' Making a noticeable effort to control herself, she continued, 'Geraint was representing *me* at that event, and it will go the way it always goes in the press when it all comes out: it will have been my fault, all of it! Because men's crimes are *always* ours in the final analysis, aren't they, Mr Strike? Ultimate responsibility *always* lies with the woman, who should have stopped it, who should have acted, who *must have known*. Your failings are really *our* failings, aren't they? Because the proper role of the woman is carer, and there's nothing lower in this whole world than a bad mother.'

Breathing hard, she pressed her trembling fingers to her temples. Beyond the net curtains night, deep blue, was inching like a veil over the glaring red of sunset and as the room grew darker, Rhiannon Winn's features faded gradually into the twilight. Soon all that would be visible was her smile, punctuated by the ugly braces.

'Give me back my wine, please.'

Strike did so. Della drank most of it down at once and continued to clasp the glass as she said bitterly:

'There are plenty of people ready to think all kinds of odd things about a blind woman. Of course, when I was younger, it was worse. There was often a prurient interest in one's private life. It was the first place some men's minds went. Perhaps you've experienced it, too, have you, with your one leg?'

Strike found that he didn't resent the blunt mention of his disability from Della.

'Yeah, I've had a bit of that,' he admitted. 'Bloke I was at school with. Hadn't seen him in years. It was my first time back in Cornwall since I got blown up. Five pints in, he asked me at what point I warned women my leg was going to come off with my trousers. He thought he was being funny.'

Della smiled thinly.

'Never occurs to some people that it is we who should be making the jokes, does it? But it will be different for you, as a man ... most people seem to think it in the natural order of things that the able-bodied woman should look after the disabled man. Geraint had to deal with that for years ... people assuming there was something peculiar about him, because he chose a disabled wife. I think I may have tried to compensate for that. I wanted him to have a role ... status ... but it would have been better for both of us, in retrospect, if he had done something unconnected to me.'

Strike thought she was a little drunk. Perhaps she hadn't eaten.

He felt an inappropriate desire to check her fridge. Sitting here with this impressive and vulnerable woman, it was easy to understand how Aamir had become so entangled with her both professionally and privately, without ever intending to become so.

'People assume I married Geraint because there was nobody else who wanted me, but they're quite wrong,' said Della, sitting up straighter in her chair. 'There was a boy I was at school with who was smitten with me, who proposed when I was nineteen. I had a choice and I chose Geraint. Not as a carer, or because, as journalists have sometimes implied, my limitless ambition made a husband necessary ... but because I loved him.'

Strike remembered the day he had followed Della's husband to the stairwell in King's Cross, and the tawdry things that Robin had told him about Geraint's behaviour at work, yet nothing that Della had just said struck him as incredible. Life had taught him that a great and powerful love could be felt for the most apparently unworthy people, a circumstance that ought, after all, to give everybody consolation.

'Are you married, Mr Strike?'

'No,' he said.

'I think marriage is nearly always an unfathomable entity, even to the people inside it. It took this ... all of this mess ... to make me realise I can't go on. I don't really know when I stopped loving him, but at some point after Rhiannon died, it slipped—'

Her voice broke.

'—slipped away from us.' She swallowed. 'Please will you pour me another glass of wine?'

He did so. The room was very dark now. The music had changed again, to a melancholy violin concerto which at last, in Strike's opinion, was appropriate to the conversation. Della had not wanted to talk to him, but now seemed reluctant to let the conversation end.

'Why did your husband hate Jasper Chiswell so much?' Strike asked quietly. 'Because of Chiswell's political clashes with you, or—?'

'No, no,' said Della Winn wearily. 'Because Geraint has to blame somebody other than himself for the misfortunes that befall him.'

Strike waited, but she merely drank more wine, and said nothing.

'What exactly—?'

'Never mind,' she said loudly. 'Never mind, it doesn't matter.'

But a moment later, after another large gulp of wine, she said:

'Rhiannon didn't really want to do fencing. Like most little girls, what she wanted was a pony, but we – Geraint and I – we didn't come from pony-owning backgrounds. We didn't have the first idea what one does with horses. As I think back, I suppose there were ways around that, but we were both terribly busy and felt it would be impractical, so she took up fencing instead, and very good she was at it, too . . .

'Have I answered enough of your questions, Mr Strike?' she asked a little thickly. 'Will you find Aamir?'

'I'll try,' Strike promised her. 'Could you give me his number? And yours, so I can keep you updated?'

She had both numbers off by heart, and he copied them down before closing his notebook and getting back to his feet.

'You've been very helpful, Mrs Winn. Thank you.'

'That sounds worrying,' she said, with a faint crease between the eyebrows. 'I'm not sure I meant to be.'

'Will you be—?'

'Perfectly,' said Della, enunciating over-clearly. 'You'll call me when you find Aamir, won't you?'

'If you don't hear from me before then, I'll update you in a week's time,' Strike promised. 'Er – is anyone coming in tonight, or—?'

'I see you aren't quite as hardened as your reputation would suggest,' said Della. 'Don't worry about me. My neighbour will be in to walk Gwynn for me shortly. She checks the gas dials and so forth.'

'In that case, don't get up. Good night.'

The near-white dog raised her head as he walked towards the door, sniffing the air. He left Della sitting in the darkness, a little drunk, with nothing else for company but the picture of the dead daughter she had never seen.

Closing the front door, Strike couldn't remember the last time he had felt such a strange mixture of admiration, sympathy and suspicion.

55

*... let us at least fight with honourable weapons, since it seems
we must fight.*

Henrik Ibsen, *Rosmersholm*

Matthew, who had supposedly been out just for the morning, still
hadn't come home. He had sent two texts since, one at three in the
afternoon:

**Tom got work troubles, wants to talk. Gone to pub with him (I'm
on Cokes.) Back as soon as I can.**

And then, at seven o'clock:

**Really sorry, he's pissed, I can't leave him. Going to find him a
taxi then come back. Hope you've eaten. Love you x**

Still with her caller ID switched off, Robin had again phoned
Tom's mobile. He had answered immediately. There was no background babble of a pub.

'Yes?' said Tom testily and apparently sober, 'who is this?'

Robin hung up.

Two bags were packed and waiting in the hall. She had already
phoned Vanessa and asked whether she could stay on her sofa for
a couple of nights, before she got a new place to live. She found it
strange that Vanessa didn't sound more surprised, but at the same
time, was glad not to have to fend off pity.

482

Waiting in the sitting room, watching night fall outside the window, Robin wondered whether she would even have been suspicious had she not found the earring. Lately she had become simply grateful for time without Matthew, when she could relax, not having to hide anything, whether the work she was doing on the Chiswell case or the panic attacks that must be conducted quietly, without fuss, on the bathroom floor.

Sitting in the stylish armchair belonging to their absent landlord, Robin felt as though she were inhabiting a memory. How often were you aware, while it happened, that you were living an hour that would change the course of your life for ever? She would remember this room for a long time, and she gazed around it now, with the aim of fixing it in her mind, thereby trying to ignore the sadness, the shame and the pain that burned and twisted inside her.

At just past nine o'clock, she heard, with a wave of nausea, Matthew's key in the lock and the sound of the door opening.

'Sorry,' he shouted, before he'd even closed the door, 'he's a silly sod, I had a job persuading the taxi driver to take—'

Robin heard his small exclamation of surprise as he spotted the suitcases. Safe, now, to dial, she pressed the number she had ready on her phone. He walked into the sitting room, puzzled, in time to hear her booking a minicab. She hung up. They looked at each other.

'What's with the cases?'

'I'm leaving.'

There was a long silence. Matthew seemed not to understand.

'What d'you mean?'

'I don't know how to say it any more clearly, Matt.'

'Leaving *me*?'

'That's right.'

'Why?'

'Because,' said Robin, 'you're sleeping with Sarah.'

She watched Matthew struggling to find words that might save him, but the seconds slid by, and it was too late for real incredulity, for astonished innocence, for genuine incomprehension.

'What?' he said at last, with a forced laugh.

'Please don't,' she said. 'There's no point. It's over.'

483

He continued to stand in the doorway of the sitting room and she thought he looked tired, even haggard.

'I was going to go and leave a note,' said Robin, 'but that felt too melodramatic. Anyway, there are practical things we need to talk about.'

She thought she could see him thinking, *How did I give it away? Who have you told?*

'Listen,' he said urgently, dropping his sports bag beside him (full, no doubt, of clean, pressed kit), 'I know things haven't been good between us, you and me, but it's you I want, Robin. Don't throw us away. Please.'

He walked forwards, dropped into a crouch beside her chair and tried to take her hand. She pulled it away, genuinely astonished.

'You're sleeping with Sarah,' she repeated.

He got up, crossed to the sofa and sat down, dropped his face into his hands and said weakly:

'I'm sorry. I'm sorry. It's been so shit between you and me—'

'—that you had to sleep with your friend's fiancée?'

He looked up at that, in sudden panic.

'Have you spoken to Tom? Does he know?'

Suddenly unable to bear his proximity, she walked away towards the window, full of a contempt she had never felt before.

'Even now, worried about your promotion prospects, Matt?'

'No – fuck – you don't understand,' he said. 'It's over between me and Sarah.'

'Oh, really?'

'Yes,' he said. 'Yes! Fuck – this is so fucking ironic – we talked all day. We agreed it couldn't go on, not after – you and Tom – we've just ended it. An hour ago.'

'Wow,' said Robin, with a little laugh, feeling disembodied, '*isn't* that ironic?'

Her mobile rang. Dreamlike, she answered it.

'Robin?' said Strike. 'Update. I've just seen Della Winn.'

'How did it go?' she asked, trying to sound steady and bright, determined not to cut the call short. Her working life was now her entire life and Matthew would no longer impinge upon it. Turning her back on her fuming husband, she looked out onto the dark cobbled street.

'Very interesting on two counts,' said Strike. 'Firstly, she slipped up. I don't think Geraint was with Aamir the morning Chiswell died.'

'That *is* interesting,' said Robin, forcing herself to concentrate, aware of Matthew watching her.

'I've got a number for him and I tried it, but he's not picking up. I thought I'd see if he's still at the B&B down the road as I'm in the vicinity, but the owner says he's moved on.'

'Shame. What was the other interesting thing?' asked Robin.

'Is that Strike?' asked Matthew loudly, from behind her. She ignored him.

'What was that?' asked Strike.

'Nothing,' said Robin. 'Go on.'

'Well, the second interesting thing is that Della met Kinvara last year, who was hysterical because she thought Chiswell—'

Robin's mobile was pulled roughly out of her hand. She wheeled around. Matthew ended the call with a stab of his finger.

'How *dare* you?' shouted Robin, holding out her hand. 'Give that back!'

'We're trying to save our fucking marriage and you're taking calls from him?'

'I'm not trying to save this marriage! *Give me back my phone!*'

He hesitated, then thrust it back at her, only to look outraged when she coolly phoned Strike back again.

'Sorry about that, Cormoran, we got cut off,' she said, with Matthew's wild eyes on her.

'Everything all right there, Robin?'

'It's fine. What were you saying about Chiswell?'

'That he was having an affair.'

'An affair!' said Robin, her eyes on Matthew's. 'Who with?'

'Christ knows. Have you had any luck getting hold of Raphael? We know he's not that bothered about protecting his father's memory. He might tell us.'

'I left a message for him, and for Tegan. Neither of them have called back.'

'OK, well, keep me posted. This all sheds an interesting light on the hammer round the head, though, doesn't it?'

'Certainly does,' said Robin.

'That's me at the Tube. Sure you're all right?'

'Yes, of course,' said Robin, with what she hoped sounded like workaday impatience. 'Speak soon.'

She hung up.

'"Speak soon",' Matthew imitated her, in the high-pitched, wispy voice he always used when impersonating women. '"Speak later, Cormoran. I'm running out on my marriage so I can be at your beck and call for ever, Cormoran. I don't mind working for minimum wage, Cormoran, not if I can be your skivvy".'

'Fuck off, Matt,' said Robin calmly. 'Fuck off back to Sarah. The earring she left in our bed is upstairs on my bedside table, by the way.'

'Robin,' he said, suddenly earnest, 'we can get through this. If we love each other, we can.'

'Well, the problem with that, Matt,' said Robin, 'is that I don't love you any more.'

She had always thought the idea of eyes darkening was literary licence, but she saw his light eyes turn black as his pupils dilated in shock.

'You bitch,' he said quietly.

She felt a cowardly impulse to lie, to back away from the absolute statement, to protect herself, but something stronger in her held on: the need to tell the unvarnished truth, when she had been lying to him and herself for so long.

'No,' she said. 'I don't. We should have split up on the honeymoon. I stayed because you were ill. I felt sorry for you. No,' she corrected herself, determined to do the thing properly, 'actually, we should never have gone on the honeymoon. I ought to have walked out of the wedding once I knew you'd deleted those calls from Strike.'

She wanted to check her watch to see when her cab would arrive, but she was scared to take her eyes off her husband. There was something in his expression that recalled a snake peering out from under a rock.

'How do you think your life looks to other people?' he asked quietly.

486

'What d'you mean?'

'You bailed out on uni. Now you're bailing out on us. You even bailed on your therapist. You're a fucking flake. The only thing you haven't run out on is this stupid job that's half-killed you, and you got sacked from *that*. He only took you back because he wants to get into your pants. And he probably can't get anyone else so cheap.'

She felt as though he had punched her. Winded, her voice sounded weak.

'Thanks, Matt,' she said, moving towards the door. 'Thanks for making this so easy.'

But he moved quickly to block her exit.

'It was a temping job. He paid you attention, so you kidded yourself that was the career for you, even though it's the last fucking thing you should've been doing, with *your* history—'

She was fighting tears now, but determined not to succumb.

'I wanted to do police work for years and years—'

'No, you fucking didn't!' jeered Matthew, 'when did you ever—?'

'I had a life before you!' Robin shouted. 'I had a home life where I said things you never heard! I never told you, Matthew, because I knew you'd laugh, like my dickhead brothers! I did psychology hoping it would take me to some kind of forensic—'

'You never said this, you're trying to justify—'

'I didn't tell you because I knew you'd sneer—'

'Bullshit—'

'It isn't bullshit!' she shouted. 'I'm telling you the truth, this is the whole truth, and you're proving my point, you don't believe me! You liked it when I dropped out of uni—'

'The hell d'you mean?'

'"There's no hurry to go back", "you don't *have* to have a degree . . . "'

'Oh, so now I'm being fucking blamed for being sensitive!'

'You liked it, you liked me being stuck at home, why can't you admit it? Sarah Shadlock at uni and me underachieving back in Masham – it made up for me getting better A-levels than you, getting into my first choice of—'

'Oh!' he laughed humourlessly, 'oh, you got better fucking *A-levels* than me? Yeah, that keeps me up at night—'

'If I hadn't been raped, we'd have split up years ago!'

'Is this what you learned in therapy? To tell lies about the past, to justify all your bullshit?'

'I learned to tell the truth!' shouted Robin, driven to the point of brutality. 'And here's some more: I was falling out of love with you before the rape! You weren't interested in anything I was doing – my course, my new friends. All you wanted to know was whether any other blokes were making moves on me. But afterwards, you were so sweet, so kind . . . you seemed like the safest man in the world, the only one I could trust. That's why I stayed. We wouldn't be here, now, but for that rape.'

They both heard the car pull up outside. Robin tried to slide past him into the hall, but he moved to block her again.

'No, you don't. You're not getting out of it that bloody easily. You stayed because I was *safe*? Fuck off. You loved me.'

'I thought I did,' said Robin, 'but not any more. Get out of the way. I'm leaving.'

She tried to sidestep him, but he moved to block her again.

'No,' he said again, and now he moved forwards, jostling her back into the sitting room. 'You're staying here. We're having this out.'

The minicab driver rang the doorbell.

'Coming!' Robin shouted, but Matthew snarled:

'You're not running away this time, you're going to stay and sort out your mess—'

'No!' shouted Robin, as though to a dog. She came to a halt, refusing to be backed further into the room, even though he was so close she could feel his breath on her face, and she was suddenly reminded of Geraint Winn, and was overwhelmed with revulsion. 'Get away from me. *Now*!'

And like a dog Matthew took a step backwards, responding not to the order, but to something in her voice. He was angry, but scared, too.

'Right,' said Robin. She knew she was on the edge of a panic attack, but she held on, and every second she did not dissolve was giving her strength, and she stood her ground. 'I'm leaving. You try and stop me, I'll retaliate. I've fought off far bigger, meaner men than you, Matthew. You haven't even got a bloody knife.'

She saw his eyes turn blacker than ever, and suddenly she remembered how her brother, Martin, had punched Matthew in the face, at the wedding. No matter what was coming, she vowed, in a kind of dark exhilaration, she'd do better than Martin. She'd break his damn nose if she had to.

'Please,' he said, his shoulders suddenly sagging, 'Robin—'

'You're going to have to hurt me if you want to stop me leaving, but I warn you, I'll prosecute you for assault if you do. *That* won't go down too well at the office, will it?'

She held his gaze for a few more seconds then walked back towards him, her fists already curling, waiting for him to block or grab her, but he moved aside.

'Robin,' he said hoarsely. 'Wait. Seriously, wait, you said there were things we had to discuss—'

'The lawyers can do it,' she said, reaching the front door and pulling it open.

The cool night air touched her like a blessing.

A stocky woman was sitting at the wheel of a Vauxhall Corsa. Seeing Robin's cases, she got out to help her hoist them into the boot. Matthew had followed and was now standing in the doorway. As Robin made to get into the car, he called to her and her tears began to fall at last, but without looking at him, she slammed the door.

'Please, let's go,' she said thickly, to the driver, as Matthew came down the steps and bent to speak to her through the glass.

'I still fucking love you!'

The car moved away over the cobbles of Albury Street, past the moulded frontages of the pretty sea merchants' houses where she had never felt she belonged. At the top of the street she knew that if she looked back, she would see Matthew standing watching the vanishing car. Her eyes met those of the driver in the rear-view mirror.

'Sorry,' said Robin nonsensically, and then, bewildered by her own apology, she said, 'I've – I've just left my husband.'

489

'Yeah?' said the driver, switching on her indicator. 'I've left two. It gets easier with practice.'

Robin tried to laugh, but the noise turned into a loud wet hiccough, and as the car approached the lonely stone swan high on the corner pub, she began to cry in earnest.

'Here,' said the driver gently, and she passed back a plastic-wrapped pack of tissues.

'Thanks,' sobbed Robin, extracting one and pressing it to her tired, stinging eyes until the white tissue was sodden and streaked with the last traces of thick black eye make-up that she had worn to impersonate Bobbi Cunliffe. Avoiding the sympathetic gaze of the driver in the rear-view mirror, she looked down into her lap. The wrapper on the tissues was that of an unfamiliar American brand: 'Dr Blanc'.

At once, Robin's elusive memory dropped into view, as though it had been waiting for this tiny prod. Now she remembered exactly where she had seen the phrase 'Blanc de Blanc', but it had nothing to do with the case, and everything to do with her imploding marriage, with a lavender walk and a Japanese water garden, and the last time she had ever said 'I love you', and the first time she'd known she didn't mean it.

56

I cannot – I will not – go through life with a dead body on my back.

Henrik Ibsen, *Rosmersholm*

As Strike approached Henlys Corner on the North Circular Road the following afternoon, he saw, with a muttered oath, that traffic ahead had come to a halt. The junction, which was a notorious hotspot for congestion, had supposedly been improved earlier that year. As he joined the stationary queue, Strike wound down his window, lit a cig-arette and glanced at his dashboard clock, with the familiar sensation of angry impotence that driving in London so often engendered. He had wondered whether it might be wiser to take the Tube north, but the psychiatric hospital lay a good mile from the nearest station, and the BMW was marginally easier on his still sore leg. Now he feared that he was going to be late for an interview that he was determined not to miss, firstly because he had no wish to disoblige the psychiatric team who were letting him see Billy Knight, and secondly because Strike didn't know when there would next be an opportunity to speak to the younger brother without fear of running into the older. Barclay had assured him that morning that Jimmy's plans for the day comprised writing a polemic on Rothschild's global influence for the Real Socialist website and sampling some of Barclay's new stash.

Scowling and tapping his fingers on the steering wheel, Strike fell back to ruminating on a question that had been nagging at him since the previous evening: whether or not the cut connection halfway through his call to Robin had really been due to Matthew snatching

491

the phone out of her hand. He had not found Robin's subsequent assurances that all was well particularly convincing.

While heating himself baked beans on his one-ringed hob, because he was still attempting to lose weight, Strike had debated calling Robin back. Eating his meatless dinner unenthusiastically in front of the television, supposedly watching highlights of the Olympics closing ceremony, his attention was barely held by the sight of the Spice Girls zooming around on top of London cabs. *I think marriage is nearly always an unfathomable entity, even to the people inside it*, Della Winn had said. Perhaps Robin and Matthew were even now in bed together. Was pulling a phone out of her hand any worse than deleting her call history? She had stayed with Matthew after that. Where was her red line?

And Matthew was surely too careful of his own reputation and prospects to abandon all civilised norms. One of Strike's last thoughts before falling asleep the night before had been that Robin had successfully fought off the Shacklewell Ripper, a grisly reflection, perhaps, but one that brought a certain reassurance.

The detective was perfectly aware that the state of his junior partner's marriage ought to be the least of his worries, given that he so far had no concrete information for the client who was currently paying three full-time investigators to find out the facts about her father's death. Nevertheless, as the traffic finally moved on, Strike's thoughts continued to eddy around Robin and Matthew until at last he saw a signpost to the psychiatric clinic and, with an effort, focused his mind on the forthcoming interview.

Unlike the gigantic rectangular prism of concrete and black glass where Jack had been admitted a few weeks earlier, the hospital outside which Strike parked twenty minutes later boasted crocketed spires and byzantine windows covered with iron bars. In Strike's opinion it looked like the bastard offspring of a gingerbread palace and a gothic prison. A Victorian stonemason had carved the word 'Sanatorium' into the dirty redbrick arch over the double doorway.

Already five minutes late, Strike flung open the driver's door and, not bothering to change his trainers for smarter footwear, locked the BMW and hurried, limping, up the grubby front steps.

Inside he found a chilly hallway with high, off-white ceilings, churchlike windows and a general suspicion of decay barely kept at bay by the fug of disinfectant. Spotting the ward number he had been given by phone, he set off along a corridor to the left.

Sunlight falling through the barred windows cast striped patches onto the off-white walls, which were hung crookedly with art, some of which had been done by former patients. As Strike passed a series of collages depicting detailed farmyard scenes in felt, tinsel and yarn, a skeletal teenage girl emerged from a bathroom alongside a nurse. Neither of them seemed to notice Strike. Indeed, the girl's dull eyes were focused, it seemed to him, inward upon a battle she was waging far from the real world.

Strike was faintly surprised to discover the double doors to the locked ward at the end of the ground floor corridor. Some vague association with belfries and Rochester's first wife had led him to picture it on an upper floor, hidden perhaps in one of those pointed spires. The reality was entirely prosaic: a large green buzzer on the wall, which Strike pressed, and a male nurse with bright red hair peering through a small glass window, who turned to speak to somebody behind him. The door opened and Strike was admitted.

The ward had four beds and a seating area, where two patients in day clothes were sitting, playing draughts: an older, apparently toothless man and a pale youth with a thickly bandaged neck. A cluster of people were standing around a workstation just inside the door: an orderly, two more nurses, and what Strike assumed to be two doctors, one male, one female. All turned to stare at him as he entered. One of the nurses nudged the other.

'Mr Strike,' said the male doctor, who was short, rather foxy in appearance and had a strong Mancunian accent. 'How do you do? Colin Hepworth, we spoke on the phone. This is my colleague, Kamila Muhammad.'

Strike shook hands with the woman, whose navy trouser suit reminded him of a policewoman's.

'We're both going to be sitting in on your interview with Billy,' she said. 'He's just gone to the bathroom. He's quite excited about seeing you again. We thought we'd use one of our interview rooms. It's right here.'

She led him around the workstation, the nurses still watching avidly, into a small room containing four chairs and a desk that had been bolted to the floor. The walls were pale pink but otherwise bare.

'Ideal,' said Strike. It was like a hundred interview rooms he had used in the military police. There, too, third parties had often been present, usually lawyers.

'A quick word before we start,' said Kamila Muhammad, pulling the door to on Strike and her colleague, so that the nurses couldn't hear their conversation. 'I don't know how much you know about Billy's condition?'

'His brother told me it's schizoid affective disorder.'

'That's right,' she said. 'He went off his medication and ended up in a full-blown psychotic episode, which by the sounds of it is when he came to see you.'

'Yeah, he seemed pretty disturbed at the time. He looked as though he'd been sleeping rough, as well.'

'He probably had been. His brother told us he'd been missing around a week at that point. We don't believe Billy's psychotic any more,' she said, 'but he's still quite closed down, so it's hard to gauge to what degree he's engaged with reality. It can be difficult to get an accurate picture of someone's mental state where there are paranoid and delusional symptoms.'

'We're hoping that you can help us disentangle some of the facts from the fiction,' said the Mancunian. 'You've been a recurring motif in his conversation ever since he was sectioned. He's been very keen to talk to you, but not so much to any of us. He's also expressed fear of – of repercussions if he confides in anyone and, again, it's difficult to know whether that fear is part of his illness or, ah, whether there's someone who he genuinely has reason to fear. Because, ah—'

He hesitated, as though trying to choose his words carefully. Strike said:

'I'd imagine his brother could be scary if he chose to be,' and the psychiatrist seemed relieved to have been understood without breaking confidentiality.

'You know his brother, do you?'

'I've met him. Does he visit often?'

'He's been in a couple of times, but Billy's often been more distressed and agitated after seeing him. If he seems to be similarly affected during your interview—' said the Mancunian.

'Understood,' said Strike.

'Funny, really, seeing you here,' said Colin, with a faint grin. 'We assumed that his fixation with you was all part of his psychosis. An obsession with a celebrity is quite common with these kinds of disorders ... As a matter of fact,' he said candidly, 'just a couple of days ago, Kamila and I were agreeing that his fixation with you would preclude an early discharge. Lucky you called, really.'

'Yeah,' said Strike drily, 'that is lucky.'

The redheaded male nurse knocked on the door and put his head in.

'That's Billy ready to talk to Mr Strike.'

'Great,' said the female psychiatrist. 'Eddie, could we get some tea in here? Tea?' she asked Strike over her shoulder. He nodded. She opened the door. 'Come in, Billy.'

And there he was: Billy Knight, wearing a grey sweatshirt and jogging pants, his feet in hospital slippers. The sunken eyes were still deeply shadowed, and at some point since he and Strike had last seen each other, he had shaven his head. The finger and thumb of his left hand were bandaged. Even through the tracksuit that somebody, presumably Jimmy, had brought him to wear, Strike could tell that he was underweight, but while his fingernails were bitten to bloody stubs and there was an angry sore at the corner of his mouth, there was no longer an animal stench about him. He shuffled inside the interview room, staring at Strike, then held out a bony hand, which Strike shook. Billy addressed the doctors.

'Are you two going to stay?'

'Yes,' said Colin, 'but don't worry. We're going to keep quiet. You can say whatever you like to Mr Strike.'

Kamila positioned two chairs against the wall and Strike and Billy sat down opposite each other, the desk between them. Strike could have wished for a less formal configuration of furniture, but his experience in Special Investigation Branch had taught him that a solid barrier between questioner and interviewee was often useful, and doubtless this was just as true on a locked psychiatric ward.

'I've been trying to find you, since you first came to see me,' Strike said. 'I've been quite worried about you.'

'Yeah,' said Billy. 'Sorry.'

'Can you remember what you said to me at the office?'

Absently, it seemed, Billy touched his nose and his sternum, but it was a ghost of the tic he had exhibited in Denmark Street, and almost as though he sought to remind himself how he had felt then.

'Yeah,' he said, with a small, humourless smile. 'I told you about the kid, up by the horse. The one I saw strangled.'

'D'you still think you witnessed a child being strangled?' asked Strike.

Billy raised a forefinger to his mouth, gnawed at the nail and nodded.

'Yeah,' he said, removing the finger. 'I saw it. Jimmy says I imagined it because I'm – you know. Ill. You know Jimmy, don't you? Went to the White Horse after him, didn't you?' Strike nodded. 'He was fucking livid. White Horse,' said Billy, with a sudden laugh. 'That's funny. Shit, that's funny. I never even thought of that before.'

'You told me you saw a child killed "up by the horse". Which horse did you mean?'

'White Horse of Uffington,' said Billy. 'Big chalk figure, up on the hill, near where I grew up. Doesn't look like a horse. More like a dragon and it's on Dragon Hill, as well. I've never understood why they all say it's a horse.'

'Can you tell me exactly what you saw up there?'

Like the skeletal girl Strike had just passed, he had the impression that Billy was staring inside himself, and that outer reality had temporarily ceased to exist for him. Finally, he said quietly:

'I was a little kid, proper little. I think they'd given me something. I felt sick and ill, like I was dreaming, slow and groggy, and they kept trying to make me repeat words and stuff and I couldn't speak properly and they all thought it was funny. I fell over in the grass on the way up. One of them carried me for a bit. I wanted to sleep.'

'You think you'd been given drugs?'

'Yeah,' said Billy dully. 'Hash, probably, Jimmy usually had some. I think Jimmy took me up the hill with them to keep my father from knowing what they'd done.'

'Who do you mean by "they"?'

'I don't know,' said Billy simply. 'Grown-ups. Jimmy's ten years older'n me. Dad used to make him look after me all the time, if he was out with his drinking mates. This lot came to the house in the night and I woke up. One of them gave me a yoghurt to eat. There was another little kid there. A girl. And then we all went out in a car ... I didn't want to go. I felt sick. I was crying but Jimmy belted me.

'And we went to the horse in the dark. Me and the little girl were the only kids. She was howling,' said Jimmy and the skin of his gaunt face seemed to shrink more tightly to his bones as he said it. 'Screaming for her mum and *he* said, "Your mum can't hear you now, she's gone."'

'Who said that?' asked Strike.

'Him,' whispered Billy. 'The one that strangled her.'

The door opened and a new nurse brought in tea.

'Here we go,' she said brightly, her eager eyes on Strike. The male psychiatrist frowned at her slightly and she withdrew, closing the door again.

'Nobody's ever believed me,' said Billy, and Strike heard the underlying plea. 'I've tried to remember more, I wish I could, if I've got to think about it all the time I wish I could remember more of it.

'He strangled her to stop her making a noise. I don't think he meant it to go that far. They all panicked. I can remember someone shouting "You've killed her!" ... or him,' Billy said quietly. 'Jimmy said afterwards it was a boy, but he won't admit that now. Says I'm making it all up. "Why would I say it was a boy when none of it ever fucking happened, you're mental." It was a girl,' said Billy stubbornly. 'I don't know why he tried to say it wasn't. They called her a girl's name. I can't remember what it was, but it was a girl.

'I saw her fall. Dead. Limp on the ground. It was dark. And then they panicked.

'I can't remember anything about going back down the hill, can't remember anything after that except the burial, down in the dell by my dad's place.'

'The same night?' asked Strike.

'I think so, I think it was,' said Billy nervously. 'Because I remember looking out of my bedroom window and it was still dark and they were carrying it to the dell, my dad and *him*.'

'Who's "him"?'

'The one who killed her. I think it was him. Big guy. White hair. And they put a bundle in the ground, all wrapped up in a pink blanket, and they closed it in.'

'Did you ask your father about what you'd seen?'

'No,' said Billy. 'You didn't ask my dad questions about what he did for the family.'

'For which family?'

Billy frowned in what seemed to be genuine puzzlement.

'You mean, for your family?'

'No. The family he worked for. The Chiswells.'

Strike had the impression that this was the first time the dead minister's family name had been mentioned in front of the two psychiatrists. He saw two pens falter.

'How was the burial connected with them?'

Billy seemed confused. He opened his mouth to say something, appeared to change his mind, frowned around the pale pink walls and fell to gnawing his forefinger again. Finally, he said:

'I don't know why I said that.'

It didn't feel like a lie or a denial. Billy seemed genuinely surprised by the words that had fallen out of his mouth.

'You can't remember hearing anything, or seeing anything, that would make you think he was burying the child for the Chiswells?'

'No,' said Billy slowly, brow furrowed. 'I just ... I thought then, when I said it ... he was doing a favour for ... like I heard something, after ... '

He shook his head.

'Ignore that, I don't know why I said it.'

People, places and things, thought Strike, taking out his notebook and opening it.

'Other than Jimmy and the little girl who died,' said Strike, 'what can you remember about the group of people who went to the horse that night? How many of them would you say were there?'

Billy thought hard.

'I don't know. Maybe ... maybe eight, ten people?'

'All men?'

'No. There were women, too.'

Over Billy's shoulder, Strike saw the female psychiatrist raise her eyebrows.

'Can you remember anything else about the group? I know you were young,' Strike said, anticipating Billy's objection, 'and I know you might have been given something that disorientated you, but can you remember anything you haven't told me? Anything they did? Anything they were wearing? Can you remember anyone's hair or skin colour? Anything at all?'

There was a long pause, then Billy closed his eyes briefly and shook his head once, as though disagreeing firmly with a suggestion only he could hear.

'She was dark. The little girl. Like ...'

By a tiny turn of his head, he indicated the female doctor behind him.

'Asian?' said Strike.

'Maybe,' said Billy, 'yeah. Black hair.'

'Who carried you up the hill?'

'Jimmy and one of the other men took turns.'

'Nobody talked about why they were going up there in the dark?'

'I think they wanted to get to the eye,' said Billy.

'The eye of the horse?'

'Yeah.'

'Why?'

'I don't know,' said Billy, and he ran his hands nervously over his shaven head. 'There are stories about the eye, you know. He strangled her in the eye, I know that. I can remember that, all right. She pissed herself as she died. I saw it spattering on the white.'

'And you can't remember anything about the man who did it?'

But Billy's face had crumpled. Hunched over, he heaved with dry sobs, shaking his head. The male doctor half rose from his seat. Billy seemed to sense the movement, because he steadied himself and shook his head.

'I'm all right,' he said, 'I want to tell him. I've got to know if it's real. All my life, I can't stand it any more, I've got to know. Let him ask me, I know he's got to. Let him ask me,' said Billy, 'I can take it.'

The psychiatrist sat slowly back down.

'Don't forget your tea, Billy.'

'Yeah,' said Billy, blinking away the tears in his eyes and wiping his nose on the back of his sleeve. 'All right.'

He took the mug between his bandaged hand and his good one, and took a sip.

'OK to continue?' Strike asked him.

'Yeah,' said Billy quietly. 'Go on.'

'Can you remember anyone ever mentioning a girl called Suki Lewis, Billy?'

Strike had expected a 'no'. He had already turned the page to the list of questions written under the heading 'Places' when Billy said:

'Yeah.'

'What?' said Strike.

'The Butcher brothers knew her,' said Billy. 'Mates of Jimmy's from home. They did a bit of work round the Chiswells' place sometimes, with Dad. Bit of gardening and help with the horses.'

'They knew Suki Lewis?'

'Yeah. She ran away, didn't she?' said Billy. 'She was on the local news. The Butchers were excited because they seen her picture on the telly and they knew her family. Her mum was a headcase. Yeah, she was in care and she ran away to Aberdeen.'

'Aberdeen?'

'Yeah. That's what the Butchers said.'

'She was twelve.'

'She had family up there. They let her stay.'

'Is that right?' said Strike.

He wondered whether Aberdeen had seemed unfathomably

remote to the teenage Butchers of Oxfordshire, and whether they had been more inclined to believe this story because it was, to them, uncheckable and so, strangely, more believable.

'We're talking about Tegan's brothers, right?' asked Strike.

'You can see he's good,' Billy said naively over his shoulder, to the male psychiatrist, 'can't you? See how much he knows? Yeah,' he said, turning back to Strike. 'She's their little sister. They were like us, working for the Chiswells. There used to be a lot to do in the old days, but they sold off a lot of the land. They don't need so many people any more.'

He drank some more tea, the mug in both hands.

'Billy,' said Strike, 'd'you know where you've been since you came to my office?'

At once, the tic reappeared. Billy's right hand released the warm mug and touched his nose and chest in quick, nervous succession.

'I was ... Jimmy doesn't want me to talk about that,' he said, setting the mug clumsily back on the desk. 'He told me not to.'

'I think it's more important you answer Mr Strike's questions than worry about what your brother thinks,' said the male doctor, from behind Strike. 'You know, you don't have to see Jimmy if you don't want to, Billy. We can ask him to give you some time here, to get better in peace.'

'Did Jimmy visit you where you've been staying?' Strike asked.

Billy chewed his lip.

'Yeah,' he said at last, 'and he said I had to stay there or I'd cock everything up for him again. I thought the door had explosives round it,' he said, with a nervy laugh. 'Thought if I tried to go out the door I'd explode. Probably not right, is it?' he said, appearing to search Strike's expression for a clue. 'I get ideas about stuff sometimes, when I'm bad.'

'Can you remember how you got away from the place you were being kept?'

'I thought they switched off the explosives,' said Billy. 'The guy told me to run for it and I did.'

'What guy was this?'

'The one who was in charge of keeping me there.'

501

'Can you remember anything you did while you were being kept captive?' Strike asked. 'How you spent your time?'

The other shook his head.

'Can you remember,' said Strike, 'carving anything, into wood?'

Billy's gaze was full of fear and wonder. Then he laughed.

'You know it all,' he said, and held up his bandaged left hand. 'Knife slipped. Went right in me.'

The male psychiatrist added helpfully:

'Billy had tetanus when he came in. There was a very nasty infected gash on that hand.'

'What did you carve into the door, Billy?'

'I really did that, then, did I? Carved the white horse on the door? Because afterwards I didn't know if I really did that or not.'

'Yeah, you did it,' said Strike. 'I've seen the door. It was a good carving.'

'Yeah,' said Billy, 'well, I used to – do some of that. Carving. For my dad.'

'What did you carve the horse onto?'

'Pendants,' said Billy, surprisingly. 'On little circles of wood with leather through 'em. For tourists. Sold them in a shop over in Wantage.'

'Billy,' said Strike, 'can you remember how you ended up in that bathroom? Did you go there to see someone, or did somebody take you there?'

Billy's eyes roamed around the pink walls again, a deep furrow between his eyes as he thought.

'I was looking for a man called Winner . . . no . . . '

'Winn? Geraint Winn?'

'Yeah,' said Billy, again surveying Strike with astonishment. 'You know *everything*. How do you know all this?'

'I've been looking for you,' said Strike. 'What made you want to find Winn?'

'Heard Jimmy talking about him,' said Billy, gnawing at his nail again. 'Jimmy said Winn was going to help find out all about the kid who was killed.'

'Winn was going to help find out about the child who was strangled?'

'Yeah,' said Billy, nervously. 'See, I thought you were one of the people trying to catch me and lock me up, after I saw you. Thought you were trying to trap me and – I get like that, when I'm bad,' he said hopelessly. 'So I went to Winner – Winn – instead. Jimmy had a phone number and address for him written down, so I went to find Winn and then I got caught.'

'Caught?'

'By the – brown-skinned bloke,' mumbled Billy, with a half-glance back at the female psychiatrist. 'I was scared of him, I thought he was a terrorist and he was going to kill me, but then he told me he was working for the government, so I thought the government wanted me kept there in his house and the doors and windows were wired with explosives ... but I don't think they were, really. That was just me. He probably didn't want me in his bathroom. Probably wanted to get rid of me all along,' said Billy, with a sad smile. 'And I wouldn't go, because I thought I'd get blown up.'

His right hand crept absently back to his nose and chest.

'I think I tried to call you again, but you didn't answer.'

'You did call. You left a message on my answering machine.'

'Did I? Yeah ... I thought you'd help me get out of there ... sorry,' said Billy, rubbing his eyes. 'When I'm like that, I don't know what I'm doing.'

'But you're sure you saw a child strangled, Billy?' asked Strike quietly.

'Oh yeah,' said Billy bleakly, raising his face. 'Yeah, that never goes away. I know I saw it.'

'Did you ever try and dig where you thought—?'

'Christ, no,' said Billy. 'Go digging right by my dad's house? No. I was scared,' he said weakly. 'I didn't want to see it again. After they buried her, they let it grow over, nettles and weeds. I used to have dreams like you wouldn't believe. That she climbed up out of the dell in the dark, all rotting, and tried to climb in my bedroom window.'

The psychiatrists' pens moved scratchily across their papers.

Strike moved down to the category of 'Things' that he had written on his notebook. There were only two questions left.

503

'Did you ever put a cross in the ground where you saw the body buried, Billy?'

'No,' said Billy, scared at the very idea. 'I never went near the dell if I could avoid it, I never wanted to.'

'Last question,' Strike said. 'Billy, did your father do anything unusual for the Chiswells? I know he was a handyman, but can you think of anything else he——?'

'What d'you mean?' said Billy.

He seemed suddenly more frightened than he had seemed all interview.

'I don't know,' said Strike carefully, watching his reaction. 'I just wondered——'

'Jimmy warned me about this! He told me you were snooping around Dad. You can't blame us for that, we had nothing to do with it, we were kids!'

'I'm not blaming you for anything,' said Strike, but there was a clatter of chairs: Billy and the two psychiatrists had got to their feet, the female's hand hovering over a discreet button beside the door that Strike knew must be an alarm.

'Has this all been to get me to talk? You trying to get me and Jimmy in trouble?'

'No,' said Strike, hoisting himself to his feet, too. 'I'm here because I believe you saw a child strangled, Billy.'

Agitated, mistrustful, Billy's unbandaged hand touched his nose and chest twice in quick succession.

'So why're you asking what Dad did?' he whispered. 'That's not how she died, it was nothing to do with that! Jimmy'll fucking tan me,' he said in a broken voice. 'He told me you were after him for what Dad did.'

'Nobody's going to tan anyone,' said the male psychiatrist firmly. 'Time's up, I think,' he said briskly to Strike, pushing open the door. 'Go on, Billy, out you go.'

But Billy didn't move. The skin and bone might have aged, but his face betrayed the fear and hopelessness of a small, motherless child whose sanity had been broken by the men who were supposed to protect him. Strike, who had met countless rootless and neglected children during his rackety, unstable childhood, recognised in Billy's imploring expression a last plea to the adult world, to do what grown-ups were meant to do, and impose order on chaos, substitute sanity for brutality. Face to face, he felt a strange kinship with the emaciated, shaven-headed psychiatric patient, because he recognised the same craving for order in himself. In his case, it had led him to the official side of the desk, but perhaps the only difference between the two of them was that Strike's mother had lived long enough, and loved him well enough, to stop him breaking when life threw terrible things at him.

'I'm going to find out what happened to the kid you saw strangled, Billy. That's a promise.'

The psychiatrists looked surprised, even disapproving. It was not part of their profession, Strike knew, to make definitive statements or guarantee resolutions. He put his notebook back into his pocket, moved from behind the desk and held out his hand. After a few long moments' consideration, the animosity seemed to seep out of Billy. He shuffled back to Strike, took his proffered hand and held it over-long, his eyes filling with tears.

In a whisper, so that neither of the doctors could hear, he said:

'I hated putting the horse on them, Mr Strike. I hated it.'

57

Vanessa's one-bedroomed flat occupied the ground floor of a detached house a short distance from Wembley Stadium. Before leaving for work that morning, she had given Robin a spare key to her flat, along with a kindly assurance that she knew that it would take Robin longer than a couple of days to find a new place to live, and that she didn't mind her staying until she managed to do so.

They had sat up late drinking the night before. Vanessa had told Robin the full story of finding out that her ex-fiancé had cheated on her, a story full of twists and counter-twists that Vanessa had never told before, which included the setting up of two fake Facebook pages as bait for both her ex and his lover, which had resulted, after three months of patient coaxing, in Vanessa receiving nude pictures from both of them. As impressed as she was shocked, Robin had laughed as Vanessa re-enacted the scene in which she passed her ex the pictures, hidden inside the Valentine card she had handed across a table for two in their favourite restaurant.

'You're too nice, girl,' said Vanessa, steely-eyed over her Pinot Grigio. 'At a bare minimum I'd have kept her bleeding earring and turned it into a pendant.'

Vanessa was now at work. A spare duvet sat neatly folded at the end of the sofa on which Robin was sitting, with her laptop open in front of her. She had spent the entire afternoon scanning available rooms in shared properties, which were all she could possibly afford on the salary that Strike was paying her. The memory of the bunk bed in Flick's flat kept recurring as she scanned the adverts in her price range, some of which featured stark, barrack-like rooms with multiple beds inside them, others with photographs that looked as though they ought to feature attached to news stories about reclusive hoarders discovered dead by neighbours. Last night's laughter seemed remote now. Robin was ignoring the painful, hard lump in her throat that refused to dissolve, no matter how many cups of tea she consumed.

Matthew had tried to contact her twice that day. Neither time had she picked up and he hadn't left a message. She would need to contact a lawyer about divorce soon, and that would cost money she didn't have, but her first priority had to be finding herself a place to live and continuing to put in the usual number of hours on the Chiswell case, because if Strike had cause to feel she wasn't pulling her weight she would be endangering the only part of her life that currently had worth.

You bailed out on uni. Now you're bailing out on us. You even bailed on your therapist. You're a fucking flake.

The photographs of grim rooms in unknown flats kept dissolving before her eyes as she pictured Matthew and Sarah in the heavy mahogany bed that her father-in-law had bought, and when this happened Robin's insides seemed to turn to liquid lead and her self-control threatened to melt away and she wanted to phone Matthew back and scream at him, but she didn't, because she refused to be what he wanted to make her, the irrational, incontinent, uncontrolled woman, the *fucking flake*.

And anyway, she had news for Strike, news she was keen to impart once he had finished his interview with Billy. Raphael Chiswell had answered his mobile at eleven o'clock that morning and, after some initial coldness, had agreed to talk to her, but only at a place of his choosing. An hour later, she had received a call from Tegan Butcher, who had not required much persuasion to agree to an interview. Indeed, she seemed disappointed to be talking to the famous Strike's partner rather than the man himself.

Robin copied down the details of a room in Putney (*live-in land-lady, vegetarian household, must like cats*), checked the time and decided to change into the only dress she had brought with her from Albury Street, which was hanging, ironed and ready, from the top of Vanessa's kitchen door. It would take her over an hour to get from Wembley to the restaurant in Old Brompton Road, where she and Raphael had agreed to meet, and she feared that she needed more time than usual to make herself presentable.

The face staring out of Vanessa's bathroom mirror was white, with eyes still puffy with lack of sleep. Robin was still trying to paint out the shadows with concealer when her mobile rang.

'Cormoran, hi,' said Robin, switching to speakerphone. 'Did you see Billy?'

His account of the interview with Billy took ten minutes, during which time Robin finished her make-up, brushed her hair and pulled on the dress.

'You know,' Strike finished, 'I'm starting to wonder whether we shouldn't do what Billy wanted us to do in the first place: dig.'

'Mm,' said Robin, and then, 'Wait – what? You mean . . . literally?'

'It might come to that,' said Strike.

For the first time all day, Robin's own troubles were entirely eclipsed by something else, something monstrous. Jasper Chiswell's had been the first body she had seen outside the comforting, sanitised context of the hospital and the funeral parlour. Even the memory of the shrink-wrapped turnip head with its dark, gasping cavity for a mouth paled beside the prospect of earth and worms, a decaying blanket and a child's rotting bones.

'Cormoran, if you think there's genuinely a child buried in the dell, we should be telling the police.'

'I might, if I thought Billy's psychiatrists would vouch for him, but they won't. I had a long talk with them after the interview. They can't say one hundred per cent that the child strangling *didn't* happen – the old impossible-to-prove-a-negative problem – but they don't believe it.'

'They think he's making it up?'

'Not in the normal sense. They think it's a delusion or, at best, that he misinterpreted something he saw when he was very young. Maybe even something on TV. It would be consistent with his overall symptoms. I think myself there's unlikely to be anything down there, but it would be good to know for sure.

'Anyway, how's your day been? Any news?'

'What?' Robin repeated numbly. 'Oh – yes. I'm meeting Raphael for a drink at seven o'clock.'

'Excellent work,' said Strike. 'Where?'

'Place called Nam something . . . Nam Long Le Shaker?'

'The place in Chelsea?' said Strike. 'I was there, a long time ago. Not the best evening I've ever had.'

'And Tegan Butcher rang back. She's a bit of a fan of yours, by the sound of it.'

'Just what this case needs, another mentally disturbed witness.'

'Tasteless,' said Robin, trying to sound amused. 'Anyway, she's living with her mum in Woolstone and working at a bar at Newbury Racecourse. She says she doesn't want to meet us in the village because her mum won't like her getting mixed up with us, so she wonders whether we could come and see her at Newbury.'

'How far's that from Woolstone?'

'Twenty miles or so?'

'All right,' said Strike, 'how about we take the Land Rover out to Newbury to interview Tegan and then maybe swing by the dell, just for another look?'

'Um . . . yes, OK,' said Robin, her mind racing over the logistics of having to return to Albury Street for the Land Rover. She had left it behind because parking places required a permit on Vanessa's street. 'When?'

'Whenever Tegan can see us, but ideally this week. Sooner the better.'

'OK,' said Robin, thinking of the tentative plans she had made to view rooms over the next couple of days.

'Everything all right, Robin?'

'Yes, of course.'

'Ring me when you've spoken to Raphael then, OK?'

'Will do,' said Robin, glad to end the call. 'Speak later.'

58

*... I believe two different kinds of will can exist at the same time
in one person.*

Henrik Ibsen, *Rosmersholm*

Nam Long Le Shaker had the feeling of a decadent, colonial-era
bar. Dimly lit, with leafy plants and assorted paintings and prints of
beautiful women, the décor mixed Vietnamese and European styles.
When Robin entered the restaurant at five past seven, she found
Raphael leaning up against the bar, wearing a dark suit and tieless
white shirt, already halfway down a drink and talking to the long-
haired beauty who stood in front of a glittering wall of bottles.

'Hi,' said Robin.

'Hello,' he responded with a trace of coolness, and then, 'Your eyes
are different. Were they that colour at Chiswell House?'

'Blue?' asked Robin, shrugging off the coat she had worn because
she felt shivery, even though the evening was warm. 'Yes.'

'S'pose I didn't notice because half the bloody light bulbs are missing. What are you drinking?'

Robin hesitated. She ought not to drink while conducting an
interview, but at the same time, she suddenly craved alcohol. Before
she could decide, Raphael said with a slight edge in his voice:

'Been undercover again today, have we?'

'Why d'you ask?'

'Your wedding ring's gone again.'

'Were your eyes this sharp in the office?' asked Robin, and he
grinned, reminding her why she had liked him, even against her will.

'I noticed your glasses were fake, remember?' he said. 'I thought at the time you were trying to be taken seriously, because you were too pretty for politics. So these,' he indicated his deep brown eyes, 'may be sharp, but this,' he tapped his head, 'not so much.'

'I'll have a glass of red,' said Robin, smiling, 'and I'll pay, obviously.'

'If this is all on Mr Strike, let's have dinner,' said Raphael at once. 'I'm starving and skint.'

'Really?'

After a day of trawling through the available rooms for rent on her agency salary, she was not in the mood to hear the Chiswell definition of poverty again.

'Yeah, really, little though you might believe it,' said Raphael, with a slightly acid smile, and Robin suspected he knew what she had been thinking. 'Seriously, are we eating, or what?'

'Fine,' said Robin, who had barely touched food all day, 'let's eat.'

Raphael took his bottle of beer off the bar and led her through to the restaurant where they took a table for two beside the wall. It was so early that they were the only diners.

'My mother used to come here in the eighties,' said Raphael. 'It was well known because the owner liked telling the rich and famous to sod off if they weren't dressed properly to come in, and they all loved it.'

'Really?' said Robin, her thoughts miles away. It had just struck her that she would never again have dinner with Matthew like this, just the two of them. She remembered the very last time, at Le Manoir aux Quat'Saisons. What had he been thinking while he ate in silence? Certainly he had been furious at her for continuing to work with Strike, but perhaps he had also been weighing in his mind the competing attractions of Sarah, with her well-paid job at Christie's, her endless fund of stories about other people's wealth, and her no doubt self-confident performance in bed, where the diamond earrings her fiancé had bought her snagged on Robin's pillow.

'Listen, if eating with me's going to make you look like that, I'm fine with going back to the bar,' said Raphael.

'What?' said Robin, surprised out of her thoughts. 'Oh – no, it isn't you.'

A waiter brought over Robin's wine. She took a large slug.

'Sorry,' she said. 'I was just thinking about my husband. I left him last night.'

As she watched Raphael freeze in surprise with the bottle at his lips, Robin knew herself to have crossed an invisible boundary. In her whole time at the agency, she had never used truths about her private life to gain another's confidence, never blended the private and the professional to win another person over. In turning Matthew's infidelity into a device to manipulate Raphael, she knew that she was doing something that would appal and disgust her husband. Their marriage, he would have thought, ought to be sacrosanct, a world apart from what he saw as her seedy, ramshackle job.

'Seriously?' said Raphael.

'Yes,' said Robin, 'but I don't expect you to believe me, not after all the crap I told you when I was Venetia. Anyway,' she took her notebook out of her handbag, 'you said you were OK with me asking some questions?'

'Er – yeah,' he said, apparently unable to decide whether he was more amused or disconcerted. 'Is this real? Your marriage broke up last night?'

'Yes,' said Robin. 'Why are you looking so shocked?'

'I don't know,' said Raphael. 'You just seem so . . . Girl Guidey.' His eyes moved over her face. 'It's part of the appeal.'

'Could I just ask my questions?' said Robin, determinedly unfazed.

Raphael drank some beer and said:

'Always busy with the job. Turns a man's thoughts to what it would take to distract you.'

'Seriously—'

'Fine, fine, questions – but let's order first. Fancy some dim sum?'

'Whatever's good,' said Robin, opening her notebook.

Ordering food seemed to cheer Raphael up.

'Drink up,' he said.

'I shouldn't be drinking at all,' she replied, and indeed, she hadn't touched the wine since her first gulp. 'OK, I wanted to talk about Ebury Street.'

'Go on,' said Raphael.

'You heard what Kinvara said about the keys. I won-dered whether—'

'—I ever had one?' asked Raphael with equanimity. 'Guess how many times I was ever in that house.'

Robin waited.

'Once,' said Raphael. 'Never went there as a kid. When I got out of – you know – Dad, who hadn't visited me once while I was inside, invited me down to Chiswell House to see him, so I did. Brushed my hair, put on a suit, got all the way down to that hellhole and he didn't bother turning up. Detained by a late vote at the House or some crap. Picture how happy Kinvara was to have me on her hands for the night, in that bloody depressing house that I've had bad dreams about ever since I was a kid. Welcome home, Raff.

'I took the early train back to London. Following week, no con-tact from Dad until I get another summons, this time to go to Ebury Street. I considered just not bloody turning up. Why did I go?'

'I don't know,' said Robin. 'Why did you?'

He looked directly into her eyes.

'You can bloody hate someone and still wish they gave a shit about you and hate yourself for wishing it.'

'Yes,' said Robin quietly, 'of course you can.'

'So round I trot to Ebury Street, thinking I might get – not a heart to heart, I mean, you met my father – but maybe, you know, some human emotion. He opened the door, said "There you are", shunted me into the sitting room and there was Henry Drummond and I realised I was there for a job interview. Drummond said he'd take me on, Dad barked at me not to fuck it up and shoved me back out onto the street. First and last time I was ever inside the place,' said Raphael, 'so I can't say I've got fond associations with it.'

He paused to consider what he'd just said, then let out a short laugh.

'And my father killed himself there, of course. I was forgetting that.'

'No key,' said Robin, making a note.

'No, among the many things I didn't get that day were a spare key and an invitation to let myself in whenever I fancied it.'

'I need to ask you something that might seem as though it's slightly out of left field,' said Robin cautiously.

'This sounds interesting,' said Raphael, leaning forwards.

'Did you ever suspect that your father was having an affair?'

'What?' he said, almost comically taken aback. 'No – but – *what?*'

'Over the last year or so?' said Robin. 'While he was married to Kinvara?'

He seemed incredulous.

'OK,' said Robin, 'if you don't—'

'What on *earth* makes you think he was having an affair?'

'Kinvara was always very possessive, very concerned about your father's whereabouts, wasn't she?'

'Yeah,' said Raphael, now smirking, 'but you know why that was. That was *you.*'

'I heard that she broke down months before I went to work in the office. She told somebody that your father had cheated on her. She was distraught, by all accounts. It was around the time her mare was put down and she—'

'—hit Dad with the hammer?' He frowned. 'Oh. I thought that was because of her not wanting the horse put down. Well, I suppose Dad was a ladies' man when he was younger. Hey – maybe that's what he was up to, the night I went down to Chiswell House and he stayed up in London? Kinvara was definitely expecting him back and she was furious when he cried off at the last minute.'

'Yes, maybe,' said Robin, making a note. 'Can you remember what date that was?'

'Er – yeah, as a matter of fact, I can. You don't tend to forget the day you're released from jail. I got out on Wednesday the sixteenth of February last year, and Dad asked me to go down to Chiswell House on the following Saturday, so ... the nineteenth.'

Robin made a note.

'You never saw or heard signs there was another woman?'

'Come on,' said Raphael, 'you were there, at the Commons. You saw how little I had to do with him. Was he going to tell me he was playing around?'

'He told you about seeing the ghost of Jack o'Kent roaming the grounds at night.'

'That was different. He was drunk then, and – morbid. Weird.

Banging on about divine retribution ... I don't know, I suppose he could've been talking about an affair. Maybe he'd grown a conscience at last, three wives down the line.'

'I didn't think he married your mother?'

Raphael's eyes narrowed.

'Sorry. Momentarily forgot I'm the bastard.'

'Oh, come on,' said Robin gently, 'you know I didn't mean—'

'All right, sorry,' he muttered. 'Being touchy. Being left out of a parent's will does that to a person.'

Robin remembered Strike's dictum about inheritance: *It is the money, and it isn't,* and in an uncanny echo of her thoughts, Raphael said:

'It isn't the money, although God knows I could use the money. I'm jobless, and I don't think old Henry Drummond's going to give me a reference, do you? And now my mother looks like she's going to settle permanently in Italy, so she's talking about selling the London flat, which means I'll be homeless. It'll come to this, you know,' he said bitterly. 'I'll end up as Kinvara's bloody stable boy. No one else will work for her and no one else'll employ me ...

'But it's not just the money. When you're left out of the will ... well, *left out,* that says it all. The last statement of a dead man to his family and I didn't rate a single mention and now I've got fucking Torquil advising me to piss off to Siena with my mother and "start again". Tosser,' said Raphael, with a dangerous expression.

'Is that where your mother lives? Siena?'

'Yeah. She's shacked up with an Italian count these days, and believe me, the last thing he wants is her twenty-nine-year-old son moving in. He's showing no sign of wanting to marry her and she's starting to worry about her old age, hence the idea of flogging the flat here. She's getting a bit long in the tooth to pull the trick she did on my father.'

'What d'you—?'

'She got pregnant on purpose. Don't look so shocked. My mother doesn't believe in shielding me from the realities of life. She told me the story years ago. I'm a gamble that didn't come off. She thought he'd marry her if she got pregnant, but as you've just pointed out—'

'I said I'm sorry,' said Robin. 'I am. It was really insensitive and – and stupid.'

She thought perhaps Raphael was about to tell her to go to hell, but instead he said quietly:

'See, you *are* sweet. You weren't entirely acting, were you? In the office?'

'I don't know,' said Robin. 'I suppose not.'

Feeling his legs shift under the table, she moved very slightly backwards again.

'What's your husband like?' Raphael asked.

'I don't know how to describe him.'

'Does he work for Christie's?'

'No,' said Robin. 'He's an accountant.'

'Christ,' said Raphael, appalled. 'Is that what you like?'

'He wasn't an accountant when I met him. Can we go back over your father calling you on the morning he died?'

'If you like,' said Raphael, 'but I'd much rather talk about you.'

'Well, why don't you tell me what happened that morning and then you can ask me whatever you like,' said Robin.

A fleeting smile passed over Raphael's face. He took a swig of beer and said:

'Dad called me. Told me he thought Kinvara was about to do something stupid and told me to go straight down to Woolstone and stop it. I *did* ask why it had to be me, you know.'

'You didn't tell us that at Chiswell House,' said Robin, looking up from her notes.

'Of course I didn't, because the others were there. Dad said he didn't want to ask Izzy. He was quite rude about her on the phone ... he was an ungrateful shit, really he was,' said Raphael. 'She worked her fingers to the bloody bone and you saw how he treated her.'

'What do you mean, rude?'

'He said she'd shout at Kinvara, upset her and make it worse or something. Pot and bloody kettle, but there you are. But the truth is,' said Raphael, 'that he saw me as a kind of upper servant and Izzy as proper family. He didn't mind me getting my hands dirty and it didn't matter if I pissed off his wife by barging into her house and stopping her—'

'Stopping her what?'

'Ah,' said Raphael, 'food.'

The dim sum placed on the table before them, the waitress retreated.

'What did you stop Kinvara doing?' Robin repeated. 'Leaving your father? Hurting herself?'

'I love this stuff,' said Raphael, examining a prawn dumpling.

'She left a note,' persisted Robin, 'saying she was leaving. Did your father send you down there to persuade her not to go? Was he afraid Izzy would egg her on to leave him?'

'D'you seriously think I could persuade Kinvara to stay in the marriage? Never having to lay eyes on me again would've been one more incentive to go.'

'Then why did he send you to her?'

'I've told you,' said Raphael. 'He thought she was going to do something stupid.'

'Raff,' said Robin, 'you can keep playing silly buggers—'

He corpsed.

'Christ, you sound Yorkshire when you say that. Say it again.'

'The police think there's something fishy about your story of what you were up to that morning,' said Robin. 'And so do we.'

That seemed to sober him up.

'How do you know what the police are thinking?'

'We've got contacts on the force,' said Robin. 'Raff, you've given everyone the impression that your father was trying to stop Kinvara hurting herself, but nobody really buys that. The stable girl was there. Tegan. She could have prevented Kinvara from hurting herself.'

Raphael chewed for a while, apparently thinking.

'All right,' he sighed. 'All right, here it is. You know how Dad had sold off everything that would raise a few hundred quid, or given it to Peregrine?'

'Who?'

'All right, *Pringle*,' said Raphael, exasperated. 'I prefer not to use their stupid bloody nicknames.

'He didn't sell off everything of value,' said Robin.

'What d'you mean?'

'That picture of the mare and foal is worth five to eight—'

Robin's mobile rang. She knew from the ringtone that it was Matthew.

'Aren't you going to get that?'

'No,' said Robin.

She waited until the phone had stopped ringing, then took it out of her bag.

'"Matt",' said Raphael, reading the name upside down. 'That's the accountant, is it?'

'Yes,' said Robin, silencing the phone, but it immediately began to vibrate in her hand instead. Matthew had called back.

'Block him,' suggested Raphael.

'Yes,' said Robin, 'good idea.'

All that was important to her right now was keeping Raphael cooperative. He seemed to enjoy watching her block Matthew. She put the mobile back in her bag and said:

'Go on about the paintings.'

'Well, you know how Dad had offloaded all the valuable ones through Drummond?'

'Some of us think five thousand pounds worth of picture is quite valuable,' said Robin, unable to help herself.

'Fine, Ms Lefty,' said Raphael, suddenly nasty. 'You can keep *sneering* about how people like me don't know the value of money—'

'Sorry,' said Robin quickly, cursing herself. 'I am, seriously. Look, I've – well, I've been trying to find a room to rent this morning. Five thousand pounds would change my life right now.'

'Oh,' said Raphael, frowning. 'I – OK. Actually, if it comes to that *I'd* leap at the chance of five grand in my pocket right now, but I'm talking about *seriously* valuable stuff, worth tens and hundreds of thousands, things that my father wanted to keep in the family. He'd already handed them on to little *Pringle* to avoid death duties. There was a Chinese lacquer cabinet, an ivory workbox and a couple of other things, but there was also the necklace.'

'Which—?'

'It's a big ugly diamond thing,' said Raphael, and with the hand not spearing dumplings he mimed a thick collar. 'Important *stones*. It's come down through five generations or something and the convention was that it went to the eldest daughter on her twenty-first, but my father's father, who as you might have heard was a bit of a playboy—'

'This is the one who married Tinky the nurse?'

'She was his third or fourth,' said Raphael, nodding. 'I can never remember. Anyway, he only had sons, so he let all his wives wear the thing in turn, then left it to my father, who kept the new tradition going. His wives got to wear it – even my mother got a shot – and he forgot about the handing on to the daughter on her twenty-first bit, Pringle didn't get it and he didn't mention it in his will.'

'So – wait, d'you mean it's now—?'

'Dad called me up that morning and told me I had to get hold of the bloody thing. Simple job, kind of thing anyone would enjoy,' he said, sarcastically. 'Bust in on a stepmother who hates my guts, find out where she's keeping a valuable necklace, then steal it from under her nose.'

'So you think your father believed that she was leaving him, and was worried that she was going to take it with her?'

'I suppose so,' said Raphael.

'How did he sound on the phone?'

'I told you this. Groggy. I thought it was a hangover. After I heard he'd killed himself,' Raphael faltered, '. . . well.'

'Well?'

'To tell you the truth,' said Raphael, 'I couldn't get it out of my head that the last thing Dad wanted to say to me in this life was, "run along and make sure your sister gets her diamonds". Words to treasure for ever, eh?'

At a loss for anything to say, Robin took another sip of wine, then asked quietly:

'Do Izzy and Fizzy realise the necklace is Kinvara's now?'

Raphael's lips twisted in an unpleasant smile.

'Well, they know it is legally, but here's the really funny thing: they think she's going to hand it over to them. After everything they've said about her, after calling her a gold-digger for years, slagging her off at every possible opportunity, they can't quite grasp that she won't hand the necklace over to Fizzy for Flopsy – damn it – *Florence* – because,' he affected a shrill upper-class voice, '"Darling, even *TTS* wouldn't do that, it belongs in *the family*, she *must realise* she can't sell it."'

'Bullets would bounce off their self-regard. They think there's a kind of natural law in operation, where Chiswells get what they want and lesser beings just fall into line.'

'How did Henry Drummond know you were trying to stop Kinvara keeping the necklace? He told Cormoran you went to Chiswell House for noble reasons.'

Raphael snorted.

'Cat's really out of the bag, isn't it? Yeah, apparently Kinvara left a message for Henry the day before Dad died, asking where she could get a valuation on the necklace.'

'Is that why he phoned your father that morning?'

'Exactly. To warn him what she was up to.'

'Why didn't you tell the police all this?'

'Because once the others find out she's planning to sell it, the whole thing's going to turn nuclear. There'll be an almighty row and the family'll go to lawyers and expect me to join them in kicking the shit out of Kinvara, and meanwhile I'm still treated like a second-class citizen, like a fucking *courier*, driving all the old paintings up to Drummond in London and hearing how much Dad was getting for them, and not a penny of *that* did I ever see – I'm not getting caught up in the middle of the great necklace scandal, I'm not playing their bloody game. I should've told Dad to stuff it, the day he phoned,' said Raphael, 'but he didn't sound well, and I suppose I felt sorry for him, or something, which only goes to prove they're right, I'm *not* a proper bloody Chiswell.'

He had run out of breath. Two couples had joined them in the restaurant now. Robin watched in the mirror as a well-groomed blonde did a double take at Raphael as she sat down with her florid, overweight companion.

'So, why did you leave Matthew?' Raphael asked.

'He cheated,' said Robin. She didn't have the energy to lie.

'Who with?'

She had the impression he was seeking to redress some kind of power balance. However much anger and contempt he had displayed during the outburst about his family, she had heard the hurt, too.

'With a friend of his from university,' said Robin.

'How did you find out?'

'A diamond earring, in our bed.'

'Seriously?'

'Seriously,' said Robin.

She felt a sudden wave of depression and fatigue at the idea of travelling all the way back to that hard sofa in Wembley. She had not yet called her parents to tell them what had happened.

'Under normal circumstances,' said Raphael, 'I'd be putting the moves on you. Well, not right now. Not tonight. But give it a couple of weeks . . .

'Trouble is, I look at you,' he raised a forefinger, and pointed first to her, and then to an imaginary figure behind her, 'and I see your one-legged boss looming over your shoulder.'

'Is there any particular reason you feel the need to mention him being one-legged?'

Raphael grinned.

'Protective, aren't you?'

'No, I—'

'It's all right. Izzy fancies him, too.'

'I never—'

'Defensive, too.'

'Oh, for God's sake,' said Robin, half-laughing, and Raphael grinned.

'I'm having another beer. Drink that wine, why don't you?' he said, indicating her glass, which was still two-thirds full.

When he had procured another bottle, he said with a malevolent grin, 'Izzy's always liked bits of rough. Did you notice the charged look from Fizzy to Izzy when Jimmy Knight's name was mentioned?'

'I did, actually,' said Robin. 'What was that about?'

'Freddie's eighteenth birthday party,' said Raphael, smirking. 'Jimmy crashed it with a couple of mates and Izzy – how do I put this delicately? – *lost* something in his company.'

'Oh,' said Robin, astonished.

'She was blind drunk. It's passed into family legend. I wasn't there. I was too young.

'Fizzy's so amazed at the idea that her sister could have slept with the estate carpenter's son that she thinks he must have some sort of supernatural, demonic sex appeal. *That's* why she thinks Kinvara was slightly on his side, when he turned up asking for money.'

'What?' said Robin sharply, reaching for her notebook again, which had fallen closed.

'Don't get too excited,' said Raphael, 'I still don't know what he was blackmailing Dad about, I never did. Not a full member of the family, you see, so not to be fully trusted.

'Kinvara told you this at Chiswell House, don't you remember? She was alone at home, the first time Jimmy turned up. Dad was in London again. From what I've pieced together, when she and Dad first talked it over, she argued Jimmy's case. Fizzy thinks that's down to Jimmy's sex appeal. Would you say he's got any?'

'I suppose some people might think he has,' said Robin indifferently, who was making notes. 'Kinvara thought your father should pay Jimmy his money, did she?'

'From what I understand,' said Raphael, 'Jimmy didn't frame it as blackmail on the first approach. She thought Jimmy had a legitimate claim and argued for giving him something.'

'When was this, d'you know?'

'Search me,' said Raphael, shaking his head. 'I think I was in jail at the time. Bigger things to worry about ...

'Guess,' he said, for the second time, 'how often any of them have asked me what it was like in jail?'

'I don't know,' said Robin cautiously.

'Fizzy, never. Dad, never—'

'You said Izzy visited.'

'Yeah,' he acknowledged, with a tip of the bottle to his sister. 'Yeah, she did, bless her. Good old Torks has made a couple of jokes about not wanting to bend over in the shower. I suggested,' said Raphael, with a hard smile, 'that he'd know all about that kind of thing, what with his old pal Christopher sliding his hand between young men's legs at the office. Turns out it's serious stuff when some hairy old convict tries it, but harmless frolics for public schoolboys.'

He glanced at Robin.

'I suppose you know now why Dad was taunting that poor bloke Aamir?'

She nodded.

'Which Kinvara thought was a motive for murder,' said Raphael, rolling his eyes. 'Projection, pure projection – they're all at it.

'Kinvara thinks Aamir killed Dad, because Dad had been cruel to him in front of a room full of people. Well, you should have heard some of the things Dad was saying to Kinvara by the end.

'Fizzy thinks Jimmy Knight might've done it because he was angry about money. *She's* bloody angry about all the family money that's vanished, but she can't say that in so many words, not when her husband's half the reason it's gone.

'Izzy thinks Kinvara must have killed Dad because Kinvara felt unloved and sidelined and disposable. Dad never thanked Izzy for a damn thing she did for him, and didn't give a toss when she said she was leaving. You get the picture?

'None of them have got the guts to say that they all felt like killing Dad at times, not now he's dead, so they project it all onto someone else. And *that*,' said Raphael, 'is why none of them are talking about Geraint Winn. He gets double protection, because Saint Freddie was involved in Winn's big grudge. It's staring them in the face that he had a real motive, but we're not supposed to mention that.'

'Go on,' said Robin, her pen at the ready. 'Mention.'

'No, forget it,' said Raphael, 'I shouldn't have—'

'I don't think you say much accidentally, Raff. Out with it.'

He laughed.

'I'm trying to stop fucking over people who don't deserve it. It's all part of the great redemption project.'

'Who doesn't deserve it?'

'Francesca, the little girl I – you know – at the gallery. She's the one who told me. She got it from her older sister, Verity.'

'Verity,' repeated Robin.

Sleep-deprived, she struggled to remember where she had heard that name. It was very like 'Venetia', of course ... and then she remembered.

'Wait,' she said, frowning in her effort to concentrate. 'There was a Verity on the fencing team with Freddie and Rhiannon Winn.'

'Right in one,' said Raphael.

'You all know each other,' said Robin wearily, unknowingly echoing Strike's thought as she started writing again.

'Well, that's the joy of the public school system,' said Raphael. 'In London, if you've got the money, you meet the same three hundred people everywhere you go ... Yeah, when I first arrived at Drummond's gallery, Francesca couldn't wait to tell me that her big sister had once dated Freddie. I think she thought that made the pair of us predestined, or something.

'When she realised I thought Freddie was a bit of a shit,' said Raphael, 'she changed tack and told me a nasty story.

'Apparently, at his eighteenth, Freddie, Verity and a couple of others decided to mete out some punishment to Rhiannon for having dared to replace Verity on the fencing team. In their view she was – I don't know – a bit common, a bit Welsh? – so they spiked her drink. All good fun. Sort of stuff that goes on the dorm, you know.

'But she didn't react too well to neat vodka – or maybe, from their point of view, she reacted really well. Anyway, they managed to take some nice pictures of her, to pass around among themselves ... this was in the early days of the internet. These days I suppose half a million people would have viewed them in the first twenty-four hours, but Rhiannon only had to endure the whole fencing team and most of Freddie's mates having a good gloat.

'Anyway,' said Raphael, 'about a month later, Rhiannon killed herself.'

'Oh my God,' said Robin quietly.

'Yeah,' said Raphael. 'After little Franny told me the story, I asked Izzy about it. She got very upset, told me not to repeat it, ever – but she didn't deny it. I got lots of "nobody kills themselves because of a silly joke at a party" bluster and she told me I mustn't talk about Freddie like that, it would break Dad's heart ...

'Well, the dead don't have hearts to break, do they? And personally, I think it's about time somebody pissed on Freddie's eternal flame. If he hadn't been born a Chiswell, the bastard would've been in borstal. But I suppose you'll say I can talk, after what I did.'

'No,' said Robin gently. 'That isn't what I was going to say.'

The pugnacious expression faded from his face. He checked his watch.

'I'm going to have to go. I've got to be somewhere at nine.'

Robin raised her hand to signal for the bill. When she turned back to Raphael, she saw his eyes moving in routine fashion over both the other women in the restaurant, and in the mirror she saw how the blonde tried to hold his gaze.

'You can go,' she said, handing over her credit card to the waitress. 'I don't want to make you late.'

'No, I'll walk you out.'

While she was still putting her credit card back into her handbag, he picked up her coat and held it up for her.

'Thank you.'

'No problem.'

Out on the pavement, he hailed a taxi.

'You take this one,' he said. 'I fancy a walk. Clear my head. I feel as though I've had a bad therapy session.'

'No, it's all right,' said Robin. She didn't want to charge a taxi all the way back to Wembley to Strike. 'I'm going to get the Tube. Goodnight.'

''Night, Venetia,' he said.

Raphael got into the taxi, which glided away, and Robin pulled her coat more tightly around herself as she walked off in the opposite direction. It had been a chaotic interview, but she had managed to get much more than she had expected out of Raphael. Taking out her mobile again, she phoned Strike.

59

We two go with each other . . .

Henrik Ibsen, *Rosmersholm*

When he saw Robin was calling him, Strike, who had taken his notebook out to the Tottenham for a drink, pocketed the former, downed the remainder of his pint in one and took the call out onto the street.

The mess that building works had made of the top of Tottenham Court Road – the rubble-strewn channel where a street had been, the portable railings and the plastic barricades, the walkways and planks that enabled tens of thousands of people to continue to pass through the busy junction – were so familiar to him now that he barely noticed them. He had not come outside for the view, but for a cigarette, and he smoked two while Robin relayed everything that Raphael had told her.

Once the call was over, Strike returned his mobile to his pocket and absent-mindedly lit himself a third cigarette from the tip of the second and continued to stand there, thinking deeply about everything she had said and forcing passers-by to navigate around him.

A couple of things that Robin had told him struck the detective as interesting. Having finished his third cigarette and flicked it into the open abyss in the road, Strike retreated inside the pub and ordered himself a second pint. A group of students had now taken his table, so he headed into the back, where high bar stools sat beneath a stained-glass cupola whose colours were dimmed by night. Here, Strike took out his notebook again and re-examined the list of names over which he had pored in the early hours of Sunday, while he sought distraction from thoughts of Charlotte. After gazing at it again in the manner of a man who knows something is concealed there, he turned a few pages to reread the notes he had made of his interview with Della.

Large, hunch-backed and motionless but for the eyes flicking along the lines he had scribbled in the blind woman's house, Strike unknowingly repelled a couple of timid backpackers who had considered asking whether they might share his table and take the weight off their blistered feet. Fearing the consequences of breaking his almost tangible concentration, they retreated before he noticed them.

Strike turned back to the list of names. Married couples, lovers, business partners, siblings.

Pairs.

He flicked further backwards to the pages to find the notes he had made during the interview with Oliver, who had taken them through the forensic findings. A two-part killing, this: amitriptyline and helium, each potentially fatal on its own, yet used together.

Pairs.

Two victims, killed twenty years apart, a strangled child and a suffocated government minister, the former buried on the latter's land.

Pairs.

Strike turned thoughtfully to a blank page and made a new note for himself.

Francesca – confirm story

60

*. . . you really must give me some explanation of your taking
this matter – this possibility – so much to heart.*

Henrik Ibsen, *Rosmersholm*

The following morning, a carefully worded official statement about
Jasper Chiswell appeared in all the papers. Along with the rest of the
British public, Strike learned over his breakfast that the authorities
had concluded that no foreign power or terrorist organisation had
been involved in the untimely death of the Minister for Culture, but
that no other conclusion had yet been reached.

The news that there was no news had been greeted online with
barely a ripple of interest. The local postboxes of Olympic winners
were still being painted gold, and the public was basking in the
satisfied afterglow arising from a triumphant games, its unspent
enthusiasm for all things athletic now concentrated on the imminent prospect of the Paralympics. Chiswell's death had been filed
away in the popular mind as the vaguely inexplicable suicide of a
wealthy Tory.

Keen to know whether this official statement indicated that the
Met investigation was close to concluding, Strike called Wardle to
find out what he knew.

Unfortunately, the policeman was no wiser than Strike himself.
Wardle added, not without a certain irritability, that he had not
had a single day off in three weeks, that the policing of the capital
while the city heaved under the weight of millions of extra visitors
was complex and onerous past Strike's probable understanding, and

that he didn't have time to go ferreting for information on unrelated matters on Strike's behalf.

'Fair enough,' said Strike, unfazed. 'Only asking. Say hello to April for me.'

'Oh yeah,' said Wardle, before Strike could hang up. 'She wanted me to ask you what you're playing at with Lorelei.'

'Better let you go, Wardle, the country needs you,' said Strike, and he hung up on the policeman's grudging laugh.

In the absence of information from his police contacts, and with no official standing to secure him the interviews he desired, Strike was temporarily stymied at a crucial point in the case, a frustration no more pleasant for being familiar.

A few phone calls after breakfast informed him that Francesca Pulham, Raphael's sometime colleague and lover from Drummond's gallery, was still studying in Florence, where she had been sent to remove her from his pernicious influence. Francesca's parents were currently on holiday in Sri Lanka. The Pulhams' housekeeper, who was the only person connected with the family that Strike was able to reach, refused point blank to give him telephone numbers for any of them. From her reaction, he guessed the Pulhams might be the kind of people who'd run for lawyers at the very idea of a private detective calling their house.

Having exhausted all possible avenues to the holidaying Pulhams, Strike left a polite request for an interview on Geraint Winn's voicemail, the fourth he had made that week, but the day wore on and Winn didn't call back. Strike couldn't blame him. He doubted that he would have chosen to be helpful, had he been in Winn's shoes.

Strike had not yet told Robin that he had a new theory about the case. She was busy in Harley Street, watching Dodgy Doc, but on Wednesday she called the office with the welcome news that she had arranged an interview with Tegan Butcher on Saturday at Newbury Racecourse.

'Excellent!' said Strike, cheered by the prospect of action, and striding through to the outer office to bring up Google Maps on Robin's computer. 'OK, I think we're going to be looking at an overnighter. Interview Tegan, then head over to Steda Cottage once it gets dark.'

'Cormoran, are you serious about this?' said Robin. 'You genuinely want to go digging in the dell?'

'That sounds like a nursery rhyme,' said Strike vaguely, examining B roads on the monitor. 'Look, I don't think there's anything there. In fact, as of yesterday, I'm sure of it.'

'What happened yesterday?'

'I had an idea. I'll tell you when I see you. Look, I promised Billy I'd find out the truth about his strangled child. There's no other way to be totally sure, is there, other than digging? But if you're feeling squeamish, you can stay in the car.'

'And what about Kinvara? We'll be on her property.'

'We'll hardly be digging up anything important. That whole area's waste ground. I'm going to get Barclay to meet us there, after dark. I'm not much good for digging. Will Matthew be OK if you're away overnight Saturday?'

'Fine,' said Robin, with an odd inflection that made Strike suspect that he wouldn't be fine about it at all.

'And you're OK to drive the Land Rover?'

'Er – is there any chance we could take your BMW instead?'

'I'd rather not take the BMW up that overgrown track. Is there something wrong with the—?'

'No,' said Robin, cutting across him. 'That's fine, OK, we'll take the Land Rover.'

'Great. How's Dodgy?'

'In his consulting rooms. Any news on Aamir?'

'I've got Andy trying to find the sister he's still on good terms with.'

'And what are you up to?'

'I've just been reading the Real Socialist Party website.'

'Why?'

'Jimmy gives quite a lot away in his blog posts. Places he's been and things he's seen. You OK to stay on Dodgy until Friday?'

'Actually,' said Robin, 'I was going to ask whether I could take a couple of days off to deal with some personal business.'

'Oh,' said Strike, brought up short.

'I've got a couple of appointments I need – I'd rather not miss,' said Robin.

It wasn't convenient to Strike to have to cover Dodgy Doc himself, partly because of the continuing pain in his leg, but mainly because he was eager to continue chasing down confirmation of his theory on the Chiswell case. This was also very short notice to ask for two days' leave. On the other hand, Robin had just indicated a willingness to sacrifice her weekend to a probable wildgoose chase into the dell.

'Yeah, OK. Everything all right?'

'Fine, thanks. I'll let you know if anything interesting happens with Dodgy. Otherwise, we should probably leave London at elevenish on Saturday.'

'Barons Court again?'

'Would it be all right if you meet me at Wembley Stadium station? It would just be easier, because of where I'm going to be on Friday night.'

This, too, was inconvenient: a journey for Strike of twice the length and involving a change of Tube.

'Yeah, OK,' he said again.

After Robin had hung up, he remained in her chair for a while, pondering their conversation.

She had been noticeably tight-lipped about the nature of the appointments that were so important that she didn't want to miss them. He remembered how particularly angry Matthew had sounded in the background of his calls to Robin, to discuss their pressured, unstable and occasionally dangerous job. She had twice sounded distinctly underwhelmed about the prospect of digging in the hard ground at the bottom of the dell, and now asked to drive the BMW rather than the tank-like Land Rover.

He had almost forgotten his suspicion of a couple of months ago, that Robin might be trying to get pregnant. Into his mind swam the vision of Charlotte's swollen belly at the dinner table. Robin wasn't the kind of woman who'd be able to walk away from her child as soon as it left the womb. If Robin was pregnant . . .

Logical and methodical as he usually was, and aware in one part of himself that he was theorising on scant data, Strike's imagination nevertheless showed him Matthew, the father-to-be, listening in on Robin's tense request for time off for scans and medical checks, gesticulating angrily at her that the time had come to stop, to go easy on herself, to take better care.

Strike turned back to Jimmy Knight's blog, but it took him a little longer than usual to discipline his troubled mind back into obedience.

61

Fellow Tube travellers gave Strike a slightly wider berth than was necessary on Saturday morning, even allowing for his kit bag. He generally managed to cut a path easily through crowds, given his bulk and his boxer's profile, but the way he was muttering and cursing as he struggled up the stairs at Wembley Stadium station – the lifts weren't working – made passers-by extra careful to neither jostle nor impede him.

The primary reason for Strike's bad mood was Mitch Patterson, whom he had spotted that morning from the office window, skulking in a doorway, dressed in jeans and a hoodie entirely unsuited to his age and bearing. Puzzled and angered by the private detective's reappearance, but having no route out of the building except by the front door, Strike had called a cab to wait for him at the end of the street, and left the building only once it was in position. Patterson's expression when Strike had said 'Morning, Mitch' might have amused Strike, if he hadn't been so insulted that Patterson had thought he could get away with watching the agency in person.

All the way to Warren Street station, where he asked the cab to drop him, Strike had been hyper-alert, worried that Patterson had been there as a distraction or decoy, enabling a second, less obtrusive tail to follow him. Even now, as he clambered, panting, off the top of the stairs at Wembley, he turned to scrutinise the travellers for the one who ducked down, turned back or hastily concealed their face. None of them did so. On balance, Strike concluded that Patterson had been working alone; victim, perhaps, of one of the manpower problems so familiar to Strike. The fact that Patterson had chosen to cover the job rather than forgo it suggested that somebody was paying him well.

Strike hoisted his kit bag more securely onto his shoulder and set off towards the exit.

Having pondered the question during his inconvenient journey to Wembley, Strike could think of three reasons why Patterson had reappeared. The first was that the press had got wind of some interesting new development in the Met investigation into Chiswell's death, and that this had led a newspaper to rehire Patterson, his remit to find out what Strike was up to and how much he knew.

The second possibility was that someone had paid Patterson to stalk Strike, in the hopes of impeding his movements or hampering his business. That suggested that Patterson's employer was somebody that Strike was currently investigating, in which case, Patterson doing the job himself made sense: the whole point would be to destabilise Strike by letting him know that he was being watched.

The third possible reason for Patterson's renewed interest in him was the one that bothered Strike most, because he had a feeling it was most likely to be the true one. He now knew that he had been spotted in Franco's with Charlotte. His informant was Izzy, whom he had called in the hope of fleshing out details of the theory he hadn't yet confided to anyone.

'So, I hear you had dinner with Charlotte!' she had blurted, before he had managed to pose a question.

'There was no dinner. I sat with her for twenty minutes because she was feeling ill, then left.'

'Oh – sorry,' said Izzy, cowed by his tone. 'I – I wasn't prying – Roddy Fforbes was in Franco's and he spotted the pair of you . . .'

If Roddy Fforbes, whoever he was, was spreading it around London that Strike was taking his heavily pregnant, married ex-fiancée out for dinner while her husband was in New York, the tabloids would definitely be interested, because wild, beautiful and aristocratic Charlotte was news. Her name had peppered gossip columns since she was sixteen years old, her various tribulations – running away from school, the stints in rehab and in psychiatric clinics – were well documented. It was even possible that Patterson had been hired by Jago Ross, who could certainly afford it. If the side effect of policing his wife's movements was ruining Strike's business, Ross would undoubtedly consider that a bonus.

Robin, who was sitting a short distance away from the station in the Land Rover, saw Strike emerge onto the pavement, kit bag over his shoulder and registered that he looked as bad-tempered as she had ever seen him. He lit a cigarette, scanning the street until his eye found the Land Rover at the end of a series of parked vehicles and he began to limp, unsmiling, towards her. Robin, whose own mood was perilously low, could only assume that he was angry at having to make the long trip to Wembley with what appeared to be a heavy bag and a sore leg.

She had been awake since four o'clock that morning, unable to get back to sleep, cramped and unhappy on Vanessa's hard sofa, thinking about her future, and about the row she had had with her mother by phone. Matthew had called the house in Masham, trying to reach her, and Linda was not only desperately worried, but furious that Robin hadn't told her what was going on first.

'Where are you staying? With Strike?'

'Of course I'm not staying with Strike, why on earth would I be—?'

'Where, then?'

'With a different friend.'

'Who? Why didn't you tell us? What are you going to do? I want to come down to London to see you!'

'Please don't,' said Robin through gritted teeth.

Her guilt about the expense of the wedding she and Matthew had put her parents to, and about the embarrassment her mother and father were about to endure in explaining to their friends that her marriage was over barely a year after it had begun, weighed heavily on her, but she couldn't bear the prospect of Linda badgering and cajoling, treating her as though she were fragile and damaged. The last thing she needed right now was her mother suggesting that she go back to Yorkshire, to be cocooned in the bedroom that had witnessed some of the worst times of her life.

After two days viewing a multitude of densely packed houses, Robin had put down a deposit on a box room in a house in Kilburn, where she would have five other housemates, and into which she would be able to move the following week. Every time she thought of the place, her stomach turned over in trepidation and misery. At the age of almost twenty-eight, she would be the oldest housemate.

Trying to propitiate Strike, she got out of the car and offered to help him with the kit bag, but he grunted at her that he could manage. As the canvas hit the metal floor of the Land Rover she heard a loud clattering of heavy metal tools and experienced a nervous spasm in her stomach.

Strike, who had taken fleeting stock of Robin's appearance, had his worst suspicions strengthened. Pale, with shadows beneath her eyes, she managed to look both puffy and drawn and also seemed to have lost weight in the few days since he'd last seen her. The wife of his old army friend Graham Hardacre had been hospitalised in the early stages of pregnancy because of persistent vomiting. Perhaps one of Robin's important appointments had been to address that problem.

'You all right?' Strike asked Robin roughly, buckling up his seatbelt.

'Fine,' she said, for what felt like the umpteenth time, taking his shortness as annoyance at his long Tube journey.

They drove out of London without talking. Finally, when they had reached the M40, Strike said:

'Patterson's back. He was watching the office this morning.'

'You're kidding!'

'Has there been anyone round your place?'

'Not that I know of,' said Robin, after an almost imperceptible hesitation. Perhaps this was what Matthew had been calling her about, when he had tried to reach her in Masham.

'You didn't have any trouble getting away this morning?'

'No,' said Robin, honestly enough.

In the days that had elapsed since she'd walked out, she had imagined telling Strike that her marriage was over, but had not yet been able to find a form of words that she knew she would be able to deliver with the requisite calm. This frustrated her: it ought, she told herself, to be easy. He was the friend and colleague who had been there when she'd called off the wedding and who knew about Matthew's previous infidelity with Sarah. She ought to be able to tell him casually mid-conversation, as she had with Raphael.

The problem was that on the rare occasions when she and Strike had shared revelations about their love lives, it had been when one of them had been drunk. Otherwise, a profound reserve on such matters had always lain between them, in spite of Matthew's paranoid conviction that they spent most of their working lives in flirtation.

But there was more to it than that. Strike was the man she had hugged on the stairs at her wedding reception, the man with whom she had imagined walking out on her husband before the marriage could be consummated, the man for whom she had spent nights of her honeymoon wearing a groove in the white sand as she paced alone, wondering whether she was in love with him. She was afraid of giving herself away, afraid of betraying what she had thought and felt, because she was sure that if he ever had the merest suspicion of what a disruptive factor he had been, in both the beginning and the end of her marriage, it would surely taint their working relationship, as certainly as it would surely prejudice her job if he ever knew about the panic attacks.

No, she must appear to be what he was – self-contained and stoic, able to absorb trauma and limp on, ready to face whatever life flung at her, even what lay at the bottom of the dell, without flinching or turning away.

'So what d'you think Patterson's up to?' she asked.

'Time will tell. Did your appointments go all right?'

'Yes,' said Robin, and to distract herself from the thought of her tiny new rented room, and the student couple who had shown her around, casting sideways glances at the strangely grown-up woman who was coming to live with them, she said, 'There are biscuits in the bag back there. No tea, sorry, but we can stop if you like.'

The thermos was back in Albury Street, one of the things she had forgotten to sneak out of the house when she had returned while Matthew was at work.

'Thanks,' said Strike, though without much enthusiasm. He was wondering whether the reappearance of snacks, given his self-proclaimed diet, might not be further proof of his partner's pregnancy.

Robin's phone rang in her pocket. She ignored it. Twice that morning, she had received calls from the same unknown number and she was afraid that it might be Matthew who, finding himself blocked, had borrowed another phone.

'D'you want to get that?' asked Strike, watching her pale, set profile.

'Er – not while I'm driving.'

'I can answer it, if you want.'

'No,' she said, a little too quickly.

The mobile stopped ringing but, almost at once, began again. More than ever convinced that it was Matthew, Robin took the phone out of her jacket, saying:

'I think I know who it is, and I don't want to talk to them just now. Once they hang up, could you mute it?'

Strike took the mobile.

'It's been put through from the office number. I'll turn it to speakerphone,' said Strike helpfully, given that the ancient Land Rover didn't have a functioning heater, let alone Bluetooth, and he did so, holding the mobile close to her mouth, so that she could make herself heard over the rattle and growl of the draughty vehicle.

'Hello, Robin here. Who's this?'

'Robin? Don't you mean *Venetia*?' said a Welsh voice.

'Is that Mr Winn?' said Robin, eyes on the road, while Strike held the mobile steady for her.

'Yes, you nasty little bitch, it is.'

Robin and Strike glanced at each other, startled. Gone was the unctuous, lascivious Winn, keen to charm and impress.

'Got what you were after, haven't you, eh? Wriggling up and down that corridor, sticking your tits in where they weren't wanted, "oh, Mr Winn—"' he imitated her the same way Matthew did, high-pitched and imbecilic, '"—oh, help me, Mr Winn, should I do charity or should I do politics, let me bend a bit lower over the desk, Mr Winn". How many men have you trapped that way, how far do you go—?'

'Have you got something to tell me, Mr Winn?' asked Robin loudly, talking over him. 'Because if you've just called to insult me—'

'Oh, I've got plenty to bloody tell you, *plenty to bloody tell you*,' shouted Winn. 'You are going to *pay*, Miss Ellacott, for what you've done to me, *pay* for the damage you've done to me and my wife, you don't get off that easily, you broke the law in this office and I'm going to see you in court, do you understand me?' He was becoming almost hysterical. 'We'll see how well your wiles work on a judge, shall we? Low-cut top and "oh, I think I'm overheating—"'

A white light seemed to be encroaching on the edges of Robin's vision, so that the road ahead turned tunnel-like.

'NO!' she shouted, taking both hands off the wheel before slamming them back down again, her arms shaking. It was the 'no' she had given Matthew, a 'no' of such vehemence and force that it brought Geraint Winn up short in exactly the same way.

'Nobody made you stroke my hair and pat my back and ogle my chest, Mr Winn, that wasn't what *I* wanted, though I'm sure it gives you a bit of a kick to think it was—'

'Robin!' said Strike, but he might as well have been one more creak of the car's ancient chassis, and she ignored, too, Geraint's sudden interjection, 'Who else is there? Was that Strike?'

'—you're a creep, Mr Winn, a *thieving* creep who stole from a charity and I'm not only happy I got the goods on you, I'll be delighted to tell the world you're flicking out pictures of your dead daughter while you're trying to peer down young women's shirts—'

'How dare you!' gasped Winn, 'are there no depths – you *dare* mention Rhiannon – it's all going to come out, Samuel Murape's family—'

'Screw you and screw your bloody grudges!' shouted Robin. 'You're a pervy, thieving—'

'If you've got anything else to say, I suggest you put it in writing, Mr Winn,' Strike shouted into the mobile, while Robin, hardly knowing what she was doing, continued to yell insults at Winn from a distance. Ending the call with a jab of the finger, Strike grabbed the wheel as Robin again removed both hands from it to gesticulate.

'Fuck's sake!' said Strike, 'pull over – pull over, now!'

She did as he told her automatically, the adrenaline disorientating her like alcohol, and when the Land Rover lurched to a halt she threw off her seat belt and got out on the hard shoulder, cars whizzing past her. Hardly knowing what she was doing she began to stumble away from the Land Rover, tears of rage sliding down her face, trying to outpace the panic now lapping at her, because she had just irrevocably alienated a man they might need to talk to again, a man who had already been talking about revenge, who might even be the one paying Patterson . . .

'Robin!'

Now, she thought, Strike, too, would think her a flake, a damaged fool who should never have taken on this line of work, the one who ran when things got tough. It was that which made her wheel around to face him as he hobbled along the hard shoulder after her, and she wiped her face roughly on her sleeve and said, before he could tell her off, 'I know I shouldn't have lost it, I know I've fucked up, I'm sorry.' But his answer was lost in the pounding in her ears and, as though it had been waiting for her to stop running, the panic now engulfed her. Dizzy, unable to order her thoughts, she collapsed on the verge, dry bristles of grass prickling through her jeans as, eyes shut and head in hands, she tried to breathe herself back to normality as the traffic zoomed past.

She wasn't quite sure whether one minute or ten had elapsed, but finally her pulse slowed, her thoughts became ordered and the panic ebbed away, to be replaced by mortification. After all her careful pretence that she was coping, she had blown it.

A whiff of cigarette smoke reached her. Opening her eyes, she saw Strike's legs sticking out on the ground to her right. He, too, had sat down on the verge.

'How long have you been having panic attacks?' he asked conversationally.

There seemed no point dissembling any more.

'About a year,' she muttered.

'Been getting help with them?'

'Yes. I was in therapy for a bit. Now I do CBT exercises.'

'Do you, though?' Strike asked mildly. 'Because I bought vegetarian bacon a week ago, but it's not making me any healthier, just sitting there in the fridge.'

Robin began to laugh and found that she couldn't stop. More tears leaked from her eyes. Strike watched her, not unkindly, smoking his cigarette.

'I could have been doing them a bit more regularly,' Robin admitted at last, mopping her face again.

'Anything else you fancy telling me, now we're getting into things?' asked Strike.

He felt he ought to know the worst now, before he gave her any advice on her mental condition, but Robin seemed confused.

'Any other health matters that might affect your ability to work?' he prompted her.

'Like what?'

Strike wondered whether a direct enquiry constituted some kind of infringement of her employment rights.

'I wondered,' he said, 'whether you might be, ah, pregnant.'

Robin began to laugh again.

'Oh God, that's funny.'

'Is it?'

'No,' she said, shaking her head, 'I'm not pregnant.'

Strike now noticed that her wedding and engagement rings were missing. He had become so used to seeing her without them as she impersonated Venetia Hall and Bobbi Cunliffe that it had not occurred to him that their absence today might be significant, yet he didn't want to pose a direct question, for reasons that had nothing at all to do with employment rights.

'Matthew and I have split up,' Robin said, frowning at the passing traffic in an effort not to cry again. 'A week ago.'

'Oh,' said Strike. 'Shit. I'm sorry.'

But his concerned expression was at total odds with his actual feelings. His dark mood had lightened so abruptly that it was akin to having moved from sober to three pints down. The smell of rubber and dust and burned grass recalled the car park where he had

accidentally kissed her, and he drew on his cigarette again and tried
hard not to let his feelings show in his face.

'I know I shouldn't have spoken to Geraint Winn like that,'
said Robin, tears now falling again. 'I shouldn't have mentioned
Rhiannon, I lost control and – it's just, *men*, bloody *men*, judging
everyone by their bloody selves!'

'What happened with Matt—?'

'He's been sleeping with Sarah Shadlock,' said Robin savagely. 'His
best friend's fiancée. She left an earring in our bed and I – oh *bugger*.'

It was no use: she buried her face in her hands and, with a sense
of having nothing to lose now, cried in earnest, because she had
thoroughly disgraced herself in Strike's eyes, and the one remaining piece of her life that she had been seeking to preserve had been
tainted. How delighted Matthew would be to see her falling apart
on a motorway verge, proving his point, that she was unfit to do the
job she loved, forever limited by her past, by having, twice, been in
the wrong place, at the wrong time, with the wrong men.

A heavy weight landed across her shoulders. Strike had put his
arm around her. This was simultaneously comforting and ominous,
because he had never done that before, and she was sure that this was
the precursor to him telling her that she was unfit to work, that they
would cancel the next interview and return to London.

'Where have you been staying?'

'Vanessa's sofa,' said Robin, trying frantically to mop her streaming
eyes and nose: snot and tears had made the knees of her jeans soggy.
'But I've got a new place now.'

'Where?'

'Kilburn, a room in a shared house.'

'Bloody hell, Robin,' said Strike. 'Why didn't you tell me? Nick
and Ilsa have got a proper spare room, they'd be delighted—'

'I can't sponge off your friends,' said Robin thickly.

'It wouldn't be sponging,' said Strike. He jammed his cigarette in
his mouth and started searching his pockets with his free hand. 'They
like you and you could stay there for a couple of weeks until – aha.
I thought I had one. It's only creased, I haven't used it – don't think
so, anyway—'

Robin took the tissue and, with one hearty blow of her nose, demolished it.

'Listen,' Strike began, but Robin interrupted at once:

'Don't tell me to take time off. Please don't. I'm fine, I'm fit to work, I hadn't had a panic attack in ages before that one, I'm—'

'—not listening.'

'All right, sorry,' she muttered, the sodden tissue clutched in her fist. 'Go on.'

'After I got blown up, I couldn't get in a car without doing what you've just done, panicking and breaking out in a cold sweat and half suffocating. For a while I'd do anything to avoid being driven by someone else. I've still got problems with it, to tell the truth.'

'I didn't realise,' said Robin. 'You don't show it.'

'Yeah, well, you're the best driver I know. You should see me with my bloody sister. Thing is, Robin – oh, bollocks.'

The traffic police had arrived, pulling up behind the abandoned Land Rover, apparently puzzled as to why the occupants were sitting fifty yards away on the verge, to all appearances unconcerned with the fate of their poorly parked vehicle.

'Not in too much of a hurry to get help, then?' said the portlier of the two sarcastically. He had the swagger of a man who thinks himself a joker.

Strike removed his arm from around Robin's shoulders and both stood up, in Strike's case, clumsily.

'Car sickness,' Strike told the officer blandly. 'Careful, or she might puke on you.'

They returned to the car. The first officer's colleague was peering at the tax disc on the ancient Land Rover.

'You don't see many of this age still on the roads,' he commented.

'It's never let me down yet,' said Robin.

'Sure you're all right to drive?' Strike muttered, as she turned the ignition key. 'We could pretend you're still feeling ill.'

'I'm fine.'

And this time, it was true. He had called her the best driver he knew, and it might not be much, but he had given her back some of her self-respect, and she steered seamlessly back onto the motorway.

There was a long silence. Strike decided that further discussion of Robin's mental health ought to wait until she wasn't driving.

'Winn said a name at the end of the call there,' he mused, taking out his notebook. 'Did you hear?'

'No,' muttered Robin, shamefaced.

'It was Samuel something,' Strike said, making a note. 'Murdoch? Matlock?'

'I didn't hear.'

'Cheer up,' said Strike bracingly, 'he probably wouldn't have blurted it out if you hadn't been yelling at him. Not that I recommend calling interviewees thieving perverts in future . . .'

He stretched around in his seat, reaching for the carrier bag in the back. 'Fancy a biscuit?'

62

The car park at Newbury Racecourse was already jam-packed when they arrived. Many of the people heading for the ticket marquee were dressed for comfort, like Strike and Robin, in jeans and jackets, but others had donned fluttering silk dresses, suits, padded waistcoats, tweed hats and corduroy trousers in shades of mustard and puce that reminded Robin of Torquil.

They queued for tickets, each lost in their thoughts. Robin was afraid of what was coming once they reached the Crafty Filly, where Tegan Butcher worked. Certain that Strike had not yet had his full say on her mental health, she was afraid that he had merely postponed the announcement that he wanted her to return to a desk job in the office.

In fact, Strike's mind was temporarily elsewhere. The white railings glimpsed beyond the small marquee where the crowd queued for tickets, and the abundance of tweed and corduroy, were reminding him of the last time he had been at a racecourse. He had no particular interest in the sport. The one constant paternal figure in his life, his uncle Ted, had been a footballing and sailing man, and while a couple of Strike's friends in the army had enjoyed a bet on the horses, he had never seen the attraction.

Three years previously, though, he had attended the Epsom Derby with Charlotte and two of her favourite siblings. Like Strike,

Charlotte came from a disjointed and dysfunctional family. In one of her unpredictable effusions of enthusiasm, Charlotte had insisted on accepting Valentine and Sacha's invitation, notwithstanding Strike's lack of interest in the sport and his barely cordial feelings towards both men, who considered him an inexplicable oddity in their sister's life.

He had been broke at the time, setting up the agency on a shoestring, already being chased by lawyers for repayment of the small loan he had taken from his biological father, when every bank had turned him down as a bad risk. Nevertheless, Charlotte had been incensed when, after losing a fiver on the nose on the favourite, Fame and Glory, who had come in second, he had refused to place another bet. She had refrained from calling him puritanical or sanctimonious, plebeian or penny-pinching, as she had done previously when he had refused to emulate the reckless and ostentatious spending of her family and friends. Egged on by her brothers, she had chosen to lay larger and larger bets herself, finally winning £2500 and insisting that they visit the champagne tent, where her beauty and high spirits had turned many heads.

As he walked with Robin up a wide tarmacked thoroughfare that ran parallel from the racetrack itself behind the towering stands, past coffee bars, cider stalls and ice cream vans, the jockeys' changing rooms and owners' and trainers' bar, Strike thought about Charlotte, and gambles that came off, and gambles that didn't, until Robin's voice pulled him back to the present.

'I think that's the place.'

A painted sign showed the head of a dark, winking filly in a snaffle bit hung on the side of a one-storey brick bar. The outdoor seating area was crowded. Champagne flutes clinked amid a buzz of talk and laughter. The Crafty Filly overlooked the paddock where horses would shortly be paraded, around which a further crowd had begun to congregate.

'Grab that high table,' Strike told Robin, 'and I'll get drinks and tell Tegan we're here.'

He disappeared into the building without asking her what she wanted.

Robin sat down at one of the tall tables with its metal bar-chairs, which she knew Strike preferred because getting on and off them would be easier on his amputated leg than the low wickerwork sofas. The whole outside area sat beneath a canopy of polyurethane to protect drinkers from non-existent rain. The sky was cloudless today, the day warm with a light breeze that barely moved the leaves of the topiary plants at the entrance to the bar. It would be a clear night for digging in the dell outside Steda Cottage, Robin thought, always assuming that Strike wasn't about to cancel the expedition, because he thought her too unstable and emotional to take along.

That thought turned her insides even colder and she fell to reading the printed lists of runners they had been given, along with their cardboard entry tags, until a half-bottle of Moët & Chandon landed unexpectedly in front of her and Strike sat down, holding a pint of bitter.

'Doom Bar on draught,' he said cheerfully, tipping his glass to her before taking a sip. Robin looked blankly at the little bottle of champagne, which she thought resembled bubble bath.

'What's this for?'

'Celebration,' said Strike, having taken a sizeable gulp of his beer. 'I know you're not supposed to say it,' he went on, rummaging through his pockets for cigarettes, 'but you're well shot of him. Sleeping with his mate's fiancée in the marital bed? He deserves everything that's coming to him.'

'I can't drink. I'm driving.'

'That's just cost me twenty-five quid, so you can take a token swig.'

'Twenty-five quid, for this?' said Robin, and taking advantage of Strike lighting his cigarette, she surreptitiously wiped her leaking eyes again.

'Tell me something,' said Strike, as he waved his match, extinguishing it. 'D'you ever think about where you see the agency going?'

'What d'you mean?' said Robin, looking alarmed.

'My brother-in-law was giving me the third degree about it, night the Olympics started,' said Strike. 'Banging on about reaching a point where I didn't have to go out on the street any more.'

'But you wouldn't want that, would y – wait,' said Robin,

panicking. 'Are you trying to tell me I've got to go back to the desk and answering the phones?'

'No,' said Strike, blowing smoke away from her, 'I just wondered whether you give the future any thought.'

'You want me to leave?' asked Robin, still more alarmed. 'Go and do something el—?'

'Bloody hell, Ellacott, no! I'm asking you whether you think about the future, that's all.'

He watched as Robin uncorked the little bottle.

'Yes, of course I do,' she said uncertainly. 'I've been hoping we can get the bank balance a bit healthier, so we aren't living hand to mouth all the time, but I love the—' her voice wobbled, '—the job, you know I do. That's all I want. Do it, get better at it and . . . I suppose make the agency the best in London.'

Grinning, Strike clinked his beer glass against her champagne.

'Well, bear in mind we want exactly the same thing while I'm saying the next bit, all right? And you might as well drink. Tegan can't take a break for forty minutes, and we've got a lot of time to kill before we head over to the dell this evening.'

Strike watched her take a sip of champagne before going on.

'Pretending you're OK when you aren't isn't strength.'

'Well, that's where you're wrong,' Robin contradicted him. The champagne had fizzed on her tongue and seemed to give her courage even before it hit her brain. 'Sometimes, acting as though you're all right, makes you all right. Sometimes you've got to slap on a brave face and walk out into the world, and after a while it isn't an act any more, it's who you are. If I'd waited to feel ready to leave my room after – you know,' she said, 'I'd still be in there. I had to leave before I was ready. And,' she said, looking him directly in the eyes, her own bloodshot and swollen, 'I've been working with you for two years, watching you plough on no matter what, when we both know any doctor would have told you to put your leg up and rest.'

'And where did that get me, eh?' asked Strike reasonably. 'Invalided out for a week, with my hamstring screaming for mercy every time I walk more than fifty yards. You want to draw parallels, fine. I'm dieting, I've been doing my stretches—'

'And the vegetarian bacon, rotting away in the fridge?'

'Rotting? That stuff's like industrial rubber, it'll outlive me. Listen,' he said, refusing to be deflected, 'it'd be a bloody miracle if you hadn't suffered any after-effects from what happened last year.' His eyes sought the tip of the purple scar on her forearm, visible beneath the cuff of her shirt. 'Nothing in your past precludes you from doing this job, but you need to take care of yourself if you want to keep doing it. If you need time off—'

'—that's the last thing I want—'

'This isn't about what you want. It's about what you need.'

'Shall I tell you something funny?' said Robin. Whether because of the mouthful of champagne, or for some other reason, she had experienced a startling lift in mood that made her loose-tongued. 'You'd have thought I'd have had panic attacks galore over the last week, wouldn't you? I've been trying to find a place to live, looking round flats, travelling all over London, I've had loads of people coming up unexpectedly behind me – that's a major trigger,' she explained. 'People behind me, when I don't know they're there.'

'Don't think we need Freud to explain that one.'

'But I've been fine,' said Robin. 'I think it's because I haven't had to—'

She stopped short, but Strike thought he knew what the end of the sentence would have been. Taking a chance, he said:

'This job becomes well-nigh impossible if your home life's screwed up. I've been there. I know.'

Relieved to have been understood, Robin drank more champagne then said in a rush:

'I think it's made me worse, having to hide what's going on, having to do the exercises in secret, because any sign I wasn't a hundred per cent and Matthew would be yelling at me again for doing this job. I thought it was him trying to reach me on the phone this morning, that's why I didn't want to take the call. And when Winn started calling me those names, it – well, it felt as though I *had* taken the call. I don't need Winn to tell me I'm basically a pair of walking tits, a stupid, deluded girl who doesn't realise that's my only useful attribute.'

Matthew's been telling you that, has he? thought Strike, imagining a few corrective measures from which he thought Matthew might benefit. Slowly and carefully he said:

'The fact that you're a woman . . . I *do* worry about you more when you're out alone on a job than I would if you were a bloke. Hear me out,' he said firmly, as she opened her mouth in panic. 'We've got to be honest with each other, or we're screwed. Just listen, will you?

'You've escaped two killers using your wits and remembering your training. I'd lay odds bloody Matthew couldn't've managed that. But I don't want a third time, Robin, because you might not be so lucky.'

'You *are* telling me to go back to a desk job—'

'Can I finish?' he said sternly. 'I don't want to lose you, because you're the best I've got. Every case we've worked since you arrived, you've found evidence I couldn't have found and got round people I couldn't have persuaded to talk to me. We're where we are today largely because of you. But the odds are always going to be against you if you come up against a violent man and I've got responsibilities here. I'm the senior partner, I'm the one you could sue—'

'You're worried I'd *sue*—?'

'No, Robin,' he said harshly, 'I'm worried you'll end up fucking dead and I'll have to carry that on my conscience for the rest of my life.'

He took another swig of Doom Bar, then said:

'I need to know you're mentally healthy if I'm putting you out on the street. I want a cast-iron guarantee from you that you're going to address these panic attacks, because it isn't only you who has to live with the consequences if you're not up to it.'

'Fine,' muttered Robin, and when Strike raised his eyebrows, she said, 'I mean it. I'll do what it takes. I will.'

The crowd around the paddock was becoming ever denser. Evidently the runners in the next race were about to be paraded.

'How are things with Lorelei?' Robin asked. 'I like her.'

'Then I'm afraid I've got even more bad news for you, because you and Matthew aren't the only people who split up last weekend.'

'Oh, shit. Sorry,' said Robin, and she covered her embarrassment by drinking more champagne.

'For someone who didn't want that, you're getting through it quite fast,' said Strike, amused.

'I didn't tell you, did I?' said Robin, remembering suddenly, as she held up the little green bottle. 'I know where I saw Blanc de Blancs before, and it wasn't on a bottle – but it doesn't help us with the case.'

'Go on.'

'There's a suite at Le Manoir aux Quat'Saisons called that,' said Robin. 'Raymond Blanc, you know, the chef who started the hotel? Play on words. Blanc de Blanc – no "s".'

'Is that where you had your anniversary weekend?'

'Yeah. We weren't in "Blanc de Blanc", though. We couldn't afford a suite,' said Robin. 'I just remember walking past the sign. But yes . . . that's where we celebrated our paper anniversary. Paper,' she repeated, with a sigh, 'and some people make it to platinum.'

Seven dark thoroughbreds were appearing one by one in the paddock now, jockeys in their silks perched atop them like monkeys, stable girls and lads leading the nervy creatures, with their silken flanks and their prancing strides. Strike and Robin were some of the few not craning their necks for a better view. Before she had time to second-guess herself, Robin introduced the subject she most wanted to discuss.

'Was that Charlotte I saw you talking to at the Paralympic reception?'

'Yeah,' said Strike.

He glanced at her. Robin had had occasion before now to deplore how easily he seemed to read her thoughts.

'Charlotte had nothing to do with me and Lorelei splitting. She's married now.'

'So were Matthew and I,' Robin pointed out, taking another sip of champagne. 'Didn't stop Sarah Shadlock.'

'I'm not Sarah Shadlock.'

'Obviously not. If you were that bloody annoying I wouldn't be working for you.'

'Maybe you could put that on the next employee satisfaction review. "Not as bloody annoying as the woman who shagged my husband." I'll have it framed.'

Robin laughed.

'You know, I had an idea about Blanc de Blancs myself,' said Strike. 'I was going back over Chiswell's to-do list, trying to eliminate possibilities and substantiate a theory.'

'What theory?' said Robin sharply, and Strike noted that even halfway down the bottle of champagne, with her marriage in splinters and a box room in Kilburn to look forward to, Robin's interest in the case remained as acute as ever. 'Remember when I told you I thought there was something big, something fundamental, behind the Chiswell business? Something we hadn't spotted yet?'

'Yes,' said Robin, 'you said it kept "almost showing itself".'

'Well remembered. So, a couple of things Raphael said—'

'That's me on my break, now,' said a nervous female voice behind them.

63

It is a purely personal matter, and there is not the slightest
necessity to go proclaiming it all over the countryside.

Henrik Ibsen, *Rosmersholm*

Short, square and heavily freckled, Tegan Butcher wore her dark
hair scraped back in a bun. Even in her smart bar uniform, which
comprised a grey tie and a black shirt on which a white horse and
jockey were embroidered, she had the air of a girl more at home in
muddy Wellington boots. She had brought a milky coffee out of the
bar to drink while they questioned her.

'Oh – thanks very much,' she said, when Strike went to fetch an
extra chair, clearly gratified that the famous detective would do as
much for her.

'No problem,' said Strike. 'This is my partner, Robin Ellacott.'

'Yeah, it was you that contacted me, wasn't it?' said Tegan as she
got up onto the bar chair, making slightly heavy weather of the
climb, being so short. She seemed simultaneously excited and fearful.

'You haven't got long, I know,' said Strike, 'so we'll get straight to
it, if you don't mind, Tegan?'

'No. I mean, yeah. That's fine. Go on.'

'How long did you work for Jasper and Kinvara Chiswell?'

'I was doing it part time for them while I was still at school, so
counting that . . . two and a half years, yeah.'

'How did you like working for them?'

'It was all right,' said Tegan cautiously.

'How did you find the minister?'

'He was all right,' said Tegan. She appeared to realise that this wasn't particularly descriptive, and added, 'My family've known him for ages. My brothers done a bit of work up at Chiswell House for years, on and off.'

'Yeah?' said Strike, who was making notes. 'What did your brothers do?'

'Repairing fences, bit of gardening, but they've sold off most of the land now,' said Tegan. 'The garden's gone wild.'

She picked up her coffee and took a sip, then said anxiously:

'My mum would do her nut if she knew I was meeting you. She told me to keep well out of it.'

'Why's that?'

'"Least said, soonest mended", she always says. That and "least seen, most admired". That's what I got if I ever wanted to go to the young farmers' disco.'

Robin laughed. Tegan grinned, proud to have amused her.

'How did you find Mrs Chiswell as an employer?' asked Strike.

'All right,' said Tegan, yet again.

'Mrs Chiswell liked to have someone sleeping at the house if she was away for the night, is that right? To be near the horses?'

'Yeah,' said Tegan, and then, volunteering information for the first time, 'she's paranoid.'

'Wasn't one of her horses slashed?'

'You can call it slashed if you want,' said Tegan, 'but I'd call it more of a scratch. Romano managed to get his blanket off in the night. He was a sod for doing that.'

'You don't know anything about intruders in the garden, then?' asked Strike, his pen poised over his notebook.

'Weelll,' said Tegan slowly, 'she *said* something about it, but . . .'

Her eyes had strayed to Strike's Benson & Hedges, which were lying beside his beer glass.

'Can I have a smoke?' she asked, greatly daring.

'Help yourself,' said Strike, taking out a lighter and pushing it towards her.

Tegan lit up, took a deep drag on the cigarette, and said:

'I don't think there was ever anyone in the gardens. That's just Mrs

Chiswell. She's—' Tegan struggled to find the right word. 'Well, if she was a horse you'd call her spooky. *I* never heard anyone when I was there overnight.'

'You slept over at the house the night before Jasper Chiswell was found dead in London, didn't you?'

'Yeah.'

'Can you remember what time Mrs Chiswell got back?'

''Bout eleven. I got a right shock,' said Tegan. Now that her nerves were wearing off, a slight tendency to garrulity was revealed. 'Because she was s'posed to be staying up in London. She went off on one when she walked in, because I'd had a fag in front of the telly – she doesn't like smoking – and I'd had a couple of glasses of wine out the bottle in the fridge, as well. Mind, she'd told me to help myself to anything I wanted before she left, but she's like that, always shifting the goalposts. What was right one minute was wrong the next. You had to walk on eggshells, you really did.

'But she was already in a bad mood when she arrived. I could tell from the way she came stomping down the hall. The fag and the wine, that just gave her an excuse to have a go at me. That's what she's like.'

'But you stayed the night, anyway?'

'Yeah. She said I was too drunk to drive, which was rubbish, I weren't drunk, and then she told me to go and check on the horses, because she had a phone call to make.'

'Did you hear her make the call?'

Tegan rearranged herself in the too-high chair, so that the elbow of her smoking arm was cupped in her free hand, her eyes slightly narrowed against the smoke, a pose she evidently thought appropriate while dealing with a tricky private detective.

'I dunno if I should say.'

'How about I suggest a name and you can nod if it's the right one?'

'Go on, then,' said Tegan, with the mingled mistrust and curiosity of one who has been promised a magic trick.

'Henry Drummond,' said Strike. 'She was leaving a message to say that she wanted a valuation on a necklace?'

Impressed against her will, Tegan nodded.

'Yeah,' she said. 'That's right.'

'So you went out to check on the horses . . . ?'

'Yeah, and when I got back Mrs Chiswell said I should stay over anyway, because she needed me early, so I did.'

'And where did *she* sleep?' asked Robin.

'Well – upstairs,' said Tegan, with a surprised laugh. 'Obviously. In her bedroom.'

'You're sure she was there all night?' asked Robin.

'Yeah,' said Tegan, with another little laugh. 'Her bedroom was next to mine. They're the only two with windows that face the stables. I could hear her going to bed.'

'You're sure she didn't leave the house during the night? Didn't drive anywhere, as far as you know?' asked Strike.

'No. I'd've heard the car. There are potholes everywhere round that house, you can't leave quietly. Anyway, I met her next morning on the landing, heading for the bathroom in her nightie.'

'What time would that have been?'

''Bout half-seven. We had breakfast together in the kitchen.'

'Was she still angry with you?'

'Bit ratty,' admitted Tegan.

'You didn't happen to hear her take another call, round about breakfast time?'

Frankly admiring, Tegan said:

'You mean, from Mr Chiswell? Yeah. She went out of the kitchen to take it. All I heard was "No, I mean it this time, Jasper". Sounded like a row. I've told the police this. I thought they must've argued in London and that's why she'd come home early instead of staying up there.

'Then I went outside to muck out, and she came out and she was schooling Brandy, that's one of her mares, and then,' said Tegan, with a slight hesitation, '*he* arrived. Raphael, you know. The son.'

'And what happened then?' asked Strike.

Tegan hesitated.

'They had a row, didn't they?' said Strike, mindful of how much of Tegan's break was slipping away.

'Yeah,' said Tegan, smiling in frank wonderment. 'You know *everything!*'

'D'you know what it was about?'

'Same thing she was phoning that bloke about, night before.'

'The necklace? Mrs Chiswell wanting to sell it?'

'Yeah.'

'Where were you when they were having the row?'

'Still mucking out. He got out of his car and went marching up to her in the outdoor school—'

Robin, seeing Strike's perplexity, muttered, 'Like a paddock where you train horses.'

'Ah,' he said.

'—yeah,' said Tegan, 'that's where she was schooling Brandy. First they were talking and I couldn't hear what they were saying and then it turned into a proper shouting match and she dismounted and yelled at me to come and untack Brandy – take off the saddle and bridle,' she added kindly, in case Strike hadn't understood, 'and they marched off into the house and I could hear them still having a go at each other as they disappeared.

'She never liked him,' said Tegan. 'Raphael. Thought he was spoiled. Always slagging him off. *I* thought he was all right, personally,' she said, with a would-be dispassionate air at odds with her heightened colour.

'Can you remember what they were saying to each other?'

'A bit,' said Tegan. 'He was telling her she couldn't sell it, that it belonged to his dad or something, and she told him to mind his own business.'

'Then what happened?'

'They went inside, I kept mucking out, and after a bit,' said Tegan, faltering slightly, 'I saw a police car coming up the drive and . . . yeah, it was awful. Policewoman come and asked me to go inside and help. I went in the kitchen and Mrs Chiswell was white as a sheet and all over the place. They wanted me to show them where the teabags were. I made her a hot drink and he – Raphael – made her sit down. He was really nice to her,' said Tegan, 'considering she'd just been calling him every name under the sun.'

Strike checked his watch.

'I know you haven't got long. Just a couple more things.'

'All right,' she said.

'There was an incident over a year ago,' said Strike, 'where Mrs Chiswell attacked Mr Chiswell with a hammer.'

'Oh, God, yeah,' said Tegan. 'Yeah . . . she really lost it. That was right after Lady was put down, start of the summer. She was Mrs Chiswell's favourite mare and Mrs Chiswell come home and the vet had already done it. She'd wanted to be there when it happened and she went crazy when she come back and seen the knacker's van.'

'How long had she known that the mare would have to be put down?' asked Robin.

'Those last two, three days, I think we all knew, really,' said Tegan sadly. 'But she was such a lovely horse, we kept hoping she'd pull through. The vet had waited for hours for Mrs Chiswell to come home, but Lady was suffering and he couldn't wait around all day, so . . . '

Tegan made a gesture of hopelessness.

'Any idea what made her go up to London that day, if she knew Lady was dying?' asked Strike.

Tegan shook her head.

'Can you talk us through exactly what happened, when she attacked her husband? Did she say anything first?'

'No,' said Tegan. 'She come into the yard, seen what had happened, ran towards Mr Chiswell, grabbed the hammer and just swung for him. Blood everywhere. It was horrible,' said Tegan, with patent sincerity. 'Awful.'

'What did she do after she'd hit him?' asked Robin.

'Just stood there. The expression on her face . . . it was like a *demon* or something,' said Tegan unexpectedly. 'I thought he was dead, thought she'd killed him.

'They put her away for a couple of weeks, you know. She went off to some hospital. I had to do the horses alone . . .

'We were all gutted about Lady. I loved that mare and I thought she was going to make it, but she'd given up, she lay down and wouldn't eat. I couldn't blame Mrs Chiswell for being upset, but . . . she could've killed him. Blood everywhere,' she repeated. 'I wanted to leave. Told my mum. Mrs Chiswell scared me, that night.'

'So what made you stay?' asked Strike.

'I dunno, really ... Mr Chiswell wanted me to, and I was fond of the horses. Then she came out of hospital and she was really depressed and I suppose I felt sorry for her. I kept finding her crying in Lady's empty stall.'

'Was Lady the mare that Mrs Chiswell wanted to – er – what's the right term?' Strike asked Robin.

'Put in foal?' Robin suggested.

'Yeah ... put in foal to the famous stallion?'

'Totilas?' said Tegan, with the ghost of an eye roll. 'No, it was Brandy she wanted to breed from, but Mr Chiswell was having none of it. Totilas! He costs a fortune.'

'So I heard. She didn't by any chance mention using a different stallion? There's one called "Blanc de Blancs", I don't know whether—'

'Never heard of him,' said Tegan. 'No, it *had* to be Totilas, he was the best, she was fixated on using him. That's what she's like, Mrs Chiswell. When she gets an idea in her head you can't shift it. She was going to breed this beautiful Grand Prix horse and ... you know she lost a baby, don't you?'

Strike and Robin nodded.

'Mum felt sorry for her, she thought the thing about getting a foal was, you know, a sort of substitute. Mum thinks it was all to do with the baby, how Mrs Chiswell's mood went up and down all the time.

'Like, one day, a few weeks after she came out of hospital, I remember, she was *manic*. I think it was the drugs they had her on. High as a kite. Singing in the yard. And I said to her, "You're cheerful, Mrs C", and she laughed and said, "Oh, I've been working on Jasper and I think I'm nearly there, I think he's going to let me use Totilas after all." It was all rubbish. I asked him and he was really grumpy about it, said it was wishful thinking and he could hardly afford as many horses as she'd already got.'

'You don't think he might've surprised her,' said Strike, 'by offering her a different stallion to breed from? A cheaper one?'

'That would just've annoyed her,' said Tegan. 'It was Totilas or nothing.' She stubbed out the cigarette Strike had given her, checked her watch and said regretfully, 'I've only got a couple more minutes.'

'Two more things, and we're done,' said Strike. 'I've heard that your family knew a girl called Suki Lewis, years ago? She was a runaway from care—'

'You know *everything*!' said Tegan again, delightedly. 'How did you know that?'

'Billy Knight told me. D'you happen to know what happened to Suki?'

'Yeah, she went to Aberdeen. She was in our Dan's class at school. Her mum was a nightmare: drink and drugs and all sorts. Then the mum goes on a real bender and that's how Suki got put into care. She ran away to find her dad. He worked on the North Sea rigs.'

'And you think she found her father, do you?' asked Strike.

With a triumphant air, Tegan reached into her back pocket for her mobile. After a few clicks, she presented Strike with the Facebook page she had brought up for a beaming brunette, who stood posing with a posse of girlfriends in front of a swimming pool in Ibiza. Through the tan, the bleached smile and the false eyelashes, Strike discerned the palimpsest of the thin, buck-toothed girl from the old photograph. The page was captioned 'Susanna McNeil'.

'See?' said Tegan happily. 'Her dad took her in with his new family. "Susanna" was her proper name but her mum called her "Suki". My mum's friends with Susanna's auntie. Says she's doing great.'

'You're quite sure this is her?' asked Strike.

'Yeah, of course,' said Tegan. 'We were all pleased for her. She was a nice girl.'

She checked her watch again.

''M'sorry, but that's my break over, I've got to go.'

'One more question,' said Strike. 'How well did your brothers know the Knight family?'

'Quite well,' said Tegan. 'The boys were in different years at school but yeah, they knew them through working at Chiswell House.'

'What do your brothers do now, Tegan?'

'Paul's managing a farm over near Aylesbury now and Dan's up in London doing landscape – why are you writing this down?' she said, alarmed for the first time at the sight of Strike's pen moving across his notebook. 'You mustn't tell my brothers I've spoken to you! They'll go mad if they think I've talked about what went on up at the house!'

'Really? What *did* go on up there?' Strike asked.

Tegan looked uncertainly from him to Robin and back again.

'You already know, don't you?'

And when neither Strike nor Robin responded she said:

'Listen, Dan and Paul just helped out with transporting them. Loading them up and that. And it was legal back then!'

'What was legal?' asked Strike.

'I *know* you know,' said Tegan, half-worried, half-amused. 'Someone's been talking, haven't they? Is it Jimmy Knight? He was back not long ago, sniffing around, wanting to talk to Dan. Anyway, everyone knew, locally. It was supposed to be hush–hush, but we all knew about Jack.'

'Knew *what* about him?' asked Strike.

'Well . . . that he was the gallows maker.'

Strike absorbed the information without so much as a quiver of the eyelid. Robin wasn't sure her own expression had remained as impassive.

'But you already knew,' said Tegan. 'Didn't you?'

'Yeah,' said Strike, to reassure her. 'We knew.'

'Thought so,' said Tegan, relieved and sliding down, inelegantly, from her chair. 'But if you see Dan, don't tell him I said. He's like Mum. "Least said, soonest mended." Mind, none of us think there was anything wrong with it. This country'd be better with the death penalty, if you ask me.'

'Thanks for meeting us, Tegan,' said Strike. She blushed slightly as she shook first his hand, then Robin's.

'No problem,' she said, now seeming reluctant to leave them. 'Are you going to stay for the races? Brown Panther's running in the two-thirty.'

'We might,' said Strike, 'we've got a bit of time to kill before our next appointment.'

'I've got a tenner on Brown Panther,' Tegan confided. 'Well . . . bye, then.'

She had gone a few steps when she wheeled around and returned to Strike, now even pinker in the face.

'Can I have a selfie with you?'

'Er,' said Strike, carefully not catching Robin's eye, 'I'd rather not, if it's all the same to you.'

'Can I have your autograph, then?'

Deciding that this was the lesser of two evils, Strike wrote his signature on a napkin.

'Thanks.'

Clutching her napkin, Tegan departed at last. Strike waited until she had disappeared into the bar before turning to Robin, who was already busy on her phone.

'Six years ago,' she said, reading from the mobile screen, 'an EU directive came in banning member states from exporting torture equipment. Until then, it was perfectly legal to export British-made gallows abroad.'

64

Speak so that I can understand you.

Henrik Ibsen, *Rosmersholm*

'"I acted within the law and in accordance with my conscience",' Strike quoted Chiswell's gnomic pronouncement back in Pratt's. 'So he did. Never hid the fact that he was pro-hanging, did he? I suppose he provided the wood from his grounds.'

'And the space for Jack o'Kent to build them – which is why Jack o'Kent warned Raff not to go into the barn, when he was a child.'

'And they probably split the profits.'

'Wait,' said Robin, remembering what Flick had shrieked after the minister's car, the night of the Paralympic reception. '"He put the horse on them" . . . Cormoran, d'you think—?'

'Yeah, I do,' said Strike, his thoughts keeping pace with hers. 'The last thing Billy said to me at the hospital was "I hated putting the horse on them". Even in the middle of a psychotic episode, Billy could carve a perfect White Horse of Uffington into wood . . . Jack o'Kent had his boys carving it onto trinkets for tourists and onto gallows for export . . . nice little father-son business he had going, eh?'

Strike clinked his beer glass against her little champagne bottle and downed the last dregs of his Doom Bar.

'To our first proper breakthrough. If Jack o'Kent was putting a little bit of local branding on the gallows, they were traceable back to him, weren't they? And not only to him: to the Vale of the White Horse, and to Chiswell. It all fits, Robin. Remember Jimmy's placard, with the pile of dead black children on it? Chiswell and Jack o'Kent were flogging them abroad – Middle East or Africa, probably. But Chiswell can't have known they had the horse carved into them – Christ, no, he *definitely* didn't,' said Strike, remembering Chiswell's words in Pratt's, 'because when he told me there were photographs, he said "there are no distinguishing marks, so far as I'm aware".'

'You know how Jimmy said he was owed?' said Robin, following her own train of thought. 'And how Raff said Kinvara thought he had a legitimate claim for money, at first? What d'you think are the chances that Jack o'Kent left some gallows ready for sale when he died—'

'—and Chiswell sold them without bothering to track down and pay off Jack's sons? Very smart,' said Strike, nodding. 'So for Jimmy, this all started as a demand for his rightful share of his father's estate. Then, when Chiswell denied he owed them anything, it turned into blackmail.'

'Not a very strong case for blackmail, though, when you think about it, is it?' said Robin. 'D'you really think Chiswell would have lost a lot of voters over this? It *was* legal at the time he sold them, and he was publicly pro-death penalty, so nobody could say he was a hypocrite. Half the country thinks we should bring back hanging. I'm not sure the kind of people who vote for Chiswell would have thought he did much wrong.'

'Another good point,' conceded Strike, 'and Chiswell could probably have brazened it out. He'd survived worse: impregnating his mistress, divorce, an illegitimate kid, Raphael's drugged-up car crash and imprisonment . . .

'But there were "unintended consequences", remember?' Strike asked thoughtfully. 'What did those pictures at the Foreign Office show, that Winn was so keen to get hold of? And who's that "Samuel" Winn just mentioned on the phone?'

Strike pulled out his notebook and jotted down a few sentences in his dense, hard-to-read handwriting.

'At least,' said Robin, 'we've got confirmation of Raff's story. The necklace.'

Strike grunted, still writing. When he'd finished, he said, 'Yeah, that was useful, as far as it went.'

'What d'you mean, "as far as it went"?'

'Him heading down to Oxfordshire to stop Kinvara running off with a valuable necklace is a better story than the trying-to-stop-her-topping-herself one,' said Strike, 'but I still don't think we're being told everything.'

'Why not?'

'Same objection as before. Why would Chiswell send Raphael down there as his emissary, when his wife hated him? Can't see why Raphael would be any more persuasive than Izzy.'

'Have you taken against Raphael, or something?'

Strike raised his eyebrows.

'I haven't got personal feelings for him one way or the other. You?'

'Of course not,' said Robin, a little too quickly. 'So, what was that theory you mentioned, before Tegan arrived?'

'Oh, yeah,' said Strike. 'Well, it might be nothing, but a couple of things Raphael said to you jumped out at me. Got me thinking.'

'What things?'

Strike told her.

'I can't see what's significant about any of that.'

'Maybe not in isolation, but try putting it together with what Della told me.'

'Which bit?'

But even when Strike reminded her what Della had said, Robin remained confused.

'I don't see the connection.'

Strike got up, grinning.

'Mull it over for a while. I'm going to ring Izzy and tell her Tegan's let the cat out of the bag about the gallows.'

He walked away and disappeared into the crowds in search of a quiet spot from which to make his call, leaving Robin to swill the now-tepid champagne around in the miniature bottle and ponder what Strike had just said. Nothing coherent emerged from her exhausted attempts to connect the disparate pieces of information, and after a few minutes she gave up and simply sat there, enjoying the warm breeze that lifted the hair from her shoulders.

In spite of her tiredness, the shattered state of her marriage and her very real apprehension about going digging in the dell later that night, it was pleasant to sit here, breathing in the smells of the racecourse, of soft air redolent of turf, leather and horse, catching trails of perfume from the women now moving away from the bar towards the stands, and the smoky whiff of venison burgers cooking in a van nearby. For the first time in a week, Robin realised that she was actually hungry.

She picked up the cork of the champagne bottle and turned it over in her fingers, remembering another cork, the one she had saved from her twenty-first birthday party, for which Matthew had come home from university with a bunch of new friends, Sarah among them. Looking back, she knew that her parents had wanted to throw a big party for her twenty-first in compensation for her not having the graduation party they had all been expecting.

Strike was taking a long time. Perhaps Izzy was spilling all the details, now that they knew what the substance of the blackmail had been about, or perhaps, Robin thought, she simply wanted to keep him on the phone.

Izzy isn't his type, though.

The thought startled her a little. She felt slightly guilty for giving it headspace and even more uncomfortable when it was jostled out of the way by another.

All his girlfriends have been beautiful. Izzy isn't.

Strike attracted remarkably good-looking women, when you considered his generally bearlike appearance and what he himself had referred to in her hearing as 'pube-like' hair.

I bet I look gross, was Robin's next, inconsequential thought. Puffy-faced and pale when she had got in the Land Rover that morning, she had cried a lot since. She was half-deliberating whether she had time to find a bathroom and at least brush her hair, when she spotted Strike walking back towards her holding a venison burger in each hand and a betting slip in his mouth.

'Izzy isn't picking up,' he informed her through clenched teeth. 'Left a message. Grab one of these and come on. I've just put a tenner each way on Brown Panther.'

'I didn't realise you're a betting man,' said Robin.

'I'm not,' said Strike, removing the betting slip from his teeth and pocketing it, 'but I'm feeling lucky today. Come on, we'll watch the race.'

As Strike turned away, Robin slid the champagne cork discreetly into her pocket.

'*Brown* Panther,' Strike said through a mouthful of burger, as they approached the track. 'Except he isn't, is he? Black mane, so he's—'

'—a bay, yes,' said Robin. 'Are you upset he isn't a panther, either?'

'Just trying to follow the logic. That stallion I found online – Blanc de Blancs – was chestnut, not white.'

'Not grey, you mean.'

'Fuck's sake,' muttered Strike, half-amused, half-exasperated.

65

I wonder how many there are who would do as much – who dare do it?

Henrik Ibsen, *Rosmersholm*

Brown Panther came in second. They spent Strike's winnings among the food and coffee tents, killing the hours of daylight until it was time to head for Woolstone and the dell. While panic fluttered in Robin's chest every time she thought of the tools in the back of the Land Rover and the dark basin full of nettles, Strike distracted her, whether intentionally or not, by a persistent refusal to explain how the testimony of Della Winn and Raphael Chiswell fitted together, or what conclusions he had drawn from it.

'Think,' he kept saying, 'just think.'

But Robin was exhausted, and it was easier to simply push him to explain over successive coffees and sandwiches, all the while savouring this unusual interlude in their working lives, for she and Strike had never before spent hours together unless at some time of crisis.

But as the sun sank ever closer to the horizon, Robin's thoughts darted more insistently towards the dell, and each time they did so her stomach did a small backflip. Noticing her increasingly preoccupied silences, Strike suggested for the second time that she stay in the Land Rover while he and Barclay dug.

'No,' said Robin tersely. 'I didn't come to sit in the car.'

It took them three-quarters of an hour to reach Woolstone. Colour was bleeding rapidly out of the sky to the west as they descended for the second time into the Vale of the White Horse, and by the time they had reached their destination a few feeble stars were spotting the dust-coloured heavens. Robin turned the Land Rover onto the over-grown track leading to Steda Cottage and the car rocked and pitched its way over the deep furrows and tangled thorns and branches, into the deeper darkness bestowed by the dense canopy above.

'Get as far in as you can,' Strike instructed her, checking the time on his mobile. 'Barclay's got to park behind us. He should've been here already, I told him nine o'clock.'

Robin parked and cut the engine, eyeing the thick woodland that lay between the track and Chiswell House. Unseen they might be, but they were still trespassing. Her anxiety about possible detection was as nothing, however, to her very real fear of what lay beneath the tangled nettles at the bottom of that dark basin outside Steda Cottage, and so she returned to the subject she had been using as a distraction all afternoon.

'I've told you – *think*,' said Strike, for the umpteenth time. 'Think about the lachesis pills. You're the one who thought they were significant. Think about all those odd things Chiswell kept doing: taunting Aamir in front of everyone, saying Lachesis "knew when everyone's number would be up", telling you "one by one, they trip themselves up", looking for Freddie's money clip, which turned up in his pocket.'

'I have thought about those things, but I still don't see how—'

'The helium and tubing entering the house disguised as a crate of champagne. Somebody knew he wouldn't want to drink it, because he was allergic. Ask yourself how Flick knew Jimmy had a claim on Chiswell. Think about Flick's row with her flatmate Laura—'

'How can *that* have anything to do with this?'

'Think!' said Strike, infuriatingly. 'No amitriptyline was found in the empty orange juice carton in Chiswell's bin. Remember Kinvara, obsessing over Chiswell's whereabouts. Have a guess what little Francesca at Drummond's art gallery is going to tell me if I ever get her on the phone. Think about that call to Chiswell's constit-uency office about people "pissing themselves as they die" – which isn't conclusive in itself, I grant you, but it's bloody suggestive when you stop to think about it—'

'You're winding me up,' said the incredulous Robin. 'Your idea connects all of that? And makes sense of it?'

'Yep,' said Strike smugly, 'and it also explains how Winn and Aamir knew there were photographs at the Foreign Office, presumably of Jack o'Kent's gallows in use, when Aamir hadn't worked there in months and Winn, so far as we know, had never set foot—'

Strike's mobile rang. He checked the screen.

'Izzy calling back. I'll take it outside. I want to smoke.'

He got out of the car. Robin heard him say, 'Hi,' before he slammed the door. She sat waiting for him, her mind buzzing. Either Strike had genuinely had a brainwave, or he was taking the mickey, and she slightly inclined to the latter, so utterly disconnected did the separate bits of information he had just listed seem.

Five minutes later, Strike returned to the passenger seat.

'Our client's unhappy,' he reported, slamming the door again. 'Tegan was supposed to be telling us that Kinvara crept back out that night to kill Chiswell, not confirming her alibi and blabbing about Chiswell flogging gallows.'

'Izzy admitted it?'

'Didn't have much choice, did she? But she didn't like it. Very insistent on telling me that exporting gallows was legal at the time. I put it to her that her father had defrauded Jimmy and Billy out of their money, and you were right. There were two sets of gallows built and ready to sell when Jack o'Kent died and nobody bothered to tell his sons. She liked admitting that even less.'

'D'you think she's worried they'll mount a claim on Chiswell's estate?'

'I can't see that it'd do Jimmy's reputation much good in the circles he moves in, accepting money made from hanging people in the Third World,' said Strike, 'but you never know.'

A car sped past on the road behind them and Strike craned around hopefully.

'Thought that might be Barclay ...' He checked his watch. 'Maybe he's missed the turning.'

'Cormoran,' said Robin, who was far less interested in either Izzy's mood or Barclay's whereabouts than in the theory Strike was withholding from her, 'have you *seriously* got an idea that explains everything you just told me?'

'Yeah,' said Strike, scratching his chin, 'I have. Trouble is, it brings us closer to *who*, but I'm still damned if I can see *why* they did it, unless it was done out of blind hatred – but this doesn't feel like a red-blooded crime of passion, does it? This wasn't a hammer round the head. This was a well-planned execution.'

'What happened to "means before motive"?'

'I've been concentrating on means. That's how I got here.'

'You won't even tell me "he" or "she"?'

'No good mentor would deprive you of the satisfaction of working it out for yourself. Any biscuits left?'

'No.'

'Lucky I've still got this, then,' Strike said, producing a Twix from his pocket, unwrapping it and handing her half, which she took with a bad grace that amused him.

Neither spoke until they had finished eating. Then Strike said, far more soberly than hitherto:

'Tonight's important. If there's nothing buried in a pink blanket at the bottom of the dell, the whole Billy business is finished: he imagined the strangling, we've set his mind at rest and I get to try and prove my theory about Chiswell's death, unencumbered by distractions, without worrying where a dead kid fits in and who killed her.'

'Or him,' Robin reminded Strike. 'You said Billy wasn't sure which it was.'

As she said it, her unruly imagination showed her a small skeleton wrapped in the rotten remains of a blanket. Would it be possible to tell whether the body had been male or female from what was left? Would there be a hair grip or a shoelace, buttons, a hank of long hair?

Let there be nothing, she thought. *God, let there be nothing there.*

But aloud, she asked:

'And if there *is* – something – someone – buried in the dell?'

'Then my theory's wrong, because I can't see how a child strangling in Oxfordshire fits with anything I've just mentioned.'

'It doesn't have to,' said Robin reasonably. 'You could be right about who killed Chiswell, and this could be an entirely separate—'

'No,' Strike said, shaking his head. 'It's too much of a coincidence. If there's something buried in the dell, it connects to everything else. One brother witnessing a murder as a child, the other blackmailing a murdered man twenty years later, the kid being buried on Chiswell's land . . . if there's a child buried in the dell, it fits in somewhere. But I'll lay odds there's nothing there. If I seriously thought there was a body in the dell, I'd've tried to persuade the police to do the job. Tonight's for Billy. I promised him.'

They sat watching the track fade gradually from sight in the darkness, Strike occasionally checking his mobile.

'Where's bloody Barclay got—? Ah!'

Headlights had just swung onto the track behind them. Barclay advanced an old Golf up the track and braked, turning off his lights. In her wing mirror, Robin watched his silhouette leave the car, turning into the flesh and blood Barclay as he reached Strike's window, carrying a kit bag just like the detective's.

'Evenin',' he said laconically. 'Nice night for a grave robbin'.'

'You're late,' said Strike.

'Aye, I know. Just got a call from Flick. Thought you'd want tae hear what she's got tae say.'

'Get in the back,' Strike suggested. 'You can tell us while we're waiting. We'll give it ten minutes, make sure it's properly dark.'

Barclay clambered into the back of the Land Rover and closed the doors. Strike and Robin twisted around in their seats to talk to him.

'So, she calls me, greetin'—'

'English translation, please.'

'Cryin', then – not to mention shittin' herself. The police came calling today.'

''Bout bloody time,' said Strike. 'And?'

'They searched the bathroom and found Chiswell's note. She's been interviewed.'

'What was her explanation for having it?'

'Didnae confide in me. All she wanted was to know where Jimmy is. She's in a right fuckin' state. It was all "just tell Jimmy they've got it, he'll know whut I mean".'

'Where is Jimmy, d'you know?'

'Havenae a scooby. Saw him yesterday and he didnae mention any plans, but he told me he'd pissed off Flick by askin' if she had Bobbi Cunliffe's number. He took a liking to young Bobbi,' said Barclay, grinning at Robin. 'Flick told him she didnae know and wanted to know why he was so interested. Jimmy said he was jus' tryin' to get Bobbi along to a Real Socialist meetin', but, y'know, Flick's not that fuckin' dumb.'

'D'you think she realises it was me who tipped off the police?' asked Robin.

'Not yet,' said Barclay. 'She's panickin'.'

'All right,' said Strike, squinting up at the little of the sky they could see through the foliage overhead, 'I think we should get started. Grab that bag beside you, Barclay, I've got tools and gloves in there.'

'How're ye gonnae dig wi' your leg like that?' asked Barclay sceptically.

'You can't do it on your own,' said Strike, 'we'll still be here tomorrow night.'

'I'm digging, too,' said Robin firmly. She felt braver after Strike's assurances that they were highly unlikely to find anything in the dell. 'Pass me those wellies, Sam.'

Strike was already extracting torch and walking stick from his kit bag.

'I'll carry it,' offered Barclay, and there was a sound of heavy metal tools shifting as he hoisted Strike's bag onto his shoulder along with his own.

The three of them set off along the track, Robin and Barclay matching their pace to Strike's, who progressed carefully, focusing the beam of his torch on the ground and making regular use of the stick, both to lean on and push obstacles out of his way. Their footsteps were deadened by the soft ground, but the quiet night amplified the chink and clatter of the tools carried by Barclay, the rustling of tiny, unseen creatures fleeing the giants who had invaded their wilderness and, from the direction of Chiswell House, the barking of a dog. Robin remembered the Norfolk terrier, and hoped he wasn't loose.

When they reached the clearing, Robin saw that night had turned the derelict cottage into a witch's lair. It was easy to imagine figures lurking behind the cracked windows and, telling herself firmly that the situation was quite creepy enough without imagining fresh horrors, she turned away from it. With a soft 'ooft', Barclay let the kit bags fall onto the ground at the lip of the dell and unzipped both. By the light of the torch, Robin saw a wide array of tools: a pick, a mattock, two pinchbars, a fork, a small axe and three spades, one of them with a pointed head. There were also several pairs of thick gardening gloves.

'Aye, that should do us,' said Barclay, squinting into the dark basin below them. 'We'll want to clear that before we've got any chance o' breakin' the ground.'

'Right,' said Robin, reaching for a pair of gloves.

'Ye sure about this, big man?' Barclay asked Strike, who had done the same.

'I can pull up nettles, for Christ's sake,' said Strike irritably.

'Bring the axe, Robin,' said Barclay, grabbing the mattock and a pinchbar. 'Some o' those bushes'll need hacked down.'

The three of them slid and stumbled down the steep side of the dell and set to work. For nearly an hour they hacked at sinewy branches and tugged up nettles, occasionally swapping tools or returning to the upper ground to fetch different ones.

In spite of the gathering cool of the night, Robin was soon sweating, peeling off layers as she worked. Strike, on the other hand, was devoting a considerable amount of energy to pretending that the constant bending and twisting on slippery, uneven ground wasn't hurting the end of his stump. The darkness concealed his winces, and he was careful to rearrange his features whenever Barclay or Robin turned on the torch to check on their progress.

Physical activity was helping dispel Robin's fear of what could be hidden beneath their feet. Perhaps, she thought, this was what it was like in the army: hard manual work and the camaraderie of your colleagues helping you focus on something other than the grisly reality of what might lie ahead. The two ex-soldiers had bent to their task methodically and without complaint except for occasional curses as stubborn roots and branches tore at fabric and flesh.

'Time tae dig,' said Barclay at last, when the bottom of the basin was as clear as they could reasonably make it. 'Ye'll need to get out of it, Strike.'

'I'll start, Robin can take over,' said Strike. 'Go on,' he said to her, 'take a break, hold the torch steady for us and pass me down the fork.'

Growing up with three brothers had taught Robin valuable lessons about the male ego, and about picking her fights. Convinced that Strike's order was dictated more by pride than by sense, she nevertheless complied, clambering up the steep side of the dell, there to sit and hold the beam of the torch steady while they worked, occasionally passing down different tools to help them remove rocks and tackle particularly hard stretches of ground.

It was a slow job. Barclay dug three times as fast as Strike, who Robin could see was immediately struggling, especially with pressing the pointed head spade down into the earth with a foot, his prosthesis being unreliable if asked to support his entire weight on the uneven ground, and excruciating when pressed down against resistant metal. Minute by minute she held off intervening, until a muttered '*fuck*' escaped Strike, and he bent over, grimacing in pain.

'Shall I take over?' she suggested.

'Think you're going to have to,' he muttered ungraciously.

He dragged himself back out of the dell, trying not to put any more weight on his stump, taking the torch from a descending Robin and holding it steady for the other two as they worked, the end of his stump throbbing and, he suspected, rubbed raw.

Barclay had created a short channel a couple of feet deep before he took his first break, clambering out of the hole to fetch a bottle of water from his kit bag. While he drank and Robin took a rest, leaning on the handle of her spade, the sound of barking reached them again. Barclay squinted towards the unseen Chiswell House.

'What kind of dogs has she got in there?' he asked.

'Old Lab and a yappy bastard of a terrier,' said Strike.

'Don't like our chances if she lets them oot,' said Barclay, wiping his mouth on his arm. 'Terrier'll get straight through those bushes. They've got fuckin' good hearin', terriers.'

'Better hope she doesn't let them out, then,' said Strike, but he added, 'Give it five, Robin,' and turned off the torch.

Robin, too, climbed out of the basin and accepted a fresh bottle of water from Barclay. Now that she was no longer digging, the chill made her exposed flesh creep. The fluttering and scurrying of small creatures in the grass and trees seemed extraordinarily loud in the darkness. Still the dog barked, and, distantly, Robin thought she heard a woman shout.

'Did you hear that?'

'Aye. Sounded like she was telling it to shut up,' said Barclay.

They waited. At last, the terrier stopped barking.

'Give it a few more minutes,' said Strike. 'Let it fall asleep.'

They waited, the whispering of every leaf magnified in the darkness, until Robin and Barclay lowered themselves back into the dell and began to dig again.

Robin's muscles were now begging for mercy, her palms beginning to blister beneath the gloves. The deeper they dug, the harder the job became, the soil compacted and full of rocks. Barclay's end of the trench was considerably deeper than Robin's.

'Let me do a bit,' Strike suggested.

'No,' she snapped, too tired to be anything but blunt. 'You'll bugger your leg completely.'

'She's nae wrong, pal,' panted Barclay. 'Gie's another drink of water, I'm gaspin'.'

An hour later, Barclay was standing waist deep in soil and Robin's palms were bleeding beneath the overlarge gloves, which were rubbing away layers of skin as she used the blunt end of the mattock to try and prise a heavy rock out of the ground.

'Come – on – you – bloody – thing—'

'Want a hand?' offered Strike, readying himself to descend.

'Stay there,' she told him angrily. 'I'm not going to be able to help carry you back to the car, not after this—'

A final, involuntary yelp escaped her as she succeeded in

overturning the small boulder. A couple of tiny, wriggling insects attached to the underside slid away from the torchlight. Strike directed the beam back on Barclay.

'Cormoran,' said Robin sharply.

'What?'

'I need light.'

Something in her voice made Barclay stop digging. Rather than direct the beam back at her, and disregarding her warning of a moment ago, Strike slid back down into the pit, landing on the loose earth. The torchlight swung around, blinding Robin for a second.

'What've you seen?'

'Shine it here,' she said. 'On the rock.'

Barclay clambered towards them, his jeans covered from hem to pockets in soil.

Strike did as Robin asked. The three of them peered down at the encrusted surface of the rock. There, stuck to the mud, was a strand of what was plainly not vegetable matter, but wool fibres, faintly but distinctly pink.

They turned in unison to examine the indentation left in the ground where the rock had sat, Strike directing the torchlight into the hole.

'Oh, shit,' gasped Robin, and without thinking she clapped two muddy garden gloves to her face. A couple of inches of filthy material had been revealed, and in the strong beam of the torch, it, too, was pink.

'Give me that,' said Strike, tugging the mattock out of her hand.

'No—!'

But he almost pushed her aside. By the deflected torchlight she could see his expression, forbidding, furious, as though the pink blanket had grievously wronged him, as though he had suffered a personal affront.

'Barclay, you take this.'

He thrust the mattock at his subcontractor.

'Break this up, as much as you can. Try not to puncture the blanket. Robin, go to the other end. Use the fork. And mind my hands,' Strike told Barclay. Sticking the torch in his mouth so that he could see by its light, he fell to his knees in the dirt and began to move earth aside with his fingers.

'Listen,' whispered Robin, freezing.

The sound of the terrier's frenzied barking reached them once again through the night air.

'I yelled, didn't I, when I overturned the rock?' whispered Robin. 'I think I woke it up again.'

'Never mind that now,' said Strike, his fingers prising dirt away from the blanket. 'Dig.'

'But what if—?'

'We'll deal with that if it happens. *Dig.*'

Robin plied the fork. After a couple of minutes, Barclay swapped the mattock for a shovel. Slowly, the length of the pink blanket, its contents still buried too deep to remove, was revealed.

'That's no adult,' said Barclay, surveying the stretch of filthy blanket.

And still, the terrier continued to yap, distantly, from the direction of Chiswell House.

'We should call the polis, Strike,' said Barclay, pausing to wipe sweat and mud out of his eyes. 'Are we no disturbing a crime scene, here?'

Strike didn't answer. Feeling slightly sick, Robin watched his fingers feeling the shape of the thing that was hidden beneath the filthy blanket.

'Go up to my kit bag,' he told her. 'There's a knife in there. Stanley knife. Quickly.'

The terrier was still yapping distractedly. Robin thought it sounded louder. She clambered up the steep side of the dell, groped around in the dark depths of the bag, found the knife and slid back down to Strike.

'Cormoran, I think Sam's right,' she whispered. 'We should leave this to the—'

'Give me the knife,' he said, holding out his hand. 'Come on, quick, I can feel it. This is the skull. *Quickly!*'

Against her better instincts, she handed over the blade. There was a sound of puncturing fabric and then a ripping.

'What are you doing?' she gasped, watching Strike tugging at something in the ground.

'Jesus fuck, Strike,' said Barclay angrily, 'are ye tryin' to rip off its—?'

With a dreadful crunching noise, the earth gave up something large and white. Robin gave a small yelp, stepped backwards and fell, half-sitting, into the wall of the dell.

'Fuck,' repeated Barclay.

Strike shifted the torch to his free hand so as to shine it onto the thing he had just dragged out of the earth. Stunned, Robin and Barclay saw the discoloured and partially shattered skull of a horse.

66

Do not sit here musing and brooding over insoluble conundrums.

Henrik Ibsen, *Rosmersholm*

Protected through the years by the blanket, the skull shone pale in the torchlight, weirdly reptilian in the length of its nose and the sharpness of its mandibles. A few blunt teeth remained. There were cavities in the skull in addition to the eyeholes, one in the jaw, one to the side of the head, and around each, the bone was cracked and splintered.

'Shot,' said Strike, turning the skull slowly in his hands. A third indentation showed the course of another bullet, which had fractured but not penetrated the horse's head.

Robin knew she would have been feeling far worse had the skull been human, but she was nonetheless shaken by the noise it had made when released from the earth, and by the unexpected sight of this fragile shell of what had once lived and breathed, stripped bare by bacteria and insects.

'Vets euthanise horses with a single shot to the forehead,' she said. 'They don't spray them with bullets.'

'Rifle,' said Barclay authoritatively, clambering nearer to examine the skull. 'Someone's took pot shots at it.'

'Not that big, is it? Was it a foal?' Strike asked Robin.

'Maybe, but I think it looks more like a pony, or a miniature horse.'

He turned it slowly in his hands and all three of them watched the skull moving in the torchlight. They had expended so much pain and effort digging it out of the ground that it seemed to hold secrets beyond those of its mere existence.

'So Billy *did* witness a burial,' said Strike.

'But it wasn't a child. You won't have to rethink your theory,' said Robin.

'Theory?' repeated Barclay, and was ignored.

'I don't know, Robin,' said Strike, his face ghostly beyond the torchlight. 'If he didn't invent the burial, I don't think he invented—'

'Shit,' said Barclay. 'She's done it, she's let those fucking dogs out.'

The yapping of the terrier and the deeper, booming barks of the Labrador, no longer muffled by containing walls, came ringing through the night. Without ceremony, Strike dropped the skull.

'Barclay, grab all the tools and get out of here. We'll hold the dogs off.'

'What about—?'

'Leave it, there's no time to fill it in,' said Strike, already clambering out of the dell, ignoring the excruciating pain in the end of his stump. 'Robin, come on, you're with me—'

'What if she's called the police?' Robin said, reaching the top of the dell first and turning to help heave Strike up.

'We'll wing it,' he panted, 'come on, I want to stop the dogs before they get to Sam.'

The woods were dense and tangled. Strike had left his walking stick behind. Robin held his arm as he limped as fast as he could, grunting with pain every time he asked his stump to bear his weight. Robin glimpsed a pinprick of light through the trees. Somebody had come out of the house with a torch.

Suddenly, the Norfolk terrier burst through the undergrowth, barking ferociously.

'Good boy, yes, you found us!' Robin panted.

Ignoring her friendly overture it launched itself at her, trying to bite. She kicked out at it with her Wellingtoned foot, holding it at bay while sounds reached them of the heavier Labrador crashing towards them.

581

'Little fucker,' said Strike, trying to repel the Norfolk terrier as it darted around them, snarling, but seconds later the terrier had caught wind of Barclay: it turned its head towards the dell and, before either of them could stop it, took off again, yapping frenziedly.

'Shit,' said Robin.

'Never mind, keep going,' said Strike, though the end of his stump was burning and he wondered how much longer it would support him.

They had managed only a few more paces when the fat Labrador reached them.

'Good boy, yes, good boy,' Robin crooned, and the Labrador, less enthusiastic about the chase, allowed her to secure a tight grip on its collar. 'Come on, come with us,' said Robin, and she half dragged it, with Strike still leaning on her, towards the overgrown croquet lawn where they now saw a torch bobbing ever nearer through the darkness. A shrill voice called:

'Badger! Rattenbury! Who's that? Who's there?'

The silhouette behind the torchlight was female and bulky.

'It's all right, Mrs Chiswell!' called Robin. 'It's only us!'

'Who's "us"? Who are you?'

'Follow my lead,' Strike muttered to Robin, and he called, 'Mrs Chiswell, it's Cormoran Strike and Robin Ellacott.'

'What are you doing here?' she shouted, across the diminishing space between them.

'We were interviewing Tegan Butcher in the village, Mrs Chiswell,' called Strike, as he, Robin and the reluctant Badger made their laborious way through the long grass. 'We were driving back this way and we saw two people entering your property.'

'What two people? Where?'

'They entered the woods back there,' said Strike. From the depths of the trees, the Norfolk terrier was still frenziedly barking. 'We didn't have your number, or we'd have called to warn you.'

Within a few feet of her now, they saw that Kinvara was wearing a thick, padded coat over a short nightdress of black silk, her legs bare above Wellington boots. Her suspicion, shock and incredulity met Strike's total assurance.

'Thought we ought to do something, seeing as we were the only people who witnessed it,' he gasped, wincing a little as he hobbled up to her with Robin's assistance, self-deprecatingly heroic. 'Apologies,' he added, coming to a halt, 'for the state of us. Those woods are muddy and I fell over a couple of times.'

A cold breeze swept the dark lawn. Kinvara stared at him, flummoxed, suspicious, then turned her face in the direction of the terrier's continued barking.

'RATTENBURY!' she shouted. '*RATTENBURY!*'

She turned back to Strike.

'What did they look like?

'Men,' invented Strike, 'young and fit from the way they were moving. We knew you'd had trouble with trespassers before—'

'Yes. Yes, I have,' said Kinvara, sounding frightened. She seemed to take in Strike's condition for the first time, as he leaned heavily on Robin, face contorted with pain.

'I suppose you'd better come in.'

'Thanks very much,' said Strike gratefully, 'very kind of you.'

Kinvara jerked the Labrador's collar out of Robin's grip and bellowed, 'RATTENBURY!' again, but the distantly barking terrier did not respond, so she dragged the Labrador, which was showing signs of rebellion, back towards the house, Robin and Strike following.

'What if she calls the police?' Robin muttered to Strike.

'Cross that bridge when we come to it,' he responded.

A floor-to-ceiling drawing room window stood open. Kinvara had evidently followed her frantic dogs through it, as the quickest route to the woods.

'We're pretty muddy,' Robin warned her, as they crunched their way across the gravel path that encircled the house.

'Just leave your boots outside,' said Kinvara, stepping into the drawing room without bothering to remove her own. 'I'm planning to change this carpet, anyway.'

Robin tugged off her wellies, followed Strike inside and closed the window.

The cold, dingy room was illuminated by a single lamp.

'Two men?' Kinvara repeated, turning again to Strike. 'Where exactly did you see them coming in?'

'Over the wall at the road,' said Strike.

'D'you think they knew you'd seen them?'

'Oh yeah,' said Strike. 'We pulled up, but they ran into the woods. Think they might've bottled it once we followed them, though, don't you?' he asked Robin.

'Yes,' said Robin, 'we think we heard them running back towards the road when you let the dogs out.'

'Rattenbury's still chasing someone – of course, that could be a fox – he goes crazy about the foxes in the woods,' said Kinvara.

Strike's attention had just been caught by a change to the room since the last time he had seen it. There was a fresh square of dark crimson wallpaper over the mantelpiece, where the painting of the mare and foal had hung.

'What happened to your picture?' he asked.

Kinvara turned to see what Strike was talking about. She answered, perhaps a few seconds too late:

'I sold it.'

'Oh,' said Strike. 'I thought you were particularly fond of that one?'

'Not since what Torquil said that day. I didn't like having it hanging there, after that.'

'Ah,' said Strike.

Rattenbury's persistent barking continued to echo from the woods where, Strike was certain, it had found Barclay, struggling back to his car with two kit bags full of tools. Now that Kinvara had released her hold on its collar, the fat Labrador let out a single booming bark and trotted to the window, where it began whining and pawing at the glass.

'The police won't get here in time even if I call them,' said Kinvara, half worried, half angry. 'I'm never top priority. They think I make it all up, these intruders.

'I'm going to check on the horses,' she said, coming to a decision, but instead of going out through the window, she stomped out of the drawing room into the hall and from there, as far as they could hear, into a different room.

'I hope the dog hasn't got Barclay,' Robin whispered.

'Better hope he hasn't brained it with a spade,' muttered Strike.

The door reopened. Kinvara had returned, and to Robin's consternation, she was carrying a revolver.

'I'll take that,' said Strike, hobbling forwards and taking the revolver out of her startled grip. He examined it. 'Harrington & Richardson 7-shot? This is illegal, Mrs Chiswell.'

'It was Jasper's,' she replied, as though this constituted a special permit, 'and I'd rather take—'

'I'll come with you to check on the horses,' said Strike firmly, 'and Robin can stay here and keep an eye on the house.'

Kinvara might have liked to protest, but Strike was already opening the drawing room window. Seizing its opportunity, the Labrador lumbered back out into the dark garden, its deep barks echoing around the grounds.

'Oh, for God's sake – you shouldn't have let him out – Badger!' shouted Kinvara. She whipped back around to Robin, said, 'mind you stay in this room!' then followed the Labrador back into the garden, Strike limping after her with the rifle. Both disappeared into the darkness. Robin stood where they had left her, struck by the vehemence of Kinvara's order.

The open window had admitted plenty of night air into what was already a chilly interior. Robin approached the log basket beside the fire, which was temptingly full of newspaper, sticks, logs and firelighters, but she could hardly build a fire in Kinvara's absence. The room was as shabby in every respect as she remembered it, the walls now denuded of everything but four prints of Oxfordshire landscapes. Outside in the grounds the two dogs continued to bark, but inside the room the only sound, which Robin hadn't noticed on her last visit, due to the family's talking and bickering, was the loud ticking of an old grandfather clock in the corner.

Every muscle in Robin's body was starting to ache after the long hours of digging, and her blistered hands were smarting. She had just sat down on the sagging sofa, hugging herself for warmth, when she heard a creak overhead that sounded very like a footstep.

Robin stared up at the ceiling. She had probably imagined it. Old houses made strange noises that sounded human until they were familiar to you. Her parents' radiators made chugging noises in the night and their old doors groaned in the central heating. It was probably nothing.

A second creak sounded, several feet from where the first had occurred.

As she got to her feet, Robin scanned the room for anything she could use as a weapon. A small, ugly bronze frog ornament sat on a table beside the sofa. As her fingers closed over the cold pock-marked surface, she heard a third creak from overhead. Unless she was imagining it, the footsteps had now moved all the way across a room directly above the one in which she was.

Robin stood quite still for almost a minute, straining her ears. She knew what Strike would say: stay put. Then she heard another tiny movement overhead. Somebody, she was sure, was creeping around upstairs.

Moving as quietly as possible in her socked feet, Robin edged around the drawing room door without touching it, in case it creaked, and walked quietly into the middle of the stone-flagged hall, where the hanging lantern cast a patchy light. She came to a halt beneath it, straining her ears, heart bumping erratically, imagining an unknown person standing above her, also standing, frozen, listening, waiting. Bronze frog still clutched in her right hand, she moved to the foot of the stairs. The landing above her was in darkness. The sound of the dogs' barking echoed from deep in the woods.

She was halfway towards the upper landing when she thought she heard another small noise above her: the scuff of a foot on carpet followed by the swish of a closing door.

She knew that there was no point calling out 'Who's there?' If the person hiding from her had been prepared to show their face, they would hardly have let Kinvara leave the house alone to face whatever had set off the dogs.

Reaching the top of the stairs, Robin saw that a vertical strip of light lay like a spectral finger across the dark floor, emanating from the only lit room. Her neck and scalp prickled as she crept towards it, afraid that the unknown lurker was watching from one of the three dark rooms with open doors she was passing. Constantly checking over her shoulder, she pushed the door of the lit bedroom with the tips of her fingers, raised the bronze frog high and entered.

This was clearly Kinvara's room: messy, cluttered and deserted. A single lamp burned on the bedside table nearest the door. The bed was unmade, with an air of having been left in a hurry, the cream quilted eiderdown lying crumpled on the floor. The walls were covered with many pictures of horses, all of them of significantly lesser quality, even to Robin's untutored eye, than the missing picture in the drawing room. The wardrobe doors stood open, but only a Lilliputian could have been hidden among the densely packed clothes within.

Robin returned to the dark landing. Taking a tighter grip on the bronze frog, she orientated herself. The sounds she had heard had come from a room directly overhead, which meant that it was probably the one with the closed door, facing her.

As she reached out her hand towards the doorknob, the terrifying sensation that unseen eyes were watching intensified. Pushing the door open, she felt around on the interior wall without entering, until she found a light switch.

The stark light revealed a cold, bare bedroom with a brass bedstead and a single chest of drawers. The heavy curtains on their old fashioned brass rings had been drawn, hiding the grounds. On the double bed lay the painting, 'Mare Mourning', the brown and white mare forever nosing the pure white foal curled up in the straw.

Groping in the pocket of her jacket with the hand not holding the bronze paperweight, Robin found her mobile and took several photographs of the painting lying on the bedspread. It had the appearance of having been hastily placed there.

She had a sudden feeling that something had moved behind her. She whipped around, trying to blink away the shining impression of the gilded frame burned into her retina by the flash on her camera. Then she heard Strike's and Kinvara's voices growing louder in the garden and knew that they were returning to the drawing room.

Slapping off the light in the spare room, Robin ran as quietly as possible back across the landing and down the stairs. Fearing that she

ROBERT GALBRAITH

wouldn't be able to reach the drawing room in time to greet them, she darted to the downstairs bathroom, flushed the toilet, and then ran back across the hall, reaching the drawing room just as her hostess re-entered it from the garden.

67

. . . I had good reason enough for so jealously drawing a veil of concealment over our compact.

Henrik Ibsen, *Rosmersholm*

The Norfolk terrier was struggling in Kinvara's arms, its paws muddy. At the sight of Robin, Rattenbury set up a volley of barking again and struggled to get free.

'Sorry, I was dying for the loo,' panted Robin, the bronze frog hidden behind her back. The old cistern backed up her story, making loud gushing and clanking noises that echoed through the stone-flagged hallway. 'Any luck?' Robin called to Strike, who was climbing back into the room behind Kinvara.

'Nothing,' said Strike, now haggard with pain. After waiting for the panting Labrador to hop back into the room, he closed the window, the revolver in his other hand. 'There were definitely people out there, though. The dogs knew it, but I think they've taken off. What were the odds of us passing just as they were climbing over the wall?'

'Oh, do *shut up*, Rattenbury!' shouted Kinvara.

She set the terrier down and, when it refused to stop yapping at Robin, she threatened it with a raised hand, at which it whimpered and retreated into a corner to join the Labrador.

'Horses OK?' Robin asked, moving to the end table from which she had taken the bronze paperweight.

'One of the stable doors wasn't fastened properly,' said Strike, wincing as he bent to feel his knee. 'But Mrs Chiswell thinks it

589

might have been left like that. Would you mind if I sat down, Mrs Chiswell?'

'I – no, I suppose not,' Kinvara said gracelessly.

She headed to a table of bottles sitting in the corner of the room, uncorked some Famous Grouse and poured herself a stiff measure of whisky. While her back was turned, Robin slid the paperweight back onto the table. She tried to catch Strike's eyes, but he had sunk down onto the sofa with a faint groan, and now turned to Kinvara.

'I wouldn't say no, if you're offering,' he said shamelessly, wincing again as he massaged his right knee. 'Actually, I think this is going to have to come off, do you mind?'

'Well – no, I suppose not. What do you want?'

'I'll have a Scotch as well, please,' said Strike, setting the revolver down on the table beside the bronze frog, rolling up his trouser leg and signalling with his eyes that Robin, too, should sit down.

While Kinvara sloshed another measure into a glass, Strike started to remove the prosthesis. Turning to give him his drink, Kinvara watched in queasy fascination as Strike worked on the false leg, averting her eyes at the point it left the inflamed stump. Panting as he propped the prosthesis against the ottoman, Strike allowed his trouser leg to fall back over his amputated leg.

'Thanks very much,' he said, accepting the whisky from her and taking a swig.

Trapped with a man who couldn't walk, to whom she ought in theory to be grateful, and to whom she had just given a drink, Kinvara sat down, too, her expression stony.

'Actually, Mrs Chiswell, I was going to phone you to confirm a couple of things we heard from Tegan earlier,' said Strike. 'We could go through them now if you like. Get them out of the way.'

With a slight shiver, Kinvara glanced at the empty fireplace, and Robin said helpfully, 'Would you like me to—?'

'No,' snapped Kinvara. 'I can do it.'

She went to the deep basket standing beside the fireplace, from which she grabbed an old newspaper. While Kinvara built a structure of small bits of wood over a mound of newspaper and a firelighter, Robin succeeded in catching Strike's eye.

'There's somebody upstairs,' she mouthed, but she wasn't sure he had understood. He merely raised his eyebrows quizzically, and turned back to Kinvara.

A match flared. Flames erupted around the little pile of paper and sticks in the fireplace. Kinvara picked up her glass and returned to the drinks table, where she topped it up with more neat Scotch, then, coat wrapped more tightly around herself, she returned to the log basket, selected a large piece of wood, dropped it on top of the burgeoning fire, then fell back onto the sofa.

'Go on, then,' she said sullenly to Strike. 'What do you want to know?'

'As I say, we spoke to Tegan Butcher today.'

'And?'

'And we now know what Jimmy Knight and Geraint Winn were blackmailing your husband about.'

Kinvara evinced no surprise.

'I told those stupid girls you'd find out,' she said with a shrug. 'Izzy and Fizzy. Everyone round here knew what Jack o'Kent was doing in the barn. Of course somebody was going to talk.'

She took a gulp of whisky.

'I suppose you know all of it, do you? The gallows? The boy in Zimbabwe?'

'You mean Samuel?' asked Strike, taking a punt.

'Exactly, Samuel Mu – Mudrap or something.'

The fire caught suddenly, flames leaping up past the log, which shifted in a shower of sparks.

'Jasper was worried they were his gallows the moment we heard the boy had been hanged. You know all of it, do you? That there were two sets? But only one made it to the government. The other lot went astray, the lorry was hijacked or something. That's how they ended up in the middle of nowhere.

'The photographs are pretty grisly, apparently. The Foreign Office thinks it was probably a case of mistaken identity. Jasper didn't see how they could be traced to him, but Jimmy said he could prove they were.

'I *knew* you'd find out,' said Kinvara, with an air of bitter satisfaction. 'Tegan's a horrible gossip.'

591

'So, to be clear,' said Strike, 'when Jimmy Knight first came here to see you, he was asking for his and Billy's share for two sets of gallows his father had left completed when he died?'

'Exactly,' said Kinvara, sipping her whisky. 'They were worth eighty thousand for the pair. He wanted forty.'

'But presumably,' said Strike, who remembered that Chiswell had talked of Jimmy returning a week after his first attempt to get money, and asking for a reduced amount, 'your husband told him he'd only ever received payment for one of them, as one set got stolen en route?'

'Yes,' said Kinvara, with a shrug. 'So then Jimmy asked for twenty, but we'd spent it.'

'How did you feel about Jimmy's request, when he first came asking for money?' Strike asked.

Robin wasn't sure whether Kinvara had turned a little pinker in the face, or whether it was the effects of the whisky.

'Well, I saw his point, if you want the truth. I could see why he felt he had a claim. Half the proceeds of the gallows belonged to the Knight boys. That had been the arrangement while Jack o'Kent was alive, but Jasper took the view that Jimmy couldn't expect money for the stolen set, and given that he'd been storing them in his barn, and bearing all the costs of transportation and so on ... and he said that Jimmy couldn't sue him even if he wanted to. He didn't like Jimmy.'

'No, well, I suppose their politics were very different,' said Strike.

Kinvara almost smirked.

'It was a bit more personal than that. Haven't you heard about Jimmy and Izzy? No ... I suppose Tegan's too young to have heard that story. Oh, it was only once,' she said, apparently under the impression that Strike was shocked, 'but that was quite enough for Jasper. A man like Jimmy Knight, deflowering his darling daughter, you know ...

'But Jasper couldn't have given Jimmy the money even if he'd wanted to,' she went on. 'He'd already spent it. It took care of our overdraft for a while and repaired the stable roof. I never knew,' she added, as though sensing unspoken criticism, 'until Jimmy explained it to me that night, what the arrangement between Jasper and Jack o'Kent had been. Jasper had told me the gallows were his to sell and I believed him. *Naturally* I believed him. He was my husband.'

She got up again and headed back to the drinks table as the fat Labrador, seeking warmth, left its distant corner, waddled around the ottoman and slumped down in front of the now roaring fire. The Norfolk terrier trotted after it, growling at Strike and Robin until Kinvara said angrily:

'*Shut up*, Rattenbury.'

'There's are a couple more things I wanted to ask you about,' said Strike. 'Firstly, did your husband have a passcode on his phone?'

'Of course he did,' said Kinvara. 'He was very security-conscious.'

'So he didn't give it out to a lot of people?'

'He didn't even tell *me* what it was,' said Kinvara. 'Why are you asking?'

Ignoring the question, Strike said:

'Your stepson's now told us a different story to account for his trip down here, on the morning of your husband's death.'

'Oh, really? What's he saying this time?'

'That he was trying to stop you selling a necklace that's been in the family for—'

'Come clean, has he?' she interrupted, turning back towards them with a fresh whisky in her hands. With her long red hair tangled from the night air, and her flushed cheeks, she had a slight air of abandon now, forgetting to hold her coat closed as she headed back to the sofa, the black nightdress revealing a canyon of cleavage. She flopped back down on the sofa. 'Yes, he wanted to stop me doing a flit with the necklace, which, by the way, I'm *perfectly* entitled to do. It's mine under the terms of the will. Jasper should have been a bit more bloody careful writing it if he didn't want me to have it, shouldn't he?'

Robin remembered Kinvara's tears, the last time they had been in this room, and how she had felt sorry for her, unlikeable though she had shown herself to be in other ways. Her attitude now had little of the grief-stricken widow about it, but perhaps, Robin thought, that was the drink, and the recent shock of their intrusion into her grounds.

'So you're backing up Raphael's story that he drove down here to stop you taking off with the necklace?'

'Don't you believe him?'

'Not really,' said Strike. 'No.'

'Why not?'

'It rings false,' said Strike. 'I'm not convinced your husband was in a fit state that morning to remember what he had and hadn't put in his will.'

'He was well enough to call me and demand to know whether I was really walking out on him,' said Kinvara.

'Did you tell him you were going to sell the necklace?'

'Not in so many words, no. I said I was going to leave as soon as I could find somewhere else for me and the horses. I suppose he might have wondered how I'd manage that, with no real money of my own, which made him remember the necklace.'

'So Raphael came here out of simple loyalty to the father who'd cut him off without a penny?'

Kinvara subjected Strike to a long and penetrating look over her whisky glass, then said to Robin:

'Would you throw another log on the fire?'

Noting the lack of a 'please', Robin nevertheless did as she was asked. The Norfolk terrier, which had now joined the sleeping Labrador on the hearthrug, growled at her until she had sat down again.

'All right,' said Kinvara, with an air of coming to a decision. 'All right, here it is. I don't suppose it matters any more, anyway. Those bloody girls will find out in the end and serve Raphael right.

'He *did* come down to try and stop me taking the necklace, but it wasn't for Jasper, Fizzy or Flopsy's sake – I suppose,' she said aggressively to Robin, 'you know all the family nicknames, don't you? You probably had a good giggle at them, while you were working with Izzy?'

'Erm—'

'Oh, don't pretend,' said Kinvara, rather nastily, 'I know you'll have heard them. They call me "Tinky Two" or something, don't they? And behind his back, Izzy, Fizzy and Torquil call Raphael "Rancid". Did you know that?'

'No,' said Robin, at whom Kinvara was still glaring.

'Sweet, isn't it? And Raphael's mother is known to all of them as the Orca, because she dresses in black and white.

'Anyway ... when the Orca realised Jasper wasn't going to marry her,' said Kinvara, now very red in the face, 'd'you know what she did?'

Robin shook her head.

'She took the famous family necklace to the man who became her *next* lover, who was a diamond merchant, and she had him prise out the really valuable stones and replace them with cubic zirconias. Man-made diamond substitutes,' Kinvara elucidated, in case Strike and Robin hadn't understood. 'Jasper never realised what she'd done and I certainly didn't. I expect Ornella's been having a jolly good laugh every time I've been photographed in the necklace, thinking I'm wearing a hundred thousand pounds' worth of stones.

'Anyway, when my darling stepson got wind of the fact that I was leaving his father, and heard that I'd talked about having enough money to buy land for the horses, he twigged that I might be about to get the necklace valued. So he came hotfooting it down here, because the last thing he wanted was for the family to find out what his mother had done. What would be the odds of him wheedling his way back into his father's good books after that?'

'Why haven't you told anyone this?' asked Strike.

'Because Raphael promised me that morning that if I didn't tell his father what the Orca had done, he'd maybe manage to persuade his mother to give the stones back. Or at least, give me their value.'

'And are you still trying to recover the missing stones?'

Kinvara squinted malevolently at Strike over the rim of her glass.

'I haven't done anything about it since Jasper died, but that doesn't mean I won't. Why should I let the bloody Orca waltz off with what's rightfully mine? It's down in Jasper's will, the contents of the house that haven't been spefi – specif – spe-cif-ically excluded,' she enunciated carefully, thick-tongued now, 'belong to me. So,' she said, fixing Strike with a gimlet stare, 'does *that* sound more like Raphael to you? Coming down here to try and cover up for his darling mama?'

'Yes,' said Strike, 'I'd have to say it does. Thank you for your honesty.'

Kinvara looked pointedly at the grandfather clock, which was now showing three in the morning, but Strike refused to take the hint.

'Mrs Chiswell, there's one last thing I want to ask and I'm afraid it's quite personal.'

'What?' she said crossly.

'I spoke to Mrs Winn recently. Della Winn, you know, the—'

'Della-Winn-the-Minister-for-Sport,' said Kinvara, just as her husband had done, the first time Strike met him. 'Yes, I know who she is. Very odd woman.'

'In what way?'

Kinvara wriggled her shoulders impatiently, as though it should be obvious.

'Never mind. What did she say?'

'That she met you in a state of considerable distress a year ago and that from what she could gather, you were upset because your husband had admitted to an affair.'

Kinvara opened her mouth then closed it again. She sat thus for a few seconds, then shook her head as though to clear it and said:

'I . . . thought he was being unfaithful, but I was wrong. I got it all wrong.'

'According to Mrs Winn, he'd said some fairly cruel things to you.'

'I don't remember what I said to her. I wasn't very well at the time. I was overemotional and I got everything wrong.'

'Forgive me,' said Strike, 'but, as an outsider, your marriage seemed—'

'What a dreadful job you've got,' said Kinvara shrilly. 'What a really nasty, *seedy* job you do. Yes, our marriage was going wrong, what of it? Do you think, now he's dead, now he's *killed himself*, I want to relive it all with the pair of *you*, perfect strangers whom my stupid stepdaughters have dragged in, to stir everything up and make it ten times worse?'

'So you've changed your mind, have you? You think your husband committed suicide? Because when we were last here, you suggested Aamir Mallik—'

'I don't know what I said then!' she said hysterically. 'Can you not understand what it's been like since Jasper killed himself, with the police and the family and *you*? I didn't think this would happen, I had no idea, it didn't seem real – Jasper was under enormous pressure those last few months, drinking too much, in an awful temper – the blackmail, the fear of it all coming out – yes, I think he killed himself and I've got to live with the fact that I walked out on him that morning, which was probably the final straw!'

The Norfolk terrier began to yap furiously again. The Labrador woke with a start and started barking, too.

'Please leave!' shouted Kinvara, getting to her feet. 'Get out! I never wanted you mixed up in this in the first place! Just go, will you?'

'Certainly,' said Strike politely, setting down his empty glass. 'Would you mind waiting while I get my leg back on?'

Robin had already stood up. Strike strapped the false leg back on while Kinvara watched, chest heaving, glass in hand. At last, Strike was ready to stand, but his first attempt had him falling back onto the sofa. With Robin's assistance, he finally achieved a standing position.

'Well, goodbye, Mrs Chiswell.'

Kinvara's only answer was to stalk to the window and fling it open again, shouting at the dogs, which had got up excitedly, to stay put.

No sooner had her unwelcome guests stepped out onto the gravel path than Kinvara slammed the window behind them. While Robin put her Wellington boots back on, they heard the shriek of the brass curtain rings as Kinvara dragged the drapes shut, then called the dogs out of the room.

'Not sure I'm going to be able to make it back to the car, Robin,' said Strike, who wasn't putting weight on his prosthesis. 'In retrospect, the digging might've ... might've been a mistake.'

Wordlessly, Robin took his arm and placed it over her shoulders. He didn't resist. Together they moved slowly off across the grass.

'Did you understand what I mouthed at you back there?' asked Robin.

'That there was someone upstairs? Yeah,' he said, wincing horribly every time he put down his false foot. 'I did.'

'You don't seem—'

'I'm not surpr – wait,' he said abruptly, still leaning on her as he came to a halt. 'You didn't go up there?'

'Yes,' said Robin.

'*For fuck's sake—*'

'I heard footsteps.'

'And what would've happened if you'd been jumped?'

'I took a weapon and I wasn't – and if I hadn't gone up there, I wouldn't have seen this.'

Taking out her mobile, Robin brought up the photo of the painting on the bed, and handed it to him.

'You didn't see Kinvara's expression, when she saw the blank wall. Cormoran, she didn't realise that painting had been moved until you asked about it. Whoever was upstairs tried to hide it while she was outside.'

Strike stared at the phone screen for what felt like a long time, his arm heavy on Robin's shoulders. Finally, he said:

'Is that a piebald?'

'Seriously?' said Robin, in total disbelief. 'Horse colours? Now?'

'Answer me.'

'No, piebalds are black and white, not brown and—'

'We need to go to the police,' said Strike. 'The odds on another murder just went up exponentially.'

'You aren't serious?'

'I'm completely serious. Get me back to the car and I'll tell you everything ... but don't ask me to talk till then, because my leg's fucking killing me.'

68

I have tasted blood now . . .

Henrik Ibsen, *Rosmersholm*

Three days later, Strike and Robin received an unprecedented invitation. As a courtesy for having chosen to aid rather than upstage the police in passing on information about Flick's stolen note and 'Mare Mourning', the Met welcomed the detective partners into the heart of the investigation at New Scotland Yard. Used to being treated by the police as either inconveniences or showboaters, Strike and Robin were surprised but grateful for this unforeseen thawing of relations.

On arrival, the tall blonde Scot who was heading the team ducked out of an interrogation room for a minute to shake hands. Strike and Robin knew that the police had brought two suspects in for questioning, although nobody had yet been charged.

'We spent the morning on hysterics and flat denial,' DCI Judy McMurran told them, 'but I think we'll have cracked her by the end of the day.'

'Any chance we could give them a little look, Judy?' asked her subordinate, DI George Layborn, who had met Strike and Robin at the door and brought them upstairs. He was a pudgy man who reminded Robin of the traffic policeman who had thought he was such a card, back on the hard shoulder where she'd had her panic attack.

'Go on, then,' said DCI McMurran, with a smile.

Layborn led Strike and Robin around a corner and through the first door on their right into a dark and cramped area, of which half one wall was a two-way mirror into an interrogation room.

Robin, who had only ever seen such spaces in films and on TV, was mesmerised. Kinvara Chiswell was sitting on one side of a desk, beside a thin-lipped solicitor in a pinstriped suit. White-faced, devoid of make-up, wearing a pale grey silk blouse so creased she might have slept in it, Kinvara was weeping into a tissue. Opposite her sat another detective inspector in a far cheaper suit than the solicitor's. His expression was impassive.

As they watched, DCI McMurran re-entered the room and took the vacant chair beside her colleague. After what felt like a very long time, but was probably only a minute, DCI McMurran spoke.

'Still nothing to say about your night at the hotel, Mrs Chiswell?'

'This is like a nightmare,' whispered Kinvara. 'I can't believe this is happening. I can't believe I'm here.'

Her eyes were pink, swollen and apparently lashless now that she had wept her mascara away.

'Jasper killed himself,' she said tremulously. 'He was depressed! Everyone will tell you so! The blackmail was eating away at him ... have you talked to the Foreign Office yet? Even the idea that there might be photographs of that boy who was hanged – can't you see how scared Jasper was? If that had come out—'

Her voice cracked.

'Where's your evidence against me?' she demanded. 'Where is it? *Where?*'

Her solicitor gave a dry little cough.

'To return,' said DCI McMurran, 'to the subject of the hotel. Why do you think your husband called them, trying to ascertain—'

'It isn't a crime to go to a hotel!' said Kinvara hysterically, and she turned to her solicitor, 'This is ridiculous, Charles, how can they make a case against me because I went to a—'

'Mrs Chiswell will answer any questions you've got about her birthday,' the solicitor told DCI McMurran, with what Robin thought was remarkable optimism, 'but equally—'

The door of the observation room opened and hit Strike.

'No problem, we'll shift,' Layborn told his colleague. 'Come on, gang, we'll go to the incident room. Got plenty more to show you.'

As they turned a second corner, they saw Eric Wardle walking towards them.

'Never thought I'd see the day,' he said, grinning as he shook Strike's hand. 'Actually invited in by the Met.'

'You staying, Wardle?' asked Layborn, who seemed faintly resentful at the prospect of another policeman sharing the guests he was keen to impress.

'Might as well,' said Wardle. 'Find out what I've been assisting in, all these weeks.'

'Must've taken its toll,' said Strike, as they followed Layborn into the incident room, 'passing on all that evidence we found.'

Wardle sniggered.

Used as she was to the cramped and slightly dilapidated offices in Denmark Street, Robin was fascinated to see the space that Scotland Yard devoted to the investigation into a high profile and suspicious death. A whiteboard on the wall carried a timeline for the killing. The adjacent wall bore a collage of photographs of the death scene and the corpse, the latter showing Chiswell freed from his plastic wrapping, so that his congested face appeared in awful close-up, with a livid scratch down one cheek, the cloudy eyes half open, the skin a dark, mottled purple.

Spotting her interest, Layborn showed her the toxicology reports and phone records that the police had used to build their case, then unlocked the large cupboard where physical evidence was bagged and tagged, including the cracked tube of lachesis pills, a grubby orange juice carton and Kinvara's farewell letter to her husband. Seeing the note that Flick had stolen, and a printout of the photograph of 'Mare Mourning' lying on a spare bed, both of which Robin knew had now become central to the police case, she experienced a rush of pride.

'Right then,' said DI Layborn, closing the cupboard and walking over to a computer monitor. 'Time to see the little lady in action.'

He inserted a video disc in the nearest machine, beckoning Strike, Robin and Wardle closer.

The crowded forecourt of Paddington station was revealed, jerky black and white figures moving everywhere. The time and date showed in the upper left corner.

'There she is,' said Layborn, hitting 'pause' and pointing a stubby figure at a woman. 'See her?'

Even though blurred, the figure was recognisable as Kinvara. A bearded man had been caught in the frame, staring, probably because her coat hung open, revealing the clinging black dress she had worn to the Paralympian reception. Layborn pressed 'play' again.

'Watch her, watch her – gives to the homeless—'

Kinvara had donated to a swaddled man holding a cup in a doorway.

'—watch her,' Layborn said unnecessarily, 'straight up to the railway worker – pointless question – shows him her ticket . . . watch her, now . . . off to the platform, stops and asks another bloke a question, making sure she's remembered every bloody step of the way, even if she's not caught on camera . . . *aaaand* . . . onto the train.'

The picture twitched and changed. A train was pulling into the station at Swindon. Kinvara got off, talking to another woman.

'See?' said Layborn. 'Still making damn sure people remember her, just in case. And—'

The picture changed again, to that of the car park at Swindon station.

'—there she is,' said Layborn, 'car's parked right near the camera, conveniently. In she gets and off she goes. Gets home, insists the stable girl stays overnight, sleeps in the next room, goes outside next morning to ride within sight of the girl . . . cast-iron alibi.'

'Course, like you, we'd already come to the conclusion that if it was murder, it must have been a two-person job.'

'Because of the orange juice?' asked Robin.

'Mostly,' said Layborn. 'If Chiswell' (he said the name as it was spelled) 'had taken amitriptyline unknowingly, the most likely explanation was that he'd poured himself doctored juice out of a carton in the fridge, but the carton in the bin was undoctored and only had his prints on.'

'Easy to get his prints on small objects once he was dead, though,' said Strike. 'Just press his hand onto them.'

'Exactly,' said Layborn, striding over the wall of photographs and pointing at a close-up of the pestle and mortar. 'So we went back to this. The way Chiswell's prints are positioned and the way the powdered residue was sitting there pointed to it being faked, which meant the doctored juice could have been fixed up hours in advance, by somebody who had a key, who knew which anti-depressants the wife was on, that Chiswell's sense of taste and smell were impaired and that he always drank juice in the mornings. Then all they'd need to do is have the accomplice plant an undoctored juice carton in the bin with his dead handprint on, and take away the one with the amitriptyline residue in it.

'Well, who's better positioned to know and do all of that, than the missus?' asked Layborn rhetorically. 'But here she was, with her cast-iron alibi for time of death, seventy-odd miles away when he was gulping down anti-depressants. Not to mention she's left that letter, trying to give us a nice clean story: husband already facing bankruptcy and blackmail realises his wife's leaving him, which tips him over the edge, so he tops himself.

'But,' said Layborn, pointing at the enlarged picture of the dead Chiswell's face, stripped of its plastic bag, revealing a deep red scrape on the cheek, 'we didn't like the look of *that*. We thought from the first that was suspicious. Amitriptyline in overdose can cause agitation as well as sleepiness. That mark looked as though somebody else forced the bag over his head.

'Then there was the open door. The last person in or out didn't know there was a trick to closing it properly, so it didn't look like Chiswell was the last person to touch it. Plus, the packaging on the pills being absent – that smelled wrong from the start. Why would Jasper Chiswell get rid of it?' asked Layborn. 'Just a few little careless mistakes.'

'It nearly came off,' said Strike. 'If only Chiswell had been put to sleep by the amitriptyline as intended, and if they'd thought the thing through right to the finest details – close the door properly, leave the pill packaging *in situ*—'

'But they didn't,' said Layborn, 'and *she's* not smart enough on her own to talk herself out of this.'

'"I can't believe this is happening",' Strike quoted. 'She's consistent. On Saturday night she told us "I didn't think this would happen", "it didn't seem real—"'

'Try that in court,' said Wardle quietly.

'Yeah, what were you expecting, love, when you crushed up a load of pills and put them in his orange juice?' said Layborn. 'Guilty is as guilty does.'

'Amazing, the lies people can tell themselves when they're drifting along in the wake of a stronger personality,' said Strike. 'I'll bet you a tenner that when McMurran finally breaks her, Kinvara'll say they started off hoping Chiswell would kill himself, then trying to pressure him into doing it, and finally reached a point when there didn't seem much difference between trying to push him into suicide, and putting the pills in his orange juice herself. I notice she's still trying to push the gallows business as the reason he'd top himself.'

'That was very good work of yours, connecting the dots on the gallows,' admitted Layborn. 'We were a bit behind you on that, but it explained a hell of a lot. This is highly confidential,' he added, taking a brown envelope off a nearby desk and tipping out a large photograph, 'but we had this from the Foreign Office this morning. As you can see—'

Robin, who had gone to look, half-wished she hadn't. What was there to be gained, really, from seeing the corpse of what seemed to be a teenage boy, whose eyes had been picked out by carrion birds, and hanging from a gallows in a rubble-strewn street? The boy's dangling feet were bare. Somebody, Robin guessed, had stolen his trainers.

'The lorry containing the second pair of gallows was hijacked. Government never took delivery and Chiswell never got payment for them. This picture suggests they ended up being used by rebels for extrajudicial killings. This poor lad, Samuel Murape, was in the wrong place at the wrong time. British student, gap year, out there to visit family. It's not particularly clear,' Layborn said, 'but see there, just behind his foot—'

'Yeah, that could be the mark of the white horse,' said Strike.

Robin's mobile, which was switched to silent, vibrated in her pocket. She was waiting for an important call, but it was only a text from an unknown number.

I know you've blocked my phone, but I need to meet you. An urgent situation's come up and it's to your advantage as much as mine to sort it out. Matt

'It's nothing,' Robin told Strike, returning the mobile to her pocket.

This was the third message Matthew had left that day.

Urgent situation, my arse.

Tom had probably found out that his fiancée and his good friend had been sleeping together. Maybe Tom was threatening to call Robin, or drop in on the office in Denmark Street, to find out how much she knew. If Matthew thought that constituted an 'urgent situation' to Robin, who was currently standing beside multiple pictures of a drugged and suffocated government minister, he was wrong. With an effort, she refocused on the conversation in the incident room.

'... the necklace business,' Layborn was saying to Strike. 'Far more convincing story than the one he told us. All that guff about wanting to stop her hurting herself.'

'It was Robin who got him to change his story, not me,' said Strike.

'Ah – well, good work,' Layborn said to Robin, with a hint of patronage. 'I thought he was an oily little bastard when I took his initial statement. Cocky. Just out of jail, and all. No bloody remorse for running over that poor woman.'

'How are you getting on with Francesca?' Strike asked. 'The girl from the gallery?'

'We managed to get hold of the father in Sri Lanka and he's not happy. Being quite obstructive, actually,' said Layborn. 'He's trying to buy time to get her lawyered up. Bloody inconvenient, the whole family being abroad. I had to get tough with him over the phone. I can understand why he doesn't want it all coming out in court, but too bad. Gives you a real insight into the mindset of the upper classes, eh, case like this? One rule for them ...'

'On that subject,' said Strike, 'I assume you've spoken to Aamir Mallik?'

'Yeah, we found him exactly where your boy – Hutchins, is it? – said he was. At his sister's. He's got a new job—'

'Oh, I'm glad,' said Robin inadvertently.

'—and he wasn't overjoyed to have us turning up at first, but he ended up being very frank and helpful. Said he found that disturbed lad – Billy, is it? – on the street, wanting to see his boss, shouting about a dead child, strangled and buried on Chiswell's land. Took him home with the idea of getting him to hospital, but he asked Geraint Winn's advice first. Winn was furious. Told him on no account to call an ambulance.'

'Did he, now?' said Strike, frowning.

'From what Mallik's told us, Winn was worried association with Billy's story would taint his own credibility. He didn't want the waters muddied by a psychotic tramp. Blew up at Mallik for taking him into a house belonging to the Winns, told him to turf him out on the street again. Trouble was—'

'Billy wouldn't go,' said Strike.

'Exactly. Mallik says he was clearly out of his mind, thought he was being held against his will. Curled up in the bathroom most of the time. Anyway,' Layborn took a deep breath, 'Mallik's had enough of covering up for the Winns. He's confirmed that Winn wasn't with him on the morning of Chiswell's death. Winn told Mallik afterwards, when he put pressure on Mallik to lie, he'd had an urgent phone call at 6 a.m. that day, which is why he left the marital home early.'

'And you've traced that call?' said Strike.

Layborn picked up the printout of phone records, rifled through them, then handed a couple of marked pages to Strike.

'Here you go. Burner phones,' he said. 'We've got three different numbers so far. There were probably more. Used once, never used again, untraceable except for the single instance we got on record. Months in the planning.

'A single-use phone was used to contact Winn that morning, and two more were used to call Kinvara Chiswell on separate occasions during the previous weeks. She "can't remember" who called her, but both times – see there? – she talked to whoever it was for over an hour.'

'What's Winn got to say for himself?' asked Strike.

'Closed up like an oyster,' said Layborn. 'We're working on him, don't worry. There are porn stars who've been fucked fewer different ways than Geraint W – sorry, love,' he said, grinning, to Robin, who found the apology more offensive than anything Layborn had said. 'But you take my point. He might as well tell us everything now. He's screwed every which w – well,' he said, floundering once more. 'What interests me,' he started up again, 'is how much the wife knew. Strange woman.'

'In what way?' asked Robin.

'Oh, you know. I think she plays on this a bit,' said Layborn, with a vague gesture towards his eyes. 'Very hard to believe she didn't know what he was up to.'

'Speaking of people not knowing what their other halves are up to,' interposed Strike, who thought he detected a martial glint in Robin's eye, 'how's it going with our friend Flick?'

'Ah, we're making very good progress there,' said Layborn. 'The parents have been helpful in *her* case. They're both lawyers and they've been urging her to cooperate. She's admitted she was Chiswell's cleaner, that she stole the note and took receipt of the crate of champagne right before Chiswell told her he couldn't afford her any more. Says she put it in a cupboard in the kitchen.'

'Who delivered it?'

'She can't remember. We'll find out. Courier service, I shouldn't wonder, booked on another burner phone.'

'And the credit card?'

'That was another good spot of yours,' admitted Layborn. 'We didn't know a credit card had gone missing. We got details through from the bank this morning. The same day Flick's flatmate realised the card was gone, somebody charged a crate of champagne and bought a hundred quid's worth of stuff on Amazon, all to be sent to an address in Maida Vale. Nobody took delivery, so it was returned to the depot where it was picked up that afternoon by someone who had the failed delivery notice. We're trying to locate the staff who can identify the person who collected it and we're getting a breakdown on what was bought on Amazon, but my money's on helium, tubing and latex gloves.'

'This was all planned months in advance. *Months.*'

'And that?' Strike asked, pointing to the photocopy of the note in Chiswell's handwriting, which was lying on the side in its polythene bag. 'Has she told you why she nicked it yet?'

'She says she saw "Bill" and thought it meant her boyfriend's brother. Ironic, really,' said Layborn. 'If she hadn't stolen it, we wouldn't have cottoned on nearly so fast, would we?'

The 'we', thought Robin, was daring, because it had been Strike who had 'cottoned on', Strike who had finally cracked the significance of Chiswell's note, as they drove back to London from Chiswell House.

'Robin deserves the bulk of the credit there, too,' said Strike. 'She found the thing, she noticed "Blanc de Blanc" and the Grand Vitara. I just pieced it together once it was staring me in the face.'

'Well, we were just behind you,' said Layborn, absent-mindedly scratching his belly. 'I'm sure we'd have got there.'

Robin's mobile vibrated in her pocket again: somebody was calling, this time.

'I need to take this. Is there anywhere I can—?'

'Through here,' said Layborn helpfully, opening a side door.

It was a photocopier room, with a small window covered in a Venetian blind. Robin closed the door on the others' conversation and answered.

'Hi, Sarah.'

'Hi,' said Sarah Shadlock.

She sounded totally unlike the Sarah whom Robin had known for nearly nine years, the confident and bombastic blonde whom Robin had sensed, even in their teens, was hoping that some mischance might befall Matthew's long-distance relationship with his girlfriend. Always there through the years, giggling at Matthew's jokes, touching his arm, asking loaded questions about Robin's relationship with Strike, Sarah had dated other men, settling at last for poor tedious

Tom, with his well-paid job and his bald patch, who had put diamonds on Sarah's finger and in her ears, but never quelled her yen for Matthew Cunliffe.

All her swagger had gone today.

'Well, I've asked two experts, but,' she said, sounding fragile and fearful, 'and they can't say for sure, not from a photograph taken on a phone—'

'Well, obviously not,' said Robin coolly. 'I said in my text, didn't I, that I wasn't expecting a definitive answer? We're not asking for a firm identification or valuation. All we want to know is whether somebody might have credibly believed—'

'Well, then, yes,' said Sarah. 'One of our experts is quite excited about it, actually. One of the old notebooks lists a painting done of a mare with a dead foal, but it's never been found.'

'What notebooks?'

'Oh, sorry,' said Sarah. She had never sounded so meek, so frightened, in Robin's vicinity. 'Stubbs.'

'And if it *is* a Stubbs?' asked Robin, turning to look out of the window at the Feathers, a pub where she and Strike had sometimes drunk.

'Well, this is entirely speculative, obviously ... but *if* it's genuine, *if* it's the one he listed in 1760, it could be a lot.'

'Give me a rough estimate.'

'Well, his "Gimcrack" went for—'

'—twenty-two million,' said Robin, feeling suddenly light-headed. 'Yes. You said so at our house-warming party.'

Sarah made no answer. Perhaps the mention of the party, where she had brought lilies to her lover's wife's house, had scared her.

'So if "Mare Mourning" is a genuine Stubbs—'

'It'd probably make more than "Gimcrack" at auction. It's a unique subject. Stubbs was an anatomist, as much scientist as artist. If this is a depiction of a lethal white foal, it might be the first recorded instance. It could set records.'

Robin's mobile buzzed in her hand. Another text had arrived.

'This has been very helpful, Sarah, thanks. You'll keep this confidential?'

'Yes, of course,' said Sarah. And then, in a rush:

'Robin, listen—'

'No,' said Robin, trying to stay calm. 'I'm working a case.'

'—it's over, it's finished, Matt's in pieces—'

'Goodbye, Sarah.'

Robin hung up, then read the text that had just arrived.

Meet me after work or I'm giving a statement to the press.

Eager as she was to return to the group next door and relay the sensational information she had just received, Robin remained where she stood, temporarily flummoxed by the threat, and texted back:

Statement to the press about what?

His response came within seconds, littered with angry typos.

The mail called the office this morning g and left a message asking how I feel about my dive shacking up with Cornish Strike. The sun's been one this afternoon. You probably know he's two timing you but maybe you don't give a shit. I'm not having the papers calling me at work. Either meet me or I'm go give a statement to get them off my back.

Robin was rereading the message when yet another text arrived, this time with an attachment.

In case you haven't seen it

Robin enlarged the attachment, which was a screenshot of a diary item in the *Evening Standard*.

THE CURIOUS CASE OF CHARLOTTE CAMPBELL AND CORMORAN STRIKE

A staple of the gossip columns ever since she ran away from her first private school, Charlotte Campbell has lived out her life in a glare of publicity. Most people would choose a discreet spot for their consultation with a private detective, but the pregnant Ms Campbell – now Mrs Jago Ross – chose the window table of one of the West End's busiest restaurants.

Were detective services under discussion during the intense heart-to-heart, or something more personal? The colourful Mr Strike, illegitimate son of rock star Jonny Rokeby, war hero and modern-day Sherlock Holmes, also happens to be Campbell's ex-lover.

Campbell's businessman husband will doubtless be keen to solve the mystery – business or pleasure? – upon his return from New York.

A mass of uncomfortable feelings jostled inside Robin, of which the dominant ones were panic, anger and mortification at the thought of Matthew speaking to the press in such a way as to leave open, spitefully, the possibility that she and Strike were indeed sleeping together.

She tried to call the number, but it went straight to voicemail. Two seconds later, another angry text appeared.

I'M WITH A CLIENT I DON'T WANT TO TALK ABOUT THIS IN FRONT OF HIM JUST MEET ME

Angry now, Robin texted:

And I'm at New Scotland Yard. Find a quiet corner.

She could imagine Matthew's polite smile as the client watched, his smooth 'just the office, excuse me', while he hammered out his furious replies.

We've got stuff to sort out and you're acting like a child refusing to meet me. Either you come talk to me or I'm ringing the papers at eight. I notice you're not denying your sleeping with him, by the way

Furious, but feeling cornered, Robin typed back:

Fine, let's discuss it face to face, where?

He texted her directions to a bar in Little Venice. Still shaken, Robin pushed open the door to the incident room. The group was now huddled around a monitor showing a page of Jimmy Knight's blog, from which Strike was reading aloud:

'... "in other words, a single bottle of wine at Le Manoir aux Quat'Saisons can cost more than a single, out-of-work mother receives per week to feed, clothe and house her entire family." Now that,' said Strike, 'struck me as a weirdly specific choice of restaurant, if he wanted to rant about Tories and their spending. *That's* what made me think he'd been there recently. Then Robin tells me "Blanc de Blanc" is the name of one of their suites, but I didn't put that together as quickly as I should've done. It hit me a few hours later.'

'He's a hell of a bloody hypocrite on top of everything else, isn't he?' said Wardle, who was standing, arms folded, behind Strike.

'You've looked in Woolstone?' Strike asked.

'The shithole in Charlemont Road, Woolstone, everywhere,' said Layborn, 'but don't worry. We've got a line on one of his girlfriends down in Dulwich. Checking there right now. With luck, we'll have him in custody tonight.'

Layborn now noticed Robin, standing with her phone in her hand.

'I know you've already got people looking at it,' she told Layborn, 'but I've got a contact at Christie's. I sent her the picture of "Mare Mourning" and she's just called me back. According to one of their experts, it *might* be a Stubbs.'

'Even I've heard of Stubbs,' Layborn said.

'What would it be worth, if it is?' Wardle asked.

'My contact thinks upwards of twenty-two million.'

Wardle whistled. Layborn said, 'Fuck me.'

'Doesn't matter to us what it's worth,' Strike reminded them all. 'What matters is whether somebody might've spotted its potential value.'

'Twenty-two fucking million,' said Wardle, 'is a hell of a motive.'

'Cormoran,' said Robin, picking her jacket off the back of the chair where she'd left it, 'could I have a quick word outside? I'm going to have to leave, sorry,' she said to the others.

'Everything OK?' Strike asked, as they re-entered the corridor together and Robin had closed the door on the group of police.

'Yes,' said Robin, and then, 'Well – not really. Maybe,' she said, handing him her phone, 'you'd better just read this.'

Frowning, Strike scrolled slowly through the interchange between Robin and Matthew, including the *Evening Standard* clip.

'You're going to meet him?'

'I've got to. This must be why Mitch Patterson's sniffing around. If Matthew fans the flames with the press, which he's more than capable of doing ... They're already excited about you and—'

'Forget me and Charlotte,' he said roughly, 'that was twenty minutes that she coerced me into. He's trying to coerce *you*—'

'I know he is,' said Robin, 'but I *have* got to talk to him sooner or later. Most of my stuff's still in Albury Street. We've still got a joint bank account.'

'D'you want me to come?'

Touched, Robin said:

'Thanks, but I don't think that would help.'

'Then ring me later, will you? Let me know what happened.'

'I will,' she promised.

She headed off alone towards the lifts. She didn't even notice who had just walked past her in the opposite direction until somebody said, 'Bobbi?'

Robin turned. There stood Flick Purdue, returning from the bathroom with a policewoman, who seemed to have escorted her there. Like Kinvara, Flick had cried away her make-up. She appeared small and shrunken in a white shirt that Robin suspected her parents had insisted she wear, rather than her Hezbollah T-shirt.

'It's Robin. How are you, Flick?'

Flick seemed to be struggling with ideas too monstrous to utter.

'I hope you're cooperating,' said Robin. 'Tell them everything, won't you?'

She thought she saw a tiny shake of the head, an instinctive defiance, the last embers of loyalty not yet extinguished, even in the trouble Flick found herself.

'You must,' said Robin quietly. 'He'd have killed *you* next, Flick. You knew too much.'

69

I have foreseen all contingencies − long ago.

Henrik Ibsen, *Rosmersholm*

A twenty-minute Tube ride later, Robin emerged at Warwick Avenue underground station in a part of London she barely knew. She had always felt a vague curiosity about Little Venice, as her extravagant middle name, 'Venetia', had been given to her because she had been conceived in the real Venice. Doubtless she would henceforth associate this area with Matthew and the bitter, tense meeting she was sure awaited her, down by the canal.

She walked down a street named Clifton Villas, where plane trees spread leaves of translucent jade against square cream-coloured houses, the walls of which glowed gold in the evening sun. The quiet beauty of this soft summer evening made Robin feel suddenly, overwhelmingly melancholy, because it recalled just such a night in Yorkshire, a decade previously, when she had hurried up the road from her parents' house, barely seventeen years old and wobbling on her high heels, desperately excited about her first date with Matthew Cunliffe, who had just passed his driving test and would be taking her into Harrogate for the evening.

And here she was walking towards him again, to arrange the permanent disentanglement of their lives. Robin despised herself for feeling sad, for remembering, when it was preferable to concentrate on his unfaithfulness and unkindness, the joyful shared experiences that had led to love.

She turned left, crossed the street and walked on, now in the chilly shadow of the brick that bordered the right-hand side of Blomfield Road, parallel to the canal, and saw a police car speeding across the top of the street. The sight of it gave her strength. It felt like a friendly wave from what she knew now was her real life, sent to remind her what she was meant to be, and how incompatible that was with being the wife of Matthew Cunliffe.

A pair of high black wooden gates was set into the wall, gates that Matthew's text had told her led to the canal-side bar, but when Robin pushed at them, they were locked. She glanced up and down the road, but there was no sign of Matthew, so she reached into her bag for her mobile, which, though muted was already vibrating with a call. As she took it out, the electric gates opened and she walked through them, raising the mobile to her ear as she did so.

'Hi, I'm just—'

Strike yelled in her ear.

'*Get out of there, it isn't Matthew—*'

Several things happened at once.

The phone was torn out of her hand. In one frozen second, Robin registered that there was no bar in sight, only an untidy patch of canal bank beneath a bridge, hemmed by overgrown shrubs, and a dark barge, *Odile*, sitting squat and shabby in the water below her. Then a fist hit her hard in the solar plexus, and she jack-knifed, winded. Doubled over, she heard a splash as her phone was lobbed into the canal, then somebody grabbed a fistful of her hair and the waistband of her trousers and dragged her, while she still had no air in her lungs to scream, towards the barge. Thrown through the open doorway of the boat, she hit a narrow wooden table and fell to the floor.

The door slammed shut. She heard the scrape of a lock.

'Sit down,' said a male voice.

Still winded, Robin pulled herself up onto a wooden bench at the table, which was covered in a thin cushioned pad, then turned, to find herself looking into the barrel of a revolver.

Raphael lowered himself into the chair opposite her.

'Who just rang you?' he demanded and she deduced that in the physical effort to get her on the boat, and his terror that she might make a noise that the caller could hear, he had not had time or opportunity to check the screen on her mobile.

'My husband,' lied Robin in a whisper.

Her scalp was burning where he had pulled her hair. The pain in her midriff was such that she wondered whether he had cracked one of her ribs. Still fighting to draw air into her lungs, Robin seemed for a few disorientated seconds to see her predicament in miniature, from far away, encased in a trembling bead of time. She foresaw Raphael tipping her weighted corpse into the dark water by night, and Matthew, who had apparently lured her to the canal, being questioned and maybe accused. She saw the distraught faces of her parents and her brothers at her funeral in Masham, and she saw Strike standing at the back of the church, as he had at her wedding, furious because the thing he had feared had come to pass, and she was dead due to her own failings.

But as each gasp re-inflated Robin's lungs, the illusion that she was watching from afar dissolved. She was here, now, on this dingy boat, breathing in its fusty smell, trapped within its wooden walls, with the dilated pupil of the revolver staring at her, and Raphael's eyes above it.

Her fear was a real, solid presence in the galley, but it must stand apart from her, because it couldn't help, and would only hinder. She must stay calm, and concentrate. She chose not to speak. It would give her back some of the power he had just taken from her if she refused to fill the silence. This was the trick of the therapist: let the pause unspool; let the more vulnerable person fill it.

'You're very cool,' Raphael said finally. 'I thought you might get hysterical and scream. That's why I had to punch you. I wouldn't have done that otherwise. For what it's worth, I like you, Venetia.'

She knew that he was trying to re-impersonate the man who had charmed her against her will at the Commons. Clearly, he thought the old mixture of ruefulness and remorse would make her forgive, and soften, even with her burning scalp, and her bruised ribs, and the gun in her face. She said nothing. His faint, imploring smile disappeared and he said bluntly:

'I need to know how much the police know. If I can still blag my way out of what they've got, then I'm afraid you,' he raised the gun a fraction to point directly at Robin's forehead (and she thought of vets and the one clean shot that the horse in the dell had been denied) 'are done for. I'll muffle the shot in a cushion and put you overboard once it's dark. But if they already know everything, then I'll end it, here, tonight, because I'm never going back to prison. So you can see how it's in your best interests to be honest, can't you? Only one of us is getting off this boat.'

And when she didn't speak, he said fiercely:

'Answer me!'

'Yes,' she said. 'I understand.'

'So,' he said quietly, 'were you really just at Scotland Yard?'

'Yes.'

'Is Kinvara there?'

'Yes.'

'Under arrest?'

'I think so. She's in an interrogation room with her solicitor.'

'Why have they arrested her?'

'They think the two of you are having an affair. That you were behind everything.'

'What's "everything"?'

'The blackmail,' said Robin, 'and the murder.'

He advanced the gun so that it was pressing against her forehead. Robin felt the small, cold ring of metal pressing into her skin.

'Sounds like a crock of shit to me. How're we supposed to have had an affair? She hated me. We were never alone together for two minutes.'

'Yes, you were,' said Robin. 'Your father invited you down to Chiswell House, right after you got out of jail. The night he was detained in London. You and she were alone together, then. That's when we think it started.'

'Proof?'

'None,' said Robin, 'but I think you could seduce anyone if you really put your—'

'Don't try flattery, it won't work. Seriously, "that's when we think it started"? Is that all you've got?'

'No. There were other signs of something going on.'

'Tell me the signs. All of them.'

'I'd be able to remember better,' said Robin steadily, 'without you pressing a gun into my forehead.'

He withdrew it, but still pointing the revolver at her face, he said: 'Go on. Quickly.'

Part of Robin wanted to succumb to her body's desire to dissolve, to carry her off into blissful unconsciousness. Her hands were numb, her muscles felt like soft wax. The place where Raphael had pressed the gun into her skin felt cold, a ring of white fire for a third eye. He hadn't turned on the lights in the boat. They were facing each other in the deepening darkness and perhaps, by the time he shot her, she would no longer be able to see him clearly . . .

Focus, said a small, clear voice through the panic. *Focus. The longer you keep him talking, the more time they'll have to find you. Strike knows you were tricked.*

She suddenly remembered the police car speeding across the top of Blomfield Road and wondered whether it had been circling, looking for her, whether the police, knowing that Raphael had lured her to the area, had already dispatched officers to search for them. The fake address had been some distance away along the canal bank, reached, so Raphael's texts had said, through the black gates. Would Strike guess that Raphael was armed?

She took a deep breath.

'Kinvara broke down in Della Winn's office last summer and said that someone had told her she'd never been loved, that she was used as part of a game.'

She must speak slowly. Don't rush it. Every second might count, every second that she could keep Raphael hanging on her words, was another second in which somebody might come to her aid.

'Della assumed she was talking about your father, but we checked and Della can't remember Kinvara actually saying his name. We think you seduced Kinvara as an act of revenge towards your father, kept the affair going for a couple of months, but when she got clingy and possessive, you ditched her.'

'All supposition,' said Raphael harshly, 'and therefore bullshit. What else?'

'Why did Kinvara go up to town on the day her beloved mare was likely to be put down?'

'Maybe she couldn't face seeing the horse shot. Maybe she was in denial about how sick it was.'

'Or,' said Robin, 'maybe she was suspicious about what you and Francesca were up to in Drummond's gallery.'

'No proof. Next.'

'She had a kind of breakdown when she got back to Oxfordshire. She attacked your father and was hospitalised.'

'Still grieving her stillborn, excessively attached to her horses, generally depressed,' Raphael rattled off. 'Izzy and Fizzy will fight to take the stand and explain how unstable she is. What else?'

'Tegan told us that one day Kinvara was manically happy again, and she lied when asked why. She said your father had agreed to put her other mare in foal to Totilas. We think the real reason was that you'd resumed the affair with her, and we don't think the timing was coincidental. You'd just driven the latest batch of paintings up to Drummond's gallery for valuation.'

Raphael's face became suddenly slack, as though his essential self had temporarily vacated it. The gun twitched in his hand and the fine hairs on Robin's arms lifted gently as though a breeze had rippled over them. She waited for Raphael to speak, but he didn't. After a minute, she continued:

'We think that when you loaded up the paintings for valuation, you saw "Mare Mourning" close up for the first time and realised that it might be a Stubbs. You decided to substitute a different painting of a mare and foal for valuation.'

'Evidence?'

'Henry Drummond's now seen the photograph I took of "Mare Mourning" on the spare bed at Chiswell House. He's ready to testify that it wasn't among the pictures he valued for your father. The painting he valued at five to eight thousand pounds was by John Frederick Herring, and it showed a black and white mare and foal. Drummond's also ready to testify that you're sufficiently knowledgeable about art to have spotted that "Mare Mourning" might be a Stubbs.'

Raphael's face had lost its mask-like cast. Now his near-black irises swivelled fractionally from side to side, as though he were reading something only he could see.

'I must've accidentally taken the Frederick Herring inste—'

A police siren sounded a few streets away. Raphael's head turned: the siren wailed for a few seconds, then, as abruptly as it had started, was shut off.

He turned back to face Robin. He didn't seem overly worried by the siren now it had stopped. Of course, he thought that it had been Matthew on the phone when he grabbed her.

'Yeah,' he said, regaining the thread of his thought. 'That's what I'll say. I took the painting of the piebald to be valued by mistake, never saw "Mare Mourning", had no idea it might be a Stubbs.'

'You can't have taken the piebald picture by mistake,' said Robin quietly. 'It didn't come from Chiswell House and the family's prepared to say so.'

'The family,' said Raphael, 'don't notice what's under their fucking noses. A Stubbs has been hanging in a damp spare bedroom for nigh on twenty years and nobody noticed, and you know why? Because they're such fucking arrogant snobs ... "Mare Mourning" was old Tinky's. She inherited it from the broken-down, alcoholic, gaga old Irish baronet she married before my grandfather. She had no idea what it was worth. She kept it because it was horsey and she loved horses.

'When her first husband died, she hopped over to England and pulled the same trick, became my grandfather's expensive private nurse and then his even more expensive wife. She died intestate and all her crap – it *was* mostly crap – got absorbed into the Chiswell estate. The Frederick Herring could easily have been one of hers and nobody noticed it, stuck away in some filthy corner of that bloody house.'

'What if the police trace the piebald picture?'

'They won't. It's my mother's. I'll destroy it. When the police ask me, I'll say my father told me he was going to flog it now he knew it was worth eight grand. "He must've sold it privately, officer."'

'Kinvara doesn't know the new story. She won't be able to back you up.'

'This is where her well-known instability and unhappiness with my father works in my favour. Izzy and Fizzy will line up to tell the world that she never paid much attention to what he was up to, because she didn't love him and was only in it for the money. Reasonable doubt is all I need.'

'What's going to happen when the police put it to Kinvara that you only restarted the affair because you realised she might be about to become fantastically wealthy?'

Raphael let out a long, slow hiss.

'Well,' he said quietly, 'if they can make Kinvara believe that, I'm fucked, aren't I? But right now, Kinvara believes her Raffy loves her more than anything in the world, and she's going to take a *lot* of convincing that's not true, because her whole life's going to fall apart otherwise. I drilled it into her: if they don't know about the affair, they can't touch us. I virtually had her reciting it while I fucked her. And I warned her they'd try and turn us against each other if either one of us was suspected. I've got her very well-schooled and I said, when in doubt, cry your eyes out, tell them nobody ever tells you anything and act bloody confused.'

'She's already told one silly lie to try and protect you, and the police know about it,' said Robin.

'What lie?'

'About the necklace, in the early hours of Sunday morning. Didn't she tell you? Maybe she realised you'd be angry.'

'*What did she say?*'

'Strike told her he didn't buy the new explanation for you going down to Chiswell House the morning your father died—'

'What d'you mean, he didn't buy it?' said Raphael, and Robin saw outraged vanity mingled with his panic.

'*I* thought it was convincing,' she assured him. 'Clever, to tell a story that you'd appear to give up only unwillingly. Everyone's always more disposed to believe something they believe they've uncovered for themsel—'

Raphael raised the gun so that it was close to her forehead again and even though the cold ring of metal had not yet touched her skin again, she felt it there.

'What lie did Kinvara tell?'

'She claimed you came to tell her that your mother removed diamonds from the necklace and replaced them with fakes.'

Raphael appeared horrified.

'What the fuck did she say that for?'

'Because she'd had a shock, I suppose, finding Strike and me in the grounds when you were hiding upstairs. Strike said he didn't believe the necklace story, so she panicked and made up a new version. The trouble is, this one's checkable.'

'The stupid cunt,' said Raphael quietly, but with a venom that made the back of Robin's neck prickle. 'That stupid, stupid cunt ... why didn't she just stick to our story? And ... no, wait ...' he said, with the air of a man suddenly making a welcome connection, and to Robin's mingled consternation and relief, he withdrew the gun from where it had been almost touching her, and laughed softly. '*That's* why she hid the necklace on Sunday afternoon. She gave me some fucking guff about not wanting Izzy or Fizzy to sneak in and take it ... well, she's stupid, but she's not hopeless. Unless someone checks the stones, we're still in the clear ... And they'll have to take apart the stable block to find it. OK,' he said, as though talking to himself, 'OK, I think all of that's recoverable.

'Is that it, Venetia? Is that all you've got?'

'No,' said Robin. 'There's Flick Purdue.'

'I don't know who that is.'

'Yes, you do. You picked her up months ago, and fed her the truth about the gallows, knowing she'd pass the information to Jimmy.'

'What a busy boy I've been,' said Raphael lightly. 'So what? Flick won't admit to shagging a Tory minister's son, especially if Jimmy might find out. She's as besotted with him as Kinvara is with me.'

'That's true, she didn't want to admit it, but somebody must have spotted you creeping out of her flat next morning. She tried to pretend you were an Indian waiter.'

Robin thought she saw a minute wince of surprise and displeasure. Raphael's *amour propre* was wounded at the thought that he could have been so described.

'OK,' he said, after a moment or two, 'OK, let's see ... what if it *was* a waiter Flick shagged, but she's maliciously claiming it was me because of her class warrior bullshit and the grudge her boyfriend's got against my family?'

'You stole her flatmate's credit card out of her bag in the kitchen.'

She could tell by the tightening of his mouth that he had not expected this. Doubtless he had thought that given Flick's lifestyle, suspicion would fall on anyone passing through her tiny, over-crowded flat, and perhaps especially Jimmy.

'Proof?' he said again.

'Flick can provide the date you were at her flat and if Laura testifies her credit card went missing that night—'

'But with no firm evidence I was ever there—'

'How did Flick find out about the gallows? We know she told Jimmy about them, not the other way around.'

'Well, it can't have been me, can it? I'm the only member of the family who never knew.'

'You knew everything. Kinvara had the full story from your father, and she passed it all to you.'

'No,' said Raphael, 'I think you'll find Flick heard about the gal-lows from the Butcher brothers. I'm reliably informed that one of them lives in London now. Yeah, I think I've heard a rumour one of them shagged their mate Jimmy's girlfriend. And believe me, the Butcher brothers aren't going to come over well in court, pair of shifty oiks driving gallows around under cover of darkness. I'm going to look a lot more plausible and presentable than Flick and the Butchers if this comes to court, I really am.'

'The police have got phone records,' Robin persisted. 'They know about an anonymous call to Geraint Winn, which was made around the time Flick found out about the gallows. We think you tipped off Winn anonymously about Samuel Murape. You knew Winn had a grudge against the Chiswells. Kinvara told you everything.'

'I don't know anything about that phone call, Your Honour,' said Raphael, 'and I'm very sorry that my late brother was a prize cunt to Rhiannon Winn, but that's nothing to do with me.'

'We think *you* made that threatening call to Izzy's office, the first day you were there, talking about people pissing themselves as they die,' said Robin, 'and we think it was *your* idea for Kinvara to pretend she kept hearing intruders in the grounds. Everything was designed to create as many witnesses as possible to the fact that your father had reason to be anxious and paranoid, that he might crack under extreme pressure—'

'He *was* under extreme pressure. He *was* being blackmailed by Jimmy Knight. Geraint Winn *was* trying to force him out of his job. Those aren't lies, they're facts and they're going to be pretty sensational in a courtroom, especially once the Samuel Murape story gets out.'

'Except that you made stupid, avoidable mistakes.'

He sat up straighter and leaned forwards, his elbow sliding a few inches, so that the nozzle of the gun grew larger. His eyes, which had been smudges in the shadow, became clearly defined again, onyx black and white. Robin wondered how she had ever thought him handsome.

'What mistakes?'

As he said it, Robin saw, out of the corner of her eye, a flashing blue light glide over the bridge just visible through the window to her right, which was blocked from Raphael's view by the side of the boat. The light vanished and the bridge was reabsorbed by the deepening darkness.

'For one thing,' said Robin carefully, 'it was a mistake to keep meeting Kinvara in the lead-up to the murder. She kept pretending she'd forgotten where she was meeting your father, didn't she? Just to get a couple of minutes with you, just to see you and check up on you—'

'That's not proof.'

'Kinvara was followed to Le Manoir aux Quat'Saisons on her birthday.'

His eyes narrowed.

'Who by?'

'Jimmy Knight. Flick's confirmed it. Jimmy thought your father was with Kinvara and wanted to confront him publicly about not giving him his money. Obviously, your father wasn't there, so Jimmy went home and wrote an angry blog about how High Tories spend their money, mentioning Le Manoir aux Quat'Saisons by name.'

'Well, unless he saw me sneaking into Kinvara's hotel suite,' said Raphael, 'which he didn't, because I took fucking good care to make sure nobody did, that's all supposition, too.'

'All right,' said Robin, 'what about the *second* time you were over-heard having sex in the gallery bathroom? That wasn't Francesca. You were with Kinvara.'

'Prove it.'

'Kinvara was in town that day, buying lachesis pills and pretending she was angry that your father was still seeing you, which was all part of the cover story that she hated you. She rang your father to check that he was having lunch elsewhere. Strike overheard that call. What you and Kinvara didn't realise was that your father was having lunch only a hundred yards away from where you were having sex.

'When your father forced his way into the bathroom, he found a tube of lachesis pills on the floor. That's why he nearly had a heart attack. He knew that's what she'd come to town for. He knew who'd just been having sex with you in the bathroom.'

Raphael's smile was more of a grimace.

'Yeah, that was a fuck-up. The day he came into our office, talking about Lachesis – "knows when everyone's number's up" – I realised later, he was trying to put the frighteners on me, wasn't he? I didn't know what the hell he was on about at the time. But when you and your crippled boss mentioned the pills at Chiswell House, Kinvara twigged: they fell out of her pocket while we were screwing. We hadn't known what first tipped him off . . . it was only after I heard he was ringing Le Manoir about Freddie's money clip that I knew he must have realised something was going on. Then he invited me over to Ebury Street and I knew he was about to confront me about it, and we needed to get a move on, killing him.'

The entirely matter-of-fact way he discussed patricide chilled Robin. He might have been talking about wallpapering a room.

'He must've been planning to produce those pills during his big "I know you're fucking my wife" speech . . . why didn't I spot them on the floor? I tried to put the room straight afterwards, but they must've rolled out of his pocket or something . . . it's harder than you'd think,' said Raphael, 'tidying up around a corpse you've just dispatched. I was surprised, actually, how much it affected me.'

She had never heard his narcissism so clearly. His interest and sympathy was entirely for himself. His dead father was nothing.

'The police have taken statements from Francesca and her parents, now,' Robin said. 'She absolutely denies being in the bathroom with you that second time. Her parents never believed her, but—'

'They didn't believe her because she's even fucking dumber than Kinvara.'

'The police are combing through security camera footage from the shops she says she was in, while you and Kinvara were in the bathroom.'

'OK,' said Raphael, 'well, worst comes to the worst, and they can prove she wasn't with me, I might have to come clean about the fact that it was *another* young lady I was with in the bathroom that day, whose reputation I've been chivalrously trying to defend.'

'Will you really be able to find a woman to lie for you, in court, on a murder charge?' asked Robin, in disbelief.

'The woman who owns this houseboat is mad for me,' said Raphael softly. 'We had a thing going before I went inside. She visited me in jail and everything. She's in rehab right now. Crazy bitch, loves drama. Thinks she's an artist. She drinks too much, she's a real pain in the arse, actually, but she fucks like a rabbit. She never bothered taking the spare key to this place off me, and she keeps a key to her mummy's house in that drawer over there—'

'It wouldn't happen to be her mother's house where you had the helium, tubing and gloves delivered, would it?' asked Robin.

Raphael blinked. He hadn't expected that.

'You needed an address that didn't seem connected to you. You made sure it was delivered while the owners were away, or at work, then you could let yourself in, collect the failed delivery card . . .'

'Pick it up, disguised and get it couriered it off to dear old Dad's house, yeah.'

'And Flick took delivery and Kinvara made sure she hid it from your father until it was time to kill him?'

'That's right,' said Raphael. 'You pick up a lot of tips in jail. Fake

IDs, vacant buildings, empty addresses, you can do a hell of a lot with them. Once you're dead—' Robin's scalp prickled – 'nobody's going to connect me with any of the addresses.'

'The owner of this barge—'

'Is going to be telling everyone she was having sex with me in Drummond's bathroom, remember? She's on my team, Venetia,' he said quietly, 'so it's not looking good for you, is it?'

'There were other mistakes,' said Robin, her mouth dry.

'Like?'

'You told Flick your father needed a cleaner.'

'Yeah, because it makes her and Jimmy look fishy as hell, that she wheedled her way into my father's house. The jury'll be focused on that, not how she found out he wanted a cleaner. I've already told you, she's going to look like a grubby little tart with a grudge in the dock. That's just one more lie.'

'But she stole a note from your father, a note he wrote while he was trying to check Kinvara's story with Le Manoir aux Quat'Saisons. I found it in her bathroom. She'd lied, told him her mother was going to the hotel with her. They'd never normally give out information about guests, but he was a government minister and he'd previously been there, so we think he managed to trick them into agreeing that they could remember the family vehicle there and that it was a shame her mother hadn't made it. He made a note of the suite Kinvara was in, probably pretending he'd forgotten it, and he was trying to get hold of the bill, to see whether there was any sign of two lots of breakfast or dinner, I suppose. When the prosecution produce the note and the bill in court—'

'*You* found that note, did you?' said Raphael.

Robin's stomach turned over. She had not meant to give Raphael another reason to shoot her.

'I knew I'd underestimated you after that dinner we had, at Nam Long Le Shaker,' said Raphael. It wasn't a compliment. His eyes were narrowed, his nostrils flared in dislike. 'You were a mess, but you were still asking fucking inconvenient questions. You and your boss were cosier with the police than I expected, too. And even after I tipped off the *Mail*—'

'That was *you*,' said Robin, wondering how she had never realised. '*You* put the press and Mitch Patterson back on us . . .'

'I told them you'd left your husband for Strike, but that he was still shagging his ex. Izzy had given me that bit of gossip. I thought you needed slowing down, you two, because you kept poking away at my alibi . . . but after I've shot you,' – an icy chill ran the length of Robin's body – 'your boss'll be busy answering the press's questions about how your body ended up in a canal, won't he? I think that's called killing two birds with one stone.'

'Even if I'm dead,' said Robin, her voice as steady as she could make it, 'there'll still be your father's note and the hotel's testimony—'

'OK, so he was worried about what Kinvara was doing at Le Manoir,' said Raphael roughly. 'I've just told you, nobody saw me on the premises. The stupid cow did ask for two glasses with the champagne, but she could've been with someone else.'

'You aren't going to have any opportunity to cook up a new story with her,' said Robin, her mouth drier than ever, her tongue sticking to the roof of her mouth as she tried to sound calm and confident. 'She's in custody now, she isn't as clever as you – and you made other mistakes,' Robin rushed on, 'stupid ones, because you had to enact the plan in a hurry once you realised your father was onto you.'

'Like?'

'Like Kinvara taking away the packaging on the amitriptyline, after she'd doctored the orange juice. Kinvara forgetting to tell you the trick to closing the front door properly. And,' said Robin, aware that she was playing her very last card, 'her throwing the front door key to you, at Paddington.'

In the wordless space that now stretched between them, Robin thought she heard footsteps close at hand. She didn't dare look out of the window in case she alerted Raphael, who appeared too appalled by what she had just said to take in anything else.

'"Throwing the front door key to me?"' repeated Raphael, with fragile bravado. 'What the hell are you talking about?'

'The keys to Ebury Street are restricted, almost impossible to copy. The pair of you only had access to one: hers, because your father was suspicious of you both by the time he died, and he'd made sure the spare was out of your reach.

'She needed the key to get into the house and doctor the orange juice and you needed it to go in early next morning and suffocate him. So you cobbled together a plan at the last minute: she'd pass you the key at a prearranged spot at Paddington, where you'd be disguised as a homeless person.

'You were caught on camera. The police have got people enlarging and clarifying the image right now. They think you must have bought things from a charity shop in haste, which might produce another useful witness. The police are now combing CCTV footage for your movements from Paddington onwards.'

Raphael said nothing at all for nearly a minute. His eyes were moving fractionally from left to right, as he tried to find a loophole, an escape.

'That's . . . inconvenient,' he said finally. 'I didn't think I was on camera, sitting there.'

Robin thought she could see hope slipping away from him now. Quietly, she continued, 'As per your plan, Kinvara arrived home in Oxfordshire, called Drummond and left a message that she wanted the necklace valued, to set up that whole back-up story.

'Early next morning, another burner phone was used to call both Geraint Winn and Jimmy Knight. Both were lured out of their houses, presumably with a promise of information on Chiswell. That was you, making sure they were in the frame if murder was suspected.'

'No proof,' muttered Raphael automatically, but still his eyes darted this way and that, searching for invisible lifelines.

'You let yourself into the house very early in the morning, expecting to find your father almost comatose after his early morning orange juice, but—'

'He *was* out of it, at first,' said Raphael. His eyes had become glazed, and Robin knew that he was remembering what had happened, watching it, inside his head. 'He was slumped on the sofa, very groggy. I walked straight past him into the kitchen, opened my box of toys—'

For a sliver of a second, Robin saw again the shrink-wrapped head, the grey hair pressed around the face so that only the gaping black hole of the mouth was visible. Raphael had done that; Raphael, who currently had a gun pointing at her face.

'—but while I'm arranging everything, the old bastard wakes up, sees me fixing the tubing onto the helium canister and comes back to fucking life. He staggers up, grabs Freddie's sword off the wall and tries to fight, but I got it off him. Bent the blade doing it. Forced him down into the chair – he was still struggling – and—'

Raphael mimed putting the bag over his father's head.

'*Caput.*'

'And then,' said Robin, her mouth still dry, 'you made those phone calls from his phone that were supposed to establish your alibi. Kinvara had told you his passcode, of course. And you left, without closing the door properly.'

Robin didn't know whether she was imagining movement out of the porthole to her left. She kept her eyes fixed on Raphael, and the slightly wavering gun.

'Loads of this is circumstantial,' he muttered, eyes still glazed. 'Flick and Francesca have both got motives for lying about me . . . I didn't end it well with Francesca . . . I might still have a chance . . . I might . . . '

'There's no chance, Raff,' said Robin. 'Kinvara isn't going to lie for you much longer. When they tell her the truth about "Mare Mourning", she's going to put everything together for the first time. I think *you* insisted she move it into to the drawing room, to protect it from the damp in the spare room. How did you manage that? Did you make up some rubbish about it reminding *you* of her dead mare? Then she's going to realise you started up the affair again once you knew its true value, and that all the dreadful things you said to her when you ended it were true. And worst of all,' said Robin, 'she's going to realise that when the two of you heard intruders in the grounds – real ones, this time – you let the woman you were supposedly madly in love with walk out into the grounds in the dark, in her nightdress, while you stayed behind to protect—'

'*All right!*' he shouted suddenly and he advanced the gun nozzle until it pressed into her forehead again. 'Stop fucking *talking*, will you?'

Robin sat quite still. She imagined how it would feel when he pressed the trigger. He had said he would shoot her through a cushion to muffle the sound, but perhaps he had forgotten, perhaps he was about to lose control.

'D'you know what it's like in jail?' he asked.

She tried to say 'no', but the sound wouldn't come.

'The noise,' he whispered. 'The smell. The ugly, dumb people – like animals, some of them. Worse than animals. I never knew there were people like it. The places they make you eat and shit. Watching your back all the time, waiting for violence. The clanging, the yelling and the fucking squalor. I'd rather be buried alive. I won't do it again ...

'I was going to have a dream life. I was going to be free, totally free. I'd never have to kowtow to the likes of fucking Drummond again. There's a villa on Capri I've had my eye on for a long time. View out over the Gulf of Naples. Then I'd have a nice pad in London ... new car, once my fucking ban's lifted ... imagine walking along and knowing you could buy anything, do anything. A dream life ...

'Couple of little problems to get out of the way before I was completely sorted ... Flick, easy: late night, dark road, knife in the ribs, victim of street crime.

'And Kinvara ... once she'd made a will in my favour, after a few years, she'd have broken her neck riding an unsuitable horse or drowned out in Italy ... she's a terrible swimmer ...

'And then all of them could fuck themselves, couldn't they? The Chiswells, my whore of a mother. I'd need nothing from anyone. I'd have everything ...

'But that's all gone,' he said. Dark-skinned though he was, she saw that he had turned ashen, the dark shadows beneath his eyes hollow in the half-light. 'It's all gone. You know what, Venetia? I'm going to blow your fucking brains out, because I've decided I don't like you. I think I'd like to see your fucking head explode before mine comes off—'

'Raff—'

'Raff . . . Raff . . .' he bleated, imitating her, 'why do women all think they're different? You're not different, none of you.'

He was reaching for the limp cushion beside him.

'We'll go together. I'd like to arrive in hell with a sexy girl on my ar—'

With a great splintering of wood, the door crashed open. Raphael spun around, pointing a gun at the large figure that had just fallen inside. Robin launched herself over the table to grab his arm, but Raphael knocked her backwards with his elbow and she felt blood spurt as her lip split.

'Raff, no, don't – *don't!*'

He had stood up, stooped in the cramped space, the barrel of the gun in his mouth. Strike, who had shouldered in the door, stood panting feet away from him, and behind Strike was Wardle.

'Go on and do it, then, you cowardly little fuck,' said Strike.

Robin wanted to protest, but couldn't make a noise.

There was a small, metallic click.

'Took out the bullets at Chiswell House, you stupid bastard,' said Strike, hobbling forwards and smacking the revolver out of Raphael's mouth. 'Not half as clever as you thought you were, eh?'

There was a great ringing in Robin's ears. Raphael was spitting oaths in English and Italian, screaming threats, thrashing and twisting as Strike helped bend him over the table for Wardle to cuff him, but she stumbled away from the group as though in a dream, backwards towards the kitchen area of the galley, where pots and pans were hanging and white kitchen roll sat, ludicrously ordinary, beside a tiny sink. She could feel her lip swelling where Raphael had hit her. She tore off some kitchen roll, ran it under the cold tap and pressed it to her bleeding mouth, while through the porthole she watched uniformed officers hurrying through the black gates, taking possession of the gun and of the struggling Raphael, whom Wardle had just dragged onto the bank.

She had just been held at gunpoint. Nothing seemed real. Now the police were stomping in and out of the barge, but it was all noise and echo, and now she realised that Strike was standing beside her, and he seemed the only person with any reality.

'How did you know?' she asked thickly, through the cold wodge of tissue.

'Twigged five minutes after you left. The last three digits on that number you showed me on those supposed texts from Matthew were the same as one of the burner phone numbers. Went after you but you were already gone. Layborn sent panda cars out and I've been calling you nonstop ever since. Why didn't you pick up?'

'My phone was on silent in my bag. Now it's in the canal.'

She craved a stiff drink. Maybe, she thought vaguely, there really was a bar somewhere nearby ... but of course, she wouldn't be allowed to go to a bar. She was facing hours back at New Scotland Yard. They would need a long statement. She would have to relive the last hour in detail. She felt exhausted.

'How did you know I was here?'

'Called Izzy and asked if Raphael knew anyone in the vicinity of that fake address he was trying to get you to. She told me he'd had some posh druggie girlfriend who owned a barge. He was running out of places to go. The police have been watching his flat for the last two days.'

'And you knew the gun was empty?'

'I *hoped* it was empty,' he corrected her. 'For all I knew, he'd checked it and reloaded.'

He groped in his pocket. His fingers shook slightly as he lit a cigarette. He inhaled, then said:

'You did bloody well to keep him talking that long, Robin, but next time you get a call from an unknown number, you bloody well call it back and check who's on the other end. And don't you ever – *ever* – tell a suspect anything about your personal life again.'

'Would it be OK if I have *two minutes*,' she asked, pressing the cold kitchen roll against her swollen and bleeding lip, 'to enjoy not being dead, before you start?'

Strike blew out a jet of smoke.

'Yeah, fair enough,' he said, and pulled her clumsily into a one-armed hug.

ONE MONTH LATER

EPILOGUE

Your past is dead, Rebecca. It has no longer any hold on you—
has nothing to do with you – as you are now.

Henrik Ibsen, *Rosmersholm*

The Paralympics had been and gone, and September was doing its
best to wash away the memory of the long, Union-Jacked summer
days, when London had basked for weeks in the world's attention. Rain was pattering against the Cheyne Walk Brasserie's high
windows, competing with Serge Gainsbourg as he crooned 'Black
Trombone' from hidden speakers.

Strike and Robin, who had arrived together, had only just sat
down when Izzy, who had chosen the restaurant for its proximity to
her flat, arrived in a slightly dishevelled flapping of Burberry trench
coat and sodden umbrella, the latter taking some time to collapse
at the door.

Strike had only spoken to their client once since the case had
been solved, and then briefly, because Izzy had been too shocked
and distressed to say much. They were meeting today at Strike's
request, because there was one last piece of unfinished business in
the Chiswell case. Izzy had told Strike by phone, when they arranged
lunch, that she had not been out much since Raphael's arrest. 'I can't
face people. It's all so dreadful.'

'How are you?' she said anxiously, as Strike manoeuvred himself
out from behind the white-clothed table to accept a damp embrace.
'And oh, poor Robin, I'm so sorry,' she added, hurrying around the
other side of the table to hug Robin, before saying distractedly, 'Oh

yes, please, thank you,' to the unsmiling waitress, who took her wet raincoat and umbrella.

Sitting down, Izzy said, 'I promised myself I wouldn't cry,' then grabbed a napkin from the table and pressed it firmly to her tear ducts. 'Sorry . . . keep doing this. *Trying* not to be embarrassing . . .'

She cleared her throat and straightened her back.

'It's just been such a shock,' she whispered.

'Of course it has,' said Robin, and Izzy gave her a watery smile.

'*C'est l'automne de ma vie,*' sang Gainsbourg. '*Plus personne ne m'étonne . . .*'

'You found this place OK, then?' Izzy said, scrabbling to find conventional conversational ground. 'Quite pretty, isn't it?' she said, inviting them to admire the Provençal restaurant which Strike had thought, as he entered, had a feeling of Izzy's flat about it, translated into French. Here was the same conservative mix of traditional and modern: black and white photographs hung on stark white walls, chairs and benches covered in scarlet and turquoise leather, and old-fashioned bronze and glass chandeliers with rose-coloured lampshades.

The waitress returned with menus and offered to take their drink order.

'Should we wait?' Izzy asked, gesturing at the empty seat.

'He's running late,' said Strike, who was craving beer. 'Might as well order drinks.'

After all, there was nothing more to find out. Today was about explanations. An awkward silence fell again as the waitress walked away.

'Oh, gosh, I don't know whether you've heard,' Izzy said suddenly to Strike, with an air of being relieved to have found what to her was standard gossip. 'Charlie's been admitted to hospital.'

'Really?' he said, with no sign of particular interest.

'Yah, bed rest. She had something – leak of amniotic fluid, I think – anyway, they want her under observation.'

Strike nodded, expressionless. Ashamed of herself for wishing to know more, Robin kept quiet. The drinks arrived. Izzy, who seemed too keyed up to have noticed Strike's unenthusiastic response to what was, for her, a safe subject of mutual interest, said:

'I heard Jago hit the roof when he saw that story about the two of you in the press. Probably delighted to have her where he can keep an eye—'

But Izzy caught something in Strike's expression that made her desist. She took a slug of wine, checked to see whether anyone at the few occupied tables was listening, and said:

'I suppose the police are keeping you informed? You know Kinvara's admitted everything?'

'Yeah,' said Strike, 'we heard.'

Izzy shook her head, her eyes filling with tears again.

'It's been so awful. One's friends don't know what to say ... I still can't *believe* it. It's just so incredible. *Raff* ... I wanted to go and see him, you know. I really *needed* to see him ... but he refused. He won't see anyone.'

She gulped more wine.

'He must have gone mad or something. He must be ill, mustn't he? To have done it? Must be mentally ill.'

Robin remembered the dark barge, where Raphael had spoken in holy accents of the life he wanted, of the villa in Capri, the bachelor pad in London, and the new car, once the ban imposed for running over a young mother had been lifted. She thought how meticulously he had planned his father's death, the errors made only because of the haste with which the murder was to be enacted. She pictured his expression over the gun, as he had asked her why women thought there was any difference between them: the mother whom he called a whore, the stepmother he had seduced, Robin, whom he was about to kill so that he didn't have to enter hell alone. Was he ill in any sense that would put him in a psychiatric institution rather than the prison that so terrified him? Or had his dream of patricide been spawned in the shadowy wasteland between sickness and irreducible malevolence?

'... he had an awful childhood,' Izzy was saying, and then, though neither Strike nor Robin had responded, 'he *did*, you know, he really did. I don't want to speak ill of Papa, but Freddie was *everything*. Papa wasn't kind to Raff and the Orca – I mean, Ornella, his mother – well, Torks always says she's more like a high-class hooker than anything else. When Raff wasn't at boarding school she dragged him around with her, always chasing some new man.'

'There are worse childhoods,' said Strike.

Robin, who had just been thinking that Raphael's life with his mother sounded not unlike the little she knew about Strike's early years, was nevertheless surprised to hear him express this view so bluntly.

'Plenty of people go through worse than having a party girl for a mother,' he said, 'and they don't end up committing murder. Look at Billy Knight. No mother at all for most of his life. Violent, alcoholic father, beaten and neglected, ends up with serious mental illness and he's never hurt anyone. He came to my office in the throes of psychosis, trying to get justice for someone else.'

'Yes,' said Izzy hastily, 'yes, that's true, of course.'

But Robin had the impression that even now, Izzy could not equate the pain of Raphael and Billy. The former's suffering would always evoke more pity in her than the latter's, because a Chiswell was innately different to the kind of motherless boy whose beatings were hidden in the woods, where estate workers lived according to the laws of their kind.

'And here he is,' said Strike.

Billy Knight had just entered the restaurant, raindrops glittering on his shorn hair. Though still underweight, his face was fuller, his person and clothes cleaner. He had been released from hospital only a week previously, and was currently living in Jimmy's flat on Charlemont Road.

'Hello,' he said to Strike. 'Sorry I'm late. Tube took longer'n I thought.'

'No problem,' said the two women, at the same time.

'You're Izzy,' said Billy, sitting down beside her. 'Haven't seen you 'n a long time.'

'No,' said Izzy, a little over-heartily. 'It's been quite a while, hasn't it?'

Robin held out a hand across the table.

'Hi, Billy, I'm Robin.'

'Hello,' he said again, shaking it.

'Would you like some wine, Billy?' offered Izzy. 'Or beer?'

'Can't drink on my meds,' he told her.

'Ah, no, of course not,' said Izzy, flustered. 'Um ... well, have some water, and there's your menu ... we haven't ordered yet ...'

Once the waitress had been and gone, Strike addressed Billy.

'I made you a promise when I visited you in hospital,' he said. 'I told you I'd find out what happened to the child you saw strangled.'

'Yeah,' said Billy apprehensively. It was in the hopes of hearing the answer to the twenty-year-old mystery that he had travelled from East Ham to Chelsea in the rain. 'You said on the phone that you'd worked it out.'

'Yes,' said Strike, 'but I want you to hear it from someone who knew, who was there at the time, so you get the full story.'

'You?' Billy said, turning to Izzy. 'You were *there?* Up at the horse?'

'No, no,' said Izzy hastily. 'It happened during the school holidays.'

She took a fortifying gulp of wine, set down her glass, drew a deep breath and said:

'Fizz and I were both staying with school friends. I – I heard what happened, afterwards ...

'What happened was ... Freddie was home from university and he'd brought a few friends back with him. Papa left them in the house because he had some old regimental dinner to attend in London ...

'Freddie could be ... the truth is, he was awfully naughty sometimes. He brought up a lot of good wine from the cellar and they all got sloshed and then one of the girls said she'd wanted to try the truth of that story about the white horse ... you know the one,' she said to Billy, the Uffington local. 'If you turn three times in the eye and make a wish ...'

'Yeah,' said Billy, with a nod. His haunted eyes were huge.

'So they all left the house in the dark, but being Freddie ... he *was* naughty ... they made a detour through the woods to *your* house. Steda Cottage. Because Freddie wanted to buy some, ah, marijuana, was it, your brother grew?'

'Yeah,' said Billy, again.

'Freddie wanted to get some, so they could smoke it, up at the

641

horse while the girls were making wishes. Of course, they shouldn't have been driving. They were already drunk.

'Well, when they got to your house, your father wasn't there—'

'He was in the barn,' said Billy suddenly. 'Finishing a set of . . . you know.'

The memory seemed to have forced its way to the front of his mind, triggered by her recital. Strike saw Billy's left hand holding tightly to his right, to prevent the recurrence of the tic that seemed for Billy to have something of the significance of warding off evil. Rain continued to lash the restaurant windows and Serge Gainsbourg sang, *'Oh, je voudrais tant que tu te souviennes . . .'*

'So,' said Izzy, taking another deep breath, 'the way I heard it, from one of the girls who was there . . . I don't want to say who,' she added a little defensively to Strike and Robin, 'it's a long time ago and she was traumatised by the whole thing . . . well, Freddie and his friends clattering into the cottage woke you up, Billy. There was quite a crowd of them in there, and Jimmy rolled them a joint before they set off . . . Anyway,' Izzy swallowed, 'you were hungry, and Jimmy . . . or maybe,' she winced, 'maybe it was Freddie, I don't know . . . they thought it would be funny to crumble up some of what they were smoking and put it in your yoghurt.'

Robin imagined Freddie's friends, some of them perhaps enjoying the exotic thrill of sitting in that dark workman's cottage with a local lad who sold drugs, but others, like the girl who had told Izzy the story, uneasy about what was going on, but too young, too scared of their laughing peers to intervene. They had seemed like adults to the five-year-old Billy, but now Robin knew that they had all been nineteen to twenty-one at most.

'Yeah,' said Billy quietly. 'I knew they'd gave me something.'

'So, then, Jimmy wanted to join them, going up the hill. I heard he'd taken a bit of a fancy to one of the girls,' said Izzy primly. 'But you weren't very well, after being fed that yoghurt. He couldn't leave you alone in that state, so he took you with him.

'You all piled into a couple of Land Rovers and off you went, to Dragon Hill.'

'But . . . no, this is wrong,' said Billy. The haunted expression had returned to his face. 'Where's the little girl? She was already there. She was with us in the car. I remember them taking her out when we got to the hill. She was crying for her mum.'

'It – it wasn't a girl,' said Izzy. 'That was just Freddie's – well, it was his idea of humour—'

'It *was* a girl. They called her by a girl's name,' said Billy. 'I remember.'

'Yes,' said Izzy miserably. 'Raphaela.'

'That's it!' said Billy loudly, and heads turned across the restaurant. 'That's it!' Billy repeated in a whisper, his eyes wide. 'Raphaela, that's what they called her—'

'It wasn't a girl, Billy . . . it was my little – it was my little—'

Izzy pressed the napkin to her eyes again.

'*So* sorry . . . it was my little brother, Raphael. Freddie and his friends were supposed to be babysitting him, with my father away from home. Raff was awfully cute when he was little. He'd been woken up by them, too, I think, and the girls said they couldn't leave him in the house, they should take him with them. Freddie didn't want to. He wanted to leave Raff there on his own, but the girls promised they'd take care of him.

'But once they were up there, Freddie was awfully drunk and he'd had a lot of weed and Raff wouldn't stop crying and Freddie got angry. He said he was ruining everything and then . . .'

'He throttled him,' said Billy, with a panicked expression. 'It was real, he killed—'

'No, no, he didn't!' said Izzy, distressed. 'Billy, you know he didn't – you *must* remember Raff, he came to us every summer, he's alive!'

'Freddie put his hands round Raphael's neck,' said Strike, 'and squeezed until he was unconscious. Raphael urinated. He collapsed. But he didn't die.'

Billy's left hand was still gripping his right tightly.

'I *did* see it.'

'Yeah, you did,' said Strike, 'and, all things considered, you were a bloody good witness.'

The waitress returned with their meals. Once everyone was

served, Strike with his rib-eye steak and chips, the two women with their quinoa salads and Billy with the soup, which was all he seemed to have felt confident ordering, Izzy continued her story.

'Raff told me what had happened when I got back from the holidays. He was so little, so upset, I tried to bring it up with Papa, but he wouldn't listen. He just sort of brushed me off. Said Raphael was whiny and always ... always complaining ...

'And I look back,' she said to Strike and Robin, her eyes filling with tears again, 'and I think about it all ... how much hate Raff must've felt, after things like that ... '

'Yeah, Raphael's defence team will probably try and use that kind of thing,' said Strike briskly, as he attacked his steak, 'but the fact remains, Izzy, that he didn't act on his desire to see your father dead until he found out there was a Stubbs hanging upstairs.'

'A disputed Stubbs,' Izzy corrected Strike, pulling a handkerchief out of her cuff and blowing her nose. 'Henry Drummond thinks it's a copy. The man from Christie's is hopeful, but there's a Stubbs aficionado in the States who's flying over to examine it, and he says it doesn't match the notes Stubbs made of the lost painting ... but honestly,' she shook her head, 'I don't give a damn. What that thing's led to, what it's done to our family ... it can go in a skip for all I care. There are more important things,' said Izzy croakily, 'than money.'

Strike had an excuse for making no reply, his mouth being full of steak, but he wondered whether it had occurred to Izzy that the fragile man beside her was living in a tiny two-roomed flat in East Ham with his brother, and that Billy was, properly speaking, owed money from the sale of the last set of gallows. Perhaps, once the Stubbs was sold, the Chiswell family might consider fulfilling that obligation.

Billy was eating his soup in an almost trancelike state, his eyes unfocused. Robin thought his deeply contemplative state seemed peaceful, even happy.

'So, I must've got confused, mustn't I?' Billy asked at last. He spoke now with the confidence of a man who feels firm footing in reality. 'I saw the horse being buried and thought it was the kid. I got mixed up, that's all.'

'Well,' said Strike, 'I think there might be a bit more to it than that. You knew that the man who'd throttled the child was the same one burying the horse in the dell with your father. I suppose Freddie wasn't around much, being so much older than you, so you weren't completely clear who he was . . . but I think you've blocked out a lot about the horse and how it died. You conflated two acts of cruelty, perpetrated by the same person.'

'What happened,' asked Billy, now slightly apprehensive, 'to the horse?'

'Don't you remember Spotty?' asked Izzy.

Amazed, Billy set down his soup spoon and held his hand horizontally perhaps three feet off the ground.

'That little – yeah . . . didn't it graze the croquet lawn?'

'She was an *ancient*, miniature spotted horse,' Izzy explained to Strike and Robin. 'She was the last of Tinky's lot. Tinky had awful, kitschy taste, even in horses . . . '

(. . . *nobody noticed, and you know why? Because they're such fucking arrogant snobs . . .*)

' . . . but Spotty was awfully sweet,' Izzy admitted. 'She'd follow you around like a dog if you were in the garden . . .

'I don't think Freddie *meant* to do it . . . but,' she said hopelessly, 'oh, I don't know any more. I don't know what he was thinking . . . he always had a terrible temper. Something had annoyed him. Papa was out, he took Papa's rifle out of the gun cabinet, went up on the roof and started shooting at birds and then . . . well, he told me afterwards he hadn't meant to hit Spotty, but he must have been aiming near her, mustn't he, to kill her?'

He was aiming at her, thought Strike. *You don't put two bullets in an animal's head from that distance without meaning to.*

'Then he panicked,' said Izzy. 'He got Jack o' – I mean, your father,' she told Billy, 'to help him bury the body. When Papa came home Freddie pretended Spotty had collapsed, that he'd called the vet who'd taken her away, but of course, that story didn't stand up for two minutes. Papa was *furious* when he found out the truth. He couldn't abide cruelty to animals.

'I was heartbroken when I heard,' said Izzy sadly. 'I loved Spotty.'

'You didn't by any chance put a cross in the ground where she'd been buried, did you, Izzy?' asked Robin, her fork suspended in mid-air.

'How on *earth* did you know that?' asked Izzy, astonished, as tears trickled out of her eyes again, and she reached again for her handkerchief.

The downpour continued as Strike and Robin walked away from the brasserie together, along Chelsea Embankment towards Albert Bridge. The slate-grey Thames rolled eternally onwards, its surface barely troubled by the thickening rain that threatened to extinguish Strike's cigarette, and soaked the few tendrils of hair that had escaped the hood of Robin's raincoat.

'Well, that's the upper classes for you,' said Strike. 'By all means throttle their kids, but don't touch their horses.'

'Not entirely fair,' Robin reproved him. 'Izzy thinks Raphael was treated appallingly.'

'Nothing to what he's got coming to him in Dartmoor,' said Strike indifferently. 'My pity's limited.'

'Yes,' said Robin, 'you made that abundantly clear.'

Their shoes smacked wetly on the shining pavement.

'CBT still going all right?' Strike asked, who was limiting the question to once weekly. 'Keeping up your exercises?'

'Diligently,' said Robin.

'Don't be flippant, I'm serious—'

'So am I,' said Robin, without heat. 'I'm doing what I've got to do. I haven't had a single panic attack for weeks. How's your leg?'

'Getting better. Doing my stretches. Watching my diet.'

'You just ate half a potato field and most of a cow.'

'That was the last meal I can charge to the Chiswells,' said Strike. 'Wanted to make the most of it. What are your plans this afternoon?'

'I need to get that file from Andy, then I'll ring the guy in Finsbury Park and see whether he'll talk to us. Oh, and Nick and Ilsa said to ask if you want to come for a takeaway curry tonight.'

Robin had caved in to the combined insistence of Nick, Ilsa and Strike himself that going to live in a box room in a house full of strangers was undesirable in the immediate aftermath of being taken hostage at gunpoint. In three days' time, she would be moving into a room in a flat in Earl's Court, which she would share with a gay actor friend of Ilsa's whose previous partner had moved out. Her new flatmate's stated requirements were cleanliness, sanity and tolerance of irregular hours.

'Yeah, great,' said Strike. 'I'll have to head back to the office first. Barclay reckons he's got Dodgy bang to rights this time. Another teenager, going in and out of a hotel together.'

'Great,' said Robin. 'No, I don't mean great, I mean—'

'It *is* great,' said Strike firmly, as the rain splashed over and around them. 'Another satisfied client. The bank balance is looking uncharacteristically healthy. Might be able to hike your salary up a bit. Anyway, I'm going up here. See you at Nick and Ilsa's later, then.'

They parted with a wave, concealing from each other the slight smile that each wore once safely walking away, pleased to know that they would meet again in a few short hours, over curry and beer at Nick and Ilsa's. But soon Robin had given over her thoughts to the questions needing answers from a man in Finsbury Park.

Head bowed against the rain, she had no attention left to spare for the magnificent mansion past which she was walking, its rain-specked windows facing the great river, its front doors engraved with twin swans.

ACKNOWLEDGEMENTS

For reasons not entirely related to the complexity of the plot, *Lethal White* has been one of the most challenging books I've written, but it's also one of my favourites. I truly couldn't have done it without the help of the following people.

David Shelley, my wonderful editor, allowed me all the time I needed to make the novel exactly what I wanted it to be. Without his understanding, patience and skill, there might not be a *Lethal White* at all.

My husband Neil read the manuscript while I was writing it. His feedback was invaluable and he also supported me in a thousand practical ways, but I think I'm most grateful for the fact that he never once asked why I decided to write a large, complex novel while also working on a play and two screenplays. I know he knows why, but there aren't many people who would have resisted the temptation.

Mr Galbraith still can't quite believe his luck at having a fantastic agent who is also a dear friend. Thank you, The Other Neil (Blair).

Many people helped me research the various locations Strike and Robin visit during the course of this story and gave me the benefit of their experience and knowledge. My deepest thanks to:

Simon Berry and Stephen Fry, who took me for a fabulous, memorable lunch at Pratt's and enabled me to look at the betting book; Jess Phillips MP, who was incredibly helpful, gave me an insider's tour of the Commons and Portcullis House and, with Sophie Francis-Cansfield, David Doig and Ian Stevens, answered innumerable questions about life at Westminster; Baroness Joanna Shields, who was so kind and generous with her time, showed me inside DCMS, answered all my questions and enabled me to visit Lancaster House; Raquel Black, who couldn't have been more helpful, especially in taking pictures when I ran out of battery; Ian Chapman and James Yorke, who gave me a fascinating tour of Lancaster House; and Brian Spanner, for the daytrip to Horse Isle.

I'd be totally lost without my office and home support team. Huge thanks, therefore, to Di Brooks, Danni Cameron, Angela Milne, Ross Milne and Kaisa Tiensuu for their hard work and good humour, both of which are deeply appreciated.

After sixteen years together, I hope Fiona Shapcott knows exactly how much she means to me. Thank you, Fi, for everything you do.

My friend David Goodwin has been an unfailing source of inspiration and this book would not be what it is without him.

The QSC, on the other hand, have just got in the way.

To Mark Hutchinson, Rebecca Salt and Nicky Stonehill, thank you for holding everything together this year, especially those bits when you were holding *me* together.

Last but never, ever, least: thanks to my children, Jessica, David and Kenzie, for putting up with me. Having a writer for a mother isn't always an easy shift, but the real world wouldn't be worth living in without you and Dad.